I0707577

Secrets of the Rainbow Bridge

Jonah, Olivia & Douglas Rosestone

Copyright © 2023 by Jonah, Olivia & Douglas Rosestone

All rights reserved. No part of this book may be reproduced or utilized in any form or by any means, electronic or mechanical, including photocopying, recording, or by any information storage or retrieval systems, without permission from the author or publisher.

This is a work of fiction. Names, characters, businesses, places, events, locales, and incidents are either the products of the author's imagination or used in a fictitious manner. Any resemblance to actual persons, living or dead, or actual events is purely coincidental.

Printed in the United States of America

Published by: Glamorium Arts, LLC

ISBN Hardback: 979-8-9880429-0-7
ISBN Paperback: 979-8-9880429-1-4
ISBN eBook: 979-8-9880429-2-1

Book Interior Design: Creative Publishing Book Design
Book Cover, Concept Art, Website Map: Arthur Bozonnet
Inside Art: Kelelowor
Inside Maps: Chaim Holtjer
Gaelic Language Consultant: Dr. Kate Chadbourne

*For Ceridwen, Inara, and Aurora who love to draw and read,
and dream and build, with dedication, grace, and courage.*

*Here — at last — from Uncle, Gram, and Grandpa
is our tale about Elves and Faeries!*

ACKNOWLEDGEMENTS

First, we would like to thank our dear friend David Solomon, for believing in us in the early years of world building and imagining what our book could be. We have come such a long way since those days, when you so patiently edited our first draft without judgments of any kind — judgments that might have made us doubt ourselves or question why we were even attempting to do this at all. Instead, you kept your opinions to yourself, and helped us to strengthen the basics of our writing, so we could keep going. And you did all of this without any pay, just out of the goodness of your heart! So, we *did* keep going, and here we are now, with a fully finished manuscript, and a real book. You're the best! Thank you again.

Next, we would like to thank Dr. Kate Chadbourne, PhD in Celtic Languages and Literatures from Harvard, and Professor of Irish Language and Folklore. All we can say is how grateful we are for all you have done to help us create an authentic lens through which to view the Elves and Faeries. Ever since we contacted you that very first day, your expert guidance and tutelage has helped us both to understand and properly communicate the *gaelic* names and terms we use throughout our book. Without your help, we wouldn't have been able to create such a full-throated rendering of *Tír na nÓg — the Undying Land.* Thank you again.

Finally, our amazing, talented editor, Jo-Ann Langseth. Wow, you took our book to another level! We knew when you began editing our book that you were a seasoned editor, but what we didn't know until we actually received your edits was what a *gifted* editor you were. We were so lucky to find you, as not everyone could have hit the ground running with us the way you did, turning out such consistently good work, chapter after chapter. What we ended up with was an integrated, well-polished manuscript, and we learned a lot from you. Buckets and buckets of thank-yous!

TABLE OF CONTENTS

They longed for Summer never to end
They were waking up to dying
As Autumn tossed her tawny head
They could feel their spirits crying

She gazed at them through amber eyes
Then beckoned with her hand
They rose to greet her foolishly
Their limbs had turned to sand

Winter buried them as they lay
And Death now made complete
Such yearning for the Selves
Which their surrender could now meet

As Mystery unfurled their shrouds
They yielded everything
And Death released itself to Life
And made the way for Spring

PROLOGUE

I remember touching the crystals in my sanctuary of Light, the cave I rested in when I sought clarity and restoration. I lay in a part of the cave I loved the most, where the crystals weren't the largest or the most exquisite, but the purest. They grew in clusters — directly from the Light — absorbing its essence and releasing its rays. When I reached for them, I gave them my colors, and when I pulled my hand back, they gave me theirs. Back and forth, back and forth we went, exchanging myriad shades of red, orange, yellow, green, blue, indigo and violet.

We traded colors for many lunar cycles, but one night when the Moon was waning, I pulled my hand away, and no Light followed. As if the tides of the sea had suddenly stopped, the ebb and flow between us ceased. I was too surprised to be afraid, so I simply stared into the crystals, waiting. After several minutes, they did not light again, so I placed my hand upon my rainbow amulet, and closed my eyes.

As always, I turned my attention within, and my vision brightened. From my heart, the rose of my soul opened. Each petal burst with Light, permeating my entire body from the inside out. I was no longer bound to the confines of my feminine form. My awareness entered the Light, and I became one with all colors of the Light.

What I was about to see would forever change not only my beloved Shiny folk, but all of Tír na nÓg.[1]

When the vision came to me, I shuddered. The images were unlike any I had ever seen: heavy like a stone fortress, noxious and cold, yielding nothing. I watched each part swirl in the ethers, until they coalesced into a methodical force — a forging shadow that seemed intent, not only on destroying Tír na nÓg, but rebuilding a mockery from its ruins.

Quickly my fear was realized, for I felt the Light — the Great Emerald Light that unites the realm — being severed.

What was once an all-embracing sphere of brilliance was being cleaved as easily as an ax rives a log for a winter Fire. The irony was impossible to ignore: I had come to the cave for sanctuary, only for Fate to grant me the ultimate vantage point from which to view the unfolding disaster.

---

[1] Pronounced [CHEER-na-NOHG] the Undying Land

I realized then, that I, Aurali,[2] Keeper of the Light, had been chosen to bear witness to what would come to be called the Great Befalling.

My vision encompassed everything. I watched — horrified — as the Great Emerald Light was torn asunder. With its harmony shattered, wave after wave of discord struck my realm. Every place the Great Emerald Light appeared was touched — no part of Tír na nÓg was left unscathed. With my senses heightened, I heard sounds of innumerable crystals shattering, as if legions of glassblowers had smashed their castings, destroying all their dreams.

Then I saw what was to come.

With the Great Emerald Light disrupted, three intertwining worlds would be pulled apart, like leaves of a shamrock being torn from their stem. Aghast, I watched the Triquetra — the Sacred Knot of the Trinity — beginning to unravel. No longer would the Shiny World know itself, or the Mortal World know the Shiny World, or either know the Luminous World. As if the land itself had been wrenched from the sea, and the sea from the sky, and the sky from the land, all three worlds would fall into chaos and misery, without hope of healing. For in the destruction would come the annihilation of Honesty, Truth and the Promise of Rebirth.

The impact of the forging shadow reverberated through me, forcing me back into my physical body. The rose of my soul closed abruptly. Instantly, I felt my body crushed into my feelings — my feelings pressed into my thoughts — my thoughts crumbled into my spirit — until I could no longer think, feel, or move.

I was stunned by the unrelenting force striking my being. Had I ever seen an anvil as hard, or an advancing guard as stalwart? Although I gathered what Light I could, and the rose of my soul reopened, the forging shadow pressed onward. I felt as if I, and all of Tír na nÓg, were behind an elven shield wall — clashing against an inexorable doom.

Yet, I was much more than the forging shadow could destroy. For I had learned long ago that my vision itself — the witness of my being — was as unwavering as the ever-Light that shines from the North Star, and as eternal as the crystal mountaintops, which stand like indomitable sentries in the Luminous Realm.

I simply would have to endure.

I do not remember how long the ordeal lasted — perhaps days, perhaps weeks. None of my Shiny folk could have withstood the agony for more than a few hours. As I struggled, I realized Fate had chosen me so I could learn more about my enemy. The forging shadow did not think or feel, yet seemed to be the foreign abettor of someone who was keenly aware of their actions. I was desperate to learn who, but the harder I pushed, the harder it pushed back.

2　Pronounced [AURA-lie]

My resolve began to weaken. The rose of my soul faded, until even my dreams disappeared, and I seemed to care less about my beloved Shiny folk. I screamed in fury, and my heart cried out in anguish. Over time, the forging shadow abated, leaving me feeling broken and powerless on the cave floor.

Gradually, my senses returned, although they were diminished. The cave was the same as before, except that I was surrounded by shattered crystals, save for a few of the purest. Perhaps they were the reason I had not faded completely. Yet, I was not myself anymore. As I waved my arms, the Light wept out of them in streams. My vessel had been cracked.

Deliriously, I reached toward the crystals, but no color flowed between us. Strangely, the shadows they cast appeared darker than usual. Had my ordeal robbed me of my powers? Frightened, I reached toward them again. To my surprise, a shadow reached back — licking my hand like a flame.

Now, instead of trading my colors with the Light, I seemed to be trading them with the shadows.

I pulled my hand away. Dreading what I might see next, I looked slowly to the side, then up, then down, and then to the other side. My heart beat wildly in my chest. I saw every shadow in the cave move in unison, as if they were living beings. They appeared to be faces — of what I was not sure. At first, they seemed like a warren of peculiar-looking rabbits, then a pack of hungry wolves, but I soon realized they were neither. A feeling of relief coursed through me. They were only birds. A host of sparrows? A cast of hawks? No — I drew back. They were an unkindness of ravens — the worst of omens — for they portend nothing but doom.

I put my hand out to invoke a simple flare to lighten my surroundings. The Light wept out of me even faster; flowing uselessly, it brightened everything briefly only to dim again.

The shadow ravens, emboldened by my helplessness, remained perched among the protruding crystals on the cave walls, watching me steadily. They cocked their heads as if to mock me, winking their beady black eyes and beating their large shadowy wings. Others opened their bills as if about to peck me full of holes, so they could simply empty the Light right out of me. Anxiously, I wondered if the forging shadow had come to finish me off.

I tried another flare, but the Light wept out of me again, bouncing here and there, and finally blinking out.

Frustrated, I bowed my head. "Why does my Light seem to play such tricks on me?" I asked.

One of the shadow ravens flew from the wall — wide dark wings, wedge-shaped tail, shaggy feathers and all — and landed on my shoulder. I froze, terrified. Coal-black feet dug into my flesh, and eerie-looking eyes, reflecting nothing, looked directly into mine.

"The Light isn't playing tricks on you, Aurali," the raven declared. "I am."

"Scannlan!"[3] I exclaimed. "Is that you?"

Instantly, the raven flapped its wings and left my shoulder, joining the others as they launched from the walls. They all then merged into one large silhouette.

I was correct. Out of the silhouette stepped my obverse: Scannlan of Scáth.[4] My hair was platinum — his was obsidian; my silk was white and lustrous — his was pitch-black and dull. I was radiant and of the Light. He was tenebrous and heavy, for he was of the Dark. Our eyes met. Ethereal beauty faced into earthly handsomeness — earthly handsomeness faced into ethereal beauty. For an instant our attraction was unalterable, but then the essence of our spirits disengaged. My glance, soulful and deep, sought purity. His glance, dry and piercing, sought to ferret out corruption. Neither of us could bear to look upon the other for too long.

"You don't seem like yourself," he announced.

He raised his arms. A veil of shadow appeared. At first, I recoiled, for the memory of the forging shadow was all too recent. Yet, I soon relaxed, as there was no malice in his dark aura. The darkness of the forging shadow was not his Darkness, as he lived not to subjugate others, but to liberate them.

"This will help you," he continued.

Dumbly, I stared into the veil, steeling myself for what was to come. His element unnerved me, yet I knew his ways could help me heal the rose of my soul.

Meekly, I looked at him. "How do you mend a broken heart?" I asked, fearing what he would say next.

Knowingly, he smiled. "By breaking it more."

His power was a bitter root that healed by poisoning first. As he touched my shoulder, I felt my Light drain out of me in waves, until all that remained was the wound inside me, open and raw. As his Darkness enveloped me, the core of my being writhed in pain.

I screamed. The remaining crystals around us brightened. Kneeling down, I pounded the cave floor, until sparks of Light shot from my fists. The wound inside me flared like burning tar.

"Enough!" I shouted.

Yet, he ignored my plea.

I wondered then if I had been a fool to trust him. Just as I thought he would destroy me, I found the strength to reach even deeper into myself. His Darkness had driven me to reclaim what I had lost. My Light came rushing back, coursing through my body, filling me to the brim. Much to my relief, I felt the rose of my soul brightening, and the tear inside me mending. My vessel had been righted.

---

[3]   Pronounced [SCAN-lan]

[4]   Pronounced [SCAW]

"That's better," he declared.

I felt my body, feelings, mind and spirit returning to harmony. "How did you know where to find me?" I asked as I rose to my feet.

"The Darkness granted me a premonition," he replied, as he folded his veil back into the shadows. "Or perhaps I had a premonition about the Darkness," he added, smiling. "I can never tell."

"You would jest at a time like this?"

"The Darkness can be quite amusing," he replied, as he looked about, studying the shattered crystals, "if you know what to look for. . ."

"Why did you come?"

"I wanted to make sure you weren't dragged into oblivion —"

"By what . . . ?" I interrupted." "Did you also. . . ?"

"Yes," he replied. "I felt a sundering shock pass through all of Tír na nÓg — a darkness that serves no good."

"When does the Darkness ever do any good?" I knew I sounded petty and ungrateful for saying that to him. He scowled.

"Didn't my Darkness just serve you?" he asked. As he spoke, the shadows swirling angrily on the surface of his skin quickly disintegrated, like murky bubbles popping in a bog.

He knew I could not argue with him. "What happened inside the cave?" he asked. "Who would dare try to break the crystals of the Keeper of the Light?"

"I came to the caves for respite," I began. "Instead I received a vision —"

"What exactly did you see?" he interrupted.

"The Great Emerald Light of the realm has been severed," I replied.

As I spoke, he did not even blink. I expected him to be horrified, but he did not flinch.

"I felt a forging shadow, bent on reforming all of Tír na nÓg," I added.

"Everyone did, but probably none as keenly as you," he replied. The more he took in my story, the more the shadows deepened upon his face.

"For weeks I faced the forging shadow, until I became too weakened to continue," I said.

"I've never seen you unable to harness your element," he replied. "What happened to you does not bode well for the Fae."

"Perhaps, we should marshal them, and strike back."

"That will fail."

"Would you dismiss me that easily?" I asked.

"I would not dismiss you, Aurali. But, you dismiss the truth within your own struggle."

"And how might that be?"

"*What you've encountered is a kind of darkness you have never known before,*" *he continued.* "*One that has invaded and will destroy our realm, the same way that a wasp enslaves an unsuspecting ladybug. You see, with the wasp's sting, the ladybug feels a new and undiminished sense of purpose. Dutifully, she continues to feed, unaware of the egg growing inside of her. In time, a young grub forces its way out of her body while eating her alive. But, the ladybug's ordeal is not over. Enthralled, she stands guard as the grub spins a cocoon beneath her abdomen. For days she remains vigilant — a servant of her tormentor. In time, the wasp hatches — abandoning her to die of madness. Such now is the Fate of Tír na nÓg.*"

"*But how?*" *I asked, unable to comprehend his words.*

"*Did you not hear me? We've been stung. No Light will be strong enough to save us!*"

"*That simply cannot be!*" *I exclaimed.*

"*You will see, Aurali. No Light is strong enough. For the first time, the darkness has grown more powerful than the Light. You simply cannot fathom that, can you?*"

As he spoke, I saw a most peculiar look upon his face, as if in speaking this truth about the darkness, he had now become both the victor and the vanquished. For an instant, I thought he might extinguish me with his force, or simply disappear entirely into the crevices of the cave.

"*I don't believe you!*" *I exclaimed. Yet, I was terrified by what my heart was telling me. I knew he had the measure of such things, for he, not I, understood the way the Darkness worked. Still, I could not concede.*

"*We must fight! The way I defeated all my enemies! I sent them all away!*"

"*You will not defeat an evil such as this, in the way you always have,*" *he declared.*

Hearing this, I trembled inside, and the rose of my soul dimmed. "*Whyever not?*" *I cried.*

"*You destroy your enemies by throwing their Light at them, until they see that their Darkness is false. The Darkness contains both good and evil, and you force them to face the latter. You banish them from their shadows with that truth, until they crumble into dust. You cannot defeat this kind of darkness in the same way, for it contains only evil.*"

"*I will. I must.*"

"*No. You won't. For this evil is <u>so</u> dark, it cannot even see its own Light. Therefore, the Light will not defeat it. You will never, <u>ever</u> win!*"

"*What kind of evil could be so impervious to its own Light?*"

"*My dear Aurali, you are so exquisitely beautiful in your intentions — but so naïve.*"

His words crashed in upon me, crushing my resolve. For the first time, I could not match him, point for point. Resigned to my failure, I simply asked, "What must we do?"

"We must find those who are brave enough to enter into the shadows. By this they will be prepared, and our fearsome enemy can be known. The brave must be honed to a strength now not found among the Fae of Tír na nÓg."

As he spoke, he smiled. For just as I had long avoided him, he had been waiting through the ages to speak these words to me.

"Only I — not you — can teach them that."

We stared at each other; neither one of us averted our gaze. Both Light and Dark had come to terms.

"Now I understand," I replied, as I studied him, perhaps truly seeing him for the first time. He was like a black swan — elegant and mysterious — shunned by his flock of brothers and sisters. Shunned and forgotten long ago by the Fae of the Light. The healing he bestowed had sustained me to bear the Darkness. I realized then that at least in his own eyes, he had been vindicated.

Then he told me what must be done next. Just as the wasp had deceived the ladybug, his plan would plant a seed, and take our enemy by surprise. Scannlan was ever shrewd and determined. What fortune that he had aligned himself with me. Yet, before we took action, we would have to make our way beyond Tír na nÓg, to attend The Splendor of the Joining Gaze.

Chapter 1

A SEARCH IN THE WATER

The month of Willow had come, and the Springs of Coventina were flowing high. Baudwin[1] reached toward the Water, spreading his fingers, taking in his element. Quickly, his senses awakened. He saw pulsing waves of blue-green color, and heard sounds of rushing Water on distant mountaintops. The icy sweet taste of the springs was on his tongue. Now there was only the moment, new and never-ending, filling him with wonder and delight. Satisfied, he took his attention away from the Water he so dearly loved, and his heightened senses withdrew. Gazing toward the marsh, he fluttered his fingers, hoping for a sign.

He was in luck.

A flock of bluethroats burst from the reeds. Happily, he watched their iridescent bibs as they sang — *chat chack, chat chack. They are indeed a rare sight,* he thought, *sharing their secrets instead of skulking in the marshes.* Surely, there was no better time to be looking for the Water. Joyously, he reached for them as they flew toward the sky.

"Today I will succeed!" he shouted.

He was grateful another chance had come. No longer did he have to huddle like a river otter in his den, waiting for the spring thaw. For now, the greening season was upon the land — the time of possibilities — when droplet and shoot became one.

Baudwin turned his gaze toward the horizon. Winter's chill was but a fleeting memory — a melting mass of ice upon distant mountaintops. Day and night had battled to a standstill, sharing the heavens in equal measure, yet slowly, the balance was tipping, for the Sun burned longer in the sky. He welcomed the changes as any Faery would. As the season of renewal burst forth, so did *Tír na nÓg — the Undying Land —* hold true to its name.

And so too, would he hold true to his search.

He touched the Water, feeling the icy wetness against his palm, bracing himself before he ventured deeper into the pool. *Will this time be any different?* he wondered.

---

[1] Pronounced [BOD-win]

Memories of countless failures filled his mind, sweeping aside his cheer, leaving him with nothing but uncertainty. *What if I should fail again?* he thought, shuddering. For then, he would feel even more alone than he already did.

For many years he had turned to the Water for guidance, standing as he did today before its daunting depths. If he dove to the bottom, would he at last find solace from what weighed so heavily upon his heart? Although he balked at the notion of giving up, he also struggled to find the courage to try again.

"What must I do?" he shouted.

A hush went over the wilds. Nowhere did he hear the slapping tail of a beaver, or the clicking buzz of a cicada. Strangely, the spring he stood before seemed to have silenced his surroundings. He stopped. A feeling of stillness crept into him. Moments became minutes, as he stood, transfixed by the Water.

From a place he could not sense, an unseen presence, which had hidden itself from him for his entire Life, felt sympathy for his plight — and in a moment turned its eye upon him. A ripple of Water lapped over the top of his hand, shot into the Air and splashed him in the face, a splash that to him seemed playfully demanding, yet alarming.

Drawing back in shock he wondered, *Am I imagining things, or did the Water just prompt me?* Such things never happened — even at the Springs of Coventina. Despite his bewilderment, he kept his palm upon the Water.

The unseen presence set to guide him. A rush of feeling coursed into his hand and up his arm, pulsing into the center of his chest like a gelid flame. Instantly, his feelings of trepidation turned into inspiration. All at once, he felt uplifted and ready to act; yet he paused, marveling at the way the Water worked: flowing ceaselessly, taking ages to reshape the contours of the rocks into cascading basins, but only a matter of moments to change him from within.

He was now ready to perform a hallowed rite — one rarely practiced by water Faeries in Deuona.

Carefully he moved his fingers, watching as rings of Water drifted away from his hand, past lily pads and lotuses, melting back into the blue-green surface from which they had formed. *The stillness of the Water guides me,* he thought. He had to remain as the Water before him, for if he did not, he would lose his intention. And there was no intention without calm.

Baudwin remembered how he had learned this lesson.

When he was one and sixty, he and his grandfather, Seamus,[2] had stood beside the river near their home, where Seamus had taught him how to practice finding his intention. "Baudwin," he said, "if you want to find the Water, this is what you must do: Take the largest breath you can. Dive all the way to the

____

[2] Pronounced [SHAY-mus]

bottom. Stay there for as long as possible and wait. Listen to your fear. When you feel you are about to burst, swim as fast as you can to the surface. Do not lose your calm."

According to Seamus, if Baudwin had a strong enough intention, something amazing could happen, something water Faeries who still practiced the old ways held to be most sacred — the Water would find *him.*

"If the Water finds you," Seamus explained over and over again, "you will hear voices of the Water, your faery tribe — moving in unison like a school of salmon swimming upstream. All of their feelings, thoughts and dreams will be speaking to you at once."

Baudwin took his grandfather's words quite seriously, so much so that he had been trying to find the Water for the past forty years. Thousands of times he dove to the bottom of the river, deftly breaststroking his arms in circles and kicking his legs, holding his breath until he felt his lungs would burst. Never in all that time had the Water found him. But, he had never stopped trying, for his reason for seeking the old ways — unlike most — came from a longing deep within his heart. He yearned for someone who was nearest and dearest to him, yet, for reasons he could not understand, someone who was also the farthest away.

He longed with every fiber of his being to find his mother.

If he simply kept looking, he was certain that one day the Water would lead him to her. Two hundred years of not knowing was enough for him. He was ready to try again — hopefully, for the last time.

I've come here so I can hear her voice amongst the Faefolk of the Water, he thought — *for that would be a greater joy than any other blessing the Water could bestow upon me.*

Despite his resolve, he couldn't forget all the naysayers who had told him to abandon his search. Even now, the willows in the distance seemed to bend ever closer to the ground, beckoning for him to accept his sorrow — to mourn her and then move on.

But how could he ever forget about his own mother? For all his Life he had wondered where she was. When he was a young one, searching for her was a game he played down by the river, imagining she would come. He looked everywhere for her, singing a song Seamus had taught him:

Find a moorhen if you can

Be careful when you do

For if you catch her, she may fly

Though you won't want her to

As he grew older, he would mutter sadly to himself, "I won't try to catch her, I just want to know why — why did she leave?"

Over the years, he asked himself the same question again and again. When he reached the age of one and thirty, he stopped singing songs and began to search for her in other ways, digging through stacks of family letters and journals, and going through drawers of keepsakes and other things — never finding anything. At one and sixty, he asked his father, Kelven,[3] outright what had happened. Kelven simply hung his head and wouldn't tell him.

"Go now, and do your chores at the dam," he said. "You need to take your mind off this." He then quietly walked away.

Baudwin *couldn't* take his mind off of her. As years went by, and the folly of his search became more and more apparent, so did his anger and frustration continue to grow. So much so, that two days prior to this one, he went again to his father, this time announcing, "If you can't tell me where she went, then I must leave Deuona[4] to look for her in other places."

Upon hearing this, Kelven snapped furiously, "You would go now, what with all there is to do at the dam and in the Water Guild? How selfish of you!"

Kelven's angry words only left Baudwin feeling even more upset and determined to act. Regardless of the difficulty, he would keep looking, until he found her.

Seamus had felt Baudwin's pain, and his newfound urge for freedom. Knowing he would never give up his search, he came to his aid.

"Stop talking to your father about all of this," he said. "I see now that your intention has never been so strong. You must go and visit the Springs of Coventina. Look for her there."

And so it was that Baudwin now stood, prepared to find the Water yet again. *Will I find her?* he wondered. *Will she speak to me?*

As if to urge him on, a nearby creek rushed even faster, a creek almost overflowing with Water that, originating in the Tadlach[5] Mountains, had tumbled and twisted for miles. Looking up, he saw them far in the distance, their icy peaks dividing *Tír na nÓg* down the middle from north to south — separating the homelands of the Fae — in the East was *Tír Éirí Sióg,*[6] and in the West was *Tír Luí Lucharachán.*[7]

The Tadlachs were blanketed with snow — Water that was theirs, but not theirs — Water they couldn't draw from a river until the spring thaw began. Water he was grateful to for bringing Life to the land for as far as the eye could

---

[3] Pronounced [KEL-ven]
[4] Pronounced [DEV-oh-na]
[5] Pronounced [TAAD-lock]
[6] Pronounced [CHEER-eerie shee-ohg] the Eastern Faery Lands
[7] Pronounced [CHEER-lee lookh-er-ahn] the Western Elven Lands

see, replenishing oak trees and blooming hawthorns, and giving the tadpoles, guppies and turtles of the marshes a place to play. Smiling, he cupped his hands over his heart, one on top of the other. "I am *with* the Water," he affirmed, making a sign of the Water. He then turned his attention to what he was about to do.

Baudwin removed his shirt, breeches and boots, and placed them on the grass. Water Faeries were a hardy lot no matter how cold the Water was, so gamely he waded into the spring, until the Water reached his waist. Taking a very deep breath, one he knew would have to last for several minutes, he lifted his arms above his head, joining his hands and linking his thumbs together. Bending his legs, he sprang up and then dove headfirst into the spring, swimming through Water many times his height, until he reached the bottom. Clinging to river rocks and plants, he floated on his side, waiting — his pale blue-green skin blending in with the currents around him.

At least a minute went by — time enough for his doubts to surface like the bubbles that rose from the bottom of the spring. *What if my intention isn't strong enough?* he thought anxiously. *What if the Water doesn't come?*

After several moments, he found himself wondering in the opposite way. *If the Water does come, will I be prepared? How will I even know if the Water has come at all?*

All these ruminations were met with an overwhelming silence. Nothing happened. Worried to no end, Baudwin turned onto his other side. Drawing his knees to his chest and holding onto a large rock with one hand, he grabbed the top of his head with the other. Closing his eyes, he pulled his head down until his every thought visualized just one thing — finding her.

In an instant, hundreds of minnows swam to the center of the pool, their silvery sides twisting and flashing in the Light. As Baudwin's senses awakened, he immediately felt their presence. He opened his eyes. Spellbound, he watched them draw nearer, forming a spiral as they advanced. When they reached him, the spiral uncurled and they merged into one large circle, swimming around and around him, as he clung to the rock.

Am I dreaming? In all his Life, fish had never come to him this way. As if to answer him, they circled around him even faster.

Remembering his grandfather's words, he centered his intention even more, for he still had plenty of breath in his lungs. He closed his eyes again.

All of his surging feelings calmed, and he entered a trance-like state. To his surprise, a dreaming came to him. He saw the school of minnows swimming inside of him, in a watery pool of blue-green Light. Their glistening bodies moved separately, yet all were joined together as one persisting creature. He then heard voices — hundreds of high-pitched utterances — whispering back and forth to one another.

Are the minnows now talking to me? he wondered.

"You must not open your eyes," they chimed in unison. "If you do, you will not hear us!" Utterly entranced by their voices, Baudwin closed his eyes even more tightly. He wondered if those were the voices of his tribe.

With that, the minnows vanished from his vision as quickly as they had appeared. *Wherever did they go?* he wondered, still motionless at the bottom of the spring. Moments passed and nothing further happened. He wasn't sure what he should do.

As he was about to open his eyes and shoot back to the surface of the Water, his dreaming continued. A vision of a water drum appeared in his mind's eye — an amber-colored gourd with large green leaves and dark roots trailing in the Water. The drum floated along the surface of a rushing river, bobbing in and out of river grass, reeds, and cattails. Someone sat in the center on a large turquoise pillow.

Who is he?

Shocked, Baudwin realized — the one he saw was himself. *Whatever is happening to me? Why is the Water showing me <u>myself</u>?*

As Baudwin watched his dream-self in the water drum, he and that dream-self become one, and he found himself inside the drum. Soon he saw a fleet of other drums drifting toward him, bumping into him. A faery lady or gent rested peacefully inside each one. The flotilla of drums continued to float down the river.

Where are we going? Baudwin thought, as he continued to watch his dreaming unfold.

"To a new beginning," an elderly-sounding faery lady announced.

A new beginning? How can you read my thoughts?

"Because we are both swimming in the same current," she replied, laughing. "You can hear me, and I can hear you."

The same current? Who are you?

"I am someone who has known you for a very long time, Baudwin," she replied.

How do you know my name? he wondered.

"You don't need to know that now," she replied. "But I will tell you this," she added. I am very old and very wise."

Why won't you tell me who you are? he wondered. *Please, you must tell me!*

"Do not concern yourself with who I am," she replied. "What you are about to discover is far more important."

Before Baudwin's eyes, the flotilla of water drums disappeared. The only thing left was his dream-self in the remaining drum, drifting down the river. *Is there nothing more to my new beginning?* he wondered.

Until now, holding his breath had been easy, but seeing his dream-self alone again, without the others, frightened him. *Is the vision I just found fading away?* He held his breath even more tightly. *When will I hear the voices of my tribe?*

"If you want to hear *their* voices, you must first hear your own," the elderly voice informed him. "Look to the young one, Baudwin."

Another drum floated by.

Baudwin looked inside and saw a tender-looking little fellow, not much older than forty, the age he had been when he first began looking for his mother.

How young I was, he thought. *I barely remember him. What does he say?*

"To find out you must listen," the elderly voice instructed.

Why must I listen to him? he thought impatiently. *Listening takes too long — all the Air will leave my lungs, and I won't find the Water.*

"If you cannot listen to yourself, you will not find the Water."

Then I will! Baudwin thought angrily. With that, he again looked at the young one resting inside the water drum, giving him his full attention. His mind opened to meet the mind of his younger self. *I can hear his thoughts, and he can hear mine,* he marveled.

"Of course you can," the elderly voice said. "What did he ask you?"

"He asked me if I had forgotten him," Baudwin replied.

"And what did you tell him?"

"I told him I had not."

"Good!" she exclaimed. "Now tell me — have your doubts disappeared?"

Baudwin took a moment to consider his doubts, only to realize that they had indeed diminished. *How did she know that?* he wondered, while noticing the ease with which he now could hold his breath.

"I know a great deal about you, but nothing you, yourself, cannot learn as well," the elderly voice said, chuckling. "And now, all those who hear Baudwin — *speak* to him."

"Do not be afraid!" a voice cried out.

"We are with the Water!" several more shouted, laughing delightedly.

With that, Baudwin's ears began to throb from deep inside his head. A cacophony of voices cried out all at once. *These are not the voices of the minnows I heard before.*

"They are your tribe," the elderly voice announced. "Those who live in Deuona and far beyond, near all the streams, rivers, and lakes of *Tír na nÓg.* Do you not hear them?"

I hear everyone in Deuona babbling incessantly, like the Springs of Coventina, he thought, rejoicing at what he heard. *We are one body — like the minnows. I hear all their longings — their hopes and fears — what they love and hate — everything!* His mind drifted to his home on the river. *My neighbor Elva dreams of having her cousin from Four Falls live near her. My father misses the times when we used to swim in the river. My grandfather wants me to lead the Water Guild. My friends Matha[8] and Criofan[9] —*

"Listen beneath the voices that you know," the elderly voice urged, interrupting Baudwin's thoughts. "What else do you hear?"

Baudwin took a moment to ponder the question. *I hear thousands and thousands of others, from every source of Water in Tír na nÓg,* he thought, *from Deuona, to Four Falls and beyond. If I want to hear any one of them alone, all I must do is listen for it.*

"Then the Water has found you!" the voice exclaimed.

The Water has found me? How could that be?

"Naturally!" the elderly voice rejoiced again.

The Water has found me! he thought deliriously. Listening even more closely to the voices of his tribe, he remembered his grandfather's words — that they would sound like a school of salmon swimming upstream.

Salmon indeed, he thought. *They sing, pipe, and cackle like a flock of exuberant birds. And I can hear them!* Despite his jubilation, Baudwin knew he could not remain much longer at the bottom of the spring, for time, like the Air in his lungs, was running out.

"Baudwin, I must leave you now," the elderly voice intoned.

No — wait, he thought. *Please, help me find her.*

"My work is done," the voice continued. "You are on your way."

If you're leaving, then Mother must be coming along soon, he thought. *Before I go, I will find her. But how? I do not know her voice.*

He paused and, remembering what Seamus had told him when he was young, gathered his wits. *I must <u>not</u> listen to my fear that I will not find her* he thought. *I must wait, and let her come to me — like the Water.* Happy with this prospect, he remained at the bottom of the spring, holding onto the last bit of Air in his lungs.

Suspended in gray cheerlessness, moments that had been bright with possibility had now abruptly vanished. Listening, he heard what he thought were chimes ringing softly in the background, and voices singing a plaintive melody. *Why does my tribe sing so wistfully?* he wondered. *Do they sing for me, or for her?* And then he heard nothing at all.

His mother never spoke to him.

An aching sadness invaded his heart, a presence that he found most frightening. *I must go back,* he thought, wanting to swim away to escape his

____

[8] Pronounced [MA-ha]
[9] Pronounced [CRI-fin]

feelings. With the remaining strength he had, he pushed off from the bottom of the spring, moving as quickly as he could.

Before he reached the surface, he heard a final voice. "Baudwin, where are you?"

Mother? Baudwin thought, shocked to hear the sound stirring fitfully inside his head. *Is that you?*

"You were supposed to meet me here," the voice said.

Baudwin realized then that the voice was not that of a faery lady. He could not listen anymore, for he was almost out of breath, so he kicked his legs harder and swam faster. As his head broke the surface of the Water, he threw his arms to the sky, arching his back and inhaling deeply. A burst of Air seared his lungs. Breathing arduously, he swam to the edge of the spring, dragged his body out of the Water, and collapsed in a heap upon the grass.

Grief-stricken, he wept. Raising his head, he looked toward the spring. "Whyever did you come to me if not to have me find her?" he cried out to the Water. "Do you not know what finding her means to me?" Minutes passed as he simply lay there, sobbing.

Never could he have imagined that his greatest sorrow would flow from his greatest joy, nor that the Water would actually will this to be so.

Chapter 2

THE RUINS OF COVENTINA

Tears streamed from Baudwin's eyes and rolled down his cheeks, falling upon the tufts of grass beneath him. Cradling his head, he squeezed his eyes even tighter, and more drops ran down his face. Oddly, he found comfort in his sorrow. The more he cried, the closer he felt to his element. For he was a Faery of the Water, and whether he cried out of sadness or joy, his feelings soothed a barren place inside of him, easing his pain.

Yet, soon he realized his bittersweet reprieve would not last.

As he wept, he had clung to the hope that the Water might give him another chance to find his mother. But now he knew this was a foolish longing; false hope would lead him nowhere. He was not as he had been moments before, swimming with the voices in the Water. Instead, he was drowning in his sorrow, and he had to move on.

"Baudwin," a voice sounded. "Baudwin!" A hand grabbed him by the shoulder, rolling him onto his back. Another hand brushed aside his hair, which was plastered to his face.

"Are you all right?"

Looking up, Baudwin saw his friend, Matha, staring down at him, shocked.

"Those tears streaming down your face rival the workings of the springs," Matha said. "Whatever is the matter?"

Hearing Matha's voice, Baudwin sat up, startled, for he was certain Matha had just spoken to him when he was under the Water.

"Did you hear me?" Baudwin asked. "Because I heard you."

"What in the world do you mean?" Matha asked, looking quite concerned.

"You asked me where I was," Baudwin explained.

"Did I?" Matha asked.

Baudwin realized that even though he had heard Matha's voice, Matha hadn't heard him. Yet, to be sure, he asked his friend what he knew.

"How did you find me?"

"I really don't know," Matha replied. "I just felt a strong urge to come here, as if the Water were whispering in my ear, but I can't say why. Are you all right? You were supposed to meet me at the cairns."

"The cairns?" Baudwin asked, confused. Standing up, he remembered that he had agreed to meet his friend to go exploring, but his ordeal with the Water had made him forget.

"That's right, I was. Only —"

"What are you doing here?" Matha interrupted.

"I came here to find Mother," Baudwin continued.

At the mention of Baudwin's mother, Matha adjusted his spectacles to better see his friend. Keenly aware of Baudwin's struggles to find her, he had long admired his relentless striving. So many had advised Baudwin to stop looking, yet Baudwin had countered them all, asking if any of them would ever give up on a loved one. To Matha, he was like a rapid fed by an ever-melting glacier, one that would wear down any obstacle before him. Yet, he worried that Baudwin's search would be in vain.

"Were you looking for a moorhen?" Matha asked, smiling. "I haven't forgotten the poem Seamus taught you."

"Yes — and no," Baudwin replied.

"Yes *and* no?" Matha asked, puzzled.

"I mean yes, I was looking for Mother, but no, not in the same way."

"What do you mean?" Matha asked.

"I came to find the Water," Baudwin said. "Or, for the Water to find me."

"I do see that," Matha said, motioning to the pile of garments on the ground. "Aren't you freezing? Tell me all of this while you put your clothes back on."

As Baudwin dressed, he shared his tale of adventure. "I wasn't sure if I was ready," he began, speaking excitedly despite his grief. "But my senses were waking, so I just dove right in. I swam to the bottom, and stayed, as I had always done. I was hoping the Water would come to me — and this time, the Water *did*."

Although Baudwin looked giddy with excitement, Matha remained stoic, trying to assess his friend.

"Then what happened?" he asked.

"First a school of minnows swam to me," Baudwin replied. "They went around me, and then I saw them *inside* me!"

Matha studied his friend. "Really? How?"

"In *here*," Baudwin replied, pointing to his head. "I heard them talking to me. They told me not to close my eyes. Then they went away. Next, I saw myself floating down the river in a water drum. For a while, I was surrounded by water Faeries — ladies and gents floating along with me. They too disappeared — and then I was alone again."

Baudwin lowered his head, sighing deeply, for the feeling of loss was more than he could bear. Looking up, he asked, "Do I sound mad to you?"

"Not at all," Matha replied. "I was compelled to find you here, so surely something is afoot."

"Or perhaps we both are mad," Baudwin said, playfully cuffing his friend on the shoulder of his well-worn blue jacket.

"Not me," Matha replied. "You just sound like you've had another one of your wild adventures. What happened next?"

"A voice told me to look into a water drum, and there I was again. Only this time, I was a Faefry[1] of about forty. The voice told me that if I wanted to hear the Water, I must first listen to myself."

"Very good advice," Matha put in, smiling.

"So, I listened to my younger self — and then the Water came to me." As Baudwin spoke, his eyes sparkled with joy. "I heard our water tribe, everyone in Deuona and beyond, thousands and thousands of them speaking to me at once. Matha, there were so many of them! If only you could have heard them."

"If only —" Matha began.

"And then," Baudwin continued, "I waited to hear her." Helplessly, he looked at his friend. "But she never came. I heard the water tribe, but I didn't hear *her* voice. She's passed on to Annwyn.[2] I know she has. Now, I'll never see her." Despondently, he stared at the nearby spring and was silent.

Matha knew he had to help Baudwin imagine other possibilities. But before he said another word, he paused. He had never seen his friend so distraught. Just a moment before, Baudwin had seemed happy and now, so quickly, he was not. A true friend wouldn't allow him to assume the worst about his mother.

"Baudwin, you don't know that," Matha said gently. "You must not —"

"Why did the Water come to me, if not to help me find her?" Baudwin interrupted.

"You mustn't blame the Water," Matha replied, taken aback. "No one can know the Water's mysteries." He removed his spectacles and wiped the dust from the lenses with the hem of his jacket. Sighing deeply, he asked, "Are you sure you should keep talking about all of this? I hate to see you —"

"What?" Baudwin interrupted.

"So *tortured,*" Matha continued.

"I'm not," Baudwin replied. "I just want to understand what happened."

"I don't think that's possible," Matha said. "At least not yet."

"I'm just not sure," Baudwin said, continuing to puzzle over why he hadn't heard his mother's voice.

"I'm not either," Matha asserted. He grabbed his friend by the shoulders. "But I believe you need me now to help restore your boundless optimism. When you are dark and despondent, you frighten me. Perhaps you should just —"

"I know what I heard!" Baudwin cut in, pulling away from his friend. "Or, should I say, what I *didn't* hear."

---

[1]   Pronounced [FAY-fry] a faery child
[2]   Pronounced [ah-NOO-vin] the faery and elven afterlife

Matha went silent. Guiltily, Baudwin realized that his friend was only trying to shield him from what was becoming obvious. Although the Water had come to him, he hadn't heard his mother's voice, so perhaps the Water was showing him that he would never find her. This realization struck him hard, leaving him shaking with distress. As the shock shuddered through him, he remained motionless, paralyzed with pain.

"Baudwin!" Matha cried. "Whatever is the matter?"

Writhing in torment, Baudwin reached for a low-hanging branch to steady himself.

"Baudwin. Speak to me," Matha pleaded. "What's wrong?"

Baudwin did not reply. His blue-green skin turned even more pale.

"Baudwin!"

Gradually, the pain subsided. As Baudwin regained his composure, he straightened his stance.

"I'm all right," he said, taking a deep breath. Tears of relief streamed down his face.

"What just happened?" Matha asked, hoping that the answer was not what he already suspected.

"I had one of my bouts," Baudwin replied.

Hearing this, Matha winced, for it meant that today Baudwin had twice been struck by ill fortune; first, it was not hearing his mother, and now the pain was from a peculiar ailment, one that had plagued him from childhood. Over the years, mystified healers had reluctantly suggested that he stay away from the Water, for these bouts always seemed to happen when he was near springs, a river, or a lake. Yet how could Baudwin do such a thing? Matha knew that telling him to give up his element would be like asking him not to breathe, lest the Air suffocate him.

"You haven't had one in a while, have you?" Matha asked.

"Not for quite a while," Baudwin replied, standing straighter and letting go of the branch.

"Why now, then?" Matha asked, pacing nervously.

"I'm fine, Matha," Baudwin said, stretching out his arms and taking a deep breath. "I just needed to —"

"I know why," Matha said. "The Water *found* you. You always have bouts when you're near the Water."

"*Now* who's blaming the Water?" Baudwin asked.

"I'm not!" Matha exclaimed.

"Yes, you are."

"No, I'm not!" Matha insisted, even louder. "You aren't listening to me. You need to —"

"You mustn't worry about me," Baudwin interrupted.

"But I'm your friend. And I *am* worried. Before you went looking for the Water, you should have thought about your bouts. Now they might get even worse."

"I appreciate your concern," Baudwin said, putting on his vest. "But you must not take such a wondrous gift as the Water finding me and turn it into some kind of dreadful curse. You know I won't stand for that."

Little did they know that as they argued, a bluethroat was hiding in the tall grasses, flitting among the twigs. Cocking its head from side to side, the gem-bibbed meddler planned its next move. As the two Faeries kept talking, the bird continued to spy on them.

Feeling Baudwin's passion, Matha conceded. "All right then," he said, happy to see that at least for now, his friend's bout was over. "I'm sure the Water isn't cursing you."

"Well, I guess that's one thing to be grateful for," Baudwin said, struggling to regain his humor. Hastily, he buttoned his vest. "I'm glad we've settled that."

As his fingers reached the bottom hole, he stopped.

"Now I've lost one my favorite buttons!" he announced, angrily.

"What kind?" Matha asked, relieved at the change of subject.

"Blue-green onyx — something irreplaceable."

"Let's look — it has to be around here somewhere," Matha said, joining Baudwin in his search for the missing button. As they scrambled about the grass, he turned and gazed at the bank of the spring.

Just across from them, Matha spotted something.

"Baudwin — look," he whispered. "A bluethroat. What a fortuitous sign. They never come out of the marshes this early in the year."

"I saw some right before I dove into the spring," Baudwin replied. "I remembered what Seamus taught me — that they're messengers of the Water — and that gave me courage."

Looking more closely at the bird, Matha asked, "What's he holding in his beak?"

"I have no idea," Baudwin replied, calming down long enough to examine the timid-looking creature.

"Nor do I," Matha replied, crouching down to get a closer look at the bird. "Let's go and see."

As the two Faeries stealthily crawled toward the bluethroat, a swarm of red and green dragonflies appeared around them, flitting playfully.

"It looks like a pebble or a piece of shell," Matha said. "No, it's —"

"My button!" Baudwin exclaimed. "Drop it, you sneaky little robber!"

Startled, the bird looked at Baudwin, its blue bib pulsing nervously. "You guided me to the Water, and now you're *stealing* from me?" Baudwin asked, as he lunged at the bird.

Without a flicker of hesitation, the bird flapped its wings and took flight. "You mischievous thief!" Baudwin shouted, jumping to his feet.

Happy to see that Baudwin had found his spur, Matha shouted, "Come, Baudwin — let's go after him!"

The two Faeries took off through the marsh, racing along the edge of the Water. Above them flew the bluethroat, which soon alighted on a branch. But as soon as they drew near, the bird flew away. Racing to keep up with the winged escape artist, they ran ever faster, their attention fixed upon the sky as they went. Together they laughed, for they knew they had no hope of catching the bird.

The bluethroat gave them a merry chase, allowing them to come close only to dart away again and again at the last moment. Still, they continued running after him, weaving in and out of tall patches of river grass, and ducking behind fallen trees whenever the bird stopped. A warm afternoon breeze enveloped them as they went, brushing their blue-green tresses away from their faces. Soon, they were sinking ankle-deep into a bog, the muddy peat wresting their boots from their feet.

Exhausted, they came to a stop.

"He's only a few yards away," Baudwin whispered, as he struggled to keep from falling into the bog. "If we can just keep after him, he'll drop it — I'm sure."

"That I doubt," Matha whispered back, trying not to laugh so he'd not lose his balance. "He must be leading us somewhere."

"Then we mustn't give up," Baudwin insisted. He then began to laugh, almost falling over.

Panting heavily, Matha stopped. "There he is — right there — between those two boulders." He pointed down the path. "In that large grove of oak trees."

The two Faeries headed toward the boulders, which towered over them on either side of the path. Above them, they spotted the bluethroat flying back and forth from boulder to boulder, still holding the button in its beak.

"He's up there!" Baudwin shouted.

"Perhaps we can climb up," Matha said.

They ran to the boulder on the left side of the path. The gigantic rock stood the height of at least five Faeries, and was covered with vines and moss. Baudwin pulled back some vines, looking for footholds, but much to his surprise, he found something else. A relief of a faery lady in profile had been carved into the rock, facing the path. Two symbols were arranged near her, a crescent Moon over her head, and a water droplet in her cupped hands. The two Faeries stood transfixed by their unexpected discovery.

"How interesting," Matha said. He then had a flash of insight. "I have an idea," he said as he darted to the boulder on the other side of the path. In the same place as the other, he pulled back some vines, and found another relief.

"Look," he called, as he brushed some dirt from the cracks. "This one is an elven gent."

The elven gent was carved in profile to mirror the faery lady on the other side of the path. Two symbols were also arranged near him, a Sun above his head — holding a hammer.

For a moment, the two Faeries forgot their pursuit, and studied the carvings.

"That hammer is the symbol of Silver Forge," Matha said.

"And the droplet is our symbol," Baudwin replied. "Whatever does this mean?"

Both Faeries had heard of Silver Forge, an elven city in the west of *Tír na nÓg*, far past the Tadlachs, but never had they seen its symbol carved into what they guessed was some kind of entrance. Although the meaning and purpose of the symbol was unknown to them, they both inferred that this was a greeting of some kind, placed there by both parties — the Faeries and the Elves.

Intrigued, they decided to continue on, for the bluethroat had already flown down the path marked by the boulders. Scanning the area around them, they talked.

"Perhaps, we'll find out more about why those symbols were carved," Matha commented, as they passed between the boulders.

"Who could have moved them here?" Baudwin asked. "They're enormous. This kind of granite had to have come from the Tadlachs."

"If the Elves of Silver Forge did this, they certainly have their ways, but I doubt," Matha added, laughing, "that the Faeries could have mustered the skills alone."

"Now Matha," Baudwin chided his friend. "You must not —"

"Must not what?" Matha cut in.

"Mock our kin."

"Why would I do that?" Matha chuckled.

"Because you like to," Baudwin replied.

"I only do that so you can see how fair-minded I really am. You know I try not to take sides between the Faeries and Elves. Doing so would be sheer foolishness. At least in my opinion. And besides —"

Matha didn't finish his sentence. Looking ahead, he tugged sharply on Baudwin's sleeve. "Over there — what's that?"

"I don't know."

Slowly, they made their way down the path through the oaks to a large area, overgrown with vines. And there, sitting atop a stone edifice was their slippery friend, the bluethroat. Baudwin's button was still in its beak. The bird studied them as they approached.

Before Baudwin could again rail at the bird, he stopped, completely forgetting his pursuit. From where he stood, he could see that the vines hid many more structures beneath them. A strange feeling overcame him, raising the hairs on the back of his neck. Something was in there for sure. What were they about to uncover?

"What *is* this place?" Baudwin gasped, taking in its look and feel as best he could.

"We'll find out only if we keep exploring," Matha replied.

In a flash of blue feathers, the bluethroat swooped down and dropped the button on Baudwin's head. As soon as the two Faeries got over their astonishment, they let loose with peals of laughter. "Looks like your thief wasn't one after all," Matha said.

Happily, Baudwin picked up his button, and they then gamely began to investigate their surroundings. The ruins formed a square. On each side were three oval granite entrances. Fieldstones placed between the ovals formed low, but level connecting walls.

After pushing through a mass of roots and vines, Baudwin and Matha stepped through an oval into the inner sanctum of the edifice. Breathing heavily, the Faeries paused to take in their surroundings. The scent of water lilies and honeysuckle enveloped them, as did the sound of Water spilling over rocks and logs.

"I've never before felt such sacred stirrings," Baudwin murmured in awe. "This must be an ancient shrine, where Faeries came for healing and renewal."

Matha stood beside his friend, enthralled. "I remember an old faery elder telling me about some ancient ruins near the Springs of Coventina," he said. "I looked for them many times, but could never find them. This must be the place."

"That bluethroat must have guided us here," Baudwin replied. "But what is the Water trying to tell us? I shouldn't have been so cross with that bird," he added, chastened. For he knew that in letting his anger get the better of him, he had forgotten the old ways — and that a bluethroat was often a messenger of the Water.

The two Faeries made their way toward the shrine, being careful not to disturb the path they walked upon. In the center of the sanctum sat a stone well, surrounded by twelve rings of seats. Four aisles, precisely crafted in both form and beauty, divided the twelve rings into quarters. Eyeing the seats from a distance, Baudwin remarked, "They seem to be made of clear white quartz. But what are they?"

Matha hurried to a seat in one quarter of the circle. Running his hands over its polished contours, he let out a peal of laughter. "Crocuses!" he announced. "Spring crocuses, large enough for you and me to sit inside, with petals full and smooth as glass."

As Baudwin went to look at them, he imagined how they might appear if they were yellow or violet. He then darted to the quarter of the circle to the right of the crocuses. "These are summer roses!" he exclaimed, laughing so hard he nearly fell over.

Seeing this, Matha raced around the circle to a seat opposite the crocuses. "These are fall acorn shells from the water oak, with leaves to rest my back against," he chortled, whereupon he jumped into an open shell.

Baudwin raced to a seat opposite the roses. "And what is left?" he asked as he sat down. "Winter holly leaves, so we may sit and rest upon this seat with ease." With that, he leaned his head against a large holly leaf. Lightly, he draped his arm on a leaf to his left, and his other arm on a leaf to his right.

The Faeries grew still. The late afternoon Sun cast ethereal Light upon their surroundings, quieting them gently from within. And there they sat, without speaking.

Matha broke the silence. "Why would the Elves of Silver Forge help water Faeries build such a place?"

Baudwin responded with a simple observation. "Perhaps for the special times when the seasons change — Ostara, Litha, Mabon, and Yule."

Baudwin sighed. So little was known about their history, and places like this contradicted what little they did remember. There were other puzzling shrines in Deuona, and this was not the first time they had stumbled upon such a mystery. All around them were fading reminders of what they didn't understand, and that most seemed happy to completely ignore. Even Matha, who took an interest in such things, seemed, at times, all too willing to discount his own discoveries.

"Perhaps you're right," Matha agreed. "But, all the Fae seem to have forgotten. Now, only the land remembers."

"My grandfather remembers things," Baudwin remarked. "He still believes there's wisdom in the old ways."

"Did he tell you to come to Coventina to find your mother?" Matha asked.

"Yes, he did," Baudwin replied sadly. "And I wish I had better news for him."

"I'm sorry, Baudwin. . ." Matha said, his voice trailing off.

Both went silent. As old friends, they could tell when there was nothing more to say, and they both knew why.

Not only was Baudwin longing to find his mother, he was also grieving for what she should have given him. Sitting quietly with Matha, his memories bubbled up inside of him. He remembered being a young faery lad of seventy, about to attend the Ceremony of the Joining. Baudwin had been excited, for his grandfather had told him that this ceremony was his first rite of passage. If he joined with his current, he would find his feelings, preparing him to one day fully understand them.

On that day, he went down to the banks of River Deuona. All the faery lads and lassies his age were there, including Matha. His own mother couldn't be with him, so he had gone with Matha's mother, Brigh.[3] She had been very kind to him that day, telling him she was certain he would join with his current. Holding her hand, he skipped down the path to the river.

The mothers stood by the shore as their little ones played in the Water, awaiting their turns. Brigh called for Matha first, and he went to her. She filled a crystal cup, and Matha closed his eyes. Cradling his neck, she poured Water over his head, and whispered into his ear; old sayings of the Water — words that only mothers knew, and young ones would always remember in their hearts.

As the Water flowed down his face, Matha's senses awakened. He raised his arms, his hands fluttered, and his whole body began to tremble. Dropping his arms, he became very still, waiting for what would come next. The Water was certainly flowing through him. Baudwin sensed that his friend could see, hear, taste, touch and smell much more of his element than he ever had before.

This was no ordinary waking. Baudwin knew this one was special, for he could tell that Matha was now joined with his current. As he grew up, he would be guided in Life by finding his feelings. Baudwin was happy for his friend. He knew Matha would always be joined with his current, through calm and rushing Water, until he passed to Annwyn.

As the Water ran off of Matha and back into the river, he opened his eyes, crying out with joy. He jumped back into the Water, cavorting in circles like a river otter. Baudwin could barely wait to be next, for how he had dreamed of joining with his current.

Brigh called to him, and just as Matha had done, he went to the shore and closed his eyes. She filled the cup and poured the Water over his head. As she did, she whispered, "The rapids are not the shallows, and the shallows are not the rapids — let neither rule you — a steady heart will always carry you through."

Baudwin waited, and like Matha, his senses awakened. Yet, he knew something was wrong. He didn't feel joined with his current — for although he could sense the Water flowing outside of him, he did not feel a change inside. His current was still unknown to him.

As he opened his eyes, he saw a look of concern pass over Brigh's face, yet, she did not speak. "The joining is complete," she simply said as she cupped her hands over her heart and made a sign of the Water. But her words were heavy with an anguish she could barely conceal.

____

[3]   Pronounced [BREE]

The time had come for the mothers to take their young ones to different spots along the river to celebrate — for they had joined with their currents. "Come, Matha. Come, Baudwin," she called.

Matha ran to her, but Baudwin remained alone on the shore, refusing to go. Brigh nodded at him as if to say, "You must come with us."

Baudwin crossed his arms in front of him and hung his head. Tears welled in his eyes. "I have no current to swim in," he blurted. "I will *never* find my feelings!"

And so it was that Baudwin never finished the ceremony. His feelings did not flow, and he could not hear the guidance of his element. Instead of a steady heart, all he knew was loneliness and confusion, always wondering who he could have been. Years later, he learned that Brigh, out of kindness, had tried to help him find his current. For if a young one's mother was absent, another faery lady could serve to join that one to their current. But for some reason that none understood, the ceremony did not join Baudwin to the Water.

Seamus, his grandfather, and Kelven, his father, argued endlessly about why this was so. For after Baudwin had sprung from the aethers, his mother had said this to them: "Should I for any reason not be here for his joining, do not take from this that the lad is doomed. I see a great future for him." Hearing this, Seamus insisted that Baudwin's Fate was yet to be decided. But Kelven believed this could not be true — how could there be a great future for one not joined to his current?

Attempting to settle the matter, they asked Brigh if she would try to join Baudwin once again. She refused, saying that the Water knew better, and that they had to wait to see what Fate had in store for him. Not to mention that if Baudwin was again put through such a failure, he might not be able to bear the disappointment.

Years passed, and when nothing changed, Baudwin became despondent. With a heavy heart, Kelven told him he was likely to remain without his current for the rest of his Life. He would have wakings, but he would never be guided by the Water to better understand his feelings.

Baudwin's problems only worsened as he grew older. At the age of one and forty, he was to attend a second rite of passage with his father — the Ceremony of the Coursing. This would teach him to further understand his feelings, so he could know himself, and in doing so, discover his true intention in Life. Only then would he begin to embrace his destiny. If he did not, he would be rudderless, unable to be guided by the wisdom of his element. Through rapid streams and shallow calm, he would remain forever adrift.

And so he did not attend the ceremony. Instead, he grew even more despondent, and for the next sixty years, he retreated to his room, playing with his toys. Fearing for the well-being of his grandson, Seamus offered him hope.

"Forget about joining with your current," he advised. "And forget about coursing with your feelings. If you simply hone your intention with patience and perseverance — the Water will find you."

Baudwin was perplexed and confused. The third rite of passage — the Ceremony of the Honing — was an endeavor that many undertook but few mastered. In this ceremony, Faeries learned that honing their intentions meant adapting their wills to the ways of Water, so they could flow into whatever forms their destinies required. However, as the ages passed, this had become more and more difficult. In Baudwin's time, few if any of the Faeries ever became fully at one with their element. Most attended the ceremonies, but achieved nothing, leaving their intentions essentially undeveloped. Instead they chose to pursue their work and the simple pleasures of Life.

Honing one's intention was daunting for any Faery, and Baudwin hadn't even succeeded with the first two rites of passage — to join with his current and course with his feelings. As far as he knew, what Seamus was asking him to do was impossible. He couldn't hone his intention, because he had no idea what his intention was. "I don't know what you mean," Baudwin had said. "You're telling me to put the cart before the grand horn."

To which Seamus had replied, "You don't *need* to know. Your intention must simply be to find the Water — or rather, for the Water to find you," he added with a wink. For Seamus knew that according to the old ways, the Water would never abandon a Faery whose intention was pure.

Baudwin could hardly believe that Seamus was telling him to do this. The third rite of passage was difficult enough to master, but the Water coming to a Faery was unheard of — something many regarded as merely legend. And if anyone were to have the Water come to them, Baudwin certainly wasn't prepared. Seamus's instructions were like asking a salmon to head out to sea and then come back and jump the falls, before so much as hatching from its egg.

Baudwin languished for a time, for he did not believe the Water could come to him, but Seamus would not allow him to give up. "If you do what I say," he added, "not only will the Water find you — but you might also find your mother. For all the voices in our tribe are carried in its currents."

And so it was that Baudwin had struggled for years, eventually succeeding at the Springs of Coventina. Afterward, he couldn't help but wonder if any of the Faeries in Deuona would believe that the Water had come to him — and in such a way that had contradicted their traditions entirely.

Sitting upon his crystal holly leaf, Baudwin snapped out of his reverie. He looked again at Matha. *Does he even believe me?* On top of the impossible, another impossible had happened. The Water had come to a Faery not joined to his current.

Still, Baudwin found himself where he was now — excited, but unsure about who would believe him. The Water had come to him, but had also left him with more questions than answers. Although he had found the Water, the Water had not joined him with its current *or* his mother, and afterward, he had even suffered a bout. He had expected that all his problems would be solved, but instead, here he was, sitting with his friend in an ancient ruin, and he wasn't even sure why.

Frustrated, his thoughts turned again to his mother. "My Life without her has been one of constant sorrow and uncertainty. My father always treated me as if the Water had somehow cursed me. Without my grandfather's kind words, I'd have had nothing to keep my spirits going." Shaking his head, he declared, "She hasn't passed to Annwyn. I know it! I just have to keep looking."

"You're right," Matha replied. "I'm glad you haven't given up hope. Certainly, that bluethroat led us here to show us what mysteries this place may hold."

Baudwin nodded. "If it was the Water that had the bluethroat guide us here, then we must take a better look around."

๛

Thus resolved, the Faeries made their way down the aisle to the center of the shrine to look more closely at the well. The masonry was of deep green Connemara marble, with eight stone pillars rising from the rim that supported a bowl-shaped vault. Together they leaned forward, peering inside. A soft blue-green Light emanated from the bubbling Water below — striking a chord within their faery hearts, one that brought them very close to their element.

They might have pondered the mysterious luminance more, but their interest quickly shifted. A dazzling new sight lay before them.

"Thousands of offerings!" Baudwin gasped. As the two Faeries leaned even farther into the well, they saw a pile of treasure bulging out of the Water. Myriad pieces of blue topaz, pearls, shards of green quartz and gold sparkled in the Light.

"I've never seen so many shades of blue and green," Baudwin marveled. "How they shimmer and sparkle in the Water!"

"Water Faeries must have come here for thousands, perhaps tens of thousands of years," Matha observed.

"Bringing their offerings, and making their wishes, I would say. But will *mine* ever be granted?" Pulling a small blue crystal from his pocket, Baudwin threw the stone on top of the glittering pile of gems. Hearing a tinkling sound, he stepped away from the well.

Matha lowered his gaze to study the base of the well. "This is rather baffling," he remarked, examining the seamless placement of the stones.

"What do you see?"

"I don't know yet," Matha replied as he circled the well. "The stones in the masonry were placed here so precisely. The walls in Deuona are built quite roughly in comparison." Bending down, he examined the base more closely.

"This shrine is perplexing. . ." Leaning over the rim of the well, he craned his neck to better see the interior of the vault. Above him, in the center, was a very large sphere made of yellow topaz.

"First," Matha began, "do you see that?"

Baudwin leaned in for a better view of the vault. "Yes," he replied. "What a fine treasure that sphere must have been — in its day. Do you see that enormous crack?"

"Of course," Matha replied. "But never mind that. What else do you see?"

Baudwin looked about. He was not always as perceptive as his friend, and Matha chuckled as he watched him peer about like a mole in a tunnel, somehow missing the obvious. Playfully, he gave Baudwin a hint. "Look at the inside of the vault, and then again at the base of the well."

Baudwin did so, but seemed unsure about what he had just seen. "Wait," he began. "I think I see what looks like sun rays and water droplets etched into the stone," he added, circling the well. "In fact, they go all the way around." He then peered inside of the vault again. "I see them in here too."

"Precisely." Matha stepped a few feet back to take in the entire structure. "The question is, what is a symbol of the Sun doing in a *water* faery shrine — one that looks like it was built by the Elves of Silver Forge?"

"That *is* the question, isn't it?" Baudwin replied. "How curious."

Baudwin knew that rarely, if ever, were these symbols seen next to each other. Water Faeries would never place the Sun next to a water symbol in a shrine such as this. Instead, they always set the Moon next to their element, for they adored the Moon, just as the Elves adored the Sun. In Baudwin's home a Moon crafted into stained glass loomed over the family shrine, and he knew that in every elven home somewhere there was a Sun crafted from a metal.

When Baudwin was young, Seamus had explained that both the Sun and the Moon were cherished by the Fae, but each in different ways. For the Elves, he had said, were the champions of *Tír na nÓg*, basking in the splendor of the Sun as they cleaved cords for the knot of eternity. And the Faeries were the dancers of *Tír na nÓg*, frolicking in the aura of the Moon, as they wove those cords into the knot of eternity. Thus was the unending mystery of Life created — by and for all.

But the mystery of the shrine contradicted the unending mystery of Life, and Baudwin had to know why. "You know as well as I do that this doesn't make any sense. I'm counting on you to figure it out."

"I really don't know," Matha replied. "But I can tell you — in all my years of talking to faery elders, I've never heard of such a thing. "

"Perhaps there's a clue here," Baudwin said, studying the puzzled look on his friend's face. "What else do you see?"

"Something quite intriguing," Matha replied, as he pointed to carvings at the base of the well. Interlocking circles, like links in a chain, were etched into the bottom. Each circle contained a glyph — first faery, and then elven, all the way around.

"The symbols would appear to suggest that both Faeries and Elves were somehow cooperating here, but I can't be sure," Matha continued.

"That means they must have joined together," Baudwin replied, "and even danced in faery rings."

"Since when would Elves be interested in faery rings?" Matha retorted. "All I know is that this ruin shouldn't be here. Never have I —"

But before Matha could finish his thought, he realized something even more important. "The boulders," he mused, his eyes widening. "Of course — the Faeries and Elves *had* to have been cooperating."

Baudwin waited for his friend to continue.

"The symbols on the boulders we passed leading to this shrine were the first clue. Remember? We saw a faery lady with the Moon and a water droplet, and across from her, an elven gent with the Sun and the hammer of Silver Forge. At first I wasn't sure what that meant, but their greeting contained a theme that is repeated here — one of cooperation. For you see, the final clue is the interlocking glyphs — both elven and faery — again indicating cooperation," Matha said, gesturing to the well.

"How could that have been?" Baudwin asked. "Today we can barely agree on where to build a simple windmill."

Matha chuckled.

"And why is there a Sun and no Moon?" Baudwin asked, perplexed.

Matha closed his eyes, concentrating even harder. "Why indeed?" he asked. "That's what makes this so unusual," he added, opening his eyes. "We water Faeries do not revere the Sun — we revere the Moon. Unless," he began, his eyes bright with excitement, "the Faeries and Elves weren't simply cooperating to build this place, but *communing* with each other by doing some kind of sun and water ritual."

Exchanging perplexed glances, neither knew how this could be. Elves seemed to have little interest in any of the elements. Always they forged their metals and stared at their clocks, tempering their efforts and measuring their lives. Never did they seek the truth of the Water, or wonder if the Moon spoke to them. But here — plain as day — was evidence to the contrary.

Baudwin gazed at the shrine. He wondered what kind of Faery would have allowed an Elve to place a Sun above a spring honoring the Water. Only one who felt great respect from such an Elve, he realized.

"We may never know for certain what their purpose was, but perhaps," he added, amazed, "they simply knew how they could benefit from cooperating with one another."

Matha nodded, smiling.

Baudwin looked into the Light of the well. Down many feet the pile of offerings was ringed with glowing blue-green Water. "One thing I do know," he said, his face brightening with hope. "You were right. All of these offerings can mean only one thing. Faeries, and perhaps even Elves, have been making their wishes here for thousands of years, so I've come to the right place."

"A very special kind of place," Matha mused. "I feel a presence here that I've never known before."

"The same one I felt when the Water came to me," Baudwin added.

"Yes, a presence that may reveal something we have yet to discover," Matha said.

Baudwin looked at the stones beneath his feet, wondering how many seasons had passed since anyone had tread on them. *What else is here?*

Matha continued to circle the base of the well, and then his eyebrows shot up. He stopped. Carefully he scrutinized the wall, kneeling in closer.

"Baudwin," he said, "you may just get your wish. We missed something."

Matha pointed to an arch-shaped niche with a scalloped top, set into the masonry of the well.

"There," he said, as he pointed to a small tablet made of blue-green agate. Looking closely, they saw glyphs etched into the center.

"Can you read them?" Baudwin asked, peering anxiously over his friend's shoulder.

"Easily," Matha replied. He then recited:

> You may wish for many things
> Or never want for much
> But that which holds the Truth you seek
> Is something you must touch

"Well," Baudwin announced, brightly, "I already gave an offering to the well, and *now* I wish to find my mother." He reached for the tablet.

"No, Baudwin!" Matha cried.

Baudwin looked at his friend, shocked. "What do you mean? I shouldn't find her?"

"No, not that," Matha replied. "You must not touch the tablet."

"Why?" Baudwin asked, angrily.

"The tablet is too special to be touched," Matha said. "Of that, I'm quite certain."

Baudwin pulled his hand away. "Well, at *least* tell me what it means."

Matha began to investigate further, but quickly stopped himself. He was worried that Baudwin would get even angrier. Everything was moving far too quickly, and the last thing his friend needed was another reason to get upset. He decided to measure his words.

"I can't say," Matha replied. "It's just a poem, Baudwin. If I were you, I wouldn't place too much meaning on the words."

"How could I *not*?" Baudwin asked, annoyed. "After that bluethroat guided us here — and we found the well — and now this?"

"Perhaps, but —"

"I wish to find out about my mother," Baudwin broke in. "If this tablet holds the truth, then why *wouldn't* I touch it?"

Determined, Matha continued to study the tablet. He knew that not being joined to his element made listening to reason harder for Baudwin. Slowly he spoke, "This symbol is your clue. Below the poem is another glyph, far more ancient-looking."

Both of them studied the glyph — two side-by-side spirals making an *S* shape, with a line beginning in the center of one and ending in the center of the other.

"Can you read it?" Baudwin asked.

"No," Matha replied, both irritated and puzzled.

"What is it that I must touch?" Baudwin asked, agitated, remembering the poem.

"Baudwin, you must stay calm," Matha said. "If I am to figure this out, I need to —"

"Matha," Baudwin interrupted, speaking in a low whisper. "Did you hear that?"

In the bushes nearby, a figure crept toward them, determined to interrupt their search. The skulking shape had followed them as they chased the bluethroat, and now lurked behind a stone pillar near the shrine, watching them. Others too crouched with the figure — hiding among the ruins — waiting. They had not come for wisdom, for they had seen the carvings on the boulders, and disregarded them with contempt. Ancient wonders held no importance for them.

Matha kept looking at the tablet. "Hear what?" he asked.

"I thought I heard a rustling."

"No one could be here," Matha said as he studied the tablet even more closely. "Be calm — no one knows where this place is."

The figure was directly behind them now, stepping soundlessly closer and closer, taking pleasure in their vulnerability. The moment had come to strike.

Suddenly, a hand grabbed Baudwin by the shoulder.

"Hey!" Baudwin yelled, as he tried to wrest his way out of the grasp. "Let go!"

"Easy, Baudwin," a deep voice commanded, chuckling. "Didn't you hear what Matha said? Be calm."

Breaking free, Baudwin faced a pair of coldly determined eyes, and a wide, malevolent grin; these features he knew quite well, but always dreaded seeing.

"Loch[4]!" he exclaimed, masking his unease. "What brings you here? How did you find us?"

"Finding you was easy," Loch replied, motioning to his gang standing behind him. "We were out looking for fallen grand horns. You leave bigger tracks than they do," he added, sneering.

"Why did you bother?" Baudwin asked. Nervously, he faced Loch, who stood half a head taller than he, wondering how long the Roiler leader had been spying on them. Baudwin could hardly remember a time when Loch and his gang hadn't tried to sabotage his every move. Season after season, their currents collided, fueled by a growing rift among the Fae of the Water. As was the custom, an elder would mediate their differences. But now, in these abandoned ruins, there would be no such one to separate them.

"Perhaps we were simply curious about where you were going," Loch replied, as he swaggered to the well.

"When do you ever do anything out of simple curiosity?" Baudwin asked.

"Perhaps then," Loch continued, as he looked at his gang, "all we wanted was to take a stroll through the Springs of Coventina. We all could use some healing, don't you think?" he added sarcastically. "Now that the Elves have come to town, we must renew ourselves and band together in the Water Guild. Would you agree, Baudwin? Are you ready to band?"

"Hardly — I would never band with a bunch of Roilers like you," Baudwin replied, his anger rising.

"Nor we with Guilders!" one of Loch's gang shot back.

"Tell us, Baudwin, why did you come here?" Loch asked.

"He doesn't owe you an explanation," Matha chided. Pulling Baudwin aside, he whispered, "Do *not* speak to him about the Water."

Hearing this, Baudwin wondered how long the Roilers had been tracking them, and whether or not they had heard him tell Matha about how the Water had come to him. The possibility filled him with dread. Staring at Loch, he tried to determine his intention, yet there was no clue beneath his steely gaze.

"Whisper all you want — I already know everything," Loch said, gesturing at the shrine. "The walls here are echoing your secrets. You're here to find your mother. Poor Baudwin. Are you still looking for her? Howling like a piteous whelp in the Woods?"

Quietly, Baudwin let out a sigh, for Loch didn't seem to know about the Water coming to him. He was just up to his usual bullying and hoping to goad

---

[4] Pronounced [LOCK]

him and Matha into a fight. To make matters worse, in his zeal to start a brawl, Loch had abandoned all deference for *gnás.*[5]

"You're the one who'll howl," Baudwin countered, "if you don't show some respect."

"Why should I respect a *liar* like you?" Loch bellowed.

Baudwin flinched. "What are you talking about?" he asked.

"You lie! The Water didn't come to you. You're not even joined to your current."

Loch fixed his eyes upon Baudwin, staring him down. Shaken, Baudwin realized the Roiler must have heard every word he had spoken to Matha about the Water.

"He's not lying!" Matha shouted back.

"He never joined *or* coursed!" Loch bellowed. It's impossible." He then stepped away from Baudwin, eyeing him up and down, examining him from every side. "Looking for the Water has finally driven him crazy!" he howled gleefully. The others joined in the fun, grinning like a pack of malicious wolves, their laughter cruel and biting.

Ignoring them all, Baudwin wondered if he should try to be honest with Loch, or just let him believe he was a liar. How much easier the latter would be, but then Loch spoke again.

"Never joined to his current — but the Water came to him anyway!" he mocked. "How desperate he must be to make up such a story!" Turning to his fellow Roilers, he added, "I guess we shouldn't be so hard on him, should we?"

Derisively, the Roilers laughed again, but Baudwin had had enough.

"I'm no liar!" he shouted. "And at least I never gave up on what mattered to me. Unlike the rest of you cowards."

"Coward, am I?" Loch shouted back, raising his fists. "Then let's have at it. We'll see who the *real* coward is."

Yet, as Loch was about to discover, the fight he wanted with Baudwin was not the fight that would be.

"What's wrong with you?" Baudwin shouted. "This shrine isn't a place for you to start one of your lowdown quarrels. We must heed the rules of concord. I will not fight you here!"

"This place, this place." Loch fired back, strutting about. "What's so special here? The old ways are gone. Stop looking for your mother in a shrine — or better yet, stop reading *glyphs* to find her."

"If you were *truly* a water Faery," you would respect the Water and the old ways," Baudwin declared.

---

[5] Pronounced [GRAHSS] tradition custom or norm

"I'll show you some respect," Loch snorted, striding to the niche.

As he reached for the tablet, his large hands clumsily gripped the sides.

"You must not touch objects deemed sacred by the Water Guild!" Baudwin shouted.

Loch handed the tablet to his gang. Quickly, they lay the relic on the ground, holding it firmly.

"What are you doing?" Matha cried out. He and Baudwin moved toward Loch, but his gang shoved them back.

"*This* is what it means to be a water Faery *now*," Loch declared triumphantly.

He opened his jacket and pulled out a bronze hammer. With one swift move, he raised his arm above his head, and then down. The hammer struck, smashing the tablet into pieces. Thousands of years of history gone in an instant.

"No!" Baudwin shrieked.

"Defilers!" Matha shouted.

"Why do you think I do this?" Loch demanded. "I do this for *you* and *you*," he continued, pointing to each of them. "One day, instead of judging me for this, you will thank me."

"*Never* will we thank you for this!" Baudwin shrieked, as he staggered several paces away from the well. Devastated, he looked at the shattered pieces of the tablet. *Had the Water willed this as well?* If so, he wondered what lesson this could serve. But before he could consider this further, he felt another feeling well up inside him — guilt. After all, it was he who had led Loch here, and as a member of the Water Guild, he had failed to protect the shrine. Greatly outnumbered, however, there was little he could do, so he motioned to Matha and turned to leave.

As they tried to move down the aisle, Loch blocked their way. "Have you not been listening? There is no truth in the Water anymore."

"There will *always* be truth in the old ways," Baudwin declared.

"You Guilders are such fools," Loch bellowed. "The only guidance you'll be getting today are my fists in your face!"

"Let us pass!" Matha shouted.

"No!" the Roilers roared back.

All at once they raised their arms as Guilders and Roilers eyed one another, brandishing their fists, sizing up their options. Out broke a scuffle, both sides meting out punches and kicks with a vengeance. One of Loch's friends tripped Matha, and the other pummeled him on the back. Loch went after Baudwin, shouting, "If you won't look to the future, then look to this!" Revolted, all Baudwin could do was defend himself.

Furiously, they fought, one side unable to retreat, the other unwilling to end the assault. Nothing could quash the ugliness they visited upon the sanctum, violating its serenity.

Until — *boom!* So distracted were they amidst all the ruckus that they did not pay heed to the noise, or feel the tremors stirring under their feet, or the ones that followed, which seemed to be coming from somewhere beneath the shrine. Blindly, they fought on.

Yet, the force below would not be ignored.

Then came another blast, this one louder. And then another, the sound reverberating from the center of the edifice through every plant, rock and crystal carving. They now felt as if they were standing on a rope bridge in a windstorm.

Suddenly they stopped — their bodies frozen like statues made of mountain ice, their fight forgotten. They would have been lucky beyond measure had the ruins stayed as still as their bodies, but this was not to be. A series of tremors struck again, far longer and louder, tremors so powerful that they seemed to have originated from the roots of the Tadlachs themselves.

In sync with the shuddering Earth, Water rose from the center of the well, filling the basin and cascading over the rim. Seeing this, Baudwin and Matha turned to flee.

"Ha!" Loch taunted. "Running away are you? Water Faeries afraid of a little Water?"

Just then, an enormous gusher blasted from the well, flooding the floor of the sanctum and the rows of crystal seats; from there, the Water rushed out of the oval entrances and spilled into the Woods.

Panic ensued.

"Matha, we must *not* fight the Water," Baudwin ordered as he lost his footing and fell into the current. He was then swept away, disappearing beneath the flow.

"Baudwin!" Matha cried.

Loch and his friends were also swept along by the surging Water. A whirlpool formed. Round and round they went, desperately grabbing at whatever came their way as they shot over seats and down the aisles. The force of the Water was about to cast them out of the shrine. Loch held fast to a crystal rose seat to keep from crashing into a stone wall.

Matha swept past Loch, barely able to keep his head above the Water. For a moment he clung to a crystal acorn seat, but then lost his purchase. The current was so strong that if he hit the wall, he knew his bones would shatter.

Still clinging to the crystal rose, Loch saw that Matha was about to hit the wall. Forgoing his animosity, he grabbed the Guilder, who, for a moment, was no longer his enemy but simply a member of his tribe. Grasping him by the collar, he gloated, "You see? The Water can't protect you, but *I* can."

But the reprieve was short-lived, for another deluge burst from the well. With that, Loch lost his hold, both upon the crystal rose and Matha. Away they went, along with the others, shooting through the portals, past the roots and vines. Tumbling and twisting head over heels, not even the Fae of the Water, so accustomed to the ways of their element, could right themselves. All believed they were doomed.

Yet, Fate was not through with them, for they still had more cords to weave into the knot of eternity.

Mercifully — just as they were ejected from the shrine — the flow subsided. The ordeal was over. There they lay upon the ground, waterlogged and wasted — scattered about like rotting twigs.

❧

Matha lifted his head from the ground. "Baudwin," he called. "Where are you? Please answer me!" Jumping to his feet and shaking the Water from his clothes, Matha searched for signs of his friend — around boulders and trees, past tufts of tall grass, and in the bushes. He saw none. "Baudwin!"

"Over here," a voice replied. Rushing to the source of the sound, Matha found Baudwin sitting on the ground, looking spent yet secure in his skin, his leg lodged between two large rocks.

"At least this time, I find you faceup," Matha joked, hoping to lighten the mood.

"Help me get out," Baudwin said, happy to see that his friend was unscathed. "As I was flailing in those currents, my leg got stuck."

Quickly, Matha grabbed a fallen branch and used it as a lever to dislodge the rock trapping his friend's leg. He jammed the branch under the large stone, and slowly lifted.

Anxious for his freedom, Baudwin tried to pull his leg out from between the rocks.

"Not yet," Matha warned as he struggled to keep the rock from rolling. "Or you'll —"

"What if the branch breaks?" Baudwin cut in.

"Don't worry, I'm far more clever than you may think," Matha teased, hoping to distract Baudwin from his worry. "I do, after all, understand how leverage and gravity work."

Working the branch between the two rocks, Matha took care not to injure his friend. He kept twisting and lifting until one of the rocks finally moved, creating just enough space for Baudwin to free his leg.

Up Baudwin jumped, surprisingly fast for one laid so low. After checking his ankle, he exclaimed brightly, "Except for a few scrapes and the fact that we barely escaped with our lives, no harm appears to have been done."

"*Barely*," Matha said, as he dropped to his knees, exhausted. "I suppose we should thank the Water that we made our way out."

Baudwin grasped Matha under his arms and pulled him to his feet. "The Water *indeed*," he said, grinning mysteriously. "Not only were we saved from the flood, but the Water also protected us from Loch and his rotten Roilers." Looking about, he added, "Where are they? What do you suppose happened to them?"

Quickly, they looked to and fro. Nowhere did they see any sign of Loch or the rest of the Roilers.

Matha thought about what Baudwin had just said. "What do you mean by *saved*?" he asked.

"Don't you see what just happened?" Baudwin continued, enthusiastically. "Loch must have upset the Water, and so the deluge came upon us. We were in danger, the shrine was in danger, and then the Water showed us mercy. We —"

"I don't know about that, Baudwin," Matha cut in. "I think what happened was simply a gusher, not some special act of the Water. They happen all the time."

"Gushers like that don't just happen in a shrine," Baudwin insisted. "Not to mention coming *just* as we all happened to be fighting. What timing. You said we should thank the Water — well, we should."

"Maybe so — maybe not," Matha interrupted again.

Baudwin sighed. "Oh, forget it — it's not like you'll listen to me anyway." Looking at the ground, he added, "The evening shadows are upon us. We must hurry home now, or risk having to find our way in the Dark."

"Aren't you at least grateful that the Water didn't send us to Annwyn?" Baudwin asked impishly, winking at Matha.

"Of course I am," Matha replied, conflicted. "I'm just not as ready as you to proclaim that the Water almost drowned us, just to save us."

With that, they made their way to the main path. Soon they were racing home, each one trying to outrun the other, being careful not to trip as the setting Sun cast ever deeper shadows upon the ground. Through Woods and fields they looked, but nowhere did they see any sign of Loch and his gang. Baudwin assumed that the Water had swept them away to some far corner of the forest, while Matha argued that they had probably chosen another path home. As they reached the outskirts of Deuona, they settled into a more leisurely pace.

Slowing his stride, Baudwin began to fume. The slower he walked, the more upset he became.

"The tablet is lost!" he said, shaking his fists. "And all thanks to Loch, and his miserable cohorts."

Matha placed his hand on Baudwin's shoulder. "We don't know if the tablet —"

Baudwin shot a cease-and-desist glance at Matha, wanting none of his friend's even-tempered talk.

"Now, I'll never find out what that glyph meant," he said. Perhaps it contained wisdom that would have led me to her."

"Whether there was or there wasn't, you must not let your anger get the better of you," Matha said. "If you do, you'll find yourself at Loch's level, in a dark place where you definitely do not want to be."

Ignoring Matha's advice, Baudwin continued to rage. "How dare he challenge me for looking for her? How dare he call me a liar? How *dare* he call himself a water Faery — what respect does *he* have for the Water? He looks down on me for not being joined, but he's the one who chooses not to try to find and understand his feelings. Instead, he turns his back on the Water. It's all so unfair! I struggle every day, but he could be a better water Faery if he wanted to be. If he were here right now, I would —"

"To defeat Loch, you must not let him draw you into the mouth of his aggression — you will be devoured," Matha instructed.

"I *will* defeat him," Baudwin said, as they approached the road to his house. "You'll see!"

"Your feelings whirl so fiercely!" Matha exclaimed. "Let your current calm you —"

Matha stopped, realizing what he had just said. Of course his friend could do no such thing. Not being joined to his current, Baudwin got riled up more easily than anyone he knew — including Loch. He simply could not find his calm as easily as most.

Matha looked at his friend, worried that his comment had upset him, but Baudwin had been too angry to notice. He placed his hand upon Baudwin's shoulder. They both stopped walking.

"Yes, he's a bullying tyrant," Matha began, "but he did save my Life."

"Oh yeah? How?" Baudwin asked.

"At the ruins he could have let me go crashing into the wall," Matha replied, "but he reached out and grabbed me instead."

"Only so he could lord his great skill over you," Baudwin retorted.

"Perhaps," Matha replied. "He does harbor the anger of a poisonous boar, but also the heart of a mother bear protecting her cubs, and he still hasn't decided which part should express his soul. As long as you see that, I say he can't really hurt you."

"He smashes sacred relics. I say he *has* decided."

"Yes, but *why?*"

"Who cares? Right now, I would like to smash his face!"

"And is that the part that expresses *your* soul?" Matha chided.

"Are you defending him?"

"No. All I'm saying is that we may not know all there is to know about him."

"Oh, we know enough," Baudwin said disgustedly. "He's the one who made the divide in our tribe so terrible."

"Baaaaaudwin, you must not lose your huuuuumor," Matha sang playfully, as he reached into his jacket pocket. "Perhaps this will cheer you up."

Matha opened his hand. A piece of blue-green agate rested in his palm. In the center was the glyph that had appeared below the poem on the tablet Loch had smashed.

"The glyph!" Baudwin exclaimed. "Why didn't you tell me?"

"In all the treachery and dire circumstances, there was no time."

"Ah, but what does it matter?" Baudwin rejoiced. "For this, I truly do thank you!"

Presently, they arrived at Baudwin's house.

"Be sure to show it to Seamus," Matha said, smiling.

"This day is over, Matha," Baudwin said. "We must now part until tomorrow."

"Yes, and what a day this has been," Matha replied.

"As you so kindly left me with this," Baudwin said, looking at the piece of agate, "I must leave you with something as well."

"And what might that be?"

"Perhaps the Water *did* save us," Baudwin began. "And this is how I know."

Matha listened with rapt attention as Baudwin spoke, explaining that if the shaking of the ground had been the result of a random gusher, they would have seen shards of topaz and quartz as well as pearls and pieces of gold strewn all over the sanctum and outside on the ground. Matha wasn't sure he believed him.

"Think about what I am saying — there were none! Not a single one."

"How can you be sure?" Matha asked.

"I noticed that as the Water flowed, *none* of those things were in evidence. Nothing swirled with us."

Seeing the look of surprise on Matha's face, he continued, "Not one offering was disturbed! Only the Water could have left such treasures untouched — so the Water must have saved *us* as well."

Baffled, Matha admitted, "I guess I was too overwhelmed to notice."

"Ha!" Baudwin cried, slapping his friend soundly on his back. "Perhaps you're not the *only* one who thinks deeply about things." He then turned and entered his home, leaving his friend to ponder this fascinating notion by the Light of the rising Moon.

Chapter 3

DREAMS OF THE WATER

B audwin slept soundly in his room that night, as his adventures from the previous day had left him utterly spent. He dreamed of voices speaking to him from the Water and ruins in faraway places. Gear-like leaves on oak trees turned into symbols he did not understand. He watched them dissolve between his fingers, streaking into mist. His visions then became even harder to hold on to, until he saw almost nothing. All he heard was a soft hum vibrating through dreary clouds that looked like melted half-forgotten shapes. The dullness he felt drained him, until he could barely move. *What must I do to find my feelings?* he wondered.

A clue came to him in another dream.

As he had the day before at the Springs of Coventina, he saw his dream-self. This time his dream-self was asleep in his very own bed — a mattress set into an oval-shaped frame made of polished oak. The frame was carved in the shape of a canal, lined with blue and green tiles, and filled with scented Water. In his dream, the Water in the frame began to stir, cycling around his dream-self.

He then heard someone speak to him.

"I call to you," the female voice said. "Do you hear me? Or must I ask the Moon to speak to you as well? Of your feelings?"

Startled, Baudwin saw his dream-self shift in his bed, almost waking from his sleep. He realized that the voice was that of the Water.

"Why do you come to me so?" he asked.

"I come to you in my sorrow," the Water replied, "for so few Faeries listen to their dreams anymore. Are you listening, Baudwin?"

"I am," Baudwin replied.

"Good," the Water said. "We found you yesterday at the Springs of Coventina, and still today you hear us, as well you should."

Baudwin wondered what the voice meant by "we." Did she mean all the voices of his tribe, or herself and someone else? There would be no explanation. He watched the canal of Water circle even faster around his dream-self, until a thin vortex of energy formed a cocoon of watery ethers around him. The ethers went into his dream-self, quickening his thoughts and feelings, until every part of him vibrated from the inside out.

I am awake in my dream. Everything he had seen before was now clear. The hum he had heard was now a flurry of whispers, and the shapeless clouds held form. The tree leaves were without gears, and he could understand the riddles of the symbols, if only for an instant. The whispers turned into the voices of his tribe. He remained on the precipice — invigorated and filled with bliss.

Once again, the Water had come to him.

The voice then spoke for the final time, saying, "The glyph will show the way."

Ecstatic, he waited, hoping the voice would explain how. But this was not to be.

Ching ching ching went a soft sound at the door.

Baudwin opened his eyes. *My dream has ended, and I am now myself, lying here in bed.* Seeing the canal of Water around his mattress, he slowly stretched his arms and legs. As always, he felt renewed after sleeping near his element.

Ching ching ching went the sound again, for Faeries never knocked at doors. Nor did they hang bells upon them. Instead, attached to the outside of every door was a lovely chime.

A voice spoke through the door, "Baudwin, do you have some extra white glowstones? I need them to light the room for the meeting tonight."

Baudwin let out a groan. "Must you borrow them now?" he asked.

"Come on now," the voice commanded, though with affection. "I'll give them back to you after the meeting. Open up, my lad. Today is Crédía[1], time to work."

Reluctantly, Baudwin got out of bed, hitting the floor with a light thud as he went. He glided across the room and grabbed the doorknob. With a whisk of his hand, he opened the door.

There stood Seamus, his grandfather — the Leader of the Deuona Water Guild — filling the doorway with his broad shoulders. He was quite tall for a Faery. Smiling down at Baudwin, his eyes bored into him. No doubt, he was measuring his grandson's mettle, looking to see how well he was facing his day. Baudwin was not surprised by his insinuating gaze. Seamus liked to get his way with others, by taking stock of them and telling them what to do.

For other Faeries in the Water Guild, this would have created constant scuffles, but not for Seamus. He was too big-hearted to make anyone angry at him for very long. Having a ruggedly handsome face also added to his advantage.

Usually everyone followed Seamus's lead. However, not all Faeries commanded the same measure of respect. Baudwin knew this all too well. As his grandfather stood before him — much to his distaste — he was reminded of Loch.

Baudwin tried to put the thought out of his mind, but he couldn't. He looked again at Seamus, who grasped his walking staff as if he were about to lead an

---

[1] Pronounced [CRAY-THEE-UH] Earthday, equivalent to Monday, the first day of the week

elven guard. Surely, he and Loch were similar in their commanding nature. However, Seamus wasn't a scoundrel, starting fights or defiling shrines. All the same, he clearly relished being in charge of his surroundings and leaving his mark upon others. The notion of him shouting orders at the Elves made Baudwin grin, for his grandfather was certainly a Faery, dressed as he was in his guild colors of blue and green.

"Why, you haven't even changed yet," Seamus said, as he stared at Baudwin's blue silk pajamas. When he spoke, his booming voice filled the entire room.

"I've changed more than you know," Baudwin said slyly, remembering what had happened the day before.

"Just look at how *I'm* dressed for the day," Seamus continued, as he pointed to his chest with his walking stick. "The Leader of the Water Guild must wear *every* color of the Water," he announced, striking the embroidered waves upon his vest. "Only then, will others see how adept he is in the ways of the Water."

Seamus pointed to his dark blue linen breeches. "The *darker* the Water, the more powerful the currents," he added. "And —"

"And the more powerful the currents —" Baudwin cut in, eager to finish his grandfather's thoughts.

"The *greater* the mastery of the Water," Seamus predictably concluded, his eyes flashing. "Never forget — you must always choose colors that impart your mastery of the Water to others."

Baudwin smiled at his grandfather. "You know I won't forget," he said, for Seamus had told him this many times — far too many to count.

"Good," Seamus said, brushing his graying blue-green hair from his eyes. He bent down to pull up a knee sock. "Now where are my glowstones?"

"Must you bother me for my last two white ones?" Baudwin asked. "I was going to grind them up for my sand painting."

"*Grind* them?" Seamus asked, smiling magnanimously. "What in all the peaks and valleys of *Tír na nÓg* are you making?"

"A dragonfly," Baudwin replied, motioning to his work table. "I need them for the highlights."

"Let's go and take a look," Seamus said.

The two Faeries approached the table. A row of jars stood on one side, filled with white river sand that Baudwin had dyed many colors, using berries, flowers, and other plants. On the other side sat a mortar and pestle that he used to crush glowstones of various colors to make highlights.

Baudwin often spent hours on end, emptying his jars to perfect his sand paintings. Some he poured into glass bottles — layer upon layer — choosing just the right color to make just the right shape. How he loved deciding what his next creation would be — flowers, mice, rabbits, or whatever caught his fancy. Others he poured onto sheets of glass, painting special water glyphs, or scenes with insects, birds, or plants.

"What fine work you have done," Seamus said, inspecting the dragonfly. "The wings look as if they were made of lace. Now I see why you're guarding your white glowstones so carefully." Baudwin beamed at the compliment.

Seamus picked up a white glowstone. "This one is a good size," he mused. "The Light should shine very brightly."

"Tap the crown, Grandfather," Baudwin said, as he rose on his toes and playfully tapped Seamus on his head.

Laughing, Seamus touched the top of the stone. In an instant, clear white Light shone from the center.

"These will do," he added, as he peered at the stone to examine the Light from every angle. "They're not like those low-quality turquoise ones we've been getting." Satisfied, he tapped the glowstone again, turning off the Light.

"One day, all we will have is the finest!" Baudwin exclaimed. "If I could, I would get more blue ones to go with Brim and Bram," he added, pointing to the nightstands on either side of his bed. On top of each one sat a sapphire-colored glowstone, carved into the shape of a nova owl.

"Those are very rare indeed," Seamus said as he put his arm around his grandson's shoulders. "You're lucky to have them. Your father loves you."

Hearing this, Baudwin pulled away from his grandfather.

"You do believe that, don't you?" Seamus asked. Baudwin looked sad. Seamus relaxed his arm, sighing heavily.

Stirred by the weight of the silence between them, Seamus strode over to Brim. He tapped the owl on the head and the stone turned on. The entire room turned a vibrant shade of blue — the color of their Guild. The two Faeries stood transfixed, staring at the Light.

"I remember the day your father brought them home," Seamus said. "He had bartered for weeks with Rian at the General Store. Blue glowstones like these were not so easy to come by. Let me tell you, there was a great deal of interest in them! A couple of Elves almost won the barter. But Kelven wore them down, until they finally gave up. And you know how hard it is to best an Elve."

"Harder than getting a Faery to keep persisting," Baudwin quipped.

"The Light was so beautiful, he couldn't resist them," Seamus continued. "He asked a friend of Rian's to do the carving, an old elven gent who had just moved to Deuona from Copper Caves. He wanted to give you something special for your one-hundred-and-sixtieth birthday."

That was the day I began to look for the Water, Baudwin thought, his memories kindled.

His grandfather's robust enthusiasm had guided him ever since that day. Year after year, Seamus had been his only champion as he dove to the bottom of the river. Sometimes he paced back and forth, waving his arms and shouting. Other times, he remained silent, calmed by simple faith in the old ways. In those moments especially, Baudwin felt his grandfather's resolve guiding him, regardless of how tired or afraid he felt. After thousands of attempts, he would return to shore, exhausted and discouraged. And although he had never succeeded in finding the Water, Seamus had never let him give up.

Now, as Baudwin looked at his grandfather's hearty face, he wondered what he would say when he heard his amazing news. He would have to wait for just the right moment to tell him, for Seamus loved to tell stories, and often rambled on and on as he spoke.

"I remember getting them," Baudwin said, as he admired the owls' striking blue color. Patiently, he listened, as Seamus continued the story.

"You were down at the river," he said. "When you came back to your room — there they were. You were *so* happy!"

Hearing the word *river*, Baudwin seized the opportunity to change the subject. "Grandfather," he began, "there's something I must tell you."

Seamus did not hear Baudwin's announcement, distracted as he was by his own story. "Let's see if this one gets any brighter," he said, as he tapped the owl harder. Instantly, the blue Light shone even more vibrantly.

"Grandfather — pay attention," Baudwin said, giving the owl a double tap. Instantly, the glowstone went back to a translucent sapphire. He looked at his grandfather.

Seamus seemed to be lost in a reverie of some kind, which often happened after the Light of their Guild touched him. Had the blue emanations brought him an old memory of the Water, or a new longing for the old ways? Baudwin couldn't say for sure. All he knew was that he was eager to tell his grandfather what had happened to him the day before.

Seamus continued in his reverie. Having lost sight of the Light, he now turned to face the large round window behind Baudwin's bed. "Look outside, Baudwin," he said.

"Grandfather —" Baudwin began again. Seamus did not reply. Rolling his eyes with annoyance, Baudwin turned to face the window.

Together, their gaze followed the luxurious green foliage and stopped at the river — a deep blue ribbon, surging with Life. On this day, golden rays glowed softly from the newly rising Sun, cloaking the trees and flowers in a mantle of blessedness and peace. They both became very still.

Baudwin could not be silent any longer. "Something happened yesterday at the springs," he announced.

"Something happened?" Seamus asked, still engrossed in the view.

"I visited them, like you told me to."

"How wonderful," Seamus replied, as he watched a hummingbird fly by. "Do tell me — what?"

"I found —"

"Do you see that hummer drinking from that foxglove?" Seamus cut in. "Such a greedy little fellow!" he added, laughing.

Baudwin gave Seamus an irritated nod. "Grandfather, something came to me."

"What?"

"The *Water* — of course!"

For a moment, Seamus said nothing, as his attention was still on the bird. Suddenly, as if he had been poked by a large stick, his eyes grew wider than an owl's. "You *found* the Water?" he asked.

"Yes, I found the Water!"

"How do you know?" Seamus asked.

"Because I heard your voice and Father's! I even heard Elva's and —"

"You *found* the Water?" Seamus interrupted, raising his walking staff. "That means the Water found *you*. Did the Water find you?"

"Yes, I heard all of your voices."

"Tell me everything that happened!"

"First I just stood by the Water," Baudwin replied. "My senses were waking."

"You had a waking first?"

"Yes, Grandfather. They've been happening more, especially when I'm near the Water. I also saw a bluethroat, so I took them both as signs that I would succeed. I dove deep down and waited, just as you always told me to."

"Just as I always told you!"

"First I saw a school of minnows," Baudwin continued. "They were all talking inside of me. I saw myself floating with other water Faeries down the river — in water drums. I was alone for a while . . . and then I heard them — the voices of our tribe. Grandfather, there were so many! I wish you could have —"

"Baudwin, dear Baudwin!" Seamus exclaimed. Excitedly, he paced around the room, past Baudwin's armoire to some shelves next to the arch-shaped bedroom door. Upon reaching the shelves, he stopped abruptly, beside himself with joy.

"I knew if your intention was strong enough, you would prevail!" he cried. "You see? You didn't need to be joined with your current."

Dancing merrily, Seamus made a grand swooping motion with his arm. As he moved, his staff hit several shelves, nearly knocking a good part of Baudwin's prized collection of steamway toys and inventions to the floor.

Baudwin looked on with horror, for he loved his collection almost as much as the Water, and his Life upon the river. "Grandfather, you must be careful," he said, as he dashed to steady him.

"Now that I am seven and eighty, I lose my balance far too often," Seamus said, aggravated. Steadying himself, he looked from shelf to shelf at Baudwin's steamway collection. The sight gave him pause.

"My goodness, Baudwin — what *is* all of this?" he asked, taken aback. For several moments, he looked at the shelves as though he had never seen what was on them before.

"Surely, you must know," Baudwin replied.

"Are those tackle tree spiders?" Seamus asked, pointing to two large spiders, with bodies the size of small birds. "*Whatever* possessed the Elves to start making them?"

How could he not remember? Baudwin thought, as he studied the mystified expression on his grandfather's face. *After so many seasons?*

"Oh, never mind," Seamus replied. "Let's talk about you finding the Water."

"Yes," Baudwin replied.

"You must tell me — did you hear your mother?"

Hearing the question, Baudwin's euphoric mood flattened, and his face became drawn with pain.

"No, I didn't," he replied, his voice heavy with sadness.

Seamus gave Baudwin a puzzled look. "How could that be?"

"I don't know." Distractedly, Baudwin picked up a bronze royal beetle, with a violet-and-amber-striped shell. Holding the insect in the palm of his hand, he looked out the window. "If the Water carries the voices of all water Faeries, why wasn't she there?"

"Perhaps next time —" Seamus replied.

"There won't be one," Baudwin interrupted.

Seamus knew very well what troubled Baudwin. He hadn't heard his mother's voice. He knew this had to be painfully hard for him to accept. Right now, Baudwin seemed to be in quite a flurry, as if all of his feelings ebbed and flowed inside of him all at once. There was nothing for Seamus to do but change the subject, or risk upsetting his grandson even further.

"What have we here?" Seamus asked, picking up a locket ladybug.

Comforted by the question, Baudwin drew closer to his grandfather. "I began collecting these when I was a Faefry. . ." he replied, his voice trailing off.

Seamus pressed on, determined to cheer him up. "That's just when the Elves began building these kinds of things," he said. "You took to all of this so quickly. I regret not spending more time with you at the river. Especially because you hadn't joined with your current."

Baudwin had heard Seamus say this many times. Yet nothing he said back to him had ever assuaged his grandfather's guilt. Over countless seasons Baudwin had told Seamus that he wasn't responsible for what had happened that day. But Seamus's way was never to accept that there was nothing he could have done.

"I've told you again and again — you spent a lot of time with me," Baudwin insisted. "You never gave up hope, even after Father stopped taking me to the river."

Smiling, Baudwin parted the red-and-black enamel wings of the copper ladybug. Beneath them, another set of wings mirrored his reflection to him like a tiny portrait. He handed the ladybug to Seamus. "Do you see your face?"

Seamus steadied himself a bit as he peered into the mirror. "Who is that handsome-looking fellow?" he asked with a booming laugh. Both of their moods brightened.

"And what is this?" Seamus asked, as he grabbed another toy from the shelf. "A chatter cricket? I haven't seen one of these in many a season!"

"Careful, Grandfather," Baudwin warned, taking the cricket from Seamus's hand. He stood the pale green legs of the polished brass insect back upon the shelf, next to the others. "If I had time, I would make them all chatter right now, so you could hear them."

Seamus gave Baudwin a perplexed look. As always, he couldn't tell if Baudwin liked steamway crickets because they were crickets, or crickets because they were Steamway. Either way, neither side made any sense to him at all.

"But the crickets in *Tír na nÓg already* chatter," Seamus replied, looking puzzled. "In the grass — in the summertime — especially in the evening."

"Now you sound just like Father," Baudwin replied.

"You know we're not the same," Seamus countered. "When I reach the Great Thousand, he'll still be a sapling!"

Hearing this, Baudwin smiled. For, unlike beings in other realms, Faeries and Elves lived to be very, very old. After they reached one hundred, they counted their birthdays in centuries, letting others know that they were, in fact, three and seventy-nine, or five and forty. He knew his grandfather still had many years before he would garner the high respect of the Great Thousand, and carve his last spiral into a stump, before he passed to Annwyn.

Seamus reached for a tremor crab, an even larger toy than the tackle tree spider. He wound up the back, but the claws didn't move, so he brought the crab closer to his eyes to see what was wrong. Suddenly, a claw clamped onto his nose, turning the end a bright, throbbing red.

"Confounded crab!" Seamus howled, as he yanked the claw away from him. The claws continued their futile clacking.

Baudwin laughed. "This is the model I'm using for my sand painting," he explained, picking up a dragonfly to show Seamus. "Don't the wings look real?"

"Perhaps for a steamway toy," Seamus remarked.

"They fly so well," Baudwin added, as he wound up the spring on the back. *Scrink, scrink, scrink.*

"Reach the sky!" he exclaimed, as he threw the tiny toy to the ceiling.

"Look at 'er fly!" Seamus laughed. "You used to play with these down by the river."

After soaring a few feet, the dragonfly glided lazily downward. Seamus watched as the glimmering wings came to rest upon the floor. "Why didn't you use a *real* dragonfly for your model?" he asked.

"A real dragonfly?" Baudwin asked. "That wouldn't be any fun."

Seamus almost wished he hadn't asked the question. In all his Life, he had never wound up a dragonfly, yet he knew what they meant to Baudwin. Growing up, nothing seemed to more easily distract his grandson from his loneliness than tinkering with his toys and contraptions. They had been his only haven then, and Seamus feared they would be his only one now. He also worried that few would even believe that the Water had come to Baudwin. For years, he had lagged behind his peers, but now it was evident that he surpassed everyone. The Water had chosen him for a reason.

"Now that the Water has come to you, you must tread carefully," Seamus said. You were never joined, and we don't know what will happen."

"What do you mean, Grandfather?"

"You're on a path never treaded by anyone before. None will know how to guide you, and that is dangerous. You always get so enthralled with things that you let yourself dream away what is real. Now that the Water has come to you, you can't be the same Faery you once were. Pay attention to what is important, and don't be foolish. These contraptions will not sustain you on your course. You must not take the Water coming to you for granted, and become taken in by the empty promises of the Elves."

Baudwin disliked being called foolish, especially by Seamus who had always been the kindest to him. How biting that the one who cared about him the most, had the most to say about what he didn't want to hear. He sorely wished to change the subject. If they kept talking, Seamus might get so upset that he would knock over more of his collection — perhaps this time not by accident. A mechanical dragonfly was certainly not worth spoiling his good news about the Water.

"Grandfather," Baudwin said. "There's something else I must tell you."

Baudwin darted to one of his nightstands. "After the Water found me," he began, as he opened the drawer, "Matha and I stumbled upon some old ruins. We found an ancient shrine filled with offerings. We also found this," he added, taking out the blue-green piece of agate. "Matha didn't know what the glyph meant, but he thought you might."

"Let me see that," Seamus said. Baudwin handed him the stone fragment.

Seamus stared at the carving in disbelief. *Indeed, the Water has never stopped speaking to the Fae!* he thought. Quickly, his fear that Baudwin would abandon the old ways was allayed. Even though he hadn't completed the Ceremonies of the Joining or the Coursing, the Water had come to his grandson's aid. The glyph was further proof. He had always hoped the Water would come to Baudwin, and so the Water had, but now something even more wonderful was happening. Holding the carving in his hand, he realized that a thread of eternity had been offered to Baudwin — one his grandson could weave into the Life he had always wished for him.

Baudwin examined the piece of agate more closely. Two side-by-side spirals were connected by a single line that began in the center of one, and ended in the center of the other. "I've never seen a glyph like this before."

"Of course you haven't," Seamus said. As he examined the glyph his face brightened and his eyebrows rose. Throwing back his head, he let out a deep, hearty laugh. "This is the ancient glyph for *Glamorium*. I haven't seen one since I was as young as you."

Baudwin had naturally heard of Glamorium, but had never seen any. He waited for Seamus to continue.

"Wherever did you find this?" Seamus asked.

"In a small alcove."

"You took this from a shrine?" Seamus asked, dismayed.

"I don't think we did any harm," Baudwin replied cheerfully. He didn't want Seamus to know about the terrible fight he and Matha had had with Loch and his gang.

Skeptically, Seamus glared at Baudwin. "You broke with *gnás!*" he exclaimed. "Whatever made you do that?"

"It's not what you think," Baudwin began. "Something happened while we were there. The ground shook, and Water came rushing up from the center of the shrine, flooding the entire place. Matha and I were swept away, into the Woods. After that, I found this at my feet."

"Ha!" Seamus laughed. "A likely story. Sounds to me like the Water was teaching you a lesson."

"I don't believe so," Baudwin said. *Perhaps Loch and his friends got taught one.* "How do you know?"

"Because nothing was disturbed, Grandfather," Baudwin explained. "None of the offerings in the shrine moved. The Water flooded out of a well, but all of the treasures stayed where they were — pearls, and pieces of gold, topaz, and blue quartz."

Seamus looked steadily at Baudwin, suspecting he was hiding something. "What that means is that the Water would never defile the sanctity of the shrine —"

"At first Matha thought that the Water had simply gushed," Baudwin interrupted, but I —"

"That was no gusher, Baudwin."

"There's more, Grandfather. Last night the Water came to me again — in my dream — and said, 'The glyph will show the way.'"

"Praise the Moon!" Seamus exclaimed. "Obviously, the Water is trying to lead you on your path."

"And there's something more," Baudwin began carefully. "I read a poem in the shrine."

"Do you remember the words?"

"Yes."

"Tell me."

Baudwin recited:

You may wish for many things

Or never want for much

But that which holds the Truth you seek

Is something you must touch

Although Seamus had never heard the poem before, he immediately understood its deeper meaning. He suspected Baudwin did not, so he paused for a moment before he spoke.

"Now you can be certain that the Water is *always* guiding you," he began, waiting for Baudwin to reply. Baudwin remained silent.

"You must contemplate the meaning," Seamus insisted. "Only then will you understand how the poem is guiding you."

"That's easy," Baudwin began. "I must find Glamorium, and if I touch some perhaps then —"

"That's *not* so easy," Seamus cut in. His suspicion was confirmed — Baudwin was overlooking the poem's meaning. How he loved his grandson, but like a little grebe, just learning to swim, Baudwin was not yet prepared to dive into deeper Water. Doing so would require work, and Baudwin preferred that Seamus find his answers for him.

Despite this, Seamus was still eager to tell him what he else he knew. "Glamorium is the most precious element in all of *Tír na nÓg*," he began, "prized by Faeries and Elves alike. Many believe that Glamorium brings blessings and good fortune to anyone who is lucky enough to own even a *tiny* piece." He then paused, reflecting on what he had just said.

"Have you ever seen any?" Baudwin asked.

"A few times in my Life, and let me tell you — words cannot do justice to this powerful, amazing metal. My memory is hazy, but when I was a lad of about one and two hundred, I remember seeing the Grand Elder himself dip a glamorium bowl into the river at a water ceremony in Deuona. The sides shimmered like green silk — as if they were alive in some way."

"What happened to the bowl?" Baudwin asked. "Does anyone in the Water Guild know?"

"I doubt that very much," Seamus replied. "Over the years that bowl as well as many other such things seem simply to have disappeared."

"Why?"

"I don't know," Seamus replied. "Many suspect that the Elves are somehow to blame, for they have always coveted our treasures."

Disappointed, Baudwin nevertheless remained intrigued. He was not about to let the greedy intentions of the Elves bar him from his quest. Seeing Baudwin's interest, Seamus remained poised to answer even more of his questions.

"Well, the Elves can't hide what they haven't yet mined," Baudwin said. "Where must I go to find the ore?"

"Glamorium can be found only in crystal deposits in the Tadlachs," Seamus replied. "To get there, you must ford rivers, travel through valleys, and scale mountains for days on end. Both Faeries and Elves alike have perished to Annwyn in the attempt."

The heights of the Tadlachs were indeed dangerous, and thinking about their snow and ice made Baudwin shiver.

"That sounds impossible," he said, his enthusiasm waning.

"But what riches come to the lucky few who succeed," Seamus continued. "For there is often gold in the veins as well."

"Gold?"

"Yes indeed," Seamus replied, his face glowing with rapture. "Legend says that Glamorium allows only those who are wise in intention and pure of heart to serve as its smelters. First, the gold must be separated from the green molten ore. When the liquid cools, what remains is a deep green metal, high in tensile strength, yet light in weight — with a wondrous sheen."

How mightily Baudwin wished to find Glamorium! Yet, his desire for adventure was diminishing. The winding road of trials would indeed be very difficult, but what frightened him even more was what he might discover at the end. He had not heard his mother's voice among the Faefolk of the Water, so he wondered if Glamorium could actually help him.

"If I touched some, could I really find Mother?"

"Only if you stay true to the Water," Seamus replied. Several moments passed. The two Faeries remained silent.

"That which holds the Truth you seek, is something you must touch," Seamus recited. Looking fiercely at Baudwin, he asked, "What *else* must you touch?"

"What else —?" Baudwin repeated, confused. For now he truly could not tell what his grandfather wanted him to say.

"Yes — what else?" Seamus insisted.

Baudwin bridled at the question, for he had assumed that finding the Water had ended the need to consider such things. He thought the poem simply meant that he should touch Glamorium, yet Seamus seemed to be saying otherwise. To Baudwin, touching meant reaching for something he could feel, not feeling for something he couldn't reach. For hadn't he reached far enough?

He believed in his heart that he had, and now Seamus seemed to be telling him that he was only at the beginning of his quest. He had endured quite enough beginnings. Every year, there had been one at the Moon of Spring, the first Moon of the season. Always, when he began to look for the Water, his hopes, like the river, rose to their highest. Then came the Moon of Summer, when his spirit was the strongest, and the land of *Tír na nÓg* was lush and full. Then, the Moon of Fall, and though the chill gave him pause, and his diving became harder and harder, he was buoyed by the beauty of the forest, the festivals at night, and the cries of Faefries as they ran through falling leaves of yellow and orange. Until finally, he could bear his struggle no longer, and his hopes, like the ice, froze under the Moon of Winter.

He and his tribe would then retreat from the Water, which was no longer theirs, until the following spring. During the cold winter months of Yule, Baudwin took solace in his room with his sand paintings and elven contraptions, for what else was he to do? He would listen to Seamus as they celebrated the Winter Solstice, and to Kelven as he spoke of matters of the Water Guild. For forty years — one hundred and sixty seasons — this was the only Life he knew. From the Moon of Spring to the Moon of Winter, he had swum with every kind of creature, in every creek, river, and lake in Deuona. Until yesterday, when the Water finally came to him at the Springs of Coventina. Yet, despite his joy, finding the Water had also left him feeling even more befuddled.

He studied Seamus, searching for clues, but his grandfather's cobalt eyes yielded nothing. The poem was guiding him to touch Glamorium, and Seamus seemed implicitly to agree, yet also seemed to be trying to make him reach for something else.

"How am I supposed to know?" Baudwin asked.

"Perhaps you won't know what else to touch — until you relinquish some of *this*," Seamus replied, pointing to the shelves.

"What do you mean?" Baudwin asked, taken aback.

"Only you can answer that."

Baudwin found the thought of giving up any of his collection quite disturbing. Attempting to change the subject, he removed a steamway sailing ship from the shelf, complete with a wind-up motor. "What about this?" he asked slyly, trying to distract Seamus from the conversation.

Grinning, Baudwin presented the ship to his grandfather. A dozen paddles protruded from bronze portholes on either side. Baudwin turned the ship around to show him the bow. A blue seahorse with orange spots and piercing brown eyes stared back at them.

"Baudwin. . ." Seamus began, intending to scold him. Instead, he decided to indulge his grandson's amusing little diversion, knowing that he would need more time to take in the lessons of the Water.

Baudwin continued trying to distract Seamus.

"Criofan gave this to me when I turned one and thirty," he said. "Do you remember?"

Seamus smiled. "Of course I do! We had a party for you down by the river. There was warm jasmine tea in small pots, and cold raspberry tea in large pitchers. The table was set with lacy white placemats and napkins, elegant-looking silverware and crystal glasses —"

"Pink and yellow cups shaped like roses, and green saucers and plates in the form of rose leaves," Baudwin added.

"And a splendid cake in the shape of a large rose with red frosting!"

"I got so many presents from my friends that day. I made them all special amulets with sand paintings to wear on beaded chains around their necks."

Coyly, Seamus allowed his grandson to continue with his diversion.

"How *is* Criofan?" Seamus asked, as he gazed above the work table. A colorful painting of Baudwin's acrobatic troupe hung on the wall — three in all. Baudwin stood with his two best friends, Matha and Criofan, one on either side of him, all wearing the same costume — shirts and pants made of cerulean satin, and indigo cummerbunds and shoes trimmed with gold braid.

"I'm going with him and Matha today to the Engineerium," Baudwin replied.

"Ah yes, the Elves are back in town," Seamus mused. "With all of their gadgets and wild inventions. Don't have so much fun there that you forget about the meeting tonight."

"The meeting?"

"The Meeting of the Water Guild. Did you forget?"

Indeed, Baudwin did remember, but only because Seamus had just reminded him. The meeting was usually held four times a year: on Furze, the

Tree of the Spring Equinox; Heather, the Tree of the Summer Solstice; Poplar, the Tree of the Fall Equinox; and Fir, the Tree of the day of the Winter Solstice. Yet, by order of the Grand Eldress herself, and due to rising discord between the Faeries and Elves, this meeting had been called during the month of Willow. Because Baudwin's father, Kelven, was the Primary of Water, and their home had been chosen for the meeting, everyone was expected to attend.

Baudwin grinned at his grandfather. "How could I forget that? The meeting will be right here at our house."

"Good."

"I promise not to let the Elves and the Engineerium carry me away," Baudwin said, laughing.

"Better that you let the *Water* carry you away," Seamus added sweetly.

Seamus was glad Baudwin seemed to remember the meeting, but he also wanted to make sure that he hadn't forgotten something even more important.

He waited for Baudwin to speak.

"I know," Baudwin began. "It's just that. . ."

"Baudwin," Seamus declared, "the Water is surely choosing you, but for what reason, I can't be sure."

"If you aren't sure, how can I be?"

"When the Water chooses a Faery, they are often the last to know the reason why," Seamus said.

Dejectedly, Baudwin picked up a steamway motor-driven carriage, a copper pumpkin resting upon two large brass wheels, with two smaller wheels in the front.

"I got this when I turned one hundred," he continued. "I used to imagine I was a Faery of noble deeds, riding inside, waving to an adoring crowd."

"You can be that Faery now — the Water has come to you. You could lead the Guilders someday."

"I heard your voice say exactly that when the Water came to me," Baudwin said. "And I heard Father tell me that he wished we still swam together in the river. . ."

"You heard us talking — the Water really did find you!" Seamus exclaimed again, swooning with delight. "Do you know how *rare* such a thing is in these times? The ways of the Water are all I ever wished for you — certainly not *this*," he continued, pointing to the steamway collection. "Here we see everything the Elves have been forcing upon us for so long."

Never had Baudwin felt himself pulled so hard, torn in such opposite directions, as he did in this moment. Intently he listened, as Seamus kept speaking.

"Whatever do you need *this* for?" Seamus asked, pointing to a periscope — a set of brass goggles, with blue lenses, attached to a rubber tube.

"I use them when I go diving."

"Why would a water Faery like *you* need a contraption like *this* to help him dive?" Seamus asked, his annoyance building. "I never used these when I swam in the river, and I wouldn't now."

"You call that diving?" Baudwin shot back. "You just don't understand. This makes everything much more interesting — and far more blue."

"Bluer than what your own *senses* tell you?" Seamus asked, glaring. "Really, Baudwin —"

"Trust me, Grandfather," Baudwin interrupted. "If you tried this once, you would *never* go back to swimming the way you did."

Seamus looked at what sat next to the periscope.

"Driving goggles?" he asked. "Tell me you aren't serious about using them, so you can drive one of *these*." Disdainfully, he picked up a miniature lumber roller.

Most Faeries found lumber rollers to be annoying nuisances, and Seamus was no exception. Throughout *Tír na nÓg*, the Elves had many uses for them, among them, mining, logging, and building. Seamus always hated hearing their loud steam whistles, and seeing the ugly marks they left on the road, not to mention all the smoke that billowed out of them.

"How would we get all of our goods from Rian without them?" Baudwin asked. "I work on lumber rollers all the time with him. If I hadn't, I never would have been able to barter with him to get that train, all those cars, and that track," he added, proudly pointing to one of his top shelves.

"Trains, eh?" Seamus replied, now somewhat calmer and mulling the idea over in his mind.

"Haven't you ever seen one?" Baudwin asked, assuming that at some time in his grandfather's long Life he must surely have spied one somewhere.

"No, Baudwin, I haven't," Seamus replied.

"Rian told me that the Elves in *Tír Luí Lucharachán* use them everywhere to haul things from place to place."

"Fine — as long as they don't bring them to *Tír Éirí Sióg*."

"But they're so much fun, and ever so useful."

"I guess I'm just an old faery fuddy-duddy who is used to wagons and a simple Life," Seamus said, sighing.

"With the train goes a clock," Baudwin continued, determined to gain the upper hand in the debate. "Rian told me that moving things long distances means they have to get where they're going right on time."

"Time, did you say?"

"Yes, this device tells me the time." Baudwin removed a watch from the shelf, and pointed to its face. "These numbers tell me the hours." Strapping the watch to his wrist, he added, "And this is how you wear one, you see?"

Now Seamus was truly worried for his grandson, for although he knew the Elves built such things, he had never seen one before.

"When I want to know the time, I just look to the heavens," he replied. Testily, he added, "But I can tell you this — if you want to find your mother, you will find her through the Water, not through *this* contraption."

Hearing this, Baudwin's anger flared, like wood shavings in a furnace.

"Yes, the Water found me," he argued, his voice rising. "And yes, what happened was wondrous —"

"Baudwin!"

"But, there are *other* kinds of wonders —"

"And you would let those elven wonders keep you from answering the Water," Seamus declared angrily.

Baudwin had heard enough.

"Look, the Water came to me, and I did not find Mother!" he shouted. "You said to look for her, and I did *not* find her!"

Shocked by the depth of Baudwin's disrespect, what remained of Seamus's exuberance all but disappeared. Quietly, he spoke, "Baudwin, let's not speak of this anymore."

Baudwin knew he had overstepped his bounds, which often happened when he didn't know how he really felt. Not being joined always haunted him, as he couldn't properly choose his words. Seeing how much he had upset his grandfather, he wasn't sure what he should say next. He put his hand on Seamus's shoulder.

"Grandfather," he began contritely.

"Yes," Seamus replied.

"Perhaps there's hope for me yet," he said. "Last night, the Water said something more to me — in my dream."

Hearing this, Seamus straightened up and held more tightly onto his staff.

"The Water wanted the Moon to speak to me — of my feelings."

"They can be challenging," Seamus replied.

"The Water also told me that few Faeries listen to their dreams anymore. Why do you suppose that is?"

"I wish I knew."

Baudwin could feel the anguish in his grandfather's heart. A look had come over his face, the look of one desperate to find something that he had lost forever. Baudwin felt terribly unsettled when he saw that look, but there was nothing he could do for him except to let the moment pass.

"Grandfather," he said, "I really must get ready. I have to do my chores before I leave."

"Yes, Baudwin," Seamus said. "I will go now. Thank you for the glowstones. You have a good day."

With that, Seamus left the room. As he made his way down the hall, Baudwin could hear his walking staff strike the floor — *tap, tap, tap.* The sound grew ever more faint, and then he was gone.

Chapter 4
EARLY MORNING MUSINGS

That certainly didn't go very well, Baudwin thought, as he hurried to his dresser. Time was growing short, so he had to find something to wear as quickly as possible. *How was I supposed to know he would get so upset?* he thought, as he opened the top drawer. *That's the problem — I <u>never</u> know.* Baudwin was glad he hadn't told Seamus about the bout he had had after the Water came to him, for surely that would have upset him even more.

Reaching inside the drawer, he ran his fingers across some silk shirts. He picked up a pair of socks and rubbed them lightly against his cheek. *Yarn from the pulp of the white fir tree,* he thought, forgetting his upset and sighing happily. Most water Faeries luxuriated in owning many kinds of fine fabrics, and Baudwin was no exception. He then removed a silk undershirt from the drawer.

"Let's see," he mused, opening the second drawer. Being a water Faery, he dressed mostly in colors of blue, green, or combinations of both. Light blue cotton shirts were stacked next to sturdy green linen breeches. Next to the breeches were everyday vests made of green or blue twilled cotton, with hints of gold or silver thread. As this was the season of Spring, Baudwin saw no need to open the bottom drawer, which was reserved for warmer clothes, along with belts, buckles, scarves, and a collection of special buttons.

This is all fine for the Engineerium, he thought, as he weighed his options. *But not for the meeting.* Although most Faeries dressed to commune with their element, they also dressed to impress other Faeries, and often commented on who wore what and looked the best. As the son of the Primary of Water, Baudwin wanted his clothes to display his devotion to the Water. And if he looked kicky and handsome as well, that was fine with him too.

As he turned to his armoire, he heard a familiar sound coming from outside his window — "coo, coo," followed by another, exactly the same — "coo, coo."

"I'm coming!" he called, darting to the window.

Faery windows in *Tír na nÓg* were mostly stained-glass circles, with a clear glass inner circle that opened with a brass handle. Baudwin's window had a glass pattern of blue irises, with green leaves and stems.

"There you are," he said, as he opened the window and peered outside. On a low branch of an elm tree sat a twilight dove, cooing softly.

"Good morning, Moonrise," Baudwin said, motioning to the bird. "Come on in."

As the dove spread his wings, the early morning Light shone through his pearl-white plumage. Azure feathers fanned out beneath them — creating a striking row of color. Unlike most other birds, twilight doves often flew at night, traveling especially long distances when the Moon was full. Once the Sun rose, they returned to their roosts to sleep.

"How was your flight?" Baudwin asked as Moonrise fluttered into the room. The bird alighted inside a small but comfortable house, on top of a wooden coat rack next to Baudwin's steamway shelves. Calmly he regarded Baudwin through large unblinking eyes.

"The month of Willow is upon us, and you still haven't found a mate?"

Moonrise turned his head away.

"You mustn't feel bad," Baudwin said. "I'm looking for someone too, and I still haven't found her."

Hearing this, Moonrise plumped himself up, and sat a little straighter on his perch. He then began preening his feathers. Baudwin couldn't help admiring his pet's elegant plumage. Sighing, he turned to his armoire, which was made of red oak, with mirrored double doors and wave-shaped brass handles.

"If you were me, which of these feathers would *you* choose?" he asked as he opened the door to examine his clothes.

"Everyone will be there," he said as he studied a number of shirts with billowy sleeves and some lacy cravats. Putting his finely tailored breeches to one side, he looked at several velvet and brocade vests, with jewel buttons.

"Perhaps these are a bit too fancy?" he asked. Smiling, he picked up a pair of pointed shoes and some canvas knee boots, wondering which would be better. On a shelf above his clothes were a number of caps decorated with feathers and carved stones, set in copper, silver, or gold. Baudwin decided against wearing a cap, as there would be dancing after the meeting, and he didn't want his to go flying off his head.

He then found the outfit he had been looking for.

"How about this?" he asked, removing a pair of royal-blue linen breeches and a light teal silk shirt. "And this?" With his other hand, he reached for a green and blue tapestry vest with gold buttons, a water glyph engraved in the center of each one. Turning to his pet, he revealed the entire ensemble.

Moonrise nodded approvingly.

"I thought so." Quickly, he began to dress. To complete his outfit, he pulled on a pair of light blue socks, tucking them into his breeches, and some dark teal canvas boots, which he knew would be better suited to the rigors of the Engineerium. He then turned to face the mirror.

"Just the right choices!" he beamed, quite pleased with what he saw. Baudwin was clearly a good-looking fellow, blessed with intelligent and handsome features: a wide forehead, high cheekbones, a well-angled nose, high rounded ears, and pale blue-green skin, which glowed ever so faintly.

"And now for the finishing touch," he said, tucking a lock of blue-green hair behind his ear. He stepped away from the mirror.

"I expect my day to go perfectly well," he proclaimed, a visionary gleam in his eye. Tapping his feet in anticipation, he continued, "For there is no reason to believe otherwise. The Water has come to me!" He flashed Moonrise a winsome, adventurous smile.

Hearing this, Moonrise turned his head away, peering at him from the corner of his eye.

"Must you look at me that way?" Baudwin asked. Frustration supplanted his short-lived euphoria. "What else *should* I think?"

Startled, Baudwin took a moment to consider the import of his question. Although the Water had indeed come to him, he hadn't found his mother. The disappointment still burned in his heart. He'd then had an ugly fight with Loch at the shrine, and the Water had flushed them all out. As Baudwin gazed around his room, he wondered if he had done the right thing by trying to defend the shrine. It seemed to him that the right thing often led to the wrong thing. And now, having told his grandfather that the Water had come to him, Seamus was pressing him to give up some of his most prized possessions. Too many things were happening at once. He had no idea what he was supposed to do. His indecision gave him pause.

"If I choose the Water, why must I lose Steamway?" he asked, facing his pet. "If I choose Steamway, why must I lose —" Baudwin stopped himself, as he found the latter consideration far too distressing.

"Coo coo," the dove responded, looking concerned.

"Could *you* choose between flying and looking for a mate?" Baudwin asked.

Moonrise leaned out from his perch, looking quite befuddled.

"Of course you couldn't!" Baudwin exclaimed.

"So you see? I don't have to choose. I can do *everything*. I'm going to find some Glamorium, and have the most fun *ever* at the Engineerium!"

Baudwin studied his reflection again. Satisfied, he announced, "Time to go!" With that, he took one last look around to make sure he had not forgotten anything. He then headed briskly out of his room, and down the hall.

❖

Baudwin stepped from his front door onto a path of green river stones. Upon reaching the front gate, he paused and looked toward the mill, adjacent to the river. The wheel that drove the mill was stopped, for he still had to raise the sluice gates. All his Life he had watched the water wheel turn, and his father and grandfather had always spoken well about the mill. Yet, when he talked about Steamway, they always scorned his interest in such things, which he found strange. How they abhorred the new ways, yet never criticized the grinding of the gears and the creaking of the mossy wooden beams.

After his chore was done, the water level would rise, pushing upon paddles that connected to wooden spokes — driving the wheel round and round. Churning sounds would then echo down irrigation troughs that led to neighboring farms. Quietly, Baudwin took a moment to consider why Kelven and Seamus respected the mill's simple harmony; the pentroughs that fed the wheel did not abuse the natural flow of the river. Never was the Water of the river disrespected.

Perhaps I'm too hard on them, he thought, as he continued on his way.

Baudwin always liked to take the left footpath, for then he could greet the river, and walk around the millpond before reaching the dam.

I don't have time to warm up this morning, he thought. *I'll just practice as I go.*

Skipping down the path, he stretched his arms as high as he possibly could, and then bent forward and kicked his legs into a handstand. For a few seconds he held the position without wavering. Satisfied with his skill, he dropped one leg and then the other, returning to an upright stance. He then took a few more steps and did another handstand. With that, he deftly continued walking down the path on his hands.

Not bad for a Faery whose muscles feel almost as cold as the river, he thought.

The path cut through a blanket of rainbow poppies — two breathtaking swaths of color. Baudwin hand-walked by them, drinking in hues of red, orange, yellow, green, blue, indigo and violet. Several flowers branched off the main stem of each plant. Only rare plants had all the colors. Even though he saw them every day, he was always enchanted by their beauty — it was almost as if their colors held a secret he would one day discover.

"Hello, my lovely ones," he trilled, keeping his balance.

Still on his hands, he remembered a song he had learned when he was very young:

> *Of all the flowers in the land*
> *When rainbow poppies bloom*
> *With colors bright they greet our sight*
> *And chase away our gloom*
>
> *Although we may not always have*
> *The faith that we must learn*

For when the Darkness steals our joy
The Light will nigh return

Of all the flowers in the land
When rainbow poppies bloom
They stir our hearts and lift our souls
Though pain and sorrow loom

So when we find the rarest ones
With stems both true and tall
The luck we feel we live as Fate
And we are one with all

Upon reaching the millpond, Baudwin arched his back and scissored his legs in the Air. He then let one of his legs down, until his foot touched the ground. Arching even more, he pushed off from his hands, so his other leg could follow the first, and he was back in an upright stance.

"Just what I wanted," he chuckled to himself. The walkover he had just performed left him standing precisely at the foot of the hill leading to the pond.

"And now for the climb," he announced, as if stating his intention would render the effort he was about to make that much easier.

Baudwin bounded up the hill to greet the river, which curved to his left toward the millpond. On the bank, cattails, rushes, river grass, and reeds mingled in a verdant display, teeming with Life. Dragonflies darted among the reeds, water spiders skimmed busily from place to place on the surface of the Water, and minnows, frogs, and turtles all swam about in the early morning Light. Seemingly unaware of their movements, the river rushed past them toward the pond, which sat like an enormous bowl waiting to be filled.

I don't have much time, he remembered, glancing at his watch.

The millpond was the size of a small meadow, with a dirt road around the perimeter wide enough for two large lumber rollers to pass each other. All Baudwin had to do was open the sluice gates at the dam, which were situated directly across the pond from where he stood. But first, he had to stop to behold what lay before him.

Two statues faced each other on either side of the river, two lady river guardians, exuding an aura of patience and serenity. Towering above the banks, their heads tilted slightly to the side, they kept perpetual watch as the river cascaded into the millpond.

"Good morning, fair ladies," Baudwin said gallantly.

Both statues were carved from deep green Connemara marble. Gowns draped their bodies from shoulder to foot. Long hair pulled back from their faces revealed graceful features, with eyes as deep and calm as the pond.

Each one stood inside a large stone octagon, lined with a mosaic of blue, green, and gold tiles. Borders of water glyphs were carved on the exterior, at the top and bottom. Both statues held water urns — one upon a right hip with a right arm, and the other upon a left shoulder with a left arm. As in an ancient water rite, Water streamed from the urns into the octagons — only to overflow back into the rushing river.

Their enduring presence often made Baudwin wonder about many things. "If you could speak, what would you say?" he asked. Looking into their eyes, he stepped closer to them. "I know what I would ask you," he continued. He thought of what Seamus had last discussed with him. "Will the Water help me understand what I must touch?"

As always, unceasing silence was their reply. *Is that your answer?* he thought, smiling. The guardians, dignified and imposing, were always a comfort to him. How easily he could forget his troubles simply by speaking his heart to them. In just a few moments, his worries about what he had to understand all but melted away.

Their silence impelled him to study them more closely. He was most enthralled with their wings, which sprang from between their shoulder blades; forewings rose majestically above their heads, and hindwings fell below their waists.

"How would they look if they weren't made of marble?" he mused. "Would the Light shine through them like the gossamer wings of a dragonfly?"

A startling thought came to him, one that stopped him in his tracks. *Yesterday, I should have asked the Water about faery wings. Why didn't I?*

Turning his attention back to the guardians, he struggled to remember his earliest memory of them. *I must have been a Faefry of thirty or so,* he thought.

His father had taken him swimming in the river. On the way back, they had stopped for a moment to look at them. He remembered asking his father — in the direct and innocently exuberant way a young one asks — "Why do *they* have wings, Father, and we do not?"

His father had answered his question with such irritation and utter finality in his voice that young Baudwin's feelings froze inside of him — as if he shouldn't have had them at all.

"You know that's just an old story, Baudwin," Kelven had replied. "Faeries don't have wings. The Elves don't have them, so why would the Faeries?" After that, they never brought the subject up again. To bury that memory entirely, he turned his attention to the mundane task of opening the sluice gates, so he could go about his business and then be on his way.

Baudwin followed the road to the spillway, where the dam barred the millpond from overflowing. Long ago, the Elves had built the dam to withstand the unrelenting force of the river. With their impressive engineering skills, they had succeeded. Baudwin skipped down the familiar steps to the sluice gates, which were lined up four in a row.

Each gate was made of solid bronze, with a large hand wheel on top, which turned a vertical metal stem. The gates were separated from each other by a wall of stone. One by one, Baudwin turned each wheel, until all four stems had raised all four gates. As he completed each task, the Water from the millpond rushed away, having once again escaped the confinement of its unyielding captor. In the distance, he could see the wheel of the mill slowly begin to turn.

That's done, he thought. *My father may not believe this, but I always try my best to do a good job.* With hardly a thought about anything else, he then raced quickly back to his house.

Baudwin went quickly down the hall to the kitchen. Upon reaching the doorway, he paused to collect himself. He wondered what his father would say when he gave him the thrilling news that he had found the Water. Although Kelven was certainly respectful of the old ways, the Primary of Water was not known for indulging in what some would consider to be the miraculous. A pang of anxiety coursed through Baudwin. He calmed himself by focusing on what he was seeing across the room.

Rays of sunlight streamed through the window into a large sink, filled with newly picked stems of red and pink hollyhocks. Other rays bounced off scores of blue and green crystals hanging from the ceiling, casting starlike patterns throughout the room. Seeing his guild colors shining so brightly, Baudwin smiled appreciatively. The sparkling reflections were a pleasant distraction. Hoping that his father would be open-minded, he turned his gaze to the center of the room.

As he did most every morning, Baudwin's father, Kelven, sat in a relaxed yet expectant manner at the round oak table in the center of the room. "Good morning, Baudwin," he said. "Breakfast is ready."

Baudwin sped to the table and sat down directly across from him. "Good morning, Father," he replied.

As always, the table was neatly set for three, with a light green mat, blue napkin, wooden bowl, and silver spoon at each place. Two green ceramic bowls sat in the center of the table. Both were filled to the brim, one with oatmeal and the other with fresh strawberries. A honey pot with a small carved bee on the lid and a dipper stood between them.

Before helping himself to breakfast, Baudwin studied his father, searching for clues that might reveal his mood. Kelven was dressed as he usually was in a blue chambray shirt, deep green linen breeches, light green knee socks, and dark blue shoes. From the look of his clothing, Baudwin could see that his father was feeling rather cheerless and worn. Neither his shirt nor his knee socks were properly tucked into his breeches, and he had chosen to wear shoes that looked shabby and frayed. His blue-green hair, pulled away from his face with a piece of silk cord, hung in tired-looking wisps on his cheeks.

"Where's Grandfather?" Baudwin asked, wishing Seamus were there to help him deliver his news.

"He said he would be late this morning," Kelven replied. "We must begin without him. I know you have plans to spend the day at the Engineerium."

As Baudwin started to fill his bowl, he held off before speaking. Knowing that his boisterous nature might overwhelm his father, he again gauged Kelven's mood by looking into his eyes, a fine-looking shade of blue, with arresting green specks. Normally wide and round, with an innocent deer-like expression, they now seemed dull and drained of Life.

"Are you all right?" Baudwin asked, worried.

"Oh yes," Kelven replied. "There's nothing wrong with me. I'm doing very well — very well indeed."

Seeing the blank expression on his father's face, Baudwin wondered how this could be true. "Are you sure?" he asked.

Kelven did not respond. As if to avoid the entire subject once and for all, he reached for the honey. Taking a deep dip, he lazily dribbled the golden stream into his bowl, saying nothing the entire time. He then picked up his spoon, and smoothly stirred the contents in circles.

Baudwin could tell that Kelven was about to broach a difficult subject. If this were not so, he would have said something by now. A regular serving of honey in his oatmeal would have been enough, and he would not have taken such a large dip.

Kelven slowly chewed and then swallowed his first bite. Apparently to collect himself, he then put his spoon back on the table. After a moment, he announced quietly, "Evan came by the dam yesterday."

"What did he want?" Baudwin asked, trying his best to seem unconcerned. Evan was an old Elve from out of town who liked to come by the farms in Deuona to barter with the Faeries.

"He had a few tools to show me," Kelven replied casually. "They weren't of much use. But, I did make him an offer on his wagon."

Baudwin shifted abruptly in his seat. "You already have a wagon."

"That one is far too small," Kelven countered irritably.

"What did you offer him then?" Baudwin asked guardedly.

"Twelve bags of flour. He's coming to collect them next week."

"Twelve!"

"I originally offered him ten," Kelven said, "but he wanted more."

Kelven described how he had offered Evan ten bags in exchange for the wagon. But Evan had insisted on twelve bags, not ten, because *he* was now without his favorite wagon to haul his tools.

"So you simply let him have his way?" Baudwin asked, feeling more exasperated by the moment.

"No, I did *not*," Kelven replied, adding quickly, "There was nothing I could have done."

"Except maybe to offer him six, and your *old* wagon. He probably would have been happy with that! Why didn't you take a stand?"

"Why do I always have to choose what makes *you* happy?" his father retorted. "Think about it. Now, instead of one wagon, we have *two*. And, all you have to do is grind a little more grain."

"Why should I have to grind *twelve* bags?" Baudwin practically shouted at his father.

"Hey! What's all the fuss I hear?" a voice boomed from outside the kitchen. In a flourish, Seamus strode through the door, looking quite perturbed. Taking a seat at the table, he began spooning strawberries and oatmeal into his bowl. "Trouble at the breakfast table? Whatever for?"

"We're simply having a disagreement," Kelven explained. "And that is all."

"Is that true?" Seamus asked, leveling his gaze on Baudwin and Kelven like a steely-eyed badger.

"Sort of," Baudwin replied. Forgetting what he had just said, he turned to his father and pounded his fist on the table. "Why can't we just get the Elves to build us a steamway grinder? Think of all the work it would save us."

How Baudwin hated the constant work of keeping the rickety old water wheel turning. Whenever there was a storm, he had to divert the river to prevent flooding of the mill. Other times, when the pond was low, the grinding took forever. Tending to the mill consumed most of their time. Yet, Kelven would not be convinced, for he did not agree with Baudwin's critical opinion of their ancestral livelihood.

"No!" Kelven shot back.

"Why not?"

"Our work is what makes us who we are," Kelven said. "We are *partners* with the Water."

"Both of you stop — now!" Seamus bellowed. With that, no one said a word; in fact, the silence was so deafening, they could just about hear a field of clover growing.

Seamus spoke again, this time striking a more conciliatory tone. "I know you both see things very differently."

"He doesn't see anything at all," Baudwin retorted.

"Baudwin," Seamus snapped. "You must try to —"

"Try?" Baudwin closed his eyes, letting a ripple of grief course through him. He struggled to choose his words. "How am I supposed to try when he —"

"You must remember —" Seamus continued.

"Remember? How can I remember when *he* can't remember?"

"What?" Seamus cried.

"What happened to Mother!" he blurted.

Baudwin's fist again struck the table. Some help *they* were. First, he had argued with his grandfather, and now his father, which made him feel even worse. All of this would mean only one thing: There would be more time frittered away in grain-grinding and guild duties, and less time for seeking his mother in new places. Despite his throbbing fist, Baudwin wasn't sorry he had gotten so angry.

Sensing his son's pain, Kelven fired back. "We lost her in the twilight of the Great Befalling," he wailed.

"But, *how*?" Baudwin cried out again.

"I don't know." Kelven replied. "And don't *ever* ask me that again!"

Baudwin and Kelven stopped shouting, aware that it would make matters even worse. All three Faeries bowed their heads and stared blankly down at their oatmeal. And there they sat, unable to speak. As always, this exchange had left them feeling sad and confused. In slow unison, they raised their heads.

Trying to smooth things over, Seamus broke the silence.

"A family as *blessed* as ours should not be indulging in such unseemly arguments."

"Blessed?" Baudwin asked testily.

"Yes," Seamus replied. "Blessed."

"How are we blessed?" Kelven asked.

"Baudwin, tell your father what happened to you."

Baudwin looked at his grandfather, knowing what he wanted him to say. "Yesterday, I went to the Springs of Coventina," he began, "to look for Mother. First, I had a waking, which I took as a good sign."

"A waking?" Kelven asked, surprised.

"He says he has them all the time," Seamus put in. "Especially, when he's near the Water. Go on, Baudwin. Tell your father the rest of what happened."

"Then, I dove to the bottom of the spring. I saw a school of minnows. They came to me, and then kept swimming around and around me."

"How did they seem to you?" Kelven asked, his interest piqued.

"At first I saw them swimming outside of me," Baudwin continued. "But then, I saw them *inside of* me. They told me to keep my eyes closed, so I did."

Kelven sat up with a start. He looked at Seamus to see what he would say and was met with a broad smile. Both turned their attention to Baudwin.

"Please do go on," Kelven said, his mood brightening.

"After that, I saw myself floating down the river in a water drum, with other ladies and gents," Baudwin continued. "The minnows went away. And then — I heard the voices of our tribe — all of them speaking to me. There must have been thousands."

With this, Kelven's eyes filled with Life. His usual lethargy was gone, replaced by a presence Baudwin had never felt before.

"Is this really true, Baudwin?" Kelven asked.

"Yes," Baudwin replied proudly. Their eyes met, and for the briefest moment all that had ever been wrong between them suddenly seemed right.

"I've never known anyone to whom the Water came," Kelven said almost reverently. "Never knew anyone who was special enough." He looked at Seamus. "Perhaps you did, though. Didn't you have a cousin?"

Seamus nodded. "Yes, I did. He was the last Faery I knew to whom the Water came after the Great Befalling. All his Life he lived on River Danu, hardly speaking to anyone, so absorbed was he in the ways of the Water."

"Perhaps there is more to you than I realized, Baudwin," Kelven said. "All I hope is that finding the Water doesn't keep you from your duties."

"This is precisely why we must all get along," Seamus declared. Hearing this, Kelven and Baudwin lowered their eyes, as if the joy they felt was almost too much to bear.

When Kelven finally spoke, he struggled to find his words. "Judging from how angry you were . . . I assume. . . that you didn't find your mother."

"No, I didn't," Baudwin replied.

"Tell him what else you *did* find, Baudwin," Seamus urged, sensing tension returning to the table.

"Is there something else?" Kelven asked.

"Yes, there is," Baudwin continued, as he fished through his pocket. "I found this." He placed the piece of blue-green agate that Matha had given him upon the table.

"This is the glyph for —"

"Glamorium," Seamus cut in. "Baudwin has been chosen by the Water. And there's more. After the Water came to him, he and Matha found this glyph at an ancient shrine. The Water also sent him a poem, which was engraved below the glyph. Tell him, Baudwin."

Baudwin recited:

You may wish for many things

Or never want for much

But that which holds the Truth you seek

Is something you must touch

Pondering this, Kelven grew quiet, his face drawn with concern. "Whatever does all this mean?" he asked, looking to Seamus for answers.

"Many things," Seamus began. "The Water has come to Baudwin. And if he is to find his mother, he must first find —"

"Some Glamorium," Baudwin interrupted.

"What must he do?" Kelven asked. "Scale the Tadlachs? That's well nigh impossible."

"No, no, he won't have to do that," Seamus replied. "The Water will help him find a way."

"Don't be so sure," Kelven replied pessimistically. "Glamorium no longer holds secrets for the Fae, and the Water probably won't —"

"Don't discourage him, Kelven," Seamus warned. "Glamorium *may* hold secrets for one to whom the Water has come." Turning to Baudwin, he added, "Glamorium is indeed very rare, but I heard that the Elves are showing a new collection of artifacts at this year's Engineerium. Be sure to ask Matha — he will know."

"I will," Baudwin replied, his enthusiasm rising.

"I can't be sure how this will help you, but you can at least go and look," Seamus explained. "You must turn over every stone."

"Maybe not *every* stone," Baudwin joked, thinking about all the ones he had seen in his young Life.

"You know what I mean," Seamus said. "When you do, you must remember, Glamorium is as elusive as Faeries dancing in river mist — first you see them — and then you don't. And then you wonder if you ever really saw them at all." He paused for a moment to collect his racing thoughts. "Glamorium is exactly like that — mysterious. Just when you think you've found some it disappears — and you wonder if your chance is gone forever."

Kelven and Baudwin pondered the import of his words.

"And then, when you least expect it — there it is again," Seamus added.

"Ah yes, Glamorium. Almost as elusive as Baudwin when I need him to do something important for me — like getting a coupler for the mill," Kelven joked, his mood lightening. "And by the way, I need you to get me one when you go to the Engineerium today."

"Baudwin, for the *love* of *Tír na nÓg*, be sure to get him his coupler," Seamus said. "But most of all, do *not* lose your faith in the Water. Your quest to find your mother is not over. You've only just begun. You must follow what the tablet says — no matter what."

"I will," Baudwin replied, buoyed by his grandfather's fiery tone. Having finished his oatmeal, he stood up and reached for the bowls on the table.

Seeing how eager he was to leave, Seamus said, "That's all right. I'll clear the table. You go along now to the Engineerium. I'll leave the hollyhocks in the sink for the meeting. Just be sure you get here early to set everything up."

"Thank you, Grandfather," Baudwin said.

"And don't forget to get that coupler I told you about," his father added. Kelven reached into his pocket and pulled out a large copper gear. "Here, take this, so you have something to trade."

"I will, Father," Baudwin said, as he placed the gear in his pocket. "Don't forget to lower the sluice gates for me."

And with every expectation for a glorious day, Baudwin left the house.

Chapter 5

TUMBLERS TIFFS AND TAILORS

Baudwin raced through the gate and down the path to the millpond. Before reaching the rainbow poppies, he veered toward the main road that would take him past the hamlet of Deuona, and then on to the Engineerium. He was glad to be getting away from home, as his feelings about his mother still weighed heavily upon his heart. Talking to his father about her at breakfast hadn't helped at all. *I won't do that again,* he thought. But, at least Kelven had been excited about the Water coming to him.

The more he ran, the more he wanted to run. "On a day like this, a way like this is a ray of bliss," he chanted cheerfully, not only to stop thinking about her, but also to divert his attention from the long walk that lay ahead. Lucky for him, the path he traveled was an enjoyable distraction.

Hundreds of years before he sprang from the aethers, the Elves had built the road without the aid of Steamway — smashing boulders, loosening rocks, felling trees, digging ditches, and filling wagon after wagon to haul away the excess. For decades they labored in teams, grading and paving the road with smooth stones to follow the natural course of the river, with all its twists and turns. On either side of the road they built walls, hauling in loads of larger stones and stacking them so they interlocked precisely, without the use of mortar. As Baudwin traveled this road, he could not help wondering how his forebears were able to persist in such a grueling endeavor.

Not to be outdone, the Faeries had added their own charming touches by covering the walls with cascades of wild roses and honeysuckle vines. Behind those walls, they planted swatches of blue forget-me-nots, yellow buttercups, lavender bell heather, and pink and white yarrow. As Baudwin passed a bend in the river, he came close enough to the border of flowers to jump the wall and pick a few blossoms. Yet, he felt himself beginning to tire of the never-ending patchwork of colors.

Why can't I just be there already? he thought. As he hurried past another jasmine vine, he spotted a dewdrop snail creeping along a leaf toward a bead of early morning dew. "At least I don't travel as slowly as you," he chortled. "If I did, the Engineerium would be gone by the time I arrived."

His friends, Criofan and Matha, had said they would meet him on the outskirts of Deuona. Eager to see them, he walked even faster. Upon reaching

Deuona proper, he noticed faery homes with dome-shaped roofs, all nestled in specially chosen places along the river. Far less frequently, he spied elven homes with peaked roofs built away from the shore, in small groves of trees, or other hilly places.

Feeling even more impatient with his progress, he turned his gaze to the land across the river. Green fields and rolling foothills merged into dark craggy canyons between distant mountains. The mountains then disappeared into muted monoliths of violet, blue, and gray. Baudwin looked again at the surging river, and felt his senses opening. He heard the rushing of Water in a faraway stream, and smelled wet moss, as if the rocks were right under his nose. Again, the moment was new and never-ending. He wondered if he would have another bout, for the last one had happened not long after a waking. But this time no sickness came to him.

His father had seemed very surprised to hear about his wakings. Baudwin was glad he hadn't told him that they seemed to be happening more and more. If he had, Kelven would have been worried. *But I do so hope that they keep happening,* he thought. For when they did, he felt so close to the Water and grateful to be alive.

Baudwin again lifted his eyes to the mountains, seeing all the colors in rich detail. For a few moments, the sight made him forget where he was going. But not for long — just then he saw his friends walking toward him.

Baudwin chuckled to himself. For such good friends, they certainly were quite an unlikely pair. Criofan strolled down the path looking as tall and confident as ever — as if he expected a crowd of admirers to surround him at any moment. Matha, on the other hand, was shorter and more circumspect. He didn't seem to care if anyone noticed him, as long as they were interested in what he had to say.

"Baudwin!" they shouted.

"Criofan! Matha!" Baudwin shouted back.

Upon meeting, they huddled in the way of teammates, their arms around each other's shoulders and the tops of their heads touching. Laughing, Baudwin lifted his head. Before either of his friends could speak, he announced, "Today is going to be such an exciting day!"

"Exciting indeed!" Criofan agreed, stepping away from his friends. He then sized up Baudwin from head to toe.

"Baudwin," he began, "aren't you a tad overdressed for the Engineerium?"

Baudwin studied Criofan's attire — an aquamarine shirt, green vest with gold embroidery and blue topaz buttons, light turquoise breeches, and teal canvas knee boots.

"I would say *you* are," Baudwin replied. "I'm just dressed for tonight's meeting."

"Really now?" Criofan chided, as he flicked at a button on his friend's vest. "I see you're wearing your guild buttons. Are you planning to impress a faery lady by showing her you're the son of the Primary of Water?"

"How silly of you to think that I wear my clothes for such things!" Baudwin replied, smiling. "I leave that to you — the son of the Primary of Commerce."

"How silly indeed," Criofan agreed, laughing, "to think that you could keep up with *me*." Fingering a button on his vest, he added, "For how often do you see topaz buttons such as these on such a —"

"On such a fabulous-looking green vest," Baudwin cut in.

"Ho! A fabulous-looking *seafoam* green vest," Criofan corrected, as he flashed Baudwin a superior smile.

"*Seafoam* green indeed," Baudwin replied. "How silly of me not to see that. You certainly know your guild colors — better than most." Criofan nodded in agreement, satisfied to have put Baudwin in his place.

Not ready to end the exchange, Baudwin stepped closer to Criofan. "Looks like you have a little something hanging there," he said innocently, inspecting the weave in Criofan's vest. Before Criofan could stop him, Baudwin puckishly tugged on a piece of gold thread.

Criofan pulled away, glaring. Baudwin laughed.

"And the sleeves of your shirt," Baudwin continued, "although billowy indeed, do seem rather *tired*-looking."

"Tired?" Criofan asked. "Whatever do you mean?"

"Lifeless and *limp,*" Baudwin replied, grinning mischievously. Although he hadn't meant a word of what he said, he knew Criofan had taken his remark poorly.

"Are you trying to insult me?" Criofan asked, stomping his foot.

Baudwin could see that he had bruised Criofan's vanity, yet he was having far too much fun annoying his friend. "Lifeless and limp like a deflated elven blimp," he added, his eyes blazing with glee.

"That's *quite* enough," Criofan said. He tried to restrain himself. "As always, you go too far."

"And as always, you know better than I do," Baudwin replied angrily.

Matha, beginning to pace, had heard quite enough. "Both of you — quit your ridiculous bickering," he demanded, glowering at both of them.

"Why do you suppose that *I* dress the way I do?" he continued, pointing to his clothes.

Baudwin and Criofan looked at Matha. He was wearing the same blue jacket that he always wore, with a moss-green shirt, and an old belt, studded with strange-looking blue and green gems. Neither of them seemed able to answer his question. Nor could they resist laughing, seeing him so agitated and upset.

"I dress the way I do to avoid ridiculous arguments about what I'm wearing with the likes of you," Matha added, shaking his fist. His scolding was enough to silence them both.

"You're right," Criofan said, sounding remorseful. "We *were* being ridiculous, weren't we, Baudwin?"

"Yes," Baudwin replied sulkily, unable to look his friend in the eye. Once again, Criofan and Matha were going about mending fences, while he continued to put up walls. Criofan hadn't gotten nearly as upset as Matha. Baudwin wondered why, and then he remembered. *Criofan's joined to his current*, he thought. *He's the lucky one.*

"Let's not discuss that — *ever* again," Matha admonished them. Happy to see that he had helped his friends make peace, he continued speaking. "Before we talk about today, we must talk about yesterday," he announced. "Baudwin, you must tell Criofan what happened."

"You haven't already told him?" Baudwin asked.

"I didn't think that would be my place," Matha replied. "You should."

"I will, of course," Baudwin replied. "But first —"

"I know you very well, Baudwin," Criofan cut in, as he placed his knee boot forward like a feisty cat. "In order for me to understand where you are going, I must first know where you have been."

Matha laughed. "You see? I was right. Tell him, Baudwin."

"All right, all right!" Baudwin exclaimed. "You win. I will tell you what happened yesterday."

Strolling with his companions along the river's edge, Baudwin again recounted the story of his trip to the Springs of Coventina: how he had gone there to find his mother, had a waking, dived into the Water, seen the minnows swimming inside of him, and heard them speaking to him. He detailed how he had seen himself as well as others floating in water drums down the river, only to hear a voice guiding him as he traveled along — until finally — the Water found him.

"And then," he continued, just as excited as the first time he had told his story to Matha, "I heard the voices of our tribe — all of them speaking to me. There must have been thousands!"

As Baudwin spoke, Criofan pranced about, so enthralled was he by what he was hearing. "You've been looking for the Water for so many years!" he rejoiced. "What made you succeed this time?"

"I really don't know," Baudwin replied. "The Water prompted me. There was something guiding me — a presence I can't describe."

Baudwin tried to explain how the Water had prompted him. Something else was at work that none of them could understand. Criofan had to know more.

"Did you recognize the voice that guided you?" he asked.

"She was a faery lady —" Baudwin replied.

"Was she your mother, then?" Criofan cut in.

"No, she sounded much older, like one of our elders."

"Did you ever hear your mother?"

"No, never," Baudwin replied, his voice beginning to falter.

"I'm truly sorry, Baudwin," Criofan said. "That must have been very hard for you."

"It was. In fact —"

"I found him on the grass after he got out of the spring," Matha broke in. "He was in quite a state — I tell you. From there, as we were chasing a bluethroat, we stumbled upon an ancient faery ruin."

"Why were you chasing it?" Criofan asked.

"He stole my button, and I had to get it back," Baudwin replied.

"Chasing after a button?" Criofan asked. "How amusing! If he had stolen one of mine, I would have been furious." Playfully, Criofan flipped one of his precious topaz buttons.

"Precisely," Baudwin agreed.

"However," Criofan countered, "as much as I like my clothes, even *I* wouldn't bother doing such a —"

"Never mind, Criofan," Matha cut in. "We saw rings and rings of crystal seats at the ruins — in the shapes of crocuses, roses, acorns, and holly. In the center was an ancient shrine to the Water, with a well that had a large sphere of yellow topaz built into the cover, and sun rays carved into the base."

"Sun rays?" Criofan asked. "That seems rather odd —"

"Criofan, you should have seen all the offerings." Baudwin enthused. "There were thousands upon thousands of them! All colors of blue and green, topaz and quartz, pearls, and pieces of gold."

Hearing this, Criofan stopped walking. As he turned to face his friends, the golden threads on his vest shimmered in the sunlight.

"Tell him what else happened, Baudwin," Matha prompted.

"If I do, you must promise not to get too angry," Baudwin implored.

"Angry?" Criofan looked at Baudwin in disbelief. "Whatever do you mean? I never get as angry as you do."

"Really, Criofan?" Matha chimed in.

"Really indeed," Criofan replied. "I can't believe that either of you would think that of me. We all know that *Baudwin* is the one who gets as angry as an Elve with his buttons cut off!" Flashing them a cool, yet charming smile, he added, "Now go ahead and tell me what happened."

Matha told Criofan about the small tablet made of agate that he had found in the niche. He also talked about the poem on the tablet, and the glyph. He then revealed that as he and Baudwin tried to figure out what the glyph might mean, Loch and his gang came storming in.

"However did they find you?" Criofan asked, his voice rising.

"They were tracking grand horns and came across our trail," Baudwin replied. "They followed us all the way from Deuona."

"Then what happened?" Criofan asked.

"They took us by surprise," Baudwin replied. "Loch was his usual nasty and overbearing self."

"He called Baudwin a liar," Matha said. "He told him the Water didn't come to him."

"He's just jealous," Criofan spat angrily. "We know how well *his* path has gone."

"We started arguing, and Loch smashed the tablet," Matha continued.

"In the shrine?" Criofan asked, incredulously.

"Yes," Baudwin replied. "And then we all got into a big fight."

"Next time I see him, I'll give him a thrashing he'll *never* forget," Criofan announced, his eyes blazing with rage.

Baudwin hurried to catch up with him. He could tell that even though Criofan was angry, he remained composed. How Baudwin envied his friend! By coursing with his feelings, Criofan could temper his resentment toward Loch, and not go to extremes.

To change the mood, a joke was in order.

"*Now* who's acting as if he just got his buttons cut?" Baudwin asked, chuckling.

Criofan did cool off, but was not the least bit amused. "I hope you gave him one," he said.

"We did — at least we tried to," Matha said. "But we all got thrashed instead by the Water —"

"How?"

"The Water rose up out of the shrine and drove us all out. We ended up scattered about in the Woods."

"If I'd been there, you wouldn't have needed the Water," Criofan said, his anger still boiling inside of him.

"Well, of course we would have welcomed your help," Baudwin said. "But as it turned out, the Water was magnificent, and gave us all the help we needed."

"What happened to Loch?" Criofan asked.

"For all we know, he might have gone to Annwyn," Matha chuckled. "We haven't seen him since."

"That would be far too easy a price for him to pay."

"Criofan," Baudwin said "That's enough. Let's not let this ruin the fun we're all about to have."

Kicking off that fun, Baudwin began racing down the road. "Beat you to the bend and around!" he shouted.

His friends ran after him, laughing and shouting. Soon they were all performing acrobatic stunts, zigzagging back and forth across the road, bouncing from wall to wall, each one trying to outdo the other. Matha and Criofan competed with each other by doing sets of roundoffs, followed by backflips, and Baudwin with them, by doing aerial cartwheels. Despite these antics, they seemed to be making better time getting to the Engineerium.

This would not be for long. As they raced around a bend, they suddenly came to a halt to avoid running into a large lumber roller in the middle of the road. An exasperated-looking Elve sat behind the wheel, trying to start the engine. Angrily, he stopped turning the key to examine the gauges on the dashboard. Upon seeing the three Faeries, he scowled at them and yelled, "Don't come any closer!" Baudwin could see that the tips of his pointed ears were scarlet with anger. He then jumped out of the cab, tools in hand, and began working under the hood.

"We just want to pass," Baudwin said, as they reached the lumber roller. "You look like you might need some help."

"How are you going to help me?" the Elve retorted. "By doing some kind of silly water dance?"

"No, I —" Baudwin began.

"You can't help me," the Elve interrupted disdainfully. "Faeries know nothing about machines."

"What do you know of Faeries?" Baudwin asked. "I work on lumber rollers all the time, with Rian at the General Store."

"I bet you haven't worked on one of *these* beauties," the Elve boasted. "This one is the newest of its kind."

"If it's so new, and it works so well, why has it stopped?" Criofan asked. Baudwin and Matha looked at each other, trying hard to keep from laughing.

"I'll get 'er going, the Elve replied, still tinkering under the hood. "I'm just working out some minor kinks with the engine."

With that, he hopped back into the cab and turned the starter key. This time, the engine turned over, and the boiler began hissing steam.

"You see?" he asked, as he flashed them all a knowing smile.

"Oh, so the engine works, but the driver can't work the engine," Matha observed.

"Very funny," the Elve replied, insulted to no end. "If you're all so clever, how come you're walking to get to where you're going, and *I'm* driving?"

"We enjoy walking," Matha replied haughtily, looking at his friends. "So we don't go daft listening to your blasted machines. Isn't that right, fellows?" Baudwin and Criofan nodded in agreement.

"Looks like you like to walk, except when you *don't* like to walk," said the Elve.

"And when is that?" Matha asked.

"When you aren't feeling so nimble and delicate that you have to rely upon all the things we Elves build," the Elve shot back. "All of you stand back, while I get this going on the road again."

With a few quick maneuvers, the Elve righted his lumber roller on the road. The way was now clear. After straightening his rear-view mirror, he pulled away from the three Faeries. Smiling affably, he tipped his hat to them, and then drove away. As the lumber roller disappeared from view, steam filled the air.

"How cheeky of him," Baudwin said. "Now that his lumber roller works again, and *his* buttons are back on, he's acting cordial."

The three Faeries resumed their walk.

"Where does that saying come from anyway?" Criofan asked.

"What saying?" Matha asked.

"Losing one's buttons?" Criofan added.

"I believe it refers to what happens when an Elve loses his job, or his position in an order or a guard," Matha said.

"Of course," Criofan replied. "The others cut the buttons off his jacket, which makes the recipient of such an act feel not only demoted, but also disgraced. For what is an Elve without his rank in the order of things?"

"What would we Faeries do?" Baudwin asked.

"Provide an extra set of buttons in case of hard times," Matha replied, laughing. "Or maybe a doublet or two."

"Yes, we certainly are different." Criofan said, amused.

The three friends knew that for thousands of years the Faeries and Elves had been at odds with each other, perhaps for even longer. Yet, there may have been a time when this was not so. Some believed that long before the Great Befalling, the Elves were far less single-minded about their gadgets, and less inclined to shut themselves away in their workshops. At the same time, before the Great Befalling, younger Faeries had been far less interested in elven inventions, and more inclined to spend time with one another, communing with their elements. Yet lately, more and more of them, including older Faeries, were breaking from tradition to enjoy elven wonders.

At first, the Elves had been happy that the Faeries were finally accepting progress. Yet, in recent years a tone of discord had been running through Four Falls and Deuona. Some Faeries wondered if the promises of the Elves could actually unite the Fae again, while many others, especially elders, remained skeptical of elven offerings.

Baudwin and his friends were no exception. At times, elven progress seemed to be an impediment to an even more important kind of progress. Of what use was a lumber roller to a Faery, if the Elve inside was cantankerous and spoiling for a fight? Most of the Fae knew that they should make attempts to get along better, but very few understood the sacrifice they would have to make to keep up such a practice. The road would indeed be fraught with misunderstanding, uncertainty, and pain, but an even greater pain awaited those who lacked the courage to begin the journey at all. At the heart of their discord, the Fae sensed a wound in *Tír na nÓg*, which if healed, would bring about a rapport they all so desperately craved. But for now, all most could do was to stumble on, and so the three Faeries looked for ways to understand what they sensed was missing.

"Something is amiss," Baudwin said, referring to the Elves. "They are cheery and bright on the outside, but to us, they seem much darker on the inside. And we . . ."

"Are the opposite," Matha replied, finishing his friend's sentence. "We are much brighter on the inside, but to them, we simply seem darker on the outside, even morose."

"Morose? Surely, not that bad," Baudwin said

"Well. . . they certainly seem more zealous and certain about the future than we do," Matha said.

"And so independent," Baudwin added. "At least we know how to cooperate!" Laughing, he began to recite a poem he learned when he was just a Faefry. Hearing him, Matha joined in:

Elves can always find the time

Faeries take the space

Elves know how to take the means

Faeries find the place

"I would much rather be a Faery than an Elve," Criofan said. "Faeries are better."

"I as well," Baudwin agreed.

"That being said, we must not let our differences allow us to forget to practice the Golden Way," Matha said, seriously. Both Faeries and Elves had been taught the Golden Way. "You do remember how it goes, don't you?" he asked, playfully.

"Of course I do," Baudwin replied. He then began:

"Always give to others what you would have them give to you, and receive from others, what you would have them receive from you."

As he went on, Matha and Criofan joined in, saying:

"For, if you balance giving and receiving, your hearts will be full, your minds will be at peace, and all will be well in *Tír na nÓg.*"

"For we are with the Water!" they all exclaimed, as they cupped their hands over their hearts, making the sign of the Water.

As Baudwin held his hands to his heart, he could not help thinking, *Who among us really understands the Golden Way anymore?* But this was not the time to ask either of his friends. For having walked several miles, they had finally reached the Engineerium.

Chapter 6

FIZZIES AND FRIENDS

There they stood in front of the entrance to the Engineerium, a large bronze ring built several yards in from the road, with two tall columns on either side. Blue and green streamers flapped briskly in the wind from the tops of the columns. Large stands of fir trees stood like silent sentinels on either side of the ring, as if they had been placed there to guard the entrance for all the ages.

Although the ring had been exposed to the elements for a long time, the surface still shone. Engraved at the top in elven letters were the words, *Elven Engineerium*. Beneath them were the words, *With Progress We Prevail*. On both sides of the inscription, elven glyphs formed a border all the way to the ground.

"How high do you think this pipe is?" Baudwin asked, as he looked at the top of the ring.

"About twelve feet, I would say," Criofan replied.

"I wonder how many Elves still know what those glyphs mean," Baudwin asked.

"Probably not too many," Matha replied.

"When progress prevails, the reading of glyphs fails," Criofan joked. They all laughed.

"Well then," Baudwin said, as he peered into the tunnel. "Now the fun begins!" For nothing pleased him more than having a good time and making sure that the fun lasted as long as possible.

The three Faeries stepped through the ring onto a wide stone path. The Elves had built the tunnel using sections of bronze pipe, attaching the flanges together to form nine joints. Inside the tunnel, they covered the seams of the joints with wide strips of copper, creating a striking effect.

Every few feet Baudwin passed sconces on the walls, that had been carved from glowstones into orange wood lilies or violet harebells. The sconces had been placed in rows on both sides of the tunnel, glowing first amber, then violet, all the way to the end. All the flowers were fastened to copper stems and leaves, and as they lit the corridor, they appeared to be growing straight out of the walls.

"Every year, we see orange and violet and orange and violet," Baudwin yelped as he dashed down the path, running his fingers along the wall. Matha and Criofan followed closely behind him.

By now, the three friends were more than three quarters of the way through the tunnel. With every step they took, the round circle of Light at the end grew larger. Baudwin could see faery families — mothers, fathers, and their young ones — skipping happily toward the opening. In the distance, he heard loud mechanical noises mixed with music, laughter, and excitement. They were almost there.

After a few more steps, they emerged from the tunnel. The entire Engineerium was shaped like an enormous flower, with four petal-shaped concourses. Standing at the tip of the South Petal, they could see the perimeter of the concourse — a long stone wall, with an aqueduct of Water flowing along the

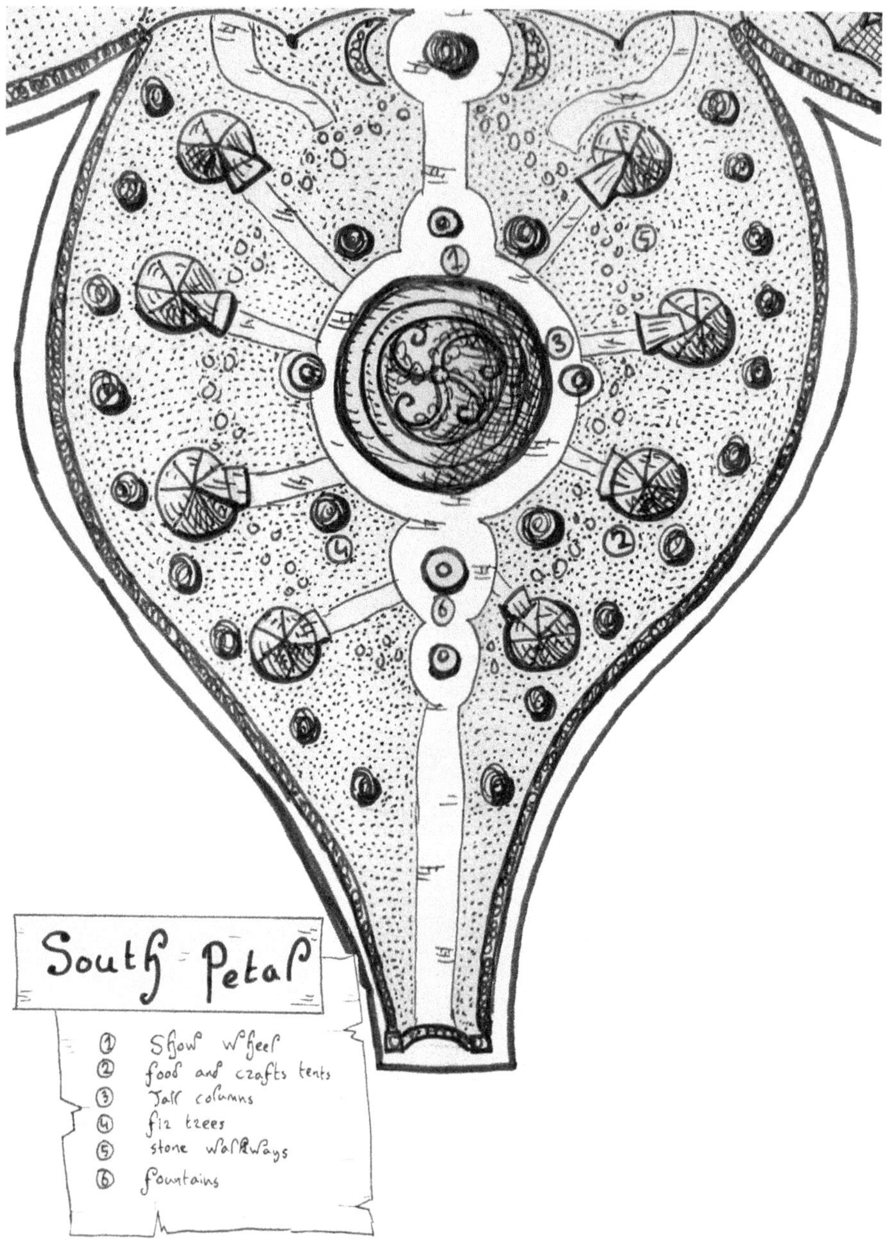

top. Evenly spaced fountains, which the Elves had built by piping Water in from the river, shot majestically into the Air.

"And now we see. . .*Water*!" Baudwin shouted.

"How beautiful the Water is!" Criofan exclaimed.

"Yes, indeed!" Matha said. "The Elves always know how to charm us water Faeries with their clever constructions."

To the left they saw the West Petal of the Engineerium, and to the right the East, with more fountains bursting from the canals along the tops of the walls. In the center of the flower was a large pavilion with a twelve-sided roof that formed a towering peak. Beyond that was the North Petal. From where they stood, the three Faeries could see scores of Elves busily attending to rides, tents, and other amusements, as well as throngs of Faeries flitting from place to place.

Finally, I'm here, Baudwin thought, scanning his surroundings. He could tell from the look of things that many Faeries had come from the city of Four Falls and beyond, no doubt to visit the colorful tents that held a marvelous array of food, clothing, jewelry, crafts, and other wares.

"What should we do?" Matha asked.

"Whatever we please," Criofan replied. "Everything is free."

"Yes, whatever we please," Baudwin agreed.

What Criofan said was true. By order of the Assembly of Progress, all food and entertainments were free.

"Don't you ever wonder what the Elves are *really* up to?" Matha asked dryly.

"What do you mean?" Criofan said.

"I don't know," Matha replied. "All of this is offered so freely to the Faeries. Why do you suppose that is?"

"We still have to barter for other things," Criofan countered.

"I know," Matha said. "It's just that —"

"Like the coupler I have to get for my father," Baudwin cut in. "Stop being such a wet lily. We're here to have fun."

"Must we follow you around?" Criofan asked, annoyed. "I want to go to the Water Park in the North Petal. And then —"

"Who said anything about following anyone?" Baudwin interrupted again.

"I want to see the collection of ancient artifacts at Curios & Marvels," Matha added. "They're extremely rare. If you join me, you might learn something you don't know about the old ways."

"Which reminds me," Baudwin said, turning to Matha. "My grandfather told me to ask you about the glamorium exhibit. Where is it?"

Before Matha could respond, Criofan interrupted him. "Glamorium?" he asked, surprised. "Why?"

"I'm going to touch some," Baudwin replied.

"You are?" Criofan asked. "What makes you think you can do that? Faeries don't just touch Glamorium simply because they've been seized by a whim."

"They do if the Water is guiding them," Baudwin replied. "This isn't just a whim."

"Sounds like a whim to me," Criofan said.

"I don't care what it sounds like to you," Baudwin countered crossly. "I believe the Water is guiding me."

"What a highfalutin thing to say," Criofan said. "Isn't it *enough* that the Water has come to you?"

"Perhaps this will answer your impertinent question," Baudwin said, as he fished in his pocket. "When Matha and I were at the shrine, we found this." Baudwin handed Criofan the piece of blue-green agate.

Criofan studied the glyph on the piece of stone. "I'm not being impertinent — just careful, so you don't end up looking like a fool. You say this is telling you to touch Glamorium?" he asked. "How do you know?"

"Because," Baudwin began, his face lighting up with excitement, "my grandfather says this is the ancient *glyph* for Glamorium. He told me that the Water had guided me to find this, and I believe him."

Matha studied the glyph. "Glamorium. So *that's* what the glyph means. We're lucky Seamus knew. Very little is spoken about Glamorium anymore."

"That's true," Criofan began. "My father has hardly spoken of it before, which means he probably never traded for any."

"Tell him about the poem that you found," Matha said. "The one we read before Loch smashed the tablet."

"Loch!" Criofan exclaimed." If I see him, I'll —"

"Forget him," Baudwin cut in. "This is more important." He then recited:

You may wish for many things

Or never want for much

But that which holds the Truth you seek

Is something you must touch

For a moment the three Faeries stood quietly, as the poem had touched their hearts and silenced their bickering.

"I wish to find my mother," Baudwin said. Earnestly, he turned to his friends. "To do this, I must know the truth about her. Perhaps Glamorium will guide me there. I need both of you to help me in my endeavor — or at least give me your support."

"What makes you think we don't support you?" Criofan said. "We are, after all, first and foremost, your best friends, aren't we, Matha?"

"Yes," Matha replied. "In fact, as I was just saying before I was so rudely interrupted, I believe you will find glamorium artifacts at Curios & Marvels in the West Petal. Word is out that they are the rarest of the rare and have never before been displayed. We should all go there together."

"How exciting," Baudwin said. "I just knew it. I *am* going to find some Glamorium and have the most fun *ever* at the Engineerium!" With that, he began hopping about on the grass, hardly able to contain himself.

"Now wait," Criofan cautioned. "Before we all get too excited, we must make a plan. Otherwise —"

"Yes, let's make a plan," Baudwin said, for he loved doing nothing more. "What should we do?"

"Something sensible," Matha interceded, in his usual laconic way, "or the Elves will find us here tonight, having never left this spot and still cavorting like a herd of rabbits around the fountains."

"I know," Baudwin said, checking his watch. "I'll go on my errand to get the coupler, and then we'll all meet up later in the West Petal." With that, he began to study the entire Engineerium, trying to figure out how he might accomplish this very important task.

As Baudwin surveyed his surroundings, a high-pitched, but pleasant-sounding voice broke his concentration. "Baudwin, is that you?" the voice called. "Would you like something to drink?"

Only then did Baudwin realize how thirsty he was after having come such a long way. Recognizing the voice, he quickly put aside his thoughts about what he was going to do. "Come with me," he said to his friends.

A few yards away, an elven lady stood inside a round tent that had a yellow-and-white-striped top with a bright red flag rising from the center. As Baudwin approached her, she was decorating the poles of the tent by tying fabric to them. She cinched a piece of red satin cord in the middle of one of the poles. The fabric at the top hung loosely, forming a semicircle, while the rest fell in a column to the ground.

Baudwin crossed his hands in front of him, his right palm facing down, and his left hand pointed up, a sign Faeries made upon meeting Elves they hadn't seen in a while. "A time for all places," he said. "Hello, Riona."[1]

"Riona made a circle with her hands, her fingers touching at the top, and her thumbs at the bottom. "A place for all time," she replied. "Hello, Baudwin!" They both stood, smiling at each other.

"Hello, Riona," Matha and Criofan said in unison as they approached the tent. "A time for all places," they added, making the same sign as Baudwin.

"A place for all time," Riona replied, as she made her sign again. "Hello, Matha and Criofan. How good to see you."

---

[1] Pronounced [REE-oh-na]

"Your tent looks very inviting," Baudwin said. "We're all quite thirsty, isn't that right?" he asked his friends. They both nodded in agreement. "What do you have this year?"

"Why, valley dew fizzies, of course," Riona replied with a toss of her head. "Made with the purest water, sweet-vine sugar, and fruit."

"We've all come a long way, and a fizzy would certainly be great," Baudwin replied, as he admired Riona's gem-studded belt. "You, I might add, look very pretty, dressed as you are in red and copper."

"Why, thank you, Baudwin," Riona said, as she adjusted the belt and smoothed her skirt. Smiling, she added, "I dressed up today hoping something special would happen, and here I am speaking with you."

The lines on Riona's face suggested that she had endured many trials, and somehow managed to weather them all. Neither her ochre hair, which curled wildly around her face, nor her rich and colorful clothing seemed to match her formal demeanor. Unlike water Faeries, who dressed to remind themselves of their element, Riona, like most elven ladies and gents, dressed to complement the luster and strength of her metal. Baudwin admired her resilience. Despite the stern side of her nature, he knew she was as malleable as Copper, for she had been hammered and bended by the struggles of her life, and had never broken apart.

Both elven ladies and gents alike enjoyed wearing jewelry — which was made from Platinum, Gold, Silver, or Copper, but had to be finely crafted — and Riona was no exception. In their view, the shinier and more polished the metal, the better. A long copper necklace hung around her neck, with many charms that flashed like sheeny autumn leaves against her pale yellow skin.

"I'm ready for my valley dew fizzy," he announced with great anticipation. Looking inside, he repeatedly pressed his lips together, as they were dry with thirst.

In the center of the tent, he spied a large green spool with wide, well-tooled ends, which Riona used as a handy work table. On top of the spool sat a smaller one, used as a shelf. The flag pole from the top of the tent ran through both spools, holding them in place.

"What flavors do you have?" Baudwin asked, as he eyed a circle of copper stands on the bottom spool. Out of each stand spiraled a vine-like stem made of clear glass, with green oval-shaped leaves and a red bell flower at the end. The petals of the flower faced down to make a fizzy tap. Baudwin wished he could drink from all of them at once. Glasses stacked two rows high rested on the top spool, ready to be filled.

"I have strawberry, raspberry, cherry, blackberry, elderberry, black currant, sarsaparilla, ginger root, peach, and apple," she replied. "Which would you like?"

"Cherry — that's my favorite," Baudwin replied.

"Cherry you shall have," Riona said, as she sprang to action. As she rose on her tiptoes to get a glass, the charms on her necklace tinkled faintly against the fizzy taps. After taking a glass from the shelf, she pulled up a flower petal on the cherry tap. A red bubbly liquid spiraled through the stem and out of the flower, and then into the glass.

"What will you have, Criofan and Matha?" she asked as she waited for the glass to fill. Back at the counter, she handed the fizzy to Baudwin.

"I'll have sarsaparilla," said Matha.

"And I'll have raspberry," said Criofan.

"Coming right up," Riona said.

Baudwin took a long, satisfying, sip. "Delicious!" he exclaimed. "However, do the Elves put bubbles in the Water? I —"

Seemingly out of nowhere, he was interrupted by the roar of a machine and a voice trying to shout over it.

"What is *that?*" Baudwin asked, as he looked down the walkway, and then back at Riona. "I don't see a thing."

"Look again!" Riona exclaimed. "And you'll see our new mono-wheels."

As Baudwin stared down the promenade, he saw a wheel, six feet high, encased by a rubber tire, spinning directly toward them. Inside the wheel sat an Elve on a seat bolted to the frame. "Watch out! Watch out!" he shouted, as he weaved in and out of the oncoming foot traffic.

"He's coming right at us!" Baudwin cried.

"All of you move — now!" Riona shouted, as she lifted up the counter. First she grabbed Baudwin by the arm, and then Matha and Criofan, pulling them all to safety inside the tent. Stumbling in haste to avoid running into each other, they almost fell down. Riona then slammed the counter back in place.

Watching anxiously, they waited as the mono-wheel sped toward the tent, making an extremely loud whirring sound. Frantically, the Elve jerked the steering wheel from side to side, forcibly placing his feet upon the ground and dragging his heels in the dirt to keep from falling over. As he screeched past the tent, he barely missed the place where Baudwin had been standing just a few moments earlier.

"There — you see!" Riona exclaimed angrily. "He would have knocked you over, and ruined my tent! They used to pedal those things themselves, but now they use steamway engines, and they go so fast they can't control them. This isn't the first time a mono-wheel has threatened me with such destruction. I don't see any use for them at all. What a charming way for us all to greet each other after a year!"

Quickly, she ran to the counter to keep the two other fizzies from spilling over, catching them just in time.

"Here you are," she said, handing the drinks to Criofan and Matha.

Seeing how distraught Riona was, Baudwin tried his best to comfort her. He knew she volunteered for the Engineerium every year, worked very hard, and rarely complained. Although she was quite sensitive for an elven lady, she wasn't afraid to speak her mind. Baudwin liked that about her.

"The mono-wheels used to be a lot of fun," he said.

"Not anymore," she countered. "They're a hazard, if you ask me. Did you hear what that Elve was shouting to everyone? 'Come see the show at the Show

Wheel. After that, step right up the Tree of Innovation.' As if anyone needed to be directed, when all they had to do was keep walking and see those places for themselves."

Seeing her point, Baudwin declared, "*You* should be running things here, Riona. Then everything would work perfectly well, and nothing would ever go wrong."

"Yes, you should," Criofan agreed, as he drained his fizzy. "That fizzy was first-rate."

"Absolutely," Matha said. Glancing at Baudwin, he said, "I suppose that Criofan and I should go now and leave you to your errand."

"That would be good," Baudwin said brightly. "We can't stay here all day bothering Riona."

"None of you are a bother," Riona assured them, again lifting her countertop. Exiting the tent, Matha and Criofan turned to thank her for her hospitality and the delicious fizzies. She watched fondly as the two Faeries disappeared into the crowd. Having decided to meet his friends at the entrance to the West Petal after he'd run his errand, Baudwin stayed behind for a few more words with Riona.

"Why did you choose to work the South Petal this year anyway?" he asked her.

Riona smiled wryly. "Perhaps, I simply wanted to be near the Show Wheel so I *too* could be entertained." With that, she let out a peal of laughter, as if she knew that nothing that had just happened mattered in the least.

Seeing that her mood had lightened, Baudwin asked, "Did you like the show?"

"Very much. And if you hurry, you'll catch the next one on time."

"I don't know," Baudwin said. "I have to get a coupler for my father. If I get into his good graces, he might agree to let the Elves build us a steamway grinder."

"A steamway grinder? What a convenience that would be for your mill," Riona said. "By the way, how *is* your father? Why haven't I seen him lately?"

"You mean *here*?" Baudwin asked, knowing that his father had little use for the Engineerium.

"No, I mean at Rian's store," Riona replied. "He used to come in all the time, to barter or just to chat."

"I don't know," Baudwin said cheerfully. Perhaps he spends too much time at the mill instead of letting a steamway grinder do the work."

Riona laughed.

"After I get the coupler," Baudwin said, "I'm going with my friends to see some Glamorium."

"Glamorium?" Riona asked. "Where?"

"Matha said there's some at Curios & Marvels," Baudwin replied.

"I know a better place," Riona said, smiling knowingly.

"You do?" Baudwin asked. "Where?"

"At the Tree of Innovation," she said, pointing to the center of the Engineerium. "In the pavilion."

"The pavilion?" Baudwin asked.

"See that banner with the sprocket, flask, smokestack, and lightning bolt?" Riona asked. "Go there."

Baudwin studied her face, catching the gleam in her eyes. He could tell that she knew how much he wanted to find some Glamorium. For she could see the deeper secrets that Elves and Faeries carried in their hearts and minds. *She can surely see mine*, he thought.

"What's the Tree of Innovation?" Baudwin asked.

"A gift from the Assembly of Progress," Riona replied, "to teach the Faeries about what the Elves are bringing to *Tír Éirí Sióg*."

"Really?" Baudwin asked, his head beginning to buzz. *Should I go to the Tree of Innovation, or get the coupler first?* he wondered.

For a moment, they were silent. "You really would like to touch some Glamorium, wouldn't you?" she asked.

There's that searching gleam again, Baudwin thought. He had to ask her another question.

"How can you tell this is so important to me?"

"Well, some Elves tinker and build," Riona replied, smiling, "while others listen deeply with their hearts."

Baudwin smiled back. "I wish I could do that," he said. "It would certainly save me a lot of trouble."

"Or perhaps get you into even more," she replied with a wink.

Hearing this, Baudwin placed his hand gently on her shoulder. "Yes, perhaps. I will go see the Tree of Innovation," he said. "Thank you for the valley dew fizzy."

"You're very welcome, Baudwin," Riona replied. "It was so good to see you again. Say hello to your father and grandfather for me. And pay my respects to River Deuona."

"That I will," Baudwin replied.

With that, he left the tent, uncertain about what he should do next. He knew he had to go as quickly as possible to get the coupler. If he didn't, he would be late for Matha and Criofan. Yet, he couldn't get what Riona had just said to him out of his mind: *'You really would like to touch some Glamorium, wouldn't you. . .?'* Baudwin decided that if he was quick enough, he could see the Tree of Innovation *and* get the coupler, so he began to hurry.

As he scurried along the promenade, he was surrounded by Faeries of all ages. Many were heading straight to the middle of the Engineerium, where the

Tree of Innovation was located. Passing a food tent, he heard a Faefry of about forty and five cry out, "Mother, I want some sweet-vine!"

"There's a little lad who knows what he likes," Baudwin thought approvingly. And he certainly couldn't blame him, for newly picked sweet-vine was delicious. He remembered picking the vines when he was a young one, alone in the Woods. They were several feet long. Much to his delight, he would suck out all the sweetness from as many as he could, never telling his father or his grandfather about what he had been up to.

Baudwin then saw that the little lad was pointing at a stand of nectar balls — delicious confections made of sweet-vine syrup, fruit, and ground nuts. He smiled to himself. Certainly, the lad deserved a nectar ball, and certainly he would have time to see the Tree of Innovation as long as he hurried.

I sure hope we both get our treat, he thought.

As he passed the stand, Baudwin could smell the sweet, fruity aroma of the nectar balls. Feeling hungry, he thought, *If I weren't in such a hurry, I would stop right now and get one.* But he knew he couldn't have a nectar ball and do everything else.

The mother began to lecture her son.

"If you eat only what you want," she said to him, "you'll never want what you need to eat."

"Mother, please," he cried again. "I *need* sweet-vine."

Amused, his mother turned her head to hide her smile. "Another bakery stand is up ahead," she proposed, hoping to dissuade him. "Let's have a potato with radish sauce first, or a flowering cabbage with leek dip."

Baudwin knew just how the young lad felt. Getting what he wanted wasn't always easy. Now, for instance, he had to get the coupler and be on time to meet up with his friends, but the Tree of Innovation was too tempting to pass up.

"Donal,[2] if you knew how to course with your feelings — like *I* do — then you wouldn't be acting like such a brat," his elder sister scolded him. "Because then you would know what you *really* should feel about sweet-vine." Spying the potato stand ahead, she turned to her mother, adding, "Next time, we should walk past the food tents from the other direction."

The mother then scolded the sister. "Be kinder to your brother," she said. "He's only just joined with his current. Give him time, and one day, he will course with his feelings as well as you do."

Hearing this, Baudwin wondered if he too should walk in another direction — away from the Tree of Innovation — toward the coupler. Like Donal,

---

[2] Pronounced [DHO-nil]

he didn't know how to course with his feelings, so he often struggled to make simple decisions, which left him feeling uncertain and alone.

"I want sweet-vine," the young one cried again to his mother.

But, if I go to the Tree of Innovation, and I do get in trouble, perhaps touching Glamorium will make everything worth it in the end, he thought. There was no need to think about coursing with his feelings any further. He simply had to stick to his plan.

"If you eat your potato, you can have a maple loaf, or a baked waffle with honey for dessert," said the lad's mother.

"No!" he shrieked.

"Donal," the sister implored, "do you know what happens to little Faeries who eat too much sweet-vine? They get lighter and lighter until they just float away, and their mothers and fathers can't catch them!"

Donal's mother nodded approvingly.

Having listened enough to the argument, Baudwin strongly hoped that Donal would get his way. But instead of waiting to find out, he decided to move past them, toward the middle of the South Petal. The Tree of Innovation awaited.

Chapter 7

NEW INVENTIONS

B audwin headed straight for the pavilion, which was situated in the very center of the Engineerium, passing several food stands along the way. The smell of freshly baked bread and herbs wafting through the Air reminded him again of how hungry he was, but he knew that food would have to wait.

I must hurry, he thought. As the leader of his acrobatic troupe, he was determined to set a good example for his friends. So when he got to the pavilion, he decided he would get the coupler first, and then look for the tree. He sped down the stone pathway, past colorful wooden planter boxes filled with spring flowers. At the end of the path, a sign on the exit door of the South Petal read:

Welcome to the Center

Baudwin went right in and stood for several moments, studying the arrangement of things. Four crescent-shaped booths divided the large circular room into quarters, each filled from ceiling to floor with elven gizmos, gadgets, and contraptions. Groups of Faeries milled around, talking and laughing, and oohing and aahing at all the elven inventions. The entire place thrummed with fun and excitement.

Now, where will I find that coupler? he thought, scanning the area. But his concentration was soon broken by what he spotted in the center of the room. His eyes grew wide with wonder.

Amazing! Flabbergasting! An enormous oak tree with winding roots appeared to be growing straight out of the floor. Four branches curved toward the center of the roof from a massive bobbin-shaped trunk. Each branch of the tree bore a symbol where the branch met the trunk — either a sprocket, flask, smokestack, or lightning bolt. The entire tree shimmered and sparkled, but he could not tell how or why.

"Whoa! he exclaimed, completely forgetting about the coupler. "This must be the Tree of Innovation!" Several Faeries standing next to him nodded in agreement.

From afar, the tree looked like any other, but up close, Baudwin saw that it was made entirely of metal. In all the years that he had visited the Engineerium, he had never seen such a well-wrought construction. *Every part looks so real — just like my steamway collection,* he thought.

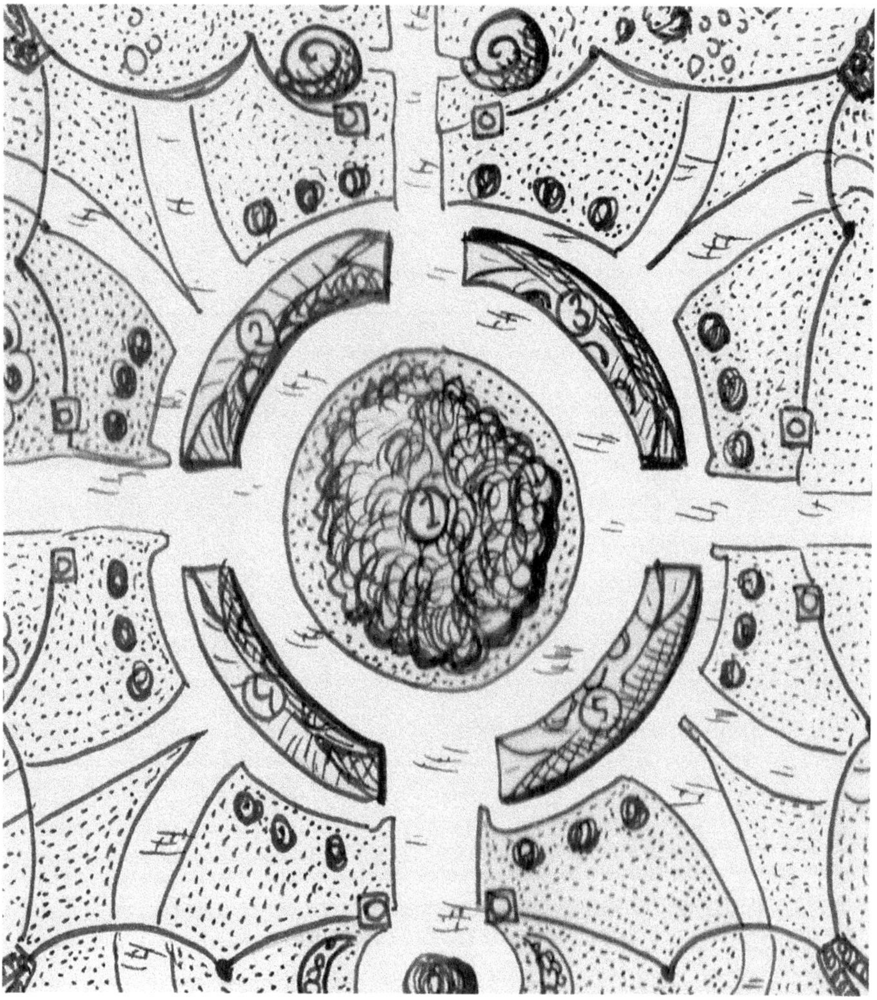

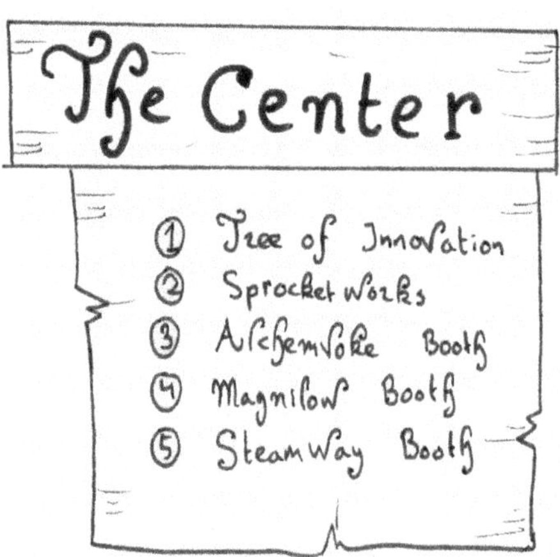
The Center
1 Tree of Innovation
2 Sprocket Works
3 AlchemVoke Booth
4 Magnilow Booth
5 SteamWay Booth

"The trunk and four main branches are made of bronze," he remarked to some nearby Faeries. "And the smaller branches are copper," he added, craning his neck to better see beneath the glimmering green canopy. "Such perfectly crafted leaves — the blades — the veins — the tips. Whatever are they made of?" he mused.

Several Faeries had overheard his question, and moved closer to him. All were "strangers," but for Faeries, this hardly mattered at all. For they often listened openly and spoke freely to one another when they talked about special or interesting things. Leaning even closer to Baudwin, they waited attentively for him to speak again.

"The very sight of those leaves takes my breath away!" Baudwin exclaimed. "They look so *alive!*"

"That's because they're made of Glamorium," a faery gent standing next to him remarked.

"Glamorium!" a number of other Faeries whispered excitedly.

"*Glamorium?*" Baudwin asked in disbelief. He then realized that indeed, this was the tree that Riona had told him about. As he continued to inspect its leaves, his thoughts about getting the coupler vanished from his mind.

"Yes, it's Glamorium, all right," the faery gent replied, motioning to the tree. "Look."

In the center of the trunk, a simple wooden sign read, *The Tree of Innovation.* Beneath the name were the words: *A trunk of bronze — branches of Copper — leaves of Glamorium. Please admire — but do not touch.*

"The leaves are made of Glamorium!" Baudwin exclaimed. His mind soared with ecstasy, and his heart thumped with joy.

"Just like I said," the faery gent replied.

"Although I haven't seen any in oh so many years," a second faery gent commented, turning to the first faery gent, "I don't remember Glamorium being so dark green in color, do you?"

"I don't know," the first faery gent replied. "But how lucky we are to be this close to such a wondrous metal." As he spoke, several other Faeries swooned with delight. "And we have the Elves to thank for this!"

"Yes! Yes!" the other Faeries exclaimed.

"Indeed, we are lucky," Baudwin said, as he fingered the piece of agate in his pocket that Matha had brought him from the shrine. *That which holds the Truth you seek is something you must touch,* he thought, remembering the inscription he had read on the tablet at the shrine. *This is my chance!*

As Baudwin reached for the nearest branch on the tree, a voice cried out, "Don't you see? The sign says 'Please admire — but do not touch.'"

"I'm only going to touch *one little leaf,*" Baudwin replied, as he reached for a shimmering green leaf. Now he would find the truth — for this was *Glamorium* he was touching! Surely the Water in all its wisdom had willed this to be so. He closed his eyes, waiting expectantly.

Several moments passed.

To his surprise, his experience proved to be flatter than lake Water on a windless summer day. Even worse, none of his senses awakened in the slightest. The moments simply remained as they were, ticking away like his watch, without depth — color — movement — or guidance of any kind.

How peculiar, he thought, shaking his head in disbelief. He certainly expected *something,* not nothing to happen.

"I don't feel a thing," he shared with the other Faeries.

"What do you mean?" the first faery gent asked, looking quite concerned.

A number of other Faeries gathered closer to the tree, craning their necks and looking from side to side to determine what was wrong. The thought that the tree leaves could be anything other than Glamorium left them worried and bewildered.

"This is Glamorium, the most precious metal in *Tír na nÓg,* prized by both Faeries and Elves alike for its amazing beauty and strength — and I feel *nothing,*" Baudwin declared. "Nothing that tells me this is Glamorium — nothing at all."

"Perhaps if you keep holding the leaf, you'll feel something," said the second faery gent, sensing Baudwin's upset. By now, several more Faeries had joined them.

"I don't believe so," Baudwin said.

"Why not?" a faery lady asked. Sharply, she jerked her head, and the long feathers on her hat bobbed in the Air.

"Because this can't be Glamorium," Baudwin insisted.

"But the Elves say it is," the first faery gent said. Speaking emphatically, he grabbed his abalone belt buckle with both hands.

"I don't see how," Baudwin said.

"Not Glamorium!" another voice exclaimed.

"Not Glamorium!" several other voices cried out in unison, as a large assortment of hats, buttons, scarves, and pointed shoes turned toward Baudwin.

"How can this be?" the first faery gent asked.

"I told you," the second faery gent said. "Glamorium never used to be this dark."

"Why would the Elves want to fool us?" another voice chimed in, shrilly.

"Why indeed?" the second faery gent asked.

"The Elves aren't trying to fool anyone," a voice cut in.

Startled, Baudwin turned to see who had just spoken. A tall elven gent approached the group, a serious expression on his face. Seeing his uniform, Baudwin wondered who this might be, for never had he seen an elven gent wearing a light violet shirt and dark violet breeches. Such colors were expensive to make, and rarely worn by guild members in *Tír Éirí Sióg.* Most Faeries preferred colors that kept them close to their element, but not the Elves, for they were always in lockstep, reaching for what went beyond the pursuit of root, droplet, breeze, or ember. Something about the elven gent's traditional-looking gray doublet, and his erudite manner made Baudwin decide to speak up.

"Glamorium should make me feel *something*," he insisted.

"You shouldn't have touched the leaf in the first place," the elven gent replied.

"But I did —" Baudwin said.

"And all you did was stir up trouble for nothing," the elven gent interrupted. You are, after all, touching glamorium leaves made by the Elves for the Assembly of Progress. And you are — after all — an *uneducated* Faery — and a young one at that."

Dismayed by the comment, Baudwin withdrew his hand. "The tree looked so spectacular, and I've never felt Glamorium before," he began. "So, naturally, I wanted to see —"

"If what you want is to *see*, first you must *hear*," the elven gent again interrupted. "I'm about to give a talk about this very subject. My name is Gavin.[1] Why don't you join me?"

Dryly, he motioned for Baudwin and the others to stand near a podium a few paces away. He then left to start his talk.

"I don't see how listening to him is going to help me," Baudwin complained to a few Faeries who were still lingering there with him. "Do you?"

"You're right!" the first faery gent exclaimed. "Uneducated Faeries indeed! If an educated Elve thinks he understands Glamorium, then isn't an *uneducated* Faery bound to know even more?"

Everyone laughed heartily.

Even though the joke actually made a great deal of sense to him, Baudwin could not help feeling worried and disheartened. Perhaps everything and everyone — his grandfather, the poem, and even the Water itself — had been wrong, and there was nothing to Glamorium. He was sorry he had gotten his hopes up, for now he seemed to be right back where he started, wanting to find his mother and not knowing how.

As Baudwin pondered his disappointment, he heard voices arguing near the podium. Some kind of hubbub had broken out to be sure. Curiously, he made his way to the commotion to see about the fuss.

The source of the trouble appeared to be several faery gents who looked to be about four and fifty. A number of other Faeries stood near the rowdy group, tittering nervously. All of them surrounded Gavin, who was about to speak.

"Maybe we're just not all that interested!" one of them shouted.

---

[1] Pronounced [GAV-en]

Indifferently, Gavin studied the faery gent, his disheveled clothes and lily hat, which sat slightly askew upon his head. "And who might you be?" he asked, trying to hide his disdain.

Angrily, the faery gent strutted up to Gavin. Placing both hands upon his hips, he announced, "I am Lugh,[2] of Four Falls, son of Donovan[3] and Leader of the Guilders of the Nechtain Quarter." Vehemently, he nodded his head, and his lily hat tipped halfway to the side, covering one eye. Quickly, he adjusted the hat, still eying Gavin.

Avoiding his scrutiny, Gavin looked past him and into the crowd, which had gathered to hear him speak. "Thank you so much for coming," he began. But, Lugh would not be stopped from heckling him even further.

"Why should we listen to you, when the leaves on that phony tree aren't even made of *real* Glamorium," he called out. Pointing to Baudwin, he added, "Just ask him — he'll tell you!"

"Why indeed?" another voice called angrily.

Baudwin realized that he was now the center of the argument. The Faeries did not seem to want to listen to Gavin, for they had seen Baudwin touch the tree, and heard Lugh's objection.

Gavin continued speaking. "As I was just saying, before I was so *rudely* interrupted," he intoned, "my name is Gavin."

Baudwin stopped listening and looked more closely at his attire. The three silver stripes on his sleeve indicated that Gavin was a Master of Silver. His graying hair and skin matched his accessories, all of which were made of silver. A medallion, featuring an artfully etched quill in the center, hung from a chain around his neck; buttons reached from the top of his standing collar to his waist, and official-looking studs were pinned to either side of his collar.

Undeterred, Gavin continued his speech. "I am a Druid of Lore, a Master of Silver, and a member of the Assembly of Progress," he informed the group, completing his introduction.

"A Master of Silver!" Lugh shouted. "More like a Master of *disaster*!" Hoping to provoke Gavin even more, two of his friends standing nearby laughed rowdily.

Unmoved by their jeers, Gavin spoke again. "My presentation is aptly named, *The Tree of Innovation — An Introduction*."

"An introduction?" Lugh spat. "An introduction to *destruction*!"

"I daresay you need not be introduced to destruction — for you are about to discover that for yourself," Gavin responded wryly. With that, he motioned to two elven guards who stood a few feet nearby.

---

2   Pronounced [LOU]
3   Pronounced [DON-oh-van]

The guards were dressed quite differently than the Druid. Studying their uniforms, Baudwin saw long-sleeved doublets made of yellow ochre, and brown pants tucked into black leather knee boots. They wore copper buttons and studs on their jackets, with only one stripe made of copper-colored silk on their sleeves, indicating that they were Apprentices of Copper. Baudwin also spotted another marking, a red star on each of their collars, but he didn't know what it meant. Immediately, they appeared at the Druid's side.

"Now if you don't mind," Gavin announced dismissively, "I must ask that you allow these Earth Guards to escort you from the premises."

"I won't be leaving anytime soon," Lugh insisted belligerently. "You with your gears, your wires, your pointless inventions, and even worse, your —"

Before he could speak another word, a hush fell over the group as an officious elven gent appeared before them. A most imposing figure, his very presence seemed too enigmatic to be a threat, yet too menacing to be ignored. Everyone seemed to have been silenced — without much effort — and seemingly against their wills.

The officious elven gent motioned toward the rowdy Faeries, pointing his finger directly at Lugh. "You *won't?*" he asked. As he spoke, the cool animosity in his tone sounded clear warning.

As Baudwin scrutinized him, he saw an intelligent-looking face, both cold and calculating, with a steady countenance; here was someone who could cleverly and contemptuously twist the facts of any subject or circumstance, thereby reducing, or increasing, their importance.

Gasping, and without even thinking, Baudwin pointed to Lugh and blurted out, "I'm sure he *will* leave, once the tree starts sprouting wrenches and bolts!" With that, the entire group burst out laughing, including the officious Elve.

This pause gave Lugh the out he so badly needed. "Well — Ferrell —"[4] he began, staring defiantly at the officious elven gent, "I wasn't interested in all of this blather anyway." With that, he and his friends turned and left.

"See that you remain that way — disinterested — on your way back to the Nechtain Quarter," Ferrell instructed them. He then turned to Baudwin, who was fidgeting uncomfortably, barely able to withstand his probing stare.

"Aren't you the rascal who just touched the leaves on the Tree of Innovation?" Ferrell asked.

"Yes — I — I — wanted to see how they felt," Baudwin stammered. "To — to see if they were made of Glamorium."

"What's your name?" Ferrell asked.

"B-B-Baudwin, son of Kelven, water Faery of Deuona," Baudwin blurted out.

---

4   Pronounced [FAIR-ell]

Hearing this, Ferrell's harsh tone abated. "I see. . . and what did you think would happen?" he asked.

Now Ferrell seemed less upset, which Baudwin found even more unnerving. The keen interest in his eyes pried into the young Faery. "I don't know," Baudwin replied, for he couldn't think fast enough to speak.

"Precisely," Ferrell reproached him. "You didn't know — did you?"

"I suppose not," Baudwin replied.

"Then try not to stir up trouble."

"I won't."

"Good," Ferrell replied. "Do *not* touch the tree — ever again."

"I won't," Baudwin replied, shaken.

Ferrell turned to Gavin. "You may resume speaking," he instructed the Druid. With that, he left the gathering, disappearing as handily as he had appeared.

After this acrimonious exchange, everyone was quite happy to direct their attention back to the talk. Despite the upset he was feeling, Baudwin decided not to let what had just happened affect his interest in hearing more about the tree.

"As I was saying," Gavin continued, "Ever since the Great Befalling, the Elves have been hard at work, performing the most vital of duties — the rebuilding of *Tír na nÓg*. Today, on behalf of the Assembly of Progress and the Engineerium, we welcome you to our newest exhibit, *The Tree of Innovation*."

As he spoke the word *innovation,* his dry voice became lilting, as though someone had tickled him quite unexpectedly with a large silky feather. As he stood behind the podium his hand rested carefully on parchment note cards. These were merely an accessory to his speech, for he had memorized what he was about to say quite some time ago.

"What you see before you are the Four Branches of Progress," he began, gesturing grandly toward the tree behind him. As the word *progress* left his lips, he sounded positively titillated. Catching his enthusiasm, the Faeries tittered expectantly, hanging on his every word.

"Over the years, we have shared many things with you," Gavin continued, with aplomb. "As you can see, our illustrious history has been artfully engraved upon this *marvelous* tree."

With that, he pointed to the first branch, which bore the symbol of a sprocket. In simple, italicized letters, the word Sprocketworks was etched into the metalwork.

"Sprocketworks provided us with the very foundation of our productivity through the making of metal — first anvils and lathes and then gears, pipes, springs, and valves. Back then, who could have possibly foreseen what would come to pass? Such a fabulous array of tools, pots and pans, utensils, and other

inventions, including much of the furniture that we all use with such pleasure in our homes."

All the Faeries nodded and murmured in agreement.

"At the same time came *Alchemvoke*," Gavin continued, pointing to the word on the second branch which also had the symbol of a flask. And with *Alchemvoke* came the making of glass in all shapes and sizes, the mixing of elements to make parchment, dyes for cloth, glazes for tiles and pottery, colors for paint, essences for medicine, cosmetics and soaps, and many kinds of thundersticks — practical ones for logging and mining, and even more extraordinary ones for our enjoyment."

All the Faeries again nodded their agreement.

"Who here has not been to a celebration at the river and seen our colorful Sky Sparks — those amazing streaks of fire that explode like blooming flowers in the night sky?" Gavin asked.

"Soon, we will celebrate the Birthdays of Our Elders with them," a young faery lad called out.

Gavin looked his way. With a smile, he removed a wooden box from beneath the podium. He opened the lid and took out a long charcoal-colored stick.

"Would you like to see one of these?" he asked, motioning to the lad to join him.

As the lad approached the podium, Gavin lit the stick with a match. The flame burned brightly with sparkling color — first red — then violet — then blue. The youngster beamed with delight.

"You may take the box and hand out the rest to your friends," Gavin instructed. He then turned back to his audience.

"And now," he continued, "*Alchemvoke* has made possible a brand-new product — Liquistone — one that you will certainly be seeing at many of our new building projects. With Liquistone, there is no longer any need for stone!"

Liquistone? Baudwin was dazzled. He certainly intended to find out more about this new invention before he left the pavilion.

"But, there is *much, much* more," Gavin continued, as he pointed to the third branch on the tree, which carried the symbol of a smokestack. "For one could inarguably say that the *real* history of the Assembly of Progress began with the advent of *Steamway*."

As he spoke, he looked directly at Baudwin.

"For many of you, this occurred around the time you were born. All of you grew up with Steamway. In addition to engines driven by steam, and a smorgasbord of tools and lumber rollers, yours was the first generation to grow up enjoying *all* the benefits of genuine progress."

Gavin paused for a moment, waiting for the Faeries to absorb the dramatic cadence of his voice.

"Knowing this," he continued, his voice building, "We now must ask ourselves, 'Is there anything *more* we can benefit from?' The elven answer is, of course — yes. Yes, there most certainly is!"

With that, Gavin pointed to the fourth and last branch on the tree which featured the symbol of a lightning bolt. "*Magniglow*."

Baudwin watched the Faeries turn this new and unusual-sounding word over in their minds. He did the same. *Magniglow,* he thought. *Magniglow!*

"Now, I'm not going to tell you what Magniglow *is*," Gavin intoned enticingly, "because words simply cannot do justice to this amazing new wonder. Instead, I want you to *see* Magniglow for yourselves." Gesturing in a clockwise direction around the pavilion, he announced, "This year, we have dedicated our booths to the Four Branches of Progress: In Booth One you will find Sprocketworks; in Booth Two, *Alchemvoke*; Booth Three, *Steamway*; and of course, in Booth Four, *Magniglow,* our newest, most exciting marvel." As he said the word *Magniglow,* many of the Faeries turned to look at the booth.

"Please visit all of our exhibits. I'm sure you'll find something in every one that will make your lives easier, not to mention far more enjoyable and filled with even greater possibilities. Thank you."

With that, Gavin smiled tensely at the audience. As the Faeries applauded politely, he left the podium. Slowly, the group began to disperse. Baudwin remained where he was, feeling deflated. Touching the tree had been an utter disappointment, and he wondered what to do next.

He then remembered.

Before I do another thing, I must get that coupler for my father, he thought. For this was why he had come to the pavilion in the first place.

◦✦◦

Knowing just where to go, Baudwin hurried to the sprocketworks booth. As he entered, he remembered Gavin's words — "the very foundation of our productivity." Curious to see the "fabulous array" of things he had just heard about, Baudwin began looking around.

As he made his way to the back of the booth, his eyes widened. Never had he seen so many different kinds of tools in one place. On the wall hung rows and rows of hammers, saws, axes, and wrenches. These were not the ordinary kinds of tools he was used to seeing. Each one was far better crafted than those he had at home.

Baudwin picked up a bronze wrench, thumbing the worm screw until its jaws opened. The action was smooth as silk. *Now the Elves are showing off,* he thought. The wrenches at his mill were like scrap metal clubs in comparison. In fact, everything he owned was like scrap compared to what was on display. He couldn't help wondering if the wrenches were meant to be hung on walls as decorations and never used.

Strolling down the aisle, his eyes skimmed the shelves, looking at utensils, skillets, pots and pans, candle holders and hooks. All had carved wooden handles, painted with oak or maple leaves.

Baudwin didn't understand how there could be so many kinds of things, and all of more superior quality than what he owned. He picked up a couple of bronze hammers. Not only were they finely crafted, but they were exactly the same. Nowhere did he see those little differences that made each one unique. Certainly, he found the metalwork impressive, but he missed seeing the little imperfections.

Individual differences were as important to Faeries as uniformity was to the Elves. Added to that, Faeries rarely, if ever, signed their work, as if doing so would somehow be an insult to their element. On the other hand, Baudwin had always seen the signatures of every elven maker on all the sprocketworks tools his family had ever owned. Yet, here there were none. *They've crafted their way out of craftsmanship*, he thought, almost laughing out loud. But he wasn't sure how.

I mustn't forget what I came here for, he suddenly thought, but this would prove impossible. Unable to course with his feelings, Baudwin often got easily distracted, especially when there was so much to see. Eagerly, he surveyed the rest of the room, eying tables, chairs, and beds with wrought-bronze butterfly backs, wall hangings made of copper and stained glass, and tables and chairs carved from wood stumps and painted with flowers of every season. Minutes flew by, and as he ambled down the aisles admiring everything, he lost all sense of time.

Lucky for him, he soon stumbled upon what he was looking for. In the front of the booth near the counter were many more shelves stacked with boxes of old nuts, bolts, cranks, gears, pipes, springs, and valves. An elderly elven gent wearing spectacles sat on a stool behind the counter, fiddling with a mechanical calculator.

The old Elve picked up an oil can, pulled the cover off the machine, and squirted some oil into a side gear. He then put the cover back on and set some numbers on the drum and the bottom carriage. After that, he turned the crank handle on the side of the drum a few times. Satisfied, he looked up at Baudwin.

"Finally, got this working again," he said, smiling. "What can I do for you?"

Instantly, Baudwin remembered his father's instructions. He reached into his pocket for the large copper gear Kelven had given him that morning.

"I'm here to trade this for a copper coupler," he said.

"Before I begin the weigh, tell me what you're looking for — an elbow, cross, cap, or ring — what?" the gent asked.

"Just a medium straight coupler," Baudwin replied.

"Choose one over there," the Elve said, motioning to a box on one of the shelves. "That's a very nice-looking gear you have there."

Baudwin went to the box and picked out a coupler. Returning to the counter, he handed the gear to the Elve. "This is from our mill," he said.

Squinting through his glasses, the old gent examined the gear. "Must have been made the same time as those," he said, pointing to a large assortment of cogs and sprockets in the glass case below the counter. "Some of them are rare and quite old. We don't make them like that anymore. Are you sure you want to trade?"

Looking inside the case, Baudwin quickly became engrossed in its contents; he could have stood there all day marveling at row upon row of cogs and sprockets, all of them made of bronze, copper, or brass. All were fashioned to look like gear-shaped, metal snowflakes — round on the outside, square, hexagonal, octagonal on the inside — with circles of holes, sharp teeth, edges, and points — each one crafted to perfection. The versatile Elves had given a purpose to every shape, one that was likely recorded somewhere in a storehouse by a starchy elven clerk. Faeries would never bother to keep track of such things, for they preferred spending their time simply frolicking in the land all around them.

"What have you decided?" the old gent asked, reminding Baudwin of his purpose.

"Uh — I have to get that coupler," Baudwin replied, images of cogs and sprockets still swirling in his head. "Please continue with the weigh."

The old gent placed Baudwin's gear on the scale. "I won't be able to trade," he announced in a businesslike way. "This gear is too light."

Now, Baudwin was beginning to feel impatient with the whole matter. He knew he couldn't go home without the coupler, and he felt the Elve was trying to cheat him by driving too hard a bargain.

"What do you mean?" he asked. "They look the same to me. You said the gear was high quality."

"Well, they're *not* the same," the gent countered, as he added the coupler to the gear on the scale. "Not double the weight. In fact, we're shy by three-eighths. What else do you have to close the trade?"

Baudwin reached into his pocket and laid several items upon the counter — a small vial of spring Water with a silver top, five brass screws, and a fair-sized, deep violet, amethyst crystal. Before he could offer him the screws, the old gent snapped up the crystal. "This will close the trade," he said appreciatively.

"Humph," said Baudwin. He put the coupler in his pocket, feeling annoyed but happy to be leaving the sprocketworks booth still wearing his shirt.

On to the alchemvoke booth, he thought. Hoping the next booth would be less of a chore and more exciting, he completely forgot that Criofan and Matha were waiting for him. Now that he had gotten the coupler for his father, he felt he deserved to see the alchemvoke booth, and especially, Liquistone.

Soon he came to a booth with a symbol of a flask and a sign that read:

Alchemvoke — Reaction Creates Action

The alchemvoke sign made Baudwin wonder what the Elves were driving at. Faeries were taught that acting out of reaction always led to greater problems.

Here, the Elves seemed to be asserting something else. Perhaps Liquistone would help him understand what that was.

If Baudwin hadn't been so lost in following his whims, he would have considered how angry his friends probably were. Not being able to course with his feelings was again driving him in the wrong direction, and all he wanted was to squeeze in more fun, seeing all the marvels there were yet to see.

Before him now were shelves brimming with bolts of silk. Stopping for a moment, he felt the richness of a butterfly brocade, woven of many shades of blue and green thread. *How fine,* he thought, sighing delightedly. Gone was all recollection of his friends, and so he continued on his way.

At the end of the aisle he found paint in canisters, and a large assortment of brushes. Lost in daydreams of painting, all he could do was imagine creating a mural in his room. *Dragonflies and butterflies to match my sand paintings,* he thought.

"Where is Liquistone?" he mused. Walking down another aisle, he saw parchment paper, charcoal, ink, wax, and seals for letter writing, but no Liquistone. Nor did he see any on the shelves bearing face powder, rouge, eye glitter, lip shine, and perfume.

Baudwin eyed the glitter greedily, like an inchworm about to devour the leaves of an apple tree. Some would certainly go well with his acrobatic costume, for he and his troupe were to perform at the upcoming Beltane Festival. He could see himself now, sparkling under the evening lamplights.

As soon as he turned the corner, he forgot all about the eye glitter. For there before him was something even more exciting — a sign reading *Liquistone* above a collection of pots, pitchers, plates, cups, and bowls.

There is no need for stone with Liquistone! he thought, his mind rushing away from his feelings like a rogue current. He then picked up a cup and saucer. At first, they seemed like any other, but there was a peculiar lightness to them. Looking further, he noticed that all the cups had identical decorations, with glazing as uniform as everything else he had seen at the sprocketworks booth. Most were blue and green with water patterns on them.

"Gather round and see the marvel of Liquistone!" a voice cried out. Enthralled, Baudwin headed straight for a U-shaped counter, crowded with clamoring Faeries and a few calmer Elves.

Behind the counter stood an Elve, about to give a demonstration. He pointed to the center of the counter at something Baudwin had never seen before; it appeared to be a large dome made of bronze with a hole in the top. "Do you know what this is?" he asked.

Puzzled faces answered him, but Baudwin spotted a few Elves nodding their heads.

"This is a casting bowl," the gent continued.

"A what?" a faery lady asked, confused.

"A mold — but not the kind of mold that means your bread is sour," the Elve chuckled.

His explanation did little to inform the faery lady, who seemed even more perplexed. "What for?" she asked.

"Watch now — what I do with the hat," the Elve replied, placing another bronze dome with a hole in the top over the first. The two domes fit snugly, one on top of the other. He then took a number of clamps and attached them to the base of the domes.

"They have to be tight," he continued, "or we won't get the right result."

With that, he reached for a copper spigot hanging above the counter, then swiveled the mouth over the hole at the top of the two domes. "In case you were wondering," he announced cheerily, "there's room between the mold and the dome-hats for what is about to come through the pipes."

He then pointed to a series of pipes leading into the single pipe that fed the spigot. All the pipes originated from a large bronze machine that had a number of valves and hoses attached to a boiler. Baudwin thought the boiler looked like one from a lumber roller.

Having gotten everyone's attention, the elven gent pointed to the Liquistone display. "What if I told you that all those pots, pitchers, plates, cups, and bowls were made without a pottery wheel or kiln?"

"I would say you were off your widget!" an old faery gent cried out. Everyone laughed.

The elven presenter smiled confidently. "And what if I said that not only were they made without a wheel or kiln, but that they also hardened almost instantly — before you knew what was happening?"

The crowd laughed again. Someone murmured, "I would say you should go back to Silver Forge and study harder."

With that, the elven gent went to the machine and turned a knob. A whirring noise came out of the device — thrumming and thrumming — as the insides churned. Baudwin could see steam pouring out of the vents on the top.

The gent put his hand on the spigot, and carefully positioned the mouth over the hole of the mold. Presently, a bright blue liquid came pouring out. Baudwin inhaled deeply, but couldn't smell a thing. Certainly, the liquid wasn't Water, even though the blueish flow looked fairly clear.

The elven gent paid them no heed as he waited for the liquid to fill up the mold. Turning to the old faery gent, he asked, "How quickly do you think the bowl will take to set?"

"Probably about as long as it takes a spider to spin a web!" the old Faery exclaimed, chuckling.

"They're pretty fast," the elven gent agreed. "I've seen a spider spin a web in about an hour — much less time than it would take to fire a bowl in a kiln."

All the Faeries nodded in agreement.

"However," the Elve continued, "I'll be a lot faster than the spider. In fact, I would say I'm *already* done."

The Elve turned off the spigot. As he pushed the mouth away from the mold, the swiveling gears on the spigot-arm grated against each other, screeching. He then removed the clamps that held the domes to the mold. Finally, he pulled them off.

The group gasped. For there before them sat a beautiful blue bowl. The semi-clear liquid had hardened into an opaque-looking wonder. The Elve held the bowl up for everyone to see.

"I would say that this one's good for a salad," he announced. "Here you go." He then motioned for Baudwin to look at the bowl.

Baudwin approached the Elve and took it reverently into his hands. The surface, while smooth and cool to the touch, felt different from either clay or stone. He turned it over and over, marveling at its look and feel. As he did, a low voice whispered in his ear, "Now we can even make our own stones to pave our roads. We just pour them like batter into any shape we want."

Startled, Baudwin almost dropped the bowl. Next to him stood Ferrell, the officious elven gent who had broken up the faery quarrelers near the Tree of Innovation. Baudwin balked at his fastidious appearance: black leather knee boots tucked into neatly pressed indigo linen pants. The standing collar on his indigo jacket had a white star, conveying an authority belonging only to an Elve of high rank.

Despite looking confident, Ferrell seemed apprehensive. His amber eyes pierced Baudwin, looking wearily calculating and shrewd. In his gaze Baudwin saw a burden of experience that seemed to wear on him, irrespective of his rank. How strange was his demeanor in contrast to his shining adornments: three gold stripes on his sleeve, gold gears on his boots and belt buckles, gold collar studs, and a large gold medallion pinned to the right side of his jacket. He wore them as if the Sun itself had bestowed them upon him, yet he was but a shadow, and they were the Light.

This elven gent, Baudwin surmised, *must be an important member of the Assembly of Progress.* Carefully, he handed the bowl back to the Elve behind the counter. The group began to disperse. Baudwin hoped that Ferrell would leave as well, but when he turned, Ferrell was staring right at him.

"What's in Liquistone?" Baudwin asked, trying to sound polite.

Ferrell was poised to respond. "The formula, which is a closely guarded secret, contains crushed rock, minerals, and water," he replied, authoritatively. Baudwin detected a hint of excitement in his voice. For a moment, Ferrell steepled his hands, and his angular, pale yellow face became a mask. Expressionless, his eyes shifted, as his mind raced through many thoughts, like a stone skipping over a lake.

"Liquid stone — Liquistone," Baudwin figured aloud.

Ferrell's face lit up. "*Precisely*," he replied, seemingly impressed by Baudwin's apt assessment. "My name is Ferrell," he added. "I am a Luminary, a member of the Assembly of Progress, and a Master of Gold."

Baudwin was right; he *was* an important member of the Assembly of Progress as well as a Master of his metal, which meant he was very accomplished for someone who appeared to be not much younger than his own father, Kelven.

"And you are Baudwin, son of Kelven, water Faery of Deuona," Ferrell replied, with a knowing gleam in his eye. "I know of your father — he's a high-ranking official of the Water Guild."

"We don't think of ourselves as officials," Baudwin replied courteously, so as not to offend Ferrell, as there was something about him that he found quite unnerving.

"Of course, you Faeries never do that — do you?"

"I've never seen anyone in these river lands wearing a uniform such as yours," Baudwin replied, trying to change the subject.

"And what is it that *you* do, Baudwin?" Ferrell asked, ignoring the comment.

"I work with my father at the dam," Baudwin replied warily, wondering how Ferrell had heard of his family. Cautious, he was determined to reveal as little as he could.

"Then you probably see many of *these* when you go near the river."

Ferrell pushed a lock of brown hair with dull flaxen streaks away from his eyes and then removed a steamway tremor crab from a nearby shelf. He wound the toy up, until the claws clacked furiously. He then placed the crab on the floor, watching intently as it scurried away. The legs banged repeatedly, as they hit the wall. Satisfied, he turned to face Baudwin.

"Your desire to touch Glamorium is highly unusual for a Faery. Isn't the *water* what you live for?"

Shaken by the question, Baudwin stepped back from Ferrell. "Perhaps I live for more than that," he replied, disguising his unease. As soon as the claws on the crab stopped clacking, an uncomfortable silence ensued.

"Ah yes, *more*," Ferrell commented, as he bent down to pick up the crab. "More to study, and even more to comprehend."

Ferrell held the claws in front of Baudwin's face. "You see," he began, as he stared unblinkingly at Baudwin, "a tremor crab, while alive, scuttles to and fro, and you never know where the fiddle-footed creature is going to end up. Very much like a water Faery looking for Glamorium, I would say. Ferrell held the crab even closer to Baudwin. "But these steamway crabs are *always* here. Do you understand?"

"I suppose I do."

"I'm sure you do. You seem like an intelligent fellow."

"Smart enough to know fake glamorium leaves when I see them?" Baudwin asked, flippantly. At first he feared he had overstepped his bounds, but the opportunity to speak up had been just too tempting.

Ferrell cocked his head at Baudwin. An arrogant smile crossed his face, which he quickly suppressed. He looked away, as if Baudwin were no longer there. Again, his mind seemed to be racing. Suddenly, he broke the silence. "Gavin said you didn't feel anything when you touched the leaf on the Tree of Innovation, but what I want to know is — what you were *expecting* to feel to begin with."

Baudwin froze. He couldn't think of anything to say. Added to that, he was beginning to feel light-headed, which he found quite unsettling. Clearly, the strange elven Luminary and his pointed questions were getting to him.

"I was just curious," Baudwin replied. "There isn't any more to it than that."

"I see," Ferrell said, his eyes narrowing.

"I'm sorry, but I really must be going," Baudwin said, as he began to step away.

"By all means, Baudwin," Ferrell replied. "I'm sure I will be talking to you again. The Assembly wants to have a good relationship with all the Primaries in Deuona. I don't want to hear that you've been giving your elders a bad name by stirring up trouble."

"I won't be," Baudwin replied. "But I do have a question."

"And that is?"

"What does that mean?" Baudwin asked, pointing to the white star on Ferrell's collar.

Ferrell seemed to enjoy the opportunity to answer the question.

"This white star represents the rank of Luminary, which is the highest of the guards. There are eight ranks in all, and each is the color of a star, as seen by our observatories in *Tír Luí Lucharachán*. We are of the Sun, just as you are of the Moon, and we discovered, much to our amazement, that every star in the night sky is a Sun, just like ours, but often different in color and temperature. And so we chose to order ourselves as the Suns are ordered."

"And what rank is a red star?" Baudwin asked.

"That is the lowest rank — of Wick," Ferrell replied. "The ranks are Wick, Spark, Flare, Torch, Lantern, Mantle, Beacon, and Luminary. And the colors, respectively, are Red, Orange, Yellow, Green, Blue, Indigo, Violet, and White."

"Like a rainbow!" Baudwin exclaimed.

"Like the *Suns*," Ferrell added, winking.

"Thank you for the explanation," Baudwin said. "I was very curious to find out."

"Good," Ferrell replied. With that, he made a circle in front of him, with his fingers touching at the top, and his thumbs at the bottom. "A place for all time, son of Kelven."

Nervously, Baudwin crossed his hands in front of him, with his right palm facing down, and his left hand pointed up. "A time for all places," he said.

With that, Baudwin decided he had had quite enough of the pavilion and this very peculiar elven gent. He hurried out of the alchemvoke booth. As he passed the steamway booth, he saw many new inventions — engines, train wheels, and boilers — but all he wanted was to go outside and get some Air.

He was about to leave through the West Exit when something caught his eye in the last booth — a bright green light attached to a round copper base, sitting in the center of the counter.

In an instant, Baudwin forgot about how faint he'd been feeling, and also forgot how late he was.

"I've never seen glowstones anywhere close to this bright before!" he exclaimed, approaching the elven gent in charge of the booth.

"That's because you've never seen Magniglow!" the elven gent replied, shifting excitedly from one foot to the other. He then pointed to a small wheel, sitting on a stand next to a glass bulb.

"I just heard about Magniglow," Baudwin said, gesturing toward the Tree of Innovation in the center of the pavilion, "from Gavin the Druid."

"What you have here is a dynamo," the elven gent cut in. "The faster you turn the crank, the brighter the bulb will shine. Go ahead — give 'er a try!" he coached playfully.

Although Baudwin had seen and used many kinds of cranks in his Life, none of them had prepared him for what was about to occur with this one. Carefully, he grasped the handle and began turning. The bulb did not light up.

"You have to go faster," the elven gent instructed, with an edge in his voice.

As Baudwin increased his speed, the bulb shined a soft red color. This, however, was not nearly enough to satisfy the elven gent. "Make the light brighter!" he insisted.

Baudwin turned the crank even faster. As he did, the bulb shined even brighter. "Faster!" the elven gent ordered. "Brighter!"

As Baudwin turned and turned, the elven gent spurred him on even more. "Faster! Brighter!" he exclaimed, with a high-pitched shriek. "Faster! Brighter!"

By now, the color was such an explosive-looking scarlet that Baudwin thought the bulb would certainly burst if he followed the elven gent's instructions a moment longer.

"Better stop, or the bulb will explode!" the elven gent shouted. Baudwin stopped.

"You *really* are good at this when you try," the elven gent encouraged. "What's your name? You should come with me for the rest of the Engineerium tour to work in the magniglow booth. I could take you to all the other faery cities and teach you all about Magniglow. Of course, you wouldn't be working for free — I would pay you."

Baudwin took his hand off the crank to take a good look at the elven gent. From the look on his face, he could see the shrewd bargain he was trying to strike with him. If he did go, the elven gent would probably pay him very little, just for the privilege of having the job, and make him do most of the work. Nevertheless, the idea of travel and the thrill of adventure was indeed tempting. Instead of working at the dam every day, he would get to see all kinds of new and interesting places.

"My name is Baudwin," he replied.

"Well, Baudwin, my name is Glas."[5]

Baudwin looked at the scarlet bulb. He had expected the light to go out when he stopped turning the crank. However, the bulb still shined.

"Shouldn't the bulb go out?" Baudwin asked.

"No," Glas replied. "This one will stay lit for hours. That's the point. Unless — of course — I do this." With that, he turned a knob on the dynamo, and the bulb went out.

Baudwin was amazed by the demonstration. Magniglow was the most exciting elven invention he had ever seen. There were so many new things for him to learn about. The bulb definitely reminded him of glowstones, but didn't work the same at all. Somehow, the Elves had made glowstones that weren't actually glowstones. Looking at the bulb, he realized that he could see right through the red glass, or at least what he thought was glass.

He couldn't help wondering which was better — glowstones or magniglow bulbs?

"Glowstones never go out, unless we tap them," Baudwin said. "So why —?"

"But *these* don't have to be mined from the earth," Glas stressed, as he paced around the booth. "They're brighter than most glowstones. And they'll be far easier to get. Plus, eventually you won't have to turn a crank at all."

---

5   Pronounced [GLOSS]

Seeing that he now had Baudwin's full attention, Glas changed the subject. "Tell me," he began, "have you ever been to the other faery cities?"

"I've heard of all of them," Baudwin replied. And he certainly had, from his father, grandfather and many others in the hamlet of Deuona. "As for going there," he continued, "I haven't been to any of them. But I want to, perhaps in the fall, after the harvest."

"Where do you work?"

"At the dam in Deuona," Baudwin replied. "With my father."

"What do you do?"

"A lot of things. I grind grain at the mill. And I also work the sluice gates."

"One day, you could have Magniglow doing all those jobs for you," Glas declared. Without waiting for Baudwin to respond, he added, "You *really* must come with me! You're just the fellow I need to convince the Faeries that Magniglow is the future of things to come."

Baudwin took a good look at the contents of the booth. Inside, he saw dynamos of various sizes, and rows of magniglow bulbs lighting up the walls. On the shelves, he saw many kinds of flower lamps — yellow daffodils, white lilies, and red-and-pink-striped tulips, all beautifully lit with the same kinds of bulbs. As he continued to gaze upon the dazzling sight, he asked, not without a sense of awe, "Do you really think so?"

"I do," Glas replied. Baudwin could not find any reason to doubt him. Instantly, he felt as if he could leave Deuona, the river, and his family — all at once. But, as soon as he looked at his watch, his dream of travel ended.

Matha and Criofan, he thought, panicking. *They've been waiting for me all this time!*

With that, he quickly explained to Glas that he would only consider his offer and nothing more. He then left the pavilion.

Chapter 8

ALLIES AND UNDERCURRENTS

Hurrying down a stone path, Baudwin soon reached the entrance to the West Petal, a double-swing wrought-bronze gate with bird and flower motifs crafted into the bars. Above the gate the words — *Wonder Show* — hung in large copper letters on a bell-curved arch. Baudwin breezed through the entrance to meet his friends.

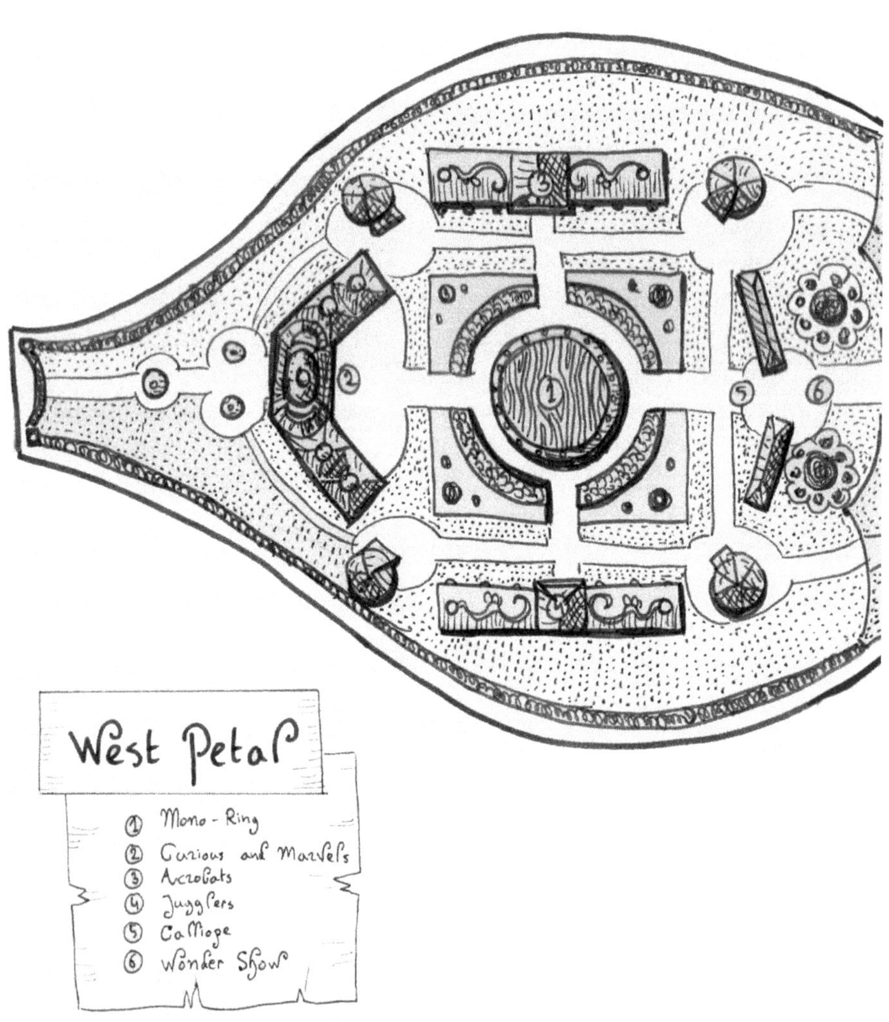

Where are they? he wondered. Fretfully, he scanned the entire place, looking through the multifarious goings-on to find them.

The entire petal pulsed with so much excitement that Baudwin could easily have gotten completely distracted, just as he had at the alchemvoke booth. Next to him a calliope in a red wagon tooted a merry tune. Gold relief carvings of elven ladies playing flutes, and elven gents pounding drums decorated the outside of the wagon. Steam puffed out of brass whistles as the melody played on — *um pah, pahpahpahpah, um pah, um pah*. Baudwin covered his ears to muffle the sound. *Did we say in the front or the back?*

Finally, he spotted them a few yards down the promenade.

"Criofan! Matha!" Baudwin shouted.

"Baudwin!" they both shouted back. All three Faeries raced to meet each other.

"Baudwin!" Criofan yelled. "*Wherever* have you been?"

"What took you so long?" Matha added. "We almost gave up waiting for you."

Guiltily, Baudwin looked at his watch. "Am I *that* late?" he asked.

"What do you think?" Criofan asked testily.

"I guess I am," Baudwin replied. "But I couldn't help it. I was detained and questioned by a high official of the Assembly. I couldn't get away." Baudwin stopped himself from saying more. He could see that Matha doubted his story.

"Sounds like squirrel droppings to me," Criofan replied. "Where *were* you?"

"I went to the Center!" Baudwin exclaimed. "You won't believe what I saw there! There's so much I have to tell you. First, I —"

"Before I listen to all of your stories," Criofan cut in, "you won't believe *this.*" Backing up a few steps, he swung his arms high above his head, and then jumped into the Air, bringing his knees to his chest while drawing his arms around his legs. Rotating once, he did a front tuck, and then landed on his feet, with a well-positioned thud.

But this was only the beginning of the trick.

Once again, he swung his arms high above his head as he jumped into the Air. Rotating once, he did a back tuck, landing again on his feet. He then performed three more tucks in succession — front, then back, then front. On the last one, he landed without so much as a wobble, smiling broadly, with his arms straight in front of him.

Motioning a few yards behind him, he announced, "While you were busy putting your fun before us, I just showed Matha I could beat that Elve back there. He could only do four." Baudwin scowled.

"Go show him you're the best, Criofan!" Matha exclaimed. "Contest, contest!"

Basking in the attention, Criofan paraded in a circle with his arms outstretched, and palms turned up. "Perhaps, a contest *is* in order," he grinned.

"I will go and arrange the terms," Matha said.

"Oh yes, the busy squirrel must arrange the contest for the peacock," Baudwin chided them. "Both of you — you're not listening! You *have* to see Magniglow!"

"Magniglow?" asked Matha. "Something magnificent that glows?"

"Like your face, when you see a new elven invention?" Criofan added with a laugh.

"Something much better than that," Baudwin replied, annoyed.

Matha shook his head. "We waited all this time," he said. "So we could all go to see some Glamorium."

Matha and Criofan exchanged irritated glances.

"Why don't you just go yourself?" Criofan said to Baudwin.

"Without the troupe?" Baudwin asked, dismayed. "I was just trying to tell you how amazing Magniglow is."

Matha had heard enough. "You said you were just getting a coupler, but obviously you got sidetracked and forgot all about us," he snapped.

"Yes," Criofan added. "You aren't acting like a member of the troupe."

Baudwin winced, for as their leader he had failed to set a good example. He wanted to make everything up to them, but before he could, Criofan took over.

"Up, up, now up, Matha!" Criofan ordered.

Baudwin knew what Criofan was up to, so he decided to play along.

Quickly, Matha grabbed Criofan's hands while standing behind him. Swiftly, Criofan lifted him onto his shoulders. As Matha stood up, Criofan let go of his hands, and then grasped both of Matha's ankles.

"Baudwin, you're next!" he insisted.

"Must I?" Baudwin asked. "We're here to see, not *be* the show."

"Of course you must!" Criofan demanded. "This is your comeuppance for being so late."

Baudwin was glad that he now had a chance to make things right.

"Then I will," he agreed, as he went to stand behind them. Quickly, he climbed both Criofan and Matha, as he would the branches of an oak tree. Having reached Matha's shoulders, he stood up. Criofan easily balanced both of them on his shoulders, one on top of the other.

"Now on the count of three — one — two — three," Criofan announced. With that, Baudwin jumped off Matha, and Matha jumped off Criofan to the ground. All three then performed a forward roll, landing in a perfectly spaced row.

"Now we're a troupe again!" Criofan announced, as he stood up, tucked his shirt back into his breeches, and adjusted his collar.

Baudwin chuckled. The acrobatic trick had worked. "Now that we're a troupe again," he began, "you have to hear what *else* happened in the Center.

I saw a huge tree made of bronze and copper, with *glamorium* leaves — only they didn't appear the way I figured Glamorium should look. So then I touched one, and I didn't feel a thing —"

"You see!" Matha exclaimed, turning to Criofan. "While *we* were waiting, he was just fiddling around with Glamorium — and not feeling a thing."

"Because the leaves probably weren't even real Glamorium," Criofan put in.

"Yes, but the sign on the tree *said* they were," Baudwin said.

"You can't believe everything the Elves say," Criofan said. "Isn't that right, Matha?"

"No, you can't," Matha agreed.

"Well, of course not!" Baudwin exclaimed. "You think I don't know that?"

Impatiently, Baudwin turned to face his friends, thrusting his hands into his pockets and stamping his foot. He wasn't sure why nothing had happened, but obviously he knew something wasn't right. Perhaps the Glamorium actually wasn't real, or perhaps Glamorium simply wasn't ready to answer him. Either way, he didn't know. Neither Matha nor Criofan were taking him seriously, and that bothered him even more. Added to that, they didn't even believe that Ferrell had detained him, or they would have questioned him on it.

Matha pointed to a shiny object on the grass. "Baudwin, did you drop something?" he asked.

Baudwin searched through his pockets, and then looked at the spot on the ground. "That's my coupler," he announced sharply. "I better not lose that, or my father will be as angry as a badger stuck in a briar patch!" Placing the piece of copper tubing back into his pocket, he remarked, "We had a big argument this morning."

"That sounds rather serious," Criofan said. "You don't argue that much, do you?"

"More of late than you might think," Baudwin replied, tersely.

Sensing Baudwin's upset, Matha quickly changed the subject. "You know, I wouldn't bother with that tree again. Who knows what the Elves did to that metal? We'll find you some real Glamorium at Curios & Marvels. That will cheer you up."

"Yes, and if nothing happens again, then we can forget all about this glamorium business," Criofan said.

Baudwin did not reply.

"Baudwin!" Criofan exclaimed. "Did you not hear Matha? Are you coming or not?"

Baudwin wasn't at all sure about what he wanted to do. What had happened with Glamorium at the Tree of Innovation had left him feeling discouraged. He didn't see any reason to look for more and get disappointed again. Added to that, Matha and Criofan didn't actually seem as if they wanted to help him. He wasn't sure what to say to them.

"I don't know," he replied.

"What do you mean?" Matha asked, annoyed. "You said you wanted to go."

Baudwin scanned the West Petal again, which was filled with countless amusements, thrilling entertainments, and lots of good things to eat. "I'm hungry," he said. "Aren't you? Let's go and get some food."

"All right," Matha said, as he shrugged his shoulders and rolled his eyes at Criofan. The three friends then headed down the promenade.

As they walked, Baudwin seemed lost in thought. Concerned, Criofan broke the silence.

"Tell us more about Magniglow," he said, hoping to draw out his friend.

"I met an Elve there at a booth," Baudwin began. "He told me I might be able to travel with him and the Engineerium — that is, if I wanted to."

Startled to hear this, Criofan stopped to study a nearby troupe of elven ladies and gents, performing at ground level on a trampoline. As they flew about in the Air, their costumes flashed like gold and silver fishes springing from a river.

"Whyever would you want to work there, when you could travel as one of *them*," Criofan asked, pointing to the bouncing acrobats.

"What do you mean?" Baudwin asked, surprised.

"Why would you be a common booth worker when you could *star* in a show like that?" Criofan asked.

Baudwin could not answer Criofan's question, much less figure out what he would do if he did join the Engineerium. He also couldn't imagine what his father and grandfather would do if he left. The son of the Primary of Water couldn't just decide to renege on his duties.

"In fact, what they're doing isn't even that hard," Criofan added, as he looked more closely at the troupe. "We could probably learn those tricks very easily, don't you agree?"

Matha nodded. Sensing Baudwin's unease, he pointed to a food tent a few yards away. "Let's go get something to eat," he said.

"What do they have?" Baudwin asked.

"Sweet potato pie, with carrots and peas," Matha replied.

"Let's go there," Criofan said, as he pointed to the center of the petal.

"I want some sweet potato pie," Baudwin announced. "Food first — fun later."

With that, they made their way to the food tent, talking loudly as they walked to hear each other above all the commotion. After ordering large helpings of sweet potato pie, they then made their way to an enormous four-sided wood and bronze scaffold in the center of the petal. A constant storm of music and shouting blared out through spaces between the beams. Faeries streamed through doors on all four sides, unable to resist the throbbing intensity of the wild attractions that awaited them.

With plates in hand, the three Faeries entered the large noisy structure. In the center sat the Mono-Ring, an enormous barrel-shaped wooden cylinder. Inside the ring, Elves raced mono-wheels at breakneck speeds horizontally along the wall, in gravity-defying circles.

"Amazing!" Baudwin exclaimed between bites of pie, as he stared at the entertaining spectacle surrounding them. High above their heads, elven ladies and gents performed spectacular feats on unicycles, riding along cables made of twisted bronze and copper. Others swung on cloud swings, with ropes made of colored silk, bending their bodies into unusual pretzel shapes, rolling and unrolling the ropes as they went.

"Perhaps we missed our calling," Matha remarked, as he watched an elven lady and gent swinging back and forth, nearly colliding and then parting again, glittering in red, orange, and yellow costumes. "However, I do believe that if I wore those colors, they would *burn* me," he added smiling.

"Better those then," Baudwin said, pointing to another Eleven couple, wearing blue, indigo, and violet.

"Better none of them," Criofan said, as he studied an elven gent riding a unicycle directly above their heads. "For I must say, I do prefer using my body when I perform, rather than all of those contraptions."

Hearing this, Baudwin and Matha laughed.

"So, if we did join the Engineerium," Criofan said, we most definitely would have to be acrobats."

"That's if we did," Baudwin agreed, feeling happier than he had in a while.

"As soon as we finish eating, let's go and watch the race," Criofan suggested, pointing toward the Mono-Ring. The three Faeries stood together, barely able to hear each other above the din of engines zooming around and around the walls.

Suddenly, everything went silent.

"They must be putting in more fuel," Matha said.

"Or, someone new is about to ride," Criofan added.

"Oh look," Baudwin said, disgusted, as he pointed at the observation ring overlooking the track. "Roilers."

The three faery friends recoiled at the unsettling sight — a band of Roilers. These gents, water Faeries by birth alone, posed alongside each other like a stand of scorched trees. Portions of their once blue-green clothing had been cut away and restitched with black leather. Strips of hide dangled like mossy strands from their bracers. The ladies gathered around them like forest maidens, their eyes darkened with midnight blue, their skirts, gloves, and hair covered with lace.

All around them, Faeries and Elves gave them a wide berth, for no one liked being too close to Roilers. One of them brazenly jutted a bracer at Baudwin — they knew they were being watched.

"Look away, Baudwin, or we're in for trouble," Matha whispered sharply.

"Too late," Baudwin replied. "The one in the middle looked me right in the eye."

"Then we have to accept the dare," Criofan announced, seemingly without concern.

"Is that —?" Matha asked, as he studied the group more closely.

"Loch?" Baudwin cut in. "Sure is. Looks like he survived the ravages of the Water."

Indeed, Loch had survived. He stood impassively, yet not without a measure of his usual defiance. The other Roilers who had been at the shrine were with him, as well as many others. Baudwin had run into most of them in Deuona, and had even known some before they abandoned the Guild. Ever since Loch changed his jacket, there had been thirty or so years of attrition; throughout that time, he had recruited more and more, until he was surrounded: The leader of his own current.

Baudwin spotted a young lad, no doubt a fresh recruit, wearing a blue jacket with hides stitched into the sleeves. As the lad turned around, black letters became visible on the back of his jacket: ROILER. The letters were written in an elven script, for the Faeries had no alphabet of their own. The young lad looked sad and tired, and strangely out of place. Baudwin wondered how much longer it would be before all the young Faeries in Deuona wore letters too.

"Why does he pick on ones so young?" Baudwin asked.

"So he can dominate them, and call his actions protection," Matha replied.

From afar, Baudwin studied Loch, wondering if the ordeal at the shrine had changed him at all. The Water could and eventually did wear everyone down. Perhaps Matha was right, and Loch could be redeemed. Yet Baudwin's sympathy could only go so far.

"Too bad the Water spared him," Baudwin joked.

"Loch!" Criofan declared angrily. "I was hoping we would run into him."

Baudwin knew why his friend was so upset. Criofan hadn't been at the shrine to stand with his troupe, so he wanted to fight now. Before either of his friends could stop him, Criofan headed straight to the observation ring. Baudwin and Matha hurried after him.

Once there, they found Loch and his friends staring into the racing pit. A Roiler sat below them inside a mono-wheel, ready to take off the instant the signal was given. Next to him, an Elve tinkered with a steamway engine.

The three Faeries stopped, Criofan at the head with Baudwin and Matha behind him. Loch and his friends raised their heads to face them, still as stone.

"Well, look what we've got here," Loch sneered upon seeing Criofan. "A fancy faery lad, all dressed up." He then looked at Baudwin, sizing up his vest. "And this one — wearing his twinkly little guild buttons," he added, laughing. "The *son* of the Primary of Water."

"Coming from someone who wears animal hides on his arms and legs, that surely is a compliment," Criofan retorted. Blithely, he eyed the gang's attire: A Roiler gent wore a rabbit skin hat, and next to him, a Roiler lady had a deer skin purse hanging from her belt. Pointing at them, Criofan joked sarcastically, "She'll carry the next fallen rabbit for you."

"Watch your tongue, Guilder!" Loch snarled.

"So are you killing animals now?" Criofan spat back at Loch. "Too impatient to wait to harvest the fallen?"

Nervously, Baudwin wondered if Criofan had gone too far. Surely, the Roilers weren't killing animals, for even at the shrine, Loch said he had been simply looking for fallen grand horns. Despite this, Baudwin could see that the ante had been raised.

Loch jousted back at Criofan, "Angry you missed the fun yesterday?" Sneering, he pointed at Baudwin. "You should have seen the look on his face when I broke his fancy tablet."

Baudwin felt his anger rising.

"There's only one thing worse than wearing fallen animals," Criofan snapped back contemptuously. "And that's wearing *letters* on the back of your jacket."

Loch's friends circled Criofan like a seething swarm of hornets, their deference to *gnás*, gone. Tensely, they waited for a signal from their leader to exchange blows. No one moved.

"That we do, don't we?" Loch declared, chuckling. As he spoke, the gents swarmed ever closer to Criofan, and the ladies clawed at him with fingerless gloves, their painted faces hissing beneath their veils.

Baudwin, Criofan, and Matha stood fast. They were outnumbered, yet would not be cowed. Criofan cocked his head and gave Loch a superior grin. "Too bad the Water didn't take you down, once and for all," he seethed.

"That wasn't the Water!" Loch yelled. "The Water doesn't take sides! And even if it did, only *we* would have been spared," he added, nodding at the Roilers who had been with him at the shrine.

"The only way the Water spares a Roiler is by washing the stench off him as he drowns in his own lies," Criofan declared, smugly awaiting the admiration of his troupe.

The Roilers scowled, their eyes slits of anger.

By now, a crowd had gathered around them. Faeries and Elves alike watched as the two sides berated each other. Some in the crowd had gamblers' gleams in their eyes, wondering which side would win, for surely the three Guilders had bitten off more than they could chew. The Elves called out for Loch to finish them off quickly, yet some faery gents jeered at the Roilers, ready to come to Criofan's aid. The ways of the Guilders would soon clash against the ways of the Roilers.

Then an older Guilder from the crowd shouted at them, "Off with you, Roilers! Spare us all from having to bear your detestable presence."

Loch welcomed the conflict. "What he calls detestable, I call necessary — *noble* even," he continued, staring at Criofan.

"Noble is something that you will never be, Loch," Criofan replied. "Crude and ignorant, more likely — but *never* noble."

Hearing this, Loch let out another bellow of laughter. "I would rather be that than inconstant and *weak*."

Enraged, Criofan lunged at Loch. Quickly, Baudwin and Matha appeared at his side, pulling him away from the fight. Around them, the crowd hooted.

"Not *here*," Baudwin insisted. "Not now."

"That's just what he said at the shrine!" Loch shouted as he circled the group, leering at the spectators. "He didn't want to fight after I called him a liar."

"Only you would want to fight at a shrine!" Baudwin shot back.

Unperturbed by the remark, Loch again lashed out at Baudwin. "He says the Water came to him. Can you believe that?"

There were mutterings in the crowd. Most seemed unsure what to think. Criofan then shouted, "The Water would sooner choose him over *you*!"

Livid, Loch shouted back, "Choose him over me? He's not even joined to his current!" Hearing this, the gang of Roilers shrieked with delight. Even some of the Guilders in the crowd laughed along with them.

"The Water *did* come to me," Baudwin sputtered. "But what do you care? You gave up on the Water years ago! Or was it the Water that gave up on *you*?"

Loch flinched, and Baudwin knew he had struck a nerve, yet the Roiler continued with his tirade. In a quavering, high-pitched tone, Loch tried to mimic Baudwin's voice, saying, "'I don't want to fight — not here, not there, not anywhere.' That's what you *always* say." Eying the three Faeries contemptuously, he added, "Wherever you are, it's the *place*, not the fight, that matters to you. *That's* what makes you weak."

"We've seen *you* weak!" Criofan shouted. "And broken! That day at the river when you gave up on looking for the Water. That's why you changed your jacket. And now you're just jealous that the Water came to Baudwin and not to you."

Furious, Loch signaled to his gang to attack, but before they could take two steps, a group of Earth Guards burst in to break up the fight. Silk trim and copper buttons flashed brightly in the Light. An elven guard with graying temples and a yellow star on his collar warned them sternly: "Disperse now, or I'll drag you to the Luminary and let him deal with you."

As Criofan raised his fists at Loch, the Earth Guard's face became a dreaded promise. The young Faeries all knew they were no match against these hardened veterans, who upheld the authority of the Assembly. Before Loch could raise his fists, the engine on the mono-wheel in the pit started up, roaring loudly. For a moment everyone was still. Guilders stared at Roilers, Earth Guards stared at the combatants, and the crowd stared at everyone.

The roaring softened. Eying the guards, Loch directed one last sneer at Baudwin and then motioned to his friends to leave. Everyone in the Roiler band broke away to go watch the race. Satisfied, the Earth Guards dispersed.

"We're lucky," Baudwin said. "We were outnumbered."

"Things were about to get ugly!" Matha added.

"Not as ugly as their presence in Deuona," Criofan replied in cheerful relief.

"Criofan — be quiet," Matha warned. "They'll hear you."

Pointing to the action beneath them, Criofan replied, "They can't hear a thing. Besides, they have too much muck and river sand between their ears." Matha laughed.

"Why do you suppose they even like racing?" Baudwin asked. As he spoke, several Roilers yelled and gestured angrily toward the pit.

"Perhaps they like circling around each other, like a bunch of wooing rabbits," Matha replied. Visualizing this, Baudwin and Criofan burst out laughing.

"You're probably right," Baudwin replied, as he leaned over the rail. "He does look like a rabbit. His rump and ears are rather large, like a rabbit's."

With his engine now fully revved, the Roiler in the pit began his ascent up the barrel. He first circled around the bottom several times. Moving faster, he shifted his position to the center. Hitting full speed, he then raced to the top. After performing several laps, he took his hands off the wheel. Holding them out to either side, he continued driving with a surly, yet victorious-looking grin on his face.

Soon, he was joined by an Elve on another mono-wheel. Together, they raced around the barrel, holding hands in the center of the lane.

"Ah yes, now he's wooing an Elve," Baudwin joked. Matha and Criofan laughed.

The two drivers then broke apart to race each other, going faster and faster as they went. The other Roilers watched from above, jeering at the Elve, and whistling and cheering for their friend.

"This would have been a lot more fun without them," Criofan said.

"Have you had enough?" Matha asked.

"Yes, let's get out of here," Baudwin replied. "We have better things to do." With that, the three Faeries left the Mono-Ring.

Chapter 9

CURIOS & MARVELS

Baudwin hurried along the promenade with his friends, exhilarated by the upbraiding they had given Loch, but frustrated that they had spent so much time at the Mono-Ring. "Well, I'm glad that's over," he said, as they made their way along. "Now let's have some *real* fun for a change."

"How about some cloud candy?" Matha asked, pointing to a stand a few yards away.

"Yes — something sweet!" Baudwin agreed.

Behind the counter, a smart-looking Elve wearing brass goggles was about to spin a new batch of candy. After placing the glass double bubble on the copper pan, he poured in sweet-vine sugar and then turned on the heat switch. As the motor hummed, he skimmed the pink candy floss with a paper cone, collecting a large puff. "May I interest you in some strawberry cloud candy?" he asked as they approached him.

"We'll have three, please," Matha replied. After taking their cones, the three friends headed toward the tip of the West Petal, eating their cloud candy and taking in the sights.

"Look!" Baudwin exclaimed. "Do you see?" Directly ahead of them, a group of elven ladies and gents ambled along the walkway on stilts. Blue silk wings rippled from their outstretched arms. Green canvas tails fanned out behind them.

"They look like flutter fish!" Matha said, delighted.

Water Faeries shared a very special kinship with flutter fish. Under Water, they swam at high speeds, aided by their streamlined bodies. When danger approached, they shot into the Air, fluttering their pectoral fins and beating their tails, gliding long distances on, or above, the Water. Water Faeries were captivated by them.

Criofan gazed at the stilt walkers. "They move down the path as if they had wings, like real flutter fish. To be one is to swim a carefree Life in the Water, but also to fly free as a bird in the Air." He paused thoughtfully. "When I see them, I feel as if I should be in another realm, flying with them, but I can't. If I could, I would be so lucky."

"Lucky indeed," Baudwin agreed, as he finished the last of his cloud candy and flipped the paper cone into a nearby basket. How he wished he could be a flutter fish and swim far away. Perhaps then he wouldn't have to worry about Glamorium, which so far had confounded him.

"I've been thinking," he began, "about what you said at the shrine."

"You have?" Matha asked.

"Yes," Baudwin replied. "You told me not to put too much meaning into the words we found on the tablet."

Hearing this, Criofan looked at them curiously.

"And you're probably right," Baudwin continued. "There probably isn't anything to Glamorium."

Matha stopped eating his treat and studied his friend.

"We didn't say Glamorium wasn't real," he said. "We only meant that perhaps the leaves on the tree weren't."

"Maybe they were, or maybe they weren't," Baudwin replied. "But perhaps," he added, "I just have to find the Water again."

"You *already* found the Water," Criofan said. "And just because you didn't find Glamorium the first time, doesn't mean you should stop trying."

"Yes, this doesn't seem like you at all," Matha said, looking worried. "Besides, what if you try to find the Water again, and you have another bout?"

Indeed, the shock of the last bout had been terribly upsetting. Yet, something frightened Baudwin even more than the thought of having another one. The Tree of Innovation had not yielded any clues. Seamus had seemed so certain that Glamorium would help him find his mother, so why hadn't anything happened when he touched the leaves? Baudwin knew Matha was worried about him, and he didn't want to frighten him even more by sharing all that he really thought. So he brushed aside his friend's concerns.

"Don't worry," he said reassuringly. "If I do have a bout, both of you will be with me. Let's go."

The three Faeries continued along their way.

"What then, about the Glamorium?" Criofan asked.

"I don't know. . ." Baudwin replied.

"You can't just give up," Criofan said, putting his arm around his friend's shoulder. "You can't give up on something that's so important to you."

Criofan's encouragement touched Baudwin's heart. "Don't worry about that," he said, as he smiled at his friends. "I'll *never* give up."

"Well, that's a relief," Matha said. "There's a mystery in that piece of tablet that we've yet to decipher."

"So then you *do* think there's wisdom in the old ways," Baudwin said.

"Of course!" Matha exclaimed, pointing down the path. "That's why we must visit Curios & Marvels to search for clues. We may not know everything about the old ways, but we will if we keep exploring their mysteries."

Now at the tip of the South Petal, they found themselves standing before three tall buildings shaped like red wagons. The Elves had placed them end-to-end — in a half circle — like cars on a train. Gold crown molding peaked gracefully along the tops; oak leaves and hydrangeas bordered the sides and bottoms.

Matha approached the center wagon, pausing in front of an arch-shaped double door with stained-glass windows. On either side of the doors, a relief showed an elven lady and gent facing each other in silhouette, welcoming visitors. Both stood with one hand reaching up toward the top of the door, palm down, and the other hand reaching down toward the bottom, palm up. Above the door, the words, *Curios & Marvels,* formed an arch.

Matha bounded up the steps. Cupping his hands to his face, he pressed his nose against the window, to better see through the red and brown oak leaves and white hydrangeas in the stained glass.

"Curious, indeed," he observed.

Grasping the handles, he slid the doors to either side, until they disappeared into the walls of the wagon. He then poked his head inside to take a look around.

"Do you see any Glamorium?" Baudwin asked.

"I don't," Matha replied, "but there must be some in here, somewhere."

As he stepped through the door, Baudwin and Criofan followed closely behind. Once inside, all three stopped forthwith, for what greeted them was not of the Engineerium. Baudwin saw no trace of Sprocketworks, Alchemvoke, Steamway, or Magniglow. Here the novel promises of the Elves had been left behind. Every corner and shelf held either an oddity or a treasure that begged examination.

They gazed around the wagon, trying to take in everything at once. Beneath his feet, Matha studied a mosaic of *Tír na nÓg* that covered the entire floor. Never had he seen such a detailed rendering of their realm. His eyes lingered upon the cities, rivers, and mountains with such curiosity that he might have remained there for the rest of the day. Criofan also stood transfixed, smiling as he perused shelves of ancient vases, bowls, and stone carvings of the Sun and Moon. Before him, Baudwin admired an edifice that seemed somewhat familiar — a stone wall circling eight stone pillars, rising to support a bowl-shaped roof. The stones reminded him of the ruins at Coventina, and Baudwin realized that the Elves must have brought them to Curios & Marvels from another shrine.

"Matha — look!" he exclaimed, as something caught his eye at the base of the shrine.

"What?" Matha asked.

"The same circle of glyphs that we saw at the ruins of Coventina," Baudwin replied.

"What glyphs?" Criofan asked.

Matha reminded Criofan about the shrine they had found at the ruins of Coventina, and then explained something he had not mentioned before. Pointing, he began, "The well in the shrine had a circle of elven and faery glyphs wrapped around the base — just like these."

"What do they mean?" Criofan asked.

"We never did figure that out," Baudwin replied, as he studied the glyphs more carefully.

"No, we didn't," Matha agreed. "They stand for cooperation — that much we know. But, what the Faeries and Elves were doing exactly — we don't know."

Baudwin studied the shrine. The very notion that the Elves must have moved these stones from somewhere made him angry. Those Elves had no right to defile and then display a shrine as if it were no more than a booth at the Tree of Innovation, but at least they had been careful. None of the stones were broken, and the entire structure appeared to have been faithfully reassembled.

Unlike the ruins of Coventina, this shrine had a wall around the perimeter that hid whatever was in the center. Baudwin guessed that what was inside probably wasn't a well. He tried to peer over the wall, but try as he might, he couldn't see what was there. Nor could he go inside, as the Elves had blocked the entrance. "Let's find a way in," he said.

"Baudwin — be careful," Matha warned. "We don't want to get into trouble."

"They're the ones who should be in trouble," Baudwin retorted. "Such nerve! Moving one of our shrines, and then blocking our way."

"He's right," Criofan said to Matha.

Determined to take in more, Baudwin looked about, making sure no one was watching. The room was empty, except for them, so he climbed onto the wall and peered inside at the center of the shrine.

"Matha," he called, "you must come here. I'm not sure what this is."

Without warning, they heard the creaking of a door opening. A series of footsteps tapped across the floor, over the map Matha had just been studying. The steps came from the west side — the Land of the Builders. This they knew was fitting, for the sound they heard was not of their kin. Faerie steps were never so precise, like the ticking of a clock. An Elve was coming.

A sharply featured face stared angrily at Baudwin, as he sat, his mouth agape, on the wall of the shrine.

"Who are you?" Baudwin asked, taken aback.

"My name is Edmund,"[1] the Elve replied. "I'm the custodian of this collection. Sitting upon an ancient marvel is strictly forbidden," he added sternly.

---

[1] Pronounced [ED-mund]

"All of you must step away, or I'll have to report this incident to the Assembly of Progress."

Edmund's uniform looked much like the one worn by Gavin, the Elve Baudwin had met at the Tree of Innovation. Both featured silver accessories with three stripes, indicating that they were Masters of Silver. Like Gavin, Edmund also had a quill on his medallion, which meant he was a Druid of Lore. The meticulously polished buttons on his jacket made him seem like the fussy sort. Baudwin thought he might be harder to fool than Gavin, but trying would certainly be fun.

Baudwin didn't want to move, but he jumped off the wall anyway. "We were just about to go," he replied, flashing Edmund a bright smile. "Which is good, because I wouldn't want you to have to take any kind of *unpleasant* action."

Hearing this, Edmund nodded, and then silently drifted a few paces away from them to examine the collection.

"Now what do we do?" Criofan whispered.

"Let's just go find Baudwin's Glamorium," Matha said.

"I just did," Baudwin said.

"What do you mean?" Matha asked.

"We have to figure out what this shrine is for," he whispered, pulling the piece of blue-green agate from his pocket. "The Water guided us here for a reason. I'm sure the symbol I just saw was *exactly* like this one — Glamorium! We have to distract that Elve, while Matha sneaks inside to take a look."

"No, Baudwin," Matha whispered. "That will just get us into more trouble. Let me take care of this."

Before Baudwin could stop him, Matha strode over to Edmund, who was busily examining some artifacts on the wall.

"Excuse me — ah — *Edmund*," he began.

Edmund turned to him. "Yes?" he replied. "Do you have a question?"

"I'm curious about the circle of interlocking faery and elven glyphs on the base of that shrine," Matha began. "And I wonder what you might think of my interpretation." Pointing to Baudwin and Criofan he added, "My friends and I are explorers, and we like to study ancient shrines in Deuona."

Edmund nodded for Matha to continue, so Matha explained how they had found similar glyphs at the ruins in Coventina. After describing them, he added, "In my estimation, the glyphs on these ruins must stand for *cooperation* between the Elves and Faeries. Certainly, they were working together for some reason, but what that is, I cannot be sure."

Edmund was only partly satisfied with Matha's explanation. "Yes, of course — cooperation," he replied. "You country Faeries have such a *quaint* way of putting things," he added smugly. "Surely they were working together, but you seem ignorant of the most relevant part."

"And what might that be?" Baudwin asked, joining the conversation.

"To help the Faeries see and appreciate *progress*," Edmund replied, as he folded his arms and stared at them. Satisfied that he had their attention, he continued speaking. "The Elves have always gifted the Faeries with these kinds of things."

"But, what for?" Baudwin asked.

"To make you understand what is possible," Edmund replied, as he pointed to the base of the shrine. "Shrines such as these were built to *excite* the Faeries."

"But this one and others like it were built *before* the Great Befalling," Matha countered. "The Assembly of Progress didn't exist back then."

Edmund shot him an irritated glance. "*Every* age has laid countless stones, paving the way for the Assembly," he replied. Matha grimaced.

"What about the glyphs inside?" Criofan asked, ignoring Edmund's comment.

"Yes," Baudwin said. "Before you told me to get off the wall, I saw the glyph for Glamorium in there."

"You must be mistaken," Edmund replied. "Those old glyphs hold little meaning."

"What's more important than Glamorium?" Baudwin asked. "You do know what the glyphs mean, don't you?"

Edmund straightened up. His back arched a little, and he fingered a button on his jacket.

"Yes," he began. "Glamorium is important, but the rest of the glyphs are not. Most of the meanings are lost, and hold little relevance now. The real purpose of the shrine is what I already told you. The Elves were trying to excite the Faeries by teaching them about progress."

Baudwin was certain Edmund was hiding something. He seemed to be bending the truth by implying that the shrine was just like the Tree of Innovation — a place the Elves had built to showcase elven wonders. Everything to this Elve was one way only, and that meant progress had to be at the center. Yet, at the same time, Edmund had admitted that the glyph for Glamorium was in the shrine, one that had nothing to do with progress. Baudwin knew that to get a better look, they would have to play along.

Glancing at Matha, Baudwin guessed that he was thinking the same thing, and was trying to trick Edmund into helping them.

"May we see the inside, please?" Matha asked, smiling politely.

"Absolutely not," Edmund replied. "Entering an ancient marvel is *strictly* forbidden."

"But you yourself just said these shrines were built to *excite* us about progress," Matha continued. "How are we supposed to get excited if we can't see what's inside?"

Firmly, Edmund shook his head *no*, but then, much to their surprise, he relented.

"I suppose you may have a point," he replied, motioning for them to come with him. "The best way to put aside your silly notions is to show you myself. It's my duty to teach you about the Assembly — so please follow me — and do *not* touch anything."

Edmund headed straight for the shrine, leaving the three Faeries grinning at each other.

"Well done," Criofan whispered. Matha smiled back.

Once there, Edmund removed the wooden barricade blocking the entrance, and they all stepped inside. Above them was a dome-shaped roof, and in the center, a round marble dais. Fashioned into the marble was a three-pointed mosaic, elegantly shaped out of green and gold tiles, forming an eternity knot. Such weaves were more ancient than anyone knew, even predating glyphs, as they were considered the original writing of the realm.

"There — you see?" Baudwin exclaimed, pointing to the center of the weave. "The glyph for Glamorium!" Matha and Criofan nodded appreciatively.

Matha inspected the weave. Indeed, there was a glyph for Glamorium in the center — two side-by-side spirals connected by a single line beginning in the center of one, and ending in the center of the other. At each of the three tips of the weave he saw the other glyphs that Baudwin had mentioned. But something else seemed even more important to him, and so his attention shifted. Baudwin and Criofan, relying upon his apt observation, followed along with him.

Matha continued to study the eternity knot, running his fingers over the interlocking lines that made up the weave. He then touched the large circle running through the three points of the weave, connecting them together as well. "I know what this is," he mused, his eyes brightening. "This is the Triquetra." Matha stared at Edmund, measuring his response. "You wouldn't dismiss *its* importance so easily — would you?"

"Yes, I would," Edmund replied. "Or at least the importance that some might place upon it. The Assembly understands this weave very well."

"Oh no. Sorry to say, you don't," Matha continued, solemnly. "The Triquetra is the symbol for the sacred trinity, which represents *Honesty, Truth,* and the *Promise of Rebirth.*"

Baudwin had heard this many times from Seamus and Kelven. All Faeries learned about the Triquetra, and tried to practice its three principles: being Honest with oneself, being open to seeing the Truth in all things, and dedicating oneself to the Promise of Rebirth.

"Well, I don't know what the Elves think," Baudwin began, "but we Faeries believe the Triquetra is sacred."

Edmund nodded impatiently. "Of course, we Elves appreciate the Triquetra," he replied. "But we don't need old weaves to remind us that we should be honest, know the truth, and ready ourselves for the afterlife. Isn't that common sense?"

"I would say that what is commonly understood and practiced by the Faeries, seems to be lost on the Elves," Matha remarked.

"Hardly," Edmund replied. "Besides, that's *not* the elven interpretation of the Triquetra. We believe what it really stands for is *Scrutiny*, *Certainty*, and the *Promise of the Future*."

Baudwin bristled. He couldn't believe his ears. How offensive that the Elves, so greedy to leave their mark upon everything, had even perverted the meaning of the Triquetra.

Edmund pointed at the glyph for Glamorium in the center of the Triquetra; it was the same one Baudwin had seen on the piece of blue-green agate from the ruins of Coventina. "As I already told you, long ago, shrines like these were made by the Elves for the Faeries. And as I also already said, the Elves wanted to *excite* the Faeries, and teach them about progress. Back then, none of your kin knew about Glamorium at all."

"If that's true," Baudwin began, tapping his fingers against the tablet fragment in his pocket, "what does Glamorium have to do with progress?"

Edmund smiled at them arrogantly. "Why *everything*, of course," he replied. "Haven't you seen the Tree of Innovation in the Center? We made that tree out of Glamorium, because someday, every branch of progress will be using Glamorium. There are great things in store for all of you," he concluded, pointing to the three Faeries.

Baudwin, Matha, and Criofan looked at Edmund, speechless.

"I know this all sounds very mysterious," Edmund continued. "Glamorium is going to be part of everything someday. I wish I could tell you more, but I've already said too much."

Baudwin had heard enough. "That wasn't real Glamorium on that tree — was it?" he asked.

"And what makes you say that?" Edmund asked, his eyebrows arching.

Baudwin thought of explaining his quest to Edmund, and why he had touched the Tree of Innovation, but he thought better of it. "Well — no — I mean — someone there said it was darker in color," he stammered. "Real Glamorium is lighter — isn't that right?"

"Ah yes — there's that. . ." Edmund stopped, carefully considering his words. "I probably shouldn't tell you this, but I also don't want to give you the wrong impression. I am after all, a Druid, and I believe our young ones should be properly instructed. So I will tell you this: Glamorium has been *enhanced* by the Elves, which is one way that we intend to make everything better for all of you. We have, after all, always been the ones to bring you new things — especially concerning metals. That's no secret." Pointing to the shrine he added, "This shrine was simply an old way of teaching the Faeries about what was to come. The faery meaning of the Triquetra may have held some relevance once, but Elves have always known the true meaning."

So, the Glamorium on the tree was enhanced, Baudwin thought. *What are they up to?* At the Tree of Innovation, Ferrell had been so eager to get him to stop asking questions. Had Baudwin and his friends not pressed this arrogant know-it-all for answers, they wouldn't have learned anything.

Now the conversation moved to what the other glyphs meant. Positioned at the tip of each point of the Triquetra was a glyph. The first was one they already knew — the glyph for *Tír na nÓg*. The second and third were unknown to them.

Edmund pointed to each of the three glyphs. "The glyph for *Tír na nÓg* is ours and will never be forgotten. Don't worry about the other two. They aren't important." He then pointed to the glyph in the center of the Triquetra, adding, "Besides, the glyph for Glamorium is all that matters."

Baudwin could see Matha smirking as they listened to Edmund's explanation. Neither of them believed what he was saying. Edmund was completely ignoring the wisdom of the old ways, as if the shrine were just a marketplace for the Assembly. Obviously, Edmund, like most Druids, knew the glyphs, but didn't think too deeply about them. How strange, Baudwin thought, that an elven Druid, who was supposed to be wise and learned, was so impervious and ignorant to the history sitting right under his nose.

Baudwin's elders were so different. He couldn't imagine Seamus or the Grand Eldress being the curator of this or any shrine, while holding its mysteries in such low regard. He glanced over at Matha who seemed ready, on behalf of the Water Guild, to present Edmund with his rebuttal.

"As we've established," Matha began, gesturing at the glyph next to the lower right point of the Triquetra, "this glyph represents *Tír na nÓg*, and the point itself represents Honesty, correct?"

"Yes, yes," Edmund replied, annoyed. "Honesty and the glyph for the realm. As if I didn't already know. What of it?" he asked, twisting a button on his jacket.

Ignoring Edmund, Matha continued, "What else we know is that the top point of the Triquetra represents the Promise of Rebirth, but we don't know what the glyph above it means. We also know that the lower left point represents Truth, but the glyph next to it is also a mystery. I would assume that if each point of the Triquetra represents a principle, then it's reasonable to assume that each glyph represents a realm. Therefore, we must ask ourselves — what realms exist beside our own?"

Baudwin could see that Matha had a point. If one glyph represented a realm, then perhaps the other two did as well. This made sense, because each of the three points of the Triquetra represented a sacred teaching.

"Don't be absurd!" Edmund exclaimed, his eyes flashing. "There are *no* other realms but ours! Those other two glyphs may hold some ancient meaning, but nothing you young ones could possibly understand."

Baudwin would not let Matha be dismissed so easily. He pointed to the top of the Triquetra. "If the Promise of Rebirth is the afterlife," he began, "then this glyph above it certainly must stand for Annwyn."

Disdainfully, Edmund shook his head.

"That's a fair enough guess," Matha replied. "But that's not a glyph for Annwyn that I've ever seen."

"And what realm stands for Truth?" Criofan asked, pointing to the glyph next to the lower left point. "I can't even guess where that might be."

"Nowhere!" Edmund exclaimed. "You're all reading into this the wrong way!"

Now Baudwin wondered. The Water had led him to Glamorium, and was now revealing something even more — that other realms could exist. What secret was unraveling before him? On the day after the Water coming to him, he had ended up at Curios & Marvels. This certainly could not have happened by mere happenstance. Yet, still, he could not tell what the Water had in store for him.

Baudwin watched Edmund's eyes narrow and then open widely. Despite his stubborn adherence to the Assembly, Matha's deduction seemed to have instilled doubt in him. Most Elves did not enjoy seeing past the established order of things. Added to this, Baudwin could tell that Edmund was about to do his best to refute everything Matha was saying.

Edmund hastily gathered his thoughts.

"Other realms do *not* exist," he asserted. "You Faeries have obviously been listening to too many faery tales. The truth is — you just don't know."

Hearing this, Baudwin saw that Criofan had had enough of Edmund's redundant dismissals.

"We don't know, do we?" Criofan asked sarcastically. "But you sound like you don't either."

"Of course I do," Edmund replied. "The Druids have recorded everything. We do not forget how far back our history goes."

"But doesn't remembering how far back things go make us eventually forget them, because they *do* go so far back?" Matha asked, smiling deviously.

"No," Edmund replied, irritated. As he spoke, his words pounced on them, like a fox on a trio of unwary field mice. "We can *always* remember the past through these and other kinds of relics, as you will no doubt see when you visit the two other wagons of our exhibit."

Baudwin wasn't going to let Edmund drive them out just yet. "As long as remembering the past doesn't upset the Assembly too much," he said flippantly. "Who knows what would happen if the Elves discovered what Glamorium was *really* for?"

Edmund glanced at the glyph for Glamorium, trying his best to ignore Baudwin's comment. As the custodian, he didn't like being challenged about what he knew, especially by a bunch of headstrong country Guilders. "Yes," he agreed, "Glamorium is the most important, more important than the rest by far. At least we can agree upon that." He then herded them out of the shrine, gesturing as he went. "To your left, you'll find a beautiful collection of relics and fineries, and to your right, the glamorium exhibit. Now leave me be."

Before Edmund had taken a step, Matha asked, "What kinds of relics and fineries?"

"One with a weave that you'll no doubt misinterpret," Edmund replied snidely. "And now, if you don't mind, I have other things I must attend to." With that, he glided out of the room in a huff, leaving Baudwin, Matha, and Criofan laughing uproariously.

"I bet he's still mulling over your observations," Criofan chortled. "I know I still am."

"If he can even follow them," Matha replied merrily.

Criofan and Matha paused to catch their breath, but Baudwin didn't notice them. He was too busy anticipating his next move. Unjoined to his current, he again struggled to find his feelings, but failed.

Quickly, he spun around to face his friends, grinning like a young one at his first festival, his eyes wild with excitement. He looked almost crazed, his gaze peering out at something he could not see but was certain was there. "I've heard enough!" he exclaimed. "Why look at a symbol of Glamorium, when we can actually see some *real* Glamorium? The Water led me here for a reason! If there *are* other realms, we're going to find them. *I'm* going to the next wagon!"

"Slow down a moment," Criofan said, as he and Matha exchanged worried glances. So many times had they heard Baudwin speak this way, his feelings tumbling inside him like a waterfall. Unable to parse them, he could not control his intense desire for gratification. Much to their dismay, they both knew what would happen next.

"*Slow down?*" Baudwin asked, staring contemptuously at Criofan. "You're just trying to stop me. You want me to fail!"

Seeing that Baudwin was behaving strangely, Matha stepped toward him. "No, he's not," he said, trying to placate his friend. "He just doesn't want you to get ahead of yourself."

"Yes, he is!" Baudwin exclaimed, eying Criofan suspiciously. "He can't see what I see. He doesn't know what I know. *I'm* the one the Water came to — not him. *I'm* the one who understands Glamorium!"

"That's enough, Baudwin," Criofan, said, keeping his cool. Both he and Matha looked nervously around for Edmund, but the Elve had not returned.

"No!" Baudwin cried shrilly. "What I'm saying is true! There's a *bigger* reason why we came here."

"Yes, of course," Criofan declared, grabbing Baudwin by the arm. "You aren't saying anything we don't already know. We just want you to calm down. You're not yourself right now."

Baudwin shook off Criofan's grasp. "Of *course* I'm myself!"

"No, you're not, Baudwin," Matha said, peering more closely at him. "You only act like this when your feelings whirl so fiercely."

Baudwin recoiled. He felt just fine, and couldn't understand why they were ganging up on him — especially as Glamorium lingered but one room away.

"What do you want from me?" he asked.

"You must slow down," Criofan replied, speaking calmly. "And the best way to do that is to give us what's fair."

"And what might that be?" Baudwin asked.

Criofan turned to Matha. "You tell him," he said.

"That you consider what *we* want," Matha replied, his arms moving up and down, like two weighing pans of a scale. "Concord requires give and take. You made us wait while you were off looking at the Tree of Innovation. Now *you* must wait for *us*. I'm sure that Criofan would love to see some of the fineries in the next wagon, and I would like to look at the weave that Edmund so snidely mentioned."

"All right," Baudwin replied guiltily, for he knew he had upset his friends. "I'll go with you to see all of that first. Besides, the Water probably wants us to learn more before we see the glamorium exhibit," he added, his eyes brightening.

Matha and Criofan rolled their eyes, relieved.

Baudwin calmed down as he accepted what his friends wanted him to do. Once again, they had to convince him to rein himself in, and all because he was never joined to his current. *How lucky I am to have such good friends,* he thought. *They pull me out of my own rapids when I need them to.* With that, he turned and headed for the fineries.

ⵣ

Soon they were in the next wagon, surrounded by artifacts whose craftsmanship was beyond any they had ever seen. There were animals carved from sapphire and topaz — wolves, deer, and hawks — as well as statues and vases with gold work so fine that Baudwin had no notion of who might have made them or where they were from. So dazzling was the sight that they paused for a moment, taking in the grandeur.

Criofan seemed the most enamored. Baudwin knew he loved finery, for was he not the son of the Primary of Commerce? Often had he visited Criofan's home, and seen goods from all over the realm: incense from Bog, carved crystals from Gleam, and windchimes from Breath Song. Criofan's family traded all of these and more, and he had grown up with an eye for the best of everything.

Criofan stared intently. The catlike gleam in his eye meant that he had spotted something special — the best of the best. Baudwin and Matha followed him to a floor-to-ceiling cabinet in the corner.

"There," Criofan said, pointing.

"A rainbow flute!" Matha exclaimed. "What a priceless treasure!"

The flute had seven segments, each one fashioned from a gemstone, beginning with red and ending with violet.

"There are no facets," Baudwin said.

Indeed, the gemstones appeared not to have been cut, and were joined together as if they had been mined from the ground that way.

"Surely, this flute must have been owned by faery royalty," Criofan remarked.

"There has never been faery royalty," a voice behind them spoke. Turning, they saw that Edmund had been eavesdropping on them.

How rude of him, Baudwin thought. *He certainly can't seem to mind his own business for very long.*

Criofan pointed to a blue diamond ring attached by a chain to a silvery arm gauntlet. "What could this silver ring be, if not for a faery king?"

"That is *Platinum*, not Silver," Edmund sniffed. "And to answer your question, there *were* no faery kings. This relic obviously belonged to a highly accomplished elven Master of the Platinum Order."

"I'm sure you're right," Baudwin declared, sarcastically. "Just as Honesty, Truth, and the Promise of Rebirth hold no real importance."

"I'll show you something of importance," Edmund retorted. "Come with me." He then led them to the rear of the wagon. "Here is further proof of why the elven interpretation of the Triquetra is the only one that matters now."

Baudwin looked at where Edmund was pointing. Very little could have distracted him from looking for Glamorium — except for what he now saw before him. Around the edge of a round wooden dais sat three porcelain faery ladies, each one beside a rosewood harp with a solid gold pillar. They reminded him of the river guardians that stood next to the millpond near his home. Like his, their skin was of the Water — the color of robin egg blue. Yet, they seemed far more celestial than any Faeries he had ever seen.

"How lovely," Baudwin murmured — spellbound — as he glided over to the faery lady sitting before him. Her expression held a bliss that he could not fathom — as if the Water had come to her and never left. For a moment, he was certain that if she could speak, she would tell him secrets that would help him understand the mysteries of Glamorium, and the Water. He wondered if the artist who had made her had been lucky enough to have known someone like her. For how moved he was by her soft caring face and sensitive deep blue eyes.

The more he studied her, the more captivated he became by her features. Her beauty was at a level far above what Faeries usually saw. Her cheekbones, fine and high, were graced by a gently smiling, rose-petal-shaped mouth. She wore a blue-green gossamer dress, more delicate than any he had seen before — very old, but not showing any signs of wear — cinched with a silver belt studded with blue topaz. A matching silver headband pulled her azure hair away from her face. *We water Faeries merely <u>play</u> at being like her,* he thought.

"Who are they?" Baudwin asked, enchanted.

"*Automatons,* of course," Edmund said proudly. "Likely built in Gleam long ago, with Sprocketworks."

"Sprocketworks is that old?" Baudwin asked, unable to take his eyes off of the faery lady.

"In its origin — yes," Edmund replied, "although that long ago, it might have been called something else."

"They look so perfectly real," Matha remarked, as he approached the dais.

"Real enough to kiss," Criofan added with a gleam in his eye. He puckered his lips and winked at Edmund.

"No mischief!" Edmund implored them.

"So where is the *proof* you were talking about?" Matha asked.

"I'll show you," Edmund replied.

Eagerly he moved to the dais and began fishing among some ornamental reeds until he found a crank, which he placed into a shaft spring and began to turn. He then darted to the other side of the dais to perform the same task. As he turned the second crank, three silver swans resting at the feet of the faery ladies began to move. Chimes inside the dais began to play a dreamy-sounding melody. Slowly, the swans turned their heads from side to side, preening their feathers. Mechanical lotuses then rose up from several lily pads around the dais. Their lavender petals opened little by little, until they were in full blossom. The swans then moved closer to each other, until only their bills and the bottoms of their necks touched, forming a heart shape. After a few moments, they broke apart, only to begin preening all over again.

All the while, Edmund kept circling the dais, opening doors, and winding up more springs. The serious look on his face had changed to a pleasant grin, and he seemed happy to perform his task. As he worked, his pointed boots tapped merrily upon the wagon floor.

All three faery ladies began plucking the strings of their harps — *plink, plink, plink.* Each one played a part of an enchanting tune, her head tilting as if she were being caressed by every note. As the music filled the room, Baudwin and his friends stood motionless, enthralled. When the tune ended, the swans reverted to their original poses, and the lotuses sank back beneath the floor. Letting go of their harps, the faery ladies then turned to face the center of the dais.

"Well, I'm glad we conducted this viewing with the proper decorum," Edmund said, smiling at them. "The ladies are very delicate — so no touching."

"As lovely as they are," Matha began, as he looked away from the automatons, "this hasn't proven anything. Where is the Triquetra?"

"I'm glad you asked," Edmund said, as he turned a final crank at the base of the dais.

They all watched the dais transform. Through a mechanical means the Faeries did not understand, a pattern emerged, rising slowly and then forming into the shape of the Triquetra. Each tip of the weave pointed to a faery lady. In the center was the glyph for Glamorium.

The three Faeries stood quietly, their mouths agape.

"Now, tell me," Edmund began, "how old do you think these ladies are?"

"They were probably built no more than a century ago," Matha replied.

Edmund laughed. "They're easily over two thousand years old. And, unlike the shrine you just saw, there are no glyphs at the points — just the Triquetra and the glyph for Glamorium — which is *no* accident."

"But why aren't the rest of the glyphs here?" Matha began.

"The shrine in the other wagon comes from very ancient times," Edmund reminded them smugly. "That's why the glyphs were there. They've since fallen out of favor. Centuries later, when these automatons were made, the Elves had a grasp on what was more important — *Scrutiny, Certainty,* and the *Promise of the Future.*"

Baudwin cringed, but then began to wonder. Could it be true that over time fewer glyphs had been included in each rendering of the Triquetra? Edmund insisted that this was so because, to his way of thinking, the glyphs held no meaning, but Baudwin didn't believe him.

"Don't be upset that the glyphs are gone," Edmund continued. "Over the centuries, they have become ever more absent. You mustn't be sorry. Your destiny, you see, is to be aware of what remains of the old ways, living side by side with the new ways. The Branches of Progress have brought fresh new meaning to the Triquetra."

"New meaning *solely* for the purpose of progress?" Matha chided him.

"Of course," Edmund replied. "What else?"

"I'm sure our kin care about more than simply living side by side with Sprocketworks," Criofan added.

"You don't *like* Sprocketworks, do you?" Edmund asked, his eyes narrowing with rage.

"Of course we do, but you go too far," Croifan replied. "The Triquetra is more than your giddy promises for the future." Smiling at his friends, he added, "We still honor its true meaning, don't we?" Baudwin and Matha nodded.

"A meaning that has lost its relevance — just like the glyphs!" Edmund exploded, pointing to the Triquetra. "Tell me, if they're so important, why weren't they included here?"

Baudwin and his friends studied the Triquetra upon the dais, noting that what Edmund said was true — the glyphs they had seen around the Triquetra not but a room away, were, indeed, absent here. Yet, there was still a glyph for Glamorium in the center of the weave.

"Just because the Elves decided not to include them, doesn't mean they're unimportant," Matha declared. Baudwin and Criofan nodded. The three Faeries all suspected that Edmund was trying to blow smoke up their bums. None of what he said proved anything. The Elves could have left the glyphs out for any number of reasons, and Edmund was only seeing things in ways that suited him.

"We don't believe you," Baudwin said.

With that, Edmund became livid. "As well you wouldn't," he sputtered. "Just honesty, truth, and the promise of *ignorance*!"

"Why do you Elves presume that nothing else matters but your gadgets and windup toys?" Matha shot back. "What else do you live for, besides making sure that everything in our realm has your mark upon it?"

Criofan then scolded, "The Triquetra should not be used to promote your achievements."

Edmund scowled.

Back and forth they argued, but oddly, Baudwin had become disinterested. He had participated in such disagreements too many times before. Just yesterday, he had argued with his grandfather about what amounted to the same thing, and now, here he was agreeing with him. Added to that, he found Edmund's overbearing arrogance distasteful. Ignoring everyone, he stared at the porcelain lady in front of him. His eyes lit up. There, in the center of her chest, was something he hadn't noticed — a shimmering green lily.

Baudwin stepped toward her, his excitement building. Could that green shimmering be *real* Glamorium? He had to find out. Looking closer, he saw that unlike the Tree of Innovation, the green was brighter in color. *Yes — this has to be Glamorium!*

Without a second thought, he touched the green lily and gasped. A stream of green Light poured out onto the dais. He braced himself for what was to come.

From behind, Baudwin heard some scuffling. "Stop that at once!" Edmund shouted, as he lurched toward him, his arms flailing.

Baudwin ignored him, as he was completely overtaken with expectation. He waited, certain that Glamorium would now bestow whatever boon was promised to him. Looking at Matha and Criofan, he exclaimed, "I just touched Glamorium!"

"No, you didn't," Matha laughed, as he approached the two other faery ladies. Deftly, he tapped the lilies on their chests. "They're just glowstones."

Baudwin looked on, crestfallen. Matha was right. How foolish he felt.

Edmund then wagged his finger at Matha. "You cut that out or I'll report the lot of you," he admonished them.

"Sure, go ahead and I'll tell them that you've been spreading false information about the Triquetra!" Matha threatened.

Just as another round of arguments was starting up, Criofan spotted something new on the dais. Where there had been only the Triquetra with the glyph for Glamorium, there were now *three* glyphs, one at each point, shining where the green glowstone Light had touched them. Somehow, the Light had made them appear.

"Baudwin — you must see this!" Criofan shouted over them. The arguing stopped, and everyone looked at the dais. Baudwin and Matha gasped, and Edmund made a strange choking sound. Clearly, he was as shocked as they were excited.

Soon, all were gaping at the discovery. Matha pointed at the lower right glyph. "That's the glyph for *Tír na nÓg*, just like the one we saw in the other wagon."

None of them understood how this was possible. Baudwin put his hand in front of the green glowstone Light, and one of the glyphs faded from view. When he pulled his hand back, the glyph reappeared.

"How can this be?" Baudwin asked.

"Are you at least *curious* about this marvel?" Matha asked Edmund, laughing.

"There's more!" Baudwin exclaimed, pointing to some lettering that had also appeared near each of the three glyphs.

"Those are elven," Matha announced, as he peered more closely at them. "Very old-looking. I'm not sure what they say."

Edmund was so excited that he forgot his anger and hastily read the letters. "These could be from the Age of Silver," he mused. "Back then, the writing was different."

Slowly, Edmund read what was written beside the lower right glyph for *Tír na nÓg*: "*The realm of the Shiny folk — As within — so without.*"

Baudwin had never heard of the Shiny folk before, but guessed they had to be the Fae, for who else dwelt in *Tír na nÓg* but the Faeries and Elves? What intrigued him even more were the words, *As within — so without.* "What do the words mean?" he asked. Expectantly, they looked at Edmund, but he seemed perplexed.

Matha then spoke. "The words are written near the point of the Triquetra that stands for Honesty, so that is how we should interpret them. My father always told me that in order to be honest with others, we must first be honest with ourselves. So in this case, honesty within leads to honesty without."

"Well said," Edmund put in. His tone and demeanor had changed in light of the discovery.

The three Faeries couldn't wait to hear more. "What do the other two say?" they asked.

For a moment, Baudwin feared that Edmund would stop reading for them. The Elve had been so adamant that there was no truth to the glyphs, insisting that was why they had seemingly been omitted. But even Edmund could not contain his Druid curiosity.

Pointing to the lower left glyph, he read, "*Danu, the realm of the Mortals — As the heart — so the mind.*"

Again they were silent, wondering what the writings meant. All knew of the River Danu, but that was not what was referenced here.

"Does the River Danu lead to another realm?" Criofan asked.

"Don't be ridiculous," Edmund replied, shaking his head. "That river is sourced in Bright Portal and empties into the Inland Sea. This speaks of some other place I've never heard of."

Baudwin's eyes then lit up, remembering something Seamus had told him. "My grandfather once told me, 'Only when your mind and heart are one, can you see the truth in all things.'"

"So, as the heart feels the truth, so then does the mind see the truth," Criofan added.

Baudwin nodded.

"I agree," Matha said, pointing to the lower right point. "That does make sense, for that glyph stands for Truth."

Now there was only one glyph left unread. They all looked at the top point of the Triquetra, which stood for the Promise of Rebirth.

Edmund then read, "*Fios, the realm of the Luminous ones — As above — so below.*"

"So that glyph is for a place called Fios, not Annwyn," Baudwin said, remembering what they had said about the glyph in the previous wagon.

"That doesn't surprise me," Matha added.

All of them waited for someone else to say more, for none of them knew what Fios was. They were excited, and rightly so, but still no one said a word.

"As we are promised to be reborn above, so will we be reborn below?" Baudwin thought out loud.

Matha rolled his eyes. "That's just silly." Turning to Edmund, he asked, "What do you say?"

"I'm not sure what the words mean or what Fios is either," Edmund replied.

Baudwin looked again at the automatons, wondering aloud, "Could *they* be the Luminous ones?" He could sense Edmund again becoming irritated. The excitement of their discovery was quickly wearing off, and too many questions were being raised.

"Do you still believe there are no other realms?" Matha asked Edmund.

"Nothing — this proves *nothing*," Edmund continued. "Remember, these old marvels are simply works of art — relics of an age long gone."

"But you said the glyphs were omitted on purpose," Matha probed, his hand circling the Triquetra. "There they are, and what's more, they're even *labeled*."

Before Edmund could reply, Criofan chimed in, "How can someone who purports to be the custodian of this collection not even know that the glyphs and writings were there? The fact is, you just saw them now for the first time!"

"Too busy lecturing to see what was right in front of your face," Baudwin chided. "Scrutiny, certainty, and the promise of *arrogance*!"

The three friends laughed, but not Edmund.

"I would prefer arrogance over *ignorance* any day. You Faeries choose ignorance, languishing your days away, pining for what will never again be, while we Elves change with the changing times!"

Baudwin and his friends stared at each other, not knowing if they should laugh out loud or rap Edmund on the head. They did neither.

Edmund gathered his thoughts. "Perhaps this exhibit has had enough visitors for today," he said. What little cordiality he had briefly displayed turned as brittle and flat as shale, and he was simply the curator again. "If you three are going to visit the last wagon, do so now, and then be on your way." With that, he tapped the glowstones off, and the glyphs vanished.

Baudwin could hardly believe that Edmund could so callously dismiss such an amazing discovery, one he would never have considered possible until this moment. He wondered then if the Elves would now hide the automatons away, their glowstone hearts remaining forever locked in the shadows.

I may never see them again, he thought ruefully, *but at least I now get to see Glamorium.* He turned and followed his friends to the next wagon.

⊙✦☉

They were greeted by a room filled with old staffs, swords, and chalices, as well as carved stones, all placed upon dusty shelves or inside cabinets.

Emblems of rulers and cities from long ago decorated the entire place. On one side, Baudwin and Matha recognized the symbol of Silver Forge, carved into a plaque on the wall. Grinning, they stopped for a moment and pointed out the silver hammer to Criofan. The three then looked at other symbols: The Sun of Gold Haven, the flute of Copper Caves, and the quill of Platinum Spires. All of them came from the capital cities of the Elves far to the west. Neither Baudwin nor his friends had ever been to these places, and they wondered how the symbols had come to be. There were also many old tablets replete with historical lore, perhaps imparting wisdom for those who sought deeper truths. Certainly, Baudwin thought, one of the many glass display cases would have what they were looking for.

Matha was just as eager as Baudwin to discover new and interesting things. "Come on, you two," he said, as he darted ahead of them. He soon found himself between two long display cases, which formed an aisle in front of the door.

Slowly, a side door opened. A young faery lad crept into the room — a shy-looking little hare with a rolled-up jacket under his arm. Furtively, he scanned the room for signs of danger. Seeing none, he stepped toward an ancient stained-glass collection in one of the cases.

Matha approached him cautiously. "Are you lost?" he asked.

Nervously, the lad shook his head *no*.

"Do you see what we have here?" Matha asked, pointing to a piece of stained glass. Curiously, the faery lad stood on his tiptoes to gaze at a river heron made of white onyx. The bird was poised on one leg, on a bed of river grass made of brown tourmaline, next to ruby lotuses and emerald lily pads.

Baudwin studied the little lad as he looked at the heron. His face brightened, as though his spirit was being watered like a thirsty plant in a desert. The little lad lifted his leg, standing just like the bird. Smiling, he then gave a small chirp.

"How strange," Matha whispered, as Baudwin and Criofan approached him. "For one so young, he seems unused to joy, but I cannot tell you why."

"Perhaps he craves seeing fineries," Criofan said. "And he has no one to take him."

"Let him be," Baudwin advised. "We mustn't forget why we came."

"I know," Matha agreed. "We wanted —"

"To see *that*," Baudwin cut in, as he pointed to the far end of the wagon.

"Glamorium!" they exulted, gazing upon the display.

"Come along with me, and we'll see what other wonders lie in store," Matha instructed the small waif, seeming to sense his loneliness. Together, the four Faeries approached the exhibit contained in three large wooden cabinets. The entire display was cordoned off with ropes, yet close examination by visitors was obviously expected.

A sign read:

Glamorium Collection
The Spirit of the Tadlachs
Please admire — but do not touch

"No faery kings, indeed!" Criofan chortled. "If that's true, then what's all of this?"

"Something else Edmund doesn't understand," Matha replied.

"Such exquisite work," Baudwin remarked, as they examined the shining collection of jewelry before them. Heavy chains with pendants made of rubies, white diamonds, and emeralds were piled next to rings, bracelets, hair combs, dishes, ornate boxes, and other precious objects — all made of polished Glamorium. Unlike the leaves on the Tree of Innovation, the metal was far more lustrous, with shimmering emanations that danced over the surface of each piece.

Matha lifted the young lad up so he could also see. The three faery friends looked into a shining plate and saw their reflections. All three appeared as they usually did, but with a verdant hue over their faces. However, when they saw the young lad, they gave a start. All traces of worry and fatigue had left his face. He looked as if he had changed into someone he had never known, a brighter, cheerier lad, one unused to pain and hardship — someone he truly wished to be.

For a moment, the young lad beamed, but then lowered his head and stared at the floor. Unlike the reflection of everyone else, his had changed for the better, and he seemed unable to bear the joy.

"How strange — Glamorium really is mysterious," Baudwin commented.

"Yes, that he would change, and we would not," Criofan added.

Matha took hold of the young lad, lifting him back up. "Come now, what you saw wasn't so bad. Have another look."

As the faery lad stared again into the shimmering green Light, his somber-looking face grew bright with excitement. Before him, two glamorium ceremonial scepters rested upon the middle shelf, with two matching diadems, one set for a lady and another for a gent. All were encrusted with white diamonds, emeralds, and rubies.

"If I could only hold them once," the little lad murmured wistfully, as he stretched his fingers toward the gleaming treasures. "I do so love beautiful things."

"The little lad finally speaks," Matha mused to himself, as he examined the collection.

"So, what's your name then?" Criofan asked.

"Teigue,"[2] the young Faery replied.

---

[2] Pronounced [TAYG]

"Well, Teigue, my name is Criofan. And these are my friends, Baudwin and Matha."

"Did these treasures really belong to a faery king?" asked Teigue.

"Perhaps they did," Criofan replied. "How else could we account for such wealth? These gems are not like those we see in the marketplace. The cut, color, and clarity are impeccable."

Baudwin looked at the glamorium diadems. "The Elves believe that all Glamorium is theirs," he said.

Matha put Teigue back down, so he could examine the case more closely.

"What are you doing?" Teigue asked, straining to see.

"Looking at what's behind the jewelry," Matha replied. "I see glamorium tablets, with different kinds of glyphs inscribed on them. Some of them seem to be as old as *Tír na nÓg* itself."

The glamorium jewelry had been stunning, but when Baudwin rested his gaze upon the tablets, his mood sobered. They were not nearly as fancy-looking as what they had already seen. At first glance, they appeared plain, neither bejeweled nor intricately made. Yet, he sensed they were far more sacred than anything he had ever seen before. Their only decorations were the borders, embossed with eternity knots and spiraling patterns that hailed from a time when all knew the meaning of such things.

"What do the tablets say?" Teigue asked.

"Many different things," Matha answered. "But the one in the middle interests me the most."

"That must have taken quite a lot of ore to make," Criofan said.

"Seeing the tablets makes me wonder," Baudwin began, "how the Elves were able to forge so many leaves to make the Tree of Innovation."

Matha looked at Baudwin, puzzled. Squinting his eyes, he said, "I haven't seen the tree, so I cannot comment upon that."

"And why these tablets seem so different from those leaves," Baudwin continued, as he leaned over the rope to reach the door of the cabinet. "I'm going to touch one to find out."

"You *mustn't* do that," Matha insisted. "Didn't you read the sign?"

"Edmund could come in at any moment," Criofan warned.

Baudwin leaned back, away from the display case, to see where Criofan and Matha were pointing. Another sign to the left of the case, read:

Property of the Assembly of Progress

Please admire — but do not touch

"I think I see another poem," Matha added, trying to distract Baudwin from further trouble.

"Another poem?" Baudwin asked. "Perhaps I'll learn something more."

Hearing this, everyone drew even closer to Matha as he examined the glamorium tablet. A large Triquetra was embossed into the top half.

"Once again, we find the Triquetra," Matha said, pointing to the weave. He then began to study the glyphs underneath. Teigue pulled on his sleeve.

"How can you read those drawings?" Teigue asked.

"I can read them because I have studied them for many years, and like milestones upon a road, I know them very well," Matha replied.

"But what do they mean?" Teigue asked.

"Everything you can imagine," Matha replied.

"Everything!" the little lad exclaimed. "That's why I like looking at them."

"As well you should," Matha continued. "These glyphs were made by our kin, and they hold all the meanings of our tribe."

"*All* the meanings?" Teigue asked. "Not even letters can do that."

"That's because glyphs *teach* and letters *preach*," Matha said.

"What does that mean?" Teigue asked.

"Glyphs teach us *how* to think about things," Matha continued, "while letters teach us *what* to think."

The little lad lit up. Baudwin could tell how eager he was to learn about his heritage. Obviously, he had been deprived of proper instruction. Smiling, Baudwin nodded at Matha to continue.

"Here is the glyph for the Sun, and this is the glyph for the Moon," Matha began. "They both have the same meaning — *bright*. Do you know why that is?"

Teigue shook his head *no*.

"Sure you do," Matha said. "Tell me, can you see the Sun in the day and the Moon at night?"

"Of course," Teigue replied.

"And what do they do?" Matha asked.

"They shine," Teigue replied, smiling.

"Yes," Matha continued. "They shine brightly. But, letters do not shine. They simply tell us what things are, not *how* they naturally arise. The Sun and Moon are bright; the *word* for bright is not. That's why I say that glyphs teach, and letters preach."

"Now I see why I like them!" Teigue exclaimed. "They're more fun than letters. They *shine* when you read them."

Baudwin was happy that Teigue had been instructed, but he was also saddened that the lad had to learn this from strangers. Whoever was mentoring him had utterly failed, yet Teigue had easily seen the truth. Obviously, the Water wanted this young one to be set upon a better course, or his current wouldn't have led him here. Baudwin could see that Teigue's interest in his heritage would only deepen.

"Now I must concentrate," Matha said. For several moments, he gave the tablet his complete attention. Having finished his task, he then spoke:

> *As within — so without*
>
> *As without — so within*
>
> *There we meet*
>
> *In the center*
>
> *From our hearts*

Hushed into silence, Baudwin, Matha, and Criofan pondered the import of the words. A look of wonder crossed their faces as they recognized that they had already seen the first line on the Triquetra near the automatons:

As within — so without

Matha read the second line:

As without — so within

"It's just as I said earlier to Edmund," Matha began. "In order to be honest with others, we must first be honest with ourselves."

"And then we meet in the center from our hearts," Baudwin concluded.

What Matha had suspected was true. Here the wisdom of the Triquetra had been made plain for all to see. The glyphs made clear that *Tír na nÓg* was a realm that stood for Honesty. The lesson to be learned was that to be honest with others, one had to first be honest with oneself. What purpose this might serve in Baudwin's quest was as yet unknown to him, but he took these words to heart, as did everyone else in his company.

The artisans who forged the tablet must have taken this wisdom so seriously that they inscribed it on the rarest metal in the realm. Baudwin wondered then if he and his friends would have known how to interpret the tablet had they not first stumbled upon the hidden writings in the previous wagon. *What an interesting twist of fate that the Water is teaching me in this manner.*

He wondered then about the other points of the Triquetra. Why wasn't the glyph for Danu, which stood for Truth, and Fios, which stood for the Promise of Rebirth, included here? Curiously, they were nowhere to be seen, and Baudwin could only guess if the wisdom of these realms was enshrined elsewhere for them to discover.

"Who then, do you suppose made the tablet?" Criofan asked.

"The Elves did, for the Faeries," Matha replied.

"We already know that," Criofan declared. "But why?"

"We can only guess," Matha replied. "This tablet was forged many thousands of years ago. The records of how this was done were, in all likelihood, lost after the Great Befalling."

Baudwin was getting bored with their deliberations. "None of this really matters," he said. "I came here to touch some Glamorium so I can find my mother. And that's *exactly* what I'm going to do!"

Before his friends could do anything to stop him, Baudwin slipped under the rope, grabbed the handle on the cabinet, and yanked open the door.

"What about Edmund?" Criofan and Matha exclaimed in unison. Teigue hopped from one foot to the other, watching nervously.

Baudwin reached into the cabinet. Straining, he craned his neck to better see through the opening. His fingertips drew closer, almost reaching the tablet. Just as he was about to touch the shining metal, he felt something catch on his arm.

Immediately, a very loud sound blasted through the room: *Clang, clang, clang, clang, clang!* And then *Clang, clang, clang, clang, clang!* over and over again. All four Faeries jumped at once, covering their ears in fright.

Horrified, Baudwin realized he had tripped a wire that was no doubt causing the clanging. Quickly, he closed the door and slid back under the rope.

"Where is it coming from?" Criofan cried.

"Above the case!" Matha shouted.

All of them looked up. Attached to the wall, a small elven automaton banged a hammer on a large brass bell. Quickly, they realized that Curios & Marvels also had a very curious-looking burglar alarm.

"Stop that!" Baudwin shouted at the automaton.

Just then, Edmund charged into the room. The shining buttons on his coat glinted like knife points. His face had turned ashen. The Assembly of Progress would have its justice.

"All of you — *stop!*" he shouted, as he raced to the cabinet and turned off the bell. Furiously, he faced the three Faeries. "Which one of you *dared* to touch the collection?" he shouted. "What were you trying to do? *Steal* from the Assembly?"

Everyone remained completely silent, until the shuffling crowds outside the wagon were all they could hear.

"Was it you?" Edmund asked Criofan. "Or you?" he asked Matha. He stopped before Baudwin. "No," he continued, as he poked his finger into the middle of Baudwin's chest. "It was *you.*"

Baudwin flinched at Edmund's touch. He hunched his shoulders and dropped his head, and then looked up, smiling sheepishly. "I only wanted to touch some Glamorium," he began, his voice quavering. "I wasn't going to *steal* any."

"Didn't you see the sign?" Edmund shrieked. "Do *not* touch!"

His voice pierced through them, until Baudwin felt cold inside.

Edmund continued his diatribe. "I suppose I can't blame you, when you Faeries can't even *read.* You're all a bunch of illiterate, untutored, simpletons!"

No one spoke.

"Here — allow me to educate you," Edmund continued again, as he pointed to the sign. He then spoke, "D-O-N-O-T-T-O-U-C-H," slowly enunciating each letter. "Didn't anyone ever teach you this?"

Again, they all remained silent.

Edmund paused for a moment. "Of *course*, no one taught you!" he exclaimed. "How unfortunate that the glyphs you Faeries are so taken with have prevented you from learning how to read."

Matha had heard enough.

"We do *so* know how to read!" he exclaimed, as he looked at Baudwin and Criofan. "Both letters *and* glyphs."

"Then you have no excuse!" Edmund shouted, shaking his fist at them. "The Assembly of Progress will hear of this! What's your name?" he asked, pointing to Baudwin.

"Here — let me spell it out for you," Baudwin replied. "R-U-N!" he shouted.

With that, all bolted for the sliding doors and pushed them open, almost tripping on the steps as they raced away. Behind them, they could hear Edmund furiously shouting after them, "Come back here — you miscreants!"

They ignored him, racing farther and farther away. "Hurry!" Baudwin shouted, breathless but laughing. "Before Edmund gets any more ideas!"

"Let's head to the Water Park!" Criofan shouted back.

"Yes!" shouted the fugitives.

Baudwin looked to his side and saw Teigue, furiously pumping his little legs to keep up.

"Are you coming with us?" Baudwin asked.

"I must go now," Teigue replied nervously. "I shouldn't have stayed as long as I did. But thank you all the same." Immediately he left, bounding over the cobblestones, his jacket still under his arm.

With that, the three Faeries took off as fast as they could, leaving the West Petal far behind.

Chapter 10

WATER SIGHTS AND SLIDES

Together the three Faeries raced away from Curios & Marvels, past the Mono-Ring, and through the West Petal entrance, toward the center of the Engineerium. As they ran they shot glances all around, fearing that Edmund may have sicced some Earth Guards on them. At any moment they could appear to reprimand them, or even worse, throw them out of the Engineerium. Yet, with every step they took, their worries drained away, like Water passing through a sieve.

They stopped to catch their breath, for they had reached the walkway around the pavilion that connected all the petals of the Engineerium.

"I can't believe he didn't follow us," Matha panted, as he stopped alongside his friends. "He was so angry!"

"What if he reports us to the Assembly of Progress?" Criofan asked.

"He won't — he doesn't know our names," Baudwin said. Frustrated, he clenched his fists. "I almost touched that Glamorium!" he exclaimed. "But just like my grandfather said, when you find some — all of a sudden — it's gone."

Baudwin remembered the Tree of Innovation, and how he had reached for the leaves, but felt nothing. Pointing over his shoulder at the pavilion, he added, "There, in the Center at that tree, and just now, at Curios & Marvels, I thought I had found some, but I hadn't. Something is keeping me away from my intention."

Baudwin wondered what his grandfather would say if he told him that he had failed not once, but twice, and both for reasons he couldn't have foreseen. The Elves had foiled him with their ingenuity, once with an apparent forgery and again, with a trap. *That confounded alarm!* he thought.

"Can you stop all your talk about Glamorium?" Matha asked, irritated. "We almost got into trouble, the kind that could have gotten us barred from the Engineerium — forever!"

"I told you — that won't happen!" Baudwin insisted. Again he scanned the area, but saw no signs of the well-regimented protectors of the Assembly. "See?"

"How do you know Edmund isn't coming?" Matha asked.

"He certainly has good reason to," Criofan added.

"You sure do know how to get us into trouble!" Matha exclaimed.

"Don't forget — I also know how to get us out!" Baudwin joked.

All of them had heard stories of Faeries who had broken the laws of the Assembly of Progress. Some were fined, and others scolded publicly, yet the punishment they feared the most was being forced to work for the Elves. The Elves were always greedy for more labor, and eager to put guilty Faeries to work to make them atone for their crimes — especially those who seemed lazy or indifferent to the Elves' goals in *Tír Éirí Sióg*. Defiance was met with crushing force, as the Elves had occupied most of *Tír Éirí Sióg* for two hundred years. Baudwin knew better than to test the patience of the Elves too often, or too long.

"I didn't mean to get us into trouble," Baudwin began. "I just wanted to see if —"

"But you *did*," Matha interrupted, fiercely, "because you think *only* of yourself!"

Hearing this, Baudwin winced. Now he didn't feel so lucky that his friends were reining him in. Angrily, he rose to his defense. "That's easy for you to say! You're *joined*!"

"That's *not* easy to say!" Criofan exclaimed. "He wasn't calling you out for not being joined! Sometimes you're just too caught up in yourself!"

Baudwin sensed that Criofan might be right. Everyone grew quiet, and an uncomfortable silence ensued. As they walked along, Baudwin picked a piece of sweet-vine from a creeper and began sucking on the end. "Matha, would you like some of my sweet-vine?" he asked.

"No, I wouldn't," Matha replied.

Baudwin glanced nervously at Matha. *He's really upset with me,* he thought, as he moved closer to his shorter companion. Matha was muttering to himself under his breath, cocking his head to one side, listening to himself as he spoke, and then cocking his head to the other. He always had pretend conversations when he thought Baudwin was being too stubborn or foolish to listen.

Seeing Matha so lost in thought, Baudwin felt even guiltier about tripping the alarm. They were right. Sometimes he attributed common problems that any Faery could have to not being joined, and Criofan was right to call him selfish. He knew he had to try something else with him.

"You know, Matha," Baudwin began, "I was really impressed with you back there."

Matha stopped muttering. "Oh?"

"Yes, quite impressed," Baudwin replied.

"With what?"

Criofan shook his head, smiling, as he watched Baudwin try to ingratiate himself into Matha's good graces.

"You deciphered the poem on the tablet so well," Baudwin continued. "I couldn't have done that."

Hearing this, Matha relaxed somewhat, and nodded to himself.

"How were you able to do it?" Baudwin asked.

"Do you really want to know?" Matha asked. "Or are you just trying to butter me up?"

"Perhaps a little of both," Baudwin admitted, grinning slyly.

"Why should I tell you if you aren't really interested?" Matha asked.

Criofan couldn't resist adding his opinion. "Just talk to the part of him that wants to know," he said to Matha. "Ignore the other part," he added, smiling.

"Why should I do that?" Matha asked, irritated.

"Because *I* want to know," Criofan said, laughing. "And I'm a much better friend. Forget him!"

Matha's mood brightened. He laughed at Criofan's joke, agreeing with him that he was, *indeed,* a better friend. He then told Criofan and Baudwin that he had visited ruins in and around the Springs of Coventina, and had, on several occasions, found many unusual glyphs. Some he had deciphered, but others he had never figured out.

"So there were more glyphs like the one for Glamorium at the shrine?" Baudwin asked.

"Yes," Matha replied. "I didn't know what that particular glyph meant, so I told you to ask Seamus."

"And you never told us about any of this?" Criofan asked, surprised. "What else did you find?"

Matha then told them that he had found many other artifacts made of stone or pottery, with ancient glyphs on them. At first he had assumed they were the same ones he saw every day, but then he realized he couldn't read them, so he studied them more closely. Some described other names for the Water, and how they related to the seasons, such as those for Summer's humidity and rain, or Winter's freeze and snow. There were also glyphs describing each phase of the Moon, most of which he barely understood.

Hearing this, Baudwin remembered the dream he had had the night before. "Do you still hear me?" the Water had asked him. "Or must I ask the Moon to speak to you as well? Of your feelings?" The questions echoed in his mind, for he suspected that hidden in the glyphs was the language of the Moon and the answers he sought. He wanted to learn to decipher some of those old glyphs himself.

"I would like to know how the Moon speaks to us," Baudwin said. "Isn't it strange that we Faeries no longer read many of the glyphs that speak to us about the Water and the Moon? Why do you suppose that is?"

Matha was pleased to hear Baudwin's question. He always seemed happy when anyone took his interests seriously. Squinting his eyes, he continued to ponder the question. He then began explaining.

"Something changed," he said. "I cannot tell you why, but I can tell you this: Ever since the Great Befalling, the Elves have become ever more zealous about using letters. Even the Faeries use them more, and the Roilers have gone so far as to abandon glyphs for letters. I believe there was a time when Faeries and Elves alike read only glyphs. Baudwin and I saw evidence of this at the ruins of Coventina, where there were only glyphs — elven and faery — on the shrine we found. And I have seen other ruins, with monuments defaced by some unknown agency. I tried to find references to them, but they, as well, had been destroyed."

"Surely, the Elves must have defaced them," Baudwin surmised. "But why?"

"I really don't know," Matha replied.

"But the real problem is," Criofan shouted as he ran ahead of Matha, "why didn't you tell us that you were visiting old monuments? Your two best friends!"

"I wanted to be sure," Matha replied, annoyed.

"Be quiet, Criofan," Baudwin insisted, as he turned to Matha. "Sure of what?"

"That the glyphs were as ancient as I thought, and they are," Matha replied. "I know, because I've been studying them for a long time."

Keeping his shoulders low to the ground, Criofan swung his arms down. He kicked one leg up, and then the other to complete an aerial cartwheel, landing in front of Matha with a well-placed plop.

"That's just like you, Matha," he announced, turning to face his friend. "You never tell us what you know, *until* you know."

Baudwin burst out laughing.

"What I do know right now is that you are being really annoying, and I am telling you that," Matha retorted, as he locked eyes with Criofan. Both Faeries stared intensely at each other.

As his friends continued bickering, Baudwin stopped for a moment. From the corner of his eye, he spotted a small faery lad with a rolled-up jacket under his arm. Upon seeing Baudwin, he froze.

"Teigue!" Baudwin exclaimed. The young lad stood a few yards away, looking timid, yet eager to see them again.

"Don't just stand there like a scared little hare!" Criofan shouted. "Come here!"

Hearing this, Teigue scooted down the path, until he reached them.

"Back already?" Matha asked.

Nervously, Teigue smiled at the three faery friends. He then turned away, as if he was about to flee.

"Come now, Teigue, don't be shy," Criofan said.

Teigue skipped toward Criofan, and then stood next to him. Grabbing him by his belt, Criofan pulled the little wisp of a lad high off the ground. "I'm going to shake you until you smile!" he said.

Teigue broke into a large grin, and Criofan set him back down.

"We're about to go to the Water Park," Criofan said. "You'll have fun there." Criofan and Teigue headed down the path toward the North Petal. Playfully, Criofan tagged Teigue on the shoulder, and ran ahead of him. Teigue ran after Criofan, darting back and forth, laughing.

"Whyever did he follow us?" Baudwin whispered to Matha.

"That I cannot say," Matha whispered back, "any more than I can say what drew him to Curios & Marvels."

"He seemed as interested in the ancient wonders as we were," Baudwin said. "Yet, he also seemed to yearn for —"

"Learning about the old ways," Matha replied. "For that, he truly seemed to pine."

"I wonder where his parents are," Baudwin said.

"Or if he has any," Matha replied. "Sadly, he seems to pine for love as well."

Baudwin remembered what Teigue had seen in his reflection at Curios & Marvels. Teigue's features had looked so much livelier in the shimmering green plate than his own. Obviously, Glamorium was offering the starving lad the nourishment he yearned for. Baudwin couldn't help feeling jealous, for wasn't he also starving? Yet, his reflection hadn't changed at all.

There was much Baudwin didn't understand. Surely, Glamorium didn't speak to everyone. Yet, at least he knew what was possible. For how many times had Edmund — the curator of Curios & Marvels — touched the glamorium regalia, without the slightest inkling of what he held in his hands? The thought made Baudwin chuckle.

Regardless of where his quest would lead, he knew one thing: Teigue was not the only one who would struggle to see what stood before him.

"His reflection in the Glamorium changed him," Baudwin said.

"Yes," Matha said. "That must be why he came back to us."

"And he probably would like you to teach him more about glyphs," Baudwin added. Having caught up to Criofan and Teigue, Baudwin shouted, "Come on, you two, I'll beat you to the water rides!"

Criofan and Teigue ran after Baudwin and Matha. As soon as they caught up to them, Criofan and Matha began joking again, having quickly forgotten their squabble. By then, they all had reached the entrance to the North Petal.

Set into the North Petal was the Water Park, an enormous oval-shaped concourse, with a stone wall at the perimeter, and fountains shooting from canals along the top. Lush groupings of river plants and trees were placed throughout the park, amid terraced stone waterfalls; piles and piles of stones stacked into steps formed pyramids with spouting tops — some dome-shaped and others pointed. Obviously, the Assembly wanted to appeal to both Faeries and Elves alike.

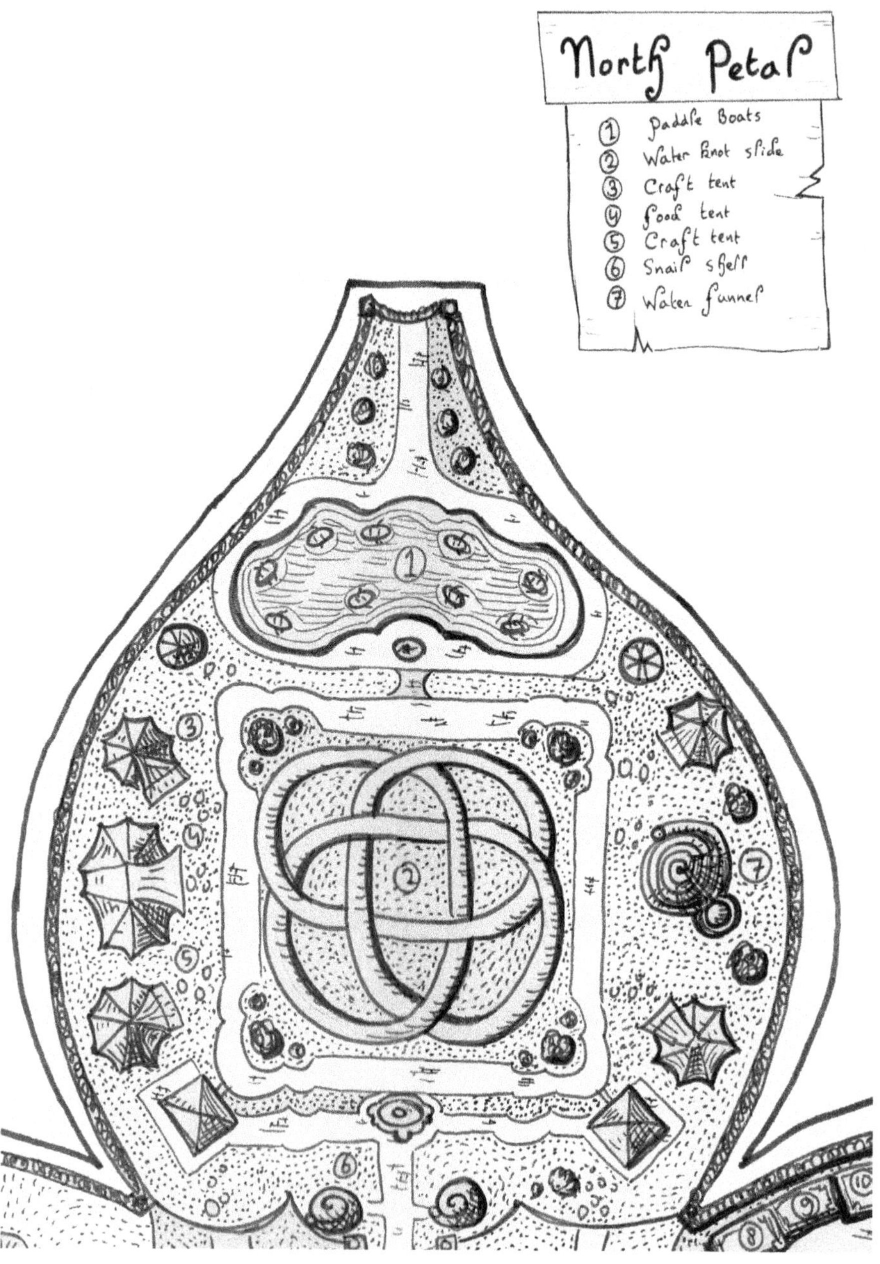

In the center of the petal, the Water Knot towered above them, a four-sided ride as tall as an ancient pine tree, with crisscrossing chutes that twisted around and around. Throngs of Faeries, mostly parents and their young ones, milled about the many other rides and tents dotting the grounds. Baudwin could hear shouts and laughter coming from the back of the petal, as Faeries played in boats that floated in an elven-made pool.

The four Faeries stood before two water snail shells, about six feet across, marking the entrance to the Water Park on either side. As Baudwin passed between them, he reached for one. "Yellow-blue, orange-violet, red-green!" he laughed, as he traced the spiral of colors from the outer edge of the shell to the center. He then proceeded into the park with his friends.

"At least we're doing something fun," Matha said, as he looked about. "I, for one, think we've had about enough discord for the day."

"Agreed," Baudwin replied. "Although I'm not at all happy that I didn't get to touch any Glamorium."

"Don't worry," Matha said. "You will."

"First let's get to the Water Knot," Criofan declared. "Are you coming?" With that, they turned right and hurried past support beams that held up the enormous slide.

"Come, Teigue," Criofan urged, as he headed toward the ride.

Upon reaching the corner, they raced up a flight of spiral stairs, all the way to the top. As they went, they heard screams of excitement, peals of laughter, and sounds of rushing Water coming from all directions.

"We're almost there!" Criofan shouted. "Baudwin! Matha! You have to see the Water!"

Matha and Baudwin burst onto the platform to join their friend. All stood — agog — staring at one of the largest lakes in Deuona — an enthralling sight for water Faeries to behold.

"Topaz Lake!" Baudwin shouted, as he reveled in the sight. The Water sparkled in the afternoon Sun like a radiant jewel. Luxuriant tufts of grass grew along the shore, shaded by pine trees. In the distance, rolling foothills gave way to the Tadlachs.

When Baudwin was a Faefry, Seamus told him that all the feelings of his ancestors rested in the lake. Earnestly following his grandfather's words, Baudwin had run to the shore and drunk all the Water he could, hoping to feel everything his kin had ever felt — but nothing happened. When he told Seamus, Seamus just laughed and told Baudwin that the way to knowing their hearts was not through his tummy.

Criofan grabbed Teigue and lifted him up so he could see over the railing. The little lad beamed, and shook with such joy that he dropped his jacket on the ground.

The three Faeries continued to gaze over the railing out toward the lake. Entranced by the splendor of their element, they fell silent, closing their eyes. Simultaneously, their senses began to awaken.

Baudwin was the first to notice. "Are we having a waking?" he asked.

No answer was needed, for all three of them realized that this was true. All felt an opening within the others as the Water passed through them. For a few fleeting moments, their senses touched the Water as a group — which used to be common among their kin, but now came far less frequently.

"I hear Water rushing," Matha said dreamily. "From so far away. Do you?"

"I hear Water rushing as well," Baudwin replied. "But from where?"

As Matha focused on the mountains, he could sense every stream from afar. "From the Tadlachs," he replied, mesmerized.

"Yes!" Baudwin exclaimed. "From the Tadlachs! The Water sounds as loud as it did yesterday when I was at the springs! Right before I saw the bluethroat," he added, laughing.

"Ah yes," Criofan joined in. "The button thief!"

Hearing this, Matha and Baudwin laughed together.

"I thought he had gotten the better of me," Baudwin said, giggling, "until he guided us to the shrine, and we found the glyph for Glamorium."

"How about you, Criofan?" Matha asked. "Do you hear the Water?"

"Yes," Criofan replied. "Snow is melting all over the Tadlachs, and the Water is rushing. I see the glittering slopes, and I hear the sound of foaming and spilling deep within my ears."

"And what about you, little one?" Criofan asked as he held Teigue.

Teigue gave Criofan a forlorn look, like a lost hare trapped in a thicket of briars. Obviously, his senses hadn't opened up. He looked at them confused, for he seemed to know what wakings meant, but didn't know how to speak about them.

"I. . ." he began sadly, shaking his head. "I don't feel anything."

"Well, don't you worry," Criofan said. "If you stick around us long enough, you will. If you want to have a waking, all you have to do is listen."

"To what?" Teigue asked, his sadness turning to hope.

"To the Water, of course!" all three Faeries exclaimed.

The three friends continued listening to the sounds of the Water. Teigue cocked his head to the side, trying to listen as well. He could not hear the Water from afar, but he did hear the spouting of the fountains below, which brought a smile to his face.

Baudwin looked at Teigue and licked his lips. "I can taste the Water too," he said, "rushing all over and around the rocks."

"The taste feels very cold," Matha said.

"Much colder than here," Criofan added.

"We're lucky we don't live in the mountains," Baudwin said, laughing again. "The Water here in Deuona is warmer."

"Quite a lot warmer," Matha said.

Suddenly, Teigue looked down and let out a nervous shudder. He was pointing at something below them. At first, Criofan paid him no heed, but the lad shuddered again.

"What's the matter, Teigue?" Criofan asked.

Criofan looked down and shuddered a bit himself. Baudwin also looked and saw Loch and a group of skulking Roilers, apparently searching for something. He watched the individual he had seen at the Mono-Ring, the one with the rabbit skin hat, peering into a waste bin, and then he saw Loch box him in the head. A few other Roilers laughed at him, and then set their gazes upon the boulders and support beams that held up the ride. With his senses still wide open, Baudwin was even more sickened by their presence.

Teigue whimpered with fright. "Oh, never mind them, Teigue," Baudwin said. "They can't reach us up here."

All four Faeries closed their eyes again, still sharing their waking.

Baudwin remembered what they had just been talking about — the warm Water in Deuona. "As I was saying," he began, "If I'd looked for the Water in the Tadlachs, instead of Deuona, I probably wouldn't have been able to bear. . ."

Suddenly, he trembled, his face grimacing in pain. Gasping, he repeated, "I probably wouldn't have been able to bear. . ."

Hearing this, Matha opened his eyes. As soon as he saw Baudwin, his senses withdrew. "To bear what?" he asked.

"The cold," Baudwin replied, again gasping. As the words left his lips, he recoiled.

"Baudwin," Matha said, "you're looking very strange. Whatever is the matter?"

". . . And the Water would never have come to me," Baudwin added. Wincing in pain, he grabbed onto the rail.

"Baudwin!" Matha cried.

Abruptly, Baudwin's senses withdrew. "Whatever is the matter?" Criofan asked.

"He's having one of his bouts!" Matha shouted. "Help him!"

Just then, they heard shouting down below. Loch and the Roilers were gesturing angrily up at them. Criofan wasn't sure what they wanted, but he could see them looking at Teigue. Teigue averted his gaze. Criofan quickly set the lad back on the ground. He then looked down at the Roilers, shaking his fist at them.

"Teigue!" Loch shouted.

Criofan couldn't imagine what they might want with the little lad, but he knew they would soon be upon them. He looked at Baudwin, now in full swoon, almost falling. Criofan and Matha grabbed him on either side to steady him.

Criofan looked down again. The Roilers were pushing their way through a line at the bottom of the stairs. If Baudwin didn't recover quickly, they would soon be overwhelmed.

"This is the second one he's had in a day," Matha said, frightened.

"The *second* one?" Criofan asked. "Why didn't you tell me?"

"I was too caught up in being here," Matha said. "I was going to tell you later."

"Why do they keep happening?" Criofan asked.

"They happen when he's near the Water, or after he's had a waking — like just now," Matha replied.

Baudwin moaned. All of his external senses appeared to be failing him. His eyes were squeezed shut, and he didn't seem to be aware of what was happening around him. Criofan and Matha struggled to hold him up.

Again, Loch shouted from down below. Criofan leaned over the rail to track his movements. The Roilers were still pushing through the line, making their way to the spiral staircase of the Water Knot.

"I have no idea what they want," Criofan said. "They were looking at Teigue for some reason."

"At Teigue?" Matha asked.

"I don't —" Criofan froze before he could finish speaking. On the ground, he noticed Teigue's unrolled jacket. Quickly, he realized what the Roilers were after. They had come to reclaim one of their own, for he could see strips of animal hide sewn on the arms.

"Teigue — you didn't tell us you were a Roiler!" Matha shouted, glaring at the jacket.

Alarmed, the little lad drew back from Matha, and hugged Criofan's leg, holding on tightly.

Baudwin moaned again and blinked his eyes.

"Don't worry about him!" Matha shouted. "We have to steady Baudwin and get out of here!"

Teigue would not let go of Criofan.

Below them, Criofan could see that the Roilers were now heading up the winding steps, their footsteps thundering as they pushed past wary, yet indignant Faeries.

"Baudwin," Matha began calmly. He placed his hand on Baudwin's shoulder to help him regain his bearings. "Listen to my voice," he said.

Baudwin did not respond.

"Take a look out there," Matha coaxed, pointing in the distance. "The Elves appear to have placed a flotilla of paddle boats on the beach. Do you see them?"

Slowly, Baudwin opened his eyes. "Yes," he muttered, closing his eyes again.

Teigue put on his jacket. The little Roiler stared at the three Faeries, uncertain of what to do next.

"Teigue!" Loch shouted from the stairs. The Roilers were almost halfway up. Hearing them, the little Roiler winced with apprehension.

Ignoring Loch, Matha continued to steady Baudwin.

"Baudwin. . ." he began. "Faeries are taking the paddle boats to the middle of Topaz Lake."

"We should go on them," Criofan said, as he grasped Baudwin's arm. "Open your eyes, Baudwin, and look."

Baudwin strained to see the boats, but he soon set his sight on something closer. The Water Funnel had caught his eye' — a cone-shaped wooden ride with rubber sides and a large hole at the top. Streams of Water ran down the sides in sheets.

Without warning, a faery lad shot out of the hole, propelled by a burst of Water — *swoosh!*

Baudwin laughed. Matha's coaxing had helped, for Baudwin's senses, which had been driven inward, were slowly returning.

"Yes. . . I see. . ." Baudwin said. Criofan and Matha were relieved to hear his voice. Teigue smiled.

Their relief was short-lived. The Roilers were almost at the top of the stairs. Loch was leading the charge — a storming mass of leather and fur. A faery lad froze — still as a mouse — clinging to the rail as they passed.

"Baudwin," Matha said, being careful not to alarm him. "Do you remember the first time we all went down that slide?"

Still groggy, Baudwin answered, "Weren't we all about eighty?"

Criofan cut in, "Yes — only eighty. Baudwin, you must wake up."

Matha nodded at Criofan, and Criofan nodded back. Neither mentioned the fast-approaching Roilers for fear of upsetting Baudwin.

"We were eighty and four," Matha clarified, steadying Baudwin.

"One time was not enough," Baudwin mused. "We went again and again, until we were sore as could be."

Matha nodded, smiling, as he gazed off into the distance. "Do you see those water drums on Topaz Lake?" he asked.

"Yes," Baudwin replied.

As Baudwin's senses continued to clear, he watched the drums in the distance, bobbing in the Water. They looked magnificent, with amazing leaves and roots. *They belong in dreams,* he thought, remembering the vision he had had the day before. Right before the Water came to him, he had seen himself floating in a water drum. The memory helped ease him back, and his senses steadied.

Listlessly, Baudwin caught sight of an indignant faery gent, shaking his fist. Startled, Baudwin grabbed the rail, trying to determine what the fuss was about. "Roilers!" he exclaimed, for Loch and his gang had almost run over the faery gent, having shoved their way past this final obstacle and reached the top of the stairs.

"We have to go!" Criofan exclaimed. "There are at least ten of them."

Baudwin knew of only one way to escape. "We'll have to ride the knot," he said. He then looked at the young faery lad. "Teigue!" he exclaimed. "Whyever are you wearing that Roiler jacket?"

Teigue could not speak.

"Why did you hide this from us?" Matha asked.

Teigue shook his head, and took off his jacket.

"Never mind all this," Matha said, looking at Baudwin. "Are you well enough to ride?"

"I'll have to be," Baudwin replied.

The Roilers were now running toward them. Baudwin could see Loch in front, waving his arms at Teigue. Quickly, they all turned to leave.

"Teigue, you better go meet him," Matha said, "so he doesn't get even angrier."

Teigue looked at Matha, utterly confused. He shot a glance at the advancing Roilers, and then back at Criofan. Back and forth he looked, not knowing what to do. For a moment, it seemed as if he would rejoin the Roilers, but then he stopped. A pulse shot through him, for his heart, not his head, had decided his course. He bounded toward the ride.

"He can't come with us!" Matha shouted.

"Perhaps not — but at least he's going in the right direction," Baudwin laughed.

The three raced after Teigue, making their way down the long walkway that ran along the top of the Water Knot. Not far behind them, they heard Loch holler, "They're not your kin!"

Once at the ride station, they were stopped by a long line of Faeries waiting to board the rafts that would take them down the winding chutes of the Water Knot. Like a well-behaved centipede, six Faeries stepped forward, taking their places behind the gate at the end of the platform. Giggling nervously, two faery ladies prepared to board the raft.

Criofan raced to the far side of the platform. "Get ready," he called. "Two more rafts are coming."

With a *whoosh*, a large violet flower-shaped raft appeared, with six wooden seats. To the right of the loading platform, an old Elve pulled a lever, releasing the gate.

Baudwin and his friends pushed through to the front of the line.

"Hey, you lousy louts!" someone yelled. "Wait your turn!"

"Sorry, but we've got a problem with those Roilers over there," Baudwin shouted, as he pointed to Loch and the mob of animal-hided hooligans that surrounded him.

Baudwin was lucky. The Faeries in line were all Guilders, and they let him by. The four Faeries scrambled for seats on the raft.

"Remember to buckle your belts before the ride begins," the old Elve called out through a brass speaker horn.

Quickly, they complied, as Loch was only a few paces away, trying to ram his way through the line. The crowd held their ground, unwilling to let a pack of rude Roilers come between them and their fun. A small scuffle broke out, slowing Loch's advance, but before long, the Roilers would surely break through.

The four Faeries waited anxiously for the Elve to pull the lever. He paused for a moment.

"What's he *waiting* for?" Criofan growled under his breath.

"Remember to keep your arms inside the flower," the Elve continued, grasping the lever.

All four Faeries pulled their arms in closer, warily watching as Loch shoved his way through the line. The Elve's fingers tightened on the lever. He then paused again, looking at Criofan. "I was *waiting* to inform you," he began dryly, "that if you fall into the Water, you're on your own. We won't be able to save you."

"You won't be able to save *yourself* if you don't pull that lever," Criofan called out. Baudwin and Matha laughed.

Just then, Loch burst onto the ride platform. "You bring him back this instant!" he yelled.

At that moment, the Elve pulled the lever. A large wheel rose out of the Water, spinning. As the wheel knocked into the back of the raft, Teigue let out a shriek. The rubber flower began to move, and they quickly floated away from the platform.

"Don't you worry, Loch!" Matha shouted. "When *we're* through with this little lad — you won't want him anymore."

As everyone in the flower raft shook with laughter, Loch shook in a fit of rage, stamping his feet on the platform.

"Here we go!" Criofan shouted. "Hold on!"

"Phew! Baudwin exclaimed. "Good riddance to bad rubbish!" No doubt Loch would follow after them, but for now, he was stuck, and they were free to enjoy themselves. Baudwin's bout had all but faded away. He looked at the slide, which was a square-shaped eternity knot made of one long interweaving chute. Each side rose to a corner, formed a tight curve, and then fell sharply to the bottom. Across from him, Baudwin could see flower rafts floating on top of the surging Water, packed with screaming and shouting Faeries.

The raft lurched forward, beginning its ascent to the first corner of the knot. After the curve it fell steeply, dropping like a rock and leaving all the passengers breathless. Round and around the flower raft spun.

"Aaaaiiiiieeeee!" they screamed.

After reaching the bottom of the first corner, the ride leveled out. Everyone relaxed. Baudwin and Criofan, who were sitting on either side of Teigue, laughed and tickled him. Having gained momentum from the drop, the raft then climbed easily to the second corner of the knot.

"Uh-oh! I see Loch — just a couple of rafts behind us!" Criofan announced, as they reached the top.

"A couple of *rats* behind us?" Matha shrieked, laughing, as he held tightly onto the sides of his seat. The raft rounded the corner. Everyone braced themselves for what was to come.

Down they went again. This time, they all screamed together, *"Aaaaiiiiieeeee!"* As before, the ride then leveled out, and the raft rose to the third corner of the knot.

"Loch is going to be so cross with me!" Teigue cried, as they reached the top.

"Then we'll just have to keep riding forever," Baudwin yelled, as they turned the corner. Seeing the look of terror on Teigue's face, he laughed. "Don't worry, little laddie! You'll be hopping out and back up the stairs in no time, like a frog after a bug!"

Baudwin's words did little to calm Teigue, for having turned the corner, the raft again dropped abruptly to the bottom. As Water shot into the little one's face, he reached for Criofan, the buckle on his harness holding him back. "We must go! We must go!" he screamed.

"But where?" Criofan cried out. Baudwin and Matha laughed and screamed, trying to take Teigue's mind off his plight. Finally, the raft reached the last corner of the knot.

"Surely, the fourth circuit will do us all in!" Baudwin shrieked. Shaking his head, he cleared the Water from his ears. The raft lurched sharply and then drifted around the final corner.

"Oh nooooooooooo!" Teigue cried, as they plummeted to the bottom. As the ride leveled out one last time, Water sprayed everywhere. Drifting a few more yards, the raft finally came to rest at the platform exit with a vigorous bump.

Everyone remained motionless in their seats, as all were dripping wet. Baudwin, Matha, and Criofan smiled brightly, exhilarated from their adventure. Teigue unbuckled his belt. Clinging to Criofan, he buried his head in his side — a sparrow huddling beneath a branch in a summer rainstorm. Criofan tried to pry him loose, but to no avail. The young lad refused to budge.

"Come now, Teigue," Baudwin began. "That wasn't so bad. What do you say?" Refusing to answer, Teigue pressed his face more deeply into the folds of Criofan's shirt.

"What he means," Criofan said, "is that if you were brave enough to ride, you must be brave enough to speak up."

For several moments, Teigue remained silent. When he turned to face them, his frown became a broad smile. "I want to go again!" he announced.

Criofan slapped him on the back, laughing heartily. "That's the way, lad! Now let's go, before Loch gets here." Everyone unbuckled their belts, jumped out of their seats, and onto the platform.

"We have to get going," Matha said, as he looked for the Roilers.

"And you should probably stay here," Criofan said to Teigue. "Although we wouldn't mind if you tagged along with us."

The little Roiler hung his head. Baudwin could tell that Criofan would have liked nothing more than to take Teigue home with him, but that was out of the question.

"Why be a Roiler if you don't even like them?" Criofan asked.

Teigue started to speak, but stopped. He sighed, struggling to find his words.

"We don't have any more time," Baudwin said, ruffling Teigue's hair. "But we certainly enjoyed making your acquaintance."

Another raft had ended its run with a large splash. Everyone froze, but then relaxed, remembering that the Roilers were still one raft behind that one. They were safe, but not for long.

The three started to leave, but Teigue looked up, having found his words. "Because he's my cousin!"

Shocked, they stopped, staring straight at him.

"You don't mean —" Baudwin asked.

"Loch," Teigue added, "He's my cousin!" Tears welled up in the little lad's eyes. He let out a sob. Teigue seemed much more Guilder than Roiler, but he was too young and would have to wait until he could make his own decisions. There was nothing they could do.

Teigue stood frozen.

"You poor little rabbit," Criofan said. "If he were my cousin, I too would jump at the sound of an acorn dropping."

"We better get out of here," Matha urged. "Loch will come shooting down that ride any moment — with more Roilers than we could ever hope to fight."

"Let's go to the East Petal," Criofan suggested.

"That's fine with me," Matha said. "Come on, Baudwin."

"I'm sorry, Teigue, but we must go now," Baudwin said, patting the young lad on his shoulder. "Don't ever take what Loch says to heart. My grandfather is the

Guild Leader of Deuona. He says that the Water is eternal, as is our reverence for the Water. Heed this, and remember that Roilers are but daylilies — gone by sunset. Guilders will always be here."

Teigue nodded, and turned to wait for the Roilers, and the inevitable scolding Loch would give him. He seemed resolute, for there was now a current of bravery inside of him that would surely carry him to a better destination.

The three hurried away from the Water Knot. Once again, Baudwin had had his fun ruined by the Roilers. Fuming with resentment, he left the Water Park with his friends.

Chapter 11

DIVIDED INTENTIONS

S oon they reached the entrance to the East Petal, which mirrored the West Petal: a double-swing wrought-bronze gate, with bird and flower motifs crafted into the rails. Above the gate, the words *Arcade and Park* hung in large copper letters on a bell-curved arch. Upon entering, they passed an Elve, who was busily handing out leaflets.

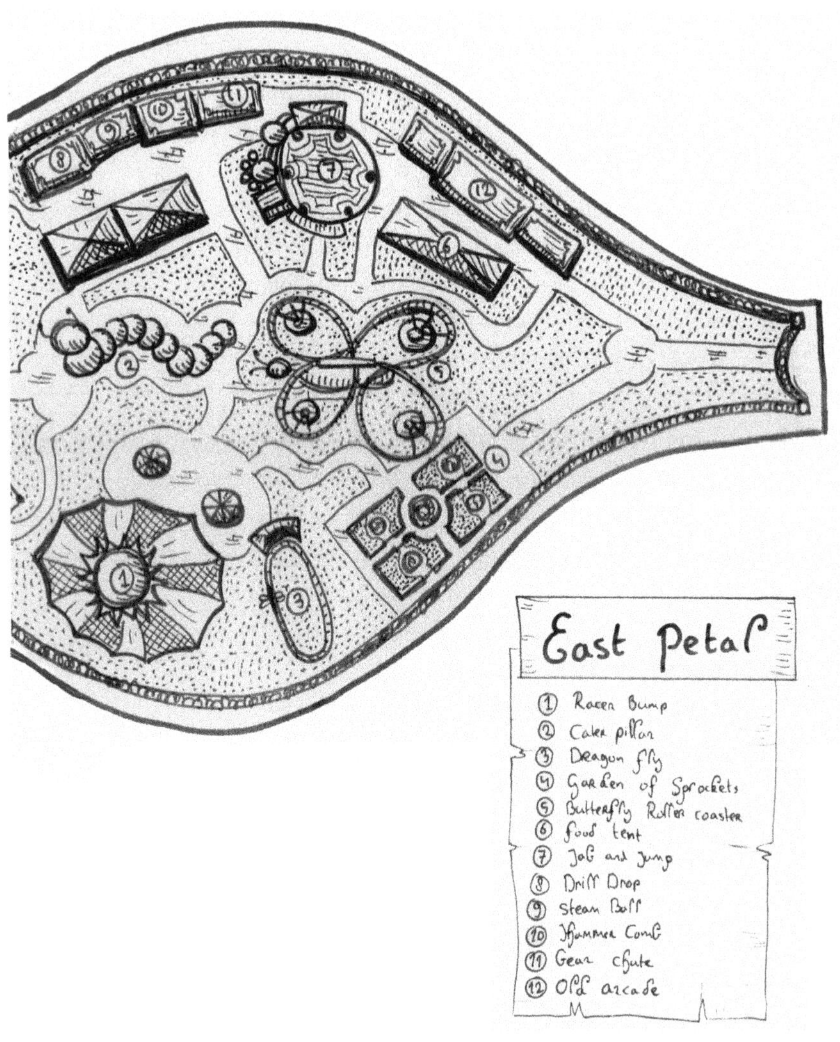

"Welcome to the Arcade and Park," he said, as he pressed a leaflet into each of their hands. "To understand the changes we have made, please take a map."

"What changes?" Matha asked.

"To the *new* Arcade and Park," the Elve replied, matter-of-factly. "Everything has changed!" he exclaimed, as he gestured toward the petal.

"I do remember things being different," Baudwin said, as he looked around.

"That's because everything *was* different," the Elve concurred. "We've changed all of this to make room for the new attraction." Pointing to the center of the petal he announced, "The Caterpillar has turned into a *Butterfly*. Isn't she a beauty?"

Impatient with the Elve's giddy explanation, Criofan grabbed the leaflet from his hand.

"Thank you for your help," he said. "I'm sure with this *amazing* map, we'll be able to figure all of this out —"

"Suit yourself," the Elve cut in. "But don't forget — you have the New Arcade to your left, and the New Park to your right. In the back, you have the Old Arcade to your left, and the Old Park to your right."

"I see," Baudwin replied, as he walked into the Park side of the petal.

"Everything old used to be in the front," the Elve called out. "But now, everything new is in the front, and everything old is in the back. Rather than looking at where we have been, we now look ahead to where we are going."

"Perhaps we should have let him explain more of this to us," Matha remarked.

"I know what I'm doing," Criofan insisted. "If we had kept listening to that gusty windbag, we'd never have gotten where we wanted to go."

Criofan took a gigantic breath. Frantically, he moved his arms from side to side, pretending to pass out leaflets. He then blew out the loudest exhalation Matha and Baudwin had ever heard.

"Will you stop that?" Baudwin asked, annoyed.

"We know you can breathe," Matha added.

"Baudwin, weren't you listening? We're not caterpillars anymore — we're *butterflies!*" Criofan shouted, laughing. He exhaled again, waving his arms at Baudwin. Matha broke into peals of laughter.

"I'm just going to ignore you," Baudwin groused.

"Suit yourself! Suit yourself!" Criofan shouted, as he blew out more Air, and staggered around in circles, gasping. Matha laughed even harder.

"You two are *far* more annoying than that Elve," Baudwin declared.

They all continued walking. "There's the caterpillar," Baudwin said. "How exciting. . ."

Directly ahead of them a long green worm with a red head and a large smiling mouth undulated up and down at high speed on a circular yellow track. Faeries sat four to a seat in body-segment-shaped cars. As the caterpillar careened sharply around a curve, they waved their arms, laughing and screaming.

"Let's do that!" Criofan exclaimed.

"No!" Baudwin said, as he angrily pressed on ahead by himself. After passing the caterpillar, he turned. Impatiently, he faced his friends.

Matha ran to meet him. "Cheer up, Baudwin," he said. "Look, that must be the Butterfly," he added, pointing to a large construction.

Before them, the Butterfly towered several stories above the ground — a huge abdomen sitting between four majestic turquoise wings, with orange and yellow spots and black wing veins. The model insect rested at an angle on a bronze support system that had been designed to resemble oak branches on a tree. From below, Baudwin could see train tracks running in loops on the edges of the four wings. The ride had been built so that passengers would travel a figure eight on one wing, and then cross the abdomen to travel a figure eight on the other, until the ride was over.

Criofan caught up to Baudwin and Matha. "Is something wrong?" he asked, seeing Baudwin's upset.

"Nothing is going right today," Baudwin pouted.

"Look, Baudwin!" Matha exclaimed, as he pointed to the right wings of the Butterfly. "Watch the car! On the track!"

Coming from the right hind wing, a car loaded with riders passed over the abdomen, and then traveled a figure eight on the other wing. Up, up, up they went, and then down and around. On any other day, Baudwin would have been enthralled, but the clacking of the wheels on the tracks was hurting his ears.

"Now they're riding on the other wing," Matha added.

"How clever," Baudwin remarked sourly. "Where else *could* they go?"

Matha and Criofan could tell that their friend wasn't happy.

"Instead of bickering, let's find something *fun* to do," Criofan suggested.

Baudwin would have none of Criofan's good-natured assuaging.

"You're good at that, Criofan," he challenged his friend. "Why don't you decide for us?"

"What do you mean?" Criofan asked.

Baudwin struggled to choose his words. "If you hadn't *made* us go to the Water Knot first, we wouldn't have run into Loch again, and we'd still be in the Water Park, having fun!"

"*Made* us?" Criofan declared angrily. "What a stupid thing to say! You're just angry that you *failed* with Glamorium! And now you're blaming me!"

"*Blaming* you?" Baudwin asked. "How ridiculous!"

"Your search is futile!" Criofan shouted. "Who knows if you actually *did* find the Water!"

"Both of you — be quiet!" Matha commanded. "I've heard enough!"

All three Faeries went silent. Baudwin and Criofan stared stonily at each other. A small part of Baudwin knew Criofan was right, but he certainly wasn't going to admit it now. Not only had Glamorium eluded him, but his efforts to have some fun had also been foiled. When he became this upset, his resentment burned so brightly that he seemed to forget that Criofan was his friend.

This wasn't the first time the two Faeries had argued this way, and Baudwin knew it wouldn't be the last. For he had known Criofan for two hundred years, and although Faeries could stop quarreling in an instant, they could also let a difference of opinion spark a feud that could last centuries. They would fight again and again, until they learned their lesson.

"Let's go our separate ways for a while," Matha suggested, attempting to diffuse the rancor between them. "We'll meet here later and then go on the Butterfly."

"That's fine with me," Baudwin replied, sounding as angry as ever.

"Good," Criofan agreed, having regained only a measure of his composure. "We'll meet back here in an hour."

Matha looked ruefully at Baudwin. "Too quickly you forget who your true friends are. We just helped you when you had a bout, and now you're accusing us of things we haven't done."

Baudwin did not reply, although he did feel uneasy about not being able to better understand his feelings.

With that, Criofan and Matha turned toward the New Park, and Baudwin headed to the New Arcade. Soon Baudwin was out of sight. Matha wondered if he had made the right suggestion. They were used to doing everything together, but with Baudwin so on edge, Matha could see his friend needed some time alone.

"That's Baudwin for you," Criofan remarked cooly, as he and Matha moved along the path. "And it's always whenever he doesn't get what he wants — especially his fun. Did you see how he treated me when we were arguing? How insulting! We were only trying to lift him out of his disappointment over not getting his precious Glamorium."

"At least I didn't catch any of the blame," Matha said with a chuckle.

"He never gets that angry with you," Criofan said. "Which makes *me* angry."

"He doesn't get that angry with me, because I know what not to say to him — and *when*," Matha said.

"That may be true, but I'm right about what I said. He didn't find Glamorium, and now he's taking it out on me. If he would grow up and think for a change, he would realize that he has bigger problems. Those Roilers will surely give us more trouble. And you, I might add, better watch your back — especially after what you said to Loch."

"You think he's that angry?" Matha asked.

Criofan cocked his head at Matha. "What do you think?" he asked, laughing. "You told Loch that when we're through with Teigue, he wouldn't want him anymore."

Criofan had a point. Loch was probably angry with Matha, but Matha figured that Loch was even more upset with Baudwin. Suddenly Matha wasn't sure that splitting up was such a good idea. But at least Criofan was still with him.

Matha glanced at Criofan and saw that he was walking away. "Wait," he said. "Where are you going?"

"Over there," Criofan replied casually, pointing at some lavender-finned dolphins and seahorses with fuchsia streaks, rising and falling to calliope music on a carousel. Nearby, a Ferris wheel, with multicolored seats, rotated peacefully around in circles.

"You're riding with the Faefries?" Matha asked, worried.

"No," Criofan replied. "I'm just heading over there."

Matha could see that Criofan was pointing past the rides at an enormous red and white tent.

"You're going to join the race?" Matha asked, surprised.

"No, I'm just going to watch," Criofan replied. "Do you want to come along?"

Matha wasn't sure what to do. Loch was on the loose, which was never a good thing. Grimacing, he paused. The Roilers may have ruined Baudwin's fun, but he wasn't going to let them ruin his. Besides, when he was in a bind, he could be the sneakiest one in the troupe. The Roilers would never catch him.

"I'm going to the Garden of Sprockets," Matha replied, "to see the newest elven automatons."

"You really like those inventions, don't you?"

"I find them fascinating," Matha replied, wryly. "And they don't get into stupid arguments."

Walking away, Criofan didn't look back. "To each his own," he said. With that, he left Matha to his own devices and headed to the track.

❦

Baudwin was furious.

So furious that he didn't know how he had gotten so upset. This always happened when he was really angry, and it happened far too often. Not being joined to his current jammed his feelings into his thoughts, until his thoughts hardened into tight little knots inside his head, burning knots that made him feel about to explode. All he wanted was to get as far away from his friends as he could. As he stomped away from the East Petal, he could barely see straight. What little he did notice gave him no comfort — at all. Instead of being full of fun and excitement, the Engineerium was now just a blur of disappointing colors, sounds, and shapes — a terrible reminder of just how disappointing his Life really was.

Aimlessly, he walked and walked, past rows of tents filled with enticing merchandise, and throngs of Faeries happily enjoying themselves. Scowling, he passed by them, not caring how fearsome or foolish he looked, so dark was his mood.

"Baaaaudwin!" A dramatic-sounding voice suddenly cried out.

Baudwin stopped, ignoring whoever had called out to him. Shocked, he realized where he was. There before him stood the Show Wheel. He was in the South Petal. *However did I get here?* he thought, for he could not remember how long he had been walking. Blankly, he stared at the large wooden stage.

"Baaaaudwin!" the voice persisted. "Can't you hear me?"

Still upset, Baudwin didn't care to find out who was calling him. Instead, his attention wandered to a fountain encircled by a pool of Water adjacent to the Show Wheel. Outside the pool, groups of Faeries were gathered on a patio made of gold and blue tiles, sipping sweet drinks and enjoying the fountain. *Perhaps I should join them,* he thought, ruefully. *At least I might get in a few moments of banter.*

But the voice wasn't going to leave him alone.

"Baaaaudwin! Oh Baaaaudwin!" he heard again. "Over here!"

Oh no, he thought. *That sounds like Elva.*[1] *Must I run into her right now?* Reluctantly, he turned to see what she wanted.

Elva was a faery lady, about four and fifty, who lived near Baudwin on a neighboring farm. She and her husband Eolann[2] worked the land, raising turnips. Although Baudwin had known her since he was a Faefry, he always found her quite annoying. There she sat at her table like a plumped-up partridge with blue-green feathers, looking very self-important in her guild apparel. "I'm over here!" she announced cheerily. "Come, my dear. Have some of my cabbage flower. I couldn't possibly eat the whole thing myself. Do sit down."

As Baudwin made his way to her table, a faery lad and lassie passed by, holding napkins piled high with cookies — sun circles with gold, and moon crescents with silver frosting. Giggling mischievously, they ran to share them with their friends. Baudwin wanted to steal a cookie from the lad, so he could

---

[1] Pronounced [EL-vah]
[2] Pronounced [OH-lan]

have at least a small moment of pleasure. He knew the lad wouldn't even notice, but Elva would, and she would tell his father, so he decided not to.

"Hello, Elva," Baudwin said as genially as he could, as he sat down next to her. "How's this year's crop?"

"Growing nicely," Elva replied. "We may have the largest one ever this year, and the biggest turnip at the fall festival."

Elva grasped Baudwin's hands, and gave them a tight squeeze. "How are you, Baudwin?" she asked, smiling brightly. "Are you coming to the meeting tonight?"

"Of course," he answered, annoyed that he had to make small talk with her. "The meeting is at our house."

"Oh yes!" Elva exclaimed cheerily. "I forgot! Quite a number of us will be there. This year, we have some very important things to discuss."

Baudwin could tell that Elva was trying to pry something out of him. If she wasn't, she wouldn't have invited him over, and offered to share her cabbage with him.

"Which way are your father and grandfather going to vote?" she asked, nonchalantly.

"On what?" he asked, realizing he was right. She *was* trying to get something out of him.

"Why, Matter *Three*," Elva replied brightly.

"I haven't any notion," Baudwin replied. "I never know what matters will be voted on until I'm at the meeting."

"You sound just like your father — keeping his buttons closed on his vest," Elva teased him. "Are you sure there isn't something you haven't told me?"

At that moment, Baudwin had an excuse not to reply, for in contrast to Elva's invasive questioning, melodious music began to sound from the Show Wheel — a very pleasant tune with a light and lively beat. As the performance was about to begin, Faeries left their places at the fountains, quickly making their way down the aisles to find seats.

"I can't share what I don't know," Baudwin replied, as he looked for an excuse to leave. "And I can't talk any longer."

"You're leaving?" Elva asked. "Aren't you going to the show?"

Although the Show Wheel sounded enticing, Baudwin knew he didn't have the time or the patience to watch the performance. He was still burning with anger, and saw no point in staying, especially if Elva was going to rope him into sitting next to her — which she certainly was. He simply didn't want to listen to her constant chattering.

"No," Baudwin replied. "I can't. I have to meet Matha and Criofan." This he knew was an out-and-out lie, but he didn't care.

Elva sensed his deception. "Why aren't they with you?" she asked. "You didn't have a disagreement, did you?"

"Of course not," Baudwin replied, annoyed at her intense prying. "I really must leave."

"Well, I wouldn't miss the show for anything," Elva said. "It's just marvelous seeing all those elven ladies and gents in their wildness for a change, instead of — you know — being so *orderly*."

Hearing this, Baudwin bristled. Elva always sounded as if she knew what was best for everyone.

"Is that so?" he asked.

"Well, yes, dear," Elva replied. "Can't you tell?"

"No," Baudwin replied, adding, "I guess I'm just not as good at seeing elven ways as you are."

Elva did not take offense at Baudwin's sarcastic inference, beaming instead at what she perceived as a compliment. As Baudwin stood up, she placed her elbows upon the table, her chin resting atop her folded hands. "Haven't you forgotten something, young gent?" she asked, batting her eyes and flashing a flirtatious smile.

Unable to avoid his duty, Baudwin stood up and pulled out her chair. Elva rose from her seat. Smiling proudly, she picked up a large bag.

"Well," she said, "if I can't have the pleasure of *your* company, then I will simply have to enjoy the pleasure of my own."

That shouldn't be too hard, Baudwin thought, for he knew just how highly Elva thought of herself.

With that, she turned and hurried to the Show Wheel. "See you at the meeting tonight," she called out gaily.

Baudwin still wasn't having any fun, but at least he had managed to dodge Elva. With that, he decided to go back to the New Arcade to find a better diversion. At least there he could count on being left alone.

Chapter 12

GAMES WITHOUT A FRIEND

*G*ood! Baudwin thought, as he passed the Butterfly on his way to the New Arcade. Since no one was with him, he could do whatever he wanted. Upon reaching the Caterpillar, he cut across the main path to a large food tent, where a number of Faeries were waiting in line to get some food.

He slowed down to watch them. An older faery gent placed his order. Behind the counter, an Elve quickly sliced a melon into pieces, fanning them into a half-circle, whistling as he worked. Next to the faery gent, a young faery couple chattered; the buttons on their coats almost popped with excitement. Everyone seemed to be enthralled with the Engineerium.

They were having the kind of day Baudwin had wanted, the kind he expected would happen. Yet all he had found was frustration. He thought then of Matha and Criofan. They didn't understand how hard he had planned to make the day go well. There was so much to juggle — getting his father's coupler, having fun with his friends, and finding some Glamorium to touch. He had almost succeeded, and yet, in the end, Loch and the Elves had managed to ruin everything.

Just then, he saw a young faery lad wearing a knitted cap tugging playfully on his mother's sleeve. He must have been about thirty, just old enough to come to the Engineerium. His mother turned, and Baudwin froze at the sight of her. She was like an apple blossom floating on a windless lake, exuding a calm that water Faeries cherished. Baudwin wondered what he would have been like, had she been his mother.

Clenching his fists, he seethed with resentment. *It matters not*, he thought. He knew he could not change his past, so he would simply have to make the best of things and accept his Life, no matter what the Water brought to him.

Yet, he could not stop thinking about what Criofan had said after he told him the Water had come to him — "What a highfalutin thing to say" — as if the Water couldn't possibly be guiding him. Did he believe that Baudwin wasn't deserving enough? Or was he simply jealous that the Water had come to Baudwin, and not to him?

And Matha. How furious he had been when they all escaped from Curios & Marvels. "You think *only* of yourself!" he had said. Didn't he know how hurtful his words were? As if Baudwin shouldn't have tried to touch the Glamorium, despite its critical importance to him.

Their words stuck in his craw.

They don't understand, he thought. *I cannot give up.* He wasn't sure if they really wanted to help him, or if they thought he was on a fool's errand. He knew he wasn't imagining the Water coming to him, yet they acted as if the Water were just playing tricks on him.

Baudwin continued fuming. Perhaps what they really thought was that he simply wasn't worthy. For they had joined with their currents years ago, and coursed with their feelings. Their intentions in Life were clear. All of his kin had been given this boon from the Water. Ironically, his intention had only been to be like them, but he knew this would never be.

Having not completed the Ceremonies of the Joining and the Coursing, he would be forever adrift. Even if his grandfather was right, and Glamorium granted him aid, without being joined to his current, he would still feel uncertain about his path.

Neither could he give up — for he feared that would mean his own destruction.

He had never told Matha or Criofan, but his bouts, that he understood simply as a strange affliction of the Water, had begun many years ago, shortly after the Ceremony of the Joining. Kelven and Seamus had been quite perplexed, for they knew that Baudwin wasn't the only Faery without a mother. None of the other young ones without a mother had suffered in this way. Yet still, Baudwin was certain that the cause of his malady had something to do with not being joined to his current.

At the Springs of Coventina, the Water had come to him. Surely, this was a great blessing. He had hoped that the Water would help him find his mother, so he could finish the Ceremony and, he fervently hoped, heal himself. Yet, neither of these things had happened. Instead, his bouts were now worse than ever, so bad in fact that he feared that unless he found her, he would pass to Annwyn.

Despite this, he knew he could not let his fears get the better of him, or he would surely remain rooted where he was, unable to choose the best direction.

Baudwin tore his gaze away from the food tent. Perhaps seeing the faery mother and her young one had helped him after all. Having contemplated his dilemma, he could feel his anger subsiding. Again he heard Seamus's words of wisdom, "You cannot hone your intention without calm."

He knew what he had to do. Regardless of how difficult his struggle proved to be, he would continue. Surely if his quest was real, Glamorium would present itself to him again. After all, the Water had come to him.

Baudwin wandered along behind the food tent. Parallel to the East Petal wall sat a long row of game booths. In large letters, a sign on the first booth read *Drill Drop*.

This better be fun, he thought.

"Want to play?" an elven gent called out from the booth. "Are you up to the challenge?"

"Of course," Baudwin replied, as he pointed at the booth. "Do I look like such a dunce that I can't play this game?"

"Go right on in then," the elven gent replied, with a good-natured smile.

Baudwin stepped inside and saw dozens of old elven workbenches, spaced in rows. Faery lads and lassies occupied most of them, playing Drill Drop. Directly ahead of him, he spotted an empty seat, so he went and sat down.

Before he began to play, he touched the smooth patina of the workbench — still lustrous after many hundreds of years. A bronze vice was bolted to one end — a simple part of the decor and a subtle reminder of the hold the Elves imposed upon the Faeries. The other end had been sawed off to make more space in the room, so more games could be played.

Despite being shortened, the bench stood solidly, with very little wobble in its cherry wood legs, scratched though they were. Before the workbench was converted into a drill drop game, some industrious Elve had undoubtedly spent years toiling over it, stalwartly measuring his cuts, and then chiseling and planing pieces of wood to make cabinets, tables, and chairs.

Such patience the Elves have when they work at their benches, Baudwin thought. And now Drill Drop was teaching the Faeries the same kind of patience, for without it, they would never develop any skill.

Smiling, Baudwin turned his attention to the game. Above the bench, he saw a large drill hanging from a sprocketworks pulley system. The drill could be aimed to fall into one of a series of evenly spaced holes on top of a sliding copper dowel. To begin the game, he turned a red knob beneath the bench one notch to the right.

On top of the workbench, the dowel began sliding back and forth. As Baudwin studied its movements, two faery lads joined him, waiting for him to make a move.

"Watch this," he said. The lads stood silently next to him.

To choose the hole he planned to hit, Baudwin grasped a lever next to the red knob. As he moved the lever from side to side, the drill hovering above the dowel shifted back and forth.

"Which one are you trying for?" the older faery lad asked, admiring Baudwin's dexterity.

"Five," Baudwin replied, fixing his attention upon the target. Years and years of trying and failing had honed his skill. Although he would never be as good as an Elve who had practiced just as long, he was nonetheless proud of his ability.

When the precise moment came, Baudwin quickly pressed a button with his other hand. Down plunged the heavy drill, like a bird of prey, impaling its tip into the center of the hole. Instantly, the sliding dowel came to a stop.

"Made the drop!" Baudwin exclaimed. A green ticket shot out from a slot beneath the workbench, which Baudwin grabbed.

"Number five!" the older faery lad cried. Of the nine holes in the line, the drill had landed precisely in the centermost one. With a click, the game reset itself, and the drill rose back to its original position above the dowel.

The two young Faeries watched, captivated.

"Are you going to play faster?" the younger lad asked. He seemed to be torn between wanting to see more of Baudwin's remarkable skill, and hoping he would vacate the stool, so he and his friend could have a turn.

"Of course," Baudwin replied. "Why do you think I'm here?" He then turned the red knob again — this time another notch to the right. Again, the dowel began to slide back and forth, moving faster this time.

"What's your lucky number?" Baudwin asked the younger lad, as he took hold of the lever.

"Nine."

With that, Baudwin withdrew into playing the game, the demands of which had increased almost twofold. In order to win, he had to concentrate even harder on the heavy drill and the dowel, which shifted back and forth, going even faster — *chek, chek, chek, chek, chek, chek, chek, chek.*

Moving his head rhythmically from side to side, Baudwin prepared himself. After carefully timing his movements, he spoke, "Ready. . . aim. . . drop." With that, the drill dove down and into the hole. Offering no time for celebration, the game reset itself, and the drill rose to click back into its original place above the dowel.

"Number nine!" the younger lad cried. Hearing all the excitement, several players at neighboring seats paused for a moment to look at Baudwin.

"How did you do that?" the older lad asked.

"By practicing since I was younger than you," Baudwin replied.

This thought struck a deep chord within him, giving him pause. For although he did not regret a single moment of fun playing Drill Drop, after so many years, he couldn't help feeling as if he had reached his limit. He had always sought out the game for pure excitement, to escape his dreary feelings. This and other distractions had carried him through countless seasons. Yet now, none of this was of any consolation to him — none whatsoever. *My time with this is over,* he thought.

With a start, Baudwin stood up. He would be out the door in a matter of moments, for the truth of his predicament was all too obvious. Despite his wanting to believe the contrary, he was simply too old for Drill Drop. Quickly, he grabbed two tickets; one was for winning the game, and a bonus ticket attested to his skill at making the dowel move faster.

"Aren't you going to play again?" the older lad asked, wheedling him to stay longer so he could gain from the instruction. "I bet you could go even faster."

"No," Baudwin replied. "I have better games to play. Here, take these tickets. Both of you — go now — and get a spirit friend," he added, as he motioned to a case near the front of the booth.

"Thank you!" they chimed in unison. Compounding the fun that most young Faeries had playing Drill Drop, Baudwin had just handed each of them a valuable prize that was not so easily won.

"One day you'll thank yourselves," Baudwin chuckled, "when you're as good as I am."

The two lads went to inspect the case that held the prizes. A number of painted wooden animals sat inside, highlighted with glowstone dust. The animals were made to lock together, so that young Faeries could collect their favorites, and by placing one on top of the other, make spirit poles.

"May I have the fox?" the younger lad asked an elven gent behind the case. In exchange for the ticket, the elven gent handed him a fox with red fur, a white throat, and gleaming amber eyes.

"How fiercely clever he is!" the lad exclaimed. "He knows much better than we how to hide in plain sight, so we cannot find him."

Hearing this, the older lad said, "I want the hawk. He can see things in great detail and remember them well." After taking his tickets, the elven gent removed a regal-looking bird from the shelf, with piercing black eyes and sepia feathers, tipped with gold highlights.

"How long has *he* been working for you?" the elven gent joked, as he handed the lad the hawk.

"Who?" the lad asked.

"Him," the elven gent replied, nodding at Baudwin.

The two lads shrugged, and then smiled at Baudwin.

"Don't forget to practice," Baudwin said, as he patted them both on the head.

"You *better* keep practicing," the elven gent said. "Otherwise, this fellow will put me out of business."

Despite winning the game and praise for his largesse, Baudwin was too deflated to laugh at the joke. With that, he left the booth.

That wasn't much fun, he thought. He wondered then what Matha and Criofan were doing. They were probably having a grand ol' time in other parts of the East Petal, and it struck him that he shouldn't have left them. Being on his own was becoming a bore. He needed to find a more exciting game to play, something more grown-up.

As he approached the next booth, he heard *whoosh,* and then *pop, pop, pop, pop, pop* — over and over again.

Steamball, he thought, as he entered the booth. Here was a game with a lot more zip.

Rather than play, Baudwin decided to watch, so he made his way straight to the front of the line. A number of players stood hunched over a counter, aiming pistols at the opposite wall. Attached to each of their pistols was a long hose.

Baudwin eyed a faery gent sitting poised and ready, grasping his pistol tightly with both hands. There was a click, and the game reset itself. Several balls rushed through the hose, driven by bursts of steam. After reaching the base of the handle, they stopped abruptly.

Promptly, the gent squeezed the trigger. Five balls shot in succession out of the barrel — *pop, pop, pop, pop, pop.* "Got four!" he exclaimed to a friend who sat next to him. "How about you?"

"Two," his friend replied.

"Only two?" the first gent asked.

Baudwin assessed the targets on the wall, which were made of various kinds of sprockets. The smaller the center holes, the more difficult the shots were to make. Despite their apparent skill, Baudwin could tell that the two Faeries were new at shooting.

Even though they had made some successful shots, Baudwin saw that the booth worker had set the targets close because they were beginners. Baudwin was very proficient at Steamball, so he decided to offer them some friendly pointers. Standing between them, he cheerfully announced, "He hit more, but you hit better."

Both Faeries relaxed their trigger fingers and took their eyes away from their targets.

"Who asked you?" the first Faery asked.

"Who indeed?" asked the second Faery.

"No one," Baudwin replied. "I just thought you might want to know the difference."

"So kindly tell us which *is* better — shooting *more* or shooting *better*?" the first gent countered, mocking Baudwin.

Laughing, the second gent pranced about, accidentally digging his heavy boot into Baudwin's foot, almost knocking him over.

Seeing this, the first gent also laughed. "That's what you get for being such a know-it-all!" he roared.

Insulted, Baudwin almost left, but stopped himself. He knew proceeding was foolish, but he felt like he didn't have a choice. How dare they meet him with such impertinence for simply trying to help them? There was nothing *grown-up* about this encounter, and he was about to let them know.

"It's just a game!" he shouted.

"Perhaps to you, but to us — it's *much* more than that!" the first gent shouted back. With a superior air, he looked back at his target.

The look on the gent's face angered Baudwin to no end. He was not about to ignore such disrespect. "*Really*?" he asked, his voice rising, as he studied their long-tailed coats and ruffled shirts. "Are you volunteering for an elven guard? You certainly appear to be! Although you look better suited to fight an invasion of katydids or tree frogs!"

"Why do you care what we do?" the first gent hollered.

"It's none of his business," the second gent replied, as he took a moment to examine his pistol. So engrossed was he in the design that he pointed the muzzle directly at his own face.

Baudwin smirked at the gent's inept handling of the pistol. "With all of your eying and misfiring," he continued, "all you'll ever be is a team of ill-trained ragtag recruits. You'll *never* be as skillful as the Elves, but that certainly seems to be lost on you."

"That's *enough!*" the first gent thundered.

"You're right!" Baudwin shouted back. "That *is* enough! And I've *had* enough!"

Enraged beyond words, he left the booth. *I hope I never end up like them,* he thought. *At least five and fifty, and waiting in line to play a game, only to fail miserably and not even know it.*

Again Baudwin had lost another chance to have fun. Flummoxed, he froze in the center of the footpath, wondering what to do next, when he heard high-pitched screams and shouts coming from the next booth. Peering inside, he spied an elven lady gesticulating wildly. The copper charms on her belt bounced madly in sync with the orange curls framing her glowing round face. A pair of violet spectacles rested at a sharp angle on her nose, having slid all the way to the end.

"Welcome to Hammer Comb!" she shouted, upon seeing Baudwin. "Hammer away, my young Fae!" she cried to a large group of Faefries.

Baudwin surveyed the chaos inside the booth; bands of lads and lassies were taking part in a melee of pounding, the likes of which he had never seen before. Many were standing at the edges of the booth, holding mallets with large rubber heads.

Vigorously, they pounded their mallets on a row of hexagonally shaped metal plates. Baudwin noticed that the plates resembled the cells in a beehive. The rows of cells, powered by steamway pistons, rose up from the ground and stopped. Lads and lassies then pounded them back down, trying to force them all the way to the ground. In this way, they could win the game, or so Baudwin thought.

Baudwin watched a lad pounding a cell. Lower and lower it went, but then something unexpected happened. Before the cell reached the ground, the piston below forced it up again. The lad pounded harder, but with each strike, instead of going down, the cell went up. Eventually, it was back where it had begun. The lad then started pounding all over again. Up and down the cell went, over and over and over, his efforts all for naught.

How ridiculous, Baudwin thought.

Whack, thump, thud, went the mallets as the Faefries struck the cells. "Wheeeee! Haaaaa! Eeeeee!" they squealed, as they delivered the blows. They acted as if they were going to win the game, but Baudwin couldn't see how.

"What's the point of all of this?" he called out above the ruckus.

"They're practicing!" the elven lady yelled back. "For the *combs,*" she added, pointing to four groups of cells in the center of the booth. "Here's a mallet."

Baudwin hesitated. "Isn't this game for young ones?" he asked.

"Oh no," she replied. "Any *rage* — I mean, any *age* — can play," she added, smiling coyly to hide her slip of the tongue.

Baudwin figured that the game in the center of the booth was where the real action was, and the game winnable. Given how disappointing Drill Drop and Steamball had been, he decided to play. He stepped toward the combs.

"Playing is simple," the elven lady explained to him, raising her voice above all the screaming and pounding. "Hit the cells, and wait for the big surprise," she said, her eyes gleaming with anticipation.

They stood before cells that had been grouped into four combs in the center of the booth. Baudwin noticed that each comb was arranged with six cells on the outside, and one in the center.

"The purpose *here,*" she began, "Is to hammer the outside cells, until they all lay flat at the same time. Only then will the wonderful workings of the center cell unlock."

"What wonderful workings?" Baudwin asked.

"You'll see," she teased. "Between one and six may play. The more players there are, the faster and easier it is for everyone to win. Wait a moment, and I'll get you some help."

The elven lady then summoned five young Faeries who had been practicing on the cells at the edges of the booth. With Baudwin, there were now six players. As soon as everyone received a mallet, the fracas began in earnest.

Each one stood before a cell that was about waist high. Fiendishly, the five young Faeries pounded their cells. Baudwin watched them curiously, for they seemed to be entranced, not thinking about what they were doing. *Whack, thump, thud,* went their mallets as they struck the cells. "Wheeeee! Haaaaa! Eeeeee!" they screamed.

Baudwin picked up his mallet and struck the cell in front of him. He too was carried away with excitement.

The unexpected then happened.

Baudwin assumed he would be able to hit his cell flat to the ground, for the elven lady had said as much. Furiously, he pounded the cell lower and lower. But, just before he could pound it to the ground, the cell began to rise again, just as he had seen the others do at the edge of the booth. Harder and harder he hit the cell, but to no avail. Looking around, he saw the Faefries weren't making any progress either. All the cells of the comb were now going up.

This game doesn't make any sense, he thought. He wondered why the Elves had built a game that couldn't be won. Not to mention, the elven lady had lied to him.

Baudwin couldn't let go of his annoyance. Agitated, he kept pounding, and the cell sank lower — stopping as if to tease him — and then started rising again.

Anger welled up inside of him as deep as a crater lake. Again, he struck downward upon the cell. He wasn't going to let the game get the better of him. Harder and harder he struck, but the cell kept rising. *I thought I was going to win,* he thought. This game was even more maddening than the practice cells had been. Unjoined as he was to his current, he could not control his anger. Screaming, he smashed down so hard that he broke off the mallet head. Exhausted, he stopped.

He leaned upon his mallet handle for support, for he had worked himself into quite a state. Unaware of Baudwin's plight, the young Faeries in the circle continued pounding their cells. Up and down, up and down they went. They shrieked with excitement, and Baudwin was glad he knew better.

The Faefries were then rewarded for their hard work.

Baudwin heard a loud whirring sound, as the steamway machinations set something new in motion.

Suddenly, steam came whistling out of the center cell. The cell then burst open like a trap door, and a frenzy of screeching pinwheels in all colors of the rainbow — red, orange, yellow, green, blue, indigo, and violet — shot upward. The pinwheels spun round and round, sparking in the Air.

Seeing this, the young ones at the edges of the booth went mad with excitement. Laughing and gesturing maniacally at the spectacle, many of them ran to the center of the comb to take a closer look, then darted back to their cells to resume their pounding, this time with even greater fervor.

For a moment Baudwin stared at the whirling pinwheels, but his interest quickly faded. His experience with the Water had led him to dream wondrously the night before, and in comparison, this display seemed empty to him. Having seen enough, he turned to leave the booth.

"Don't you want to see the other workings?" the elven lady asked. "The pinwheels will go higher and higher, until even more rainbows of Sky Sparks come shooting out."

"What's so wonderful about that?" Baudwin retorted. "All of the hammering and the noise —"

"The hammering and noise are foremost parts of the game," she cut in, pushing her spectacles back to rest upon the bridge of her nose. "Young Faeries need games such as these to hone their skills, and prepare them for life."

"More likely to prepare them to *fail*," Baudwin shouted above the din.

"Are *you* prepared?" she shouted back.

"Better than they!" he shouted again. "And I didn't need a pointless game like this to teach me!"

With that, Baudwin exited the booth, ruminating about what he had just said. When the elven lady had asked him if he was prepared, he had simply shot her an angry answer. Now he knew he had to slow down and think.

How would I really know if I'm prepared or not? he wondered. He assumed that the Water coming to him meant that he was. But after playing Hammer Comb and feeling so blisteringly angry, he no longer had the comfort of that certainty.

In a daze, Baudwin went to sit on a low stone wall next to the promenade, his head swirling. *What did all that pounding teach me?* he asked himself. Only that he was far angrier than he knew, which he found quite frightening.

Baudwin thought and thought, trying to understand why this was so.

He then remembered the words of the poem at the ruins of Coventina: *That which holds the Truth you seek, is something you must touch.* He remembered too what his grandfather had asked him: "*What else must you touch?*"

With a start, Baudwin realized what Seamus had been trying to tell him — that to answer the question, he had to solve the riddle. He had been looking for answers outside of himself, "wishing for many things," but now he realized the answer — something he had to touch — was within him. And if he did, he might be able to unlock the secrets of Glamorium.

A Light as bright as a glowstone then went off in his head.

Getting angry at Hammer Comb had been a blessing because only now could he sense that there was something beneath that anger, something that went to the heart of the matter. If he could only learn more about what that was, he was certain his quest would succeed. No longer would he be ruled by a roiling pool of rage that he couldn't control. But would he ever find what that something was?

He sat on the wall, dispirited, yet somehow calmer.

Despite his realization, he still had no idea how he would find what he was looking for. Gazing past throngs of happy revelers, he felt wracked with uncertainty. *This is the price I pay for not being joined with my current,* he thought. Truly, he felt doomed. If only he had understood what his grandfather had asked him *before* he had seen the glamorium collection at Curios & Marvels, perhaps something special might have happened. Perhaps instead of only changing Teigue's reflection, Glamorium would have changed his as well, and he would have found his deeper self. Now his chance to touch some Glamorium and to find his mother could be lost for a long time — perhaps forever.

Chapter 13

CONCORD AND DISCORD

Matha left the New Park quite perturbed with Baudwin and Criofan and their silly fight. *What a couple of obstinate goats they are,* he thought. *Butting heads the way they did.* Ever since they were Faefries, they had argued the same way. Sometimes Baudwin was right, and sometimes Criofan, but judging by their stubbornness, neither of them were half as smart as they thought they were.

Obviously, neither of them understood concord. If they did, they would have listened to him when he told them enough was enough. After all, wasn't he the son of the Primary of Concord? When things went wrong, as they had when Loch saw them at the Water Knot, he believed friends shouldn't fight over who was right. Instead, they should figure out what needed to be done to set a better course.

Matha knew that he would have to be careful on his own. Loch would be looking for the three of them, but as he was alone, he was much less likely to be spotted. *At least we aren't running around — feuding like fledglings — attracting attention,* he thought.

He was still frustrated by what had happened. Not only did he have to listen to their foolish arguments, but he would likely have to help them resolve their disagreement. They certainly couldn't show up at tonight's meeting of the Water Guild still upset with each other. The sons of the primaries were expected to conduct themselves reasonably, with manners and decorum.

How tired he was of having to place their concerns above his own. With that, he took his map out his pocket.

"Let's see," he mused, as he proceeded toward the Old Park. "In the middle is the Butterfly. . . which means the Dragonfly must be right *there.*"

Peals of laughter and screams of panic confirmed his estimation. A green dragonfly with wire mesh wings towered before him, suspended from a large platform. As the giant insect swung back and forth, groups of Faeries in the wooden abdomen looked tremblingly down on the ground beneath them. When the insect reached the midpoint of its swing, Matha spotted some acquaintances. "Come fly with us!" they shouted.

"Later!" Matha hollered back. He then continued on his way.

The shimmering green sides of the dragonfly reminded him of the glamorium tablet he had just seen at Curios & Marvels, which irritated him even more. How could Baudwin possibly know how meaningful the tablet was to faery history? All he could do was go on and on about his mother. Many other artifacts in the case were also very important to him. But he had no chance to look at any of them, because Baudwin had ruined everything by getting them all chased out of the place. *I never get to study what I want to study, when I want to study it,* he thought.

Much to his delight, this was about to change, for he had reached the Garden of Sprockets, a large park enclosed by a well-manicured laurel hedge. Behind the hedge stood a wrought-bronze fence. On every rail, copper sprockets alternated with bronze flowers from top to bottom. Matha stepped through the front gate, eager to explore what awaited him there.

Before him was the haven he sought from all the discord. Around him were flowers, both real and mechanical, and not a soul to break the tranquility. He walked past a row of red roses, planted next to another row of roses with bronze stems and copper blooms. He couldn't help thinking that the Elves who built the garden must have understood the core tenants of concord. For how else could they have created such a pleasing balance between nature and machines? He remembered what his father had told him: Without balance how can there be harmony, and without harmony how can there be balance? Smiling to himself, he recited a poem about harmony he had learned from his mother:

> If I do half the work and let you play
> You must do the other half next day
> Therein we find amity and peace
>
> If what you do is play, forgetting work
> Knowing that your duties you will shirk
> The harmony we share will surely cease

Matha wished that he could lock both Guilders and Roilers in one room, and make them recite the poem until something changed for the better. Perhaps then, Baudwin and Loch would finally broker peace. Although first, Loch would have to learn some basic respect for *gnás*. At least Baudwin knew that much.

His thoughts shifted to finding the Sprouting Patch. As he scanned around and then looked at his map, he was interrupted.

"Excuse me, please, excuse me," a voice called out. Looking down the path, Matha saw an elderly faery lady hurrying toward him, with a young faery lad in tow.

"Is that a map you have?" she asked.

"Yes," Matha replied.

"How wonderful!" she exclaimed. Breathing quickly, she added, "I seem to have misplaced mine, and I do so need to know where everything is. My name is Ida,[1] and this is my grandson, Conor."[2]

"Hello, Conor," Matha said, as he studied the round-faced, intelligent-looking little lad. "My name is Matha."

"Hello," Conor replied, eying the map. Matha could tell that Conor was even more interested than his grandmother to learn about where things were.

"What is it that you want to know?" he asked, finding their interest in the park and all of its workings refreshing. *For once I am talking, and someone is actually listening,* he thought.

"Mostly how things are arranged," Ida replied. "I know the Sprouting Patch is in the center of the garden, but I don't know about the four gardens. I really want to see the dahlias, but I don't want to miss the tulips either, and Conor simply has to ride as many insects as possible."

"You mean *automatons,*" Matha corrected her.

"Au-tom-a-tons?" Ida replied.

"Obviously, the insects here aren't really insects," Matha explained. "Just sprocketworks machines that have been made to look like them."

"How fascinating!" Ida said. "I didn't know the Elves could build such things."

"*I* knew!" Conor exclaimed. "Which is why I want to ride them. Only my grandmother doesn't know where they are."

"Never mind that, Conor," Ida said. "Aren't we lucky to have found Matha? He seems to know so much about these kinds of things."

"You can find automatons on most any path that goes through the garden," Matha continued, as he looked at the map. "When you see one, just ask a garden keeper to wind the spring. Then, off you go."

"What about the rest of the garden?" Ida asked. "Please do tell us more."

"Why don't you just come with me to the Sprouting Patch?" Matha offered. "We may find some automatons there. If we do, I'll tell you more about them. I myself am looking to see if there are any new ones in the garden."

"That would be wonderful!" Ida exclaimed. "Come now, Conor," she added, motioning to her grandson.

Matha had invited them not only to be kind, but also because they were a welcome distraction. Certainly, a grandmother and her grandson would be easier to deal with than Baudwin and Criofan, as well as less noticeable to Loch and his gang than a single Faery walking alone. Soon they were standing in

---

[1] Pronounced [EE-da]

[2] Pronounced [KON-ner]

the very center of the garden, looking at a large bronze sprocket lying flat on a wooden platform. The sprocket had a large center hole with a bronze cover on top. Around the sprocket was a ring of smaller sprockets, and around that ring was another ring, and around that was another.

"So, this is the Sprouting Patch," Ida remarked, as she examined the sprockets from several angles.

"Unlike other sprockets in the corners of the garden, this one has no real flowers," Matha said.

"Why is that?" Ida asked, as she continued looking about.

"The Elves believe that mechanical inventions can be just as beautiful as living things."

As Ida gave Matha a sustained puzzled look, he continued speaking.

"We Faeries say that elven inventions are second to living things, but they put their inventions before everything else. Here, in this garden, the Elves have made them equal — at least in their eyes."

Ida shook her head. "They couldn't be *that* equal," she opined. "A sprocket, no matter how well polished, is just a sprocket — just a piece of copper or bronze — with strange-looking teeth at the edges."

"Well," Matha continued, not wanting to discuss the subject any further, "you're in luck." As he spoke, he looked at his watch. "We're about to see something much more interesting than that. We're at the middle of the hour. Look, Conor — something fun is about to happen."

Just then, sounds of violins, flutes, drums, and other instruments streamed out from somewhere inside the sprocket.

"Music!" Conor exclaimed.

Suddenly, a whirring noise came from the large center sprocket. The bronze cover on the center hole slid out of sight. Green metal shoots then rose out of the hole, rising taller and taller. As other whirring noises began, mechanical leaves sprang from the shoots. Somehow, the Elves had built a series of parts that could pop out of each other. Soon, mechanical buds sprang from the metal shoots as well. The buds opened like blooming Suns, with brass foil petals and dark brown centers. All the flowers then began turning on their stalks, like giant pinwheels.

"Spinning sunflowers!" Conor exclaimed, barely able to contain himself. "What else is going to happen?"

"That's up to you, Conor," Matha replied, as he pointed to a large crank protruding from the base of the sprocket. "Go ahead — start turning."

Conor grabbed the crank. "This is too hard!" he cried. "The handle is stuck."

"Let me help you," Matha said, not wanting Conor to get more upset than he already was.

Matha grasped the handle and began cranking, slowly at first, and then faster and faster. Instantly, a number of other things began happening in the rest of the sprocket.

More whirring noises came from the first ring of sprockets that surrounded the large center sprocket. Matha saw that all the covers on all the sprockets were now gone. The whirring sounds grew louder. Soon, shoots of dog rose with green metal stems began rising out of each one. The stems sprouted leaves with sharp prickles, and buds that bloomed into pink metal flowers with yellow centers. The entire circle of sprockets then began to rotate around the sunflowers in the center sprocket.

Seeing the blooming dog rose, Conor shouted, "I want one! I want one!"

"They're not to pick," Ida said. "Only to see."

"What else is there to do?" Conor wailed.

"Just grab the crank and keep turning," Matha instructed.

"Don't forget your manners, Conor," Ida said. "Say please."

"Please, oh please!" Conor said, as he reached again for the handle.

The workings of the Sprouting Patch continued to unfold in ways that took everyone by surprise. The second ring of sprockets produced dozens of yellow and orange daisies, with gold centers, all rising from the center holes. After all the daisies had opened fully, the second ring of sprockets began to rotate around the ring of dog rose, going in the opposite direction. Mechanical meadowlarks then rose from the center holes of the third and final ring, with beige wings, bright yellow bodies, and streaks of black across their throats. All the meadowlarks sat perched on poles, nodding their heads and warbling in time to the music.

"I want one! I want one!" Conor cried again, upon seeing the birds. All the while, the dog rose and daisies rotated in time to the music, and the meadowlarks sang ever more loudly. Conor watched the unfolding of the Sprouting Patch, beaming brightly. Matha and Ida stood on either side of him, also smiling at the sight.

Without warning, a voice behind them declared ominously, "We couldn't take down that tree, but we sure can take *this* down."

"Looks like those three will be the last to see it in all of its mechanical refulgence," another voice added, sarcastically.

Turning, Matha saw a water Faery with two friends in tow. He had never met their kind before, but he had heard of them. What struck him first was their appearance — knotty-looking and unkempt, as if they had been out netting seaweed for far too long. Their clothing was a tangled mess, with strings of shells and small water drums hanging from their waists. Around their necks were vials filled with Water. Matha had never seen so many worn at once. He wondered if they couldn't choose between which spring to honor, so instead they had chosen them all. Even for Guilders, they seemed extreme in their devotion.

The one who had spoken first approached. As he strode closer to the Sprouting Patch, shells around his waist swished back and forth. He stopped, but still the shells swayed as he shifted his stance this way and that. For someone who had just spoken so toughly, he seemed unusually agitated. Peering out from under a water lily hat that covered his brow line, he regarded Matha.

"Take down what?" Matha asked.

"That sprocketworks abomination," the Guilder replied, raising his arms. Strings of shells hung from his sleeves like curtains of protection, warding off all he abhorred.

"Who are you?" Matha asked.

The Faery strode closer to Matha, until he was inches from his face. "My name is Lugh, of Four Falls, son of Donovan. I am the Leader of the Guilders of the Nechtain Quarter," he added, as if he was about to convey a secret that only he knew. He then made the sign of the Water, leaning closer to Matha. Cupping his hands even more tightly he said, "I am *with* the Water."

When Lugh uttered the word *with,* he gave Matha a knowing look, as if they were both members of a very informed group. His eyes bore intently into Matha's, searching to see where he stood with him. Matha found those eyes unnerving. Surely, he was a Guilder, and they were on the same side. Yet Lugh seemed like a wolf that had broken from his pack, and started his own.

Uncomfortably, Matha pulled away, and made the sign of the Water. He then un-cupped his hands. Lugh smiled amiably at him, a smile that went on for too long, as if he expected Matha to stop everything, and join him in his cause. Seeing no such response, he dropped his hands as well.

Matha's resistance did not deter Lugh from espousing more of his opinions. "Good!" he exclaimed as he motioned to everyone present. "We're all Guilders here. That's what really matters." Warily, Ida and Conor took a step closer to Matha.

"One question remains," Lugh continued. As he spoke, he raised his voice to be heard above the din of the mechanical construction. He then pointed to the large center sprocket, with all the sunflowers still spinning. "What are the Elves *really* sprouting?" His two friends laughed at the question.

"They're sprouting fun!" exclaimed Conor.

"Whimsy, perhaps," said Ida.

"Concord," said Matha.

"No, no, no!" cried Lugh, as he angrily stamped his foot. His two friends shook their heads from side to side. "That's what they *want* you to think. I was just at the Tree of Innovation, where they want you to think the same thing."

Lugh looked away for a moment, agitated. Holding onto his nerve, he continued, "But, *I* know that what they want you to think is really just a cover for what they *don't* want you to think."

"And what might that be?" Matha asked.

"For two hundred years the Elves have occupied *Tír Éirí Sióg*. They came with their swords, laws, and contraptions, caring for little other than to impose their ways on us. All the while they pretend to hide this fact, as if we are too stupid to see what they're doing, and you know what? I'm beginning to think more and more that we Faeries really *are* too stupid, so I'm sounding the alarm!"

Amused, Matha began to reply, but before he could, Lugh and his friends leapt toward the Sprouting Patch. They raised their arms again, as if to ward off what was before them.

Swiftly, they scrambled over a low rail circling the perimeter of the Patch.

"You can't do that!" Matha cried out. "You'll break them!"

"Exactly!" Lugh shot back. "I'm going to free all of you from your prison of assent!"

Stomping a number of daisies, and bending several dog roses beyond repair, they soon reached the center sprocket. One of them smashed a meadowlark. All three then shimmied their way up three of the sunflowers, until they reached the tops. Vengefully, they stopped the spinning flowers, snapping them from their stems, and throwing them to the ground.

"Not the sunflowers!" Conor wailed.

"You whiny little poltroon!" Lugh spat, looking at Conor. "One day you'll see who the truly brave are."

"You can't be Guilders!" Ida yelled, shaking her head at them. "No leader of the Nechtain Quarter behaves this way!"

"I have to!" Lugh shouted, glaring at Ida.

Matha knew that he had to try to diffuse the situation. "Why are you upsetting this elderly faery lady and her grandson? Shame on you! This is not following concord!"

"And who might you be?" Lugh asked.

"Matha, son of Niall, water Faery of Deuona."

Lugh stopped to consider Matha. His two companions did the same.

"The son of the Primary of Concord," Lugh said. "I have always respected your father, and for years I listened to him. But then, one day my eyes were opened, and that's when I saw that I had to take matters into my own hands."

Matha knew this was his chance to keep Lugh distracted. As he talked, he inched his way closer to the machine. "Then you miss the point of concord entirely," he began. "What you're doing will not stop the Elves, and who's to say that what they're doing is so wrong? This was a beautiful place before you came."

Matha was now close enough to act. Quick as a flash, he grabbed the crank, turning with all his might. In a matter of moments, the ring of sprockets and all of their parts lowered in succession, back to where they had come from.

"Oh no you don't!" Lugh shrieked. Instantly, he raced away from the center sprocket and then tried to wrest the crank from Matha's grasp. Back and forth they wrestled, like two beavers tussling over a log. Lugh's lily hat fell off in the struggle, and lay trampled in a pulpy heap upon the ground.

"Make them stop!" Connor cried out.

"Find a garden keeper!" Ida shouted.

Lugh's two friends broke them up, prying him and Matha apart. As Matha held on tightly to the crank, seaweed from their sleeves slopped onto his shirt. Up close, he thought they smelled like rotten mossy river pools.

Matha turned to assess the damage to the sprockets. The birds and flowers had lowered back into their holes, and the covers were closed. All that remained were three broken sunflowers, piles of dog rose leaves, daisy petals, and a smashed meadowlark.

Matha was furious.

"You three fools have done nothing but harm here!" he shouted.

"The Elves are the foolers, and you the fooled!" Lugh shouted back.

"Pray tell me, Lugh," Matha asked, "which Elves do you think made this place?"

"Probably a bunch of meddlers from Silver Forge, or perhaps Gleam," Lugh replied.

"Where they're from is beside the point," Matha said, as he picked up a dog rose leaf. What they *are* is what matters. This leaf was handmade by a craftsman who wished to create harmony between the Elves and Faeries, and you destroyed that with your crazy zealousness."

Matha dropped the leaf to the ground. It fell between them.

"That leaf is not what they built at the Tree of Innovation," Lugh persisted. "I was *there*. The Elves want to trick us with their contraptions."

Matha remembered what Baudwin had told him about the Tree of Innovation, and knew enough to say, "That may or may not be, but you have ruined the good to destroy the bad. You are discordant, and I ask that you leave this place."

Lugh puffed up, looking even more insulted. Taking full measure of Matha, who was clearly younger by a couple of centuries, he started to speak, but then thought better of it. Retrieving his smashed lily hat, he instead turned away with his friends.

"The Elves will ruin *Tír Éirí Sióg*!" he shouted. "Mark my words — this isn't the end of it. I will state my case at the meeting tonight." With that, he and his companions left, their mossy green boots tramping away in disgust.

"He'll be quite amusing at the meeting," Ida said, as she straightened her hat and put her arm around Conor. They both turned to face Matha.

"I can only imagine the look on the Grand Eldress's face when this Lugh character pulls out one of his nutty claims," she added with a laugh. "That is, when he spouts — or should I say, *sprouts* — off."

Matha looked more closely at Ida and Conor. Although both were putting on a brave face, he could tell they were extremely upset by what had just happened. Taking out his map, he began, "Now where were we before that most unpleasant interruption? Is there anything else I may help you with?"

"Do you have time to tell us about the rest of the garden?" Ida asked, looking at the map.

"Here we are in the center of the Garden of Sprockets — at the Sprouting Patch, which is a circle," Matha said. "You see?"

"Yes," Ida replied.

"Now," he continued, "four paths lead to the Sprouting Patch from the north, south, east and west."

Matha showed Ida the map. "I see," she said. "The four paths divide the garden into four parts."

"Correct," Matha replied, happy to see that she appreciated the design. "In each part, you will find sprockets filled with various kinds of flowers."

"I certainly hope so!" Ida exclaimed brightly.

Matha traced a large rectangle with his finger. "This path goes around the entire garden. There are four entrances — one on each side. The four paths leading to the Sprouting Patch begin at these entrances."

"And the flowers?" Ida asked.

"Where are the automatons?" Conor demanded.

"Conor, I'm speaking to your grandmother," Matha warned. "If you interrupt me again, I may not tell you." Having explained the layout of the garden so precisely to Ida, he was beginning to lose his patience. Hearing this, Conor waited silently.

"As I was saying —" Matha resumed. Seeing that Conor seemed confused, he stopped. "Why don't you just come with me," he, suggested, "so I can show you what I mean?"

"May we?" Ida asked. "I hope we're not too much of a bother."

"You're not," Matha replied. "I can show you where the flowers are, as we look for the automatons."

"What kinds of automatons will we see?" Conor asked, as they left the Sprouting Patch.

"Mostly ladybugs, beetles, and spiders," Matha replied.

"Tell me what they look like!" Conor exclaimed.

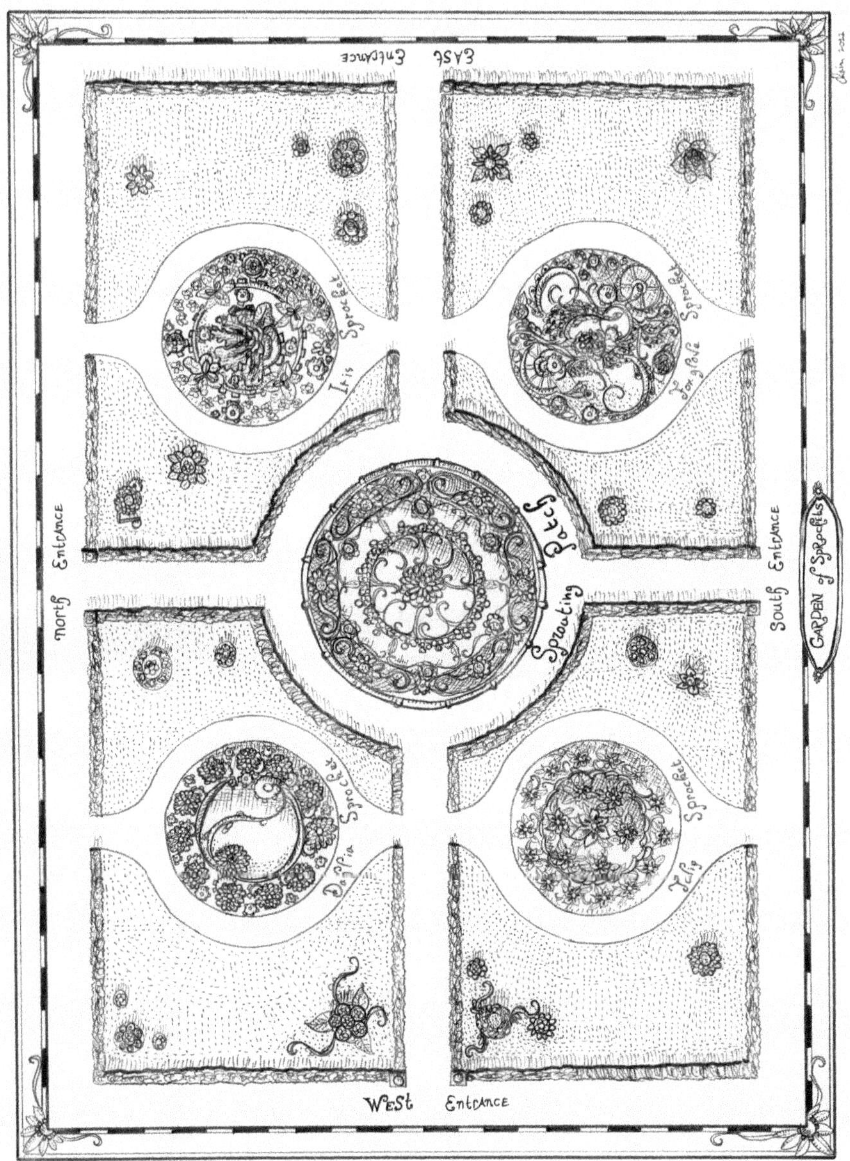

"Do you have any steamway toys?" Matha asked.

"Of course."

"What kind?"

"Snails, ladybugs, and some spiders," Conor replied.

"The ones here look a lot like them, only they're much bigger, so you can ride them," Matha said. "Mechanically speaking, they're a lot more complicated than your toys."

"How do you know so much about them?" Conor asked. "You're a *Faery*."

"Just because I'm a Faery, doesn't mean I can't learn about the way Elves build things," Matha replied. "I like to understand the way things work."

Matha remembered the first time he had seen a sprocketworks toy. Back then the Elves didn't call them Steamway because most of them weren't driven by steam, but as he grew up and the toys became more sophisticated, the name changed. Some toys were still just Sprocketworks, but a lot of the newer ones were Steamway. Baudwin and Matha used to go to Rian's store to barter for them. They would ask lots of questions, such as how the toys were made, and how the winding gears worked. Baudwin always seemed more intent on playing with them, while Matha liked to take them apart in his mind. By watching Rian tinker at his workbench, he learned how all the pieces fit together.

His favorite toy of all was the chatter cricket. The best ones came from Gleam, an elven city far away in *Tír Luí Lucharachán*. The shipments arrived only once a year, for Deuona was much smaller than Four Falls, and there were many other cities that wanted them as well. So every year, he competed with all the other Faeries in Deuona to acquire them, especially Baudwin, who was always more clever at talking Rian into getting what he wanted. Nevertheless, Matha was still able to get some for himself, and he learned more than he ever let on.

Having come a quarter of the way around the Patch, they turned and strolled down the long stone path which led to the westernmost garden entrance. Farther down, Matha could see a number of automatons strewn about, and a few garden keepers assisting Faeries to ride the insect of their choice.

"Ladybugs, beetles, and spiders! Ladybugs, beetles, and spiders!" Conor sang out. "Ladybugs, beetles —"

"Maileeeeeee!"[3] a voice cried out. "You give that chatter cricket back to your brother right now, or I'll tell the garden keeper to unwind him!"

With that, a giant sprocketworks grasshopper flew toward them — emerald with purple wings. A young faery lassie rode on its back, holding on for dear Life. As she passed, her hair streamed behind her like a pale blue cotton cloud.

"Watch out, Conor!" Matha exclaimed, as he grabbed the young lad and whisked him from the path. Both fell to the ground.

Raising his head, Conor groaned, "You didn't tell me there were crickets."

"I said we would find *mostly* ladybugs, beetles, and spiders," Matha replied.

Matha and Conor turned toward the faery lassie who had landed just a few feet away. She leaned toward the grasshopper's head, her face aglow with

____

[3] Pronounced [MAY-lee]

excitement. Lightly, she pressed her hand against its thorax. Like a well-trained pet, the grasshopper drew its hind legs closely into its body. Suddenly, they straightened out. Hop, hop, hop, they went, landing right next to Conor.

Matha took a moment to collect his thoughts. "This," he began, pointing at the stunning replica, "is *not* a cricket. *This* is a grasshopper. Crickets are pale green, and grasshoppers are much deeper green."

Hearing this, the faery lassie giggled mischievously. "I know," she said. "I took this one from my brother, because the steamway ladybugs can only crawl. The spiders walk, but this one *flies*."

"She's correct, Conor," Matha added, chuckling at the young lad's lack of knowledge. "Unlike most crickets, grasshoppers can also fly."

Matha paused for a moment, intrigued. *The Elves have certainly outdone themselves,* he thought. For they had created an insect that could glide — an automaton far more advanced than any he had ever seen. Thus far, the automatons had been impressive. Just by winding them up, they could do much of what living beings and things can do. And now, this one could also carry a passenger — as it leapt. In Rian's store, he had learned a great deal, but the workings powering this machine were a mystery to him.

Matha wondered what had driven the Elves to improve their inventions so quickly. Recently, Sprocketworks, Alchemvoke, and Steamway had become much more sophisticated, and this year, the Elves were unveiling something new — Magniglow. To him, they seemed like acrobats, saving their most alluring tricks for the grand finale of the show. This was probably why they had rolled out so many new inventions in just a few short years. Clearly, they were trying to *enchant* the Faeries. Likely they had even greater marvels hidden away that they would showcase in the coming years. Matha didn't trust their intentions, and he wondered what larger scheme they had for the *Tír Éirí Sióg*.

The lassie looked down the path. "Here they come!" she exclaimed.

"Maile!" the lassie's mother called out again, as she and her son approached the disheveled-looking group.

"You must be her mother," Ida surmised, having also caught up to them. "Do tell me, do you think my grandson is ready to ride a grasshopper, or should he try a beetle first?"

"Good luck talking him into riding a beetle," the mother joked. Ida laughed.

"I promised I would find him a grasshopper," Matha declared.

"But where are the flowers?" Ida asked, concerned.

"Go down this path to the center. To the right, you will see dahlias, and to the left, tulips," Matha instructed. "The foxgloves and irises are on the other side of the Sprouting Patch."

"Thank you," Ida called out to Matha, as she ventured out on her own. "Conor likes the mechanical flowers, but I do so love the *real* ones. Go now with this nice gent, Conor, and find yourself a grasshopper. I'll be with you shortly."

"Conor, I see some automatons ahead. Perhaps, we can find you a grasshopper," Matha said, as he and the young lad made their way to the dahlia sprocket. Conner skipped over the cobblestones. Willow trees lined the pathway on either side, with red and purple azaleas circling their trunks. The Sun was still high, shining through the clouds, blanketing their surroundings with a golden hue.

Soon they reached a cluster of insects. Some of them appeared to have been recently used, as they had not run down completely and were still making low whirring sounds.

Conor rummaged through them. "Here's a ladybug, some beetles, and a couple of spiders, but no grasshoppers," he announced. "What do you see?"

"Everything but a grasshopper," Matha replied.

"What if we don't find one?" Conor asked. But then his concern changed instantly to jubilation.

"Wow! A super-long rolly-polly!" he exclaimed, as he pointed to an orange centipede with red and brown stripes, and at least twenty black legs on either side. "I want to ride *this*!"

"Quite remarkable indeed," Matha said, as he turned the centipede over to examine the way in which the legs connected to the trunk segments. "But you would need to have someone else with you to ride this one, or you might lose control of the back."

"What about you?" Conor asked.

"I must go soon," Matha replied. Seeing the disappointment on Conor's face, he added, "Let's go and see what else we can find." Hope restored, Conor followed Matha around the corner, and then up the stone path.

Before them was a boxwood hedge, manicured into the shape of a large sprocket. Deep purple dahlias sprang from the center, followed by circles of red blooms with pink, lavender, or violet tips.

"This must be what my grandmother wanted me to see!" Conor blurted, as he goggled the circles of living blooms.

"Haven't you ever seen flowers before?" Matha asked.

"Not like these," Conor replied.

"Then you are very lucky that your grandmother brought you here," Matha said.

Shocked to hear that Conor had never seen such flowers, Matha wondered how this could be so. Perhaps Conor had spent many more years than he had as a young lad, immersed in steamway toys and other elven inventions. Were there no flower boxes or plants around his home? Had no one ever shown him the joy of watering flowers or picking vegetables in a garden? Although Matha enjoyed a lot of what the Elves had to offer, he could not imagine growing up without seeing lots of flowers and other living things.

What if all Conor ever learned about such wonders would come only from *mechanical* likenesses? He knew the Elves used real flowers to entice the Faeries to come to the Garden of Sprockets, yet a strange thought occurred to him. He wondered what *Tír na nÓg* would be like if the land was covered only with mechanical plants. Chuckling, it dawned on him that the Elves would run out of metal before that happened.

"These *real* flowers look so different from those," Conor said, as he pointed to other parts of the garden.

Matha followed Conor's gaze as it scanned the yard. Smaller bronze sprockets shined like garden sculptures; dahlias with copper leaves and stems sprang from the centers, flashing petals made of red, orange, yellow, or rust-colored foil. Small cranks protruded from the bases which, when turned, made the flowers rotate, like whirling gears.

Perhaps this is nothing but a garden of metal weeds that will one day choke all breath out of the living, Matha thought, shuddering. "Come, Conor," he said, trying to banish the thought. "I see a grasshopper." They made a beeline for the automaton.

Matha was so lost in thought that he barely noticed a Roiler approaching from the other side of the sprocket. He paused, hoping he was just one of Loch's hapless underlings. Much to his dismay, he realized that the height and arrogant gait could mean only one thing — Loch himself was heading straight toward them. He cursed himself for getting so distracted.

"L-o-ch-?" he stammered. "What are you doing here?"

"I suppose I could ask you the same thing," Loch replied. "Aren't you rather far away from your friends?"

"I thought you were. . ."

"A garden keeper?" Loch asked, smirking. "Perhaps I am," he gloated, bending down to snap the antennae off a ladybug automaton. "There — that's better."

Conor stepped closer to Matha. "Don't be scared, Conor," Matha said, putting his arm around the lad's shoulder.

"He's right," Loch said to Conor, as he planted himself in front of Matha's face. "But *you* should be," he added, staring steadily into Matha's eyes.

"Why did you follow me?" Matha asked.

"You should know," Loch retorted.

"Well, I don't," Matha replied, his anxiety mounting.

"Such poor judgment," Loch declared with a surly tone, "for someone who thinks he's *so* smart."

Before Matha could respond, Loch's raving continued. "You know, I don't really hate you. At the ruins of Coventina, you did exactly what I would have done. Baudwin said he wasn't lying about the Water coming to him, and you stood up for him. You also called me a defiler at the shrine, but I don't hate you for that either. I have my reasons for what I did." Loch pumped his fist in the Air. "I'm a Roiler through and through!" he proclaimed. "We have to be true to what we are."

"Why did you come after me then?" Matha asked.

"Because I'm being true to who *I* am, and that means looking out for my kin," Loch replied vehemently. "Do you *really* think I would let you get away with teaching Teigue about glyphs?" Seeing the fear on Matha's face, he smiled. Mockingly, he imitated what Matha had said to him, "Don't worry, Loch. When we're through with this little lad — you won't want him anymore!"

Despite his apprehension, Matha spoke up. "What I *really* meant," he began, "was that we'll *never* be through with him, because there's so much you've cheated him out of learning."

Loch's face became a hardened mask. "Don't lecture me with your pious guilder rot!" he bellowed. Matha shook inside.

"Is anyone here in need of a wind?" a voice asked. A garden keeper had entered the dahlia garden, a burly elven gent, who was looking to see what all the commotion was about.

Matha saw his opportunity. "Conor," he said, "this garden keeper's come to help us with the grasshopper. He'll wind it up for you."

All three measured the situation. A battle of stares began. The garden keeper eyed Loch. Loch eyed Matha. Matha eyed the garden keeper. The garden keeper spoke first to Loch. "Are you giving these Guilders trouble?" he asked.

Loch scowled. The garden keeper continued, "This is a place of peace. Please take your quarrel elsewhere."

Loch sized up the garden keeper. He was half a head taller, with broad shoulders and strong arms that obviously came from years of doing hard work.

Loch relented. "We were just having a small disagreement." Smiling phonily at Conor, he added, "Go now, and learn from the Elves."

Uncertainly, Conor approached the garden keeper, who helped him mount the grasshopper. All the while, the garden keeper kept his eyes on Loch.

Matha relaxed a bit. Now, he only had to worry about how he would get away from Loch. He knew what he had to do. Turning to the garden keeper, he said, "This Roiler can't be trusted. My disagreement with him isn't small, and he's not as peaceable as he's trying to appear."

Loch clenched his fists, but checked his rage.

Noticing this, the garden keeper spoke. "If you bring any further trouble here, I'll have the Earth Guards come." Loch was silent.

Matha then made his move. "Conor, I really enjoyed meeting you. I'm late to meet my friends."

"Goodbye," Conor said rather sadly. "Thank you for finding me this grasshopper."

"You're welcome, Conor," Matha replied. "Have fun."

As Matha turned to leave, he could feel Loch's eyes boring into his back. How long would the garden keeper's warning keep him at bay? Matha had gotten no more than thirty paces away when he heard a high-pitched whistle. Looking back, he saw Loch beckoning to some Roilers, who had been lurking nearby.

He knew he was in trouble.

Now three Roilers had joined Loch. Their eyes flashed with delight as they began to run down their quarry. *What cowards*, Matha thought. He chuckled to himself, for surely they would think the same of him for what he would do next. Totally outnumbered, there was only one choice.

He bolted.

"Come back, you gutless weakling!" Loch yelled.

"You're the one who whistled for help!" Matha shouted back.

The Roilers were after him. Glancing behind him, Matha saw the garden keeper grab a bronze hoe and trip one of them running past him. Soon the others were nipping at his heels.

What now? he thought, as he raced out of the dahlia garden and onto the main path. He knew they wouldn't stop until they caught him. Loch was never one to let go of a grudge. Looking over his shoulder, Matha saw them gaining on him. One of the skinnier lackeys was fleet of foot. His heart beat wildly in his chest. A quick decision was in order.

Matha thanked the Moon that he had explained the map of the Garden of Sprockets to Ida. For now he knew all the paths and exits that would lead him to safety. As usual, his big mouth had gotten him into trouble, and his head would have to get him out.

Behind him, he could hear the Roilers shouting; two were closing in on him. The pounding of their feet grew louder. However, they couldn't chase what they couldn't see. If he took a shrewd route, with only two turns, he would be out of their sight.

The closest entrance to the Garden of Sprockets was the South Entrance. To get there, he would first have to race through the tulip sprocket and turn left. Matha shot across the path and into the sprocket, past a blur of red, pink, violet, coral, yellow, and white. The Roilers were now way too close for comfort — only some kind of diversionary tactic would save him. Diving behind a maze of high hedges, Matha found the escape routes he needed. Their quarry now out of sight, the Roilers stopped and began searching for him. Meanwhile, Matha crept stealthily away. Upon reaching the exit, he turned left.

The South Entrance was just ahead of him. If he could only get to the exit quickly, they wouldn't know which way he went. Still in grave danger, he raced along the path. He was almost there, but his game of chase was not yet over. Just as he was about to turn right, to go through the exit gate, a large group of Faeries stepped inside to tour the garden. He stopped short to avoid crashing into them.

Panting heavily, he looked to his left, back toward the Sprouting Patch, in the center of the Garden of Sprockets. *Banjaxed yet again!* he thought. Loch and one of his underlings were advancing on him. They had taken a different route, no doubt to head him off. He shot a glance behind him, and saw the other two Roilers catching up to him.

All four were closing in, ready to clobber him. There was no escape. In front of him and to the right was the faery crowd. They had slowed him to a near standstill. All he could do was push through the throng, and hope that he could stay ahead of the Roilers.

Angry mutterings greeted him as he elbowed his way through the crowd. The exit to his right was close. He was almost there, but then another large group began to enter the South Exit. They pushed in front of him. Like a cluster of logs jamming a river, the throngs merged, slowing him down even more. Certain that he was trapped, he waited helplessly.

Fortuitously, a faery mother and father chose this time to pick up their young ones and set them on their shoulders. A small opening appeared next to them. This wasn't what he had planned, but the Roilers were now pushing through the crowd. He had to keep going straight. He stepped into the gap, then burst with all his might out of the gaggle. Looking back, he could see all four Roilers fused together in the middle of the throng, arguing furiously about where he had gone.

As he had failed to get through the South Entrance, he now had to run toward the East Entrance. At least he had a bit more time to get away.

After running several more yards down the path, he turned left into the foxglove sprocket, which was near the East Entrance. Tripping over an automaton that was blocking his way brought curse words to his lips, but then an idea came to him. He knew he had enough time to escape, but Loch deserved to be dealt with. Lucky for Matha, Loch was a skilled tracker, so he would show up right on time.

Quickly, Matha dragged a few snails and ladybugs, and a number of tackle tree spiders to make a pile. He then paused for a moment, listening intently. Sure enough, the Roilers were on their way. He had only a few moments left.

Not far away, he spotted a number of grasshoppers, and dragged one of them off the path. Frantically, he searched its thorax and beneath its hind wings. *The key,* he thought, *where is the key*? As he continued his search, his heart beat faster and faster.

In the distance, he heard one of the Roilers holler, "He's not getting away!"

"We'll find him!" Loch exclaimed, laughing.

The first Roiler burst into the foxglove sprocket. As if on cue, he tripped over the automatons Matha had piled on the path, and then stumbled again. Losing control, he fell flat on his face. When Loch and the other two caught up to him, they laughed maniacally.

"There's Earc,[4] crippled by a couple of ladybugs!" Loch shouted.

Shaking with fury, Earc stood up. He then spotted Matha, taunting him from the other side of the foxglove sprocket in the center of the garden. "There he is!" he roared. But, before any of them could reach him, they had to clear a path through the pile of automatons blocking the entrance.

In the meantime, Matha had found the winding key beneath the grasshopper's forewing. Quickly, he sized up the Roilers' situation. He knew they couldn't run through the dense foliage of the sprocket. He predicted they would go around the side. He was right, but the four of them had split into pairs, each rounding a side of the foxglove sprocket. If he didn't think fast, soon they'd be pounding him with their fists.

Matha hadn't expected them to come from both sides, but he knew just what to do.

The spring, he thought, as he frantically searched for the keyhole. Lifting up the other forewing, he felt around for the hole. *Where? Where?* And then finally, *Here!*

Madly, he wound up the first grasshopper and then the other. Groaning, he turned one of them, aiming at the place where he thought the first pair of Roilers would cross. Again, he did the same, aiming the other grasshopper at the second pair. Breathlessly, he waited.

Snarling and huffing, Loch rounded the path, followed by Earc. Matha could see they were nearly upon him. The Roilers had almost converged. The sprocket was now behind them. His risky gamble had brought them dangerously close to him.

Matha mounted one of the grasshoppers. Pressing the thorax, he heard the coils wind. Seeing him, they all began to laugh.

"Is that how you're going to fight? By *hopping* over us?" Loch taunted.

"You'll see!" Matha shouted. Quickly, he dismounted and pressed another button.

---

[4] Pronounced [EARK]

Hop, hop, hop, went the automaton, until its wings were fully extended. Riderless, the giant insect took flight, crashing a few seconds later into Loch and Earc. The force of the collision sent them sailing into the sprocket, their faces buried deeply in a hedge of red and purple foxgloves.

"He got me!" Earc screamed.

With one quick move, Matha pressed a button on the second grasshopper. Instantly, the insect took off, and soon crashed into the other two Roilers. They too stumbled and fell into the hedge.

Seeing Loch and Earc tangled in the thick foliage of the sprocket, their arms and legs flailing, Matha howled with laughter — as the Roilers screamed with rage. "Am I correct in assuming you won't be touring the lovely irises today?" he shouted, laughing. Without a moment to lose, he turned and quickly ran out of the foxglove sprocket to the East Exit.

Chapter 14

RACES AND ROILERS

Angrily, Criofan strode across the field toward the Racer Bump tent. *Baudwin!* he thought. *I'm a <u>much</u> better friend to him than he is to me!* Hadn't he encouraged Baudwin to search for Glamorium? How unfair of Baudwin to blame him for choosing to go to the Water Park. The Roilers could have shown up anywhere. And no one had the slightest idea that Teigue was a Roiler. Too easily Baudwin forgot how much he owed his friends, especially on a day like this. Such selfishness! After all, Baudwin was the one who had gotten them in trouble at Curios & Marvels, not he.

When Criofan felt rejected by someone, his anger burned so hotly that all he wanted was to even the score. But Baudwin was his dear friend. How would that look? Certainly not good. There was nothing he could do — which made him even angrier. Now, all he wanted was to blow off some steam at Racer Bump.

The fact was, he was very glad they had all gone their separate ways. Now he could have fun without Baudwin or Matha finding out. Neither of them knew about his interest in racing, for he hadn't told them that he had learned how to drive. Just like them, he was trying out new things. Baudwin liked to collect gadgets for his own pleasure, and Matha wanted to understand how they worked, but Criofan's interest in Racer Bump was neither of these. As the son of the Primary of Commerce, he knew that driving machines were a big part of the future for Faeries. They had to change with the changing times, and stop using wagons.

The more he considered the shape of the future, the more he wondered what his friends would think of what he intended to do. *Probably that I'm going to turn into a Roiler,* he thought. Yet, the Roilers knew a thing or two about driving that the Guilders didn't. If they were going to keep up, the Guilders had to compete, which was why he had come to the track.

As he made his way to the tent, he wondered how his skills would compare with the others. *Certainly, I'll be great,* he thought, smiling to himself. *I'll probably win.*

Before him stood the Racer Bump tent. The top of the tent had two enormous peaks, with bronze rails and wooden fencing supporting the perimeter. As Criofan studied the tent, he noticed the racer bumpers parked outside. They were painted red, green, yellow, or blue, with four wheels, and built low to the ground for quick turning. This year they looked different. He noticed they had more exhaust pipes but he didn't know why.

Criofan hurried toward the entrance of the track.

"Come and try Racer Roller — the new Racer Bump!" an Elve shouted through a megaphone.

Criofan went to stand in line.

"What's Racer Roller?" he asked a faery gent standing next to him.

"That's what the Elves call the cars and the track now," the gent replied. "The new racer rollers are a lot faster than the old racer bumpers."

"How much faster?" Criofan asked.

"They used to go at the pace of a hedgehog," the gent explained. "But, now, with the new vapoflame engines, they run as fast as a hare."

"Vapoflame?" Criofan asked.

"Yes," the gent replied, his voice charged. "*Vapoflame.* A gas the Elves pump from deep within the ground. The racer rollers go so fast, you can crash and hurt yourself. So, be careful."

Criofan now knew why they had changed the name of the track. Elven pragmatism led progress. Bumping into each other was fun, but that was for Faefries. The time had come for older Faeries to challenge themselves in a new way. He knew that racer rollers would teach Faeries to appreciate not only the excitement, but also the efficiency of driving. Only then would progress lead to more commerce, and commerce to more progress. Neither could happen without the other. As he waited, a poem he had learned from his father went through his head:

> We must not fault our friends the Elves
> For all that they invent
> For if they did not make such things
> Our lives we would lament
>
> Instead, we must applaud the Elves
> For guiding us to learn
> That commerce comes from what they make
> So, we may work and earn

The line began to move forward. Moments later, Criofan was inside, gaping at two huge bronze columns that held up the tent. They towered like monuments, with relief work of Faeries dancing on one, and Elves holding hammers on the other. The columns were built upon an oval strip of grass. Around the grass was the racetrack. Nearby, a sign read:

Racer Roller Track — Courtesy of the Assembly
of Progress — Built with Liquistone

Criofan inspected the track, which looked very different from last year's track. Gone was the dirt, replaced by something he had never seen before — a seamless slick of slate, as if a road of cobblestones had melted together. He was intrigued.

Teams of Elves wearing work-clothes waited in their pits, as the racer rollers whizzed by on the Liquistone track. Groups of Faeries watched the race from the stands, cheering on their favorite drivers.

As Criofan waited for his turn to race, an Elve in work-clothes approached him. "A new contestant. Do you want one or two seats?" he asked.

"Just one," Criofan replied, coolly hiding his nervousness. He could never have imagined that the racer bumpers, which were more like large toys, would be replaced. The Elves had upped the stakes, but he wasn't about to back out now. *Driving a racer roller can't be all that different,* he figured. He would learn, no matter what.

"One moment please," the Elve said, as he held up his index finger and whistled to another Elve.

Within moments, a red beetle-shaped racer roller zoomed up to them. The driver turned off the engine and jumped out.

Criofan opened the door, sat in the driver's seat and studied the strange vehicle: four wheels, no roof — and obviously lots of pep — set inside a solidly crafted bronze frame. Criofan saw that the speedometer on the dashboard looked different from the ones he had seen inside lumber rollers.

"Not so different from a racer bumper!" he exclaimed, as he ran his hands over the steering wheel, dashboard, and seats. Looking in the rear-view mirror, he admired his reflection.

"Ever race before?" the Elve asked.

"Some," Criofan replied, which was not altogether true.

The Elve appeared to be sizing him up, and Criofan could tell that he didn't believe him.

"These rollers can bolt like a grand horn stung in the rump by a hive of bees," the Elve laughed. "Put your foot on the brake," he added, as he leaned toward the steering wheel. "Now, turn the key."

Criofan twisted the key in the ignition, and the engine roared to Life.

"Now release the hand brake," the Elve yelled, as the engine revved up. Energized by the sound, Criofan flashed him a confident smile. Floundering, he searched for the hand brake. Grinning, the Elve pointed. "Not there — *there.*"

"Of course," Criofan replied with a toothy grin. He released the hand brake.

"Listen closely," the Elve yelled above the roar of the track. "You see that lever? Push it forward and the racer will be ready to go."

Criofan pushed the lever forward. The Elve smiled. "Step on the pedal to go, and on the brake to stop," he instructed. With that, he pointed to the starting line of the track, which was only a few yards away. "Don't forget to steer," he added, chuckling.

Criofan stepped on the pedal. The racer roller took off with a neck-snapping jerk.

Behind him he heard the Elve yell, "And watch that speedometer!"

This was certainly much faster than the racer bumper he had driven just last year, and far more exciting. He wanted to be the best driver on the track. To keep from losing control, he backed off the pedal, and then turned the wheel from side to side to get a feel for the steering. At the same time, he sized up the competition heading for the starting line. Eleven other racer rollers were also jostling for position to begin the race.

I've got to get to the innermost lane, he thought. He had only a few yards to drive, but before he could make his move, a bright green racer roller zoomed past on his left. With a rush of speed, the driver adroitly took the best position.

While this was happening, Criofan jammed his foot on the pedal, narrowly missing another racer roller. To keep from crashing, he yanked the steering wheel, and then pulled in next to the green racer roller. As he came to a stop, his wheels screeched loudly. Angrily, he glared at the driver who had outmaneuvered him.

To his surprise, a faery lady who looked to be about two and twenty turned to face him. Although she seemed apologetic about cutting him off, she also looked quite satisfied with her place in the lineup. In an effort to smooth things over, she smiled at Criofan.

He found her appearance charming. Seeing her almond-shaped green eyes and wavy blue hair, he forgot how annoyed he was. "Hello," he called out. "Are you the only one?"

"The only what?" she asked.

"The only lady?" Criofan replied. "Racing?"

"Yes, I believe so," she called back. "And if you win, which I doubt you will, *you* could be the only gent," she added flirtatiously. As she spoke, she let out a high-spirited, silvery laugh. Her pale blue skin flushed brightly, and her hair cascaded in deep blue ripples farther down her back.

"What's your name?" he asked.

"Carina,"[1] she answered. "And you are?"

"Criofan." Momentarily, he felt so smitten that he almost forgot the race was about to begin.

---

[1] Pronounced [Ka-REEN-ah]

An Elve wearing overalls and an engineer's cap stepped out from behind the fence. Holding a speaker horn under his arm, he approached a large boiler near the starting line. He opened the door and fed the fire more wood. Licks of red and orange flames and rushes of heat came blasting out. As the flames burned fiercely, more smoke billowed out from the boiler's smokestack.

Closing the door, the Elve placed the megaphone to his mouth. Gesturing toward the track, he announced, "Twelve racer rollers in three rows — four to a row. Because a lot of you Faeries are new to the wheel, please pass each other only on the right. That will keep the race fun, safe, and fair. At the sound of the whistle, whoever crosses the finish line after completing ten laps, wins."

The Elve stepped toward the copper steam-chime whistle attached to the boiler and pulled a brass lever. A blast of steam poured from the steam slot. With that, a long low sound like a train whistle reverberated across the starting line. The drivers took off, their engines going *vroooooom,* and clouds of vapoflame smoke blasting from the exhaust pipes.

"The race is on!" Criofan shouted, as he took his foot off the brake and stomped on the pedal. His racer roller shot forward; finally, he would have his chance. Yet, his flirtatious exchange with Carina had left him distracted, and he almost crashed as soon as the race began. To make the race more challenging, the Elves had placed three bales of hay diagonally across the track — to the left, in the middle, and to the right.

Criofan slowed to avoid hitting the middle bale. To his left, Carina noticed the left bale almost too late. As she sped around the track, another large heap of straw suddenly loomed in front of her. She panicked, swerved sharply to the right, and came straight at Criofan.

Criofan was forced to slow down. He could have tried to speed up and pass her, but he let her by through the opening in front of him. This bit of gallantry cost him quite a lot. A racer roller behind him zipped past him on his right, speeding behind Carina. More drivers also took advantage, careening past him, and going around the bales. Out of twelve racers, Criofan was now in eighth place.

Despite his poor position, he was determined to retake the lead. He stomped even harder on the pedal, making the vapoflame engine roar even louder — *vrrroooommmmm.* He saw the pack ahead of him. Carina had dropped behind them and was now in front of Criofan. He sped up next to her.

"Hello again!" he called out. With a sunny smile, she waved back. Without warning, three more bales appeared at an angle across the track. The six racer rollers in front of Criofan and Carina wove skillfully around them.

"Until next time!" Criofan shouted to Carina. Approaching the right bale, he found his opportunity to pull out ahead of her. Before she could catch up to him, he shot around the side, smiling broadly as he went. She didn't wave back, but as she looked at him, he could tell she was pretending to be snubbed.

Seeing how lovely she was, he almost lost his concentration again. But he hadn't gotten into this race to lose. More than anything, Criofan hated losing. Forcing her out of his mind, he turned his attention to the four racer rollers that had just passed the starting line ahead of him.

The first lap was over. *The next time we cross, I will be ahead,* he vowed.

Criofan steered adroitly around the next set of bales. After that, he passed two of the racer rollers. Catching up to the next two would prove far more challenging. His racer roller was ever so much faster than the racer bumpers he was used to, but the rules of the track were almost the same.

Starting his second lap, Criofan came upon a yellow racer roller with blue stripes. The driver was a faery gent, who appeared to be about three and eighty. Steering steadily, he took a moment to size Criofan up. He then zeroed back in on the track.

Criofan could tell that this gent was older and more experienced, and that beating him would not be that easy. As they approached the first set of bales, he prepared to drive by the bale on the left. But first, he had to get past the yellow racer roller.

Remembering that Carina had almost gotten trapped in the same place, he pressed even harder on the pedal. As he did, Air rushed past his face, blowing his hair in all directions. He shot past the left of the yellow racer roller, nodding smugly at the driver.

This was a big mistake.

Angered by Criofan's arrogance, the driver of the yellow racer roller sped up, going even faster. Before Criofan knew what was happening, the driver approached the middle bale, and then passed him on the left — breaking the rules. To avoid crashing into him, Criofan stomped on the brake, and turned his steering wheel sharply to the left.

"Cheater!" Criofan shouted. His quick maneuver made him lose control of his racer roller. Careening past the bale, narrowly missing a pile of tires, he found himself on the grass, where he came to a violent stop. Quickly, he righted his racer roller, and re-entered the track. Much to his frustration, the yellow racer roller was long gone — headed toward the finish line.

☙❦❧

As he ran away from the Garden of Sprockets, Matha knew he'd still not shaken the Roilers. Ducking in and out of the crowd, the terrible prospect of Loch and his friends catching up to him spurred him on. *I must find Criofan!* he thought, as he reached the Dragonfly ride.

Down the path he ran, dodging in and out of a throng of Faeries who had gathered to ride the Dragonfly. Having reached the Ferris wheel, he raced across the field to the track. Looking over his shoulder, he saw all four Roilers closing in on him. *Where is he?* he thought.

Once inside the tent, Matha ran onto the grass strip near the starting line. Several Elves were scattered about near the track, tinkering with engines and changing tires. Groups of Faeries stood admiring racer rollers and congratulating the drivers. Desperately, he searched for Criofan.

He had almost reached the starting line when he heard a voice call out, "Matha, over here!" A few yards away, Criofan sat slouched in his racer roller, sipping some tea — obviously enjoying himself. Carina was nearby, talking to another young faery lady.

"I say we race again," Criofan bantered to the driver of the yellow racer roller who had cut him off and was now parked beside him. "Then I'll beat you."

"Really?" the other driver asked good-naturedly. "You're newer to driving than morning dew." With the race over, their rivalry had quickly ended, and there were no hard feelings between them.

Matha didn't know what was going on between Criofan and his new friend.

"Criofan —" he began, but Criofan ignored him and continued talking to the other racer.

"I understand racing," Criofan boasted, "and especially why lumber rollers are so important to the Faeries. I am, after all, the *son* of the Primary of Commerce of Deuona."

"Well, well, then," the other driver quipped. "I guess that being such an expert in affairs of that nature makes you a racing force to be reckoned with."

"Yes, you better watch out," Criofan agreed, laughing. So engrossed was he in his own story that he failed to notice how upset Matha was.

"They're coming for us!" Matha shouted.

"Who?" Criofan asked.

"Loch and three of his lackeys! We have to find Baudwin!"

"Loch?" asked Criofan. "We left him at the Water Park."

"No!" Matha exclaimed, as pointed to the entrance. "They're right out there, hunting *me*."

Just as Matha finished his sentence, he caught sight of two Roilers, searching through the tent. Methodically, they moved through the crowd, past this one and the next. As Matha watched them coming toward him, he shivered. *They seem more like automatons than Faeries,* he thought.

"I told you Loch was angry with you!" Criofan exclaimed.

"You were right," Matha replied, ducking behind a nearby racer roller to hide. "And he's even more angry after I flew an automaton into them — a big grasshopper."

Criofan turned to Matha. "You don't have to hide," he began. "We aren't going to fight them right now." Criofan looked at the yellow racer roller next to him, seeing two seats. He then faced the driver.

"May I trade?" he asked. "My friend needs a seat."

"Is he in trouble?" the faery gent asked, having spotted the Roilers, who were still searching through the crowd. "With them?"

"Yes," Criofan replied. "Roilers never let go of a grudge."

Criofan gestured toward the first two Roilers. Loch had been joined by a fourth Roiler, and they were halfway through the throng, still scanning.

"They sure do look angry," the gent said, speaking the obvious.

"Yes," Criofan replied warily. "When they aren't skinning fallen animals, all they like to do is fight."

"Take the wheel," he said. "I'll find another racer roller." The gent then faced Criofan and Matha. With a spirited nod, he cupped one hand over the other in the center of his chest, palms down, his elbows lowered. "My name is Brecc,"[2] he affirmed.

Matha and Criofan acknowledged the gesture. The ancient water sign meant one thing, "I am with the Water," but also, "I am with you." In response, they nodded and laced their fingers the same way. Each of them spoke:

"I'm Matha."

"I'm Criofan."

All three Faeries made the sign again — in unison — proclaiming as they did, "We are with the Water!"

"Get in, Matha," Criofan instructed. "Another race is about to begin."

Matha dove into the back seat. Criofan jumped into the driver's seat and turned on the motor.

"Do you know what you're doing?" Matha asked.

"You're not in any danger," Criofan replied.

"I'm not?" Matha was incredulous. "Since when do you know how to drive?"

"This will be more fun than fighting them, trust me," Criofan insisted, with a roguish grin.

It occurred to Matha that he wasn't the only one who was secretive. But, visiting old monuments didn't seem half as outrageous as learning to drive and not telling his two best friends.

Criofan then turned to Carina. "Are you racing again?" he called to her.

---

2 Pronounced [BRECK]

"No," she replied. "I'll watch you from here." She turned and whispered something to her friend. They both giggled and waved at Criofan. Smoothly, he waved back, and then took off the brake.

Out of twelve racer rollers ready to begin the second race, three had already taken their positions. Criofan drove to the middle place in the second lane.

"Where are Loch and his lackeys?" Matha asked.

"Who cares?" Criofan remarked as he studied the rest of the racer rollers. "They won't be able to catch us with me at the wheel." Gleefully, he added, "Besides, it's too late now to enter the race!"

Suddenly, the chime-steam whistle sounded. The race was on.

As the three racer rollers in front of him sped away, Criofan followed closely behind them, watching for the first set of hay bales, which came quickly into view. As soon as he navigated around them, the driver to his left pulled ahead of him.

Just then, he and Matha felt a sharp bump. Matha turned around to see what had happened.

"Roilers!" he yelled.

"That can't be!" Criofan exclaimed, speeding up. Leaning out of his racer roller, he looked back. "They've stolen three racer rollers!" he shouted. With that, he jammed the pedal flat against the floor.

Matha saw that Criofan was right. Breaking the rules, the Roilers had driven three racer rollers onto the track.

"We better keep our distance," Matha advised. Despite Criofan's obvious skill, he wondered if the Roilers were better drivers. They had caught up quickly to the race pack. Criofan accelerated sharply. He was learning quickly how to better time his pedal work.

"Here they come again!" Matha shouted.

Suddenly, another bump jolted them, which almost sent Criofan flying out of his seat. Matha saw Loch grinning devilishly at them from behind. Criofan tugged on his seat belt. "Tighten up!" he yelled to Matha.

"Get us out of here!" Matha shouted.

Matha held the back of Criofan's seat, looking for the three racer rollers. "They're getting closer!" he shouted. "Now they're all in a row!"

Criofan looked in his mirror and saw Loch driving in the middle racer roller, with one of his gang in the back. The other two were in separate racer rollers, one on either side of him.

"Good!" Criofan shouted back, as the second set of hay bales appeared in his way. "One of them is in for a big surprise."

With that, he carefully hit the brakes, letting the Roilers catch up. Taken off guard, one of them didn't have time to react. Criofan turned the wheel and slammed into him. The Roiler spun out of control, twirling onto the grass.

Seeing the look of panic on the Roiler's face, Matha let out a shriek of laughter. "You sent him flying like a weasel quilled by a porcupine," he chortled.

Now there were only two Roilers racing on the track. Trying to stay ahead of them, Criofan's skills were pressed to their limit. Behind him, he saw Loch was just one racer roller length away. Criofan had caught up to the other drivers, who were packed together ahead of them. He was forced to slow down.

The first lap was over, and they were about to cross the starting line. He looked over his shoulder at the two remaining racer rollers. Loch sat in one of them, seething with anger.

"Ha!" Matha shouted. "I bet he didn't know you could drive like this."

Criofan beamed.

"You're *so* right!" Criofan cried out. As he crossed the starting line, he was shocked to see the Roiler he had knocked onto the grass speeding directly at him, driving the wrong way down the track. As the Roiler came straight at him, many other drivers had to swerve out of the way. Instantly, Criofan turned to the left to avoid crashing into the Roiler.

"They're going to knock us off the track!" Matha shouted.

"No, they aren't!" Criofan shouted back. "We'll do that ourselves!" With that, he veered to his left toward the grass strip in the center of the track. His tires met grass, and their racer roller started bumping up and down.

A number of Elves on the sidelines had gotten wind of the chaos. Gesturing frantically, several of them signaled for the race to stop. The pack of racer rollers complied and pulled over, but the Roilers did not obey, and instead drove after Criofan. A number of Faeries watched fearfully from a distance.

"Loch's crazy!" Matha shouted. "If we stop, he'll probably run us over!"

Criofan nodded his head. "You're right; we better find a way to lose him."

Matha gave Criofan a puzzled look. How was he going to lose them on a racetrack?

They whizzed past the great central columns in the tent. The Roilers were hot on their heels. Matha could see what Criofan intended to do. Ahead of them, he saw the entrance gate of the track.

"Go through!" Matha shouted.

Criofan sped from the grass back to the track. As the tires met the liquistone pavement, he slammed the pedal, steering toward the gate. Frantically, Faeries waved their arms at them, but they couldn't stop. The Roilers were right behind them. Tearing down the exit lane, Criofan honked his horn as they zipped past Faeries and Elves, who scrambled out of the way, and then through the exit.

Frantically, Criofan sped away from the tent, shooting between the carousel and the Ferris wheel. "We made it out!" Matha yelled. A number of faery lads and lassies were in their way, lined up for the rides.

"Watch out!" Matha shouted.

Swerving sharply this way and that, Criofan plowed down the main path of the Old Park, weaving in and out of several more groups of Faeries. A sudden jolt shook their bones. Loch had rammed into them from behind, nearly sending them flying into a row of mono wheels parked nearby.

"That deviant, wrench-loving gear gobbler!" Criofan shouted. He pressed even harder on the pedal. The vapoflame engine roared, but the Roilers remained close behind. He then turned quickly away, onto a side path, wheels drumming on the cobblestones.

Matha looked straight ahead, his face frozen with fear. A wooden fence blocked their way. As they crashed through, the slats went flying, but this was the least of their worries. Directly ahead, the Dragonfly swung like an enormous blade that was about to slice them in two. "We'll never make it!" he yelled.

"Neither will they!" Criofan yelled back, looking at the three racer rollers behind him. Criofan timed the movement of the sweeping Dragonfly, slowing to watch the ride scythe back and forth.

"Go around!" Matha shouted, pointing to another path that led away. Just as he spoke, a group of Faeries stepped onto the path, blocking their best escape.

Criofan looked in his rear-view mirror. "They're almost here!" he shouted. "We'll have to take a chance." Seeing the look of terror on Matha's face he added, "What's the worst thing that could happen?"

Shuddering, Matha looked at the ride.

Like an enormous pendulum, the head of the Dragonfly rose skyward, followed by the long abdomen, packed with screaming Faeries — oblivious to the danger below them. The head was about to reach the peak of its swing. Momentarily, they were lifted off their seats. Raising their arms high above their heads, they gawked breathlessly at the sky.

The green metal tail then began to drop, followed by the abdomen and head — rising in the other direction. As soon as the head cleared the center, Criofan announced, "Now we go!" They sped forward. Just as the Dragonfly began its backward fall, Matha let out a yell. But, Criofan's timing was exact, and they narrowly escaped being obliterated by the sweeping head.

"We're through!" Matha exclaimed deliriously.

Behind them they heard a crash. The two Roilers behind Loch had collided — probably to avoid hitting the Dragonfly. Loch had stopped next to them.

"That should slow them down," Criofan joked. Soon they passed the Garden of Sprockets. All around them they heard shouts of Faeries and Elves, demanding that they stop. Criofan ignored them.

He turned westward.

"Where are we going?" Matha asked.

"Loch's roller still rolls," Criofan replied, speeding across the path.

"We'll get in trouble," Matha said.

"Don't worry, Matha," Criofan replied smoothly, as he scooted beneath the giant Butterfly ride. "If anyone noticed us, they're all having way too much fun to care."

As they drove beneath the colossal turquoise and orange structure, loud noises blasted down upon them. Looking up, Matha saw chains of cars tearing around the contours of the wings, their wheels going *clickety-clack, clickety-clack* on the rails. To muffle the sound, he covered both ears with his hands.

Criofan was far too busy steering to be concerned about the noise. He continued to weave in and out among the support posts, until he reached the place where the fore and hind wings of the great ride met. He stopped abruptly and turned off the engine.

"Now what?" Matha yelled above all the clattering and screeching.

"We hide for a little bit, and then we go," Criofan yelled back. "Or, we just leave the racer roller here," he added as he looked around at the huge support beams.

As they considered what to do, they heard the roaring of an engine. "What's that?" Matha yelled.

"Probably just —"

"They're here again!" Matha shrieked. Looking back, he saw Loch's racer roller quickly closing in.

"They haven't seen us yet," Criofan said, starting the engine. "I'm going through to the other side." He then pulled away.

"Yes, they have!" Matha shrieked again.

In a matter of moments, Criofan steered in and out around the posts, until he reached the other side of the Butterfly. As he was about to turn onto the main path leading back to the New Arcade, Loch pulled up beside him, blocking the turn. The Roiler in Loch's back seat reached into Loch's jacket and pulled out a pistol. In a flash, he aimed the muzzle directly at Criofan, and pulled the trigger. A torrent shot him in the face.

Criofan cried out in pain. "He got me in the eye!"

"With a geyser pistol!" Matha shouted.

Rubbing his eye, Criofan instructed, "You have to drive."

Enraged, Matha jumped from the back of his racer roller. Lunging at the Roiler behind Loch, he punched him in the face and grabbed the pistol from his hand. As he did, Loch tried to grab hold of his arm, but he was too late. Quickly, Matha jumped into the front seat of his racer roller, and Criofan climbed into the back.

"Put your foot on the pedal and drive!" Criofan commanded. With that, Matha grabbed the wheel and pressed the pedal. Inching forward, he turned to the left, scraping Loch's racer roller, which was still blocking the way. There was barely room, but they made it past them. He then took off, with Loch in hot pursuit.

As he drove, Matha gripped the steering wheel until the knuckles on his blue-green skin were pale as birch bark. In his entire Life, he had never so much as seen a racer roller, much less driven one. Heading down the path toward the New Arcade, he struggled to keep from careening into all the tents and throngs of roving Faeries.

Without warning, an old faery lady stepped out in front of them, holding a number of parcels in one hand and a large yellow parasol in the other. As she glared at him in disbelief, Matha tried to avoid her. A number of things then happened all at once.

He slammed on his brakes. The racer roller almost grazed her. Terrified, she let go of her packages, which flew in all directions like a pile of rocks blasted by a charge of explosives. The racer roller stopped just inches from her pointy faery shoes.

Furiously, she shook her fist at Matha. "Are you trying to give me an early passage to Annwyn?" she shouted. Her high-pitched hysteria captured the attention of a number of onlookers. Mesmerized, they watched, appalled.

Matha turned the wheel hard, and hit the pedal. As he did, she threw her parasol at them. The parasol flipped over twice before smashing into the very center of the windshield. The stretchers inside broke apart, and the canopy split in half. The resulting mess looked like a flattened yellow bird with splayed legs.

"Annwyn doesn't call you yet!" Matha yelled back as he drove away from the old faery lady. "This *chicken* you call a parasol will send *me* there instead." Maniacally, he started laughing.

"I can't see!" he shouted at Criofan. "Clear the window!"

Holding his eye with one hand, Criofan struggled to climb over the seat, into the front of the racer roller. As he did, he pressed himself into Matha, squeezing him against the driver's door, like a melon about to burst.

"Be careful!" Matha shrieked, as he struggled to keep his hands on the wheel.

"I'm doing my best!" Criofan shouted back.

Still holding his eye, Criofan reached over the windshield with his other hand, peeled off and then tossed the splayed parasol away.

"Keep driving!" he shouted, as he turned to look behind them. "Loch is behind us!"

"I don't know what I'm doing!" Matha shouted.

"That's obvious!" Criofan shouted back. He looked at the geyser pistol Matha had stolen from the Roilers.

"Why did you take that?" he angrily interrogated. "Now we'll *never* get away from them."

"Because!" Matha shouted again, seething with anger. "They shot you, in the eye! With *Water*!"

Chapter 15

A GAME WITH A FRIEND

Baudwin didn't know how long he had been sitting on the wall, watching the meandering crowd. He was supposed to meet his friends, but he hadn't even bothered to check the time. Hammer Comb had shown him that there was something beneath his anger that he had to find. Seamus had also said as much. But he'd not be learning what that was now, because he had no idea where to begin. Filled with doubt and conflicting desires, he couldn't decide what to do next. *Perhaps I should just go home,* he thought.

An elven worker approached him, but Baudwin didn't look up. Aimlessly, he picked at some withering moss on the wall. Out of the corner of his eye he spotted some jugglers. They looked so carefree, tossing their rings into the Air, the bells on their wrists jingling. Nearby, a small faery lad shouted and clapped. *Lucky for them,* Baudwin thought.

"Cheer up," the elven worker said, trying again to get his attention. Baudwin didn't reply. "Come now," the Elve continued, holding out a wooden box. "Things can't be that bad," he added, smiling. He then removed a cloth bag from the box. "Play a game of Gear Chute?"

Looking up, Baudwin took the bag and turned it upside down. The contents clinked, and ten small copper balls fell into his palm. A bit of a smile crossed his lips as he rolled them around. *Perhaps when all is lost, something new appears,* he thought.

He thanked the Elve and hurried toward the Gear Chute booth. Upon entering, he was greeted by a steady stream of sounds. *Ping, ping, ping,* went the machines, like myriad drops of rain falling on copper roofs in a storm.

Gear Chute machines were rectangular in shape, made of Wood and bronze, and loaded with copper balls. Throughout the booth Faeries sat perched on stools, playing. Baudwin took a stool in a less crowded row and prepared to join in the play. In front of him was a glass window set into a square bronze frame. Two wooden trays were placed beneath the frame, one above the other. Large red and gold letters at the top of the game read:

Gear Chute Treasure Box

Mounted behind the glass was a large bronze ring, which contained the workings of the game. The goal was simple: Turn a knob that shoots balls into the ring and watch them fall through different contraptions, eventually going toward the collection tray.

This better go well, he thought.

Baudwin set his ten copper balls into the top tray. He then turned a knob, and the tray turned end over end. Through the glass, he saw all the balls dropping quickly. *Ping, ping, ping* they went, hitting the spinning gears. Some went into chutes that faced different directions, shooting up and down, hitting more and more spinning gears. Others fell into catchers that opened and closed. Soon, they reached the bottom, but instead of dropping into the treasure box, as Baudwin hoped they would, they disappeared into the exit chute. *I have to pay better attention,* he thought. Next time, he would turn the knob more carefully, so the balls would feed more slowly. In that way, they wouldn't go down the wrong chute, and some would go into the catchers.

As Baudwin continued playing, a hand squeezed his shoulder.

"Find a gold one yet?" a low voice asked, with a gentle twang.

Baudwin looked up. Serenely, a face smiled down at him — one he knew quite well — rather old and wrinkled, with lustrous pale blue eyes and bushy gray eyebrows.

Baudwin had been so unhappy that he forgot that his good elven friend might be here. "A time for all places — hello, Rian!"[1] he exclaimed. Rising from his stool, he crossed his hands in front of him, with his right palm facing down, and his left hand pointed up.

"A place for all time — hello, Baudwin," Rian replied, as he made a circle in front of him with his fingers touching at the top, and his thumbs at the bottom. They then gave each other a warm hug.

Every year Rian worked in the Gear Chute booth at the Engineerium, taking time off from the General Store in Deuona. Seeing him in his blue and white striped overalls and black work boots with silver buckles, Baudwin chuckled. Rian always looked the same wherever he went.

"Is this your first game?" Rian asked. As he spoke, a series of balls went *ping, ping, ping,* disappearing down the exit chute, never to be seen again.

"Yes, and I haven't won so much as one copper ball," Baudwin replied. "Never mind silver, or gold."

"Such things happen, when you let an Elve such as myself break your concentration," Rian replied, laughing.

Baudwin smiled at Rian. Theirs was a special friendship going back many years. They had first met at the General Store, when Baudwin was a Faefry and the Engineerium was little more than a festival. As each petal was built,

---

[1] Pronounced [RY-an]

every fountain filled with Water, and all the games and amusements were added, Rian mentored Baudwin in elven ways. In all that time, Baudwin had never spoken ill of the Elves to Rian. Neither had Rian spoken ill of the Faeries to Baudwin. Baudwin appreciated Rian's quiet strength, and Rian, Baudwin's inquisitive nature.

"No matter," Baudwin replied. "How are you?"

"I'm well," Rian replied, as he pulled up a stool and sat down. "Gear Chute keeps me very busy."

"Of course — my favorite game," Baudwin said, trying to hide his discomfort, for he was still reeling from his ordeal with Hammer Comb.

"How are you, Baudwin?" Rian asked.

Baudwin didn't know what to tell his friend. There he was, struggling in a way he never had before, feeling hopeless and discouraged. What was the point of even talking? Rian probably wouldn't even know what to say.

"I'm all right, I suppose," Baudwin replied.

"You suppose?" Rian asked.

"I don't know," Baudwin replied, shifting uncomfortably on his stool. "I just went to the hammer comb booth, and I feel quite —"

"Unsettled?" Rian asked.

"Yes," Baudwin replied.

"I'm not at all surprised," Rian added, chuckling. "Hammer Comb can be *quite* unsettling."

Hearing this, Baudwin relaxed a bit and turned back to his game. He wasn't surprised to hear that Rian was not a fan of Hammer Comb. Rian was not the kind of Elve who believed in all the promises put forth by the elven hierarchy, for he had a mind of his own.

Baudwin knew that Rian could tell he was very troubled. He expected his friend to try and comfort him somehow. Rian cleared his throat and nodded his head. The Elves were great storytellers, and the Faeries were avid listeners. Baudwin sensed that Rian was about to help him in the best way he knew how — by telling him a story.

"Did I ever tell you how this game was invented?" Rian asked, pointing about the booth.

"No," Baudwin replied. In all of his many visits, he had never thought to ask.

"I knew the Elve very well," Rian continued. "His name was Daibhi.[2] He was a clockmaker. One day, his wife, Una,[3] dropped a ruby earring he had given her into a clock he was repairing."

----

2 Pronounced [DAY-bhee]
3 Pronounced [OO-na]

"How did she do that?" Baudwin asked, as a number of balls suddenly fell into the treasure box. Happy with his progress, he kept playing.

"As he took off the back," Rian replied, "she was talking right next to him, which she always liked to do, and fiddling with her hair. Needless to say, she got very upset when her precious earring fell off, and disappeared into the workings."

"Then what happened?"

"He wanted her to be happy, so he picked up the clock, which was rather large and heavy. Holding the back close to his ear, he turned the sides around and around, listening as the earring made its way through the gears. When it finally dropped out, he got very excited. 'I can make a game out of this!' he exclaimed."

Hearing this, Baudwin looked around at the motifs on the machines. "All of these came from a clock?"

"Yes," Rian said as he pointed around the booth. "Of course, being an expert clockmaker, Daibhi's first games worked like clocks. Then he tried his hand at steamway puzzles, with lots of gears, rods, and flippers. When he got tired of those, he made trees with apples, cherries, and peaches falling into baskets. And hazelnuts, acorns, and walnuts rolling into holes near ground squirrels. Then lots of special eternity knots, with complicated twists and turns. And finally, all of these beautiful treasure boxes," he added, pointing to the game in progress.

With that, several bells and whistles sounded from inside Baudwin's game. A large number of balls fell into the treasure box, going *ping, ping, ping*.

"I won!" he exclaimed.

Baudwin slid a lever on the lower tray, and the balls dropped inside. He scooped them into his hand, and then put them in a basket beneath the tray. "Your friend was quite the inventor."

"He certainly was," Rian replied, nodding. "I know how interested you are in all of this. Elves like to make games from things that are practical in nature," he continued. "Take Drill Drop, for instance. Anyone can see that game comes from drilling for ore, or making furniture. Steamball comes from riveting to make lumber rollers, or other kinds of steamway machines.

Rian's story cheered Baudwin up. A thought then struck him. "What about Hammer Comb?" he asked. "What's practical about that?"

"Nothing," Rian replied. "Just meaningless entertainment."

"Doesn't seem very elven to me."

"We use hammers, but only for building," Rian added, as he picked up Baudwin's basket. Changing the subject, he looked inside. "What did you win?"

"Mostly copper, maybe a silver, but no gold," Baudwin replied, studying the contents of the basket. He then sighed deeply.

"Are you disappointed?" Rian asked.

"No, not about this — but yes," Baudwin said. "I don't know. . . It's just that. . ."

"Baudwin," Rian asked, putting his hand on his young friend's shoulder, "what has you so upset?"

Baudwin wasn't sure where to begin.

"I came to the Engineerium to have fun and to find some Glamorium . . ." he began. "I didn't get to touch any, and I'm not having any fun, either. I got into a fight with my friends. Then I got into another fight at Steamball. But the very worst thing happened after I played Hammer Comb. The more I pounded, the angrier I got. The game was so nonsensical! When the elven lady in charge of the booth asked me if I was prepared for Life, I realized that I wasn't. There's something inside me that I need to touch, before I can complete my quest. But I don't know —"

"Why are you interested in Glamorium?" Rian interrupted.

"You may not believe me, but I think the Water is guiding me to touch some, so I can find my mother," Baudwin replied.

"Really?" Rian asked. "Why do you say that?"

Baudwin appreciated the respect Rian was giving him. Unlike Matha and Criofan, he was taking what Baudwin said at face value, with no reservations. This inspired Baudwin to tell him even more about what had happened.

"Matha and I found an ancient glamorium glyph in a ruin not far from the Springs of Coventina," Baudwin began. "When I showed it to my grandfather, he said the Water was guiding me to touch some."

"Then you came to the right place," Rian said. "Have you seen the tree in the Center and the display at Curios & Marvels?"

"No — I mean, yes. I mean —"

"What *do* you mean, Baudwin?" Rian interrupted, smiling.

"Yes, I did see the tree, but no, nothing happened. That is, when I touched the leaves," Baudwin replied.

"How disappointing that must have been."

"Yes, it was," Baudwin said. "Very disappointing. So I went to Curios & Marvels. When I tried to touch a tablet in the collection, a thunderous ringing shocked me and my friends. Then the curator kicked us out. He was furious."

"A thunderous ringing?" Rian asked, amused. "You must have set off an elven alarm. We're masters at building them."

"Yes," Baudwin replied ruefully. "They probably heard it in the Clock City."

"You should have known better than to try to put one over on the Elves," Rian said, laughing. "There are better ways to find Glamorium. But you must hurry."

"Why is that?" Baudwin asked.

"I know the Elves have been gathering all they can find — throughout *Tír na nÓg* — no matter how big or small the pieces are," Rian replied, worried.

Hearing this, Baudwin sat up straighter, surprised. "Whatever for?"

"I don't know," Rian replied. "I suspect for reasons that are quite different than yours. Of that I can assure you."

"If the Elves are collecting all the Glamorium, I'll probably never find any," Baudwin said. "I certainly can't scale the Tadlachs —" he added sadly. "That's what my father said I'd have to do. And my grandfather said finding Glamorium is as mysterious as Faeries dancing in river mist."

"Or faery ladies playing harps around the Triquetra?" Rian asked, again laughing.

"What do you know about them?" Baudwin asked, wondering why Rian had brought up the automatons in Curios & Marvels.

"Who do you think keeps them playing?" Rian asked. "I've even replaced a gear or two to keep the Triquetra moving."

Baudwin still didn't understand why Rian had mentioned the faery ladies, much less the Triquetra. "What about them?" he asked.

"Exactly," Rian replied. "You tell me — what does the Triquetra have to do with Glamorium?"

"I don't know," Baudwin replied, perplexed.

Laughing, Rian tousled Baudwin's hair. "Why, *everything* of course," he replied. "Didn't you see the symbol for Glamorium in the center of the Triquetra?"

"Yes, I did, but. . ." Baudwin replied, not knowing what to say next. He had spent most of his time in Curios & Marvels arguing with Edmund about the history of the Triquetra, and the meaning of the other glyphs. Now, Rian seemed to be saying that they hadn't discussed what was most important, and he felt angry that Edmund had wasted so much of their time.

Ruefully, Baudwin smiled at his friend. "Edmund kept trying to convince us that he was right about everything," he began. "He did say Glamorium was important, but he never discussed what it had to do with the Triquetra."

Rian shook his head. "Edmund!" he exclaimed, sharply. "Of course he didn't teach you anything of *real* importance. Except, of course, what the Assembly wants you to know. You know. . ." Rian paused for a moment, looking around. "I shouldn't tell you this," he whispered slyly in Baudwin's ear, "but I've heard that back in Platinum Spires, when Edmund was going through his initiation to become a Druid, he nearly didn't gain entrance."

"What happened?" Baudwin asked, surprised.

"Ho!" Rian replied, merrily. "He failed the oral history exam."

Baudwin's eyes grew wide as Rian continued to spill all the beans. "That's probably why they put him to work in Curios & Marvels. He could easily memorize only a limited number of things. That way, they could play to his strengths and be certain to promote their account — lecturing everyone about the Triquetra — *Scrutiny, Certainty, and the Promise of the Future.* That's about all his memory could hold."

Rian laughed until his belly shook. "They know full well that their interpretation isn't valid!" he exclaimed. "Never was, and never will be, but the Assembly has grown more and more rigid over the years. So, what else did Edmund have to say?"

Baudwin described everything that had happened at Curios & Marvels. Edmund had insisted that the shrines had been built to excite the Faeries, and teach them about progress. Matha had posited that the three glyphs set near the points of the Triquetra represented *three* realms — *Tir na nÓg,* Danu, and Annwyn. And Edmund had also opined that Glamorium was the most important symbol, only because he claimed that the Elves were enhancing it.

Finally, Baudwin mentioned the automatons. How the Triquetra had risen out of the dais through a mechanical wonder, and how the glyph for Glamorium had been present, but that the other three glyphs had been missing. "Edmund," Baudwin began, "said that that those three glyphs had fallen out of favor — but he was obviously wrong."

Baudwin then explained that when he touched the green lily on one of the lady automatons, glowstone Light had shone upon the dais. The missing glyphs had then appeared, much to Edmund's surprise.

"How remarkable!" Rian exclaimed. "I never knew that. I've oiled the gearbox under the dais many times, but I never thought to touch the green lily."

"Do you suppose that no one has ever noticed them before?" Baudwin asked.

"Likely not," Rian replied. "Although perhaps an Elve or two in Gleam knows the secret."

"But, what does it all *mean?*" Baudwin pressed.

"I can't say anything for sure about those other glyphs," Rian replied, "but if Matha surmised that they are symbols for other realms, I wouldn't be surprised if he was right. I would trust his judgment over Edmund's story any day — that's for sure. One day you may discover their true meaning. However, the *real* lesson — the one that Edmund could never tell you — was staring you right in the face."

Baudwin waited breathlessly for Rian to continue.

"Baudwin," he began, "I've known you your entire life. You've come into my shop in Deuona for hundreds of seasons, full of curiosity, always asking about elven ways and contraptions. You, Matha, and Criofan were so interested, but, as you were young, this was not unexpected. I believe that in the future, Faeries will grow ever more accepting of our inventions, and that's not necessarily a bad thing. But I do object to how the Assembly is erasing the past. Edmund did you a great disservice — one that I'm going to remedy."

Rian paused for a moment to collect his thoughts. "You say you wish to touch some Glamorium," he began. "Many touch Glamorium every day and nothing happens, but it sounds like Glamorium is trying to touch *you* — a rare calling — especially in these times."

"Could Glamorium really help me find my mother?" Baudwin asked.

"Indeed it might," Rian replied. "Glamorium could bestow great boons upon you. Some say this wondrous metal has the power to heal sickness of body, heart, mind, and spirit, to restore balance in the metals and the elements, and may somehow bring Elves and Faeries into greater harmony. Unquestionably, Glamorium provides visions — but only to one who is *ready*."

Intrigued, Baudwin studied Rian as he continued speaking.

"A long time ago many understood the teachings of the Triquetra — that in order to wield Glamorium, one had to be Honest, know the Truth, and be open to the Promise of Rebirth. This wisdom was learned only after undergoing numerous trials, and in the case of Faeries such as yourself, only after they had joined with their currents, coursed with their feelings, and honed their intentions."

Hearing this, Baudwin wondered if Kelven and Seamus understood all of what Rian had just explained to him. Strangely, his elven friend seemed to know more about the Triquetra and Glamorium than his elders. Baudwin saw no reason why they wouldn't have told him everything they knew. Surely, Seamus would have, but clearly he didn't, so perhaps he and Kelven just didn't know as much as he thought they did.

Rian was far more learned than Baudwin had ever imagined.

"I bet you're wondering how a mere shopkeeper knows all of this," Rian said, as he pushed out his chest and tugged on his overall straps. Baudwin nodded, and he continued, "As you know, I'm a Master of Silver, but what you don't know is that I'm *also* a Druid of Guidance."

A Druid of Guidance, Baudwin thought. Surely Rian trusted him a great deal to share such a significant secret with him. He had always felt that Rian was an unusual Elve, and now he knew why. Added to that, this was the third time that day that Baudwin had met a Druid; two of Lore and now one of Guidance. He much preferred how Rian was using his insight to help, rather than to mislead him. Eagerly, he listened, hoping his friend would share even more with him.

Rian continued, "I used to live in *Tír Luí Lucharachán,* where I studied and became a Druid. After the Great Befalling, I felt a need to make my way east. I grew weary of the unwary path my kin were taking. I had a strong desire to share whatever truths I could, but I had to do so away from the rigid reach of the Assembly. That's how I ended up as the proprietor of the General Store in Deuona — and you and I became friends." Baudwin beamed, and Rian continued, smiling all the while. "But, know this — we Masters of Silver read our friends the way sea turtles sense the tides of the Moon. Something has called to you, and I intend to assist you on your path."

Baudwin regarded Rian.

Always, the Sun touched the Elves, and every Elve, whether of Copper, Silver, Gold or Platinum, had a shine about them. These glimmerings were illuminated by the Sun, and while subtle in nature, could be seen anywhere, whether deep beneath a mountain, or high upon a ridge.

Baudwin watched as Rian's presence grew stronger and stronger. His silver Light was shining more brightly than ever. Awed, he wondered if all Elves could shine this way. *Perhaps,* he thought, *only those as wise as Rian.*

"*Draíocht!*"[4] Rian exclaimed, throwing his arms high above his head and almost falling over. Like an arrow sent from the sky, the Master was indomitable in his purpose. With a flourish, he produced a pendant hidden beneath his shirt. On the surface was a lantern finely etched onto untarnished Silver, a symbol Baudwin had never seen before. Rian was much more than he had ever imagined. Raptly, Baudwin readied himself for what the Druid of Guidance would say next.

Rian sat down next to Baudwin. Leaning toward him, he placed his hands on Baudwin's shoulders, giving them an earnest shake. "Are you prepared to honor the lessons of the Triquetra — to be Honest, know the Truth, and prepare yourself for the Promise of Rebirth?" he asked.

Hearing the question, Baudwin was filled with trepidation. "How can I answer you, when I never joined with my current?"

"Baudwin," Rian replied, "take heart. I understand guidance. The Water of your tribe is clearly aiding you, or you wouldn't now be here with me. Forget that you're not joined. Just tell me and think deeply before you answer — what does it mean to be honest?"

Baudwin thought as hard as he could, and then exclaimed, "I am honest!"

"Honest with others?" Rian asked.

"Yes," Baudwin replied. "As much as I can be."

Rian smiled. "How about *yourself*?" he asked.

Baudwin stopped. No one had ever spoken to him about this difference, and he wasn't sure where he stood. He thought then of what his grandfather had said about touching something inside himself. *Perhaps,* he thought, *honesty with myself is the key.*

Seeing Baudwin struggling, Rian then asked, "They aren't the same, are they?" Baudwin nodded. "Don't be disheartened that this never occurred to

---

[4] Pronounced [DREE-oct] that which is unseen or alchemical and mysterious, denoting the secret lore and arts of the Druids

you," Rian continued. "You're at the very beginning of your quest. Lessons such as these can take a lifetime to master. Now, come with me. I have something to show you."

❦

After leaving the Gear Chute game, Rian led Baudwin to a door at the back of the booth. "In here," he said, as he turned the doorknob.

They entered the room. Next to the wall was a workbench, with a large chest sitting on top. Screwdrivers and wrenches were strewn about, along with other tools and a number of Gear Chute machines in need of repair.

"If I remember correctly, what I'm looking for is over there," Rian said, pointing to a large wooden case opposite the bench.

Rian and Baudwin made their way to the case through a maze of machines, chairs, and wooden boxes.

"What's in all of these boxes?" Baudwin asked.

"Mostly parts to repair my machines," Rian replied. "And prizes to give to the winners," he added, pointing. "Like those wind-up butterflies."

"I remember them!" Baudwin exclaimed. "When I was a young one, I used to play with the blue and green ones, near the river reeds."

"Watch your step — don't trip," Rian cautioned his friend. Having reached the case, he examined the shelves. "Let's see now," he mused.

"What are you looking for?" Baudwin asked.

"A very old box," Rian replied. "Not very big." As he stooped down to examine the bottom shelf, Baudwin joined him in the search.

"That one's too small," Rian said.

"How about this one?" Baudwin asked.

"Not old enough," Rian replied, as he continued looking. After a few moments, he stopped. "Here it is," he said, as he removed the box from the shelf.

"That looks like one of the boxes that I saw at the sprocketworks booth," Baudwin said. "I went there to get a coupler for my father."

"The box is nothing special," Rian said, as he removed the lid.

"What's *inside* is," he added, smiling.

"Red silk?" Baudwin asked, eying the contents.

Rian then removed the ball of silk from the box, separating the folds, until they lay flat against his palm. "There," he said. "As beautiful as ever."

On top of the silk lay a shimmering green egg. Baudwin could barely believe his eyes. "Is that *Glamorium?*" he gasped.

"Yes," Rian replied. "I haven't shown this to anyone in a very long time."

"About the size of a duck's egg!" Baudwin exclaimed. "How exquisite!" Instantly, all discouragement about his day dissolved into pure exuberance. He couldn't believe his good fortune. Despite his failure to touch Glamorium, the opportunity was now right before him. *How could the Water <u>not</u> be guiding me?* he thought, wanting to press the egg to his heart and dance in circles.

"Baudwin," Rian began, "you may not have learned all the lessons of the Triquetra, but if you touch this egg, Glamorium may still grant you a boon. Glamorium can speak to anyone, even one who is not yet a master but still an apprentice. Take this — but beware! If all you seek is light without the shadow, then all you will find is shadow without the light." Rian offered Baudwin the egg. "This now belongs to you."

"Rian," Baudwin began, "I simply can't accept this."

Rian set the glamorium egg upon the table. "I hope my words didn't alarm you."

"I'm not alarmed," Baudwin replied.

Rian chuckled. "Are you sure?" he asked.

"I would like nothing more than to take that egg from you, but . . ." Baudwin hesitated. He wanted to be honest with his friend, but he struggled with what to say. Recalling the first lesson of the Triquetra he began, "There is something I must be honest about, but I don't want to seem like a fool."

Rian laughed. "One who is honest is never a fool. If you're being honest with me, then perhaps you're learning to be honest with yourself, and that is very good — for that is the *fire* of honesty."

Encouraged by Rian's words, Baudwin continued, "I'm alarmed, but not because of shadows. I've been chasing after Glamorium all day, worried that I might fail to find some. Now, here is some before me, and I wonder — what if I touch Glamorium and nothing happens? Then I will be deemed unworthy, and that frightens me more than anything. Besides, I'm not even joined to my current, and my intention remains unknown to me, so why *would* Glamorium speak to me?"

As Rian studied Baudwin, Rian's subtle silver glow grew more intense, until even his blue eyes had a silver sheen upon them. Obviously, Rian was reading him, and Baudwin wondered what his friend was about to say. "You are more worthy than you know. I can see into you. Your element seems to have changed you. You are not as you were when last we met."

Just as Rian had shared his secret with Baudwin about being a Druid of Guidance, Baudwin now wanted to share his secret with Rian.

"After years of searching, the Water finally came to me," Baudwin said. "At the Springs of Coventina, I heard all the voices of my tribe. That's how the Water set me upon my path."

"The Water finally came to you!" Rian exclaimed. "How remarkable. You've been searching for at least forty years. What more proof of your worthiness do you need? Now you *are* acting like a fool! Cast aside your doubts."

Again, Rian offered Baudwin the glamorium egg. "Because you were willing to practice the true meaning of honesty, you deserve to have this," he began. "Glamorium will answer you, if you are deemed worthy. I feel in my heart that this is true, and I have no finer friend in all of the realm that I would rather give this to."

Hearing Rian's words of praise, Baudwin's eyes filled with tears. As Rian held the egg out to him, he looked at his reflection in the metal. *How curious,* he thought, seeing his tears shine. They seemed to be made of Light. He blinked several times. *Is Glamorium calling to me?* he wondered.

"My reflection is different," Baudwin said, breathing deeply.

"Good," Rian said. "You must sit down," he added, pointing to a chair.

Baudwin sat, waiting expectantly, his tears still fresh upon his face, for he did not want to brush away any of what he had just seen. He took the egg, leaving the silk in Rian's palm.

"Legend says that for Glamorium to speak to them, both Elves and Faeries must hold Glamorium close to their hearts," Rian said.

Baudwin closed his eyes, holding the egg to his heart. All was still for several moments. He wondered if anything would happen. But, having seen his tears turn to Light, he remained hopeful. And so, he sat — waiting — for what seemed to be a very long time.

Nothing happened.

Worried, his mind began to race. Was he not worthy? Why would the Water lead him down this path, if only to fail? With each passing moment, he felt more and more stricken.

The poem written on the tablet at the Springs of Coventina then came to his mind:

That which holds the Truth you seek, is something you must touch.

He knew he had done his best to be honest, but had he been honest enough? He wasn't sure. Sighing, he wondered if he should give up. He then looked at Rian. "I know not what else I should touch," he said.

"Then you must let the truth touch *you*," Rian replied.

As Rian spoke, an understanding came to Baudwin. Although he felt his anger keenly, he didn't know what lay beneath it. What was so important that he had to touch? All he could sense was frustration and pain. His chest was a lime kiln, burning with rage. But he knew stoking the Fire would not make the pain cease, for it had always haunted him. Ever since he was a young one, he had carried embers within him — memories of deprivation — being raised by only his father and grandfather — not being joined, and always feeling like an outsider amongst his peers. The Faery who was not *truly* a water Faery.

He grimaced. In following these thoughts fully, he had finally been honest with himself — more so than ever before. He then thought again of Seamus's words, "What *else* must you touch?"

That's it! What lay beneath his anger was his pain. Contemplating this, he felt the embers within himself cooling. The burden he carried was now lighter. In a moment his mind emptied, allowing his heart to fill. The fear that Glamorium would not grace him gripped him again, but this time, he did not avoid the feeling. Somehow, he knew he had to hold fast, and so he did. Eventually, the fear melted away, leaving only the bliss he had felt moments before.

Remembering what the voices of his tribe had told him at the Springs of Coventina, Baudwin kept his eyes closed. Just as when the Water had come to him, his inner sight opened. Gradually, a warm sensation entered his fingers, and then, a ripple of green Light flashed from the glamorium egg. His inner sight allowed him to see everything, as if his eyes were open, but Rian did not share in the vision. Scintillating rays of Light streamed from the middle of his chest. A shudder of excitement coursed through his body, almost knocking him out of his chair.

When the Water came to him, he had seen minnows and heard the voices of his tribe, but this seemed very different. *This seems* — but, before Baudwin could finish his thought, the green Light exploded in starlike beams inside of him, and then went shooting in all directions out of his body.

Rian watched carefully, wondering what Baudwin was seeing. Baudwin remained in his seat, his eyes closed. Soon, he relaxed into a trance-like state. All of his senses grew still. *This seems almost like the opposite of a waking,* he thought. *As if my senses are waiting for something beyond the Water.*

A voice then spoke to him that seemed to come from somewhere deep within him, a voice he had never heard before:

"As within — so without, as without — so within. There we meet, in the center, from our hearts."

The poem. . . on the tablet. . .at Curios & Marvels, he thought, enthralled. *Is that what I just heard?*

The green Light grew even brighter, filling his heart with a blissful warmth. Waves of energy poured through him, until he thought he might burst with happiness. Never had he felt so complete. He almost could not bear the rapture.

Baudwin found what happened next to be even more unexpected. The sparkling green Light continued to shine. Everything he saw and felt within himself merged with everything he saw and felt outside of himself, until he could not tell which was which.

As within, so without, he thought, remembering the poem. *So this is where feeling through my pain takes me.* Unable to resist the emanations, he remained motionless in his chair. All the while, he held the glamorium egg close to his heart.

After a few moments, the green Light began to fade. In its wake, a vision appeared. A faery lady stood before him, delicate and refined in her beauty. Dressed in a light turquoise gown, she rested in an estuary of Light. Her pale blue-green skin was soft and smooth, like the petals of a river lily. She had watery blue-green topaz eyes. As she beckoned to him, rivulets of Light streamed from her body, undulating softly, like liquid ether.

Who is she? he thought, gazing at her features. *Is she my mother?*

Baudwin looked at her more closely, searching for a clue. She stood in a stream of Water, and like the tears he had just seen on his face, she seemed to be of both the Water and of the Light. Startled, Baudwin wondered how two very different elements could be seen as one.

As he continued looking at her, again she beckoned for him to come to her. He went toward her slender, light-filled arms. When he reached her, he stopped. She took his hands, and then wiped the tears from his face, saying, "Do not weep, my young one, for we have found each other."

They embraced, and he felt her arms holding him gently. His heart swooned with joy. *Finally, I am with her*, he thought. How long their embrace lasted, he could not tell.

"Are you my mother?" he asked. "Are you?"

Who or what was he really holding so close to his heart?

He looked at her again, but now her arms were covered with dark brown feathers, ragged and molting. Her lovely face had a pointed orange beak, and small, dull, brown eyes, dark and despondent.

What happened next was strangest of all, consuming him with dread.

The odd-looking lady-bird made a peculiar noise, as if she were being smothered. Tentatively, Baudwin held her, but she wrested herself away from him. She then turned completely into a bird and flew away, leaving him stunned and horrified.

Shuddering with fear, he waited to see what would happen next, for he could sense that something truly terrifying was coming. The river of Light that she had been standing in became a stifling force, choking all the Water, rocks, and plants, until they turned into something ominous — a surging mass of tarnished silver, noxious and cold — yielding nothing.

Baudwin panicked. He began to run, fearfully looking over his shoulder as he went. Sensing his helplessness, the noxious river flowed ever faster, chasing him, becoming darker and darker with each surging twist and turn. Feelings of doom consumed him. Soon, he would be of the realm no more. He was desperate to get away, for the surging mass was about to engulf him.

Gasping, Baudwin bolted up in his chair. Grimacing with fear, he gripped his seat until his fingers ached. With a ring, the glamorium egg hit the floor, as if a somber bell had been struck. Baudwin let out a groan and opened his eyes.

Rian stood quietly, waiting for him to speak. "What happened, Baudwin?" he asked.

"The most wonderful and terrible of things. . ." Baudwin replied, his words trailing off.

Baudwin strained to find his voice. "Begin with what was good or right," Rian said, seeing his friend's tortured demeanor.

"I saw everything," Baudwin began. "A green Light went shooting through me, and I felt *everything* — and a peace that I have never known."

Hearing, this, a look of wonder came into Rian's eyes. He, as well, could barely speak.

"Baudwin," he began, smiling, "you were touched by the *Dúrúnghlas*."[5]

"What's that?" Baudwin asked.

"Legend says that the *Dúrúnghlas* appears only to a lucky few who touch Glamorium," Rian replied. "I, myself, have never had such a blessing."

Rian stepped toward Baudwin and took his hand. "But I, myself, am fortunate indeed to have a friend, such as yourself, who has."

"I was no longer *divided*," Baudwin went on, his face glowing with feeling. "In any way."

"What do you mean?" Rian asked.

"My thoughts no longer stood against my heart; my heart no longer shrank with fear from what I knew was true," Baudwin replied. "Such freedom! I can't say anything more than that."

"Then what happened?" Rian asked.

"I saw *her*."

"Who?"

"A faery lady," Baudwin replied. "Perhaps she was my mother. At least, she seemed like she could have been."

"Go on."

"She seemed to be of two elements," Baudwin continued.

Rian remained silent, listening carefully.

"Two?" he asked.

"Yes, of the Water and of the Light."

"The water *and* the light?" Rian asked, puzzled. "How could that be?"

---

[5]   Pronounced [doo-ROON-ghlass] profound green mystery

"I really don't know," Baudwin replied. "She was beautiful, like a water lily. When she smiled at me, Light poured out of her — from her face, arms, and body. The Light was like glowstone Light, only much more. . ."

Baudwin stopped speaking, so absorbed was he in the feeling of what he had seen.

"More *what*?" Rian asked.

"More *soothing*. . ."

"Yes, I see," Rian mused. "What you saw was indeed something of great import."

Baudwin then grimaced at the memory.

"Baudwin," Rian began, "I saw your pained expression when you were entranced. What happened next?"

"I went toward her," Baudwin began, "and she reached for me." He took a breath to keep from choking with emotion.

"Go on," Rian said.

"Her arms, so long and slender, were filled with Light. She embraced me. But then, I saw her change. She became covered in feathers, from head to toe. She had a beak, and small unhappy-looking eyes. She made a sound as if I were crushing her. And then. . ."

Baudwin stopped speaking. Tears welled in his eyes.

"Go on, Baudwin," Rian said.

"She turned into a moorhen," he replied. "I watched her fly away. For a moment, I almost had her — and then she was gone."

The two friends remained silent for several moments. Neither could alter the doleful nature of what Baudwin had just experienced.

"You mustn't take this as a bad sign," Rian said, trying his best to comfort his friend. "She was, after all, a river bird. You're of the river. And you at least did get to embrace her."

"Yes, but then something else happened, something even more strange and terrifying."

Now Rian grimaced, steeling himself to hear the rest of the story.

"She had been standing in a river of Light," Baudwin continued, "a river filled with beautiful plants, river grass, and rocks, all shimmering in the Light. As soon as she flew away, the river turned into something unspeakably ominous, a surging mass of tarnished silver, dark and ugly, and bent upon my destruction. The river rushed toward me, as if to drown me."

Baudwin shuddered. "And then I opened my eyes, and saw you."

Baudwin was so agitated he could barely speak. Twice now, he had been both blessed and cursed. First, when the Water came to him, he had heard the voices of his tribe, and he was overjoyed. But, he hadn't heard his mother's voice, which left him bereft. And now, Glamorium had granted him a *Dúrúnghlas,* which was a great blessing, followed by a terrifying dream.

"There was such wonder, but then such unbearable torment. Why?" Baudwin asked, choking with emotion. "Why does this keep happening to me?"

Rian's blue eyes melted empathetically into Baudwin's. Seeing what his friend needed, the Druid of Guidance then poured out his knowledge. "Legend has it that Glamorium once bestowed only great blessings upon those lucky enough to own even a tiny piece."

"That's what my grandfather told me," Baudwin said, his mood brightening.

"He's correct," Rian said. "But that is what *used* to be." As Rian spoke, Baudwin saw his consternation grow.

"Now *you* seem upset, Rian," Baudwin said. "Why is that?"

"I've also heard that Glamorium may bring a great shadow upon those who are *unlucky* enough to touch even a tiny piece."

"A *shadow*?" Baudwin repeated, shocked. "How can that be?"

"No one knows for certain, but some believe this occurred as a result of the Great Befalling," Rian replied. "What was once pure and sacred is now befouled — but how and why, I cannot say."

Rian pointed to the empty box. "This is why I kept the egg safely tucked away. For, should the wrong kind of Elve or Faery touch it, who knows what would be unleashed?"

Baudwin wondered if this was why the Elves were collecting all the Glamorium they could find. Perhaps they knew how dangerous it had become, so they were hiding it away, or locking it up in plain sight at their exhibits. The Glamorium at Curios & Marvels had been cordoned off, and the Glamorium on the Tree of Innovation wasn't real Glamorium. Despite this, Baudwin wouldn't be deterred. "Can Glamorium still be used for good?" he asked.

"Only by those who can see its shadow, and not be corrupted by it," Rian replied. "If you remember, I warned you that if all you seek is light without the shadow, then all you will find is shadow without the light. You're lucky you saw both the beautiful and the ugly. Do not seek the light of Glamorium without deep consideration of its shadow, or next time you could be met with only shadow and no light."

Hearing this, Baudwin shuddered. *What if I had seen only a surging mass of tarnished silver, bent upon my destruction, and not also the faery lady?* he wondered. *Then there would have been only shadow without the Light. Rian's right,* he thought. *I am a lucky fool.*

"I'm glad you told me as much as you did," Baudwin said, searching the floor. "Rian!" he exclaimed. "There's the egg — right as ever."

"Of course," Rian said, as he carefully scooped up the egg with the silk. "When worked by a master, Glamorium can become malleable, but once forged, the form Glamorium takes is nearly indestructible."

"As is our friendship," Baudwin warmly added.

Baudwin and Rian could feel the emanations coming from the shining green egg. The two friends sat quietly, unable to speak, filled as they were with feelings of deep happiness and peace.

Rian wrapped the shimmering treasure in the piece of silk, and gave it to Baudwin.

"Thank you, Rian," Baudwin said, as he buttoned the egg in the inside pocket of his vest. "Wherever my Life takes me, I will always hold this close to my heart."

"Once Glamorium has granted a vision, one cannot know where their path will lead," Rian said. "But, of this I am certain — if you heed and honor the lessons of the Triquetra, you will eventually discover the truth about your mother."

Baudwin wondered if the egg would ever again grace him with its Light. Glamorium was so unpredictable, and would not bend to his will. He would have to be patient and learn what he could. Honesty, Truth, and the Promise of Rebirth. He had learned some of the first lesson, but what of the rest?

"What of Truth and the Promise of Rebirth?" he then asked Rian. "How will I learn these lessons?"

"We Elves must go to life," Rian replied, "and take action just as a tracker tracks, or the forgemaster hammers. As a Faery, you must wait for life to come to you."

Baudwin then thought about Loch, who was clearly a tracker. "I don't understand. We Faeries also track in the forest."

"Yes, but the difference is in the *doing*. For wisdom to be gained, a Faery has to float down a river, rather than swim against the currents as an Elve would. You will learn your lessons, not by shaping an ingot, but by staring at the fire that lights the forge."

Baudwin believed he understood. "That's exactly what happened when the Water came to me. Yes, I swam in the Water, but my swimming isn't what made the Water come to me."

"Yes, you were *floating*," Rian said. "You were waiting, as any Faery would, to have the Water come to you. I imagine that if we swapped places, I would have found my mettle mid-stroke. Don't forget — we are of the Sun, and you are of the Moon."

"And so what now?" Baudwin asked.

"Continue on," Rian replied. "Do as you normally would. Don't fight the current; just let the current take you where you need to go."

"I will do my best."

Baudwin checked his watch, wondering where Matha and Criofan were. He couldn't wait to tell his friends about what had happened. Seemingly, his day had gone all wrong. And yet, if he hadn't gotten angry and then split up with them, he might not have stumbled into the New Arcade.

"I suppose I have Hammer Comb to thank for this," Baudwin said. "How ironic."

Rian cocked his head. "What do you mean?"

"Hammer Comb made me so angry that I was forced to look within. This is what my grandfather was trying to get me to do. How amusing that I'm now more honest with myself, because I played that elven game! In the end, I did follow my grandfather's advice, by giving up on elven contraptions — or at least Hammer Comb."

"Well, at least some good came from that game," Rian said, sarcastically.

"Tell me," Baudwin began, "why you don't like Hammer Comb."

"If you want to understand Hammer Comb," Rian replied, "ask yourself this question: Do the Elves want the Fae to play, or to *obey?*"

"To play or to *obey?*" Baudwin asked, trying to grasp the sense of the question. "The elven lady in the hammer comb booth told me that young ones needed to hone their skills and be prepared."

"That sounds just like Cristin!"[6] Rian exclaimed. "Making everything she does into a cause, without seeing what she's causing. Call me old-fashioned, but if a game has you hammering, you should *learn* something."

"What do you mean?" Baudwin asked.

"All of the old game machines were designed to teach something," Rian said.

"Teach?" Baudwin asked.

"Of course," Rian replied. "Drill Drop teaches timing and dexterity. Steamball, aiming and shooting. And of course," he added, gesturing to the front of the booth, "Gear Chute teaches patience and fortitude in the face of loss."

"Also the fun of winning," Baudwin added.

"But Hammer Comb," Rian declared, "is just ridiculous nonsense. At first they tell you to hammer the plates down, so you'll win the game. Then you find out you can't do that, because the plates only go willy-nilly. This comes after you've torn your hair out trying to figure out what you're doing wrong. And finally, you discover that no matter *what* you do, the game can't be won. But then you win anyway — for no reason. How harebrained is that?"

"Why is the game so pointless?" Baudwin asked.

Rian became serious. "I fear that the Assembly has lost its way," he replied. "Originally, we strove to inspire *Tír Éirí Sióg*, but as of late, we seem more intent

---

6   Pronounced [KRIS-tin]

upon driving the Faeries to distraction. Did you notice something odd about Hammer Comb?"

Baudwin thought. "Other than that there was no point?"

"Hammer Comb doesn't *reset* itself," Rian replied. "There's no real goal, so the game doesn't cycle its inner workings back to the starting point. Never forget, good elven machines like Drill Drop, Steamball, and Gear Chute all reset once the player has won or lost. This is because we Elves revere the cycles of time and progress, by counting and measuring things, and building clocks. So, I ask you: What good is a machine that cannot tell when a job is done, and ready itself for its next use?"

Baudwin mulled over Rian's words. Everything he said made sense. He wondered then why the Elves would invent such a game. Remembering what Rian had said moments before, he asked, "How does Hammer Comb make the Faeries *obey* instead of play?"

But before Rian could explain, there was a crash, the loudest one Baudwin had ever heard, along with a great deal of shrieking and hollering. Both dashed out of the room to the front of the booth. Looking out, they saw that directly across from them, a good part of the food tent had collapsed.

Chapter 16
A FIGHTING CHANCE

Amidst shrieks of anger and yowls of pain, Baudwin and Rian raced toward the tent. "Tell me — what am I to do?" a voice cried out. Anguished, the elven proprietor stood before them, dripping from head to toe with apple pie. Behind him, several wooden shelves lay on the ground, surrounded by jars of raspberry and peach preserves, all of them smashed to smithereens. Blackberry and cherry pies were everywhere.

"A season of growing. . . weeks of canning. . . and *all* the baking!" he wailed as he surveyed the mess, wringing his apron with his hands. Rian stopped to console him, and Baudwin made his way into the partly collapsed tent. Faeries were freeing themselves from a twisted mess of poles and canvas, and piles of ruined bread, cookies, and cakes.

"Are you all right?" Baudwin called out to them.

"Yes," they all nodded, bobbing their heads like robins searching for early morning worms.

Baudwin turned toward the center of the tent. *How ever did this happen?* he wondered, as he made his way through the knocked over tables and chairs. Eager to find the cause of the destruction, he could barely contain his astonishment at what he found.

"Matha! Criofan!" he shouted. There they were, his best friends, covered in blackberry pie, having crashed their racer roller through the side of the tent. Matha sat in the front seat in an apparent state of shock, pasty ooze dangling from his chin. Criofan sat in the back, a stricken look on his face. Sloppy sweet clusters had slithered down his chest and into his lap. Seeing that neither of his friends was hurt, Baudwin fell to the ground, rolling from side-to-side, laughing until his sides hurt.

"You think this is funny?" a voice snarled above the turmoil.

Looking up, Baudwin saw a face peering down at him, one with a broad forehead, steely deep green eyes, and a formidably square jaw, all framed by an oily mane of blue-green hair. *So he's the cause of this,* he thought. "Loch!" he exclaimed, jumping to his feet.

"Guess who just ran your friends into the fruit pies?" Loch asked with a prideful smirk.

The look on Loch's face — a tough-minded grin, tinged with wanton conceit — made Baudwin wince. *Not even a punch in the mouth would change that smile*, he thought.

Baudwin was not about to let Loch get the better of him. Before speaking, he dusted himself off and adjusted his belt. "So, Loch," he taunted, "is this what you Roilers do for fun when you're not destroying shrines? Smashing into cakes and pies like stupid fools?"

"I'd be careful if I were you," Loch replied, pointing to the wreckage. "That's the kind of thing Matha said about me — and you can see what just happened to him."

Baudwin ignored him. "Or are you training for Racer Bump?" he laughed. "If so, you're certainly on your way to becoming a champion."

"How would *you* know anything about driving?" Loch asked, as he looked at his friend, who was still sitting in the back seat of the other racer roller. As the Roilers exchanged conspiratorial glances, Baudwin took a closer look at the wreckage. Matha and Criofan were still hemmed in by shelves of bread and other baked goods, unable to extricate themselves from their seats.

Baudwin approached Criofan, who sat with his hand covering his face. "Are you all right?" he asked, as he began clearing the debris.

"He shot me a ways back. . . in the eye. . . with a geyser pistol," he sourly replied, pointing at one of Loch's Roilers.

"He did *what*?" Baudwin asked. Angrily, he dropped the shelf he was holding, which landed with a loud thump. He then turned to face Loch.

"Such disrespect!" he shrieked. "For the *Water*!"

"He deserved what he got," Loch replied. "It was his just deserts for letting *Matha* do the driving." He then strutted closer to the crash scene, assessing the damage.

"As for the Water," he continued, sneering at Criofan, "I would say it served him well — coming as it did, straight out of my geyser pistol."

"One day, you'll atone for those words!" Baudwin exclaimed.

"Only if you bow to them first," Loch replied. He then moved to free his friend, who was sitting in the back seat of the other car, still quite stuck. "Wouldn't you agree?" he asked, as he began clearing the rubble.

Casting a contemptuous look at Baudwin and Criofan, his friend nodded *yes*.

Outraged, Baudwin turned his attention back to Criofan, and working even harder to free him from his prison.

With that, several more Roilers came bursting into the tent. *What a miserable lot*, Baudwin thought. *Always getting their thrills at the expense of others.*

Looking more closely at them, he spotted a young faery lad. Frightened, the young lad ran to Loch. *Teigue!* Baudwin thought. *I hope he's all right.* Teigue looked at Baudwin, and then quickly turned away.

By then, Criofan had freed himself from the car, and was helping Matha out as well. Both began picking chunks of pie off their bodies, leaving dark wet stains all over their clothes. Several Roilers formed a circle around them, mocking their efforts.

"Leave them alone!" Baudwin shouted.

"They do what *I* tell them to do!" Loch shouted back, raising his hand in a tight fist above his head.

"Come on, Matha!" Criofan exclaimed, as he hurried to Baudwin. Seeing this, all the Roilers quickly joined Loch.

Both sides met in an aggressive face-off, with everyone itching to come to blows. Loch pressed himself closely to Baudwin, until Baudwin could feel and smell his putrid breath on his face. Bracing for the worst, Baudwin raised his fists.

However, the skirmish was not to be.

"All of you! I order you — stop now!" a voice commanded above the fray. The uniform the Elve wore meant only one thing: They had better watch their step. Scowling fiercely, he stood with his arms folded squarely across his chest.

Instantly, Both Guilders and Roilers went quiet.

"Ferrell," Baudwin muttered under his breath. "Such timing."

"Who's Ferrell?" Criofan whispered.

"I can't tell you now," Baudwin replied, as he looked warily at Ferrell. "But we certainly could do without him."

"He's more of a threat than a bunch of nasty Roilers?" Matha questioned. "Why?"

"You'll see," Baudwin replied.

Projecting an aura of calm superiority, Ferrell swaggered toward the group, a number of Earth Guards behind him. Upon reaching the group, he paused, surveying them carefully.

"My, my, such enmity," he began. "Such loathing among those who all purport to be of the same *ilk* — the water Faeries. I find this fascinating — truly fascinating indeed. Do tell me. What is all of this about?"

No one spoke for several moments, cowed as they were by Ferrell's disarming presence.

"He had no right," Loch began.

"And *you* are?" Ferrell asked, with a mixture of curiosity and sarcasm.

Baudwin watched Loch take in Ferrell's manner and appearance. *Now he meets someone far more powerful than he is,* he thought, elated. For if Loch did not watch his words and deeds, he would find himself tasting a poison for which there was no antidote.

"I'm Loch," Loch replied, his voice sounding flat, rather than its usual dominating tone.

"*Loch,*" Ferrell repeated. "A strong name for someone so young — and with such *strong* opinions." With that, the two locked eyes. Loch looked steadily at Ferrell, then averted his gaze.

"Do tell us more," Ferrell prompted. "For starters, what has you *so* upset?"

"Him," Loch replied, pointing to Matha. "He had no right to teach my little cousin about old glamorium tablets at Curios & Marvels, or about —"

"You would question the value of learning about our most ancient history?" Ferrell interrupted.

"No. . . I mean, yes. . ." Loch stammered, as he pulled Teigue closely to his side. "He told me at Curios & Marvels that Matha told him about glyphs." As Loch spoke, Teigue closed his eyes, grimacing.

"How endearing," Ferrell replied. "Two cousins, who hold such affection for each other. And the rest of you?" he asked, turning toward Baudwin and his friends. "What do you have to say?"

"*He,*" Baudwin replied, pointing angrily at Loch's lackey, "had no right to shoot my friend in the eye with a geyser pistol — Water is *sacred.*"

"So I've been told by many in the Water Guild," Ferrell replied. "However, none of this explains why you crashed into this tent."

"I didn't crash," Baudwin said, pointing to Loch and his friend. "*They* did, after running down my friends." Baudwin then gestured toward Matha and Criofan.

Ferrell narrowed his eyes, studying the three Faeries. "I see," he began. "I received a report that three young water Faeries were causing trouble at Curios & Marvels, but. . ." Ferrell stopped, as he continued glaring at them. "We'll get to that later."

Baudwin and his friends tried to hide their nervousness, as Ferrell sized up Matha. "So you're the cause of all of this?" he asked. "For teaching glyphs?"

"What's wrong with knowing glyphs?" Matha asked, perturbed.

"Nothing, I suppose," Ferrell replied. "If one is interested in outworn forms of knowledge — especially ones that are fundamentally irrelevant to our current age."

Loch took Ferrell's comment as a cue to take control of the debate, and score a point or two in the process.

"Exactly," he countered. "Glyphs are slow, and dumb, and *stupid,* that's what they are. Letters are much faster and better."

"Why not know both?" Matha asked. "Or are *you* too slow, dumb, and stupid?"

Hearing this, Loch could maintain his composure no longer. He pushed Matha to the ground, knocking off his glasses. Matha landed with a heavy thump, and the promise of several scratches and a bruise or two. Baudwin and Criofan then jumped Loch from behind, pummeling and punching him in the back and sides. Several Earth Guards went for them instantly, but Ferrell called them off, as he appeared to be enjoying the fracas.

Baudwin, Criofan, Loch and the other Roilers tumbled to the ground, kicking and thrashing. As they rolled over each other, the contents of Baudwin's pockets spilled onto the grass. Baudwin grabbed the brass screws and vial of spring Water and sprang to his feet. Frantically, he looked for the coupler, searching through broken pieces of Wood and chunks of pie.

"Missing something?" Loch asked, as he dangled the shiny piece of copper in Baudwin's face.

"Give that back — now!" Baudwin yelled, lunging at him.

"Why should I?" Loch asked. To further taunt Baudwin, he dangled the coupler even closer to his face. As Baudwin tried to grab it back, Loch jerked his hand away. He turned to his friends, laughing. Seeing this, Criofan and Matha rejoined Baudwin, ready to take up the fight.

Ferrell had seen enough.

"All of you — stop!" he shouted, signaling the Earth Guards. Quickly, they stepped toward the rancorous band, grabbing hold of the combatants. Everyone stopped fighting.

Ferrell turned to face Loch. "Now, give me that coupler," he ordered.

"Not until we get our geyser pistol back," Loch declared.

"What geyser pistol?" Ferrell asked.

"The one he stole from us," Loch replied, pointing angrily at Matha.

"Where is it?" Ferrell asked Matha.

"Tell them to check in the racer roller," Matha replied disdainfully.

"Go, then," Ferrell said. With that, one of the Roilers went to retrieve the missing pistol, and then handed it to Loch. Ferrell snatched the coupler from Loch, and handed it to Baudwin.

"Well," Ferrell began, striking a more conciliatory tone, "*I've* always thought that while glyphs tell us where we have been, letters tell us where we are going, *neither* of which tells us —"

"Letters preach, while glyphs teach," Matha recited heatedly, as he wiped off his glasses and put them squarely back on his nose. Hearing this, Loch scowled.

Annoyed by the interruption, Ferrell spoke again. "Now if I may complete *my* sentence: Neither of which, tells us, where. . . we. . . are. . . *now*."

Everyone remained silent, stymied by Ferrell's inference. Seeing this, he continued speaking, obviously delighted with his superior position and his audience's seeming lack of insight.

"You see," he continued, "none of this talk about letters and glyphs, or couplers and geyser pistols, has anything to do with the real matter at hand, which is the crash. And now," he added, motioning toward the Earth Guards to contain the others, "if you will all kindly accompany me outside, we will deal with the truly serious matter — *that.*"

The entire group filed out of the tent like a line of dutiful ants. No one wanted to upset Ferrell any further, for fear of being accosted by the Earth Guards. Once outside, they were met by an agitated throng of Elves and Faeries. Rian was among them, trying to calm the crowd, many of whom were gawking at the damage and commiserating with the proprietor. There he stood like a tragic bard in a play, left to tell his tale of woe to anyone who would listen.

"Who will pay me for my losses?" the proprietor kept asking.

"Who indeed?" an older faery lady in the crowd exclaimed.

"Perhaps those ruffians, over there!" an elven gent cried out, as he gestured angrily toward Criofan and Matha. "I saw them drive their Racer Roller right into the tent." Hearing this, Loch and his friends smiled knowingly at each other.

"They rammed *us* into the tent!" Criofan exclaimed, pointing at Loch and his friend. "*They* should pay. Without them, none of this would have happened."

"None of what?" Loch asked. "Without your incompetence, you mean! We could have ended the drive at any time without so much as a scratch!"

"Like you did at Racer Roller?" Criofan asked indignantly. "Ha! Such skill!"

"What about the tent?" an angry Elve called out from the crowd. "Someone must pay!"

"Yes! Someone must pay!" another voice cried out.

"Silence!" Ferrell exclaimed. "I will not tolerate this asinine bickering any longer! Obviously, someone must pay," he added, as he studied the feuding group of Guilders and Roilers. "The question is," he added, his eyes gleaming, "*Who?*"

"Let them fight it out at the Jab and Jump!" an elven voice cried out.

"Ah, yes, of course, the Jab and Jump — why didn't *I* think of that?" Ferrell asked. Not only did he greatly enjoy basking in the hostility between the Guilders and Roilers, but also his role as the arbitrator.

The Jab and Jump that Ferrell referred to was the contest of quarrel staffing, a means by which Elves and Faeries settled their differences. Frequently, but not always, these contests took place in various arenas throughout the realm.

"You mean the Hop and Hit!" a faery gent cried out. "The winner stays — and the loser pays!"

"Of course," Ferrell concurred, dismissing the faery gent. "Let us not forget, shall we? According to the time-honored custom among Elves and Faeries, should such a duel take place at the Jab and Jump, the winner shall stay in the good graces of those who witness the fight, while the loser must pay whatever price is owed. Now that is *eminently* fair, don't you all agree?"

Rian turned to Ferrell. "Yes, your *eminence*, you of all authorities would know what that is," he said, eyeing the gold buttons on Ferrell's indigo jacket.

Ferrell nodded at him. Baudwin could tell that the two knew each other, but he wasn't sure what Rian had meant by what he said.

"Yes, yes!" many Elves and Faeries shouted their approval.

Ferrell pretended to ignore Rian's remark, instead looking right past him. "The Assembly *always* makes sure things are fair," he replied. Subdued by Ferrell's tone, all parties nodded in agreement.

Seeing this, Ferrell made one final demand, much to everyone's chagrin. "And, I might add, should either of you lose and not be able to pay, said loser will be indentured to *me.*"

Hearing this, Baudwin flinched. "Then we must win," he muttered to Matha and Criofan. Solemnly, they all nodded, trying to appear strong in their resolve, despite their apprehension.

"The Jab and Jump!" a number of Elves chimed in joyous solidarity.

"The Hop and Hit!" some other Faeries shouted.

"The only thing left is to choose who fights," Ferrell declared. "Are there any volunteers?"

"I will fight," Loch announced gruffly.

"Who else?" Ferrell asked.

"I will," Criofan replied, pointing to one of the Roilers. "Since he's the one who shot me in the eye."

"And your name is?" Ferrell asked.

"Criofan."

"Good!" Ferrell exclaimed. "Criofan versus Loch."

◌◈◌

With that, Ferrell ordered the Earth Guards to follow the group. One and all then traipsed toward the arena, which was situated directly between the Old and New Arcade. Rian followed along. As Baudwin and his friends made their way along the path, they were surrounded by rambunctious bands of Faeries and Elves, clamoring to see the fight.

"I've never been to this arena before," Criofan said to Baudwin and Matha as they hurried along. "Have you?"

"No," Baudwin replied. "The Elves built it just this year. Don't worry, it can't be that different from the other ones."

"Baudwin," Matha said, "I've heard this arena is *nothing* like the other ones." Turning to Criofan, he added, "You're in for quite a shock."

"Why?" Criofan asked, his concern mounting.

"We usually quarrel staff on wooden platforms, but here the Elves have built something far more ingenious," Matha explained, trying his best not to frighten his friend. "Each contest is staged differently, so you never know what to expect. As the fight proceeds, the workings of the arena constantly shift. Things get tumultuous. At any given time, anything can change, and you won't know what to do."

Hearing this, Criofan's confidence began to plummet. Baudwin knew he had to act. "Let me fight!" he exclaimed. "I can beat him."

"But I'm the one who got us into this mess," Criofan declared. "I should fight him. Besides, I would really like to wipe that cocky smile off his face, once and for all."

"Actually, I'm the one who crashed," Matha put in guiltily. "I should be the one."

"You must leave this to me," Criofan said, having regained a measure of his confidence.

"Yes," Baudwin added. "From what you just told us, this doesn't seem like a task for the son of the Primary of Concord." Before Matha could respond, they reached their destination.

There before them sat an enormous wooden tub, filled with Water. Its walls reinforced with bronze slats and copper rings, the entire structure looked like an oversized barrel that seemed ready to burst. Imagining how this ominous-looking contraption might behave made Baudwin terribly nervous. As they approached the entrance, a group of Faeries rushed by, pressing them tightly against the side of the wall.

"Go carefully," Matha admonished them, but to no avail. They headed pell-mell toward the bleachers, looking for seats, which rose in staggered concentric circles round the huge basin of Water.

"Let's watch that Roiler lose!" one of them exclaimed gleefully.

Matha slapped Criofan on the back. "See that? If you lose, you'll at least have some disappointed fans."

"Yes," Criofan agreed, trying to appear confident.

"Let *me* disappoint them instead," Baudwin insisted, trying again to talk Criofan out of fighting.

As they spoke, Ferrell appeared behind them, seemingly from out of nowhere. Like a calculating blue heron, he had been stalking them, patiently picking his way through the crowd to keep up with them, and listening intently to every word they said.

With no provocation, he lunged at Criofan, as if to devour him. With his lips slightly parted, he hissed, "Yes! Let Baudwin fight."

Criofan shuddered. Eyeing Ferrell warily, he said, "Perhaps I should wait for a more compelling adversary. Besides, I wouldn't want to rob Baudwin of his chance for glory."

"I will fight," Baudwin declared calmly.

Criofan took in Ferrell's demeanor. The Elve was master of a game, with rules that none could even guess at. Baudwin could sense that Criofan didn't want to back down, but the force of Ferrell's will was far more than he could defy. He watched his friend's resolve crumble into a feeble gesture of good intentions. Ruefully, Criofan looked at Baudwin, and then nodded a simple *yes.*

"Good," Ferrell replied. "Baudwin, you will enter from the right, and meet me in the center island. See that you go quickly." Leaving Baudwin to his own devices, he then turned and strode toward the entrance.

For an instant, Baudwin wanted to bolt from the entire scene. Yet he knew he couldn't, for then the responsibility would fall upon Criofan, or even worse, Matha, which he simply could not allow. Seeing his friends smiling at him, he quickly found his courage again.

"Baudwin, use your acrobatic skills to your advantage, and beat that bully!" Matha exclaimed.

"Good luck!" Criofan and Matha shouted. They then went to find their seats.

Baudwin hurried along the bottom of the bleachers, searching for the entrance. A quarter of the way around, he reached a high wooden door supported by a wide stone arch. He flung open the door and raced up a long flight of steps, until he finally reached the top. Panting, he crouched with his hands on his thighs, taking in the sight.

Before him sat an enormous tank of dark blue-green Water. *How strangely like the millpond this is,* he thought. Shielding his eyes from the Sun, he looked anxiously at what lay before him. *The Elves were good at trapping the Water. Just as I now am trapped,* he thought. *For if I don't win, I will . . .* He didn't want to think about what would happen if he lost. Indentured servitude to an Elve, especially to one of Ferrell's stature, would be truly dreadful. No doubt he could expect long hours of hard labor that would make working at the millpond seem like going to a festival.

A long narrow walkway stretched from where Baudwin stood to a large bronze island in the middle of the giant tub. Ferrell stood in the very center, obviously a longstanding veteran of these events, holding a bronze speaker horn in his hand. Looking across the tub, Baudwin spied the menacing silhouette of his opponent — Loch.

Seeing that Baudwin had reached the edge of the tub, Ferrell turned first to him, and then to Loch. "Come to the center, now Baudwin, now Loch!" he shouted. Despite the horn's unwieldy size, he seemed to enjoy speaking and hearing his own voice, which blasted into the stands like a bellowing moose.

Baudwin made his way along the long bronze walkway leading to the island, moving cautiously to avoid falling into the Water. In his relatively short Life — a mere two hundred years — he had done his share of quarrel staffing, but never at an arena like this, mainly because until now, he hadn't been involved in any great altercation. With every step he took, the crowd roared with anticipation, spurring him on, despite his apprehension.

He looked at Ferrell and Loch, unsure of whom he should fear the most: *the one who would dominate me with what he knows, or the other, who would do so with his blows?* However, he had little time to ruminate any further, for he had reached the center of the island. Loch stared directly at him. Both stood just a few feet away from each other, on either side of Ferrell.

"Welcome, one and all!" Ferrell shouted through the speaker horn.

Scanning the crowd, Baudwin spotted a number of Faeries and Elves sitting in the first row of bleachers, laughing and cheering. "Quarrel staffing at the Jab and Jump!" an elven gent shouted above the din.

"No, the Hop and Hit!" a faery lady shouted back.

"The Jab and Jump!" the Elve cried out even more insistently. Instantly, choruses of "Hop and Hit" followed by "Jab and Jump" broke out among the Elves and Faeries. As the argument intensified, each side tried to outshout the other, much to everyone's amusement.

After several moments, the shouts sounded less humorous and more bellicose. Ferrell pressed the speaker horn even closer to his lips. "Now! Now!" he shouted. "That is quite *enough!*"

"Whose side are you on?" an angry Faery screamed.

"Yes!" an irate Elve shouted. "Whose side?"

"Must I always be the perfectly balanced scale, to weigh all of your petty differences?" Ferrell shouted, trying to control the crowd.

"Who but a Master of Gold could handle the weighing of such a hefty treasure?" an Elve shouted back. Hearing this, the crowd settled down somewhat.

"Who indeed?" Ferrell asked, smiling. "How I do so love the Jab and Jump, or should I say, the Hop and Hit!" Hearing this, the crowd roared its approval.

Pointing to Baudwin and Loch, he added, "Now, instead of me having to serve as balancer, these feuding Faeries must do so themselves, for our entertainment." As large numbers of Elves and Faeries jumped to their feet, again the crowd roared, "Jab and Jump!" and then "Hop and Hit!" over and over again.

"Sit down! Sit down!" Ferrell shouted. Ignoring his order, they remained standing. Once again, both sides appeared to be on the brink of violence.

"Sit down, I say!" Ferrell commanded. Strutting around the island, he made another attempt to rein in the crowd. "Do you even *know* the story about this Jab and Jump, or Hop and Hit, that you're all arguing about?" he shouted through the horn. "Probably not — you rabble — so I am *now* going to tell you what you should know."

Hearing this, a ripple of expectant silence coursed through the audience. Everyone sat down and prepared to listen.

Basking in the crowd's submission, Ferrell shouted, "A story, I might add, that is as comical as it is tragic!" He then paused to gather his thoughts.

"Let's hear it then!" a voice shouted. Ferrell began speaking:

"The Jab and Jump, or the Hop and Hit, is an ancient custom that began as a game, a game the Elves invented as a clever way to resolve disputes of almost any kind. Legend says that in those times, Elves and Faeries fought mostly to settle their disagreements, and not to injure or to take each other to Annwyn."

Ferrell paused for a moment, as if to consider the import of what he had just said.

"I myself cannot fathom such maturity of spirit," he declared, grandly gesturing toward the crowd, "especially after witnessing the entrenched and overarching rivalry before me today — a rivalry, I might add, that could be contained only by someone such as myself, someone with a fair-minded attitude, and all the proper finesse."

Fair-minded indeed! Baudwin thought angrily to himself. *How self-serving of him. Surely he is joking.*

In response to Ferrell's grandiose assertion, a large group of Elves began laughing and cheering. To counter their enthusiasm, a small yet vocal number of Faeries shouted out insults, booing him repeatedly. Ferrell nodded in both directions, seemingly to maintain the entertaining, if not instructive, hold he now had upon the crowd.

"Never mind," a voice called out. "Get back to the story!"

Thus, he continued:

"As I said, in those times, Elves and Faeries fought mostly to settle their disagreements. Although the Elves invented the game, over time, the Faeries joined in, improving it a great deal, both with their staff fighting expertise as well as with rules for how the game should be played." As Ferrell spoke, both Elves and Faeries alike cheered at the mention of their respective contributions. Ferrell continued speaking:

"For generations, a story was passed down in towns and hamlets throughout *Tír na nÓg* about how Laserian,[1] the Elve who invented the game, had fought with Rohan,[2] the Faery who improved the game.

"Then, one side — no one remembers which — noticed the game did not yet have a name," Ferrell continued. "Elves and Faeries alike coined a phrase,

---

[1]   Pronounced [La-ZER-ee-an]
[2]   Pronounced [RO-hawn]

each side claiming that their name was more suitable, and should therefore be the standard."

"The Jab and Jump!" some Elves called from the crowd.

"Yes," Ferrell continued. "believing their claim to be superior because —"

"We *invented* the game!" an irate elven voice shouted out from the crowd, interrupting him.

Ferrell nodded his agreement before speaking again.

"The Hop and Hit!" some Faeries called out.

"Yes, yes," Ferrell continued. "Feeling their claim was appropriate because —"

"We *imagined* what the game could be!" another angry Faery shouted, interrupting him again.

"Such idiocy," Ferrell muttered under his breath as he turned toward Baudwin. "That I must be the arbiter between these recalcitrant mules and their ridiculous tug-o-war."

Yet, he continued:

"Once the argument began, each side wanted their way to the bitter end, which brings us again to the story of Laserian and Rohan."

Ferrell adjusted his collar and straightened his stance, before resuming:

"The Faeries called Laserian the 'lamebrain,' while the Elves called Rohan the 'milksop.' This, indeed, was highly amusing, because if either of these monikers had been truly descriptive, neither of them would have been able to fight each other for hundreds of years — which they both did, as incredible as it may sound. When they finally tired of the contest, everyone believed they would come to a reconciliation, but on the exact day they were to announce the compromise, something happened." Ferrell then fixed his eyes on a group of Elves in the bleachers.

"Do any of you know what happened?" he called out to them. Lowering his voice, he snickered to Loch and Baudwin, "None of them will know."

But, as he was about to discover — someone *did* know.

"I remember!" an Elve shouted to Ferrell from a few rows away. "Laserian's son said, 'Father, you must not stop! Show that milksop what a goldbricking weakling he really is!'"

Hearing this, the Elves in the crowd roared with laughter, jeering and cheering.

"That's correct," Ferrell replied. "Both Bran,[3] the elven son of Laserian, and Liam,[4] the faery son of Rohan, had gathered that day with a crowd of onlookers

---

[3] Pronounced [BRAN]
[4] Pronounced [LEE-am]

to watch their fathers lay down their staffs. Yet, both ended up accusing their fathers of giving in to the other."

Ferrell then turned his attention to a group of Faeries. "Do any of you recall what Liam said back?"

"We Faeries know our history — yes, we do!" a Faery shouted. "Rohan's son said, 'Do not listen, Father! Beat that oafish halfwit within an inch of his Life, until he finally sees the error of his ways!'"

Hearing this, the Faeries in the crowd rose from their seats, laughing and jeering.

"There is even more to this story," Ferrell called out, determined not to let either side take control of the debate.

"And so it went," he continued, "that Laserian passed his well-worn staff on to Bran, and Rohan passed his on to Liam. The feud over the name continued for at least another seven hundred years, before they too passed on to Annwyn, neither side ever conceding to the other."

Hearing this, the crowd fell silent. Having gained their full attention, Ferrell smugly strutted back and forth, preparing to speak.

What a long-winded dissertation this is turning out to be, Baudwin thought, sighing with disgust.

"Why did such a foolhardy endeavor continue for so long?" Ferrell asked. "Was it simply Bran and Liam's mutual mistrust of each other that made them follow in their fathers' footsteps? And why did countless Elves and Faeries take up the dispute, engaging in what many believed was the same willful, ugly, and senseless conflict for thousands of years?"

Again, the crowd was silent, for few, if any, knew what Ferrell was about to say.

Standing between Baudwin and Loch, Ferrell whispered, "Just as I thought. They're nothing but a bunch of ignorant dimwits, filled with endless cravings for excitement, and utterly devoid of discrimination." Loch nodded in agreement.

Ferrell then turned toward the crowd, and repeated the question he had just asked them:

"Why then, *did* they engage in such a conflict for so long?" Before answering, he paused one last time for dramatic effect.

"Because!" he shouted. "Because the game *represented* them so well! For you see, a game to settle a conflict is one thing. But a never-ending conflict over the *name* of the game ensures that we never *ever* tire of playing — or fighting!"

The crowd erupted in laughter, cheering, and clapping.

Outrageous! thought Baudwin. *How blithely he used that story to make us all look like bickering simpletons.*

Echoing Ferrell's sentiment an elven gent shouted, "Then let us play!"

Ferrell nodded at the Elve and then summoned help. In an instant, two young elven gents appeared before him. Each one held a staff made of red oak. As was the custom, they handed one to Baudwin and the other to Loch, making sure they received them at exactly the same moment.

Ferrell then declared, "According to the time-honored custom among Elves and Faeries, the winner of this duel at the Jab and Jump, or should I also say the Hop and Hit, shall *stay* in the good graces of those who witness the fight. The loser must *pay* whatever price is owed. Should either side be unable to meet their obligation, said loser will be indentured to me, the arbitrator, until the price is paid."

Hearing this, the crowd hummed with anticipation.

"A level start, but not for long!" Ferrell shouted. "Let the water decide who wins this quarrel. The first to fall off the platform loses. Beware of the steps you take!" He and the two Elves then swiftly exited the island, leaving Baudwin and Loch to their fate. The walkways leading to the center island quickly retracted out of sight.

"The winner stays, the loser pays!" a faery lady screamed at the top of her lungs, laughing hysterically.

Distracted by her antics, Baudwin's eyes went toward the crowd. Matha and Criofan had managed to find seats in the very front row, with Rian sitting in between them. All three were cheering him on.

Despite Matha's enthusiasm, Baudwin could tell that he was worried. Perhaps he was afraid that Baudwin might have another bout, for the Water was right below him. This, however, was the least of Baudwin's concerns.

Far more frightening was the prospect of losing the contest. For then, not only would he be bound to Ferrell, but he would have to spend all of his free time working off his debt, unable to explore the path where Glamorium might lead him.

Baudwin put his hand over his vest pocket, feeling the egg that was buttoned securely inside. He wondered if the *Dúrúnghlas* would bring him luck. However, he let go of the thought, for he didn't want to jinx himself. Glamorium deserved respect.

This fight was his own. *I must beat him,* he resolved, as he turned toward Loch.

Defiantly, Loch stared back at him. "So, *you,* not Criofan, are the one I face," he sneered. "I can easily beat any one of you. Before I toss you in the Water, I will crush you like the helpless worm that you are!"

"Not on this day!" Baudwin shot back.

"You'll be mewling for your mother while you shovel grand horn droppings for Ferrell," Loch added, laughing.

"*You're* the one who'll be shoveling grand horn droppings," Baudwin retorted, as he gripped his staff in front of him, his hands shoulder-length apart. "And, you'll have no time to steal their hides!"

Instantly, they came to blows. As Loch lunged at Baudwin, Baudwin stepped aside and shoved the center of his staff into Loch's flank. Loch staggered but quickly struck back — one, two, three, times — while Baudwin vigorously defended himself. On the third strike, as Baudwin lifted his staff high above his head with both arms, Loch got in a decent jab. Baudwin stumbled. A cry of "Jab and Jump!" rose from the stands. Loch then smashed down on Baudwin, but it was a glancing blow — *whack!*

Baudwin stumbled and then recovered. As their staffs locked together, they struggled, until Loch gained the upper hand. He placed his foot in the center of Baudwin's chest and shoved hard. Baudwin staggered backward several steps. For a moment it looked like he would fall over, but — quick as a cat — his years of acrobatic training helped him regain his balance. The crowd roared appreciatively, like a pod of hungry seals tossed a bucket of live fish.

Without warning, an ominous rumble emanated from the center of the island. Vibrations rippled in circles toward the perimeter, shaking the very foundation upon which they stood. As the force of the tremors shot up their legs, Baudwin and Loch lost their footing, and were sent tumbling away from each other.

The entire island shifted violently, tipping from top to bottom, bottom to top, until it seesawed so high that neither of them could stand upright. Both slipped down, heading toward the Water. Shocked, Loch stumbled as he tried to regain his footing, and scrambled up the pitching platform. He then darted toward the top of the island, gaining less and less ground as the angle steepened. With his last step, he barely managed to grab the edge to keep himself from slipping back toward Baudwin. At the same time, Baudwin teetered precariously, splaying his legs as wide as he could. Wedging his staff into a crack, he managed to keep from falling off the bottom of the platform and into the Water.

As both clung to opposite sides of the island, they struggled to hang on. Loch groaned, holding his staff with one hand, while clamping onto the edge with the other. Seeing his distress, Baudwin shouted delightedly, "Before you crush me, the Water will surely take you down!"

Slowly, the island lowered, becoming level again, and still. Both opponents crouched down to study the other — wondering if the movements would suddenly start up again. Satisfied that the wild rumbling and tilting had stopped, Loch headed toward the center. Grasping his staff in front of him with both hands at shoulder level, he planted his feet firmly on the island in a wide stance, his knees slightly bent. He then boldly thrust out his chest, hunching his shoulders as high as he could.

The bear has his methods, and he is very strong, but he is also heavy and slow, Baudwin thought. *Now I will make my move.*

Baudwin ran to meet Loch, holding his staff in front of him. Standing before his opponent, he assumed his own stance, with both hands at shoulder level, legs apart, and knees slightly bent. Stepping forward onto his right leg, he bent his knee deeply as he went. He held that position for a moment, then brought his leg back to center. He then stepped back with the same leg, again bending his knee deeply, and holding his staff in front of him at shoulder level.

The stag is not as powerful, but he is agile, faster, and more alert, he affirmed to himself.

With that, their staffs cracked again and again, as each sought an opening that would lead to a winning blow. However, a grinding sound of metal upon metal signaled that this was not to be. Before either of them could make another move, the island began rocking again with great force. As Baudwin slid to the left, he noticed a bronze plate rising out of the Water — about four feet across. Scanning the perimeter, he noticed eleven more plates had risen to form a ring around the island — like numbers on a clock. The distance from each plate to the center island was near enough to attempt a jump, yet spaced so dangerously that any miscalculation would end in disaster. From afar, Baudwin saw that each plate was marked with a number.

Seeing this, Baudwin thought angrily, *Will this confounded machine just stop and let us fight?*

But again, this was not to be. Before his eyes, another ring rose out of the Water featuring twelve platforms, each one about eight feet across and marked with a number. The platforms made an even larger ring around both the center island and the inner circle of plates. Excited by the dangerous uncertainty the players now faced, the crowd began to chant, "Baudwin! Baudwin!" Others cried out, "Loch! Loch!"

As the tumultuous rocking began to subside, Baudwin placed his full attention on what to do next. Beneath his feet, the island was descending into the Water, and would be gone in a matter of seconds. Whirling around, he watched Loch race all the way to his right.

Baudwin nearly panicked. Matha had warned him that the game would change in unpredictable ways, but he could not have known that the center island itself would disappear. Beating Loch would be much harder than anticipated.

Loch broke right, jumping onto the nearest inner plate. Quickly, he calculated his next move, struggling to master the grinding gears and lurching plates of the ever-shifting Hop and Hit arena.

Instinctively, Baudwin turned to his left, raising his staff, until the tip pointed toward the sky. As he sped to the outer edge of the island, he could feel his feet sinking toward the Water.

I will not end this as the fool! he vowed, taking less than a second to plot his next move.

The crowd went wild. If Baudwin did not act quickly, he would lose.

As the Water reached his ankles, Baudwin had little time to escape. He ran to the edge of the island and wedged the tip of his staff into a deep crack. Leaning forward, he nearly slipped, but was able to push off, and then vault into a flying leap. He soared to safety, first over the inner ring of plates, to the outer ring of platforms, where he landed, with a heavy thud, on the third one.

Narrowly, he had made the jump — by only a few inches. Looking back, he saw that the center island where he and Loch had begun their fight was now submerged. Loch stood diametrically opposite him on the ninth platform of the outer ring, brandishing his staff high above his head.

The crowd roared with excitement, cheering them on.

Despite their considerable fighting skills, neither Baudwin nor Loch was prepared to deal with the ever-changing arrangement of the plates and platforms. With a distance between them and less pressure to fight, both took a few moments to regain their composure.

Baudwin flourished his staff busily, twirling it in a wide circle with his left hand, as he shifted forward onto his left leg. Passing his right hand under his left forearm to grab the center of the staff, he then continued to twirl in a wide circle with his right hand, shifting backward onto his right leg. He then repeated this sequence, passing his staff from left to right hand, over and over again.

Baudwin's *stag* flourishing brought cheers from the crowd.

From the corner of his eye, he saw Loch performing a similar sequence. But, instead of shifting his weight from front to back, he stepped forward with his left leg, then his right, turning halfway around as he went to face the opposite direction. He stepped back onto his left leg as he came out of the turn, tapping his staff on the ground near his right foot as he paused. He then repeated the sequence over and over again, moving rhythmically, and twirling his staff with even greater skill.

Loch's *bear* flourishing brought even more cheers than his own had. Baudwin scowled.

"When are you both going to stop your fancy dancing and *fight*?" a voice jeered from the crowd.

Another voice shouted, "Let's see the fight! C'mon, you timorous boars! Fight!" More rowdy voices joined the chorus, heckling and hooting at them.

Enough! Baudwin thought. *Now I must act.*

Provoked by Loch's flamboyant moves, and the taunts of the crowd, Baudwin jumped to plate number four of the inner ring. He leapt again, landing on the fourth platform of the outer ring. Loch mirrored him by jumping to plate number eight of the inner ring, and then the eighth platform of the outer ring.

They were now closer to each other. In only a few more jumps they would meet. Baudwin felt his confidence rising. The plates and platforms were indeed challenging, but he was more agile than Loch, and skillfully passed his way along them.

Without hesitating, Baudwin jumped toward the inner ring, landing on plate number five. He then did an aerial cartwheel, landing directly on the fifth platform of the outer ring.

Racing to confront Baudwin, Loch jumped from plate to platform four more times — inner, outer, inner, outer — until he ended up on the sixth platform of the outer ring. From there he advanced forward, aggressively swinging his staff while practicing a number of sequencing targets — head on the right, then left, ear on the right, then left, followed by side, ankle, belly, and groin.

Staring across from Baudwin, Loch growled, "All right, you fancy-toed, glyph-wearing lout, now we'll see how tough you are."

Undeterred, Baudwin catapulted onto the sixth *inner* plate and then the sixth *outer* platform. At last, the two adversaries stood face to face.

"Six six, they're in a fix!" Ferrell shouted from the crowd.

"Six six, they're in a fix!" the crowd roared back.

The fight now began in earnest. *Clack, clack, clack* went their staffs, with such steady intensity that the sound itself became an insulating bubble between them and the noisy goings-on of the crowd. They attacked each other fiercely, striking and guarding, jumping and ducking, blocking and thrusting with naught but one thought in mind: to drive the other to the edge of the platform and shove him into the cold, unforgiving Water.

Loch whirled around suddenly, swinging his staff at a low angle as he went. With a sharp whipping motion, he attempted to sweep Baudwin's feet out from under him. To avoid the strike, Baudwin jumped high into the Air, with his knees pressed tightly against his chest.

As he dropped toward the platform, Loch whirled around again, this time swinging his staff higher and faster as he went. Baudwin retaliated with a downward smash. Their staffs met and remained tightly pressed against each other, testing and taxing the strength of both combatants.

In an effort to seize the upper hand, Loch shoved away and then struck. Baudwin quickly struck back, locking his staff on top of Loch's. Using his greater strength, Loch pushed Baudwin's staff upward, forcing him to stretch higher and higher. The bear was overpowering the stag. Both continued struggling against each other, until with one last push from Loch, Baudwin was forced to pivot to his side.

Loch had forced his staff downward, over Baudwin's, locking them both in place.

"Six six — what a fix!" Ferrell shouted. The crowd roared with delight.

There they stood, side by side, breathing heavily, looking as if they had been nailed together like boards in a fence — at the shoulders, ribs, and hips — with their staffs crossed and their legs spread apart. Loch had placed his right leg over Baudwin's left, to block him from moving. As he pressed his right shoulder into Baudwin's side, he grunted, "Soon you will see just who the Water chooses."

Loch's greater size and strength almost made Baudwin topple over. If he did, he would then be easy prey. However, luck was with Baudwin and the platform began to rumble. Slowly, it lowered. Loch continued to press harder.

Obviously, he hoped to knock Baudwin off before he jumped away from the platform. Yet, a sudden jolt made Loch lose his footing. Baudwin escaped, running and jumping to plate number seven of the inner ring. Loch regained his footing and followed.

The plate was half as wide as the platform, with much less room to fight. Even Loch seemed intimidated. Baudwin and Loch eyed each other steadily, waiting for the other to make a move.

But, the game would make the move for them, for the plate they stood on began to descend as well.

"The seventh plate — they must not wait!" Ferrell shouted.

But it wasn't just the seventh plate. The entire circle of plates quickly lowered. Baudwin jumped to the seventh platform. Loch followed. Now only the platforms were above the Water, but all of them were still slowly sinking. They struck blows, but stopped, their eyes darting here and there. Time was running out.

With no plates to jump to, Baudwin knew he had to get away from Loch. He vaulted to another platform. The distance was farther, but he made the jump. Where would he go if all the plates and platforms were under Water? To his relief, he saw that the inner ring of plates was again rising out of the Water. Quickly, he jumped to the eighth plate. Now the platforms were under Water.

"Stop running, you coward!" Loch yelled as he vaulted after him.

His footing steady, Baudwin chose to fight again. However, the narrow plate had little room to maneuver, giving Loch the advantage. Rushing Baudwin, he used his greater strength, pressing his staff against him, twisting his torso, and leaning in with all his might. He pushed Baudwin across the plate, right up to the edge. Baudwin stumbled. With the end of his staff, Loch then shoved Baudwin hard.

Baudwin dropped his staff and careened off the plate.

I'm done for, he thought. Desperately, he grabbed for anything he could.

The audience jumped to its feet, roaring. Loch gloated gleefully. As Baudwin's feet touched the dark icy Water, he recoiled in shock. A hush came over the crowd.

"The fight is not over until the blade is *fully* quenched," Ferrell's voice boomed.

All was not lost.

In the midst of the chaos, Baudwin had managed to cling to the edge of the plate. Up to his knees in Water, he kicked his legs, splashing frantically, holding onto the rim. Pain shot through his fingers as he tried not to let go.

"*Now* are you afraid?" Loch asked. Grinning, he leaned over Baudwin. Beads of sweat dripped down his face and into the gloaming pool, which held their fate. Raising his arm high above his head, he readied himself to deliver the blow that would knock Baudwin completely into the Water.

As Baudwin looked up at him, his fingers felt as if they would shatter from grasping the cold bronze plate. Unwilling to concede defeat, he remembered his training. *If the stag does not flee to higher ground, he will surely lose his Life,* he thought.

As Loch's blow fell toward Baudwin's head, Baudwin let go of the plate with his left hand. Dangling from the ledge with his right hand, he swung his body around, until his back was facing the plate. Still hanging from his right hand, he then grabbed the plate with his left.

Wham! went Loch's staff. Missing Baudwin by a hair's breadth, the blow hammered the edge of the plate. Baudwin then let go of the plate with his right hand, and swung his body over, until he was again facing the ledge.

His acrobatic trick — shimmying with a twist — had worked. Before Loch could strike again, Baudwin pulled himself up onto the plate, grabbing his staff. The crowd cheered, amazed by his dexterity.

The inner ring of plates was descending again, so Baudwin devised a new strategy. *The stag must tire out the bear,* he thought.

"Start fighting, you lummox!" he shouted. Enraged, Loch came at him.

Baudwin turned tail and then leapt onto the ninth, tenth, and finally, the eleventh plate. Looking back, he could see Loch lumbering toward him, noticeably winded.

"*Now* who's afraid?" Baudwin taunted.

"Not I!" Loch bellowed, as he reached Baudwin, who waited for him. Quickly, Loch struck, but Baudwin countered easily. His plan had worked, for Loch's blows had weakened.

Baudwin seized the moment. *Crack!* He landed a blow on Loch's shoulder. Loch winced, but countered much faster than Baudwin expected, striking his thigh. Pain shot through his leg. Baudwin couldn't believe his rival's endurance. *Will I ever beat this putrid boar?* he thought.

Baudwin then noticed that the outer ring of platforms was beginning to ascend. As he readied himself to jump again, something caught his attention. The inner ring of plates had almost descended into the Water, but the center island where they had begun their fight was rising out of the Water. *Why is this happening?* he wondered.

"Baudwin!" someone shouted.

Scanning the crowd, he saw Matha, Criofan, and Rian, cheering him on. Waving his arms, Rian stood up and then pointed at the center island. Baudwin remembered what he had said:

Good elven machines always reset.

Baudwin then knew what he had to do — he jumped to the outer ring of platforms and turned around. His ruse was working. Loch was on his heels. Running toward Loch, he feinted to one side and then darted to the other, causing Loch's blow to glance off him.

Now that Baudwin was close in, he made his move. He tripped Loch with his staff, and Loch fell upon the platform. Baudwin would have liked nothing more than to try to shove Loch off the platform, but he had something much better in mind for the Roiler. Firmly holding his staff, he raced several paces ahead. Upon reaching the edge of the platform, he performed a roundoff into a front aerial, landing on a plate of the inner ring — almost at water level. He then vaulted to the center island, which was still rising, barely making the jump. The crowd gasped and Guilders cheered as Baudwin's plan became clear.

Smiling gleefully, he turned to face Loch.

Loch didn't know it yet, but Baudwin had outsmarted him.

Winded from his fall, Loch took a few moments to catch his breath. He stood up awkwardly, and noticed that all the platforms were sinking. He ran to jump, but stopped. The entire inner ring of plates had already disappeared into the Water. Desperately, he vaulted toward Baudwin, but the distance was too great. With a look of rage and bewilderment on his face, he fell short of his target and landed in the Water.

Seeing his rival's defeat, Baudwin raised his staff high above his head. "Now we know who's going to pay for all those pies!" he shouted. Hearing this, the audience laughed uproariously.

Both walkways then extended to the center island, one on either side. Within moments, Ferrell had made his way toward Baudwin, accompanied by a number of Earth Guards. Several Elves joined Baudwin on the island to reclaim his staff and congratulate him, as was the custom. As they did, Ferrell shouted above the din of the crowd, "Baudwin is the winner!"

"You just got lucky after you tripped me!" Loch shouted from below, spitting out mouthfuls of Water.

"Luck indeed." Baudwin scoffed. "I knew if the center island rose, the inner and outer rings would descend — completing the cycle!" Gratefully, he saluted Rian. "Just as the Moon must go through all of its phases, so too do all good machines reset themselves!" Rian shouted his approval.

"Well then," Ferrell shouted, as he gestured toward Baudwin and then Loch, "we can certainly see who the smarter one is, can't we?" The entire audience roared with laughter.

"So smart that he searches for what doesn't exist!" Loch yelled, pointing up at Baudwin.

None in the crowd knew what Loch meant, and Baudwin paid his words little heed. "*Fool!*" Baudwin shouted triumphantly. "You've been beaten twice today — by my skill and by your own lack of wits!"

With that, Ferrell turned his attention to Loch, who was still spluttering and thrashing about, as he tried to find a way out of the Water. Several of his gang had gathered on the stairs next to the giant tub, yelling at him to come to them. One of them threw a rope into the Water.

Angrily, Loch refused the help, determined to get out of the Water all on his own. He swam to the center island and climbed up a ladder. Two Elves attempted to help him up, but he shoved them away. There he stood before Ferrell and the others, dripping wet and trying his best to ignore the mocking taunts of the crowd.

Seeing his glowering face, Ferrell shot him a scornful look. "Not only did you lose, but now you must pay."

"I cannot repay such a debt," Loch replied insolently.

"Well then, according to the law of *Tír na nÓg*, you are now indentured to me," Ferrell declared curtly.

Loch opened his mouth to speak, but seeing the phalanx of Earth Guards who were ready to follow Ferrell's every command, he remained silent. Turning to Baudwin, he muttered, "*This* time, the Water saved you."

Having just made their way along the path and onto the island, Matha and Criofan ran toward Baudwin. Hollering and laughing, they grabbed his legs, hoisted him off the ground, and up onto their shoulders. As the crowd continued to chant, "Baudwin! Baudwin!" they paraded him in a circle around the edge of the bronze island for all to see.

Baudwin took in the entire sight, uplifted by his victory and sharing in the euphoria of the crowd. Looking at the Water below, he wondered if Loch was right. Had the Water saved him? *No*, he thought. This time an Elve had saved him — a Druid of Guidance.

Chapter 17

A VERY SWEET RUCKUS

G iddy with excitement, Baudwin and his friends left the Engineerium through the East Petal tunnel. Having decided not to take the main road, they made their way through the Woods, laughing and talking as they went.

"Baudwin!" Criofan exclaimed. "You must tell us! How did you know the machine would reset at the Hop and Hit — and that you would gain the upper hand?"

"I will tell you," Baudwin replied, "but first you must explain to me why you kept your driving a secret."

"I simply didn't want you to think I had placed my interest in driving above the ways of the Water Guild," Criofan replied.

"Good," Baudwin said, slapping his friend on the back. "Because I'd hate to have to call you out for teasing me about my interest in Magniglow — especially since you were so busy racing around with the Elves, and getting into trouble with the Roilers."

"We sure did get into trouble," Matha added. "So much that I wasn't sure we would prevail."

"But we did, thanks to Baudwin," Criofan beamed, as he draped his arm around Baudwin's shoulder.

"I'm happy to see you two are friends again," Matha said. "Concord has prevailed, as I knew it would." Baudwin and Criofan nodded at him and smiled.

"Is your eye all right?" Baudwin asked, turning to Criofan.

Lightly, Criofan touched his eye. "Yes," he replied. "But answer me this: Since Matha and I were the ones who crashed, why did you insist on fighting Loch?"

Baudwin started to speak, but stopped. Surely, the answer was simple. Loch was certainly asking for someone to put him in his place. Baudwin wanted to say just this, yet no words left his lips and he wasn't sure why. He was like a flooding stream, one that forked in too many directions, running this way and that, never finding its tributary. Remembering how being honest with Rian had served him, he decided to heed the lesson of the Triquetra.

"Everything was my fault," Baudwin replied. "If I hadn't gotten so angry, we wouldn't have gone our separate ways, and none of what happened after that would ever have taken place. So, the fighting was up to me. I always learn too late what my feelings are trying to tell me."

Hearing this, Criofan smiled appreciatively.

Matha looked at his friends. "How did you know?" he asked.

"What?" Baudwin replied.

"That the machine — the Hop and Hit — would reset?"

Baudwin then explained to his friends how when he was at the Gear Chute booth, Rian had told him that well-designed machines always reset. When the center island rose again, he saw the pattern of how the machine was working. The plates and platforms moved in a sequence — eventually resetting — so the pattern would start over again.

"That's how I got the advantage, and bested Loch," he said with a wink.

"So, you were able to think ahead for a change?" Matha asked, playfully boxing his friend on the shoulder.

"Watch out," Baudwin said, rubbing the spot. "Loch got me there." Wishing to give credit where credit was due, he continued, "I'm lucky Rian mentioned this before the fight, or I might have lost."

Thoughts bubbled in Baudwin's mind. Perhaps Loch was right and the Water did save him, for in leading him to Rian, he had discovered how the machine worked. And then he had won the fight.

"That was very lucky for you," Criofan said. "Not that Loch got you, but that you knew what to do to get him."

"You actually beat that abominable bully!" Matha exclaimed.

"And what a roaring fight it was — to the very end!" Criofan exclaimed. "I don't think I've ever seen a better one," he added, beaming with satisfaction.

"Did you see Loch's face as he sank into the Water?" Matha chortled gleefully. "He looked so defeated! And I loved how you tripped him on the platform and then vaulted off! All of our rigorous training paid off!"

"In that way, we *all* beat him," Criofan agreed.

"He deserved to be knocked in twice," Matha chuckled.

With that, Baudwin ran several yards ahead of them until he reached a large boulder. He scrambled to the top, and then stood up.

"Now Matha," he said, looking sternly down upon them both, with his fists resting firmly on his hips. "According to the Faery Code of Manners, one must not revel in triumph after defeating an adversary, but remain honorable, respectful, and above reproach."

Matha and Criofan looked incredulously at Baudwin, but this did not stop him from continuing to admonish them. "Didn't you learn this when you were Faefries?" He then recited:

A Faery must not gloat

Or he may find himself afloat

Drowning in anger

In a sea of blame

Without a friend or a boat

Kelven had taught Baudwin this poem when he was very little. Growing up, he had heard many times that when a Faery gloats he may feel that he's afloat, but actually, he's sinking. "The sea of blame drowns everyone," Kelven had said.

Criofan obviously knew the meaning. Exasperated, he ran his fingers through his pale blue hair, tugging on the ends. "I can't believe you're saying this!" he exclaimed. "Really, Baudwin!"

"Why not? It's the faery *way*."

"But surely that disgusting lout deserves our. . ." Matha began. Seeing the look of intense disapproval on Baudwin's face, he stopped speaking mid-sentence.

Baudwin folded his arms squarely across his chest. He lowered his head, and tapped his foot repeatedly on the ground, demonstrating his displeasure. No one said a word.

Abruptly, he raised his head and flashed them both a wide, impish grin. He then finished Matha's sentence. "But doesn't that disgusting lout deserve our contempt? Of course he does! And if not *contempt*, then why not trade all of our gleeful boasting for pure disdain? You saw the way he treats his little cousin."

As Baudwin continued speaking, he turned his face to the sky, his arms stretched above his head. Lowering his voice, he imitated Loch. "You must not read glyphs, Teigue, for they are slow and stupid, which makes them worthless — and positively *evil*!"

"Baudwin, you're such a slyboots!" Matha chortled.

Baudwin jumped off the boulder to the ground. He then went running down the path, chuckling with delight for having tricked them both so easily.

Matha and Criofan ran after him, laughing and shouting, "Baudwin! Wait up!"

"He certainly seems pleased with himself," Criofan commented as they raced along the path.

"Well, he did just beat Loch in what many would consider to be the contest of the season," Matha said. "Wouldn't you?"

"I suppose I would," Criofan said. "But he does seem *awfully* pleased."

"Wouldn't you feel that way if you were him?" Matha asked.

"I don't know," Criofan replied. "Perhaps I —"

"Are you sure you aren't just jealous?" Matha asked.

"Of course not," Criofan replied. "I just think there may be more going on with him than he's letting us know."

"Perhaps," Matha agreed. "But, that's Baudwin." The two Faeries laughed.

As soon as they caught up to Baudwin, Criofan asked, "Did you see Loch's rage and how he couldn't accept defeat? What's the matter with those Roilers?"

"Perhaps their heads are turned inside out from reading only letters, which scrambles their brains and makes them a little lopsided," Matha added mischievously. They all laughed.

"More than a little!" Criofan exclaimed.

While the three of them did know how to read letters, they weren't sure they liked them all that much. The idea to study them had been Matha's, who had learned from an old Elve in Deuona. Matha worried that if they didn't learn them, there would be a lot they wouldn't know about the ways of the Elves, and what they were up to. At first, neither Criofan nor Baudwin showed much interest in them, but then Criofan realized that all the new commerce would eventually use letters. Baudwin also surmised that he'd be unable to work the new inventions if he couldn't read the instructions.

However, they all agreed that when they read letters, they didn't feel the same as when they read glyphs. Glyphs always made them see everything at once, as if they knew without knowing. Letters made them see things one at a time, leaving them feeling cluttered and overloaded after reading them.

"Roilers obviously respect letters more than glyphs," Baudwin declared. "And all things Steamway are far more interesting to them than anything the Water Guild has to offer. Because of that, the ways of the Water are no longer sacred to them," he added, cupping his hands in front of his chest to make the sign of the Water.

Seeing this, Matha and Criofan joined him in making the sign. "We are with the Water!" they affirmed in unison, feeling decidedly better.

"And, we certainly know who the smarter ones are!" Baudwin exclaimed, laughing. "Don't forget what Ferrell said."

"By the way, who *is* Ferrell?" Criofan asked. "I've never seen him before today."

"Have you?" Matha asked, turning to Baudwin.

"Me neither," Baudwin replied. "I must admit that when I met him, he gave me quite a start."

"What happened?" Matha asked.

Baudwin explained how Ferrell had appeared from out of nowhere to break up a squabble between some Faeries and a Druid named Gavin at the Tree of Innovation.

"What were they fighting about?" Criofan asked.

"Gavin was giving a talk, and some Faeries seemed quite suspicious of his intentions, so they kept interrupting him."

"How rebellious of them," Matha joked.

Baudwin thought then of what had happened when Ferrell ambushed him in the alchemvoke booth — whispering in his ear about Liquistone. Ferrell had seemed like such a zealot. He didn't just appreciate the Four Branches of Progress, he was *driven* by them, oblivious to how others might interpret his manner. Baudwin wondered if the Elve was simply a stranger to these parts, or simply strange. The fact that he knew so much about his family made Baudwin nervous.

"Ferrell is quite peculiar," Baudwin said. "I found his manner disturbing."

"To say the least," Criofan agreed.

"When we saw him at the crash," Matha added, "he took such pleasure in making his observations and ordering everyone around. And that speech at the Hop and Hit. What are the Elves up to? I've never heard of a Luminary coming to Deuona, especially a Master of the Order of Gold."

"Do you even know what a Luminary is?" Criofan asked.

"I certainly do," Matha replied.

"How do you know he wasn't just another member of the Earth Guard, there to keep the peace?" Criofan asked.

"He had the white star on his collar," Baudwin added.

"Didn't you also see the medallion he was wearing?" Matha countered.

"I don't believe I did, what with the arguing and fighting going on, and all those fruit pies flying through the Air," Criofan replied sarcastically.

"Well, if you had, you might also have noticed the elven symbol for the city of Gold Haven in the center — a golden sphere, with rays of Light around the edges, and a large eye in the middle. An eye which, despite its intimidating stare, is meant to convey fairness, like a beacon of impartiality," Matha lectured.

"Perhaps I did then," Criofan replied. "But what does that have to do with being a Luminary?"

"Because," Matha continued, sounding as if he were speaking to a Faefry of about thirty, *"all* the elven Luminaries originally came from Gold Haven, which is where they received their training. And many now still do."

"All right!" Criofan exclaimed. "But what does he do?"

"He's obviously a high official in charge of the Engineerium," Matha explained.

"Which is odd, because Rian never mentioned him to me," Baudwin said. "Although he seemed to know who Ferrell was."

"Perhaps Rian is too low in rank to be of importance to Ferrell," Matha added. "Regardless, I do believe that before the Great Befalling, the symbol on his medallion meant something quite different than it does now —"

"Now, the eye simply means that he has his eye on us," Baudwin broke in, laughing.

"Well, he certainly was watching *you*, Baudwin," Criofan agreed. "He didn't want me to fight, and I still don't understand why."

"Nor do I," Baudwin said. "But enough talk about him. Let's go find some rainbow honey to celebrate our victory."

"That's the best thing you've said all day!" Criofan exclaimed.

For a moment, Baudwin thought he should head right home. The meeting would be starting soon. Seamus and Kelven were no doubt already preparing everything, and they would need his help. Yet, winning at the Hop and Hit made him feel like he deserved more time to enjoy himself. Looking up at the sky, he saw the Sun was not that low yet. Added to that, the Rainbow Glades were just too tempting to pass up.

With that, they all went bounding through the Woods, ducking in and out among the trees, which had begun to cast late afternoon shadows upon the ground. The Rainbow Glades were a treasure of Deuona, envied by all the other faery cities. Here among the purest Waters, rainbow bees made their hives, for here not only were there rainbow poppies, but flowering trees of every color of the rainbow.

Looking at the glade, Baudwin saw grists of bees flying around, their iridescent wings flashing like jewels in the Light. As the three Faeries ran through the trees, the bees buzzed around them, yet none were afraid of being stung. Rarely did they frenzy away from their hives. As one landed on Baudwin's shoulder, the hairs on its abdomen shimmered in a prism of color.

"Tell me, little one — where is your home?" he asked.

"We must find an oak," Criofan yelled. "The bees like them the best, to build their nest." As the search went on, they crisscrossed back and forth along the path. They then went their separate ways into the Woods, calling out to one another as they ran.

"I found one!" Criofan shouted several yards ahead of his friends. "Here!"

Moments later, they stood before an enormous oak tree, hoping to see a hive built among the branches.

"This oak looks just like the hand of a great faery elder," Baudwin said. As he spoke, he pointed to four branches stretching like aged fingers toward the sky, and to another branch, large like a thumb and with knotted joints, reaching all the way to the side. "Do you see?"

Exhausted, Matha dropped to the ground. "Perhaps," he replied, "but what I don't see is a hive."

"There must be one somewhere around here," Criofan insisted. "Baudwin! Stop gawking at that tree and help us look."

"That's what I'm doing," Baudwin said, tilting his head to peer through the branches. After circling the base, he joined Criofan and Matha, who were sitting against the trunk, looking tired and annoyed.

"I can usually tell where the bees are," Criofan declared. "This always happens when I spend too much time in the elven world, with all of their gadgets and machines."

"So, now you're blaming the Elves for your lack of skill?" Baudwin jested.

"No," Criofan replied. "But if we want *rainbow* honey, we'll have to find bees that have just collected some nectar and follow them back to their hive." He then stood up.

"That's right," Matha agreed.

"Let's go then," Baudwin replied. Looking at his watch he added, "But we have to hurry — there isn't much time." The Sun was setting quickly, and Baudwin wondered if stopping was a mistake, but with all the bees around them, finding a hive probably wouldn't take too long.

As soon as Baudwin spoke, Criofan began to run down the path. "The first one to find bees that lead to a hive wins. And that will be me! The others have to climb the tree to get the honey. That will be both of you!" he yelled. Soon, they all were running through the Woods, searching for trees with colorful blooms.

"I see a golden rain!" Baudwin shouted as he stopped to look at a handsome tree with a broad dome-shaped crown, adorned with clusters of yellow flowers. "But, no bees."

"I told you I would find them!" Criofan shouted back. "I see a lilac dark star with the deepest blue flowers, and —"

Before he could finish his sentence, Matha called out from farther afield, "A flame tree — swarming with bees!"

With that, Baudwin and Criofan raced to find him. Soon they all descended upon the leafless tree, which stood almost one hundred feet high, with scarlet, bell-shaped flowers hanging from every branch — a thrumming umbrella of bees. The three friends stood gaping at the magnificent sight.

"Bees indeed!" Criofan exclaimed, as he watched them buzzing busily in and out among the flowers.

"You mean *rainbow* bees," Matha corrected him, excitement ringing in his voice.

"We must follow them!" Baudwin shouted, as he pointed to a grist, which was buzzing away from the tree. Off they ran, making sure to keep sight of them as they tore in and out among the bushes. Finally, they came to another great oak.

"See — they're entering the hive, laden with honey!" Matha exclaimed. He pointed to a bearding mass, hanging from a lower branch. Turning to Criofan he announced, "I'm ready for my honey now."

"Let him get his own honey," Criofan said coolly to Baudwin, as he leaned on the trunk.

"You're such a sore loser," Baudwin said, as he scrambled up Criofan's back and onto his shoulders.

"Now be still, while I check the hive." Criofan groaned, holding him up.

"I need three sticks," Baudwin announced.

Matha searched the ground, picked up three branches, stripped them of their leaves, and handed them to Baudwin.

"Very good," Baudwin said, taking the sticks. Steadying himself on top of Criofan, he leaned in closer to the hive. "And now," he said, speaking to the bees in a calm, pleasant voice, "do you mind sharing some of your honey?"

"How many colors do you see?" Matha asked.

"Red, orange, yellow. . ." Baudwin replied as he carefully examined the buzzing comb. "They have done their job well. Every color is here."

"Good," declared Criofan. "You know what they say: When every color is present, they all taste better!"

"Get me some red," Matha said.

"Easy now, I have to see whether the bees mind if we take some." With that, Baudwin took a stick, and gently reached into the hive. "We're in luck," he announced. "They don't seem to care." Carefully, he spun the stick to get as much honey as he could. He then handed the red dip to Matha, who grabbed appreciatively for the delicious treat. "What color do you want, Criofan?"

"Purple," Criofan replied.

"Good, and I'll have green," Baudwin said, as he dipped the two remaining sticks into the purple and green sections of the comb.

"Mine tastes like strawberry, with a touch of red poppy," Matha said, sampling his honey. "Delicious!"

Hearing this, Baudwin simply had to taste his as well. "Green apple!" he exclaimed.

"What about mine?" Criofan asked. "Baudwin, where are your manners? In your belly?"

"Sorry, Criofan," Baudwin laughed, as he handed him his stick.

"Mine tastes like plum," Criofan replied, as he took a lick of his stick.

The three Faeries then sat down beneath the tree to enjoy their honey. Baudwin knew the moment had come for him to share his astonishing account of what had happened to him with Rian at Gear Chute. As soon as he finished his honey, he spoke.

"I have something more to tell you both, something *wonderful*." He fished into the inside pocket of his vest and pulled out the ball of red silk.

"What is that?" Matha asked, intrigued.

"You'll see," Baudwin replied. Carefully he unwrapped the silk, making sure not to touch its contents. "This, my friends, is an egg made of Glamorium." He placed the silk on the ground, still careful not to touch the egg.

"Wherever did you get that?" Criofan asked, stunned. He then nodded knowingly at Matha. "You see?" he asked. "I *told* you there was something more going on with him."

"What do you mean?" Baudwin asked, trying to appear more innocent than he was.

"What I mean is that I know you very well," Criofan replied. "I could just tell that you had something else up your sleeve."

"Or should we say, in your pocket," Matha added, smiling. "You're very lucky that you didn't lose that in the fight."

"Luck had nothing to do with it," Baudwin replied. "I'm sure that the Water prevented me from losing it."

Upon hearing this, Criofan and Matha rolled their eyes, and exchanged looks.

"Baudwin, what are we going to do with you now?" Criofan asked. "First, you beat Loch, and now you actually have some Glamorium! What if your head gets as big as that hive?" he added, pointing to the buzzing hub above them.

"Don't worry," Baudwin laughed. "If that happens, I won't be able to stand up."

"You must tell us how this came to you," Matha insisted.

Baudwin explained that when he had met Rian, he told him how dismal his day had been. Instead of having fun, he had gotten into fights with his friends, and with strangers at Gear Chute. Even worse, he had twice failed to touch some Glamorium. Taking pity on him, Rian had escorted him to the back of the Gear Chute booth. Hidden away in a small box was the glamorium egg.

"Did you *ask* him for it?" Criofan asked.

"Of course not," Baudwin replied. "He insisted that I take his gift."

"Why?" Criofan asked.

"Because I practiced the true meaning of Honesty — as the Triquetra instructed at Curios & Marvels," Baudwin replied.

Baudwin then explained how he and Rian had discussed how to properly wield Glamorium. The first step was to master the lesson of Honesty, which was contained in the Triquetra. Only then, Rian had said, could Baudwin use Glamorium to find his mother.

"Does this mean you'll stop tricking everyone into getting what you want?" Matha joked.

"Baudwin, you're really lucky," Criofan said, trying hard to contain his envy. He then looked at Matha. "None of our elven friends have ever given us such a priceless treasure, have they, Matha?"

Matha nodded in silent agreement before he spoke. "What would happen if Criofan or I touched it?" he asked, as he reached toward the shimmering green egg.

"I don't know," Baudwin replied. "But I can tell you this: The first time I did, something both wonderful and terrible happened to me."

Hearing the word *terrible*, Matha quickly withdrew his hand.

"Come on, Matha," Criofan said, laughing. "Don't be so skittish. Touch the egg!"

"Not before Baudwin tells us what happened to him," Matha replied.

"I will then," Baudwin said. "But you must be prepared. The story is both wondrous and terrible — at least to me."

Baudwin then told his friends what had happened when Rian gave him the egg, how when he clasped the treasure to his heart, green Light exploded in starlike beams inside of him, and then went shooting out of his body.

"And then I heard a voice — one I had never heard before — speak from deep within me," he explained.

"What did it say?" Criofan asked, staring intently at Baudwin.

"The voice recited the poem that was on the tablet in Curios & Marvels — the one we all read when we were there." As Baudwin spoke, Matha and Criofan listened quietly — hanging on his every word.

As within — so without

As without — so within

There we meet

In the center

From our hearts

Once again, they were hushed into silence, until Baudwin spoke again. He told them that after the Light had gotten very warm and even more brilliant, something truly amazing happened. The Light brought together everything he saw and felt inside of him with everything that was outside of him, until he couldn't tell one from the other. The peace he had felt was indescribable.

"That truly does sound wondrous," Matha said. Criofan nodded in agreement.

"What else happened?" Matha asked.

Baudwin told them what else he saw — something that was even more wonderful — a faery lady, standing in a river that seemed to be made of both Water and Light. He described how beautiful she was, and how, when she beckoned to him, Light poured from her entire body. He thought she might have been his mother, so he went to her, and she embraced him.

"And then. . ." As Baudwin's voice trailed off, he shuddered with sadness.

"Baudwin," Matha said. "What else did you see?"

"I — I — don't know," he stammered.

"Take your time," Matha said, as he put his hand on Baudwin's shoulder.

"When I looked again at her arms, she was covered in feathers," Baudwin said. "Her face had a beak. She seemed so small and dark. . . and. . ." Baudwin could not speak any further.

"And what?" Criofan asked, alarmed.

"*Befouled*," Baudwin replied, shaken. "She turned into a moorhen, and then she flew away."

Matha and Criofan looked at Baudwin, not knowing what to say.

Baudwin spoke again, his fear mounting. He described how the river of Light she had been standing in turned into something horrible — a rushing stream of tarnished, ugly silver. Wave after wave came after him, until he thought he would surely drown.

"Did it seem like Water?" Matha asked, shaken.

"No — I mean, yes — I mean no, it couldn't have been," Baudwin replied. "It seemed more like a molten *shadow* that wanted to destroy me, but what kind of shadow, I cannot say. Everything felt so dark and cold. I was so alone. I had such a feeling of dread. There was. . . there was. . . no help for me."

"Of course there's help," Matha said. "We're with you now."

"I know, but. . ." Baudwin's voice trailed off again. He then continued speaking. "And then, I opened my eyes, and Rian was right there."

"Just as *we* are now," Matha put in warmly.

"The end of my vision was so terrible," Baudwin said, still frightened.

"How could such a beautiful occurrence become so ugly so fast?" Criofan asked, visibly shaken.

"I don't know," Baudwin said. "But, when I told Rian everything I just told you, he said that through Glamorium, I had been touched by the *Dúrúnghlas*, which is a great blessing."

"What kind of blessing I wonder," Matha mused.

Baudwin smiled for a moment, and then his face became full of consternation. Seeing how distraught he looked, Criofan asked, "Tell us, Baudwin. Did Rian say anything else?"

"He said that for reasons he did not understand, Glamorium may also bring a great shadow upon those who touch even a tiny piece."

Both Criofan and Matha looked at Baudwin with concern.

"A great shadow?" Matha asked, frightened. "How can that be?"

"Rian said it had something to do with the Great Befalling," Baudwin replied. "Which is why my vision was both so wonderful and so horrible. What was once a sacred source of renewal is now itself befouled, but how and why, I cannot say."

All three Faeries sat against the tree, eating their honey, hardly speaking. As soon as Baudwin finished his, he scooped up the glamorium egg, touching only the silk. He then extended his hand to his friends.

Jokingly, he asked, "Now that you have heard my story, do either of you want to touch this?"

Matha looked at the egg. "How do I know what will happen? Something wonderful, or terrible?"

"Or neither," Criofan added.

"Better we should talk to our elders first," Baudwin said. "Otherwise, we may be sorry."

But before either of them could say anything more, something hit the tree with a very loud *thwack,* followed by three more: *thwack, thwack, thwack!* The hive tumbled off the branch, landing on the ground like a split melon, with multi-colored streams of honey oozing from all sides.

Scores of angry bees swarmed out. The bees had been willing to share some of their honey, but an assault on their hive was another matter.

"How ever did this happen?" Baudwin shouted, as he jumped to his feet and stuffed the glamorium egg into his pocket.

"Over there!" Matha exclaimed. Apprehensively, he looked toward the tree line.

"They're coming for us — lots of them!" Criofan exclaimed.

"Bees?" Baudwin asked.

"No! Roilers!" Criofan yelled. "They're over there — near those oak trees — with slingshots!" At least twenty yards away, a group of Roilers sat crouched among the bushes, grinning menacingly.

Above the faery friends, a flurry of bees had formed a furious cloud, ready to avenge the loss of their hive. The Sun shone on their glistering bodies — scores of sharp rainbows — ready to strike.

"Ouch! One got me," Matha exclaimed. "Now the bees are after us too!"

"Run!" Baudwin cried.

With that, they began racing through the Woods, licking their fingers and shrieking with laughter at the mess they now were in.

Seeing them flee, the Roilers gave chase, racing past the tree where the hive had fallen. Instantly, the bees descended upon them, buzzing and stinging them so ferociously that the Roilers forgot their prey, and scattered, screaming.

"We must get to the river!" Criofan shouted. "Follow me!"

All three Faeries ran as fast as they could. As soon as they reached the shore, they dove into the Water to escape, not only the Roilers, but the livid swarm as well. Moments later, they bobbed to the surface, catching their breath, shaking their hair out of their eyes, and treading Water.

"They haven't seen us yet," Baudwin whispered, pointing. By then, a group of Roilers had reached the river, and were holding their heads in pain, swatting at the bees and yelling.

"That's because the bees are smarter," Matha noted, trying hard not to burst out laughing.

"Isn't that Loch, jumping into the river with his jacket pulled over his face?" Baudwin asked, snickering uncontrollably.

"Yes," Matha snickered back, adding, "and if we don't keep our heads down, they'll soon spot us."

"Like the bees, they have us outnumbered," Criofan warned. "We have to go downstream, and hide in the reeds. If we swim as fast as flutter fish, we can avoid them altogether."

"Then all we get is one breath," Baudwin declared.

With that, they inhaled deeply and dove beneath the Water. Moving their arms in wide circles and kicking their legs behind them, they swam stealthily underwater to the reeds. The Fae of the Water easily held their breath, waiting for the right moment. Baudwin was the first to rise to the surface. Slowly and cautiously, he crouched to avoid detection by the Roilers, who were fast approaching. He then made his way around a number of slippery-looking rocks, which jutted sharply out of the Water. For several moments, he turned away from shore to look for his friends.

Without warning, two arms with large red welts on them grabbed him from behind, almost squeezing the Life out of him. "Because of *you*, I have to meet Ferrell at Four Falls and do his bidding," a low voice snarled. Twisting around, Baudwin found himself face to face with Loch. Gasping, Baudwin struggled to break free of the crushing hold he had upon him. But before he could move a muscle, Loch lifted him up and, with all his might, threw him into the Water.

Baudwin was driven down until his feet hit the bottom. He pushed upwards, until he broke the surface, shaking the Water from his eyes and ears. Seeing Loch's face again, he retorted, "Because of *me*? Because I won, and *you* lost." As he ducked to the side, Loch grabbed him again, this time twisting his arm around his back. *Is there no way to get this stupid oaf off me?* Baudwin thought. Furiously, they thrashed about in the Water.

As if to answer his question, two arms suddenly grabbed Loch from behind, dragging him several paces toward the shore. Surprised at his sudden freedom, Baudwin looked to see who had come to his aid. "Criofan!" he exclaimed. "How good of you to save me from this ungrateful hooligan. Without me, he never would have formed such a close alliance with Ferrell," he added, laughing sarcastically.

Incensed by Baudwin's words, Loch broke Criofan's grip, and spun around. He grabbed Criofan tightly around the neck, holding him in a headlock. Criofan remained stuck in this position, helplessly facing the sky with his arms flailing about in the Water. Not missing a beat, Baudwin sloshed his way through the current to come to the aid of his friend.

Criofan's feet found a boulder. With that, he pushed backwards with all his might. The force broke Loch's grip and Criofan was free. Now on his feet, he punched Loch in the gut, knocking the wind out of him. With his other arm, he grabbed Loch's face, poking him in the eye with his thumb and shoving him down at the same time. Pressing his other hand into Loch's chest, he dunked him in the Water. As Loch went under, Criofan sputtered furiously, "Tell me now, is this how you felt when the Hop and Hit took you down?"

Weakly, Loch pushed himself up, struggling to breathe.

"Criofan — that's enough!" Baudwin barked, as Criofan shoved him under the Water again. "You wouldn't want to send him to Annwyn and have his unhappy soul on your conscience, would you?"

Abruptly, Criofan let go of Loch, who lay limp in the Water, gasping for Air. He then looked at Baudwin, and they both laughed triumphantly.

"Let the river have him," Baudwin said. "We have to find Matha."

"I sure gave him a dousing!" Criofan rejoiced, as they pressed on through the Water to get to the shore. "That's for the shrine!"

As soon as they reached the reeds, a voice called out, "Baudwin, Criofan!"

"Matha!" they shouted back. Matha placed his forefinger to his lips to quiet them, pointing through the reeds at a group of Roilers who were making their way along the shore.

"We must get to the main road," Baudwin whispered to Matha as soon as he and Criofan caught up to him. After passing silently through the reeds, they all began to run.

Looking over his shoulder, Baudwin saw at least fifteen Roilers chasing them. "Head for the trees!" he yelled. On the other side of a small hill, several yards in the distance, sat a large grove of pine trees.

Upon reaching the trees, all went their separate ways, looking for the tallest ones. With great acrobatic dexterity, each then shinnied up a trunk. *Shoosh, shoosh, shoosh,* went their pant legs against the bark, as they ascended higher and higher. Swiftly reaching the top, they perched among the branches — hiding, watching, and waiting.

Cresting the hill, the Roilers paused to survey the turf, then rushed to the bottom like a pack of hungry wolves, hunting their prey. Moments later found them beneath the pine trees, howling and roaring, oblivious to Baudwin, Matha, and Criofan, relaxing in the branches high above them. Just as quickly, they disappeared, their voices fading into the distance. In and around the surrounding trees, everything became eerily silent.

As soon as he was sure that the Roilers were gone, Baudwin gave a low whistle. "Down we go," he whispered.

With that, they descended the trees like a trio of lively squirrels, and went dashing through the Woods, occasionally running up other trees to make sure the Roilers would not find their trail. Jumping from tree to tree, and bounding from boulder to boulder, they finally reached the stone wall that separated the Woods from the main road.

"What about the Faery Code of Manners?" Matha shouted as he sprang onto the wall. With that, he ran along the top, doing aerial cartwheels over the honeysuckle and wild roses as he went.

"A Faery must not gloat," Baudwin began, laughing, "or he may find himself afloat, drowning in anger in a sea of —"

But, before he could finish the rhyme, Criofan cried out — "Roilers!"

Matha stopped short. As he turned to look behind him, he almost fell off the wall. "That can't be!" he shouted. From where he stood, he could see the Roiler band running through the Woods, hooting and hollering.

"What can't be — often *is!*" Baudwin exclaimed. "They've jumped the wall to the road. We have to get on the other side!" To avoid being seen, all three of them climbed over the wall, landing in a sweaty heap on the ground.

Panting heavily, Matha spoke in a low tone. "What are we to do? Whether we stay or go, we risk getting caught."

"And being the objects of their wrath," Criofan gratuitously added.

Looking up, Baudwin exclaimed, "What is, often can't be! *That* can't be!" His excitement was understandable, for a lumber roller was chugging steadily toward them, having made a wide turn onto the main road. A sign on the side of the cab read, *Rian's General Store.* They bounded over the wall, and raced to catch up with the driver.

"Rian!" Baudwin shouted, as he ran alongside the passenger door. "We need a lift!" Seeing Baudwin, Rian slowed down, and tipped his cap in a smiling *hello.* He then motioned for them to get inside.

As Criofan and Matha scrambled onto the tender, Baudwin jumped into the cab. The look on Rian's face, while amused, also was concerned. "Looks like you're in quite a hurry," he shouted above the roar of the engine.

"We sure are lucky we ran into you!" Baudwin exclaimed.

Rian glanced into his rearview mirror, nodding. "Looks like you've got lots of admirers trying to catch up with you — or catch you" — he joked, driving steadily. As Baudwin leaned to look out his window, he saw Loch gaining on them, along with several other Roilers.

"Take a look behind you!" Baudwin shouted to Criofan and Matha. "They're coming up fast!" He then slumped angrily down in his seat. "Will we ever lose them?"

"No need to get upset," Rian replied. "Just tell your friends to stoke the firebox. Once we build a head of steam, they won't have a chance of catching us."

Baudwin opened the back door of the cab, joining Matha and Criofan in the tender. "Throw some more Wood into the firebox!" he shouted.

As he spoke, Loch came charging alongside them, with two of his friends. Matha opened the door and threw several pieces of Wood onto the Fire. Just as Loch was about to jump onto the tender, Baudwin pointed to a cord of Wood. "Unbuckle the straps!" he shouted to Criofan.

Criofan immediately undid the buckles, releasing an avalanche of Wood onto the floor. And just as Loch landed on the tender, a few of the jostling logs rolled under his feet, tripping him. Flailing his arms every which way, he tumbled onto the road. Flat on his back, he continued his flailing like a felled turtle, trying to avoid the falling Wood.

Rian opened the accelerator vent, flooding the furnace with air. The fire roared, and the lumber roller took off in a burst of speed. As Loch and his friends were left floundering in a cloud of dust and steam, Baudwin, Criofan, and Matha watched, elated.

But their amusement was short-lived. As the vehicle sped away, Loch pulled a shiny object out of his pocket, which he waved victoriously above his head. For an instant, a streak of copper flashed brightly in the setting Light.

"Whatever is he doing?" Matha asked.

With that, Baudwin began poking frantically around in his pockets with both of his hands. "*That* can't be!" he shouted furiously. Much to his dismay, he realized that somewhere amid all the fighting, Loch had somehow managed to steal his coupler.

Chapter 18

AN IMPORTANT MEETING

The ride back home proved to be uneventful, a welcome relief from the day's hectic goings-on. Baudwin's search for Glamorium had been daunting, but a glimmering green gift had come to him in a very unexpected way. Now that the egg was his, his hopes of finding his mother were high. He wondered then what he would tell Seamus. Was he ready to talk about the wonderful but dark vision Glamorium had shown him? Regardless, Glamorium would have to be put aside while he helped prepare for the meeting. His duty now was to his family and the Guild.

Now Baudwin was almost home. He dreaded speaking to his father, for Loch had stolen his coupler. Even though he had defeated him at the Hop and Hit, Loch had still managed to ruin his day. No doubt the brute had guessed how necessary the coupler was when Baudwin dropped it in their skirmish at the food tent.

Curse him! he thought.

As the lumber roller came to a grinding halt in front of his house, Baudwin and his friends jumped off the tender.

"Thank you for the ride, Rian!" Baudwin shouted. "You came right —"

"Before the shadow hit the dial," Rian cut in, pointing to the horologe in Baudwin's yard. "What about this mess of wood you and your friends left me with?"

"I'll re-belt the whole stack tomorrow," Baudwin replied.

"I'm going to hold you to that," Rian declared. He then tipped his hat and drove off.

"Come on, you two," Baudwin yelled to Matha and Criofan as he ran toward his dome home. "We have to make up for lost time!"

"We're coming," they called out, as they hurried to catch up with him.

Unlike square, sharply pointed elven homes, Baudwin's dome home was built upon a round foundation of river stones, with walls made of straw bales plastered with river mud. As soon as they got to the gate, Baudwin stopped for a moment to look at the stone wall encircling the house. There among the vines, he saw a cluster of yellow stars with bright orange centers, closing for the day. Smiling, he recited:

Morning glories,
You are done
Say good-bye
To the setting Sun

Next to them, he saw a cluster of blue stars with bright purple centers, opening for the night, so to them he said:

Evening glories
Don't start too soon
Wait a bit
For the rising Moon

"Baudwin, you're late!" Seamus exclaimed. There he stood outside the front door, leaning on his staff, looking quite perturbed. Seeing how distracted his grandson seemed, he added, "Well, at least tap the gate!"

Hearing his grandfather's displeasure, Baudwin swept his fingers across the doors. In a flash, glowstones covering the lily pads and stems shone with sparkling blue-green Light. Baudwin opened the gate, and he and his friends went to greet Seamus.

"Hello, Grandfather," Baudwin said. Matha and Criofan both nodded *hello*.

Seamus took a moment to adjust his spectacles. "Am I just an old Faery who is simply seeing things, or did all of you just go for an evening dip in your clothes?" he asked. "What a bunch of scatterbrains!" Noticing Baudwin's sheepish smile, he added, "Now you have to change, lower the sluice gates, and prepare for the meeting. There's hardly any time."

"Father said he would lower them," Baudwin declared. "This morning."

"Well, he hasn't," Seamus replied. Bristling, he straightened his tall frame, until the hair on his head almost touched the arch-shaped lintel above the door.

"Why not?" Baudwin asked, upset.

"Perhaps you should ask him," Seamus said, raising his staff and shaking the tip at Baudwin.

"With all the time I have left?" Baudwin asked.

"Baudwin, we'll help you with this," Matha said. "Won't we, Criofan?"

"Of course," Criofan replied. "What has to be done?"

"The cushions have to be placed in the meeting hall, and the tables set in the dining room," Seamus replied gruffly. "Other than that, hardly anything at all."

"Baudwin, go and speak to your father," Matha said. "We'll help your grandfather."

"Where is he?" Baudwin asked Seamus.

"Down at the mill," Seamus replied.

"I'll be right back," Baudwin said. He turned, and then ran from the gate and down the path.

Before him was the mill, which was also a dome-shaped construction. Upon reaching the door, he went inside and bounded up the stairs. There he found Kelven, slowly pouring rye into a funnel-shaped hopper. Several burlap sacks sat next to him on the floor, some filled with flour and others with grain. To his right, a large glowstone rested on a simple worktable, filling the entire room with soft white Light. Before him, two millstones ground noisily against each other — one on top of the other — like two enormous sandstone pancakes.

"Hello, Father," Baudwin shouted above the din. "I just got back from the Engineerium."

Kelven paused for a moment to look at Baudwin. He then pulled a lever to raise the top millstone, stopping the noise.

"Hello, Baudwin," Kelven said.

"What are you doing?" Baudwin asked, wondering what kind of mood his father was in.

"Grinding Evan's grain, so you won't have to," Kelven replied.

"I didn't say I wouldn't," Baudwin said, taken aback by the anger his father's soft-spoken voice belied.

"You also didn't say you would," Kelven replied, barely changing his tone. "How was your day at the Engineerium?"

"Good enough," Baudwin replied, not wanting to recount all the ups and downs of what had happened. "I thought you said you would lower the gates."

"First, I wanted to see if you remembered the coupler," Kelven countered, half-jokingly. With that, he pulled the lever to lower the millstone again.

Soon only the grinding of the millstones could be heard. Neither of them spoke a word. They stared at each other, and Baudwin hated Loch even more. "I lost the stupid thing," he blurted out above the grinding.

Kelven raised the millstone again. "Come here, Baudwin," he said.

As Baudwin approached his father, Kelven looked at him for several moments.

"Baudwin — you have to do your own growing — no matter *how* tall your grandfather is," he said sternly.

"Whatever is that supposed to mean?" Baudwin asked, again taken aback.

"You'll have to figure that out for yourself," Keven replied. "Now, go back to the house. There's a lot to be done. I will lower the gates."

"All right!" Baudwin exclaimed. Without saying another word, he left the mill.

He tells me things, and then doesn't bother to explain them, he thought angrily, as he hurried back to the house. *What does <u>he</u> know about growing? He hasn't grown a day in his Life!* But, before he could think any further about his father, he ran into his grandfather again. Seamus was busily sweeping the walkway from the gate to the front door.

"Light the path," Seamus said, handing Baudwin his staff. Baudwin darted to the gate. Moving quickly toward the house, he tapped a line of white glowstones on either side of the walkway, going back and forth, back and forth, until they all sparkled brightly. He and Seamus stood for a moment, admiring the shining effect.

"Good, that's done," Seamus said as he rubbed the border around the front door with a damp cloth. Pressed into the plaster were tiles, seashells, and bits of colored glass. "Did you clean the borders around the back door, and the windows on both sides of the house?" he asked Baudwin.

"I already did that yesterday," Baudwin replied, pleased to inform his grandfather that he had done something without being told to.

Seamus could not help noticing the smile on Baudwin's face. "You seem rather happy," he said. "How was your day at the Engineerium?"

Baudwin *was* happy, or at least he was in the moment. Ups and downs were normal for him, but he had had enough of them at the Engineerium, and didn't want any more.

"Quite honestly," Grandfather," he replied, his voice trembling with uncertainty, "I don't know where to begin."

"Then begin somewhere," Seamus said, looking intently at him.

Baudwin hesitated before he spoke, as he had no idea how to explain his tumultuous day to his grandfather. "I saw Riona," he began.

"Did you now?" Seamus asked.

"Yes, she had a valley dew fizzy tent in the South Petal. We were very thirsty after walking all the way to the Engineerium, so she gave each of us one. They were very good."

"How kind of her," Seamus said.

"Yes, it was," Baudwin said. "She said to say hello to you, and to Father, and the river." He then paused, not sure of what to say next.

"What else did you do?" Seamus asked.

"I saw Elva at the Show Wheel," Baudwin replied. "She and Riona wanted me to see the show, but I couldn't, as I had to meet Criofan and Matha. We went to see Curios & Marvels, and then we went on some rides. I also played some games." Again Baudwin paused, unable to decide what next to say.

Seamus sensed his grandson's discomfort. "Baudwin," he said, as he put his arm around his shoulder, "is there something else you want to tell me?"

Baudwin looked at his grandfather, eager to begin explaining everything that had happened. He wanted him to know about all the strange and wonderful experiences he had had, as well as his struggles and triumphs. *I want to tell him how I beat Loch,* he thought, *but if I do, he'll pry everything else out of me.* He didn't want his grandfather to know that he had found some Glamorium, even though Seamus had been right — it *was* as elusive as Faeries dancing in river mist.

Before he could say another thing, he stopped. No words came to his lips, for oddly, much to his dismay, thinking about Glamorium only filled him with dread. Neither of his friends had wanted to touch the egg. He had been so sure that finding Glamorium would solve his problems, but it had only revealed an even larger one that he didn't understand. Eventually he would have to tell Seamus, but now was not the time.

Baudwin looked again at his grandfather. He was glad that Seamus was so preoccupied with all the preparations for the meeting. For now, he could simply change the subject.

"No," Baudwin replied, trying his best to sound cheery. "There isn't anything more."

Seamus looked skeptically at Baudwin, but then took him at his word. "Well then," he said, his voice booming with anticipation, "let's go and finish preparing for the meeting." With that, he opened the door, and Baudwin followed him inside.

The interiors of faery homes in *Tír na nÓg* were laid out in concentric circles, like radiating ripples on a pond. In Baudwin's home there were four such ripples: a ring of outer rooms, a circular hallway adjacent to the rooms, a meeting hall adjacent to the hallway, and a shrine in the very center of the house.

"We must go to the kitchen," Seamus said, as he and Baudwin stood in the greeting room.

Baudwin glided down the hall with Seamus and then into the kitchen. The red and pink hollyhocks that had been lying on the counter earlier that morning were now arranged in two tall vases. Two decorative brass lanterns sat next to them. A white glowstone rested inside each one.

"Let's see," Seamus said, musing to himself. "The flowers go outside the front door. I always like a bit of color," he added, pointing to the bright red and pink blooms, which were not the traditional green or blue. He then picked up a lantern to examine the sides. "And these —"

"Are my glowstones!" Baudwin exclaimed. Seamus had borrowed them earlier that morning. "What are you going to do with them?"

"They're mine for now," Seamus replied with a wink. "You'll see." With that, he set the lantern down. "How did the talk with your father go?" he asked.

"The talk —?"

"About the gates, and the coupler," Seamus cut in.

"Do we have to discuss this now?"

"Not if you don't want to," Seamus replied tersely. "But, we do have to talk about Matter Three."

"What's so important about Matter Three?" Baudwin asked, agitated. "This is the second time today that I've heard about it."

"Who else spoke to you?" Seamus asked.

"Elva did," Baudwin replied.

"Did she now?" Seamus asked, as he dropped several flowers on the counter.

Baudwin could tell that Elva annoyed Seamus, but in all fairness, Elva annoyed everyone. At the Engineerium, she had tried to poke her nose into Kelven's business, digging into Baudwin like a chipmunk after a flower bulb. If she hadn't been so pushy, then perhaps he would have asked her what Matter Three was about. Instead, he got away from her as quickly as he could.

"She didn't say anything useful, except she seemed to be very interested in how you and Father were voting," Baudwin replied. "What is Matter Three anyway?"

"Was she now?" Seamus asked, arching his eyebrows and adjusting his spectacles.

"Yes, but what's all the fuss over Matter Three?" Baudwin asked.

"There isn't time to explain," Seamus replied, "what with all there is left to do around here. All you must know is that your father and I want you to vote *no*."

"I don't always vote," Baudwin said, perturbed. "You and Father both know this. I didn't vote last year on Matter One when they wanted to ban stinky radish stew in all the eateries, because that one was just too silly. And, I also didn't vote on Matter Five, to allow the Elves to build yet *another* windmill in the North Bend, because every time they do, the Faeries just have them tear it down, and then they just build another one, which is just too stupid, if —"

"Baudwin, this time you *must* vote," Seamus declared.

Feeling troubled by his grandfather's tone, Baudwin changed the subject. "When I spoke to Father, he said he would lower the gates for me."

"Good," Seamus said. "And did you bring him the coupler he wanted?"

"I meant to, but I —"

"You *forgot*?" Seamus asked.

"Yes," Baudwin replied, unable to admit what had actually happened.

He could tell his grandfather was upset with him. Without the coupler, he couldn't make up for the fight he had had with his father that morning. He knew what was coming next. Always, when he made a bad mistake, he would get the same lecture.

"Baudwin," Seamus began, "we all struggle in this realm, but I feel that your actions aren't your own."

Baudwin cringed. Seamus always began this way.

"Everyone makes mistakes," he replied. "I —"

Seamus cut him off. "Yes, but this isn't the kind of mistake you should be making!"

Seamus had said this so many times to him. So had his father. Baudwin almost picked the flowers off the counter and threw them across the room. They always blamed him for things he couldn't help, and even when he did make things right, they blamed him anyway. Everyone else was joined to their current, so following through on their intentions was easy for them. Whatever mistakes they made were quickly forgiven and forgotten. *How wonderful that must be,* he thought.

"I don't feel the current of the Water the same way everyone else does," Baudwin reminded Seamus.

Seamus sighed. "I know how hard this is for you, but once you get joined, and you *will* get joined, everything will become clear."

In that moment, Baudwin would have liked nothing more than to show Seamus the glamorium egg, for he knew whatever hopes he had lay within the *Dúrúnghlas,* but he was too upset.

Sensing his grandson's unease, Seamus insisted, "You *must* vote no on Matter Three, if only to make up for not bringing him the coupler."

"Then I will," Baudwin replied. He wanted to ask what the matter was about, but just as quickly, he decided he didn't care, for this was a convenient way to make amends. "Should I set the flowers outside the front door?"

Before Seamus could respond, a voice exclaimed, "There you are!" Baudwin turned and saw Matha standing in the doorway. "We've been looking for you. Come and help us finish with the meeting hall."

"Go ahead, Baudwin," Seamus said. "I'll put the flowers outside." With that, he took the vases off the counter. With one in each hand, he walked out the door and down the hall.

Baudwin was more than happy to go to the meeting hall with Matha. "I'm glad you came when you did," he said, as they stepped into the hallway.

"Was your grandfather working you too hard?" Matha joked.

"No, too *seriously,*" Baudwin replied.

"What do you mean?" Matha asked.

"Just another lecture about my current," Baudwin replied.

Hearing this, Matha flinched. Baudwin appreciated his friend's empathy, for Matha had been at the joining so long ago, and knew more than any other the deprivation Baudwin had endured.

"Did you tell him about the Glamorium?" Matha asked.

"No," Baudwin replied.

"Why not?" Matha asked, surprised.

"I wanted to," Baudwin replied, flustered. "But then I thought better of it. Besides, there wasn't any time."

"You have to," Matha said.

"I know I have to," Baudwin replied. "Let's not talk about this anymore."

"Well, all right," Matha said, happy to drop the subject.

"How much is left to do?" Baudwin asked, as he gazed around the room. Round cushions covered in blue and green silk sat in evenly spaced circular rows along the red oak floor.

"Only two more parts, on the other side of the shrine," Matha said. With that, they went around the hall until they reached the remaining empty sections. There they found Criofan, holding three cushions under his arm, as he placed a fourth one on the floor with the others.

"Criofan!" Baudwin exclaimed.

"Baudwin," Criofan replied, chuckling as he set all the cushions on the floor. "I'm so glad you decided to help us!"

Criofan then approached a tall cabinet next to the washing room. As he opened the door, several cushions tumbled off the shelf and onto the floor. "Don't just stand there," he said, as he picked up a few and slung them at his friends.

Baudwin and Matha caught them as they flew. They barely had time to place them on the floor before two more came winging their way. Two more came, and then two more, as Criofan kept throwing them, and they kept setting them down where they belonged. Very quickly, the remaining sections of the meeting hall were covered with rows of well-placed cushions.

As they stood admiring their work, Seamus appeared in the hallway. "The meeting hall looks very grand indeed," he said. "Baudwin, don't forget to light the shrine."

Baudwin darted to the edge of the walkway, down the steps, and into the circle. A crystal bowl sat in the center, nearly five feet across, resting on a three-legged marble stand, like a flower in the palm of a gracefully cupped hand. A fountain of Water burst from the center of the bowl, which was filled with carved turquoise glowstones.

Many years before, Kelven had asked Baudwin to place some blue and green glowstones in the fountain as a decoration. And what fine glowstones they were! Without hesitating, Baudwin arranged them in a ring around the inside of the bowl near the rim. And there they stayed to this day, part of the natural order of things. For to a Faery, arranged in a ring should all things be, and how they should remain — without a second thought on the matter.

Baudwin reached behind a tall vase and picked up a long wooden stick with a copper tip. He circled the shrine, tapping all the glowstones around the rim as he went. Soon, the entire circle glowed brightly. After that, he tapped the center pile, until the spray of Water shooting from the fountain sparkled with turquoise Light.

Seamus as well circled the shrine. "Is there any clutter?" he asked. "Have any of the flowers wilted?"

In Deuona, giving gifts to the Water was almost as cherished to water Faeries as being near the Water itself. Gifts were a way of expressing how much they adored their element, and also a way of saying thank you to the Water for the blessings they received. In Baudwin's home, everyone expressed their gratitude for the Water by placing special offerings around the family shrine: blue and green crystals and colorful flowers in glass vases, pieces of tourmaline and topaz, gold bells, finger cymbals, chimes, and other whimsical-looking objects.

"No," Seamus said, having completed his walk. "Everything looks quite fresh and very festive." He then glanced up at the ceiling. "Looks as if we'll have to clean the dome crest by the end of the summer."

In the center of the ceiling, another kind of jewel sparkled brightly above the fountain — a round stained-glass window — about the size of the circle on the floor below. Baudwin went to stand near Seamus, as he too, looked up at the crest.

Baudwin was determined not to talk about Glamorium quite yet. With Criofan and Matha standing right there, he feared that if Seamus brought up the subject, he would not be able to hide the truth from him. He knew how much his grandfather liked to talk about history, so he decided to ask about the crest, even though he knew the story very well.

"How ever was that made?" Baudwin asked.

"You don't know?" Seamus asked. "I've told you that story — many times."

"Perhaps I've forgotten in my two hundred years," Baudwin replied, chuckling. Seeing the annoyed look on his grandfather's face, he added, "Or perhaps I simply like hearing the story."

Or, he thought, *perhaps I can slow him down just enough, so he won't ask me anything more about my day.*

"Then I will tell you again," Seamus declared. "As the son of the Primary of Water, you must know your family history."

Seeing that Seamus was about to launch one of his long-winded stories, Criofan and Matha slipped away to work on other things. Seamus almost all but forgot the hurry he was in, as he thought about what he was going to say. Leaning on his staff, he craned his neck to look again at the ceiling. "As you know," he began, "every faery family in Deuona has a crest at the top of their dome home. My memory is hazy, but I believe in order to have ours made, your great-great-great-grandparents — or so — on your father's side had to travel a very long distance indeed."

"Where to?" Baudwin asked.

"To meet with a tribe of gifted stained-glass artists in Ember Chasm."

"Were they Faeries or Elves?" Baudwin asked.

"Faeries, of course," Seamus replied.

"Ember Chasm," Baudwin mused. "That's so far away. How did they afford such a long trip?"

"They went by grand horn and cart, which was quite an undertaking, I must say," Seamus replied.

"Grand horns took them all the way to Ember Chasm and then back, with the crest in the cart?" Baudwin asked.

"Yes," Seamus replied. He was most happy to tell Baudwin about this part of the story, as he himself had had many great adventures with grand horns.

"According to the story," he continued, "after the spring mating season, two male grand horns presented themselves to your great-great-great-grandfather — or so — for service, as they often did to the Faeries and Elves."

"Service?" Baudwin asked. "What made them do that?"

"Perhaps if you didn't spend so much time fiddling with elven gadgets and diversions, you would know the answer," Seamus replied, amused at Baudwin's apparent lack of knowledge. "Grand horns *always* present themselves to Faeries and Elves after the spring mating season."

"Where were they when that happened?" asked Baudwin.

"In the field next to Elva's farm," Seamus replied. "Back then, she wasn't around to scare them off." They both laughed. "In those times," Seamus continued, "as they do now, they presented themselves to both Faeries and Elves. The Elves used them mostly for hauling and trading," he continued.

"And the Faeries?" Baudwin asked.

"The Faeries favored them for farming and traveling," Seamus replied. "Grand horns are indeed quite stubborn. They never let themselves get coerced into service. But, if given the proper time and treated with respect, they do volunteer. An extra offering of privet berries never hurts either."

"Did our ancestors offer them privet berries?" Baudwin asked.

"Indeed they did," Seamus said. "In return, as the story goes, before your great-great-great-grandparents — or so — traveled to Ember Chasm, they hung many things on their racks — bells and chimes, beads of all shapes and sizes, cups, pots and pans, pieces of fabric, flowers, dried herbs, and glowstones. They traded as they went, which helped them to pay for their journey. The grand horns would shake their heads, bellowing loudly, when they heard the sounds of the bells and chimes."

Baudwin looked again at the ceiling. "Did our great-great-great-grand Fae also help to design the family crest?"

"You couldn't have forgotten that," Seamus replied, cuffing Baudwin on the head. "As they were newly bonded in the aethers, they wanted both sides of the family to be represented. One side preferred the color blue, and the other green, so they combined both throughout. This is also why those hues are so popular in Deuona today. You come from a well-born lineage, Baudwin."

Hearing this, Baudwin looked again at the dome crest on the ceiling. As was the custom, every water faery family in Deuona had a Moon in the center of their dome crest, made of crystal with beveled sides. Around the Moon was a green glass eternity knot with many weaving patterns. They wove outward — ending in a square shape that framed the Moon. Finally, around the eternity knot was a blue glass ring, segmented into quarters. Four waves of blue Water were placed in the ring, one to a quarter, with green glyphs on either side of the waves, all emblems of Baudwin's family history.

"The Moon shines ever so brightly," Baudwin said, nodding appreciatively at the ceiling. "What fine work they did."

"Fine indeed," Seamus agreed, beaming with pride. For a moment, he and Baudwin gazed at the Moon without speaking.

Good, Baudwin thought, as he looked at Seamus. His plan had worked. He already knew the story of the dome crest, but getting Seamus to talk about family history was the distraction he had hoped for. Now his grandfather had forgotten all about Glamorium and the coupler. But not for long. As soon as Kelven spoke to Seamus, Baudwin knew he would have to tell them both what had really happened.

"Well now," Seamus asked, "where's Matha?"

"I don't know," Baudwin replied. "Matha!" he called out.

"Here I am," Matha replied, hurrying toward Seamus. "Criofan and I were just making sure that the meeting hall was all set."

"Did you also finish the dining room?" Seamus asked.

"Not yet," Matha replied.

Hearing this, Seamus could barely contain his frustration. "Why did you insist that I tell you that story?" he asked, turning to Baudwin. "Now, there simply is *no* time left!"

"I didn't," Baudwin protested. "Grandfather, you mustn't get so upset. Come with me now!"

With that, Baudwin sped with Matha around the hall, past Seamus's sleeping room and the sitting room. Upon reaching the dining room, he burst inside to take a good look around.

"Everything has been done," he announced happily, as Seamus, Criofan, and Matha caught up to him.

"We were just fooling you!" Matha exclaimed. "We finished all the work."

"You mean you were just trying to provoke my grandfather," Baudwin said, laughing. "I will deal with you both later."

Seamus looked askance at Baudwin, shaking his head. They all stood together, taking in the look and feel of the room.

Before them was a long wooden table, covered with a white lace tablecloth. A silver candelabrum with five white candles sat on either side. Behind the table, stacks of plates, trays of silverware, and rows of carefully folded napkins were neatly arranged on a sideboard. Two smaller tables on either side of the room held glasses. Several ceramic pitchers, soon to be filled with either tea or juice, stood behind the glasses. When the guests arrived, they would cover the main table with their favorite dishes and desserts.

"Thank you, Criofan and Matha," Seamus beamed, as Criofan caught up to them. "What I began, you finished very well." He then paused for a moment to collect himself.

"You're welcome," Matha and Criofan said at once, happy to have been of service.

"I hear the chime," Seamus announced. "Our guests have begun to arrive!"

⁂

With that, they rushed out of the dining room, around the hall, and into the greeting room. Seamus strode briskly toward the door and flung it open.

"Blessings from the Water!" he exclaimed, his voice booming.

"Blessings from the Water!" a number of voices replied back in unison.

There stood several members of the Water Guild — a group growing larger by the moment — faery ladies and gents of all ages, dressed in shades of blue and green, holding plates of food in their hands, and musical instruments — violins, lutes, fifes, reed pipes, and drums.

As the others waited patiently, one faery lady pushed her way through the group, saying, "Excuse me, excuse me," as she went. Upon reaching the door, she added cheerily, "Such a fine-looking group of faery gents! May we please come in?"

Upon seeing her, Seamus cupped his hands over his heart, exclaiming, "Blessings from the Water, Elva! Where's Eolann?" Elva had put on a large blue hat, but was still dressed in the same outfit Baudwin had seen her wearing at the Show Wheel that day.

"Blessings from the Water, Seamus," Elva replied. "Where *is* Eolann?" she asked. "He was right behind me."

Just then, Eolann appeared beside her, excited as a groundhog who had just bored his way through a tunnel of dirt and then popped through. "There you are!" she exclaimed, and proceeded to adjust his jacket collar.

"Blessings from the Water, Eolann!" Seamus exclaimed.

"Blessings from the Water, Seamus!" Eolann replied, smiling brightly. "Blessings from the Water, Baudwin," he added, bobbing his head up and down as he spoke.

"Blessings from the Water!" Baudwin replied.

Elva removed her coat, which she did rather awkwardly as she was also holding a large pie. "Eolann, dear, please do take this pie, will you?" she asked.

"Yes, yes, of course," Eolann replied. He stuffed the flute he was holding into his pocket, and then reached for the pie with both hands.

"Elva, is this your famous potato and leek pie?" Seamus asked, bending down to take a big sniff.

"Famous not only in Deuona, but as far as Four Falls and beyond," Elva replied. "Eolann, dear," she said, turning to her husband, "will you please hang my coat in the greeting room so I can take this pie to the dining room?"

"Yes, yes!" Eolann replied, as he handed the pie back to her, and took her coat.

"I see you brought your flute, Eolann," Seamus said. "After the meeting, we must play together."

Before Eolann could respond, a voice called out, "Are you going to let us come inside, or are we going to stand here all night like a mischief of silverdew mice?"

Everyone laughed, and for good reason. Blue-eyed, silver-coated silverdews were known to be very intelligent mice. They were also known to be quite silent, living as they did beneath fields of milk thistles in underground communities throughout *Tír na nÓg*. They came out only at night.

"We certainly are smart enough," another voice called out. "And some of us have been known to eat a milk thistle or two to cure a touch of indigestion, but none of us will ever be *that* quiet!" Everyone laughed even harder.

"All of you, please do come in!" Seamus called out, smiling broadly.

With that, the entire group filed into the greeting room, nodding and smiling, and saying to one another as they went, "Blessings from the Water!" Many went to hang their coats and hats on hooks, while others sat upon benches, chatting gaily. Some darted around the room, greeting friends they hadn't seen in a while, while others simply stood where they were, laughing and talking. Although the room was quite cramped for space, no one seemed to mind, as everyone was having such an enjoyable time.

Now that the guests had arrived, Baudwin went to his room to change his clothes, which were still damp from the river. Minutes later, he returned to the back of the room, ready to lend a hand whenever he was needed.

"Baudwin, darling, do join us!" a voice exclaimed. To his right, he noticed a small circle of Faeries. Among them were Matha's father, Niall,[1] and his mother, Brigh, the faery lady who had just called to him. Next to them were

____
[1] Pronounced [NIEL]

Criofan's father, Congal,[2] and his mother, Moira,[3] who were talking to Kelven. Criofan and Matha were not with their parents, as they had raced home to change their clothes.

The three Primaries, Baudwin thought, as he watched his father, Niall, and Congal chatting amiably with one another. Theirs was a friendship that went back many hundreds of years, with many shared responsibilities in the Water Guild. Kelven, as the Primary of Water, concerned himself with the well-being of the river. Congal, as the Primary of Trade, saw to commerce, crops, and goods. Niall, as the Primary of Concord, made sure Faeries in the Water Guild got along, both with one another and with those in other elven and faery towns. With that, Baudwin went to say hello to everyone.

"How good to see you, Baudwin," Brigh said. As she touched him on the cheek, Baudwin remembered the moment when she had whispered to him at the Ceremony of the Joining. His entire Life since then had been the same, until yesterday when the Water came to him. Although he hadn't heard his mother, he at least still had Brigh. Eventually, he would confide everything in her, for she held a special place in his heart.

"And you as well, Brigh," Baudwin said.

"Baudwin!" Niall exclaimed. "You must tell us all about the Hop and Hit!"

"Now, Niall," Brigh said, "you mustn't ask him that. What if he doesn't want to talk?"

"Of course he does," Niall replied. "He won!"

"How did you hear about the Hop and Hit so soon?" Baudwin asked, bemused.

"Why *everyone* has heard of your victory over that nasty Roiler," Niall replied. "I heard from Aengus.[4] He heard from Gobán,[5] who heard from Càel.[6] Aengus said there hadn't been such quarrel staffing since his cousin Finn[7] fought with Rian's brother Fraech[8] over a building dispute. And that was over two hundred years ago."

"What happened?" Baudwin asked, wondering why Rian had never told him this story.

---

[2] Pronounced [CONN-ell]
[3] Pronounced [MOY-ra]
[4] Pronounced [ANG-us]
[5] Pronounced [gub-BAWN]
[6] Pronounced [KALE]
[7] Pronounced [FIN]
[8] Pronounced [FREK]

"An Elve named Artgal[9] had agreed to build them each a home, but he made a big mistake when he did. Instead of building a faery home for Finn, and an elven home for Fraech, he did quite the opposite.

"He built Finn an elven home, and Fraech a faery home?" Baudwin asked, amused.

"Precisely," Niall replied. "Needless to say, they were both quite upset."

"How did the fight begin?" Baudwin asked.

"Artgal told them he had an easy answer for their problem. All they had to do was trade houses. Fraech was most willing so he could have his house right away, but Finn did not want to leave his ancestral land. So, I had to step in to help them settle their differences. I told them that if they wanted to resolve their dispute, they would have to fight things out at the Hop and Hit. If Finn won, both houses would be torn down and rebuilt, but if Fraech won, they would simply swap houses. What a contest that was! The fight lasted half a day."

"Who won?" Baudwin asked.

"Why, Finn, of course. Which made Artgal very angry at Fraech. He said that if Fraech had fought harder and better, he wouldn't have had to tear down the houses. After that, they quarrel staffed for *years* over who was right!"

Hearing this, Baudwin said modestly, "I'm sure there have been other contests since then that were more impressive than mine."

"That I rather doubt!" Congal exclaimed. "You really did show that Roiler just who was with the Water. Or, who the Water was with!" he added, laughing. He then turned to Baudwin's father. "What do you think, Kelven?"

"I will tell you what I think," Kelven replied with a gleam in his eye that Baudwin had never seen before. "I think my coupler is at the *bottom* of the Hop and Hit." He then smiled, and let out a strange-sounding laugh, which Baudwin had also never heard.

"What does a coupler have to do with Baudwin's victory?" Moira asked.

"Do tell us," Brigh chimed in.

As Kelven stopped laughing, Baudwin glanced uneasily at him. "Nothing, I suppose," Kelven replied as he looked at Baudwin. "I was only joking."

All eyes turned to Baudwin. "Is he?" Niall asked.

"Of course," Baudwin replied, not knowing what else to say. He then felt a sharp tap on his shoulder. "If you will excuse me for a moment," he added, feeling quite happy to turn his attention away from the conversation.

As he looked behind him, Baudwin found himself face to face with a pair of shifty eyes, nervously scanning the room for danger, like a brown hare wary of a badger. "Do I know you?"

---

[9] Pronounced [ART-ghal]

"You do and you don't," a voice answered back. "My name is Lugh, of Four Falls, son of Donovan. I am the Leader of the Guilders of the Nectain Quarter." Seeing that Baudwin seemed to recognize him, he added, "I'm the one you saw in the Center at the Engineerium."

Baudwin noticed that he was dressed more formally for the meeting. Gone were the strings of shells and water drums hanging from his waist, as well as his lily hat. His hair was combed, and pulled away from his face, and his clothes, while rather odd-looking, were clean and well pressed.

Certainly, Baudwin did remember who he was. "You're the one who tried to —"

"Stop the talk that elven Druid was giving," Lugh replied. "Such a nasty business!" Tensely cupping his hands to make the sign of the Water, he added, "In case you thought I wasn't, I am *with* the Water. I came to tell you and everyone else that for the sake of the Water, we must stop them — we must vote *no* on Matter Three!"

"Stop who?" Baudwin asked. "Perhaps you should talk to my grandfather," he added, pointing across the room at Seamus.

"We *all* must stop them," Lugh added, sounding as if the very room in which they stood was about to be invaded by an elven force. "This is just another poisonous gift from our occupiers."

Before Baudwin could say anything more, a voice cried out, "The Grand Eldress has arrived!" The room fell silent — she was the one for whom they had all been waiting. A faery gent opened the door, and everyone streamed out of the room and into the front yard to greet her and her procession.

Chapter 19

THE GRAND VOTE

The Grand Eldress held the highest office in the Water Guild. To get elected by the general membership, a faery lady (or in the case of the Grand Elder, a gent) had to be at least eight hundred years old, of sound body and mind, wise in spirit and caring of heart. Above all, such a one had to have the integrity to hold members of the Water Guild to the highest of standards, and to honestly conduct the affairs of the Guild by being fair to all and partial to none. Tonight, the Grand Eldress would preside over the important meeting — but first she was to lead the processional — a formal celebration where everyone in attendance gathered to commune with one another and their element.

Baudwin could see her emerald robes fluttering in the warm evening breeze. Her large green eyes pensively surveyed the membership — eyes set deeply into a face that had been striking in youth but was now wrinkled and wizened with age, like a well-dried prune. Beneath her robes she wore a blue silk skirt and blouse, with a handsomely woven brocade sash around her waist. A gold necklace hung from her neck, with numerous water charms attached to the links, many of which had been given as gifts over the years. Her graying, blue-green, waist-length hair and pale blue skin offset a remarkable-looking countenance — both compassionate and fiercely determined.

"Blessings from the Water!" she cried, her outstretched arms welcoming each and every member of the Water Guild at once.

"Blessings from the Water!" they cried back.

Wherever she traveled, the Grand Eldress found herself surrounded by a lively, devoted entourage: faery lads and lassies holding baskets of flowers, which they eagerly strewed along her path, musicians playing fanciful tunes, and dancers prancing in time to the music, the bells of their silky costumes tinkling from their waists and ankles.

This evening, two attendants also waited beside her. On one side, a faery gent held a large turquoise parasol above her head, with dragonflies and water lilies embroidered on the sides. On the other side, a faery lady carried a large ceramic pitcher, painted blue and green, with gold Water Guild crests in the design.

"To River Deuona we go!" the Grand Eldress announced.

Everyone filed through the gate, forming a processional behind her. Seeing that Matha and Criofan were approaching the house, Baudwin quickly hopped over the wall and ran toward them. He knew he should not start a conversation during the processional, but just couldn't help himself. Grabbing onto Matha's sleeve, he signaled for them to step away under a tree, so he could talk to them about his dilemma.

Baudwin lowered his voice, so that none nearby would hear. "I just spoke to a rather strange character named Lugh," he said. "He says to vote *no* on Matter Three. How are you both voting?"

"Let's talk about this later," Criofan said. "The processional is about to begin."

Baudwin knew they should be in line, headed toward the river, but he had to understand why Matter Three *mattered*.

"Just tell me if you agree with Lugh."

"Lugh?" Matha asked. "Was he wearing a lily hat?"

"No," Baudin replied. "Why?"

"I met a water Faery named Lugh at the Garden of Sprockets," Matha replied. "Wild, unpredictable and *determined* to save the Faeries from the Elves. In fact, I had to stop him from tearing down the Sprouting Patch."

"Really?" Baudwin asked. "I wonder if —"

Before Baudwin could finish his sentence, Criofan interrupted him. "I haven't heard of Matter Three," he said. "Have you?" he asked, turning to Matha.

"Not until this moment," Matha replied.

Looking over his shoulder, Baudwin could see the musicians joining the processional. He had to speak quickly.

"This is the third time today that I have," Baudwin said. "What's going on? This important matter seems *very* important, and I don't know what to do. My grandfather wants me to vote *no*; in fact, he insisted that I do."

"I don't know," Matha replied, "but I'll probably vote the way my father does. He says that concord is more crucial to our well-being than anything else in Deuona."

"My father always votes the way yours does," Criofan said, "because without concord there can be no trade." Turning to Baudwin, Criofan asked, "You aren't worried about this, are you, Baudwin?"

"I suppose not," Baudwin replied. "But three times in one day makes me want to know what is so —"

"Then stop thinking about what you heard, and just vote *no*," Criofan said, trying not to laugh.

"That's what I was planning to do," Baudwin replied, irked.

Turning his attention back to the meeting, Baudwin saw the Grand Eldress motion to the musicians to begin to play. As he turned to join the processional, Criofan put his arm around his shoulder. "Did you tell him?" he asked.

"Tell who, what?" Baudwin asked, looking quizzically at his friend.

"You know," Criofan replied. "Seamus. Did you tell him about the glamorium egg? Since we talked?"

Uncomfortably, Baudwin looked down at the ground.

"You didn't tell Seamus?" Criofan asked. "Why not?"

Baudwin knew that he had some explaining to do. The last time he and his friends had spoken about Glamorium, they had agreed to talk to their elders about the egg. However, Baudwin had avoided the subject with Seamus. Looking at his friends, he knew he wasn't going to fool either of them. If he told them Seamus had been too busy to listen, they would know he was lying.

"We haven't spoken about it yet," Baudwin replied, "what with all there was to do to get ready for the meeting."

"Really now," Criofan said. "How *responsible* of you."

"I told him he had to," Matha chimed in. "But he didn't."

"All I'm interested in now is how the meeting will go," Baudwin said. "Especially Matter Three."

"Oh, sure," Criofan chided him. "You're *so* interested that you don't even know which way you're going to vote."

"Which is why I want to give my complete attention to the meeting right now," Bauwdin replied, grinning. *Now I have them where I want them,* he thought. "Are you saying I shouldn't pay such close attention to the *Matter* at hand?" he asked.

"Don't put words into our mouths, Baudwin," Criofan said.

"I'm not," Baudwin replied. "Any more than you're putting your words into mine. Let's go, shall we?" He gestured toward the gate.

Before his friends could respond, a series of drum rolls, accompanied by flutes and trumpets, sounded the call that the processional was about to begin. The Grand Eldress began leading the walk to the bottom of the hill, everyone singing and clapping as they followed behind her. An ancient faery hymn filled the Air:

The Earth abides to hold my body

To fill my soul with vigor

The Water abides to heal my heart

To fill my soul with feeling

The Air abides to touch my mind

To fill my soul with vision

The Fire abides to feed my spirit

To fill my soul with fervor

The Woods abide to bring me Life

To fill my soul with rapture

The Light abides to show me truth

To fill my soul with Being

Having reached the river, they paused for a moment. Twilight was upon them, as were the stars and the rising Moon. Everyone became very still. The faery lady in attendance handed the sacred pitcher to the Grand Eldress. Reverently, she bent down to dip the spout into the rushing stream, holding the handle with one hand, and steadying the bottom with the other. Her long hair trailed upon the surface of the Water like silken strands of river grass. When the vessel was full, she rose and presented her offering to the group. "May the Water always flow through us!" she proclaimed.

To which they all replied, "And may we always flow with the Water!" As they spoke, the wind picked up, and sounds of tinkling chimes could be heard, as if myriad pieces of glass were clinking together at once — although none were anywhere to be seen. The ceremony had opened their hearing. Carefully, they cocked their heads to one side — listening — becoming lost in the arguing of blackbirds in the trees and the whispering of fish in the Water, while understanding every word they spoke. And all the while, currents flowed beneath the surface, leaving luminescent trails of blue, green, and gold Light. All watched — transfixed — unable to look away, or to take their leave. For they had forgotten themselves by remembering the Water.

The Grand Eldress raised her arms. "Now, we must go," she announced, for if she hadn't, they would have remained there all night. Reluctantly, they came out of their waking, bonded as they now were to one another. They then made their way back to the house, their legs wobbly, minds still, and hearts full — so absorbed in their element had they been. The Grand Eldress held the pitcher before her as she went, the musicians and dancers played and danced along, and the others followed behind them, singing and clapping. All in all, they were as festive a group as any that could be found in *Tir na nÓg*.

Baudwin followed behind his father and grandfather, happy to have shared the waking with them, for he hadn't had another bout and everything seemed to be fine.

Upon reaching the house, everyone filed through the gate, down the path and into the greeting room. The Grand Eldress made her way to the shrine, and the others went to sit upon the cushions in the meeting hall. The musicians and dancers seated themselves in the first circle around the shrine. None of the youngest Faeries were to be seen, as they had been whisked away by their elder siblings to go home to bed.

As Baudwin and his friends searched for a place to sit, Lugh approached him. "Mind if I join you?" he asked.

"Not at all," Baudwin replied. "In fact, I would like you to meet my friends. Lugh, this is Matha and Criofan; Matha and Criofan, this is Lugh, the faery gent I was telling you about."

"We've met," Lugh said, eyeing Matha suspiciously.

"I almost wouldn't have recognized you without your lily hat," Matha quipped. "Or a broken meadowlark," he added snidely.

"A broken meadowlark?" Baudwin asked, raising his eyebrows at Lugh.

"Not a *real* one," Lugh replied, smiling.

"Just one that probably took an Elve weeks to make," Matha admonished him.

Lugh stopped smiling, and Baudwin began laughing. He then remembered more about who Lugh was. "You're Lugh of Four Falls, son of Donovan, Leader of the Guilders of the Nectain Quarter," he said. Baudwin placed his hands on his hips, as Lugh had done the first time Baudwin had seen him. He then looked sternly at Matha. "They kicked him out, you know."

"Where?" Matha asked.

"At the Tree of Innovation!" Baudwin exclaimed. "In the Center. At the Engineerium. So tell me, how do you know this lily-hatted troublemaker?"

"From the Garden of Sprockets," Matha replied dryly. "When he tried to demolish the Sprouting Patch."

Amused, Baudwin was now certain that the Lugh he knew, and the Lugh Matha knew were indeed one and the same. "*Really* now?" he laughed, boxing Lugh on the shoulder. "You're quite the rabble-rouser, aren't you?"

Lugh smiled, obviously pleased with his infamy. Nodding amiably at Baudwin and his friends, he cupped his hands in front of him, saying, "I am *with* the Water."

Matha decided not to provoke Lugh any further with his comments. Instead, he made the sign, saying, "I am with the Water," as did Criofan. Most of the Faeries in the meeting hall had by now found their seats, so hurriedly they all sat down.

⚭

Standing before them at the fountain, the Grand Eldress was about to start the meeting. A hush came over the room as, pitcher in hand, she slowly began her customary walk clockwise around the circle. As she went, she poured the Water from the river into the sparkling turquoise fountain of the shrine. "May the spirit of the Water guide us always — in good times and bad — to heal our hearts and fill our souls with feeling," she spoke as an invocation. "Blessings from the river."

To which everyone replied, "Blessings from the river."

The Grand Eldress then took leave of the walkway, sitting down in a circle nearest to the shrine, so she could continue the meeting, her two attendants on either side of her.

"And," she affirmed, "may we give thanks to every puddle, spring, brook, stream, creek, river, pond, lake, or sea, which *is* the Water, for nourishing us with Life, healing our hearts, and bringing feeling to our souls. Thank you to the Water," she added, as a blessing.

To which everyone replied, "Thank you to the Water."

Standing up, the musicians and dancers then formed a circle around the shrine. As the musicians played a stirring melody, the dancers pranced and whirled in circles around the fountain of Water. *Ching, ching, ching,* went their waist and ankle bells, in rhythm with the lilt of the music. Everyone in the meeting hall joined in with them, singing and clapping. When the music was over, the performers returned to their places, and the meeting hall fell silent.

All the preparation ceremonies were now complete, but the meeting could not begin until the rest of the Faeries arrived. Something entirely unexpected then happened. A faery gent stood up, a member of the Channel of Concord who served under the Primary. "And may the river also bring us prosperity," he announced, "for this evening we have come together to consider two Matters of great importance to Deuona — Matter One, pertaining to Concord, and Matter Three, to Commerce. Should we vote *yes,* Matter One will most assuredly bring our community closer together, and Matter Three will most certainly enrich our coffers."

Upon hearing this, a ripple of rancor coursed through the entire hall, along with gasps of incredulity. A voice cried out, "This is simply *outrageous*! Such things are not to be spoken of now! We must wait until after the Eddies and the Roilers arrive!"

The distress among the members was completely understandable, for according to *gnàs,* worldly affairs of the Water Guild should not be addressed alongside those considered to be sacred. Announcements — before, during, or after — were *never* to be given at ceremonies. This particular custom — observed by the Water Guild for as long as anyone could remember — had now been violated, snapped in two like a brittle branch of kindling before a roaring balefire.

Seamus then spoke. "Sit down. We must wait for the Eddies and Roilers to arrive before we discuss these matters."

With a blush, the faery gent sat down. In his haste to sway the gathering, he had forgotten *gnàs*, which had to come before all else. Waiting ensured respect not only for missing parties, but even more importantly — for the Water itself. In this way, both reason and decorum would prevail among the rills of the Water Guild — the Guilders, Eddies, and Roilers.

Great importance was put upon ensuring that these three groups of Faeries got along, for each had very different views about how the affairs of the water Faeries should be run. The Guilders had always tended to be rigidly for, and the Roilers recklessly against *gnàs*, while the Eddies had been exclusively neither, vacillating between being both for and against *gnàs*. Often, the Eddies found themselves in the conciliatory middle, affording them influence which they greatly enjoyed.

"Did you hear that?" Lugh whispered, incensed by the gent who had spoken out of turn. Leaning closer to Baudwin, he added, "He sounds like Gavin at the Tree of Innovation. Bringing us together, so he can assail us with his manipulations. Since *when* has the Water Guild ever included announcements in their ceremonies? I tell you, something is afloat — as offensive as a rotting school of beached garfish!"

The meeting hadn't even begun, and already sentiment in the room had turned sour. This surprised Baudwin, for although the gent who had spoken out of turn had been rude, the Faeries seemed particularly upset. Now he wondered even more what the matters were about.

"Outrageous!" several other voices cried out in unison. "Outrageous!"

"Now, now!" the Grand Eldress called out, as she pounded loudly upon a water drum with a wooden mallet. "We must have order in the meeting hall! The Eddies and the Roilers have arrived." Hearing the thrumming sounds of the water drum, everyone became silent.

The entrance of the Eddies and the Roilers did nothing to lessen the tension in the Air. Arrogantly, the Roilers pushed into the hall past the Eddies, who were all too willing to let them by. As both rills sat down, Baudwin feared they might only make everything worse, for he had never seen them arrive in such numbers. *Matter Three must be tremendously important,* he thought. He then looked at the Roilers in their darker shades, the Eddies in their medium shades, and the Guilders in their lighter shades. All were much too different for a meeting like this — from the clothing on their backs, to their views about the Water, and even how they read. For the Guilders preferred glyphs, the Roilers letters, and the Eddies both glyphs and letters. Too long had these rills drifted away from one another, and Baudwin feared that this meeting would only underscore their differences.

All of the rills were almost seated. As Baudwin turned his head, surveying the crowd, a deep frown crossed his face.

"What's wrong?" Matha whispered, seeing his friend looking so perturbed. Baudwin simply nodded toward the back of the meeting hall. There stood Loch, looking surprisingly composed as he surveyed his surroundings, dressed as he was in dark green and blue, with black leather boots.

"I don't recall him ever attending a Water Guild meeting," Matha said. "Do you?"

"He's not wearing bracers," Baudwin replied.

"I almost didn't recognize him in such elegant-looking clothes," Matha said.

"What could he possibly be up to?" Baudwin asked.

"We'll find out soon enough," Matha replied.

Hearing this, Lugh leaned closer to Baudwin and Matha. "*He's* not the one you should be worried about."

Before either of them could reply, the Grand Eldress announced: "Welcome, one and all, to this impromptu meeting of the Deuona Water Guild. Due to the challenging issues that have arisen, I have called this meeting, so we can reach a consensus on some very important matters. I see that the Eddies have arrived, and many more Roilers than usual, which is good. The Guild wants all of the rills to be properly represented."

Hearing this, Baudwin scowled. Angrily, he began tearing the stitching out of the silk pillow beneath him.

"Stop," Matha muttered to him, "before all the stuffing comes out." Sulkily, Baudwin withdrew his hand.

"Let us now open up the circle," the Grand Eldress continued. "Before we consider the matters at hand, are there any new announcements?"

"If anything is left *to* say," Lugh muttered.

A rather portly-looking faery lady stood up. Slowly, she made her way toward the shrine. "Please remember," she began as she ambled around the circle, "this year for Ura — the Night of Heather — we will gather by the river at the North Bend. All are welcome. The celebration begins at dusk. We hope to see you there. If you would like to help with food, drink, or merrymaking, you may speak to me, Almha,[1] or to Finola."[2] As she spoke, Finola stood up, nodding brightly at the group.

As soon as Almha sat down, Seamus rose and approached the shrine. "As the Leader of the Deuona Water Guild, I say welcome." Strolling around the circle and nodding to his friends, he added, "We're happy to be your hosts this evening. Please do join us after the meeting in the dining room. After that, you may come to the sitting room, where we will be dancing and making

---

[1] Pronounced [ALM-ha]
[2] Pronounced [Fin-O-lah]

music. Be sure to bring your instruments!" As he finished speaking, everyone clapped appreciatively.

"And I see that we have another Guild Leader with us tonight," Seamus added, gesturing toward Lugh. "I thank you for coming all the way from Four Falls."

"I'm glad to be here," Lugh replied. Baudwin was surprised that Seamus knew him, for he had never mentioned him before, as he rarely spoke of other guild leaders outside of Deuona.

Seamus then sat down.

"Are there any more announcements?" asked the Grand Eldress. No one rose. "Very good. Are there any announcements from the three primaries?" she asked, smiling benevolently at Kelven, Niall, and Congal, who sat a short distance away. Smiling back, they shook their heads *no*.

The Grand Eldress pounded her drum, laughing merrily. "May I take this to mean that you're saving your words for the matters themselves? Let us then commence with the meeting. May we hear from the Primary of Concord?"

With that, Niall stood up. After making his way to the circle, he began speaking. "Please allow me to introduce Matter One, which has been penned by members of the Channel of Concord on behalf of the Roilers. As you know, the Roilers have no primaries, so they are exercising their right to put this matter before the Guild. Matter One is primarily a building project to enhance the beauty of the Township of Deuona, which could also draw even more visitors and travelers to our fair hamlet."

Hearing his father speak, Matha scowled, and Baudwin surmised that Niall had been forced by the Roilers to bring the Matter forward.

"And now," Niall continued, "Allow me to introduce my friend and fellow guild member, Liber.[3] Most of you know Liber not only as an Eddy, but a very successful trader in Deuona."

As Liber stood up, Lugh muttered to Baudwin, "He's a *traitor* — not a trader. My own brother!"

"Your brother?" Baudwin whispered.

"Yes." Lugh replied. "I can't believe he's turning away from the Guilders about this Matter." With a frown, he went silent.

Liber made his way to the front of the meeting hall to stand before the group. He was rather tall, and very fashionably dressed in a light turquoise shirt, blue breeches, and a green brocade doublet, with an elegant *L*-shaped pin fastened on the lapel. As he walked around the circle, he pressed his hands tightly together, making a sign of the Water. Nodding at the members, he flashed them

---

[3] Pronounced [LEE-ber]

a well-polished smile, as if to say, *I regard all of you, most certainly, as my close personal friends.* This assumption, upon closer examination, did seem rather grandiose, as Liber did not know everyone in the hall *that* well.

As he spoke, his voice sounded suave, yet invitingly superior. "Imagine, if you can," he began, speaking slowly yet adamantly through his nose, "a beautiful garden of river plants and animals made of glowstones and other wonderful materials, a garden built with help from our elven friends — both on land *and* Water — a beautiful *glowstone* garden, built into the cove at South Bend, a garden simply called — *River Shine.*"

"River Shine!" a number of voices sang out in unison.

"Yes, *River Shine,*" Liber continued, even more slowly and adamantly. Despite their apparent interest, he spoke to them as to a group of dullards, who were too thick-headed to understand the importance of what he was saying.

"River Shine!" a number of other voices responded again in unison.

"Is this really necessary?" an agitated Guilder piped up from behind. "Do we really need more large glowstones in South Bend?"

"What we *need* is fewer Guilders telling us how to light our town!" a Roiler exclaimed.

"Or fewer Roilers determined to replace our scenery with glowstones!" the Guilder shot back.

"These are not *simply* glowstones," Liber replied condescendingly, as he adjusted the pin on his doublet. "This is a *garden* of glowstones, perfectly carved into river grasses, cattails and lilies, with sea stars, perch, flutter fish, river otters — and much more."

"Indeed!" another Roiler exclaimed. "Think of all the trade this would bring to Deuona. Even the Elves would come — just to see the Light."

"Precisely," Liber affirmed.

"I say we don't need Water Shine at all!" the Guilder shouted back, more angrily.

"That's *River* Shine," Liber replied, caustically.

As the arguing continued to bounce back and forth among the rills, the entire hall pulsed with emotion. "This is quite enough!" the Grand Eldress called out above the din, as she pounded loudly on her water drum. "Please stop, so we may hear from some others."

With that, a Guilder rose from the center of the hall, a faery lady who looked to be about six and fifty. "Shouldn't we be using our resources more wisely?" she asked. "The glowstones could be used in other parts of the city to light our roads at night. Perhaps, instead of building Water Shine, we could simply spend more time with each other down by the river."

Liber scowled. "That's *River* Shine —"

Another voice then cut him off. "Glowstones won't change the river that much," a younger faery lady, an Eddie, said as she stood up. "Besides, what could be better than improving concord with other faery cities? What harm could come of that?"

With that, the tension in the room mounted, as the Guilders worried that the Eddies would vote with the Roilers. Faery ladies and gents chattered furiously back and forth with one another.

Then another Eddie, an older gent, spoke. "I see the young lady's point, but the river is sacred, and we shouldn't forget that glowstones are a gift from the Elves. We don't want them decorating our entire way of Life. Perhaps we should vote *no*."

Now the Guilders calmed some, and the Roilers seemed upset, for they couldn't tell what the Eddies would do.

The Grand Eldress pounded her water drum. "We are now finished with this discussion, and we must vote. All those in favor of Matter One, the building of River Shine, please rise and say *yea*. When you rise, remember to allow the official counters to complete their tasks. They must bring me the results before you sit down, or you will risk losing your vote."

With that, all the Roilers, and some Eddies stood up, shouting "Yea!" as loudly as they could, clapping and cheering. A number of counters checked the rows where they stood, making note of all the *yeas* and writing the results on parchment cards.

Baudwin tried to count the Eddies, wondering if they had swayed the vote for the Roilers.

"Remain standing," the Grand Eldress ordered the group. As soon as the counters completed their task, they met in groups to compare notes. Having added up the tally, one of them delivered the final count to the Grand Eldress.

"Thank you," she said as she received the card. "And now, all those who are opposed to Matter One, please rise and say *nay*. As you do, remember to allow the official counters to complete their task. They must bring me the results before you sit down, or you will risk losing your vote."

Now every single Guilder stood up, determined to block the Roilers from winning. Baudwin stood too, hoping that Kelven would notice his respect for the Guild. They all shouted, "Nay!" as loudly as they could. They remained on their feet, clapping and jeering, until all of their votes were tallied. As soon as the counter turned in the vote, they sat down.

The Grand Eldress examined both cards carefully, reading the results. Holding the winning card in one hand, she pounded the water drum with the other — *boom, boom, boom*. To the sounds of both cheers and jeers, she announced, "77, yea, 63, nay — the yeas have won the vote — Matter One has passed. River Shine will be built."

These results set off a chorus of shouting, as well as a great deal of squabbling among the members.

"Sold to the membership by the slippery eel that you are, Liber!" Lugh yelled at his brother. "You don't care about the river — you just want more trade!" He then stood up and angrily stamped his foot.

"Sit down — why don't you?" a Roiler gent shouted behind him.

As Lugh took his seat, Matha leaned toward him, saying, "We lost this Matter, but we'll win the others."

"Your father should never have let the Roilers put this forward," Lugh replied, glaring at Matha.

"You *know* he had no choice," Baudwin interjected. Hearing his displeasure, Lugh became silent.

"May we hear from the Primary of Water?" asked the Grand Eldress.

With that, Kelven stood up. After making his way to the circle, he began. "Please allow me to introduce Matter Two, which has been penned by members of the Channel of Water — again, mostly Roilers, I presume," Kelven added. As he spoke, he looked disdainfully at a group of Roilers who were sitting in a row of the meeting hall. They glared back at him.

"Matter Two will allow geyser pistols in the town of Deuona proper, at all times of the day or night. As the Primary of Water," he added scornfully, "I hope this Matter sinks like a boulder to the bottom of the river." With that, a chorus of guilder cheers filled the room.

Taking notice of his father's words, Baudwin turned his attention to Loch, who had risen to speak. "Despite the position the Primary has taken on this," Loch began, "I believe the time has come to allow those of us who like to carry geyser pistols to be able to do so, *wherever* and *whenever* we want to." Snidely, he shot Baudwin a glance, which only reminded Baudwin of how Criofan had been shot with a geyser pistol that very day. Although geyser pistols were used mainly for recreation, all Guilders were nevertheless appalled by them.

"And by what right should you?" Criofan retorted as he stood up. "When you can't even use them properly? Your Roiler friend shot me right in the eye at the Engineerium!" Hearing this, ripples of outrage coursed through the hall.

"That never happened!" Loch shouted. Gesturing to groups of Roilers on either side of him, he turned to face Kelven. "To answer his question," he continued, pointing to Criofan, "it's by the right that I am, as of this evening, the newly elected leader of the Roiler rill, and also, I might add, its first and *only* leader." He then smirked contemptuously at Baudwin and his friends, who could only look incredulously at each other.

"I can prove that what my friend Criofan says is true — *I was there!*" Matha exclaimed, as he stood up.

Hearing this, Loch smiled boldly. "Well, if this did happen, and I say *if*, I'm sure my friend was only playing. Accidents do happen, especially at the Engineerium." Hearing this, a number of Roilers clapped loudly in support.

"Your callous disregard for the Water is no accident," Baudwin sputtered angrily, as he stood up. "We must not allow him to steer us away from our path," he implored the group, "by allowing these defilers of the Water to *play* with what we all hold to be most sacred." As Baudwin sat down, chattering groups of rills began arguing and shouting.

"Now, now," Loch declared above the din. "We do all of this simply in the spirit of enjoying the Water, as you yourselves do, and having fun. You take our actions way too seriously."

"Yes!" a Roiler called out. "You're just a bunch of staid, humorless, clodpoles!"

"Clodpoles indeed!" a Guilder called out. "You're just a rill of rowdy, rebellious rascals!" A sizable part of the hall then lit up with laughter, whistling, and clapping.

With that, Kelven stood up. Looking past Loch and his entourage and out to the general audience, he began, "I must add my thoughts about this very important matter. Every day, we see more and more of our townsfolk gathering in groups and carrying on with these geyser pistols, interrupting what should be the natural harmony and flow of our everyday lives. Just now, when I heard someone shout, 'rebellious,' I became concerned. Some of our kin may be acting out of impulse rather than harmony with the Water. This is why, before we consider our vote, we should first ask ourselves, *rebellious* to what end? There are times when resistance is called for, but I must question the intentions of some who would regard themselves as being *above* our ways. For I believe that when we engage in rebellious behavior without having proper reverence for the Water, we are very much like water lilies trying to grow in a dry, barren riverbed. There can be no such thing! Therefore, I say, enough is enough! For the good of all, we must keep certain restrictions concerning the use of geyser pistols in place."

Kelven's words struck a strong chord throughout the hall, and Baudwin beamed with pride at his father. So infrequently was he resolute, but tonight he had found his spur.

A voice then cried out, "Hear, hear, for the Primary of Water!" Amid a flurry of protests and applause, which reverberated throughout the entire hall, Kelven sat down, looking pleased with himself.

Baudwin glanced again at the Eddies, for they ultimately would decide the vote.

"Thank you for your comments — and now we must vote." Again, the Grand Eldress beat her drum, and everyone became silent. "As you know, my duty is to remain impartial. I do not and *will* not take sides in this matter. That being said, I caution you all to make the right decision. For you will have to live with both the merits *and* the consequences of your vote, no matter which of the rills you are with. And, I myself thank the Water that as the Grand Eldress I do not have to stoop so low as to trifle about what is sacred and what is play, for the only course in my view, is to truly flow *with* the Water!"

She then brought the vote forward.

"All those who are in favor of Matter Two, allowing geyser pistols in Deuona at any hour of the day or night, please rise, and say *yea*." With that, a large number of Faeries stood up, many of them young, shouting "Yea!" as loudly as they could. As they continued cheering and clapping, the counters began to tally all of their votes.

"Remain standing," the Grand Eldress warned. Having completed the task at hand, the counter brought her the final tally. Upon receiving the card, she called out, "And now, all of those who are opposed to Matter Two, please rise and say *nay*."

Once again, a large number of Faeries stood up shouting, "Nay!" as loudly as they could. As they continued jeering and clapping, the official counters quickly tallied the vote, which they presented to the Grand Eldress.

Again, Baudwin tried to count the Eddies, but he wasn't sure how they had voted. *Have they drifted too far from the Water?* he wondered. Perhaps too many seasons of circling in their own currents had made them indifferent to the flows around them.

The Grand Eldress carefully examined the two cards in her hand. Everyone in the hall tried to read her expression, but her prune-faced wrinkles were still as granite, and her steely eyes revealed nothing.

"The count is 68 yea and 72 nay — this time the nays have won the vote. Matter Two has *not* passed!" she cried out, as she pounded her drum.

"Yes!" Baudwin shouted, staring jubilantly at his father. The entire hall became a crucible of shock and fury, with voices jabbering and shouting, and emotions reaching an absolute fever pitch. Kelven nodded happily at Baudwin, and then glared at the Roilers across the hall. Baudwin looked at Loch, who scowled back at him. His false air of sophistication had quickly melted away, and Baudwin wondered if the Roiler would charge at him.

Baudwin wasn't going to let a sore loser get the best of him. He rose to defend himself, but immediately a hand grabbed his arm, pulling him down. "Baudwin — calm yourself!" Matha exclaimed.

"Listen to him," Criofan declared, "or you will surely regret your actions!" Having said that, Criofan chopped Baudwin in the back of the knees with both his hands, until they buckled.

"You beat him once —" Matha continued.

"Once is not enough!" Baudwin countered.

"This isn't the Hop and Hit!" Matha exclaimed. "Now sit!" Hearing Matha's insistence, Baudwin reluctantly sat back down on his cushions.

Smugly, Loch sneered at Baudwin, happy that he had gotten a rise out of him.

"The Matter has *not* passed," the Grand Eldress repeated fiercely, as she pounded her drum. "All of you now — be *silent!*" She then shook her mallet at the hall, like a conductor who, by waving her baton only once, could simply make the entire orchestra disappear. Instantly, all voices in the hall fell silent.

"Good," she continued. So as not to completely dampen their spirits, she asked, cheerfully, "May we please hear from the Primary of Trade?"

With that, Congal carefully approached the circle, looking as if he were about to hang a bell around the neck of a wild boar. Once there, he got right to the point. "Please allow me to introduce Matter Three, which has been put forward by members of the Channel of Commerce in cooperation with the Assembly of Progress." Struggling to conceal his exasperation, he added, "For some of you, this will be a very contentious issue, as Matter Three will allow our elven friends to provide Deuona with a newly created source of power, which will be used in our homes and businesses alike — *Magniglow.*"

"You see?" Lugh whispered hotly into Baudwin's ear. "*This* is what I meant." As he spoke, Liber made his way toward the circle, accompanied by another faery gent. Seeing his brother, Lugh declared, "It's not just the Elves, but the Eddies who are behind this, along with those awful Roilers. What a bunch of hornswogglers!"

Upon reaching the circle, Liber turned to face the members. Invitingly, he announced, "Please allow me to introduce my friend, Lachtin,[4] a faery gent who has come all the way from Four Falls to explain what Magniglow *is*, and why you must vote *yes* on Matter Three."

Hearing this, Lugh jumped to his feet. "I've listened to all I care to hear!" he shouted. "I've already learned enough about Magniglow, the *Fourth* Branch of Progress — as if we needed another!" he scoffed. "I tried to warn everyone about Magniglow, but the elven Druid, Gavin, wouldn't listen to me, and then his crony, Ferrell, had his guards escort me from the Center of the Engineerium."

"Too bad he didn't escort you back to Four Falls," Liber said. "so you can whisper to your lilies that the Elves mean to ruin us all."

---

4   Pronounced [LOCK-tin]

Laughter broke out in the hall. The Roilers hooted, and some of the Eddies jeered at Lugh. None of the Guilders said a word.

"Yes, and too bad the Water sent me a profane coward like you for a brother!" Lugh shouted.

The Grand Eldress hammered on her water drum, and eyed both of them sternly. Lugh and Liber bit their tongues. Lugh then continued. "By the way, Liber, don't you find it curious that a Luminary like Ferrell would arrive in Deuona just as we are voting on this?"

"Whatever do you mean, Brother?"

Lugh then became agitated, nervously shifting his eyes from side to side, as if he wasn't sure he wanted to speak the truth. The entire community was before him, and he didn't seem to want to challenge their authority.

Yet, he did.

"He's too high up on the elven ladder to have just come here by coincidence!" he exclaimed. "Obviously, he means to meddle in our affairs by offering us a glittering promise that's too good to be true!"

"I wouldn't know," Liber replied smoothly.

"Yes, you do!" Lugh shouted. "The Elves are out to get us! Magniglow will poison the Water!"

The hall went silent. Everyone looked at Lugh, wondering what he meant. Baudwin had never considered that Magniglow could poison anything. Lugh sounded addled, but there was an earnestness to him that made Baudwin wonder all the same. Seamus nodded at Lugh, agreeing with him, yet Baudwin could tell his grandfather wasn't entirely sure of what he meant.

"Now you certainly are being absurd," Liber added breezily.

Baudwin could see that Liber was pretending to be calm so that he could make his brother look like a raving fool. He also sensed that Lugh was fuming inside, but had checked himself, being careful not to lose any more credibility with the gathering.

"You'll see someday — mark my words," Lugh concluded.

"Calm down — both of you," the Grand Eldress commanded, leaning toward them. "Now, Liber *and* Lugh," she continued, "I've known you for far too many seasons to count. As of late, I have presided over a number of your disputes, and I must say, you certainly were *much* more fair-minded with each other when you were young lads, not to mention better-behaved!" Hearing this, everyone began to laugh. "Now, if you will *please* stop your arguing, we will get back to the Matter at hand." Petulantly, Lugh sat back down.

"Thank you, Grand Eldress," Liber continued suavely. "Now, if we may please give Lachtin the opportunity to explain what Magniglow *is*, including all the amazing uses of this marvelous new invention, I'm sure all of our concerns will be put to rest."

Lachtin made his way to the circle and began to speak. "There's nothing to fear about Magniglow, for this invention is the most *exciting* Branch of Progress yet. It's entirely new — but not new at all — something the Elves call *power* — very much like bolts of lightning that flash across the sky during a summer rainstorm. Magniglow power will provide us with a reliable way not only to light our homes, but also to operate our machines. Imagine a realm where you no longer need a water mill to grind grain!"

Hearing this, a number of Faeries gasped in awe.

"Now, the Elves know how to bottle lightning?" an Eddie cried out.

"Lightning in a bottle!" a number of other Eddies whispered excitedly.

"Not exactly," Lachtin replied. "While Magniglow is similar to lightning, there are other things about this amazing new power that are quite different. No one knows how the Elves make Magniglow, and I don't know if the Assembly of Progress is planning to tell us."

"And why do you suppose that might be?" Lugh whispered to Baudwin and Matha, deeply agitated.

"I can't say," Matha whispered back, "as I haven't even seen Magniglow." As he spoke, he looked at his father, who was shaking his head vehemently from side to side. "But from what I can see, I will probably vote *no*."

"Well, I've seen Magniglow," Baudwin began, his eyes shining. "I tried to tell you and Criofan, but there wasn't any time."

"I don't know —" Matha replied skeptically, as he looked again at his father.

"Keep listening," Lugh cut in, "and then you *will* know." Hearing this, the three of them turned their attention back to Lachtin.

"You must not let any of this worry you," Lachtin continued to explain. "I myself was skeptical at first. But the Elves in Four Falls assured me that we have nothing to be concerned about. Magniglow is completely safe and reliable. Wait until you see the demonstration!"

Feeling the tension in the hall subsiding, Lachtin said optimistically, "Some of you have seen the magniglow booth at the Engineerium. With Magniglow, our homes will run more easily, we'll have brighter, more dependable lights, less need to mine glowstones, as well as the promise of many future comforts and economies to come. I've heard that in the Clock City, all of the homes run on Magniglow."

After the first two Matters had been settled, Baudwin had assumed he wouldn't like the third. Much to his surprise this wasn't the case, for he found Magniglow to be very exciting. He wondered then how he would vote.

"You see?" Baudwin whispered to Matha. "You should have seen Magniglow at the Engineerium. All the bulbs glowed so brightly — much brighter than glowstones! The Elve at the booth told me that one day we could have Magniglow doing all of our jobs at the mill and the dam. I wouldn't have to do all that boring grinding, and the gates would just raise themselves!" Hearing Baudwin's enthusiasm, Matha decided not to comment, choosing instead to listen to the debate. Baudwin gave up trying to engage him.

"I just don't know about this!" a faery lady exclaimed as she suddenly rose, holding tightly onto her sister's arm. Both of them were long-standing Guilders, and well over eight hundred.

"What I mean," she continued, "is that a lot of things were much better when we were young." Smiling fondly, she added, "We worked very hard — my sister with weaving, and I with pottery. We traveled together by grand horn in our wagons, traded for other goods, and then brought them home. Things were much better then between the Faeries and Elves. . . although I'm not exactly sure when that was," she added, rambling absentmindedly.

Catching herself, she continued, "The work was hard, but we didn't mind because there was much less noise. All these inventions are too loud. I just don't —"

"*Understand*, my dear," Lachtin interrupted, "You don't understand. With Magniglow, there will be *less* noise, not more. You'll see." Upon hearing this, a ripple of approval coursed through the meeting hall.

"Yes, instead of being noisier," Lachtin continued to the general membership, "Magniglow will make things *much* quieter. For one thing, we won't have all of those loud, annoying steamway engines, pumping and grinding. Even our lumber rollers will be quieter."

Hearing this, the faery lady stood a bit straighter. "Well, I certainly don't know much about Magniglow, young gent," she asserted, "but I do know something about the Elves, and I can tell you this — if we allow them to do *whatever* they want in Deuona, there may be less noise, but there will be lots of wires. In fact, I think there will be wires, and wires, and even *more* wires."

"Exactly!" Lugh exclaimed, as he suddenly put his arm around Baudwin's shoulders, squeezing them tightly. Seamus gripped his staff, nodding his head.

"Perhaps," Lachtin replied, as he turned to face the old faery lady. Speaking efficiently, he continued, "However, I am *quite* confident the Elves will be able to handle the wires, and in fact —"

"Now you listen to me!" the old Faery interrupted, as she stood even straighter, holding more tightly onto her sister. "Wires are like little worms, except they are much, *much* longer. Imagine an earthworm several yards long, burrowing and twisting under the ground — getting longer and longer, until the entire body takes over your garden, squeezing the Life out of your flowers, and ruining your summer vegetables. *That's* exactly what you will have!"

Momentarily, her tirade silenced the entire meeting hall, giving her sister a chance to speak. "My sister is right," the second sister began. "Do we really need this new invention? At the Engineerium today an Elve named Glas claimed that his new magniglow bulbs were much better than my glowstones. Do we *really* need such blindingly bright lamps in our homes? I can do my work just as well with what I have. And, if I need more Light, all I have to do is to place more glowstones next to each other."

"I was there when my sister told him just that," the first sister added emphatically. "All he said was, 'Don't you get tired of lugging around all those heavy glowstones? Just imagine how much more easily you will be able to light your rooms if you use magniglow bulbs.'"

Upon hearing this, another faery gent stood up, wizened and stooped, the eldest by far in the room. "I am a proud member of the Eddies," he began. "Unlike my lady friends," he added, as he winked in their direction, "I myself could use brighter lights. When I tap the crowns of my glowstones, they don't glow as brightly as I want them to. Perhaps, I am getting too old to see properly, and some of them are quite heavy."

"Ho! Then we have *just* the solution for you!" Lachtin exclaimed. "Faeries like yourself who are getting on in years need not worry about constantly reaching for glowstones, because now you will be able to use *switches*!"

Hearing this, a flutter of excitement coursed through the hall, and several voices murmured "Switches!"

"A switch," Lachtin continued, "can be put on any wall in your home. When you move the switch either up or down, the bulbs in the room will go either on or off." He then flipped his finger up and down, showing how a switch would work. As he finished his explanation, several Faeries gasped in astonishment.

"Older Faeries aren't the only ones who are having trouble lighting their glowstones," Lugh whispered tensely to Baudwin and Matha. "I've spoken to Faeries as young as two and fifty who are having the same kind of difficulty. Why do you suppose that is? Shouldn't we be paying attention to *that* instead of this?"

"I can't really say," Matha replied. "Perhaps —"

Before Matha could finish his sentence, Seamus stood up and grabbed the two lanterns he had brought with him and strode toward the circle, holding one in each hand. Inside were the white glowstones he had borrowed from Baudwin that morning. "All of this is complete and utter nonsense!" he exclaimed, as he set the lanterns down. "If I want Light, I simply *make* the Light that has always been here in *Tír na nÓg*."

He then reached inside one of his lanterns, and tapped the glowstone sharply in the center. Instantly, rays of Light beamed throughout the meeting hall. After that, he picked up the other lantern and tapped the other glowstone. "And," he went on, "if I want *more* Light, I simply *make* more." With that, he tapped both glowstones, until they shined brighter and brighter.

"My glowstones *always* work for me!" he exclaimed. Seeing the demonstration, several groups of Guilders laughed and jeered.

Seamus beamed, and Baudwin wondered if his grandfather had just swayed the vote, the same way Kelven did on the previous Matter. Baudwin wondered what Seamus would do if he voted for Magniglow. *I better not*, he thought.

The Roilers, who had been silent through Seamus's demonstration, now had a gleam in their eyes. Baudwin couldn't tell why they seemed so confident.

"Whatever are they doing?" Matha asked.

"Who?" Baudwin replied.

"Loch and his friends — over there," Matha said, motioning to the far right of the hall.

Baudwin knew the Roilers had to be up to something. He and Matha watched Loch make his way down the aisle toward Lachtin, who smiled approvingly. Two Roilers followed behind him, each one holding a large wooden box.

"What are they carrying?" Criofan asked.

"Nothing good — of that I can assure you," Lugh replied.

As soon as the Roilers reached him, Loch motioned for them to set the boxes down and open the lids. Each one then removed a large bronze object, one from each box.

"What strange-looking machines — what are they?" Matha asked.

"Strange indeed," Criofan agreed. "I've never seen one before."

"I know what they are," Lugh replied angrily. "They're —"

"Dynamos!" Baudwin cut in. "I saw them at the Engineerium. An Elve at the magniglow booth showed me how to use one."

"And now they're going to show us," Lugh said disdainfully.

With that, Loch motioned for his lackeys to place the dynamos directly across from each other, one on either side of the circle.

"What nerve," Baudwin remarked as he watched them set up their display. Yet, despite his disgust, he also could not keep from staring appreciatively at the dynamos. They then placed a lamp fitted with glass bulbs next to each one.

"Watch what happens!" Baudwin exclaimed. With that, Kelven and Seamus gave Baudwin a concerned look, as he seemed far too excited for their taste. Everyone in the hall then turned their attention to the bulbs. Even the Grand Eldress raised her eyebrows, cocking her head to one side. Seamus stared angrily at the Roilers as they started cranking the dynamos.

"Faster!" Loch exclaimed, waving his arms. Hearing his command, both of the Roilers turned their cranks more rapidly. As they did, some of the bulbs began to glow a soft green color, and the others red. Seeing this, groups of Faeries throughout the hall giggled and clapped with delight.

"Faster!" Loch shouted, waving his arms from side to side. "Brighter!"

"Ooooooh!" swooned the Eddies, as the light radiated more brightly. "Ooooooooooooh!" they swooned again, as the Roilers cranked even faster, and the light grew even brighter. "Ooooooooooooooooooooooooooh!" they swooned again, this time without restraint. The Roilers were now turning the cranks as fast as they could, and all the bulbs radiated a bright green or red, overwhelming the glowstones that Seamus had left on.

Seeing this, the Guilders were not as excited as the Eddies, yet a few wore smiles on their faces.

"You see, Seamus," a faery lady called out, "perhaps *you* see no need for this new invention, but some of us must, politely, disagree."

As Seamus turned around, there stood Elva, Seamus's neighbor, appearing quite pleased with herself as she spoke. "I for one as a proud Eddy, and this includes my dear husband, Eolann, believe that Magniglow is *just the thing* for our growing turnip farm." A number of Eddies sitting next to her nodded in agreement.

"I believe that a lot of our neighbors feel the same way," she added, basking in the attention she was receiving, like a queen bee in the center of a busy hive. "With Magniglow, we will be able to pump more Water to our farms, and raise even bigger and better crops. Isn't that true, Liber?"

"Elva, you are completely correct," Liber replied, vainly pushing his hair to his temples with his two middle fingers. "Not only will Magniglow help us to better light our homes, and irrigate our crops, but we will also be able to use this amazing new invention to light parts of River Shine. A new display such as this will soon open in Four Falls, where Magniglow is about to be approved."

"Not if I can help it!" Lugh shouted.

Hearing this, Seamus double-tapped the glowstones on the walkway, putting them out. Angrily shaking his head, he picked up his lanterns and left the circle. Seeing the look on his face, Elva called out, "Seamus, you mustn't let our disagreement about what is best for Deuona ruin our friendship!"

Seamus ignored her. The Roilers then stopped cranking, and the bulbs dimmed somewhat, as the charge from the dynamos had kept them lit. Liber continued speaking.

"As I was saying," he added, nodding at Elva and Seamus, "in addition to new lights, the very next invention you *both* could be enjoying in your homes is a new spice grinder for your kitchen. And then a new pump for the fountain in your shrine. Magniglow pumps are much quieter." Hearing this, groups of Faeries began chattering excitedly throughout the meeting hall.

"We must keep up with Four Falls," Lachtin added, gesturing humorously toward Elva and Seamus. Elva smiled and Seamus scowled.

"What we *know* about Magniglow — power, wires, and switches — is not what we have to worry about!" Lugh shouted. As he stood up, his voice blasted through the entire hall, squelching the euphoria. "What we have to worry about is what we *don't* know. All of you won't be so happy when you find out what that is!"

"Such as?" Liber asked, sounding almost sinister.

"Why, whatever else is a closely guarded secret of the Assembly of Progress. And why, if Magniglow is so safe, do its workings have to be kept a *secret*? Really, now, Liber, at least tell us the *truth*!" He then lurched toward the circle, as if ready to come to blows with his brother.

"That is *quite* enough," the Grand Eldress warned. "If you do *not* stop your senseless squabbling, I will have you both removed from the meeting hall. Never have I seen such acrimony on display over a matter of the Water Guild! I thought the opinions about Matter Two would surely blow the plaster off this dome home, but this is beyond the pale! Now, I'm sure we've heard enough debating from all sides. We must vote."

Baudwin turned to look at Loch. Loch stared back, smiling through a sneer and looking as if he had already won.

"Ignore him," Matha said under his breath to Baudwin. "You know what you have to do."

"Yes. . ." Baudwin replied, as he looked again at Loch, and then his father, who was sitting with Niall and Congal, nodding expectantly at him. As he did, the red and green light emanating from the bulbs fused with the tense excitement of the meeting hall. *What should I do?* he wondered.

"All those in favor of Matter Three, rise and say *yea!*" the Grand Eldress cried. Scores of Roilers, some Eddies, and a few Guilders rose to vote. His choice had to come now, and he wasn't at all sure which one was right. At first he thought he would remain where he was, but much to his surprise, his legs pushed him to rise. Friends and family looked on with shock, as he separated — like a lone wolf from his pack — and then stood up.

"Yea!" he shouted.

☙❧

A short time later, Baudwin found himself standing alone in the dining room, chewing a bite of potatoes with vegetables and currants, and thinking about everything that had just transpired. Around him, groups of Faeries filled their plates and chatted amiably. All were careful not to break with *gnàs,* by expressing either their satisfaction or displeasure about the votes. Regardless of how they might be feeling, all in attendance were expected to set aside their differences, and simply enjoy one another's company. Nevertheless, as Baudwin glanced around the room, he could not help wondering what his vote on Matter Three might have cost him.

Before he could ponder his concerns any further, a voice exclaimed, "Baudwin dear, I bet you didn't think you would be agreeing with someone like *me* about something as *important* as Matter Three!" There stood Elva, smiling smugly, holding a plate of lentil and cabbage stew. Knowing that they both had voted *yes,* Baudwin was for a change happy to see her.

"Yes, indeed, Elva," he replied. Thinking out loud, he added, "The vote was seventy-one to sixty-nine. . .which means that if I had voted *no* —"

"The vote would have been seventy to seventy, and the Grand Eldress herself would have had to break the tie," Elva explained, before Baudwin had a chance to finish his sentence.

"She almost certainly would have voted *no,*" Baudwin continued thought-fully. . . "So instead of passing, Matter Three would have —"

"You voted for what you believed was right," Elva interrupted again. "You must not let what your father or grandfather have to say about this matter wither away your spirits."

Hearing her supportive words did not make Baudwin feel any better, as his thoughts continued to plague him, like a dust funnel swirling inside his head. Feeling his discomfort, Elva patted him on the back and said, "I'm going to have some blackberry pie. Would you like me to get you some? You'll feel better."

Before he could reply, a voice exclaimed, "*Whatever* were you thinking?" As Baudwin looked behind him, there stood Matha and Criofan, looking quite perplexed.

"No thank you, Elva," Baudwin said, as they came toward him. "If you will excuse me."

"Of course, dear," she replied, smiling happily. "Remember — you did the right thing!"

"I thought you said you were going to vote *no,*" Criofan complained.

A few Faeries looked at them crossly, shaking their heads.

"I changed my mind," Baudwin replied. "And you're breaking with *gnàs.*"

"But, *why?*" Criofan said, undeterred, lowering his voice so none nearby could hear.

Baudwin wasn't about to tell his friends the truth. He knew they wouldn't understand. They didn't have to work a mill and constantly juggle the tiresome tasks of a dam. Magniglow was going to make his Life easier. He remembered what Glas had said at the Engineerium — that one day he could have Magniglow doing all his jobs for him.

Baudwin was sure that eventually his grandfather and father would come around to the truth of this. After all, he wouldn't have argued with Kelven if they had a steamway, or better yet, a magniglow-powered grinder at the mill. With Magniglow, he would have more time to pursue the old ways with Seamus. Surely, there could be no harm in making their lives easier.

Baudwin kept silent.

"How are you going to explain all of this to your father and grandfather?" Matha whispered, worried.

"I don't know," Baudwin replied. "How do you explain to your father that you read both glyphs and letters?"

"That's different," Criofan replied. "We read glyphs and letters, and for the most part, our parents tolerate that."

"Then my father and grandfather will have to be even *more* tolerant."

"I don't see how they will," Matha said.

"Whyever did you vote *yes*?" Criofan asked.

"I — I — " Baudwin stammered.

"You what?" Criofan asked.

"Don't ask me to explain," Baudwin said. "You wouldn't understand."

"I'd rather you didn't use that excuse," Criofan said, insulted. "I'm your friend. Tell me anything but that."

"I feel the same way," Matha said. "You can't just —"

With that, the sound of music and laughter swelled out of the next room. "Let's not talk about this anymore and break *gnàs*," Baudwin insisted. "What's done is done. I'm going to the sitting room to have some fun. Are you coming?"

Criofan and Matha had no choice but to drop the subject. The three friends set their empty plates on the table and left the dining room. As they entered the sitting room, the festivities were in full swing. All the revelers seemed to have forgotten the contentious meeting, much less having been at odds with one another in any way. Most of the furnishings had been moved to accommodate the musicians and make room for the dancers.

On one side of the room, a large overstuffed green and blue silk sofa had been pushed in front of a stately-looking wooden bookcase, which reached from floor to ceiling. Many old books rested upon the shelves, bound by hand with fine fabrics. Surrounding the books were a number of elegant crystal goblets, plates and vases, along with exotic curios.

On the other side of the room, two comfortable-looking chairs had been pushed just below a grouping of delicately painted river scenes hanging on the wall. A number of other furnishings in the room were scattered about: silk and brocade cushions, wooden cabinets, and end tables with carved glowstone lamps. Various musical instruments were strewn about on the floor, including violins, trumpets, flutes, tambourines, and drums. All in all, the disarray only made the room appear that much more inviting to anyone who wanted to celebrate with the utmost pleasure and abandon.

Directly across from where Baudwin stood with his friends, Seamus had found his place in a half circle of musicians near the window. There he stood, playing his flute to his heart's content. Next to him was Eolann, accompanying him on his flute as well, and in such perfect tune and time that it seemed as if he might burst with joy.

In the center of the room, a number of ladies and gents, wearing ankle bells and finger chimes, had formed three circles, one inside the others. Dancing a spirited step dance those in the innermost circle moved clockwise, the next circle counterclockwise, and the outermost one clockwise again. Round and round they went, their arms linked at the elbows, or around one another's waists. As their feet flew faster and faster, the glowstones on the table shone brighter and brighter, until the entire room was bathed in shimmering blue and white Light.

Seeing the room so full of excitement, Baudwin sighed with relief, knowing that at least for now, he could relax and take pleasure in the celebration. Although he was concerned about his grandfather and father, he knew they would wait for another time to express their disapproval.

"Let's go and join the circles," he suggested to Matha and Criofan. With that, they dashed to the center of the room.

As he approached the outermost circle, Baudwin stopped short, almost stumbling. There directly in his path, stood Loch. Startled as he was to see him, Baudwin could not help blurting out, "Tell, me, Loch — who advised you to lead the Roilers?"

"Ferrell," Loch replied, without as much as a flicker of emotion. Seeing the look of shock upon Baudwin's face, he added, "And to think my meeting Ferrell would never have come about if I hadn't run Matha into the food tent. Or if Criofan hadn't been shot in the eye with a geyser pistol. Perhaps the Water *is* with me."

"That I truly doubt," Baudwin countered, barely able to contain his disgust. He then took in a breath to steady himself, as he was determined not to break with *gnàs*, and upset the room.

"Really now," Loch replied, as he took in the frivolity swirling around them. Smiling, he stepped closer to Baudwin, grabbing him by the shoulder. "Why be so upset? I won on Matter Three, and so did you. Although I must say, I am surprised that a Guilder such as yourself would do that. Nevertheless, the rills have spoken."

"My reason for voting for Magniglow was not the same as yours," Baudwin snapped, pushing Loch's hand away. "This new gift the Elves have given us is not for you, but for *Deuona*, something you and your Roiler friends don't seem to understand."

"Ah, but I *do* understand," Loch countered, as he motioned grandly at the dancers whirling around in circles. "Why do you suppose everyone is dancing? Because they have a new source of power, or because they now *have* power?"

"Anyone who still has respect for the Water can see that they're dancing for joy," Baudwin replied. "Don't judge the Fae of Deuona, simply to justify your notions of power."

Hearing this, Loch flashed Baudwin a menacing look. "Don't *you* tell me what to do!"

"Now, now, Loch," Baudwin declared with a laugh. "You must watch your temper! As the newly elected leader of the Roilers, you wouldn't want to be seen breaking with *gnàs* at your very first guild meeting, would you?"

Loch composed himself.

"And you wouldn't want to be seen as too craven to accept the changes voted in by the rills," Loch replied, reining in his anger as he spoke. "Perhaps you should decide whether or not you have the courage to remain in the Water Guild. For if you do, you'll have to meet me halfway, accepting both your victories *and* your defeats."

As their eyes locked, suspicion fouled the Air between them. Guardedly they stood, as if expecting the next round of the Hop and Hit to begin. "I suspect I would be better at that than you," Baudwin replied. "I'm not afraid to face the Darkness in my own heart."

Having spoken his mind, he turned and quickly disappeared into the circle.

Chapter 20

VERY ODD OCCURRENCES

When Baudwin woke up the next morning on Uiscedía,[1] he was so groggy he could barely open his eyes. He didn't want to think about the previous night and wasn't ready to get up, so he rested in his bed, looking out the window. A thick layer of mist rose from the river, pouring in and out among the rocks, disappearing into patches of cattails and reeds. Baudwin watched the vapors form into plumes and vanish in the Air. Sighing, he closed his eyes. *The mist comes and goes — like the thoughts in my head, — but my River Deuona is always there.*

From outside his window, he heard a noise.

With a start, he opened his eyes to take a look. A young faery lad was running toward the river, laughing and talking to himself, nearly tumbling head over heels as he went.

Whatever is he doing? Baudwin wondered. *Surely, he must be lost.* He jumped out of bed, threw on his clothes, and went dashing out of his house to chase after him.

Ahead he saw the veering silhouette of the lad, cartwheeling down the hill.

"Hey there!" Baudwin shouted as he ran through the wet morning grass. "Where are you going?"

Ignoring Baudwin's call, the lad raced even faster toward the shoreline, trying to avoid clumps of blackberry brambles as he went.

Exasperated, Baudwin shouted, "At least stay on the path!"

But the young lad did no such thing, so Baudwin tried even harder to catch him, dodging in and out among the brambles as he raced down the hill. By the time he reached the river, the lad had disappeared into the mist.

That was a wasted effort, Baudwin thought.

As he stopped to catch his breath, he noticed a blueish glimmer of Light, shining from a hollow in the twisted trunk of an old hawthorn tree. Curious to see what it was, he ran to the tree and hoisted himself up into the branches. He reached into the hollow, grasped something smooth, and lowered himself back down to the ground.

---

[1] Pronounced [ISH-KUH-THEE-UH] Waterday, equivalent to Tuesday, the second day of the week

Baudwin opened his hand. A blue-green piece of quartz rested in his palm, cut and polished into a sphere. He held the gem up to the Sun. Rays of sparkling color shone from its sides.

How beautiful, he thought. *So like the river in color.*

As Baudwin continued to examine his newfound treasure, he gasped. Hardly able to believe his eyes, he peered into the crystal sphere. Trapped in the very center was a tiny faery lady, dressed in white silken clothes and holding a Triquetra. Beseechingly, she stared at him, pressing her face against the sides of her prison. He stared back, shuddering.

What to do? Before he could decide, the sphere turned burning hot. "Ouch!" he shouted, dropping it onto the ground. Licking his scorched fingers, he watched the sphere tumble away from him, rolling over and over toward the river.

Before he could chase after the disappearing faery lady, he stopped. Again, he heard the sound of laughter and talking. A short distance away, Baudwin saw the young faery lad emerge from the mist. Quickly he forgot about the mysterious crystal sphere. "Please stop!" he yelled as he ran toward the shore.

Paying him no attention, the lad waded into the river. The rushing stream rose above his ankles and then up to his knees. He reached into the Water, felt among the rocks, and picked up a bowl carved from a beryl green river stone. Holding the bowl to his chest, he carefully made his way out of the Water, beaming with joy. Baudwin ducked behind a clump of river grass to see what he would do next.

As soon as the lad reached the shore, an Elve appeared, seemingly from out of nowhere. Baudwin noted his blue-and-green uniform — faery colors that Elves never wore — with gold buttons and black boots.

That Elve can't be older than one and seventy, Baudwin thought.

Still holding the bowl to his chest, the young lad turned to face the Elve. Streams of Water flowed like a miniature waterfall over the rim of the bowl, and then to the ground. "What is this for?" he asked, showing him his prize.

"Nothing of any use," the Elve replied, laughing. He then reached into his pocket and pulled out a coupler made of solid Gold.

Seeing the coupler, the lad dropped the bowl onto the sand. Grinning, the Elve handed the coupler to the lad, and picked up the bowl. He then hurled it as far as he could — back into the river. Mesmerized, Baudwin remained still, watching from behind the river grass.

Instantly, a large shadow moved through the Water, turning the river black. Something emerged from the current, a creature neither male nor female, with a sallow green face, hollow-looking eyes, and long misshapen limbs that undulated eerily in the morning mist. As the creature grew in size, the river rose, until the waves were so large that they swept over the young lad and then over Baudwin, pulling them down into the undertow. Helplessly, they swirled together. Baudwin grabbed at the lad to keep him from being carried away. To his horror, he couldn't save him. Terrified, the young lad slipped away from him, into the mad, rushing stream.

Baudwin waited for the vortex to carry him under, but then he heard a howling. Looking up, he saw the creature towering above him. Sunken green eyes stared down upon him, emanating a sickly incandescence. At that moment, a very strong wave enveloped him and pushed him toward the bank. The creature howled again, and gave a gargling laugh. Struggling to the shore, Baudwin choked on mouthfuls of bitter-tasting Water. Surely the creature would strike him, tear him apart, or send another wave to drag him down.

What is happening? he thought, terrified. As he pulled himself onto the land, he gasped for Air.

He turned to face his enemy, again towering over him, but was stopped by a sound.

"To understand, you must wake up," a mysterious female voice instructed him. "You must wake up, you must wake up," the voice kept insisting, over and over again.

"I *am* awake!" Baudwin cried out, shaking in his delirium. With that, he opened his eyes, only to find himself in his own bed, with a very loud banging coming from his door.

"Baudwin, why aren't you answering?" Seamus exclaimed, pounding repeatedly on the door. "Morning has come! You must wake up!"

☉┼☉

A short time later, Baudwin found himself in the kitchen, sitting across from Seamus and Kelven, eyeing a stack of blueberry pancakes at the breakfast table. Having gotten up early to clear out the meeting hall and rearrange the furniture in the sitting room, Seamus and Kelven were already eating.

As Baudwin helped himself to breakfast, an angry silence greeted him at the table. He looked at his father, but Kelven would not return his glance, preferring to stare absently out of the window. Sipping a cup of tea, he repeatedly shook his head in disbelief.

Seamus seemed even more perturbed. Repeatedly, he banged his foot against the leg of his chair. Baudwin knew they were very upset about Matter Three. Instead of speaking to either of them, he sat in his chair, quietly eating his pancakes.

"Would you please pass the honey?" Kelven asked, as his gaze returned to the table. "And," he added, testily, "While you're at it, will you also please explain where my coupler is?"

"Certainly not at the bottom of the Hop and Hit," Baudwin replied, passing the honey to his father.

"Do you really believe I don't know that?" Kelven asked.

"The coupler was taken," Baudwin replied, as he spread more butter on his pancake.

"Then why didn't you take the coupler back?" Kelven asked, his anger rising.

"We have other more pressing things to talk about this morning," Seamus interrupted. He'd stopped tapping his foot.

"Yes, we do," Baudwin agreed. While relieved that Kelven and Seamus were speaking to him, he wanted to avoid discussing last night's meeting, especially Matter Three.

"I had a dream," he began.

"The one where the Water spoke to you about your feelings?" Seamus asked. "How unfortunate for you and for us that you didn't listen, or you might have voted differently —"

"That was the night before," Baudwin cut in. "Last night, I had another dream, one I simply cannot fathom."

"Another one?" Seamus asked.

"Yes," Baudwin replied.

"Go on then," Kelven said, piqued.

Baudwin was relieved that they were willing to listen to him. In keeping with faery *gnàs,* he needed them to share the burden of his dream with him, for better and for worse.

Throughout *Tír na nÓg,* Faeries had a very special affinity with dreaming, and whatever took place in their dreams. Dreams were usually shared in groups or tribes, each faery at home in his or her own bed. Then when they awoke the next morning, they would share what had happened with one another. At the market or some such place, one of them might say, "I had a dream last night that the lily pads in Topaz Lake had grown to the size of tabletops, and the water lilies were even larger."

"Did you, now?" another one would ask. "So did I! And the lilies, instead of being white, were bright red and yellow."

"I did too!" another one might exclaim. "The lilies were striped, and the pads were so large that faery lads and lassies were riding them like boats on the Water."

More and more Faeries would then join in, adding detail after detail, until everyone present agreed that they had all had the very same dream. This was almost always how their dreams went, except for those that were strange or unusual, like the one Baudwin had just had.

Baudwin looked at his grandfather. Already, he could tell that Seamus hadn't seen his nightmare from the night before. Nor had Seamus spoken of the dream that Baudwin had shared with him yesterday morning — when the Water had spoken to him of his feelings. At the time, Seamus had been too hurt by their argument to ponder who else might have had the dream. But now Seamus was angry, and Baudwin knew he would demand to know much more.

"Did anyone else have this dream?" Seamus asked, looking directly into Baudwin's eyes to read his face.

"I don't know," Baudwin replied, "as I haven't seen anyone besides you and Father. But I do rather doubt that anyone else did, as this dream was so disturbing."

Seamus did not take his eyes off Baudwin. "What do you mean by *disturbing*? Baudwin, speak the truth — plainly."

"You have to give me a chance," Baudwin said, unnerved by his grandfather's tone.

All three Faeries stared at each other, unable to speak.

"Give him a chance," Kelven said, looking at Seamus. They both then sat for several moments, waiting for Baudwin to resume his story.

"At first my dream seemed wonderful," Baudwin began. "And then it became strange and terrifying." Baudwin lowered his eyes.

Seamus and Kelven exchanged worried glances.

"Kelven, did you have any dreams last night?" Seamus asked.

"Only that Eolann, our neighbor, was playing his flute," Kelven replied, smiling. "He was his usual irrepressible self, until the flute turned into a sky sparkler and exploded," he added, chuckling.

"You don't say," Seamus chuckled. "I did too. His face was covered in soot, which bothered him greatly."

"Even more than his wife, Elva?" Kelven snickered.

Baudwin wasn't happy that they had shared a dream. Now, there were two shared dreams, both merry, contrasting with his one, making him feel even more alone. Added to that, their dream had been humorous, and his had been dreadful. Resentfully, he glared at his father.

"You just don't like her because she voted *yes* on Matter Three."

"Don't be insolent with me," Kelven countered, his anger returning.

"Both of you — stop your bickering and pay attention!" Seamus exclaimed. Baudwin and Kelven went silent.

"Well then," Seamus continued, "what could Baudwin's dream mean?"

Seamus posed the question in accordance with ancient faery *gnàs*. For, if a faery lady or gent ever dreamed outside of their group or tribe, intimates of that particular Faery were obliged to pay special attention to the dream *itself*. Seamus seemed determined to pry the details of Baudwin's dream out of him, no matter how uncomfortable this would be.

"What appeared in your dream?" Seamus asked.

"A young faery lad, a bowl carved from a green river stone, an Elve about one and seventy, and a gold coupler," Baudwin replied hesitantly.

"A gold coupler!" Kelven exclaimed. "Well, that certainly is —"

"Now, Kelven," Seamus cut in. "We must listen to *all* of his dream before we comment upon what any part may mean." Remembering this requirement, Kelven became silent.

"Was there anything else?" Seamus asked.

"A faery lady, trapped in a beautiful crystal sphere, was holding a Triquetra," Baudwin added, sensing that this admission would surely add to their concern. Generally speaking, Faeries did not dream about unpleasant things, and if they did, such things were worrisome at best.

"Trapped?" Seamus asked, concerned.

"Yes," Baudwin replied glumly.

"Like *we* are now trapped, what with Magniglow coming to Deuona," Kelven snapped. "And we have *you* to thank for this!"

"You told me to do my own growing — so I did!" Baudwin shot back angrily.

"Both of you — keep your tempers," Seamus ordered, visibly upset. "We must not let our differences cloud our reflections upon this very crucial matter. What exactly happened in your dream, Baudwin?"

Baudwin then recounted his dream to them, including how he had chased the young lad until he ran into the mist at the river's edge, found and then lost the crystal sphere that was in the tree, and how he saw the lad again — holding the bowl as he stood in the river — with Water overflowing. He described how the Elve handed the gold coupler to the lad, and tossed the bowl back into the river. After he finished speaking, Seamus and Kelven looked uneasily at each other for several moments.

"So, you stopped trying to save the lady holding the Triquetra, and instead, you went chasing after a gold coupler?" Seamus asked. Baudwin didn't answer.

"Is there anything else you want to tell us about your dream?" Kelven asked.

"I saw a strange apparition in the river," Baudwin replied.

"You see?" Kelven argued, his voice cracking with frustration. "Not only did you vote *yes* on Matter Three, but you spoke in anger with that Roiler in the sitting room after the meeting. This is *exactly* what happens when you break with *gnàs!*"

"That Roiler's name is Loch!" Baudwin shouted. "And I was angry with him! He's the one who stole your coupler!"

"And now he's the official leader of the Roilers?" Kelven asked. "This has never happened before. Why *ever* did you let him get the best of you?"

"Best of me?" Baudwin asked, indignantly. "I beat him at the Hop and Hit!"

"You should have listened to your new friend," Kelven countered.

"And who might that be?" Baudwin asked.

"Lugh," Kelven sputtered disgustedly. "The one who spoke against Magniglow and the Four Branches of Progress at the Engineerium. You see, I still know a *little* something about the ways of the rills, even if you don't."

"What else do you have to tell us?" Seamus asked.

"The river rose against me and the boy," Baudwin replied, shaken. "I tried very hard to save him, but I couldn't."

"*Against* you?" Seamus asked, his usually hearty face looking pale and drawn. "Baudwin, what have you gotten yourself into? Why didn't you —"

"And then a voice told me that I had to wake up," Baudwin interrupted, trying to hide his anxiety.

"Well, we know who *that* was," Seamus said, relaxing somewhat.

"No — the voice was a *lady's* voice," Baudwin said. "Mysterious. I know I've heard that voice before, but I'm not yet sure who she was."

"So, *I* wasn't the one who saved you from the river?" Seamus asked, remembering how he had awakened Baudwin from his sleep.

"No."

"Why did you even bother to tell us about this dream?" Kelven asked, distraught.

Baudwin didn't answer. Being cornered about Matter Three by Matha and Criofan had been bad enough, and now Kelven and Seamus were rubbing salt into the wound. Blaming his nightmare on how he had voted seemed so unfair. He had only wanted to bring Magniglow to the mill to make their lives easier. No doubt, they thought this was his only motive because he wasn't joined to his current. How weary he was of being misunderstood.

He wondered then if he had voted *yes* simply to defy his father. Surely he had reason to, for over the years Kelven seemed to take less and less of an interest in his struggles. As he sat fuming in his chair, he knew he had to show Kelven something he wouldn't be able to ignore.

"You didn't listen to us about Matter Three, so why would having such a terrible dream be a surprise?" Kelven began.

"I told you about my dream because of this," Baudwin replied, as he reached into his vest pocket. Quickly, he removed the wrapped egg, peeling the silk away. He then placed the egg on the table, careful not to touch it.

Seeing the shimmering green treasure, Seamus instantly forgot his anger. "Baudwin!" he exclaimed, his eyes shining with amazement. "Is that —?"

"Glamorium?" Baudwin interrupted, his mood lightening. "Yes."

"Kelven!" Seamus exclaimed again. "Do you see? Glamorium! Never in all my years have I seen such a marvel in our home! Have you?" he asked.

"I have not," Kelven replied stoically. Baudwin was startled to see the look on his father's face. Kelven appeared as if he didn't know whether he should laugh with delight, or cry woefully, so surprised was he by the sight. Instead, he simply stared at the green egg, without blinking an eye.

"Let me hold it!" Seamus exclaimed, as he reached across the table toward Baudwin.

Icy fear welled in Baudwin's stomach, going up his spine. If his grandfather touched the egg, would he also receive a dreadful vision like the one he had seen in Rian's backroom? After telling them about his dream, he now had even more to explain. Some who touched Glamorium saw nothing as they moved sleepily through their mundane lives. The fortunate ones saw the *Dúrúnghlas,* and the unlucky ones, a great shadow. Baudwin had seen both. Deep down he worried that the shadow of Glamorium had not only befouled his vision at Rian's, but also last night's dream — and perhaps every dream thereafter.

"No!" Baudwin shouted, pushing his grandfather's hand away. "Please!" he implored. "You must not!"

"Really, Baudwin, there can't be any harm in Glamorium," Kelven said.

"You don't know that," Baudwin replied. He wanted to explain what he already knew, but he simply couldn't. He was afraid that if he was honest with them, they would assume his story was a fabrication — brought about by wild imaginings because he wasn't joined to his current. Even worse, they would treat him like a Faefry when all he wanted was their respect. The more he thought about Glamorium, the more uneasy he became. Quickly, he pulled on the silk, sliding the egg toward him.

Sternly, Kelven looked at Baudwin. "Are you so enamored of this priceless possession that you can't bring yourself to share it with anyone?" he asked.

"No!" Baudwin replied, stricken, unable to course with his feelings. Fear, confusion, and anger flooded his heart. "Of course not!" he exclaimed. "How could you even *suggest* such a thing?"

"How could I not?" Kelven asked, looking at Seamus. "When you don't even trust your own grandfather?"

"Trust has nothing to do with it!" Baudwin insisted. But he was mistaken. Baudwin could tell that his grandfather knew he hadn't been truthful the day before, when he had come home from the Engineerium. He also saw the disappointment in his eyes. Obviously, Seamus realized that all their talk about the dome crest had simply been a distraction. His grandfather was old, but he could see through Baudwin's evasions, no matter how clever they were. There was no fox, however sly, that Seamus couldn't track.

Seamus's disappointment turned to anger. "You hid the egg from me!" he shouted.

"I was going to tell you," Baudwin said. "But I just couldn't."

Baudwin knew Seamus almost as well as Seamus knew him. He could never keep anything from his grandfather for very long. Nor could he mollify his anger after fooling him — especially now, after he had also broken his trust. *He's so upset with me,* he thought. *Surely this is worse than not saying anything.*

Baudwin wondered what would have happened if he had told Seamus the truth from the beginning. His grandfather always stood by him no matter what, but Baudwin had been torn between choosing to regain his approval and facing further ridicule. Still, Baudwin knew in his heart that he could have spared them both a great deal of pain. He thought then about the important meeting. *Perhaps if I had been honest no matter what, my grandfather and I would have had a better rapport and talked more openly about Matter Three. Perhaps I wouldn't have voted* yes, *and then been cursed last night, by such a horrible dream.*

Only now could Baudwin see the chain of events that his dishonesty had made even worse. *Of course,* he thought, remembering what Rian had told him. *If I'm to wield Glamorium, I will have to be honest, regardless of the pain I must feel.*

Just then he felt as if he could tell them anything, but before he could speak, Kelven began, "I know things have been difficult for you. I'm also guessing you know that whatever story you're about to tell us is unnecessary, because it's a foolish lie. You don't have to lie anymore, Baudwin, but you *do* need to start doing your own growing."

He <u>*does*</u> *just see me as a Faefry,* Baudwin thought, scowling at Kelven. Now all thoughts of honesty fled, and only anger at his father remained.

"Baudwin, you must tell us," Seamus pressed, "why can't I touch the egg?"

Without answering, Baudwin scooped the egg off the table. Kelven and Seamus stared in disbelief. "Because," he replied, haltingly, his eyes tearing, "there's a *shadow* in Glamorium."

Their questions came quickly, too many for him to answer at once.

"A *shadow*?" Seamus asked. "In *Glamorium*? Whatever do you mean?"

"How do you know?" Kelven asked. "This doesn't sound like the truth."

"Where did you get the egg?" Seamus demanded.

Baudwin put the egg back in his vest pocket. They were acting just as he expected. "I simply cannot tell you!" he exclaimed. "Not now!" Before Seamus and Kelven could reply, he stood up and bolted from the room.

⚭

Baudwin couldn't remember the last time he felt happy to be going to the dam to raise the sluice gates, but this morning certainly was one of them. For the second day in a row, breakfast had been very unpleasant, and all he wanted was to forget his troubles. He had hoped that showing the glamorium egg to his father and grandfather would prove to them that he hadn't failed at everything — after all, the Water *and* Glamorium had come to him — but instead he had upset them even more. He also wasn't sure that they would ever believe him about the shadow in Glamorium. After all, he was just an orphan of the Water, never joined with his current and never understood.

As he headed down the path to the millpond, he could barely contain his thoughts, which buzzed inside his head like a swarm of bottle flies. *Magniglow — Roilers — Glamorium —* there was so much to consider. Deuona was changing quickly, and less and less made any sense at all. Since when did so many Roilers attend meetings of the Water Guild? And why were the Elves pushing so hard for Magniglow? What dreadful luck that all of this would happen on the heels of the Water coming to him, now that he finally had reason to believe he was closer to finding his mother. Surely, the lessons of the Triquetra were the key, yet he needed time to become adept at them. Rian had said as much. Baudwin still believed the Water was guiding him, but after talking to his father and grandfather, his confidence was shaken.

Soon, he found himself in front of the first sluice gate at the dam. Moodily, he had passed the river guardians without even noticing them. Whatever secrets they held were of no help to him now. There he stood, gazing carelessly at the river, ruminating about his dilemma.

As Magniglow rushes toward me, the river flows away, he thought. He reached for the hand wheel and began turning. The wheel squeaked sharply, and the gate stem hardly moved.

Now I have to oil the stupid thing! he thought. Irritated, he tried even harder to turn the wheel. His knuckles strained, turning even paler blue. With his eyes on his task, he didn't notice that the river was flowing much faster and higher than usual. Nor did he see a number of other curious things, all happening at once.

Beneath the surface of the Water, scaled and slippery creatures, both webbed and finned, had gathered among the river plants. Puffed up to several times their size, the plants swayed in the river like wavy curtains of gossamer floss.

Downstream, a large school of golden trout pivoted suddenly, and then jumped — high into the Air. They did so in unison — without reason — for none were rising to feed.

Along the shores, schools of silvery minnows spiraled around in circles, and then snapped into lines, only to resume swimming in spirals all over again. Had Baudwin seen them, he would have noticed that some were shaped like eternity knots.

Soon, the river sang even more.

Schools of green and yellow sunfish slapped their bright orange tails repeatedly, as if to greet each other for the very first time.

Frogs hopped from lily pad to lily pad, jumping higher and higher into the Air, as they traveled through the marsh.

Turtles retreated in groups to escape the chaotic goings-on, rearranging themselves in tight circles on large rocks and logs, with their heads and legs pulled into their shells.

The wheel still locked in his hands, Baudwin fumed about how breakfast had gone. Somewhere behind him, an unseen presence was about to make itself known.

Without warning, a voice broke the silence — a sensitive-sounding female voice. "Hello, Baudwin."

The voice — serene and soothing — seemed to be coming from everywhere at once — from both shores — above and beneath the Water — and from every rock, plant, and river creature.

Stunned, Baudwin let go of the wheel. The voice enveloped everything, yet seemed to pass right through him. He dropped his arms to his sides.

"Elva?" he asked. "Is that you? If so, please show yourself!"

He knew that Elva couldn't possibly sound this way, but he asked anyway. He then thought that perhaps he had heard the voice in his dream of the night before. But the voice wasn't the one he had heard at the Springs of Coventina the day the Water had come to him, the one that said, "I am very old and very wise." He waited, hoping to find out. For several moments, a calm yet ever-deafening silence greeted him. All he could feel was the terrified thumping of his heart in his chest. All he could hear was the sound of his own breath, and the river's timbre rushing ahead of him.

Yet, the abeyance from this strange, yet beguiling happening would be fleeting.

The voice then spoke again, insistently, yet gently, "Hello, Baudwin."

Now he was certain that this voice was the mysterious one from his dream the night before, and also the voice he remembered from another dream — the one he had had the night after his visit at the Springs of Coventina. The voice that had spoken to him about his feelings. He wondered why two different female voices had spoken to him, and why one of them now spoke to him again.

Baudwin scanned his surroundings, wondering where the voice might be coming from. Much to his dismay, he discovered that the source was nowhere to be found — not ahead of him down the river, not near the mill on his right, not toward the sluice gates on his left, and not behind him in the millpond.

Helplessly, he asked, "Who of all the mischievous jokers in *Tír na nÓg* is playing such a dreadful trick on me?"

"Baudwin — are you *feeling* all right?" the voice asked again. Like a stream of Water slowly sinking into a pile of sand, her voice enveloped him — first his body, then his feelings, and then his mind. He struggled to make sense of the voice.

"Of course I'm all right," he boldly affirmed, if only to find his courage. The voice was soothing, but his thoughts were not. He could see them, dancing among the ripples in his mind's eye. In flashes, he saw Faeries arguing at the Tree of Innovation, Loch striking him at the Hop and Hit, and Kelven pounding his fist on a table.

He shut his eyes to block what he was seeing, and the voice spoke again.

"Of course! You would know better what you are feeling than *this* river." With that, the Water behind him in the holding trench rose several feet higher — lapping loudly against the stone wall.

"Am I dreaming?" Baudwin blurted out. *At least, I hope I am,* he thought.

"Why would you think you were dreaming?" the voice asked, sounding caring, yet amused.

"I don't know, except that as of late my dreams have been rather —"

"*Unexpected?*" the voice interrupted, as the word echoed playfully from place to place along the shore.

"Well, yes, except. . ." Baudwin groped awkwardly. . . "How would *you* know?"

"What makes you think I know?" the voice asked again, this time sounding dreamy and rather distant.

"Well, I don't, except. . ." Baudwin stopped himself. He wouldn't utter another word until he discovered who was playing this trick on him.

"Who *are* you?" he asked.

There was no answer, and the delay gave him pause. The voice sounded like a faery lady, but her tone was curious — certainly not like those of his tribe — and imbued with a presence that confounded him. She seemed not to be beholden to the toils of the Fae, yet her voice contained all the wisdom of the Water.

He looked around, scanning rocks, bushes, and the river, but he didn't see anything. *Why can't I see her?*

As if she could read his mind, he then heard her speak again, "I am *this* river." And with her words the river trembled, rippling with the timbre of her voice.

Baudwin froze, for he now knew he was being visited by something he couldn't fathom. He wondered then if a spirit was speaking to him.

Growing up, he had heard stories of water spirits, but neither Kelven nor Seamus ever said they were actually real. Sitting beneath their dome crest, he had heard of the mischief these beings created when an Elve disrespected the Water, or a Faery forgot to leave an offering on the full Moon. Sometimes, the stories ended well, with blessings, and other times, with ill fortune. Baudwin wondered how his story would end.

Again she said, "I am *this* river," and the sound of rushing Water became louder.

"River Deuona?" Baudwin asked, perplexed.

"That's what you Shiny Faeries call me, but I am *this* river," the voice repeated, sounding even more amused, as the sound of rushing Water became even louder, crashing against the banks.

"*This* river," Baudwin repeated uneasily, as he mulled the word *this* over in his head. Did the voice mean that *she* was the river, or did the river simply have a voice? The spirit, or whatever she was, was certainly playing tricks on him now. The harder he tried to understand her, the more anxious he became. The truth was, the more she spoke, the more she terrified him.

He resolved to act as bravely as he could. "Why must you pester me now?" he asked, trying his best not to stutter. "I have a job to do."

"Now, now, let *this* river help you," the voice replied.

"Before I let you help me, you must show yourself."

"First you must let *this* river pass," the voice replied, still amused.

Baudwin didn't know what she meant. Whoever or whatever she was, she didn't seem to care that she was frightening him. Quickly, his fear turned to anger.

"Pass wherever you want," he declared. "I'm not stopping you."

"Nor could you, even if you wanted to," she replied, laughing.

With that, the Water rose behind him in the holding trench, and then went pouring over the wall of the dam and onto the stone walkway where he stood. Baudwin froze. The Water then subsided, flowing slowly toward his feet. *This can only be a downstream surge,* he thought — *nothing to be frightened of.* Shocked, he watched as the Water then did something he had never seen before. Rising like a snake, it struck at him, covering his legs, torso, and neck in a flash. Panicking, he tried to run but couldn't move. His muscles felt heavy, as if they were buried in sand. The Water had him trapped and was about to smother him. He took a long, deep breath.

"Why are you holding your breath?" the voice asked brightly. "I would never hurt you, Baudwin." The Water stopped moving short of his mouth. Baudwin did not make a sound.

Cheerfully again, the voice asked, "Have you forgotten that you were born — of *this* river?"

Baudwin exhaled through his nose.

"And you call yourself a *water* Faery?"

After several moments, the Water, which had encased him like a cocoon, slowly receded down his entire body and back into the holding trench, leaving him perfectly dry. Baudwin was astonished that his clothes weren't wet.

"Now, will you let *this* river pass?" the voice asked. "Out of your wretchedly confining millpond?"

"Of course you can leave! Please do!"

"Why are you so upset, water Faery?" the spirit asked.

"I could have —"

"Drowned?" the voice interrupted. "By the spirit which feeds *this* river? Who comes only when *this* river has fallen too low?"

Helplessly Baudwin pleaded, "Right now, the river is too high, and I must lower these gates."

"*This* river will help."

Once again, Water streamed out of the holding trench, across the walkway, and up the stone wall to the four hand wheels. Snakelike tendrils of Water then appeared. As the tendrils spiraled over them — all at once the wheels turned around and around — until the gates were completely raised.

Baudwin could not believe what he had just seen. That the Water could move this way seemed impossible to him, but there, right before his eyes, this had happened. The spirit also seemed intentionally provocative, and he wasn't sure what she was after. He decided then that the best course of action would be to get in her good graces and then try to escape.

As he watched the tendrils of Water retreat and cascade into the river only to disappear, his frown turned into a smile of satisfaction.

"How marvelous!" he exclaimed, pretending to be pleased that his job was done. This was his chance to flee. Not knowing whether the spirit would ultimately help or hurt him, he saw no sense in sticking around to find out. Coyly, he turned.

"I really must go now," he said.

"Must you?" the voice asked. "Without so much as — ?"

"Well, I do thank you," Baudwin hastened to add. "And I will be sure to leave an offering to you, good spirit. My family leaves the finest ones of blue topaz and honey milk."

"*This* river requires far more than your offerings," the voice replied, sounding quite offended.

With that, the tendrils of Water quickly returned. The hand wheels began spinning in the opposite direction. In a matter of seconds, the sluice gates were completely lowered. Seeing this, Baudwin realized that the spirit would not be easily fooled. This did not surprise him, as the stories of these beings often portrayed them as clever. Always those tales ended with the spirit bestowing either a trick or a boon, and he wondered if he would be able to steer the outcome at all. She certainly wasn't helping him now.

Playing his next step coolly would have been prudent, but as he was not joined to his current, he could not hear the guidance of his element, which meant he couldn't listen to his feelings. If he had, he would have known that he could choose to be respectful. To escape his fear, he instead drew upon his anger. "You said you would help!" he shouted.

"Perhaps *this* river was a bit duplicitous," she replied.

"A bit? I would say much more than that. How am I to finish — ?"

"Poor, poor, Baudwin," the voice interrupted, sounding droopy and sad. "Your feelings go up and down, just like the gates. When things go well, you are *so* bright and happy, and when things do not, you are *so* dark and despondent."

With that, the tendrils of Water turned the hand wheels in the opposite direction, until the gates were again raised, but this time only halfway up. "Why not find the middle course between the two? Only then will you be *truly* happy."

"Why should I believe what you say?" Baudwin asked, his exasperation growing. "I did not ask for this."

"Because, only then will you find *yourself*. Such is the plight of one not joined to his current."

Baudwin was shocked that she could know his history. Had she been spying on him since the Ceremony of the Joining? *If so, this spirit is worse than a trickster,* he thought, *for now, she plays on my fears as easily as a faerie reveler toots a fife.* He was determined not to let the spirit intimidate him. Quickly, he thought out what he'd say next, speaking as formally as he could.

"Tell me, spirit, who seems to know me *so* well," he began, "why I should listen to you, when you won't reveal yourself? Are you the spirit of the dark Waters that makes grand horns stampede, smashing windmill, gate, and barn? Or are you the one that dances over the gleaming pools of the harvest Moon, bringing cheer and good fortune to all in *Tír na nÓg*?"

"Such clever questions," she replied. "But why do I have to be either?"

Stillness followed, but not for long. As the tendrils of Water quickly disappeared into the pond, Baudwin hoped that she had gone. But then — Water! A new burst of Water from the holding trench shot across the walkways and up the stone wall. Again, the sluice gates were raised, but this time the Water continued past them, cascading into the river.

What madness is this? he thought. Standing behind the gates at the top of the dam, he looked below. Again, the Water was still.

But then, slowly, waves began to form and rise, coalescing into a swirling mass of ethers, as layer upon layer of Water rose higher and higher. Out of those ethers appeared a form apparently made of the currents — a form comprised of neither Water nor flesh — but something in between. Like the womb of a whale, the Water fluxed and gave birth. Soon a head appeared, and then the rest of the form took shape. Two eyes appeared on the face — eyes serenely closed, as if sound asleep — yet awareness emanated from beneath their lids.

A slender neck then appeared between two softly curved shoulders — a flawless form that all water Faeries extolled in their hearts. Now, as the form became more solid and the ethers coalesced, two hands emerged, folded softly over the being's heart. Soon the willowy feminine body was mostly complete, yet still the ethers swirled around her.

She was expressionless as a statue, yet her presence asseverated all the wisdom of the Water. As Baudwin felt this wisdom pass through him, his fear of her abated. A soothing sensation came over him. He wanted then to trust her, yet there she was, hovering over the river, watching him through closed eyes and speaking to him without even opening her mouth. Who knew what she was capable of, or what her true purpose was?

"What kind of strange and fearsome apparition are you?" he cried. "Have you come to haunt me straight from the very bowels of Annwyn?"

Now he heard her speak again, yet still her lips did not move.

"*Haunt* you?" she asked. "Hardly. *This* river has watched over and protected you from the time you were but a tiny Faefry." Baudwin stood agape, wondering how this could be so.

She laughed at him, a flowing laugh that babbled madly like a brook in the Spring thaw.

"Why are you laughing?" he asked, unnerved.

"Because you have met me — many times — and still you do not know me."

Baudwin was dumbfounded.

"Tell me this, Baudwin, son of Kelven, water Faery of Deuona," she continued. "Who prompted you at the Springs of Coventina? Taught the Roilers respect at the shrine where the Sun meets the Water? Whispered to you in your dreams of your feelings? And who speaks to you now?"

Could she truly have done all of this? he wondered. *Yes, she could.* Now Baudwin knew that this was indeed the same voice that had spoken to him in his dream about his feelings, and also the voice that had spoken to him in his dream last night. Amazed, he realized that she had done all these things. How incredible!

Baudwin then remembered what had happened when the Water came to him at the Springs of Coventina. A ripple from the spring had splashed him in the face, and he had wrongly assumed that the Water itself was answering him. Now he could see that he was mistaken. For *she* had prompted him. Commanding the Water, she had splashed him first and then ushered in the visions and voices he had then seen and heard. Surely the Water had come to him, but not without her guidance.

Gazing upon her watery form, he wondered what she would do next. At the ruins of Coventina, both Guilders and Roilers had been but twigs scattered in her wake. How easily she could crush him if she wished! Her assurances did little to calm him, for her mood could change quickly if he displeased her. Already, he regretted having tried to slip away from her. She would not be moved by his ruses. Desperately, he thought of how he could appease her. He knew that being of the Water, she could easily feel whatever he was feeling. There was no use in trying to hide his fear from her. Still, he waited for her to act.

She smiled — her eyes still closed — and then outstretched her willowy arms. *Perhaps she is trying to comfort me*, he thought. Yet, he could not help wondering if she would turn into the terrible apparition that had visited him in his dreams the night before — the moment she embraced him.

Baudwin cowered behind the hand wheel to protect himself, should he be struck down simply for speaking. "Tell me, spirit of the Water," he implored. "Have I displeased you?"

"No, Baudwin, you have not," she replied.

"Then, I am at your mercy," he said. After that, he waited, feeling certain that if he uttered another word, something truly terrible might happen to him.

In response, for the first time, she opened her eyes. Baudwin gasped at what he saw: two opalescent orbs, shimmering like the inside of an abalone shell, with dark blue pupils, eyes filled with caring and compassion. She seemed incapable of harming him, but he was still frightened. Overwhelmed, he stumbled back several steps, almost falling as he went.

"*Must* you stare at me so?" he asked, as he stood, shaking.

"Must *you* stare at *this* river?"

With that, she turned her hands over, and Water began spilling from her palms, cascading in streams into the river. Her body shifted, becoming more pellucid, until he could barely see her physical shape.

"Please be as the Fae, for I cannot fathom you," he implored.

As if to answer him, the clear rivulets of Water shaping her form became more solid. Soon he saw hair that looked like satiny locks of river moss, with gold beads and pearls braided into the tresses. Her skin turned blue-green, appearing even more lustrous than his. The Water then wove itself into sea-green silk, until patterns of fish scales and lilies covered her body. Jewelry appeared — a gold belt set with mother-of-pearl and aquamarine — and a delicate conch shell hanging from a gold chain around her neck. He couldn't help but wonder how the Water had shaped these illusions, for they appeared to be so real.

Her body continued to transform, until finally, he saw her face — no longer swirling in the ethers, or translucent in the sunlight. Again, he gasped. Standing before him on a large rock was the most beautiful faery lady he had ever seen.

Her enchanting beauty and calm demeanor reminded him of the automatons at Curios & Marvels, for certainly her form appeared to be as flawless. He couldn't help but wonder if spirits such as she had been the inspiration for the elven artists who had created them.

Instantly, he forgot his fear. "Why do you show yourself this way to me now?" he asked.

"So as not to frighten you any further," she replied, unmoving upon the rock. Extending one arm high, and the other low, palms facing each other, she then brought her arms together until her hands were almost touching. Quickly, she separated them again, swapping them at the same time, so the low hand moved high, and the high hand, low.

With that, she repeated the entire sequence several times more. In response, the river surged faster and rose higher. The impossible then happened: The entire Watercourse divided into two distinct currents — coinciding with the motions of her arms. On one side of the river the current rushed upstream toward the millpond, and on the other, the current rushed downstream, and away from the dam.

As the river continued dividing in two, the Water around her feet began swirling in circles, going faster and faster.

"Until you join with your current, and find the still, strong, voice inside of you, like *this* river you will always flow in two directions," she explained.

Baudwin did not understand what she was saying. From the dam he looked down at the river, which moved like two long pikes, passing each other in opposite directions. *Which of them moves the right way?* he thought. Surely, the current moving backwards was wrong, yet he suspected that this was not what she was trying to teach him. He thought then about Matter Three, and wondered if his choice had been backward or forward. Had he merely chosen the current that he found more exciting? Before he could consider this further, his reverie was interrupted.

Again she showed him the impossible.

Out of the swirling currents at her feet crawled dozens of tiny sprite-like creatures — first onto the rock, then up the folds of her skirt, and onto her torso and arms. Their small bodies were blue-green, with fine features and piercing eyes. They covered their protector like a shawl of Water, moving in unison with their tiny arms and legs. Before they reached her neck, she playfully brushed them away in clusters. They fell back into the Water, only to begin climbing out to reach her again.

Baudwin could hardly believe his eyes. What beings were these that looked like tiny sprites and carried such loving mischief in their eyes? He watched as they formed two lines at her feet, one moving upstream, and the other downstream. As he watched them, a question slowly escaped his lips. "I flow in two directions?"

"Ah, now you see it!" she exclaimed. "You must find your place between the two and take a stand. Watch me as I do."

Forcefully, she extended her arms, and the flow of the river changed again. Now the river that was divided — flowing in opposite directions — stopped. The entire river behind her began to flow downstream, as was normal. However, the river in front of her gushed upstream, splashing over Baudwin, the sluice gates, and the walkway — and then over the dam and into the millpond. As he ducked for cover, she laughed and motioned with her arms, sending even larger waves toward him.

Soon the waves subsided, and the river resumed its normal course.

Bringing her hands together, palms up, in front of her, she asked, "Why do you suppose *this* river came to you right now, and in such a way?" As she spoke, waves streamed at her feet, swirling around the rock where she stood. Into this rushing circle of Water swam a school of golden trout, their scales flashing in the sunlight. The small sprites played among the trout, carefree as they swam.

"I know not why you have come," Baudwin replied.

"After seeing *this* river, how could you not know? Have the Shiny Faeries forgotten so much? There was a time when your kind visited these currents, yet now they are mere messengers to a tribe of unknowing fools."

As she spoke, the fish raised their glistening heads out of the Water. They continued rising, until they formed a circle around her, standing on the ends of their brown-spotted tails.

"I really cannot say," Baudwin replied uneasily, as he studied the peculiar, yet striking arrangement of the fish. "Why must you ask me such —"

"*Difficult* questions," she interrupted. As she spoke, she turned her gaze to the fish, which remained poised around her — on the very tips of their tails. "Are such questions *so* difficult, my young ones?"

With that, the fish began writhing vivaciously, as if the very sound of her voice enticed them even closer to her. Laughing, she asked, "What do *you* say, my little merlings?"

Transfixed, Baudwin watched as the top of each fish began to morph from a scaly head into a faery-like one, until all the heads had changed. The upper half of each fish then became a torso, with arms, chubby and supple. Locks of tangled sea-green hair curled softly around their large eyes and glowing cheeks.

Baudwin drew back in alarm. As the metamorphosis was now complete, the entire circle of newly formed creatures sprang onto the rock, only to rest at the water spirit's feet, with their eyes fixed upon her.

Nervously, Baudwin asked, "Half fish, half Faery — what *are* they?"

"Why, *merlings,* of course," she replied. "Rather young ones, all of them around the age of ten or fifteen. Did you not hear *this* river call out to them?" she asked.

"I—I— suppose I did," Baudwin stammered as he watched the young ones cavort around her, their pale blue-green fingers happily picking at clusters of river moss. Despite his confusion, he found them adorable in their demeanor. They reminded him of a pod of baby seals. He wondered then why he had never seen them before, for surely they would be a welcome presence in his Life.

"I was —"

"So busy going in two directions — up and down — that you didn't notice?"

"Didn't notice what?" Baudwin asked, his bewilderment mounting.

"This is what," she replied, as she pointed at the dam. "*This* river rises, but you say, '*I* make the river rise.' *This* river falls, but you say, '*I* make the river fall.' All this is the power of *this* river, yet you say, '*I* power the river.' What are you claiming? The power belongs to *this* river. You have no place in the rising and the falling of *this* river, but once you are there, standing before it, you presume to overrule *this* river —"

"How?" Baudwin interrupted, defensively.

"With your *gates!*" she declared.

Seeing the confusion on his face, she paused for Baudwin to get his bearings. She then continued, "If you take a moment to ask yourself — *honestly* — you see that you cannot overrule *this* river. Then, *this* river simply rises and falls. When you are separate from the rising and falling of *this* river, you suffer. When you are *with* the rising and the falling of the river, you do not suffer. Do not separate yourself from *this* river!" As she spoke, other kinds of river creatures began gathering around her — schools of tadpoles and minnows, a romp of river otters, and swarms of dragonflies.

Silenced by her words, Baudwin nevertheless did not want to consider their meaning too deeply. And while his ignorance pained him, he couldn't admit this to himself. Added to that, she had to know he wasn't joined, so why would she harass him so? After several moments, he declared, "I am *not* separate from this river. These gates do not *really* separate me, for —"

"*You* separate yourself!"

"I don't see how," Baudwin replied, offended by her accusation. "Perhaps in reeling off all of this, you expect too much from me." As he spoke, he made the mistake of cocking his head — which only made him seem foolish — while eyeing her defiantly — which only made him seem arrogant.

"Perhaps, my insensible young friend, you expect *far* too little from yourself!" she exclaimed. "Come, my young ones."

Before Baudwin had a chance to reply, the water spirit stretched her arms by her sides, until they grew three times in length. Bending down, she scooped up the entire ring of merlings, holding them tightly to her breast. She then began whirling around and around, going faster and faster. As she did, her body began to dissolve, until she and everything she held turned into a clear column of Water.

Overcome, Baudwin cried out, "For the love of all Water — *please* stop!"

But his entreaty came too late, for he had unleashed her fury. "*Stop*, you say? The way your dam stops *this* river? There was a time when we had no need for such things."

"How then, did we water our crops?" he asked, meekly hoping to escape the stirring of her rage.

"*This* is how!" With that, the column of Water whirled toward him, tearing him off the ground and into the Air, spinning him around and around until his limbs felt as if they were going to be torn from his body, and his eyes sucked from their very sockets.

As the column turned into a swirling black cone, Baudwin remembered the dark funnel of Water in his dream. *Am I to meet the same fate as the little lad?* he wondered in despair.

Around and around the Water whirled, carrying him across the walkway, and then up and over the dam. "Please!" he shouted. "Let me go, let me go!"

With that, the angry funnel of dark spinning Water dissipated into a cloud of heavy mist, dropping Baudwin into the very center of the millpond. Down he sank, straight to the bottom.

As he bobbed to the surface, he looked around frantically, only to see that the cloud of mist above him had turned into a whirlpool of dark ethers. He knew she was changing — yet again. Staring at him through the murky vortex were two glowing yellow eyes. Her head then shot forward, stopping within inches of Baudwin's face. Her body was now covered in scales, her skull stretched long and deadly, like a weever fish.

Through a small mouthlike orifice, a voice taunted, "Do you *really* believe you are honest enough to wield Glamorium?" Panicked, Baudwin began to swim as hard as he could to the bank of the millpond.

Two arms shot out, with thumbs and fingers that opened like unfurling ferns. A long, scaly body then twisted toward him, its fins covered in spines. Now she was the monster he had so feared in his dream.

She circled around him, her serpentine body barring his way.

"Let me go! Let me go!" he pleaded.

In a flash, a long arm reached out and plucked him from the Water, lifting him high into the Air until again he was but inches from her face. Frozen dumb in that closeness, he waited for her to shred him limb from limb, and then perhaps devour the pieces. What else would such a creature do?

Instead, she regarded him calmly. Surprised, he saw a small tenderness in her eyes, woven into the fabric of her fury. Hypnotically, those eyes drew him in, calming him slightly. "You're not such a bad fellow," she began, "but you're honest only when it suits you — which isn't honesty at all."

Baudwin tried to twist out of her grip. "Rian said I was honest!" he exclaimed.

"Bah!" she spat, still holding him firmly. "You couldn't even tell your friends why you voted for Matter Three. Now the Elves will bring even more of their fascinating contrivances to Deuona."

"They wouldn't have understood," Baudwin whimpered. "And neither do you."

"I understand much more than you could *ever* imagine," she retorted. "I saw you that day at the Ceremony of the Joining as you watched — crestfallen — while your friend Matha frolicked in the Water." Looking into his eyes, she added softly, "I felt your suffering then, and I feel it now when you cannot make the same choices that others take for granted. In your heart you know when your words are wrong, but you cannot draw upon the well inside of you to make them right."

Baudwin recoiled, and he didn't know why, for now her fearsome form no longer frightened him. But still, there was something he found terrifying — it was the *way* she spoke to him. Never before had anyone so easily breached his defenses and come this close to his feelings. She was right — he couldn't make the choices that others who were joined took for granted. Yet others had mothers and the Water itself guiding them, and he did not. He trembled, not wanting her to know his feelings, even though he knew she did.

She continued to regard him. As the black pupils of her eyes narrowed into slits, the scales on her face quivered. "You certainly are brave, despite your ignorance," she hissed. "I can see you standing up against the shadow in Glamorium — but only as a fool would, not as someone who is guided by the Water."

"If I'm such a fool, why did the Water even come to me?" Baudwin asked angrily.

"Because the Water knew you much better than you knew yourself."

Baudwin was dumbfounded.

"A foolish question from such a fool," she added. "Are you *really* the one who would wield the talisman — cross the bridge — and leave this realm behind?"

She appeared to be weighing his worth, and clearly, she was unimpressed. Baudwin had no idea what she meant by the talisman or leaving the realm, and he didn't care. He was tired of being her captive. "That doesn't sound so hard," he flippantly replied. "Release me, and I'll go to any realm you desire."

Her glare could have halted a charging boar. "Last night a dream came to you," she began. "You saw a lad, a young Elve, as well as a faery lady trapped in a crystal. You spoke of them with your father and grandfather. Tell me now, what do they mean?"

Baudwin shook his head. "None of us could say."

Sharply, the clawed hand shook him like a rattle, back and forth, back and forth, until he feared he would pass out. The mouth hole opened, and she shrieked, "*Who* is the little lad?"

"I don't know — really, I don't!" Baudwin shouted, flailing futilely.

"*Who*, then, is the Elve?" she shrieked again, ignoring his suffering and holding him a hair's breadth from her sharp fangs. Her anger boiled the Water inside of her and steam hissed off her scales.

"I don't know that either!"

With that, she lifted her other hand out of the Water and showed him what it held. On her palm was a mass of Water that quickly molded to her will.

"What is *this*?" she bellowed.

Baudwin stared in astonishment at what he saw. Before him was the crystal sphere from his dream, with the faery lady still imprisoned inside.

"A faery lady imprisoned in a crystal," he replied.

"No!" she screamed again.

"I don't know!"

"These are your *feelings*, Baudwin," she declared. "Trapped inside of you, lost and forgotten. *Now* do you see what comes from not being joined with your current?"

Before his eyes, the crystal then turned into a large coupler — shaped exactly like the one in his dream.

"Would you trade a bowl overflowing with Water from *this* river for a golden coupler?" she snapped.

Baudwin knew then that the water spirit had not only witnessed his dream, but must have shaped every part of it — which gave him the opportunity to make a choice. All along, she had been leading him to just this point, offering him riddles but never giving him any answers. No doubt his freedom, perhaps even his very Life, depended upon what he said next.

Closing his eyes, he searched inside himself, just as he had done at the Ceremony of the Joining, so long ago. He felt her attention on him soften, for she sensed and respected his inquiry. A calmness washed over him. The answer was clear.

He opened his eyes. "*I* must be the little lad."

"But you do not know the Elve!" she exclaimed, continuing her admonishment. "If you had, you would not have dropped the bowl upon the sand and reached for the coupler. That vessel is far more precious than you realize. If you cannot see what is truly valuable, you will never conquer the shadow in Glamorium, and find your mother."

Baudwin was silent.

"You chose the coupler over the bowl because you don't see what the Triquetra is truly telling you," she continued. "You're only honest when it suits you — which as I just told you, isn't Honesty at all. Did you not see the faery lady in the crystal, holding the Triquetra, beseeching you to pay attention? She was trying to help you be honest, so you can find your feelings."

Baudwin could not speak. He had dreamed more dreams than he could remember, but never had he dreamed a dream that had caused him so much pain. Nor could he understand how she could decipher his dream, yet be so indifferent to his helplessness. He shuddered, waiting for what she would do next.

With that, her now long fingers quickly tore at his jacket, searching.

"You're not ready for the *Dúrúnghlas!*" she screeched.

Baudwin watched in horror as his glamorium egg fell from his pocket, which she snatched out of the Air. She then dropped him into the icy cold Water of the millpond. As he surfaced, choking and coughing, he cried, "Please! I must have that to find her!"

He looked this way and that, but the spirit was gone.

Fighting exhaustion, he swam to the bank and crawled out of the Water. His strength was for once failing him. Finally he made his way to the dirt road along the edge of the pond. As he lay on his back gasping for Air, his chest heaved painfully.

For a time, his senses left him, and he passed out.

Slowly, he opened his eyes. From afar, he could see a large figure, watching him steadily. He feared the spirit had returned, but the gaze upon him never wavered. Neither did the head nor the rest of the body move.

"Who are you?" he moaned. "Speak to me now, or send me to whatever fate you choose."

Groaning, he lifted himself onto his elbows, bravely facing the looming figure, which he feared had not only the means, but the urge to crush him.

"Have you no mercy?" he cried out in his delirium. He then collapsed again upon the ground, barely able to keep his eyes open. Madly, he tried to make out who or what the figure was. All he could see was something green and solid.

"Are you the *Dúrúnghlas* come to save me?" he cried.

His vision cleared, and his exhaustion faded. With a jolt of surprise, he looked again at the face. This time, the figure did not stare, but seemed to be calmly watching him. Two wings were spread, like a butterfly in flight. Water cascaded from two large urns to the ground.

Baudwin recognized one of the statues at the dam — a river guardian, rising above him. "Such protection," he mumbled, "wasted upon one without a current."

Chapter 21

A FORK IN THE RIVER

Shivering with shock, Baudwin stumbled home, mud dripping from his clothes. Crossing his arms and gripping his shoulders as tightly as he could, he tried to calm himself. As he lurched up the path, he dreaded the prospect of running into his father or grandfather. *No matter what happens, I must not let them see me,* he thought.

Rather than going to the front of his house, he headed around back. Scuttling through the gate, he looked furtively around before going inside. He scurried into the sitting room and then down the hall. Upon entering his room, he staggered to his work table and collapsed in a heap upon his chair. Leaning forward, he held his head in his hands for several moments to steady himself. Still struggling, he sat up and began removing his shirt.

"Now look what I did," he fumed. Large drops of muddy Water had fallen onto the table, ruining the dragonfly sand painting he had so diligently been working on. "And all of this is because —"

Before he could finish his sentence, he heard a loud fluttering, followed by a startled-sounding "coo, coo," and then another sharp "coo, coo." Perched inside his birdhouse, Moonrise stared at him, his large eyes filled with consternation.

"Moonrise — did I wake you?" Baudwin asked.

"Coo, coo," was the reply.

"Are you all right?"

"Coo, coo, coo," went the bird, his eyes growing even larger.

"I know — I'm a shocking mess," Baudwin said, bracing himself to stand. "The truth is, I'm not sure what just happened to me. For all I know, I might have been dreaming."

Why then, are you so wet? the worried look on the dove's face seemed to be asking.

"I know — this whole thing does seem quite unbelievable," Baudwin continued. "I wish I could explain it to you better." Seeing that Baudwin was not himself, Moonrise bobbed his head in all directions, almost falling off his perch.

"Careful, Moonrise," Baudwin exclaimed brightly. "Things aren't that bad. I mean, if everything was a dream, then *what* a dream I had!"

Baudwin's words did little to convince his pet that he really was all right. His hands shook as he tried to remove his boots. Fumbling with the laces, he finally pulled them off, as well as his socks, which he dropped on the floor. Seeing how alarmed his pet looked, he turned away from him. Droplets continued to drip from his clothes onto the floor, gathering in ever-growing pools.

For the first time in his Life, Baudwin, who always had something to say about everything, had nothing more to say. He simply could not believe what had just happened to him. That spirit, or whatever she was, couldn't be real. Certainly nothing in the tales he had heard had prepared him for this encounter. Those old stories depicted creatures like her as wild and dumb, but her intelligence was far greater than his. What she saw and felt was more than he could fathom. He was little more than an unsuspecting mouse that had been toyed with by a cat — no, a lion! — one that seemed to have little use for him, but hunted him down anyway. And now all he could do was cower in his wet hidey-hole, trying to make sense of everything she had said and done. Minutes passed as he stared blankly out the window at the rushing river. Moonrise waited patiently.

A look of wonder then came into his eyes, and he began to speak. "She was so *beautiful*. . . her eyes. . . her hair. . . her clothes. . ."

Hearing the word *she*, Moonrise relaxed, as if Baudwin was talking about a special faery lady he had just met. Expectantly, the dove inclined his head toward him, attending to his every word.

"She was so . . . *powerful!*" With that, Moonrise nodded and began preening himself.

"She could move the river in both directions — at the same time!" Hearing this, Moonrise stood tall, darting his head back and forth, looking to and fro, with a rather bewildered look upon his face. He then settled back down on his perch, plumping his feathers.

"She was just so. . . *unpredictable*," Baudwin continued. "First, she simply spoke to me. . . and then. . . she appeared *right* there before me. She made the river rise and fall. . . and lots of creatures appear as well."

Baudwin paused and was quiet for several moments.

"I saw *merlings*," he added with delight. "Have you ever seen one, Moonrise?"

Hearing the question, Moonrise looked at him strangely. Baudwin then became quiet again.

"You look as if you know what I'm talking about," he mused, as he continued to watch the rushing river. "And yet you don't. . . "

As Baudwin continued to ponder what had happened, he remembered what else she had done, and his eyes narrowed with rage.

The glamorium egg was gone. He had worked so hard, undergone so many trials, and then *she* had come — telling him he didn't know his own feelings, and then taking away what he cared about most. Glamorium was the key to finding his mother, and only she could join him to his current and restore him to wholeness, but this was now impossible. The spirit had judged him unworthy, snatching away from him the very means by which he could have made right what she saw lacking in him. *Without the egg, I'll never find Mother, but without my mother, the spirit will never give me back the egg,* he thought.

Sighing, he put his head back in his hands.

Perhaps she was right, and he didn't know his own feelings. What Faery would in his place? *How unfair that she refused to see this*, he thought.

What she had done made no sense — none at all. Perhaps she wasn't a spirit of the Water, but only a mad spirit, even worse than those of the dark pools in the stories he had heard. Baudwin lifted his head, perplexed. Yet she had also seemed so wise and caring. . .

Now everything was ruined. He was back to where he had started from, without the slightest notion of what to do next. The water spirit had been guiding him the entire time, only in the end to take away his precious egg. The irony of it all stabbed him bitterly. All those years, she had watched him from afar as he struggled, looking and waiting for the Water to come to him. She had also been the one who prompted him at the Springs of Coventina, made the Water erupt at the ruins, and visited him in his dreams. She had shaped his destiny, stringing him along, and then had stolen all his hope.

Without Glamorium, Baudwin could see no reason to learn the lessons of the Triquetra. Even if he found more Glamorium, he feared that would draw her right back to him. Now he would have to decide his own fate. Nevertheless, she had left him bewildered, not knowing what to do next.

Moonrise resumed his staring, his large round eyes filled with concern.

Baudwin stood up. "Beautiful — powerful — unpredictable!" he muttered, as he paced around the room, gesturing wildly. "But, SO. . . cruel! I hope I never, *ever* meet her again!!!"

ଓୡଡ଼

A week passed until Aerdía[1] arrived, and as the soil drank in the rising Water, the month of Willow bloomed. But Baudwin could not enjoy the rainbow poppies, or other delights of the season, for he was too consumed by the anger in his heart. At every turn, he avoided Kelven and Seamus. When necessity forced him to see them, no one mentioned Glamorium, or Matter Three. They ate their meals in silence, regarding each other stonily, waiting for one side or the other to speak, but Baudwin was not ready to say anything.

Every day seemed the same. He did his chores, raising the sluice gates, grinding grain, and taking care of their home. At first, revisiting the dam made

---

[1] Pronounced [AIR-THEE-UH] Airday, equivalent to Wednesday, the third day of the week

him nervous and wary. Cautiously, he would approach the sluice gates, worried that the spirit would return, but when he looked at the rushing river, she was nowhere to be seen. Near the millpond all he could hear were the usual sounds of the Water, and the splashing of river creatures as they frolicked.

Hoping to distract himself, he turned to his sand paintings and steamway collection, but they gave him little comfort. Soon, he lost interest in his hobbies. Moonrise cooed at him with concern, but Baudwin only stared gloomily at him, unable to be comforted, or to reconcile the harsh judgment of the spirit.

Listlessly, he wandered among the reeds by the river, considering another visit to the ruins in Coventina. Perhaps there he would find another clue. Quickly, he dismissed this idea as foolish. He had already reached his goal, and then his prize had been taken away — gone in the clutches of a mad serpent who dwelt somewhere in the depths.

Eventually, his anger all but subsided, leaving him simply frightened and confused. The water spirit had, in the end, deemed him unworthy. Her words echoed in his mind:

"These are your feelings, Baudwin," she had said. *"Trapped inside you, lost and forgotten. Now do you see what comes from not being joined with your current?"*

Again and again, he thought about the dream she had sent him. This dream had been his alone, and therefore he knew this meant there was a special meaning. He had seen a young one dropping a bowl upon the sand, in exchange for a gold coupler, and the young one was, as she had said — *himself,* throwing away what was sacred.

Yet, he felt cheated, for he had not been the one to control the dream — she had. Or had she? She certainly had set the stage, but how unfair she was to judge him for a choice he wasn't sure he had made. She told him that he did not know what was truly valuable, but why, then, could she not help him see what was?

Of course he hadn't wanted to drop the bowl, but how *else* could he hold on to the coupler? Yet, surely, if given the chance, he could have carried them both — couldn't he?

If she were truly a steward of the Water, he expected more from her. She could have been more patient with him. He was, after all, a Guilder. He could have grasped her wisdom, if she had given him more of a chance. Not even his father had ever judged him so harshly. Added to that, whatever future guidance Glamorium may have offered had now vanished.

He seethed, for he knew the value of Glamorium. In time, he would have understood everything that she saw lacking in him. *Or so he thought.* However, deep down, he suspected she was right: without his current, he couldn't know his feelings, and without his feelings, he couldn't find his way. Yet, despite all of his shortcomings, hadn't he *always* persevered? The spirit pushed him to feel something that she had said was impossible for him to feel. How cruel.

"What then, *am* I to feel?" he cried.

He thought then about speaking to his grandfather, but Seamus was still upset with him. Ruefully, he remembered all the years that his grandfather had guided him to find the Water. In the end, Seamus's advice hadn't worked. Glamorium had not helped him find his mother. His grandfather had always prized the old ways, but now Baudwin saw them as nothing more than the dreams of an old fool. And he had no further use for dreams, whether they came from a mad spirit, or an old gent's unrelenting hopes.

Now, he would have to chart his own course. No longer would he vainly hope that the Water would teach him what he had to learn for himself. Glamorium and all its mysteries seemed of little importance, and he didn't have time to wait for further guidance. He had already spent too much time waiting for Life to come to him. Now he would go and make his Life happen on *his* terms.

Baudwin thought then of visiting Matha and Criofan. Talking to them might inspire him, but he decided not to go. Seeing them would only make him feel worse, for their currents bubbled in their hearts, a reminder of what he would forever lack. Still, he had to speak to someone about his plans.

Quickly, he decided to visit Brigh, Matha's mother, the one who had tried to join him with his current so long ago. He had already finished his chores for the day, so the time was right to see her. Perhaps she could help him sort out his feelings.

As Baudwin walked over the hill toward Matha's house, his mood lifted. He hadn't seen Brigh since the important meeting, but she could always be counted on to cheer him up when he was feeling poorly. He wondered if Matha would be home in his room, looking at glyphs, or debating some aspect of concord with his father. He hoped to avoid him if at all possible.

Shortly, Baudwin found himself there. Their home wasn't much different from his own, except for the presence of a smaller building nearby called the Weighing Dome, where they mediated disputes. Faeries came from all over Deuona seeking help from Matha's father and mother in settling their differences. In exchange, visitors made a donation of goods, or performed some kind of service for them.

Baudwin reached the door and rang the chime. A window opened, and out leaned Matha's little sister, Caitlin,[2] hanging like a possum over the ledge.

"Baudwin!" she exclaimed, as she straightened up. "You're just the one I wanted to see."

---

[2] Pronounced [KATE-lin]

"I can't imagine why," Baudwin said as he mimicked her face. They had always done this since they were young ones. She pretended to be a field mouse or a rabbit, while he tried to outdo her with his silly contortions.

"Matha is *so* angry at me," she called from her window. "I told him that his old glyph for lion is probably for cat, because lions don't live in these parts of *Tír na nÓg*."

Baudwin was amused. Matha was not the only one who knew a lot about animals. Caitlin was also very well-informed. No doubt Matha was looking through his glyphs, over and over again, trying his hardest to prove that he was right.

"Are you two arguing again?" Baudwin asked, chortling. "You and I both know your brother. I hope you're ready to be wrong."

"This time, I'm sure I'm right," Caitlin said, winking mischievously. She was an irrepressible one, always butting heads with Matha and trying to get the better of him and Baudwin when they went on adventures together.

"Let me guess," Baudwin said. "He's in his room."

"Of course," she said. "Come right in. You must go and cheer him up for me. He'll need you, when he sees how wrong he is." With that, she shut the window, laughing.

Baudwin decided to go inside and was soon at Matha's door. He had only wanted to see Brigh, but he suspected that she was at the Weighing Dome. For now, he would put aside his upset, and see his friend.

"Matha," Baudwin said, ringing the chime. "It's me, Baudwin. May I come in?"

Baudwin put his ear to the door, waiting. Hearing nothing, he rang the chime again.

Eventually, Matha called out, "She's wrong. There *were* lions here once."

"I believe you, Matha," Baudwin said. "Come on — let me in."

Baudwin heard the door unlock. Matha hadn't turned the knob, because he wanted Baudwin to let himself in. *He's always so stingy when he's upset,* Baudwin thought as he opened the door. Inside, he saw his friend back at his desk, sulking over the glyph. His face looked like a dreary blue cloud.

"Look," Matha insisted. "I'm *sure* it says lion."

Knowing how seriously Matha took his work, Baudwin approached the desk and carefully studied the glyph. The usual glyph for *lion* was different, yet this one didn't seem like *cat* either. He understood how Matha would think it was for lion, but he agreed with Caitlin — there were no lions in this part of Deuona, although oddly the glyph had been crafted there.

"I hate to say it," Baudwin began, "but this looks like it's probably the old glyph for cat."

"Now you sound like Caitlin!" Matha exclaimed.

"Matha, there are no lions here," Baudwin said.

"There *were* once," Matha retorted. "This glyph is clear proof."

Baudwin realized that arguing with Matha was futile, so he tried to cheer him up. He looked again at the glyph.

"You know, you could be right," he said. "I recall my grandfather telling me that long ago, a lot more animals lived here, including large cats. Some of them were gigantic. Perhaps this is the glyph for one of them."

Matha perked up. "Indeed," he said. "After the Great Befalling, a lot of animals left. Some were quite unusual. They even say that certain kinds of spirits were more common too. Although no one knows for sure."

At the mention of the word *spirit*, Baudwin felt a coldness pierce his heart. Thoughts swirled chaotically in his head. He could see the serpentine water spirit towering over him, ready to swallow him whole.

"You seem upset," Matha said, seeing the fear in Baudwin's eyes. "Whatever is the matter?"

Baudwin wanted to tell him everything. Surely, he could trust his dear friend, for Matha seemed to have more respect for and open-minded interest in what most would deem impossible, but no words came to him.

"Nothing. . . I was just thinking. . ." Baudwin mused out loud, "about when Loch chased us in the honey fields."

"Ah that," Matha said. "He's such a coward — always attacking when he has us outnumbered."

"Indeed," Baudwin said, masking his fear. "Where's your mother?" he asked. "In the Weighing Dome?"

"Yes, I think she and my father are speaking with farmer Declan[3] and Finbar,[4] arguing, yet again, over Finbar's milk cows that stampeded through Declan's cabbage field. They never settle anything, but they are always kind enough to donate milk and cabbages."

"Which is very good, else you would starve."

They both laughed. Matha then said, "Luckily, we receive goods in harmonious times, as well as inharmonious ones."

Baudwin agreed. Matha's family was given goods in both times of accord and discord. The community supported them regardless, which had been their way for as long as anyone could remember.

Just then, they heard the front door close.

"They must be finished," Matha said.

____

[3] Pronounced [DECK-lan]
[4] Pronounced [FIN-var]

"Good, I really need to talk to her," Baudwin said, giving his friend a look. Matha nodded his head, for he knew that Baudwin had come for advice or consolation. Baudwin nodded back, because he knew that Matha wouldn't try to pry anything out of him.

"Go right on in then."

Baudwin went down the hall, looking for Brigh. He found her in the sitting room, arranging a vase of light green lilies on a table. Matha's father, Niall, was not there, likely finishing up with the farmers at the Weighing Dome, but as soon as Brigh saw Baudwin, she smiled. Her long hair was braided and pinned into a bun, with blue cornflowers and small silver bells that jingled softly as she turned her head.

"Baudwin," she said, looking up from her flowers. "How good to see you."

Baudwin approached her, surprised at how ready he was to talk, for he hadn't spoken to anyone about anything of importance in quite a while. "There's something I must tell you," he began.

Brigh went to sit on a large sofa. As Baudwin joined her, he noticed the silk pillows he used to fight Caitlin and Matha with, wondering how they had managed to survive. He waited for her to speak.

"Is this about Matter Three?" Brigh asked gently, for she regarded him not just as Matha's good friend, but also as her own son.

Baudwin wasn't sure how to begin. He knew that just about everyone in Deuona had heard about him casting the deciding *yes* vote for Magniglow. What he had done had probably seemed very strange to her, as it was to Kelven and Seamus. Yet, Magniglow was the farthest thing from his thoughts. He had not come to talk to her about that or the meeting.

"No. . ." he replied, his words trailing off, just as they had with Matha.

"Are you sure?" she asked.

"Well, I did fight with my father and grandfather about it," Baudwin said. "I tried to tell them that Magniglow would make our mill work much easier. I even told them about a dream I'd had, but instead of listening, they just got more and more upset. My father can be such an uneasy, worrying moaner. . . Well, perhaps not *that* bad. I probably could have —"

"*Weighed* your words more carefully," she cut in, laughing.

"I suppose you could say that," Baudwin replied, as he struggled to speak about what was really bothering him. He simply couldn't find the courage to talk about the spirit. For how would she believe such a thing?

Brigh looked at Baudwin with concern, for she could see right into him. Water faery ladies like her felt the feelings of others as if they were their own; it was as if, when they swam in a rushing river, they were themselves that river — without boundaries, or separation of any kind.

"Tell me, Baudwin," she asked, "what has you so upset?"

Slowly, he searched for the right words, hoping she would understand. He began by recounting the tale of how he and Matha had found the glyph for Glamorium at the shrine, and how he had wanted to touch some Glamorium, and then failed twice at the Tree of Innovation and Curios & Marvels. And then how, after suffering the consequences of his many shortcomings, his elven friend Rian had surprised him with an amazing treasure — a glamorium egg.

He then went on to explain what had happened the morning he went to do his chores at the dam. When he described the water spirit, Brigh's eyes grew wide, not with fear or disbelief — but awe. Even when he spoke of the spirit's rage and contempt — when she took the egg away from him — tears streamed down Brigh's face, as if she could not bear the truth of what she was hearing. But, she did not interrupt him. Instead, she waited for him to tell his entire story before she spoke. And tell he did — every moment of joy, mystery, and horror. In the end, she seemed to be at a loss for words as well.

They both sat, quietly looking at each other, and then she spoke. "So the stories are true," she began. "Baudwin, you have been chosen for something. For what, I cannot say, but the water spirit was trying to show you the way."

Baudwin was greatly relieved that she was so open to hearing him out. She hadn't challenged him, but she would have if she felt he was lying. Surely, she did believe him, but what surprised him the most was how easily she accepted that a being such as the water spirit could exist. Tales of such spirits were considered little more than entertaining stories, used to teach young ones lessons about Life. Baudwin had never heard of anyone who had seen a being like this, and he doubted that Brigh had either, but she seemed to accept his story completely. He wanted to know why.

"You believe me?" he asked.

"Now I do," she replied.

"Why is that?"

"Because you just told me."

Baudwin smiled. In *Tír na nÓg*, everything that wasn't, could be. Even when the Fae didn't know something, somewhere inside they knew anyway. Would that all of them could be as wise as Brigh — and as accepting — for she was the wife of the Primary of Concord, and shared his duties as the weigher of tales and of truth.

"You should have seen her!" he exclaimed. "She was so amiable at first, but then I think I must have scorned her, and she acted as if she was going to destroy me."

"She wouldn't have done that," Brigh said.

"But she almost did!" Baudwin replied fiercely.

Brigh closed her eyes for a moment, and as she felt Baudwin's words, her empathy seemed to him to run deeper than the Springs of Coventina. She shook her head and then spoke. "No, that is *never* their way — no. To terrify you perhaps, but not to harm you."

"Isn't that the same thing?" he asked angrily. Surprised, he stopped, for he had never raised his voice to her. Brigh was unperturbed by his tone.

"From what you told me," she continued, "that spirit was trying to help, not harm you. The stories say that they can seem underhanded, but they are not the same as us. They move more like the weather in their actions. We must not judge them. For they are free, and we are not. She knew that you were not joined, and so she took your glamorium egg, for she did not deem you worthy of wielding its power until you come to a better understanding of yourself."

"But that's not fair!" Baudwin exclaimed.

Brigh took his frustration in stride. "I understand how unfair this all seems, for how could you feel something she claimed you could not, if you are an orphan of the Water? Her actions seemed cruel to you, of this I am sure, but there is a deeper purpose at work here. You are being called to have fortitude and not act rashly."

"Then I'm leaving!" Baudwin exclaimed fiercely.

His words took him by surprise. For days he had been stewing, determined to take hold of his Life after the water spirit had turned it completely upside down. Now, he was surprised by his own candor.

Brigh shook her head. Baudwin expected her to implore him to stay, but she surprised him, saying, "Even if you leave, this will follow you wherever you go."

Sadness then crossed her face. Wistfully, she spoke. "This must be terribly hard for you. If you were joined to your current, you would have already felt the lesson, and made a better choice, but you cannot, and so you flounder." She sighed heavily. "I am so sorry."

Baudwin was deeply bothered by what Brigh said, so much so that he shook his head and clenched his fists in frustration. Yet, he knew that she meant the best for him, so he kept listening.

"I cannot say why the spirit took the egg away," she continued, "but if you remain on your path, it will come back to you. Instead of being angry, you must contemplate this. You must be the calm pool that holds the swirling fishes, as if they were nothing but still reeds, anchored to the bottom."

"I've tried that!" Baudwin exclaimed, as he stood up and paced about the room. "I *can't* anymore. If only you had seen her. She was nothing like the tales we were told. At first she was cordial — compassionate even — but then she was all rage and fury. She took from me the very thing I needed, leaving me with only emptiness and fear."

Brigh went to Baudwin and hugged him. "The answer will come," she said. "The spirit is angry now, but perhaps someday she will deem you worthy. The fact that she took any interest in you at all should give you hope."

"I don't feel worthy of anything," Baudwin said. "And I never will."

Gently, Brigh touched Baudwin's cheek. "Your time for reconciliation will come," she said. "All things become clear, once we see how they were meant to be. Even though I feel it was a very big mistake, I understand why you voted for Matter Three. I know you were trying to reconcile the Faeries and Elves, but the Elves are not being forthright with us. Many times in the Weighing Dome, we have dealt with their deceit. There is much that they are hiding from us."

Pondering this, Baudwin wondered if telling Brigh about the water spirit had been a mistake. He knew that she meant well, but his story about the spirit had nothing to do with Magniglow. This was not how he wanted their conversation to end. Matter Three had passed for good reasons, and Magniglow was nothing to fear. He had learned as much from Glas at the Engineerium. Magniglow simply made light and moved machines. If Brigh was going to hold that against him, then perhaps he didn't want her help after all. For hadn't his own father told him that he needed to do his own growing?

"I'm sorry, Brigh," he began. "I thank you for your kind words, but I just don't see things the same way."

"What then, will you do?" she asked.

"I'm not sure."

"Whatever you decide, make good with your father and grandfather," she said. "Many times in the Weighing Dome, I've seen what happens to those who cannot tell the truth and make amends."

Baudwin had spoken the truth the best he knew how. He didn't know what he would do next, but after giving Brigh a hug, and asking her to promise not to tell anyone about their talk, he left for home.

⚬◆⚬

As Baudwin headed home, the Sun was low on the horizon, and the hush of twilight blanketed his path. He was relieved that he had told Brigh about the water spirit. Even though they had disagreed about Magniglow, she believed his story, and now he didn't feel as alone. His pace lightened a bit. Playfully, he kicked a pile of rocks down the path, racing after them as they bounced. Now he had to speak to his father and grandfather. Brigh was right — he had some fences to mend. Yet, he wasn't sure what he would say.

Rays of Light shone through a canopy of oak branches on either side of the path. Azure butterflies flitted over the grass, and a rabbit hopped alongside him, for there was never any fear between him and other creatures of the Woods when they crossed paths. Baudwin was amused that they trusted him more than he trusted his own family. He remembered a poem Seamus had taught him when he was a young one, walking with him through the forest:

> The lark lands on my shoulder
> The mouse runs near my feet
> The timid deer comes closer
> When our paths and eyes do meet
>
> Such freedom as they linger
> For moments when we pass
> As they are never frightened
> Of the Fae — aye, lad or lass

How he wished to be free like the woodland creatures. They trusted the Fae, because the Fae trusted them. *Perhaps there is nothing to fear if I tell the truth,* he thought. *Then all will be made right.* He reached for the sky as he walked, smiling. Now he knew what he would do.

Having arrived at home, he went looking for Kelven, and found him quietly reading a book in the sitting room. The Sun was down, and the glowstones were lit.

Kelven looked up for a moment, and went back to his reading.

"Father," Baudwin began.

Kelven looked up again. The serenity on his face turned to irritation, which he quickly suppressed. He smiled.

"Baudwin, good to see you."

His father seemed cordial enough. Encouraged by his civility, Baudwin blurted out, "Father, I want to tell you what happened."

Kelven nodded his head. Perhaps he had been waiting for Baudwin to come to him — perhaps not. Baudwin wasn't sure. He could never tell if his father meant what he said, or just said what he wanted Baudwin to hear, but he did seem placidly available.

"Father, I want you to know about Magniglow," Baudwin continued. "I realize that I might have been hasty when I voted *yes* on Matter Three, but you told me to do my own growing, so, I thought you would respect me if I took a stand and —"

"It's all right, Baudwin," Kelven interrupted.

When he spoke, Baudwin couldn't tell whether or not he was still reading his book. He seemed distracted, which was often his way.

"It's all right?" Baudwin asked. "Really?"

"Yes."

Baudwin had expected his father to be upset, but he wasn't. There he sat — determinedly quiet — as if smoothing things over was more necessary than actually speaking his mind. Baudwin wondered if he could really trust what he was saying.

Kelven spoke again. "I talked to Seamus about you and Matter Three. We both can see that you're getting older. We know how difficult things have been for you, especially what with finding the Water, and how long you've been searching for your mother."

Baudwin was relieved that his father seemed so understanding. No doubt Seamus had talked to him, taken his side, and finally won Kelven over. The last few days had been an awful mess, and Kelven must have realized this.

"We can control Magniglow!" Baudwin exclaimed, his spirits rising. "And, if we don't like what it does, we'll just tell the Elves that they can take their new invention back across the Tadlachs to the Clock City."

Again, Kelven nodded his head. "Yes," he agreed. "Already, there has been talk of this. Now we must judge whether or not we truly want this *gift* — as the Elves put it — in our community."

Baudwin was happy the conversation was going well, so happy that his head was buzzing. "I must tell Grandfather what we've talked about," he said.

Kelven gave Baudwin a solemn look, searching for the right words to speak. "I know you never felt comfortable sharing your dreams with me — Seamus was the better one," he began. His eyes grew distant and heavy with sadness. "And I cannot fault you for that, as he was only too willing to fill the emptiness that my Shaela left behind."

Baudwin wondered how many years had passed since his father had spoken his mother's name in this very room.

"Why did you stop looking for her, Father?"

Kelven shook his head. Baudwin felt the pain that had been growing inside of his father — for years — like a creeping blight.

"I did look, but I lost count of how many full Moons passed, until I believed that like your grandmother, she had passed to Annwyn."

"Annwyn!" Baudwin exclaimed. "Of course that's not true!" Kelven did not reply.

Baudwin couldn't believe that his mother had passed, so he quickly changed the subject. "What dreams did Grandfather tell you of?" he asked.

Kelven paused, weighing his words. "He spoke of his dreams for you and the old ways — that Glamorium will guide you to find what you're looking for."

Baudwin froze, for instead of soothing him, his father's openness only pained his heart. He thought then not of Glamorium, but of being with Kelven so long ago, as they stood before the river guardians. The memory struck him like a hammer.

"Why do *they* have wings, Father, and we do not?" he had asked. Such a simple question, and the only time he remembered sharing his innermost feelings with his father. The moment was made even more poignant, because he had never done the same with his mother.

Dismissal had been Kelven's reply.

"You know that's just an old story, Baudwin," he said, annoyed by his young one's foolish question. "Faeries don't have wings. The Elves don't have them, so why would the Faeries?"

After that, Baudwin had retreated, never speaking to Kelven again about anything that truly mattered to him — until this moment. And now his father expected him to accept his kindness as if no history existed between them. Resentfully, he thought of all the years that Kelven had treated him so coldly. All the seasons he had tried to talk about his mother — but couldn't — and all the times he had sat alone in his room, playing with his gadgets instead of joining Kelven and Seamus at the family shrine, gazing with them upon the Water.

Sadly, just after Baudwin's quest had failed, Kelven had decided to be candid with him. Now he wasn't sure what he felt about anything. A reckoning began to flow through him like half-thawed ice. He wasn't accidentally trapped; his father had trapped him. Or rather, he was the one who didn't know his feelings because his father had never allowed him to have any. The water spirit had told him as much.

Not being joined to his current was a terrible burden, but Kelven's reticence had made everything worse.

What do they know about my dreams? he thought. The morning the water spirit had attacked him, Kelven and Seamus had been unable to help him understand the meaning of his dream. Instead, they had recoiled in fear when he told them the river had risen up against him. After that, the conversation had deteriorated.

They had failed him, so he would not waste his time explaining that his hopes were fading. No longer did he care about Glamorium or the old ways. He then decided to keep the whole thing a secret — no matter what.

Kelven was again silent, looking down at his book. Baudwin had tried to make amends, with some success. At least now they could put Matter Three behind them, but he was still resentful that his father had taken so long to be open with him. He almost ended the conversation there, but before he did, there was one last thing he wanted to say.

He looked at Kelven then, making sure that now was the right time. The blight inside of his father seemed to have lessened some, for he seemed happy that he had confided in his son. Baudwin seized the moment.

"It's funny that you mention Glamorium," he began brightly. "You know how Grandfather talked about how elusive it is? The strangest thing happened. That glamorium egg I showed you and Grandfather at breakfast just *vanished.*"

Kelven sat up with a jolt, dropping his book. "Are you sure?" he asked. "That it simply vanished? How could that be? Perhaps it's somewhere else, and you have simply forgotten where."

Baudwin was cornered by the question. Now what could he say? Again he thought of how he had felt, standing as a young one with his father — how much he had needed his father to be kind and caring. And now, how much he wanted to tell him that the spirit had come and taken away the egg. But if Kelven didn't believe him, the humiliation would be unendurable. He couldn't take that chance. His father often accused him of not telling the truth, when he actually was. And, even if Kelven did believe him, he probably would accuse him of not being worthy, just as the spirit had. Brigh had also told him as much. He could not bear to hear this again, especially from his own father, never mind, his grandfather.

"Yes," Baudwin continued. "It just vanished. Perhaps our argument at breakfast about the shadow in Glamorium made it disappear," he added, his voice trailing off. "I don't know. . ."

Baudwin looked again at his father. His heart sank, for he knew what he was thinking. The answer came swiftly, without compassion.

"I don't believe you," Kelven said, his placid tone of voice turning cold and distant.

Baudwin knew he had to protect himself from his father's ire. "Why not?" he asked, innocently.

"Because I know when you aren't being honest with me," Kelven retorted. "This whole thing is far more serious than Matter Three. This goes to the heart of what you care about most — and you're a very bad liar."

Terrified of admitting his lie, Baudwin exclaimed, "I didn't lose it! The shadow took it!"

Angrily, Kelven continued speaking. "You lost it! And, I might add, if Rian *did* give it to you, then you have failed him, and failed us as well. Glamorium is very rare, and very precious."

"I told you — the shadow took it!" Baudwin shouted.

"What nonsense!" Kelven shouted back. "There's no shadow in Glamorium — just your own irresponsibility!"

"I am *not* irresponsible!"

"You've *always* been!" Kelven fired back. "Although I can't say that I blame you entirely, for if your mother were still here, you would be calmer — like the rest of us."

"Your words are harsh, Father," Baudwin retorted, stricken. "Why bring *her* into this? Perhaps she left because of *you*! The only thing more terrible than the Elves rampaging through Four Falls is your own bitterness!"

"Baudwin!" Kelven yelled.

"You say you don't remember!" Baudwin yelled back. "That's because she left without a word — didn't she? *You* were the reason!"

"What you say isn't fair *or* true!" Kelven raged. "You don't know what things were like back then. The elven guards were marching to Four Falls — there was desperation in the land. She was sensitive — your mother — almost as if she didn't belong among us to begin with. The Great Befalling barred us from the Water, and we couldn't feel our currents. The Water had no guidance for us then. The times were truly terrifying!"

"*I don't believe you!*" Baudwin shouted, louder than he ever had at anyone in his entire Life. Shaking with rage he then turned and left, storming down the hall to his room. As he passed the dining room, he caught sight of Seamus silently studying a portrait of Baudwin's grandmother, whom they never spoke of either, for she had passed to Annwyn in the Great Befalling. Sensitive as she was, the ordeal had been too much for her. No doubt, Seamus had overheard their argument and, stricken with grief, could say nothing.

Baudwin slammed the door to his room. Moonrise sat on his perch, madly preening his feathers.

Baudwin had had enough. Of everything. He was tired of searching, tired of his family, tired of the discord and animosity — tired of being tired. He flung open his drawers, grabbed a backpack from his armoire, and began packing. Traveling clothes, dark blue and green and dull, the kind he would have to get used to wearing. He looked at his steamway collection. There would be no taking any of that. He would have to find Steamway elsewhere. Yes, that's what he would do. Glas at the Engineerium had offered him a job, and that was exactly where he would go.

Moonrise flew out of his cage and nervously alighted from place to place.

There was no sense in staying, for as his father said, he had grown up. Now was the time to make his own decisions. The Guild and the Water had failed to help him find his mother, but perhaps the Elves had other answers for him — perhaps with the Four Branches of Progress. He knew that the Engineerium would be in Four Falls, and that was where he would go.

After finishing his preparations, he waited. He looked over at Brim and Bram, and tapped them on. As the moonlight shone through his window, all was silver and blue, somber, yet alive. He then wrote a note, which he left on his desk for them to find:

Gone to find Glamorium. Don't worry — I'll be safe.

He left his room, creeping quietly down the hall and out the door, with Moonrise on his shoulder and not a soul in the house hearing him leave.

Chapter 22

AN OFFICIAL VISIT

Loch tramped up the winding street of the steep hill, feeling weary and annoyed. How he hated having to follow through on Ferrell's demands. Especially when he had spent so long traipsing up and down the hills of Four Falls to find him. Here there was no trail to follow, only cobblestone streets. As a tracker, he had never been so lost, asking for directions from a bunch of city Faeries, who didn't even know their own neighborhood, much less where the building was.

"Tell me, where is the Chamber of Water?" he asked one of them.

To which the faery gent replied, pointing, "Just go up the winding path."

"This path?" Loch asked, confused.

"Yes," the faery gent replied, his eyes gleaming. "Don't you know? The path that winds! Of course this path, and not the other ones."

"What other ones?" Loch asked, turning to what lay before him. "This one? Or that one?"

"This one," the faery gent replied, as he gestured up the hill. "Which becomes that one, and then that one, until you're there." Loch's threatening glance did nothing to silence his jabbering. "Yes, the winding path. The street of streets! Just like our rivers and canals, each one is joined to the next."

Frustrated to no end, Loch took matters into his own hands, and grabbed him by the collar. "Tell me where to find the Chamber of Water," he bellowed, as he gestured to a nearby park, "or I'll throw you so hard into that fancy fountain that you'll forget you ever knew how to swim!"

"*Wherever* are your manners?" a voice called out. Loch turned and faced not a faery gent, but a lady staring contemptuously at him. Usually those that looked at him had fear in their eyes, but she had none, and her looks were striking. Remembering his manners, he quickly let go of the faery gent, who scuttled away from him.

"My manners always present themselves when someone as lovely as yourself is present to receive them," he replied with a cavalier grin. Looking askance at the faery gent he had just dropped to the ground and was currently making his getaway, he added, "He certainly wasn't."

"So the brute is a gent after all," the faery lady said. "Tell me, am I to be swayed by your compliment?"

"No," Loch replied, "but perhaps by the bind I'm in, for I can't seem to find the place I'm looking for — the Chamber of Water. Everyone gives me riddles. Are simple directions that hard for you city folk?"

"The winding street isn't a riddle," she replied, "but a lesson. We in Four Falls live among a web of canals, all fed by four great rivers. These canals lead us to the rivers, just as this street spirals to the Chamber of Water, whence we are governed. Seeing how each street is joined to the next reminds us to appreciate how each of us is joined by the Water to the greater whole."

"Yes, fine, but where is the *building*?" Loch moaned.

"At the top, of course!" she exclaimed. "Where *else* would it be?"

Loch looked up the hill, but could not see anything, as there were too many domed buildings and trees in the way. One street spiraled up and forked, and spiraled up and forked again. He could not tell where all the spirals ended. Spirals were sacred to Faeries, and no doubt these streets had been efficiently — yet madly — laid out for them long ago by the Elves. There was indeed a lesson here to learn, but Loch still didn't understand.

"I see nothing," he announced, vexed.

"You're much closer than you know," said the faery lady, smiling. "The building you are looking for is right at the top of this hill. Come with me."

Together, the two took another spiral, continuing up the hill. Upon reaching another fork, the faery lady stopped.

"There — you see," she said, pointing to a building. "Perhaps you got exactly the help you needed to get here."

She had shown him an opening in the view, and now Loch could see that at the top of the hill there was indeed a large building, sitting among the trees and other structures.

"All I was told was to keep walking!" he exclaimed. "There's no sense in these streets," he added, exasperated.

The faery lady smiled again at him. "Just keep going up. You're at the last fork now. And do be polite. We *city* faeries have our ways, and do not appreciate rudeness of any kind."

"Forgive me," Loch said. "This place wears on me, like none I've ever seen before. I'm far more accustomed to winding dirt paths, and the bubbling springs of the country." As he spoke there was an unfamiliar kindness in his voice, for she had disarmed him, and soothed his rankling.

Taking his leave of her, he then continued up the hill, traveling the last spiraling fork — up and up — until finally, he reached the top, where he now stood. Turning sharply, he saw the place he had traveled to find — a grand-looking edifice, built not only from which to govern, but to impress visitors and guests from faraway places. The structure towered before him like an enormous diadem, with one tall building in the center, and others that got lower in height — one by one — on either side. Before him stood the Chamber of Water in the Danu Quarter — where much of the business of Four Falls was conducted, and where he had been forced to go. The sight before him rekindled his frustration.

Why am I at such an official-looking place for such an unofficial reason? he thought. He looked more closely at the center dome — five stories high. On either side stood another dome — four stories high. Then came three more on either side of those, each standing three, two, and then one story high. The dignity and grace of the design was indeed impressive. How much more interested would he have been, had he come here of his own accord, rather than being forced to leave his Roiler gang behind. Resentfully, he bounded up the steps.

He then stood before the largest door he had ever seen — over two stories high — enormous and grand — carved from white oak — with ornately wrought bronze fixtures. A silver plaque on the door read, *Four Falls Chamber of Water.* On either side of the door stood a blue-green statue of a faery lady in a flowing gown, with calla lilies entwined in her hair and seashells circling her waist. Both statues held a large bowl of Water in their arms — an offering to visitors.

Drawn to their lifelike mien, Loch slowed his stride to a stop, for they were so unlike him. Their patience was unalterable, whereas his did not exist. They held their bowls without faltering, yet all he wanted was to retreat, to shirk his duty, for having lost to Baudwin at the Hop and Hit. His Roiler band needed him. The thought of simply not showing up had occurred to him, but running from Ferrell was out of the question.

Hurriedly, he dipped his hands into one of the bowls. Cupping them in front of him, he made a sign of the Water. "I am with the Water," he declared under his breath. He then grasped one of the handles, and pulled open the door.

Inside, he was met by a resplendent offering to the Water: An atrium reaching to the ceiling, with a circle of silk ropes hanging like a curtain from a large stained-glass dome. Every rope was strung with blue and green jewels that shimmered like waves of Water as they stretched to the ground. Some of the ropes hanging from the ceiling stretched to the walls, creating a glimmering crystal canopy. The rest hung in a column toward the floor, reaching a large pool of Water.

Seeing the display, Loch forgot his displeasure. The climb up the hill had only annoyed him, but seeing this hall was worth the effort. He wondered then about the Faeries who had dreamed this place into being. The Great Befalling had changed everyone, and now the Elves were bringing new wonders to *Tír Éirí Sióg*, but when would halls like this be built again? Gazing up at the ceiling, ambition pricked him. Someday, *he* would build a hall for the Roilers, even grander than this, to represent the coming age. This age would not be stagnant like a shallow pond tainted by the trailings of an elven mine, but bursting with Life, like the runoff from the Tadlachs in the Spring.

Loch approached the pool. Studying his reflection, he thought about his future. He was Ferrell's servant now, but he was learning quickly: How to be diplomatic, work the crowds, implement the finer points of strategy, and govern. Already, he had Magniglow coming to Deuona and soon, all the faery cities would have it as well. He then visualized what he would put in *his* hall — magniglow lights, of course — like the glowstones in this one, and not simply a curtain of pretty ropes, but statues of powerful leaders, just as the Elves had in their halls. A leader was due the respect of his followers, for all of his hard work and protection. He would help the Faeries understand what the Elves already knew.

In the center of the pool four salmon crafted out of silver leapt toward a bursting fountain, their bodies twisting in midair. Staring into the Water, Loch spied blue and green carp swimming among polished river stones. As he ruminated further, bending down to run his fingers through the Water, a voice broke his reverie. "Excuse me, young gent."

An old faery gent toddled toward him, hunched over a large stack of ledgers. His faded breeches looked as if they had been worn down by years of bumping into punishing edges. Although he seemed agile for his age, Loch couldn't tell if he was naturally stooped, or if the ledgers were simply weighing him down.

"What do you want?" Loch asked.

"For you to please take some of these, before they get away from me," the gent replied, as he struggled to steady himself.

Loch removed several ledgers from the pile, placing them under his arm, except for one. Opening the cover, he rapidly began turning the pages, studying its contents.

"Hey! I didn't ask you to read them," the old gent snapped. "They're from the Assembly of Progress. I'm to deliver them to the proper offices." As he spoke, he tried to grab the ledger from Loch, almost dropping the others he was holding.

"Now, now," Loch countered, as he continued to peruse the contents of the ledger. "What makes you think I'm interested in lists and lists of numbers?" Snapping the cover shut, he announced, "What I want are directions to the Assembly of Progress, and you're just the one to tell me."

"Come along then," the old faery gent replied. If you want *my* help, *you* must help *me*." Eyeing the letters on Loch's jacket, he added, "You *do* read letters, don't you?"

"Perhaps," Loch replied. "But, isn't that your job? Why can't you read them?"

"That certainly is *not* my job," the gent snapped. "I'm the assistant to the Primary of Concord, not Trade. As such, these are not my regular duties, nor do I need to read letters to conduct them,"

Amused by the old gent's temerity, Loch grabbed several more ledgers from the top of the pile. "Where are we going?" he asked.

"To one of those offices," the gent replied, nodding his head at the four quarters of the room. "Just look at the front of the ledger."

Hearing this, Loch took a moment to study the rest of the hall. Four offices were visible, one in each quarter. The windows were tinted blue, and the floor leading to them had wavy blue-green marble paths, each one slightly different from the next. Loch had some inkling of what the offices were for, so wanting to confirm his suspicion, he decided to help the old faery gent.

"Read the letters," the gent insisted.

"River Nechtain,"[1] Loch replied, looking down at the ledger.

"How many?" the gent asked.

"Five," Loch replied, as he shuffled through the pile.

"Over there," the gent announced.

Together, they approached the office to the left of the front door. A sign read, *River Nechtain*. Just as Loch had thought, each office conducted the affairs of one of the four rivers in Four Falls.

"If you please, you may deliver them to the front desk," the old faery gent instructed, as he juggled the remaining ledgers in his arms. "Hurry!"

Loch opened the door and entered the office. The room was abuzz with Faeries tending to the affairs of River Nechtain. Lines of wooden desks, arranged in neatly spaced rows, filled the room. Faery ladies and gents sat busily writing, with glowstone lamps illuminating their work. On each desk sat a silver cup.

Loch's attention quickly wandered to something else. On a wall behind them was a mural of an enchanting-looking faery lady, with lustrous blue-green skin and a delicate conch shell hanging from a gold chain around her neck. She leaned in profile over a vaulted well. Where her legs should have been was nothing but watery ethers. In the distance a white cow stood calmly in a pasture. Next to her were three attending cupbearers, holding cups identical to the ones on the workers' desks. *Perhaps they keep cups on their desk to honor her,* he thought.

Loch counted nine hazelnut trees surrounding the cupbearers, their branches reaching toward them like open fans. The rendering moved him, for not only did the faery lady appear wise and determined as the Light radiated softly around her, but powerful as well.

"Who is she?" he asked a young faery lady sitting behind the counter.

---

[1] Pronounced [NECK-ten]

"Who are *you*?" she asked, eyeing him with surprise.

"Why is a meretricious-looking Roiler such as yourself asking such a question?" a faery gent next to her asked, as he took note of Loch's jacket.

"I ask what I want," Loch replied.

"They certainly don't school you Roilers in your history, do they?" the faery gent countered. "Or your manners, I might add."

"History is for those who dwell in the halls of leaders long past, not for those who attain leadership themselves," Loch replied with a snarl.

The faery gent laughed, amused by the answer. Winking cannily at the faery lady he said, "I will instruct the upstart." He then pointed to the mural. "She is Boann,[2] who, after drawing from a sacred well, created all the rivers in *Tír na nÓg*. Through this act of devotion, Water was gifted to our realm. Always she has watched over the water Faeries. She is the spirit who guides us in joining with our currents, coursing with our feelings, and honing our intentions, and when one is deemed worthy, she is the one who sends them the Water."

As Loch studied the mural, he scoffed. The old ways held no place in his heart any longer, yet he couldn't take his eyes off her. She certainly seemed great, but in a way he wasn't used to seeing — she was one whose power over the Water called her to lead, not one whose leadership made her powerful. He had almost disregarded the rendering completely, but something else besides the lady startled him.

The well itself had captured his attention.

He realized the design was identical to the one in the shrine at the Springs of Coventina. The masonry of both wells was made of deep green, Connemara marble, with eight stone pillars rising from the rim to support a bowl-shaped vault. Both stood with vines encircling their pillars. *Why were they the same?* he wondered.

Smiling, he thought about what had happened that day at the shrine. How he had relished his battle with Baudwin, sneaking up on him so easily. The two Guilders had been overwhelmed, but he respected them for fighting against the odds. They could never have won, outnumbered as they were, but he would have let them go anyway — just as he always did — for he was the one who decided when the game was over.

Remembering more, he eyed the mural again, staring at the well.

Had he not been the one to end the fight that day? No — the Water had flooded the shrine and ruined his plans. How shocking that had been. At the time, he thought that the eruption had been only a gusher, but as the days passed, doubt had slowly eaten away at his conviction. And now, here he was,

---

2   Pronounced [BOH-un]

standing before the mural, reminding him that the old ways and the Water were not so easily forgotten.

A flash of guilt pierced his heart. He had defiled the shrine in Coventina, but what fight was he really fighting, and to what end? He looked again at the mural. Perhaps if Boann had been standing at the well that day, he would not have broken with *gnás* — and would have thought twice before smashing the tablet. This gave him pause.

Seeing Loch so deep in thought, the faery gent interrupted him, this time, curiously. "What is the mural telling you?" he asked.

"I was just feeling the Water. . ." Loch replied. Fixing his gaze upon the cupbearers, he thought of the time long ago when his mother had poured Water over his head and he had joined with his current. Such freedom he had felt. Such joy! *At one time, I even looked for the Water as well, hoping it would come to me,* he thought. *On River Nechtain. . .* As he studied the mural, his memories tumbled inside of him. Back to a time before he was a Roiler, a simpler time, when he had just been a young one, swimming amongst the reeds.

"The mural touches many in this way," the faery gent said. "That well is — after all — sacred to our kin, and it is found on River Nechtain."

Hearing this, Loch's memories again went to his time on the Nechtain, the river that flowed north from Lake Aidmid to Four Falls. When he was a Faefry, he had spent more time there than on River Deuona. The Nechtain had drawn him then, and was now speaking to him again.

Still, he did not know why.

Looking again at the mural, he wondered, *Why didn't I find this well on the Nechtain?* For if he had, perhaps the Water would have come to him, and he would have taken the blessing. But like so many, he had given up his search, and his intention had carried him in another direction. For a fleeting moment, his heart lifted in a way that he hadn't felt in many years, and he was a young one again, swimming in the reeds.

Loch turned to the gent and spoke. "I saw a well just like this one in Coventina. The Water there erupted, and I was carried away."

"That's a lesson that only such a well *could* teach a Roiler," the faery gent said, chuckling.

Loch ignored the joke. "I thought it had been only a gusher, but perhaps it was more."

"More than you'll probably ever understand," the faery gent replied, but there was no rancor in his voice.

"I know more than you think!" Loch boomed, his anger returning. "Without my leadership, Deuona would never have accepted Magniglow."

A number of workers looked up from their desks, smirking at him. He expected them to argue or laugh at him, but instead each of them raised a silver cup to him. He couldn't tell if they were toasting or mocking him. They then recited:

Leaders do not choose the Nechtain
To the Water we are sworn
Aye, the Nechtain chooses leaders
From the Water we are born

Leaders do not choose the Nechtain
From the Water we are born
Aye, the Nechtain chooses leaders
To the Water we are sworn

Loch had no idea why they were inspired to recite the poem, but he could tell they were amused by him. "You Guilders don't think I understand because I'm a Roiler, but I do!" he shouted. "We haven't forgotten who we are! I, too, once tried to find the Water, and I'm sure I got a lot farther than any of you!"

"You mean you tried to get the Water to come to you?" one of them asked, setting down his cup.

"Yes!" Loch yelled. "And I know what that means too!" With that, he slammed the ledgers onto the desk and exited the offices of River Nechtain.

The old faery gent was outside, waiting for him. "That sounded like quite a *roil* in there," he said, smiling, as Loch approached him.

"Just a bunch of arrogant Guilders is all," Loch declared. Pointing through the window, inside the office, he shouted, "He's no better than me!" Glaring at the old faery gent, he added, "Just tell me where the office of the Assembly of Progress is. I'm here to meet with Ferrell."

Hearing this, the old gent's eyes grew wider. A hint of fear crossed his face, then quickly vanished. "Well," he began, as he shuffled through the remaining ledgers, "If *that's* the case, we can skip the rest of these. Rivers Danu, Cyhiraeth, and Condatis will simply have to wait."

They headed to the stairs, climbing them until they reached the landing to the third floor. The old faery gent then paused for a moment to look at Loch. "What business does a Roiler such as yourself have with the Assembly of Progress, and with Ferrell no less?" he asked.

"What concern is it of yours, old one?" Loch replied. "You're wasting my time with your stupid questions."

"At least *you* have time *to* waste," the old gent replied. "I know *I* certainly don't. But, to answer your question, Ferrell does not deal with just anyone."

Having gained Loch's full attention, he added, "And those with whom he *does* deal often regret that they ever met him."

Hearing this, Loch wondered to what extreme Ferrell would go if he reneged on paying his debt. He wasn't sure, but he could tell that this old faery gent certainly feared Ferrell. Together, they walked around the circular hall, past walls lit with glowstone lamps, and stained-glass windows with cattail and dragonfly motifs.

Loch shook his head. "Don't worry about me," he said. "I've already seen the worst that he can do."

The old faery gent stopped again. Loch could see the lines on his face, furrowed with concern.

"Don't underestimate the Elves," the old faery gent said, "for they are the sword swingers — the *cogadh*[3] makers — and the ones who hold our fates in their hands. The Assembly runs everything now, and Ferrell is thinking farther ahead than you could ever imagine. His authority comes from one who has bound this realm to his will, and all those who opposed that one have long since passed to Annwyn."

"Who do you mean?" Loch asked.

The old Faery straightened his stance. "I mean — Govannon[4] — the King of the Elves," he said. "You're too young to know much about him, but I lived through those times."

Like most Faeries his age, Loch knew little of the elven king, except what was generally understood in the realm. Govannon had been the one who triumphed at the end of the Great Befalling. He had won the *cogadh* of succession against his brother, Belanus,[5] and defeated the Faeries who allied with him. The battles had been catastrophic, especially in *Tír Luí Lucharachán*. Gold Haven, ruled by Belanus, had clashed with the Clock City, ruled by Govannon. On the River Dagda, beneath the Fallen Peaks, their guards had met. Brother battled brother, and across the land all the way to the Clock City, the clashing of swords knelled a thunderous chiming. Both sides fell in droves and passed through the gates of Annwyn.

Many called the *cogadh* the struggle between the Eternal Movement and the Rise of Time. For the Elves under Belanus wished to count time by gazing into eternity and tracking the movement of the stars, while the Elves under Govannon wished to build a machine that would count the eons for all eternity. Theirs was a *cogadh* not only for dominion of the kingdom, but also for how they would embrace all that they held sacred.

---

[3] Pronounced [KUG-ah] war or conflict
[4] Pronounced [GO-VAAN-ahn]
[5] Pronounced [BELL-UN-US]

Eventually, the *cogadh* escalated, and other elven cities were called to fight, some favoring Belanus, and others Govannon. *Tír Éirí Sióg* was also brought into the conflict, and after much debate about the danger of coming between the Elves, eventually, the Faeries sided with Belanus. They were unsympathetic to the *cogadh*, but feared the conflict would spill over into the faery lands, and so they found their fury, swearing to protect their elements. Soon their fighters swept through the forest of Gwydion,[6] flanking Govannon's Clock City. All colors of the Faeries were dreary and ashen, an unkindness of ravens flew over their banners, and the howling of the shadows was their only joy. They carried their fates with them, as though they were but trinkets to be sold for a pittance, for they would never let their beloved lands be defiled.

Govannon found himself hopelessly outnumbered, but then destiny intervened. Out of nowhere struck the Great Befalling, and all found themselves lost in a paralyzing stupor. Either through luck or guile — none could tell — he then turned that uncertain time to his advantage. He smashed through his brother's ranks and defeated him. With the armies of Gold Haven beaten, and all the Faeries left in torment and confusion, Govannon pressed his advantage, and ruthlessly destroyed all of his enemies. Pursued by his forces, the Faeries retreated back to *Tír Éirí Sióg*, and Gold Haven surrendered.

Having won, Govannon become conciliatory, and promised to restore both Elves and Faeries to their former greatness. As such, for the past two hundred years the Assembly had kept a light grip upon *Tír Éirí Sióg*, attempting to woo the Faeries with clever inventions and outright wonders, many of which Loch and others in Deuona enjoyed and benefited from as well.

Ferrell, of course, had worked tirelessly in this endeavor, but Loch wasn't sure in what capacity. Did he report directly to Govannon? If so, that would truly be impressive, if not fortuitous, for it would mean that Loch himself was closer than he could ever have imagined to the most powerful Elve in the realm. He thought this was likely, for Ferrell was, after all, a Luminary, and a Master of Gold, an honor reserved only for those who were most favored under the Master of Platinum — Govannon himself.

Loch wasn't sure why Ferrell hadn't spoken of Govannan. Perhaps Ferrell was simply the secretive sort. He certainly appeared to be. Or perhaps he simply couldn't be bothered to speak to an indentured servant about his own master. If Loch had been in Ferrell's place, he wouldn't have either. As much as he hated his servitude, he would have to bide his time and remain in Ferrell's good graces.

Quickly, Loch abandoned any more thoughts of fleeing. Govannon's eye was on Ferrell, whose eye was on him. There was no escape — to anywhere.

---

[6] Pronounced [GWID-ee-ohn]

He could not run, so he would have to tread carefully, for he was far more vulnerable than he had imagined, which he hated. Loch realized then that the old faery gent was right to caution him, for in speaking the truth, he had done him a favor. Despite his annoyance, Loch was glad that he had carried the ledgers for him.

He spoke one last time to the old faery gent. "I thank you for your warning," he said.

"You're welcome," the old faery gent replied. "Go around the hall, until you reach the next office. Ferrell will be waiting for you there." With that, he shuffled away.

☙

Loch hurried down the hall to the office. He now knew that Ferrell was holding many things back from him. He had many questions, but feared Ferrell would turn them against him. The best thing would be to keep his curiosity to himself.

Clang, clang, clang went the bell on the door, as Loch pulled the clapper. *What a dreadful sound*, he thought, wondering why the Elves didn't use door chimes instead.

"Come in," a voice directed.

Loch entered the office, taking in the entire room. Here the Assembly's mark was obvious. Gone was any reverence for the Water, and all shades of blue and green. Everything was arranged for the sake of utility and order. Despite this, he was drawn to the look of things, trying to understand Ferrell by studying what he saw. Much was plain — wooden cabinets packed with books and ledgers. A bronze safe caught his eye, with a steamway horse on top, rearing up on its hind legs. Faeries didn't revere horses the same way Elves did, this he knew. Horses were never ridden in *Tír Éirí Sióg* either, for they would throw their riders as soon as they crossed the Tadlachs. Once there, they could roam freely — as did all the other creatures — instead of being bound to their riders.

Smirking, Loch thought of Ferrell being thrown from his horse, should he attempt such a crossing. He studied the wall. From across the room, a bust of an elven gent glared sternly at him. *Is that Govannon, or a relative of Ferrell's?* he wondered. Hanging from a large wooden wheel in the ceiling was a Sun, sculpted from solid gold. Carved white glowstones hung from the spokes. What finally captured his attention was a clock made of gears, with brass and copper tubes and odd-looking dials. He couldn't understand why the Elves were so fascinated by time, but the workings interested him nonetheless. Beneath the clock was an inscription:

The clock remembers what time forgets

Loch pondered the meaning. Had this been written after Govannon won the *cogadh*? He wasn't sure, but he wondered if Govannon had said this after his victory, or perhaps someone else had in the Assembly. The phrase did seem odd to him, as though clocks alone could be relied upon to remember the history of the land.

He looked again at the inscription. Forgetting was necessary, for only then did stillness take hold. That was the way of the water Faeries. This much Loch knew. But as the words implied, the Elves were always busy remembering, and could never be still. *How strange to be an Elve,* he thought.

There sat Ferrell at his desk, studying, thinking, and planning. For a moment Ferrell reminded him of Matha, the strangeness of which caught him by surprise. Yet, the two were oddly similar, always so lost in their heads, consuming facts and ideas. But there the comparison ended, for Ferrell, unlike Matha, seemed never to gain any pleasure from his knowledge. In fact, Ferrell never seemed to take pleasure in anything, and he was certainly far more dangerous than Matha.

Growing up, Loch had never feared Matha for his physical prowess, but surely, he could not disregard Ferrell the same way. Elves were adept with swords, especially elven commanders with experience leading guards. Despite this difference, one thing was certain — both were very intelligent, for Matha had outwitted him in the Garden of Sprockets, and Ferrell always knew how to turn everything to his advantage. How he hated that about both of them.

Loch approached him. Seemingly oblivious to being watched, Ferrell read a page, and then looked up. "You're late," he snapped. Loch would have countered anyone who spoke to him in this way, but already, he had learned not to talk back to Ferrell.

"Sit down," Ferrell said.

"I became lost finding this place," Loch said, taking a chair in front of Ferrell's desk.

"A tracker, lost?" Ferrell asked, picking at Loch with his words. "Such irony. However, the winding streets in Four Falls can be confusing. As a newcomer to this city I find them —"

"Not lost for long," Loch interrupted.

"As I was saying," Ferrell continued, eyeing him sharply, "I find them to be *too* connected."

"What do you mean?" Loch asked, confused.

"You Faeries just don't seem to get it," Ferrell replied. "There's no sense of separateness among Faeries. You're always trying to *join* everything together, as if that should always be the way. All the canals connect to the rivers, and the streets are made in the same way, but it's all so unnecessary."

"The Water is our *Life*," Loch said defensively. The streets and canals merely remind us of that."

"Perhaps the Roiler *is* a Guilder after all," Ferrell said, chuckling.

Loch bristled. "We Roilers have our own reverence for the Water."

Ferrell disregarded him and went on speaking. "There's just *too* much water here for my liking. I much prefer the wind. I'm from the Chinewilds, where gales rush through the canyons until most of the trees are blown over and twisted like roots. The wind bores into you, until your bones feel as if they will break and impale themselves upon your very soul. In those places, alone and challenged with the imperative of survival, you must find your own strength."

Loch had never been to the Chinewilds, but he knew what a chine was — the backbone of an animal. As a tracker, he had seen many. Ferrell no doubt had become very strong in those wilds. All the Elves likely found their strength alone, and to Loch this seemed strange.

"Here we find our strength together," Loch said.

"Indeed," Ferrell replied dismissively. "Let's discuss the meeting of the Water Guild."

"Matter Two didn't pass," Loch declared. "We still can't have geyser pistols in Deuona, whenever —"

"Forget about Matter Two," Ferrell cut in. "*I* am now interrupting *you*. Matter Three is what I'm interested in, not some silly geyser pistol law." Smiling willfully, he added, "I've already heard the reports — Magniglow is coming to Deuona. What I told you to do worked. Your new leadership position is amounting to something."

"How else might you instruct me about leadership?" Loch asked, for although he hated admitting this to himself, he knew that without Ferrell, he probably would not have won either Matter One *or* Three. In fact, if Ferrell hadn't forced him, he probably wouldn't have shown up at the meeting at all. Roilers hardly ever attended such events.

Ferrell collected himself before speaking, as though he had been waiting for just this moment to begin his instruction. "Let me ask you this," he said. "What makes a Faery, or even an Elve for that matter, follow a leader?"

"Courage, skill?" Loch put in vigorously.

"No," Ferrell replied. Leaning forward, he peered intently at Loch, pressing his arms onto his desk. "They follow leaders because they believe they possess the same qualities that they do. So, if the leader is clever, they believe this means that they are clever. If the leader is shrewd, they believe they are shrewd. What do you think they see in you, Loch?"

"That I am bold?" Loch asked.

"Perhaps," Ferrell replied. "But if they also suspect that you are arrogant and stupid, perhaps they follow you blindly in order *not* to see that they too are arrogant and stupid. Then they don't have to see their own shortcomings."

Hearing this, Loch flinched. Ferrell then leaned even closer to him, almost lifting himself off his chair as he spoke. "Do *not* think you did this all yourself," he hissed. "Without my counsel, you would never have known what to do to win."

The room went silent. Ferrell spoke again, this time without emotion. "I heard that even your guilder rival, Baudwin, son of Kelven, helped you win the vote."

"Yes," Loch replied, nodding his head. "Magniglow is coming to Deuona."

"Although I do indeed wonder *why* Baudwin helped," Ferrell continued. "The Guilders were against Magniglow from the start. He's quite an interesting character."

"He's just a conniver, and a clever one at that," Loch said disdainfully.

"But, he certainly bested you, didn't he?" Ferrell asked. "Used the Jab and Jump and all of your quarrel staffing skills against you."

Loch grimaced as he thought about what Ferrell was saying. He was always so used to getting his way, to having his way, to holding his way. And now he was being forced to learn a *new* way, something he wasn't used to doing. Ferrell was right, again. Always he was right, and Loch knew there was still a lot that he would have to learn, for Ferrell, not he, was the one now in charge.

"He's a troublemaker, that Baudwin," Loch began. "He won't be easy to control. Neither will his father, Kelven, or his grandfather, Seamus. The Guilders still don't trust you, or the Assembly, and especially not me. You'd be better off kidnapping Baudwin and dumping him in Bog than you would be in recruiting him to your cause. If you want, I could take him there, and do the job for you."

Ferrell laughed, slapping his desk. "And then another would simply take his place, and another after that. Don't you see? You can't win every *cogadh* by fighting. The Elves need the Faeries to understand that we are not their enemy. I will take no action that isn't in accordance with the laws of the Assembly." Ferrell beamed for a moment, and then added, "And what fine laws they are!"

Loch could tell from the look on Ferrell's face that he was about to digress into another long-winded dissertation, just like the one he had given at the Hop and Hit to the Faeries and Elves. Already, Loch had endured many of these. Ferrell then began:

"Law Number One: You shall not take from others without their permission, for if you do, other things will be taken from you.

"Law Number Two: You shall not receive from others that which you do not deserve, for if you do, you must forfeit any and all of such things.

"Law Number Three: Whether or not you are justified in taking or receiving from others is not for you to determine, but only for those who are higher in rank, stature, and experience."

How interesting, Loch thought, for he could hear that all the laws Ferrell recited were merely nuts-and-bolts representations of what sounded like the Golden Way — all reason without spirit.

Idly, he began playing with a glass globe on the table that had a shining green stone suspended in the center. As the green Light caught his attention, he stopped listening to Ferrell and inwardly recited the Golden Way: "Always give to others what you would have them give to you, and receive from others what you would have them receive from you. For, if you balance giving and receiving, your hearts will be full, your minds will be at peace, and all will be well in *Tír na nÓg.*"

"Have you no manners?" Ferrell barked, stopping his recitation. "Don't touch that! It's *not* a glowstone."

"I didn't think it was," Loch replied, sulkily removing his hand. Yet, he remained curious. "I saw something that looked just like this at Curios & Marvels. What's in the center of the sphere — Glamorium?"

"No," Ferrell replied. "These are mere oddities. The secret is lost in antiquity."

How amusing, Loch thought, *for an Elve to own something and not know exactly what it is.* Yet, he didn't believe Ferrell, so he continued to press him. "I know it's not a glowstone," he said, "but it certainly does resemble Glamorium."

"It's *not,*" Ferrell announced flatly. "Although we believe that before the Great Endeavor, and the founding of the Assembly of Progress, stones such as these had very special properties."

"You mean the *Great Befalling,*" Loch corrected.

Ferrell rolled his eyes. "If that's what you Faeries want to cling to, yes. You call that time the Great Befalling, yet none of you can say why the times we live in now are so terrible. Why are you so up in arms? We have made things so much better. You're always claiming things are worse, but you can't say *why.*"

Loch ignored Ferrell, and looked again at the sphere. "Was this an award?" he asked. "Some kind of honor bestowed upon you?"

Ferrell grew quiet. His usual piercing gaze was gone, and for a moment, he no longer stood like a sentinel in his head, armored by his words. Loch could feel a sadness in him, one that Ferrell usually kept well hidden.

"No, this was given to me by . . . a very old friend," Ferrell said. "Stones such as these used to be given by the Elves as gifts, mostly for sentimental reasons. Green ones like this are said to bring healing."

"What kind of healing?" Loch asked.

"Never mind," Ferrell replied, annoyed.

Loch decided to turn the vulnerability he sensed in Ferrell to his own advantage. Choosing his words carefully, he began, "There's something I've been meaning to tell you."

Ferrell shot him a suspicious look, for he knew Loch was up to something.

"I've learned a great deal from the Assembly, and from you," Loch continued. "I will pass everything to the Roilers, and you will see this as a great boon to your efforts in *Tír Éirí Sióg*."

"And?" Ferrell asked, his eyes narrowing.

"And so I was wondering — at what point will the Assembly be satisfied with my service?" Loch asked.

"I don't understand your inference," Ferrell replied.

Loch held back a scowl, clenching his fists behind the desk. "When will the Assembly judge my debt repaid?" he demanded.

"*When*?" Ferrell asked, standing up. "How long does a field of wheat take to grow and be harvested, and then ground into sacks of flour to make a slew of pies?"

Pies! Loch remembered chasing Matha and Criofan in the Racer Roller, and crashing into the food tent full of pies at the Engineerium. There were so many witnesses that almost everyone in Deuona knew what had happened. No doubt, the story would be told for a hundred years. Even worse was the humiliation of losing to Baudwin at the Hop and Hit. He slammed his fists upon the desk.

"What you say is an injustice!" he yelled, sputtering with rage. "Baudwin is the one who should have paid! When I see him again, I'll make sure he —"

"Calm yourself, and don't forget who you're talking to!" Ferrell interrupted. He paused to collect himself. "Why do you hate him so much? You really aren't that different. Except for the fact that you wear animal hides, you're both brothers of the Water."

"Brothers indeed," Loch replied. "Baudwin is a fool — always chasing after a silly dream."

Ferrell sat back down in his chair. Looking at Loch, his eyes gleamed with curiosity, like a raccoon's. "A dream?" he asked. "What dream?"

"The dream of looking for the Water — so he will find his mother," Loch replied. As he spoke, he wondered if Ferrell would use what he was learning against Baudwin. If so, he was pleased to tell him more. For if he had to keep working for Ferrell, then Baudwin would have to pay as well.

"To many water Faeries, there is no greater joy in Life than finding the Water," he continued. "Baudwin searched unceasingly, and for that, I hate him."

Hearing this, Ferrell turned in his chair, his gaze going out the window. "Of course, that does make sense. We Elves are searchers as well, for we must separate with our metal — that is, before we forge and temper." As he spoke, a look of satisfaction crossed his face.

"Tell me, Loch," he continued, "if finding the Water brings such joy to water Faeries, how could searching for the Water be a mistake? Although most in the Assembly consider such things to be utterly foolish, we Elves nevertheless don't get in the way of such endeavors."

"What you call foolish, I call stubborn," Loch replied.

Ferrell then regarded Loch. "*How* stubborn?" he asked.

"Forty years of stubbornness — ever since we all first saw him swimming in the creeks of Deuona, with his grandfather standing over him."

"That is quite a long time — especially for one so young," Ferrell conceded. "Why do you suppose Baudwin has persisted so long?"

"I told you," Loch almost shouted. "He's always pining for his mother."

"Where is she?" Ferrell asked.

"Gone now, for two hundred years," Loch replied. "She was lost during the Great Befalling."

Ferrell took a breath. "Ah — now I understand," he said. "That was no doubt a heavy loss for him. And, if I understand your ways correctly, that also means that he never joined to his current either."

"That's right," Loch replied. "Unlike me, he never did."

Loch studied Ferrell's demeanor, hardly believing what he saw. Ferrell seemed sympathetic to Baudwin's plight. How Baudwin stoked his ire, with all of his determination to find the Water, for he had persisted long after Loch had given up his own search on River Nechtain. Loch didn't believe that the Water had come to Baudwin. There was *no* Water to find, and there probably never would be. The old rituals were empty. Once Loch had assumed that Baudwin, Criofan, and even Matha would also become Roilers, but that hadn't happened, and their rivalry had only gotten worse and worse. His fury erupted all over again.

"You needn't feel sorry for him!" he exclaimed. "He just got lucky at the Hop and Hit. His only problem is that he needs to get over the old ways. He's frozen in the past — like a block of ice. As an Elve, you should see what I am saying. Out with the old! In with the new! I really showed him the other day at the Springs of Coventina. Baudwin and Matha feared for their lives."

"Oh, do tell," Ferrell said sarcastically, as he again gazed out the window.

Loch then told Ferrell about his encounter with Baudwin and Matha: How he and his Roiler friends had crept up on them at the ruins near the Springs of Coventina. They all had argued — as they always did — about the old ways in front of an ancient well. Loch could tell that Ferrell was bored with the story, but he continued speaking, if only to impress him with his disregard for forgotten relics. When Baudwin had refused to fight, he grabbed a sacred tablet, hidden in a niche, and smashed it to bits.

Having heard the end of the story, Ferrell was now entirely interested in what Loch had to say. "Do you know what was written on the tablet?" he asked, spinning away from the window to face him.

"No," Loch replied, "but I could tell that they were quite fascinated. Matha seemed to want to take it home with him, to study it at his leisure. But I know he wouldn't have," Loch continued, smirking. "No Guilder would take such a treasure away from what they considered to be a shrine to the Water."

"Well, if that's the case," Ferrell said, "then you were right to smash it. The last thing we need is more Guilders studying old tablets and getting lost in the past." Deviously, he shifted his eyes to the side and back again, saying, "I probably shouldn't tell you this, but we do from time to time restore such places to get in the good graces of the Faeries."

"You probably would have had a very hard time restoring this one," Loch said. "In the center of the vault above the well was a huge sphere made of yellow topaz — with a very large crack."

Hearing this, Ferrell snapped to attention. "A sphere made of yellow topaz? What else did you notice?"

"An unusual circle of carvings at the base of the well," Loch replied. "But I didn't have time to look any further. After I smashed the tablet, we all got into a fight. I had them both beat. They aren't nearly as strong as I am, but they were lucky fools."

Loch then finished his story. "There was a shaking in the ground. Then the oddest thing happened. You see, the spring suddenly ran high, and we all got washed away." Loch hesitated.

"Washed away?" Ferrell asked.

"You heard me," Loch replied. "There was a huge eruption. The Water flooded the place, and we all got separated."

Loch hoped his story had impressed Ferrell. No doubt, he had fought many battles himself, winning great victories for Govannon, and could appreciate hearing such an unusual tale. Yet, a serious look had crossed Ferrell's face, and Loch wondered why.

"The Water flooded the place, you say?" Ferrell asked. "In the middle of the shrine?"

"We were caught off guard," Loch replied.

"The shrine was a sacred place?"

"The Guilders believe so — the fools."

"Did you notice anything else, perhaps around the base, or near the carvings?"

Loch thought for a moment and then answered. "I saw a circle of sun rays."

Ferrell stood up abruptly and began pacing around the room. "Just what I suspected," he declared. "A Sun made of topaz in the vault, and a circle of sun rays at the base. Not the usual kind of water faery shrine. In fact —"

"Very similar to the well on the mural in the office of River Nechtain," Loch interrupted.

"*Exactly!*" Ferrell exclaimed. "This is a shrine we would never restore. They attract all the wrong kinds of attention."

"How do you know the difference?" Loch asked, smirking.

"I know what truly serves the Fae, even if they don't," Ferrell replied. "There is good in the past, but we must choose what should be remembered. Just as you must choose as well." Loch could feel Ferrell studying him, which he detested, for he was reminded of how easily Ferrell could read him.

"The timing of the flood was surely interesting," Ferrell said, "erupting just after you broke the tablet. Added to that, you were all carried in different directions, almost as if you were being separated. What are the chances of that, I wonder?"

Loch did not reply, resisting what came next out of Ferrell's mouth, for he could not stand the inference.

"Baudwin may be a much more interesting character than you give him credit for," Ferrell said. "You must understand, our realm harbors many dangers — forces of ill will toward the Assembly, forces threatening to destroy all the progress we've made. Our duty is to protect everyone from them."

"What forces?"

"Forces that are dangerous and wild — forces that ignore the laws of the Assembly. If I'm right, that eruption was more than you could imagine."

Loch then saw something in Ferrell he had never seen before. The Elve was afraid. Did he really believe that a spirit in the well had caused the flood? Loch couldn't help himself. "Perhaps it was Boann herself," he blurted out.

Ferrell's eyes narrowed, and he laughed manically, for he recognized the name. "So you stopped in at the office of River Nechtain, did you?"

Loch nodded.

"Then you've met her twice," Ferrell said, "although it sounds like you weren't properly introduced the first time. They can be quite aggressive when they want to be, especially when they feel they're being disrespected."

Loch couldn't believe his ears. Ferrell had to be putting him on. How could an Elve believe in such a thing? He expected Ferrell would tie off the joke, but instead he became even more serious.

"We'll need to learn more about this," Ferrell declared. "She has taken an interest in Baudwin, it seems. Oh, and you, by the way, are of no use to her. I'll need to learn more. But rest assured — I will find out — and you will help me, by being less belligerent, keeping your eye on Baudwin, and your nose out of trouble. Magniglow is coming to Four Falls, and we must be prepared."

Chapter 23

ROADS, RIVERS, AND QUARTERS

As Baudwin trudged down the winding road leading to Four Falls, the Sun flamed in the sky, parching his skin. He had never been to Four Falls, and already the road felt far too long, and painfully dry and dusty. There was no way to escape the heat. How he wished he were traveling near a river, so he could dive into the Water and cool off.

Moonrise didn't seem to mind, as he was fast asleep in an open pocket of his backpack. Baudwin reached for his pet to make sure he was there. Fondly, he smoothed his feathers. Moonrise didn't move. Had he brought sunflower seeds for him? Reaching into his jacket pocket, he smiled. Yes, he had.

Today was Adhmaddía[1] and already, Baudwin had been walking for a day and a half. Hours ago he had eaten the last of the few provisions he had packed as he left his house. He did have things to trade once he arrived in Four Falls, and if he needed to, he could forage in the Woods for nuts or berries. The city was still many hours away, and he would simply have to hold out until then.

The road curved sharply to the right. Coming out of the turn he saw a grand horn, pulling a wagon on a side road. The wagon was painted green with yellow trim, with large red wheels and straw spilling through slats in the sides.

Baudwin looked more closely at the front of the wagon. The driver was a Faery, but what kind, he wasn't sure. His clothes looked far too worn and faded to be much of any color. And his skin seemed different as well, not blue-green, but some other shade — Baudwin couldn't really tell. From where he stood, he could see crates in the back of the wagon. No doubt, this Faery had just made a delivery and was coming back to the main road.

Baudwin raced toward him, for here was his chance to save some time. Dust burst in small clouds from beneath his boots as he ran. He held his pack straps firmly so Moonrise wouldn't get too shaken. Approaching the wagon, he shouted, panting, "Hey there! Please stop — would you?"

The driver pulled on the reins, and as the grand horn stopped, four hooves pounded the ground like large mallets. Copper pots hanging from two large

---

[1] Pronounced [EYE-MUD-THEE-UH] Lifeday or Woodday, equivalent to Friday, the fifth day of the week

antlers clashed into each other, clanging loudly. The driver then turned to Baudwin.

"What can I do for you?" he asked, grinning with interest.

Up close, Baudwin could see he was well past six hundred, but he still wasn't sure what kind of Faery he was. He didn't want to ask, for fear of seeming ignorant. Wishing to make a good first impression, Baudwin tried to appear as charming as possible.

"Might you tell me where this fine wagon is headed?" he asked, bowing his head. Looking up, he asked, smiling, "Are you going to Four Falls?"

"That I am," the gent replied.

"Would it be possible for me to ride with you then?" Baudwin asked. "The road is long."

"Anything is possible," the driver replied, as he looked Baudwin up and down. "But what will *you* do for *me*?"

Baudwin bounded to the wagon, and hoisted himself up to take a look. Inside, he saw cases of rainbow honey — color after color — sitting on piles of straw to cushion the ride. From what he could tell, there were still many more to be delivered. "Would you like me to unload these for you?" he asked. "They look cumbersome to carry. Why not let a younger one like myself ease your burden?"

Again, the driver regarded Baudwin. "What's your name?" he asked.

"Baudwin, of Deuona."

"Hello, Baudwin, of Deuona. I'm Earnan,[2] of Wood Fern. I think we've made a bargain — do you?"

Baudwin nodded *yes.*

"Hop in then," Earnan said, as he motioned to the inside of the wagon. "Just sit there, and when I make my stops, you can unload the cases and deliver them. If you do good work, I'll even feed you at the end."

Baudwin was overjoyed at the first bit of good luck he'd had since leaving Deuona. "Thank you so much!" he exclaimed. "You can count on me!" Quickly, he went to the back of the wagon, and undid the latch on the tailgate. Setting down his backpack, he hopped inside and secured the gate with a click.

"Ready?" Earnan called out, to which Baudwin replied *yes,* and they were off.

Wood Fern, Baudwin thought. He had met a few Faeries from there, which meant that the driver was probably a wood Faery. Water Faeries had sea blue-green skin, and Earnan's was green like the trees and plants of the Woods. They didn't come to Deuona too often — except to trade — and Baudwin had never spent much time around them.

---

2   Pronounced [ERN-nan]

The wagon was covered by a wooden top, protecting Earnan and his haul from the Sun. Otherwise, the honey would certainly be too runny. Baudwin relaxed and stretched his arms, resting his back against a pile of straw. Moonrise hopped out of his backpack and found a niche amongst the cases of jars, where he roosted happily.

"Now you've found comfort and can get some *real* rest," Baudwin told his pet. Feeling how much he loved him, his heart grew tender, for Moonrise was now his only friend.

Baudwin reached into his pocket, took out some sunflower seeds, and offered them to him. Busily, Moonrise pecked at them.

"You must not fear, Moonrise," Baudwin whispered to his pet. "It's just us now. I brought enough to trade for a nice cage for you — if need be — and we should have enough provisions to last us until I find work."

Happily, the dove cooed at him.

As the grand horn lumbered along the road, Baudwin watched the wide antlers of the large beast, strung with apples and strange-looking roots. "How long has that grand horn presented herself to you?" he asked.

"She has done so for the past six years," Earnan replied, "ever since she got a taste for rainbow honey!" he added, chuckling.

"Grand horns don't eat honey, do they?" Baudwin asked.

"*This* one does," Earnan replied merrily. "And I'll tell you why. Years ago, I had a delivery of honey and apples to make, but nothing to pull the wagon with. My other grand horn had passed away, you see, and I could find no other to help me. Cursing my luck, I spilled a jar of honey, right where you're sitting. I went to fetch some Water from the well to clean it up. When I came back, there she was — the grand horn you see pulling my wagon. She was eating an apple, covered in honey."

Baudwin laughed. "A grand horn with good taste, for I love apples and honey too!" Earnan smiled.

"What do you call her?" Baudwin asked.

"Belle," Earnan replied. "She presents herself every spring and works right through the fall harvest. As long as I give her honey apples and oats, she always comes back."

Ahead of them, Belle shook her head, and the copper bells on her antlers rang.

"Does this honey come from the glades?" Baudwin asked.

"Of course!" Earnan exclaimed. "Every spring I make the trip and fill the jars myself. Deuona has the best honey in all of *Tír na nÓg*. This load will be worth quite a lot in barter."

"Who's your next customer?" Baudwin asked, for they had been traveling for a while.

"Funny you should ask," Earnan replied. "Our next customer is named Tárlach.[3] He's an Elve — a bit of a hermit, I would say. He dwells not far from here, near a creek. He likes to measure the Water, and other such things."

Baudwin thought this was quite peculiar. Why would an Elve want to measure the Water? What difference did it make if the Water went up or down? For a few moments, he thought about this. On the other hand, why *wouldn't* an Elve measure the Water? They certainly measured most things — time, distances, and just about everything else.

"He keeps to himself," Earnan continued. "But he loves honey as much as anyone. The Elves may laugh at our ways, but they certainly can recognize quality, and the finer things in life."

Earnan pulled on a rein, and the wagon turned and headed down a side road.

"This road is such a pleasure to travel in the spring," Earnan said, pointing to a small meadow. "Do you see? The yew trees are in bloom."

Baudwin looked at the trees. They had stout trunks and wiry branches, with green blades and clusters of white blooms on the stems.

"I hope I reach the Great Thousand and live as long as they," Earnan continued, with a lilt in his voice. "For they are everlasting, and teach us so much."

Hearing this, Baudwin was now sure that Earnan was a wood Faery. He could tell that Earnan's love of the Wood was the same as his own love of the Water. He wanted to know more. "What do they teach you?"

"They are bestowers of Life and messengers of Annwyn, for although they live thousands of years, their berries are poisonous, even to us wood Faeries. They teach us the old ways — that Life and the passage to Annwyn are inseparable."

Baudwin winced when he heard this, for mention of the old ways made him think of Seamus. What might he be doing now? Quickly, he put the thought out of his head, for the pain was more than he could bear. The wagon rolled on.

Ahead of them he saw the house of an Elve, with a steepled roof, set into a sleepy hill.

"Now, when we get there," Earnan cautioned Baudwin as he turned up the driveway, "let me do the talking. He's a persnickety fellow, and gets upset quite easily."

They approached the house and came to a stop. Leaning out of the wagon, Baudwin could see how different this house looked from his own home. The foundation was rectangular — not round — with very large peaks rising from the ground that looked like shingled pieces of gingerbread. The peaks stretched

---

3   Pronounced [TAR-lock]

all the way to the roof. In the center of each was a rectangular window, or a door with a round top. Seeing this, Baudwin chuckled. *At least something here is round,* he thought. In all, the entire house looked like one large roof, made up of many peaks, all of which he found quite charming. Hazel trees and rose bushes surrounded the house, all carefully tended.

Together, Earnan and Baudwin walked up the stone path, bordered with harebells and periwinkles, until they reached the front door. Earnan rang a large brass bell. Hearing this, Belle shook her head and pawed the ground with her hoof. Out came an elven gent, wearing a coat that looked too warm for the day, and a wool cap.

"So, my honey is finally here!" he announced. "Late as usual!" he added with an impish grin. Baudwin noticed that he seemed rather pudgy for an Elve. When he smiled, his teeth meshed together, making him look like a clever, yet impudent, woodchuck. He seemed quite pleased with himself.

"I'm on time, as usual, Tárlach," Earnan replied. "I was to deliver your honey today."

"Perhaps so, perhaps not," Tárlach said, as he strutted down the walkway to Belle and patted her on her neck.

"So tell me, Belle," he asked, "what's it like to serve a driver who can't remember what day it is?"

"As if she'll answer an Elve!" Earnan shot back, as he and Baudwin followed Tárlach to the wagon.

Undaunted, Tárlach gestured to a nearby tree. On the ground, several squirrels were busily cracking open nuts. "I can talk to any creature!" he boasted. "Just watch me!"

Tárlach approached the squirrels. "Candy, Bandy, and Dandy!" he called out. As he spoke, the three squirrels perked up their ears, and looked at him.

"Tell me — do you like those fine walnuts that I left for you?"

At first the squirrels didn't respond. Earnan laughed, but Baudwin looked to see if Tárlach could tell what they were saying, the same way he could with Moonrise. Water Faeries could feel what creatures said, but as far as he knew, Elves could do no such thing. Curiously, Baudwin looked at Candy, Bandy, and Dandy. He could feel their gratitude for the walnuts. He could also tell that Candy had taken too great a share, and that Bandy and Dandy were upset with her.

Tárlach nodded his head at them. "So, Candy, you've been feeding again at the trough, haven't you?" Playfully he put his hand out, and Candy jumped onto his palm.

Gleefully, Tárlach smiled, gnashing his teeth. "You're such a greedy little one," he continued, "but you better watch out — come winter you'll be *way* too fat, and you won't be able to scurry around to find the acorns that you've already stashed." Impishly, he pointed to the other two squirrels. "Then these two will get everything," he added.

Hearing this, Bandy and Dandy rose up on their hind legs and nodded. Tárlach put Candy back down and turned. "You see?" he asked, his eyes squinting delightedly. "You Faeries aren't the only ones to talk to them. We Elves do as well."

Baudwin smiled, surprised. Tárlach did seem to have a way of knowing what the squirrels were saying. He certainly was unusual for an Elve.

"Which jars should I give him?" Baudwin asked Earnan, as he approached the wagon.

"All of those," Earnan replied, pointing to a stack of cases. Baudwin opened the tailgate, and began loading one onto a dolly.

Tárlach would not be silenced, as he wanted to provoke Earnan even further. Patting Belle again on her cheek, he said, "I bet you think she's working hard for you, but she's not. She has you believing how hard she works, but she gets apples and honey for doing very little compared to foraging in the woods for food."

Earnan laughed again. "She's not fooling me. She likes pulling this wagon."

"Perhaps so, perhaps not," Tárlach said. "Just you wait! When you're not looking, she's gonna make off with a whole sack of apples, and a jar or two."

"Oh no she's not," Earnan countered. "We've been together for six years! Why would she steal what she gets for free?"

"Why indeed?" Tárlach asked, smiling maniacally at the thought.

Hearing this, Belle shook her head, loudly ringing the bells on her antlers. Earnan grimaced at the question, and the squirrels grew alarmed and raced up the tree.

Tárlach continued speaking to Belle. "Why do you suppose that he hangs those bells on you, Belle? I know — so he can hear where you're going, and you won't be able to steal his honey!"

He then turned to Earnan, asking, "And why do you think she lets you hang those bells on her? So you'll believe that she won't sneak up on you, because then you'd hear her stealing apples from you!"

Madly, Tárlach paced the ground, before he laughingly shouted, "*Who* lets *who* wear those bells, anyway?"

With that, Baudwin sensed amusement coming from Belle and the squirrels, and soon, he and Earnan and Tárlach were all laughing together. Tárlach really did know what the animals were saying. Baudwin wondered how and why, so having finished his job, he wheeled his dolly closer to speak to him.

"How do you know such things?" he asked. "I've never met an Elve who did."

Tárlach did not answer him, for despite his amusement, he seemed very much like the secretive sort.

Earnan looked at the Sun, and nodded at Baudwin, saying, "The time has come. We must leave."

"So, Earnan," Tárlach continued, as he pointed at Baudwin, "finally got yourself a helper? Good! Maybe *he'll* pull the wagon, after Belle runs off with your honey!"

Tárlach laughed again, and then regarded Baudwin, for he had decided to share a little more of himself. "When I came to *Tír Éirí Sióg*," he began, "I couldn't hear the animals, but after spending many seasons here, measuring the currents and the weather, the lesson came to me. Soon, I was talking to every creature in the woods." As he spoke, Baudwin could feel a certain joy in Tárlach's heart.

"What do you measure?" Baudwin asked.

"I keep a log of the water — a record — because the Elves in Four Falls like to know such things so they can predict a harvest, or a possible flood. This year, I'm not sure what to tell them. For the water is moving strangely. I saw a water geyser shoot up out of my neighbor's well, and then, just as suddenly, stop. And I've heard similar reports from all around the four rivers. They all seem to lead to Four Falls."

This made Baudwin wonder. Water erupting out of wells meant that the water spirit might be causing trouble for other Faeries. How disconcerting for him that she could also be heading to Four Falls. Baudwin tried to put the water spirit out of his mind, for he disliked thinking about her.

"Perhaps there is some large underground spring that's creating all of this havoc," Tárlach said. "Whatever the case, I'll keep measuring!"

Baudwin sincerely hoped Tárlach wouldn't run into her.

Earnan and Tárlach continued their banter as Baudwin loaded the dolly into the wagon. They all said their goodbyes, and then Baudwin and Earnan were off again, down the road.

They made several more stops, and Baudwin helped with the deliveries — a case to a family of Faeries — then more Faeries — and an Elve or two. Baudwin was hungry, so he asked when they would eat, and Earnan told him they would on the last stop before Four Falls, which was coming up.

The thought of food made him think of home. By now, they must have been eating lunch, perhaps some of his grandfather's delicious barley stew, or walnut apple crumble. He wondered how Seamus and Kelven were doing. Were they angry? Were they afraid for him? The thought pained him, but he knew they would find the note he left. Everything had happened so quickly. He could have told them of his intentions, but he hadn't wanted them to stop him. He doubted they would have respected his wishes. His search for Glamorium had been far too much trouble. All he wanted now was to get away from Deuona and explore new possibilities. Traveling with the Elves would be so much simpler. If he wanted to find his mother, he would have to look in other places, and joining the Engineerium would be the best way.

A pang of fear then jolted Baudwin. He had been so preoccupied with leaving, that he hadn't considered whether or not there would be a place for him at the Engineerium. At the magniglow booth, Glas had offered him the job only in passing. If Glas wasn't even there, he had no idea what he would do.

Yet he had to hope for the best, not fear the worst. Four Falls was the city of his kin — surely he would find a way to live there. He had, after all, brought a few things of value to trade, although they probably wouldn't keep him going for long. Nevertheless, he cast his doubts aside, for his adventure was only just beginning.

"Everything we hope for will be there!" he exclaimed, as he looked at Moonrise. Calmly, the dove blinked at him.

The road twisted and turned, and then began heading down a large incline. Baudwin looked out at a cluster of dome-shaped buildings. Banners flew from the roofs, and glowstone carvings of water birds and river otters lined the cobblestone streets.

"Is that Four Falls?" he called out to Earnan.

Earnan chuckled. "No, that's just a small hamlet, much like the one you come from. Four Falls is far bigger. Trust me — you'll know it when you see it."

As they approached the hamlet, Baudwin saw a sign that read, "Welcome to Blue Springs." He felt foolish, for he could see how small the buildings actually were, and the river that flowed nearby.

Earnan pulled on the reins, and the wagon came to a stop. He went around to the back and opened the tailgate. "Hungry?" he asked.

"More than you could imagine!" Baudwin exclaimed.

The two sat on the back of the wagon. Earnan opened a bag, took out some muffins and strawberries, and handed them to Baudwin. Ravenously, Baudwin began eating. He gave a piece of his muffin to Moonrise.

"So tell me," Earnan asked as he sat eating his muffin, "what business do you have in Four Falls?"

"I am going to join the Engineerium," Baudwin replied, his mouth full.

"That sounds like quite a plan," Earnan said, nodding. "How are you going to convince the Elves to hire you?"

"One of them already offered me a job," Baudwin replied confidently. "He said I could work in his booth."

"What made you leave Deuona?"

"Well. . ." Baudwin paused to choose his words. "I think it's high time I made my own decisions, instead of being guided by others."

"Then you'll be in good company — you already sound like an Elve," Earnan laughed.

"Who says a Faery can't do things like an Elve?" Baudwin asked. "We just met an Elve who speaks to animals."

Earnan gave him a wry smile. Quietly they sat, staring at the trees and finishing their food. Looking out into the distance, Baudwin stood up and stretched his legs. He thought he saw the faint outline of buildings and clouds, but he wasn't sure.

"Well, we're almost there," Earnan said. "Just this delivery, and then a final one at the Four Rivers Faire in Four Falls."

"Four Rivers Faire?" Baudwin asked.

"Yes, the place where you'll meet just about any kind of Elve or Faery, and find all kinds of goods as well." Earnan regarded Baudwin, chuckling. "They come from all over *Tír na nÓg*. You won't believe all that you will see — so be ready!"

Hearing this, Baudwin jumped back into the wagon and closed the tailgate. Soon they were off. The downward slope of the land made the wheels turn faster. Belle moved along at a lively clip. Right after Baudwin made the next delivery, they were back on the road again. The cart bumped up and down, and up and down. The ground became more even and the bumping stopped — a sign that they were getting closer.

Baudwin thought then of Criofan and Matha. How excited he would have been if they had all come here together. *So* excited! He had wanted to tell them he was leaving, but what would they have done? Surely, try to convince him not to go. This was his problem to deal with, not theirs. Seamus and Kelven would have to be the ones to tell them that he left. Everyone would be upset, and they would probably search for him. But he had left without a clue, so they would have no idea where he was. And Earnan, the driver, didn't even live in Deuona.

Now the cart was reaching the crest of another hill. Baudwin looked below. This time, he was certain that he was seeing Four Falls. In the distance were four great rivers, all converging on a large expanse of dome-shaped buildings. To the north was River Condatis,[4] and to the south, River Nechtain. Coming from the northeast was River Cyhiraeth[5] and from the southeast was River Danu. Baudwin had heard of all of them many times.

Each of the rivers taught an essential lesson — one that flowed from a long and rich history. Lessons that were like the rivers — emboldening, yet daunting,

---

[4] Pronounced [COHN-da-tice]
[5] Pronounced [CY-hi-reth]

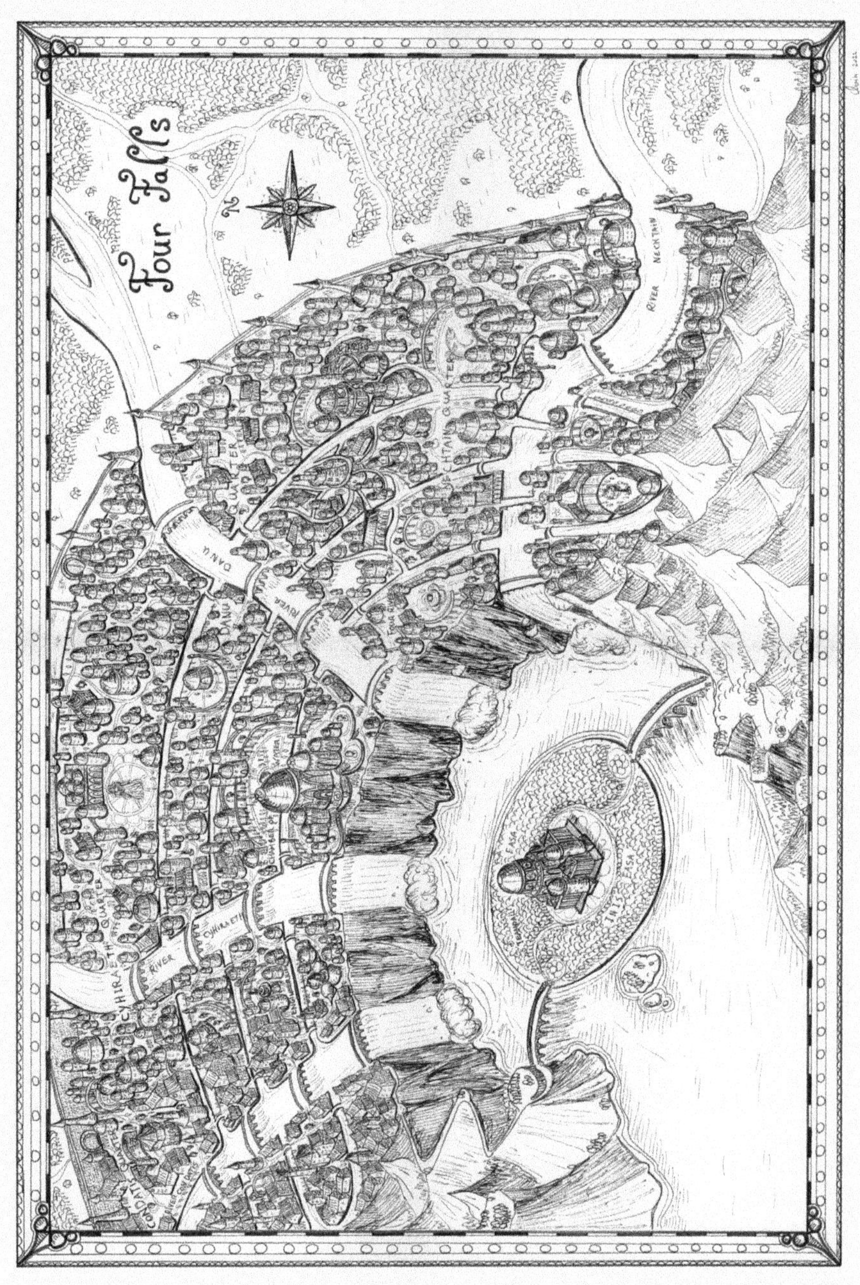

forceful, yet steady. Searching for guidance, water Faeries in Deuona visited River Nechtain the most, and less often, River Danu. Baudwin had done so as well, but not where they converged in Four Falls. Yet, few water Faeries from Deuona traveled to River Cyhiraeth anymore, which flowed from the dark lands in the north, and was fed by Lake Aife.[6] And even fewer visited River Condatis, the only one that came from *Tír Luí Lucharachán* — the land of the Elves. For this river flowed through the only opening in the Tadlachs — the Col of Lonrúil[7] known only through stories from water Faeries who had made the journey.

As Baudwin rode in the wagon, his senses opened. A waking came upon him, unlike any he had ever had — four powerful rivers coursing inside of him, all joined together. The feeling was so exhilarating he could barely keep from falling over. Were these rivers calling out for him to join with their currents? How he wished that were so! For he could taste them all rushing through his body, see their tumbling shades of green and blue, smell their watery essence, and hear them as they crashed into each other, all merging into one huge, thrashing Waterfall. As he reached out — as if to touch them — they filled his heart, overcoming him with joy.

"Magnificent — aren't they?" Earnan asked, as they rolled along, shaking the dragonflies from Belle's neck with the reins. Although he couldn't see Baudwin from the front, he could tell that he had found his yew trees.

"Oh, my, yes!" Baudwin replied — speaking through his waking — entranced as he was by his element. A thought struck him hard. *Why did my father never take me here?* he wondered, confounded. *To this grand and wonderful city?* How strange — and how very sad — that the work at the dam never ceased, and the work of containing the Water had contained *them* for so long, limiting their lives so. On top of that, his father's heart had been heavy for Baudwin's entire Life, weighing them both down with sadness and regret. Now, they were parted, and gone was any chance to enjoy this moment together. Having abandoned his home, the Water now embraced him, a gale-force reminder of his past on the eve of his independence.

In the midst of his waking, he thought then about his grandfather, and doubt began to gnaw at his heart. He had dismissed the old ways as unimportant and Seamus as a fool long in years, but now the Water was calling to him again. Indeed, *haunting* him again. *Fine*, he thought. He may have left home, but he was still a water Faery, and he would learn about Four Falls on his own terms.

"I'm going to visit all four of those rivers!" he announced to Earnan, as his senses withdrew and his waking subsided. "Each one. And not only am I going to learn the lesson of each river, I'm going to get to know all of my kin as well!" Earnan nodded, and Belle shook her antlers, ringing the bells.

These thoughts filled Baudwin with trepidation, for he wasn't sure he had the fortitude to achieve such a goal. Yet, he also felt delighted, for what

---

6 Pronounced [IFE]
7 Pronounced [CALL of LON-rule] the luminous col that shines in the dark

a powerful intention he now had — almost as powerful as his intention had been to find the Water. For the first time since the water spirit had stolen his glamorium egg, he felt alive.

Would the Water approve of my intention? he wondered.

He was about to find out, for they were now close to the city. As the wagon rolled on, Baudwin balked at the buildings. They were much taller than any he had ever seen before. *How could they be so high and not topple over?* he wondered, as he craned his neck to see the tops of the domes. He couldn't wait to see the falls, but he would have to, for they were a lot farther ahead — out of sight.

Soon they approached the gate leading into the city alongside River Nechtain. Baudwin gasped, for on one side of the river was a blue marble statue of a water faery lady, and on the other, a water faery gent. They faced each other with their arms extended. Each held a large wild salmon — an offering to travelers — and a gesture of hospitality and peace. *They have wings — like the guardians at the dam,* Baudwin thought, as he passed them. *Never have I seen a faery gent with wings!*

After passing through the gates, they headed down the Upper Nechtain Road beside River Nechtain. The cobblestone street bustled with activity. In one place, bands of young ones played tag with one another. In another, an Elve changed the glass on a window. Other wagons rumbled by, loaded with goods flowing into and out of the city — lumber, carpets, sacks of grain, barrels of pickles, sweet-vine, and every kind of fruit and vegetable.

Next to the river, Baudwin spotted some grand horns hauling away pieces of a razed building, and a group of water Faeries arguing on a street corner. Curiously, he listened, but could make out little of what they were saying. The city was a cacophony of voices, each one vying to be heard above the others. There was so much of everything! The rivers and canals spoke to him like a chorus of babbling creeks, and there he was, at the very center, surveying all the goings-on like a visiting dignitary, peering through the curtains of a palanquin.

His eyes went to the buildings. The early evening Sun was low, and the Light glittered brightly on their walls — buildings painted all the colors of the Water — azure, sapphire, and turquoise. Great golden domes capped the buildings, with dome crests in the centers, all of them many times larger than his own family crest. Symbols of the Water were everywhere. Here and there, statues of water Faeries stood atop the domes — in the centers of the crests — each one resting upon a circle of stained glass that told a story of its own.

Baudwin wanted to stop to see each one, listen to the home dwellers as they spoke about their heritage, play with their young ones, and explore all the side streets. The wagon slowed as they approached an arched stone bridge.

Belle proceeded carefully. What he saw next intrigued him even more, for they were crossing the first canal off of the Nechtain. As the wagon creaked over the cobblestone arch, Belle's hoofs went *clack clop, clack clop.*

Captivated, Baudwin looked down from the bridge at dozens of flat-bottomed boats, sailing to places where the streets never went. Water Faeries dressed in blue and green silk stood at the sterns, peacefully paddling their oars, steering their boats. One carried a delivery, another a wealthy passenger in a cabin. They had no care for busy streets, for theirs was a Life on the Water — always connected to their element — in contrast to the stone and plaster city around them.

With all the sights surrounding him, Baudwin was quickly forgetting about Deuona, taken in as he was by the city. "Where is the Four Rivers Faire?" he called to Earnan.

"Near the center of the city," Earnan replied. "We're on the outskirts. The city is laid out in four quarters, divided by the four rivers. We're in the quarter named after River Nechtain."

Baudwin realized then that there had to be three other quarters to see, each with a river that flowed to the falls, all very close to where they were going. He was learning that the city of Four Falls was laid out like a giant fan, divided into four parts, all connected by rivers and canals.

Soon, they passed over another arch-shaped stone bridge, with a canal beneath them. They were now in the center of the Nechtain Quarter. Here the Faeries were better dressed, and as Baudwin looked about, they seemed very different. They certainly were of the Water, yet they had a busyness about them quite unlike water Faeries in Deuona. And there was something else. As Baudwin spotted a faery gent walking down the street, he noticed a symbol of a salmon on his jacket.

Baudwin looked at a nearby building. Carved on the front was a statue of a salmon, and flying from the top was a salmon banner. Obviously, they were very important to the Faeries in this quarter.

"What does the salmon mean to them?" he asked Earnan.

"Faeries in this quarter revere the salmon," Earnan replied, smiling. "The salmon stands for wisdom."

"What kind of wisdom?" Baudwin asked, intrigued. Although he had swum with salmon many times in the river, apart from appreciating their persistence and agility, he had never considered much else about them.

"The wisdom that all the Fae should possess — even the Elves," Earnan replied. For they are born joined to their currents — coursing, and knowing their intentions. Before they are even alevins, salmon know that their fates lie with their home river — whether the Nechtain, Cyhiraeth, Danu, Condatis, or any other river in *Tír na nÓg*. They grow until they are large enough to swim out to sea. When the time is right, and they are big and fat, they come back, but always to their home river. How this is so, no one knows, but it is for this reason that wisdom is attributed to the salmon. Is that not what we all seek — to be true to our element and always return to our Source?"

Earnan paused, and Baudwin noticed his gaze grow even more intense than when he had spoken of the yew trees.

"I've never heard this told before," Baudwin said. "Such wisdom must be as deep as the ocean, for that is where they go." *Unlike those who never find their currents,* he thought, wistfully.

From the back of the wagon Baudwin could see Earnan nodding his head. Although Baudwin knew that the Nechtain was known as the bearer of wise lessons, he now knew why. He had many more questions to ask, but they would have to wait, for they were approaching the final bridge that led to the Four Rivers Faire.

As they passed over the bridge, Baudwin looked again at the canal below them. Boats loaded with goods were traveling to and from the docks. Turning right, Belle plodded along. In the distance, he saw four large wooden poles, each with a banner flying from the top. After traveling for hours, they had finally reached the entrance to the faire.

Baudwin studied the banners. On the first was a fine rendering of a salmon with silvery scales flashing in the Light. *That must be for River Nechtain,* he thought. The second had a Moon, full and bright — the third a wizened faery lady, ghastly-looking and frightening — and the fourth a spring, with steam rising from the surface of the Water.

"Do you know about the other banners?" Baudwin called out to Earnan.

"Of course!" Earnan replied. "The Moon is for River Danu, the banshee for River Cyhiraeth, and the hot spring — that's for River Condatis, which comes from the land of the Elves. Even *they* bring us Life and healing," he added, chuckling. Considering this, Baudwin smiled, and then wondered more.

"The Moon and the hot springs I know very well, and love," he said. "But the *banshee* I find —"

"Eerie and unsettling?" Earnan interrupted, chuckling. "As well you should. Particularly if you visit that part of the city."

Baudwin did not respond, but instead looked ahead to where they were going. The wagon lurched through the entrance of the faire, which was nestled in a large grove of oak trees, covering many acres. Everywhere, Baudwin saw tents of many colors — not only the blues and greens of Deuona — for here both Faeries and Elves of many different metals and elements traded freely. Most tents had symbols on their tops. Some, he recognized instantly — the elven hammer of Silver Forge — and the Sun of Gold Haven. Others he had never seen before. On a green tent was a symbol of a tree, which must have been from Wood Fern — the home of the wood Faeries. And on a sky-blue tent was a symbol of a cloud, which must have been from Breath Song — the home of the air Faeries.

Heading along, they passed merchants peddling their wares. A fragrant aroma wafted toward Baudwin. Turning, he spied an elven gent shouting, "Incense — the finest from Bog! Our bouquets are as fair as our city is foul!" Laughing, the elven gent held up several sticks he had already lit, and waved them at Baudwin.

Nearby, another elven gent sat inside a tent, between two large wooden cases with glass tops. Dressed in opulent-looking robes, he eyed Baudwin through an oversized monocle. "Color — clarity — karat!" he shouted, as he pointed to the cases. "Get the finest jewels from the best cutters in *Tír na nÓg*!" Seeing him, Baudwin thought again of Criofan, wondering what he would think of the display.

"You there!" another voice sweetly called out. "With the dove! Come and hear this chime! Bless your pet with fine Air as he flies!"

Looking for the source of the voice, Baudwin spied a faery lady unlike any he had ever seen, tall and breezy as a cloud, with pale blue skin and vapory gray eyes. Around her hung chimes of every kind and size. Seeing she had Baudwin's attention, she continued, "The chime of the season is Spring! Bring in the warm winds, and keep your mind blissful and sharp!"

Taken as he was with her, Baudwin did not know what to say. Sensing something akin to a breeze passing through her, he assumed she was an air Faery, and that she probably hailed from Breath Song. Excitedly, Moonrise hopped from side to side as they passed. *Is she speaking to him about the wind in ways I never have?* he wondered.

As Earnan steered the wagon to a large tent, filled with crates of honey, Baudwin spied a flag on top, bearing a symbol of the Water, and stitching obviously done by his kin. For a moment he thought of Deuona, and his heart was heavy, but he quickly set aside his feelings.

After unloading the wagon one last time, Earnan turned to Baudwin. "Here's a bonus for you," he said, smiling. He then handed Baudwin three blue topaz crystals — a lucky prize.

"What will you do now?" Earnan asked. For in the short time they had traveled together, he seemed to have grown quite fond of Baudwin.

As usual, Baudwin wanted to do everything at once. Every part of the Four Rivers Faire was calling to him, waiting to be explored. But he knew this plan would not do, as the day was ending, and he had no idea where to find the Engineerium. Quickly, he checked himself. "Do you know how to get to the Engineerium?" he asked.

"The Engineerium is between the River Cyhiraeth and Condatis Quarters," Earnan replied. "Just go there," he added, pointing to the center of the city. "Follow the canal we last crossed until you get to the north side of the city, and then pass the great hill where the Chamber of Water is located. If you keep going, you can't miss it."

Baudwin thanked Earnan, adding that he was on his way. He had earned his ride making the deliveries, and the wood Faery had been kind to him. After they said their goodbyes, Baudwin picked up his backpack. Moonrise hopped onto his shoulder, and together they went to explore the faire.

❧

Walking among the tents, Baudwin felt excited, yet uneasy. His choices were now completely his own to make. How could he be sure which ones would be right? He would have liked to spend the rest of the evening and well into the night at the faire, but the most prudent thing would be to trade for the provisions he needed. Again, he thought of Criofan. Certainly, his family knew of this place. Criofan's father had probably traded here before. Suddenly, he missed Criofan sorely. But if he was going to succeed with his plan, he had to forget Deuona and follow the intention he had chosen.

Ahead, he saw a food tent. He decided to get what he could that wouldn't perish in his pack. In the tent he found various kinds of dried fruit, nuts, and seeds. "Good," he said, "Moonrise, this will do for both of us." Quickly he traded, put a large sack of nuts and seeds into his pack, and then continued on his way.

As he ambled down the path, looking at all the wares, an elven gent motioned for him to enter his tent. Looking at the top, Baudwin saw a flag in the center, with a symbol of Gold Haven — a shining Sun. He noticed that the elven gent was surrounded by peculiar-looking clocks. Intrigued, he stepped inside. Looking about, he saw hourglasses of all shapes and sizes made of paired glass bulbs filled with sand and set into wooden, bronze, or silver frames. He turned one over and watched the sand fall through its narrow neck into the bottom bulb. Next to the hourglasses were sundials made of stone, with lines and numbers carefully etched into them. *How remarkably the Elves measure the passage of time,* he thought. For just as the hourglasses measured the hours of the day, many of the sundials measured the seasons themselves.

He turned and stopped. Before him was a clock he had never seen before, a bronze cone marked with lines and numbers, set into a two-column frame.

Seeing Baudwin's interest in the timepiece, the elven gent approached and spoke to him. "A water clock for a water Faery," he announced, his calm voice sounding measured, yet precise.

Baudwin jumped, surprised, and then laughed. "Indeed," he replied. "Is that what I'm looking at?"

As he spoke, he looked more closely at the elven gent, for he had never met anyone from Gold Haven before. Certainly, his attire was as finely made as the clocks in his tent: a light-yellow silk shirt, with breeches to match — both amply trimmed with gold braid — and an hourglass clock made of gold and hanging from a heavy gold chain around his neck. Baudwin wondered if this elven gent was a Master of Gold. If so, he was impressed by how different he seemed from Ferrell — the only other such Master Baudwin had ever met. This elven gent was less regimented and more elevated in his demeanor, as though, in his pursuit of time, he aspired to achieve something even more essential. Ferrell had seemed interested only in keeping order and dispensing justice.

Baudwin looked again at the contraption. Water dripped from a small hole in the bottom of the cone. A bowl sitting beneath the cone caught the drops.

"*Time* for a demonstration," the elven gent announced, chuckling at his joke. He took out a vase of water and poured some into the cone. The bottom of the cone dripped slowly and steadily.

"As the water level goes down," the elven gent continued, "you see how much time has gone by. And unlike sundials, they also work at night."

Baudwin had never seen a water clock before, and was instantly taken with its workings. So much so, that he looked at his own watch to see how the times compared. *Water tells the time*, he thought, happy to see the results.

"You'll find that a water clock is far more reliable than a watch," the elven gent said.

"No, they aren't!" declared a nearby voice. Looking up, Baudwin saw another elven gent a few paces away, hanging a flag on another tent. Apparently, he had been eavesdropping. Wondering where this elven gent was from, Baudwin studied the flag and saw a symbol of the Clock City — a clock.

The elven gent tied off the flag, working his fingers with seamless precision. Deftly, he jumped to the ground, as if he didn't have a moment to lose. Storming toward Baudwin and the Gold Haven Elve, he chided them both. "What this Faery needs is an *accurate* clock! Not those old relics!"

Hearing this, the Gold Haven Elve bristled. "Spying *again*, Fearghus?"[8] he asked, his voice low, yet steady. "You stay out of this — this is *my* customer. Can't you see he's a guild Faery, and doesn't want any of your *clinking* contraptions?"

As Fearghus approached them, Baudwin took in the look of his clothing — purposefully severe — dull gray silk with tightly stitched black trim, no jewelry, and high black boots that laced up the front with far too many eyelets.

---

[8] Pronounced [FER-gus]

He thought then about Tárlach, whom he had just met, and how he spent his days measuring the Water. Perhaps this elven gent from the Clock City did the same kind of thing, measuring time as he laced his boots, counting the seconds with each eyelet. Why else would he spend so much time lacing them every day?

This notion gave Baudwin pause. He certainly did find the Elves perplexing. *Even for this Elve, time couldn't be <u>that</u> interesting,* he thought, amused.

Fearghus neared them, leaning forward as he walked, his eyes to the ground, as if he were counting his every step. He stopped abruptly and then shot his head up at the other Elve.

"Oh, I wouldn't be too sure about that, Seanán,"[9] he declared, his eyes blazing with certainty. To Baudwin he seemed ready to explode, so fixed was his opinion. Yet he also seemed afraid of his own words, as if, despite their ferocity, he couldn't trust himself to speak them. "I sold a watch to a guild Faery in the Condatis Quarter just the other day," he added. "Just like the times, the way we *keep* time is changing!" he added, chuckling at his joke.

Baudwin groaned. These elven gents certainly seemed to enjoy clashing — being for this and against that.

Seanán and Fearghus regarded each other, sneering contemptuously.

Seanán turned to Baudwin. His ire had been stoked, yet his manner seemed calm to Baudwin, like his father's — almost soothing, his anger hidden. Yet who could say how dangerous he might become if his anger was entirely provoked? Baudwin wasn't sure if he wanted to find out, so he stood where he was, waiting.

"So, which *do* you like more?" Seanán prodded. "You came to my tent first. Therefore, I assume you like my clocks better."

"And yet," Fearghus added, as he looked at Baudwin's wrist, "I see that you're wearing a *watch*." As he spoke, he stepped closer to Baudwin, seeming like both a close friend and a dangerous enemy.

The two elven gents stared at Baudwin, waiting expectantly.

Nervously, Baudwin looked from side to side. "Well. . . I'm not sure. . . I mean. . . I do have a watch of my own, but this water clock is. . . of course . . . hard to resist. . . of course."

"And?" both elven gents asked at the same time, surprising Baudwin with an unexpected moment of unity.

"Well," he replied anxiously, "I suppose I like them both."

"No, no, no!" Fearghus exclaimed. "That simply won't do!"

"You *have* to choose!" Seanán insisted.

Right then, Baudwin decided that he didn't like either of these elven gents, and certainly wasn't going to let them force him to choose anything. He suddenly

---

9 Pronounced [SHAN-awn]

felt as though he was right back at that important meeting, and the magniglow vote. He had to think quickly.

"I don't know enough to decide," he said. "I need more. . .well. . ." Exhaling slowly he added, "I. Need. More. *Time.*"

Hearing this, Seanán's eyes lit up. "I know what he means!"

"Yes!" Fearghus agreed.

"What he *needs* is a debate!"

"Yes, a debate!" Fearghus exclaimed.

Baudwin looked askance at both of them. Seanán continued speaking, unflurried. "If what you want is *more* time — then *time* is what you shall have. Elven debates *create* time, and they are the only way that Elves can really settle their differences anyway. So, let us —"

"And you're in luck," Fearghus interrupted, "for the Clock City boasts the finest debaters!"

"Hardly the finest," Seanán countered. "Why then, is Gold Haven still carrying the Golden Scroll Trophy from last season?"

"The judges were biased!" Fearghus shouted. "But this *time,* they won't be," he added, laughing.

"Come with us," Seanán said. They headed out of the tent.

All of their talk about time was wearing thin, as were their silly jokes, and Baudwin wished he could simply leave. But something told him that he should see the debate through, so he wouldn't upset either of them any further.

Baudwin watched them race back into their tents. He had no idea what they were doing. Each of them came out holding a large wooden crate, which they placed side by side on the ground. They hopped onto the tops.

Moonrise cooed with nervous anticipation, and then flitted over to Baudwin's other shoulder.

"Don't worry, my feathered friend!" Seanán laughed. "This is all in good fun!"

"Now, young Guilder," Fearghus began, "let me introduce myself — I am Fearghus, son of Mochuda,[10] of the Clock City —"

"And," Seanán, interrupted, not to be outdone, "I am Seanán, son of Berach[11] of Gold Haven."

"Who might *you* be?" Fearghus inquired.

Baudwin hesitated, unsure if he should tell them who he was, lest word of his whereabouts get out to his father. But Four Falls was very large, and they were, after all, Elves who probably wouldn't mention him again. "I am Baudwin, son of Kelven, of Deuona."

---

[10] Pronounced [MUK-oo-da]
[11] Pronounced [BAR-ock]

"Well then, Baudwin, you must decide who starts the debate. So please — kindly take this seal of mine — which is perfectly balanced — and give it a flip. Seanán will call it in the air."

Fearghus handed Baudwin the seal, which he then turned over in his hand. On one side was the symbol of the Clock City, and on the other a rather charming, yet sinister-looking Elve, with pursed lips, a calculating gaze, and a decidedly haughty manner. Baudwin didn't know who he was. He wanted to ask, but didn't. Instead, he flipped the seal high into the Air.

"City or face?" Fearghus asked.

"City!" Seanán called.

The seal hit the grass — face.

"Ha — Govannon wins again!" Fearghus exclaimed gleefully.

Seanán grimaced. He wasn't pleased with the result, and Baudwin could tell that wasn't the only reason he was upset. He clearly didn't like seeing the face, which Baudwin realized belonged to Govannon.

"Should have used my seal instead!" Seanán exclaimed.

"Never mind that," Fearghus snapped. "Do you want to begin, or should I?"

"I will," Seanán replied.

Baudwin looked around and saw that a number of Elves had gathered to watch the Gold Haven vs. Clock City debate. Obviously, they had done so many times before. Some cried out for Fearghus, and others for Seanán to win. The wind picked up, rustling the trees, and whipping the flags on the tents. A reckoning of sorts was in the Air, and as both sides clustered around their leaders, they seemed like two distinct forces — called to battle and ready to fight — boots on the ground and swords raised.

Yet, there were no swords — only words.

As Seanán spoke, his calm demeanor shifted, and he seemed heightened in his resolve. Baudwin noted the change. "In order for our guilder friend to choose which clock is better," he began, as he looked at Baudwin and the crowd, "we must first understand what each one measures. And so, I begin with a question: What *is* time?"

No one in the crowd answered.

Undaunted, Seanán continued. "Time is best understood as the Eternal Movement. As such, it stems entirely from the cosmic constant — that which moves the cosmos forward — through eternity." Again, Baudwin noted the change in Seanán's demeanor, duly impressed with how the topic brought out his vigor, making him seem indomitable.

Having found his spur, Seanán turned to Baudwin and said, "Behind the wooden counter in my tent, you'll find a rod. Go now. Get it and pass it to Fearghus."

Quickly, Baudwin went into the tent. As Seanán had described, the rod was behind the counter. Baudwin gasped at the sight, for it was made of red oak and tipped at both ends with bands of copper, silver, gold, and platinum. He raced back and presented the rod to Fearghus.

Fearghus took the rod and began to speak. "There's no need to ask such questions, because we already know the answers. Time is what is *measured*. Time arises from what we ourselves can measure, and how accurately we perform such measurements. Even eternity is just another word for that which we haven't yet measured. Therefore, our *only* challenge is to accurately observe."

Fearghus then passed the rod back to Seanán, for it was now his turn to talk. For a moment, they each held an end, staring disdainfully at each other, each of them refusing to release his grasp. Seeing this, Baudwin shivered, for this debate seemed to be getting more serious than either of them had let on.

Fearghus let go of his end.

As they continued to debate, Baudwin could see the Elves on the Clock City side fold their arms and nod their heads in agreement, while the Elves on the Gold Haven side strutted back and forth, with their hands on their hips. Obviously, one side did not agree with what Fearghus had said.

Seanán took the rod and spoke again. "As Fearghus pointed out, my clocks may not seem as accurate, but that's because they need not be. The cosmic clock lives within all Elves. To know what time it is, all we must do is peer inside ourselves. Clocks are merely *symbols* of what we already possess when we live pragmatic lives, in tune with the cosmic clock." Again, he passed the rod, and the debate continued.

Emphatically, Fearghus shook his head. "Mere *symbols* — indeed!" he exclaimed, taking the rod. "Nowadays, what few Elves can even *tell* time without a watch? Such days are *over*! We must now turn to Sprocketworks in order to know the time. Your old clocks are as outdated as the old ways!"

"You miss the point entirely," Seanán countered, his voice rising, as he took the rod. "Surely accuracy matters, but the tracking of the stars can be done simply by watching the movement of the heavens. If we weren't following the constellations, we wouldn't know the solstices from the equinoxes!"

"Our observatories in the Clock City do that too!" Fearghus shot back.

"All that really matters," Seanán replied confidently, "is that the Eternal Movement has *no* beginning and *no* end. All you care about is measuring beginnings and endings! The true lesson of time, is that it is *relative*."

"Rubbish!" Fearghus shouted.

"Now, now," Seanán said, holding tightly to the rod, "I haven't passed the rod yet."

"Time is not relative!" Fearghus shouted, his frustration having reached a fever pitch. "Our clocks are becoming more and more accurate. Soon, all the clocks in *Tír na nÓg*, will be synced to such precision that we will know what time it is down to the tiniest fraction of a second."

Both elven gents had now completely forgotten about the rod.

"And what about the space between the tiniest part of the second?" Seanán shrieked.

"We will measure that as well!" Fearghus roared.

"And after that?"

Fearghus went silent.

"The old ways of the Elves are clear," Seanán insisted. "When you embrace the cosmic clock, you vibrate with the intensity of the heavens, and move so quickly that you see that time is, in fact, relative. The cosmic clock is the only thing that matters — for *it* never changes!"

"And what time is *that* constant?" Fearghus shouted.

"The time beyond knowing," Seanán replied.

"What is the use of knowing *that*?" Fearghus exclaimed. "Preposterous! How *inept* can you be?"

"Inept?" Seanán shot back. "I would say we are far more *adept* than you at knowing the time."

"Adept at being utterly muttonheaded dimwits!" Fearghus exclaimed.

"Hardly," Seanán insisted. "I myself have known Elves who can tell the time without even *looking* at a clock."

"Careful now," Fearghus said. "Such claims are frowned upon by the Assembly!"

"The Assembly doesn't frighten me!" Seanán shouted. "We are not —"

"You *should* be!" Fearghus interrupted. "Now give me that rod. It's been my turn to speak for *quite* some time!"

Baudwin wasn't sure whose turn it was, for as their bickering escalated, they had stopped passing the rod altogether.

"Don't give him the rod!" an elven gent shouted from the crowd. "It's still your turn!" Many more shouted in agreement. Others then shouted in defiance.

"As I was saying," Seanán went on, shaking the rod at Fearghus. "I'm not frightened by the Assembly — not frightened at all! Gold Haven may have lost the *cogadh*, but we will not be robbed of what we know to be true. The Clock City has lost its way! Time is not solely in the measurement — and *never* will be!"

Baudwin had heard enough. The debate was wearing on his nerves. "Please stop!" he cried.

"Yes, we're being terribly rude," Seanán declared, as he turned to look at Baudwin. "We forgot all about him. He is, after all — our patron."

This was not the response Baudwin had wanted. Seanán continued speaking, handing Baudwin the rod. "Tell us now," he began, "who do you think is right? We will never agree, but we'll let you settle this one."

Baudwin thought for a moment and began to panic. He didn't know which side to take, much less what would happen if he did choose. He almost wished he was back in Deuona. "I don't know whose side is right," he replied. "But I do know that just as between the Faeries and Elves — the Elves must find concord."

Hearing this, Elves on both sides of the debate began laughing and jeering. "This isn't about Elves and Faeries!" an elven gent shouted.

"How do you know?" Baudwin asked. As he spoke, he remembered the poem that he, Criofan, and Matha had recited before they reached the Engineerium — the poem about faery and elven concord — which he then repeated:

Elves can always find the time

Faeries take the space

Elves know how to take the means

Faeries find the place

"How amusing!" another elven gent in the crowd cried out.

"Gold Haven can find the time — and the Clock City will take the space!" another elven gent shouted. Both sides laughed uproariously at the notion of the Elves finding such concord between themselves.

An irate elven gent then cut in. "This isn't about time and space!" he shouted. "This is about *time*! Why bring *space* into the debate?"

"Maybe you can't understand one without the other," Baudwin politely suggested.

"He thinks we need *space* to understand *time*!" Fearghus laughed.

"I'm sure he means well," Seanán declared, taking a more even-handed position. "He's trying to settle this debate. Let him speak more."

Baudwin assessed the crowd, flinching. He knew he had to weigh his words carefully, but the growing animosity from the Elves made him nervous, so he blurted, "Because! When one is lost, one must consider not just time, but time *and* space!"

"We're not lost!" an elven gent in the crowd shouted.

Seanán again intervened. "Dear me," he began, "I think we're all being too hard on him really —"

But Baudwin was determined to speak his piece, so he cut Seanán off. "But you *are* lost!" he exclaimed. Why *else* would you argue about time if you weren't? Faeries *never* argue about space!"

"How dare you tell us that we're lost!" Fearghus growled.

"But you *are*!" Baudwin blurted, laughing nervously. "You're as lost as I am!"

For a moment the crowd went silent. Baudwin hoped that his equalizing point had lessoned their ire, but he was about to be sorely disappointed. Within moments, any chance of reconciliation vanished, and the crowd began to roar. Baudwin's kind and simple wisdom proved to be too much for them, and soon the crowd broke out in a rage.

Baudwin feared they would soon be after him, but then Seanán pointed at Fearghus, shouting, "If we *are* lost it's *your* fault!" The crowd then quickly forgot about Baudwin, all too eager to turn on one another again.

Baudwin watched as the Elves from Gold Haven began brawling with the Elves from the Clock City. Within seconds, they were a flailing smear of gold and gray, pushing and punching each other. Somewhere, a Clock City Elve had his jacket ripped to shreds. Elsewhere, a Gold Haven Elve had his nose broken by a punch. All seemed well practiced in their rancor, and Baudwin wondered which of them had seen action as guards, marching into battle.

Seanán jumped off his crate, and pointed the rod at the crowd. "We'll show you!" he shouted triumphantly. "The Rise of Time will *fall!*"

"Enough!" Fearghus commanded, jumping off his crate. He tried to wrest the rod away from Seanán. The two struggled back and forth, back and forth, while the fighting around them worsened.

Baudwin stood agape, as clocks of all designs became weapons of choice. Suddenly, he ducked, narrowly missing a hurled sundial. Mechanical clocks were thrown at Seanán's tent, and hourglasses shot through the Air, their bulbs smashing to bits as they hit the ground. More rioters piled into the tents, tearing them down and destroying the contents.

As others poured in, the chaos intensified. Faction joined faction. Soon Elves wearing symbols of Suns, who were from Gold Haven, were joined by those wearing symbols of four beetles, who were from Pine Reach. They clashed against Elves wearing symbols of Clocks from the Clock City, who were joined by Elves wearing symbols of cracked mountains, from the Fallen Peaks. Baudwin was curious about these alliances, but there was no time to ponder.

Incensed at the recklessness of the Elves, a group of water Faeries stormed into the fight, tripping the Elves with quarrel staffs, trying to break them apart. All the while they shrieked, "Leave us now! Go back to *Tír Luí Lucharachán!*" Other Faeries joined in, screaming, "Begone!"

Terrified, Moonrise dug his talons into Baudwin's shoulder, cooing and shaking. Baudwin decided he had better make haste and leave while he still could. Quickly, he turned to go, but directly in his path was a group of water Faeries. They moved together as a band, and many wore the symbols of their quarters — salmon, Moon, banshee, and hot spring.

One of them stepped forward, a Moon on his jacket. He was a Guilder — handsome and tall — and he reminded Baudwin of Seamus.

"Stop this at once!" he commanded. "You Elves forget that you're our guests here!"

The riot continued despite his protest. "Go back to your canals, Ayamonn!"[12] Fearghus called out to him. Many laughed when they heard this.

Ayamonn grimaced. "River Danu provides the Four Rivers Faire with abundance, and will surely take it away if you continue this nonsense!"

Again they ignored him, continuing the fight. The brawl would not stop, and now, even more Elves came pouring in. Several tents were torn to the ground as the rival elven factions continued rioting.

"Someone call the Earth Guard!" a Faery shouted from the sidelines. "Let the Elves sort out their own quarrel!"

Many Faeries shouted in agreement. The water Faeries with Ayamonn waited expectantly for help to arrive. Looking to and fro, Baudwin saw a troop of Earth Guards pushing their way into the riot, which had now grown to hundreds of Elves and scores of Faeries. Somewhere nearby a tent caught Fire, and screams sounded all around.

"You fools!" Ayamonn shouted. "You disrespect the rivers! You disrespect Danu, Cyhiraeth, Nechtain, and even the river that carries your own kin — the Condatis!"

This time no one answered. Instead, a crazed-looking elven gent from the Clock City, on his way to put out the Fire, threw a bucket of Water over Ayamonn's head. The Water splashed over him and everyone near him.

Enraged, Ayamonn stood, dripping wet. Baudwin knew what a desecration this was — as insulting as the Elves throwing clocks and sundials at each other. *Gnás* had been forgotten, and there would be no more coming together now — whether to travel or trade, dance or debate.

Ayamonn charged into the crowd, his followers behind him. Those wearing symbols of Moons, salmons, banshees, and hot springs soon clashed against the Elves — those battling for the Eternal Movement or the Rise of Time.

The riot was now truly out of hand. Somewhere a cart was broken, and a grand horn stampeded, smashing through a tent of incense. The elven gent from Bog howled with rage. Elsewhere, the wind chimes of the air faery lay smashed upon the ground. Seeing her fine things destroyed, she joined the fight, as did several other wood and earth Faeries. Charged with fury, no one seemed willing to give up.

---

[12] Pronounced [AY-mon]

The upheaval grew, until Baudwin couldn't tell who was fighting who. Seeing an opening in the riot, and holding his backpack tightly, he said, "Moonrise, fly and meet me on the other side of the canal!"

Quickly, Moonrise flew out of harm's way. How Baudwin would love to have flown with him, above the petty brawl, but this was not to be. Frantically, he turned to leave.

Racing down the path, he passed the Earth Guards, who were fighting to contain the turmoil. Overwhelmed, they tried to stop a grand horn from smashing more crates. Weaving in and out, Baudwin managed to avoid them — but then he felt a sharp pain in the back of his head. Something had struck him. Dizzy and bewildered, he turned to see what it was. He stumbled and fell. Panicked, he feared a grand horn had hit him.

"Ha — got him good!" a harsh voice shouted. Baudwin thought the voice was elven, for who but an Elve would speak in such a way to a Faery?

"That one's for the Clock City!" another voice agreed, laughing.

Looking down, Baudwin saw a piece of Wood on the ground with blood on the end. Shocked, he realized that it was his blood. He stood up but stumbled again, still dizzy from the attack. He looked at the Elves who had struck him, stupefied by their malice.

Painfully, he knelt down. Frightened that his wound could be serious, he touched the back of his head.

"Quick!' the first voice said. "Grab his pack, before he comes to his senses."

Their actions were cruel — not even Loch had ever treated him this way — taking such delight in his pain and defenselessness. He felt a sharp pull on his pack, but he still had enough strength to pull back.

"Strong one here," the other voice snickered.

Baudwin turned and looked at the Elve. His vision was still hazy. The Elve stared back at him, his eyes slant, his grin fierce.

"Let go!" Baudwin shouted, but then he felt a blow to his side from the other Elve, and he doubled over. They tore his pack from his back. As they ran off laughing, their cries were low and raspy, like two conniving vultures.

"Into the canal it goes!" the first Elve shrieked, as he tossed the pack into the water. "This is what you get for all your nonsense talk about time and space!"

Baudwin wanted to cry out in anguish, but he did not. He would not let them steal his dignity. He tried to track them, but they had already disappeared into the crowd. He put his hand to the back of his head again. The wound wasn't serious, and he had to keep going, so he stood up and stumbled forward as fast as he could.

Soon his vertigo lessened, and he was an acrobat again — an angry, watery jet, shooting through the faire.

He vaulted over a broken wagon, jumped over a barrel, and grabbed a rope dangling over a smashed tent, swinging himself over a pile of burning trash. He ran farther and then turned back onto the Upper Nechtain Road, heading away from the falls.

Ahead he saw a canal. On one side was the riot, and on the other were crowds of calmer Fae, their mouths agape as they watched the spectacle before them. He wanted to catch the cowards who had attacked him, but they were long gone. Instead, he raced, weaving and ducking, and then rushing like a river, escaping to the sea.

Finally, he reached a bridge and was over the canal, back in the heart of the Nechtain Quarter. Above him he saw Moonrise circling. Quickly, he dove down, flying faster than most would have thought possible. Again, he was on Baudwin's shoulder. Together, they fled as far away as they could.

ʘ

Baudwin ran even faster. He wanted to get away from this horrendous place. A torrent of feelings churned inside of him. He wanted to go back home, but he also didn't want to be at home. He wanted justice, but he also didn't care. Racing alongside the canal, he moved across the Nechtain Quarter to the next one.

Upon entering the Danu Quarter, he saw Moons everywhere — on streets and buildings, and the clothes of many of his kin. For a moment the symbols brought him comfort. They were lustrous and full, and they reminded him of the crystal Moon in the dome crest above his family's shrine to the Water.

He turned onto the Lower Danu Road, going toward the falls. Breathing heavily, he crossed another bridge over the canal. Deliriously, he kept running, not sure of where he was going.

Next to the canal bridge, he saw another bridge running perpendicular to the Lower Danu Road. This one was supported by three stone arches stretching beneath the deck. On a pillar at the entrance was a symbol of River Danu — another large shining Moon. As he raced across the bridge, the river flowed soothingly beneath him. He wanted to dive into the rushing currents, to forget his torment and be with his element.

All manner of thoughts swirled inside his head.

How could these noble Faeries — followers of the Water and all they held sacred — allow this to happen? He would never understand why the Elves had fought so bitterly, but he knew what they had done was wrong, and he was angry. *This is, after all, our city*, he thought. A simple debate had turned into a deluge of acrimony, crimes, and misery.

Soon he reached the Upper Danu Road. Turning toward the falls, he then crossed another bridge over the canal. Running alongside the canal to the

Cyhiraeth Quarter, he passed tall buildings with domes and fountains and large pools, grander than any he had ever seen — but he didn't care. What difference did any of it make if there was no peace to be found?

Still he ran, until he reached the Lower Cyhiraeth Road. He crossed yet another bridge going over the canal to the falls.

Next to the canal bridge, he saw another bridge running perpendicular to the Lower Cyhiraeth Road. A pillar at the entrance bore the symbol of River Cyhiraeth — a wailing banshee.

As he raced across the bridge, Baudwin saw water Faeries, dressed in deep greens and blues, with long blue-green hair, mysterious and mournful-looking. He would have liked to meet them, but instead ran down some steps, taking refuge under an arch of the bridge.

With nary a soul to hear or help him, he collapsed by a small dock. There was no solace to be found next to the dirty stone walls and worn wooden pilings. Moonrise alighted near him on a barrel, cooing with concern.

Baudwin touched the back of his head again. The wound was tender. He knelt next to the river. Cupping his hands, he poured Water over his head. The wetness stung, yet soothed his wound. He felt a change coming over him.

This Water carried Darkness. The Water in Deuona brought joy. *Why is the Water this way?* he wondered. *What murky springs and dank temples in the north were home to the Cyhiraeth?*

No answer came.

Baudwin's vision then shifted, and he saw only shadows and ashes. Moonrise resembled a rawboned raven. His senses awakened, and he could hear the Water wailing at him, telling him not to flinch, but to embrace his pain.

He recoiled from the river. What strange guidance was this river giving? Why would the Water ask this of him now? Escaping to this place had been a mistake. He should have gone to the Condatis Quarter instead — to the healing of the Elves. He would not accept any more pain on this day.

This river is cursed, he thought, as he feebly rose to leave.

But before Baudwin could place both feet on the ground, a shock jolted through him. His eyes went wide. A new pain coursed through him, one that made the cut on his scalp seem trivial. He rolled over on his side, writhing. Through unspeakable pain, it yet occurred to him that he himself had ushered in this torment. Too readily, he had overlooked the danger of coming too close to the Water. Cursing his foolishness, he steeled himself, waiting for the shock to pass.

His arms and legs shook violently. Never had a bout been this disabling. Terrified, he wondered if Annwyn was taking him — pulling him through the inky Water of the Cyhiraeth — into oblivion.

He tried to look for Moonrise, but couldn't turn his head. He wanted to cry out, but his lips wouldn't move. There he lay, for how long he didn't know — alone — as the Darkness washed over him.

Baudwin then found himself floating in a void. Vaguely, he felt his body, but he could not marshal his senses. Time passed, and then within him, he heard a voice.

"Baudwin, I am here for you."

Baudwin recognized the voice — the same faery lady voice he had heard at the Springs of Coventina.

"Who *are* you?" Baudwin muttered, as his senses slowly returned.

At first, she did not respond to him in the Darkness, but then he heard, "I am the one who is pledged to watch over you. Take heart, and do not be discouraged by the fighting you witnessed this day. The Fae have been at odds with one another for many hundreds of years, and this debacle was unavoidable. In time, you will better understand how their hearts became so hardened, because your own feelings will not always be trapped inside you — lost and forgotten."

Astonished, Baudwin realized that before she had judged him unworthy to wield Glamorium, the spirit at the dam had spoken these very same words about his feelings. He wondered if that spirit and this other voice were somehow related. *Is the spirit an accomplice of the voice now speaking to me?* he wondered. That seemed possible, but he found the manner of this voice very different from the spirit's — less critical and far more soothing. Nevertheless, he didn't want to be controlled by her.

Regardless of who this being was, hearing that he was still under scrutiny angered him greatly. "I have left that path!" he shouted. "The spirit took my egg! I will make my own way now!"

"Only along your own path will you find yourself, and in finding yourself will you know your true path. Do not lose heart. Throw yourself into your own choices."

"Good!" Baudwin exclaimed. "I'm joining the Engineerium! And neither you nor anyone else can stop me!"

Reassuringly, the voice replied, "That is good. Do not fear, for I will see you soon and care for you. Now sleep, and tomorrow you will know the healing of the Cyhiraeth!"

Baudwin then fell into a deep, dreamless sleep.

Chapter 24

BACK TO THE ENGINEERIUM

Baudwin awoke with a groan. Morning had come, and his body ached from lying under the bridge all night. He opened his eyes and stretched his arms, surprised to find himself in these surroundings. Sitting up, he remembered the past awful night. *Why am I still here?* he wondered. He wasn't sure when he had finally passed out, but he still felt sore from the tremors that had possessed him. He recalled that someone had spoken to him. Her words had been soothing and he wanted to believe that she cared that much about him, but without knowing who she was, he couldn't. Right then, he wished he had a dream to share with someone, so he would not feel so alone. But this was not to be, as his sleep had been dreamless, and no one was in sight.

Despite this, he smiled. There was at least one thing to be grateful for — Annwyn had not yet taken him. He was still alive — and breathing. He had been fearful that another bout would be his last, but somehow last night he had hung on. Perhaps the voice that had spoken to him had saved him.

Baudwin looked around. Moonrise was nowhere to be seen. He knew the twilight dove had probably gone foraging, no doubt after seeing him fall asleep.

The river rushed past him, appearing lighter in the early morning hours. Still, he felt the uncanny Darkness rippling beneath its surface. Against his will, the Cyhiraeth had pulled him under, forcing him to succumb to a bout unlike any he had ever suffered. Although the pain had been severe, he was surprised to find himself feeling stronger than he had just the day before.

"What a *strange* river you are," he said aloud. He wondered then if his bouts would be any different with each river he visited. Never had he considered this before — but never had he been near so many rivers in one place.

Looking down, he grimaced at his wrinkled, dirty clothes. He thought then of his dresser at home, wishing he could change into a clean pair of breeches. Anxiously, he looked for his pet, putting the thought out of his mind.

"Moonrise," he called. "Come, my shooting star!" Moments went by and still there was no sign of him. Now Baudwin began to worry, for Four Falls had proved to be as inhospitable as it was unpredictable. Twilight doves had little trouble finding those that they were bonded with, but still Baudwin worried.

Standing up, he took in his surroundings. The dock near the bridge was a creaking mess of planks, a stale-looking waypoint, forgotten by ferriers and passersby alike. Sleeping under the bridge had been a torment, yet being near the river had left him changed, although he had no idea how or why.

He remembered the previous day — the pleasant ride with Earnan, seeing Four Falls for the first time, and then the unseemly riot at the Four Rivers Faire. Those Elves had gotten the best of him. Back in Deuona, he could have taken revenge or sought justice, but how could he find his attackers here, among so many? No doubt they singled him out for this very reason. How easy for them to spot a vulnerable country Faery.

"Cowards," he muttered, seething.

Placing his hand on the back of his head, he touched the place where they had hit him. The cut had closed, and was already healing. Surprisingly, the pain was not as strong as he expected. A wound like that would normally throb the next day. Was this also a gift from the Cyhiraeth, he wondered?

Baudwin gazed at the river rushing past him. Now he was certain. Here in his isolation, the Water had made his pain worse, giving him no escape. However, the healing meant that the Cyhiraeth had also helped him, perhaps because he had stopped running, and accepted his suffering, if only for a time.

"Moonrise!" he called again.

Soon he saw a flash of white and blue feathers, and his dove alighted on a barrel nearby, cooing softly at him.

"I'm so glad you decided to come," Baudwin joked, smiling. "As you can see, I'm still here."

Moonrise cooed thankfully.

"Did you find anything to eat?" Baudwin asked.

Moonrise nodded at his friend and began preening his feathers.

"Lucky for you," Baudwin said. "We have to get to the Engineerium. There are no provisions, and I'm awfully hungry." As he spoke, Baudwin's eyes lit up. "I almost forgot!" he exclaimed.

Searching his pockets, he found the three topaz crystals. "We still have Earnan's pay! Thank the Water that I didn't put them in my pack."

Moonrise jumped off his perch to the ground, and strutted back and forth, puffing out his chest feathers.

"With these, we can get what we need," Baudwin said, tapping the crystals. "Now let's get out of this miserable place."

As Baudwin turned to leave, Moonrise quickly alighted on his shoulder. Together, they bounded up the steps, and across the Cyhiraeth River bridge. Soon, they reached the Upper Cyhiraeth Road. They crossed a bridge over a canal and then turned to follow that canal to the Engineerium. Ferriers were beginning their morning errands, carefully steering their boats.

As if for the first time, Baudwin saw the Cyhiraeth Quarter — streets, alleyways, and buildings, with symbols of banshees everywhere. A sound then caught his ear. He looked for the source.

Across the street, he saw a group of young Faeries singing and playing. They were chasing each other — weaving in and out — twisting and turning like threads of an eternity knot — each one following the other. They wailed as they moved, their voices rising and falling, echoing back and forth, as if they were mourning a loved one. The lassies pretended to weep and wash their clothes in the Water, while the lads poured them glasses of pretend Water, which they drank.

Baudwin looked again at the young Fae. Suddenly, they streaked like a swarm of bees to a patch of wild lilies near the canal. They stopped, as if hearkening to sounds that none but they could hear. They all began singing again, seemingly lost in a trance, waving their arms and swaying from side to side like river rushes in the wind. Some of their greens were so dark that they looked blue, and their blues so dark that they looked black, all of which made them seem eerily out of place and ready to float away, should the wind pick up and catch them by surprise.

An old faery gent strolled by, listening to their cries.

"Pardon me," Baudwin asked, stopping him. "What song are they singing?"

"The song of the banshee's search," the old one replied. "For when she finds you, you know the end is near."

"What end?" Baudwin asked.

"*The* end — the lesson that everyone learns," the gent continued, seeing that Baudwin did not understand. "The end that everyone must face."

Hearing this, Baudwin felt a shiver run through him. He didn't want to know any more about endings — only beginnings — so he thanked the gent and then moved on.

Baudwin soon stopped to look toward the west, where the four rivers met. Although he couldn't see the falls, he could hear them roaring in the distance.

"Moonrise," he said, pointing toward them, "in your travels last night, did you see the Engineerium?" The dove nodded.

Baudwin headed a bit farther to the border where the Cyhiraeth and Condatis Quarters meet. In the distance, he saw a familiar sight — two tall posts with blue and green streamers flying from the tops. Between the two posts sat a large bronze ring.

"There!" Baudwin exclaimed. "The Engineerium!" Grabbing Moonrise, he raced toward the ring. As soon as he got to the posts, he stopped and looked up. Engraved at the top of the ring were the words, *Elven Engineerium.* Beneath them more words proclaimed, *With Progress We Prevail.* Other elven letters formed a border from the top of the ring, all the way to the ground.

Baudwin wasn't sure which petal he was entering, but he couldn't wait to find out, so he stepped through the ring onto a long stone pathway. Inside, the tunnel was built exactly like the one in Deuona, with wide strips of copper covering the seams of the joints. Only the sconces on the walls were different. Instead of orange wood lilies and violet harebells, there were red tulips and green chrysanthemums.

Racing through the tunnel, Baudwin's spirits lifted. This was indeed a familiar place. He wondered how different this Engineerium would be from the one in Deuona. He still didn't know where he was, but as the round circle of Light at the end of the tunnel grew larger and larger, he knew he would soon find out.

"Moonrise — look!" he shouted, as he emerged from the tunnel. "The East Petal!"

Unexpectedly, a pang of sadness pierced his heart. This time, as he surveyed the wondrous sight, neither of his two best friends were by his side. Today he would not hear Matha chiding them to stop lingering at the fountains, cavorting like rabbits. Nor would he hear Criofan insisting that he did, indeed, support Baudwin's mission to touch some Glamorium. If his friends had been here, they would have taken off in a frenzy to explore everything, laughing and shouting. Matha would have known what to study, and Criofan what to admire. And they still would have had time for other, more serious pursuits.

Quietly, Baudwin took his time, taking in the look and feel of the place as best he could. From his vantage point, he could see the entire perimeter of the concourse, a long stone wall, with fountains shooting from a canal of Water flowing along the top. To his left was the South Petal of the Engineerium, and to his right the North, with low stone walls, canals, and more shooting fountains. A short distance away, a blue and green banner flying from the top of a post read: *The Engineerium Welcomes the Summer Solstice.* "Litha, the high holiday is approaching," he said to Moonrise, holding him on his shoulder.

Unlike Deuona, this Engineerium had not only throngs of water Faeries, but wood, earth, and air Faeries as well. Just as at the Deuona Engineerium, everywhere he looked he saw scores of Elves wearing copper, silver, and gold, all busily attending to rides, tents, and other amusements. *Those Elves look like they need a hand,* he thought. *For sure — I'll get a job!* Despite missing his friends, he knew he had to turn his attention to the task at hand. Baudwin headed through the East Petal, determined not to waver, but he'd not gone far before the sadness of missing his friends turned to guilt. Here were many of the places they had been, right after they had gone their separate ways.

Matha had left for the Garden of Sprockets, and once there, fled from Loch and his Roilers. Criofan had gone to Racer Roller to get away from Baudwin's ire. Later, they both had barely escaped with their lives, driving their Racer Roller under the Dragonfly, again to escape from Loch and his Roilers. *If only I hadn't gotten so angry,* he thought, *none of that would have happened. We all would have been much better off just staying together.*

He stopped. Towering before him was the Butterfly, its turquoise wings and black abdomen resting like an enormous leaf on the branch of an oak tree. Ruefully, he smiled. *Instead of arguing and fighting like fools,* he thought, *we would have gone on that and had a fine old time.*

As if to mock him, riders in cars on the looping tracks whooped and hollered as they passed from wing to wing. Frustrated, Baudwin walked away. He hadn't ridden the Butterfly then, and he certainly wasn't going to now.

What a great friend I am, he thought guiltily.

He hoped his admission of guilt would soothe him, but instead he was reminded of something he had been avoiding ever since he left Deuona.

I wasn't honest with them, he thought. *They don't even know why I left.*

Baudwin thought then that perhaps his friends deserved not knowing where he was, for surely they weren't always honest with him either. Looking at Moonrise he declared, "No one's *always* honest, you know. . ."

Moonrise looked sharply at Baudwin, and then cooed irritably, as if to say, "Stop fooling yourself."

Baudwin knew his pet was right. How lucky he was that the heart of a dove was guiding him. His friends weren't dishonest with him — ever — or if they were, not for very long and for good reason. In the end, Criofan had explained why he'd kept his driving a secret; he hadn't wanted Baudwin to think he had placed his interest in driving above the ways of the Water Guild. When pressed, he had answered Baudwin honestly. Yet, Baudwin had decided not to tell either him or Matha why he voted *yes* for Magniglow, or how he had been visited by the water spirit.

Baudwin wondered why he hadn't been more forthright. Criofan and Matha were, after all, his two best friends, but he didn't have the time to think about them right now. He was on a mission to get a job, and nothing else mattered. Ignoring his dirty, wrinkled clothes, he bent down to brush off his boots. He then stood up, adjusted his belt, and continued on his way.

Reaching the heart of the Engineerium, he saw the twelve-sided roof of the pavilion. In there was the Center — not far away. He didn't want to talk to Glas on an empty stomach, so he stopped at a nearby food tent. He was ready to trade one of his topaz crystals for a vegetable pie and sweet-vine, expecting several small blue quartz crystals back in return. Happily, he then remembered the food was free.

Eating as he walked, he offered Moonrise small bits of the pie crust. Hungrily, his pet devoured them. Before he reached the Center, he passed the New Arcade. Again, he was reminded of someone he wanted to forget. Across the way he saw the Gear Chute booth, the game his friend Rian operated. He knew he couldn't possibly begin to explain to him what had happened to the glamorium egg. The thought almost made him laugh. Once again, he had gone only a few paces before he was reminded of his shortcomings. He paused, shaking his head.

"What would I even say?" he asked aloud. Moonrise nodded but offered no advice.

Baudwin knew that fate would grant him another chance to speak with Rian, but not now. "In the end, I'm going to make *everything* all right," he vowed, his mood brightening. Moonrise looked askance at him, but Baudwin didn't even notice.

Soon, he reached the entrance to the Center of the Engineerium. He went through the door, then paused, looking about the room. The same crescent-shaped booths conformed to the walls — Sprocketworks, Alchemvoke, Steamway, and Magniglow — all filled with elven gizmos, gadgets, and contraptions. Quickly, his gaze went to the middle of the room. There stood the Tree of Innovation just as before — a trunk of bronze, copper branches, and glamorium leaves shimmering in the Light. The Center looked exactly like the one in Deuona, but the Faeries here were different.

Instead of the usual guild colors from Deuona, they wore emblems of every quarter — the salmon of the Nechtain — the Moon of the Danu — the Banshee of the Cyhiraeth — and the hot springs of the Condatis. Every water Faery wore greens and blues, but every piece of clothing had a symbol stitched to a pocket, sleeve, or skirt. These divisions did not exist in the other water faery lands, for most had only one river, and none had four in such close proximity.

Baudwin could see that some of them were Guilders such as himself, and others were Eddies, but missing were the Roilers. Certainly, there had to be some in the city, but perhaps they didn't look the same. He wasn't sure, but he remained vigilant, in case he ran into any.

Most of the water Faeries seemed to keep to their own kind, but here and there he could see that different groups did mingle, for they were, after all, water Faeries first, and loyal to their quarters second. Having the longest history, Baudwin knew that the Guilders hailed from all the quarters, but he wasn't sure what quarters the Eddies and Roilers had allegiance to.

He looked again at the Tree of Innovation. Many unhappy memories of Glamorium still lingered in his heart. Touching the leaves on the tree had only gotten him into trouble, and even worse, nothing he had hoped for had come to pass. Later at Curios & Marvels, he had tried to touch the tablet, which had gotten him and his friends chased out. Both times the Elves had admonished him for his actions. Nervously, he looked about, expecting to see Ferrell, but there was no sign of him. Again, he thought of his friend Rian at the Gear Chute booth and the glamorium egg Rian had given him. Holding the egg to his heart, he had seen the *Dúrúnghlas*. Such a rare experience — and what a joy! He had thought that Glamorium had truly blessed him, yet the vision had ended so terribly.

As Baudwin remembered what had happened next, his mood darkened. There he had been, simply going about his chores at the dam. And then *she* had come — overwhelming him with her powers and finally betraying him — stealing his glamorium egg and ruining his plans to find his mother. She was the reason he had failed and the reason he was here now, trying to find a job, so he could begin anew. Even the Elves had cost him dearly, fighting one another, wounding him, and then stealing his pack. There was nothing left for him to do but to go and see Glas.

Once at the magniglow booth, he spotted the Elve. Glas was busy twisting some copper wire into a cable. Steadily he worked, fixed on his task, his gaze unmoving, not noticing Baudwin.

Baudwin waited for him to be finished. Glas wound the cable around a spool, set it in a box, and then looked up. "Hello," he said. "What may I do for you? Have you come to preview Magniglow?"

Baudwin hesitated. To his dismay, Glas did not recognize him. He had been so certain that he would.

"I've actually seen this before," Baudwin began. "We've met. I ran your dynamo in Deuona, and you offered me a job."

Glas studied Baudwin, his gray brows furrowing.

"Faster — brighter, faster — brighter!" Baudwin exclaimed, hoping to jog Glas's memory. "That's how you told me to crank."

Glas's eyes lit up. "Oh yes, of course!" he exclaimed. "I remember you now. The one with the quick hands."

"Yes," Baudwin replied, bowing and smiling. "And I'm ever so eager to be of help! I came all the way from Deuona. I made a stupid mistake by not accepting your offer right then and there."

Glas suddenly seemed quite uncomfortable. His eyes shifted nervously from side to side. He looked down at the spool in the box, and then back up.

"Well, you see," he began. "The thing is. . ."

Baudwin knew the news was bad.

"I've already found an assistant."

Baudwin was crestfallen. Moonrise cooed sadly.

"I see," Baudwin said, trying to hide his disappointment. "Could you use another one, by any chance?"

Glas shook his head. "I only keep one assistant on at a time. If only you had been here a few days ago. I'm sorry you came all this way for nothing."

Baudwin didn't want to make things any worse. "That's quite all right," he said. "I only had to travel for a couple of days."

Glas looked as if he felt sorry for Baudwin. "Here," he said. "Since you came all this way, take this." He went to a box and took out a small coil of copper wire. "As a memento," he added, handing the coil to Baudwin.

Baudwin thanked him, and then left. He wandered past the steamway booth and back to the Tree of Innovation, and then sat down on a wooden bench near the tree, staring listlessly into the crowd. Moonrise perched idly on the arm of the bench.

Baudwin then remembered an old elven saying that Rian had taught him: *If you plan and do not think, what you plan will surely stink.*

Rian had often said this to Baudwin when he was helping out in the general store — especially when he was too lazy to move the chairs around before he swept the floor, and then had to sweep it all over again, after finally moving them.

Now what have I done? Baudwin asked himself. Riding in the wagon with Earnan, he had only briefly considered that he might not get the job. He was so excited about the future that he hadn't even thought about what would happen should he fail. And now here he was, stuck at the Engineerium, with hardly anything left and no job at all. For sure, he would have to get used to sleeping under bridges. Either that, or he would have to go back home. Kelven and Seamus would be very angry with him, but they would count this as just another one of his foolish adventures, and all would probably be forgotten within a week.

Looking at the tree, he reached for a glamorium leaf, not expecting anything to happen. The leaves were not as lustrous as his egg had been. *If only I still had that egg,* he thought. *Everything would be different.* Never in his Life had he felt so despondent.

"Nothing helps me, Moonrise," he said to his pet. "Not the Water, not Glamorium — not even the Elves."

Not knowing what to do next, he slowly lost track of time. The Sun dropped over the horizon, and the bustling of the Fae around him turned into a dreary hum. He no longer cared about what might happen next. Sitting where he was seemed just as good as going anywhere.

Listlessly he sat, and then he heard some commotion — shrill voices engaged in loud arguing. Disinterested in looking for the source, he continued to stare blankly ahead. The shouting grew louder, and he felt Moonrise turn on his shoulder. Finally, he looked to see where the noise was coming from.

"It's no good I tell you!" a faery gent yelled. "No good!"

The voice sounded familiar. Baudwin stood up, took a few steps, and peered into the crowd.

"Those branches don't belong in Four Falls!" the voice shouted. "Take them back to the elven lands!"

Baudwin recognized the gent. It was Lugh, the water Faery who had argued with Gavin the Druid in front of the Tree of Innovation in Deuona, and also tried to destroy the Sprouting Patch at the Garden of Sprockets. The same water Faery who had come to the important meeting at his house. Baudwin chuckled when he saw him. Again, he was wearing his lily hat.

Curiously, Baudwin walked toward Lugh to hear what was going on. Once again, he saw Gavin the Druid there. No doubt, Lugh was again interrupting his talk about the Four Branches of Progress.

"That's enough out of you," Gavin snapped. "I'm tired of you obstreperous Guilders spoiling this event. I put up with you in Deuona — but not here!"

"We don't want your inventions," Lugh countered.

"Oh, I beg to differ," Gavin shot back. "Magniglow is coming to Deuona, and is coming here as well!"

Baudwin then saw another faery gent speak. Immediately, he recognized him — Ayamonn from River Danu, the water Faery he had seen at the riot.

Trying to defuse the situation, Ayamonn spoke up. "Lugh, you have a right to protest, but this is neither the time nor the place."

"But we *must* protest!" Lugh shouted. "The Elves are deceiving us!"

"Lies!" Gavin shouted back. "We have been nothing but honest!"

Ayamonn strode over to Lugh and Gavin, and stood between them. He raised his arms, pressing his large palms into their chests. "Lugh," he commanded, "as a fellow Guild Leader, I must ask you to stop. We don't want another riot." Ayamonn looked Lugh in the eye, and for a moment, the two regarded each other with respect. Baudwin could tell they knew each other very well.

"Fine!" Lugh said. "But I must say, the quarters and the rills will speak of this again!"

With that, Lugh began to leave and Baudwin intervened.

"Lugh!" Baudwin shouted. "Lugh!"

Ignoring him, Lugh stomped away from the Tree of Innovation, his lily hat flapping wildly as he moved. Obviously, he mistook Baudwin for a heckler.

Without looking, he waved back in disgust. Aching to speak to a familiar voice, Baudwin ran to catch up with him.

"Lugh — stop!" Baudwin shouted again. "It's me — Baudwin!"

Lugh turned around, surprised. Recognizing Baudwin, he smiled.

"Baudwin!" he exclaimed as the two approached each other. "How good to see another Guilder amongst these traitors and invaders." He walked up to Baudwin and gave him a big hug, not noticing Moonrise perched on his shoulder. Instantly, Moonrise jumped up onto Baudwin's head to avoid being hit.

"Sorry, my feathered faery friend," Lugh said, laughing, as he lightly touched the dove on his wing. "I didn't see you there."

"That's quite all right, Lugh," Baudwin said. "You're not fast enough to hurt him."

"Lucky for him, and for me," Lugh said amiably. He then looked away from Baudwin and scowled at the tree. "Do tell me, Baudwin," he began, "why are you here? Shouldn't you be in Deuona?"

Baudwin hesitated, not wanting to mention that he had tried to work for Glas, for he knew Lugh would not approve. "I just came to visit," he replied. "I've never been to Four Falls before."

Lugh looked at him in disbelief. "Never?" he asked. "In two hundred years you've *never* been to your capital city? Kelven should be ashamed of himself! A young promising Guilder such as yourself, the Son of the Primary of Water? You should have come here a hundred years ago."

Baudwin considered this, and realized he agreed. Kelven's reluctance to experience new and different things was indeed unfortunate. "You're right," he said, nodding at Lugh. "But in my father's defense, I must say that we Deuona Faeries do tend to stay pretty much in one place. The springs are so soothing, and the land is so lush. I'm wondering if he's ever been here."

"He must have been," Lugh said. "Probably before the Great Befalling, but that was long ago. And Seamus must have come as well."

Baudwin looked down, trying to hide his unhappiness at the mention of his grandfather's name.

"Where are you staying?" Lugh asked, eyeing Baudwin up and down. "Who are you with? Have you seen the guild houses? Of course, each quarter has their own."

Again, Baudwin wasn't sure what to say. First, there was the matter of working for Glas, and now the riot. "Well," he began, "I'm alone. . . You see. . . The thing is. . . I was robbed."

"Robbed?" Lugh asked. "Where?"

"There was a riot at the Four Rivers Faire, and some Elves stole my pack."

"I heard about that riot," Lugh said fiercely. "Those Elves! Such thieves!"

"Those metal-headed gear scrapers," Baudwin added, clenching his fist. "I hope Annwyn calls for them soon."

Close by, Ayamonn, who had been eavesdropping, exclaimed, "I remember you! You were the one who set them all off!"

Baudwin froze. He hoped that Ayamonn didn't mean him, but when he turned to look, sure enough — Ayamonn was staring right at him. Nervously, he shifted his stance. Already, he had been in Four Falls for just one day, and two Guild Leaders had him in their sights. Before long, word would get back to Deuona to his father and grandfather, which was the last thing he needed. Regardless, he had to defend himself.

"I did not!" he exclaimed. "They set themselves off with their ridiculous debate! I was just trying to help. Instead, I got caught between their currents."

"You told them they needed space to understand time, which was bad enough," Ayamonn continued. "But then, you added insult to injury by saying they were as lost as you were."

"What's so wrong with that?" Baudwin asked.

"Because, you *never* speak to an Elve that way."

Ayamonn paused to look at Gavin, the Elve Lugh had just been arguing with. He then lowered his voice. "Because an Elve must *always* think he knows better than a Faery, even when the Faery knows that *he* knows better." Ayamonn winked and then leaned closer to them. "I should know," he whispered, chuckling, "because in my long Life I've dealt with *many* liverish Elves."

"Well, I haven't!" Baudwin exclaimed. "And so," he chortled, "I said what seemed right at the *time*." As he spoke, he couldn't help wondering what the Elves would have thought of his little joke.

Lugh laughed, but Ayamonn was not amused.

"You better be careful in Four Falls, young Guilder. This isn't Deuona. Already you've gotten yourself into a heap of trouble."

"I did nothing wrong!" Baudwin practically shouted.

"Lugh could see that Baudwin was overwhelmed, so he said, "Ayamonn is just trying to set you straight for your own good. I'm sure that you meant well, but in Four Falls tensions are running high."

"Yes," Ayamonn agreed. "There's more to worry about here than just Roilers."

"There are Roilers here?" Baudwin asked.

"Of course," Lugh replied. "They're everywhere the Elves go now. They ruin everything, but we'll stop them and the Elves too," he added, looking about the pavilion, and then again at Baudwin. "So, you have nowhere to go?" he asked. "Where will you stay?"

Baudwin shook his head. "I had planned to barter for a place to stay, but I have little left. I was considering what to do when I heard you shouting at Gavin."

"I've heard enough," Lugh said, as he put his hand on Baudwin's shoulder. "You're staying with me."

"I don't want to be any trouble," Baudwin said.

"That's enough, young gent!" Lugh exclaimed. "The son of the Primary of Water will not go homeless. Especially here in your own capital. Why, I doubt there would be a single guild house that would turn you away, if you weren't so stubbornly self-reliant. You act almost like an Elve. You must get that from Seamus."

Ayamonn then spoke. "So you're the son of Kelven, the Primary of Water of Deuona? I know everything about you except your name. Who are you?" He then let out a hearty laugh, which reminded Baudwin of his grandfather. Tall and forceful, Ayamonn certainly seemed more like Seamus than Baudwin, even if Lugh thought Baudwin was stubbornly self-reliant like Seamus.

So much for staying low to the hill, Baudwin thought, sighing. "I am Baudwin, of Deuona, son of Kelven," he replied.

"The son of the Primary!" Ayamonn exclaimed. "No wonder you took such liberties with the Elves and got yourself into such a nasty mess!" Forcefully, he slapped Baudwin on the back. "Well, Baudwin, son of Kelven, I am Ayamonn, of Four Falls, son of Tassach,[1] leader of the Danu Quarter. Go now with your friend, and I will see you both another time." Turning to Lugh he said, "Be sure to bring him to the Moonstone Rushes to visit me when you come to the Danu Quarter." Lugh nodded.

⚘

The matter was settled. Baudwin followed Lugh to the Nechtain Quarter. As they made their way, the Sun was setting, and the golden hour had arrived. Red and orange rays of sunlight painted the city, covering its domes and arches. Most of the Fae were heading home now, traipsing down the sidewalks, flowing in lines like currents in a river. In the distance, Baudwin could see the Tadlachs, much closer than they were in Deuona. He could even make out the opening where the river Condatis flowed from *Tír Luí Lucharachán*.

They reached Lugh's dome home, modest in size yet quite similar to Baudwin's. The walls were made of straw bales, set upon a circular foundation of river stones and plastered with river mud. Blue and green tiles and silver salmons bordered the doors and windows. Vines covered many parts of the dome home, especially in places where sunlight hit the walls.

Baudwin and Lugh went through the front gate and up a stone path. Before them was an atrium leading to the front door. Lugh opened the door. Seeing the inside of the atrium, Baudwin could see where Lugh's lily hats came from.

---

[1] Pronounced [TASS-ock]

There were scores of them, in every possible shade of blue and green, growing in a well-kept garden, with dangling leaves hanging in tiers. On the ground were pools, with pond lilies growing on the surface of the Water.

"Meet my milliner," Lugh chortled, as he pointed to the array of six-pointed blooms. He picked a turquoise-colored lily out of a pool, flicking the Water from its petals. He then placed the flower on Baudwin's head.

"You, sir, have arrived," Lugh announced, laughing.

As he spoke, some water droplets fell onto Moonrise. The dove launched from Baudwin's shoulders, perching on a nearby plant. Quickly, he began preening himself.

"What is your twilight dove's name?" Lugh asked.

"Moonrise," Baudwin replied.

"Moonrise," Lugh said, "the Water won't harm you. The pools here are pure."

Moonrise stopped preening himself. He looked at Lugh and cooed.

"You're welcome to stay in the atrium, Moonrise," Lugh said, smiling. "You'll be safe and warm. There's even a small window, if you want to go flying," he added, as he motioned to a round stained-glass pane. "I'll leave it open for you."

The window reminded Baudwin of the one in his room with the blue irises and green leaves. *What am I doing here*, he wondered, *when I could be in my own room in my own house*? Except, there was no longer a house he could call his home. He was but a wayfarer now. *I had better get used to it,* he thought.

Moonrise cooed again, and Baudwin forgot his troubles. He adjusted his lily hat and followed Lugh.

They entered the house through the greeting room, went around the hall and then into what seemed like a sitting room. Baudwin was struck by the curious yet tidy arrangement of things. In addition to sofas, tables, and other colorful furnishings, there were wooden chests everywhere. Some were big, and others were small. Some were ornately painted, while others were plain, but all of them had hinges, corners, and hasps made of copper or bronze. The Elves had to have made them. They were sturdy, attractive, and designed to hold just about any kind of useful object or treasure.

Among them were blue chests, green chests, engraved chests, and locked chests — *many* locked chests. Baudwin wondered why Lugh needed so many. What was *so* important that he needed to hide away, and in so many different places? Surveying the room, he had to ask the obvious question.

"Whatever are all these chests for?"

"An unusual habit of mine," Lugh replied, as if he never tired of answering the question. "Everything must be sorted and secure." Seeing the puzzled look on Baudwin's face, he added, "It's also a hobby. I have a chest from every corner of the realm." Pointing at one, he said, "Here, look at this one."

Lugh led Baudwin to an oak table. There sat the most beautiful chest Baudwin had ever seen. The top had a border, its edges set with red, orange, yellow, green, blue, indigo, and violet gems. The chest itself was carved out of cherry Wood, and polished to perfection.

"This certainly is beautiful," Baudwin remarked, his eyes lighting up. "These gems remind me of a rainbow flute that I saw at the Engineerium in Curios & Marvels."

Lugh nodded at Baudwin. "Yes, I know the one you mean. Very possibly, both were made by the same crafters in Gleam."

Baudwin had heard of Gleam, but knew very little about the city. Criofan's family knew a lot more, for they traded there for the best gems in *Tír na nÓg*.

"Why do the gems make a rainbow?" he asked.

"Many old artifacts from Gleam have rainbow patterns," Lugh replied. "They say the Elves used to have a fascination with rainbows."

This struck Baudwin as odd. Few Elves except Rian seemed to care at all for such things, especially rainbows. In fact, even if Rian did admire them, Baudwin had never heard him mention them before.

"I've never met an Elve who liked them," Baudwin said.

"That doesn't mean they don't," Lugh said. "According to some, rainbows used to bring the Faeries and Elves together, and take them across a bridge to another realm."

Another realm? Baudwin thought, startled. He then remembered the water spirit's question: "Are you *really* the one who would wield the talisman — cross the bridge — and leave this realm behind?" He wondered if Lugh and the spirit were talking about the same thing. If they were, would he ever find such a bridge? No, he wouldn't — for he had left that path behind.

Baudwin stared at the chest and thought of his own treasures at home. He missed his sapphire glowstone owls — Brim and Bram.

"The chest is very beautiful," he said, wondering when he would see his owls again. "I must travel to Gleam someday. There must be treasures like this everywhere."

"Oh, there are," Lugh said. "There's also a throne in Gleam, which has been there since Sitric ruled the Elves thousands of years ago. They say it outshines any other kind of opulence. When you gaze upon it, you lose your senses. Perhaps when the Elves see it, they have their own kind of wakings."

Hearing this, Baudwin let out a laugh. Lugh laughed as well. Baudwin couldn't imagine what a throne like that would look like. He wondered why the Elves would build one, for they certainly wouldn't do that now. Not even Ferrell would want to sit on such an ostentatious-looking object. *Or would he?* Baudwin wondered. For he knew there was a lot about Ferrell that he kept hidden.

Lugh showed him more of his home.

They entered his sleeping room — cozy, clean, and well-appointed. Here Baudwin saw the fate of Lugh's discarded lily hats. On one side of the bed was a long table. Rows of withered lilies were stacked on one side. On the other was a wooden flower press made of oak, with a long bolt and a wingnut at each corner. Next to the lilies and the press was a large book, filled with parchment pages.

"So this is where all your lilies pass to Annwyn," Baudwin said, joking.

"Not if I can help it," Lugh said.

"What do you mean?" Baudwin asked, stifling a laugh. He knew how easily Lugh might interpret a joke as an insult.

"Come see for yourself," Lugh said proudly.

Lugh opened the book. Baudwin watched over his shoulder as he began turning the pages. In the center of each page was a dried lily. Underneath each lily was a poem.

Lugh turned the pages until he came to one particular lily, still very green despite being withered and dry. "This is my favorite one," he said. He then began to read:

In Life you perish

Yet you always bring me joy

In Death I cherish

What my loss cannot destroy

Lugh looked up from the poem. Baudwin could see traces of tears in his eyes.

"Such devotion," Baudwin said. "I didn't know you were a poet, Lugh."

"Nor did I," Lugh said, "until I began losing my lilies. I had to dedicate myself to them in some way, or the pain would have been too much to bear."

"I understand," Baudwin said. "What flower other than the lily reminds us so of the Water?" He then removed his lily hat and placed it on the table. "You must keep this," he said. Lugh solemnly bowed his head.

The two water Faeries stood quietly for a moment. Baudwin looked about the room and saw more locked chests, but fewer in number.

"Do you live alone, Lugh?" Baudwin asked.

"Yes, I'm not attached to anyone — at least for now. When I joined my current and found my intention, I knew that would be my fate in Life, but I have no regrets. For some, such things are the way they must be. Living alone has made my fight for the Water easier to pursue. Faery ladies are wonderful, but my current is wild, and cannot be tamed."

"I never joined with my current," Baudwin said, surprised at his own candor.

"I learned of your misfortune at the meeting," Lugh said, as he put his hand on Baudwin's shoulder. "Your actions have always been irregular, which is why you must have voted for Matter Three. At least that is what I, and others I have spoken with about you, believe."

Startled, Baudwin looked at Lugh. Although Lugh had been adamantly against Matter Three, he did not seem to judge Baudwin for voting *yes* on it.

"Aren't you angry with me?" Baudwin asked.

"Not at all," Lugh replied. "You're a pure spirit, Baudwin. You did what you thought was best, not what others thought was best. You will always come back to the Water. You're a Guilder — through and through."

Baudwin wasn't sure this was so. He had tried this very day to work for the Elves, wanting to learn what they know — binding copper wires to make Magniglow. But, Lugh seemed so earnest when he spoke that Baudwin did not want to challenge him.

"Tell me, Baudwin," Lugh asked, "are you hungry? I make the best noodle squash and vegetables in the Nechtain Quarter."

"That sounds very good," Baudwin replied, for he hadn't had a good home-cooked meal since he left Deuona.

"Good," Lugh said. "I will prepare dinner. Why don't you go to my shrine and look at my dome crest? The glass is quite beautiful."

Baudwin went from the sleeping room to the center of the house, where he found the shrine. It was a circular pool of Water with blue and green lilies growing from the bottom, and orange and blue carp swimming among polished river rocks and pieces of tourmaline and topaz. In the center sat a large blue glowstone carved in the shape of a salmon. Vases of flowers were placed around the shrine, along with shells and gold bells, and other kinds of offerings. Water dripped from stone to stone, soothing his heart as he listened. For he hadn't been near a shrine in what seemed to be a long time.

Looking up, he saw the dome crest. Just like the one in his home, this one had a Moon in the very center, surrounded by an eternity knot. Around the knot was a beveled glass ring. Set into the ring were water glyphs and family symbols. Along with them were salmon and walnuts, finely crafted, all representing River Nechtain. Baudwin admired the way they sparkled as the Light shined through them.

Soon, Lugh called him for dinner. The table in the dining room was set for two. A loaf of bread and a butter dish sat between them, along with a bowl of noodle squash and vegetables. As soon as Baudwin sat down, they both filled their plates and begin eating.

"How do you like Four Falls?" Lugh asked.

"I've never seen such a place," Baudwin replied. "It's wonderful, to be sure, but also, overwhelming. There's so much of everything, and so little of what I'm used to. I didn't know the quarters were so different. It's nothing like Deuona. Everything there is the same."

Having said all of that, Baudwin could think of nothing further to add. The noodle squash was so well seasoned that he decided to stop talking and just keep eating.

"You're right," Lugh said. "Four Falls is nothing like Deuona. The four rivers come from very different places, and they influence the Faeries in many different ways. Here, the Faeries are divided not just among Guilders, Eddies, and Roilers, but each of those groups also claims a river as its own. They tend to stay in their own quarters, with their own customs. As you can see, I am of the River Nechtain. The wisdom of the salmon is what I hail. Like the salmon, we water Faeries swim on reverse currents, beneath the surface of the Water. In this way, we learn not to battle the currents of Life. No matter where we are, we are always on our way home."

"I saw the salmon in your dome crest," Baudwin said. "They're beautiful. Their scales glisten like jewels."

"Thank you," Lugh said, smiling.

"But what of the other quarters?" Baudwin asked.

"Each quarter of the city learns a lesson from its own river, and imparts this lesson to all members of the water faery tribe. In the Danu Quarter, they follow the Moon, as do all Faeries, but theirs is a special affinity. They feel the pull of the Moon more keenly than the rest of us, and know what they feel more than you or I. This makes them lucky, but also quite changeable, as their feelings wax and wane like the phases of the Moon. Next, there are the Faeries in the Cyhiraeth Quarter, gloomy and mysterious, but also more alive than we in some strange way. For they know of the banshee, and the stark lessons she sings of, when Annwyn calls."

"I saw some young ones this morning in the Cyhiraeth Quarter, singing about the banshee," Baudwin said. "They wailed and danced like old ones, washing clothes and pouring Water for each other."

"Yes, they seem like old ones, and their parents behave as if they have partly left for Annwyn. They're a strange lot, but if they let you get close to them, they will share their secrets with you. For they understand the path a Faery must walk in order to prepare for Annwyn. If you are not prepared, you will not understand the truth that Annwyn reveals."

Considering this, Baudwin sat quietly. He realized he had a great deal more to learn, not only about Four Falls, but also his own kin.

"And finally," Lugh continued, "you have the Condatis Quarter. These Faeries understand healing, for their river is sourced from an ancient network of hot springs, where a long soak is said to cure any ailment. Oddly, the source of this healing comes from the land of the Elves, which many Faeries find perplexing. Why would such a wonderful thing come from another land? What lesson is being taught? I believe the Condatis Faeries are here to teach us to understand the Elves as well as we understand ourselves. For this reason, they're the only Faeries in *Tír na nÓg* whose purpose has yet to be fully revealed. Their destiny flows from *Tír Luí Lucharachán*, between the only opening in the Tadlachs — the Col of Lonrúil."

"Are there other kinds of water Faeries here?" Baudwin asked.

"Yes, there are sea Faeries, who sail from the port below the falls. They're an independent lot, always going their own way. They are said to have originally dwelt on the Island of Baranthus in the Inland Sea, which is not too far from here by boat."

Baudwin was curious to hear more about the sea Faeries, as the ocean was beyond his imagination. Unlike a river, there was no beginning and no end. The sea Faeries had to be bold and skilled, like his grandfather. How else could they navigate such a vast body of Water?

They continued their meal. Baudwin took a second helping, and another slice of bread. As they finished, he could tell that Lugh was about to say something serious.

"I fear you've come to Four Falls on the eve of great trouble," Lugh revealed. "Not since the Great Befalling have the tensions been this high. The Elves are insufferable. They would turn this place into the Clock City, if we let them. Which brings me to the matter at hand. What exactly happened at that riot? I don't believe that Ayamonn was right to blame you for starting it."

Baudwin then told Lugh everything he knew about the riot, including how he had been there when Seanán and Fearghus began arguing about hourglasses and watches. A simple debate about the Eternal Movement and the Rise of Time had turned into a heated argument and then a fight. Clocks were thrown, tents torn down, and Elves were beaten. Both sides unleashed destruction upon the other, until even the Faeries joined in, and everything got worse and worse.

Having finished his story, Baudwin sat quietly.

"So that's what started it," Lugh said, sobered by the news. "You were the spark that ignited the Fire. Ayamonn has a good heart. I'm sure he only wanted you to be more wary."

"Well, he sounded as if he believed I was the Fire — *not* the spark."

Lugh paused, marshaling his thoughts.

"Baudwin," he said firmly, "when you take your father's place someday, you'll have to fight for the Water. The Elves seem reasonable and even-handed, but they're not. Nothing is ever enough for them. Magniglow will ruin us."

As Lugh spoke, Baudwin became quiet, for there would be no taking his father's place. He had abandoned his home, and Lugh was none the wiser.

"What's wrong, Baudwin?" Lugh asked. "You seem troubled."

"Nothing," Baudwin replied, putting his thoughts of home aside. "Tell me, why are you so afraid of something that will only make our lives easier?"

Lugh looked at Baudwin, considering him closely. "I think it's time you learned the truth," he began. "Everyone has some objection to Maniglow. They say glowstones have always been enough for them. Or they say Magniglow will complicate our lives, or distance us from the old ways. These reasons are all relevant, but they are not the primary concern."

"And what might that be?" Baudwin asked with great curiosity, for he could not imagine the answer.

Lugh clasped his hands, and took a deep breath.

"The Elves mean to *control* our intentions!" he exclaimed, his eyes flashing.

"Whatever do you mean?" Baudwin asked.

Lugh paused, looking for his words. As he did, he removed his lily hat, placing it carefully upon the table so as not to crush the petals.

"Baudwin, have you ever heard the tale of *The Ladybug and the Wiley Wasp*?"

"I'm not sure I have," Baudwin replied moodily, sounding bored.

"Then I must tell you," Lugh said, "to show you what I mean." He paused, gathering his thoughts, and then began:

"Once there was a ladybug, who lived beneath a long, slender leaf of a sweet alyssum plant. She loved to smell the lively fragrance of the purple blooms, and to feast contentedly upon the leaves. She also loved fine things, and had a collection of jewelry that she enjoyed wearing. One day, as she rested beneath her leaf, a wasp appeared.

"Spying her spindly black legs and open jaws, the ladybug grew frightened, for wasps were known to sting ladybugs and lay their eggs inside of them. When the wasp came near, she hid even further under the leaf, so she could not reach her."

Lugh looked to see if Baudwin was listening, and then continued.

"The wasp then spoke, her singsong voice, low and pleasant-sounding. 'Why are you hiding beneath that leaf?' she asked.

"To which the ladybug replied, 'Do you think I'm a fool? You've come to sting me.'

"'How rude of you to say that,' the wasp snapped. 'I'm not that kind of wasp. I'm a stingless wasp — a friend to all. I would never hurt you.'

"But the ladybug did not trust her, so she remained where she was, safely hidden beneath her leaf, smelling her flowers and admiring her jewelry.

"'I don't believe you!' she cried out.

"'Then I will simply have to convince you of my good intentions,' said the wasp, as she flew away. Later, she returned with a glittering object in her jaws, which she placed on the ground, right outside her hiding place.

"'Now you must come out,' she said, 'for here is a gift — one I'm sure will delight you.'

"Cautiously, the ladybug peered out from beneath her sweet alyssum leaf. 'I don't see anything,' she said.

"'Then you must come closer,' said the wasp. 'If you do, you will not be disappointed. Something wonderful awaits you.'

"Cautiously, the ladybug looked out from under her leaf. She gasped. The wasp had told the truth, for she could see a golden aphid on a lovely chain. Enthralled, she exclaimed, 'How beautifully it shines in the sunlight!'

"'How beautiful indeed,' the wasp agreed, 'but even more beautiful if it were shining in the sunlight on *you.*'

"Forgetting her fear, the ladybug crawled out from under her leaf, for now she had to have the golden aphid. No sooner had she put it on, than the wasp flew at her, stinging her fiercely. Now she would be her slave, dutifully carrying her egg until a young grub hatched inside of her, and then bore its way out of her abdomen. Possessed, she would remain its slave, as it spun a cocoon beneath her, only to hatch into another wasp — leaving her to die of madness."

"How dreadful," Baudwin said, shaken to the core.

"Yes," Lugh replied, "which only goes to show what happens when we let our selfish desires erode our common sense, especially when we are offered something that seems too good to be true."

"Still, I don't see how this relates to the Elves," Baudwin said.

Lugh nodded, leaning closer to Baudwin. "What you don't understand, my friend, is that the Elves are *just* like that wasp. Magniglow is simply a golden aphid, and we know what happened to that ladybug. The Elves say they are giving us a gift, but they really mean to trick us. Using Maniglow to control our intentions is a very clever way to do this."

Baudwin was taken aback by Lugh's certainty. "But how?" he asked. "Magniglow simply makes light and moves machines."

"Yes," Lugh replied, "but through some guise, their control of this *perfidious* invention will slowly bend us to their wills. Their first step has been occupation and their next will be domination."

"What proof do you have?"

Lugh shook his head. "I don't need any. I just *know.*"

"But how?" Baudwin asked. "Have you felt your intention changing?"

"Why is that important?" Lugh asked.

Baudwin had to suppress a smile. "Why? Because then you have a fact, some proof about what you're saying."

"What I know *is* the proof!" Lugh exclaimed defiantly.

Now, Baudwin did smile.

"Don't laugh at me," Lugh warned.

"I'm not," Baudwin said.

"Yes, you are!"

"No, I'm only laughing at —"

"See — you *are* laughing!"

"At how you confuse your own opinion with *actual* facts," Baudwin said.

"It's rude of you to say that," Lugh said, concealing his anger. "I could just as easily say that perhaps you don't understand what I'm saying because you aren't joined to your current. That your mind won't let you listen to your feelings, like I listen to mine. It's not always a question of facts, as this poem will prove." Lugh then recited:

The mind seeks facts and lances

And only wants to know

The heart feels facts and dances

And only beats to grow

Baudwin looked at Lugh, stunned. Slowly, he chose his words. "Perhaps," he said, "Your talent for poetry outshines your ability to know the ways of the Elves. . . and as for me not being joined to my current, you sound just like my father. He always says that, which is why I left Deuona. My opinion about Magniglow has nothing to do with not being joined. I truly believe that the Elves are not trying to deceive us, and that only they can help me find my mother — with their knowledge and devices."

Lugh paused for a moment. "Please forgive me," he began. "I spoke unkindly. I know little of your family —"

"She went missing long ago," Baudwin cut in, "after the Great Befalling."

They both grew very quiet, and then Lugh broke the silence.

"If you're trying to find your mother," he said, "only the Water will help you. You must trust me on this."

Baudwin stifled a groan. "I've tried that before."

"Don't give up."

"I never will," Baudwin said. "Although my methods may change."

Lugh shook his head at Baudwin. "Like I said before, you are more Guilder than you know."

"Why do you say that?" Baudwin asked. "Just because of who my father is?"

"No." He looked at Baudwin with calmness and certainty. "You are not like other water Faeries. Something flows differently inside of you."

"Yes, because I was never joined," Baudwin insisted, sarcastically.

"No, that's not it," Lugh said again, as he leaned even closer to Baudwin. "Your Water is purer somehow, more *ethereal*. Perhaps not joining with your current was an act of destiny, so that you would find another path."

Hearing this, Baudwin felt puzzled and piqued. He shook his head. "Yes, my destiny. To go nowhere."

"Not nowhere," Lugh corrected. "You're here, aren't you? You say you never joined your current, and now here you are in the one place in *Tír na nÓg* where the Water flows the strongest. Only the Island of Baranthus has stronger currents."

Baudwin still didn't understand. Lugh's fanciful consideration simply annoyed him. "What are you trying to say?" he asked.

Now, like a canny salmon dodging an eagle's strike, Lugh countered him, quick and wise. "What story are you telling yourself? Why come to Four Falls now? You said your father drove you away, but you could have searched for your mother anywhere."

"I just had to get away," Baudwin replied, shaking his head, for he would have liked to explain more about what had happened. Lugh would have been fascinated hearing about the water spirit, and how the *Dúrúnghlas* had touched him. Yet, none of this would have answered his question. And then Baudwin realized that Lugh was right. He hadn't fully considered why he had come to Four Falls, except perhaps to forget his failure.

He also knew that this answer would never do.

"As I said, I came to get help from the Elves," Baudwin replied.

"I doubt they have any answers, Baudwin," Lugh retorted. "How could they? You saw what they just did at the Faire."

Baudwin shook his head. Of course he had to hope the Elves would help him. What other recourse did he have? Certainly not the Faeries, the Water, or Glamorium. There was no other reason to be here. Why, he wondered, was Lugh making this so hard?

Lugh shook his head as well, almost as if he were giving up.

"They're not *all* like that," Baudwin insisted. "My friend Rian has always been good to me. Glas, who works at the magniglow booth, was quite friendly."

Looking at Lugh, Baudwin realized what he had to say next.

"I know you don't trust them, Lugh, but I will prove that I am right. I will find a way to work for the Elves in order to discover if they truly want to control our intentions. If you're right, then I will forgo believing that they can help me."

"And more importantly, you'll come back to the Water," Lugh nodded, smiling. "What then, is your ploy, young Guilder?"

"Somehow, I will find a way to get Glas to hire me," Baudwin replied. "When I gain his confidence, I will ferret out whatever information I can, for he works with Magniglow every day."

"Well, at least that's a start," Lugh chortled. "Will you be digging underground, or spying from the rooftops?"

Lugh seemed happy that Baudwin was taking him seriously, even if Baudwin's plan seemed rather far-fetched. The rest of the meal was cheery. They talked more about the quarters, and the history of Four Falls. Baudwin told Lugh about how he had searched for the Water for years, never succeeding in his quest. He wasn't sure why, but he didn't want to tell Lugh everything too quickly. They traded stories until the Moon was high, and shone through the dome crest with silver Light.

Once they finished their meal, Lugh led Baudwin to the guest room.

"Tomorrow we can see about getting you that job," he said. "Sleep well."

Lugh left, and Baudwin peered out the window. Outside, he could see the upper tier of the atrium.

He opened the window.

"Moonrise, are you there?" he called out.

The dove flew through the window to him.

"Did you explore any more of the city?"

Moonrise cooed sleepily.

"Done so early?" Baudwin asked. "Well, you *have* been awake much of the day."

The dove nodded his agreement.

"I'm sorry," Baudwin added, stroking his feathers. "Soon, I expect you will be on your own time."

The dove cooed, bobbing his head in delight.

"Come then, let us sleep," Baudwin said, as he headed to his bed. "Tomorrow, I will find out if I've gotten myself into even more trouble."

He took a pitcher from a nightstand and poured Water into the canal that lined the bed. He didn't know where the Water had come from, but assumed that it had to be from the Nechtain. Would he dream of salmon? He hoped that he would at least wake up a little wiser the next day.

He tapped the glowstone on the nightstand, and the room went Dark.

☙❦❧

Baudwin awoke. After sleeping in a proper bed, he was refreshed, and thanked his lucky stars that he hadn't had to sleep under a bridge again. Moonrise was already awake, gazing intently at him, as he often did. As Baudwin got out of bed, he realized that he hadn't even bothered to undress. His pack had been stolen, and he had nothing else to wear.

A chime rang at the door. "Breakfast is ready," Lugh called. "C'mon down — I've come up with a plan for you."

Baudwin was relieved. He still had no plan of his own, and felt that he had lied to Lugh to appease him. Now, at least he wouldn't have to feel guilty.

As Baudwin opened the door, Lugh looked at his rumpled clothing and shook his head.

"You can't go to ask for a job like that!" he exclaimed. "You have to look your best."

"But, I have nothing left to wear," Baudwin said.

"Yes, I know," Lugh said. "Those nasty Elves stole your pack! Well, don't you worry. Not one bit. I have plenty of clothes for you."

Lugh led Baudwin to a closet and pulled open the door.

"Do you think any of these will fit?" Baudwin asked. "I'm taller than you."

Lugh looked at several pairs of breeches. "True," he replied, "but you aren't the first one to stay here. Over the years, many have left things behind."

Lugh rifled through the closet, pushing this and that out of the way, until he found a pair of seafoam green breeches, a jacket with blue and gold embroidery, and a light blue shirt. The formal-looking clothes were nicely tailored and the right size.

"Now change into these, and leave your other clothes on the bed, and I will have them washed."

Baudwin did so, and then headed to the dining room. Before leaving, he took a quick look in the mirror, and was surprised to see how good he looked in the clothes. They seemed like the kind of garments a guild leader would wear to a ceremony.

As they ate breakfast, Lugh's spirits seemed high.

"I went to sleep last night thinking about what we talked about," Lugh said. "You're right — a little subterfuge would be of great benefit to us right now. And then I had a very curious dream," Lugh added, amused. "I'm sure you didn't dream what I did."

Baudwin was very interested. If this was so, then he had better pay close attention, as this dream was likely to be special.

"What did you dream?" Baudwin asked.

"I was on a raft, in the ocean," Lugh began. "There was a great storm. The waves were so high that I was carried up and down, and I feared I would be tossed into the sea."

"Were you too afraid to swim?" Baudwin asked, as he leaned closer to Lugh.

Lugh nodded before he spoke. "In the ocean we can swim very far — yes, we can — but the ocean is not like a river or a lake. A great storm can send even our best swimmers to Annwyn, although we would last longer than any other kind of Faery."

The ocean must truly be a sight — like a boundless lake, Baudwin thought.

"But then on that raft," Lugh continued, "I saw a ship. Not one of ours, but of the Elves. They came and rescued me, and I was carried onto the deck. The captain looked like he was from Clearport, the elven port city. And then he said that I had to crew his ship, or he would throw me back into the ocean."

Baudwin started to giggle.

"Yes, I know!" Lugh exclaimed, as amused as Baudwin. "So I crewed his ship for him, and while I was on deck, my arms turned into two great oars. I plunged them into the ocean, and I was able to row the ship back to land. Then, I escaped."

"Oars for arms?" Baudwin asked. "Whatever does that mean?"

Lugh thought for a moment and then smiled. "I know," he said. "It means that if you are forced to work for them, then you will be able to steer your destiny. Which, I might add, will help us resolve our dispute about what the Elves are really up to."

"But that was *your* dream, not mine," Baudwin said, smiling. He knew he hadn't seen that dream. Yet, the story was very funny, and the dream certainly seemed special.

"Yes," Lugh replied, "but I believe it was meant for *you*, of course. I am but the messenger of the dream." He then recited another poem:

When friends need guidance

They first must see

The Water's meaning

Fate's decree

A channel is chosen

That one is me

Lugh laughed heartily, and Baudwin joined in the merriment. The poem was indeed charming, so he decided not to challenge Lugh about being a messenger. Instead, he spoke more about how he might steer his destiny.

"But how might I be forced to work for them?" he asked. "Do Glas and Ferrell crew boats now?"

"No," Lugh replied. "Not by crewing on a boat — by becoming an indentured servant of theirs."

Now Baudwin went silent. Immediately he thought of Loch, who had been forced to work for Ferrell for smashing into the pie vendor, and losing at the Hop and Hit.

"But that means I will be a slave," he protested. "That could last for years."

"Only if the crime is too great," Lugh said. "We'll make sure it's not. All you need to do is get caught committing some petty crime. The punishment should be light enough to remain in their employ, but certainly not as severe as one that would result from, say, burning down the Clock City," Lugh added, chuckling.

This was not what Baudwin had expected. He had thought Lugh would use the influence of the Guild to find him a job, not tell him to do this. He wasn't sure he liked the idea.

"I don't know, Lugh," Baudwin said. "This all sounds —"

"Don't you worry," Lugh interrupted. "We'll make everything innocent enough. The punishment will be mild, and won't tarnish your reputation. Surely a week or two of service will do it, and then you'll have your foot in the door."

"But what should I do?" Baudwin asked.

"I have something in mind, something so trivial that you will receive the lightest possible punishment for it."

Eagerly, he explained his plan to Baudwin — something about stepping on someone's foot, and getting them so angry that they punched him, and then everyone falling onto valuable displays.

Baudwin didn't think the plan was good enough — and then his memory was stirred by a warning that an Elve had once given him. He knew then what had to do. The plan would be risky, but not too difficult to achieve. He told Lugh, who agreed — Baudwin's plan was much better than his own.

They finished eating and headed off to the Engineerium.

Chapter 25

THE PLOY

As Baudwin headed back to the Engineerium, the back of his head began to throb. Only a day had passed since his bout under the bridge. The bitter touch of the Cyhiraeth had run its course, granting him a reprieve that had been all too fleeting. And now his head ached worse than ever. Just when he needed to be clear and sharp, the Water had left him to shoulder his own burden. This irritated him to no end. *Fine,* he thought, as he touched the tender lump. *I'll just go it alone.*

At face value, the plan seemed needlessly reckless. Why would he go to such lengths before he had even bothered to ask the Elves for help in finding his mother? The worst they could do was to say no. However, the plan had one key advantage. If it worked, it would satisfy both of his goals at once, saving them a lot of time. By getting closer to the Elves, Baudwin would find a way to gain their help, while also determining whether or not their management of Magniglow was safe and sane, so he could put Lugh's fears to rest. The plan had a good chance of success, for he and Lugh had gone over every detail.

They were already through the Nechtain Quarter, walking alongside the canal on their way to the Engineerium. Soon they were in the Danu Quarter. Over bridge after bridge they crossed, first the Lower Danu Road, and then River Danu. As they made their way through the Cyhiraeth Quarter, Baudwin thought about what he should say. He would have to be upbeat, yet persuasive, or Glas would see through his ruse. They reached the Upper Cyhiraeth Road, and came to the bridge, and soon they were over the Cyhiraeth River.

Baudwin looked down, his head still throbbing.

The Water certainly has its whims and ways, he thought. *But why abandon me now?* He knew there was no sense in staying angry, but still he resented the dark river below for bringing on a bout, easing his pain, and now seemingly discarding him to his fate.

Now that they had crossed the bridge, there wasn't much farther to go. High in the sky, a flock of birds passed over them.

Baudwin thought then of Moonrise. He had left him in the atrium to catch up on his sleep. He hadn't wanted to burden his pet with any more trouble, and the atrium was a fine refuge. Who knew how much longer before they found another? This at least gave him some comfort.

The Engineerium was now within sight. Soon they reached the ring, and then they were passing through the tunnel along the stone path. Baudwin was pensive, and Lugh said nothing, his lily hat bouncing under the Light of the flower sconces. What had been a welcome return for Baudwin yesterday, was now an unsure beginning, yet Lugh seemed composed. Perhaps years of rebellious encounters with the Elves had prepared him for whatever they might do. Baudwin tried to act the same, but inside, he was struggling to find his courage. Nervously, he twisted his watch. Lugh glanced at him.

"You mustn't worry," Lugh said. "The worst that can happen won't be that bad, and the best that can happen is bad enough," he joked.

"You're a lot of consolation," Baudwin replied, chuckling. "But perhaps you're right."

"We have to see it that way," Lugh said. "Otherwise, our fears will corner us."

Once they got through the tunnel, the trip through the East Petal went quickly. Soon, they were back in the Center, full of bustling Faeries talking and shopping, and busy Elves attending to the booths and attractions.

The magniglow booth was just a few paces away. Baudwin could see Glas sitting behind the counter, busily examining some elven magniglow plans. He and Lugh approached him.

"Hello, Glas," Baudwin said.

Glas looked up at him, surprised.

"Well, hello there," Baudwin," he said. "What brings you here again?"

Baudwin was relieved to see that Glas recognized him this time.

"What can I do for you?" Glas asked.

"This is my friend, Lugh," Baudwin replied. "We've come to see your magniglow inventions."

"I know you," Glas said, as he studied Lugh, frowning. "You're the one who's always upsetting Gavin. Don't think I haven't heard about your constant troublemaking!"

Baudwin took a deep breath and tried not to panic. From the corner of his eye, he could see Lugh, fidgeting nervously.

Of course, Baudwin thought. *How stupid could I be?* Lugh was indeed a troublemaker, and Baudwin hadn't considered the possibility that Glas might already know him. He had to think fast.

"I had to bring him here," he began, smiling brightly, "to prove to him that the Elves are not a threat to the Faeries. I'm actually trying to get him to *stop* making trouble."

"Is that why you're dressed like such a dandy?"

Baudwin looked down at the clothes Lugh had loaned him. "These aren't the clothes of a dandy, but an ordinary Guilder."

"They don't look ordinary to me," Glas said.

"That's because you haven't seen my *other* clothes," Baudwin joked.

Baudwin nudged Lugh in the ribs. Lugh then bowed to Glas, a deep formal bow that Faeries often give when they're trying to make amends.

"I've come to offer my sincere apologies," Lugh said. "My friend Baudwin has told me that I've misjudged Magniglow. He made me promise to see for myself that it can do no harm."

Glas didn't seem convinced. Frowning, he tapped his fingers on his work table.

"Want to see for yourself, do you?" he asked. "Fine. Then allow me. I'll crank the bulbs for you."

Baudwin saw his chance. "Wait!" he exclaimed. "Do you think I could? I greatly enjoyed cranking them before."

Glas nodded, dropping his irritation. "All right then. I suppose it's the least I can do since I wasn't able to hire you." Glas pointed at some flower lamps on a nearby shelf. "Which one do you want to try?" he asked. "How about one of these daffodils?"

Baudwin pointed to a higher shelf. "Actually," he replied, "I was thinking about one of *those*." There sat a lamp, with twenty finely crafted stems, resting on a bed of leaves, all made of bronze. Attached to each of the stems was a lily shade of blue and green stained glass, with a clear glass bulb inside.

Glas looked at the lamp, smiling. "Now aren't you the confident one! Sure, but cranking those to their peak brightness will require some real elbow grease. I'll tell you what, though. I have a new dynamo, with some very powerful coils inside. I'll hook it up for you."

With that, Glas went to the back of the booth, and began rummaging through his stock. Baudwin grinned, barely able to contain himself. Glas came back to the counter and plugged the dynamo into the lamp. Up close, Baudwin could see how finely the shades were made. They seemed real, bending gracefully from their stems to face the counter. But the bulbs were what interested him the most.

"Where were the bulbs made?" he asked.

"In the Clock City, of course," Glas replied. "I made the cable, but the dynamo is also from there. The shades were made in Gleam, by some excellent stained-glass artists."

"They're very finely made," Baudwin said, as he reached for the crank. He hoped his plan would work, for otherwise he wasn't sure what he would do. He began turning, but the bulbs barely let out a glow. This was going to be harder than he thought.

"You see?" Glas said. "I told you it wouldn't be easy. You have to go faster."

Baudwin turned the crank more, and noticed that this dynamo was indeed powerful, for all twenty bulbs were beginning to light.

"Faster!" Glas exclaimed. "Brighter!"

Baudwin cranked harder and harder, until the bulbs got brighter.

"You see?" Glas said, turning to Lugh. "No harm done. Your lily hat hasn't wilted either," he chortled. Baudwin kept cranking.

"Now go faster!" Glas exclaimed, jumping from foot to foot. "You're almost there!"

Baudwin and Lugh exchanged glances, smiling coyly at each other. Baudwin then cranked really hard, harder than he ever had before. The bulbs shone brilliantly with gleaming white light.

"Okay — that's enough!" Glas shouted. "Time to wind 'er down!"

Baudwin ignored him, cranking harder and harder.

"I said — that's good enough!" Glas shouted again.

Still Baudwin cranked, until he felt his arm would fall off.

"Stop, or you'll blow the bulbs!" Glas shrieked. "I told you this before in Deuona! Don't you remember?"

As a matter of fact, Baudwin *did* remember. "No way!" he exclaimed. "I trust the inventiveness of the Elves. Besides, I want Lugh to see the absolute limit of this machine!"

"You've already made your point!" Glas cried out.

Baudwin shifted his body weight and kept cranking. Blinding light shone from the center of each bulb, until they looked like small Suns.

"There — Lugh!" Baudwin exclaimed. "You see? Maginglow can't hurt you."

Glas grabbed Baudwin by the arm to force him off the machine. But he was too late. Suddenly, all twenty bulbs exploded in a flash of light, and then faded into sparks, sending shards of glass flying all over the booth.

"You *stupid* fool!" Glas hollered. "I told you this would happen! Get out!"

"Oh no!" Baudwin exclaimed, playing dumb. "I'm *so* sorry! I only wanted to prove to Lugh that Magniglow wouldn't hurt him, no matter how bright the lights got."

Glas was furious. "I told you to stop! Why didn't you listen?"

Again Baudwin played the fool. "I just wanted to help. I know how difficult the divide has been between the Faeries and Elves — all the arguments between Guilders and the Assembly. I'm *so* sorry."

Glas was not persuaded by Baudwin's entreaties. "Those bulbs were expensive!" he shouted. "That display was meant to go up at the Grand Unveiling! And you've gone and *ruined* it!"

Now, the commotion had drawn the attention of a number of Elves and Faeries, who watched in spellbound disbelief. Word quickly spread through the crowd about the altercation. Soon some Earth Guards appeared on the scene, ready to sanction the guilty parties so as to maintain peace and preserve order. As they approached Baudwin, one of them recognized him.

"*You* again," he said, as he looked disgustedly at Baudwin. "I remember you! You and some Roilers crashed into the food tent in Deuona."

Baudwin couldn't believe his bad luck. "That wasn't me," he said. "But I did fight a Roiler named Loch at the Hop and Hit — and I won."

An Elve in the crowd then shouted, "He's the one who started the riot!"

Now Baudwin became very cross, for not only had Ayamonn — a Guild Leader — blamed him, but also an Elve. Mumblings went through the crowd as more and more recognized the rabble-rouser from the Four Rivers Faire.

"I was the one who tried to *stop* them from fighting!" Baudwin exclaimed. "And I almost succeeded too!"

The Earth Guard glared at him, unimpressed.

One of the hecklers in the crowd began shouting, "Elves can always find the time, but this Faery doesn't know his place!" They all shrieked with laughter.

Baudwin was beginning to wonder if he had thought his plan through carefully enough. He couldn't believe he had grown so infamous, so quickly. He wondered if Seanán and Fearghus had blamed him afterwards, and perhaps they had. Judging from the looks on their faces, the guards seemed eager to take extreme measures. Perhaps the punishment for breaking the bulbs would exceed the crime.

"What's all this about?" the guard asked.

Glas, Baudwin, and Lugh explained everything that had transpired. Neither Baudwin nor Lugh refuted anything, and Glas did not embellish his account. At the end, Baudwin added that he had simply wanted to prove to his friend that Magniglow would do him no harm.

"I was overzealous," he admitted. "I'm really sorry."

The guard shook his head at Baudwin. "You may have won the Hop and Hit last time, but you won't escape justice this time." He then turned to another guard. "Get Ferrell."

Baudwin's stomach began to churn. He looked at his friend. Lugh seemed as if he was going to pass out with apprehension, for both had thought that the dispute would end with Glas, and neither of them expected that the Luminary would come.

An uncomfortable time later Ferrell arrived, the gold medallion shining against his freshly pressed, indigo jacket. So much had changed for Baudwin since the last time he had seen him. Yet, here they were again — at the Engineerium — and Ferrell didn't seem any different — at all.

"Gotten yourself into yet another jam?" Ferrell asked.

Baudwin wasn't sure, but beneath the admonishment, Ferrell seemed almost entertained. Baudwin felt even more uncomfortable, wondering if he also knew about the riot.

Ferrell studied the exploded remains of the bulbs and then laughed. He looked at Glas. "You know, Glas," he began, "there are means to stop those bulbs from exploding. That problem has been solved already. Don't you have any current throttlers?"

Glas shook his head. "No, the Clock City has been too stingy with them. Besides, these are just for demonstrations anyway."

Ferrell shook his head. "What exactly happened here?" he asked.

The guards told their story. When they got to the part about how Baudwin had not stopped cranking, Ferrell glanced at him.

"Got a little carried away, did you?" Slyly, Ferrell paced around Baudwin like a cat about to pounce. Baudwin shook inside. *Now he'll make short work of me,* he thought.

"Well, I suppose accidents *do* happen," Ferrell said, seeming not to care. Idly, he picked up a bulb from the counter and examined the filament. The sudden shift in Ferrell's manner caught Baudwin by surprise. But this did not last for long.

Ferrell studied Lugh, stripping him apart with his gaze. "What a coincidence," he began. "Or is it? Just when another one of our inventions breaks — here *you* are."

As Ferrell spoke, Lugh thrust his hands in his pockets in an effort to steady himself. Sweat broke out on his brow. He then bowed to Ferrell, trying to ease the tension. "As the Guild Leader of the Nechtain Quarter, I offer my most sincere apologies for this unfortunate incident," he said, smiling amiably. "Baudwin was only trying to help me see the error of my ways. It's my fault for being so stubborn."

Ferrell cocked his head at Lugh. "The *error* of your ways?" he asked. "Lugh, son of Donovan, Leader of the Nechtain Quarter? Have any wise salmons been speaking to you in your dreams? I think not. You're not the type to *ever* change." He put down the bulb and took a step closer to Lugh. "Are you lying to me?"

Lugh took a breath. "W—w—wisdom can be found most anywhere," he stuttered. "In this case, I'm not lying. I was only trying to heed the wise counsel of my friend."

"Indeed," Ferrell said, for the interrogation was now over. Apart from dunking Baudwin and Lugh in the river, there was little more that he could do to extract the truth from them. Straightening his collar and adjusting his medallion, he spoke to everyone at once. "Well, accidents do happen, don't they?" he asked. "And, as in this case, overzealousness is often involved," he added, with a hint of sarcasm.

The crowd gathered around, waiting expectantly to hear his pronouncement. They all knew what was coming. Some Elves called out for Ferrell to punish the two of them severely. One heckler shouted that Baudwin deserved what he got, since he had caused the riot the day before. Ferrell ignored them, which was a relief to Baudwin. Hopefully, he knew this was a lie, but Baudwin wasn't sure. The guards surveyed the crowd, readying themselves, in case his judgment brought about another riot right then and there. Lugh looked nervously about, his eyes shifting from place to place. Glas listened eagerly, impatient to get on with his day.

As Ferrell turned to speak to him, Baudwin braced himself, wondering what his fate would be.

"So, tell me, Baudwin," Ferrell began, "I heard you voted *yes* on Matter Three? Did you not?"

"Yes, that's true," Baudwin replied. At least Ferrell hadn't asked him if he was lying as well.

Hearing the answer, Ferrell changed his tone. "If only for that reason, your punishment will not be as severe," he began. "It is a matter of public record that you — the son of the Primary of Water — supported Magniglow, so there must be *some* truth to your story. Two weeks service to Glas is appropriate as punishment."

Glas thought for a moment, and then nodded his head, seemingly satisfied. Baudwin hid his excitement and his immense relief. The plan had gone perfectly, and Ferrell didn't seem to care about the riot.

"And, as for you," Ferrell said, turning to Lugh. "I heard someone vandalized the Sprouting Patch in Deuona. If I find out it was you, then you'll be indentured far, far longer than that."

Lugh bowed again. "I assure you, that certainly was *not* me. I —"

"Save it," Ferrell said.

"You know what to do with this," Glas said, as he happily handed Baudwin a broom.

Straightaway, Baudwin began sweeping glass up off the floor. As he worked, Ferrell studied his every move.

"After you've finished for the day, I want to speak with you," he said.

"Certainly," Baudwin replied, looking up from his work. He had no idea what Ferrell wanted, but he didn't like the sound of his voice. All of this had seemed too easy. Ferrell had basically accused Lugh of smashing the Sprouting

Patch, and then dropped the accusation. What was the Luminary up to? Baudwin put his head down and went back to his work.

Lugh left Baudwin with a wink and a smile, and the day continued. Glas informed Baudwin that the work would be tedious, and that he was not allowed to touch a dynamo without his permission. As he spoke, his usually amicable tone was that of an annoyed taskmaster. First, Baudwin had to fetch a large bundle of copper wire, some spools from the back, and a wire cutter. He had to cut and wind, and cut and wind, filling spool after spool. Then there was polishing, and more sweeping, and sorting boxes in the back.

Baudwin didn't seem to mind. For now, he had the time he needed to study the Elves, and see whether or not they were actually up to something. Lugh's story sounded crazy, but he would do his best to find the truth. Perhaps he would find a clue about how they planned to control the Faeries' intentions. Better yet, he might learn if the Elves knew anything about how to find his mother.

Later in the day, another assistant arrived — a stocky-looking Elve who brought a bag of snacks to eat. The day before, he'd tossed most of his wrappers on the floor, and Baudwin had to clean them all up. Glas began teaching the assistant how to run the demonstrations up front. Baudwin felt slighted, but at least he had gained employment — of a kind.

Eventually the clouds became pink and gold, and as the Sun set most of the Faeries left. Only a few lingered, bartering for whatever they could get in a bargain exchange. Baudwin had never seen the Engineerium so empty, nor been alone with so many Elves. They all seemed so self-contained as they tinkered in their booths. They were an independent lot — each one working alone — a simple cog in a well-oiled machine. Next to him, he saw an Elve polishing a boiler in the steamway booth. Across the way, another was putting away some tools in the sprocketworks booth. Nearby, another Elve, was cleaning glass vials in the alchemvoke booth. As they completed their tasks, their day came to an end.

Finally, Glas approached him. Baudwin had just finished brushing some corrosion off a copper lug. Glas inspected his work.

"Not bad, I suppose, for a Faery," he said, smiling. "You're lucky Ferrell was in such a good mood. He can be quite severe at times."

"Why is he like that?"

Glas paused and then spoke. "Some say he always had the heart of a rapacious kite ready to strike its prey. But I think the Great Befalling changed him, turning his heart bitter and cold. Whatever happened, he was never the same. So many weren't — you see? I remember what he was like before. He still reduced every little thing to a set of off-putting facts, but he was cheerier. He could feel *affection* — but not anymore."

Baudwin had heard stories like this so many times before, about many others. He did not comment, but instead changed the subject.

"I'm to meet him after I'm finished working," he said. "Do you know where he is?"

"He's likely in the North Petal, in the guard office. They keep that office out of sight."

Glas explained the way to Baudwin, and told him to come back the next morning. Baudwin then left the Center and headed to the North Petal to meet Ferrell.

֍

With the Sun setting, the Engineerium was indeed a wonder to behold. Baudwin had never seen the grounds this late, for Faeries weren't usually allowed in Engineeriums after dark. Set against the evening sky, much of his surroundings were covered in magniglow bulbs that looked like dew-spangled spider webs — all glittering brightly — in every color of the rainbow. Baudwin gasped at the sight.

Seeing lights coming from the East Petal, he took a detour.

Before him was the Caterpillar. Yellow lights sparkled in rows along the contours of the head, and green lights along the body segments. Moving closer to the front of the ride, he examined the beguiling smile on the face, lit with red lights. *They look so much better than the glowstones on the gate at home,* he thought. *Or on any such thing.* He wondered how there could be so many of them placed on such a long, undulating creature, or if they would take as long to make if they were glowstones.

"That's Magniglow for you," a voice said.

Baudwin jumped. Next to him stood an old Elve, beaming with pride.

"Yes," Baudwin agreed, sizing up the Elve. He seemed friendly enough, and there was something familiar about him. Looking him up and down, Baudwin realized that he was the same Elve who had stood near the entrance to the Arcade and Park in Deuona — passing out leaflets — when he and his friends had gone to the East Petal after the Water Knot. A pang of regret coursed through him, for how he wished Matha and Criofan could be with him now — taking in all the lights.

"What are the lights for?" he asked.

"Don't you know?" the old Elve asked, laughing playfully. "The Engineerium will soon be open, not just in the day, but also at night. Soon, the entire place will be ablaze with light — every color you can imagine. If I know the Faeries, they'll come here in droves."

"I see," Baudwin said, awed. What a surprise this would be for the Faeries. For the Elves had invested a great amount of time and materials, lighting every fountain, tree, building, path, and ride.

"Yes, indeed," the old Elve replied, dancing a little jig. Suddenly, he grabbed Baudwin by the arm, and pulled him to one side of the Caterpillar. "Now watch this!" he commanded, as he looked at his watch. "We're right on time."

Baudwin followed the Elve's finger, as he pointed in the distance.

"The Butterfly is about to take wing!" the old Elve exclaimed.

They stood waiting, and all of a sudden the black abdomen was ablaze with thousands of violet lights. The wings then lit up with turquoise lights, and their spots, with orange and yellow. Finally, the black wing veins lit up with more violet lights.

"I've never seen such a spectacle of light," Baudwin marveled.

"Wait!" the Elve exclaimed. "There's more."

And there was, for then the leaves of the branches the insect rested upon lit up with green lights, and the other branches with amber. Baudwin and the Elve stood admiring the sight. Baudwin sighed. Now, after all he had been through since he left Deuona, he felt much better about having come to Four Falls. His ordeal had certainly tested his resolve, yet here he was standing before an elven marvel, one that filled him with joy and hope. For if the Elves could create these kinds of wonders, they must also know of others as well. He felt his guilt slipping away. He had been right all along to vote for Matter Three. When his water faery tribe beheld this engineering feat, perhaps even those most attached to the old ways would appreciate the new.

He could have stood there all night admiring the Butterfly, but then responsibility pricked him. *I must see Ferrell,* he thought. He thanked the Elve for his time, and then went on his way.

Eventually, he found the guard house in the North Petal, well hidden around a corner of the Water Knot behind a small shop. He knocked at the door, and an Earth Guard let him in.

Inside, Ferrell was talking to another Earth Guard. Baudwin recognized his uniform; a long-sleeved doublet made of yellow ochre, and brown pants tucked into black leather knee boots. But this one had silver buttons, studs, and silk trim. He had to be a Master of Silver, for he had three stripes on his sleeve. There was also a green star on his collar, which Baudwin remembered meant he had the rank of Torch — Ferrell had told him this. Baudwin had expected Ferrell to be sitting behind a desk, but the guard was there instead, and Ferrell was merely commanding him.

Upon seeing Baudwin, Ferrell smiled, taking Baudwin by surprise. "So, you've come," he said. "How was your first day?"

"There were too many contraptions in the back," Baudwin replied, joking. "Don't ask me what they were all for. I couldn't tell you."

"You'll know — eventually." Ferrell said.

Hearing this, Baudwin felt as if he were being enlisted for a tour in an elven guard, a sobering thought.

Ferrell changed his tone. "Although I must say — I don't know either. Yet, we can always learn, can't we?"

"I suppose so," Baudwin replied. As usual, he found Ferrell puzzling at best, if not disquieting.

Ferrell's next confession only added to his confusion. "I just want you to know that it's a good thing you're here."

"A good thing?" Baudwin asked, feeling his spirits rise. "Why is that?"

"It's good that a Guilder like yourself is learning our ways. I think it will help promote concord, and improve future relations."

Baudwin hadn't expected Ferrell to be so diplomatic. He searched for what to say, but before he could utter a sentence, Ferrell spoke again. "In time, if everything goes well, I hope that you and I will learn to trust each other."

"Yes, I would also like that," Baudwin replied.

"Good," Ferrell said, smiling. "I believe the Assembly has a lot to offer you, as you're curious about us, aren't you?"

"Yes, I am," Baudwin replied.

"And I will make it my duty to enlighten you. I am, after all, a Luminary. Believe it or not, my job is not simply to lord things over everyone."

Baudwin relaxed, smiling, yet his relief was short-lived. Ferrell gave him a serious look.

"So — on the subject of riots," Ferrell began wryly, with a cavalier smile. Centuries of experience stared him down, and Baudwin felt totally overpowered. He went silent, waiting for Ferrell to continue. "There's been talk in the city that a young Guilder, the son of Kelven, started an argument between two Elves, Fearghus and Seanán, stirring up the crowd."

"That's not what happened!"

"When I heard about this," Ferrell continued, "I had my guards do some investigating. Your whereabouts were unknown, so I sent them to Deuona, and they learned that you had run away. Seems as if a lot of the community there is worried about you."

"It wasn't me who started the riot," Baudwin insisted. "The Elves did it!"

"No matter," Ferrell replied. "In time the truth will come out, but I'm discovering that you're quite an interesting character."

"Am I?"

Ferrell steepled his fingers, and grinned at Baudwin, "Oh yes, I've learned a lot about you, from speaking to your rival, Loch. He was more than willing to talk about you, after you defeated him at the Hop and Hit."

The guard who had been sitting behind the desk slowly shook his head at Baudwin, regarding him as if he were a lamb, about to be taken by a pack of wolves.

"You can't trust Loch!"

"No, you can't — can you?" Ferrell replied, grinning again at Baudwin, his fierce gaze honed by years of battle. "But he did say you had an encounter at the Springs of Coventina. Something about a well erupting."

Baudwin tried to hide his fear. *How much did Loch know and what had he told Ferrell?* "It was just a gusher — I'm sure," he replied. "They happen all the time."

Ferrell nodded. "I've been to many old shrines," he began. "They contain knowledge of the old ways, much of which the Assembly and I frown upon. But, what I find especially *spectral* is that while exploring these places, I've often felt as if something was frowning *back* at me — something I couldn't see." Ferrell then wriggled his spine, nodding his head from side to side, grinning. "Do you know what I mean?"

Baudwin went cold, for Ferrell had never spoken to him this way. *Why is he trying to scare me like this?* he thought. *What does he want?* Shocked, he realized that the only thing that could have frowned back at Ferrell would have been *her.* Desperately, he tried to figure out what to say next.

Steeling himself, he replied, "Perhaps the old ways, themselves, are frowning at *you.*"

Ferrell regarded Baudwin, measuring his demeanor. "Have you seen the Show Wheel?" he asked.

Baudwin thought that Ferrell had changed the subject awfully quickly. He then remembered that he had seen the Show Wheel, but not the show. That day at the Engineerium, after he had left Criofan and Matha, he had met his neighbor Elva there. There she had been, eating her cabbage flower in front of the fountain, waiting for the show to begin. She had almost persuaded him to go with her, but his adventure in the Engineerium had led him elsewhere.

"No, I haven't yet," Baudwin replied.

"Excellent," Ferrell said. "Then I would like to take you there — to give you a proper introduction to *Tír Luí Lucharachán,* and the ways of the Elves."

"Oh, I'd like that very much," Baudwin said, as he adjusted his cuffs, for he was willing to do anything to avoid Ferrell's strange interrogation about the water spirit.

"It's settled then," Ferrell said. "I will collect you in a few days. You'll have a fun diversion from your duties."

Baudwin had never seen Ferrell acting so cordially. Perhaps Glas was right, and there was another side to him. In time, Baudwin hoped that he might be able to let his guard down and trust him more. As he turned to leave, Ferrell did something quite unexpectedly. He made a circle in front of him, with his fingers touching at the top, and his thumbs at the bottom.

"A place for all time, young Guilder," he said.

Baudwin crossed his hands in front of him, with the edge of his front hand facing Ferrell, and the palm of his back hand facing down. "A time for all places," he replied. He then left Ferrell and the Engineerium and headed back to Lugh's dome home.

⚶

Later at dinner, Lugh asked Baudwin how his day had gone. Baudwin told him that the work had been boring, but he was glad the plan had worked so well. They chuckled about how upset Glas had been when the bulbs burst, and how lucky they were that Ferrell was lenient with them. Both of them agreed that this seemed irregular, but they didn't know why. Lugh told Baudwin to watch his step around Ferrell. He then gave Baudwin an idea for how to investigate Magniglow. There had to be some kind of clue inside one of the devices, he said, but this seemed silly to Baudwin. Nevertheless, Baudwin did not want to offend his host, and he had promised to help, so he agreed to look inside one of the dynamos. He was actually eager to give the idea a try, so he could put Lugh's worries to rest.

"Just a few quick turns of a wrench, and you'll find it," Lugh said.

"Find what?" Baudwin asked.

Lugh thought for a moment. "I can't say for certain," he replied. "Look for things that are unusual, or don't belong — things that don't have to be there."

Obviously, Lugh didn't understand anything about Magniglow, much less what was inside of a dynamo. Baudwin was amused. Perhaps if Lugh spent more time studying the Four Branches of Progress, rather than trying to sabotage the Tree of Innovation, he would discover his fears were unjustified. In the corner, Baudwin spied a locked chest, and wondered what was inside. Perhaps something strange and unwieldy, like the thoughts in Lugh's head.

He told Lugh he would do his best.

The next morning, he was back at the booth. Glas had given him a box of glass bulbs to clean. They already seemed clean enough, and Baudwin wondered if Glas did this simply to toy with him. But he thought better than to talk back, for that might lead to even more work.

Around mid-morning, Glas's assistant arrived again, a heavyset Elve with fleshy jowls, pink cheeks, and a cheery smile that easily turned into a hostile glare if the wrong thing was said. With every step he took, his breeches strained under the effort, and his belt buckle looked ready to burst. Tightly, he clutched a bag with sweet-vines popping out of the top. He shuffled through the door, plopped his bag on the workbench, and pulled out a vine.

Sucking on the end, he addressed Baudwin. "Oh — *sluurrrp* — you must be — *shluurrrp* — the new — *sluurrrp* — helper."

Baudwin looked askance at him, but decided to ignore his terrible manners. "I'm Baudwin," he said. "Pleased to meet you."

"I'm — *sluurrrp* — Olaf," he said. "Yesterday, I didn't introduce myself. I was too busy."

"I'm sorry — what?" Baudwin asked.

Olaf stopped sucking on the vine. "I'm Olaf," he replied, as he watched Baudwin cleaning the bulbs. "Heard you got into a little trouble, and now you have to clean everything."

"That's right," Baudwin said, without looking up. "It was just a silly accident." Already, this Elve was getting on his nerves.

Olaf took out another sweet-vine and started sucking on the end. "Well — *shluurrrp* — don't forget to — *shluurrrrp* — polish up the tools after I'm done." As he spoke, he pointed at a row of wrenches hanging on the wall.

Again, Baudwin ignored him, deciding instead to be diplomatic. "Sure thing, Olaf," he said.

At least he slurped less, so I could understand more of what he said, Baudwin thought, exasperated. He didn't like Olaf's pleasant, yet superior tone, as if he were the master, addressing his servant.

The work continued. At the front of the booth, Glas did some magniglow demonstrations for a gaggle of curious Faeries. Baudwin kept cleaning the bulbs, and Olaf began his work, although Baudwin still wasn't exactly sure what that consisted of.

Olaf took out a dynamo, grabbed a wrench, and began removing the bolts. Soon they were spread all over the work table, like the snack wrappers had been on the floor the day before. He then began taking the machine apart.

Baudwin looked over Olaf's shoulder, searching the insides, to see if anything seemed odd or amiss. Frustrated, he stopped. He wasn't sure what he was looking at — at least not completely. He saw copper coils inside, and gears that attached to a hand crank. There was also something else, darker in color than the surrounding coils.

"What's that?" Baudwin asked, pointing.

"Don't bother me," Olaf replied, annoyed. "I'm trying to concentrate."

"I just have a question," Baudwin replied. "I'm trying to learn about Magniglow."

Olaf took out another sweet-vine and began sucking on the end. "One — *sluuurp* — question — and *shluurrrp* — no more, okay?"

Baudwin nodded.

"This — *sluurrrp* is — *shluurrrp* — a cobalt magnet."

"A what?" Baudwin asked, even more exasperated, for now this Elve's unpleasant habit of slurping was preventing him from learning about the dynamo.

"I said — *sluurrp* — a cobalt magnet."

"What?" Baudwin asked again, ready to grab the bag of sweet-vine and throw it out of the booth. How he wished he saw a group of young Faeries, so he could do just that! For then, this disgusting distraction would be gone instantly, and he could get his questions answered.

Olaf pulled the sweet-vine out of his mouth.

"It's a cobalt magnet," he said. "And that's all I'm saying."

Baudwin didn't know what a cobalt magnet was, but the part sounded important. None of his steamway toys had them, but there it was — at the heart of the machine. Carefully, he looked inside. The magnet had a dull gray luster, and didn't seem dangerous at all. He wanted to ask more, but thought better of it.

Olaf took out another another dynamo, which he also took apart. He did this twice more, and soon there were four of them strewn about. His pudgy hands greased up the parts as he placed them on the workbench.

Just then, Glas appeared, unannounced. "Olaf, have you got those new coils put into the dynamos yet?" he asked, as he stood over his shoulder.

Olaf turned and clumsily knocked over parts of one of the dynamos. Bearings, screws, and fittings jangled and bounced all over the floor.

"Be careful!" Glas yelled.

Olaf stuck another sweet-vine in his mouth. "Baudwin, help me *sluurrrp* — pick them up."

"He has work to do," Glas interrupted. "*You* pick them up. And stop sucking that sweet-vine!"

Resentfully, Olaf stopped slurping and began picking up the dropped parts. Glas berated him more. "Don't take them all apart at once!" he shouted. "Just do one at time."

With that, Glas left, and Baudwin tried not to laugh.

"He thinks I'm stupid," Olaf began, "but my way is faster."

Baudwin expected Olaf would change the coils in the dynamos and put them back together, but instead, he started another task. In the corner of the booth, he pulled back a canvas cover. Underneath were many threaded objects that looked as if magniglow bulbs could fit right into them. Olaf took them to another workbench. He pulled back another canvas cover and took a bunch of brass items over to the bench as well. He then began to attach the brass items to the threaded objects.

Looking up, Olaf saw Baudwin staring at him. "Okay, I'll explain this too," he said, pointing to the threaded objects. Baudwin could tell that Olaf relished proving what he knew about something.

"These are magniglow sockets." He then pointed to the brass items. "And this is called a socket shell. After I put them together, I can screw the magniglow bulbs into the sockets."

"But, what is it for?" Baudwin asked, determined to pry the answer out of the oafish Elve.

"Too many questions," Olaf said.

Baudwin smiled coyly at him.

"Okay, fine," Olaf replied. "These are for the big display coming up at the falls. We're getting the sockets ready." Olaf started sucking another vine. "Now — *sluurrrp* — stop asking me — *shluurrrp* — questions. I'm *sluurrrp* — busy."

Baudwin was happy with what he had learned so far. There were no clues about what Lugh was worried about, but now he knew more about Magniglow, and he wondered what the big display was for.

A few days went by. Baudwin was still given all the menial work, but he did manage to glean a few more lessons from Olaf. He learned how to attach the cables to machines, and how to put a socket together as well. As much as he tried, though, he couldn't find any clues as to how Magniglow might control the Faeries, so he stopped looking.

Eventually, Glas gave Baudwin a long lesson in the workings of Magniglow. He told him that the dynamo creates current, and Baudwin wondered if this was like water currents, but that just made Glas laugh. "No," Glas said. "This current is like lightning, and it's the source of how Magniglow works." He told Baudwin that Magniglow actually exists in everything — even potatoes.

"Potatoes?" Baudwin asked.

"Yes, and now I'll show you," Glas said.

Glas took out a potato and placed a copper washer into one end and a zinc spike into the other. He then took out another potato and did the same thing again. Next, he attached the spike of one potato to the washer of the other potato with a cable. Another washer and spike remained, not attached to anything. Almost finished, he took out another cable and attached it to the remaining washer. Finally he took out a third cable and attached it to the remaining spike.

"Now comes the fun part," Glas said, grinning. He took out a magniglow bulb, and attached it to the washer-cable. Nothing happened. Finally he attached it to the spike-cable. Faintly the bulb began to glow.

Baudwin was amazed.

Indeed, a potato had Magniglow in it! He knew then that he had to tell this to Lugh, for how could Magniglow be dangerous if it was already in the food they ate?

Glas smiled at Baudwin. "You're probably the first Faery to ever see this demonstration. Our machines don't just work on their own. They follow natural laws. There's nothing mysterious about Magniglow — or anything in the Four Branches of Progress."

Baudwin thought for a moment, and then said, "Except where the current comes from in the first place, and how it gets inside the potatoes."

Glas let go a big laugh. "I can see where this is going," he said. "We actually don't know anything, when we really think about it. But, don't tell anyone in the Assembly — it makes them nervous."

Baudwin was pleased that Glas was again being friendly toward him. Looking at his watch, he saw the time was almost noon. He was hungry, and wanted to go get some food.

As he was about to leave, a voice called out, "Baudwin! Baudwin!"

Turning, Baudwin saw his friend Rian standing right outside the booth. Only weeks had gone by since Baudwin had seen him at the Deuona Engineerium, but they seemed like months.

"Rian!" Baudwin exclaimed. "How good to see you!"

Baudwin was delighted to see his friend, but a pang of guilt coursed through him. He had forgotten to visit him at Gear Chute, so busy had he been with Glas and the magniglow booth.

Baudwin went to Rian. "A time for all places!" he exclaimed, as he crossed his hands in front of him, with his right palm facing down, and his left hand pointed up.

"A place for all time — hello, Baudwin," Rian replied, as he made a circle in front of him with his fingers touching at the top, and his thumbs at the bottom. They gave each other a big hug.

"What are you doing here?" Baudwin asked.

"I suppose I could ask you the same thing," Rian replied, laughing in disbelief.

Hearing Rian, Glas came out of the booth. "The Gear Chute operator," he said. "Hello, Rian."

"Hello, Glas," Rian said. Baudwin laughed as the two Elves greeted each other. "I heard you got a new assistant," Rian began, "but I didn't know it was Baudwin."

Embarrassed, Baudwin grabbed a bolt off of the workbench, turning the nut at the end around and around with his fingers.

"Yes, he's paying his debt back nicely," Glas said. "I assume you heard?"

"Yes, through the rumor mill," Rian said, giving Baudwin a wry grin. "Mills are built for milling, but rumors are milled for spilling." Seeing Baudwin's upset, he added, "But that isn't why I'm here. I've come because I wanted to see if the new magniglow gear chute machine has arrived yet."

"Not yet," Glas said. "But it should be here soon. The engineers in the Clock City have almost completed their work.

Rian nodded. "Well, if that's the case," he began. "With your permission, I would like to borrow your assistant."

"You came at good time," Rian said. "He's about to take a break. Baudwin, don't be more than one half hour."

With that, Rian and Baudwin left the booth. As they strolled through the Center, Rian took his friend by the arm. "What I really want to know is —"

"I'm sorry I didn't visit," Baudwin cut in. "I would have, but —"

"*Whatever* are you doing in Four Falls?" Rian asked.

Baudwin could barely speak, as the shock of seeing his friend was overwhelming. "I should have come to see you," he said, lowering his eyes.

"Don't worry about that," Rian said. "I can see you've been quite busy. The Engineerium isn't that big a place. Eventually, we would have found each other."

Rian let go of Baudwin's arm, and peered into his eyes. "You must tell me," he said, "why are you here?"

Baudwin didn't know what to say. The glamorium egg was gone, and with that, he had simply left, hoping to forge a new path amongst the Elves. He could easily have explained what had happened, but he hesitated. Rian was one of the few friends he had who would understand, but Baudwin could not bring himself to tell him the truth. Again, he was failing the first lesson of the Triquetra — he couldn't be Honest.

Instead he spoke about something else. "Do you remember the *Dúrúnghlas*?"

"Of course I do," Rian replied. "How could I forget?"

"So wonderful, and so fleeting," Baudwin continued, with a catch in his voice. "Almost as if it never happened."

Rian stopped walking and regarded Baudwin. "Did the *Dúrúnghlas* come to you again?" he asked.

"No, not exactly, "Baudwin replied, remembering the spirit. "Something else did."

Rian put his hand on Baudwin's shoulder. "Where is the egg?" he asked.

Baudwin stopped walking as well, struggling to find his words, unable to look his elven friend in the eye. "My pack was stolen at the Four Rivers Faire," he replied. "The egg was in there."

"You mustn't feel bad," Rian said. "Glamorium will find you again."

Baudwin was surprised at how readily Rian accepted his news. The Druid of Guidance didn't seem the least bit alarmed or disappointed that the treasure was lost.

"I'm so sorry, Rian," Baudwin said.

"Nonsense!" Rian exclaimed. "You must not feel badly about this. For once you see its inner light, Glamorium has decided your fate."

Baudwin wanted to tell Rian about the water spirit, but he was too ashamed to explain the real reason he had lost the egg. She had judged him unworthy, which hurt more than anything his father had ever said. He could have withstood countless admonishments from Kelven, but the spirit had brought a devastating end to his quest. Her fury had chased him down a path of desperation. And now here he was, before the Elve who unwittingly had set everything into motion.

"I wanted something new," Baudwin began uncertainly. "Something to do differently. So I decided to find a way to work for the Elves."

"I understand," Rian said. "*Completely.*"

As Rian spoke, Baudwin saw that he was without judgment of any kind. *He knows I lost the egg,* he thought. *Yet, he still believes in me.* How grateful Baudwin was that his friend understood how difficult his struggle had been.

"All I've ever known is Deuona," Baudwin said. "I was there far too long and have never even been to my own capital city before. What if you had never been to the Clock City?"

"I have been there," Rian said, laughing. "But I wouldn't want to go back. Gold Haven is my home."

Baudwin and Rian went to get some food, and as they ate, Baudwin told him about how Seanán and Fearghus had started the riot at the Four Rivers Faire with their silly argument. He explained how some of the Fae had blamed him for everything, even though he was only trying to prevent a bad situation from getting worse. He then told him more about how the Elves had stolen his pack.

Rian was furious, especially when he learned that Baudwin had had a bout under the bridge. He was also mystified that the Cyhiraeth had given Baudwin such a bittersweet healing. Over the years Baudwin had told him about his bouts, and Rian expressed his concerns. Now he asked if Baudwin had ever been healed this way after a bout. Baudwin shook his head *no,* choosing not to mention the voice that had spoken to him. He was afraid Rian would pry too much out of him, and he would find himself talking about the spirit.

"Perhaps the Cyhiraeth has more to teach you than the Elves — as does Glamorium," Rian said.

"But the egg is gone," Baudwin replied weakly.

"Just because the egg is gone doesn't mean you can't practice honesty, and in doing so, learn to wield Glamorium. In time, Glamorium will come back to you. And then you won't need anyone else's help — much less the Elves," he added seriously.

Baudwin was taken aback. If Rian was correct, he never should have left Deuona, and simply practiced honesty while searching again for Glamorium. How long would that have taken? Already, Baudwin had searched for decades, found the Water, and then been thwarted. He was out of patience.

"I found a new path."

"And I believe in my heart," Rian replied, winking, "that whatever path you choose will eventually lead you to the *right* one — if you are willing to learn from your mistakes."

Rian's words reminded Baudwin of what the voice had said to him after he had had his last bout: "Along your own path you will find yourself, and then in yourself you will know your true path. Do not lose heart. Throw yourself into your own choices."

Now both of them had told him a similar thing. Rian was an old friend who was wise, and she was an old, wise Faery — *but their advice isn't making me any wiser*, he thought. He didn't want to hear any more, from anyone, so he changed the subject.

"You'll never guess who I ran into when I came here."

Baudwin then told Rian that he had met Lugh at the Tree of Innovation. When he explained how he and Lugh had plotted to trick Glas into hiring him, Rian cuffed Baudwin playfully on the back.

"Ha!" Rian exclaimed. "Lugh is such a trickster! So you're helping him find out how Magniglow is going to control us all? He's a fine fellow, but I think being so locked into the old ways has addled his mind."

"Funny you should say that," Baudwin said, "because he keeps *everything* locked away."

"Oh?"

"Yes," Baudwin replied. "His house is full of locked chests. He's so peculiar. But, he was nice enough to let me stay with him."

Hearing this, Rian's blue eyes softened. "You know," he began, "if you had come to me, I could have gotten you a job — of some sort."

"I don't know why I didn't come to you," Baudwin said. But the truth was that he *did* know why, and he simply wouldn't say.

Seeing his upset, Rian quickly added, "But, you found your own way. My hat's off to you. Already, you've become quite the Elve!"

Baudwin smiled. They headed back to the booth. As they approached the door, they saw Ferrell had arrived, and was talking to Glas. Baudwin almost tripped at the sight, for despite their new rapport, Ferrell's presence always unnerved him.

"I see your punisher is here," Rian said, barely masking his disdain. "I must say hello."

Baudwin noticed that Rian didn't seem to fear Ferrell. Neither Ferrell's stature nor his rank made Rian blink. Although Rian never wore his stripes, he was a Master of Silver, which meant he was as established in his metal as Ferrell was in his. Brazenly, Rian headed over to greet him.

"Ferrell," he said, feigning cordiality. "Come to check up on the Assembly's latest recruit?"

Instantly, Ferrell turned to Rian. "Yes, and what a fine recruit he is," he replied, with controlled indifference. "Why, Glas was just telling me that he's already learned some of the basics about Magniglow."

Beneath their facades, Baudwin could see that just like Seanán and Fearghus at the Four Rivers Faire, they didn't like each other at all.

"How fortunate for you," Rian continued. "The son of the Primary of Water. What an asset — I mean what a great *assistant* he'll be."

Ferrell hid a scowl. "Yes, a fine assistant. . ."

Rian then spoke, "Ferrell, perhaps you should reconsider his punishment."

"And why is that?" Ferrell asked, sharply.

"Well," Rian replied, "because Baudwin was just telling me that some Elves attacked him at the riot the other day. He was there when it all began."

"Really, now?" Ferrell asked, shooting Baudwin an interested glance.

"Yes," Rian replied. "Seanán and Fearghus were up to their usual petty debates — it seems. They got the entire crowd all worked up. Which isn't fair, because Baudwin got the blame, though he was just a bystander."

"Actually, the guards already told me all about it," Ferrell said impatiently. "I'm sure Seanán was the instigator."

"I'm sure he wasn't!" Rian exclaimed, angrily. "Those who follow the Eternal Movement don't start fights."

"Gold Haven never started a *cogadh* before?" Ferrell scoffed.

Several Earth Guards standing near Ferrell began to laugh, but Baudwin wasn't sure what the joke was about. As he listened to Rian and Ferrell, they reminded him of Seanán and Fearghus at the Four Rivers Faire.

"If Govannon had followed the council's ruling, that cursed *cogadh* would never have begun," Rian insisted.

"And who were they to say he couldn't build his city?" Ferrell asked. "Ha — you stepped right into that one!"

"Who were they indeed!" Rian exclaimed, looking as if he might come to blows. "Has two hundred years completely robbed you of memory? They were the leaders of the realm — peerless, wise, and benevolent. And your master sent most of them to Annwyn, and drove away the rest."

"Oh, I remember it well," Ferrell said, shaking with rage. "Those fools thought they knew what was best for everyone. Have you forgotten how we languished then? There were no more dreams coming from the Faeries, and there hadn't been for a long time. The council had no guidance for us, just empty platitudes that our lives would improve out of thin air. Govannon gave us a new purpose. He wasn't the one who started the *cogadh* — he only *finished* it."

Rian was silent. Baudwin expected him to say more, but he just shook his head and changed the subject. From their exchange, Baudwin could tell that Rian, who hailed from Gold Haven, upheld the Eternal Movement, and he knew that Ferrell's loyalties were to the Clock City and Govannan, which also meant he upheld the Rise of Time. *No wonder they don't like each other,* he thought.

"You'll never understand," Rian said, glowering. "Besides, the Earth Guards at the riot *must* have seen Baudwin. He even got hit over the head for his trouble. It's a travesty of their station that they didn't come to help him."

"The riot was utter chaos," Ferrell said, "for both Elves and Faeries alike."

"Indeed it was," Rian agreed. "Yet, can't you see he's already been punished enough? Perhaps you should commute his sentence."

As Ferrell regarded Rian, his gaze could have torn the face off of a badger. He had no intention of losing the argument, much less backing down. Turning to Baudwin he said, "That won't be necessary. He's enjoying the work so much — aren't you, Baudwin?"

Dumbly, Baudwin nodded in agreement.

"You see?" Ferrell asked, edging a few steps toward Rian. "He's having *fun.* Let's not spoil it." He stopped just short of Rian, but Rian held his ground, and didn't move.

"Just like a Master of Gold — too *superior* to be concerned about the plight of those beneath him," Rian snapped.

Ferrell shot back, "Just like a Master of Silver, too *inferior* to see his own strengths, so he attacks those he considers his betters."

Baudwin had never seen two Masters of any metal speak to each other this way. He sensed the paths they had taken were quite disparate. Ferrell had no doubt seen too many battles, and Rian too many injustices, making them both too hardened in their views to yield to the other. He wondered then about all the Elves of the four metals — and whether they too clashed this way.

The argument was finished and, turning to Baudwin, Ferrell then spoke. "Before I forget, today is a special day. The Show Wheel begins soon, and I've got a coach ready to take us there." Veiling his antipathy, he continued, "You see — I didn't intend for him to work *all* the time. Come with me, Baudwin — now."

As Baudwin prepared to leave, he saw Rian watching him, looking very concerned. Baudwin would have liked to reassure his friend that nothing terrible was going to happen. After all, the Show Wheel was only an entertainment. Confidently, he waved goodbye to Rian. Ferrell motioned for him to move along, and Baudwin followed, his steps hard upon the heels of the Luminary's shadow.

Chapter 26

THE SHOW WHEEL

Baudwin left the Center, heading toward the North Petal. Ferrell was in front of him, moving quickly. The Luminary's strides were long, and as his boots clacked upon the cobblestones, his steps conveyed an unmistakable resolve — building the future was in the hands of the Elves. As he walked, the crowd mirrored his purpose, parting as if an unknown force had moved them as soon as he approached, and then closing just as soon as he passed. Struggling to keep up, Baudwin increased his pace, zigging and zagging around other Faeries and Elves blocking his way.

"Isn't the Show Wheel in the South Petal?" Baudwin called out, beads of sweat dotting his brow.

"Yes," Ferrell replied without looking back.

"Why, then, are we going this way?" Baudwin asked, perplexed.

"To give us time to talk," Ferrell replied, without slowing down in the least.

Baudwin had no idea what Ferrell had in mind. He could barely keep up with him, much less hold a conversation; nevertheless, he followed along. Soon they reached the North Petal tunnel, hurrying along the stone path until they got to the end. Baudwin went right through the ring. Once he got outside, he saw Ferrell standing next to a stately-looking coach, parked near another path.

"This will take us to the Show Wheel," Ferrell said, as he looked at his watch. Baudwin wondered if he had been timing him as he sped through the tunnel.

"Jump, or should I say *hop* right in," Ferrell instructed him. He then let out a peculiar laugh, surprised by his own joke. Baudwin got the humor right away and laughed as well, so as not to put a damper on Ferrell's levity. Obviously, the word *jump* referred to the Jab and Jump, and the word *hop* to the Hop and Hit. The Elves used the former, and the Faeries the latter, and Ferrell wanted Baudwin to see that he found humor in the difference.

Before getting in, Baudwin studied the coach. There were no grand horns at the front, but there was a large copper steamway boiler in the back, shining like new, as well as magniglow lights set inside glass lanterns on all four sides. The carriage was painted indigo with gold trim. There were four large spoked wheels, and a cab with windows and curtains. *Indigo and gold,* Baudwin thought, impressed by the grandeur. *Colors fit for a Luminary and a Master of Gold.* A coach Elve sat in the driver box waiting for instructions, and a foot Elve stood on the rear boot, ready to close the coach door as soon as he got the signal. Baudwin could see the carriage was far smaller than a lumber roller, yet probably a great deal faster. He couldn't wait to find out, so he quickly climbed inside.

Sitting down, he ran his hands over the upholstery, remembering his steamway carriage at home, a copper pumpkin sitting on two large brass wheels — just a young one's toy. He also remembered showing it to his grandfather, telling him he wanted to be a Faery of noble deeds, waving from his coach to an adoring crowd. Seamus had been pleased to hear this, for Baudwin had also told him that he had found the Water — just the day before. "You can be that Faery — the Water has come to you," Seamus had said, unable to contain his joy.

Baudwin wondered what kind of water Faery his grandfather would see now, sitting with an elven Luminary and heading for an entertainment which he knew nothing about. Looking out of the window, he saw the foot Elve close the door. So then did his mind close on the memory of his grandfather's hopes for him. The coach Elve began driving, and the coach rolled away, taking the long route toward the South Petal.

Ferrell sat across from him, pouring a drink from a flask. "Roseberry libation?" he asked, offering Baudwin a glass.

Baudwin hesitated, for he didn't know what Roseberry was, but the name sounded good.

"Never heard of Roseberry?" Ferrell asked, bemused. "You really must travel more. Roseberry comes from Mist Valley in *Tír Luí Lucharachán*. Have some."

Ferrell thrust the glass at him. Timidly, Baudwin took a sip, enjoying one of the most delicious beverages he had ever tasted. The drink was finer than a valley dew fizzy — perhaps not as sweet — but the rose and berry flavors were distinct, and they complemented each other well.

"*Roseberry*," Baudwin said, savoring every sip.

"Roseberry bushes grow only in Mist Valley, you know. They like the fog. It's also a fine place to grow grapes."

Ferrell appeared more relaxed than Baudwin had ever seen him. The Elve had already poured himself a glass, and was staring out the window at the throngs around them approaching the Engineerium.

"I've never heard of Mist Valley before," Baudwin said.

"Yes, that doesn't surprise me." Ferrell replied. "Govannon, our leader, is from there. Before he built the Clock City, that was his home."

Hearing the name, Baudwin recalled the argument Rian and Ferrell had just had in the magniglow booth. They had spoken of the *cogadh* that had taken place before the Great Befalling, but Baudwin knew only a few details. The *cogadh* had claimed many lives, but beyond that, he had heard little talk of it growing up in Deuona. Not wanting to seem like a fool, Baudwin continued the conversation as best he could.

"I heard he fought with Belanus of Gold Haven," Baudwin said. "And after that, he built the Clock City and founded the Assembly of Progress."

"Not exactly," Ferrell said. "The Clock City was built before then, and was one of the big reasons the *cogadh* began in the first place. The Assembly was founded afterward — Govannon's great gift to the realm."

With that, Ferrell raised his glass high: "A toast to the Clock City!" he exclaimed. Baudwin didn't want to be rude, so he raised his glass as well. As they clinked them together, Ferrell affirmed the faery way to Baudwin by saying "To the Moon," which was the custom. Baudwin affirmed the elven way to Ferrell by saying "To the Sun." Smiling, they both then drank.

Ferrell leaned closer to Baudwin, as if about to share a secret that few knew. "He saved us all, Baudwin. Before the *cogadh*, life was miserable. *Tír Luí Lucharachán* was not as it is now — thriving — with apprentices, experts, and masters building the new dream he founded. No — everything was tarnished, run down, and falling apart. There was even famine. So many lives had passed to Annwyn, and we had no direction. He put an end to all of that. We had no dreams of our own, but he gave us a new one. Everything you see around you now is because of him."

Baudwin looked at the inside of the coach, and then outside at the Engineerium. He wondered how this could be true.

"Rian said that he destroyed the council," Baudwin said. "What did he mean?"

Ferrell put his glass down on a tray, built into the seat.

"Before I answer that," he replied, "we must start at the beginning. It's time you were given a true account of what happened."

The carriage was now going down the winding path that ran alongside the Engineerium toward the East Petal. Outside, Baudwin saw groups of Faeries, waving and shouting at the coach. *There's my adoring crowd,* he thought, amused. *Yet, I have not performed any noble deeds — at least not yet.* These thoughts gave him pause, for he realized he had another question to ask Ferrell.

"What did you mean when you told Rian there were no more dreams coming from the Faeries?"

"How can you ask me that?" Ferrell asked, shocked at Baudwin's lack of knowledge. "Don't you know that once — long ago — in *Tír na nÓg* the Faeries were the dreamers of all that was to be? That they were the ones who gave the Elves the inspiration for what to build?"

"Neither my father nor grandfather ever spoke of that," Baudwin replied, confused by his own ignorance. "Our ways are those of the Water," he added, defending himself.

Ferrell picked up his glass again, giving Baudwin a wry smile.

"Yes, the water, of course — but there was once more — much more," Ferrell added. "I must confess, though, that I don't exactly know *what*. You know of the Golden Way, don't you?"

"Of course," Baudwin replied, his mind racing, as he remembered the words:

Always give to others what you would have them give to you, and receive from others what you would have them receive from you. For, if you balance giving and receiving, your hearts will be full, your minds will be at peace, and all will be well in Tír na nÓg.

Ferrell could tell that Baudwin was pondering his mention of the Golden Way. He continued his explanation, saying, "Those times were harmonious like the Golden Way, because cooperation flourished between the Elves and Faeries. Many say that during this time there was great equanimity between us. We lived with strong accord, no one wanted for anything, and our ways were in balance."

Ferrell's face clouded with strain. "But then, something changed," he added, as he looked out of the window. He seemed to be considering something deeply, and then quickly turned his gaze back to Baudwin.

"Everything began to decline, you see," he said. "No one knows for certain why. Our history goes back many thousands of years, and much has been lost. Only the Elves have kept fragments of the written records, and archived other remaining artifacts."

"You mean like the ones at Curios & Marvels?" Baudwin asked.

"Yes, those things, and far more than you can imagine. The original four great cities: Copper Caves, Silver Forge, Gold Haven, and Platinum Spires were different then. Perhaps greater in some ways. And those marvels weren't marvels. They were just everyday parts of the lives of the Fae, although those on the Assembly can't make up their minds as to what they were actually for."

Baudwin remembered arguing with Edmund at Curios & Marvels about the true meaning of the Triquetra. Edmund was positive that it was *Scrutiny, Certainty,* and the *Promise of the Future,* while Matha had argued for *Honesty, Truth,* and the *Promise of Rebirth.* Baudwin thought about asking Ferrell about this, but before he could, Ferrell spoke.

"The decline made everything worse in the realm, and the Elves nearly stopped building. We languished for centuries, and then Govannon was inspired to build the Clock City, to provide us with a new sense of purpose. The council was fearful. They represented everything that we now abhor. They despised change. They spoke of things they didn't even understand, so desperate were they to save us. Govannon built his city without their permission, and that sparked the *cogadh* with Belanus, his brother. Of course, I marched with Govannon.

I fought by the river Dagda, beneath the Fallen Peaks. Thank the metals that we won that day. Otherwise, the Elves would have remained rudderless and desperate. Our cities would be crumbling, even now, and the council would have ruined us all."

Ferrell raised his arms to his chest, clenching his fists. "The Rise of Time was the rise of the Elves," he declared.

Never before had Baudwin heard this account of history. Always, Kelven and Seamus had given him very few details, focusing and lingering instead on the Water, or the Guild, with little concern about the world outside of Deuona. They rarely mentioned the Assembly, and he had barely heard of Govannon, until he came to Four Falls. He wondered about this leader of the Elves, and also if what Ferrell said was even true.

Quietly, he looked at Ferrell. The Elve did seem utterly earnest when he spoke. Gone was his calculating gaze, as if he were testifying before a meeting with the primaries and the Grand Eldress herself — where few would dare to tell a lie — for just as the Water flowed, so too would the truth of one's intent be laid bare.

Neither of them spoke, and then Ferrell broke the silence. "You must tell me, Baudwin," he began, "what is *your* story? Why are you here?"

The carriage was now halfway past the East Petal, heading toward the South Petal. Outside, a small group of Faeries ran toward the coach, trying to hitch a ride. They were turned away by the foot Elve. Laughing, they stopped in their tracks. In back of the coach, the boiler hummed. Like the wheels beneath them, Baudwin's Life was being propelled forward, but he didn't know the whys or wherefores.

Baudwin wasn't sure where to begin. "My story?" he asked, struggling for an easy answer. "I wanted to see the Engineerium. I heard this one was better than the one in Deuona, and then I ran into Lugh, and I had to prove to him that Magniglow was safe."

Ferrell looked askance at Baudwin. "Come on," he said, almost laughing. "I know you both were lying. Lugh would never entertain having someone, especially someone younger than himself, try to prove something that he will never believe."

Uncomfortably, Baudwin shifted in his seat, almost knocking the glasses onto the coach floor. "Careful now," Ferrell said. "Those are made of a rare crystal." As he spoke, his calculating gaze returned, searing Baudwin's face. "Whatever you two were up to," he continued, "is of little consequence. I'm glad you broke the bulbs, as I was planning on meeting you again anyway — you see?"

"I swear to you," Baudwin said, trying his best to sound sincere. "What I said is true. Lugh really believes Magniglow is dangerous — but, he can't say why."

"And he'll never be able to," Ferrell said. "Guilders like him are fools. You young ones will carry the torch into the future — those with enough sense in their heads, that is."

"He has some sense," Baudwin said. "He's kind. He let me stay with him after I was attacked."

"I'm sure he doesn't mind taking care of his own when he's not wreaking havoc upon our inventions," Ferrell countered, scowling. "In time, everything will become clearer. For a Faery, you are far more forward-thinking than the rest of your kin. You must not have any illusions about this. Whatever you need most in life, the Elves are the ones who will help you — not the Faeries."

As the coach sped along, Ferrell then asked one more question. "Tell me, Baudwin, what is dear to your heart? What can I help you with that matters most?"

Baudwin thought then of his mother, and the quest he would never abandon. He looked at Ferrell, wondering if the Luminary could help him where both the Water and Glamorium had failed. "After the Great Befalling, I lost someone very dear to me," he replied.

"Yes?" Ferrell asked.

"I was born right after the Great Befalling and my mother — she went missing. Losing one's mother is a terrible thing for my kind — for it means that we cannot join with the Water. This has burdened me all of my Life."

Sighing deeply, Baudwin set his glass upon the tray next to him. Never would he have imagined telling this to Ferrell, but now it made perfect sense. If he hadn't broken the magniglow bulbs, he wouldn't now have the chance to directly ask a Luminary for help. His fate recently seemed cruel, but now appeared to be fortunate, which was strange. The water spirit had taken away the egg, but perhaps something better was about to happen.

Ferrell gave Baudwin an imposing look, almost the way Seamus would have done. "Baudwin," he began, "the Assembly will help you find her. We have resources beyond what you could ever imagine. Machines that make this carriage look like a simple steamway toy." Leaning closer, he said, "Wherever she is — if I were to give the command — the guard would find her."

The coach stopped. Outside, Baudwin could see the Show Wheel a few yards away.

"Now let me show you who the Elves *really* are," Ferrell said, as he waited for the foot Elve to open the door. With that, they exited the coach.

◦✦◦

Before them was the Show Wheel, a circular wooden stage, even larger than the one in Deuona, sitting in the round and mostly empty. "That's the wheel," said Ferrell.

"What does it do?" Baudwin asked.

"Oh, I won't spoil it," Ferrell said. "You'll see soon enough." As they walked closer, Baudwin examined everything.

Circles of seats surrounded the wheel, wrapping all the way around, with aisles dividing them into wedges, like pieces of a pie. Next to the stage, a cheerful-looking Master of Ceremonies stood on a small platform, with bronze rails and an orange and blue canvas top. Waiting patiently, he seemed poised to pull a large bronze lever, which undoubtedly would transform the Show Wheel into an Engineerium marvel. "He's the one I must see," Ferrell said, pointing to the Elve, who wore a maroon tailcoat with a white ruffled shirt, and black shoes with golden buckles. "Come with me."

Baudwin followed Ferrell down an aisle, past many rows of seats, which were already filled with excited Faeries. They seemed to know what the show would be about, as they waited with untiring delight, but Baudwin still had no idea. Ferrell had made a big point of bringing him here, but he wasn't sure why. Baudwin still didn't know if he could trust him or not, but Ferrell had been kind enough to offer him his help, so he decided to withhold his judgment.

As soon as they reached the row nearest the stage, they were led by an usher to their seats. "You may wait here," Ferrell said, "for there is something that I must do." Baudwin sat down and watched as Ferrell headed up the steps to the platform. Soon he was standing next to the Master of Ceremonies. Seeing Ferrell, a hush came over the audience. They all knew what his uniform meant. After checking his watch, the Master of Ceremonies pulled out a large bronze speaker horn, which he handed to Ferrell.

Ferrell took the horn, and as he spoke, his voice carried throughout the audience. Baudwin remembered the last time he had seen Ferrell so in his element, speaking just before Baudwin had fought Loch at the Hop and Hit. Certainly, Ferrell relished addressing large crowds of attentive Faeries.

"Welcome to the Show Wheel!" he exclaimed. "As you can see, we're here to open the show, but before we do, I want to speak to all of you about the future of our beloved *Tír na nÓg*. What you are about to see is far more than mere entertainment. This show is a demonstration of what we must all remember as we strive together in our shared realm. As the performance unfolds, you will see that the old ways of the Elves truly are as undying as the old ways of the Faeries. We too cherish our history. Just as there is still a great deal that the Faeries hold in high regard about the old ways, there is still a great deal that we Elves remember about them as well. As you will see, the old ways are *not* separate from the new ways. Therefore, we must continue to see our history not as the result of a Great Befalling, but as the *beginning* of a Great Endeavor!"

Hearing this, groups of Faeries in the audience stood up, whistling, cheering, and clapping. Ferrell stood smiling, letting the applause continue, for he did so enjoy basking in their enthusiasm. "And now," he continued, "if you will allow me, I will pass this speaker horn to our Master of Ceremonies."

Ferrell then handed the horn to the Master of Ceremonies, who eagerly grabbed the handle. "Welcome to the Show Wheel!" he exclaimed. "An exciting extravaganza, where the performers will never leave the show but — as you are about to see — the show will *certainly* leave *you*." He then motioned to Ferrell to pull the large lever next to him, which Ferrell did, making a very loud *keeeeeeerunk*.

Once the lever was pulled, a lively tune began to play, emanating from somewhere beneath the stage. The wheel then began rotating in a clockwise direction, turning like an enormous gear. Baudwin was duly impressed, and then thought, *Of course — the <u>Show</u> Wheel.* Looking at the platform, he could see that Ferrell had already left, and was making his way back to him.

As soon as the Show Wheel had made one complete rotation, Baudwin heard whirring noises beneath the stage. Soon, a second stage rose from the wheel, smaller than the first one, but large enough to hold a row of benches around the perimeter, facing the audience. The benches were painted salmon, cream, and turquoise, with golden accents.

After the wheel had made another complete rotation, a large bronze column rose from the center of the smaller stage. A sprocketworks canopy unfolded from the top of the column, painted the same colors as the benches. As the two stages and the canopy rotated with the music, the Faeries happily clapped their hands. Baudwin began to clap. He then looked over and saw that Ferrell had sat down and was clapping as well.

Door-shaped slits then appeared in the column, and soon Baudwin realized that there were hidden doorways. The door panels slid down into the wheel, until there were now four open doors, each one facing a different quarter of the stage. The music grew louder. Dozens of elven musicians — both ladies and gents — streamed out of the doors, playing violins, mandolins, melodeons, trumpets, drums, tambourines, hand cymbals, and chimes. They all paraded merrily to the wooden benches and then sat down.

"Oh, oh!" the Faeries cried out. As the musicians kept playing, they swooned with delight.

"And now — behold the Four Elven Guards," the Master of Ceremonies announced. Out streamed four lines of shimmering color, one from each door.

"Behold the Earth Guard — protectors of the land — in colors of yellow and brown," the Master of Ceremonies called out.

The Faeries rose from their seats, stomping their feet, for they loved and respected what the Elves protected. "The Earth, The Earth!" they sang out, clapping.

"Behold the Water Guard — protectors of the shores — in colors of teal and sea green," the Master of Ceremonies called out.

The Faeries remained standing, their arms rippling like waves. "The Water! The Water!" they sang out, clapping.

"Behold the Air Guard — protectors of the sky — in colors of royal and sky blue," the Master of Ceremonies called out.

The Faeries remained standing, murmuring like the wind. "The Air! The Air!" they sang out, clapping.

"Behold the Fire Guard — protectors of the hamlets — in colors of red and orange," the Master of Ceremonies called out.

The Faeries remained standing, swaying back and forth. "The Fire! The Fire!" they sang out, clapping.

The audience was in an uproar, cheering with rapturous excitement. They then all sat down, eager to see what would happen next. Looking closely, Baudwin saw that the guards were moving two by two, and that each pair featured a lady and a gent. Ferrell caught him noticing this and said, "Yes, there are ladies in the Guards as well."

Baudwin counted that each guard line had eight couples.

As each guard made their way to a quarter of the stage, they were truly a sight to behold. The ladies wore skirts and blouses, and the gents doublets and breeches, all made of the finest silk. Topaz jewelry sparkled from their boots, belts, and necks; the Earth Guards wore yellow and brown gems, the Water Guards, green and blue, the Air Guards, light and dark blue, and the Fire Guards, red and orange.

The Show Wheel was still rotating, and Baudwin watched as the lines of guards came in and out of view. "As you can see," Ferrell pointed out, "there aren't just Earth Guards, but three other kinds of guards as well. You've probably seen only the Earth Guards in Deuona, but soon you will have knowledge of all of them."

Baudwin nodded, completely taken in by the sight.

"The Earth Guard is right there, in front of us," Ferrell continued. "And the Water Guard is there," he added, pointing to his left. "To the right is the Fire Guard, which means the Air Guard is behind the carousel on the other side of the stage," Ferrell explained.

All the while, as the Show Wheel kept turning, the audience watched all four orders of the Guards begin their performance. Having taken their assigned places in a quarter of the stage, each began to perform a spirited step dance.

With arms at their sides, legs flying high, and their feet tapping out intricate rhythms on the floor, they began to chant:

Guardians
Of home, field, and hearth
With boots on the land
We all serve the Earth

Guardians
Of sand, shell, and otter
With boats on the shores
We all sail the Water

Guardians
Through lenses we stare
With spyglass in hand
We all watch the Air

Guardians
Of wood, farm, and pyre
With steam pump and hose
We all stop the Fire

Earth
Water
Air
Fire
Earth
Water
Air
Fire

"You see," Ferrell said, as he leaned in closer to Baudwin, "they all perform the same dance in all four parts of the stage as it rotates."

Baudwin nodded again, quite impressed, for he had never seen such a well-coordinated effort. Although Faeries liked to dance in circles, one inside another, each going a different way, the Elves liked to perform the same dance in different parts of a large place, while rotating around and around. *The Show Wheel,* he thought again. *Very entertaining indeed.*

As the music ended with a flourish, all the guards ran to form a circle at the edge of the stage, eight couples to a quarter. There they stood for several moments facing the audience, with one leg crossed behind them, and their arms held high above their heads. They then turned, and quickly exited the stage, back into the column.

This ending only marked the beginning of another part of the show.

⊙⸾⊙

Four round stone pedestals rose from beneath the floor, one in each quarter of the stage. Eight couples sat in a circle around the base of each pedestal — two couples wearing shades of yellow, two in green, two in blue, and two in red.

"However did they do that?" an old Faery sitting next to Baudwin asked, as she cocked her head to the side, to better see the rising circle.

"Tunnels under the stage," Ferrell replied. "We have used our steamway expertise to construct a system of passageways." Baudwin fixed his eyes upon the pedestal in front of them.

Ferrell then focused on Baudwin. "This is my favorite part. Look closely at the pedestals."

Baudwin looked at the four stone pedestals and saw that each one had eight stones upon them. The eight couples on each pedestal rose and danced in circles around the pedestals, holding hands as they went. Next, they turned away from the pedestal and danced in a circle, this time in the opposite direction. They repeated the circle dance three more times — facing the pedestal, turning away, and then back. After that, each of the eight gents picked up one of the stones.

The couples then turned away from the pedestals one last time. As they did, the stones they were holding slowly turned from pitch black to pearl white. Silence fell over the audience.

"How did they change color like that?" Baudwin asked. "They don't look like glowstones."

"That's because they aren't," Ferrell replied. "They're moonstones."

"Moonstones?"

"Yes," Ferrell replied. "They turn a soft milky white — when touched by the Fae. They're especially valued by the Elves. According to the old ways, moonstones were first given to them as gifts from the Faeries. Which is why I always try to remind the Faeries about the strength of our bond, and the length of our shared history. Watch now, and you will see what moonstones actually do."

Baudwin could hardly believe that Ferrell was speaking so kindly about the old ways. Did he truly mean what he was saying, or did he have some other intention?

With that, the dancers broke the silence by leaving the pedestals, and running to the edge of the stage, eight couples to a quarter. As the music continued playing, they danced another marvelous step dance for several minutes. The music stopped, and the dance ended. A hush went over the audience. And all the while, as the Show Wheel kept turning, the audience watched the circle of dancers waiting at the edge of the stage.

"And now a song to stir our hearts," the Master of Ceremonies announced, cheerily.

Holding the moonstones, the gents stepped between the ladies, facing the audience. With mandolins, drums, and chimes playing softly in the background, they sang:

A moonstone I did give my friend
To help him find his strength
So he could take the ways he chose
To almost any length

A moonstone I did give my foe
To show him of my mettle
That I could wait or carry on
And he would have to settle

A moonstone I did give my love
To share with her my heart
So she would know both time and space
Could n'er keep us apart

A moonstone I did give myself
So I would not forget
To live with feelings good and bad
And be without regret

The ladies then stepped forward toward the audience. After handing them the moonstones, the gents stepped back. The ladies sang the entire song again:

A moonstone I did give my friend
To help her find her strength
So she could take the ways she chose
To almost any length

A moonstone I did give my foe
To show her of my mettle
That I could wait or carry on
And she would have to settle

A moonstone I did give my love
To share with him my heart

So he would know both time and space
Could n'er keep us apart

A moonstone I did give myself
So I would not forget
To live with feelings good and bad
And be without regret

As soon as the song ended, all the couples joined hands and ran to the edge of the stage, holding their moonstones. As the Faeries clapped and cheered, the players took a bow, and then quickly exited the stage into the column doors. The music came to a pause.

Baudwin sat quietly, touched by the song. He turned to look at Ferrell, and could see that he was unusually quiet as well. Perhaps the Elve did have some genuine respect for the old ways after all.

"As I was saying," Ferrell began slowly, "the emanations from a moonstone allow those who hold them not only to find, but to understand their feelings."

"Is that why the Faeries gave them to the Elves?" Baudwin asked.

"Yes," Ferrell replied. "Which is help I'm sure you Faeries would agree we need," he added.

Baudwin smiled, taken in by Ferrell's honesty. Perhaps there was more to him than he realized, but he still wasn't sure if he could trust him.

"Have you ever held one?" Baudwin asked.

"As a matter of fact, I have," Ferrell replied. "They are also said to contain the feelings and memories of previous owners. But I never experienced this myself. Long before we were born, the Faeries gifted these stones to the Elves, which does seem to make sense."

"Why did they do that?" Baudwin asked.

"Because so little has really changed. Just like today, the Elves built many things for the Faeries. The moonstones were gifts of gratitude, given by the Faeries to the Elves. For the Elves helped build the faery shrines. They are quite distinctive. You may have even stumbled upon one near Deuona." Ferrell turned to Baudwin and gave him an odd look, one that Baudwin found quite unsettling. "Usually there is a Sun and a well together," he continued, "and you might even have seen water gushing everywhere."

Baudwin flashed back to the ruins of Coventina — the place where Loch had smashed the tablet, and the Water had come gushing out. He looked at Ferrell, who regarded him with cool suspicion. How could Ferrell know about this? He thought then of Loch — yes, of course — but why had Loch told Ferrell?

Ferrell continued, eyeing Baudwin carefully, "The shrines were known as sun circles, places where the Faeries found renewal. And legend says that the Elves would sometimes bring their moonstones as well."

"To do what?" Baudwin asked.

"I'm not sure," Ferrell replied. "But, the performance is based upon the clues we have. The meaning is in the poetry, I suppose."

Baudwin wondered how Ferrell knew all of this. How surprising that he did, since no one in Deuona had ever spoken to him about such things. He was also alarmed that Ferrell seemed to know about what happened at the ruins of Coventina. Ferrell was being awfully coy, and that made Baudwin wonder what he was up to. He would have liked to have asked more questions, but there was no time, for suddenly, the entire Show Wheel came to a grinding halt. Billowing clouds of steam came hissing out of cracks in the floor, and especially from the central column.

⚜

A door in the column opened, and the Master of Ceremonies burst out, this time wearing a burnt orange tailcoat, eggplant breeches, a gold belt, brown stockings, and dark chestnut shoes, with a hat to match. The Master of Ceremonies circled the perimeter of the stage, smiling at the audience. "We hope you're enjoying the show!" he shouted from a brass speaker horn. "How pleased we are that you're here!" Baudwin was certain that his words could be heard throughout the South Petal of the Engineerium.

"Before we continue on," he announced, "allow me to tell you about all the thrilling places that you must visit at this year's Engineerium —"

"We didn't come here for a speech," a voice called out. "Stop your selling!"

Everyone in the audience looked to see who was starting the commotion. A few rows away, Baudwin spotted a faery gent wearing a mask of leaves, lilies, and bark. Sitting next to him were several other Faeries wearing similar masks.

"Be quiet, you!" the Master of Ceremonies shouted back, as he strutted about the stage.

The masked Faery then stood up and threw a potato at him. "We know all about the Engineerium!" he shouted, as he hurled several more potatoes at the stage. A few of the other masked Faeries joined him. Instantly, a storm of vegetables went flying at the Elve — cabbages, broccoli, and bunches of rotten leeks.

"We know all about the show!" the gang of masked Faeries continued to shout. Hearing this, Baudwin wondered why they were so angry.

"Stop interrupting!" Ferrell shouted back.

Seemingly unconcerned by the uproar, the Master of Ceremonies continued on — "In the East Petal, see the Arcade and the Park, in the West, the Wonder

Show, in the North, the Water Park. And, in the Center, do not overlook our newest, most amazing exhibition."

"Hey! Take a look at this!" another masked voice cried out. With that, a mechanical boomerang whizzed through the air, emitting a long, low whistle. Upon reaching the apex of its flight, the copper projectile arched back toward the audience, narrowly missing the Elve's head. As he ducked to avoid being struck, he was hit by a rotten red tomato. The audience laughed uproariously.

"Let him speak," a member of the audience cried out. He's not *selling*, he's *telling*!"

"He's not doing *either*!" the leader of the masked Faeries yelled. With that, he bounded over the seats and up the aisle to the platform, where the Master of Ceremonies stood. A ripple of surprise coursed through the audience. He climbed the steps and wrested the speaker horn from the Master of Ceremonies, shoving him out of the way until he went careening off the platform. There the masked Faery stood, holding the speaker horn and looking like a sea Faery blowing on a conch shell. For now he had the means to speak to a very large audience, and nothing would stop him from making the most of the opportunity.

Soon, the rest of the gang had come forward, jeering at the Master of Ceremonies and blocking the steps, as they hung off the rails of the fence.

Ferrell stood up, furious. "Stop this at once," he shouted, "or I will call the Earth Guard!"

The gang of Faeries ignored him as they waited for their leader to speak. "The moonstones should not be used as entertainment, he shouted, "and especially not displayed on a platform such as this!" With that, he ground his heel into a tomato that had been hurled onto the stage.

"The Show Wheel is deserving of respect!" Ferrell shouted.

Mimicking Ferrell's voice, the rest of the gang called out, repeating earlier parts of his speech: "As you will see, the old ways are *not* separate from the new ways." Over and over they repeated this, all the while swinging from the platform fence, jeering and laughing.

In the aisles, Baudwin could see Earth Guards approaching. Obviously, they had heard the uproar. "That's enough!" Ferrell shouted again. "Stop him — *now!*"

With that, the rather portly Master of Ceremonies slipped past the faery gang, and then shimmied back up onto the platform. He lunged at the faery leader, and ripped the mask from his face. Baudwin was shocked, for there stood someone he knew quite well.

"Lugh!" he gasped, wondering why his friend would have taken such a chance.

Anxiously, Baudwin looked at Ferrell to see what he would do next. Surprisingly, Ferrell did nothing more.

"Get off the platform, you hooligans, Ferrell shouted, "or I will have the lot of you arrested!"

At Lugh's signal, all of his friends exited the platform, shot down the aisle, and disappeared from the Show Wheel as fast as they could. Ferrell motioned for his Earth Guard to desist. He seemed more intent on getting on with the entertainment than pursuing Lugh. With ill-concealed agitation, he tightened his bootstraps, waiting for the show to resume. Baudwin hid a smile, for again Lugh had gotten away with his subversive shenanigans.

Steam came hissing out of the floor of the stage, and the Show Wheel began turning again.

The Master of Ceremonies pressed his horn to his lips. He then paraded around the entire stage, shouting at the top of his lungs, "Play fun and challenging games at the Arcade! Go on thrill-packed rides at the Park! See ancient, highly prized artifacts at the Wonder Show! Ride chutes in the Water Park that are faster and more exciting than the river! And, whatever you do, you *must* visit the Center, to see our newest, most spectacular display — *The Tree of Innovation!*"

Baudwin looked at the faces in the crowd. They seemed slightly less entertained than they had been earlier — almost as if all the mechanical wonders were beside the point. Ferrell seemed to notice this also, and scowled. Lugh had left his mark. Baudwin kept quiet, being careful not to fuel Ferrell's ire.

The Master of Ceremonies removed his cap and bowed deeply. "Thank you, one and all." To the sounds of both cheers and jeers, he turned briskly and exited the stage.

Above the din of all the cheering and clapping, Baudwin couldn't help but wonder, *Could the Elves possibly do anything more grand?*"

☙❧

As if to answer his question, four sets of staffs rose from beneath the floor, one in each quarter of the stage. All the staffs were hewn from red oak and gleamed brightly, for they were trimmed in the middle and at both ends with one of four metals: Platinum, Gold, Silver, or Copper.

Seeing them, Baudwin remembered the debate rod he had fetched for Seanán and Fearghus at the Four Rivers Faire, trimmed with all four metals at both ends. How different this charming display had been from that brutal altercation. For here, the Elves still respected and honored what their staffs meant to them, and would not let their actions get out of hand.

"And now, behold the Four Elven Orders," the Master of Ceremonies announced, seeing the staffs appear. Out of the four doors streamed the four orders, their costumes shimmering like wheat gilded by the summer Sun. All four orders wore the finest silk, in the same shade of light yellow ochre.

Once again, Baudwin counted the number of couples in each order: Eight from the Platinum Order, the Gold Order, the Silver Order, and the Copper Order. Each order dashed to a set of staffs that matched the metal they were wearing, removed them from the stands, and then formed a circle in a quarter of the stage.

As they made their way to their places, each was a sight to behold. The ladies wore skirts and blouses, and the gents, doublets and breeches. Chains, medallions, and buttons flashed from their clothing, and the buckles of their boots were crafted from Copper, Silver, Gold, or Platinum. Seeing them in their regalia, the indefatigable audience cheered and then clapped loudly in time to the music.

Resuming their places in a quarter of the stage, all four orders began to perform yet another step dance, their staffs held high. As they danced, they sang:

> If you seek learning about other realms
> Come to Platinum Spires, my friend
> Our Druids speak of ancient truths
> Of the Light their words portend
>
> If you seek riches or a good name
> Come to Gold Haven now, my friend
> Our rulers hailed from every age
> To their reach there was no end
>
> If you seek a sword, chain, or sprocket
> Come to Silver Forge now, my friend
> Our smithies pound on every metal
> On their skill you can depend
>
> If you seek music, song, or dance
> Come to Copper Caves now, my friend
> Our artists will send your spirits soaring
> Their many gifts you will commend

Everyone performed the same dance in all four parts of the rotating stage, and then something new happened.

Four cauldrons made of red obsidian rose from beneath the floor, one in each quarter of the stage. Each one rested upon a three-legged stand, crafted from the four metals.

Baudwin watched closely as the eight couples of the Copper Order moved toward the cauldron directly in front of him and Ferrell. As they did, flames shot into the air from the center of the vessel.

Fire, Baudwin thought with a shudder. For although Water could douse a Fire instantly, this was small comfort to a water Faery, as Fire could also boil Water into oblivion.

"Do not flinch, Baudwin," Ferrell said, noticing his discomfort. "The Elves know what they're doing. Everything they build begins with metals and ends with fire, which is their way."

As Baudwin shifted uncomfortably in his seat, Ferrell continued to speak:

"We do not join with our elements the same way you do. In fact, we don't join at all, we *separate* with our metals, and then we forge our individual paths. And finally, we temper our intentions. The Four Orders facilitate this process. For the metals are as sacred to us, as the elements are to you."

"Separating, forging, and —?" Baudwin asked.

"*Tempering,*" Ferrell finished.

"We water Faeries join, course, and hone."

"Yes — I know. And, just as you Faeries must hone your intentions, so must we temper ours."

Baudwin found it curious that both Faeries and Elves ended with their intentions, even though the way they discovered their life paths was so different. There had to be a reason why, but he had no idea what that could be.

"We certainly are *not* the same," Ferrell continued, seeming to know what Baudwin was thinking. "And yet, we complement each other so well. Which is why we must rediscover our common past through the Great Endeavor. Only then, will *Tír na nÓg* heal."

Baudwin turned to watch the fire dance unfold. One of the ladies held her staff in the center of the cauldron, until the top became a flaming torch. Turning toward her partner, she touched her staff to his, lighting the top. He then turned to the next lady to light her staff. From there, the flame was passed from lady to gent, to lady to gent, until all sixteen torches were lit. The cauldron then receded back into the floor.

As the Show Wheel kept turning, all the orders continued dancing. Baudwin could see the Silver Order coming into view. He waited, spellbound, as he watched them move.

All eight couples of the Silver Order stood in a circle, holding their staffs above their heads, first lady, then gent, first lady, then gent, and so on. The circle began to rotate. The ladies pointed the flaming ends of their staffs toward the center of the circle, and the gents pointed their flaming ends away from the center. The gents then took a step forward. They pressed their staffs against the ladies' staffs, igniting both their own and the ladies' unlit ends. Soon, everyone in the circle held a staff with both ends flaming.

All the orders kept dancing, and the Show Wheel kept turning. Soon, Baudwin saw the Gold Order coming into view.

The circle continued turning, like a blazing hoop. All eight couples of the Gold Order moved away from each other, giving everyone room to dance. They whirled in circles, twirling their staffs faster and faster as the flames burned brighter and brighter, leaving undulating trails of Light. The sound of the music and the movement of the Fire reached a fever pitch, imbuing not only their spirits, but those of the audience as well, with Fire and Light.

All the orders kept dancing, and the Show Wheel kept turning. Finally, Baudwin saw the Platinum Order coming into view.

At the same time, the center column descended beneath the stage. The Show Wheel now allowed the audience to see all four orders performing at the same time — Platinum, Gold, Silver, and Copper — each of them twirling lighted staffs, faster and faster. All danced their final steps, ending with such a flourish that the Faeries could not contain their enthusiasm. They jumped to their feet, waving their arms, clapping and cheering.

"Now you have seen the roots of our ways," Ferrell declared, as he also jumped to his feet, clapping. Baudwin joined in as well, nodding and smiling.

The show having ended, the audience began to leave. Baudwin followed Ferrell up the aisle. Soon they were back riding in the carriage. Baudwin thought about all he had seen: the Earth, Water, Air and Fire Guards, protectors of the elements, moonstones that changed from black to white and showed the Elves their feelings, and finally the four Orders — Copper, Silver, Gold, and Platinum.

More than anything, Baudwin was fascinated with the Orders. For they were surprisingly similar to the ways of his tribe. He had to know more.

"Do the Elves struggle to temper their intentions?" Baudwin asked. "We Faeries struggle to hone ours."

Ferrell nodded his head. "Yes, in that way we are not so different."

"But, why is that?" Baudwin asked.

He studied Ferrell, searching for clues, wondering if perhaps the Luminary could shed some light upon the subject. Quietly, he waited for Ferrell to speak.

"Before the Great Befalling," Ferrell began, "and before the *cogadh*, there was a long period of decline. According to legend, thousands of years before we came to be, the Fae did not struggle with their intentions at all. Then something happened, but no one is sure what. The Great Befalling came at the end of the decline. *Tír na nÓg* fell into utter disarray. Then Govannon rose up, and our Great Endeavor began. My belief is that under his leadership, we will all be healed."

Ferrell's explanation left Baudwin with many more questions than answers. For, if the Elves were now the builders of the Great Endeavor, why then did they struggle to temper their intentions? If they were so uniquely capable of building great wonders, it seemed strange to Baudwin that they would be struggling with their intentions at all. Unless, that is, their capacity to build cities and temper their intentions truly had nothing to do with each other. And if the Faeries had once been the dreamers of *Tír na nÓg*, why then could they not hone their intentions, if only to rise above what they claimed was a Great Befalling? He had to know, so he asked:

"It can't merely be coincidence that both of our kind were struck down in the same way? — can it?"

"No," Ferrell replied. "Yet, there must be a reason for why things went the way they did. You Faeries are of the Moon, and spring from the elements, and we Elves are of the Sun, and spring from the metals. Perhaps these celestial bodies have cursed us all for our transgressions — the Sun with anger, and the Moon with anguish, so that we Elves cannot properly temper our intentions, and you Faeries cannot properly hone yours. I cannot speak for your tribe, but this is what our clan believes. For the Elves have always known that all the metals come from the Sun and the stars in the sky. So why wouldn't the Sun have its way with us for all of our failings?"

Baudwin had never heard the beliefs of the Elves before. They were so unlike those of the Faeries, who were said to have been born of the moonlight that shone on the elements in *Tír na nÓg*. Had the Moon become morose, watching the tribes flailing and failing? And had the Sun become angry? Were the Faeries as cursed as Ferrell said, never to hone their intentions and find fulfillment in their lives?

"So the Elves are really just as lost as the Faeries," Baudwin said. *Which is what I unwittingly told the Elves at the Four Rivers Faire,* he thought. "My kin barely speak of this anymore."

"Indeed," Ferrell replied. "Your kin probably can't even tell the difference between a gusher and a water spirit either."

Hearing this, Baudwin nervously looked away, becoming silent. Again, Ferrell seemed to be baiting him, but he had no idea why. After a while, he looked out the window of the coach. Again, he was in the Nechtain Quarter.

"This is where I must get off," he said.

"We can ride further," Ferrell said. "I know where Lugh lives."

"Thank you all the same," Baudwin replied, "but I would rather walk the rest of the way. I need space to consider what you so graciously spoke about to me. I hope you understand."

Ferrell looked askance at Baudwin, as though their previous conversation had meant nothing. "Have it your way then, Son of Kelven. Take your space, for I have all the time I need."

The coach came to a stop, and Baudwin got out. "Thank you for taking me to such a fine entertainment," he said. "I certainly understand more about the Elves now than I did before."

"You're welcome," Ferrell replied, staring blankly ahead. As the coach sped away, he suddenly stuck his head out of the window, smiling. "Prepare yourself," he announced. "I have one more surprise for you tomorrow. See you then."

"I look forward to it," Baudwin replied, masking his unease. Walking back to Lugh's he thought, *All this talk about intentions, and I still have no idea what Ferrell's intention is for me.*

Chapter 27

A TOUR OF THE CITY

The next day was Dorchadía,[1] the second-to-last day of the week. Baudwin was in the atrium, helping Lugh tend to his garden. As Lugh tipped his watering can, a shower of droplets soaked a row of ferns. He then placed some soil into a large glazed pot. Baudwin could see the plants were having a calming effect on him, and that his usual dithers were gone. All was well in the early afternoon sunlight, and lunch had been delicious. Not wanting to ruin Lugh's pleasant mood, Baudwin hesitated before sharing his experience of the Show Wheel. He decided to weigh his words carefully, for Lugh, like the lily he was about to plant, required careful handling — especially if what he heard sounded contrary to what he believed to be true.

Baudwin remembered the Show Wheel. How surprised he was that the old ways of the Elves ran as deeply as those of the Faeries. Perhaps if Lugh had spent more time watching the show, rather than creating a ruckus, he would have seen the truth of this. Baudwin again wondered why Ferrell had been so lenient when the uproar erupted. He was, after all, a Luminary, and a commander under Govannon — King of the Elves — and Lugh had escaped with only a warning. Perhaps Ferrell was waiting for a more opportune time to dispense justice, or hopefully, he merely looked at Lugh as a petty annoyance.

Baudwin thought about Ferrell. He certainly had been more forthright as they witnessed the elven show. In a way, Baudwin couldn't blame Ferrell for having seemed so cold and imperious when they first met. Baudwin and his friends had, after all, created a lot of trouble at the Deuona Engineerium, crashing into the food tent and fighting with Loch. Even in the past few days, he and Lugh had fooled Glas into giving him a job, believing they could also fool Ferrell. Of course, Ferrell hadn't been taken in, and he had told him as much when they were riding to the Show Wheel. Knowing this, could he really blame Ferrell for reining them in? Baudwin decided to give Ferrell the benefit of the doubt.

Baudwin wasn't about to tell Lugh any of this. He knew Lugh regarded him as a promising successor of the Water Guild. Lugh assumed Baudwin would

---

[1] Pronounced [DORCHUH-THEE-UH] Darkday, equivalent to Saturday, the sixth day of the week

eventually see everything his way, including his nonsensical claim that the Elves were trying to control the Faeries' intentions. Yet, Baudwin wasn't sure that Lugh was the kind of Guilder he should aspire to. For someone joined to his current, Lugh was simply too rash for his own good. Added to this, Baudwin doubted that Lugh saw any virtue in the Elves. Lugh struck Baudwin as someone who was fighting something he didn't really understand. Having mulled all this over, Baudwin knew he couldn't let Lugh plant another lily before asking him a very serious question.

"Did you know that the Elves must temper their intentions the same way that we must hone ours?"

"Why are you asking me that?" Lugh asked, fixing his eyes on his planting.

"Although, unlike us, they don't seem to take the old ways very seriously anymore."

Lugh remained silent, and kept working.

"Isn't that interesting?" Baudwin asked. "About their intentions? I keep wondering why that is. I never would have guessed that the Elves struggle just as we do. It's also surprising that I learned this from an Elve, and not from my own father. How very odd."

"You seem different," Lugh declared, annoyed. "Now you're even more easily taken in by everything you hear."

Baudwin did not reply.

Sighing, Lugh put down his trowel. "All I mean is that you're willing to be even-handed with the Elves — not just your own kind. Perhaps I should as well."

Encouraged, Baudwin pressed on. "The Elves have four Guards that protect the Earth, Water, Air and Fire. Just as we love the elements, they try to protect them."

Hearing this, Lugh shook his head, forgetting what he had just said. "They've fooled you, but they haven't fooled me!" he exclaimed. "Don't you know? Before the Great Befalling there *were* no Guards."

"No, I didn't," Baudwin replied.

"There's a lot you don't know," Lugh continued. "What they're really trying to do is to *control* the Earth, Water, Air, and Fire, just like they try to control everything else. Since when are the Elves interested in the elements? They don't protect the Fire; they protect us *from* the Fire."

Baudwin wasn't sure what to say, for Lugh had changed his opinion so quickly. Still, he was determined to convince him otherwise.

"Yes," he persisted, "they do protect us from the Fire, but perhaps once upon a time such things meant more than that. Perhaps they were also trying to protect the Fire *itself*, somehow."

Lugh stood up, finished with his planting. "The Elves never wanted to protect the Fire, and their moonstones have never made them feel anything but the jealous hatred in their own hearts. They covet *everything*, especially *Tír Éirí Sióg*, which is why they've come here. I'm surprised you —"

"How unfortunate that you didn't see the whole show," Baudwin cut in. "After you ran away, the Four Elven Orders appeared, and their fire dance was truly inspiring."

"Was that before or after Ferrell's lickspittle came to sell us on the wonders of the Tree of Innovation?" Lugh asked.

Baudwin stopped speaking, amused, yet taken aback by Lugh's outburst.

"And by the way," Lugh continued, "what, if anything, did you find out about Magniglow?"

Exasperated as he was with Lugh for not taking an interest in elven culture, Baudwin yet decided to be patient with him. *A straight answer,* he thought, *is best.* "I watched Olaf take apart a dynamo," he replied.

"Yes?" Lugh asked, his interest piqued.

"The inside had a cobalt magnet," Baudwin said. "He told me magnets create current."

"Current like the Water?"

"No," Baudwin corrected, smiling. "Not that kind. Current coming from a dynamo *is* Magniglow. The magnet turns around the copper, and makes Magniglow somehow."

For a moment Lugh appeared to be taken in by Baudwin's description. Smiling faintly, he stared at the pool of lilies. Quickly, his mood changed.

"What else did you notice," he asked with great suspicion, "when you opened the device? Did you feel changed in any way?"

Baudwin was irritated by the question, but decided to remain civil. "Actually, no," he replied. "I didn't feel any different."

"Then you must keep looking," Lugh insisted. Furtively, he scanned the atrium, as if they were being watched. "We're very close. That device holds a dark secret."

Baudwin had heard enough. "Actually, Lugh," he began, "I must object. Olaf showed me that the power of Magniglow also comes from ordinary things — even *potatoes.*"

Lugh gave Baudwin an incredulous look, and then let out a peal of laughter.

"Potatoes!" he exclaimed. "That's ridiculous!"

"Ridiculous or not," Baudwin said sardonically, "I *saw* it."

Again, Lugh was caught off guard, which only demonstrated to Baudwin how little he actually knew about the Elves.

"Oh, come now, Baudwin," he implored. "He was just putting you on."

Baudwin smiled, for he knew that what he said next would stifle Lugh's ignorance, if only for a moment.

"No," he began, pausing before speaking further, for he wanted Lugh to absorb the full impact of his words. "He plugged wires into them and they turned on a magniglow bulb." Facing Lugh, Baudwin smiled again, for he could see that upon hearing the news, Lugh appeared to be listing to one side of his lilies, having run aground in the conversation.

"I don't believe it," he said flatly.

Unperturbed, Baudwin dealt him the final blow. "In fact, you've been *eating* Magniglow your entire Life."

With that, Lugh stabbed at the soil in another pot with his trowel. "I had my reservations about fooling Glas into hiring you," he said. "Obviously, you didn't take your responsibility seriously."

Lugh's upset did not dissuade Baudwin from pressing him even further. "Don't you see?" he asked earnestly. "They *can't* be controlling our intentions, because they can't even master their own. They're *just* like us."

"What I *see* is that this was all a mistake," Lugh said.

Baudwin became resentful. They had, after all, made a bargain. He had held up his end and investigated Magniglow, and now Lugh was being stubborn. "A *mistake*?" he asked. "Like that stunt you pulled at the Show Wheel yesterday? You knew I was going to be there. What were you trying to prove?"

"The Show Wheel is an abomination," Lugh replied. "Ferrell just wants to demonstrate the old ways so he can *hypnotize* you with the new ones!"

"Oh, come now, Lugh —" Baudwin began.

Before he could continue, a coach pulled up in front of the dome home, right next to the atrium. Immediately, Baudwin knew who had to be riding inside, for he recognized the color and the coach Elve from the day before.

"Who in all of *Tír na nÓg*, could *that* be?" Lugh asked, as he opened the atrium door. As Ferrell stepped out of the coach, Lugh became still, looking very tense.

Baudwin stepped up to his friend. "Don't worry," he muttered under his breath. "If he's come for you, I will defend you. We are — after all — with the Water."

"Lugh!" Ferrell shouted through the atrium, as he strode toward them. "So good to see you. Why so pale? You mustn't look so agitated. I haven't come to haul you off to work the mines of Copper Caves."

Lugh relaxed somewhat. "What a surprise, Ferrell," he said, smiling amiably through his upset. "Have you come alone — with just a driver and a coach Elve?"

"Not completely alone," Ferrell replied. Baudwin was surprised to hear a lilt in Ferrell's voice, but he couldn't imagine why he was so cheery. He hoped that Ferrell wasn't planning to punish Lugh for interrupting the Show Wheel.

"Before I tell you why," Ferrell continued, "let me begin by saying: on this *wonderful* day, I thought I should. . ." He paused for a moment, stretching his arms to the sky, taking in the Sun's rays. In so doing, he looked as if he might burst with confidence. For Elves always enjoyed taking in the light of the Sun, and he was no exception.

"I thought I should *visit*," he said, completing his sentence.

"Then you should have informed us first," Lugh said. "We're watering our plants right now, which is how we water Faeries tend to our element."

Ferrell ignored Lugh's insulting tone. As he was about to speak, Moonrise shot over Lugh's shoulder and out of the atrium, cooing happily. Everyone's eyes followed the bird. Baudwin wondered what had gotten into his pet, until he saw two forms hop out of the coach. He gasped. This had to be Ferrell's surprise. *No*, he thought. There were *surprises*, and then there were shocks of fate — ones that struck swiftly like lightning bolts.

"Criofan! Matha!" he shouted. "*WHATEVER* are you doing here?"

The three friends stared at each other in disbelief, and then raced toward one another. Upon meeting, they huddled like teammates — as was their custom — with their arms around each other's shoulders and the tops of their heads touching. Laughing, they remained linked together for several moments. Finally, Criofan spoke.

"Ferrell sent for us," he said.

"Ferrell?" Baudwin asked. He then raised his head to look at Ferrell, who seemed to be very pleased with himself.

"Baudwin!" Matha exclaimed. "We were so worried! You must tell us everything!"

"But before you do," Criofan said, studying Baudwin's appearance, "I must point out that your travels haven't been very kind to your clothes. The colors look so dark and dingy. You must let us get you some new ones while we're here."

"They certainly aren't as old and worn as Matha's jacket," Baudwin said, chortling. He then hugged Matha saying, "You certainly are a sight for sore eyes!"

"I would say that Criofan's eyes are sore, looking at what you're wearing," Matha quipped. "Isn't that right, Criofan?" he asked.

"Indeed!" Criofan exclaimed, grinning. "Now tell us about what brought you here and why."

Baudwin didn't know where to begin, for he didn't want to reveal too much in front of Ferrell. He hadn't expected to see his friends so soon, and under such unusual circumstances. Added to that, he wasn't sure whether he was more shocked or excited. Ferrell stood next to them, smiling, and Lugh seemed quite surprised as well. Criofan and Matha just seemed genuinely happy to see him. All the while, Lugh studied Ferrell with considerable mistrust.

Again the friends greeted each other, hugging and laughing. As yet, there was no time for long explanations, just smiles and simple questions.

"We're so happy to see you're safe!" Matha exclaimed.

"All you left us was a piddling note," Criofan chided him.

Baudwin felt a pang of guilt. Had the hastiness of his departure been ill-considered, perhaps even heartless? He thought then of Kelven and Seamus, and quickly turned his mind away from them. All he could do was make the obvious small talk.

"How did you get here?" he asked.

Hearing the question, Ferrell took the opportunity to seize the moment. He stepped toward them, looking again like a blue heron, just as he had when he followed them to the Hop and Hit, before Baudwin fought Loch. "Getting these two here was easy," he continued, smiling slyly at Baudwin. "I only had to send a few Earth Guards to fetch them. Turning to Lugh he said, laughing, "Perhaps I simply took pity on them." He then turned to Matha and Criofan, continuing his thought. "Or perhaps I simply didn't want you to wonder any longer what had happened to him."

"I would say that was very noble of you," Baudwin said brightly.

Lugh looked suspiciously at Ferrell. "Noble indeed," he sniffed.

They all talked quickly. Baudwin spoke of his trip to Four Falls in the back of Earnan's wagon, the riot at the Four Rivers Faire, and sleeping by the docks in the Cyhiraeth Quarter. He then told them how he had run into Lugh, and gotten a job with Glas. Finally, he mentioned seeing the Show Wheel.

"The show was astounding!" he exclaimed. "The Elves are just like us. We love the elements, and their four Guards protect them. And they struggle as well — to find their intentions."

Hearing this, Ferrell nodded approvingly. Criofan and Matha gave Baudwin a puzzled look. Baudwin seemed surprisingly different to them after such a short time. They both sensed a breach among them — where none had existed before — and they struggled to understand why.

"What an interesting way to speak of the Elves," Criofan said.

"Interesting indeed," Matha added. Neither of them sounded convinced of their own remarks.

Ferrell then spoke, pouring honey into the conversation, instead of more salt. "Extremely interesting," he said. "For as you must know, we all have much in common, and much to heal in the realm. It is for this reason that I brought you all together," he added, as he looked at Lugh. Watching him, Baudwin could tell that Lugh was also unconvinced.

"Perhaps we don't need you to bring us anywhere," Lugh replied, "for one does not bring the currents of a river together — they simply flow."

Annoyed by the comment, Ferrell continued, "The Elves are not your enemy, Lugh. In fact, we want you to be part of the Great Endeavor."

Criofan and Matha were caught off guard by the conversation, for they had been intent only upon reuniting with their friend, and now seemed to be caught up in a strange consideration. Baudwin could tell that they were wondering what they were getting themselves into. Yet, he could also tell that they were very happy to be with him again.

Determined to win them over, Ferrell continued, "Soon, we will have the Grand Unveiling in Four Falls. I've arranged for all the great families of the water Faeries to come see the wonders of Magniglow." Ferrell then pointed to Baudwin, Matha, and Criofan. "I'm also planning for these three to be the first faery acrobats ever to perform at such an event."

"Not without their agreement you won't!" Lugh exclaimed hotly. Seeing the menacing look in Ferrell's eyes, he went quiet.

"Of course — it's up to them," Ferrell countered. "Yet, do tell me — why do you find my invitation so terrible?"

"I'll be glad to tell you —" Lugh began, but Baudwin interrupted him.

"Please, Lugh, say no more," he said. Looking at Matha and Criofan, he happily announced, "We'll do it — won't we? And I will help with the Grand Unveiling. Anything to heal the divide between the Faeries and Elves."

Matha and Criofan nodded agreeably, not wanting Ferrell to know any more about what they really thought.

"You don't know what you're agreeing to," Lugh countered. "How can you, when you don't even know your own roots? All of you must come with me. I will show you the rivers and their quarters. After that, you will be able to decide between them and what this *mountebank* is offering."

"I would say your words are rather harsh," Baudwin said, looking nervously at Ferrell. If Ferrell was insulted, he wasn't revealing any of it to the four Faeries.

Seeing this, Baudwin continued, "But perhaps we should also go with you, just for the sheer adventure of it." Looking at Matha and Criofan he added, "And for concord and commerce, isn't that right?" Again, his friends nodded in agreement, and Baudwin could see how much they wanted to speak to him more privately, away from Ferrell's persistent probing.

Everyone became silent, and then Matha spoke. "I for one don't know what the Grand Unveiling is, but I certainly would like to see this magnificent city. I'm not sure what Lugh has in store for us, but knowing concord, it's always good to hear both sides of a story before coming to conclusions."

Hearing this, Criofan had to offer his opinion as well. "It's always best to learn about a place from someone who actually lives there, wouldn't you say?" As he spoke, he looked at Ferrell, not averting his gaze.

"Let Lugh show you your history then," Ferrell said. "I have no objection to that. Afterward, I will reveal my plan to help find Baudwin's mother."

Lugh stifled a sneer. Baudwin beamed with excitement. Looking at Criofan and Matha he could tell they had no idea what was going on.

Matha then put in, "We must thank the Moon for Baudwin's good luck." Criofan nodded, adding, "And we're lucky as well. Without Ferrell, no one would have known where to find Baudwin."

Moonrise dropped onto Baudwin's shoulder, cooing earnestly.

As if to echo their sentiments, Baudwin said to Ferrell, "And I would be most grateful for any help that you could give me in this regard." Matha and Criofan nodded yet again.

"Very well," Ferrell said. "Then the matter is settled. We will all be friends, won't we? All of you, go and see the city, and we'll make other arrangements later at the Engineerium."

With that, Ferrell straightened his jacket and briskly walked to the coach. As he rode away, the four water Faeries could hear the wheels striking the cobblestones, going *clackity clack*.

Lugh shook his head, muttering, "There's nothing lucky about getting *his* help."

⚬✦⚬

A short time later, the faerie friends were exploring the Nechtain Quarter, running through fountains and around corners, laughing and shouting. Baudwin, Criofan, and Matha did roundoffs and backflips, almost knocking into apple carts as they went. Bystanders jumped off the sidewalk to avoid the three rambunctious acrobats.

Lugh had already told Criofan and Matha that of course, they were going to stay with him. He also pilloried Ferrell for not bothering to tell him that he would be bringing them to his house. "He should study the Faery Code of Manners," he grumbled. He then recited:

A Faery must not visit uninvited

For he may leave his loved ones feeling slighted

Or find his name and reputation blighted

And all his foes and enemies delighted

"That does seem rather harsh," Baudwin said, "to have one's reputation blighted simply for being a party crasher."

"Not if you know what purpose the manner serves," Lugh said, "which is to protect Faeries from such things. For who could fault a faery lady or gent for being involved in a dispute if they were *invited* to an affair, but chose not to interfere? Whereas if they were *uninvited*, they certainly could be blamed."

"I've certainly never heard of that manner," Matha said, "and my father is the Primary of Concord. But I do see its merit."

Hearing this, Lugh smirked. "This is why the Elves are always causing so much trouble, storming into this and interfering with that. I for one believe they are given far too much rein, imposing all their rules and regulations upon us without following them as well. Something must be done about it. Don't you agree, Baudwin?"

Much to Lugh's displeasure, Baudwin did not reply. Nor did his friends. They were all having too much fun enjoying the sights of the city, and did not want to belabor the issue. Lugh did not press the subject, and the four Faeries continued on their way.

Criofan and Matha were a flood of questions. For although they had been to Four Falls before, they hadn't gone since they were very young, and mostly on short trips, when their parents were doing business for the Guild. Criofan seemed to remember the most about the city, as his family was so involved in commerce. As usual, Matha wanted to know everything about the history. Lugh began with what he knew best.

He pointed to a statue of a Faery holding a salmon.

"Salmons are considered wise, because they always know to return to the river whence they were born."

Hearing this, Baudwin perked up, saying, "That's what Earnan told me, the wood Faery who drove me here. He said that salmons are born joined to their currents — coursing and knowing their intentions. Before they are alevins, they know their fates lie with their home river, and so they always return there before they pass on."

Lugh nodded, adding, "Yes, but the wisdom of the salmon goes far deeper than that. Tell me, what is the significance of a salmon returning home and always knowing its course?"

The three Faeries flashed quizzical looks. None were sure.

"That home is most meaningful," Matha guessed.

"That forgetting the way will make you look foolish," Criofan said.

"No, you've forgotten what matters most," Lugh replied. "When a salmon returns to its spawning grounds, what happens?"

"The salmon passes to Annwyn," Baudwin said.

"Yes!" Lugh exclaimed. "What then, is so important about a salmon understanding this when it is born?"

None hazarded a guess.

"Because all salmons know that Life in *Tír na nÓg* is only a preparation for a passage, which begins when they return to the source of a river, so that they can pass to Annwyn and be reborn."

"And they also give birth before they pass," Baudwin added.

"Indeed," Lugh said.

None said anything after this, for each understood how sacred the salmon was, and the lesson they were being asked to ponder. Lugh explained to them that the Source salmons returned to was much more than the mouth of a river. The Source was beyond words and could not be named. The lessons of the four rivers only alluded to the Source's meaning because ultimately, all the lessons of the rivers were also beyond words and could not be named. Yet the lessons of joining, coursing, and honing were always named — if one was to conquer the personal challenges within one's own nature.

Baudwin wondered then what Source he would ultimately return to. Perhaps someplace far away. His friends sensed what he was thinking.

Criofan gave Baudwin a mischievous grin, saying, "Then there's hope, even for you, Baudwin. Perhaps one day you'll return — to your home river — in Deuona."

Baudwin glanced at Criofan. Beneath his friend's humor, he could feel the pain in his heart. Quickly, Baudwin looked away, not wanting to lock eyes with him, as he once would have done.

"Yes," Matha agreed. "There is hope — for we know you're as wise as a salmon."

"He certainly is wise," Lugh chuckled, "for he knows how to trick an Elve into giving him a job, even when there isn't one."

"What does he mean, Baudwin?" Criofan asked.

Baudwin knew that he hadn't actually tricked Ferrell into telling Glas to give him a job at the magniglow booth. Ferrell had seen right through him. But he didn't want to look like a fool in front of Matha and Criofan, so he said nothing more. "Enough about salmons," Baudwin said. "Let's see the Danu Quarter."

Lugh raised his hand and shook his head. "We've only just begun in the Nechtain. We must stay a while longer. This is — after all — my home." As he spoke, Lugh pointed to the Nechtain, saying, "This great river is sourced from Lake Airmid,[2] near the home of the wood Faeries, which is likely why your friend, Earnan, knew of its history."

Ambling along the Upper Nechtain Road next to the river, they passed small shops, alleyways, and large dome-crested buildings. The Sun was still approaching its zenith. Finally, they reached a square with a very large domed building, and an enormous salmon before its entrance, carved from green Connemara marble. Baudwin stopped and gazed at the giant fish, remembering the river guardians at the dam where he lived. Like them, the salmon seemed to speak to him of deeper mysteries that he could not even begin to understand. *Whatever am I doing?* he wondered. For unlike salmons, who knew where they

---

[2] Pronounced [AHR-ih-ved]

were going, he knew no such thing. He and his friends stood without speaking, gazing at the herald of the Water that rose before them.

Lugh broke the silence. "This is the Nechtain guild house, where we conduct the affairs of this quarter. That is," he added, smiling, "when I'm not shut away in my home with my lilies. There's a building like this in each quarter of the city."

"What if we had buildings like these in Deuona?" Croifan asked, looking appreciatively at the tall dome-shaped edifice. "Then our affairs would seem very far-reaching indeed."

Baudwin could tell that Matha was not as impressed with the grandeur of the architecture. "Perhaps then, the history of Deuona would seem equally great," Baudwin said, trying to elicit a comment from Criofan.

Lugh ignored their banter. "I brought you three here so you would understand that your history *is* as great. Living in Deuona, you never get to see what our tribe has really accomplished. This guild house, and the other three in the Danu, Cyhiraeth, and Condatis Quarters, are just as much yours as any other water Faery's. All of us are brothers and sisters of the Water. My quarter understands this better than any other. For we never forget the common folk."

Baudwin and his friends looked again at the building, taking in what Lugh had said. The ways of the Water displayed there were also their own ways, and they felt less separate from their surroundings.

Lugh then spoke again, making sure he had their full attention. "All of this is much more than a tour." Looking at Baudwin, he added, "The lessons of the Water are all that really serve our kind. We must never relinquish our loyalty to the Water and the old ways."

Baudwin didn't like his tone. Lugh seemed as if he were trying to trick Baudwin into giving up on the Elves before he had barely learned anything from them.

"Yes, loyalty comes from what we already know," Baudwin countered, "but it also comes from what we have yet to discover. I believe the Elves can help us as well."

Now Lugh became cross. "You barely understand the lessons of the Water," he scolded. "You don't yet know its full wisdom, which is why I've started you off here — where such things naturally flow."

"I know enough," Baudwin blurted. "For forty years, I searched for the Water, until it finally came to me. And then, it led me nowhere. Even its agents were of little help. . . " His voice trailed off as he thought then of the water spirit and her wrath.

Criofan and Matha became concerned, while Lugh was astonished by Baudwin's outburst.

"The Water came to you?" Lugh asked. "How could that possibly be? You told me you were never joined to your current."

"Is that *so* hard to believe?" Baudwin asked, incensed. "Just ask Matha. He was there right afterward. The Water touched me in a way that is rare — but it didn't help me find my mother. All I got was pain and disappointment. Tell me — what would *you* do if you strove so long and had *nothing* to show for it?"

Lugh was still taken aback, but the Guild Leader had many seasons on Baudwin, and so he replied, "I know you aren't a liar. I believe you, as spectacular as your claims seem. I know you must be telling me the truth. I'm even a little jealous — who wouldn't be? But what I don't understand is this: After all that has happened, why would you abandon the Water — for the *Elves*?"

"I *haven't*," Baudwin insisted. "I'm here, aren't I? I just believe that they may have a solution to my problem."

"With *currents* and *potatoes*?" Lugh asked, incredulously.

"I'm sure Ferrell has more to offer than that," Baudwin replied angrily.

Baudwin and Lugh stopped speaking, and Matha then chimed in.

"Come now," he began, "we've only just been reunited. I'm sure Baudwin would never abandon the Water entirely. He's just been through a lot, and hasn't fully found his way."

Criofan nodded in agreement, for he wanted Baudwin to see that he was also on his side. "Do you work in this quarter?" he asked Lugh, hoping to change the subject.

Baudwin decided to stop arguing.

"Yes," Lugh replied, "off and on, when I'm needed. We have primaries here of concord, commerce, and Water — just like you do at home."

"Back home, we have only one Guild Leader — Baudwin's grandfather — but he doesn't have a large building like this," Criofan said. "And as for how he leads, he usually defers to the primaries — or at least he tries to," he added, smiling.

"The way we conduct our affairs is not so different," Lugh added. "If Seamus lived here, he would be in one of these buildings as well, and would probably be doing a better job than any other in Four Falls."

"You think so?" Baudwin asked, his anger all but gone.

"I *know* so," Lugh said. "Don't shrug off your heritage so easily. Your family has both a guild leader *and* a primary, which is likely why Ferrell has taken such a keen interest in you."

Baudwin knew that questioning Lugh about this would only start another argument, so he said nothing. Yet, he did take issue with him. For if all Ferrell was interested in was his family's influence in the Water Guild, then Ferrell was indeed playing him for a fool. This idea was not one that Baudwin wanted to entertain, especially after Ferrell had said he would make a plan to find his mother.

Satisfied with what he had shown them, Lugh proceeded westward toward the Danu Quarter. They took the Lower Danu Road, passing over a bridge, and then they were there. Where they had been seeing salmons, they now saw Moons — shining balls of Light, woven into tapestries, carved on buildings, and set into tree branches.

"This is the Danu Quarter," Lugh announced proudly. "Some say this quarter is the crown jewel of the water Faeries. For the Danu River flows from Lake Belanus, which is sourced from the mountains around Bright Portal. This ancient city is said to be where the Light of the realm was once the strongest. The light Faeries used to dwell upon its shores, and bring riches to our ports — the first and foremost being moonstones."

Baudwin had heard of Bright Portal, but in scant detail, for that city was remote. Few, if any, were said to live there anymore. Added to this, ever since the Great Befalling had struck, the fate of the light Faeries was unknown.

Everyone waited for Lugh to say more, as he was far more knowledgeable than they were. He continued speaking to Baudwin. "As Ferrell probably told you at the Show Wheel, moonstones were gifted to the Elves — by the Faeries — and still are to this day. Some say it serves as a way to help the Elves find their feelings. Or perhaps," he added, smiling, "to simply make them more agreeable."

"Speaking of feelings," Matha said indignantly, as he stopped and glared at Baudwin, "perhaps *you* should touch one of those moonstones, so you can feel all the pain that you've caused us."

Matha's remark cut into Baudwin like a knife. No doubt he had waited for just the right moment to express his displeasure, catching Baudwin completely off guard.

"So much for concord," Baudwin replied angrily. "You don't even know what happened."

"Oh, we know *very* well," Matha continued. "You told Kelven you lost the glamorium egg, because the shadow of Glamorium came and stole it from you. And when Kelven blamed *you* for losing it —"

"I only told him what I thought he would believe," Baudwin snapped. "And I would do it again, if I had to!"

Neither Criofan nor Matha were convinced.

"No," Matha said. "You were careless, and fought with him. You'll have to apologize when you return."

Baudwin thought then of the water spirit — the true reason why the egg was gone. She was a bitter memory in his mind, tearing at his thoughts everywhere he went. And now that the rift she had created was beginning to mend, here she was again, making a new tear — in his friendship with Matha and Criofan.

How he wanted to tell them that she had taken the egg, but he was afraid they wouldn't believe him. No one ever saw water spirits. They only appeared in poems or stories taught to young ones.

Baudwin, Matha, and Criofan stopped speaking.

Lugh wasn't sure what they were talking about. He knew of Baudwin's mother, but nothing about what had happened to Baudwin with Glamorium. Yet, he could not let their argument become even more contentious.

"Stop your bickering!" he exclaimed. "You should be kinder to one another. And, what's all this about a glamorium egg?"

Baudwin said nothing.

"Baudwin was given a special gift," Matha began, "a glamorium egg from Rian, who works the gear chute booth at the Engineerium."

"Yes, I know who he is," Lugh said, looking utterly perplexed. Staring at Baudwin he asked, "Whyever would you consort with the likes of someone like Ferrell when you have an elven friend like Rian, who gave you such a treasure?"

Hearing this, Matha and Criofan glared accusingly at Baudwin.

"Ferrell might have done the same," Baudwin insisted. "You don't know him."

"You sound like you put more trust in him than you do in us!" Criofan exclaimed. "For all you know, he could be playing you like an elven flute."

Baudwin lowered his head and stared at the ground. "I didn't mean that he's a better friend, or even a friend at all. All I was saying was that —"

"Well, that's what it sounded like," Matha added. "At least to us."

"What I meant to say was that Rian gave me the egg because he wanted to help me find my mother."

"And then you lost it!" Criofan exclaimed.

"And now it seems Ferrell is more than happy to help you find her," Matha continued. "Why would you trade the help of someone who accepts you as you are, for a graceless inquisitor, who is probably trying to use you to his advantage?"

Hearing his rebuke, Baudwin continued to stare at the ground. The three water Faeries from Deuona did not speak.

"Now, now," Lugh said, smiling at them. "Let's not be so harsh. We must remember concord, mustn't we? You're here to reconcile with one another. And you are doing just that." Turning to Baudwin, he grabbed him by the shoulder, saying, "Besides, if your path is to find more Glamorium, then more will come to you."

At the mention of Glamorium, Baudwin winced. Lugh studied him carefully. "I've heard of the shadow of Glamorium before, from some Guilders in the Nechtain Quarter immersed in the old ways. They told me there are some who have touched Glamorium, and felt a sinister presence. This came about after the Great Befalling, yet none can say why. Tell me, Baudwin, when you held the egg, did a horrific vision come to you?"

"I saw a faery lady," Baudwin replied. "Perhaps she was my mother, but before I could find out, she turned into an ugly moorhen and flew away. And the river she was near turned ominous and dark, like molten silver. The currents rushed toward me, as if to drown me."

Lugh nodded. "Yes, I've heard stories such as that, but they are few and far between." He looked at Matha and Criofan. "I think we must be kinder to Baudwin. There is truth in what he says. There is surely some kind of strange affliction in Glamorium that we do not understand. We must not let our judgments get ahead of us." With that, Lugh began to recite:

Our minds must remain open
When we do not understand
So our hearts will still find hope in
What seems lost or out of hand
A friend who does not falter
When the truth is hard to see
Has a strength that will not alter
What the truth then proves to be

After Lugh spoke, Matha and Criofan nodded their heads, chastened.

"I will give you the benefit of the doubt," Matha said. "For right now, that's all I can do."

"So will I," Criofan added. "But I'm still very angry at the way you left us. What if you had passed to Annwyn in that riot? None of us would have even known."

Baudwin hung his head as well, not speaking.

"What started that mess anyway?" Matha asked.

Baudwin explained how the riot had begun at the Four Rivers Fair. He told them that he had seen two Elves, both selling different kinds of clocks — older, and newer mechanical ones. One wanted to sell him a water clock, and the other a metal clock with gears of all shapes and sizes. The two Elves then began to argue — each over the merits of his particular timepiece.

"So both of them wanted to prove his clock was better?" Criofan asked, smiling. "In a way, I can't blame them. For who doesn't want to win over a customer in the marketplace?"

"No," Baudwin replied, shaking his head. "Their disagreement was much farther-reaching than that."

"You mean the competition for the sale went much deeper?" Matha asked, taken by the thought.

"Absolutely," Baudwin replied. "In fact, I was shocked when I saw how deep their ill will went — deeper than any mountain lake I've ever swum in — and I have in many."

Processing this, Matha and Criofan listened intently to Baudwin's account. He told them about how the elven disagreement had turned into a debate. He described how the two merchants had both stood on wooden crates, passing an ornamental talking-stick back and forth. Before long, instead of talking about the merits of their clocks, they were angrily discussing the differences between the Eternal Movement and the Rise of Time.

"The *what* and the *what*?" Matha asked, looking intrigued. Criofan as well seemed quite taken with Baudwin's account.

"Having forgotten the initial subject — clocks — they then began to discuss what time *itself* was — which they did with great relish and no regard for each other," Baudwin continued. "*Gnás,* as we know it, was completely absent. In fact, they sounded far worse than Loch ever has, when he rants about the old ways. Fearghus, the Elve who sold the mechanical clocks, said time was only what is measured. He thought that eternity was just another word for what they hadn't yet discovered. The only challenge, as he put it, was to understand the *unknown.*"

"And then Seanán, the Elve who sold the older timepieces — water clocks and sundials — spoke, saying that time lives within all Elves, and that clocks are just symbols of what they *already* should understand."

"How did you get mixed up in such a strange elven debate?" Criofan asked, bemused.

"They saw my watch," Baudwin chortled. "I was the buyer — the one who needed to be convinced. And yet, they ended up going to terrible extremes, trying to convince each other."

Matha's eyes lit up with interest. "What happened next?" he asked. For he greatly appreciated the nature of the debate, despite not understanding all of the particulars.

Baudwin then explained how the debate had quickly gotten ugly — how the two merchants had turned on each other and eventually gotten the crowd worked up. And then, how the riot had erupted. "Fearghus kept saying that time was not relative, but Seanán insisted that it was. I have no idea why they became so angry over that."

The three Faeries looked at Lugh, expecting he would have something to add.

"That's a hoary argument that the Elves keep having," he said. "I'm guessing that Fearghus was from the Clock City, and Seanán was from Gold Haven. They don't agree about the nature of time. It's as if we Faeries were to argue over what space and the elements were, until we came to blows. Such foolishness — but they are, after all, the Elves."

"Just like we argue with the Roilers," Criofan said, smiling at Lugh. "And I must say, I'm impressed with your knowledge of these things."

"As am I," Matha agreed. "I've learned a lot that I didn't know before."

Lugh grimaced. "Yes, but sometimes I wish I didn't know quite so much about the ways of the Elves. Living here, I'm exposed to a great deal. I long for a quieter Life, in a more peaceful place."

"Perhaps you should move to Deuona then," Criofan suggested.

"There's still more to tell," Baudwin continued. "Everything became even worse until a water Faery named Ayamonn arrived."

"Ayamonn!" Lugh exclaimed, looking at Baudwin. "We saw him the day we met at the Engineerium. I was protesting the Tree of Innovation, and you were wandering around, wondering what to do, since you'd lost your pack."

Baudwin nodded and continued speaking. "All the guilder Faeries in the quarter then began fighting as well. That's when I tried to get away — that is, before I was hit in the back of the head, and my pack was stolen and thrown into the river."

"Those cowards!" Criofan exclaimed. "If I'd been there, I would have thrown them in as well, and not let them get out until they made right what they had done — even if they were Elves!"

"Especially if they were Elves," Matha added, amused. "For an Elve swimming in the river is such a laughable sight — compared to a water Faery."

"I heard that Ayamonn eventually ended the riot, with the help of the Earth Guard," Lugh said. "He managed to contain the Elves, so they didn't spread their nasty upheaval throughout the rest of the city."

"He reminds me of my grandfather," Baudwin said.

"Yes, he is quite bold — both as a leader and an upholder of the old ways," Lugh said. "In fact, we're in his quarter right now. Talking about him must not be a coincidence. At the Engineerium, he told us to come see him. I think the Water wills that you meet him."

Baudwin wasn't sure he wanted to do anything of the kind. Despite the interesting things they had discussed, the arguments had left him still very angry with his friends for being so hard on him.

"I don't think so, Lugh," he said. "I'm just going to turn in. Perhaps Criofan and Matha would like to turn in too, as they've traveled so far."

Hearing Baudwin's refusal, a lofty look of loyalty crossed Lugh's face. Earnestly, he implored, "Baudwin, I'm not trying to influence what you should do, but I must say this: Not being joined to one's current is not common. Only rarely do mothers fail to do this. But what is even rarer is for the Water to come to someone — especially one not joined to his current — and rarer *still* is for that one to be put upon a quest for Glamorium. There is something at work here — the ways of the Water tell me. So, before you go see Ferrell, you must at least come to the Moonstone Rushes, for I have a surprise for you there."

Now Baudwin was intrigued. *What is Lugh playing at?* he wondered. But before he could reply, Criofan and Matha decided for him.

"Of course we'll go!" Matha exclaimed, looking at Criofan.

"Yes, we must see them!" Criofan agreed, looking at Matha. "I'm sorry, Baudwin — but we just outvoted you."

Baudwin relented. He didn't want to upset his friends, and he could see that Lugh really only wanted what was best for him.

Everyone agreed that they should visit Ayamonn, for Lugh knew that on Dorchadía he was likely to be at the Moonstone Rushes. He led them up a hill until the city streets began to narrow, and they reached the walls of ancient stonework at the top. At the entrance they looked this way and that, stepping over winding waterways that flowed down the hill. Some ran into gutters, while others zigged and zagged through gardens and around dome homes, all the way to the canals. Baudwin wondered where so many streams could come from, and then Lugh spoke.

"These are the Moonstone Rushes," Lugh said. "All of these streams flow from a spring that wells up at the top of this hill. Their source is a mystery."

"Why do Faeries come to the springs?" Baudwin asked. "Healing, I hope, for I could surely use some."

"You'll see," Lugh said.

With that, they entered a large edifice, which reminded Baudwin and Matha of the ruins of Coventina. Enormous pieces of granite carved into portals led to an open area, surrounded by a circle of rocks. Inside the circle, they saw a large pool, glimmering in the Sun. Many small streams flowed from the pool.

"Ayamonn!" Lugh exclaimed. "How good to see you."

Near the pool, a guilder gent raised his head and gestured for them to come. Baudwin recognized the arm — lean and strong — wearing a gold band set with blue azurite mixed with green malachite — a rare combination in one stone. So was his nature both hard and durable — yet arresting — like a well-polished gem. He appeared to be quite calm, and Baudwin wondered if he could be having a waking.

"Well met, Lugh!" Ayamonn said, as he stood up and took his friend by the shoulders. "I see you've brought friends. Quickly he sized up the other three Faeries, stopping at Baudwin. "Ah, Baudwin, we meet again."

Baudwin regarded Ayamonn, struck by how much he reminded him of his grandfather. "Yes," he replied sardonically. "I'm the one who started the riot."

"Glad to see you survived," Ayamonn said, as he threw his head back, laughing.

"And who have we here?" he asked, looking at Criofan and Matha. Neither spoke for a moment, as they were too taken by Ayamonn's hospitality.

"What a fine jacket," Ayamonn complimented Criofan. "Sharper-looking than an icicle from the Glittering Tundra. Sure to impress."

"And this one looks more worn than a road through the Vanishing Moors," Ayamonn said to Matha, giving him a sharp box on the shoulder.

Both Criofan and Matha grinned.

"I am Ayamonn, son of Tassach, Leader of the Danu Quarter," he said. Forcefully, he raised his arms, and then made the sign of the Water over his heart, which they returned.

"I am Baudwin, son of Kelven, of Deuona."

"I am Criofan, son of Congal, of Deuona."

"And I am Matha, son of Niall, of Deuona."

Ayamonn nodded his acknowledgment. "Three sons of Deuona come to visit!" he exclaimed. "Such an honor." He then pointed to the streams.

"Tell me then," he began, "is this your first time visiting the Moonstone Rushes?"

"This is their first time visiting most anywhere," Lugh said, chuckling.

"Then they must learn what this place *is*," Ayamonn affirmed, as he knelt down and thrust his hand into the pool. Grabbing a moonstone, he then held the glossy black orb to the Light. The moonstone turned white, casting a prism of rainbow colors off the walls and trees.

"This is a moonstone — as I'm sure you know," Ayamonn began. "But this one and others like it have been renewed."

"By the Water?" Matha asked.

"Yes indeed, sharp one," Ayamonn replied, smiling. "The Water renews them — empties them out — so they can be gifted again."

"But how?" Baudwin asked.

"By washing away the feelings — both good and bad — that previous owners have left in them — feelings that have fed their memories." Ayamonn paused for a moment to make sure they were listening, and then continued. "Some memories are better left forgotten, just as others are worth remembering. The Water flushes both kinds out. Then, when a moonstone is re-gifted, new memories can be made. For this to happen, moonstones must first help us to *feel* what we feel. And, this we all must do."

"Does this happen for the Elves as well?" Matha asked.

"Yes, of course," Ayamonn replied. "For they are also enamored of these stones, as well they should be."

With that, Ayamonn gazed into the rushes. Several moments passed. To Baudwin, Ayamonn seemed to be searching for hidden treasure that only he could see.

"The Elves should thank me for my dedication to their welfare," Ayamonn said. "An Elve who cannot feel is an Elve who cannot heal, and we cannot have them poisoned with rage and clogged with bitterness about the past. For that does not bode well for us either."

Ayamonn then turned to Criofan. "Hold this," he said, handing him the moonstone. "Tell me, what do you feel?"

Criofan held the moonstone, expecting something to happen. All paused, waiting. Criofan then said, "I feel nothing."

"Very good," Ayamonn said. "This one is ready for a new owner."

Criofan handed the stone back to Ayamonn, but Ayamonn refused it.

"Keep it," he urged. "You must let this moonstone guide you to your feelings. Only then will you be able to appreciate your good memories, and let your bad ones go."

Quickly, Ayamonn turned and gathered two more stones from the streams. He gave one to Baudwin and the other to Matha.

"There and there," he said. "Good. Young Guilders should always have their own moonstones. How else will they be able to tell what the Water is trying to teach them?"

Lightly, the three Faeries turned their moonstones over in their palms, running their fingers along their smooth, rounded edges. Touching his, Baudwin remembered the Show Wheel — how the elven ladies and gents had sung so beautifully as they held their moonstones, their costumes glimmering in the Light, the music playing sweetly in the background. Moved by the memory, he sang the last verse:

I gave myself a moonstone

So I would not forget

To live with feelings good and bad

And be without regret

Softly, Baudwin continued humming the tune. *Will this moonstone really help me feel my feelings, so I can let go of my memories?* he wondered. He had suffered so greatly looking for his mother — always to no avail. His memories had only haunted him, leaving him torn and bitter. How he longed to get even with others because they were joined to their currents, and he was not. Who were they to judge him? To tell him they knew better? To speak of their pain? Their pain was nothing compared to his. Yet, he knew he had let his feelings fester into anger and disrespect for his grandfather and father, when he should have told them how he really felt, without fear or rancor.

If I do feel my feelings, will I then be without regret? he wondered. The thought provoked such uncertainty in him that he could not contain his unease. What if his friends saw how powerless he really was? For to be without regret, he would first have to feel *so* many feelings, and face *so* many memories. He wasn't sure he would ever have the fortitude that such an undertaking would require. Perhaps it would simply be better to put the moonstone aside.

Or perhaps the moonstone in his hand was already showing him his feelings, and there was nothing he could do but listen to them. They couldn't *all* be bad. Quickly, he changed his mind, asking brightly, "Can we keep these?"

"Of course!' Ayamonn exclaimed. "They aren't just for the Elves. Even if they may believe so."

All three Faeries smiled gratefully at Ayamonn.

"There is one last thing we must do," Lugh said, as he motioned to a low stone wall, overgrown with ivy. From where he stood, Baudwin could see a row of small doors with rounded tops and with a keyhole in each one. As they approached the wall, Lugh removed a bronze key from his pocket. Upon opening one of the doors, he reached into a dark cubbyhole. What he touched none could tell, until he pulled out a green silk bag. Opening the drawstrings, he produced a moonstone, just like the one Baudwin had been given.

"This moonstone belongs to me," he said. "We guild leaders keep ours here in case we should disappear, so that others may use them to gain clues as to our whereabouts. This also keeps a record of our memories, so history does not rewrite itself should a tyrant conquer the realm. Ayamonn, Padhra,[3] and Donagh[4] have theirs here also, as well as other guild leaders from the past."

"Do the primaries keep their moonstones here as well?" Matha asked.

"Indeed," Lugh replied, "and also the Grand Eldresses and Elders."

"How interesting," Matha mused. "How far back do these moonstones go?"

Lugh then looked somber, as did Ayamonn.

"Sadly, most of the oldest moonstones were lost over time," Ayamonn replied. "We only have ones that go back a generation or two. The rest are lost to history. What ancient few remained went missing after the Great Befalling."

All the Faeries then hung their heads at a loss they recognized as greater than they could ever imagine.

"But enough about that," Lugh said brightly, turning to Baudwin. "My moonstone is still here. And Baudwin, I have a surprise for you, for this moonstone was given to me when I was but a Faefry — the day I was joined to my current."

Lugh then offered the moonstone to Baudwin. "Hold this," he said, "and let the memory of that day ease your suffering."

Hesitantly, Baudwin took the moonstone. At first he hardly felt anything, just a smooth round stone in the palm of his hand, like any other he had

---

[3] Pronounced [PAR-ra]

[4] Pronounced [DUN-na]

skipped across the surface of a river. The moonstone had already turned white. He waited for a few moments, and then slowly, he felt a stirring inside himself, like warm Water swirling in his heart.

"Close your eyes," Lugh whispered, "and wait for the memories to come."

Baudwin did as he was bidden, and the swirling inside of him grew stronger. The Darkness behind his lids then turned a bright blue, and he saw a vision of a young one holding the very same moonstone near a river. The river had to have been the Nechtain, and the young one a much younger, more tenderhearted-looking Lugh. Much to Baudwin's amusement, he was also wearing a lily hat.

Lugh's mother then appeared in the memory. She looked just like her son, dressed as she was with seashells and vials of Water round her neck, and having the same hands and feet and blue-green eyes and hair as he. Baudwin could hear her voice, just as if he were standing there.

She poured Water over Lugh's head and whispered in his ear, just as Brigh had done so many seasons before, first with Matha, and then with him. Lugh's senses then awakened, as they did for every Faery who partook of the ceremony. Just as Matha had, Lugh trembled with anticipation — and then he was joined. What joy Baudwin felt as he experienced Lugh's memory. For instead of failing as he had, Lugh had found his current.

Holding the moonstone, Baduwin didn't simply see the memory — he *became* the memory. For the first time ever, he felt the stir of the Water inside of him, as if he too were being joined to his current. Jubilantly, he cried out, just as Lugh had done. And then, he watched as Lugh ran and dove into the Water, just as Matha had done. For Lugh — then and always — all would be right with the Water.

Now Baudwin knew where Lugh's loyalty to the Water came from, for in this joining was a fierce reverence for the Water itself, which rushed like a great tide into Lugh's soul.

Tears came to Baudwin's eyes, for now he felt the joy of a young one being touched by the wonder of the Water, with no heavy current of sadness and despair pulling him down. Such was a moment that all water Faeries who were joined to their currents carried for the rest of their lives, and now as Baudwin felt the meaning of Lugh's joining firsthand, his birthright seemed restored.

The memory ended.

Baudwin opened his eyes and saw his friends, and the Guild Leaders, looking at him.

"What did you see?" Criofan asked.

"I saw Lugh being joined to his current on the Nechtain, and I saw his mother."

Abaigeal[5] was her name," Lugh said.

"Yes, and then I felt. . ." Baudwin paused for a moment, overcome. "And then I felt the *anchor* I've missed, which has left me searching my whole Life."

Baudwin was happy, but the moonstone's memory was bittersweet.

"Though I am grateful for this, Lugh," he began, "I must admit that I am also saddened, for I still don't know what this memory would mean if it had been my own."

Lugh was not surprised by Baudwin's words. "Of course, Baudwin," he said. "I shared this with you so you could in some way feel what joining your current is like. You must not falter in your quest. Just remember, when you find your mother, this and much more will be yours. You must never abandon your course — let the *Water* guide you!"

"The Water is your destiny, Baudwin," Ayamonn agreed. "If you don't swim, you'll be dragged down."

*Dragged down. . .*The thought reminded Baudwin of that terrible day at the dam, when the water spirit had attacked him. Caught in her violent fury, he feared he would drown. How kind she had seemed at first, until she judged him unworthy. Knowing what he felt now, he wondered if she would have taken his glamorium egg if he had already been joined with his current. Brigh had said as much, but Baudwin had not wanted to believe that fate could be so cruel — until now. For in feeling the moment that Lugh had joined his current, he now understood in greater depth what he himself lacked.

This made Baudwin despair even more. But if Brigh was right, then perhaps there was still hope. But was there? He needed to be joined to be worthy of Glamorium so he could find his mother, but he could not be led by Glamorium because he wasn't joined.

There was no clear path for him.

How sick and tired he was of everything. So much so that he wanted to declare the truth right then and there. Two Guild Leaders now stood before him. Who better to reveal his story to — as well as to his two best friends? The moment had arrived to tell them everything. The first lesson of the Triquetra was, after all — Honesty.

Nervously, Baudwin looked at their guileless faces. As he touched the moonstone, his fingers trembled. Now that he had witnessed and vicariously experienced the joining of another, perhaps they would believe his tale about the water spirit. *Yes, I must tell them,* he thought. He waited before speaking, but then, to his dismay, confusion set in, muddling his feelings. *No — I mustn't,* he thought, because if he did, they might tell him that the moonstone had addled

---

5   Pronounced [ABI-gale]

his mind — that he was speaking nonsense. He couldn't take the chance of suffering the latter, so he said nothing. Criofan and Matha had already accused him of heartlessly disregarding their feelings, and he feared being ridiculed again.

"This is all so much to consider," he said, as he wearily handed the moonstone back to Lugh.

"Yet," Lugh began, taking the moonstone, "there is so much *more* to consider."

Baudwin could tell that Lugh seemed happy with how the moonstone had affected him, but this did not stop Baudwin from asking, "Isn't this enough for one day?"

"No," Lugh countered. "The wonders of Four Falls will not allow you to abandon your kin. There is more I have yet to show you. There are two quarters left to see, and I know we can visit at least one more today. The Cyhiraeth calls to us."

Criofan and Matha seemed excited, and Baudwin decided that he could not let them down. He would have to do Lugh's bidding. Still, he was unconvinced that any of what he might learn could actually help him in his quest. Still, he lingered on Ferrell's promise.

Ayamonn then spoke up. "These three must learn what the Guild is *really* about before the Assembly muddies their currents."

Everyone laughed.

"Be sure to take them by the crumbling streets," he added. "They must see for themselves what happened."

"Yes, I already had that in mind," Lugh replied, nodding.

With that, they all set out for the Cyhiraeth, wondering what Lugh had in store for them.

Chapter 28

THE CYHIRAETH QUARTER

They stood on top of a hill, gazing down upon the Cyhiraeth Quarter, its river a turbid pool of ink spilling into an otherwise azure city. Below them they sensed a wavering chill drifting through shops, throngs, and alleyways, like clouds of mist rising along a turgid river. Nothing seemed to remain the same for very long. From afar they saw candles being snuffed out behind windows. Others were then lit — for no apparent reason — as the Sun's Light had not yet left the streets. Perhaps, Baudwin thought, they were honoring something, but he didn't know what that could be.

A group of Faeries speaking on a corner dispersed, and then regrouped quickly at the next one. Over and over they did this, each place seeming to beget a new conversation. Baudwin saw a gaze of raccoons standing on top of a fence, peering out at bystanders. All at once they jumped into a garden fountain, splashing and drinking. They then became very still, looking as if they saw nothing at all. Beneath their masks, they seemed to be witnessing passings to another realm.

These happenings were evidently what the Water willed, and the moody stirrings of the Cyhiraeth River made them seem even darker, yet Baudwin wasn't sure why. He remembered the bout he had had near the docks — the worst one ever, with terrifying visions. Yet despite the fear that his next bout would take him to Annwyn, the aftermath had left him feeling stronger. What lesson might this river be trying to teach him? Whatever the answer, he knew that here he would have to tread lightly.

He took a breath to prepare himself, and down the winding road they went. With each block, the cobblestones looked darker and the buildings more somber. The Moons of the Danu Quarter disappeared, replaced by images of the banshee. Baudwin stared, mouth agape. She was everywhere — pallid, red-eyed, and wailing, her wraithlike body gaunt and terrifying. He shivered, for he had never seen anyone like her. *Except, perhaps, for the water spirit in her wrath,* he thought.

"I saw some young ones in this quarter the day after the riot," Baudwin said, as they continued down the hill. "On my way to the Engineerium."

"You went to the Engineerium without us?" Criofan chided him. "You forgot us again!"

"Indeed!" Matha exclaimed.

"I know you're both just joking," Baudwin said. "Had you been here, I surely would have had you with me." Matha and Criofan smiled in agreement.

"As I was saying," Baudwin continued, "I saw some young ones here, singing and swaying, pretending to wash their clothes and drink Water. Why do they play such strange games?"

"They're honoring the banshee," Lugh replied. "For she washes the clothes of those who will pass to Annwyn, and sings to them. In return, she is offered drinks of Water for her trouble."

Baudwin thought then that the candles must have been lit and snuffed out in her honor. "Even the young ones know of such things?" he asked, surprised.

"Yes," Lugh replied. "Even they know about the song of the banshee's search — the song of ending."

"For when she finds you, you know the end is near," Baudwin said, remembering what he had been told that day. Looking at Matha and Criofan, he noticed their suddenly halting steps. They had never heard such happenings spoken of regarding the Water. No doubt Lugh had many times, but not they. River Deuona had kept them both close to their currents like tadpoles, where beginnings, not endings, were all they ever knew.

Soon they reached the bottom of the hill. The Cyhiraeth Quarter was all around them, encased in a mist-like shroud that seeped from canals, down streets, and around corners. Faeries shuffled gloomily as they went about their business, their dreariness masking a deeper, more mysterious kind of vigor. It was the same vigor Baudwin had felt the day after his last bout. *What kind of tenebrous potency did the Water bestow here?* he wondered. *One that weakened from the outside, yet strengthened from within?*

Baudwin shuddered.

The Danu Quarter had been much more boisterous, but as he looked more closely at his somber cousins of the Cyhiraeth, oddly, they seemed far more alive.

How could this be?

Together they looked about the quarter. None of them spoke any further about the banshee. As they came down the hill, Baudwin noticed something that caught his attention.

A short distance away, an old faery lady stood before an easel, painting the scene before her. Lightly, her spindly fingers held her paintbrush, the hairs at the tip moving like tiny spider legs across the canvas.

His curiosity piqued, Baudwin moved closer to her. Politely, he peered over her shoulder to take a look. He gasped. Before her were rose bushes, alive and well, yet the ones she had painted were withered and spent, their Life and color completely gone.

Seeing Baudwin's upset, she tried to soothe him. "They are better off for this, you know," she said.

"But they're *lifeless*," Baudwin said, trying to conceal his dismay.

"No," she said as she pointed to the bushes. "You see, they are still *very* much alive."

He had no idea what she meant, so he said nothing.

"Their Water will leave them one day" she continued, pointing to the roses growing in front of her. "This painting avows their journey, and those of many such others."

Baudwin tried to make sense of her words. Behind him, he could see that Criofan, Matha, and Lugh had come to look, taking in the wisdom of the Cyhiraeth Quarter as best they could.

"I think I understand," Baudwin said. Solemnly, his friends nodded their agreement. For Baudwin had realized that the strength of these Faeries came both from the embrace of loss and the rapture of letting go. Pondering further, he wondered if this was what had left him feeling stronger the day after his bout.

The four Faeries were off again. Intrigued by what the faery lady had said, Lugh began to explain. "Faeries here are the most unusual in all of the water faery lands. The reason for this is that their river — the Cyhiraeth — is sourced far to the north, from Lake Aife, which is fed by the rivers and streams of Mount Arawn,[1] and the mountains of Scáthach.[2] It is at the foot of those mountains that the dark Faeries are said to dwell, though few are seen anymore — if at all. At one time they visited this quarter regularly, leaving their mark upon all that you see around you."

"Why are they gone?" Matha asked.

"No one is sure," Lugh replied, his anger rising. "Another casualty of the Great Befalling, I would assume. But they're actually lucky. They don't have to witness what the Elves have done to this city. Likely, they went missing for the same reasons that the light Faeries are gone as well."

"I've only seen earth, air, and wood Faeries before," Criofan said.

"Yes, you would be too young to have met the other ones," Lugh replied. "But I'm not. I remember them well, and also the fire Faeries."

At the mention of *Fire*, the three Faeries instantly recoiled. For that element always made them heedful of their surroundings, as if they could be boiled away at any time, leaving not a trace of themselves.

"There are four tribes accounted for, and three missing," Lugh continued. "Or rather two missing, and one sealed away. The fire Faeries were never

---

[1]   Pronounced [OUR-owwn]
[2]   Pronounced [SCAW-huck]

conquered. They've maintained a stalemate in Ember Chasm with Govannon's forces for the past two hundred years."

"What were they like?" Baudwin asked. "Kelven and Seamus told me about them, but never said they were sealed away. The elders barely spoke of them at all."

"They are of the Fire, as we are of the Water," Lugh continued. "They are our opposite, so our ways have always been conflicting, but oddly transforming. The dark Faeries, on the other hand, held us closer to them than any other faery tribe. The evidence of that can be seen over there."

Lugh pointed to an older-looking building, with less ornamentation than the others, and very sturdy masonry. "That building is known as the Onyx Shell Keep. It was here two hundred years ago that the Guild Leader of the Cyhiraeth Quarter stubbornly refused to surrender to Govannon's forces. He fought alongside one of the few dark Faeries who still remained here, whose name was Cairbre."[3]

"What happened?" Matha asked.

"You already know," Lugh replied. "We lost. One small shell keep had no chance of victory. That was the last time a dark Faery was ever seen in our city."

"Why did he refuse?" Baudwin asked. "Ferrell said that Govannon liberated us."

Lugh could have ground his heel into a tomato, as he had done on the Show Wheel, but instead he held his anger in check. "You're wrong!" he exclaimed. "That's *not* what happened! Govannon destroyed the council and then went on a rampage to conquer *Tír Éirí Sióg* — at least in part. We were the first to fall, you see. As we were the largest city near the Col of Lonrúil, the Elves took Four Falls as soon as they went through the pass."

Baudwin didn't want to upset Lugh any further, yet he had to know more. "But Ferrell said that the Faeries were no longer sending dreams to the Elves," he began, "and that the older kings of the Elves had failed them, leaving *Tír Luí Lucharachán* wasting and impoverished. Surely he was trying to help his subjects."

"By splitting his own clan into two opposing sides?" Lugh countered, sputtering. "By driving off *three* of our tribes? He was not helping at all! He had absolutely *no* right to come here and proclaim himself leader of *Tír Éirí Sióg*!"

"But we supported his enemy, did we not?" Baudwin asked.

"Yes, and we had chosen the *right* side," Lugh replied. "We stood with Belanus."

Baudwin decided to end the debate right there. He and his friends were so taken by their exploration of the Cyhiraeth Quarter that he didn't want to

---

[3] Pronounced [KAR-bra]

infuriate Lugh, who was, after all, their guide. While realizing that the *cogadh* had made victims of many Faeries, he also wasn't willing to simply blame Govannon.

"Well then, next time we meet Ferrell, we must ask him to extend his cordiality to the dark, light, and fire Faeries," Baudwin said, chuckling.

"Bah!" Lugh exclaimed. "Follow me, Baudwin, son of Kelven, water Faery of Deuona. I will show you what the outcome of that *cogadh* was."

The tone of Lugh's voice cut short their levity, and soon the three Faeries were rushing to keep up with him as he busily stomped through the streets of the Cyhiraeth Quarter. As they followed him, they noticed that the buildings were becoming more and more dilapidated. The masonry was cracked, and the domes of the roofs broken. No Elves were in sight, and the remaining Faeries looked poorer than any Baudwin had ever seen.

Huddling in groups, gaunt-cheeked and grimy, it seemed that not even the Water could cleanse them of their ills. Their clothes were ragged, and none seemed to have any business to call their own. Despite this, they were present in their suffering — their eyes calling for help, their mouths twisting soundlessly while not uttering a word. Near a fountain, Baudwin saw them filling bottles of Water, and then aimlessly pouring the contents over their heads. Another strange ritual of the Cyhiraeth, perhaps, but their mood never seemed to change. Always they looked wounded and downtrodden.

Baudwin had never seen such poverty before. Once in Deuona a family of water Faeries had come to live in the South Bend. Their clothes were tattered and worn, and they looked as if they hadn't had a meal in over a week. Quickly, they were helped — given new clothes and a warm place to sleep. Almost overnight, the color returned to their faces. The young ones sang and played in the river, and their parents smiled with joy. But no such thing had happened here.

"What is wrong with them?" Baudwin asked Lugh.

"They lost their intentions," Lugh replied.

"What do you mean?" Baudwin asked. "They never joined with their currents?"

Lugh shook his head. "They're not the same as you and me. They joined with their currents, and they once knew their intentions. But after the Great Befalling, their intentions were stripped away, as if they had never joined, or coursed with the Water to begin with."

Baudwin looked at the wretches scattered in groups along the sooty streets. If they had lost their intentions, then somehow they were the same as he, but unlike him, there seemed to be no spirit left in them. He wondered then how the Fae of Four Falls could allow them to live this way. Surely, they all deserved at the very least clean clothes on their backs, and food whenever they were hungry. In Deuona no one ever went hungry. Certainly, something could be done for them.

"Why don't other water Faeries help them?" Baudwin asked. Looking at Matha and Criofan, he could tell that they were wondering the same thing.

"Because they cannot help themselves," Lugh replied.

Criofan scowled. "But commerce and concord always ensure everyone has a place to live and can work," he said. "That is our way."

"We do feed them," Lugh replied, "but frequently they barely even eat. We house them, but they always leave and come back here. No one knows why, but I think that whatever happened during the Great Befalling struck the Cyhiraeth Quarter harder than the other ones."

"But why?!" Baudwin exclaimed.

Normally, a loud outburst like this would have attracted attention, but none of the Faeries near them seemed to notice. This upset Baudwin even more. Determined to find an answer, he broke away from the group and headed for a faery gent, an older one, graying at his temples. His dark blue coat was pocked with holes.

"Excuse me," Baudwin began. "You there — please."

The gent barely seemed to notice that he was being called. Only when Baudwin placed his hand on his shoulder did he raise his head and look him in the eye.

"I'm sorry," Baudwin began. "I'm new to this quarter, and I wanted to know — why do you choose to live here without proper food and shelter?"

Hearing this, the gent stiffened. As he spoke, his face was ashen, and Baudwin could barely catch his words.

"This is my home," the gent replied, pointing to the ruin of a dome home across the street.

"That's not a home any longer," Baudwin said, concerned. "Why hasn't it been rebuilt? It's been two hundred years!"

Now the gent became even more distressed. He shook his head, choosing not to reply.

Matha, Criofan, and Lugh caught up to them, and Lugh then spoke. "Please stop, Baudwin!" he exclaimed. "He doesn't know how to answer your questions. Pressing him will only upset him further."

Baudwin looked again at the gent, who had already turned away, staring listlessly ahead at nothing. Again, Baudwin sought to get his attention.

"I also have struggled with my intention," Baudwin said, taking him by the arm. "You must not give up hope!"

Hearing the word *hope,* the gent spoke, not looking at either Baudwin or his company. Instead, he stared out — just as the raccoons had done earlier — as if he were witnessing passings to another realm.

"They sent us onward," he began, his voice a dull whisper. "And then we sent *them* onward. But afterward, the path was not one that any of us could travel again."

"What path?" Baudwin asked, grasping the gent by the shoulders. "What happened?"

The gent did not answer. Instead, he looked out again — at nothing — way past Baudwin. "The path the banshee wailed about," the gent whispered again. "All listened, but afterward, none of us could *hear*."

Baudwin didn't know what the gent was talking about. Before he could ask anything more, the gent began to weep. His tears, dark and pitiful, streaked his cheeks like rain stirring the ashes of a charred garden.

"The swords came for us, but they did not take us to Annwyn!" the gent wailed.

Perplexed, Baudwin gaped at him. "Whatever do you mean?" he asked.

"Because only *we* could take ourselves there. Those of us who'd had enough of vying, and were ready to embrace the art of dying."

Baudwin wondered what had happened to make this gent speak in such riddles. He decided he better stop asking. Lugh was right. He felt a pang of guilt, for he had only worsened the gent's distress.

He wondered then if this gent could have been at the Onyx Shell Keep with Cairbre. Perhaps all the Faeries in this place had also been there, and the pain of that final battle had broken them from their intentions. Whatever the reason, Baudwin pitied them, for their lot was even worse than his. He at least had not completely given up, despite what the Water had willed for him.

Baudwin would have liked to somehow console the faery gent, but he then heard a commotion down the street. A group of Earth Guards was arguing with some Faeries. "The Assembly has marked this area for redevelopment!" their leader shouted. "Everyone here is to be relocated!" Seeing the two silver stripes on his sleeves and the blue star on his collar, Baudwin knew he was an Expert of Silver, with the rank of Lantern.

"We are the ones to decide when to rebuild, and how!" an outspoken faery gent shouted back at him, seemingly more coherent than the others. Baudwin noticed that his clothes, while worn, weren't as badly frayed. Added to this, he appeared more confident than his peers.

"You'll be well provided for," the Expert of Silver declared, shaking his head. Why would you want to remain here? This place is in ruins!"

"You aren't rebuilding our homes!" the outspoken gent shouted back. "You're just building whatever suits *you*!"

Lugh frowned at the scene. "Now do you see, Baudwin?" he asked. "This is why Ayamonn sent us here. The only help the Elves offer the Faeries is help that benefits *them*."

Before Baudwin could reply, the Expert of Silver strode closer to the Faeries, shaking his fists. "I'm not the one who makes the decisions!" he declared angrily. "If you don't like being moved, speak to your guild leader!"

"As if that will do any good," the outspoken faery gent shouted, "when we have to deal with the likes of *you!*"

The Expert of Silver continued speaking, unmoved by the uproar surrounding him. "All of you must come to the shelter — now — or we will forcibly relocate you!"

Baudwin had heard enough. Watching Matha and Criofan, he could tell that they had as well. Together they approached the Expert of Silver. Many in the crowd took notice of them, for their clothing was not in tatters, and they obviously hailed from somewhere else.

"And who might you be?" asked the Expert of Silver.

"I am Baudwin, son of Kelven, of Deuona," Baudwin replied. "I've come to offer my assistance."

"I know who your father is," the Expert of Silver replied, as, with furrowed brow, he studied Baudwin. "Perhaps you can be of assistance — if you can get them to understand. We're not their enemy. We just have orders to rebuild this place."

"After you destroyed everything?" Lugh chided. "How *considerate* of you!"

The Expert of Silver regarded Lugh. "You're Lugh, Guild Leader of the Nechtain?"

"That I am," Lugh replied.

The guard became more conciliatory. "Yes, there was a great battle here, long ago. But that *cogadh* is over. Now we must rebuild, for the time has come for greater things."

"Rebuild what?" the outspoken faery gent exclaimed. "You didn't ask us what we wanted! Just look around you! Do you think any of them are ready to leave? This isn't about rebuilding. You simply cannot stand the sight of those who would besmirch your vision of *progress* — for in your eyes they do nothing but tarnish your endeavors!"

Hearing this, the Expert of Silver clenched his teeth, and Baudwin could tell that he was getting more impatient by the moment.

"Two hundred years is time enough," the Expert of Silver declared. "I know you don't want to leave this place, but I can't speak for the plans our leaders have made. I am, myself, but a servant — don't you see?"

"Did Padhra make this decision?" Lugh asked.

"I believe so, yes," the Expert of Silver replied.

Lugh shook his head, disgusted. Baudwin assumed Padhra was the Guild Leader of the Cyhiraeth.

"If you want us out, you'll have to force us!" the outspoken faery gent exclaimed, pointing to the scores of street urchins around them. "And if you do, you'll only terrify them. You'll see! Their panic will stir the banshee! She'll awaken them, and then you'll know terror as well!"

The Expert of Silver nodded. Resigned to the task before him, he signaled. Soon several steamway wagons arrived, their wooden wheels creaking to a stop. Seeing the guards jump out of the wagons, scores of Faeries began to flee. They scattered away from the square — terrified — running to side streets and alleyways. Unmoved by their panic, the guards formed into rows, advancing steadily, their faces vacant but determined. In the center of a row, Baudwin spotted one of them holding what resembled a geyser pistol, but much larger. He aimed at a group and fired.

Baudwin expected to see a burst of Water, but instead a net of rope shot through the Air, opening into a large square, pulled by a weight at each corner. In an instant, the net had covered a group of Faeries. They struggled to get free. The remaining guards moved to subdue them. Piteously, the Faeries cried for help.

"Stop!" Baudwin shouted. "Think about what you're doing to them!"

"You're disrespecting the Golden Way!" Lugh cried. "By the authority of the Water Guild, I command you — stop!"

"You have no such authority in this quarter," the Expert of Silver declared. "Speak to Padhra, or the Assembly."

"This has nothing to do with authority!" Lugh shouted. "Just common decency!"

Ignoring Lugh's protest, the Expert of Silver motioned for the guards to continue. One of them grabbed a young faery mother, separating her from her young ones. As the guard dragged her out from beneath the net, she wailed with anguish. Her scream rang through the square. Many of her kin then began to cry as well, until all that could be heard was a dirge of voices, mourning a heap of unkept promises.

If Baudwin stopped the guards, he feared what Ferrell might do. If he didn't, he worried that he would look like a coward and lose his friends' respect. The Elves' methods were cruel, but certainly they were stymied, having tried to bring order to the area for countless seasons. Perhaps the Elves were right, but perhaps they didn't belong here in the first place. He couldn't decide which stance to take. Lugh seemed ready to burst upon the guards in a rage. Matha and Criofan seemed ready to do so as well. *How easily I could join them,* he thought.

Before Baudwin could act, a voice shouted above the din. All looked up.

From afar, Baudwin could see the ruins of a many-storied domed building, with shattered stained-glass windows, and pediments and columns cracked and broken. Up high, standing upon the rafters of the collapsed roof, a figure looked down upon them, his face shrouded by a cowl.

"Take your hands off of them — you tyrants!" he commanded. "You have no right here!" The voice sounded familiar to Baudwin.

The Expert of Silver stared up at the figure, unmoved by his protest. "Govannon is the law here!" he shouted. "Begone, or I will arrest you as well!"

Hearing this, the hooded figure laughed. "Then you'll have to come up here and get me yourself!" he shouted. "A pity that your elven guards are clumsier than a sleuth of bears, as they try to steer those wagons of yours!"

The Expert of Silver did not flinch. "We'll see who's clumsy, after the mines break you," he snarled. "Arrest him!"

Several guards moved to subdue the hooded figure, but before they could reach him, he whirled a sling over his head. A stone flew at one of them, striking him with a crack directly on his bronze helmet. Stunned, the guard cried out and stumbled.

"The mines are no place for me, you arrogant, metal-marching, drone!" the hooded figure cried.

The Expert of Silver grinned. "You'll know your place soon enough," he said, gesturing disdainfully at the crowd of destitute Faeries. "Just as *they* will."

The insult hit its mark. The hooded figure was still for a moment, and the tension in the Air mounted. Enraged, he suddenly tore off his disguise. "From the Water we are born!" he shouted at the guards.

The face was one Baudwin knew very well, as did the others. Never would they have expected to see Loch upon the roof. His defiance was reckless, even by his own standards. But there was no time to wonder why he had come.

From below, a guard aimed one of the net shooters at Loch, but Loch quickly took aim, hurling another stone, cracking the guard on his hand. The guard dropped his weapon, cursing.

Now many more guards joined to stop Loch. Baudwin wondered what chance he had against so many. His aim was true, but he would not be able to beat all of them.

Loch, however, was not deterred. He slung another stone and then another. The guards shielded their faces as the stones rained down upon them.

All Baudwin and his companions could do was watch. *Loch certainly is acting bravely,* Baudwin thought. *Or he's just strikingly stupid.*

The guards had reached the bottom of the building. Piles of rubble slowed their advance. A few of them tripped, and Loch laughed at them. Nimbly, he straddled the rafters, slinging more stones. *The bear is not easily frightened,* Baudwin thought, remembering their fight at the Hop and Hit. *But he should be careful, for he cannot keep this pace up for much longer.*

Baudwin could hear one of the guards shouting as they entered the ruined building. "The stairs are broken!"

"Then find another way up!" the Expert of Silver shouted back.

"C'mon now!" Loch exclaimed. "Go ahead — up and at 'em! Let's see how agile you are!" Slinging more stones at them, he laughed, a deep bellowing laugh, and Baudwin surprised himself by smiling.

By now the guards had climbed a pile of broken marble and some beams leading up to the rafters. Loch appeared to be trapped, but he didn't back down. Defiantly, he hurled a piece of marble at them, striking the lead guard with a thud. He stumbled backward. Other guards tried to steady him, but Loch threw yet another marble chunk at them, and they lost their footing. Soon they were all tumbling down the pile of rubble to the floor, their bronze armor clinking and crashing all the way.

The Expert of Silver gave a signal, and a few net-shooting guards took aim at Loch. There were too many to avoid. Loch stepped behind a broken column, exposing his back to the guards below. *He's done for now*, thought Baudwin.

The seemingly miraculous then happened. The crowd of destitute Faeries had taken notice of Loch, his courage striking a chord in them. Emboldened, they began shouting at the guards. Soon other Faeries flooded back from the alleyways and side streets, joining those who had remained in the square. The mob advanced. They pulled off the nets from those who were still trapped, or too befuddled to free themselves. Outnumbered, the guards retreated.

"From the Water we are born!" Loch shouted triumphantly. Baudwin found himself also shouting. Carried away by the turn of events, Criofan and Matha joined in as well. Lugh began to cheer.

A change had come over the crowd of Faeries, their indolence fast forgotten — bravery remembered. Just as they had once fought for Belanus — their armies sweeping through the forest of Gwydion, flanking Govannon's Clock City — they would now fight for themselves. From an army long disbanded, both ladies and gents formed a new line. A dire warning replaced their cries of anguish. Three then shouted in succession:

The banshee wails!

The dread wind gales!

Her song impales!

Baudwin had never heard a chant such as this before, but the words were obviously a cry for *cogadh*. Looking about, he saw not faces of a downtrodden crowd, but of warriors. They seemed possessed by a fury — fearless in their resolve — just as they must have been two hundred years before. Several began searching the ground, and soon a rain of stones fell upon the guards, causing many to shield themselves. Emboldened, Loch slung more stones at them.

The Faeries in the square advanced on the guard, their numbers having grown one hundredfold.

Seeing this, the Expert of Silver shouted, "Fall back!" Quickly, the guards retreated from the building, back to their steamway wagons.

Lugh shrieked with delight, and Criofan and Matha cheered. The guards continued their retreat. They jumped into their wagons, which rolled away down the street, picking up speed as the crowd continued chasing them.

"The banshee wails!" someone shouted again.

Soon the wagons were out of sight, and the crowd fell silent. Baudwin expected them to cheer, and spread word of their triumph, but with their fury fading, their wits left them as well. *Why do they forget themselves so easily?* he wondered with dismay. How maddeningly impossible that after their unexpected arousal and victory that they would fall right back into apathy — as if years ago they had burned their candles to the bottom, and what he had just witnessed was simply the last of their wicks sparking, before they sputtered out. Once again, they were pained and lost. He spotted the gray-templed gent staring at a broken fountain. The Faerie spokesman who had argued with the guards simply shook his head and walked away. Slowly the crowd thinned around them, shuffling back to the ruins.

Knowing the guards would no doubt return, Baudwin worried about the Faeries. What would be their fate without someone to inspire them? *Loch*, he then thought, wondering what strange purpose might have brought him here. He looked at the rafters where Loch had stood moments before, but he was gone.

"From the Water we are born," Criofan repeated, mulling over what Loch had said.

"Whatever is he up to?" Matha asked.

"Fighting the right fight for a change," Lugh replied, adjusting his lily hat.

Baudwin had no idea, but whether accidentally or on purpose, Loch had inspired the crowd to defend themselves. Looking at them now, Baudwin was deeply saddened. All they had needed was a leader to remind them of their intentions. Loch was a Roiler through and through, and the poor Faeries around them were all Guilders. What had compelled him to stand for them this way?

Baudwin then thought of their fight weeks ago at the ruins of Coventina. There Loch had saved Matha from the water spirit's wrath, and now he had helped the Faeries drive the Elves away. He certainly was becoming an interesting puzzle. Baudwin knew that Loch was still indentured to Ferrell, just as he was, and that by coming here, he was probably defying him.

"Seems like Loch is off Ferrell's leash," Baudwin said.

"And you're still on," Matha said, laughing.

"Just for now," Baudwin replied, irritated.

Matha and Criofan rolled their eyes, not speaking.

Lugh was in high spirits, taking less notice of the crowd's disposition. "That was excellent!" he exclaimed.

"But what will they do now?" Baudwin asked.

"What does it matter?" Lugh replied. "They showed those Elves what they are made of!"

Baudwin shook his head. "Without Loch, they wouldn't have."

"Perhaps he inspired something they will find again," Lugh suggested.

"Something *we* should have shown them," Criofan said. "We're better than Loch, and yet we just stood here, with our mouths agape, while he fought."

Criofan's words upset Baudwin, for he knew his friend was right. While they were debating whether they should fight, Loch had taken charge of the situation. Meanwhile, Baudwin hadn't done anything at all, because he didn't want to lose Ferrell's help. Loch owed the Assembly a debt, yet the well-being of his kin had come first — he didn't care about the consequences of his actions. Baudwin feared that Loch's current might be carrying Loch down a more honorable path than his own. Compared to Loch, Baudwin saw himself as nothing but a skittish water bug, skimming from place to place, always looking for a better spot, but never finding one.

"Who's really the brave one — Loch or me?" Baudwin asked aloud.

His friends balked at the question. Criofan placed his hand upon Baudwin's shoulder, saying, "You pay him too much regard."

"No, I don't," Baudwin replied. "He just did more for our kin than I ever have."

"That's not true," Matha objected. "You forget what a bully he is."

"And how little respect he has for *gnás* and the old ways," Criofan added.

Baudwin didn't know what to say, as he was still confused and upset by what Loch had just done. Without a word he went to sit upon a broken column. The square was now mostly deserted, with a few Cyhiraeth Faeries lingering around. Nervously he bounced his heel against the ground. Around him, the mists of the Cyhiraeth were still as dank as a tomb. Matha and Criofan called to him, but he wouldn't look at them. Soon they crowded around him, worry blanketing their faces.

"What's wrong?" Matha asked.

Baudwin didn't reply. The memory of his vision at the Moonstone Rushes weighed heavily upon his heart. Lugh's moonstone had given him a glimpse of being joined, but the vision hadn't eased his burden. So much had gone wrong since the spirit had crushed him, and he had left Deuona. Abandoning his friends had been his only recourse. And now Loch was proving to be the *real* hero, which was a far cry from Baudwin's triumph at the Hop and Hit.

He struggled to see why his path was so difficult. There seemed to be no pattern or purpose to his Life. Rian had instructed him to be honest so he could learn the first lesson of the Triquetra and wield Glamorium, yet his Life had been so unfair, he didn't see any use in trying.

A pang of regret then struck Baudwin, for he realized that he had barely tried at all.

"At least Loch is honest when he's a bully!" he shouted. "All I ever do is lie!"

Lugh cocked his head at him. "Whatever do you mean?" he asked.

Baudwin opened his mouth, tripping over his words. "I . . . I . . . just don't know."

Patiently, his friends waited for him to continue.

"I lied," he said.

"About what?" Criofan asked.

Baudwin hesitated, and then finally spoke. "I was scared to tell you what really happened before I came here," he began. "I didn't think you would believe me — and I still don't — but it doesn't matter anymore."

Before he began his tale, he remembered what Ferrell had asked him at the Show Wheel: "Don't you know that once — long ago — in *Tír na nÓg*, the Faeries were the dreamers of all that was to be? That they were the ones who gave the Elves the inspiration for what to build?"

Baudwin didn't know why that memory had come to him, until he realized that Ferrell's words had touched upon a mystery he now felt compelled to explain. He sensed that long ago, the Faeries and Elves *had* been closer to one another — witnessing wonders that then were commonplace but now seemed unimaginable. Looking at the night sky, the Faeries may have seen not simply a milky-white saucer, but the Moon — alive — gazing *into* them, each phase emanating specific wisdom for them to absorb. Hawthorns weren't merely trees — they were storytellers, whispering the tales of every ring that formed their trunks. Twilight doves may have spoken — not of their travels, but of their longings to be one with the heavens. From what little Baudwin understood, the realm *had* changed, and he didn't know how his story would ever make sense in the kind of world the Elves were building.

Glumly, he shook his head. All he could do was start at the beginning and not spare a single detail. And so he told them the truth about what had happened to the glamorium egg. When he recounted the dream he had had with the green bowl and the gold coupler, and how the river had risen against him, they looked concerned. After that, he explained how he had woken up that day and gone to the dam. When he told them he had heard a voice that seemed to come from everywhere, they looked baffled. He then described how the water spirit herself had appeared. Matha wiped his spectacles on his sleeve,

Criofan's confident gaze turned to disbelief, but Lugh slowly nodded his head, taking in everything Baudwin said.

"She grew so angry with me," Baudwin continued. "And then she took the egg. She said I was unworthy, and then she whirled me around in the Water, until I thought I would drown."

After he finished telling his tale, everyone remained silent.

"I've never heard of such a thing," Lugh began. "There are the old stories, of course, but I've never heard of anyone being visited by such a being. Are you sure that's what happened? Were you perhaps in some kind of daze?"

Baudwin shook his head. "I know what I saw."

Matha then put in, "I've known Baudwin his entire Life. I don't believe he would lie about something like this." Looking oddly at his friend, he added, "Yet, I'm still not sure I believe this — and I'm a Guilder!"

"I agree," Criofan said, studying Baudwin.

"So *this* is why you left us," Matha said, "and why you visited my mother? You had to tell someone, and you didn't trust us."

"I didn't think you would believe me," Baudwin replied. "But she did."

"She did?" Matha asked.

"Yes."

A change then came over Matha and he said, "Then what you say must be true."

Lugh then grabbed Baudwin by the shoulders. "I'm not sure I believe your story. Perhaps you saw something while you were lost in a waking."

Criofan didn't seem sure either. "Have you ever had a waking like that?" he asked.

Baudwin was disappointed that only Matha seemed to believe him.

"Perhaps the Water just chose for me to suffer," he said.

"No, no!" Lugh began. "You're seeing this the wrong way! If you didn't have a waking, then she took your egg for a reason, but the egg will come back to you. None of us may understand that spirit, but she *is* of the Water, and just as the tides may carry out a boat, eventually they will draw it back to shore."

"But my egg is gone!"

"Well, perhaps you lost it some other way," Criofan said.

"Yes, and if you did have a waking, the waking must have made you misplace the egg," Lugh added. "Surely, it will come back to you."

Baudwin realized there was no use in trying to convince them, so he decided to play along. He remained still, sitting stooped upon the column. "She was so horrible, Lugh. . . I can't begin to explain."

"And yet she spared your Life — didn't she?" Lugh asked.

This thought had never occurred to Baudwin. Lugh was placing importance upon something that only a wiser Faery like himself could understand. If only Lugh really believed him.

"What of it, then?" Criofan asked. "Perhaps she just wanted to toy with you."

"No!" Lugh exclaimed. "You tell us she said you weren't worthy — which is the clue. She's waiting to see something more from you."

"I don't *have* anything more," Baudwin replied, frustrated. He hadn't realized until now how exhausted he was. Beleaguered, he held his head in his hands. Only Matha seemed to believe his story was true. Around him, the Cyhiraeth sounded like nothing but a dark, droning hum. He had nothing left to say.

Lugh then shot a glance at Matha and Criofan. "I know what we need to do to lift Baudwin's spirits," he began. "There's someone in this quarter I want you all to meet. She may be able to help Baudwin see what other steps to take on his path."

"*Another* adventure?" Baudwin groaned.

"The last stop before we turn in — I promise!" Lugh replied.

Sighing, Baudwin stood up. Taking a final look at the squalor around them, he was relieved to be leaving, but sorry that he hadn't been able to ease the Faeries' plight.

Lugh slapped him on the back. "Don't fret, old chum," he said. "The Elves have done us all a great favor today."

"How is that?" Baudwin asked.

"Don't you see?" Lugh replied. "They totally ignored what the Faeries really wanted, revealing just how *little* they actually care about them. Using nets? Degrading! They would *never* do that to their own kin!" Having found his stride, Lugh continued, his eyes blazing. "I couldn't have hoped for more today. I thought you would simply see how poor the Faeries were, but now you see how mistreated they are as well."

"Yes, and you should do something!" Criofan exclaimed.

Lugh shook his head. "The Expert of Silver was right — I have no authority here. But, if they had tried this in the Nechtain Quarter, we would have had a thousand Faeries at our backs. Here, all we had was Loch."

Hearing this, they all laughed.

"Baudwin," Lugh offered earnestly, "you must never forget what you just saw — and you must *never* trust the Elves!"

"But Ferrell said he could help me find my mother," Baudwin insisted.

"Bah!" Lugh replied. "Only the Water will help you. No self-respecting Faery, who's also the son of the Primary of Water, should *ever* depend upon an Elve over his own element!"

The words pierced Baudwin to his core. Lugh had made his point, but Baudwin still wanted to give Ferrell the benefit of the doubt. The Elves weren't the only ones to blame. Padhra, the Guild Leader of the Cyhiraeth, had supported the removal of the street urchins. Baudwin wondered what Padhra was really like. Shouldn't he at least have come to observe the relocation? Perhaps he and other guild leaders were not as noble as Lugh.

"Come now!" Lugh exclaimed, running. "Let's be off, while we still have the Sun."

◦✛◦

Leaving the ruined neighborhood behind, they headed deeper into the Cyhiraeth Quarter. All conversation ceased as they reflected upon the events of the day. They turned onto the Lower Cyhiraeth Road, and then crossed a bridge over the canal. Soon they saw another bridge running perpendicular to the Lower Cyhiraeth Road. On a pillar at the entrance was a symbol of River Cyhiraeth — another wailing banshee. Together they traveled across the bridge, looking all around for signs of trouble. But all was silent and still.

Just before they reached the border between the Cyhiraeth and Condatis Quarters, Baudwin heard a voice singing. The voice carried through the alleyways, rising and falling like a dirge in Winter — desolate, yet strangely comforting. Listening more closely, he tried to make out the words, but there were none, only a mesmeric keening that drew them in — closer and closer.

Matha looked to and fro, his spectacles glinting in the afternoon sunlight. "Who is that?" he asked, cocking his head to the side. Baudwin saw curiosity in his face, mixed with apprehension.

"Just another wailer," Lugh replied, listening. "This quarter is full of them."

"Certainly a lady's voice," Criofan said, closing his eyes to better hear.

Baudwin nodded, and then ventured into an alleyway to find the source of the singing.

"There's no time!" Lugh called, but Baudwin ignored him. Soon everyone was following him, as he turned down one street and then another, the rooftops of the buildings drawing closer and closer, forming a latticework that nearly blocked out the Sun.

They took one turn and then another. As sunlight streamed through the narrow spaces between the buildings, the streets grew darker, and the Air more pungent. Walking faster, they almost tripped over piles of broken cobblestones, and then a mischief of rats scuttled past them, their yellow eyes gleaming eerily in the shadows. Baudwin quickly jumped out of their way.

The wailing grew louder, and Baudwin pressed on harder, unperturbed by Lugh's persistent protests. Finally they rounded one last corner. Across from them, they found the source of the wailing.

Criofan had been right. The wailer was indeed a lady, and a water Faery at that, sitting on her front porch in a high-back chair, knitting. Next to her was a lighted glowstone, for this far into the alleyway, the Sun was almost gone. The colors of her clothes, like the wrinkles on her face, were deep and darkened with age. Baudwin could sense that she knew they were there, but still, she did not look at them. Busily, she kept knitting. A raccoon lay at her feet, keeping her company.

She stopped wailing, and then sang in a low, melodious voice:

How do you die before you die?

What does the banshee say?

How do you face what you can't deny?

When will she come your way?

As the words left her lips, they stared at her, speechless. Returning their gaze, her eyes pierced into them. Having taken their measure, she went back to her knitting. Ivy green hair streaked with gray hung in wisps over her work, as her pallid, bony fingers steadily stitched.

Lugh recognized her. "Esther!" he exclaimed.

Baudwin expected her to say something, but she was silent. Strangely, while much about her seemed fresh and vibrant she also seemed spent — as if her Water had already left her, like the painted withered roses he had seen when he entered the Cyhiraeth Quarter. As he remembered this, she looked at him and laughed, and he suspected that she could read his thoughts. A shiver went up his spine.

"What then, are the answers," she asked, "to *all* the questions in my song?"

Baudwin said nothing. Matha and Criofan looked at Lugh, expecting him to speak first. Much to their surprise, Lugh stared blankly back at them. Laughing, she set down her knitting needles, and turned to face them.

They took a half step back.

"No, I am *not* a banshee!" she exclaimed, laughing even more.

Gathering his senses, Lugh said, "Of course not. You're the one I wanted Baudwin to meet. I was so busy leading him that I didn't realize *you* were the one doing the leading." Eying her home, he added, "I see you have moved."

Esther[4] laughed again. "Perhaps I moved, or perhaps the *Cyhiraeth* did the moving."

"Your wailing mesmerized us," Lugh said. "My friend, Baudwin, came running at the sound."

"That is its purpose," she replied, nodding her head and reaching for her raccoon. Gently, she began stroking its fur. The raccoon stared back at her, lazily

---

[4] Pronounced [EIS-tir]

swishing his ringed tail. She then looked directly at Baudwin. "Why have you answered my call?" she asked.

Nervously, Baudwin explained, "I was drawn to your wailing, but when I heard your song, the words reminded me of someone I just met."

"*The swords came for us,*" she recited, as she sat up straighter in her chair, staring at him. "*But they did not take us to Annwyn.*"

Hearing this, Baudwin jumped, the hairs on his neck prickling. For those were the *exact* words the old faery gent had spoken before the guards had arrived to take him away. Had she been spying on all of them? The idea was absurd, for she was old, perhaps eight hundred years or more, and the destitute Faeries were far from here. She couldn't possibly have been watching them, yet he was curious how she could know what had been said.

"How did you hear those words?" he asked.

"Yes," Lugh said, stepping toward her. "I too would like to know."

"*Because, only we could take ourselves there,*" Esther continued, repeating the rest of what the old faery gent had said. "*Those of us who'd had enough of vying, and were ready to embrace the art of dying.*"

Hearing the riddle recited again in its entirety, Baudwin also stepped toward her. Perhaps she knew what the faery gent meant. "Where could they take themselves that the swords could not?" he asked.

"To the place I sing of in my song," she replied, "where only *you* — not elven swords — will end your Life."

Her explanation seemed strange to them. Why would anyone end their own Life? The Faeries in this quarter were indeed peculiar, if not mad. Baudwin pondered her song; dying before dying seemed impossible. Yet her words burrowed into his mind, demanding that he see a deeper meaning that he could not yet fathom.

An uncomfortable silence ensued.

Lugh had heard enough. "Esther," he began, "I've brought Baudwin so that you could help guide him. He's lost his way."

"I've known of his coming," she replied. "Allow me to introduce myself. I am Esther, and this is my companion, Washer."

"Hello, Washer," Baudwin said.

"Say hello, Washer," Esther said, stroking her pet. "A Guild Leader and his friends have come to visit."

Washer looked up at Baudwin, his eyes gleaming from his black fur mask.

"Are you curious why we're here?" Lugh asked, amused. Washer chittered back at him.

"Did you earn your name by cleaning clothes for the banshee?" Baudwin asked. Nodding, Washer rubbed his paws together. Lugh chuckled.

"And you're Baudwin?" Esther asked.

"Yes, Baudwin, son of Kelven of Deuona."

"Criofan, son of Congal, of Deuona."

"Matha, son of Niall, of Deuona."

They then made the sign of the Water.

Standing up, Esther clapped her hands. The greatness of the wisdom she bore made her seem taller than she was. Her clothing was tattered with age, yet she remained dignified. She had a shyness in her countenance that had been tempered through hundreds of years meeting the challenge of her station.

"Good!" she exclaimed. "Now it's time for me to hear about why you came." Turning to Baudwin, she continued, flaring her hands on either side of her face as she spoke:

"Long ago, before the Great Befalling, I was a young one like you," she said, pointing her bony finger at Baudwin. "In those days all the Faeries in the realm traveled to this city. And in this quarter, the dark Faeries visited most frequently, bringing us wisdom to end all that is false before healing," she continued.

Hearing this, Baudwin was reminded of his bitter night under the bridge in the Cyhiraeth. He had certainly felt that he was dying. Was the Cyhiraeth trying to show him that he was more than his fear? He had, after all, taken in the bitterness of the inky Water, and felt stronger, so perhaps he had been dying before he died.

"They taught us what very few Faeries could face, and we in turn taught them what we knew about the Water. We understood them better than any other faery tribe — you see?"

"Why is that?" Baudwin asked.

"The dark Faeries were shunned by many," Esther replied. "They had been greatly misunderstood, but we water Faeries never faulted them for seeing the realm differently. So in kind, they took a liking to us, and shared their secrets. They also gave us gifts. I was one who was fortunate enough to receive a great boon from them. Hundreds of years ago, after I joined with my current and coursed with my feelings, I was taken to a special ceremony."

All of them were captivated, hanging upon her every word. Washer sat up on his hind legs, with his front paws clasped together, staring at her.

"I was about your age — two and ten — and I was frightened," she continued. "You see, even water Faeries become uneasy around dark Faeries. Yet, we feel a special kinship with them, for our wisdom teaches us about our feelings. We know how to navigate the darkest places within. And they know how to face the Darkness itself."

Esther stood for a moment before speaking again. "They took me deep inside the Onyx Shell Keep to a chamber. I had coursed well with my feelings, enduring my darkest ones, far more than most my age. For this reason, I was touched by the banshee and granted the Sight."

"The Sight?" Baudwin asked.

"Yes, the ability to see the past — the present — and the future — while knowing that all we will ever have is the present moment."

If I could see the future, I certainly wouldn't need the present, Baudwin thought to himself. As if she knew what he was thinking, Esther smiled at him. "You *are* a young sprout," she said as she picked up Washer and began stroking his fur.

"Why are you telling us all this?" Lugh asked.

"I know of your search, Baudwin," she replied. "Come inside, and I will guide you."

With that, she disappeared through the door of her modest dome home. The rest of them remained outside, wondering what might await them should they follow her.

Baudwin wasn't about to spend another moment wondering what to do. He wanted to know his future. Quickly, he moved to the door. As he did, Matha tugged at his sleeve.

"You aren't going in there, are you?" Matha asked.

"Of course I am!" Baudwin exclaimed. "I would be foolish not to. Did you hear what she just said? She knew what that poor gent said at the ruins of the Cyhiraeth Quarter. If she has the Sight, perhaps she can help me find my mother."

Soberly, Lugh looked at Baudwin. "Be careful," he said. "I've known her for many seasons, and while I can guarantee she means no harm, I don't know what effect her words will have on you, or your path."

"Have her use the Sight to find you something better to wear!" Criofan added, pointing at the old-fashioned clothes Lugh had lent Baudwin.

"Fashion is for the vain," Lugh retorted.

"He's right," Baudwin said, laughing. "I must not let vanity interfere." Gesturing toward the door, he added, "Come now — aren't you curious about what she has to say?"

Baudwin's friends considered what to do next. Eying each other, they hesitated. The open door taunted them to steel their courage and enter. None wanted to be the last to go forward, so they all did at once.

Inside there was no sign of her, just the smell of incense and water lilies. Around the circular hallway they went, with just a few glowstones to light the way, past paintings of creatures of the night — red foxes, flying squirrels, and beavers — gathered near trees and along riverbanks.

"Pass the painting of the large beaver and turn right," she called out.

As they proceeded, the floorboards creaked under their weight. No doubt, the old home was rarely visited by so many at once.

Entering a small room, they found her sitting behind a round wooden table facing the door. Stuffed chairs with purple velvet upholstery contrasted boldly against green velvet curtains that stretched from ceiling to floor. Woven patterns of seashells and eternity knots in the carpet hinted of mysteries only she could decipher. Washer rested next to her, curled up in a ball on a pillow. A simple crystal bowl filled with Water sat in the center of the table, lit by a circle of violet glowstones.

"Please do sit down," Esther said. As they took their seats, she dropped willow leaves into the bowl, stirring them gently with her fingers.

"Has anyone ever scried for you?" she asked, looking at Baudwin. "And told you what they see?"

Baudwin shook his head *no*.

"You must state your intention," she continued. "What do you desire to know?"

"I want to find my mother," Baudwin replied, trying to remain calm, for he earnestly hoped she could help him.

Hearing this, she closed her eyes and then recited:

Sacred stirrings of the Water

Night so dark and day so bright

Join together as we summon

All that frees our inner Sight

Inner Sight, he pondered. Was Esther finally going to give him the answers he so desperately needed? As he looked at her, she said nothing, remaining calm and quiet like a tide pool reflecting the full Moon.

Baudwin waited, and Esther stared, transfixed, into the bowl. The leaves moved this way and that, touching each other and drifting apart. Quietly she sat, reading a language only she could understand. After a time, she looked up at Baudwin.

"You'll find one who will send you to her, but before you do, you must first travel as the salmon does."

Taking her words to heart, Baudwin could barely contain his excitement. If Esther was right, his mother had to be alive — somewhere! All he had to do was to understand her riddles. What did she mean when she spoke of salmons? he wondered. Was she speaking of the Nechtain, where the salmons made their home? He sneaked a glance at Criofan and Matha, who also seemed to be puzzling over her words.

He had to know more.

"Travel as the salmon does?" he asked. "You mean swim — isn't that right? How fortunate! We're all excellent swimmers!"

Esther ignored Baudwin and continued her scrying. "Your travels will be forced upon you, by one who is of your tribe, and one who is not. Both will also bring a perilous tide upon your kin."

Whoever does she mean? he thought, his mind racing.

"You will choose an ally who is actually your enemy," she continued. "And then save an enemy who is really your ally." Fiercely, she looked at him. "But through the gate you will go — alone!"

"An ally who is *actually* my enemy?" Baudwin asked. "*What* gate?"

Seeing his confusion, Esther gave him a warning: "Do not try to choose between the old and the new. You must let the currents decide for you. If you don't — you will surely drown."

Baudwin had no idea what she meant by *old* and *new*. Thus far, little of what she said made any sense at all.

Esther waved her hand, and the scrying was over. Washer sat up, chittering. Baudwin had a torrent of questions to ask. Matha and Criofan looked puzzled, and Lugh seemed strangely composed, as if he understood the deeper meaning of what she had just said, but couldn't explain it.

Baudwin asked her many more questions, but Esther only shook her head, saying that she saw nothing more. He would have to puzzle the rest of it out for himself, she explained. Baudwin persisted, but she said that seeing the future was never as clear as seeing the past, and he needed to remain in the present.

"What more will happen I cannot say," she continued. "I can only describe what is shown to me."

Irritated, Baudwin felt he had wasted his time.

"What good is it, then?" Criofan asked, frustrated.

Matha tried to ease the tension. "There must be more to figure out," he said. "We must look for a clue in the words."

"I do see one more thing," Esther added, surprising all. "When I spoke of the gate, I saw an image of a rainbow."

"A rainbow?" Baudwin asked.

"But this one doesn't come from the sky," Esther replied.

"What kind of rainbow doesn't come from the sky?" Matha asked.

"A rainbow. . ." Lugh mused. "A most auspicious sign — is it not?"

Ignoring their comments, Esther continued. "Yes, and the rainbow will be the key, but how and why, I do not know."

"What am I to do *now*?" Baudwin asked, more confused than ever.

Esther took his hand. "You need not do anything. Your fate will carry you forward."

Baudwin was disappointed. "None of this makes any sense!" he exclaimed. "We've wasted our time!" He pounded his fist on the table, shaking the Water in the bowl.

"Baudwin," Lugh said sternly.

"An ally who is *actually* my enemy?" Baudwin continued. "An enemy who is *really* my ally? What does that even mean?"

If Esther was offended none could tell. She looked at Baudwin, expressionless, waiting from him to finish his reproach.

"And a gate?" he asked. "Gates are everywhere! I might just as well wander through the city, hopping through every one I see!"

"Baudwin, you're being rude," Matha chided.

"Rainbows!" Baudwin bellowed. "While I wander, I may as well just look at the sky, and save myself some time!"

Esther then said, "The rainbow of which I speak isn't in the sky."

"Then — where is it?" Baudwin shouted, again pounding his fist on the table. Everyone but Esther was embarrassed. The Water in the bowl shook again, and then, ever so slowly, began circling in a small whirlpool. None noticed.

"You are weary from your journey," the scryer concluded. "I do not control what the Sight reveals to me, but I can tell you this. Your current challenge will soon seem a mere trifle, having been eclipsed by what is yet to come."

Baudwin opened his mouth to speak, but then saw everyone staring at the bowl on the table. The Water was now circling very rapidly. The room fell silent.

"Esther — is this *your* doing?" Lugh asked, shocked.

Esther looked as surprised as Lugh, but before she could speak, she fell into a trance, no longer seeming to be among them.

"What's the matter with her?" Baudwin asked nervously.

"I don't know," Lugh replied, alarmed. Uneasily, they watched the bowl. They had all seen whirlpools in rivers, driven by opposing currents, but they couldn't fathom what was happening now.

The Water in the bowl then circled even faster. Baudwin gasped. None of them knew what moved the whirlpool, but they did know that faster currents could mean a storm was brewing. Fearing what might happen next, Lugh steadied himself, remembering that the Water was their strength. Protectively, he cupped his hands over his heart, and the others followed suit. Bowing their heads they affirmed, "We are *with* the Water."

As if to challenge them, the Water in the bowl circled faster yet, rising to the ceiling in the shape of a spout. Curtains on the windows whipped, and floorboards rattled beneath them. As the glowstones lighting the room began to flicker, Washer scuttled beneath a chair to hide. A waking then seized them all but this one was unusual. There was no feeling of bliss, and they could not see, hear, or taste the Water. Instead, they felt another whirlpool spinning *inside* of them, like the spout of Water in the Air. They struggled to steady themselves. Nausea then overcame them, and with it the feeling of a presence watching them. Suddenly, the whirling inside them stopped, for something had seized hold of their element. Paralyzed, they waited.

Esther stared straight at Baudwin, but her eyes were not her own.

Panicked, they realized they could not move their mouths to speak. She smiled at them, and the hold the presence had upon them subsided. She then spoke, but with a voice that none but Baudwin had heard before. "Are you *really* the one who would wield the talisman — cross the bridge — and leave this realm behind?"

Baudwin recoiled. The one who had spoken these words was one he hoped never to meet again.

Lugh regarded Esther. "*What* talisman?" he demanded. "Esther, stop with your tricks! You're frightening us!"

Baudwin knew this was not Esther speaking to them any longer. *What is she doing here?* he thought. He wanted to reveal who she was to them right then and there, but stopped himself. Filled with dread, he waited to see what she would do. Their last encounter had ended horribly.

Everyone eyed Esther warily. Criofan gave her a distant stare and Matha was mute. "I will not be ignored," she said.

Possessed, Esther snapped her fingers. The spout in the Air burst, drenching them. Just as quickly, the wetness retreated, leaving them dry again. The Water then coalesced into a sphere, which rose into the Air — spinning. Everyone remained deathly silent, for none knew of anyone who could command the Water in this way.

"Tell me, Guild Leader," Esther began — her words deepening, her voice overtaken by an unknown being — "has this young one stopped *lying* to himself?"

Matha and Criofan were too shocked to reply, but Lugh steeled his courage. "Esther. . ." he began.

She laughed and then shook her head at him. "Esther," she replied, "cannot hear you — you leader of dolts."

"Who are you to mock me?" Lugh asked.

"Certainly not Esther," she replied. With that, she pointed into the Air, and a bubble appeared, and then another, and another. With a puff, she blew them at Lugh.

Lugh brushed the bubbles aside. "Why are you so interested in Baudwin — *whoever* you are?" Lugh asked.

"If you could see as a water Faery should, you would know," she replied. "But you are blind — as are all the Fae in *Tír na nÓg* who serve the *King* of Platinum. Again, tell me — has your friend stopped *lying* to himself?"

"Why should I answer your question?" Lugh asked.

"Because I can help ease his burden," she replied. "That is, *if* he has the character to be deemed worthy."

Lugh looked at her with suspicion, but she paid him no heed. "Take this as proof that I mean him no harm," she said.

A trickle of Water then flowed out of the sphere of Water that was still spinning midair. Swirling toward Lugh, the sinuous tendril turned into the shape of a water lily. She then spoke:

In Life you perish

Yet you always bring me joy

In Death I cherish

What my loss cannot destroy

Lugh could not fathom how the voice possessing Esther — whosoever it was — could have recited to him his favorite poem — one he had shared only with Baudwin a short time ago at his home. Whoever this being was seemed to have incredible *cumhachtaí*.[5] Challenging her any further would be foolish, if not downright dangerous.

Baudwin wondered what Lugh would say. The last time the spirit had spoken to him had been at the dam, just before she almost drowned him — chastising him for his feeble understanding of the first lesson of the Triquetra.

Transfixed by the water lily, Lugh relented. "I believe he has stopped," he replied. "Lying to himself, that is."

"And why do you say that?" she asked.

"Just today," Lugh continued, his voice quavering, "he confided in us that he did not believe himself to be honest. He then informed us about how he had *really* lost something precious to him — a glamorium egg. From what he told us, I believe a waking must have come to him — guided by the Water — for he said he had seen a vision of a water spirit, one he thought was real."

The possessed Esther grinned. "So, he *lied* about a water spirit coming to him," she asked, "by telling you he had a waking?"

Baudwin could sense how confused everyone was by her questions, but he knew who she really was. He wondered when she would reveal herself, and remained fearful of what she might do.

She stared at Lugh, her amusement quickly fading. The water lily in the Air disappeared.

"N — not — not on purpose, no," Lugh stammered. "I believe the Water was teaching him some kind of lesson, and that in a daze, he must have misplaced the glamorium egg."

---

[5] Pronounced [COO-uck-tee] powers

"Indeed," Esther replied, laughing. "The Water *was* teaching him a lesson, but not in the form of a waking."

Lugh regarded Esther with extreme annoyance. "How would you know?" he asked. "You weren't there!"

"Is that *so?*" Esther replied, her voice shifting into an unearthly timbre. Flinching at the sound, Lugh became silent. Esther then went completely still. For a moment, all they could hear was Washer wriggling nervously under the chair.

"*Esther* wasn't there — but *I* sure was!" she exclaimed merrily.

The sphere of Water spinning in the Air then transformed into the visage of the water spirit. Only her face appeared to them. She looked exactly as she had at the dam, the morning Baudwin first met her. She was beautiful again. Her opalescent eyes were framed by satiny locks of hair resembling river moss, with golden beads and pearls braided into the tresses.

Seeing her face, Lugh gasped, trembling. "So it is true — Baudwin *was* visited by a water spirit!"

Matha and Criofan were struck dumb.

Saying nothing, the water spirit regarded them. Ever so slowly, a smile formed on her lips. "Tell me, Guild Leader, would this young one trade a bowl flowing with Water from *this* river, for a gold coupler?" As she spoke, a translucent hand appeared and scooped the bowl up off the table, suspending it in the Air.

Lugh's face went pale. "You must tell me, spirit!" he exclaimed. "Who *are* you?"

"I am the babbler in the brook," she replied. "I'm the whisperer in the well, the rusher of the rivers, and the one who guides the Shiny ones to join with their currents, course with their feelings, and hone their intentions. Throughout the ages, all water Faeries knew my name, but no longer, so I will tell you now lest you forget — I am Boann."

So — she has a name! Baudwin thought, wonderstruck. He had never heard of her before, but she sounded older than the rivers, and from a time long ago when the old ways were revered.

"B—Boann!" Lugh stammered, his mouth agape. "Are you *really* she?" Struggling for words, he continued, "Unless you're just some nefarious imposter spirit, your presence must portend the dawning of a new age! Is that so?"

She reframed his question. "The counting of the ages belongs to the Elves. I am but the steward who prepares the Shiny ones for what is to come."

Lugh nodded, but Matha was not convinced. "We just saw you commanding the Water as the legends of Boann have told, but can you truly prove that you are *she?*" he asked.

Baudwin wasn't surprised that Matha knew of Boann, but he was worried that Matha's challenge would evoke her wrath.

"I can show myself to you," she said, "but you will not see who I truly am until you understand how *little* you know of yourselves."

Everyone was befuddled. None knew what to say, until Criofan broke the silence.

"Why have you come?" he asked. "And what have you done to Esther?"

The face of the water spirit then scowled, her watery teeth sprouting into fang-like protrusions. "*You* do not command *me* — son of the Primary of Commerce!" she snarled.

Hearing this, Criofan blenched and struggled to regain his composure, while the others remained silent.

The bowl dropped to the table — shattering — but the Water caught the shards of glass before they went flying.

The visage then spoke: "It is as you have said. Baudwin has at least become *somewhat* honest — but despite this, you did not believe in him. What good are you as friends?" As she spoke, she smiled at Matha. Lugh and Criofan looked down at the floor, for they had not believed Baudwin's story.

"I am living proof of his honesty," she continued. "For I am the one who took his glamorium egg — the only means by which he could achieve his goal — which then caused him to abandon his home and wander off. Set upon a new path, he was eventually forced to tell his friends the truth. In doing so, he learned Honesty — the first lesson of the Triquetra — which was always my intention."

"You *foresaw* all of this?" Baudwin asked, incredulous.

"Indeed," Boann said, "I initiated your journey, but didn't need to know every step you would take. In time, you would either be compelled to be honest, or prove yourself *truly* unworthy."

"I *did* prove myself worthy — didn't I?" Baudwin asked. "Now will you give me back my glamorium egg?"

"Getting ahead of yourself, as usual?" she asked.

Baudwin bit his tongue, for he had learned that it was better not to talk back to her.

The visage of the water spirit glowered. "You have taken a single step, but still many more challenges await you. Only when these are overcome will you be ready to be reunited with the one you seek. Take heed, for if you are strong enough to meet her, your longing to be joined will be replaced by a duty none should ever have to bear."

"But aren't I honest enough now?" Baudwin asked, as politely as he could.

"Perhaps so, perhaps not, but you have yet to learn the second lesson of the Triquetra — Truth. The gate will open only when the talisman is wielded by one who has sufficient command of the first two lessons. Only then will you cross the bridge."

"What bridge?" Lugh asked. Boann ignored him.

Thinking hard upon the words Esther had spoken earlier, Baudwin then asked, "Are you my *ally* or my *enemy*?"

A look of scorn crossed Boann's face. The Water around her eyes darkened. "Ask yourself *honestly*, and you will know the answer!" she declared.

Baudwin had no answer.

She then recited:

How do you die before you die?
What does the banshee say?
How do face what you can't deny?
When will she come your way?

"What are you trying to tell me?" Baudwin asked.

"What *truth* are you still denying?" she railed.

Baudwin remembered the devastating moment at the dam when she snatched his glamorium egg and then dropped him into the icy cold Water of the millpond. "I don't know!" he exclaimed, stricken.

"What is the truth that would tell you whether I'm your ally or your enemy?" she asked sharply.

"I barely understand the lessons of honesty!" he implored. "Why must you excoriate me with your demands that I know the *truth* as well?"

"The Water led you through this quarter so you could answer that very question," she replied. She then recited: "The swords came for us, but they did not take us to Annwyn! Because only *we* could take ourselves there."

Exhausted, Baudwin braced himself for what she might say next.

"Have you had enough of *vying* — and are you ready to embrace the art of *dying*?"

"What does that *mean*?" Baudwin asked. He hadn't understood *then* what the gent had meant in the ruins, and now he felt as if his entire future hinged upon grasping the riddle.

"Baudwin," she began, "through the lessons of honesty you must face this truth: That to truly *see* who you are, you must let go of who you *think* you are!" Waiting a moment for him to absorb the blow, she then added, "And *that* is how you die before you die!"

Her answer shook him to his core. He would have asked another question, but before he could, the sphere of Water and shards of glass fell back onto the table.

And then, whispering, she spoke one last time. "Perform not for fools, lest you become one." With a roar of rushing Water, her presence then vanished. The room was still.

The scrying bowl was back in place, as good as new. Baudwin suspected that the broken bowl had been an illusion all along, but that the Water had been real. Esther came out of her trance and asked them what had transpired. All they could tell her was that Boann had made her presence known. She had challenged Baudwin to find the truth that was *already* inside of him — truth that only honesty could lead him to see.

Chapter 29

THE CONDATIS QUARTER

Once again, Loch was on his way to meet Ferrell. Time was short, but the route was simple — just down the Lower Condatis Road and over the bridge, and he would be there. Ferrell had demanded that he report to him about what he had learned by following Baudwin. At first Loch had enjoyed spying on him and his friends, feeling as if he were back in the forests of Deuona, tracking grand horns. But after a time of skulking behind fountains and eavesdropping in alleyways, it had grown tiresome. As the excitement wore off, he felt more like a scullion, trudging after Baudwin in the quarters of Four Falls for hours on end. How he despised being forced to do this.

Heading down the road, Loch turned his gaze to the Condatis, the only river that flowed from *Tír Luí Lucharachán* through the Col of Lonrúil. *Time be cursed,* he thought. Wanting to feel something familiar, he knelt for a moment and thrust his hand into the current. This river Water was unlike any he had grown up around. It was foreign and wild. Pulling his hand away, Loch then tasted a droplet. Closing his eyes, he waited for his senses to speak to him. There was something more — a healing force — one he knew had to come from the hot springs that fed the river near Lake Aife.

To his surprise, he smiled.

The Condatis stirred his memories. He remembered being a young one on the Nechtain, riding the rapids in a water drum, and throwing pinecones at his friends. He wished he could be back there again, before he had known what the Assembly of Progress was, or he had ever been a Roiler — back to when he had had his last waking. *How long ago was that?* he wondered.

The Condatis coaxed him to remember. He wasn't sure, but likely his last one had been not long after he stopped looking for the Water. After that, he had never had another. Now, he could scarcely remember what a waking felt like — to be inside the Water and the Water *inside* him — as he flowed down creeks, over rocks and through rushes, completely in the moment. Back then, the Water was all he ever needed. But the Water had turned its back on him, so he had blazed a new trail of his own.

"And so it must be," Loch said, the smile leaving his face. Now he had better things to do.

Standing up, he left the river and made his way back to the main road. Ferrell was waiting, no doubt counting the seconds until his arrival. *That Elve is a drill, boring through stone*, he thought.

Ever since Loch had told him about his fight with Baudwin at the Springs of Coventina, Ferrell seemed different — agitated and perplexed — asking him question after question about the flood. How long had the eruption lasted? How high was the flow? But what Ferrell kept repeating over and over again was, "You're a water Faery. And you can't tell the difference between a gusher and a spirit?"

Loch had told him everything he knew. He had not seen a spirit — just Water — and probably a gusher, but Ferrell insisted he knew better. Surely Ferrell knew that gushers could rise very high and last a long time. Loch knew Ferrell was far too smart to be this stupid, which made Loch wonder even more about him. Ferrell maintained that the flooding of the shrine at the ruins of Coventina had been the work of a spirit, due to the fact that the flood had erupted right after they broke the tablet. The Water had separated Roilers and Guilders, yet Loch didn't believe a spirit could have done such a thing.

Ferrell was so certain that the spirit had caused the flood that he had become increasingly obsessed with Baudwin, which was probably why he had given Loch the chore of tracking him. Ferrell was searching for some link between Baudwin and the spirit. Loch had hidden his surprise when he learned that Baudwin had gotten himself indentured to Ferrell by breaking an expensive lamp. What was that fool up to? He must have known what the consequences would be. *And now he's jumped into Ferrell's lap*, Loch thought, amused.

Soon he reached a bridge running perpendicular to the Lower Condatis Road. On a pillar at the entrance was a symbol of the river — a hot spring rising from a circle of stones. Crossing quickly, he passed a number of Faeries, noting their steps. How much louder theirs were than his. He laughed. Unlike him, they didn't need a reason to be quiet. City Faeries would never hide behind trees, motionless, lest they break the silence around them, as they waited for their quarry to appear. No — they simply clacked upon the cobblestones, shifting about, shouting over one another, their gazes always landing at the next corner.

Having crossed the bridge, he wasn't far from where Ferrell had told him to meet — the place in the Condatis Quarter where the Elves were building their display for the Grand Unveiling. Not far away, he saw long stretches of bronze and wooden scaffolding, cranes and pulleys and large crates piled high upon the ground with elven markings on the sides. This quarter had the most elven influences of them all, for here River Condatis brought together *Tír Luí Lucharachán* and *Tír Éirí Síóg*. Around him he saw more pointed roofs than he could count.

Looking up, he saw an elven worker on a scaffold, bolting a large socket to a panel. Loch didn't know much about Magniglow, but he figured a huge bulb would be placed there, along with many more.

Rounding a tall stack of crates, he spotted Ferrell speaking to an elven gent he had never seen before. Oddly, the gent had a squirrel perched on his shoulder. Loch thought he looked strange wearing a knitted cap that was too warm for the day. His breeches were covered in river mud, and his shoes spotted with water stains.

As Loch approached them, Ferrell nodded at him. He continued speaking to the elven gent. He seemed happier — his usual cynicism gone. He motioned for Loch to wait.

"The Water's not right," Loch heard the gent say. "Not following any pattern that I have on record. The level goes up, and then down again, and then up, but at this time of year, it should be slowly receding."

"Tárlach," Ferrell asked, "has there been a flood?"

Tárlach shook his head. "The Condatis flows from Lake Dian Cècht,[1] which as you know is fed by the snows of Mount Breasal.[2] This year was not unusually wet. The water should get lower, bit by bit by bit," he added, gesturing with both his arms toward the ground. "And then rise again in the fall," he continued, smiling with delight, his arms lifted high.

Ferrell looked askance at Tárlach — a look Loch knew only too well. He then gazed past Tárlach, lost in thought. Loch wondered what lingered in the recesses of his mind. He imagined Ferrell had countless thoughts, all of them stored away in jars by a mad but methodical alchemist, who constantly shifted through them, unscrewing their lids, examining their contents, adding others, and then screwing the lids tightly back on.

"So is there nothing that explains why this is happening?" Ferrell asked, staring blankly at the water's edge. Loch could see how annoyed he was, and how much he disliked his own ignorance.

"Nothing I've seen before," Tárlach replied. "We're lucky the river isn't totally out of control. A while ago, the water rose so high I thought the quarter would flood." Tárlach stood for a moment, thinking. When he spoke, he seemed amused.

"Perhaps the Condatis *itself* is angry. There have, after all, been riots in the city, or so I've heard." Seeing that he had Ferrell's attention, he continued, his pudgy face grinning mischievously. "Or perhaps the spirits in the Chinewilds are simply restless, sending us their restless waters."

---

[1] Pronounced [JEE-un kaycht]
[2] Pronounced [BRESS-ill]

"I'm from the Chinewilds," Ferrell said, bristling. "What you call *spirits*, I call the wind. Wind that blows from Mount Breasal, a place so high that birds won't even fly there. This river is simply wild — as it should be."

Loch could sense that Ferrell was holding his suspicions back from Tárlach.

"Besides," Ferrell added, chuckling, "if there *were* spirits in the Chinewilds, I doubt they would bother placing their attention here. We couldn't be that interesting to them."

"I agree, you aren't," Tárlach said mockingly. "Which is why I prefer living in the woods."

Loch was surprised that Ferrell wasn't insulted. Instead, the Luminary grinned and put his fist over his heart, head down. Raising his head, he saluted Tárlach by placing four fingers to his temple. "You've done a great service to the Assembly, coming all this way," he said. "I'm sure the ride wasn't all that pleasant. On behalf of us all, I thank you."

"My pleasure indeed," Tárlach said, bowing. "Taking the water's measure is what I do. Will you be needing any more assistance? If not, I must return home to my pets. I'm sure they miss me. Isn't that right, Candy?"

As Tárlach stretched out his arm, Candy ran from his shoulder down to his hand, chirping loudly. Tárlach reached into his pocket and pulled out a treat. "Mustn't give you too much, or you'll get even fatter, my little friend," he said, beaming. "We don't want that."

Ferrell gave Tárlach a strange look. "You aren't one of those squirrel huggers, are you — like the Faeries?" he asked.

"Not at all," Tárlach replied, grinning. "But I do like talking to them. They understand exactly what I say." He then motioned to his pet. "Come, Candy, back into the pocket. We're going home."

Having eaten the treat, Candy scurried back up Tárlach's arm and into his pocket. "You see?" Tárlach asked. "She knew just what to do."

Now Loch was impressed. Elves weren't known for speaking to animals, much less telling them what to do. Tárlach was an interesting one. Perhaps when he went back to Deuona, he would visit him, and get him to spill his secrets.

Tárlach finished his farewells, and then was off. As he left, Ferrell handed him a piece of paper, probably a promissory note for his service, Loch thought. Ferrell then turned to watch some Elves above them on the scaffolds, busily twisting wrenches and pounding hammers.

"You better have something for me," Ferrell said without looking at Loch.

"I did exactly what you told me to do," Loch replied, bridling at Ferrell's tone. "I followed them all day, through the Nechtain, Danu, and Cyhiraeth Quarters. As you said, the lot of them were together — with Lugh."

"And?" Ferrell asked, his attention still fixed on the Elves as they worked.

"In the Nechtain Quarter, they spoke about the ways of the salmon. In the Danu Quarter, they met Ayamonn, the Guild Leader of the Danu Quarter, at the Moonstone Rushes. He explained to them about how the Faeries give moonstones to the Elves to help them find their feelings. Then he gave them all moonstones. I was a bit jealous, as I would have liked one for myself. Ayamonn seemed like a strong leader. I rather liked him. He seemed like an older version of myself, except for —"

"Enough!" Ferrell interrupted, impatiently tapping his foot. "What about Lugh? What did he say to Baudwin?"

"He told him that the reason you were so interested in him was that Baudwin had both a guild leader *and* a primary in his family."

Hearing this, Ferrell seemed taken off guard by the comment. Loch paused before speaking again, wondering how Ferrell would take what he would say next.

"He also spoke of Rian, asking Baudwin in no uncertain terms why he would consort with you when he has Rian as a friend. He said Rian was a *true* friend, but you were nothing but a graceless inquisitor."

Having said his piece, Loch expected Ferrell to explode, but Ferrell kept his anger in check. How Loch relished sharing such a vexing tidbit with him and watching him seethe. Ferrell said nothing.

"There was even some talk before that about a glamorium egg," Loch continued. "Matha and Criofan had been arguing with Baudwin. Matha said that Rian had given him the egg, and then Criofan said that Baudwin had lost it."

Suddenly, Ferrell shifted his eyes from the workers to Loch. "They talked about a glamorium egg?" he asked. "Do tell."

"Yes," Loch replied. "It seems that Rian gave Baudwin the egg to help him find his mother."

"Such nonsense!" Ferrell exclaimed. "*I'm* the one who will help Baudwin find his mother — and no one else." Hearing this, Loch went silent. Ferrell raged on.

"You're not keeping anything from me, are you?" Ferrell shouted. "If you are, I'll —"

"No!" Loch exclaimed. "Why would I do that and risk extending my servitude?" Changing the subject, he continued, "After that, they spoke about the riot. It seems Baudwin had been there from the beginning. A couple of Elves started the whole thing, arguing about the Eternal Movement and the Rise of Time. Chaos ensued, and even Ayamonn was unable to end the fight."

"Good," Ferrell said, his humor returning. "At least Baudwin got to see firsthand what truly matters in elven culture." As he spoke, his Luminary medallion glinted brightly in the sunlight. "What else did you see or hear? Anything strange or out of the ordinary? Did Baudwin ever leave them?"

"No," Loch replied, hoping to end the conversation. Ferrell's volatile questioning was wearing on him. "Nothing you wouldn't expect."

"What then, is Baudwin *up* to?" Ferrell asked. "He has to be up to something." Loch couldn't tell what Ferrell really wanted to know. Again, he went silent.

"And *so?*" Ferrell asked, his voice prodding Loch, as if Loch were a hedgehog curled into a ball, his spines popping back at Ferrell.

"After leaving the Danu Quarter, they headed to the Cyhiraeth. Tracking them was much more difficult. Even in the daylight, the streets were strange and dark. They stopped to watch a faery lady painting roses. She told them peculiar things — how she was painting their journey to Annwyn. On the canvas, the flowers looked withered and almost dead. I could tell Baudwin and the rest of them had no idea what she was going on about." Loch paused before speaking. "That was mostly everything."

"Mostly. . ." Ferrell mused, his voice trailing off. He then began pacing. Loch steeled himself as Ferrell seemed poised to strike.

"My guards," he began, sounding accusatory, *"my* guards say there was *another* riot — in the Cyhiraeth. They were trying to relocate some indigent water Faeries to a better place. Some kind of misunderstanding arose, and then a fight broke out."

Ferrell continued, glaring at Loch. "They also told me someone intervened — a water Faery who brazenly tore off his disguise and shouted at them. Tell me, Loch, what were those words?"

Loch tensed, the stitches on his patchy coat stretching. "I don't know," he replied. "For a time, I was separated from my quarry."

"Allow me to help you remember," Ferrell said, stepping closer to Loch, until their faces almost touched. "*From — the — water — we — are — born,*" he intoned, riveting his gaze upon Loch.

A jolt went up Loch's spine. "Ah yes," he replied. "*That's* the line."

Ferrell stepped away from him, again studying the handiwork of the Elves. Steadily, they sawed and pounded. Loch waited, uttering nothing. Was Ferrell intending to ridicule or punish him?"

Ferrell weighed his words before speaking. "You're a courageous idiot," he said flatly, much to Loch's surprise. "But an idiot nonetheless. Slinging stones at so many is ridiculous. You didn't have a chance, but you attacked them anyway. I should send you to the mines and be rid of you, or better yet send you to Bog, just as you once said you would do to Baudwin. Certainly, that would be fitting. What kind of tracker are you — making yourself known to your quarry? When my guards told me about your nonsensical exploits, I almost believed you were trying to work against me, but I know you couldn't be *that* stupid — could you?"

Ferrell looked again at Loch. Unexpectedly, he began laughing.

"You want to be a leader — isn't that right?"

"I *am* a leader!" Loch shouted, his hesitancy gone.

Ferrell shook his head. "You can't lead because you choose battles you can't win."

"I was helping my kin," Loch declared, his passion returning at the memory of what he had done.

"Ah yes, helping them to fail — and needlessly so. After you left, they went right back to where they were before — choosing to live in squalor in the aftermath of Govannon's triumph."

"You had no right to shoot them with nets and then cart them away like trumpery."

A heavy silence fell upon the construction. A number of workers looked down upon them, wondering who would be so foolish as to shout at the Luminary. Nearby, some Earth Guards studied them as well, prepared to act, wondering how Ferrell would respond.

"*My* right?" Ferrell shouted back. "Who do you think gave the order?" he asked, smirking. "None other than one of your own kin, Padhra, the Guild Leader of the Cyhiraeth Quarter. He knew the Elves were rebuilding the area, as well as what was best for the Faeries."

Ferrell waited for Loch to take in his words.

"Even more to the point," he went on, "what do you suppose Baudwin thought about *you*? That you were brave, or up to something questionable? Pulling off your disguise was stupid. You should have kept it on, but you couldn't help yourself, could you? If you want to be a leader, you must learn to play the long game."

Loch remained silent, for he knew Ferrell had a point.

"Next time use some sense," Ferrell added. "Weigh your actions before you take them. Think beyond your own arrogance."

Gruffly, Loch turned away. He didn't care what Ferrell said, or if he was right, for he had acted for the benefit of his kin. *Just like Boann would have done,* he thought, remembering the mural he had seen in the office of the Nechtain. Although tearing off his mask had complicated matters, what kind of leader hides himself? No — that was not his way.

Sensing Loch's displeasure, Ferrell pointed at the construction.

"Look around you. What do you see?" he asked.

"I see preparations for the Grand Unveiling," Loch replied.

"And do you know what could ruin it all?"

"Faery riots?" Loch replied, joking. "Large swarms of flying beetles? A stampede of wild boars?" As he envisioned a sounder of swine overrunning the city, he couldn't help laughing.

Ferrell drew closer to Loch than he liked. Close to Loch's ear he whispered, so that not a single worker could hear, "At the ruins of Coventina, are you *sure* you didn't see a spirit?"

Loch suppressed a laugh. He had already told Ferrell many times that all he had seen was Water, and nothing else. Ferrell's insistence on this being otherwise was becoming ridiculous.

"Just the Water," he replied.

"That flowed so high that you nearly drowned, carrying you and your Roilers away from Baudwin — so far, in fact, that you couldn't find him again? Water that came from a *sacred* well, cherished by the Faeries, yet long since forgotten? Water that you and your kin now simply call a *gusher*?"

Ferrell paced about as he spoke further, keeping his voice low. "Do you *really* believe ancient water Faeries would build a well over an underground gusher?"

Loch reflected on this for a moment. Everyone knew that the Waters in Coventina were a huge tangle of springs, many of which gushed from new places from time to time — until the ice came. Yet, Ferrell had a point. Loch decided to find out exactly what Ferrell meant.

"If not a gusher, then what?"

Ferrell studied him, measuring him carefully. Still speaking in low tones, he said, "A *spirit* of the water."

Loch would have laughed had Ferrell not seemed so ingenuous. Surely the Luminary couldn't believe in such things, for Loch certainly didn't. Yet Ferrell seemed as if he did. Loch decided to test him further. He would pretend to believe in spirits and see what else Ferrell had to say.

"If the Water flowed from a spirit, why would it come for us?" Loch asked.

As he spoke, Loch wondered if Ferrell could tell that he was putting him on.

"You're more like Baudwin than you know," Ferrell replied, frowning. "A naive pair of bumpkins — filled with credulity."

Now Loch really wondered what Ferrell would say next.

"Neither of you knows your own history," Ferrell continued. "At the Show Wheel, I had to explain to Baudwin about moonstones, and now I have to teach you about your own spirits. They say such ones used to initiate Faeries at shrines like those, so they could teach them special wisdom about the elements. They would perform hidden rituals — now long lost — that would bestow boons. But first, they would have to find those who were worthy of such instruction."

"What kind of boon?" Loch asked, his curiosity piqued.

"I don't know," Ferrell replied.

"If this is true, why then, would such a one attack us?"

"Because you weren't *worthy*!" Ferrell exclaimed. "You were fighting in a sacred place — you fool. Defiling the shrine." Pointing to the scaffolds, he added,

"You couldn't have done any worse if you took out your slingshot and attacked one of my workers. You angered it by disrespecting the old ways."

The workers around them pretended not to notice Ferrell's outburst, unaware of what he was talking about. Ferrell composed himself again.

Loch still wasn't sure what angle Ferrell was playing. But he did remember the warning Baudwin had shouted as they were all swept away: "We must *not* fight the Water!" If a spirit had come for them, then perhaps Baudwin was less of a gullible bumpkin than Ferrell knew.

"If you're right, the spirit must have chosen me, to teach me a lesson so I would become a better leader," Loch said, grinning at Ferrell.

Ferrell started laughing, and Loch wasn't sure what to say next. "Who else would such a spirit come for?" he asked. "Why, Baudwin — of course!" Ferrell exclaimed, answering his own question. Do you always believe everything is all about *you*?" Loch appeared shaken, having been dealt a rattling blow.

"Surely not!" Loch shouted. Now he understood. All this talk of spirits was just a roundabout way for Ferrell to remind him of his place by making him feel inferior to Baudwin.

"Baudwin still searches for the water, isn't that right?" Ferrell asked. "He's of the Water Guild. You, on the other hand, are a mere Roiler, and while you seem to pine for the water, you turned your back on its sacred promise, did you not?"

Ferrell's reasoning cut him to the bone. How he wanted to pound Ferrell into the ground for his biting judgment. How outrageous that Ferrell would make up such a story simply to humiliate him.

"So you think he's worthy, and I'm not!" he bellowed.

"Yes, I do," Ferrell replied, unmoved by Loch's outburst. "However, you must not take what I say the wrong way. You're much better off as a Roiler. We Elves welcome your kind, for you see more clearly what the future holds."

Ferrell's words gave Loch little comfort. Still, he seethed with anger. He was, after all, proud to be a Roiler, but jealous that Baudwin seemed more worthy of the Water in Ferrell's eyes than he. Even if Ferrell was making up stories about spirits to prove his point.

"Why *not* me?" he asked.

"Because you gave up on the water!" Ferrell exclaimed. "And that's not such a bad thing."

Ferrell had shouted again, and still the workers pretended not to notice. He then whispered, "These spirits are *dangerous*. They're from another time and place. They don't belong in the future we envision. Look what happened to you. All you did was break an old tablet in a crumbling shrine, and you were almost sent to Annwyn for your trouble. None of us knows what will happen next, so we have to be ready."

"You can stop now," Loch said crossly. "No one believes in spirits. You know that."

Ferrell nodded slowly, as a moment of warmth breached his calculating veneer. Carefully he spoke, "I knew you wouldn't believe me, so I summoned you here to prove it."

Loch bristled, but part of him wondered if Ferrell might be telling the truth.

Ferrell smiled as he explained, "That Elve that was just here — the peculiar one with the squirrel. Do you know why I had him measuring the water level?"

Loch waited for Ferrell to continue. "The water level has been going up and down — and madly so. This isn't normal for the Condatis, or any of the other rivers. None of them should flow this way. That spirit is still after Baudwin — of this I am certain. Once they turn their attention on someone, they're relentless, you know."

"Well, I wouldn't know."

"Until you *did*," Ferrell replied, again lowering his voice. "But then, you might be sent to Annwyn if you did too. I've seen them. I've fought them before. I know you don't believe me, but someday you will."

Loch couldn't believe what he was hearing. An Elve and a Luminary of the Assembly of Progress had just admitted to him that not only did he believe in spirits, but he had *seen* and *fought* them. Could all of this be true? Loch knew Ferrell was calculating, and would go to any length to achieve his aims, but would he also lie — and so elaborately — about something like this?

Loch turned away from Ferrell, taking in his demeanor from the corner of his eye. He could usually gauge the guile of an Elve or Faery quite easily. Like a wolf, he could tell a friend from a foe just by glancing at them. But Ferrell was different. He didn't seem like either, which bothered Loch even more. What if he couldn't figure him out? What then? Not knowing was even worse than knowing. A strange kind of panic set in, one that made him want to escape to another place. But he knew there was nowhere else to go. At least for now, running away was out of the question.

Thus far, despite his enforced servitude, Ferrell hadn't punished him too severely, either by beating him down or locking him away. So for now, Loch would wait and see. Yes — that was the best idea. Perhaps Ferrell's bark was worse than his bite, and his threats of being sent to the mines were empty. Even better, perhaps he did want to broker some kind of peace between the Faeries and Elves. And that worked for him, for Ferrell was leading *Tír na nÓg* toward a future that Loch wanted to embrace.

Not knowing what to say next, Loch simply asked, "Why are you telling me all this?"

"To be forewarned is to be prepared," Ferrell replied, staring into the distance. "We all must be. If Baudwin needs our help, I expect you to join me in protecting him." Seeing the look of surprise on Loch's face, he added, "Come with me. There's something more I have to show you."

Ferrell led Loch to a gated area with two guards at the front. Inside a high fence sat stacks of supplies near barrels, and other sophisticated magniglow machinery. On the ground Loch saw a few crates with black sprockets painted on the side — a symbol he had never seen before.

"That symbol marks secrets the Assembly is not yet ready to share with your kin," Ferrell began, adamantly. "You won't know what's inside until I tell you to deliver one of those crates to me." Ferrell paused, staring intently at Loch. "The black sprocket must *not* be taken lightly. Crates marked with the black sprocket are used *only* in times of dire emergency."

Loch studied the crate, wondering what could be so important.

"My guards will keep these crates close, but should they be unable to deliver one, then you must fetch it for me."

⚜

The month of Willow had ended, and with the flourishing of spring came Hawthorn — the sixth Moon of the year. The days were bursting with sweetness and warmth, yet Baudwin had little time for fun, as he was working very hard. By day he assisted Glas, his fingers callused from twisting copper wire onto spools, and by night he practiced his acrobatic tricks with Criofan and Matha, his muscles begging for rest. *The show is almost here,* he thought. Soon the hard work would end, and hopefully, Ferrell would give the command to search for his mother. He hadn't begun yet, but Baudwin expected that he would.

Baudwin still wasn't sure upon whom he could rely. Boann had told him that to truly see himself, he would have to let go of who he thought he was. But who *did* he think he was? He had hoped that Boann would provide clearer guidance, but she hadn't. The lesson of truth was to him still an enigma, and he had only begun to be more honest. If Ferrell did help him, then Baudwin wouldn't have to master the lesson of truth, or wield whatever strange talisman Boann had hinted at. She still seemed to believe that he was unworthy of such a task. And even worse, if Ferrell reneged on his promise, then where would he be?

Lugh, Criofan, and Matha were left breathless after seeing her, shocked that she was real. Lugh surmised that her arrival, two hundred years after the Great Befalling, meant a great change was coming to *Tír na nÓg.* Criofan and Matha wanted to tell everyone about her, but Lugh cautioned them not to speak, for fear that none would believe their story. Baudwin was reminded of the bystanders at the Deuona Engineerium. None had believed that the Water had come to him. Faeries were now living in an elven realm, Lugh had said, where progress left no room for spirits. However, Lugh had counseled Baudwin to heed the words of Boann, and no other.

Baudwin wondered what Esther's riddle had meant: "You will choose an ally who is actually your enemy, and then save an enemy who is really your ally." Was Ferrell his ally? Boann certainly didn't seem to be. Pondering more on the riddle, he wondered who the ally was that he would save. The thought of rescuing either Ferrell or Boann seemed absurd to him. Again, he wasn't sure which path to take. *Should I listen to the currents swirling inside of me?* he thought. *Or should I attend to the gears whirling outside of me?*

Perhaps the easier choice was simply to accept Ferrell's help — once and for all — as his ally. Again, he decided to visit him, and so he did. Later that day, he met with Ferrell in his office at the Engineerium. Ferrell promised Baudwin that if he worked hard for Glas, and performed well at the Grand Unveiling, he would command the Water Guard to search for his mother. Baudwin took his words to heart:

"I can search the entire realm for her. My fleet will sail out from the Reach of Rhiannon[3] to Sea Thoir[4] off the coast of the faery lands, and then down to where the Tadlachs touch Sea Theas,[5] near the Mouth of Lyr.[6] From there, they will go up the Bracing Reach, toward the Island of Baranthus[7] where the sea Faeries live. Then through the Calming Reach out to Sea Thiar[8] — the elven sea — and up past Pine Reach to Sea Thuaidh[9] above the Glittering Tundra. And if we still don't find her, we'll go past the Northern Faery Lands to explore the Island of Avallach,[10] which holds many unknown wonders and dangers."

"You would do all this for me?" Baudwin asked.

"Yes," Ferrell replied.

"Then I am indeed fortunate."

Ferrell was in good spirits. He asked if Glas was being too strict and told Baudwin not to be nervous when he performed at the Grand Unveiling. "Your performance should be themed to bring Elves and Faeries together," he said, and Baudwin nodded yes, understanding his intent.

And then Ferrell asked Baudwin something that took him completely off guard.

---

[3] Pronounced [RHEE-ah-nin]
[4] Pronounced [HEHR] east
[5] Pronounced [HAAS] south
[6] Pronounced [LEER]
[7] Pronounced [BAR-an-thus]
[8] Pronounced [HEE-er] west
[9] Pronounced [HOO-ey] north
[10] Pronounced [AVAL-lack]

"Tell me, Baudwin," he began. "When you fought Loch at the ruins of Coventina — did you hear a voice before the water started gushing?" As Ferrell spoke the word *voice*, Baudwin's thoughts raced like river rapids inside his head. How he wished he was joined with his current, for then he would feel steady.

"A voice?" Baudwin asked, startled. "Where?"

"At the Springs of Coventina — when you fought Loch."

"A *voice*?" Baudwin asked again, hoping Ferrell meant something other than what he had said.

"Yes," Ferrell replied, his tone low and fierce.

Dismayed, Baudwin realized that Ferrell was not going to give up. At the Show Wheel Ferrell had spoken of a gusher at the ruins of Coventina, and now he was after the truth of the matter.

"Surely you know what I'm talking about," Ferrell continued.

Conflicted, Baudwin tried to push Ferrell's question out of his mind. He wanted to be honest and tell the truth, but despite Ferrell's willingness to help him, he still wasn't sure he could trust him with such a vital secret. He was hoping Boann would leave him alone, but now Ferrell was asking about her, which made him nervous. The truth was, he *had* heard her voice — at the dam — not at the ruins of Coventina.

Baudwin studied Ferrell, trying to remain calm. How terrible it would be if Ferrell had heard her speak. For then, he would know *everything*. Baudwin shivered at the possibility.

But of course he wouldn't hear her, he thought. *He may be a Luminary, but he's <u>only</u> an Elve. She wouldn't speak to him.*

Baudwin didn't want Ferrell to know that Boann had spoken to him. Ferrell was too interested, and Baudwin didn't trust his urgency. *I should keep my cards close to my vest, so they can't be used against me,* he thought.

Yet, he also didn't want to lie to Ferrell and risk losing his help. Struggling for an answer, he took too long to reply. Finally, he blurted, "Loch broke my tablet — that scoundrel — and for that the Water sent a gusher at us. Served him right."

Ferrell's eyes narrowed. "You're *sure* you didn't hear anything?"

"Not a thing," Baudwin replied. "Just ask Matha."

As Ferrell studied him, Baudwin was certain that Ferrell knew he wasn't telling the complete truth. After all, Ferrell had seen through his plan when Baudwin tricked Glas into hiring him. Feeling a queasy cold knot in his stomach, he wondered what to say next.

"I want to believe you," Ferrell began, "but tell me — does the water do such things? Or could the gusher have been a *spirit*, acting of its own accord?" Ferrell stared at him, waiting for his reply.

Now Baudwin was very nervous. He squeezed the arm of his chair and then quickly let go, worried that Ferrell would notice. Ferrell's expression didn't change.

"Well, no," Baudwin began, struggling to find an answer Ferrell would believe. "I mean — who *really* believes in such things? How could a spirit drown us when only the Water has that power? No, there's only ever been the Water — flowing of its own accord. The elders always say that when the Moon is high, the springs flood — not from the will of an angry being — but senselessly — like a landslide smothering a hamlet."

"So you believe your element *alone* is to blame?" Ferrell asked. Baudwin nodded, waiting to see if Ferrell believed him.

"I cannot find fault in what you say," Ferrell continued. "We Elves believe that the metals also do such things — but in different ways. Some believe that Gold brings luck and good fortune, but that if you lie, you will receive lead and misfortune, blearing the luster that brings us joy, making our sorrows intolerable."

Baudwin hid a sigh of relief, wondering how he could further conceal the truth from Ferrell. At the ruins of Coventina, at first he had assumed that the Water, not a spirit, had sent the gusher. Later Boann had told him that she had been the one. But Baudwin wanted Ferrell to believe that the *Water* was the one. For blaming the Water would be like blaming the weather — Ferrell could do nothing about it. And that suited him just fine. Baudwin also found Ferrell's interest in Boann strange and unnerving. Why was he so obsessed? Elves didn't believe in spirits.

Baudwin decided to push back. "How would an Elve even know the difference between the Water and a *water* spirit?" he asked. "Not even my kin seem to know. I believe I deserve an explanation."

Baudwin expected Ferrell to accuse him of being insolent, but Ferrell surprised him. "Yes," he replied. "I agree. You do deserve an explanation. I haven't been forthcoming."

Ferrell steepled his fingers and then looked away, his gaze recalling a past long gone. "I was not always a Luminary," he began. "The title was given to me after the *cogadh* with Belanus. Until then, I was merely Govannon's staunchest ally. No one was surprised when he gave me the title, but there was one battle where I distinguished myself, which is why I was rewarded. For until that day, we Elves thought we were masters of the fire. Although that would later prove to be arguable, everyone in the Assembly nevertheless knew of my exploits."

Looking directly at Baudwin, Ferrell then asked, "Do you know of the final battle in *Tír Éirí Sióg* after the Great Befalling?"

Baudwin shook his head.

"There were two *cogadhs,* you see. The first was between Belanus and Govannon — the Eternal Movement against the Rise of Time — but the second was the liberation of *Tír Éirí Sióg,* which the Elves called the Renewing of Dreams. We liberated every faery city, and those who fought us didn't understand that we were on their side, trying to share our own dream with them after they had shared theirs with us for so long. Govannon had always told me that in the past the Elves had taken too much from the Faeries and that now was the time to give back."

Baudwin wasn't sure what Ferrell meant by *giving back,* but he was reminded of the Golden Way. *For if you balance giving and receiving. . .* he thought. Yet somehow, something didn't quite ring true — but what, he wasn't sure. Perhaps Govannon meant well, but from the way the Elves had treated the indigent Faeries in the Cyhiraeth Quarter, hearts did not open that way. Neither did minds come to peace.

"We liberated every faery city," Ferrell then continued, "but the last one we came to, which we never conquered, was Ember Chasm."

"You fought the *fire* Faeries?" Baudwin asked, his eyes widening.

"Yes, being of the metals, Govannon sorely wanted to triumph at Ember Chasm. He thought that as surely as the Elves forged the metals, so too should they possess the fire of the Faeries — and so we fought. But we failed to liberate the city. Ember Chasm was the only faery city that thwarted us. We were beaten that day — not by the fire Faeries — but by the fire *itself,* spurred on by something we could not fathom."

Ferrell paused for a moment and spoke again.

"Govannon then told us all that the fire should not be liberated, but held in abeyance. 'Let them all remain in there,' he declared, 'until they extinguish the *very* air they breathe. Such fire is of no use to the metals.'"

"I don't see how the Elves could have believed they could capture the Fire, when they can't even capture the Water," Baudwin objected. "Perhaps you should have entered Ember Chasm peacefully."

Ferrell took time before he responded. "I understand that you believe we were tyrants," he began, "and I can't blame you either. We did go in by force, but what you don't understand is that the Faeries were failing *Tír na nÓg.* Do you even know what happened when the dreams of your kin no longer came to us?"

"You told me there was poverty and famine," Baudwin replied, as he knew little about the decline that led to the Great Befalling, and didn't want to seem ignorant.

"For as long as anyone can remember," Ferrell continued, "the Faeries sent us their dreams, and we built them, but when the dreams stopped coming, the consequences were catastrophic. You saw those Faeries in the Cyhiraeth Quarter that Loch defended — did you not?"

He must have known we were there, Baudwin thought. *Nothing escapes him.* He could feel Ferrell prying into him, looking to see how he was taking his question.

"Yes," Baudwin replied, trying to remain calm. But Ferrell seemed not to care, as he was after something else.

"Now, imagine a realm where almost everyone was as despondent," Ferrell said.

Baudwin thought then about the water Faeries in the Cyhiraeth Quarter. They had been so downtrodden, yet fighting for their freedom when Loch appeared, and then simply giving up as soon as he left. Could the entire realm have once been like that? He had never heard of this before. Perhaps like the Faeries in the Cyhiraeth Quarter, all the Faeries had lost their intentions, and even their dreams. And perhaps they had become inured to Life as it was and had never questioned why.

Or perhaps Ferrell was wrong.

"But I thought the *cogadh* caused them to be that way," Baudwin said.

Ferrell shook his head. "Not exactly — no. The fact is, *Tír na nÓg* was like that in many places before the Great Befalling. While it's true that the Befalling rent a wound in us all, there had been a steady decline long before calamity struck. No one knows what caused the Great Befalling. We Elves are blamed by you, but I served in Govannon's guard. Never did I see a plan that would leave the Elves and Faeries severed from one another, with so little remaining of our bonds — us to our metals and you to your elements. Govannon waged *cogadh* to stop the decline and was just as shocked as anyone when the Befalling struck, which is why we refer to the Great Befalling as the Great Endeavor. That was his way of remaining defiant. We Elves do not accept defeat. Govannon took charge of rebuilding the realm, and for that we are all in his debt — you see?"

Baudwin couldn't grasp all of what Ferrell had explained. The Faeries in the Cyhiraeth Quarter had seemed stricken by the *cogadh*, but now Ferrell was saying that their illness had been present everywhere, before the *cogadh* even began.

"Before the *cogadh*, were *you* like those Faeries in the Cyhiraeth?" Baudwin asked.

"Yes, but perhaps not as much as other Elves, for I was in good company. But many, as I said, weren't as fortunate. They were losing their way, deprived of food and shelter, unable to work, their limbs too feeble to grasp what little life would grant them — their intentions weakened beyond hope. As I told you at the Show Wheel, the Elves were struggling to temper their intentions, and the Faeries to hone theirs."

"If that was so," Baudwin asked, his eyes narrowing, "why invade *Tír Éirí Sióg*? Surely this didn't help the Faeries, did it?"

Ferrell smiled knowingly. "But it *did*."

Baudwin couldn't believe what he was hearing. Surely, none of the Faeries in the Cyhiraeth Quarter had been better off after the *cogadh*. "But those Faeries in the Cyhiraeth —"

"Are the exception," Ferrell interrupted. "We liberated thousands more in other faery cities. Gradually the malaise we had suffered before the Great Befalling lifted. Now, Govannon is trying to heal the wound that the Befalling itself has inflicted. This part of the story is not popular among your kind — but it is the truth. Too readily, they blamed us for the decline, but that began before the cogadh, and was made worse by the Befalling. Over the past two hundred years, the Faeries have begun to regain what they had lost in the decline, and we have been given little thanks."

"But the Faeries no longer send the Elves their dreams —"

"*We* make the dreams now," Ferrell interrupted, his eyes flashing.

Baudwin fell silent.

"Do you even know what caused the decline to begin with?" Ferrell asked.

Baudwin shook his head.

"The decline began when the dreams of the Faeries stopped coming to the Elves, and went on for hundreds of years. After that came the Great Befalling itself, a time of horrific shock and travail. Yet, the Befalling was only the peak — the high-water mark — like waves bursting over a dam. I'm sure you understand what *that* means."

Being of the Water, Baudwin could feel that Ferrell believed what he said was true. All he had heard from Seamus and Kelven was that the Great Befalling had been terrible, but they never spoke to him about just what had occurred. He wondered if they even knew.

"So Govannon ended the decline?" Baudwin asked.

"Did he ever," Ferrell said. "We built a stronghold north of Ember Chasm, which he named the Aerovent, near the Reach of Rhiannon. If Govannon couldn't have Ember Chasm, he would at least build a gleaming spire of metal in the heart of *Tír Éirí Sióg*. That was almost two hundred years ago, where to this day, we've been in a stalemate with the fire Faeries."

Ferrell paused, extending an arm, palm up. He then pulled up his sleeve. "And at that final battle, I earned *this*." On his forearm a burn scar coiled around his arm like a snake. Carefully, he continued rolling up his sleeve — more and more. Baudwin could see that the scar ended at his shoulder.

"Curious-looking — no?" Ferrell asked. "You're the first Faery I've ever shown this to." The unusual scar appeared to be painted on his arm, but the reddish rope-like marks were unmistakably caused by fire.

"When I earned this," Ferrell continued, "I first heard a voice. That's their way — you see? They always speak before you see them. And this one was not of the water — but of the fire."

"A *fire* spirit?" Baudwin asked. "Why did it attack you?"

"They protect, which is their nature," Ferrell replied. "This one certainly didn't want us breaching Ember Chasm. Until that battle, we were confident, but when the spirit came, all we saw was a wall of fire. Our machines melted into slag, our ranks broke, and I called for a retreat. The bravest warriors I'd ever known could barely turn around before they disintegrated into vapor and passed to Annwyn." Without speaking, Ferrell rolled his sleeve back down, and carefully buttoned the cuff.

"So many perished," he continued, "and I was certain that I would be punished for our defeat. But Govannon surprised me by proclaiming victory, for had we not prevailed against a foe that could have melted any metal into rivulets? The Guards weren't equipped for such a battle, and I had brought him many victories prior, so he named me a Luminary, and then put me to work learning about these spirits, so we could better fight them in the future."

"Why fight them at all?" Baudwin asked, aghast at Ferrell's story.

"Haven't I *already* told you?" Ferrell snapped. "They are chaotic and lawless — a threat to all of the Fae."

Baudwin was confused. He didn't know enough about fire Faeries to judge the fire spirit. Perhaps the fire Faeries had misunderstood the Elves' intentions, or perhaps not. The Elves had forced their way into *Tír Éirí Sióg*, but the Faeries had sided with Belanus, who lost the *cogadh* against his brother Govannon. And after two hundred years, Govannon seemed to want to make things right in the realm — or at least Ferrell believed so. Not to mention, who knew if the fire spirit had even acted at the behest of the fire Faeries? Boann certainly hadn't been acting at his behest when she stole his glamorium egg.

Now Baudwin understood Ferrell's fascination with spirits. He knew Ferrell would never stop investigating them, so he decided to further conceal his lie about Boann with a half-truth.

"I'm sorry for what happened to you," he began. "The fire spirit must have been truly fearsome. The Great Befalling was indeed ugly and chaotic, and I feel many may have acted out of fear, not malice. There is more I must tell you." Straightening in his chair, Baudwin struggled to speak. For he was about to tell a lie.

"Before I tell you what I know, you must promise to keep what I say a secret."

Solemnly, Ferrell nodded his head. He then said, "By the Assembly, your words will not leave this room."

Baudwin then began.

"For years I searched for the Water, so that it would come to me and help me find my mother. And one day the Water did come, but I did not hear her voice. So I grew forlorn, and with my friend Matha, I traveled to the shrine at the ruins of Coventina. There we found a tablet, inscribed with a riddle of Glamorium, and then Loch and his friends came, and he smashed it to pieces. Then we fought, and the Water rushed from the well, and we were all thrown out of the shrine."

Hearing this, Ferrell's burnished-looking countenance turned leaden. This was not what he wanted to hear.

"When the gusher flooded the shrine, I heard no voice," Baudwin stressed, determined to hide the truth of what he really knew. "That is the truth. I thought then that the Water coming to me that day was the reason for the eruption at the shrine — and nothing more."

"So you're *completely* sure the water caused the gusher — and not a spirit?" Ferrell asked.

Baudwin could see how dissatisfied Ferrell was with his answer, yet he continued, "So then I began to search for Glamorium, for Seamus had told me that I'd not simply come upon the tablet by chance. The next day I searched, and that was the day that you and I met. And just as Seamus had predicted, I came upon some Glamorium at the Tree of Innovation, and then it was gone again. Always, Glamorium is elusive. Even at Curios & Marvels, I was unable to touch any."

"Ah yes," Ferrell smiled. "Edmund told me that a group of Faeries had stirred up trouble. So that was you."

"And then Rian," Baudwin continued, "whom you know well, took pity on me and gave me an egg of Glamorium."

"A generous gift — from a generous friend," Ferrell noted. Baudwin caught what appeared to be a look of envy upon Ferrell's face, as he hung upon his every word.

"And so I took the egg," Baudwin continued, "still not sure of what meaning it held. I took it home with me, and later, as I was holding the egg near the dam, I *did* hear a voice, whose source I could not see."

Ferrell's eyes lit up, the luster in his countenance returning. "What did it say?"

"The voice said to me:

You unworthy of the shrine

Still not ripe upon the vine

Don't deserve a prize so fine

So my friend the egg is mine"

"And then what?" Ferrell asked, his excitement mounting.

"The Water rushed at me, and a torrent went over me until I passed out. When I awoke, the egg was gone from my pocket."

"So it *was* a spirit!"

"I thought then that it was only the Water speaking to me, and I didn't believe anything else, but as you say, perhaps it was something more — yet, why it took my egg, I'll never know."

Ferrell nodded. "Yes, that is understandable."

Baudwin studied Ferrell's face, delighted beyond measure to see that he had successfully tricked him with a half-truth. Above all, he did not want Ferrell to know that Boann was trying to guide him, and especially that she had recently visited him. No good would come of Ferrell knowing that she was instructing him in the lessons of the Triquetra. Baudwin wanted Ferrell to believe that she had lost interest in him, and that Baudwin would turn only to *him* for help.

"They can be terribly vengeful," Ferrell mused, as he stood up and moved closer to Baudwin. "Likely this one was not through with disciplining you and Loch."

"Perhaps," Baudwin said," but I never saw anything but the Water. I'm still not sure why."

Ferrell nodded, saying, "They're known to take on different forms, so it's no wonder you thought that the water itself spoke to you, but taking your egg was quite unusual." Ferrell's eyes gleamed. "Perhaps there was some kind of jealousy that you had been given such a treasure by an Elve, and not by a Faery."

"Perhaps," Baudwin replied. "Yet, why take such an interest in me — at all?"

"You were chosen for a reason," Ferrell replied, "but for what, I have no idea."

Out of the blue, Ferrell grabbed Baudwin's hand. "You must believe me," he implored. "That spirit is *not* your friend. They play tricks on the unwary and are full of wrath. They do not reason like we do. Instead, they spew anger like the volcanoes of Ember Chasm. They erupt seemingly without warning, giving little heed to the cries of those who perish in their wake. They are not so unlike their element, perhaps not as senseless as you say — as when a landslide smothers a hamlet — but calculating and dangerous all the same."

Ferrell took away his hand. "It is my duty to protect you, so if you see anything unusual, do not hesitate to come to me."

Baudwin thought then of his lost egg, and replied, "Of course, I will. Thank you for your help and protection."

Chapter 30
DREAMERS AND BUILDERS

Solasdía,[1] the day of the performance had finally arrived, and Baudwin was still in a terrible quandary, not knowing who to trust. His friends were awed by Boann, holding her in high regard for her wisdom, but Baudwin remained doubtful. At Esther's reading, he had sensed less antipathy in her than he had at the dam, and she seemed more earnest in her desire to guide him. Yet, in the end, she had given him only another riddle: "To truly see who you are, you must let go of who you *think* you are!" Lugh had taken her words to heart, but Baudwin simply didn't know what she meant. Even more important, Esther — not Boann — had been the one to reassure him that his mother was still alive.

Baudwin recalled the coiling scar seared into Ferrell's arm by the fire spirit, and Ferrell's warning to him about Boann: "That spirit is not your friend." Was Ferrell right? Baudwin couldn't tell. *Perhaps,* he thought, *water spirits aren't as dangerous.* But she was certainly unpredictable. When Criofan asked her what she had done to Esther, she admonished him, saying, "*You* do not command *me* — son of the Primary of Commerce!" Obviously, she didn't care about Criofan's concern for Esther's welfare.

She then had frightened them, by breaking a bowl and sending shards of glass flying everywhere. *What kind of <u>friend</u> would frighten them so?* At least in the end the broken glass had been an illusion. And although she had been more restrained, Baudwin feared what she would do if, despite all his efforts, he couldn't measure up to her expectations. He hoped she would merely abandon him. Otherwise, he would remain fearful of her wrath. He imagined her attacking him again in all her fury, tendrils of Water coiling around him, squeezing the very Life out of him — such an unspeakable end for a water Faery.

Much to his dismay, his friends continued to speak reverently about her. They had not seen her at her worst, and saw more benevolence in her than he did. He had tried to tell them how ferocious she could be, describing in even greater detail how she had transformed into a serpent and snatched away his glamorium egg, leaving him to drown. Still, they remained unswayed by his story, insisting that she would never have put him in mortal danger. When

---

[1] Pronounced [SOLACE-THEE-UH] Lightday, equivalent to Sunday, the seventh day of the week

they asked him if he could feel her in his heart, he looked at them blankly and shook his head. They then tried to reassure him by reciting the ancient faery hymn they had sung at the important meeting when Magniglow was voted on:

> The Water abides to heal my heart
> To fill my soul with feeling

Singing instead:

> *Boann* abides to heal my heart
> To fill my soul with feeling

Having met her, they felt uplifted as never before.

Their words failed to stir his heart. *They see only the honeyed merlady,* he thought, *but I know the monstrous, merciless serpent.* Matha implored Baudwin to try to understand her riddles. After rehearsals, he poured through Lugh's books, looking for clues about talismans and bridges, hoping to discover more about the true nature of Baudwin's quest. Criofan drilled Baudwin in the lessons of the Triquetra that they had discovered at Curios & Marvels, convinced that if Baudwin remembered them fully, all would come to fruition. He saw Boann as the pinnacle of the water faery tribe, and even chided Baudwin for not respecting her more.

But respect was not something Baudwin had ever felt he owed her.

When he confided all of this to Lugh, Lugh was even more adamant that he call off the performance, arguing that Ferrell had turned him against his own kind in a most insideous way. As everything stood, Lugh believed that nothing good would come of Baudwin trying to unite the Faeries and Elves by putting on a show. Matha and Criofan weren't as quick to abandon Baudwin's plan. All they wanted was to support him in doing what he thought was right. Yet, they kept praising Boann — in all of her beauty and power. That such a being could even exist was beyond anything they could ever have imagined. The stories of the old ways had come alive! They seemed to trust her, but only because they hadn't seen her wrath — or so Baudwin thought. Only he knew how cruel she could be. Still, he found himself trusting Ferrell more than her, simply because Ferrell had never treated him like an enemy.

Added to this, in the days leading up to the performance, Baudwin had trouble paying attention while he practiced. He kept fumbling some of his most basic tricks, until both Criofan and Matha became worried. When they asked him what was the matter, he didn't know what to tell them. Finally on the eve of the performance, he had again confided in Lugh.

"Who should I believe?" he lamented.

"You must follow the Water — always," Lugh had said.

"She gave me no help — just riddles. I can't trust her."

"Then you must come with me," Lugh began, "and I will show you her creation, formed in the mists before time was measured by the Elves and before Faeries sang their first songs."

Later that day Lugh led them from the Nechtain Quarter around hills and over canals to the top of the falls. Standing next to Baudwin, he pointed down to Inis Easa,[2] a large oval-shaped island. After making their way down a long flight of wooden stairs, they reached a stone bridge at the bottom that led to the island. As they crossed the bridge, Lugh explained that there was another staircase on the opposite side of the island that led up to the Condatis. Carefully they made their way onto the island, an expanse of grass, patches of wildflowers, and groves of ancient oaks. In the center of the island facing the falls they saw the Teampall Easa[3] — a giant dome of translucent blue-green marble, appearing weightless in the perpetual mists surrounding the island. Baudwin and his friends approached the temple — the most sacred of all places for water Faeries — said to have been shaped by the Water itself. Here the confluence of the four rivers formed the An Bhanna[4] — the great river that flowed from the temple.

During his descent, Baudwin had heard the falls — a cacophony of sounds, dampening his thoughts and stirring all his feelings at once. Upon entering Teampall Easa, the mix of sounds blended into a single tone, made up of all the sounds of the falls vibrating together — *aaaah-nnnn*. The walls of the temple shimmered softly with blue-green Light. Having ended their journeys, the Nechtain, Danu, Cyhiraeth and Condatis sang out to them — a chorus of triumph and transformation. Having run their course, their combined wisdom now gave birth to the An Bhanna which continued through a natural tunnel in the Tadlachs and then out to sea. The four Faeries stared in wonder at the Light shining through the translucent walls, luminance that seemed to shift the ground beneath their feet. The feeling was discombobulating.

Only Lugh was not alarmed. "Your unsteadiness will pass," he said. "This is how the temple greets you."

Soon they regained their balance, and with that came a feeling of bliss, as they now could feel the temple inside of them.

Lugh again sought to calm them. "The temple disarms you, and then places itself within you, washing away your past and preparing you for what is to come. For millennia water Faeries have come here to join with their currents, course with their feelings, and hone their intentions. According to legend, long ago the temple even served to prepare them for the passage to Annwyn."

---

[2]   Pronounced [INISH ASS-uh] Island of the Falls
[3]   Pronounced [TYAHM-pull ASS-uh] Temple of the Falls
[4]   Pronounced [UH wahnah]

As they continued to study the temple, their eyes came to rest upon the chamber in the center. A spiraling ramp made of dark blue marble descended in a circle beneath their feet. At the bottom of the ramp spun a whirlpool of Water — fed by the four rivers.

"Here there are many mysteries," Lugh began, "but what always makes me wonder is how the temple was crafted. Look closely, for you will not see any trace of how it was made."

What Lugh said was true. Nowhere were there signs of saw or chisel marks. The ground was devoid of tile work. Only smooth stone met their feet.

"Before our decline everyone knew that Boann, like a master sculptor, hollowed and hallowed the entire temple," Lugh continued reverently. "Look around you. Do you see any glyphs? Who but she would not bother to write down a single one? For only in her greatness could she be so humble as to not leave any sign of her work behind."

Baudwin wondered if what Lugh said was true. He and his friends looked for markings and glyphs, but could find none. Seamless walls curved into the floor, and the floor curved just as seamlessly into the domed ceiling. None of them could imagine how Boann had crafted this wonder.

"This pool holds the Water of the four rivers," Lugh said, gesturing to the Water beneath them. "Here they find their end and are reborn as the An Bhanna," he added, his eyes tearing. "So much like my lilies. In Life these rivers perish, yet they always bring us joy. In Death we cherish what our loss cannot destroy. And so, after the four rivers leave us, we and the Ah Bhanna live on, cherishing them always."

Moved by Lugh's words, everyone was silent, waiting for him to continue.

"This is the place of our origins," Lugh began. Seriously he spoke, awed by the hierarchy of purpose that surrounded them. "In an age long past, this was where we water Faeries were born. Like the An Bhanna, we too sprang from these four rivers, created by Boann herself. She brought forth this temple to teach us the four lessons."

Lugh paused before continuing:

"From River Condatis we learned to strive for wholeness and healing. But how does one strive for healing?"

Lugh waited for them to reply. Dumbstruck, they merely stared at him. Happy to explain, he continued.

"We cannot strive for healing without learning from River Cyhiraeth that we must surrender that which is false within us. To do this, we must hold on to what is true. But how is that done?"

He looked at them, awaiting some response. Matha then spoke. "We must follow the wisdom of the Nechtain. . ."

"Yes!" Lugh exclaimed. "Very good. We must go back the way we came — like the salmon — to the Source of our being, owning what is true within us and letting go of what is false."

Baudwin and his friends nodded their heads, waiting.

"And finally," Lugh continued, "as there is only one river left, we must learn from River Danu to understand our feelings. Which means River Danu is the *first* step to how we can understand the lessons of the four rivers."

Baudwin watched Matha pondering Lugh's words, his eyes squinting behind his spectacles.

"So if it begins with Danu, then we must understand our feelings, go back the way we came, and let go of all that is false within us," Matha recited. "Only then will we find wholeness and healing."

"Very good," Lugh said, nodding.

"Wholeness and healing from what?" Baudwin asked.

"Our suffering," Lugh replied. "We spend our lives moving away from the Source, and as we do, we forget the truth of our element."

Lugh could tell that they didn't really understand what he was saying. Intensely, he asked, "Do you know why I *really* hated River Shine?"

"River Shine?" Matha asked. "What's that got to do with it?"

"Just listen," Lugh urged.

Baudwin remembered River Shine, the glowstone project Lugh's brother, Liber, had proposed at the important meeting — Matter One. Much to Lugh's disgust, Liber had suggested that they build a glowstone garden at the South Bend, made of sea stars, perch, flutter fish, and river otters. Normally this wouldn't have bothered Baudwin, for he did appreciate fine craftsmanship. But River Shine wasn't being built by the noble inspiration and aspirations of artists, but rather as a spectacle in a place that should have remained sacred. The truth was, River Shine distracted from the river, rather than showing Faeries how to *be* with the River.

"Whenever we move away from the Source, we suffer," Lugh continued. "Just as we did when we voted at the important meeting to build that monstrosity out of glowstones. We disregarded our most precious source — River Deuona. Boann gave us the four rivers, so that instead of moving away from them, we could remain steady on our paths, and return to the Source."

Hearing this, Matha and Criofan were once again awed by Boann, her creation of the temple, and the lessons of the four rivers. Softly, Matha began to sing:

Boann abides to heal my heart

To fill my soul with feeling

"Like the salmon, we too can return to the Source," Criofan affirmed.

"But how?" Baudwin asked.

Lugh led them down the spiral ramp to the pool below. Pointing to the Water, he said, "You must drink."

Puzzled, Baudwin regarded him.

"The Waters in this pool form the An Bhanna," Lugh began. "Just as the four rivers become the An Bhanna, so must their lessons become one in us. You fear Boann because you do not understand why she has appeared. Even I had once questioned whether she was real or merely legend. We cannot know what her intentions are, but now that she has made herself known to us, we must pay her heed."

"But Ferrell said such spirits were dangerous," Baudwin declared.

"Perhaps to an Elve she would be, but not to us," Lugh corrected.

"She almost drowned me! She hasn't done a thing to help me."

"That's because you don't understand her *or* the lessons of the four rivers. Drink, and more will become clear."

Baudwin hesitated.

"What a pity it is that the son of the Primary of Water was not brought here as a young one," Lugh said. "Sadder yet is that you were never joined. You can thank the Elves for that. If they hadn't invaded *Tír Éirí Sióg*, your mother wouldn't have gone missing in the Great Befalling. Now, here is your chance to recover what was taken from you."

Baudwin knew Lugh was right. How unfortunate that he had never been to the most sacred of all water faery temples — the very place from which his tribe had sprung. Kelven should have taken him long ago. Certainly the Primary of Water owed his son as much. The journey to Four Falls was not that difficult or long. Baudwin understood how losing his mother after the Great Befalling had devastated his father. In his grief, Kelven had lost himself in his duties — in the toil of running the dam and giving speeches to the Water Guild. For two hundred years his father had languished in Deuona, his heart broken. And throughout Kelven's malaise, Seamus had been the one to guide him.

Baudwin also knew that his grandfather's unwavering faith in him had brought him to where he now stood. Seamus had championed who he could be, for years insisting that he find the Water — until he finally did. And ironically, Seamus had also brought Boann to him. For if he had not told him to search for the Water, Boann would not have brought forth the Water to him at the Springs of Coventina. His greatest supporter had brought him his greatest obstacle. Afterward, Seamus had told him to look for Glamorium, and in doing so, he had learned of the Triquetra. Boann had then taken a keen interest in questioning his honesty and his ability to tell the truth. Unnerved, he couldn't tell who had shaped his destiny more.

Lugh gestured toward the pool. "Drink from this shrine. Only then will you be granted a true vision of Boann, so you will finally trust her."

"Can I *really* trust her?" Baudwin asked.

"Drink," Lugh insisted.

Baudwin peered into the pool at the whirling nexus of the four rivers. All their currents had coalesced here, so much so that he worried he might have another bout. Sensing the moody stirrings of the Cyhiraeth, he remembered his last bout under the bridge. Feeling tortured and alone, he had simply passed out. Thankfully, here at the pool, he could also feel other things. As the Waters of the Nechtain, Danu, Cyhiraeth, and Condatis whirled together, they spoke to him as never before. A wholeness was waiting for him — calling to him as the Water had at the Springs of Coventina. Kneeling down, he cupped his hands and drank.

Lugh motioned to Criofan and Matha, and they drank as well. Lugh then drank.

Baudwin closed his eyes and waited. At first nothing happened, but soon he found himself contemplating the lesson of the Condatis. He then realized that the healing he sought would come if he could trust — deep down — in his own wholeness. Such a possibility had never occurred to him before. Thoughtfully, he smiled, and then he began to contemplate the lesson of the Cyhiraeth, knowing that to trust in his wholeness he would have to sacrifice his fear and anger and hold on to the strength of his fortitude, so he could embrace his joy. Now he felt uplifted. As he felt the currents of the An Bhanna quickening in him, he couldn't help believing that Lugh was right — he was going to understand *everything*.

Glancing at Matha and Criofan, he wondered what wisdom the four rivers were imparting to them. He then began to contemplate the wisdom of the Nechtain, seeing that if he was to continue on his journey, he would have to go back the way he came. He would have to see and feel all the ways his pain had overrun his heart, preventing him from trusting and understanding himself. Finally, he contemplated the last lesson, that of River Danu. Expecting to fully understand his feelings for the first time, he became even more excited. He knew the words to this lesson, but as he tried to feel them, there was nothing — only a void. Patiently he waited, but soon realized that his reflections were over. Just as the Water had come to him at the Springs of Coventina, but not his mother's voice, there was no greater experience awaiting him now — only more travail.

A voice cried out and Baudwin opened his eyes. Across the pool, a young one had partaken of the Water and joined with his current. As his mother smiled, he gamboled about, laughing and splashing.

Baudwin was furious. Again, the lessons of the old ways had brought him to the precipice, only to fail him. *Why, did this happen?* he thought, raging.

And then, of course, he knew. As always, the reason was the same — *always* the same. He was not joined with his current, and he had never coursed with his feelings. To understand the lesson of Danu, he first had to understand the lessons of joining and coursing.

The lessons of the four rivers are of no use to me, he thought. Looking at Lugh, Criofan, and Matha, he saw them in a state of bliss. So absorbed were they, that they didn't notice his disgust.

"Baudwin," Matha chortled, "do you feel the An Bhanna? How wondrous!"

Criofan then joined in, "I must sacrifice my vanity. That is what's false within me. I mustn't collect so many shoes," he added chuckling.

Lugh regarded Baudwin. "Baudwin," he began, "Boann has given us —" but he then stopped short. So absorbed were they that they hadn't noticed Baudwin's anger. Looking into his eyes, Lugh could see something was terribly wrong, but before he could ask him what, Baudwin declared:

"I feel *nothing.* The old ways have failed me for the last time. No longer will I look to them for guidance."

And so he left the temple, more determined than ever to find something that would grant him a result upon which he could rely.

☙❦❧

The falls churned ceaselessly as they had long before the city was built, when the Fae of the Water had first come out of the ethers and gazed up at the Moon. When the only language they knew was the song of the luminous tides. The falls still sang these songs, but the Fae no longer listened. They had forgotten whence they came, so lost were they in an illusion constructed by a desperate mason. So lost that they didn't know they needed to be found. The granite and soil of the island that once supported the temple and the oaks now upheld a new dream, one that came not from the luminous tides, but from *Tír Luí Lucharachán* and farther still — from a place foreign to all of *Tír na nÓg.* A place not of songs and wonder, but of the blunt forge of reason — smelted by those who had also forgotten their purpose long ago.

Yet *she* had not forgotten. In the Falls she waited, bound by one greater than herself to never abandon the Shiny ones. There she bided her time as a *ceirean* — a beast of the Water — seething in mists that rose in bursts, going up and up and then over the island where the Fae had now congregated. The Faeries of the Water were her body — as they had always been. As the vapors dropped like a canopy over *Teampall Easa,* cascading over the great stage that had been erected in the center of the island, she wanted to embrace them all. They were hers until Annwyn returned them to the Source. What hopes she had for each of them. Even now she sensed that mothers had brought their young ones to *Teampall Easa* to join with their currents — a gesture of good faith to the Assembly of the Elves. She let out a bellowing shriek, but none heard her. There was only the churning of the Falls, relentlessly plunging onto the granite below.

On this day she would not show them her devotion. The Fae of the Sun — the Elves — had chosen this place to build their contraptions, but certainly not the wonders of Gleam, which had heralded a golden age long forgotten. Not the wonders built from the dreams of her children, either. They were but contrivances, mere shadows mocking the ambitions of masters long passed to Annwyn. The Elves had grown far too arrogant and wild, seeking to supplant the most sacred of all places of her tribe. On this day she would make them remember who they really were. But first she would wait for her novice to begin — one who was yet to fathom what destiny had in store.

East of *Teampall Easa* he readied himself upon the stage, about to perform his own illusion for the masters of illusion. He was both determined and lost, but she knew he would find his way, and in doing so heal the rift between the Faeries and Elves. The Sun, still bright, was setting as the day neared its end. The performance would begin at the golden hour.

Baudwin adjusted the sleeves of his costume, pulling on the cuffs until they were even. As he peeked out from behind the curtain at the audience below, his stomach tightened into a knot. Seamus and Kelven were sitting in the front row. Ferrell must have invited them as well. No doubt they were worried and still upset with him. Baudwin wondered what Ferrell's guard had told them about him. How he wished he could slink away, for they were bound to object to what he was about to do.

Criofan and Matha were standing right behind him. Silver moon crescents and water droplets shimmered on their indigo cummerbunds. Three elven lady acrobats, whom Baudwin had recruited from the Engineerium, waited on the other side of the stage for their cue. Baudwin waved to them, and they smiled back. Masks of glitter and tiny jewels shone on their faces. They stood ready to perform. Golden Suns and hammers of Silver Forge sparkled on their orange cummerbunds, complementing the moon crescents and water droplets. When Baudwin first told Matha and Criofan that Ferrell wanted the performance to promote harmony between the Faeries and Elves, Matha suggested that they use the symbols they had seen on the boulders at the ruins of Coventina — a tribute to a concord long forgotten.

Peeking through the curtain, Baudwin wondered how his performance would promote harmony among such disparate attendees. Seeing the Grand Eldress, he imagined her hosting a grand tea party, and inviting them all. "Help yourselves to crumpets and marmalade," she would say as she poured the tea. He spotted Seanán and Fearghus, the two Elves who had started the riot at the Four Rivers Faire. They had bickered about the Eternal Movement versus the Rise of Time: time that was relative versus time that was measured only by machines.

Baudwin imagined her scolding them: "The two of you are trying to make a clock from gears that will never mesh, measuring time in two contradictory ways — *only* to further your debate. One of you has hold of the hour hand and the other the minute hand, and you're pulling them in opposite directions. A cantankerous scurry of chipmunks has a better chance of building a sundial than you will *ever* have of understanding each other!"

Baudwin chuckled. How similar these Elves were to Lugh and Liber, the faery brothers who had argued about Magniglow at the important meeting. They had been just as uncompromising, forcing the Grand Eldress to silence them both. When provoked, both Faeries and Elves could be so utterly muleheaded. His task seemed impossible.

Looking further into the crowd, Baudwin was disgusted to see Loch and overjoyed to see Rian. Again, what common ground would *they* find as they drank their tea? A faery tracker and an elven Druid might speak about the forest, but if they discussed the Eternal Movement and the Rise of Time with Seanán and Fearghus, Loch the Roiler would no doubt side with Fearghus, and Rian, the Druid of Guidance, with Seanán. Both sides of the argument would then become even more contentious, the divide between them growing ever larger. Unbuttered crumpets would no doubt start to fly, until the Grand Eldress herself would end up thwacking someone on the head with a wooden spoon, or worse yet, a teapot.

Spotting Ferrell, Baudwin felt himself blanching as he imagined the great delight that Ferrell would take in such a mad party — if the Grand Eldress was credulous enough to invite him. At first Ferrell would no doubt charm them all with his plans for the Great Endeavor. But if anyone took offense — as Lugh, Rian, and Seanán surely would — he would probably bait both sides into a Hop and Hit, until everyone ended up quarrel-staffing on the table. The Grand Eldress would watch — horrified — and Ferrell would laugh as everyone slipped and slid on pastries and pie, smashing plates, bruising bodies, and blackening eyes — turning the entire party into an all-out melee

"Whyever did I agree to this performance?" he muttered, as his palms began to sweat, and hives broke out on his high, rounded ears. What would Ferrell say if the performance didn't go well? he wondered. Would he still help him find his mother, or would he cast him aside like an old broken saw?

Regardless of what happened, Baudwin wouldn't abandon his kin. He knew they were depending on him. Hesitantly, he gave the crowd a final look. They had come not only from Four Falls, but other neighboring hamlets: Blue

Springs, Babble Brook, Dark Creek, and of course, Deuona. Each hamlet had had its own important meeting, similar to the one Baudwin had attended in Deuona. The Guilders seemed weary and anxious, wondering what their votes had brought them. He saw fear in them, for they didn't know if what was coming to the realm was for good or ill. The Roilers didn't seem as frightened, but they remained on guard. Baudwin wondered if any of them had heard about Loch's fighting in the Cyhiraeth. He surmised that the Eddies had come to see what would happen next, for they, like channel currents, only became stronger when the wind picked up. Baudwin could sense the winds of change most definitely blowing. Through guile and diplomacy, the Assembly had finally gotten its way. For better or for worse, Magniglow was on the rise, and the Grand Unveiling was nigh.

The curtain was about to open. From afar, Baudwin saw Moonrise perched on a hawthorn tree, nervously cocking his head from side to side. Just below the dove sat Esther from the Cyhiraeth Quarter, swaying to and fro, her emerald gray hair blowing in the breeze. He wondered why the scryer had come, and then he remembered her words: That he would travel as the salmon does, and by so doing, find someone who would send him to his mother. Her predictions all seemed so ridiculous to him. He was now on the elven path, and he would not fail.

An elven stagehand motioned for Baudwin to begin. The audience then hushed as a line of musicians filed into view, playing violins, horns, cymbals, and chimes as they made their way to the orchestra pit. The curtains parted, and Baudwin's training took over. He forgot all about the crowd.

Out he tumbled with Matha and Criofan, rolling and jumping, twisting and turning, doing roundoffs and front flips. Two decorative oak trees adorned the stage. Deftly they tumbled, until they reached a tree opposite from where they had entered, with a large orb suspended in its branches. They climbed the tree as easily as squirrels and then tapped the orb. Cool silvery Light shimmered from the center. Quickly, they jumped to the ground to admire their work.

Upon seeing the glowstone Moon, the Faeries in the crowd cheered and clapped, and the Elves smiled.

Out then tumbled the three elven ladies from the other side of the stage, rolling and jumping, twisting and turning, doing roundoffs and front flips. Deftly, they tumbled, until they reached a tree on the other side of the stage, with a larger orb suspended in its branches. Quick as cats they climbed the tree and then tapped the orb. Warm golden Light glowed from the center. Like the Faeries, they jumped to the ground to admire their work.

Upon seeing the glowstone Sun, the Elves in the crowd whistled and stomped their feet, and the Faeries smiled.

Seeing what the elven ladies had done, Baudwin, Matha, and Criofan then performed a series of aerial walkovers and other acrobatic tricks, going clockwise in a circle around the Moon in the tree. The music played faster and faster. The elven ladies did the same, going counterclockwise in a circle around the Sun in the tree. Again, the music played faster and faster. Two more groups of acrobats joined them, wearing Moons or Suns on their costumes. Around and around the trees they danced. The circles of Suns and Moons expanded out from the trees, until both sides crashed through the other, and everyone went spinning off the stage.

The music stopped and all was quiet.

Slowly, the music began playing again. Only the three elven ladies returned. Each one held a silver hammer in her hand. Sneaking up to the Moon on the other side of the stage, they proceeded to circle the base of the tree. Smiling mischievously, they climbed the branches and reached for the Moon. *Tap, tap, tap,* went their hammers against the Moon — *tap, tap, tap* — and then the Moon went out.

The Elves whistled and stomped, for now the Moon no longer shined and day had come.

Baudwin, Matha, and Criofan then returned. Criofan was holding a large pitcher. They sneaked up to the Sun on the other side of the stage. Matha pulled himself up onto Criofan's shoulders. Baudwin then vaulted both of them and stood on Matha's shoulders. Criofan passed the pitcher to Matha, and Matha to Baudwin. Baudwin poured Water over the Sun. *Clank, clank, clank* went the pitcher against the Sun — *clank, clank, clank* — and then the Sun went out.

The Faeries cheered and clapped, for now the Sun no longer shined, and night had come.

Baudwin, Criofan, Matha, and the three elven ladies then exited the stage. The music again stopped and all was quiet. Everyone in the audience wondered what would happen next.

The rest of the acrobats then tumbled back onto the stage, Faeries on one side and Elves on the other. The Faeries lay down on the floor in concentric circles, while the Elves remained standing in lines, holding hammers and wooden pegs.

Circle by circle, the Faeries rose, their bodies swaying, arms reaching toward the sky, and eyes closed — dreaming. The Elves stood, motionless, listening. Back and forth the Faeries swayed, their arms moving in circles, as if they were capturing clouds. The Elves remained still as stones. The Faeries then fell back to the floor, lying quietly as the Elves darted about the stage, pounding their pegs with their hammers — building, building, building.

The three elven lady acrobats tiptoed to the center of the stage, holding a large sun-shaped lantern — two spans wide — above their heads. Hammers of Silver Forge shined on their orange cummerbunds, as they paused — waiting.

Baudwin, Matha, and Criofan then glided to the center of the stage, holding a Moon — two spans wide — made of finely polished silver leaf. Water droplets shimmered on their indigo cummerbunds as they paused — waiting.

Criofan and Matha then passed in front of the elven ladies, holding the Moon in front of the Sun, while Baudwin waited to the side. Seeing this, the Faeries in the audience lit up, cheering and clapping, for the Moon had now eclipsed the Sun. The Elves remained stoic, not certain that they liked what they were seeing.

Criofan and Matha then pulled the Moon away from the Sun. The Elves lit up, whistling and stomping, for the Sun was now shining alone, without the Moon. The Faeries became quiet, wondering what this meant.

Baudwin then stepped to the front of the stage and spoke:

"Many have said that long ago, the Faeries were the dreamers, and the Elves were the builders of *Tír na nÓg.*"

Baudwin saw a few nods of understanding in the crowd and many blank stares, so he continued. "What this means is that the Elves once built all the dreams for *Tír na nÓg* that the Faeries had sent to them. Thus, our realm remained in balance and at peace."

Baudwin paused, gathering his courage before he spoke again. "Then, for reasons none can remember, a period of decline began. The Faeries stopped sending their dreams to the Elves. Thus, our realm fell into a state of disarray and decay. This brought forth the Great Befalling — sowing strife throughout our realm."

Everyone in the crowd nodded their heads, seeming to understand what Baudwin had said, and so he continued.

"But now, a new beginning has come, and there is a solution for our woes."

Baudwin gestured toward the golden Sun on the stage. The Moon was now absent, having been carried away by Matha and Criofan. The crowd remained still, waiting. Emboldened by their silence, he spoke again:

"No longer do the Faeries need to send the Elves their dreams. The times we live in are like a parting eclipse, where the Moon has left the Sun, and the Sun now shines alone. For now, Govannon — the King of the Elves — has told his kin to build *his* dreams. The Elves are now both the dreamers and the builders."

With this, the Elves in the crowd began to cheer, and Ferrell smiled, but the Faeries were deathly silent. Baudwin tried to ignore the shocked looks on Kelven's and Seamus's faces.

"Our duty as Faeries is to take heed of what the Elves require of us," he continued, "and to allow them this time to reforge the destiny of *Tír na nÓg*. To do this, we must be open to the elven interpretation of the Triquetra — Scrutiny, Certainty, and the Promise of the Future." Ferrell nodded, beaming with pride.

Hearing this, the Faeries began booing, and Baudwin's worst fears were quickly realized. The Guilders shook their heads disgustedly, their mouths sneering with contempt. The Eddies seemed uneasy, as they waited to hear more, and the Roilers grinned smugly at each other.

Boldly, the Grand Eldress stood up, angrily whipping her robes about her, as she shouted over them all, "This will leave the Faeries in the shadows!"

"No!" Baudwin shouted back. "Please! All of you must understand."

But the Faeries did not want to understand, and so they scoffed at him even more.

Ferrell then stood up. "Silence!" he shouted. "All of you! Let him finish."

An unpleasant tension came over the crowd, and not an utterance could be heard. Baudwin hastened to fill the void.

"We Faeries will not be left in the shadows," he proclaimed. "We will *always* have a place in *Tír na nÓg*. Whatever dreams we had, whether for gardens, dome homes, or shrines, were sent long ago by Faeries who have long since passed to Annwyn. How can we be so sure that the dreams of the Elves won't benefit us all? Consider the leisure time that Steamway and Magniglow will afford us. We'll have fewer responsibilities, and more time to commune with our elements. Instead of scrubbing and grinding, we'll have more wakings and festivals!"

Hearing this, some of the guilder Faeries perked up. Obviously, they enjoyed the notion that the Elves might make their lives easier and more pleasurable. The Grand Eldress, however, was not having any of Baudwin's flowery promises.

"You do your kin a dangerous disservice, son of the Primary of Water!" she exclaimed. "You speak of things that you know nothing about, misled by those who seek to reshape our destiny based upon falsehoods, from a time they *barely* understand."

"But the Guild barely understands them either," Baudwin retorted. "How can we demand that the Elves not share their dreams with us, when we've forgotten how to share ours with them? We can't blame them for losing our own way, and then demand that they lose theirs as well — while we sit and do nothing."

The Grand Eldress fell silent, as did the Faeries, for Baudwin's words had subdued them. Kelven and Seamus were stricken, having recognized a truth they had long avoided facing.

Ayammon, the Guild Leader of the Danu Quarter, then stood up, shouting, "The Moon may have eclipsed the Sun, but the Rise of Time will *never* eclipse the Eternal Movement!"

At first Ayammon's words surprised the crowd. Rows of Faeries and Elves, including the heads of Four Falls society, looked perplexed. Baudwin took this moment to ponder why Ayammon would say this. The last time there had been talk about the Eternal Movement and the Rise of Time was right before the riot at the Four Rivers Faire.

"Indeed!" Seanán shouted, as he stood up. "How amusing that a *Faery* must point out what an Elve is too addlebrained to see. Time is much more than the movement of a gear."

"Can't keep from spewing your antiquated nonsense, can you Seanán?" Fearghus said as he stood up. "The Rise of Time teaches that time is only that which we can measure, and without it we cannot scrutinize, be certain, or build a stable or promising future."

Baudwin could see Ferrell nodding, as Ferrell seemed certain that Fearghus would win the argument. The crowd waited for Seanán's rebuttal, as tales of their disagreement had spread throughout the city. All listened — fascinated — riveted to their seats, wondering what would happen next.

"Time is not just the meaningless movement of a gear!" Seanán exclaimed. "A tick or a tock on a clock has no value beyond knowing when something starts or stops. Only when you go beyond binary processes do you truly understand time, and see that the *very* act of measuring is, in fact, an illusion."

"The act of measuring *is* time!" Fearghus shouted. "And you call yourself an Elve!"

"No!" Seanán shouted back. "Time is a paradox — a paradox that at its *root* helps us to contemplate the mystery of our own existence!"

"No, it is not," Fearghus retorted. "Time is *conceptual!* Strictly the result of measurement!"

Seeing the vainglorious smile upon Ayamonn's face, Baudwin surmised that he had deliberately tried to turn the Elves against each other. Baudwin looked then at Ferrell, who at first had welcomed the argument, but now was poised to intervene. The Luminary stood up to speak, but he was too late, for Ayammon begun shouting again, his commanding voice carrying through the entire audience.

"The Elves can't agree on time, so why should we let them influence our young ones?" Gesturing toward Baudwin, he added, "And let them dictate what should or shouldn't be? The Moon *always* has a place in the heavens. Night comes after every day, just as the Sun rises every morning. We must heed the natural balance that has always existed!"

"Stop your blathering, Ayammon!" Fearghus shouted. "Pay attention to Baudwin. The Sun now shines *alone!*"

If Ayammon was angry at Fearghus, none could tell. Wantonly, he smiled at him, baiting him further. "You don't say!" he exclaimed. "How in your misguided view of the heavens does only the Sun shine? Do you agree with him, Seanán?"

Ferrell then tried to intervene, exclaiming, "Of course he does!" But his entreaty fell on deaf ears. The chance for harmony had passed.

Seanán then spoke. "I understand the plight of the Faeries. Their Moon is very much like the Eternal Movement. They are misunderstood and bullied by those who believe they shine brighter and carry more significance. Rubbish! The Rise of Time and the Sun are no more or less important!"

Fearghus then said, "Baudwin is right. The Faeries stopped sending us their dreams nearly a thousand years ago. Once their dreams guided our aspirations, which led us to build wonders that have long since been lost. The wise among us say that this exchange was foremost in our existence, sowing purpose in the lives of all the Fae — but that time is *gone*."

Seanán had other ideas. "What is foremost in our existence can *never* pass," he said. "And if you truly understood time, you would agree."

Fearghus laughed dismissively. "You sound as sentimental as a dove who's lost his mate. Will the Moon now weep for us as well?"

Elves, Roilers, and Eddies in the crowd laughed, and Seanán became red with anger.

Fearghus then tried to sum it all up. "The long decline and the Great Befalling led us here, and the Elves must now fend for themselves. Who's to say that the Sun and the Rise of Time cannot change things for the better and heal the realm? When Baudwin unmasked your hypocrisy, you Guilders were all silent. Face it — you have no dreams left for us, and even if you did, you wouldn't know how to go about sharing them. Time has moved on and so too must we, lest we fail to embrace our destiny and realize the Promise of the Future."

Ferrell then stood up to intervene. "Enough!" he shouted. "Let us not forget the purpose of this gathering. The Assembly of Progress and Govannon himself instructed me to sow harmony — not discord — by bringing the Elves and Faeries together. Even if you cannot agree upon the Sun and the Moon, or time itself, at least allow yourselves to see and enjoy the practical benefits of elven wonders. Let us now get on with the Grand Unveiling, which will commence after a brief intermission."

With that, he turned and left the gathering.

Chapter 31
THE GRAND UNVEILING

A thousand years had passed since the Faeries stopped sending their dreams to the Elves, a thousand years since the wood Faeries last came from Wood Fern to *Inis Easa*, bearing gifts of saplings — mere sprouts of acorns that carried the strength of the greatest oaks in *Tír na nÓg* — trees they named *An Lucht Buan*.[1] The wood Faeries were delighted to bring their saplings to *Inis Easa*, for only there did the Water of the An Bhanna provide them with the same life-force as the great forests of Wood Fern. Here also did the trees flourish, bearing the weight of the ages as their trunks and branches grew into giant canopies over the island.

On this day, the trees all bore witness to what had just transpired, whispering through their roots to one another, murmuring their dismay that the Faeries — no longer the dreamers of *Tír na nÓg* — were conceding their dreams to the dreams of the Elves. Unlike the trees, the Faeries had forgotten their purpose. The trees had always provided shade and shelter, just as the falls had fed moisture to the moss that grew in wispy festoons from their branches, forming curtains of protection for the birds as they feathered their nests and nurtured their young. The birds sang sadly as they perched among the branches, for they felt the same as the trees. Their songs carried through the hanging moss, mourning all that had been lost.

None of the Faeries mourned, except for those who did so with a lingering sentiment about the past. They sensed that long ago their dreams had held far more significance, but no longer did they understand how this could be true. Baudwin's performance had only demonstrated how few, if any, were guided by the dreams of long ago. And now most of his peers remained conflicted. They didn't want the Elves to exert more influence by doing both the dreaming *and* the building. At the same time, most didn't understand what purpose their dreams had actually served and that once they had shaped the entire realm.

The Elves were giddy and ready to rebuild *Tír Éirí Sióg*. As they filed out, heading for the magniglow exhibits, many slapped each other on the back, for they had certainly demonstrated their superiority over the Faeries. After

---

[1] Pronounced [UN LOOKHT Boo-un] the enduring ones

all — this was now *their* time. For now, they would share their dreams — Govannon's vision — with the Faeries, and build whatever they saw fit. All the displays were west of where Ferrell stood waiting at the shoreline. And so, toward the booths they went, all of which were arranged along the cobblestone paths. Signs read, "Health" "Wealth" and "Jubilation" for the Elves had provided each invention with a theme to better educate the Faeries about the promise of Magniglow.

Baudwin believed he had won the day, but when he smiled at some nearby Guilders, they shook their heads, scoffing at him. No longer was he the same as they. In their eyes he was now just another fool, who would no doubt soon become a Roiler — or at best an Eddie. He then regarded Criofan and Matha as they made their way through the dispersing crowd, a few paces from the bottom of the stage. They were still wearing their costumes, as was he. The elven lady acrobats were with them as well, receiving admiring glances from some Elves. Criofan seemed to be as unruffled as ever, but Matha, seeing the scorn of the Faeries around him, looked visibly shaken. Apprehensively, he scanned the crowd for some form of reassurance and found none.

"Baudwin — dear Baudwin!" a familiar voice then called out.

"Grandfather!" Baudwin exclaimed, turning.

Seamus smiled and they ran toward each other. The tall Faery hugged his grandson, his arms strong as oak branches. Despite his grandfather's joy, Baudwin sensed vulnerability in him that he had never felt before.

"Father!" Baudwin exclaimed, his arms still around Seamus. There behind them stood Kelven, happy to have found his son. For now, their angry parting was forgotten.

"What a solid performance!" Seamus boomed, as he let go of Baudwin. "I've never seen you do a double flip with a half twist before. Wherever did you learn that?"

Baudwin smiled at his grandfather's apt appraisal. "From my new friends," he replied, gesturing toward the lady Elves. "They taught me a trick or two."

All three Faeries regarded the lady Elves, who nodded back at them. One of the ladies pointed to the golden Sun on her cummerbund, and the other gestured as if she were pounding a hammer. Baudwin chuckled, for he had been working with them for weeks. When he first asked them to join his performance, they had been skeptical. Since when did Elves ever perform with Faeries? But after they learned that Ferrell had requested the performance, they immediately agreed.

"You're lucky they aren't faery ladies," Seamus quipped. "Otherwise you'd be bonded in the aethers before a fortnight." Baudwin could tell that Seamus would have liked nothing better than for him to go back to Deuona, bond with a faery lady, and settle down.

Kelven gave Baudwin a hug, saying, "We would have come sooner, but Matha and Criofan told us to wait, because Ferrell wanted them to see you first. We assumed you were all right."

"And we weren't sure you wanted to see us," Seamus added, lowering his eyes. Baudwin couldn't bear to see his grandfather's pain.

"Of course I did!" he exclaimed.

"I see you've done a lot of work," Kelven said. "More than I could get out of you."

Baudwin was so happy to see them that he ignored his father's remark. Besides, Kelven looked truly relieved to be there.

Soon Criofan was hugging his parents, Congal and Moira, and Matha was hugging his, Niall and Brigh. Completing their joy, Moonrise alighted nearby on top of a post on the stage. Everyone began talking all at once.

"The Rise of Time has risen," Congal joked. As he spoke, his face lit up and he danced a little jig. Baudwin laughed, seeing how Congal's sense of humor seemed so like his own.

"And the Eternal Movement is no longer eternal," Moira chimed in, more seriously. Reserved by nature, she said nothing more. Baudwin wondered how the Elves' difference of opinion might lead to more rancor in the realm.

"Concord among the Elves seems to have perished — officially," Brigh added, sounding forlorn. Baudwin saw disappointment etched into her face.

"When concord falls away, commerce saves the day," Congal said brightly.

"Until someone feels cheated and gags on their cabbage," Niall added. "Then they come to the Weighing Dome for our help. Now the Elves have no such recourse — or so it seems."

Everyone nodded.

With the time they had before the Grand Unveiling, Baudwin suggested they visit some of the elven exhibits. He could tell his elders weren't that interested, but in the spirit of concord, they all decided to take a look. Before they left, he and his friends changed out of their costumes.

Down the cobblestone path they went, toward the eastern end of the island. The spring evening was balmy, the fragrance of elder hedgerows wafting through the Air. Tents scattered about resembled a festival like none Baudwin had ever seen. Rather than glowstones, magniglow lights were strung everywhere — upon oak trees, like sparkling spider webs, and around painted signs, making the letters jump right out at them. Everything looked curiously alive. Canopies shimmered like pinwheels of glossy taffy, and on the ground, shadowy hues of red, green, and yellow bounced off the booths, as they glowed in the fading sunset.

In the back of the group were Baudwin, Criofan, and Matha, and in front of them were their elders — first Kelven and Congal, then Moira and Brigh, and finally Niall and Seamus in the front. Everyone walked cheerfully, reminding Baudwin that he hadn't been in a procession like this since the important meeting, when they had voted on Matter Three. He was pleased to see everyone getting along, and hoped they would understand the path he had decided to take.

Ahead of them was a booth with a sign that read, "Wealth," They stopped for a moment to look at some bronze drills. An Elve flipped a switch and magniglow energy made the drill whirl. The drill bit bored easily through the rock. Satisfied, the Elve pulled the drill back. Gleaming specs on the tip of the drill bit shone brilliantly.

Curiously, Congal, Criofan's father, asked, "What are those shiny bits on the end of that thing?" To which the Elve replied, "Diamonds."

"Diamonds to find diamonds," Congal quipped. "How very clever. I wonder if I drilled with diamonds for a gusher, if I could wash away the Assembly." Everyone but Baudwin laughed.

"You have to be careful around gushers," Baudwin added. "They can be quite unpredictable."

"True wealth isn't mined from rocks beneath the ground," Seamus said, "but is found in hollows where springs flow, and the Water nourishes all creatures that lurk and dig."

Hearing this, none of them wanted to consider elven notions of wealth any further, so they left the booth. They soon reached another, labeled, "Jubilation." There they saw Elves lighting Sky Sparks, drawing attention to a large collection of lanterns and steamway toys, all powered by Magniglow. "Come enjoy the jubilation of Magniglow!" the Elves shouted, as the Sky Sparks exploded like blooming flowers in the evening sky. Baudwin stopped, amazed to see so many steamway toys lit up this way; birds and other forest creatures glared with magniglow eyes, and flowers glowed with radiant magniglow petals and leaves. None of his toys ever shined like these.

Enviously, he thought of all the young ones who would get to enjoy them. How much he would have loved to have owned some of them himself. They weren't simply wind-up toys. They all moved with the energy of Magniglow. On a table, he spotted a bronze frog hopping up and down, attached to a copper cable.

Sharply, he felt a tug upon his sleeve. "Come on, Baudwin," Matha whispered. "You mustn't get too distracted. There are other sights to see." Looking away from the toys, Baudwin saw that everyone was already several yards down the path at another booth, labeled "Light Up Your Health." He and Matha ran to catch up with them.

"All we need is the Water for health!" Seamus exclaimed, raising his arms to the sky.

Kelven, Niall, Brigh, Congal, and Moira all nodded, smiling.

"So this is the dream of the Elves," Kelven said, as he began to inspect what appeared to be a walk-in closet large enough for a single Elve or Faery to stand in. A sign read, "Magniglow Light Cabinet." The inside was arrayed with magniglow bulbs from stem to stern.

Criofan, Matha, and Baudwin went to inspect the cabinet, while their relatives stood behind them.

"What does it do?" Criofan asked.

"It seems you stand inside," his mother, Moira, replied.

"The outside is elegantly made," his father, Congal, put in, touching the wall of the cabinet. "The wood paneling is of the finest spruce that comes only from Pine Reach in the elven lands. And the work on the fixtures was done by a master coppersmith."

"Indeed it was!" a voice exclaimed. Turning, Baudwin saw Glas a few paces away. Baudwin had helped him prepare the exhibits, assisting only with menial tasks. Never had Glas allowed him to see what the assembled equipment was for, so Baudwin wondered what he would say next.

"Before I begin my demonstration, I'll need a volunteer," Glas continued. None of the Faeries responded, so he pointed to Seamus, asking, "How about you, tall one? I'm sure the cabinet is high enough. And, you seem old enough to gain the most benefit," he added, chuckling.

Nervously, Seamus looked inside the cabinet. Set squarely into bronze sockets, the round white bulbs might just as well have been rows of teeth. He grimaced at the device, an expression Baudwin rarely saw. The lines on his face were tight with strain, and his usual steely gaze was a mix of vehemence and revulsion. He couldn't have been less inclined to step inside.

"*Scared*?" Glas asked.

"Of course not," Seamus replied.

"Just some explanation first, please," Kelven added.

"Certainly," Glas began. "What you have here is what we Elves believe to be a new way for everyone in *Tír na nÓg* to stay as healthy as possible. To receive the benefit, all you must do is stand inside. I will flip this switch and then the healing will begin."

Glas pointed to a switch that was on the counter. Baudwin could see wires running from it to the cabinet.

Seamus balked at Glas. "So this is a switch," he said. "If you ask me, it's more like a *hitch*." Baudwin knew Seamus would probably never trust switches. Most everyone there had learned about them just weeks ago at the important meeting, and Baudwin could tell that they weren't impressed seeing one. After all, he was the only one present who had voted for Magniglow.

Seamus tapped the switch with his finger. "It's hardly an improvement over the smooth beauty of a glowstone." Baudwin could tell how galled his grandfather was. "How will flipping this thing help me?" Seamus asked, eyeing Glas sternly.

Nervously, Glas looked at the group. In front of him were not one, not two, but five guild primaries, their sons, and a guild leader from Deuona — a formidable lot to be sure. Although he was soured by the question, he was uncertain about what to say, so as not to upset them. Amiably he intoned, "Through the fortuitous fusion of the element of light and our marvelous invention — a very well-conceived and executed fusion, I might add. I'm sure you're aware of the healing powers of light, yes? Light is one of your elements — is it not?"

Glas had now regained at least some of their attention. Slowly, they nodded, and then Kelven said, "Yes, of course. Light is not our element, but it does heal in its own way, just as Earth, Water, Air, and Wood do. Every element is said to heal something, somehow, which is why we Faeries look to the Water for such things when we join and course. Some even say that our elements provide healing, so we may better hone our intentions, whatever they may be." Hearing this, all the Faeries nodded again.

"Of course," Glas replied brightly. "And this means that magniglow light can do the same. As you will see, this cabinet will provide you with renewed vigor. The Elves hope that soon every faery home will have one of these in their washing rooms."

Gazing around, Baudwin could tell that the Faeries weren't so sure they liked where Glas's explanation was going.

"But that's not *real* light," Brigh said, shaking her head.

"Oh — it's not?" Glas began. Spotting Baudwin, he craftily continued. "Baudwin, did you not learn that magniglow currents are found in potatoes?"

Baudwin nodded. "Yes, it's true. I saw Olaf plug copper wires into potatoes, connecting them and then lighting a bulb."

Kelven and Seamus looked unconvinced. Niall and Brigh weren't sure, but Congal and Moira seemed at least warm to the idea.

"Perhaps so," Seamus said, shaking his head vehemently. "But that isn't the Light of a glowstone, *or* the Light of our lost cousins, the light Faeries."

"Light is light!" Glas exclaimed. "Come now, step in and stand inside, and see for yourself. It won't harm you."

Baudwin seized the moment to speak. "Grandfather, you can trust what Glas is saying. I've been working with him for weeks, paying off my debt. The light cabinet is safe, in fact —"

"Debt?" Kelven interrupted. "Whatever did you do?"

"Never mind that, Kelven," Seamus said. "That can wait." He then paused, looking directly into Baudwin's eyes. "Safe?"

"Yes — I promise," Baudwin replied.

Seamus didn't need to hear another thing. He trusted his grandson, and so he went and stood inside of the cabinet — the lights still off — while everyone watched.

Glas then pointed to a switch on one side of the device.

"Before I turn this on," he began, "I'm going to have him put on these spectacles to help shield his eyes from the healing beams."

"If the beams are healing, why do I need these?" Seamus asked.

"The light is brilliant," Glas explained. "So bright that the sensitive parts of your body need protection."

Glas handed the spectacles to Seamus, who then put them on. His hair hung over the rims in straggly clumps. Impatiently, he brushed them away.

Glas then went and flipped the switch. Soon all the magniglow bulbs were shining brightly on Seamus's blue-green skin.

"Once, when I was a lad, I went to Bright Portal," Seamus said. "The glowstones were the brightest I've ever seen, but not like these."

"Yes," Glas agreed. "Nothing glows as brightly as magniglow light. Tell us now — do you feel a change coming over you?"

Baudwin had no idea what Seamus would say. He wasn't even sure the light cabinet worked, and if he was skeptical, he was certain that Seamus would be even more so.

"Well, you know," Seamus replied, closing his eyes, "I *do* feel a tingling sensation over my skin."

"Yes?" Glas asked, hanging on his every word.

"Yes. . ." Seamus replied. "How curious. Perhaps these old bones do, somehow, feel lighter."

Now all the Faeries were paying close attention, for they hadn't expected that Seamus would feel any different.

"What else?" Glas asked.

"Kelven," Seamus asked, "what was it that we ate today?"

Kelven gave Seamus an odd look. "I think it was mushroom stew. . ."

"Yes, the brown-cap mushrooms. . ." Seamus mused. "Drat! They always give me the tingles."

Now Glas was clearly annoyed. "Very funny!" he exclaimed, flipping off the switch. Grumpily, he concluded, "Obviously, you aren't fully accustomed to the light — as yet."

"I don't trust this machine at all," Niall spoke up. "You Elves always have some kind of trick up your sleeves. What will you think of next? Water machines, so we won't need the rivers, or mechanical trees so we won't need the forests? You just want us to go along with you, and you're using this silly machine to charm us. What kind of a *dream* is this, anyway? You're just trying to trick us." Glaring at Glas, he went on, "You offer us roses, so we offer you peace, but if your roses are only thorns, then you can go back through the Col and never return."

"Now, now, Niall," said Brigh. "We must heed concord. I'm sure Glas doesn't mean any harm with this contraption." Matha nodded in agreement with his mother.

"You'll see," Glas said, smiling. "This machine *will* bring health. Just as much as the light of Bright Portal once did."

"Why should we replace the Light of Bright Portal with this booth?" Seamus interrupted, angrily. "We don't need this!"

Glas was shaken. Short as he was for an Elve, Seamus towered over him. Quivering, he looked up at the tall Faery, and then lowered his head.

Now Baudwin intervened. "Grandfather," he began, "he means no harm. Come now."

Kelven then spoke. "Yes, enough of this. Let's at least attempt to be amicable."

And so they left and took a break, visiting a confection tent to grab a pastry before going to the Grand Unveiling.

Criofan, Matha, and their parents went to stand in line, and as Baudwin followed them, he felt a tug upon his sleeve.

"Baudwin," Seamus said. "Wait a moment — please. Kelven and I must speak to you in private."

Baudwin dreaded dealing with what he knew would happen next. Surely they meant to question his leaving, and his allegiance to the Elves. How he wished he could just vanish into the mist of the falls, but there was no avoiding this conversation.

They all stopped beneath an oak tree, lit by lanterns above them, not far from the confection booth.

Before Kelven or Seamus could speak, Baudwin blurted out, "I know the performance must have been incredibly shocking to you, but please — you must listen."

"Baudwin — the Elves' dreams *alone* cannot guide this realm," Seamus said.

"But, it's as I said," Baudwin insisted. "We have no dreams of our own to send their way. Not that we would know how to send them, even if we did."

"Perhaps," Kelven said, remaining calm. "Yet now it seems we're deadlocked. We all know our realm used to be more balanced — when our kin sent their dreams to the Elves — but we don't remember how this sacred harmony was achieved. I never spoke of this to you, and I now see that this was a mistake."

"Why didn't you?" Baudwin asked.

"I didn't want to compound your misery," Kelven replied. "You were burdened enough not having your mother, and not being joined."

"Do you even know how the Faeries sent their dreams to the Elves?" Baudwin asked.

Kelven went silent. Seamus then spoke. "I suspect it was through the joining, coursing, and honing that we were able to gain wisdom and achieve feats far greater than we do now, and that Glamorium played an essential part in this, but exactly how, I cannot be sure."

Baudwin could hardly believe his ears. All his Life they had tried to teach him the old ways by molding him into the Guilder they expected him to be. Yet, never had they told him the truth — that they knew more about what had been lost than they had said. And now they wanted him to believe that they had done this to spare him. He couldn't help thinking that they were mostly sparing themselves, so they didn't have to feel the pain that the truth might cause them all.

"What good does hearing this do me now?" he asked. "You held back too much from me. I learned of this from Ferrell who isn't even a Faery."

"You can't trust that one," Kelven said.

"He's done nothing but help me," Baudwin replied curtly. "We're fallen, so we must heed those who have an answer, rather than none at all."

Gravely, Kelven shook his head. "Your performance made that official to the entire city of Four Falls and to all the hamlets. The Elves now lead because nothing is there to stop them — for better or for worse."

"You must understand," Seamus added, "that this is all quite a shock to us, Baudwin. To be honest, we've known for some time that the Elves have been pursuing their own dreams, but that's not really what concerns us right now."

"It's not?" Baudwin asked, surprised.

"No," Seamus replied.

"What, then?" As usual, Baudwin was so taken by his own thoughts that he skipped over the surface of things, failing to see what really mattered.

"Why have you allied yourself to Ferrell?" Seamus asked. "What could you *ever* possibly hope to gain from him?"

"He promised to help me find Mother," Baudwin replied. "He commands a fleet that can search the entire realm."

Kelven and Seamus now became quite serious. "Promised?" Seamus asked. "Why would he do that?"

"Perhaps he wanted to reward me, for giving the performance, and. . . "

"And?" Seamus asked.

"For being open-minded about Magniglow. . ." Baudwin continued. "And for voting *yes* on Matter Three."

"Certainly, for voting for Magniglow," Kelven added.

"Well — yes — he does seem to have taken a liking to me — and to Criofan — and to Matha," Baudwin stammered.

"I wouldn't put your trust in him — so quickly," Seamus cautioned, visibly shaken.

"He's sincere — I'm sure he is," Baudwin replied.

"If he gave you his word, perhaps you can trust him, but that's not what *really* concerns me," Kelven said.

"Then what is it?" Baudwin asked.

"Baudwin, the search you've been on all these years has given you a purpose — which is very important. So important that we never had the heart to tell you that your Life could be even more than this — so much more."

Baudwin expected a lecture, but instead his father surprised him.

"You searched so long for the Water, until finally the Water came to you, and then just as soon, you were off to find Glamorium, and then Glamorium was gone, and now it seems that Ferrell will whisk you off to yet another adventure before you've barely finished the last."

"It's my choice —" Baudwin began.

"That we know," Seamus cut in. "Which is the point — isn't it? You're two hundred years old now. The choice is yours to make. But, before this night is over, and the Elves have finished showing us their gadgets, you should consider the Life you could still have in Deuona."

"How can you say that?" Baudwin asked, shocked. He then stared at them, and they stared back.

"Do you see *Teampall Easa* behind you?" Seamus asked, gesturing past them.

Baudwin looked beyond the exhibits, where the great temple loomed. The Sun's rays were low as they danced over the great dome. No doubt mothers were inside, joining their young ones with their currents in the great basin of Water, whence sprang the An Bhanna.

"*Teampall Easa* is your future," Seamus said. "Someday, after we have passed on, you will lead young ones, just as we do now."

"The future you never bothered to show me!" Baudwin exclaimed.

"You weren't ready," Kelven said.

"What's that supposed to mean?" Baudwin asked.

Gently, Seamus placed his hand on Baudwin's shoulder. "We were waiting to see if your affliction would pass."

Hearing this, Baudwin was filled with dismay. *So <u>that</u> is why,* he thought. They had sheltered him his entire Life, hoping his bouts would subside, but they never did. Little did they know he had already been inside the temple, but he had failed, and not for the reason they thought. The truth of the matter broke his heart. A lump rose in his throat and his eyes teared up. Kelven and Seamus regarded him, wondering if he would weather the storm he now was in, or capsize.

"Can you forgive us?" Seamus asked. "Your bouts might have —"

Sent me to Annwyn, Baudwin thought, shuddering. But perhaps they only had his best interests at heart.

"We only wanted to make your Life easier. You've had to carry such a burden," Kelven struggled to explain.

"I will try to forgive you," Baudwin said. But the truth was, he didn't know if he could. In the temple, the An Bhanna had not helped him, and the lesson of River Danu had eluded him. Confusion, anger, and sadness rushed through him. Forgiveness would have to wait.

Baudwin shook his head. "No matter, I'll return to *Teampall Easa* after I have found her."

"Baudwin," Kelven implored. "You could spend the rest of your seasons looking."

"I will if I must!" Baudwin exclaimed.

"Yes," Seamus replied. "But you don't have to. You can stop anytime — after Ferrell sails you around the realm, or even after tonight. The choice is yours. No one will judge you — regardless."

Baudwin pondered what Seamus said. He had spent so long searching, and never thought about quitting, but as he contemplated his grandfather's words, he wondered. What if Ferrell wasn't able to help him at all? What if he spent another hundred years looking — or two hundred? The time would go by, and Life would leave him behind. Criofan and Matha wouldn't always follow him, would they? Perhaps when they set sail, but eventually they would head back to their lives in Deuona, perhaps to become primaries themselves. Then what would he do? Looking at his father and grandfather, he could tell that they knew their words had reached him. Nervously, he began, "Well, I don't know. . . I mean. . . I don't have to accept Ferrell's offer — do I?"

"You have to do your own growing," Kelven replied.

Hearing this, Baudwin remembered the last time his father had spoken these words to him — the day of the important meeting, when he had returned home empty-handed, without the coupler. *No matter how tall your grandfather is,* he thought, remembering the rest of what his father had said. Seamus looked at him, smiling, as if he knew what Baudwin was thinking.

"And I *will* do my own growing," Baudwin replied. "But I'm not satisfied yet. I'll go with Ferrell — at least for now."

"And we stand by your choice," Seamus said, as he hugged Baudwin soundly around his shoulders. "But this time, we are saying our goodbyes properly. If you leave a note again, we'll strap you to the millwheel until we've dunked some sense into your head."

They all had a hearty laugh.

"So, tell me," Kelven asked. "Did that glamorium egg *really* disappear?"

"Well. . . it was taken. . . I. . ." Baudwin replied.

"You can tell us when you're ready," Seamus said. "We don't want to corner you like a muskrat in a dried-up swamp. We're just happy we were able to speak with you about all of this. We were terribly worried before Ferrell's guards told us where you had gone."

Baudwin sighed with relief. The explanation about Glamorium would have to wait. So much had happened this evening, and there was still the finale — the Grand Unveiling — which would certainly lighten everyone's mood.

And so they left the confection booth, silent as they headed toward the easternmost part of the island, where the shore faced the base of the falls. There a great U-shaped stage had been erected for the Grand Unveiling. Between the falls were scaffolds, catwalks, and rigging, and among them large canopies, covering up the surprise. Even Baudwin, who had worked closely with Glas to help spool the wire for the hidden display, didn't know exactly what was there. As the falls churned, he could feel mist, cool and damp, like the Air at the Springs of Coventina. He and his friends and their families went to sit on seats near the stage that had been reserved for them. The Grand Eldress was there with her entourage. As Ferrell stood center stage, prepared to give a great speech, the last rays of the Sun faded into the horizon.

⊙╬⊙

Imperiously, Ferrell scanned the crowd. To Baudwin, he looked positively pompous. Baudwin knew how tirelessly Ferrell had worked to persuade Four Falls and the outlying hamlets to agree to allow Magniglow into the water faery lands. Winning them over had not been easy, for he'd had to overcome thousands of years of *gnás*. After months of planning, Ferrell's hard work was about to bear fruit, and he didn't seem the least bit concerned about the fiery quarrel that had broken out after Baudwin claimed that the Elves alone were now the dreamers. Even though the Fae were at odds with each other, Ferrell acted as though soon, none of their bickering would matter — the Elve definitely had a trick up his sleeve.

Next to Ferrell and secured to a post was a magniglow control unit with a large knife switch. Baudwin also knew that Ferrell was relying on this contraption to ensure that the Elves forgot their rancor, and the Faeries fell in line. At the moment of his choosing, he would flip the handle down to connect the main contact blade to the copper knife clips, freeing the magniglow current to trigger the Grand Unveiling.

The eye on Ferrell's medallion glinted brightly under the magniglow stage lights, reminding Baudwin of what Matha had said to him — that the eye, despite its intimidating stare, was meant to convey fairness, like a beacon of impartiality. *Will he be that,* he wondered, *or just the arrogant, metal-marching, sprocket-kisser my grandfather believes he is?*

As Ferrell placed his hand upon the knife switch, his elation was palpable. With one motion, he would change the entire realm — forever. The crowd waited for him to speak.

"Welcome to the Grand Unveiling," he began. "I hope you enjoyed the displays of Health, Wealth, and Jubilation as much as we enjoyed building them for you." Gesturing to Baudwin, he continued speaking. "If you would kindly allow me, I would like to explain more about Baudwin's claim that we must now heed the dreams of the Elves. Baudwin, as you may know, is from Deuona, the son of the Primary of Water." Hearing this, Baudwin glanced at his father and grandfather, but they did not return his gaze. Instead, they stared coolly at Ferrell.

"In Deuona," Ferrell continued, "the Faeries do not regard the Triquetra the same way we Elves do. They still follow the old meaning — Honesty, Truth, and the Promise of Rebirth. However, Baudwin has recently discovered the new meaning of the Elves — Scrutiny, Certainty, and the Promise of the Future."

As Ferrell spoke these words, Baudwin saw Lugh bare his teeth. The Grand Eldress scowled, and Rian waited stonily for Ferrell to continue.

"Being eager to learn new ways," Ferrell continued, amiably, "Baudwin first *scrutinized* the past, seeing that the Faeries had not sent their dreams to the Elves for at least a thousand years. During this time, the Elves had no dreams to build on. And, I might add," he said, chuckling, "making this simple, yet obvious deduction was quite a bold step for a young Faery to take."

Ferrell smiled patronizingly at the crowd, as many of the Guilders shook their heads in annoyance. He then continued, "Only after scrutinizing the past could Baudwin become *certain* in the present that the Faeries weren't going to send their dreams to the Elves ever again. He now recognized that the Faeries had forever lost these abilities, and that they were never going to return."

Ferrell paused, waiting to see how the Faeries would respond. Hearing not a feather drop or a gear grind, his confidence grew. "Being the upstanding young Faery that he is, he took it upon himself to convince his kin that they should accept the *promise of the future* — by allowing the Elves to be both the dreamers *and* the builders of what is to come."

Baudwin then saw Seamus grip his seat, as if he were about to rise, but the Guild Leader held fast. Sensing the stillness of the crowd, Ferrell delivered one last comment. "So you see — in summary — our young faery friend *scrutinized* the past, became *certain* in the present, and therefore saw the *future* more clearly."

Hearing the old meaning of the Triquetra so brazenly supplanted by the new one, Baudwin watched as a ripple of unease ran through the crowd. Groups of Faeries shook their heads, and others blurted out their dismay. Only the Roilers and the Elves took Ferrell's comments in stride. *However will the eye seem impartial now?* he wondered.

Despite the crowd's obvious displeasure, Ferrell continued, undaunted. "But, just as surely as the purest gold ingots come from Gold Haven, I know that you will never accept what I'm saying, unless you yourselves *scrutinize* the Grand Unveiling, become *certain* of its value, and then accept Magniglow as the *promise* of the future — for Elves and Faeries alike. I challenge you all. Don't take my word for it — come to your own conclusions!"

The Guilders in the crowd murmured, seemingly pacified for the moment.

"The gifts we bring you of Health, Wealth, and Jubilation are indeed the dreams of the Elves," Ferrell continued, "and we offer them to you freely, with the utmost sincerity and goodwill. As a veteran of *cogadh*, I know the hardships we have all faced — all the souls that faded to Annwyn, the ruined shops and homes, and the tremendous fear and uncertainty. The Great Befalling took something from each and every one of us — that unspeakably terrible time when all we could do was to stare dumbly at the ground, barely able to stand, feel, or think. Elves and Faeries alike feared that our suffering would never end, and indeed, our helplessness and hopelessness seemed to go on forever, until we finally regained our senses — all with a feeling that somehow, along the way, we had lost something of very great importance."

Ferrell saw now that he had the attention of the Guilders. Attempting to bolster their regard, he spoke further. "I remember the day that the Great Befalling struck. The warriors among us were lost in a daze, their once fierce faces clouded in stupor, their limbs, shaking. I myself could barely speak, as I was severed from a great font within me that even now I fear is forever lost. All in the realm sensed that this last link had been broken, which made honing or tempering our intentions well-nigh impossible. All were confounded and weighed down by vexation, uncertainty, and abandonment. I wondered if I had fallen into a permanent state of melancholy, or if I had simply lost my connection to the metals and to time itself. Today I do not care to know if this is true, as Govannon has given me a new purpose."

Baudwin glanced at the Grand Eldress, who nodded her head. For now, she seemed to be taking Ferrell's speech as an indication of goodwill.

Ferrell stamped his boot upon the stage. "But we Elves did *indeed* rise up, and although some might say that our methods were at times too severe, we fought — but not against the Faeries after Belanus was defeated, for that was never our real intention. We fought against the *true* enemy — the malaise of the Great Befalling. That stupor terrified us all, and I would argue that it terrified the Elves the most. And do you know why?"

Ferrell then looked squarely at the Grand Eldress, who regarded him with a wry look.

"Because," Ferrell continued, "we Elves take ourselves and what we do very seriously. When we cannot think straight, when we can barely act, we are entirely lost. The Great Befalling seemed to end something in our very souls. Whatever link we had to the ancient ways of our ancestors was all but severed. Even though the decline of our realm had long since begun, after the Great Befalling, we all sensed that separating from our metals, forging our paths, and perhaps most important of all, tempering our intentions, was well-nigh impossible. And so, we charted a new course."

Ferrell then placed his hand upon the knife switch, saying, "So let a *new* time now begin. I promise that the Elves will *always* respect the ways of the Faeries. We are but beasts of burden — toiling grand horns — carrying you forward, so that you will flourish and understand how we came to see the Great Befalling as the Grand Endeavor!"

Ferrell then paused, and everyone remained riveted to their seats.

"With a flip of this knife switch, I shall sever the barrier between us!" he proclaimed.

Ferrell then pulled the knife switch.

Baudwin heard a large hollow grinding sound, as levers, cogs, and pulleys began to move. All the while, the churning of the falls continued to roar. Limb-like mechanical arms that held up the great canopies hiding the surprise also began moving. The arms pulled back the canopies exposing a huge array of magniglow lights, each bulb the size of a Faery's head. The lights were arrayed in columns between the falls, beginning at the base and going almost to the very top.

Suddenly, the bulbs went on, and a spectacular light show of all colors of the rainbow illuminated the falls. The crowd gasped, and Baudwin saw that even the Guilders were in awe of the beauty. Red lit the base of all four falls, making the Water glow bright crimson. As Baudwin lifted his gaze, he saw orange — then yellow — green — blue — indigo and violet. Ferrell turned a knob on the magniglow controller and the lights reversed. Red was now at the top of the falls, and violet at the bottom. The Faeries cheered, oohing and aahing, and the Elves whistled and clapped.

Baudwin then remembered what Esther had said when she scried for him, that "a rainbow will be your goal," and that "the rainbow of which I speak isn't in the sky." The rainbow before him certainly wasn't in the sky, but near the Water.

Was this evidence, he wondered, that he had chosen the correct path by joining Ferrell? *Is this the rainbow that will help me find my mother?* he wondered.

The rainbow of lights then turned one solid color — red. The Faeries in the crowd oohed and aahed even louder, clapping and swooning. Some jumped out of their seats and danced in the aisles. All the lights then turned orange — yellow — green — blue — indigo — and violet. With each change of color, the Faeries grew more and more excited. *The Faeries are even happier seeing this than the magniglow dynamos at the important meeting,* Baudwin thought. *Ferrell has certainly won the Promise of the Future.*

All who gazed upon the falls were captivated beyond measure — some by the array of beautiful colors, others by the ingenuity of the builders, and many by the precedent that the Grand Unveiling had set. Four Falls was no longer simply Four Falls, but something much greater, though perhaps, for some, something far less.

The water Faeries stared into the mists, tinged with rainbows of color. As the clouds wafted over them, suddenly all felt the Water keenly. Something was drawing them in, and they realized they were having a waking — a group waking — far larger than any had ever experienced.

Baudwin looked about and saw stares much like his own. Yes, all were taken in, but they seemed just as confused as they were amazed. He looked toward his father and grandfather, and they had no words. The Grand Eldress sat surrounded by her entourage. She alone seemed fearless, without confusion, almost as if some small part of her had known this would happen. Her eyes stared steadfastly at the mists, waiting.

The Elves sensed that the water Faeries were especially entranced, as did other Faeries, who had visited out of respect — wood Faeries from Wood Fern, air Faeries from Breathsong, and earth Faeries from Locus Keep. They all sat quietly, waiting.

The Grand Eldress then spoke. "The Water speaks to us all!"

Baudwin could feel the thoughts of his kin. Even the Roilers had been pulled into the waking, which almost never happened to them anymore. He sensed Loch's wonder and confusion. *Had the Roilers actually been longing for this?* he wondered.

The sheer size and force of the waking caused the Faeries to sense the Water many leagues away from them — all the way to places Baudwin could scarcely name. He could taste the icy Water under the frozen streams of Mount Breasal, the largest mountain in the entire realm, which rose on the eastern side of the Tadlachs, south of the Glittering Tundra. The waking grew and grew, until every water Faery in Four Falls was in its grip — and, he suspected, most water Faeries in *Tír na nÓg* as well.

Ferrell, who had been quietly admiring his magniglow display, now looked upon them as they swooned. "To the new ways *and* the old!" the Luminary shouted. Baudwin could tell that Ferrell interpreted the waking as a good sign. In his glory, the Luminary assumed that the Water was now accepting the dreams of the Elves. All seemed right and good, and for a moment there was not a murmur of dissent. Yet, even though Baudwin supported Ferrell's vision, he was doubtful that the Water would deliver a waking simply to benefit the Elves.

For a short time, few shared Baudwin's doubt. There was only the joy of the display, rainbows of light refracting on the Water — a spectacle fit for the triumph of the Elves. The Luminary stood tall — his will had prevailed. Now the masses swooned with delight. But just as surely as the first leaf falls in Autumn, there was then a subtle shift.

The waking fluxed, and the excitement that had been so evident dissipated as quickly as a cloud swirling in a thunderstorm. There was a sullenness in the Air — a sudden reversal — as if a fawn had been snatched away from a doe before she could even lift an ear.

A piercing fear then struck Baudwin. Being so close to the Water, he panicked that he was about to have another bout. All around him the waking was growing ever more powerful. Terrified, he worried that the intensity would bring on a bout that would surely send him to Annwyn — a fear that had haunted him ever since he had collapsed in pain beneath the bridge at the Cyhiraeth. Breathing deeply, he tried to calm himself.

Just as his fears seemed to ease, a gelid shadow enveloped his heart, filling him with dread. *A bout!* he thought. *Now — surely — I am doomed!*

But was he?

No, he thought, *this is something far different.*

As he waited, the gelid shadow then stirred a memory in him. He remembered his time at the Springs of Coventina. Before he found the Water, a gelid *flame* had coursed up his arm and into his chest. The flame was similar to the gelid shadow he now felt, but opposite in purpose. Baudwin flinched, stricken with fear. *The gelid shadow — icy and scythe-like — wants to <u>harm,</u> not heal me,* he thought. Instead of inspiration, he now felt only trepidation, as if the dawn, helpless and besieged, had fled in terror from the banshee's wail.

Something else — much worse than a bout — was arising.

Still in the grip of the waking, he sensed his tribe feeling this as well. Something dire had smothered their euphoria. Baudwin gazed at the Grand Eldress. Instantly, he knew her mind. Through the waking she passed a thought to him: *The Water has not yet finished judging the dreams of the Elves.*

Baudwin steeled himself, waiting for what was to come.

The gelid shadow passed through the crowd, halting the breath of thousands. The benches upon which the Fae sat shuddered, as if an unseen weight was pressing down on them, and the rainbow lights flashed haphazardly. Everyone froze, and all would have screamed in terror if not for the eerie silence that filled their ears. In the blink of an eye, an impenetrable fog had enveloped them. No longer could they hear the euphony of the falls.

Peering into the miasma, all were petrified.

The gelid shadow wrenched them away from one another, putting a cruel end to the largest group waking they had ever known. Piteously, they all cried out. Row after row of water Faeries sat, tears streaming down their faces. Baudwin felt the depth of their grief.

Many Faeries rose to their feet and went stumbling down the aisles. Frightened and confused, even more from every quarter followed them. The Elves called out to them as they went, asking them what was the matter. Ferrell shouted for them to stop — to regain their composure. Ignoring him, they flailed their way toward the edge of the island, to see for themselves what their ears could no longer hear.

Once there, hordes of Faeries stared blankly into the fog. Head after head of blue-green hair stood motionless. All were aghast, unable to comprehend what was happening.

"Ready yourselves!" The Grand Eldress shouted. Baudwin did not know what she meant. None did, for the fog was so thick that nothing could be seen.

As if to answer her, the fog then parted. To everyone's horror, they saw that the Water of the four rivers had stopped flowing. Only the sight of smooth rock greeted their eyes, slimy with algae, for the Water had been torn from its usual place, like a sail ripped from a mast. *They are joined to their currents,* Baudwin thought, *so this must terrify them even more than me.*

Panic spread through the crowd.

"The falls have stopped flowing!" Lugh shouted, crazed with fear. "What is happening?" many more shouted. "No longer are we joined to our currents!"

Ayamonn then cried, "I cannot course with my feelings!"

Indeed, what he said was true. The water Faeries' most sacred bond with their element had somehow been severed. Like Baudwin, they were no longer joined to their currents. Nor could they course with their feelings — leaving their intentions dulled.

The crowd became a torrent of chatter. Bleating piteously like herds of shorn sheep thrown into an icy river, they cast around for an explanation. Baudwin spied a faery lady dropping to her knees, her mouth open, as if to scream. She uttered not a sound as she stared at the barren falls — forsaken — her gaze beseeching the Water to please come back.

Baudwin was horrified to see so many dignified water Faeries undone in such a disturbing manner. They were so much worse off than he, for they, having been attuned to their currents for so long, were now being torn from them. The Great Befalling had taken their ability to hone, but now, unjoined, coursing was also beyond their grasp. They shook with fright until their skin sallowed, but Baudwin remained as he was, as this affliction was all he'd ever known.

Wild-eyed, the water Faeries turned to the Grand Eldress for answers, but she remained silent, determined not to lose her composure.

"Do not panic!" Ferrell shouted over his speaker horn. "There must be some kind of logical explanation. Perhaps the rivers have been dammed upstream."

"Preposterous!" Ayamonn shouted. Those around him were quick to agree.

All knew this simply couldn't be. Who or what could dam four separate rivers at the exact same time? Everyone could tell that the Luminary was as desperate for an answer as they were.

Baudwin looked to see how his friends were faring. Matha and Criofan stood near the edge of the island, gripping the railing, reeling with shock.

"You must be strong!" Baudwin exclaimed. "You will stumble as I do, but not being joined does become more bearable."

Helplessly, they stared back at him. "*However* do you live this way?" Criofan asked. "With nothing to guide your feelings?"

Matha then spoke. "All that guides me is gone — all that helps me understand the sorrow, fear, and anger I've ever endured." Baudwin noticed that like a water skeeter, Matha's attention flitted everywhere, looking this way and that. "Now I must know everything — *do* everything — because there *is* nothing!"

Baudwin was shocked to see his friend filled with such despair. "Matha —" he began.

"Something is coming for us — can you feel it?!" Matha exclaimed. Apprehensively, he looked about, as if sensing a monstrous animal lurking nearby. Wailing, he shouted, "She's gonna get us all!"

Baudwin did not know how to calm his friend. Beside himself with grief, Matha cried, "When I was joined, I could feel through my fear, but now. . ." He stopped, his attention flitting faster and faster. "But now, everything is changing so quickly that I can't — and I'm simply going to be *devoured!*"

Baudwin pulled his friend closely to him. "Do you remember the Ceremony of the Joining when we were young ones?" Sadly, Matha nodded his head. They both recalled that day, so long ago, when Baudwin had failed to join with his current. Now Matha found himself suffering the same plight.

Baudwin then saw Kelven and Seamus. Kelven spoke first. "I deeply regret that you've lived this way all your Life. The falls have stopped, and we are all scared witless, but at least I now understand what a burden this has been for you." Seamus did not speak, but instead hugged Baudwin, as this was all he could do. During their embrace, Baudwin felt hundreds of years of pain piercing his grandfather's heart.

Ferrell shouted shrilly over his speaker horn, the magniglow device giving his voice a metallic twang: "Please remain calm! The Assembly will make this right!"

Hundreds of Faeries replied to him, crying out in anguish. Now they were truly terrified, falling to the ground, writhing back and forth, wailing in pain. Scores jumped over the rail into the pool beneath the falls, many shrieking, "We must join back with the Water!" Others held tightly to each other, stricken with grief. Ferrell looked on, his face dark with puzzlement.

"It's gone," Seamus said, his face heavy with sadness. Baudwin turned to his grandfather.

"What is gone, Grandfather?" Baudwin asked.

"The Water. . ." Seamus replied. "The Water is gone. . ."

Baudwin understood. Matha then explained, "No longer do I feel the Water as I did before."

"I don't feel joined, and my feelings won't course," Criofan added.

"Yes, both have left me as well. . ." Matha replied, his voice a whisper, his eyes wide with horror beneath his glasses.

"Just like me," Baudwin replied, astounded. Looking for the falls he saw only bedrock. Nothing moved. Not a sound could be heard. Thousands of murmurs from all over the island and above them at the edges of the city then broke the silence, for all could see Water rising from the large pool at the base of the falls. The Water formed four columns — one in front of each wall of bedrock. Eerily lit at odd angles by the magniglow bulbs, the columns of Water seemed as if they might collapse, leaving only chaos in their wake. Yet, strangely, they remained unwaveringly where they stood.

What everyone saw before them was impossible to fathom. Had circumstances been otherwise, many might have seen the cessation of the falls and the rising of the columns as a miracle of sorts, but this was not the case. Both Faeries and Elves alike could only gape, their gazes fixed with dread, wondering what would happen next. Baudwin looked at Ferrell, whose grip had slackened on his speaker horn. Loch was surrounded by a few Roilers — speechless — as was the Grand Eldress, and all the Guilders. Lugh then gave Baudwin a knowing glance, filled with alarm, as did Criofan and Matha. Instantly, they all knew what had to be the cause.

Not the Banshee, as some may believe, Baudwin thought. *Someone far more terrifying — one who wields the gelid flame <u>and</u> the gelid shadow.*

For a moment the columns of Water towered over them, reaching almost to the top of the falls. One by one, they changed forms. In front of River Nechtain, the column of Water compressed into a floating sphere and then into the shape of a salmon, writhing and jumping. The crowd cried out in wonder and horror.

"Is this *your* doing?" an Elve in the crowd shouted at Ferrell.

Ferrell shook his head. "Everyone must leave — now!" he shouted.

No one listened to him.

In quick succession, the column of Water in front of River Danu changed into the shape of a Moon, the column in front of River Cyhiraeth into a banshee, and the column in front of River Condatis into a hot spring rising from a circle of stones.

Reverberating from the columns, a menacing voice broke through the agony of the Faeries, enveloping all who stood upon the island. "Who among us should be joined to *this* Water?"

The force of the question coursed through Baudwin's body like a perilous riptide, almost drowning him in fear. He shook, as did most in the crowd. None dared to speak, cowed as they were by the accusatory tone, and the truth silencing them all. Now for certain he knew who had spoken. Boann had come again. Immediately he thought of Esther scrying for him. <u>*This*</u> *must be the perilous tide,* he thought.

Boann spoke again, this time with annoyance. "WHO among us should be joined to *this* Water?"

The Elves did not reply. Instead, they looked expectantly at the Faeries. Even Ferrell, trying to maintain his composure, waited for the answer.

The Grand Eldress then spoke. "We Faeries of the Water — the ones who draw strength from *Teampall Easa* — we should be joined."

"*Indeed*?" Boann asked, the timbre of her voice softening to a whisper.

The Grand Eldress squarely faced the falls, her usual vigor laced with fragility. "Our nature is to follow and be one with the Water. Just as the eagle flies, or the spider spins, the Water nurtures our very souls."

"*Grand* one," Boann began, her voice sounding more intense. As she spoke, a wisp of Water shot out of the pool, circling the place where the Grand Eldress stood. "Perhaps," she continued, "you know the truth of this in your heart, but I find the same conviction lacking in those who look to you for guidance."

The Grand Eldress sighed, as if she knew the truth of Boann's judgment all too well.

Boann then continued. "I have deemed all of you — my most cherished ones — as unfit to be joined to your element, as you seem to have chosen the dreams of others to guide you, rather than your own. However, if you choose to persuade me otherwise, I will allow you all to rejoin your currents, save for those who never were."

Baudwin wasn't sure if her last comment was meant for him, or as a slight to the Elves.

Ferrell then spoke over his speaker horn, a jarring intrusion. "What trick is this?" he shouted. "Why should any of us trust this formless voice?"

With that, an ominous-looking tendril of Water shot from a column and quickly wrapped around Ferrell's chest, pulling him high into the Air. "Do not interfere — *Goldclanger!* Or I will make sure that you and your kin witness the price of your meddling. Perhaps then, you will *all* learn something."

The Luminary dangled in the air like a marionette. Seeing one so powerful now so powerless engendered terror in the now vulnerable crowd. Baudwin at least knew who she was, and had already tasted her wrath, which made her seem somewhat less terrifying.

"An evil spirit!" Ferrell shouted back, his legs kicking wildly. "Everyone — you must run! She will send you all to Annwyn!"

Much to Baudwin's surprise, the tendril of Water placed Ferrell back down upon the ground unharmed. The tendril then dissipated.

"I have not come here to send anyone to Annwyn," Boann continued. "My duty is to the Water and to another who dwells in a realm far beyond this one. And I should not be a mystery to those who dwell here. The Faeries of the Water and their cousins who now stand in attendance know me already. I am the steward of the falls and the An Bhanna — the one who guides the Shiny ones to join with their currents, course with their feelings, and hone their intentions."

All were quiet, and then she declared, "I am Boann."

Her claim seemed impossible to most, yet not an utterance of protest was heard. Baudwin peered at Loch, whose usual steely gaze was now one of befuddlement and wonder. *What does he know?* Baudwin wondered, seeing a look of recognition upon the Roiler's face, a look far too certain for Loch not to have known who she was. Baudwin decided to puzzle that out later.

He then studied the crowd.

The old ones were overawed, for they recognized the presence of an ancient being. Gripped by the significance of her appearance, they swayed back and forth, nodding their heads. Seamus, Kelven, the Grand Eldress, Rian, and the Guild Leaders all were hushed, as their knowledge of the past was now eclipsed. No more were the stories they had heard merely legend, but a living attestation, tearing away skepticism and revealing a truth that none could refute. In the crowd, the Elves listened to her with guarded skepticism. They remained mistrustful, for she was not a steward of their kin, they who dwelt in the cities of metal, where the forges pounded and the Craft-Elves toiled.

"You were away from us for so long, we could only believe you were merely a legend!" Ayamonn cried out.

"Indeed," Boann replied, her voice echoing from a place none could see. "Now let us discover whether or not you *really* understand the lessons of that legend." Another tendril of Water then shot out of one of the columns, pointing at Lugh.

"You," Boann began, speaking to him. "Tell me now what I ask you. And remember that if you answer me wrongly, your kin will *not* be rejoined with their currents. Instead, they will be forever lost, like the acrobat from Deuona, who now parrots the dreams of the Elves, and tells falsehoods upon a stage of fools."

Baudwin shivered, for Boann was obviously speaking of him. Clearly, she was scornful of his performance. He said nothing. Some in the crowd regarded him with suspicion, and he felt the judgment of many Guilders fall upon him.

Lugh pondered Boann's words. As her form was still elusive, he spoke to the Air, "I will answer to the best of my ability."

"Good," Boann replied. "Now tell me, Guild Leader of the Nechtain, one who is so fervently against the dreams that the Elves bring: How does going back the way we came, take us forward?"

Lugh rose immediately to the challenge. "When we go back the way we came, we travel as the salmon does. We return to our spawning ground, to the Source of our being. Once there, we are able to own what is true within us and let go of what is false."

"And how does that take us forward?" Boann asked.

"If we return to the Source of our being, then we must indeed be going forward. The Source of our being is our *true* nature, when we are like alevins, newly hatched, swimming in the Waters of innocence."

Lugh paused, happy as a duckling that had deftly taken its first bob in a lake. No doubt he expected praise for his answer, but Boann remained formless, saying nothing.

The Water at the base of the falls then churned, splashing wildly. *Surely, she will flood this place and send us all into oblivion,* Baudwin thought. The crowd cried out in fear, but then the Water ceased moving.

"Yes. . . that is true. . ." Boann replied. "But, now tell me this, Guild Leader. How do *you* fare in your progress? How well have you traveled this path?"

Lugh was determined not to give up. "I believe I've learned to return to the Source. I am, after all, the Guild Leader of the Nechtain. Many times have I swum in the Waters of this great river and pondered its mysteries."

"You *have*?" Boann asked, her displeasure crashing like a flash flood over everyone watching.

"Yes. . . I. . . I mean, yes. . . of course," Lugh replied.

"I would say that you know *nothing* of the cleachtadh[2] of which you speak."

"That's not true," Lugh retorted. "When I really want to ponder this wisdom, I look to my lilies and my poetry. They help me to reflect upon such lessons."

"Ah yes. . . your lilies. . ." Boann began. "I hear all the dreams of my kin, and I know of your obsession with your lilies. They do not provide you with wisdom. They are but a trifle, a mere diversion. You, like so many of your kin, have memorized the words, but you do not practice what you speak. All that separates you from the Elves are but a few shreds of understanding, for ways you say you respect, yet do not follow. You are lost to me."

The tendril of Water that had been pointing at him then dissipated.

Hearing this, Lugh winced with shame, and the water Faeries in the crowd lost all hope. The excitement of meeting one such as Boann had quickly turned to chagrin. They of the Water had been burdened by a long decline brought about by their failure to understand the old ways. Having hoped that the Great Befalling was the last shock they would ever have to endure, they now suffered ridicule from one they had revered and believed would bring them only joy. Hundreds upon hundreds of Faeries hung their blue-haired heads, as did their cousins from the outlying lands. The Elves were perplexed, but seeing the Faeries so bereft, they waited stoically.

Baudwin wondered if Boann would make good on her threat to leave them all unjoined to the Water. He almost hoped she would, for then he wouldn't feel as alone, yet he knew this was a terrible thing to wish for. Ashamed, he too hung his head, waiting.

Snarling, Ferrell shook his fist at the mists, his voice blaring over the speaker horn. "They — your kin — may be lost to *you*, but they are *not* lost to their friends, the Elves!"

"The Faeries don't need a scheming friend like you, *Goldclanger*," Boann retorted.

"What you call a scheme, I call a purpose," Ferrell replied. "Because I won't forsake them. Or should I say, Govannon won't. You say you're a steward, but you're *no* friend of the Fae!"

The Waters at the base of the falls began to churn again, yet still she remained formless. "I am their *only* friend!" Boann shrieked.

Large tendrils of Water then shot into the air, thick as oak trunks, their tips almost reaching the tops of the falls. Ferrell held fast. "You come here and spread panic!" he shouted back. "After being silent for so long, appearing out

---

[2] Pronounced [CHLAHCK-too] sacred practice

of nowhere, you speak in riddles, and then expect everyone to agree with your pronouncements. You ridicule their ways, but offer them no real guidance!"

The tendrils then crashed into the Water at the base of the falls. The Water rose, and an enormous wave rushed toward the island, which would have swept them all away had Boann not held the wave in place, high above their heads.

"Long ago, my arrival was guidance enough!" she roared. "The old ways were a cleachtadh, which took the Faeries home to themselves. They didn't need words. They *already* knew how to join and course with their currents, and hone their intentions. All of that prepared them to practice the lessons of the Triquetra: Truth, Honesty, and the Promise of Rebirth. Now they know *nothing*! Which means they will *never* understand the mysteries of Glamorium. They, like you and the Elves, are fallen, which means you are *all* doomed!"

Ferrell looked at the wave above them, and Baudwin saw him tremble. Thus far, the Luminary had been brave and bold, but against her, what hope did he have?

Ferrell then bowed before her. Laying his speaker horn on the ground, he declared, "If you think we're all unworthy, then have at it! Drown your kin and what the Elves have built, and be done with it."

Tendrils of Water then shot out, directly at the magniglow lights. "Do you *really* believe I've come to drown them or your silly inventions? I remember in an age long past when Sitric of Gleam ruled the elven lands, building wonders that make your Branches of Progress look like petty trifles. Sitric *truly* lived the old ways, using the power of crystals, so naturally, his creations were in balance with what mattered most."

Myriad tendrils of Water then shot out at all of them — both Faeries and Elves alike. "*None* of you understand the true purpose of your lives! Your missing of the mark is a far greater atrocity than whether or not you use a glowstone or a magniglow bulb."

Crashing into them, her words came as more of a threat than her tendrils. Only the Grand Eldress seemed to fully understand Boann's criticism, yet she did not speak up. Seamus and Kelven nodded their heads, yet all appeared to be lost. Absent understanding of what she meant, Baudwin knew that everyone was wondering exactly what they should be practicing, which Lugh had also failed to explain.

Ferrell stood up and grabbed his speaker horn. "Even if you tried to instruct them, they wouldn't trust you."

"And why is that, *Goldclanger*?" Boann asked. The large wave above them inched closer to Ferrell.

Ferrell flinched, and Boann stopped its advance. Coyly, he continued, "If you want them to be as wise as you say they once were, then you must show yourself to them. They cannot trust what they cannot see."

Everyone stared with trepidation at the colossal wave, which could have snuffed them out in an instant. Baudwin couldn't tell what Boann would do, as his own experiences with her had been so unpredictable. Would she help them, or deem them unworthy and destroy them?

"Perhaps you're right," Boann replied. To his relief, the wave then retracted back into the base of the falls. The columns in the Air dissipated.

The tendrils of Water then coalesced, and just as when she had first appeared to Baudwin, the Water fluxed and gave birth. Boann took form again, as she had at the dam, but this time, when her head appeared, her enormous opalescent eyes were wide open, piercing everyone in the crowd. Seeing her tower above them — at least four stories high — the awestruck crowd gasped. She was beautiful, her blue-green skin lustrous, her demeanor calm. Night had come, and the magniglow lights shone brightly upon her willowy form. As the Faeries stared up at her, she gazed down upon them, smiling benevolently.

Some of the Guilders from the Nechtain Quarter shouted, "The stories are true. Boann, our spirit of the Water, has returned!" They then knelt down to her, as did Lugh, and the other Guild Leaders. All at once, everyone else followed, save the Elves, who resisted the urge to kneel and remained standing.

Baudwin could see crowds of Faeries at the top of the falls staring down at her, their silhouettes lit by the magniglow lights. News of her presence had passed through the entire city, as quickly as a tidal wave. He knew this moment would be remembered by all for at least a thousand years. Like a black swan, she had appeared out of nowhere, and now nothing would ever be the same.

This is all my fault, Baudwin thought. *If I hadn't been looking for the Water, she would never have come.* And now she had taken away their currents. Hoping to assuage her wrath, he looked up at her and asked, "Please tell us — what is this cleachtadh of which you speak?"

Staring down at him, Boann replied, "The Fae who stand before me now are not the Fae I once knew. You are *all* out of balance!" Joining her hands in front of her, as if she were holding them all in her palms, she then continued, "You Elves *overuse* your wills, obsessing over your inventions, while you Faeries *underuse* yours, languishing by the wayside, forgetting the purpose of your dreams. No wonder the Elves have usurped the mantle of the Faeries — by doing both the dreaming *and* the building!"

Fiercely, she threw her arms to the sky. "This abomination of the natural order of things will be the ruin of *Tír na nÓg*! None of you are able to *properly* practice the old ways. The Faeries are joined with their elements, and they may course with them, but they cannot hone them, because they don't have the wills to do so. The Elves separate from their metals, and they may forge them, but they cannot temper them, because their wills are overwrought."

Slowly, she brought her hands to her heart, and then let her arms drop to her sides. Smiling, she continued, "Why do you suppose both Faeries and Elves live in *Tír na nÓg*? Neither of you is complete without the other! To dream, the Faeries must have the Elves build; to build, the Elves must have the Faeries dream. When you work together, you renew our realm. When you do not, you defile our realm. So, the cleachtadh of which I speak should already be taking place, but you cannot or will not understand your roles, such as you are."

Baudwin could see from the blank faces that none were entirely certain what Boann meant. Still determined to discover how this could be fixed, he asked, "How might we balance our wills?"

To which Boann replied, "You must abide as the other does, in a concord once learned in the ancient temples, where the Great Emerald Light was received. There, the East and the West came together as one. But the temples are long lost, so I doubt any of you could do this now."

At the mention of concord, Baudwin saw Matha taking a keen interest. He would ask his friend later if he knew anything more. But there was no time for that now.

"They come to you, humbly seeking answers, and all you do is confuse them!" Ferrell shouted.

"And what answers do *you* have, *Goldclanger*? A false Triquetra to mislead them with?"

Hearing this, ripples of indignation coursed through the Elves, and many scowled at Boann.

"At least the Elves offer the Faeries something workable," Ferrell exclaimed. "Instead of nonsense from an age long passed!"

Boann bridled at Ferrell's words, and for a moment her serene form flickered into that of a ceirean, before changing back.

"I see my efforts here are to no avail," she said.

Baudwin wondered what Ferrell was driving at. Surely Ferrell knew what would happen if he continued to antagonize her, yet he remained undeterred. Pivoting toward Baudwin, he shouted, fiercely, "You tell her — son of the Primary! Tell her how well you understand her! How useful her words are to you now!"

All eyes shifted to Baudwin. Boann peered down upon him, awaiting his response. The burden of expectation was more than he could bear. How he wished he were back in Deuona, so he could hide inside a water drum and drift away.

"Well. . ." he began, "I don't see what you mean about our wills. They don't seem to be imbalanced. I know that we struggle to hone our intentions, but our wills are working fine. We Faeries still dream, even if we don't share those dreams with the Elves. Until our dreams return to us, the Elves are happy to keep building. And we shouldn't judge their dreams until we've had a chance to see what they build."

Boann hissed, and the Water around her towering form twisted into a cyclone.

"No matter what you believe about your wills, as long as you cannot receive the Great Emerald Light, they will be out of balance. Not to mention that you haven't even learned how to hone and temper your intentions."

"The Great Emerald Light?" Baudwin asked. "What do you mean?"

"That which was torn asunder in the Great Befalling! That which must be healed! That which sustains *Tír na nÓg*, and is watched over by those who dwell in a realm beyond this one!"

"More nonsense!" Ferrell shouted.

Baudwin couldn't help but side with Ferrell. Always had the old ways let him down, depriving him of the satisfaction he craved. He wanted something he could count on, not another futile trial he couldn't understand. The Water, Glamorium, the An Bhanna, and even the dreams of his kin had all failed to help him. "We Faeries will no longer uphold that which we cannot practice. We will now do as the Elves do."

"You are young and naive," Boann replied. "Goldclanger has misled you. You can't sense what will serve your better interests, let alone understand what I'm saying. Now do you see why I took away your glamorium egg? You weren't ready then, and you *still* aren't ready to bear the egg."

Boann's words humiliated Baudwin as never before. *How dare she single me out this way,* he thought, *in front of everyone?* He glanced at Kelven and Seamus who now knew that she had taken the egg. How he wished to speak to them right then and there, but he couldn't.

His anger rose.

"I no longer care about that silly egg! Our wills are hardly a concern of yours, and we don't need your guidance! The Fae will forge their own path!"

Baudwin stopped short, unable to believe what he had just said. Ferrell smirked defiantly, preparing for the worst.

Boann stretched out her arms. "Very well then," was all she said. A nexus of Water began to whirl inside of her, until her body vanished from sight. She had shown them her beauty and her power, but now, like a tempest, she would show them how unpredictable she really was. Soon all they saw was a torrent of Water topped by a ceirean head, with yellow eyes and gnashing teeth. She shrieked at them, and they recoiled, horrified.

Two enormous arms reached out from the nexus of whirling Water and began tearing down the magniglow lights, wreaking havoc upon the edifices the Elves had erected. Baudwin saw Ferrell signal to Loch, who quickly ran away from the shore to the exhibits. "Everyone must leave the island!" Ferrell shouted through his speaker horn. "This evil spirit will doom us all!"

Boann continued to tear down the lighting. Raging, she sent a wave of Water toward the island. The crowd turned to run, but the torrent accelerated, washing over them and continuing to the center, crashing into the exhibits. Loch held fast to a post. Pieces of Wood and canvas shot by, as the Water flooded tents and walkways, dislodging statues that had been placed among the oak trees in the Temple Circle.

The Water drew back as Boann's form continued to tear at the lighting. She didn't bother looking down upon them, as in her rage, they were as inconsequential as a colony of ants. *We're lucky,* Baudwin thought. *If she wanted to, she could send a tidal wave and drown us all.*

Forcefully, her ceirean tail slapped the Water, sending another wave even larger than the last. Again, the crowd turned to run, shrieking with terror, as they attempted to gain purchase before the wave washed over them. From afar Baudwin saw Loch reach a stack of crates. The Roiler tried to grab one, only to have them all wash away. Loch deftly swam after them, and Baudwin wondered why.

The Water then began receding back toward Boann. Harnessing her etheric might, she drew the tidal forces back to her in a vortex, pulling scores of Faeries and Elves toward her. Gnashing her teeth, she released the vortex, pushing them away. The vortex then sent a third wave — larger than the last — forcing many of the Fae onto the rim of *Teampall Easa*. *Is this a small mercy on her part?* Baudwin wondered. Swimming toward an oak tree, he saw that the temple dome had remained above Water. Pulling himself onto a branch, he then stood up to survey the chaos.

Boann's treacherous waves had swept many Elves off the island. Some ended up scattered at the base of the falls. Across from the island, a lucky few had reached the shore, while others were left flailing desperately in the water. The water Faeries were not as frantic as the Elves, as even the old ones were strong swimmers. They grabbed onto their faery cousins, and as many Elves as they could, to help them reach safety. The remaining light was bright enough for Baudwin to spy Loch swimming in the distance, apparently still searching for something — but for what, he couldn't tell.

Baudwin then caught sight of the Grand Eldress, who was on the roof with the others. "Please, A chroí istigh[3] — show us mercy!" she cried out to Boann. The name she spoke to address her was unknown to Baudwin, but the words seemed ancient, and the respect they carried soothed her fury.

---

[3] Pronounced [UH-chree ish-tee] my darling - oh heart within

Much to Baudwin's surprise, Boann ceased her destruction and regarded the Grand Eldress. "If not for you, all of your kin would be lost beyond hope. Yet even *you* do not truly understand whereof I speak."

Baudwin felt his kin struggling to make sense of her actions. *Perhaps, if their intentions were better honed*, he thought, *they could better understand a spirit such as she.* Yet even after considering this, he wondered if that was even possible. Her will ebbed and flowed, just as the Moon pulled the tides to and fro. Was she trying to protect them or annihilate them? As if to echo his sentiments, the top half of her body turned back into that of a beautiful faery lady, while the bottom half remained a grotesque-looking ceirean, covered in scales.

Wrathfully, her tail lashed at more lights, leaving only the ones at the top of the falls remaining. As she did, she stared down at them, her face implacable as she destroyed all that the Elves had built. She was both guardian *and* tormentor, which had the most unnerving effect on both Faeries and Elves alike. Wood and bronze scaffolds crashed into the Water, forming enormous piles of debris, madly blinking color after color.

Baudwin then spied some Elves floundering in the Water near a row of submerged magniglow lights. All were out of Boann's sight. As the current brought them closer, they shrieked — terrified — at the approaching danger. Sparks flew — and then they were silent, their bodies facing down, as they drifted upon the surface of the Water.

"They've been shocked!" an Elve called out. "Someone GO — save them!"

"No — you fool!" Glas shouted. "You'll be shocked by the magniglow currents! The fallen rigging has turned the pool into lightning. Woe and alas — there's nothing we can do!"

All stared at the elven gents, now drifting helplessly. Much to the horror of the onlookers, their bodies vanished — passed to Annwyn — as all the Fae who perish do. Many in the crowd had never seen this, but all knew that those who passed away would disappear into the afterlife, each one's body and soul traveling together, as one. All that remained were their garments, floating upon the river.

"Nooooo!" Baudwin cried. "How could you do this?"

Boann then turned, her body that of a ceirean towering above him. She lowered herself until her gigantic head was but a few feet away from him. Her glowing yellow eyes would have made even the Banshee flee.

The gravity of her apparent crime was inconsequential to her. She was the flood that suffocated colonies of ants, and destroyed the abodes of burrowing creatures. Turning all to mire and mud, she left the soil fertile for new seeds to grow.

"You are *such* a fool!" she hissed at Baudwin through her teeth. "But I have not given up on you yet. I have plans for you. Let my torrents be a lesson to *never* turn your back on what matters most, even as you flail in its wake. And let those who have passed to Annwyn lead a purer, more peaceful Life."

With that, Baudwin saw the falls begin to flow again. As Boann sliced the icy Air with her claws, the rushing Water of the four rivers seemed to strengthen her. She reached toward the branches where Baudwin stood, petrified. As she grabbed hold of him, her arms turned into smothering tendrils of Water, raising him higher and higher, until he almost reached the very top of the falls. There, only the few unbroken lights illuminated his ascent.

"Go now — and find your *true* destiny," she said. "Know that even if you do not succeed, your failure will not be of my doing, but rather from the falseness which has seeded itself within you."

Sick with terror, Baudwin rose even higher. At the top of the falls she entwined him in her grasping tendrils, swirling him into a vortex, whirling and whirling. He heard Seamus and Kelven cry out to him, horrified to see him so helpless. The Water then pulled him up and over the falls. She had enveloped him like a cocoon, and all he could sense was that he was traveling very fast, surging up River Nechtain, far away from friend and foe alike.

❧

From the roof of the temple, Matha watched, bewildered at what had just transpired. Boann had ensnared Baudwin in her elongated arms and delivered him to the top of the falls, where he had disappeared. *What has she done with him?* he wondered. Her plans for Baudwin were an utter mystery, and this uncertainty frightened Matha the most. *And she doesn't seem finished yet*, he thought.

Boann skimmed closer to the island, her ceirean form towering over them. She glared down at the Faeries and Elves on the roof of the temple, their upturned faces clamoring piteously for her mercy. Angrily she raised her scaly arms as if to smite them, but then she stopped. *Will she answer their pleas?* Matha wondered. Indeed, the falls had begun to churn again, so perhaps she did intend to rejoin them to their currents. He wasn't sure. Perhaps she had simply allowed the falls to flow again to show her strength, before she consigned Baudwin to the current.

Matha watched as most of the water Faeries huddled together on the rim of the roof, the Water almost reaching their feet. "The falls move again!" several of them cried. "She means to rejoin us!" Quickly, they prostrated themselves before her, many others joining in the fervor. Matha hoped their enthusiasm would be well received.

Boann gazed down upon them, but did not scowl or gnash her teeth. Instead, she studied them, her face still. What she would do next was unknowable.

"Please, rejoin us! O please!" they implored her. "We will heed your guidance!"

Her yellow eyes widened, but she did not respond to their pleas. Instead, she raised her arms majestically above her. Behind her, Matha saw the Water of the falls shift. As she drew the four falls toward her, the Nechtain, Danu, Cyhiraeth, and Condatis rose into the Air, and coursed into her beckoning claws. Like a hooded cloak she drew them up and over her head and shoulders, and then over the front of her torso, holding them against her, her arms crossed. Her body grew many times larger, until her gargantuan form blocked out all the remaining lights at the top of the falls.

A gasp went through the crowd, as her scaly body began to change again.

They watched — awed — as her scales faded into pale blue skin, appearing even more lustrous than before. Her neck was slender and her shoulders softly curved. Soon her hair appeared, resembling satiny locks of river moss, with gold beads and pearls braided into the tresses. With her hands she folded the Waters of the four rivers over her heart. The rivers then wove into sea-green silk, with patterns of fish scales and lilies covering her body. Jewelry appeared — a gold belt set with mother-of-pearl and aquamarine — and a delicate-looking conch shell hanging from a gold chain around her neck. Her body continued to transform into faery-like flesh, until finally, they saw her face — no longer that of a fearsome ceirean, but of a majestic queen, serene and powerful. She remained expressionless as a statue, yet her presence asseverated all the wisdom of the Water.

And then she proclaimed,

"The Water wills, the Fae divide for worse,

Whence comes the fog, will they know their curse!"

At her feet a fog crept out of the An Bhanna, unlike any they had ever seen, blanketing the Water with an eerie chill. The murky mist grew steadily, smothering the base of the falls in gloom and misery. The crowd waited, shrouded in dread. On the roof of the temple, most of the Elves and many of the Faeries were gathered around Ferrell. As the fog thickened, both Faeries and Elves felt a pain well up inside them.

A shudder went through the crowd. Boann's watery cloak flowed, but she remained implacable. The effect of the fog grew, and as their pain increased, many put their hands to their temples. Matha could sense that the wracking pain was affecting all of the Fae — Elves of every rank, as well as all the water, wood, air, and earth Faeries in attendance. Matha gazed at the Grand Eldress, who seemed as shaken by the unfolding events as everyone else.

Matha then heard the Grand Eldress whisper to herself, "Whence comes the fog, will they know their curse. . ."

What does she mean? Matha wondered. And then, as if he had spotted a white hare trapped in a black bramble bush, he realized why they were afflicted. *Of course,* he thought. She was cursing them.

"She's cursing us!" Matha exclaimed. His words reached the ears of those nearest him, spreading quickly through the entire crowd. Matha's observation was now obvious to most, yet they had been slow to face the truth. *More than likely,* Matha thought, *because she had just unjoined them.* The pain of the curse was too much for them to bear, and many water Faeries found themselves unable to even speak. The other Fae were faring somewhat better.

"She's cursed us all!" An Elve cried. Many stared — frozen — at Boann. The Faeries waited to see if she would show them mercy, and the Elves regarded her defiantly.

In the dim light Matha spied Ferrell, who appeared ready to burst a coil. Matha recognized the same disturbance in him that was affecting everyone. Yet Ferrell was an Elve, and he seemed determined to get control of his surroundings. The Luminary had been staring at the clothes in the water, where the bodies of his kin had vanished.

With a deadly stare, he grimaced at Boann.

Looking over his shoulder, Ferrell stepped sideways on the rim to see past the dome in the center of the roof. Quickly, he signaled to a figure in the water. Turning to better see, Matha spied Loch signaling back. To stay clear of the magniglow exhibits, the Roiler had managed to pull himself onto some floating debris, keeping himself safe from harm. As he drew closer to Ferrell his body was strangely lit by the submerged lighting beneath the Water, haphazardly strewn about.

Matha strained to see what Loch was up to. In the chaos most of the island had been flooded. Large pieces of the Grand Unveiling floated everywhere — beams, scaffolding, and containers — but for some reason, Loch had searched through the entire mess for only one thing — a crate. Grabbing onto a strap, he towed the crate behind him as he paddled on his makeshift raft. Remarkably, despite his exertion and the torment befalling everyone, Loch was keeping his composure. Matha saw what appeared to be a black sprocket marked on the side of the crate. He wondered what the ominous-looking symbol meant.

Loch paddled closer to the temple and pushed the crate up onto the rim of the roof. Quickly, he hoisted himself up, and then tore open the top of the crate. The rim of the roof was wide and flat, making it easy to bound around the edge, past the high dome, and reach Ferrell. He tossed him a contraption that he had removed from the crate, something Matha had never seen before — similar to a crossbow, but without the bow. The device had a wooden stock and a trigger, but where the flight groove should have been, there was a magniglow coil, with a metal protrusion at the tip. Loch also lobbed a pair of goggles to Ferrell.

Before Matha had time to ponder what the contraption was, Ferrell caught it and put on the goggles. Taking aim at Boann, he shouted to everyone, "CLOSE YOUR EYES!" Everyone hesitated, confused and frightened.

"DO IT!" Ferrell shouted.

Many Elves, who seemed to know what Ferrell meant, then shouted, "DO IT!" And so Matha clamped his eyes shut, as did everyone else.

"There will be no curses on *my* watch!" Ferrell shouted.

Boann's large yellow eyes stared curiously down at him. The Water of the four rivers adorning her torso did not cease to swirl, still free of the granite walls they normally flowed over. For a moment, Matha opened his eyes and believed he saw a look of acceptance cross her face. *Now we must face the folly of the Fae and where their lack of concord has taken us,* he thought.

A bolt of lightning shot from his weapon, tearing into Boann. Reflexively, Matha shielded his face with his arm. As the force ripped through her, everyone heard an agonized shriek. Matha could see the pattern of the bolt sear the back of his closed eyelids. Opening his eyes, he saw the coils on the contraption glowing. By some means, Ferrell had shot her, but how he had done so seemed impossible for the Faeries to understand. He then heard an Elve shout, "Got her with a shocker, Ferrell has!"

"Give her another volley!" Glas shouted.

As Ferrell readied for another shot, Matha saw Boann reeling in torment. Whatever a shocker was, the magniglow contraption had done its work. Quickly, she shrunk in size, her pale blue-green skin turning ashen. Now weakened, she relinquished her grasp upon the rivers. A look of disbelief crossed her face, and all the water Faeries could feel how deeply shaken she was. Unjoined to the Water, they felt her pain tenfold. Many cried out in sorrow for her. She remained unable to speak or make sense of what had harmed her. Despite having seemed to accept the violence that she would meet, Matha sensed that she was nevertheless unprepared for the intensity of what would befall her. Her clairvoyance was merely an impression, without the assurance of experience.

Never before had anyone wielded such an aberrant and brutal weapon in Four Falls.

The shocker had torn a fissure in her, and she was now lost to herself. All the water Faeries watched, feeling her torment as she diminished, until only her primordial nature remained. She shifted into a mass of watery vapor, with an ethereal head like a banshee. Incredulously, she peered at Ferrell, gazing at the roof where he stood.

"Close your eyes!" Ferrell shouted, and again, everyone did so.

Another bolt of lightning shot from the shocker at her, but this time she dodged out of the way, and went barreling down at Ferrell. He pulled the trigger in quick succession and two more shots came out, striking her once, as she flailed at him.

Matha opened his eyes.

Upon her body he saw two gaping holes, all glowing a phantasmal blue. The spectral flesh surrounding them was ripped aside, and when Matha peered into the wounds, the blue appeared fathomless. Before Ferrell could fire another shot, she raised a shimmering appendage and a torrent of Water shot out, forcing him to the ground and his shocker from his hand.

Deep in pain, she shrieked again, her cry causing such grief in the water Faeries that they could not bear to look upon her. They covered their ears. Unjoined as they were, they were overwhelmed by how gravely she had been wounded.

"As was foretold — the Fae will divide!" she cried out.

Weakened by the shocker, her strength waned, and the murky mist smothering the bottom of the falls dissipated. She let out another shriek, and the Faeries watched — devastated — as she withdrew into the cavernous drain works between the falls. As she went, her phantasmal form shrank into a blue wisp, vanishing from sight.

In her absence, all stared into the haze surrounding them. The miasma thinned, and so did their pain subside. A sparse fog still lingered.

Ferrell rose triumphantly, his shocker back in hand. By some fluke or artifice he had beaten her. Matha had never seen such a device — a secret well kept by the Elves — until now.

"We're saved!" an Elve shouted out to Ferrell. Many of his kin sent cheers his way. In their eyes, the bravery and ingenuity of the Elves had driven the violent spirit away and halted her curse.

But not everyone was ready to pronounce Ferrell a hero. The Grand Eldress seemed ready to bite off his head. Rising to stand apart from the water Faeries huddling nearby, and whipping her cloak around her shoulders, she faced Ferrell, outraged. "Fool!" she chided. "You've breached ancient *gnás* by lighting a Fire that no Water will *ever* quench!"

"*I myself* have quenched the fire," Ferrell replied. "Didn't you see?"

They would have continued arguing had Matha not intervened. "Stop!" he demanded as he scanned the top of the falls, his eyes filled with worry. "No more fighting. We have to find Baudwin!"

The Grand Eldress cooled herself, but Matha knew she wasn't finished with the Luminary.

Adroitly, Ferrell slung his shocker over his shoulder. Brushing past the Grand Eldress, he walked down the sloping roof. "You're right," he replied, studying the drain works where Boann had disappeared.

"Now what do we do?!" Kelven shouted at the Luminary.

"I don't know about any of you, but I'm going to find my grandson," Seamus declared.

Everyone now regarded Ferrell. The Guilders looked at him with disdain, but the Elves and Roilers, already singing songs of his victory, seemed ready to celebrate. Matha couldn't tell where most of the Eddies stood on the matter, whether they would turn their backs on Ferrell or demand that he help find Baudwin.

Ferrell then spoke to the assembled Fae. "We will look upriver, but first I must settle this. She has made her move, and now I shall make mine."

With that, the Luminary signaled to his guards, who had already gathered several boats. Soon he was with them, rowing toward the drain works in pursuit of his quarry. The Faeries watched — overcome with grief — as he too disappeared into the cavernous passages beneath the city. Bereft of hope, all they could do was struggle to make sense of what Boann's wrath had wrought.

Chapter 32

ASSEMBLED AND UNJOINED

Throughout *Tír na nÓg*, near every creek, river, pond, lake, or sea, water Faeries could sense that the wellspring that had always nourished them had vanished. They were unjoined, and just as the Great Befalling had torn away the essence of what had bonded both Faeries and Elves to one another, every water Faery was similarly torn from their element. All had entered into the great waking the day before, which had called them together and in their ecstasy guided them to embrace a joy that had long been dormant. But as soon as their senses opened, Boann had come, and now, bereft, all they knew was the foreboding emptiness.

The Water had indeed abandoned them, and without their currents they could only lament. On the Isle of Baranthus, a water Faefry wailed as his father smashed a pot upon the ground, angered by the tediousness of his craft, a feeling that had, until now, been unknown. The succor that Water had always provided was gone, his reverence for the temples he cared for was far from his heart, and all he had left were his burdens.

Far to the south in the Mouth of Lyr, a water faery captain sailed his merchant vessel. He had always navigated his ship, weathering the storms that broke against the rocks of Clearport, all the way to the shores of Pine Reach. On his steamway cutter that sailed without the wind, he had felt a momentary sweetness pass through him — a delight amidst a voyage of salty spray and bitter work — but now he was unjoined. When the next storm came to him, his courage faltered. He feared the gales and mistrusted the stars, as they — like his current — no longer guided him. He was alone upon the waves.

Near many bodies of Water in both the faery and elven lands, small tribes of water Faeries who did not call Four Falls their home knew a great scourge had befallen their kin. Many thought they saw an impression of Boann's likeness upon surging rivers, and in the wake of her fury the elders had proclaimed these images to be of her. None knew why she was filled with such wrath, and could only hope that all would soon be rejoined. Surely, their kin in Four Falls would find a way to appease her and return them to the Water.

Frantically, they asked their cousins, of Earth, Wood, and Air, if they too had been unjoined from their elements. From the Earth, they heard that the ground was still fertile, from the Wood that the plants still sprouted, and from the Air that the wind still carried pollen. All were still joined. Only the Water had left, and all that the other faery tribes had to offer was their sympathy. Yet, many feared that their elements might abandon them as well.

News from Four Falls had not yet traveled very far. The Elves had delivered messages, sending signals of light from their relay stations over the Tadlachs and across the plains to the Clock City. There the Assembly of Progress tried to make sense of what had happened. All had witnessed a water spirit — said to have been Boann herself — who in her fury had attacked the city and torn down important elven gifts to the Faeries. Handily, she had been forced into retreat by none other than a Luminary in their ranks — Ferrell — a Master of Gold. All were relieved to hear of his triumph, but remained cautious as to what this would mean for their plans in *Tír Éirí Sióg*. Quickly, they would get the news to Govannon, their king, and await his orders.

❧

Matha gazed upon the Temple of the Falls, which had weathered Boann's deluge and was now shining resplendently in the rising Sun. Throngs of Faeries huddled on the steps, struggling to take stock of what they had lost, seeking comfort in each other's company. Their hopes of being rejoined to their currents had disappeared with Boann into the drain works of Four Falls, somewhere deep within the labyrinth of its ancient water courses.

Turning his attention to the base of the falls, Matha saw three openings leading into the drain works. Elven masons had built them long ago to control the overflow of the rivers and the many underground streams of the city. Boann had fled into the middle one, located between the falls of Rivers Danu and Cyhiraeth. Stricken, Matha wondered how far Ferrell and his guard had ventured into the tunnels. He could almost hear their boots stomping upon the stonework, their faces grim as they tried to shoot her again with one of their shockers.

Matha couldn't imagine that Boann would ever forgive such a hurt, and Ferrell was clearly not intent upon reconciliation. After Ferrell had entered the tunnel, many guards had followed on longboats, more and more, until the center opening was ringed by moored vessels. From afar, he spied some guards unloading a large tubular-shaped contraption, which they wheeled into the tunnel. *What is that Elve about to do?* he wondered, alarmed.

Matha knew the arrival of more guards meant only one thing — Ferrell's search would not end until he achieved his goal. He wondered if the Luminary would catch Boann. She was very fast, but he suspected that her wounds had made her vulnerable. He imagined her now, cornered somewhere with shockers pointed at her. As more and more elven forces spilled into the tunnels, the hope that the water Faeries would be rejoined became ever more remote. Overcome with grief, the sadness of his kin filled the Air, heavy like the ever-thickening mists around them.

Nearby stood the Temple Circle, a ring of oak trees with a statue of a water faery lady in the center. A white-necked raven landed on her shoulder, cawing bleakly. In response, an unkindness of ravens arrived, alighting on moss-covered branches. Arguing, their caws echoed off the temple walls. Nervously, the white-necked raven hopped closer to the statue's head, flitting its wings. Some of the other ravens then flew to the plinth of the statue, staring up at the white-necked raven, arguing even louder. Matha could see that thousands of years of mist had eroded the statue. Looking closely, he made out the faded features of a merlady with large oval eyes, a scaly tail, and hands tenderly reaching out to him. A raven cawed, breaking his concentration. *An unkindness of ravens*, he thought, shaken. *Coming after Boann's deluge, this could only portend unimaginable hardship.*

Matha's thoughts raced as he looked for a certainty he could not find. Desperately, he wondered what had happened to his friend. Had Baudwin drowned? Under the magniglow lights, everyone had seen the Water snatch him high into the Air and carry him to the top of River Nechtain. There he had disappeared from sight, presumably following the river's course. Boann had sent a terrifying surge against the unvarying current of the river. Accounts from the Faeries of the Nechtain Quarter confirmed what everyone who had been on the temple roof suspected. All had seen a great torrent of Water move quickly up River Nechtain — with Baudwin probably trapped inside — but where the current stopped along the great river, none could be sure.

Thankfully, drowning a water Faery was well-nigh impossible, yet this was Boann's doing, and he had no idea what she had done with his friend. Even if Baudwin hadn't passed to Annwyn, perhaps she had sent him so far upriver that he wouldn't know where he was. The Nechtain reached all the way to Lake Airmid, but also forked off to River Deuona, which had many other tributaries that eventually arrived at Wood Fern, or even farther south to Lake Nodens.[1] Baudwin could be in any of those places, smashed upon rocks or wedged between logs. Even now he could be wandering along some shore, lost and alone. At least he might be safe, but what if Boann's powers could still reach him? If the stories were true, then anything was possible. She could have sent *Cuachag*[2] after him, an evil river sprite who haunted the dreams of Faefries, or turned him into a vile mertoad, so all creatures would flee at the sight of him.

----

[1] Pronounced [NO-dens]
[2] Pronounced [COO-uck-ahn]

But as much as he worried about Baudwin, he was even more frightened for the water Faeries around him. For most of his Life he had seen Baudwin behave strangely, unjoined as he was, but at least Baudwin had friends he could rely upon for help. They always offered him a steady hand. Now everyone suffered the same affliction, and Matha imagined the city falling into chaos. Despondently, he looked around him.

Nearby, young ones who had recently been joined wailed piteously, clinging to their mothers who held them tightly, trying to assuage their terror. So soon after being joined, their currents had been torn away from them. The young ones couldn't understand why a servant of the Water — the one their parents called *Boann* — would punish them this way. They pleaded for comfort, but their parents could offer them none.

"We must be strong," a mother said to her young son, as she struggled to keep hold of herself. Kneeling down to meet his eyes, she said, "We are, after all, water Faeries. The Water will return. Now come close." As she hugged him, Matha wondered who would be the one to console *her*.

Many Elves sympathized with the Faeries' plight, knowing that if Sitric of Gleam himself had appeared, telling them that they knew nothing of the metals, they, as well, would have felt forsaken. A forlorn faery lady sat weeping upon the steps, her hands cupping her face. An elven gent placed his hand upon her shoulder, whispering words of solace.

Matha watched her, wondering why she cried so. Perhaps because Boann was right, and water Faeries simply didn't understand the Water anymore. *Or, perhaps,* he thought, *she weeps because she relinquished her dreams to the Elves, one of whom now consoles her.* Puzzled, he shook his head, not sure of how concord would transpire between Faeries and Elves under such trying conditions.

Gazing upon the fallen faces of his kin, he spotted Lugh sitting on a stone bench, staring absently out at the falls. They flowed haphazardly, as if they too had suffered a wound, as had Boann the night before. The Water gushed, but then streamed oddly to a trickle, and then gushed again. Matha sensed that Lugh struggled to course just as the falls did, his usual pluck and courage replaced by an unfathomable fear.

Matha then looked to Criofan, one of his two best friends. Usually, Criofan seemed so sure of himself, but now he just roamed about — as if in search of his lodestar. His usual charm was lacking, and he seemed consumed with grief. Matha worried that Criofan, who could be cool even in the best of times, might become callous now that he couldn't course with his feelings.

The ravens on the plinth kept cawing, until the white-necked one took flight, disappearing over the great dome of *Teampall Easa*. They then appeared to be turning on each other, cawing incessantly. Annoyed, some faery elders shook their heads with displeasure at the unwelcome invaders, and even some nearby Elves shouted at them to go away. Matha worried that everything was becoming too chaotic. The ravens finally quieted down, as did the Faeries and Elves.

Perhaps, Matha thought, *the elders have more faith that we will be rejoined.* They certainly seemed less beset by the calamity. Being joined for so many years had fortified them from within, instilling in them the endurance of the Water. Despite this, Matha could see that while most were better able to weather their distress, some struggled to maintain their composure.

Seamus looked about anxiously, but remained quiet, taking stock of everyone. He then spoke to Kelven in rushed sentences, doing his best to sound reassuring. Kelven seemed to be faring worse than his father, his face unmoving, a vice of fear and pain clutching his body.

"Boann wouldn't just abandon us!" Kelven exclaimed. "If Ferrell hadn't driven her off so savagely, she would have rejoined us."

"Perhaps you're right," Seamus replied, nodding. "But we still don't know her whereabouts. Surely the Water meant for her to make us whole again."

"Indeed," the Grand Eldress put in. Of all the water Faeries, she seemed the least beset by the calamity that had struck them. Benevolently she added, "Boann is not yet finished with us, and the Water would not forsake us."

"Tell me, Grand Eldress," Seamus then asked, "who *is* Boann? Why did she come?"

"She is the first wave that rises when the tide has ebbed, flowing from a time beyond memory. When I was a young one, most believed she was merely legend, but many elders who long ago reached the Great Thousand spoke of her, passing what they knew to me. They said that she was once very close to us. Some say she appeared regularly at *Teampall Easa,* gracing our ceremonies. Every faery tribe has a living brilliance like her to help and guide them along their paths. She is responsible for tending to and keeping water Faeries in right relationship to their element. Her long silence and angry arrival speak to how fallen we are, which does not surprise me in the least."

"Thank you, Grand Eldress," Seamus said. "You have confirmed what I suspected all along."

Now the ravens flew from the plinth and began circling in the sky. Round and round they flew, cawing madly. Soon they were joined by scores of other ravens. Louder and louder their cries became. Distressed by the ravens, many Faeries crowded around the Grand Eldress. They strained to hear her every word, desperate to better understand their predicament. The Elves stood farther back, listening stoically.

"I fear Ferrell has created an irreconcilable breach of *gnás,*" the Grand Eldress began, "as he and his kind have not been taught the proper respect that one such as she deserves. But I don't believe he has the power to drive her away for good."

Hearing this, the Elves jabbered irately among themselves. Matha expected them to challenge her, but she was the Grand Eldress, standing upon the water Faeries' most sacred ground. For now, they remained respectful.

"I do hope the plan she has for my dear son ends well," Kelven began. "I fear this may be all too much for him. We've been unjoined less than a day, and he, for his entire Life. And now he must endure trials beyond his ability, without his friends, who have also been his companions for his entire Life. The Water has been too unkind to him."

Protectively, Seamus put his arm around Kelven's shoulder. "Grand Eldress," he asked, "What do you suppose has happened to Baudwin?"

All were silent, waiting for her to speak. Most acknowledged that Baudwin had been taken by the Water, and then lifted up and over the falls. Others who dwelt in the Nechtain Quarter said they saw a torrent of Water shoot up River Nechtain, going under bridges, leaving the city gates. A number of nearby Elves insisted that he had been swept down the drain works beneath the An Bhanna, pulled under by Boann and probably drowned. Perhaps, they added, Ferrell would save him while he hunted her. Most Faeries believed that the latter speculation was wrong, but as time passed, more and more were unsure, as they realized that Boann's command of the Water could have driven Baudwin anywhere.

"She has called upon him, but for what purpose I do not know," the Grand Eldress replied. "I have always wondered about Baudwin, and feared for his wellbeing. He suffers such a wound, yet he always forges on. The fates of those who do are often significantly tied to the rest of us."

"And now we also carry the same wound," Seamus said, his eyes filled with tears.

"Which cannot be mere coincidence," the Grand Eldress added.

With that, all fell silent again, as they considered what everything meant. Baudwin's friend Rian, the Master of Silver and Druid of Guidance, then approached them. He was wearing his blue-and-white-striped overalls, wrinkled from being soaked in Water and dried in the morning Sun. Around his neck was his silver pendant, with the symbol of a lantern visible for all to see.

"Pardon me," he said, as he bowed before the Grand Eldress. Seeing him, she seemed charmed by his deference.

"I believe I have a clue to the puzzle that is Baudwin," Rian began. "He is a dear friend to me, you see. For most of his life, he visited me at the general store in Deuona. This year he met me at the Engineerium, quite distraught, claiming that the Water had put him on a quest for Glamorium. He seemed to have lost his way, and I couldn't bear to see him fail, so I gave him a small egg of Glamorium. As some may know, Glamorium will not reveal its secrets to just anyone. The Assembly is said to have large stores, but such hoarders never know the true wonder of this amazing metal, blinded as they are by their own selfish greed. I thought that because the Water had set him upon this path that destiny had to be involved. To my joy and surprise, the egg answered him."

Awed, the water Faeries turned toward the temple making the sign of the Water, while the Elves listened respectfully. At the mention of Glamorium they curtailed their usual dismissal of faery concerns. As metalworkers, they took themselves to be the forgers and the keepers of glamorium lore. Therefore, because the egg had spoken to a simple water Faery such as Baudwin, it meant that something rare, and perhaps even unprecedented, was afoot. While the Faeries were fascinated with the tale, they were even more taken that Baudwin had received the attention of a water spirit — the significance of which was still unknown.

"What a remarkable story," the Grand Eldress declared, looking kindly at Rian. Matha could see how highly she approved of him, as he was not an Elve of the Assembly, but one loyal to the ways of Platinum Spires. *No doubt*, he thought, *the Water must also have willed Baudwin to stumble upon him that day at the Engineerium.*

"Yes, the *Dúrúnghlas* answered him, giving him a vision both of wonder and of shadow," Rian continued.

Looking about, Matha heard many voices utter all at once, "Shadow?!"

"The *Dúrúnghlas* is a rare blessing, especially for one so young, but I do not know what you mean by *shadow*," the Grand Eldress said.

"Shadow!" Seamus exclaimed, perplexed. Looking at Kelven, he added, "Baudwin tried to explain this to us, but at the time, we didn't listen."

"Yes, indeed," Rian replied. "We Elves are masters of metals, and of course, Glamorium is the pinnacle of metals, which the Druids of Platinum Spires have studied well. Ever since the Great Befalling, many of us have detected the presence of a shadow, penetrating and corrupting Glamorium. After the egg revealed the *Dúrúnghlas* to Baudwin, a vision of wonder, and then shadow, came to him. His mother appeared to him in a field of water and light. Strangely, she turned into a moorhen, and then she flew away. After that, a silvery-black morass came upon him — a cold, unrelenting force, bent upon his destruction. And then his vision ended."

"A black morass?" the Grand Eldress asked. "That must have been the shadow of which you speak. Wasn't Baudwin terrified?"

"He was," Rian replied. "But he didn't blame me, or the egg, which is why I value him so as a friend."

"Baudwin showed us the egg," Kelven added, downcast. "But he wouldn't let us hold it, for fear that we might be harmed by the shadow. Days later, he told me he had lost the egg, and I accused him of lying. We got upset with him, and he left."

Kelven lowered his eyes in shame, unable to speak another word.

"He didn't lose the egg," Matha said. "He told you that because he was afraid you wouldn't believe the real story. The egg, in fact, was snatched from him by Boann herself, at the dam."

"*Boann* took the egg?" the Grand Eldress asked, captivated. "How curious."

"Even curiouser," Matha added, "because she was the agent by which the egg came to him to begin with."

"What Matha says is true!" Lugh exclaimed, a newfound courage flaring within him. "Baudwin told us the story in the Cyhiraeth Quarter, just before Boann visited us at Esther's."

Kelven stared at them, nodding sadly. "I wouldn't have believed this yesterday morning, but now I know it must be true. I wish Baudwin could have trusted me enough to tell the truth."

Matha could see his mother, Brigh, nodding her head in agreement. With his father at her side, she had been attending to every word.

"But what does all this *mean*?" Seamus asked, his brow furrowed with concern. "I told Baudwin to find some Glamorium, and the Water led him forward, but as soon as Rian gave him the egg, Boann stole it away, and then followed him here to Four Falls. And now she has sent him onward, to what fate none of us can say — alone and without help. Why would she do this?"

"None of us can fathom why," the Grand Eldress replied. "Perhaps she wants him to be worthy of such a powerful treasure. Or she is trying to aid him in ways we can't imagine. But one thing is clear — like the threads of an eternity knot, Glamorium has been woven into his quest. And although Boann has deemed him a fool, clearly, she is not yet finished with him."

The Grand Eldress's words rang true.

"So if she set him upon this path, then perhaps my Shaela has not yet passed to Annwyn?" Kelven asked, his voice trembling.

"Yes," she replied. "I have a strange feeling that Baudwin had to vanish so that Shaela could eventually be found."

Without warning, Loch stormed toward the group, ready to wallop them all with a single blow. Like a school of salmon escaping the claws of a vicious bear, everyone darted away from him.

"If it weren't for Baudwin, we'd all still be joined to our currents!" he shouted. "I hope he's paying for his foolish deeds — wherever he is! He should never have gone looking for the Water."

Everyone stared at Loch in disbelief. "How can you say that?" Matha asked, appalled.

"What a bunch of idiots!" Loch shouted. "How stupid can you be?"

"Show some respect, Roiler!" Seamus bellowed.

"Why should I?" Loch fired back. "Don't you see where your reverence for the Water has gotten you? If it weren't for Baudwin, we'd all still be joined!"

Criofan lunged at Loch, unwilling to listen any further to his ugly tirade. "And now that *you're* not joined," he hissed, "you hate him even more. Because now you're *just* like him, and *still* the Water would never come to you!"

Looking at Criofan, Matha sensed a block of ice had frozen his feelings, yet he could not disagree with his words.

"What *I* hate," Loch continued yelling, pacing back and forth and gesturing at everyone, "is the way you let your love for Baudwin *weaken* your hearts!"

"Loving your kin *never* weakens your heart!" Seamus shouted back. "What's wrong with you? Being unjoined sure has destroyed what was left of *your* heart — if you ever had one to begin with."

Everyone gasped. Unjoined, there was little to guide them as they spoke. Feelings were immediately inflamed, adding to their resentments and leaving their anger to poison them like a festering wound. All feared that from now on, there would be only more of the same.

Matha was unnerved. Despite Loch's ravings, he could see that many in the crowd seemed sympathetic to him, mostly Elves and Roilers, but also some Eddies.

"You attack Baudwin because you are more frightened than we are," Kelven said boldly. "We are, after all, still Guilders, but after seeing Boann, how can you still call yourself a Roiler?"

"How can you call yourself a Guilder after what she's done to us?" Loch shouted.

Now the ravens still on the plinth began cawing vociferously. Snappishly, they ruffled their feathers, and Matha saw them leaning in closer, ready to peck at each other. He wondered what else they might have a mind to do, and whether his kin were paying any more attention to them. Many seemed not to be.

Matha considered Loch. The unjoining had been excruciating for everyone, but for the Roiler, losing his current seemed to have stripped away what little was left of his empathy. *Baudwin was never like this*, he thought. The loathing Loch carried was immense. Seething, he seemed like a rancid gourd about to burst. The lines so deeply etched into his face signaled pure disdain, and he wore his Roiler jacket like a pall of malice.

"The Primary of Water," the Grand Eldress began, gesturing at Kelven, "calls himself a Guilder, because even as the Water has left him, still in his heart he has not left the Water." Angrily, she glared at Loch. "A lesson you would do well to learn."

She then drew herself up face to face with Loch, a badger about to scale a rampart. As short as she was, she seemed to loom above him when she spoke. Defying her stature, Loch looked down upon her, his eyes unflinching daggers.

The Grand Eldress met his gaze, unperturbed. "What a disappointment you are to the Water," she began, dismissing him with a wave of her hand. "You were so busy hauling Ferrell's lightning spitter that you didn't even consider the consequences of your actions."

"I considered *enough*," Loch shot back, mocking her. "Come to think of it, though, I should probably thank Baudwin for his misdeeds. Without him, we Roilers would not be as we were always meant to be — unjoined, and not beholden to the sappy Water." As Loch raised his fist, some Roilers and Elves behind began hooting and hollering.

The Grand Eldress, unswayed, continued speaking. "First you say that you are upset that we are unjoined, and then you say that you are happy not to be beholden to the Water. You zig and you zag like a crazed boar, running from a pack of wolves, yet all the while running away from yourself." Peering intently at him, she asked, "So are you Roiler *zig*, or are you Roiler *zag*?"

The crowd broke into laughter, and Matha took note that this was the first bit of humor he had heard since Boann had stopped the falls and taken away their currents.

Recoiling from this insult, Loch looked as if he had been lashed across the face. At first, he appeared ready to strike her, but instead jumped onto the plinth where the ravens had been. Raising his leg, he pressed his boot against the statue. With all his might he pushed, until the ancient stone cracked, split in two, and went tumbling to the ground. The head broke off, rolling away from the body.

The crowd was appalled. All the Guilders and Eddies, and even some Elves shouted at him. *Unforgivable! Insolent! Horrendous!* they cried, again and again. Seamus looked as if he would wallop Loch right then and there, but much to everyone's surprise, the Grand Eldress restrained him.

"Here is the price we will all pay for being unjoined, and the harbinger of what's to come if we falter even more!" she cried above the din. "Now more than ever, we must not abandon the Water, since the Water appears to have abandoned us." Pointing to Loch she continued, "We must now be truer than ever — or fall as low as this one has."

Scowling, his face a mask of irreverence, Loch jumped down from the plinth. Landing next to the statue's head, he kicked it toward the Grand Eldress, chuckling viciously as he watched it roll along the stones, stopping at her feet.

Undaunted, she continued, "Why do you all suppose the Water never came to this one? Did he not try hard enough? For years, he searched on River Nechtain. We all knew this, but he wouldn't let his guard down enough to tell us what happened. We watched him try for a very long time, until he finally gave up."

"The Water never comes to most," Loch shot back contemptuously.

"Indeed, but in your case the Water found that your heart was not in the right place."

Matha expected Loch would counter this, but instead the Roiler appeared to be hanging upon her every word, as if desperately craving the truth of which she spoke, even as he tried to hide it from himself.

"You are strong, and brave," the Grand Eldress said. Seamus told me once that you would make a fine guild leader, but that your heart is split in two. One part seeks to embrace the Water, just as the other part seeks to master the Water for its own purposes."

"That is *not* true!" Loch bellowed.

"Oh, but it *is*," she replied, her face as calm as his was livid. "The Water will not come to one whose loyalty hinges upon an outcome. You would not serve the Water if the Water failed to give you what you thought you deserved, so the Water remained silent and you drifted away, with nothing left of yourself but the urge to destroy statues and hurl insults at your elders."

"You're *wrong*!" Loch bellowed again, this time baring his teeth and clenching his blue-green fists until his knuckles were pale with rage. "I was meant to be a Roiler, as are many of my kin, because we are on the *right* side of the future. And you should be more grateful. Ferrell saved you all!"

"Ferrell has likely doomed us!" Seamus shouted back.

"The Roiler speaks the truth," a voice declared. Everyone looked into the crowd and saw an Elve approaching, looking dull in appearance but measured in his step. Matha recognized Fearghus, who had been arguing about the Rise of Time with Seanán after Baudwin's performance. "Who needs conniving spirits like her coming to our city and terrifying us? She destroyed our inventions and sent our kin to Annwyn. I say listen to Loch. You don't need to be joined."

"And I suppose you Elves don't need your metals either?" the Grand Eldress declared, glowering at Fearghus. "Boann will restore our currents, once we see the error of our ways."

"No, she won't!" Loch shouted. "She's a deranged spirit, an aberration from a time we'd all do well to forget. If our currents don't return, then we are as we should be. The day of the Roilers has arrived!"

Despite Loch's bluster, Matha detected a note of doubt in his voice.

"No!" the Grand Eldress shouted back. "She was only trying to show us what we have lost. The Faeries are not in balance as they once were — and neither are the Elves."

"Perhaps so, or perhaps not," Fearghus replied. "But what are we to do now? She offered us no solutions, only vague notions about ancient temples and the Great Emerald Light — mystical ramblings from a long-forgotten age."

Hearing this, the already agitated crowd began grumbling and arguing, and some even got into scuffles. Matha saw some young Eddies knock over some of the Health and Wealth displays remaining from the Grand Unveiling. Many Faeries sided with the Grand Eldress, excited that the legend of Boann was true. Even though they were now unjoined, they had faith that she would make everything right again. Most adamant were the Faeries from the Nechtain Quarter, with Lugh chief among them.

Yet most of the Elves seemed intent on trying to persuade the Faeries otherwise. Matha suspected that they were taking advantage of the Faeries in their weakened state so they could seize the opportunity to be both the dreamers and the builders. Among them were some Earth Guards who, on Ferrell's orders, had stayed behind. "Govannon cares about your welfare as much as he does ours," Matha heard one proclaim. "Now is the time to put your trust in our leader."

"I would sooner trust a sprocketworks grasshopper built by a Faery than *him*," Lugh retorted. "The last time we trusted the Elves, they took over the city. We'll have no more help like that — thank you."

The guard who had spoken up then shook his head. "We are not your enemy. Let us share the wonders that Govannon has bestowed upon us, and let this unfortunate event bring us closer."

For years, Matha had seen his parents settle disputes in the Weighing Dome, which had honed his ability to sense deception. In his estimation, the guard was speaking what he believed to be true, even if those in greater authority had deceived him. Matha wanted to help Lugh understand this, but he knew that, being unjoined, Lugh would certainly be more mistrustful than ever.

"I shall never trust your king of lies!" Lugh shouted, and with that the discussion ended.

Matha then saw Seamus arguing with Loch. "You've gone too far!" he exclaimed. "I often thought that Baudwin would become the next primary and you the next guild leader, but now I see how foolish I was."

"I am with the Elves now," Loch replied. "I don't want a title from you. Unless," he added mockingly, "I could become the first faery Luminary."

Seamus shook his head in derision. "You addle-brained ass! Everyone knows elven Luminaries aren't the adepts they used to be. That said, you'd still be half as smart as they are, and less than half as useful."

Both looked as if they would come to blows. Loch balled his fists, ready to swing, but some Earth Guards pulled him back. "Why tarry here?" Seamus shouted. "Leave us! The Tadlachs call to you. Go now, and be with the Elves."

"Perhaps I will," Loch shot back, "but not before I've taken half the city with me!"

Looking about, Matha saw discord everywhere. *How will we mediate so many disputes?* he thought. Some young, unjoined Faeries had gone wild, and were taunting the Roilers. One Roiler had tied a screaming young Faery to a tree, prompting an Earth Guard to box him in the head. He then cut the Faery loose.

As the young faery onlookers cheered the Earth Guard, Loch shouted, "You see? Only the Elves can save you now!"

The Grand Eldress stepped into the fracas to calm everyone down, but they ignored her with impunity. Seeing her treated thus, Rian the Elve sat brooding on a stone bench, hopelessly shaking his head.

Above them the ravens continued to wheel — a cacophony of shrill rasping caws spewing from a whirlwind of feathers. As if attesting to the chaos below, they circled back and forth, landing in trees, prompting others to take to the sky. Higher and higher they flew, swirling up into the mist, screaming ever more insistently. Many set down upon the remains of the statue, strutting back and forth across its torso, pecking at the merlady's tail.

Matha watched — aghast — unable to understand what had possessed them to do such things. He sorely wanted to find a way to calm them, as they were upsetting everyone. Like the ravens, his kin badly needed calming. At the Weighing Dome, he had witnessed such rancor many times. His mother, Brigh, always liked to remind him that when two rams butt heads, they won't see the wolf that is stalking them, about to sharpen its teeth on their bones. And now if the Faeries kept fighting each other, they'd not see their real problem — until it was too late. Being unjoined, all would surely drown in Water they could neither know nor navigate.

Fearfully, he looked for his parents, Brigh and Niall, and saw them conversing with some wood Faeries. Waving his arms at his parents, he shouted, "We have to do something!"

"And we are," Brigh replied. Beside her stood a wood faery lady with pale green skin. When she looked his way, Matha sensed a great oak tree staring into him. Next to her was a wood faery gent with mossy green hair and extra-long limbs, waiting for her to speak.

Palms together, both of the wood Faeries interlaced their fingers and pointed them up. "Blessings from the Wood," they said.

In response, Matha made the sign of the Water, cupping his hands over his heart. "Blessings from the Water," he replied. The wood faery lady then spoke. "The ravens cry for what the water Faeries have lost."

"And as they cry, they also attest," the wood faery gent added. "They speak for other creatures as well, for they are the devourers of the fallen and are able to endure the aftermath of Boann's calamity."

"The ravens are clearly troubled," Matha replied, perplexed, "but how do we calm my kin?"

"Shhh," Brigh scolded Matha, as she waited for the wood Faeries to continue. Matha went silent.

"We of the Wood do not fathom the Water as you do," the wood faery lady spoke, motioning kindly. "But we do sense that if our friends, the ravens, are to properly attest to this place, they must be calmed."

Unjoined, Matha could only blurt, "Why bother with all of that? Let them get as upset as they want, until they peck each other blind! The *crowd* is what must be calmed."

The wood Faeries looked at each other, unsure of what to say. The wood faery gent strained for words, as if he were searching for a particular plant among many that held the remedy he sought. "If the birds are not calm," he replied, "they will not attest properly. The spirits of the Wood will then not be satisfied. Nor will the ancient ones who dwell beyond this realm."

Hearing this, Matha looked dubiously at the wood faery gent, even though the gent appeared to know a great deal more than he about such things. Agitated, Matha removed his spectacles and repeatedly inspected the lenses, before wiping them clean.

Seeing Matha's discomfort, the wood faery lady spoke again, her voice light as a breeze in a linden tree. "Boann came here not simply to warn the water Faeries, but to remind all of the Fae that they must remember the lessons of the elements. Before we look to calm the unjoined, we must pay heed to the old ways, and so, as wood Faeries, we will calm the ravens as a token of respect to spirits greater than ourselves, and also to alleviate the suffering of your kin. For, without a calm forest, we cannot find peace."

With that, the wood Faeries, lady and gent, raised their arms and approached the ravens.

"Shrill ones, with feathers of coal," the lady began.

"Peck not another hole," the gent followed rhythmically.

"Feast not upon watery bones," the lady continued.

"But fly away from these stones," the gent concluded.

The ravens on the toppled statue and on the plinth cocked their heads at the wood Faeries, but did not stop reveling in the upheaval they had created. Some Elves and Faeries in the crowd looked at the wood Faeries, unsure of what they were witnessing. Matha expected the Roilers to hurl insults, but they were remarkably quiet as they watched.

"Dark ones, with pointed beaks," the lady began.

"See now what your chaos wreaks," the gent followed.

"Let the Fae's folly be a balm," the lady continued.

"And let this forest now be calm," the gent concluded.

"Assert as a sentinel does — alight on yonder branches!" they both cried out, raising their arms higher.

To Matha's amazement, the ravens flew to join the others twisting in the sky, and then, like a black cloud parting, they swept down to the circle of trees. Soon the branches were filled with black ravens, watching silently.

"The ravens are well settled," the wood faery lady said, turning to Brigh and Niall. "No longer are they pondering ill omens, but are ready to attest."

"The rest is up to you," the wood faery gent added.

Matha sensed that the grounds of the temple were now calmer. No longer cawing, the ravens spied keenly upon the Faeries below them. He then regarded his parents as they stood beside each other, prepared to speak. Brigh looked poised and lovely in flowing blue-green silk, and Niall was quiet, yet ready to take up the cause. Each had a necklace with a half-moon around their neck. Primaries of Concord — usually couples — always wore half-moons as symbols of unity to bring feuding Faeries together. "When both sides come together, only then are they complete," Niall would always say to Matha. *But making this Moon full,* Matha thought, *will be very difficult indeed.*

His parents certainly had their work cut out for them. Ever since he was a young one, Matha had been impressed by how skilled they were at settling differences. Both were rather withdrawn by nature, but this could change in an instant, as Brigh's feelings went deep as a lake, and Niall's sense of purpose and responsibility was as strong as river rapids. Matha knew that they complemented each other, as they were a formidable team when they mediated as a couple. Countless times had he seen them bring conflicting factions together, often among those who would sooner grab a quarrel staff than resolve their differences peaceably.

Looking at his mother, Matha chuckled to himself. Despite her considerable skill, he could tell that she was feeling more shy than usual. Whenever she was, she shook her head nervously, repeatedly ringing the silver bells in her hair. His father seemed simply more irritated, as if resenting the extra strength he would have to draw upon to run the rapids he was about to encounter. Like

Baudwin's father, Kelven, he often seemed ready to quit before he began, and yet, when sufficiently roused, he could stop a badger in its tracks.

"Thank you," Brigh began. "You have tended to this forest, and now we must tend to our own kin. Everyone — please," she called out. Although some of the tension in the crowd had indeed diminished, they paid her no heed.

"All of you — listen," Niall then insisted." We are here to help." There was some response to this, as many addled water Faeries turned to him — rows of pale blue-green faces, mixed in with the light cream, ochre, gray, and orange hues of the Elves. Gazing at Niall, many harbored a strong expectation, looking as if they would rend him in two were he to fail them.

"If we want our pain to lessen," Niall continued, carefully, "then we must do as Boann has instructed — we must balance our wills."

Loch, who had been sitting with some Roilers on a stone bench, then shouted back, "What does that even mean? Go back to Deuona!"

"Silence!" the Grand Eldress commanded. "Let him continue."

"What I'm saying," Niall began, "is that we must abide as the other does."

Stares of confusion met him, and Matha began to worry. He knew his parents were adept mediators, but he wondered how they would be able to interpret and communicate the will of Boann when they weren't even sure what she meant.

Brigh didn't falter. "I may not know what ceremonies Boann spoke of," she began, "or what was once taught in the glamorium temples, but I do know this much." She then beckoned to Seamus, and also to Rian. "Come, please, and stand side by side before us."

Undaunted, Seamus strode up, his wide frame blocking the view of those he passed. Rian, who had been sitting despondently, then perked up, eager to be of service. Soon they both stood before Brigh and Niall, the crowd forming a half-moon around them.

"Please address the crowd," Brigh began, directing her words at Rian, "and tell them who you are."

"I am Rian, son of Martin,[3] a Master of Silver and a Druid of Guidance. I live in Deuona, but I made my way there from Platinum Spires."

With that, some of the Elves in the crowd and the guards looked respectfully at him. Rian enjoyed some notoriety, and they viewed him favorably. Matha could see that Brigh had chosen wisely, for Rian was pleasant-tempered and loved by both Elves and Faeries.

She then asked Seamus to do the same, and he replied, "I am Seamus, son of Conn,[4] and the Guild Leader of the water Faeries in Deuona."

---

[3] Pronounced [MAIR-tin]

[4] Pronounced [KON]

Almost everyone knew of Seamus, for he too was held in high regard. Even the Roilers grudgingly admired his strength.

"Good," Niall began. "To abide as the other does and be true to our nature, we must balance our wills. I will ask Seamus what dreaming means to him, and then I will ask Rian what building means to him, and then ask them how they might respect the other and work in harmony."

"Please tell us," Brigh prompted Seamus, "what *dreaming* means to you."

Seamus looked toward the Sun, which had not yet reached its zenith, and then at the giant grotto in the Tadlachs through which the An Bhanna coursed its way to the sea. He regarded the statues and stonework, and the ancient foundations his kin had walked upon for millennia. Matha knew Seamus was reaching deep inside himself for an answer only a Guild Leader could provide. If Seamus was troubled by being unjoined, it didn't show.

Boldly, Seamus began to speak. "My dreams have always been for the Fae — and not just the Faeries, mind you — that they truly understand that their real cleachtadh comes from within. My dream for everyone who gazes upon this temple is that they will feel this greatness within themselves. These rivers and this city are not separate from them, but a part of who they are — down to the last *fiber* of their being. Faeries share their dreams for a reason. I believe we wake each day and share ours because we are each but a piece in a puzzle that must be joined in order to make sense of the mosaic of our lives."

The few hecklers in the crowd had stopped their heckling. Loch was silent, and the Elves seemed impressed with what Seamus had said. Eagerly, they awaited what Rian would say.

"Please, tell us," Niall then queried Rian, "what does *building* mean to you?"

In a reserved but eloquent manner, Rian explained, "For us Elves, building is the means by which we create a glorious monument that is enshrined in the mind's eye of our benefactors. Always we strive for greater achievements, but not for the sake of our vanity. We build for the mutual benefit of all, which is immediately palpable in the faded shrines of the ancient ones, built so that *both* Elves and Faeries could find greater unity. We build not only for ourselves, but out of love for those who lack our means. We create an expression that is shared by all."

With this, the Elves beamed with pride. None in attendance could have spoken these words more sincerely than Rian. *The Elves of long ago must have lived to serve the wishes of those they met in other lands,* Matha thought. What greater evidence of this than Four Falls — not fashioned like *Teampall Easa* by Boann — but erected long ago, by elven masons, to fulfill the dreams of the Faeries.

For some, all of this talk was heresy. "Fine words!" Loch shouted. "But now the Elves will do the dreaming *and* the building."

"Will they — indeed?" Rian calmly replied.

Loch guffawed at Rian, gesturing as if he didn't care. "We're all still unjoined, and all of your balmy words are of no use to us. They won't help."

"But there is more to consider," Brigh put in. Now was her moment to prove all doubters wrong, her chance to perhaps alleviate even a small part of their sudden misery, and so Matha clung to her every word.

"Tell me, Seamus," she began. "After you dream, does your will flow swiftly, like a river in springtime, or slowly, like a creek before the rains?"

Seamus spoke hesitantly, seemingly reluctant to reveal his admission, yet confident in his clarity. "I would have to say that it flows slowly. I do not share my dreams as I should, and they do not come to me as I would wish them to come, nor do they impress me as they did when I was a younger Faery."

"Thank you," Brigh said, as she gently placed her hand upon his chest.

"Tell me, Rian," Niall then continued. "You own the General Store in Deuona, and there you build and trade many things. You also operate the Gearchute booth at the Engineerium, do you not?"

"That I do," Rian replied.

"Tell me, then," Niall began, "when your steamway boilers hiss, and your gearchute gears turn this way and that, driving the balls through the chutes, does your will pound madly, like a steam hammer in overdrive, or would you say it putters steadily, like a well-oiled lumber roller?"

"Honestly?" Rian replied, regarding the Elves in the crowd. "My will seems to run faster and faster. You all know whereof I speak. We go faster and faster, and while the Assembly says that we can and should always go faster, I wonder if that's even true. As for me, I feel as if I will *never* be fast enough."

"So then, it looks like Seamus's will is too weak, and Rian's will is too strong," Brigh said. Smiling, she pronounced, "What Boann told us is true. We are *not* in balance."

She turned to Seamus. "Now tell me. Do you see this in yourself?"

Seamus hesitated, but then spoke. "Yes, I now see what Boann meant."

Without being asked, Rian then added, "I do as well."

"Because we have forgotten the ancient rite of balance," Brigh continued, "we cannot balance our wills. From centuries of mediating disputes at the Weighing Dome, I have come to understand that recognition of the heart of the matter in a personal dispute is the first step toward healing."

Matha looked at Seamus and Rian and the crowd, sensing that his mother was right. Yet, recognizing that their wills were weak, the water Faeries were despondent. Growing up at the Weighing Dome, he remembered seeing the same kind of dynamic. When Brigh and Niall diffused a conflict between two parties, they first had each side speak honestly about their grievance, without blaming the other. The difficulty in doing this usually brought about much teeth-gnashing, until the rounds on their ears turned red. But Matha knew that self-honesty was the only way to achieve true resolution.

Brigh clapped her hands, signaling for attention. "Yes, your wills are out of balance. But you must not wallow in the pain of seeing this. Instead, you must enter into and pass beyond your pain. Only then will you be able to see yourself in the other."

Matha worried that, coming upon the heels of the calamity, this step might be too much to ask. But here, at *Teampall Easa* among the wisest water Faeries in the land, he saw much courage. A change had come over them. All at once they were calmer, as if they had been on a perilous voyage, their ship leaking, a storm splitting the mast, yet now on the horizon they could make out the faint outline of a lighthouse.

"I do feel more balanced," Seamus said with a wink. "I feel as if my dreams could grab me by the collar and show me fancies to make me young again. I'm not afraid. Tell me what else I must admit to, so that I can become as great as the headwaters of the Danu."

"And that you will!" the Grand Eldress exclaimed, turning to Matha's mother. "Thank you, Brigh, for your wise words. As I said before, Boann and the Water have not forsaken us. And, I might also add, for simply practicing the first step of the Triquetra — Honesty — we have been duly rewarded."

"Perhaps it's our only step. . ." Loch said solemnly.

Matha was surprised by the seriousness of his tone. Brigh's wisdom had reached even him, as if, in some small part of his heart, Loch understood that honesty could indeed usher in healing, even if he didn't want such things to be true.

"But what of it?" Loch asked, his tone hardening. "If our wills are not as they should be, then we will have to fend for ourselves. There is no other choice."

If anyone wanted to rebut Loch, they didn't bother. Across from the temple grounds, near the center drain work, a horn blared.

Broooooooooom, went the horn, again and again, until an Eleven guard announced, "Ferrell returns!"

❧

A dozen or so longboats came into view, loaded with guards. Victoriously, they worked their oars as they made their way over the headwaters of the An Bhanna toward the island. Ferrell stood at the bow of the lead boat, silent and still as stone, surveying the crowd.

Inside one of the longboats, Matha spied the strange contraption he had seen earlier. Straining to see, he detected a tubular object made of large bronze plates, welded into place. Vaguely he could also make out small pressure pipes running along the top and sides. Again he wondered what Ferrell was up to. Oddly, this boat broke away from the other ones, heading toward a lift the Elves had built for the Grand Unveiling near the Condatis Quarter. He tried to see more, but the contraption was too far away. Soon the other boats were beached, and the crowd rushed from the temple to greet Ferrell.

Ferrell hopped smartly off the boat, splashing his boots noisily in the Water. His dress uniform was wet and torn, the lines on his face were drawn, but if he was tired, he didn't miss a step. Stalwartly, he faced the crowd and was immediately surrounded by Elves and Faeries, all squeezing in closer to find out what had happened. Speaking all at once, they questioned him, until Ferrell exclaimed, "All of you — be quiet!" All fell silent.

"The tunnels beneath Four Falls are very numerous," he began. "We ventured into them, our marvelous magniglow torches lighting the way. Some of the masonry had collapsed, and we found ourselves at many a dead end. The tunnels were cold and damp. Throughout our mission, we could hear an eerie wailing, but from where we couldn't tell. She was in there — somewhere. Despite our trepidation, we pressed on. Eventually, the forks in the tunnels became so numerous that, despite the danger, I decided we should split up, which meant we could provide only one magniglow torch per group."

Ferrell raised his torch and lit the bulb at its tip. The crowd was captivated.

"We were now three parties, traveling deeper and deeper, our shockers in hand, determined to subdue the beast."

"That beast is a *divine* spirit," the Grand Eldress declared.

Ferrell ignored her and kept talking. "The sound carries well in these tunnels — hollow and smooth as they are — and although we couldn't see where everyone had gone, we could hear one another from quite a distance. After working our way even further into the tunnels, I heard one of our groups cry out. Their yells were horrifying. Then came the sounds of shockers firing, but there was nothing I could do. Not knowing if they had fallen, all we could do was press on."

"Then what happened?" Loch asked.

"Eventually we came to a large chamber, where many of the tunnels converged. The other two groups had also reached this chamber, and one of them reported that they indeed had spied the beast, and fired volleys at her, forcing her to retreat even deeper. I was relieved that none of our guards had been harmed, but as I looked around me, I wondered if we had been drawn into a trap."

Ferrell paused before continuing.

"The chamber was circular, with a ceiling that must have been as high as twenty Elves. There were many stone pillars inscribed with glyphs, worked by masons from a time beyond memory."

"You must have found the old water temple, built by the Elves before the city we now know existed," Seamus informed them. "There the Faeries would venture into the murky Waters and gaze at the sky through giant holes in the bedrock. By the Light of the Moon, they would sing, their voices weaving into the knot of eternity."

"Indeed," Ferrell replied. Matha sensed his surprise that Seamus knew such things about the temple. "Interestingly, there were also elven symbols. And murals that depicted the Elves cleaving chords of some kind —"

"For the knot of eternity!" Seamus exclaimed, interrupting him. He gave the Grand Eldress a knowing smile.

"All the old temples have that in common," she added.

"Yes," Ferrell replied. "But even more staggering was a pool of Water we came to. Its surface was dark — black even — and when we shined our torches upon that surface, light could not penetrate."

"The Water of the dark Faeries," Lugh said. "That pool came from them, a gift from long ago, fed by an underground stream from the Cyhiraeth."

"Perhaps," Ferrell replied. "Or the Water was simply filthy and stagnant. We would have taken more time to study the ruins, but soon I heard a guard yell. I turned to see who had uttered the sound, pointing my light, but all I could see was a shocker, lying on the temple floor. Looking up, I saw that she had him."

Some gasped, but Matha could tell many Guilders were too skeptical to take Ferrell's account seriously.

"She was as we all saw her before, towering above us, her scaly face stretched into a snarl, teeth like daggers, yellow eyes glowing in the dark. Seeing my guard so desperate, I ordered, 'Release him!' But she did no such thing, and then, with a snap of her jaw, she had swallowed him whole."

"Impossible!" the Grand Eldress exclaimed. Matha understood why she said so. The Fae never ate animals, and to many present, the notion that a spirit would devour someone was unthinkable.

"Ridiculous!" Seamus and Lugh both shouted at once. Obviously they did not believe him, and Matha wasn't so sure he did either.

"Of course, I ordered my guards to open fire. Their shockers tore into her, and she sure did bellow. Disoriented by the bright flashes, my guards were defenseless as, her claws flailing every which way, she tried to send us all to Annwyn! I ducked behind a stone pillar, evading her blow just in the nick of time. And then, crouching low, I peered from behind the pillar, aimed at the beast, and fired."

Reenacting the scene, Ferrell crouched low, wielding his magniglow torch like a shocker, aiming the tip to the sky. "The bolt was blazing in the dark," he began, "and without shocker goggles, I was momentarily blinded. Without my vision, I could only huddle behind the pillar, hoping I had hit my mark. I then heard one of my guards cry out."

One of the guards who had been with Ferrell then picked up the story. "He hit his mark all right, square in her chest, and then she just vanished."

"Yes, and I had previously wounded her, as you all witnessed," Ferrell added solemnly. "Then I finished the job."

Almost spontaneously, the crowd found itself dividing into two groups. One group believed Ferrell's story, and, not to Matha's surprise, the believers included some Eddies, all of the Roilers, and almost every Elve.

The Grand Eldress did not believe Ferrell at all. "You couldn't have defeated a being like her in that way. She would merely have changed forms."

"But I saw Ferrell's bolt hit," the guard insisted, "and then her body flashed bright and vanished."

Ayamonn, who had been listening with all the other guild leaders, then concluded, "If she vanished, that is further proof that she changed form."

"Nah! She just gave up the fight," Loch added. "She wouldn't stop if she hadn't lost."

"*Lost* doesn't mean passed to Annwyn," Seamus corrected. "Most likely, she simply retreated to fight another day."

The debate worked into a frenzy, and soon the combatants seemed almost on the verge of being at each other's throats. Matha could tell that his parents were worried, especially given that this relapse had happened so soon after they had successfully eased those tensions. Ferrell also seemed concerned, Matha observed, but not in the same way that Brigh and Niall were.

The Grand Eldress rounded on Ferrell, "*No* Faery would violate the sanctity of a spirit such as she. You used your vile contraption on her, and made the lesson she was trying to teach us *far* harder for us to bear!"

"Lesson?" Ferrell spat. "You mean *curse!* But the pain and torture she made us endure is no more."

The Grand Eldress pointed at the fog. "Why then, do Boann's mists linger so? They will not leave us until her work is done. Even after the next sunrise, you will see this fog upon us."

"Nonsense!" Ferrell exclaimed. "The fog will vanish as it always does. Even now, the mists are thinning."

"The fog will *not* vanish, as you will certainly see," the Grand Eldress declared. "This is all your fault — *Goldclanger.*" As she repeated Boann's insult, Ferrell glowered at her. "You brought her wrath upon us, threefold — first by meddling into that which is held sacred, then by leading Baudwin astray, and finally by bringing violence upon the steward of the Water who formed this sacred place."

"You water Faeries brought this upon *yourselves!*" Ferrell shot back, enraged.

"Perhaps we did — by ignoring the old ways. And so she unjoined us — but you have cursed us further by wielding that lightning spitter!"

"She murdered *innocent* Elves!" Ferrell shouted. "She had to be stopped!"

The Grand Eldress ignored his rebuke. "You're just an ignorant pawn of Govannon's — nothing more. He'll bring chaos to our realm, and by the time you realize what he's done, our efforts will have been too late. He'll have us *all* bowing down to him."

"Govannon heralds a new age of peace!"

"Discord — *not* peace." She stepped closer to Ferrell, and for a moment Matha thought he saw him flinch.

The Luminary did not respond, choosing instead to gaze off into the mist.

"Answer me this then," she continued, undeterred. "What would *you* do if someone cracked the old crystals you keep in the stellarary[5] in Gleam?"

At this, Ferrell looked the Grand Eldress directly in the eye, and Matha wondered what a stellarary was. He had never heard of one, but he could tell that Ferrell knew very well what she was talking about.

"Why would someone do that? That stellarary is *hardly* a threat to anyone," Ferrell declared. "There would never be a cause to destroy one."

The Grand Eldress stared back at him. "The Elves are said to have once communed with the heavens through them — at least *I* know that the stars are as alive to you as the elements are to us. The stellararies are sacred to your kind, are they not?"

"Yes — of course they are," Ferrell replied tersely.

"Then I'm sure you know of the legend of Sitric,[6]" the Grand Eldress continued, "who ruled during the Golden Age." Seeing the look on Ferrell's face, she laughed, adding, "Even we water Faeries have heard of Sitric's accomplishments. Legend says that he endured many trials while constructing the Lea Torch, and that he drew up his plans in the stellarary in Gleam. Many say his quest was divine — given to him by beings beyond this realm — and that he created the Lea Torch to bring healing to all. What if a group of Faeries, suspicious of elven ways, had sabotaged his efforts, and destroyed his stellarary?"

"No Faeries in the Golden Age would have broken the stellararies."

"Indeed, for they were not prone to violent outbursts and ruled by ignorance."

Matha didn't know of this story, but the Lea Torch sounded like a very important artifact. And if Sitric, Matha surmised, had not been so noble, then

---

[5] Pronounced [STELLA-rare-ee] sacred elven observatory
[6] Pronounced [SIT-ric]

perhaps someone would have sabotaged him, — exactly what the Grand Eldress was now accusing Ferrell of doing to Boann.

"Again — I don't understand your inference," Ferrell replied, stoically. "Sitric achieved greatness, but I don't see how you can compare his ingenuity to the chaos that Boann just wreaked upon us. She spoke in riddles, and then in a fit of rage, tore down everything we worked so hard to build. And now you claim that the mists will thicken, and that this is all *my* doing? Nonsense!"

"What you call chaos, I call a form of protection that we must respect. Just as Sitric's plans were not challenged, Boann's words of wisdom should not have been challenged either. Sitric was a just king, but if you were in his place, I'm sure someone would have tried to thwart your efforts — probably out of desperation, because they would know you weren't fit to heed the voices in the heavens."

"Such utter rubbish," Ferrell snarled.

Both then commenced with another round of altercation. Matha watched — transfixed — as the Grand Eldress explained to Ferrell how she saw the truth. She shared her insight into the workings of the Water — subtleties he could barely fathom — as he countered with convoluted objections that made no sense to her at all. Without concrete *evidence* that Boann was being helpful, Ferrell explained, he could not accept her arguments. And so, the Grand Eldress argued even more strenuously, so that he would accept her claims *as* evidence.

Like the immeasurable distance between the stars and the river at night, the chasm between them only grew. Back and forth they wrangled, and Matha could see that the real tragedy between them was that they would *never* come to terms; their sparring only reinforced the unresolvable stalemate between them. This was the usual way of Faeries and Elves, who often disagreed and fought every time there was a problem to be solved, forgetting about *gnás* and blaming one another for their differences. This only made their problems much worse.

And then Matha remembered what Boann had said to them:

"The Water wills, the Fae divide for worse,

Whence comes the fog, will they know their curse!"

And so it was that they *were* dividing, and as they argued, Matha wondered then if the fog around them did seem just a little bit thicker, enough perhaps for Faeries to detect, but not enough for Eves to notice, most of whom had probably forgotten how thin the fog could be. And if one side couldn't even explain itself to the other, how then could they *ever* meet in the middle and reconcile? *And this absence of concord,* Matha thought, *is just as terrible as the tragedy of the Faeries losing their dreams, and the Elves building their own instead.* Without concord, the Elves would do only as they saw fit and, unable to understand the Grand Eldress, Ferrell would only continue fighting her.

What difference does it make if Boann cursed us or not? he wondered ruefully. *For we are <u>already</u> cursed.*

Tired of arguing, the Luminary then spoke. "What of Baudwin?" he asked. "Has anyone found him yet?"

"No one knows where he is," the Grand Eldress replied resentfully.

Ferrell looked to his guards, who confirmed with a nod that this was so.

In measured tones, Ferrell concluded, "Let us all put this speculation about the spirit's fate behind us. What really matters now is how we are going to find Baudwin."

"How very high-minded of you," Seamus said. "But since you did such a first-rate job of incensing Boann, she sent him far away, where none of us can find him."

Hearing this, Ferrell looked alarmed, as more and more Guilders appeared to be turning on him.

"You chased our steward of the Water, and you shot her not once, but *twice!*" Ayamonn shouted.

"Go back to your Clock City!" Criofan shouted.

"Luminary of *doom!*" Lugh added.

Matha saw a look of apprehension cross Ferrell's face that he had never seen before. The proud arrogance he bore had melted away, for his conquest of Boann had turned into a liability he had not expected.

"Come now!" Ferrell exclaimed. "I offer my service. I alone have the resources to send my guards all over the realm to find him."

"Good, and while you're at it, you can find Baudwin's mother as well!" Criofan shouted.

All the Guilders laughed, especially those from Deuona. Unjoined, they delighted in Criofan's spiteful remark.

Lugh couldn't help himself. "I doubt they will," he declared angrily. Turning to Ferrell he added, "Take all your guards with you back west, before you do any more harm."

At this, there was more laughter. The crowd began jeering at Ferrell and his guards, who grimaced back at them. Just as all seemed about to ignite into a riot, Matha heard a familiar birdcall coming from above — *coo* — followed by another *coo coo.*

Moonrise alighted upon Seamus's shoulder, greeting him with yet another *coo coo.* Some in the crowd seemed not to notice or care, but Seamus was over-joyed to see the dove. "There, there," he crooned. "I'm glad you came through this awful night." Matha watched as Seamus listened intently to what the bird was telling him. Uncharacteristically, Seamus then sneaked away, avoiding the Roilers and Elves as he went. Wondering what was going on, Matha quickly made his way to Seamus, until they stood together, mostly amongst a group of Guilders.

"What did Moonrise tell you?" Matha asked.

"Of course, I should have thought of this myself," Seamus whispered, trying to conceal his sudden elation, "But in all the terrible upheaval, I didn't. *Moonrise* knows where to find Baudwin."

Instantly, Matha knew that this was true. *Why didn't I think of this?* he wondered.

But their joy was cut short, for Ferrell had spied them sneaking off. Like a calculating heron about to pounce, Ferrell spoke loudly so all could hear: "Baudwin's whereabouts need not be difficult to determine, and I won't have to send guards everywhere to look for him. Baudwin is in one place, and I know exactly how to find him."

Seamus was not happy that Ferrell had cut in, and neither was the Grand Eldress.

"*Lies!*" she exclaimed.

"Facts," Ferrell intoned adroitly, his demeanor now calm. Taking a biscuit from his pocket, he approached Seamus, and then offered a piece to Moonrise. Hungrily, Moonrise pecked at the treat.

"As we all know," Ferrell said, "twilight doves are keenly attuned to the ones they bond with, and always return to their masters. Moonrise will find Baudwin for us."

After a quick pause, the water Faeries acknowledged that this was so, as did the wood Faeries, who especially knew it to be true.

"Don't act like you were the first one to figure this out," Seamus snapped. "Moonrise just told me that he could sense Baudwin — and we don't need your help."

Undaunted, Ferrell continued. "I deduce that Boann sent him somewhere up the Nechtain, for the guards of that quarter saw him disappear there. Being of the water, she could not have sent him over land, so he is no doubt somewhere on the river. Unluckily for us, the Nechtain forks in many places, even joining with River Deuona, which runs upstream all the way past Wood Fern to Lake Nodens. Even if Moonrise can lead you there, you will still have to navigate many twists and turns, and the distances are vast. Water Faeries can't swim *that* far. If you wish to reach him faster, you'll need Steamway."

"Moonrise is *all* we need," Seamus retorted.

"Perhaps," Ferrell replied smoothly, "but if you are heading upriver, I *still* say you will need my steamway vessels to do so."

Seamus and Ferrell locked eyes for several uncomfortable moments.

Ferrell then cut through the tension. "I'm as concerned for Baudwin's safety as you are, so I will lead this expedition. Whoever wishes to come along, may do so. Our steamway vessels will navigate the currents with ease, until Moonrise can find him."

"I'll accept," Seamus said reluctantly, "but only because we will get to Baudwin faster."

And so, all came to agree that whoever wished to would travel with Ferrell, escorted by his guard, and follow Moonrise wherever the dove took them.

Chapter 33

THE TWO BOATS

At the edge of the Nechtain Quarter, lines of steamway boats waited for inspection at a water floodgate before entering or leaving Four Falls. There were four gates — one for each quarter of the city — each one made of massive wooden beams, braced with bronze. Many years of currents sloshing against the gates had left a mint-green patina on them — a carpet of moss against an ochre field. *Beautiful,* Criofan thought, *but also destructive — like Boann.* He knew the corrosion would eventually make the gates inoperable, which is why the Elves had to refit them every hundred years or so. But the Faeries didn't question their methods, for bronze had long ago been deemed most appropriate for building in *Tír Éirí Sióg.*

As the gates opened and closed, they controlled not only the boats, but also the flow of the river. Early that morning a crew of Faeries turned a large wheel, and the Nechtain gate opened. The vessels went through and then docked, waiting to be loaded or unloaded. The goods they carried were then either traded upriver, or hauled through the city, down to the An Bhanna and out to sea.

Criofan now stood upon one of the docks, gazing pensively at the Water. Only a day and a half had passed since everyone had made hasty preparations to find Baudwin. In that short time, he had become more and more unsure about whether they would succeed. Rather than hoping things would go their way, he could imagine only his own failure, which filled him with lethargy. Before the Grand Unveiling, he had been ready to conquer anything, like a mountain goat bounding up the side of a cliff. But now he stood shocked at his own hesitancy. How he hated losing his mettle. The worst thing in Life was failing to succeed, which meant he *had* to find his friend. *The Faeries must be the ones to take home the prize — not the Elves,* he thought.

Seamus hadn't liked the notion of cooperating with Ferrell, but as the Elve had an expeditious steamway vessel and the Water Guard at his command, he had no choice but to accept his help.

"I don't like the plan," Seamus griped, as he stood next to Criofan on the dock. He was dressed in his traveling attire, a dark blue woolen coat with a blue and green plaid hat and scarf, and gray canvas knee boots. Moonrise sat perched upon his shoulder, having never left him since Baudwin disappeared.

As Seamus stared disapprovingly at the Timewaker — the steamway paddle boat they were about to board — he seemed ready to explode with frustration. "If we take Ferrell's boat," he continued, "then he outnumbers us, and his crew can pounce upon us at a moment's notice."

Criofan knew Seamus was right. The Timewaker was an elven-crewed vessel. No place onboard would be safe if Ferrell suddenly decided he had other plans for them. If they angered him in any way, he could order his crew to seize and haul them back to an elven court. The Luminary seemed sincere, but what his intentions really were for Baudwin, no one could say.

"He'll certainly take us to him," Lugh remarked, "but don't forget that the Assembly is deciding things now, even as we speak. And we and our lands be damned!"

Criofan couldn't argue with Lugh. Ever since Boann's arrival, the four quarters had been abuzz with speculation. Although the Elves remained tight-lipped, word was that their relay stations had been working furiously, sending signals of light back and forth from Four Falls to the Clock City. Everyone in Four Falls knew that the towers had been flashing almost nonstop since the Grand Unveiling. And Ferrell, he surmised, was obviously the main sender and receiver of the information. None but the Elves knew what the light signals meant, but Matha had told Criofan that they were a code, made of long and short flashes, which the Elves used to send messages over long distances.

"If the Assembly turns on us, we'll be trapped, unable to defend ourselves," Lugh muttered, his voice edged with dread. Despite being recently unjoined, Criofan could tell how unbearable the condition was for him. Criofan felt the same way, as did every water Faery he had spoken to. Yet most also felt that they had no choice but to soldier on through their pain, or be dragged into oblivion by fear and sorrow.

"Ferrell can't be trusted," Criofan continued, turning to Seamus. "We shouldn't have agreed to accept his help. Why don't we just take one of our own vessels?"

They had all discussed the matter the night before. Seamus had insisted that they take a faery ship, but Lugh had countered that since they didn't have a steamway ship like the ones the Elves used, they'd be unable to keep up as they traveled against the river currents. Still perturbed, Seamus conceded, adding, "We're screwed as tightly as a rusty elven lockbox."

Down the dock Criofan spotted Matha lugging a large duffel bag, with Kelven next to him. Of the two, Criofan could tell that Matha was faring better at being unjoined. He at least smiled when Criofan approached them. Kelven stumbled, exhausted, and set down his bag. Everyone had been up all night long, preparing for the journey. Despite having all of the guild resources at his disposal, Criofan knew Kelven felt ill-equipped to embark upon the expedition. Most of the older ones were leading by example, but Criofan knew that, having lost Shaela and now Baudwin, Kelven was struggling.

"So — there she is," Matha began, duly impressed. "The Timewaker."

Surveying the ship, Criofan had to admit that she was an amazing feat of elven engineering — at least fifty feet long, with two large paddle wheels, one port and the other starboard, and an even larger wheel at the stern. Two decks, upper and lower, were lined with well-wrought brass railings, both sturdy and stylishly Steamway. The first deck toward the stern housed an engine room, filled with a maze of brass pipes, dials, knobs, and levers, all worn by the sweat of many hands; midship, on the second deck, stood the wheelhouse. Behind the engine room hung a skiff, suspended by a sprocketworks crane above the stern. The Timewaker had a shallow draft, designed for river navigation.

"Let's hope she gets us there," Criofan remarked.

"Oh — she may — but there's another that would be much truer to yer purpose," a loud, heavily accented voice boomed behind them.

All five of them turned, and Moonrise did a quick hop-turn on Seamus's shoulder to see who had spoken.

A water Faery stood before them, unlike any Criofan had ever seen, about four and eighty. His coat, weathered and worn, appeared to have been battered by more than one hundred storms. Like his counterparts from Deuona, he had pale blue-green skin, yet his was more leathery and wrinkled, and his hair, although groomed, was, upon closer examination, matted with salt. Strings of seaweed, shells, and silver beads were woven into his braids. His piercing and deeply set blue-green eyes made his demeanor seem much wilder in nature than that of any Faeries he had ever seen. Criofan wondered if he always looked this way, or if being unjoined had made him so.

"Will ye be needin' a bit o' help?" the wild-looking Faery asked, smiling at Seamus.

Behind the newcomer, an elven Water Guard wheeled a crate of provisions to be loaded onto the Timewaker. They had been doing so all morning, the only task left before their departure. Craning his neck at the guard, the wild-looking water Faery quipped, "Now be sure to bring plenty of caulkin', cause yer goin' to need it." The Water Guard ignored him.

"Caulking?" Criofan asked.

"Sure, for when them Elves run aground, 'cause they be too busy polishin' gears to rightly navigate the river," the outspoken Faery shouted at the guard.

Before Seamus could open his mouth to speak, the strange Faery spoke again. "Sorry I say, but could ye be usin' a bit o' help?"

"Help — with what?" Seamus asked gruffly.

"Now given that them Elves are gettin' the jump on ye. Ye bein' the *real* kin of the missin' party, I'd be thinkin' ye might want to get to him first. If he'd be *my* grandson, that would be right, and ye bein' his father's father, are ye not? And given, I'm guessin', ye not trustin' them schemin' Elves," the Faery added, winking.

Seamus stopped him there. "Been listening to our conversation, have you?" he asked, shaking his staff at the Faery. "Just what are you up to? I have no time for eavesdroppers!"

"So then, Seamus, if you won't be needin' a friend, guess I can just mosey right along," the Faery replied. "But ye should listen to *that* one," he added, pointing to Criofan. "*He* knows ye can't trust them Elves."

Behind them, a Water Guard was making his way back with an empty dolly. Thumbing his nose at the rambunctious Faery, he shouted, "We can't trust you either — you dopey, water-loving, fools!"

Criofan expected the wild Faery to be insulted, but instead, he started laughing. "Sure — that be right! And don't ye forget it!"

The Water Guard just shook his head and wheeled away the dolly.

"How do you know my name?" Seamus demanded. "You're no friend of mine."

"I'd be yer friend if ye'd let me," the unknown Faery replied. "And a friend is what ye need, if I've spied yer predicament rightly." Respectfully cupping his hands over his heart, he made a sign of the Water. "My name is Loingsech,[1] and I'm *with* the Water, and I'd be listenin' to ye and yers half the night as ye scrambled about these docks. And the more I listened, the more I saw there be reason for my listenin'. I know it be non-polite, but this be an urgent matter, and I'll forget all I've heard, if ye wish it to be so."

Seamus furrowed his brow. "You're a sea Faery, aren't you?"

"Indeed," Loingsech replied with a flamboyant bow. "That I be."

A *sea* Faery. Criofan knew little about them, but he did know a lot about what they did, for they were consummate traders on the Water. They brought goods from as far away as Pine Reach in the Northern Elven Lands, and Bog in the Southern Elven Lands, and shipped them to the inland sea, past the Island of Baranthus — which was their home — and then into the sea tunnels that ran under the Tadlachs to Four Falls. Criofan's parents had told him they were called *salties*, and that they were a rebellious and mysterious lot.

"After the Befalling, you salties were a rare sight," Seamus said.

"Sure, ye can thank the Assembly for that!" Loingsech exclaimed. "They blamed us for the entire mess."

---

[1] Pronounced [LUNG-shuk]

Criofan didn't know what Loingsech meant. Seeing his puzzled look, Loingsech spoke again. "Now ye were nothin' but a Faefry then," he said pointing to Criofan. "We of the sea were the ones that helped the defenders of Four Falls. We kept their mouths fed when Four Falls was starvin' for grain, and the buildins were burnin', and the Shell Keep was a-fallin.'"

"And my thanks for that," Seamus said. "So, as you are now here, I suppose the Assembly lifted the embargo?"

"Sure, they had to win everyone over, didn't they?" Loingsech asked. "It's no matter anyway. We never left the sea. They kept chasin' us back to Baranthus, and we would just leave port again, under cover of Darkness. We being the *real* masters of the sea," Loingsech added, chortling. "They'll be sure to chase us again someday, but for the time bein', this river will certainly suffice." He then shifted his weight back and forth, the habit of one who has spent most of his Life on the sea.

They all laughed.

"Ye see, everyone knows what *really* happened," he added, stamping his boot on the creaking dock. "Our guardian, whom ye call Boann and we call Lí Ban,[2] we bein' of the sea, and ye of the rivers, well, she's the Water's Life — wherever there be enough to cry even a tiny tear. Well, she whisked yer lad away, and then that scoundrel, Ferrell, shot her with that abominable contraption after she tried to bring some wisdom to them addle-brained freshies — no offense."

Loingsech then stopped himself.

"No offense taken," Seamus chuckled, "but as we see it, Water is *always* fresh, unless you add salt."

Everyone laughed.

"So now," Loingsech continued, "seein' Lí Ban, or *Boann,* at yer Grand Unveilin' wouldn't have surprised us nearly as much as it did ye freshies. We hold rites long forgotten to ye river dwellers, and she has saved many of our kin, in storms they nary ought to have survived. On the Island of Baranthus she's well respected, and her bein' savagely shot by that deranged dolt — who calls himself a Luminary — must not go unavenged." He'd whispered the last part in a low voice, so none nearby could hear him.

Criofan was taken aback by how combatively Loingsech spoke about the Elves. Surely Loingsech's struggles had taught him to see Life through different eyes than those of the Deuona Faeries. The pain of being unjoined pulled them into disturbing rages, but Criofan sensed that this sea Faery, having ceaselessly clawed and fought to keep his kin fed and his loved ones safe, seemed better able to endure his discomfort. Unlike the others, his anger fortified him.

---

[2] Pronounced [LEE Bahn]

"And so, if not avenged, then at least he should not be the instrument by which ye find yer son again," Loingsech continued, looking at Kelven.

"I agree," Seamus said. "But we made a deal with Ferrell, and he's the only one with a steamway boat fit for the journey."

"The only one — now is it?" Loingsech asked. "No, not the *only* one — not by a league." As he spoke, he circled around them. "Ye see, we're traders, and we go everywhere. Our travels have made us a great deal of bounty, bein' as we buy and sell things everywhere — before yer eyes even behold our goods."

"What kinds of things?" Criofan asked, trying to imagine all the riches they had amassed over so many years.

"Now ye know — furs — only from fallen animals, of course," he added, smiling. Incense from Bog — always more incense — the finest scents from the dankest place in *Tír na nÓg*. Lumber — not every tree grows everywhere — especially ironwood from the Vanishing Moors, which makes the strongest keels ever built. Wool and silks, glassware and pottery, and most of the gadgets and tools the Elves make for yer dome homes, crystals and tapestries, gems and jewelry from Gleam, barley, oats, wheat, and apples, and even your famous Rainbow honey — the easiest thing to trade in the elven lands, as them Elves can never get enough." Loingsech paused for a moment before continuing. "But the dearest thing we ever traded them Elves for was the *Beal Inse*," he added, gazing fondly up the docks.

"The *Beal Inse*?"[3] Criofan asked.

"Sure, she's our treasure of the rivers," Loingsech replied, nodding. "Ye see, we trade on the sea, but these fresh Waters are also a love of ours, and she's the finest vessel here. Built by them Elves — but dreamed up by us better 'n any of them could — and rightly suited for the river."

Loingsech then pointed down the docks at another steamway ship that looked somewhat like the Timewaker. Instead of elven motifs, the bronze railings were distinctly faery, with sea stars, salmons, and dolphins crafted into the design, surrounded by painted wooden waves of blue, green, and gold. On the foredeck were two side-by-side spirals worked into the railings — making an *S* shape — with a line beginning in the center of one and ending in the center of the other.

"I've seen those spirals before," Matha said.

"Where?" Criofan asked.

"On the glamorium tablet in the shrine at the Springs of Coventina."

"The same one that Baudwin showed me," Seamus added. "On a piece of blue-green agate."

---

[3] Pronounced [BAYL Insheh] entrance to the island

Criofan remembered that Matha had mentioned this. The sea Faeries were becoming ever more interesting.

"That be the symbol of our lost temple on Baranthus," Loingsech said, pointing to the *S* on the foredeck. "Where once all feelins were felt, and we wound and unwound the spirals until we saw the other in ourselves, so the dreams and the forges were then set rightly."

Criofan remembered what Boann had said, that Faeries and Elves should abide as the other does. *"Seeing the other in ourselves" must mean the same,* he thought. Surely the temple on the Island of Baranthus was one that Boann had spoken of, and Loingsech certainly seemed to understand what such temples were for — to receive the Great Emerald Light. The verity in Loingsech's words struck him deeply, and he couldn't help hoping that one day he would be able to uncover more of their meaning. How he wished Baudwin was there to ponder their import with him.

"You speak with the wisdom of the Grand Eldress," Seamus said, beaming. "So it is true that the dwellers of Baranthus still know of the teachings of Glamorium and the old ways?"

"Sure we do!" Loingsech roared. "Now if ye come along with me, I'll be tellin' ye about that and much, much more. So after we rescue yer grandson, we can all sail to Baranthus together." He then gestured toward the *Beal Inse.* "She'll faithfully be the one to take ye to yer lost kin. We commissioned an elven shipmaker to build 'er. She's got all the improvements, and even a steamway engine, just like that bloated whale over there," he said, pointing at the Timewaker. "She's not as fast when the river is easy, but when the Water winds, she is the nimblest in her class, by far."

Criofan could see that the Timewaker was about as long, but sat deeper in the Water, which could only mean the vessel was heavier than the *Beal Inse,* perhaps because there was so much bronze work all over the ship. *There's no such thing as too much metal for an Elve,* he thought, amused. Many sharply pointed angles merged into curious-looking curves, and then back into angles again, and at the bow was the large copper figurehead of a rabbit playing a flute, which Criofan thought was a very strange choice for Elves to make. Later, he would have to ask what the rabbit meant.

"Yes, I agree your ship seems better suited to the river," Criofan said.

"Sure she is," Loingsech replied. "Sorry, so what do ye say? How about ye scuttle yer plans with Ferrell and join our crew?"

Everyone seemed buoyed by the idea. Lugh was the easiest to persuade, as he had quickly taken a liking to Loingsech, but Kelven and Seamus were uncertain, for they feared that breaking a previous agreement would bring the wrath of the Assembly down upon them.

Seamus then said, "We should explain that we want to bring another vessel along with the first, so they'll have a harder time believing that we want to exclude them."

And so, they all moved forward with the plan.

Criofan soon found himself walking up the ramp with his kin to the bow of the Timewaker. All were steeling themselves as they prepared to give Ferrell the news. Upon reaching the bow, a crewmember notified Ferrell, who then appeared from the quarterdeck. At first the Luminary greeted them cordially, but upon seeing Loingsech, he looked ready to spit a rancid nut out of his mouth.

"We are loaded and ready to embark," Ferrell began, "but I see you've brought someone else with you. . ." He then regarded Loingsech coldly, who did the same in kind.

Not one to mince words, Seamus got right to the point. "We've decided upon a new course of action," he began. "Loingsech has generously offered us the use of his ship, so we had to ask ourselves, why not take both? If one runs aground in the fog, we'll at least have another to keep going."

Seeing how Loingsech's proposition was affecting Ferrell, Criofan hid a grin. Now Ferrell looked as if he had not a single rancid nut to spit out, but a whole mouthful. "Yes, I suppose the fog could be a problem," Ferrell conceded, "but surely we can all communicate better on one ship."

"Surely ye may," Loingsech spoke up, staring Ferrell in the eye, "but this be no ordinary fog. This fog be Boann's dark breath, which carries her curse whether she be near or far away — and all thanks to harsh measures that were taken by ye, I be thinkin'. And surely ye know that since her arrival, strange-lookin' fogbanks have been poppin' up all over the rivers." Leaning in closer to Ferrell, Loingsech added, "Now this be a thick soup of a fog that flows harder than the gasps of a heavin' grand horn. This fog ain't the pleasant kind that ripens the rose berries in Mist Valley, but a shadowy, skulkin' specter of a fog that means to envelop ships as they go through the tight corners of the forks. It's the kind that comes after a heavy rain, but far deadlier — to enshroud juttin' rocks, break hulls, and crack skulls, as crews stumble and fall." Looking sternly at Ferrell, he continued, "Bein' of the Water — unlike ye — if I could take ten boats, I would. To take only *one* boat, when ye can take two, is sheer folly."

Hearing this, Ferrell frowned. "I suppose only *you* would know that," he countered.

"Surely I do," Loingsech replied. As he continued speaking, Criofan could see how pleased he was to have taken the upper hand in the debate. "'Near Copper Caves is the Calmin' Reach, but that reach be anythin' but calm. A poet, not a mariner, must have named it that! When we be shippin' goods to Pine Reach, we came to the middle passage where it narrows and the sea surges somethin' fierce. So there's a fog on the rivers now that I've been hearin' stories about, but the fog I'm talkin' about was from some other spirit of the Water — one even wilder than Boann and much more unreasonable — movin' on its own whims without regard for anythin'. I couldn't see any of the rocks juttin' out of the Water 'til it was too late. We glanced off a giant rock, and if we had been but a foot to starboard, we'd have been a-flounderin' and thrown into the sea. And that's why we need two boats — in case one of 'em runs aground."

Criofan could see Ferrell straining for a way to put Loingsech in his place. "Well, there's a hole in your plan," Ferrell blurted. "If the fog is as treacherous as you say, we won't be able to see each other anyway, so two boats would not be an advantage, but a liability."

"Good of ye to think of that," Loingsech replied brightly, pointing to the top of the Timewaker. "If knowin' where we're goin' is what concerns ye, we'll use the signalers on the wheelhouse pole." Criofan spotted a bronze box on top of a pole, fitted with a clear lens. The box looked like a smaller kind of signal tower used by the Elves.

"I doubt your vessel is fitted the same," Ferrell declared, his temper flaring.

"The *Beal Inse* is a ship of yer makin'," Loingsech replied, grinning. "Surely ye know she has the same fittin's. The signalers can easily cut through the fog, distances on the river bein' much shorter than they are on the sea. That'll do the trick."

Criofan could see that Ferrell wanted to keep debating, but uncharacteristically, he had been taken unawares and didn't have a solid rebuttal. His only recourse was to grudgingly agree. "I welcome your expertise in these matters," he declared. "Two ships it is then! In the interest of mutual cooperation and good will between the Assembly and Four Falls, I accept."

"And in the interest of mutual cooperation with Baranthus as well," Loingsech replied with a grin. Ferrell snorted.

"*However* will we get on without the Faeries?" a female voice queried from behind Ferrell. Out from the quarterdeck stepped an elven lady — a fearless flash of metal and determination, with striking features, both alluring in their beauty yet dubious in their intentions. Stunned, the gents all took a step back, staring at her. As she raised her arms, Criofan saw gold bracers, with Suns etched into them. He couldn't tell why she wore them — for added protection when she fought, or simply for show. Perhaps all she wanted was attention, if only to advance her standing with others. Certainly she seemed as if she would use any means possible to achieve her goals. On her sleeve were three gold stripes, marking her as a Master of Gold, and on her collar an indigo star, the rank of Mantle. She wore the uniform of an Earth Guard, but to Criofan her bearing seemed to indicate that she was far more capable than most rank-and-file Elves.

"The Luminary illuminates the Mantle," she said to Ferrell. Criofan had never heard the guards speak so formally before. From what he had seen, Ferrell usually barked orders at his underlings, but he guessed that as a Mantle, she had to properly address him.

Ferrell then replied, "The Mantle kindles the Luminary." They saluted each other, placing their fists over their hearts, head down, and then raising their heads, putting four fingers at their temples.

"Ferrell," she began, authoritatively, "you've missed something. The signal codes aren't taught to the salties. They'll have to accept a member of our crew. We can't have our boats out of communication in the fog, can we?" she asked, giving Loingsech a wry smile.

"Surely basic signals will suffice," Loingsech replied. "And those we know."

"Perhaps," she replied, "but in the event of unexpected circumstance, we'll need *precise* communication."

"Maeve[4] is correct," Ferrell said. "You should take one of our crew with you."

"Accepted," Loingsech replied. Congenially, he smiled at Maeve. "I be knowin' him," he said, gesturing toward Ferrell. "But sorry, I don't believe I've had the pleasure of meetin' ye before."

Maeve regarded Loingsech. "I am Maeve of Gold Haven, daughter of Eibhlin,[5] here at the request of the Assembly to help Ferrell find Baudwin as well as ensure that the voyage is secure. Everyone is quite concerned about him, and we all want to see him home safely."

"That we do," Loingsech replied.

"Good," Maeve added, looking at Ferrell. "And it's also good that I'm here, because crucial details might otherwise get missed."

"Crucial details," Ferrell replied, stonily. "Like what happens when you drive desperate ones to even greater desperation? Your exploits in the Cyhiraeth have not gone unnoticed by the Assembly."

Maeve seemed offended, but as Ferrell was her superior, Criofan was not surprised to see her bite her tongue. He knew what Ferrell was referring to, as he had been in the Cyhiraeth with Baudwin, met the destitute Faeries, and witnessed their helplessness. Now he wondered how Maeve might have made things even worse. Judging from her manner, he would need to be careful and not let down his guard.

"What were ye up to in the Cyhiraeth?" Loingsech asked Maeve.

"Helping to deal with a difficult situation," she replied coldly.

---

4   Pronounced [MAYV]
5   Pronounced [EV-leen]

"Aye," Loingsech retorted. "I'm sure what ye call *helpin'*, I call *meddlin'*."

Now Criofan really wanted to know what Maeve's dealings had been with the downtrodden in the Cyhiraeth. The Assembly must have tried again to relocate them, and she must have been the one in charge. If she had used harsher measures, she certainly was not the kind of Elve Criofan wanted anything to do with.

Maeve then sauntered nearer to Loingsech. Leaning in closely, she quickly produced a small gold canister from her pocket, and then blew some of the contents into his face. The powder was orange. Clutching his throat, Loingsech began coughing violently.

"What you call meddling, I call *serving*," Maeve declared. "How do you like my fragrance?" Looking closely at her, Criofan noticed several other canisters hanging around her neck from rings on a thick gold chain. He wondered what was in each one.

"Maeve!" Ferrell exclaimed. "That's enough!"

Loingsech stopped coughing. "If that be poison," he snarled, "ye will soon know the justice of Baranthus! And yer punishment will be a lot less lenient than what the Assembly would give ye!"

"It's just a fragrant powder to help you relax, you silly goose," Maeve retorted.

Loingsech straightened up. "A silly goose am I?" Keenly, he glared at her. "Well now, speaking of details," he added, shooting Ferrell a glance, "there's one that both of ye missed. Which ship will lead — eh?"

"The Timewaker of course," Ferrell replied. This operation is still ours."

"Is it now?" Loingsech replied, looking at Seamus. "Did ye make that agreement?" Seamus shook his head *no*.

"Now then, looks like we're at an impasse, aren't we?" Looking at Maeve, Loingsech added, "The one with more experience on the Water should lead of course — which be me. You don't look like ye'd be much use on the Water. With those skinny legs, ye'll probably fall overboard as soon as things get rough, and we'll be slowed down fishin' ye out of the river."

"I'm more than capable of handling myself with these legs," Maeve replied.

"Then prove it!" Loingsech exclaimed, pointing toward the bow of the boat. "If ye can climb the signal pole and tie this scarf to the top — as the fog flows — then the Timewaker will be the one to lead. And if not, then the *Beal Inse* will."

"Is *that* all?" Maeve asked snidely.

Loingsech handed her the scarf, and she made her way to the quarterdeck entrance. The pole was located one deck above, at the top of the wheelhouse. Criofan wondered if Loingsech had chosen too simple a challenge. For an acrobat, scaling the pole would be easy, and not much harder for an Earth Guard.

As Maeve began climbing the ladder to reach the pole at the top of the wheelhouse, Loingsech shouted, "I said — *as* the fog flows!"

Turning around, she saw that he had produced another scarf. "Tie this," he said, "to cover yer eyes."

Maeve hesitated, looking at Ferrell, who nodded for her to continue. "He's right," Ferrell said. "The fog's the real challenge we face, so you must put on the blinder."

Criofan sensed that Ferrell was playing along, because secretly, he enjoyed watching Maeve being put on the spot. Perhaps Ferrell was also curious to see if she could pull off the challenge. He could feel the animosity between them, which made him wonder what kind of history they had.

"Fine!" Maeve exclaimed, as she grabbed the scarf and tied it across her eyes.

"No peekin'!" Loingsech warned. "I can tell when my crew cheats, and ye're no exception."

Maeve turned to ascend the ladder on the side of the quarterdeck. Slowly, she placed one hand forward, reaching for another hold. Her progress was steady and methodical, and Criofan was impressed with her agility. One foot up, then another hand forward, then one foot up again. Despite her confidence, she seemed tense. And perhaps she would get even more so as she neared the top of the wheelhouse, where the real challenge awaited.

She had almost reached the roof of the wheelhouse, when Loingsech picked up a nearby bucket of Water, used for scrubbing the deck. He heaved the contents at her. The Water hit her squarely in the back and splashed all over the railings. She almost slipped, but didn't cry out. Instead, she froze.

"Sorry, ye never know when a wave will hit ye — do ye now!" Loingsech shouted, laughing. "That's for dousin' me with yer *fragrant* powder!"

Criofan expected Maeve to get upset, but instead she ignored him. Confidently, she continued up the ladder, and soon pulled herself onto the top of the wheelhouse roof. She had now reached the signaling pole, which was at least thirty feet high, with bronze rungs that looked quite narrow. Climbing them would indeed be tricky. Ferrell beckoned to everyone, and they quickly followed him inside the quarterdeck, up the stairs to the wheelhouse, and then through the hatch at the top to watch her progress. By the time they reached the roof, she was already several rungs up the pole.

Instead of going with them, Loingsech stepped to the side of the deck and grabbed a fire hose, which he then aimed in her direction. Ferrell watched, hiding his glee, taking no issue with the extra challenge she would have to face.

Maeve was now halfway up the pole, her arms and legs in sync with the task as she kept climbing. Again, Criofan was impressed with her skill.

Loingsech opened the valve. Suddenly, a surge of Water struck her with such force that she nearly lost her grip.

"You scoundrel!" she shouted, as she shook off the soggy assault. "You're a traitor to your tribe, using your element for your own gain. An Elve would never use a metal for such an odious purpose!"

Criofan looked down over the railing at Loingsech, and they grinned at each other. He could easily see an Elve using a metal for any kind of purpose. Ferrell suppressed a laugh by pretending to cough. Loingsech looked back up at Maeve.

"Now, don't ye be telling me that," Loingsech, retorted, as he set down the hose. "If ye can't handle the docks, then ye'll never handle the river."

"I can handle the river, but can *you* handle your own precious water?"

"When it comes to testin' high-handed Elves, I never hesitate to call on the Water — no matter *how*."

Maeve remained calm and still. Not enough spray had struck her to undermine her progress, and she wasn't about to give up. Instead, she simply waited for the water to drip off of her. Making sure that her grip was steady, she began climbing again, determined to reach the top. Once there, she untied and victoriously waved the scarf. She then slid back down the pole to the roof.

In short order, she presented the scarf to Loingsech, saying, "The Timewaker will lead!"

And so the contest was decided, and if Loingsech was disappointed, his face hardly bore a clue. Bowing to her, he replied, "And so it shall be, my lady."

⚶

The *Beal Inse* steamed steadily up the Nechtain. A day and a half had passed since she and her crew had left the docks of Four Falls. If Criofan hadn't felt so morose, he would have been quite excited to be traveling with his friends, upriver, on such a marvelous ship. There was little for him to do but gaze over the gunnel at the rushing river, or try to occupy himself with idle conversation. Added to that, he hadn't expected the trip to be so plodding. Thus far they hadn't encountered fog, or run into anything of note — only marshes and trees, birds wheeling in the sky, and deer and other forest creatures gazing at them from along the shore.

He remembered being in the Temple of the Falls with Baudwin, Matha, and Lugh when they had talked about the lessons of the four rivers, before all the trouble had started. *If I weren't so out of sorts, I could heed the lesson of River Nechtain and go back the way I came — to the source of my pain — like the salmon,* he thought despondently. *But now all I am is a salmon without a current.*

The Air grew hotter as they moved south and further inland, parallel to Deuona and closer to the Tadlachs. So far, Loingsech's crew had been orderly, attending to their duties and little else, and Loingsech himself had been very welcoming, spending hours telling them stories of Life on the Isle of Baranthus and at sea. Everyone had taken a liking to him, and Criofan was glad that they'd had the good fortune to meet him, especially after the terrible misfortune when Baudwin had vanished and they had been unjoined from their currents.

As Criofan made his way to the bow of the *Beal Inse*, he could see the stern of the Timewaker. On the back of the wheelhouse, he spotted several Elves, but through the curtain of spray churned up by the rear paddle wheel, he couldn't make out Ferrell or Maeve. Worried about their intentions for the Faeries, he had been trying to keep an eye on them. Seamus and Kelven were certainly no match for two Elves who had the Branches of Progress at their disposal. Criofan sensed that in their eagerness to help, they probably intended to control everything, and he seriously doubted that they had Baudwin's best interests at heart. Fortunately, Loingsech had been able slow them down.

After Maeve tied the scarf to the pole, Loingsech immediately confided to Criofan that he knew she was going to win the contest. Coming aboard the *Beal Inse*, the Faeries, hadn't lost anything, he chuckled. And all he wanted was for Ferrell to believe that the Elves had won *something*. Added to that, he had actually wanted the Elves to go first. Criofan was impressed with Loingsech's craftiness. After years of locking horns with the Assembly, Loingsech had managed to smuggle himself into their good graces and gain the upper hand — at least for now.

"Now Ferrell controls our pace and where we stop, but goin' first is more dangerous," Loingsech told Criofan. "If that river swine runs aground, only the *Beal Inse* will still be afloat. That Master of Gold be *no* master of the river."

Criofan was happy that Loingsech had taken an interest in him. He was also glad that Loingsech was so chipper, because being unjoined from the Water was becoming ever more distressing. Having confided his upset to Matha, Matha agreed that he as well felt mired in misery. Neither of them had slept well the night before, and being on the river hadn't renewed them the way they had hoped. Instead of feeling calm and uplifted by being on the Water, they felt injured and alone, as if floating upon a darkish void — an endless chasm that was vastly indifferent to them.

Criofan heard the door of the engine room open, followed by sounds of salties stoking the furnace. There was a sudden *vronk*, as the heavy bronze door shut. Soon the paddle wheels were churning up more spray, as the ship picked up steam along the river.

"Moonrise returns!" he heard Seamus cry out. Looking ahead, he spotted the bird gliding first over the Timewaker and then the *Beal Inse*. With a flutter, he alighted upon Seamus's shoulder.

"Tell us, Moonrise," Seamus began, "are we on the right track?" Moonrise bobbed his head. "Good," Seamus said. "You must tell us if something is wrong."

Moonrise then cocked his head at Seamus, making a most peculiar *coo*.

"What's that you say?" Seamus asked. "A ruckus up ahead?"

Moonrise cooed again.

"Flutter fish?" Seamus asked.

Again Moonrise cooed, hopping from side to side.

"We'll keep a lookout for them," Seamus said. "Now you must go and take a well-deserved nap." He then opened the door of a cage Loingsech had bolted to the side of the wheelhouse. Moonrise hopped inside, and Seamus covered the cage with a blanket.

"He's sticking his beak out for us," Seamus declared. "Flying so much by day, instead of at night. We better make sure he rests."

"Yes, and soon we'll be sticking our beaks out as well," Lugh added, laughing.

At this, everyone was silent, and Criofan remembered something Seamus had told him. Just the night before, Loingsech had ordered the elven crew member they had been forced to include on their boat to polish the pipes near the engine room. After the Elve left the wheelhouse, Seamus had overheard Loingsech and Lugh speaking in a hush. According to Seamus, they were scheming about how they might take revenge upon the Elves for dishonoring Boann. Hearing this, Seamus had barged into the wheelhouse, making them swear to scuttle whatever plans they had until Baudwin was safely aboard. There had been some gnashing of teeth, but eventually both Lugh and Loingsech promised Seamus they wouldn't do anything — yet.

"*Our* beaks are better left in our bird seed," Seamus now said to Lugh.

"Fine," Lugh replied, impatiently. "But, I don't believe the salties will stand down forever. The Faeries of Baranthus will see Boann avenged."

Criofan knew this had to be true, yet he hoped the salties would stay in line, at least until they had a chance to find Baudwin. Looking ahead at the Timewaker, he wondered if the Elves had other, more nefarious plans in mind.

One of Loingsech's lookouts then called out, "Ahead — off the starboard bow!"

Criofan barely had time to take cover before a thick jumble of scales and tails went whizzing overhead. Whatever they were was so dense that he couldn't make out what he was seeing, until Loingsech cried out, "Looks like the flutter fish are a-flyin'. Cover yer faces!"

Peeking out, Criofan saw an entire school of flutter fish fly toward them — thousands of them, soaring out of the Water and over the deck of the *Beal*

Inse on large wing-shaped fins. Some fell short and flopped about, terrified, near Criofan's feet. Taking pity on them, he tossed them back into the Water.

"I've never seen flutter fish so frightened," Criofan said.

"That's because they're bein' chased," Loingsech replied, pointing upriver. "And they don't want to be supper."

Looking ahead, Criofan saw still more flutter fish swarming around the Timewaker. On the port side, he also saw flashes of pink in a mass of frothy bubbles.

"What are they?" Criofan shouted. "Otters?"

"No!" the lookout exclaimed. "They're pink river dolphins — a whole pod of them."

Now Seamus, Kelven, Lugh, and Matha came to see what all the fuss was about.

"Bring us up slow, alongside 'em," Loingsech called up to the wheelhouse. "There's somethin' I must ask 'em."

Soon the flutter fish had passed, and the pink river dolphins were approaching the boat, frolicking and spinning like acrobats, shooting high into the Air and back into the Water. Criofan had heard of pink river dolphins, but had never seen them before.

Loingsech then let out a loud, high whistle. As the pod approached the boat, they poked their heads out of the Water — one, two, three, four, five — like petals of a flower, whistling and clicking. Everyone laughed appreciatively, and Criofan noticed that the burden of being unjoined seemed far less in the company of these delightful creatures.

Leaning over the gunnel, Loingsech whistled even louder at the matriarch. "Seen anythin' out of the ordinary?" he asked. She whistled back, her lime green eyes staring playfully up at him.

"Well then, go and feed," Loingsech replied. "We'll wait for ye."

The pink river dolphins then dove into the Water, chasing after the flutter fish that were now downstream. Swimming even faster, they raced ahead of the school, and timed their leaps to snatch the fish right out of the air. While the crew watched them feed, Loingsech spoke. "The matriarch was tellin' me she has news, and when she's had her fill, she'll tell us more."

"I've seen pink river dolphins only a few times in my Life," Seamus said.

"Sure, they're extremely rare," Loingsech replied, "and seein' them on the Nechtain means that Boann's comin' must have drawn them here, for they're bound to her for a special purpose."

"They do have a strange way of speaking," Seamus said. "Not like birds, or rabbits, or grand horns. I can't understand them."

"I only know their speech from talkin' to their cousins, the pink sea dolphins," Loingsech remarked. "They all speak the same — whistlin' and clickin' and singin' songs of Boann — for dolphins are her messengers, in all the Waters."

"Don't they breathe differently than fish?" Criofan asked.

"Yes," Loingsech replied, laughing. "They breathe the same Air as you and me, 'cept you and I don't have noses on the tops of our heads, as I've heard some Elves do. Some say that water Faeries were once dolphins, but I don't know if I be believin' that."

"But how did they get here?" Matha asked.

"So the legend says that Boann brought them to the realm when she created *Teampall Easa*, so she would always have a way to speak to water Faeries. Them bein' so shy, they only come around when Boann has a message for the Fae. That said, water Faeries haven't been listenin' to her, so they've stopped comin' around. That's why they're seen so rarely. But we salties still revere them. On Baranthus there be a ruby statue of a pink sea dolphin to honor the many times they've saved many a mariner."

From afar, they heard a whistling. The dolphins, having had their fill, were swimming back, and soon the matriarch was again speaking to Loingsech. Criofan tried to hear what she was saying, and although he could make out some of the words, most were still too difficult to understand.

"So that's all?" Loingsech asked the matriarch. "Well then — thank you very much." Loingsech clicked and whistled, and the pink river dolphins dove down into the Water. He then relayed the message to everyone about what they had seen. Recently they had been called to witness a great roiling upon the river — a calling Loingsech assumed had come from Boann herself. When they arrived at the scene, all the river creatures appeared to be frightened. A maelstrom of Water could be seen surging upriver at incredible speed. None of the dolphins knew how or why, but their special sense detected a Faerie lad shooting past them, trapped inside a watery bubble. They had no time to save him, as they were swept aside.

"Does this mean that Baudwin is farther upriver?" Seamus asked, his face brightening.

"For sure," Loingsech replied. "This is certainly a good sign for us. Baudwin is within Boann's torrent, sent onward by her."

The news uplifted the crew, and everyone felt a renewed sense of hope.

"We will find him," Seamus declared, placing his hand upon Kelven's shoulder. Kelven nodded, his eyes tearing up.

"The Timewaker is signaling us," the lone elven crew member shouted to Loingsech. "Wants to know what the holdup is about."

"Then signal back," Loingsech replied. "Tell them that we stopped for tea with some pink river dolphins, and they told us they had seen Baudwin heading upriver."

Loingsech laughed, and the crew joined in.

Criofan also laughed, but quickly became downcast. He wasn't sure why, but the news of hearing that Baudwin had been sighted hadn't raised his spirits. *Why am I not overjoyed?* he wondered, glumly. Baudwin was no doubt upstream somewhere, and the river would eventually end, so surely they would find him in a matter of time. How he wished his mood, like the river, would end as well.

Slowly, he made his way to the bow of the ship. Gloomily, he placed his elbow upon the rail and, resting his chin upon his fist, looked out at the Water. Life stood colorless and still — until he saw Loingsech coming toward him.

"What's ailin' ye?" Loingsech asked, as they stood side by side, surveying the scene.

"I wish I knew," Criofan replied. Unable to look Loingsech in the eye, he kept looking outward — and seeing nothing.

Loingsech waited.

Criofan finally spoke. "Baudwin may be safe, but I've already failed him."

"What's that yer sayin'?" Loingsech asked. "You're *here*, are ye not?"

"Baudwin was unjoined long before the rest of us were," Criofan continued. Hearing this, Loingsech seemed startled, yet curious, so Criofan went on. "Whenever he struggled to do something — and he was so hampered by not being able to course with his feelings — I always told him to just try harder. But I didn't see just how hard he *was* trying. I remember a season ago when we were at Topaz Lake, and I wanted him to race me to shore, but he was having a really hard time. He'd been feeling ill earlier in the day, and just wanted to go home. You see, being near the Water sometimes makes him feel ill — no one's sure why."

"Really now — is that so?" Loingsech asked, but he didn't press Criofan too hard for details about Baudwin. Instead, he said, "Please do go on."

"I told him," Criofan continued, "that if he worried less and worked harder, he probably wouldn't have a bout, but now I see how hard-hearted that must have sounded to him. Matha told me to back off, and then I got angry at Matha. I didn't care how I looked to either of them, because I just wanted Baudwin to make *me* look good. Don't you see? I wanted to win the race. And I was using him to win, instead of feeling the pain he was already in. That's how I failed him then — and am *still* failing him now!"

Criofan took a breath. Being unjoined was difficult, and he was less tolerant of those who upset him, but he did notice that he was also oddly more empathetic with those who, like Baudwin, deserved his support.

"I'm sure ye only meant to help him the best ye could," Loingsech said, measuring his tone.

"No!" Criofan, exclaimed, his voice choking with remorse. "At the lake, I should have stood by what he needed from me, not what I *wanted* from him. All those times I dismissed his feelings for not being joined, expecting him to be different than he was or could be."

"Why do ye suppose yer seein' this now?" Loingsech asked, studying him carefully.

"Because now *I'm* not joined," Criofan replied ruefully. "Now I'm just like him — so I can finally feel his pain."

"And why *else*?" Loingsech asked, leaning toward Criofan, his eyes boring wildly into his.

Criofan sensed that Loingsech wanted him to crawl even more deeply into the mire of his anguish, no matter how punishing the journey proved to be. Loingsech, who clawed and fought to survive and provide for his loved ones, knew the value of facing the truth, even when doing so meant risking even greater pain or abandonment by others. Criofan flinched, seeing that what he hadn't shown Baudwin, Loingsech was now showing him — never to turn away from those who suffer, no matter how hobbled they are by their pain.

"Sorry, I can see how hard this is for ye," Loingsech said, his tone gentle, but firm.

Hearing this, Criofan felt his sorrow twist into a searing knot of heartache, which he feared might simply do him in right then and there. Not to mention how he might look to Loingsech if he broke down, sobbing like a helpless Faefry. And yet, perhaps because Loingsech had weathered so many of his own storms, he seemed already steady and untouched by what Criofan might say next. Seeing this, Criofan was determined not to fail again. He would simply tell the truth.

"I'm a *fake*!" he blurted out, stricken with guilt. "As fake as a glass ruby from Gleam. Until I was unjoined, I couldn't even practice the first lesson of the Triquetra — Honesty. But I sure liked to believe I did!" With that, tears streamed from his eyes and down his face. Detecting an emotional exchange, the crew looked to see what all the commotion was about. Seamus, Kelven, Matha, and Lugh looked as well, but stayed where they were. They knew there was nothing they could do. Before their eyes a dam of suffering had burst, and like a circle of forest creatures surrounding a wounded traveler in the Woods, they could only sadly watch, their eyes wide with sympathy.

A smile then crossed Loingsech's face. *Perhaps,* Criofan thought, *he's happy to see me up to my neck in my own mire.*

"What must ye do then, goin' forward?"

"I wish he were here right now," Criofan mused, "so I could just tell him that I understand — and that I'm sorry."

"Ye'll be havin' yer chance."

"Only because I'm not joined!" Criofan exclaimed. "I feel such regret that I had to lose my own current to *finally* feel what Life was like for him. Only now do I understand the first lesson of the Triquetra — that to be honest with others, one must *first* be honest with oneself. I wish I had known this then."

"But now ye *do* know," Loingsech said. "Which is all that matters. Boann unjoined us for this very reason. Only when we learn again what we have forgotten, do we feel all feelins', and see the other in ourselves." Thrusting his finger into Criofan's chest, he added, "And yer doin' splendidly."

"You're being too kind," Criofan replied, chastened.

"Nay!" Loingsech exclaimed. "I'm sure that if Boann herself were here, she'd be overjoyed at yer discovery, and be beamin' with pride at what a fine friend ye *truly* are."

Criofan wasn't so sure. It was a relief to finally admit to someone how he had failed Baudwin, but he wasn't sure where to go from there. If and when he met Baudwin again, he certainly would tell him, but after that, then what? He had learned to be more honest under duress, but wasn't at all certain he would do better otherwise. "Perhaps I'm a little more honest, but I'm not sure of what to do next," he said.

Loingsech placed his arm on Criofan's shoulder and grabbed his chin to meet his gaze. "Ye must find in this what will make ye strong. Forget about bein' more honest. You've been honest. Forget about how ye failed him. Stop hangin' yerself from the yardarm, and figure out what ye must do goin' forward."

Criofan took a breath, as if he was about to take a deep dive into the river. He closed his eyes, searching, and then the answer quickly bubbled up. "I must *care* more, not only about what ailed Baudwin, but about others as well."

"*Care?*" Loingsech asked, smiling. Criofan could feel a deep sense of loyalty in his saltie friend, braced by the courage to face things just as they are.

"Yes," Criofan replied. "I must care for others, not just myself. I cared too much about how Baudwin made *me* feel, instead of caring about how I looked to him."

"How did ye look?"

"Cold and silent too much of the time, when I should have listened to him more and loved him just the way he was."

"So that's what ye'll do," Loingsech replied.

Criofan didn't say anything else. He knew Loingsech was right, and that from now on, whether he was joined or not, he would have to be honest.

Beneath the ceaseless churning of the Timewaker's paddle wheels flowed River Nechtain, meeting the wood and bronze blades like a quicksilver shield. Loch steadied himself upon the deck, studying the expanse of Water with an elven spyglass. Scanning as far as he could, he looked for patches of fog, even though there wasn't a cloud in the sky. Ferrell had heard reports that the fog would come suddenly. Loch imagined finding a bank of fog in defiance of the hot Sun — a miasma with a will of its own. He wondered what would happen if they did run into such a thing. *What swirling strangeness awaits us in the mists?* he wondered.

Being unjoined, Loch's usual confidence had diminished. Sensing his vulnerability, the Grand Eldress had lambasted him for zigging and zagging — turning against the Water, while also speaking of its importance. *Curse her*, he thought, clenching the rail. She had forced him to feel the crooked path he was on, and now he was no longer sure about where he stood with the Water. Added to that, he would also have to learn to withstand its absence — as Baudwin always had — and he wondered if he could. He had a grudging respect for that Guilder, who somehow, despite being unjoined, had even managed to best him at the Hop and Hit. *Perhaps*, Loch thought, *being unjoined will actually make me stronger, and I will rejoin with the Water on _my_ terms.*

Yet no matter how strong he got, he doubted that he could ever equal a spirit like Boann. He was still reeling from what he had seen. There she had been — the one in the mural at the Chamber of Water, leaning over a vaulted well — the one who had also shaped *Teampall Easa*. At the falls she had towered over his kin, and they had all faced an immediate reckoning, for she had unjoined them to punish them for their ignorance. *What power she has*, he marveled, surprised at the depth of his envy. *She'd probably have been unstoppable if Ferrell hadn't caught her off guard.* How he wished he could wield such power! To control the Water was supreme mastery — something he very much wanted for himself.

He remembered Ferrell's description of his triumph over Boann in the drainworks. Ferrell had no doubt managed to find her, but Loch was sure he had exaggerated his victory. He couldn't imagine a being like her devouring anyone. That was the only flaw in Ferrell's story — probably a fabrication to stoke the imagination of the gullible. What exactly had happened there remained a mystery, and Loch was keen on figuring it out.

He wanted to blame Ferrell as much as he did Baudwin for all of this. Perhaps if Ferrell, like Baudwin, hadn't been so insolent, she might have spared everyone such an intolerable burden, but at least Ferrell had dispatched her. *What a marvel those shockers are*, he thought. Ever since he saw the first one, he kept wondering how they were made, and what he could accomplish if he had just a few at his disposal. Ferrell had turned the battle so quickly, and Boann had seemed so weakened and bewildered. As he suspected right along, the Elves were hiding many things from the Faeries — and in this instance, a very powerful weapon. He wanted to know more, but as usual, Ferrell was tight-lipped.

Having nothing left to consider, he peered over the bow at the Water. Unjoined as he was, he couldn't sense the currents the way he always had, and this bothered him to no end. Added to this, he was the only Faery on the ship, and he certainly didn't want the Elves to know of his discomfort. Again Ferrell had placed him in an uncompromising position, and he had also been assigned to lookout duty, because there was no other job for him to do.

Thus far, the Elves had been wary of him. No longer required to accommodate other faery passengers, they gave him little deference, treating him simply as Ferrell's drudge. Often the butt of their derisive jokes, he chose to eat his meals alone, and sleep on top of a pile of ropes. Only the Elve Tárlach had been cordial, trying to make him feel welcome. Loch remembered meeting Tárlach at the falls, when he was measuring the Water for Ferrell, and Ferrell was bossing him around. What a brickbat that Elve was! Trying to avoid Ferrell now, Loch spent more time with Tárlach, who didn't mind talking about the Water, while he cheerfully played with his squirrels, Candy, Bandy, and Dandy.

As Loch continued his rounds, Tárlach stopped him.

"Tell me," Tárlach asked, "do you see any fog ahead? Anything strange on the Water?"

"No, I do not," Loch replied.

"Since the spirit's departure, the water has been unpredictable," Tárlach continued. "I see more eddies than usual."

"There are always more Eddies than I would like," Loch replied, joking. "They always mess with my plans. But you wouldn't understand that, would you?"

"I'm taking about eddies in the water," Tárlach replied. "The ones I measure there."

"And I'm talking about the ones on shore that take measure of *me*, so they can interfere in whatever I do," Loch added, waiting to see if Tárlach got the joke. Tárlach considered Loch's words. His eyes lit up, and he smiled.

I guess he did, Loch thought, nodding at Tárlach. *He's more akin to me than the others, perhaps because he talks so much to his squirrels.*

Loch was impressed with Tárlach's ability to read the Water. He wondered what part of the elven lands he was from, and why he was so unusual.

"If we keep going, the river may become unnavigable for this vessel," Tárlach continued. "And if the spirit's wrath returns, we could even capsize."

"If things get that rough," Loch said, "I'll leave you Elves to your fates, and swim ashore by myself."

"Indeed," Tárlach agreed, chortling. "Better you do that than drown with this lot. You, at least, would likely make it to shore."

Loch hadn't seriously considered that this could occur. Elves were notoriously ill at ease in the Water. He wondered then if he would be thanking the Water for an early release from his servitude. Chuckling out loud, he was struck by the irony of swimming out of the Nechtain, freed, but still unjoined.

"What makes you so different from them?" Loch asked Tárlach, gesturing toward the crew.

"I come from a hamlet beneath Pine Reach, near River Ard Greimme,"[6] Tárlach replied. "I grew up near a tribe of wood Faeries, and they taught me some of their ways."

"So that's why you live alone in the Woods and talk to animals while you measure the Water!" Loch exclaimed. Tárlach grinned, nodding.

"You're full of surprises, aren't you?" Loch said. "I wish the rest of the Elves were more like you."

"Once they may have been," Tárlach said. "Boann was right about one thing — our wills are not as they once were."

"Then you believe she was right?" Loch asked.

"Certainly, for if I hadn't stayed with the wood Faeries, I would never have lived as the other does and watched my will unwind."

Loch couldn't argue with what Tárlach had said. He detected no deception from him, but more questions would have to wait. "I'm sorry to end our conversation, Tárlach, but I must continue my rounds." He left the Elve and headed for the quarterdeck.

Along the way, he noticed several signs on the Timewaker. All had elven letters, and none had glyphs. As a Faery, being able to read letters made him feel less subservient to the Elves and their ways. How he disliked being ordered around by them. He missed being in charge of his band of Roilers — the ones he had been forced to leave behind — and he couldn't help wondering how they were faring without him. They had all been so aimless and unsure of their intentions when he first recruited them, much like the Faeries he had fought for in the Cyhiraeth Quarter. Yet, unlike those wretches, his Roiler band was held together by a greater purpose. Now that he was gone, and without being joined, would they remain true to their intentions, or simply drift away? He had explained to them that the burden of being separated from their currents was Baudwin's fault, but shouldering their futures was up to them.

---

[6] Pronounced [AHRD Gremmeh]

As Loch entered the quarterdeck cabin, he came upon Maeve and Ferrell, squabbling. *Those two are always butting heads*, he thought. For a subordinate, Maeve talked back to Ferrell far too often, and he was surprised to see Ferrell ignore her impudence as much as he did. He couldn't help wondering about Maeve. Surely, she wasn't an ordinary guard. Her bearing and training seemed to suggest she was much more than that, but what, he had no idea. Moving past them, he pretended to be interested in going through the quarterdeck to the stern, but as soon as he got through the rear door, he stopped, then pressed his ear against the wall — listening.

"Traveling to Lake Airmid would take at most seven days," Ferrell said. "We should find him before then."

"We'd better find him before that spirit does," Maeve warned. "And get him to the Clock City."

"That spirit isn't going to find him," Ferrell said.

"How can you be so sure? You said you shot her, and she vanished."

"She *has* vanished," Ferrell replied.

"Where?" Maeve asked, peering intensely at him. "Into the mist? The reports coming down the Nechtain say the fog is thickening, just like the Grand Eldress said it would."

"The shocker did its work."

Ferrell said nothing more, and Loch imagined the two of them eying each other suspiciously. There was certainly more to the story, but Ferrell wasn't telling her what that was.

"I'm sure it did — but how do we stop panic from spreading? Many of the Fae still believe she's at large, and the Elves fear retribution."

"There won't be any."

"Then let's find the lad, and get him to the Clock City."

"No — the Faeries will never accept that!" Ferrell exclaimed. "All of our well-conceived plans would go directly to Annwyn. We'll return him safely to Four Falls, and look like the heroes we must be."

"But wouldn't he be much safer in the Clock City?" Maeve asked. "You saw what she did in Four Falls — tore down our rigging as if it were cobwebs. And we both know she was holding back."

"Yes, but she won't. . ." Ferrell trailed off, absentmindedly.

"Ferrell, your attention seems elsewhere," Maeve snapped. "The Clock City is the safer place."

"We must weigh popular opinion against the safer *unnecessary* solution," he replied. "If we took him to the Clock City, the Faeries would distrust us even more. They already blame us for Boann's wrath."

"Well, if she comes to Four Falls, you can shoot her again with the shocker," Maeve declared. "And they can blame you again — except for the Roilers, who at least seem sympathetic to us."

Loch heard Ferrell scoff. "They remain at the fringe of their tribe. We need to win *all* of them over — Guilders, Eddies, and Roilers — and then our plans will not be foiled."

"That one — Loch — when did he become your fawner?" Maeve asked.

"He's paying off his debt — indentured directly to me."

"Shouldn't he be cracking rocks somewhere?"

"No."

Loch listened — outraged — as Ferrell explained the story of how he had crashed into the food tent at the Engineerium. Maeve began laughing. "My, my! He is *quite* the bold fool, isn't he? I don't know why Govannon chose this course for the Faeries. They all seem totally incapable of accepting our ways, or even behaving civilly."

"Unlike the Elves of Gold Haven, the Clock City sees all the Fae as uniting under Govannon's banner," Ferrell replied.

An uncomfortable silence then ensued, which Loch secretly savored.

"The Elves of Gold Haven still remember their place," Maeve replied icily.

"And what place is that?" Ferrell asked. "Remember why you're here, and whom you serve."

"I never forget," Maeve replied, undaunted by Ferrell's tone. "Gold Haven will find its place again, and we will all rise high under Govannon's new order."

"Good," Ferrell said. "Just don't forget that Govannon is the one to whom we owe our allegiance."

"Yes," Maeve replied. "And you advanced your station by understanding that — didn't you?"

"I know how to serve the Master of Platinum," Ferrell retorted, "unlike those who take the liberty of running *experiments* while they're on duty."

"That's not true —" Maeve began.

"Oh — but it is!" Ferrell exclaimed angrily. "You plied the Faeries in the Cyhiraeth with one of your alchemvoke mixtures. In the report I received, the Assembly said as much — some kind of concoction to make them more docile, so you could relocate them more easily. I also heard that when Govannon learned of your actions, he slammed his fist so hard on his selector that half a dozen of his automatons went haywire."

"There's more to what happened than —"

"Perhaps," Ferrell interrupted. "But that doesn't change what you did. You violated our rules. Only approved technologies are to be shown or used on the Faeries."

"Like wielding shockers in front of the entire elite of Four Falls?" Maeve spat back.

"That was a *unique* circumstance," Ferrell declared. "Govannon has already pardoned me."

"That's no surprise to me," Maeve declared peevishly. "You always *were* his favorite."

"That's because I follow orders," Ferrell snapped. "And you need to follow yours as well. Obey the letter of the law, and keep your personal priorities out of this. Gold Haven will have its time again — don't you worry."

The chatter died down, which suited Loch fine. He had heard enough. Certainly, Maeve was more than just a guard. She seemed to be quite familiar with Ferrell, and when she accused him of being Govannon's favorite, she sounded as if she knew both of them very well. As he made his way to the aft, Loch couldn't stop thinking about what he had just heard. Maeve had plied the Cyhiraeth Faeries with some kind of alchemvoke concoction to calm them down, and for this, he despised her. Of the two, Ferrell seemed more honorable, and he was glad he was indentured to Ferrell and not to her. She would have had him grinding gravel somewhere, toiling in obscurity, instead of being on lookout duty, trying to find Baudwin.

Then there was Baudwin. Out of everyone in Deuona, Boann had chosen him — a good-for-nothing, circle-hopping fool. Baudwin, who, when he was only one hundred, had riled up the honey bees in the Rainbow Glades so mightily that the entire harvest had to be put on hold, while the Faeries spent days calming them down. Baudwin — who had none of his grandfather's wisdom — and had triumphed over Loch in one moment at the Hop and Hit, and in the next moment impulsively voted to support Matter Three. Baudwin, the unreliable one, and now the runaway, who even did such a poor job of that that he dragged everyone along with him.

At least Baudwin isn't here on this ship serving the Elves, like me, he thought. *So I don't have to see his asinine face.*

Loch headed away from the door, this time making his way along the walkway on the starboard side of the quarterdeck. Upon reaching the bow, he saw that they were approaching a bend in the river. He couldn't see very far upriver, but as the Timewaker began to round the bend, he looked through his spyglass and saw something. *That just shouldn't be,* he thought.

On both sides of the sharply narrowing river along the banks, many trees had been felled. Their trunks seemed to have fallen into the Water, but Loch knew this didn't make any sense. If the trees had simply fallen over, many would have landed crowns first into the Water, but the opposite had happened — only trunks had landed there. Even stranger, this had occurred on both sides of the river. Oddly enough, there weren't just a few trees on either side, but stacks of them, layered on top of each other. Coming from both sides of the river, they formed a V shape, stretching out into the Water, blocking the way.

There was little time to take action. Even though the current was against them, the steamway engines propelled the boat with a great deal of force. If they hit the trees at this speed, the hull of the Timewaker would indeed rupture.

"Ahead! Ahead!" Loch shouted, cupping his hands to his mouth. "Something is blocking the way!" he yelled up at the wheelhouse, waving his arms. "Full stop! We're going to crash!"

An Elve in the wheelhouse saw him through the window and began ringing a bell. Soon a foghorn blared, warning the crew. Loch heard a loud *clack* as the throttle slid backwards. The paddle wheels began to turn in the opposite direction, and the Timewaker slowed. Looking ahead, Loch saw that the jutting V of tightly packed trees was getting ever closer. Whoever had blocked the river had done a clever job.

Ferrell was soon abreast of him. "What's the problem?" the Luminary shouted.

"Someone blocked the river!" Loch exclaimed.

Ferrell looked ahead without emotion. *He's as cool as a skunk cornered by a band of coyotes,* Loch thought.

"We aren't stopping fast enough!" Ferrell shouted. "Quickly — come with me! You too!" he barked at Maeve, who had appeared alongside him.

Ferrell shouted up at the wheelhouse, "Signal to the *Beal Inse*! Tell them — full stop!"

An Elve headed to the signal tower. Several more bounded toward the bow of the boat, grabbing boat hooks to stave off the trees that were about to crack open its hull. The engine room engineers had already opened the furnace and were throwing wood into the flames.

"They won't burn fast enough!" Ferrell cried. "We need more fire!"

"She's already at maximum!" an engineer shouted.

"Get the accelerant!" Ferrell shouted back.

The engineer gestured for Ferrell to stop. "If you use too much, the engine could blow," he warned.

"Do it anyway!" Ferrell shouted.

The engineers were deathly still, terrified of what might happen if the plan backfired.

"Just go!" Ferrell shouted. "All of you — out! I'll throw in the charges!"

Soon the engine room was empty, leaving Ferrell, Loch, and Maeve alone with the hissing of the engine, wondering whether Ferrell's plan would doom their mission.

"Open the hatch!" Ferrell shouted to Loch, who quickly yanked a handle on the door. Inside were canvas bundles that looked like small flour sacks, each one marked with an alchemvoke symbol.

Ferrell turned to Maeve. "One or two?" he asked.

"One — then two!" Maeve exclaimed.

"What do you mean?" Ferrell asked.

"Throw one — wait for my signal — then two more," she replied.

Ferrell didn't ask why, as he seemed to implicitly trust Maeve's judgment. The engineers had left the furnace door open, and he put on a pair of goggles. As Ferrell threw a bundle into the furnace, Loch heard a tremendous roar erupt from inside. Ferrell slammed the door shut, and Loch felt heat come pouring out of the bronze work. The pipes were much hotter than Water feeding a boiling hot spring, and the steam more scalding. The searing shift in temperature made him clench his teeth. How he wanted to escape into the river! Soon the rising heat made the venting steam hiss even louder, and then a jolt of force propelled the turbines, making the paddle wheels churn even faster — until the brass bolts on the ship jangled violently. They were almost out of time, and the timbers blocking the passage were approaching the ship like tusks on a boar.

A collision was imminent. Ferrell primed himself to throw in two more bundles.

"Wait!" Maeve shouted.

"There's no time!" he shouted back.

"A little more!"

Maeve looked at the temperature gauge. As the heat increased, the arrow on the dial reached the red line. The charge burned out in the furnace, and the arrow reached the white line again.

"Now!" she shouted.

Ferrell yelled at Loch to pull the latch. He then threw in two more charges and Loch slammed the furnace door shut. As the latch closed, they felt a jolt, and the paddle wheels began rotating even faster. The arrow on the temperature gauge rose sharply, reaching all the way to the top of the red line. The vents on the boiler belched a torrent of black smoke tinged with red, which Loch figured was the color of whatever alchemvoke mixture had been inside the charges.

The boat was now slowing. Bounding to the bow and peering ahead, Loch saw that the starboard side of the bow of the Timewaker was about to ram into the logjam of fallen trees. As he steadied himself, the Elves near him strained to stave them off. Ferrell soon joined them, pole in hand, barking orders. "Brace for impact, Wicks!" he shouted.

Watching Ferrell, Loch shouted, "If we sink, and I save your elven rump, will you free me?"

Ferrell laughed, as he also braced for impact. "You better save hers," he replied, pointing to Maeve. "Everyone knows Gold Haven Elves would rather bathe in the Sun than swim."

Hearing this, Maeve scowled at Loch. "If you do, Govannon will make you the first Roiler Wick."

As the Elves at the bow jammed their boat hooks into the jutting trees, the vessel came to a full stop. In the wheelhouse, the crew shouted with relief.

"Well done, Wicks!" Ferrell exclaimed. "Let's go have a closer look."

They made their way to the bow. On the starboard side of the Timewaker some paint had been stripped off, as the ship had scraped against the cluster of logs. The lower branches on the trees looked to Loch as if they had been sheared off. *How strange*, he thought. Whoever had done this had also skillfully interlocked the remaining branches, hooking the trees together so they'd hold fast. *How clever. But whatever for?* Felling and moving this many trees would have taken a huge team, and he couldn't figure out who stood to gain from the effort. Not to mention the ingenious engineering — the location had been carefully chosen at a sharp bend, where the river narrowed. And the entire construction had been built out from both banks to the center, which was very deep. Whoever had done this had almost managed to block the entire river.

Soon the *Beal Inse* pulled up beside them. The ship was now along one side of the V of trees, and the Timewaker, the other. Seeing Loingsech on the port side of the *Beal Inse*, Loch shouted over to him, pointing at the V formation. "Now we'll have plenty of extra timber for the furnaces!" Loingsech shouted, laughing.

"We'll have to split into two teams to clear the trees," Ferrell yelled. "We'll take this bank, and you take the other."

"So now we have *another* contest?" Loingsech asked.

"Indeed," Ferrell replied, furrowing his brow. "But since there's hardly a chance that you'll beat us, I'll give you a head start. You can load your longboat first."

"We'll not be needin' any head start!" Loingsech shouted, raising his fist at Ferrell.

Loch watched the two crews untie the rigging that held up the longboats on each ship. Two cranes swiveled the boats over the aft paddle wheels, lowering them both into the Water. Soon a crew of Elves sat in one longboat and a crew of Faeries in the other. From afar, Loch saw that Criofan and Matha had joined Loingsech and his crew. Ferrell ordered him, Tárlach, and Maeve to board the longboat on their side.

Once they reached the shore, Ferrell and his crew waded into the river to tie ropes onto the trees so they could unjam the logs. Some of the elven crewmembers carried Vaposaws from the Timewaker. Loch figured Ferrell would beat Loingsech, as the Faeries didn't have saws of their own.

The Vaposaw brattled, and the chains around the guide bars began to rotate.

"Diamond tipped," Ferrell declared, gloating. "We'll be assisting them on their side before evening."

The noisy Vaposaws clattered on. Soon enough, the elven crew had managed to unjam a portion of the logs, tie them with ropes, and pull them to shore. Their job, however, was far from over. Loch assumed they would have to work until nightfall to make the passage navigable. Looking across at Loingsech's crew, he saw that they hadn't made as much progress as the Elves.

On top of the logjam near the shore, Loch noticed something quite peculiar. At first all he could make out was a furry mass, like a muskrat, but much closer in size to a black bear. The mass scampered down the logs, heading right for the crew. Loch saw furry legs, a big snout, and huge reddish teeth. *Of course,* he thought, chiding himself for being so slow to figure out the puzzle. He had gathered pelts from their fallen ones so many times before. *But what are they doing here on the river — so out in the open?* he wondered.

"Beavers!" he yelled to Ferrell. "Beavers!"

Startled, Ferrell looked up. The giant beaver was now close enough to be seen by the crew — two huge rust-colored incisors protruding from a fiercely charming, yet industrious-looking face. "Maeve — look!" Ferrell exclaimed. "We've found our culprits."

Maeve gaped at the beaver. "This is *not* their way," Tárlach informed the group. "Beavers are very shy, and don't dam rivers this large. They live up in the tributaries, making ponds for their dens, which are tucked far away from places like this."

"Why are they doing this," Maeve asked testily.

Before Tárlach could reply, Loch shouted, "Look!"

Near the bank, a dozen or so beavers had crawled onto the logjam and were heading straight for the Elves. Loch saw the same thing happening on the other side of the river — another dozen or so, all heading toward the Faeries. Furiously, the beavers stood on their hind legs, gnashing their teeth and screaming at the crews — a terrible din. An Elve near Loch was unable to dislodge a log that a beaver, weighing at least three hundred pounds, was sitting upon. When he shouted, commanding the creature to move, the beaver let out a piercing whine. Holding his ears in pain, the Elve abruptly quit his task.

On the other side of the river Loch saw that the Faeries weren't faring any better, although they seemed less distressed than the Elves. More at home in the Water, they were trying their best to communicate with the beavers.

"We don't have time for this!" Maeve exclaimed. Grabbing a boat hook from the longboat, she attempted to prod one of the beavers into retreating. Deftly, the creature wrenched the boat hook from her grasp, snapping the pole in two as if it were a toothpick.

"Careful!" Tárlach warned Maeve. "They're very strong, and not the least bit happy that we're trying to tear away their logs."

"Well — I'm not happy with *them*," Maeve retorted. Grabbing a Vaposaw from one of the Elves, she menaced one of the animals. The beaver stared at the spinning blades, barking madly. The Elves were still standing in the water. As she inched closer, the river deepened, and her footing became more precarious.

"Stop her, Ferrell!" Tárlach exclaimed. "We must not harm these creatures."

Loch wondered what Ferrell would do next. He knew the beavers were nothing but a petty nuisance to him, but harming them would surely alienate the Faeries. Even the Elves didn't generally take such measures, unless they were under extreme duress.

"Stop!" Ferrell shouted to Maeve. She pretended not to hear him.

"I said — stop!" he shouted, this time so loudly that Loch couldn't believe she would continue with her insolence.

Maeve relented, and turned off the Vaposaw. "Well then, how do you propose to make these beasts move?" she asked.

"With my superior dexterity — of course," Ferrell replied. Grabbing another boat hook from the longboat, he carefully climbed on top of the logs and moved toward the beavers. There were many of them, and Loch admired Ferrell's courage for approaching them this way. He saw Ferrell's tactic. Lined up on the log as they were, they couldn't attack him all at once.

"Show them, Ferrell!" some of the crew cried out to him. "Send them back to where they came from!"

The Luminary struck a beaver on the shoulder. The blow had little effect upon its thick, tough skin. The beaver growled, barring its teeth.

Ferrell deftly struck again. The beaver snapped at the boat hook, but Ferrell avoided the giant incisors, landing a blow to its front leg. "Hurrah!" cried his crew. But just as Ferrell seemed as if he might be able to drive the beaver away, Loch noticed that some of the others had slipped off the log, under the Water, out of sight.

Skillfully, Ferrell had forced the beaver to retreat, but suddenly, a number of them shot out of the water near him. One mounted the log behind him, and another came at him from the side, below him.

"Behind you!" Maeve shouted.

Before Loch could blink, Ferrell pivoted, placed the tip of his boat hook into the log, and vaulted over the beaver. Retreating down the logs, he rejoined his crew. Most were now in the water. On the other side of the river, Loch could see the Faeries still vainly trying to communicate with the beavers.

"Your superior dexterity saved you, but unfortunately it also rallied the beavers," Maeve declared, laughing. Ferrell glared at her.

Before Ferrell could act again, the beaver colony made their next move. They swam right up to the crew and slapped tails — the size of tabletops — upon the water, sending out an ear-splitting shockwave. Instantly, everyone covered their ears. Ferrell ordered them to hold fast, but they were too overwhelmed to obey his command. They stumbled out of the river as fast as they could. The beavers seemed delighted, as their angry screaming turned into a cacophony of chuckles.

Ferrell retreated, bounding down the logs. "Everyone — back onto the longboat," he called out. "I have an idea." The Elves had loaded the longboat and were heading back to the Timewaker. The beavers stopped slapping their tails, and barked happily to each other as they began undoing the damage the Elves had done to their barrier.

On the other side of the river, Loch could see the Faeries trying their best to talk to the beavers. They swam up to them, offering tree buds and hoping to coax them into coming closer. All their attempts failed, as the beavers remained mistrustful. Seeing this, they fetched Seamus and Lugh to help reassure the animals, but their efforts also failed.

Ferrell was now ready to put his next plan into action. Once aboard the Timewaker, he ordered some of his crew to tie ropes to the bow. He then threw the ropes to the Elves in the longboat. "Tie each one to a log!" he shouted, pointing to the logjam.

As soon as the Elves had tied all the ropes to the logs, Ferrell shouted up to the wheelhouse, "Reverse — steady and slow — and then giver 'er all you got!"

The paddle wheels dug into the river, and the Timewaker began to move backward. The slack lessened more and more, until the ropes pulled tight and the heavily laden steamboat bellowed black steam.

Loch wasn't sure that Ferrell's plan would work. The beavers had done an impressive job of interlocking all the trees, and he worried that the ropes would snap. But a small part of the V began to give way, and the river currents swirled.

"It's working!" Maeve shouted.

Ferrell looked at his handiwork, satisfied. "Good!" he shouted back. "This is the best solution."

"We should thank the metals that *he's* here," Tárlach declared, glaring at Maeve. She ignored him.

Further down the logs, the beavers glowered at Ferrell, their whiskered faces disapproving of what he had just accomplished. A troop of them bounded down the logs, paws front, legs back. They screamed at the Timewaker and then jumped into the water.

Loch couldn't see where they had gone, presumably beneath the logjam. As the Timewaker continued to reverse, some of the logs were pulled apart, but then one of the ropes attached to a log came loose. Angrily, Ferrell pulled up the loose rope and saw that the end had been gnawed off.

"They're biting the ropes off — underneath!" he shrieked.

There was nothing they could do. Helplessly they watched as every rope was quickly severed. The forceful shift in tension made the Timewaker list to the port side. Maeve screamed, and several of the crew went flying across the deck. Under the water, the Beavers remained safely out of reach, having completed their task.

"Full stop!" Ferrell commanded, as the paddle wheels came to a halt.

"They'll ruin whatever we do!" Maeve shouted, as she scrambled to her feet. "We have only one choice. Get the shockers."

Ferrell looked askance at Maeve. Loch didn't know that the Elves had brought shockers. Until now, the secret had been kept very well, something Ferrell obviously preferred. "That is *completely* out of the question!" he exclaimed.

"They won't pass to Annwyn, if we set the dials low," Maeve insisted.

Ferrell paused to consider the idea, and then Tárlach spoke. "Ferrell — please. You must not allow her to do that to them! They may not pass away, but the shock will addle them even more. They're *already* so distraught."

"And why is that?" Ferrell asked.

Tárlach paused. "I can't be sure why they won't speak to us, but I know they're doing this because they're frightened — feeling a deep terror. Shocking them would upset them even more, and I don't know what else they might do. We must respect their fears — not add to them."

"But what other choice do we have?" Ferrell asked.

"There *is* another way," Tárlach replied. "Something even *she* will accept — I'm sure. We can feed them beaver brew. They'll calm down and go back to their lodges to sleep. Being awake during the day is unnatural for them. They're creatures of the Moon."

"*Beaver* brew?" Ferrell asked, perplexed.

"Yes," Tárlach replied, happy to see Ferrell's interest in his plan. "Near my home there are many beavers. They're always trying to build dams where I take measurements, so I give them beaver brew to calm them down. Then I can lure them away to other parts of the river. When they're drunk on brew, they can't resist the lure of birch bark laced with sweet-vine."

"And you can make this beaver brew — here?" Ferrell asked.

"Of course," Tárlach replied. "We only need to gather the roots and herbs. They're abundant in these parts. We'll brew them a batch, and then see what happens."

"That's only more lost time," Maeve argued peevishly.

Ferrell studied the Faeries, who had already given up on their side and were boarding the *Beal Inse*. They looked at the Timewaker, chuckling at the gnawed-off ropes dangling from its bow, and the beavers barking at them from the bank.

The Luminary considered both of his choices, and then made his decision. "Very well," he announced. "Let's tell Loingsech about this new plan so we can spread out to gather the herbs more quickly. This, I believe, is our best option."

Loingsech and the Faeries quickly warmed to the idea. Many joked about how the beavers had bested Ferrell, saying they had outsmarted him at every turn, and how Ferrell's swordsmanship had been no match for their gnashing, six-inch incisors. Now, the only way he could save face was by looking as if he had their best interests at heart. As the group met ashore to go searching for the herbs, Lugh called out to the beavers:

"Conquerors of the Elves — I salute you!"

"We needed ye at the siege!" Loingsech shouted.

Everyone let out a chorus of howls and guffaws. The Elves pretended not to hear. Maeve busied herself on the riverbank with Tárlach, attaching a bronze cauldron for brewing to a cooking stand. They had already collected kindling and chopped a pile of logs from the fallen trees. Seeing that Maeve had finished her work, Loch decided to seize the moment. Ever since he had overheard her conversation with Ferrell on the Timewaker, she had been an even greater puzzle to him. She didn't seem beholden to Ferrell, making her the only Elve of the crew who wasn't. He could sense that she had her own plans, which meant her authority had to come from someone higher than Ferrell. This could mean only one thing. He then decided to learn more about her.

"What got you interested in Alchemvoke?"

"I suppose I can tell you," Maeve replied coyly, looking up from her cauldron. "You don't strike me as an informant."

Loch stared back at her, bemused.

"When I was young one, I had a pet rabbit named Radish. She was white with reddish spots, a gift from my father. Father expected me to work very hard, but could also tell that I needed a companion, as he was frequently attending to his duties in Gold Haven. I often played with Radish in my garden, and although I couldn't speak to her like Faeries do, I nevertheless felt very close to her. I was her sole guardian in the realm, and she was my best friend."

Maeve paused for a moment, sadness crossing her face.

"Then one day Radish grew ill. Rabbits don't whine the same way other animals do, so I was late to discover her sickness. She stopped eating, and I couldn't make her drink. Abruptly, my father decided that her time had come, but I was determined to save her. Against his orders, I wrapped her in her special blanket, left home, and took her to the apothecary."

As Maeve told her story, Tárlach paid close attention, and Loch noticed other ears in the group were also turned to her.

"The apothecary told me that Radish showed all the signs of having been poisoned, and asked me about my garden. Eventually we concluded that she had nibbled on some widow vine — a weed common to Gold Haven — which is poisonous. There was, however, an antidote, but only if it was given quickly."

Tárlach, who had been hanging upon her every word, then asked, "Surely you were there in time?" Sitting upon his shoulders, Candy, Bandy, and Dandy gave worried chirps.

Maeve shook her head. "No, I was not. Radish passed to Annwyn and I blamed myself. If only I'd had the means to create my own antidote, I could have saved her. That is what attracted me to Alchemvoke, and of course I should note that my father always had an interest in such things. He is, after all, a high-ranking member of the Assembly of Progress, and an alchemvoke engineer."

"Did you train to become an apothecary?" Loch asked.

"My studies in Alchemvoke cover many topics, both in medicine and explosives. I was also inclined to learn how to create elven inventions, such as Sky Sparks and charges, and learn the formulas for their production. My father approved most of those things," Maeve said.

"I would never have suspected that there was such a soft-centered reason for your ambitions," Loch said. "When you were climbing up that signal pole, it seemed like all you wanted to do was go as high as you could — as fast as you could."

Maeve ignored Loch's comment.

Sharply, Tárlach rapped a wooden spoon against the lid of the cauldron. "Well, if you cared so much for that rabbit, then I would hope you'd do the same for these beavers," he said crossly.

"My rabbit would never bar my path, or try to slice me in two with its teeth," Maeve fired back.

"Still, you should care the same for *all* animals," Tárlach said, wagging his finger at her.

"I'm sure she will," Ferrell chimed in. "And thanks to you, we have a plan to help her get there. Now please, let's get a move on — everyone to their assigned group. Let's cover the ground quickly, get what we need, cook up the brew, and then hopefully, be underway tomorrow morning. Baudwin awaits us."

They moved in squads. Loch was in one group with Ferrell, Matha, Seamus, and Tárlach, while the other group had Loingsech, Criofan, Lugh, Kelven, and Maeve. The remaining crew stayed to guard the camp and the ships.

All had been given instructions to find black alder bark, chamomile, sage, lavender, and the last ingredient, bone truffles, which grow only in the roots of the white oak. Tárlach informed them that finding most of the ingredients wouldn't be hard, but he had some concern about the bone truffles. They had to keep their eyes peeled for a white oak.

Loch liked being on land again, as he hadn't been back in the forest since he left Deuona. He was quick to spot a deer trail, and so they all went behind him single file. Luckily, the trail moved up a ridge that had several white oak trees. Loch scanned their trunks looking for knots that indicate the presence of bone truffles, but didn't see any. The trees above them formed a canopy of green, golden afternoon Light spilling through, and the moist smell of moss filled the Air. He then spotted a black alder, and soon they were stripping away its bark, and picking pieces up off the ground.

"Fill the bags up — there's a lot of brew to be made," Tárlach instructed.

Ferrell put some bark into a sack and then spoke. "Tell me, Tárlach, do you ever miss *Tír Luí Lucharachán*? You've lived here for so long now."

Tárlach, who still had his pet squirrels hopping about on his shoulders, didn't hesitate. "No, I like *Tír Éirí Sióg* better, especially here. The land feels calmer, even in the wilds, and I can be just as I truly am more easily."

"But don't you miss your family?" Ferrell asked. "And all the elven festivals, food and games, and the parades? The crafting holidays and the invention competitions are so exciting — nothing like here. Besides that, you're smart enough to rise high in the Assembly, should you ever choose to do so."

Tárlach just shook his head. "Such competitions hold no interest for me. I'm content, and I like a simple life. Besides, Candy, Bandy, and Dandy would be crestfallen if they had to leave their forest behind."

Ferrell finished stuffing another bag with bark. "I've never felt at home here. If I had to live in a forest, I would go back to the Chinewilds."

Seamus, who had been listening, then asked, "You're from the Chinewilds?"

"Yes," Ferrell replied. "An even wilder place than this, and much more dangerous."

"What's so different?" Seamus asked.

"The Chinewilds are like living on the back of a porcupine. Yes, this place is wild, but there, boars are as tall as we are. Just one charge and their tusks will end you. Not to mention the great shale hills that will slice you to pieces should you fall, and wind that rips through the valley so brutally cold that it will crack your teeth on a winter's night. This place is too soft for me."

"And are *we* so soft?" Seamus asked. "You seem to believe that we water Faeries haven't a care in the world, and that all we do is just swim about, sucking on sweet-vine all day long."

"I know you can be a tough lot when you have to be, but you seem to be living a more cosseted life than I have."

Seamus then took stock of Ferrell as if he were seeing him for the first time. Intensely, he peered at him, and Loch wondered what the Guild Leader would say next. "The problem with *you*," Seamus began, "is that you don't strike me as loving anything in your Life, except for following the orders of that Assembly of yours."

Ferrell cinched his bag closed, his fingers tight. "Indeed," he replied, "I have loved."

"You have?" Seamus asked. "Yet, not anymore?"

"No," Ferrell replied. "Not for a long time. With the Befalling, I too, lost a great deal."

"Is that so?" Seamus asked. "I did as well, and of course, as you know, so did Baudwin, who took us upon this course."

"He told me his story," Ferrell said. "And I offered him my help."

"And you're sincere?" Seamus asked.

"Yes," Ferrell replied. "I gave him my word — and I keep my promises."

Seamus nodded at Ferrell. "Well then, good. The last thing we need is for Baudwin's heart to be broken again. When the time comes, I would like to hear more about your loss."

Ferrell agreed that at a more opportune time he would share his story with Seamus. Loch wondered what Seamus was trying to pry out of Ferrell. Perhaps, he thought, Seamus only wanted to be sure that he could trust him.

Soon they reached the top of the ridge. Above them the sky was an open vault of blue, with wisps of clouds streaking into a vast tapestry of white and gold. Before them was a large meadow. Seeing this, Tárlach became quite excited.

"Chamomile flowers!" he exclaimed. "Gather what you can — quickly."

They filled more sacks, and Loch then suggested that they go back and see what the other party found.

"We still need bone truffles!" Tárlach, exclaimed, agitated. "They're the most important ingredient."

"We'll have to look on the way back," Loch replied. "Let's go."

As they made their way down the ridge, a falcon dove behind the crest of a hill. Looking toward the top, Loch spied a stand of white oaks he hadn't seen earlier.

"I see some white oaks," he said, as they all joined him. "Let's take a closer look."

"I see some knots!" Matha exclaimed, approaching the oaks. Quickly, he made his way to the base of the largest, then stopped, stooping over. As Loch made his way to him, Matha was already at work, digging into the ground with a spade. He turned around smiling, holding a bone truffle in his hand.

"We're in luck," Tárlach said. "Let's gather more and get to brewing."

Back at camp they met the other group, who had also succeeded in finding the ingredients, except for the bone truffles. All had been waiting and worrying until Loch informed them that they had found some. Everyone was relieved, and soon Maeve and Tárlach were busy lighting a fire beneath the cauldron and adding the ingredients. As the water boiled into a grey-brown froth, the stewing bark filled the air with an earthy aroma. Tárlach then added the bone truffles, and a stronger odor wafted into their noses, one that smelled more like musky limes, with a chestnut aftertaste.

"We must let this brew overnight," Tárlach began, "so we can attend to the beavers in the morning and then be on our way."

"*All* night?" Maeve asked, annoyed. "Surely there must be a way to speed this up."

"There's no need to do that," Tárlach explained. "We have nothing to gain by rushing things."

Maeve kept arguing with Tárlach, until Ferrell told her to stop. Having been mixed with great care, they left the brew to simmer, and then began to set up camp on shore, so they could guard against any unwanted visitors. After the Sun had set, the campfires were their only illumination, except for a few glowstone lamps brought from the *Beal Inse*.

Everyone sat in a circle around the largest fire. At first, smoke wafted toward them, but then Maeve sprinkled some powder onto the fire. The flames flared up and the smoke thinned, blowing straight up into the air, allowing everyone to move closer to the heat.

Their spirits were now lighter, as most believed that Tárlach's plan would work. In just a few hours, they would wake up, feed the beavers, board their boats, and head back upriver. Feeling unusually chipper, the Elves brought out their flutes, drums, and various other instruments, which they began to play — vibrant tunes that made them stomp their boots into the dirt. Some even danced around the circle, locking arms, singing, and laughing. The Faeries joined in, and for a time the pain of being unjoined lessened and all of their cares were forgotten. Loch remembered that the last time he danced was at the important meeting. He and Baudwin had argued about Magniglow, and Baudwin had accused him of being afraid to face the Darkness in his own heart. Mulling that comment, which had stayed with him, he looked down at his feet, moodily scratching marks into the ground with a twig.

"Whatever is the matter?" Seamus asked him.

"I was just remembering the important meeting," Loch replied, "when I traded harsh words with Baudwin."

"Ah yes," Seamus said. "I remember as well. You two were so consumed with anger, you forget about *gnàs*."

"Yes," Loch replied, "and now that we're all unjoined, I'm wondering if our arguments about Magniglow and its proper uses were beside the point."

"Being unjoined has also made me consider some things differently," Seamus said. "And I imagine the same is true for you."

Loch could see Seamus was being affable, so he reciprocated. "As a Roiler, I've been at odds with the Guild, and I still am. I want more change, and you want less, but I also wonder if this new path we're on will twist our fates in ways we never could have imagined."

Seamus furrowed his brow. "You mean what Boann told us at the falls, don't you?"

"Yes," Loch replied. "She challenged us to live as the other does, and Baudwin told me I wasn't facing the Darkness in my own heart. Now I can see that if I do face that Darkness, I could live as the other does. Perhaps all of us were unjoined to help us decide what stand to take."

Hearing this, Seamus gave Loch a friendly slap on the back. "You may be onto something, lad. Boann is showing us the way, and there will probably be far more pressing matters ahead than squabbles over Magniglow."

Sitting on a log next to Lugh, Loingsech chimed in, "Aye, she sure be leadin' us — that's her way."

"But to where?" Loch asked. "I believed in the promise of the Elves and Magniglow, but now all of that seems beside the point."

Ferrell then cut in, saying, "Magniglow will have a place no matter where this adventure leads."

Maeve, who was sitting across from them with Ferrell, nodded. "The Four Branches are our future. This is but a diversion."

"Perhaps," Seamus replied. "But if I've learned one thing — right now — nothing is for certain."

Implicitly, the Elves seemed to agree, and all went silent for a few moments as the fire crackled.

Seamus then turned to Ferrell, saying, "Please tell me and the rest of us, if you don't mind, more of your story. I'm curious to know about your triumphs and your losses in the Great Befalling."

Ferrell didn't shy away from the question. Instead, he replied eagerly, and Loch took this to mean that he simply wanted another chance to promote the

Assembly. "I served under Govannon, from before Belanus fell, until the Great Befalling," he began.

Seamus and the others leaned toward him, listening intently.

"In the siege of the Clock City, the future of the realm was decided," Ferrell continued. "We had fought valiantly against Belanus's army, pushing his forces back from the Clock City, as their directive had been to raze the city to the ground. By then, we had suffered many losses. We defended Govannon because we believed he had the right to build the city, and create a monument to the Rise of Time. The Rise was our business — not theirs — and the council that hailed from Gold Haven had ruled unfairly that the city was unlawfully built. I remember fighting in the spring. The ground was muddy, miring us in place, and as we clashed, a brown sludge churned beneath us. The earth then began to sprout blades of grass, as the fallen passed to Annwyn. With so many departing, their life force had fertilized the ground. As thousands disappeared before our eyes, only tattered clothing and empty armor remained. One of our banners had fallen into the sludge, and I remember a young Elve from Green Plain running to prop the pole back up. For his trouble, he was impaled with arrows, but the banner stood high."

As Ferrell stared ahead, his eyes were bright with the light of the fire and the tale he was telling.

"We believed we could keep them at bay," he continued. "The Clock City was in the early stages of construction, but we assumed our outer fortifications and rations were sufficient for a siege. But then, enemy reinforcements came from *Tír Éirí Sióg*, and everything changed. The Faeries had joined Belanus, wearing their battle colors and wielding the spears they favored so highly. A spear, which is much like a quarrel staff, could often win against a sword given its length, and the Faeries were experts at wielding them. At the time I regret not having taken them more seriously. There hadn't been an incursion of so many from *Tír Éirí Sióg* in many hundreds of years, going far back to the time when Bethaill[7] ruled from Mist Valley."

Loch shot a glance at Lugh, who smiled knowingly at Ferrell's admission. Ferrell ignored them both. "They clashed against our eastern flank," he continued, "and we began to buckle. The ground around the outer fortifications was bare earth, and the Faeries were nimble in the mud with their lighter armaments. Their spears gave them leeway to better choose their engagements. We also had spears, but not as many, and our greatest asset, our horse riders, had already been decimated. Back then we didn't yet wield magniglow shockers, and the Four Branches were still being organized by our master engineer, Sprin."

---

[7]   Pronounced [BEV-el] former Queen of the Elves

Loch had never heard of Sprin before, and he wondered who this genius was — the one who had made so much possible that the Elves now took for granted.

"They pushed us back to the inner-city gates," Ferrell continued. "The walls were still unfinished, but we had placed several rows of spikes into the ground to cover exposed areas, and so we refortified ourselves, and by doing so, the difference in the size of our forces meant less. They had only a few ways to breach the walls, unless they attempted to clear the spikes and risk volleys of arrows. They had to attack us on our terms, and the ground in the inner city was much firmer, with even stone to stand on. We were in a better position, but all we had done was to buy ourselves time."

Ferrell paused to fully take in the memory, before speaking again. The fire flickered brightly, and the group waited, as silent as the trees around them.

"It was then that Govannon turned to me," Ferrell said. "I remember him now. His uniform was in shambles, pocked with mud and blood, and half his forces were gone. We were stuck in defense of a hopeless siege, but he was somehow unconcerned. He had caught wind of something, and had a plan that he seemed completely confident of — so much so that he simply looked at me and told me that he was leaving his remaining forces in my hands. He intended to slip by the enemy with nothing but an honor guard and bring reinforcements from the towns around the Fallen Peaks and the Chinewilds."

"Why not just send messengers?" Loch asked, mesmerized by Ferrell's story.

"Although those towns were sympathetic to him," Ferrell replied, "they also believed our cause was hopeless, which meant he had to go there personally to persuade them. I'm sure there was something he wasn't telling us, so he just left, and I had to hold out through many more days and nights. It was easily the most exhausting battle I've ever known. I didn't think we would prevail."

"But ye *did*," Loingsech said. Loch sensed that despite the animosity Loingsech held for the Luminary, he nevertheless appreciated hearing the tale.

"Yes, we did," Ferrell went on, "although we were brought to the breaking point. Our morale was being cut down as if a scythe were slicing through a field of wheat. They were hauling logs and constructing siege machines outside, and we could only watch — hopelessly — as, nail by nail, they ensured our impending doom."

Ferrell paused again, this time drawing in his breath ever so slowly, until it seemed as if he might simply merge — without resistance — into the stillness of the night.

"And then from out of nowhere," he continued, "we felt a great shock pass through our ranks — one I had never felt in all my years, and hope to never again. At first I thought the Faeries had effected a clever ruse." As he spoke,

Ferrell hunched toward the fire, clutching his chest with his arms, his eyes closed. "I remember vividly — standing upon a high wall, one of the few that was nearly built. I clutched my chest, steeling myself and almost falling over the battlement. After that, I could barely tell what was going on, but I do remember looking at the enemy ranks and seeing that they too were in disarray."

"Yes!" Seamus exclaimed. "We *all* felt the shock. The shock that hit everyone throughout all of *Tír na nÓg* that day."

"Indeed," Ferrell replied. "The shock stopped the entire battle. No one was untouched. We had all lost our senses, and were rendered feeble and confused. I remember raising my sword, wondering what use it could possibly have. I had forgotten why I was even there. In the days that followed, I could barely remember to eat, drink, or sleep."

"Was that the Great Befalling?" Loch asked.

"Most definitely," Ferrell replied. "You would have been too young to remember, or perhaps not yet sprung from the aethers, but when the stupor finally lifted, Govannon returned soon thereafter with reinforcements, and immediately took the initiative. A siege is very easy to break when attacked from the rear. He could have routed them with half the troops he brought. Govannon won the day."

Hearing this, Maeve pumped her fist in the air, exclaiming, "After that, Govannon saw that the future was ours! The Great Befalling was actually a gift to us."

"*Was* it, though?" Ferrell asked. "After that, we were never the same. We were severed from something — from what, no one could say — not unlike the way in which the water Faeries are now unjoined, but, back then, all the Fae — both Elves and Faeries — suffered a similar plight."

Loch had never been satisfied with the explanations he had heard of the Great Befalling, and now seized the opportunity to learn more. "But *how*?" he asked. "The elders never give us straight answers. What changed so much?"

At first there was no response, and Loch wondered why. The Elves were all reticent, and the Faeries, oddly disengaged.

Kelven, who had been gazing at the stars, then faced the group. Haltingly, he found the words. "Before the Great Befalling there was a greater sense of oneness without distinction. I used to feel this the most when I gazed upon the shimmering green auroras that sometimes painted the night sky."

"I've never seen those," Loch said.

"They vanished after the Great Befalling," Kelven added.

Loingsech spoke, "Aye, those auroras were of the Great Emerald Light, dancin' in the sky."

"The Great Emerald Light?" Kelven asked.

"Aye," Loingsech affirmed. "The Great Emerald Light wasn't somethin' that most could touch, but everyone felt its presence — the vital source that held our realm together, givin' us wisdom that was beyond words. When the Great Befallin' struck, we sensed that the door to that wisdom had been slammed shut. After that, everyone suffered the absence of this vital force, which we had taken for granted for far too long."

Pondering Loingsech's words, Kelven nodded his head.

Rian then added, "You must be speaking of the *Dúrúnghlas*."

Loch could see how perplexed the Elves were, except for Rian, but the Faeries, especially Loingsech, also nodded their heads, and so Loingsech continued. "They be one and the same — the *Dúrúnghlas and* the Great Emerald Light. You Elves have yer way of talkin' about it, and we have ours. Thousands of years before your smiths were smithyin' and studyin' Glamorium, the Great Emerald Light, or the *Dúrúnghlas* as you say, would grant them a vision of oneness without distinction and then place them on a quest. On Baranthus, we still revere the Great Emerald Light. Once we held great rites to commune with Glamorium, before the shrines were shattered and the rites forgotten."

Loch wanted to know more. "But why did the shrines shatter, and how did the Great Befalling make the Great Emerald Light vanish?"

"Nobody knows," Kelven replied. "Most of what we do now is to commune with the Water. Just as we are now unjoined from our currents, so too did the Great Befalling wrench us away from a mystery that held the hope of great joy and bliss."

"Yes, but what *was* it?" Loch asked.

Again, Loingsech tried to explain. "As Kelven said — oneness *without* distinction. Long ago, when we were imbued with the Great Emerald Light, the Elves didn't wield their metals like swords, and the Faeries didn't wield their elements like shields. Faeries and Elves have often had difficulty getting along, but back then, I believe that the Great Emerald Light helped us to overlook what we saw as differences. But then came a long decline, capped by the Great Befallin', which made our loss permanent."

"The Elves have *always* wielded swords," Maeve scoffed.

"Yes, but over time the wieldin' has become less about swordplay and more about upholdin' our differences, by fightin' about what we believe we are and what we believe we are not," Loingsech said.

Hearing this, Maeve cooled herself, as she seemed to be out of her depth. To Loch, what Loingsech said rang true. He also saw that Loingsech's words were not completely lost on the rest of the Elves.

Ferrell stirred himself to speak. "In the past, conflicts rose up like great fires, ignited by lightning — fires that burned the forest to ashes, so that the soil beneath our feet would again become fertile. Now we don't abide by the natural order. Instead of waiting for lightning to strike, and allowing the forests to naturally burn themselves out, we light our own fires."

"Even worse," Kelven added, "evermore, we light Fires by fighting to change others — so they will believe what *we* believe."

Loingsech continued, "We once revered the elements and the metals, and didn't allow them to create a split between us." Loingsech leaned closer to Ferrell. "For ye see, underneath it all, I'm more than a water Faery, and *you* are more than a Master of Gold."

"I've never heard it explained in this way," Kelven said. "Truly, you Baranthus Faeries are unusual."

Loingsech continued, "Long before the Great Befallin', we knew very well that the roles we were given were not all that we were. But now that the Great Emerald Light is lost, we all be taken in more easily by appearances."

To Loch's surprise, Ferrell then joined in. "Something closed forever on that day. After that, I remember very well that the Elves seemed more driven in their efforts, and somehow more dense, like glowing ingots being folded in on themselves."

"And they were *meaner*," Lugh remarked.

"And the Faeries?" Maeve asked, arching her brows.

"The Faeries seemed more scattered in their efforts, as if they were disappearing, like dandelion puffs floating in the wind," Seamus replied.

"Which was very good for the Elves, and the Grand Endeavor," Maeve chortled. "The Faeries were *weaker*."

Hearing this, everyone fell silent.

"Which reminds me, we have an endeavor that we must deal with tomorrow — the beavers," Seamus said.

Loch remained unsatisfied. "But, what caused it all to happen?"

"You ask too many questions," Ferrell snapped. "My belief is that the Great Emerald Light broke of its own accord, after the Fae underwent a long decline that ended in a terrible battle."

Hearing this, Seamus shook his head, but didn't offer anything more.

"Some things simply cannot be explained," Rian added.

Loingsech chimed in, "Yes — no explanation, and I wouldn't look to the Elves for deep answers. The secrets of the Great Emerald Light certainly aren't known by the Assembly, or a brainy oil-sniffing tool-licker like Govannon!"

"Watch your tongue," Maeve snapped.

"Enough!" Seamus exclaimed. "We didn't come all this way to fight over the Great Befalling. Tomorrow we feed the beavers, and then we'll go and find Baudwin."

Chapter 34

THE SHRINE OF THE NECHTAIN

Matha awoke the next morning, bundled up in his bedroll. There hadn't been any disturbances during the night, but as he got up, he heard Ferrell dressing down one of his guards.

"Spark!" Ferrell shouted. "The fog has come — why didn't you raise the alarm?"

Matha looked about in the dim morning Light, and noticed that a thin fog had entered the camp, creeping over the trees and tents.

"I'm sorry, sir," a guard with the rank of Spark replied to Ferrell. "The layer was so thin — nothing like what we saw in Four Falls — that I assumed it wasn't the foul brume of Boann."

Matha suspected that the Spark might be right, but Ferrell seemed especially concerned, as had everyone else, about running into any kind of fog. Boann's warning had indeed been ominous. Apprehensively, he remembered her words:

"The Water wills, the Fae divide for worse,

Whence comes the fog, will they know their curse!"

The Elves were dismissive, but Matha knew the Faeries were filled with trepidation about what would have happened at Four Falls had Boann's curse fully taken hold. Nor could he imagine the Fae banding together in the case of a dire circumstance. *Far too often,* he thought, *we divide for worse, because we would rather fight about who is right than simply try to do better.*

"Fool!" Ferrell barked at the Spark. "My instructions were clear. Any sight of the fog — awaken everyone!"

The Spark hung his head, and Ferrell said no more. *If there is to be a punishment,* Matha thought, *Ferrell will no doubt mete it out later.*

"Everyone — up!" Ferrell ordered. "A fog is coming in!"

Soon everyone in the camp was awake, stretching and shuffling about. Lugh, Seamus, and Kelven readied themselves, resigned to another day of worry and struggle. After removing his sleeping hat, Rian took a salt biscuit from a tin and began nibbling the edges. Matha saw that Criofan had already put his boots on, and was eying Maeve, who had just come bursting into camp a moment earlier. Criofan studied her suspiciously as she stuffed something into a bag. *Perhaps some kind of herbs,* Matha thought, gazing across the smoldering Fire at her. He could tell that Criofan was wondering the same thing — where had she been in the early morning hours, and why hadn't she informed the guards about the fog?

As if aware that she was being scrutinized, Maeve announced, "The fog is thin — just a haze before the Sun embraces the realm."

Ferrell scowled. "If you're wrong," he declared, "our clothes could be empty piles before the day is over."

Hearing this, Loingsech squinted his eyes, waiting, a carrot sticking out of his mouth. Carefully he studied the fog — like a sailor looking far out to sea from the deck of a ship. Still clenching the carrot between his teeth, he responded, "Ithhsss thiickennenn."

"What?" Ferrell asked, annoyed.

Ferrell waited impatiently as Loingsech chewed and swallowed the carrot. "It's *thickenin'*," he repeated. "We must hurry. If this be Boann's fog, then we've brought her wrath upon us. From now on, instead of dividin' for worse, we must try to live as the other does — impossible as that may seem."

"And how *exactly* are we supposed to live as the other does?" Ferrell asked.

"Well, for now, by tryin' not to disrespect one another. That will likely keep the fog at bay, for since we treated *her* with disrespect, she's been keen on teachin' us a lesson with her curse."

Matha then remembered what Baudwin had said about Boann the first time he had met her at the dam. *She must also have sent the gusher at the Springs of Coventina,* he thought, *to teach us a lesson.* Nothing else made sense. "What he says is true!" he exclaimed. "When I was with Baudwin at a shrine near the Springs of Coventina, she sent a gusher at us when we started fighting — fighting with *you,*" he added, turning to Loch. "And I tell you this now — further discord will only bring about more suffering."

Loingsech nodded his head, and Matha saw a look of recognition cross Loch's face.

Maeve was not impressed with Matha's admonition. "You think she's trying to teach us something, but I say she simply wants to destroy us," she snapped. "Her fog doesn't scare me!"

"Well, ye *should* be scared!" Loingsech said, his temper flaring. "Since the happenin's at the falls, the fog may have faded once she fled, but now it's comin' back, probably stronger than before — and wilder."

Maeve scoffed, but Matha could tell that Ferrell had a better measure of the situation. "Spirits are unpredictable!" Ferrell exclaimed. "Never forget that — *Mantle,*" he added, glaring at Maeve. "If this fog is hers, then it is following her will. To be prudent, we should cooperate with one another. None of us like being disrespected, spirits most of all."

"I don't see why we should care," Maeve said.

"We should *care* because if Loingsech is correct, we may find ourselves defenseless," Ferrell replied. "You can't use shockers on a fog."

Hearing this, Maeve snickered, and the Faeries glared disgustedly at Ferrell.

Seamus then spoke. "All Faeries, please respect Loingsech's words. We must not bring the curse of the fog upon us. Behave as if you were at a guild meeting. Remember *gnàs*, and be civil."

Diplomatically, Ferrell then added, "We Elves must follow *gnàs* as well. Act as if Govannon, your king, were watching your every move. Govannon has said many times that Elves and Faeries must usher in a new era of respect and cooperation. I see no reason why we shouldn't at least be even-handed. The fog may or may not act as Loingsech says, but we must err on the side of caution."

And so, as they prepared to leave, all agreed that they would behave with respect and decorum.

"Now, move out," Ferrell snapped at his guards.

From a distance, Matha observed Ferrell, always the calculating heron. But now he seemed more like a jittery egret, sensing that a red-tailed hawk was circling above. Matha knew that Ferrell was similar to him in some ways — both being more intelligent than most — but too often filled with a jumble of thoughts chasing each other, thoughts fueled by an all-engulfing dread, which usually led him to imagine the worst. So far, the Luminary had been hiding his apprehension well, putting on a strong face to his guards, but Matha could tell that Ferrell was also smart enough to understand the danger they were really in. Likely he believed what Loingsech had said far more than he let on to the Elves. Govannon's decree, which Ferrell had often used to sway the Faeries by convincing them of his good intentions, was at this point simply a useful distraction.

The camp then turned into a mess of Elves and Faeries racing about, breaking down tents, rolling up bedrolls, and packing what was left of their supplies. After they doused the embers of the Fires, crewmembers of the *Bael Inse* and the Timewaker began hauling the gear and equipment to their ships. The rest of the group formed a circle around the beaver brew, steaming in the cauldron.

Matha's stomach rumbled as he smelled the brew. Looking at Rian's salt biscuit, he wished he were back home in Deuona with nourishing, tasty food — certainly not this. The Elves didn't seem to mind salt biscuits as much, but to him they were disgusting. Baked twice at low heat, they were as dry as sand, like eating chalk. Rian had offered him one, but instead he took a carrot from Loingsech's bag. Hungrily he chomped the top, watching as Tárlach sniffed a ladle of beaver brew. There was something appetizing as well as off-putting about the aroma. "Very good," Tárlach announced, smiling. "The bone truffle has settled in. This will do the trick."

"Then let's feed those obnoxious beasts and clear the trees," Maeve said, jumping to her feet. Tárlach shook his head, disgusted.

"These *obnoxious beasts*," he began, "built this dam because they were frightened. When precious creatures of our realm are filled with fear — due to the doings of the Fae — they act not of their own true nature. Ever since the happenings at Four Falls, the water has been wild and unpredictable, and I believe these occurrences have put the poor creatures into a terrible panic. Building this dam was their way of coping, so they could feel that they at least had *some* ability to control the water."

The water Faeries all sensed the truth of this, and Maeve opened her mouth to speak, but Ferrell looked at her sharply and she thought better of it.

With the help of some of Ferrell's crew, Tárlach then began filling a number of troughs they had hewed from logs the day before to hold the brew. As he did, he sang a song for all to hear:

Beavers are the keystones
For creatures large and small
In rivers creeks and ponds
They lift them one and all

As they build their lodges
They must dam the Water well
Behind the dams are many ponds
Where creatures love to dwell

Trout and salmon lay their eggs
Dragonflies find their mates
Ducks and geese raise their young
Grand horns feast on watery cates

The Fae must always cherish
Their purpose great and tall
In rivers creeks and ponds
They lift not one but all

Hearing this, all the Faeries clapped delightedly, and the Elves nodded appreciatively. "Tárlach," Seamus said, "I didn't know that you were such a poet."

"When I'm not measuring the water, or playing with my squirrels, I like to write songs," Tárlach said. "I also play the flute."

"Then you must play with us sometime," Seamus said.

"When we are not feeling so beset," Kelven put in, smiling.

Everyone then turned their attention to the task at hand. One by one, an elven guard filled a bucket of brew from the cauldron, and then poured the contents into one of the troughs. Soon they were all filled, and at Tárlach's command the Fae waited a respectable distance away for the beavers to smell the aroma.

Worried that they might alarm the beavers, Tárlach asked Ferrell to tell everyone to lie side by side in a line as they waited. At Tárlach's request, Ferrell ordered everyone to do so, and Loingsech ordered his crew to do the same.

Soon the Fae were lying flat on the ground — like peas in a pod — on a small bluff overlooking the beavers. The industrious animals were still busily repairing the damage from the day before, and adding even more trees to the hulk. The troughs had been placed near the shore, on grassy damp Earth that met the stones and sand of the river.

All were quiet and still as they peered through the slowly thickening fog, waiting for the beavers to take notice.

At first nothing happened. Matha and the others were concerned, but then one of the beavers raised its whiskered head, black nostrils twitching. The large creature then lumbered over to the trough and began drinking.

"Aye," Tárlach whispered under his breath, chuckling. "They must have liked my song."

Soon many more beavers had reached the troughs, and Matha saw that they were all drinking the brew.

"How much longer?" Maeve asked, as she turned her head down the line, glaring at Tárlach.

"An hour at most for the brew to settle in their stomachs," Tárlach replied, "and then they'll calm down and mosey on back to their ponds."

Maeve stood up. "We haven't the time," she declared. "This will make the brew take hold faster," she added, producing the herbs from her pocket that Matha had seen her bring into camp earlier that morning. She also took out a jar of powder. Stuffing the herbs into the jar, she quickly shook up the contents.

"No!" Tárlach exclaimed. "You fool! Your alchemvoke concoction will spoil the brew."

"I trust Maeve's expertise," Ferrell declared. "She's well-schooled in the ways of Alchemvoke." Gesturing at the fallen trees, he added, "Don't forget how she used the charges to save the Timewaker from crashing into this ridiculous blockade."

Ignoring Tárlach, Maeve made her way down the bluff toward the river and the beavers. Instantly, Tárlach jumped to his feet, crying loudly, "Stop!"

Maeve froze, but then turned to Tárlach. Bowing, she said, "I'm certain this will work." Smiling slyly she added, "Govannon will pardon me in any case — I'm sure."

"Sorry, but *I* won't pardon ye!" Loingsech shouted at her.

Maeve ignored him, choosing instead to move toward the beavers so she could pour the contents of her jar into the troughs. Quick as a hare, Loingsech was charging down the bluff after her, and soon Ferrell was off too, and as Loingsech was clearly outnumbered by the Elves, Lugh charged down as well. As they ran, their boots sent chunks of turf flying. Bushes were trampled, pinecones stomped flat.

Now quite a spectacle was in motion as both Elves and Faeries were close to tussling near the beavers' whiskers. Neither side wanted to lose, and surely more Elves and Faeries would have joined in the skirmish had Rian not managed to rise quickly, before a mass of guards could race down the hill to join Ferrell. He threw his hands up at them — the Druid of Guidance mustering all his authority — and so they halted. Just as this happened, Kelven and Seamus also rose up in front of Loingsech's crew and stopped them as well, before they could storm to the bottom of the bluff.

Soon the beavers turned their heads, curiously watching Loingsech pounce on Maeve, who until then had been stepping lightly, surreptitiously easing her way toward them. Loingsech tackled her, and they wrestled in a ball of fury on the ground. He managed to wrest her alchemvoke concoction from her, smashing the jar against a rock. Soon Ferrell and Lugh were upon them — a brouhaha of Fae — with Ferrell pulling Maeve away from Loingsech, and Lugh preventing Loingsech from further fighting.

Amidst the clamor of yelling and cursing between Loingsech and Maeve, Matha watched, horrified and afraid that the beavers would stampede the interlopers. Luckily, the brew was beginning to take hold, leaving the animals somewhat docile and disinterested in the spectacle unfolding before them, though not yet ready to leave their blockade.

After Ferrell had managed to pry Maeve off of Loingsech, Lugh and Loingsech simply watched, scowling. Saddened by what a fine mess they had made of the whole affair, Matha retreated to a stump to puzzle out what their next move should be. Much to his chagrin, the group had not succeeded in getting back to the river without coming to blows. Shaken, he realized that no one was paying attention to what really mattered.

The creeping fog was indeed thickening.

Knowing that the beavers would not be leaving anytime soon, Matha gave Tárlach a worried glance. Tárlach only shook his head in frustration. They then spotted Loch, who had been distancing himself from the entire event all morning. If the Roiler was concerned, no one could tell as he remained stoic, but Matha knew that Loch could also see the mist thickening. Everyone was stuck there, and soon the fog would test their resolve.

Ferrell, Maeve, Loingsech, and Lugh made their way back to the bottom of the bluff. The four of them looked up at the line of Fae who were still prone on the ground, watching their every move.

Seamus spoke first. "A fine mess we've made," he groaned, pointing at the mist. They all knew he was right — more and more, the fog was thickening.

"We may as well drive them off and be on our way," Maeve countered.

"Don't forget your place," Ferrell retorted. "Govannon will not forgive incompetence, especially that born of childish impatience." The rebuke was enough to silence her. Ferrell then continued, "Even if we drove the beavers off, our plans wouldn't change. Clearing the logs will take hours, and if this fog is as dangerous as the Faeries say, then it's already too late. We can't abandon the ships either." Squinting his eyes, Ferrell then looked as far as he could into the distance. "There's no way of knowing where this fog ends, so there's no getting away."

Matha knew that Ferrell was right. Now they could only watch and wait, hoping that Boann's curse would not worsen the severity of being unjoined for the Faeries. Turning to Criofan, Matha said, "I wish I could calm those poor animals further. They don't deserve to be the victims of our trifling squabbles. What they need is our compassion."

To which Tárlach replied, "Soon, we may be the ones needing *their* compassion."

"Aye — he be right," Loingsech said. "It's thickenin' somethin' fierce now." Sweeping his arms toward the encroaching fog, he continued, "See now how it creeps upon us — brought about by all of our petty bickerin'."

The fog was now so dense that just ahead of Matha the trees had vanished from view. He could hear the river, but couldn't see the Water surging by them. The Sun had dimmed into a large clouded blur. He could still see his companions, but only those who were a few feet away.

"Careful now," Loingsech warned. "Ye don't know what lost is — I'm telling ye — till ye all be turned 'round by Boann's fog. This isn't the same fog that she whips up on the sea when she's in a rage. This fog — I fear — is here for a *reckonin'*."

Matha feared that this reckoning would complete what Boann had begun at Four Falls, and that this time her will would not be thwarted. He could only wait to see what she would rain down upon them.

☙❧

Loingsech's words had so startled the Faeries and Elves that they began stumbling about in the fog. In response, Ferrell barked orders for his guards to remain still. "Do as the Elves do — for in this moment we must rely upon one another!" Loingsech shouted. Matha heard quick shouts of affirmation from Loingsech's crew. All became still, but cries of shock then broke the silence.

"What's this all over my skin?" Lugh bellowed.

Touching his face, Matha felt something strange on his fingers. From what he could gather, the pale blue-green skin of his cheek was covered with a gray substance, cold and clammy. Repulsed, he touched other parts of his body. Like the shifting fog around them, he felt the substance cover him in spidery webs, then puff up like sickly patches of rising dough. Whatever this was, it had spread very quickly. The gray substance then took a very nasty turn, penetrating his skin. Terrified, he sensed a rush of dark energy pouring into his veins, invading first his organs and then his head. *I'm cursed,* he thought. Vertigo overcame him, and he stumbled — disoriented.

Close by, Matha heard a scramble of footsteps. Someone ran into him, almost knocking him over. Peering closely, he recognized Tárlach. On impact, Tárlach fell to the ground in front of him. Matha saw the same substance on Tárlach's skin as on his own.

"Are you hurt?" Matha asked. Tárlach was slow to respond. As Matha reached to pull him up, he noticed a compass on the ground — no doubt having slipped from the Elve's pocket. The needle in the center was spinning madly.

Matha helped Tárlach to his feet, then handed him his compass. Both watched, slack-jawed, as the needle continued going round and round in a counterclockwise direction.

"Loingsech!" Matha shouted. "The compass needle won't stop spinning!"

"Aye!" Loingsech shouted back. "I told ye — ye don't know what lost is!"

"Remain calm," Matha heard Ferrell cry out to his guards. "Remember your training and steady as you go."

The vertigo then changed to pain, one that none should ever have to bear, a pain he imagined only a greater being like Boann could properly endure, for he could not fathom what purpose this might serve one as insignificant as he. Nor could he imagine what intention he could ever hope to pursue, thus afflicted. Writhing in agony, he thought then of Baudwin. Had the same fog found him — far away and alone — without Loingsech to offer some kind of guidance? *And not only Baudwin,* he thought, wondering what had become of all the water Faeries in the realm. *Was this truly Boann's will, and if so, who would they turn to?* How fortunate he was to have so many wise ones with him — and so some small comfort was his.

Looking about, he realized that the Elves were also suffering terribly. Next to him, Tárlach was writhing in pain, and he wondered what Boann's plan was for them as well. Who was wise enough in their ranks to offer succor to those suffering this aberrant ailment? The Faeries had Loingsech, but the Elves had only the platitudes of the Assembly. How glad he was then to be a Faery, and not an Elve.

The pain continued to worsen, and as he was unjoined from his current, Matha feared that he would be taken to a breaking point. From afar, he heard Moonrise cooing frantically in his cage on the *Beal Inse*. From all around him came groans and cries of anguish, but in the smothering fog, he couldn't make out Elves from Faeries. Gasping, he dropped to his knees, and Tárlach did the same. Bile rose in his mouth, and he retched.

"We shall prevail," Tárlach said stoutly, placing his hand firmly on Matha's shoulder. Matha saw him wince, and then also retch.

Why would she subject us to this? Matha thought, his strength waning.

Surely his fellow Faeries were wondering the same. While he couldn't read their faces through the fog, he suspected that they too were questioning Boann's judgment. For with a pain so great, how could they not decry their tormentor?

Matha's suspicion was confirmed when Loingsech then spoke, his voice measured, yet drawn. "Do not forget — her curse, while horrendous, is but a way to guide us back to what we've lost." In response, some simply groaned, and others wailed, yet he continued. "Remember — as if you were in quicksand — that if you do not struggle, the grip of her curse will not tighten." Hearing this, the group stilled their cries.

Matha tried his best not to struggle, but could find no relief. He could feel his muscles tensing up, but knowing this would only make matters worse, he took a long, deep breath. Closing his eyes, he imagined himself floating blissfully on Topaz Lake in Deuona. He felt the dark energy gradually abating.

"Once ye calm yourselves, remember the true wisdom of the Fae!" Loingsech shouted. "Concentrate on the coursin'. And if ye'r an Elve — on the forgin'. Only by followin' the old ways will her grace return to us!"

"I shall *never* submit myself to her!" Maeve shrieked through the fog. "What does *she* know about the old ways — this mad spirit who capriciously felled my kin at Four Falls?! The nerve of her judging us all!"

Matha wasn't surprised at Maeve's rebuke. He'd not expected that she or any of the other Elves would heed Loingsech's advice, but as he trusted the sea Faery, he kept trying to course with his feelings.

Still kneeling on the damp Earth, Matha closed his eyes and tried to center his attention. Looking inward, all he could sense was the chasm Boann had rent inside him. Without the Water's renewal, his travels from Four Falls had left him exhausted. How easy it would be to simply give up. Instead, he clung to remembering better times when he was a young one, and imagined what being a Faery millennia ago might have been like. Because all could easily hone their intentions back then, continuously guided to join and course, misery such as this could never have taken root. How he wished he could now hone his intention, adapting his will to be like the Water. Surely that was the way to overcome this wretched curse.

But this, he knew, could not be. For the unjoined, coursing was out of the question, and honing impossible. *How ironic,* he thought, *that I now long to hone my intention, just as Baudwin had longed to hone his when honing was also out of his reach.* He who had ventured to the river countless times, hoping for the Water to come to him. *If only Boann would grace me now by rejoining me.* That was his only intention — to be rejoined, and to course again.

As Matha continued his journey inward, the fog did not abate. His legs were cramping from remaining still for so long. Sensing that the Faeries were losing their mettle, he feared that the burden of the curse was his alone to lift. He knew that the Water had impelled him to this place for a reason, so he placed his attention on his intention, just as Baudwin had done for so many years. Moments later he noticed a small shift occurring within himself. An easing was setting in, a respite that did not lift Boann's curse but did bring a measure of relief. *Of course,* he thought. Using his intention had now granted him grace, just as Baudwin's use of his intention had graced him at the Springs of Coventina.

Time passed, and the dark energy of the curse steadily subsided. Feeling somewhat renewed, he informed the Faeries, "You must heed what Loingsech says. Look inward, and as you do, try to remember the coursing — but even more importantly, have right intention. This alone will stave off the worst of your torment. Her grace will come to you just as it did to Baudwin when the Water came to him. Know that for years, Baudwin wasn't joined, nor could he course, and neither now can we. Yet we must hold fast to our intention, which must be for the Water to heal us."

The Elves scoffed at Matha, and Tárlach shook his head, but the water Faeries heard the wisdom in his words. Most had heard the tale of how Baudwin had found the Water. Seamus and Kelven now made their assurances known to everyone.

"If Matha feels the curse subsiding," Seamus cried out, "then do as he does. Throw your heart into your reflections and pay attention to your intention. Surely, this is what Boann meant for us to do."

Matha remembered again all the years that Baudwin had searched for the Water. How courageous he had been — all the while suffering so terribly for not being joined — yet he had not succumbed to bitterness, nor allowed torment to warp his intention. Nor had he ever relinquished his purpose until success had finally come his way. *Thanks to Seamus,* Matha thought, his feelings welling up inside of him. How lucky Baudwin was to have always had his grandfather at the river, ever poised with the heart of a lion to encourage him when Baudwin was too despairing to continue. Seamus's strength lived in Baudwin, and that had kept him going.

How Matha envied the sneaky bluethroat that had stolen Baudwin's button at the Springs of Coventina. *If only I had that bird's skill,* he thought. Then perhaps he could have stolen some of Baudwin's courage that day, so that just like his friend, he could now endure the unendurable even more. Perhaps, if he did, he could also ride the coattails of those braver than he. *Yes. Thanks to Seamus,* he again thought, this time allowing tears to stream from his eyes. All along, Seamus had known that the greatest lesson of the Water — pure devotion — could bring about the grace they needed. And for Seamus, this had always meant devoting himself to Baudwin, his grandson — his orphan of the Water — so that Baudwin would always carry the same devotion in his heart.

"Seamus," Matha cried out, his heart beating fervently, "you were right to guide Baudwin as you did. You taught him well, and now I can only hope that the same grace comes in turn to us."

"Indeed, follow my father's words," Kelven directed. "Dwell not upon how you have been wronged, or how you have been made to suffer. Make your intention known to yourself, and in this very moment, you may turn your pain into strength."

And so the water Faeries did heed his words, and soon Loch announced that even he had found some small comfort, even as the curse continued to rage inside of them.

The Elves were perplexed, muttering about what to do next, while Rian, the Druid of Guidance, mustered up his courage. "We are all suffering the torment of Boann's curse," he began. "The Faeries cannot course because they are not joined, yet they bravely attempt to hone their intentions anyway. We Elves are not at such a disadvantage. We can still separate and forge. I know that many of you have turned your backs on such things, but I implore you now to try. Each of you must find the anvil inside yourself — feel the heat and then forge. In this way you will feel less strained, and more able to bear your torment."

Tárlach — the only Elve Matha could see through the fog — knelt on the ground and began to place his attention on his intention. Never had he seen an Elve attempt to use the old ways. He assumed they never did, but surmised that the practice wasn't outlawed, for the Elves still had reverence for the old ways, even if they didn't properly understand them. As Matha gazed at Tárlach, he wondered about his metal.

"What's your metal?" Matha asked him.

"Master of Copper," Tárlach replied.

Matha didn't expect Tárlach to properly harness his metal, but then to his surprise, he sensed something shift inside of the Elve.

"When we forge," Tárlach began, "we feel our metal inside us — its shape changing in accordance with our heart's desire. This is not so unlike the coursing of your kin, but for us, it's not to understand our feelings, but to harness our thoughts, so we can shape our metal into what our destiny requires."

Matha sensed a stronger sense of purpose in the Elve, and a feeling that his metal was being formed, which Matha assumed bolstered him in some way, although he wasn't sure exactly how.

Tárlach then turned to him, grinning. "I'm lucky Copper is my metal, for I do feel a cleansing effect."

So that's what copper can do, Matha thought. "So you're cured?" he asked.

Tárlach grimaced as a jolt of the curse moved through him, his nausea having only somewhat abated. "Just a little," he replied. Turning away from Matha, he focused again on forging.

Matha then heard reports from the Elves. "Nothing has changed!" a guard shouted through the fog. "I feel *nothing*!"

Next to Matha, Tárlach shouted, "I feel a little better and my thoughts are clearer, but I'm of Copper, so naturally, I would. And I doubt you Wicks know what you're doing anyway."

"Well, *I* don't feel any better," Maeve retorted. "Why should we listen to you Faeries?"

"What else then should we do?" Tárlach asked.

Matha then heard Seamus shout out to the Elves, "I know we don't always see eye to eye, but in times past, surely we did — when our forebears honed our intentions, just as surely as yours tempered theirs. Back then, the Elves built the true wonders of their clans. Forget what you believe you know and find the place within yourselves that stands for cooperation. Be like my grandson — he honed for the sake of honing — so now, you must temper for the sake of tempering."

Matha saw Tárlach next to him, still kneeling, uncertain of what to do, his hesitancy palpable. No one spoke. Matha expected that Seamus's words had fallen upon deaf ears.

Rian broke the silence. "We've all learned the rudiments of tempering, even if none of us have ever mastered them. See your metal as a part of yourself, growing hot and hotter still, seeming as if it will melt away." Rian paused, waiting for his kin to catch up to his words, before continuing. "Now feel *through* that heat. Then quench that place inside of you in the snow of your resolve and do so — again and again!"

Matha could see that Tárlach was confused. He suspected that the act of tempering for an Elve was as daunting as honing was for a Faery. To his great surprise, he then heard Ferrell speak, a note of subtle desperation in the

Luminary's voice. "I command you," Ferrell ordered, "I command *all* of you to obey. The Assembly still considers tempering to be a valid part of Elven ways. Remember now your king Govannon — and draw strength from him. For it was he who must surely have tempered his intentions to bring us back from the brink of our own annihilation. See the forges of the great cities, and all the tempered metals in the foundries of the Clock City — how spark and flame built and fulfilled the new dreams he has given us!"

Tárlach appeared to be concentrating with great intensity. If Ferrell's words were new to Tárlach's ears, Matha didn't know, but his encouragement certainly had helped Tárlach redouble his efforts. Despite this, Matha could tell he was still struggling along with all the others.

Ferrell noticed this as well, and so he shouted, "We must rally ourselves! Druid of Guidance, will you lead our calls to temper?"

Commanded by the Luminary, Rian affirmed, "Bethink the forging of our glimmering Platinum Spires! Remember Sorcha[1] who built the great academies there. Embrace the wisdom we cherish from that inspired city. If you are of Platinum — temper!"

"Remember Grania!"[2] Ferrell put in. "Remember our Queen of Silver Forge, from a time of legend before Sitric ruled in Gleam. Remember the cosmic clock that she built, which oscillated perfectly and was the envy of the realm. If you are of Silver — temper!"

"And don't forget Mor[3] of Copper Caves!" Tárlach added. "Hear her melodies deep in the caverns where she lived and reigned. The rabbit plays a copper flute. If you're of Copper — temper!"

Criofan then chortled maniacally, his voice slipping through the fog like the call of an unseen owl. "So *that's* where the rabbit on the bow of the Timewaker comes from!"

Encouraged by his friend's voice, Matha joined in, "Exactly! The Elves need more rabbits to help them temper!"

There was a chorus of laughter, and the levity, however brief, seemed to be welcomed by all.

"Indeed — you circle hopper!" Maeve exclaimed. "But the *best* has yet to be announced. Remember Étain[4] of Gold Haven — the just and the fair. The first ruler of the Elves, and our great queen. The most blessed, and the bearer of the Golden Orb. If you are of Gold — temper!" she urged.

---

[1] Pronounced [SOR-ka]
[2] Pronounced [GRAN-ya]
[3] Pronounced [MORE]
[4] Pronounced [AID-een]

Matha was surprised to hear Maeve speak so admiringly of a queen from so long ago. How contradictory the Elves were, who so adamantly upheld the Assembly, yet when strife and hardship came, swiftly recounted their origins with unwavering pride. Still, he wondered if their entreaties would do any good at all. Could Boann's curse be mitigated by venerating past rulers? Or had the Elves unsheathed — just barely — a font of virtue that could renew them?

Matha could see that Tárlach was still kneeling alongside him, his eyes tightly closed. "When I focus on the tempering," Tárlach mused, "I do feel an easing of this burden."

"As do I," Ferrell shouted. "How do you fare, Maeve?"

"The edge does seem to have been taken off," Maeve replied, "but perhaps I'm simply uplifted by Criofan's marvelous levity."

Matha sensed a renewed vigor in the Elves, upliftment that must have made the curse abate somewhat. He was beginning to make out the figures of more and more of those around him. The fog was certainly thinning. As the clouds continued to slip away, the gray substance on his skin was already flaking off.

"'Tis as I predicted," Loingsech declared. "Boann meant for us to do this."

Matha had no way of knowing if this was true, but he did remember that Boann had scolded the Fae for not understanding who they were; now, by embracing what was lost, they had found a measure of relief. Minutes later, the fog had vanished almost completely. Around him, Matha saw Faeries and Elves in states of repose. Many of the Elves were kneeling, and he assumed that this must be how they observed their metals. Some of the Faeries were sitting on stumps left over from the beavers, and others were on the ground, lying on their sides. Everyone's situation had improved, yet even with the fog gone, the uncomfortable pain lingered, and Matha wasn't certain how they all would be able to continue on.

"The bind we're in is as Loingsech said," Rian declared. "Boann seeks to rekindle the old ways in us, until only our faith in such things ends up easing our burden."

"Perhaps so," Ferrell said, as the Elve stood up, "but I still feel a wound inside of me. And I wonder what old ways has she *really* rekindled by forcing us to revere that which we already hold in high regard?"

"Nay," Loingsech countered. "She's makin' ye use it as ye were meant to, so that Elves and Faeries alike would renew their interest in what is lost."

"What's the use of using something that's no longer useful?" Maeve asked, as she smiled at the newly emerging sunlight reflecting off of her bracers. Matha could tell how happy she was to return to her former posturing. "Don't you understand?" she asked. "Our forging and *supposed* tempering has barely changed anything." She then inspected the other guards around her. "They look as if they've been lost at sea for months. I wouldn't count on them for anything in this condition."

Matha looked at the Elves. The teal and sea green uniforms of the Water Guard were dingy with the grime the fog had left, and the yellow and brown of the Earth Guards were also soiled from their labors. Most had bags under their eyes from the ordeal they had just endured.

Turning to the Faeries, Maeve asked, "Are any of you rejoined to your currents?" None responded.

"Nay," Loingsech replied. "I'm not rejoined, but when I intoned from within, I felt the curse easin' its grip on me. Simply respectin' that the old ways still have a place within us is the first lesson most of us must learn."

"Loingsech is probably right," Lugh said, "but how will any of this help us to find Baudwin?"

Baudwin, Matha thought, *desperately needs our help, and all we can do is argue about the old ways.*

More words were bandied about — a crushing exchange of doubts, opinions, and accusations. All were unhappy that the torment of the curse lingered on. Some of the Elves again knelt, attempting to invoke the pride of the cities they held dearest, or the metals they most revered. The water Faeries did the same with their element, but while this had previously eased their burden, both Elves and Faeries now found that their attempts had no effect. Everyone was quite perplexed, as most were sure that intoning the old ways had indeed been of value, but why they could find no further succor was a puzzling mystery.

"Come now!" Ferrell exclaimed, as he surveyed the river. The logjam was still intact, and as River Nechtain rushed past them, dragonflies flitted among the reeds over the cool clear water. They stood on the inside of the riverbend where the land formed a small peninsula. Across the river the hills sloped away from them, and to their left, the view upstream remained obscured — a taunting mystery. Everyone was eager to move on, but unsure that the fog was really gone for good.

"The beavers have left," Ferrell announced. "We can't just stand around. Guards! Make preparations to clear the trees from the river."

Matha could see that Ferrell was correct. While the Fae had struggled in their agony, the beavers, just as Tárlach said they would, had all left and gone back to their dens — up the small creeks, back to their ponds.

Standing up, the Elves made their way to the *Bael Inse* to unload their Vaposaws from the hold. Ferrell and Loingsech agreed that together, they would clear the side they were presently on before going across to the other shore, for having just struggled in the fog, none were inclined to compete any further.

Now the Fae would work together, for the Faeries knew that in any case, they couldn't work faster than the speed of the Vaposaws.

All trudged toward the river, tired and weighed down from the ordeal they had just endured. Matha noticed that most of Boann's affliction had passed, with only some lingering discomfort. Despite his nagging doubt, he hoped that with the fog's retreat, her curse was gone for good. If this was truly the end of her castigation, what purpose had the curse actually served?

Matha felt no different than he had before the fog had struck him. Pondering this, he watched the Elves begin to set up their Vaposaws for cutting the trees. Most everyone else was standing near him. Among them was a cluster of Faeries about ten feet away from a group of Elves, while elven guards with Vaposaws stood by the river, almost twenty feet away.

For no apparent reason — none at all — the Elves by the riverbank suddenly began to stumble. They could barely keep their legs under them. Several of them were tossing their Vaposaws aside before their bodies hit the ground, so they wouldn't fall on the teeth and cut themselves.

"Be careful with those," Maeve called from afar.

The Elves stood up, each one wobbling to and fro. As if walking a tightrope, all stretched their arms out to their sides to keep steady, but their efforts were in vain, and they kept falling over.

"What a bunch of bumbling, cack-handed anvil-pounders!" Lugh shouted at them. "Come on now — one foot after the other. Walking couldn't be that hard!"

The Faeries, especially Lugh and Loingsech's crew, jeered at the Elves, and the guards who had been stumbling weakly returned the taunt.

Ferrell ordered Loch to go and see what was happening. The Roiler approached the bank, offered his hand to an Elve sitting on the ground, and pulled him up. When close to Loch, the Elves looked to be steadier on their feet. None were now falling over, and Matha wondered how this could be. Was it mere coincidence that they found their footing once Loch had come near them, or was something else going on?

Matha saw Loch and the Elves speaking, but from where Matha stood, he couldn't make out what they were saying. All shook their heads — perplexed — as they spoke to the Roiler, and they appeared to be repeating the same thing again and again. Loch simply shook his head back at them, looking equally perplexed. Intensely, they all stared at each other, talking even more. An Elve next to Loch cuffed his own ear, and Loch likewise did the same.

"They can't understand me!" Loch shouted back at the group standing near Matha.

"What do you *mean* they can't understand you?" Ferrell shouted back to Loch. "I can hear you perfectly."

"I know," Loch shot back, "but *they* can't!"

"They're probably on strike," Lugh snorted. "Govannon must be too stingy with their pay."

"Govannon provides *all* when retiring with land and bounty," Maeve snapped at him.

"From the looks of them, I'd say they're ready to retire right now," Lugh added, chortling.

Hearing this, Loingsech's crew guffawed, but as Loingsech studied the Elves, he grew increasingly concerned. The sea Faery then drew closer to Ferrell, moving away from the crowd of Faeries who were within ten feet of the crowd of Elves.

Matha heard Loingsech declare, "I don't believe the curse is yet lifted."

"What did you just say?" Ferrell asked Loingsech. "I can't hear you."

Matha's eyes grew wide. He could hear Ferrell, but he could see that Loingsech could not, which made no sense, because Loingsech was standing right next to Ferrell. Maeve also tried to exchange words with Loingsech, but failed, as did Rian and Tárlach, who were now both standing close to him.

Matha then realized what was happening, so he shouted over to Ferrell, "This is just what happened to Loch! When Elves and Faeries are standing near to one other, they can no longer *hear* each other."

Every Elve who could hear Matha, whether in the group near Ferrell, or the one farther away at the shore, saw that he was right. Every Faery had also heard what Matha had said. Great confusion ensued, as everyone wondered what to do next. Matha saw Loingsech pick a long stick off the ground. The sea Faery began to draw on the sand in front of him. Puzzled, Ferrell looked down at the ground.

Matha approached them, and saw that Loingsech had scratched out a glyph which depicted a Fire trapping a Fae in a cave, and another glyph depicting one hand cupped over the other — the symbol of the Water — with waves of Water rising above. Matha knew the first glyph was for curse, and the second was for water spirit.

Ferrell nodded his head to indicate that he understood the glyphs. The Luminary rested his chin on his hand as he studied them more, lost in concentration. Maeve opened her mouth to say something, but Matha couldn't hear a word she uttered.

A shout of recognition then coursed through the group. "*This*, my friends, — must be the *real* curse!" Matha turned to see Seamus pacing in circles, frantically waving his arms as he spoke. "We all believed that the torment we just endured was over, but apparently that was merely the seed of the curse being planted in us — a harbinger of things far worse!" Matha noticed Seamus and Lugh heading for the outer edge of the camp to get their packs. Soon, they too stumbled and fell over.

Loingsech tapped Ferrell on the arm, and then pointed through the trees at Seamus and Lugh. Loingsech then pointed to where Loch still stood near the Elves. Hastily, he began to scrawl more glyphs on the ground.

One by one the glyphs were drawn, and Matha read them: "Boann has cursed the ears and the legs."

Another of Loingsech's glyphs meant "walk to them." Matha pointed at Seamus and Lugh.

Rian did exactly that, and as soon as he reached Seamus and Lugh, they immediately regained their footing. Yet confusion still remained, because Rian didn't seem to hear what Seamus and Lugh said to him, and they couldn't hear him, either.

"Thank the Water," Seamus shouted, "that a Druid of Guidance came near us — otherwise, we'd *all* be falling over!" Although Matha knew Seamus liked Rian, he wasn't certain that being a Druid of Guidance made much difference.

Loingsech's glyph stick continued to scrawl more glyphs. Matha knew their meaning, and for all who could hear him intoned: "When physically close, Elves and Faeries cannot hear one another, and when alone and far away from each other, neither Elves nor Faeries can walk."

Hearing this, Ferrell's pale yellow skin turned ashen. Maeve said something inaudible to Matha. From afar, Lugh had picked up what she said, and shot back, "I'm sure his glyphs make sense. We don't need your dunce-like letters to communicate!"

"Glyphs are for dunces because they're slow and stupid!" Maeve snarled.

Ferrell ordered an experiment so that he could verify Loingsech's explanation. He ordered some Elves to walk away from the group. When they began to stumble, Criofan went to them and their balance was restored.

Matha had watched everything. Criofan had gone — like a rabbit gingerly approaching a nursery of skittish raccoons — trying to reach them, so they wouldn't topple over into a nearby patch of nettles. Matha had noticed Criofan stumbling a bit when he was halfway near them — too far from the Elves he had just left, and still not close enough to those he wanted to reach. Once with the Elves, Criofan shouted to Ferrell and Loingsech that their balance was restored.

Now, however, they probably won't be able to speak to each other, Matha thought ruefully.

Eventually, either by using glyphs or simply shouting, everyone was informed of what was going on. Working together, Ferrell and Loingsech decided that the Faeries and Elves should form lines about ten feet apart from one another. Soon both sides were facing each other, just far enough away to keep their balance, but close enough for their shouting to be audible.

"This is the curse of Boann," Loingsech informed the two groups. "She used the fog to bring this upon us, and I fear that it likely has reached all of the water Faery lands, perhaps going even farther."

"But that would mean —" Ferrell shouted back.

"*That* would mean," Loingsech interrupted, "that right at *this* moment, in Four Falls, Elves and Faeries may be stumblin' around, bewitched and bewildered — unable to speak to each other or walk, while they try to figure out what's happenin'."

"That's *if* the fog has reached there," Maeve added.

"Sure," Loingsech replied. "We don't know how far the fog has traveled, but we do know that she meant to teach us *all* a lesson — so assumin' —"

"And what *lesson* might that be?" Maeve interrupted testily.

"That we can't live *with* or *without* one another," Seamus declared. "She has forced our hand to make us come to terms."

"Come to terms?" Maeve asked. "By turning us into a bunch of witless speakers and stumbling fools? How do we come to terms with *that* — much less carry on?"

"Well, at least you won't have to listen to us, when we stand close." Lugh shot back. "For you that would certainly be a welcome change."

"Perhaps you're right," Maeve added, glaring at Lugh, "although I would prefer that the Faeries hear us, but we not them."

Both sides jeered heartily. Both Elves and Faeries seemed to be at once upset and cynical about their circumstance.

"If I'm using the washing room on the *Bael Inse*, I won't have an Elve chaperoning me there!" Lugh shouted. Hearing this, everyone laughed.

"And if I'm doing my rounds on the Timewaker, I won't be followed around like a mother duck the whole time!" Loch shouted.

More and more grievances came spewing out. Neither side liked the idea of having to rely upon the other, so Ferrell cut in, "As much as this may irk you to your bones, both Elves and Faeries are going to have to depend on one another, until the curse lifts."

"That's all well and good," Loingsech said, "but the curse won't be liftin' unless we do somethin' to make it so." At this, everyone fell silent, wondering what he or she would say next. Loingsech continued, "When Boann came to Four Falls, I knew somethin' was afoot. She spoke of a curse, which led me to offer my help to all of ye. I wasn't sure what I was meant to do, but I knew that the wisdom of us Baranthus folk would be needed, and I was right. Now her intent has become crystal clear to me. She cursed us to force us to reconcile and heed the old ways."

"I won't be forced by that *creature* to do anything," Maeve snapped.

"Sure, but even *your* stubborn rump will have to," Loingsech interjected, his eyes narrowing. "We must travel to a shrine not far from here, and invoke a sacred rite to call upon Glamorium, which will require *both* Elves and Faeries to cooperate."

"That's *completely* impossible," Ferrell said, greatly annoyed. "The Assembly prohibits exploration of the temples. Only Druids of Lore or others who are authorized are allowed to enter a temple, much less move anything that's there."

"Sorry — and why would *that* be?" Loingsech asked Ferrell.

"Those sites are dangerous!" Ferrell exclaimed. "Evil spirits roam them, and the artifacts therein are dangerous as well. Loch told me that a gusher almost drowned him at Coventina. Not to mention that old shrines stir up false memories of the past."

"Nonsense," Loingsech replied. "The shrines are places where Faeries and Elves have communed for ages, and by our reckonin', have only done so to bring greater harmony into their lives. There's no danger there, unless ye be disrespectin' the place."

Matha could tell that Ferrell hardly believed Loingsech, but rather than press the point, Loingsech said, "Ye think ye have a choice right now, but ye don't. Even with yer mighty guards, and yer mighty Branches of Progress, and yer mighty Assembly, ye're powerless now. If you don't come to the shrine to restore *gnàs*, surely ye'll be forever cursed. Boann will not cure our difficulty hearin' and walkin' until ye have heeded her lesson."

"We don't have to do *any* such thing," Maeve insisted, glaring at Loingsech.

"But ye *do*," Loingsech replied, his eyes bright with certainty. "If ye don't, ye'll be stumblin' all the way back to Four Falls, and all practical exchanges between the Fae will cease to be. In fact, ye might not even make it. I don't know if the fog has gone beyond the water faery lands, but if it has, then eventually, the entire realm will grind to a halt. We *have* to go to the shrine. My elders spoke of one upriver that's hidden away — the Shrine of the Nechtain."

At this Loch asked, "So the shrine *does* exist?"

"Aye," Loingsech replied. "Out of sight, but I know where to look. All Faeries of Baranthus know of them. They're tucked away, but as the elders often told me, one day I might be needin' one of them — and if there ever was such a needin', that be now."

"Surely, you don't expect us to understand what we must do there," Ferrell remarked coldly.

"But ye *already* do," Loingsech replied. "Earlier ye forged, and ye even tried to temper, and yer pain lessened. The way was shown to ye."

"Such a way can't be *that* simple," Ferrell retorted.

"The rite isn't that difficult to perform, but it does require mutual respect, without makin' one side or the other more important — a part of *gnàs* that hasn't been practiced for a very long time. I can't remember the last time anyone among the Fae has even tried to do this."

Matha saw Ferrell pause, obviously deep in thought as he weighed his options. Wearily, he bent his arms, running his fingers over his sleeves to pick at bits of grime. As he stared at Loingsech, the lines on his face were etched with strain.

"You say there is no other way?" Ferrell asked.

"None," Loingsech replied. "Don't ye see? She be the one in control now. She has been since the falls."

"Yes," Ferrell replied stoically. "I suppose that even in her defeat, she had more surprises for us."

Matha could see that Maeve had heard enough. "You aren't seriously considering this — *are* you?" she asked. "What you're planning goes against everything the Assembly stands for!

Matha didn't see how Ferrell could possibly accept the plan, but then again, what choice did the Elves have? Both sides of the line now eyed each other. Faery regarded Elve, and Elve regarded Faery. They were now inexorably tied to one another — tethered by a leash of necessity, and pulled together to face each other fully. Of all the Elves, Rian and Tárlach seemed the most open to the proposal, but the rest of them seemed reticent, to say the least.

On the other hand, the Faeries seemed shocked, but not surprised, by the turn of events, wondering just what this rite was, and whether or not such a thing could actually help them. If Ferrell had truly defeated Boann, his victory had been utterly hollow, as her curse had left the Elves completely impotent. At this, the Faeries beamed with pride. For the first time in two hundred years an unexpected protector of the water Faeries from *Tír Éirí Sióg* had bested Govannon and the Assembly.

And so Ferrell relented, agreeing that they would adjust their crews and make their way to the hidden shrine. All the while, Maeve tried her best to get Ferrell to change course, but reminding her of their stark and stuck predicament was enough to quell her objections. The Elves would attempt the rite for its own sake, though few believed in its efficacy. All the same, some did wonder — just a bit — if the rite would work, for earlier they had eased the torment of the curse by resorting to the old ways.

Soon the trees were cleared, and when the last Vaposaw stopped blaring and the logs were hauled away, mixed groups of Elves and Faeries boarded the *Bael Inse* and the Timewaker, then headed upriver to find the shrine. All the while, Matha worried about how Baudwin was faring, as after the beavers, they were beset with yet another delay.

◈

As they voyaged to the shrine, the crews of the *Bael Inse* and the Timewaker were full of trepidation and uncertainty. None were sure that Loingsech's plan would work, and whatever inspiration they may have felt was beginning to fade. In order to keep themselves from again stumbling, many Faeries had boarded the Timewaker. More than once, Loch had seen a Faery move too far away from an Elve, or vice versa, making them start to slip and slide, almost falling off the deck and into the river.

"A fine lot we are," Tárlach grumbled, "walking about topsy-turvy and then keeling over like a bunch of fools."

"Perhaps we're a finer lot for not falling overboard — yet," Loch quipped. As he spoke, he made sure he was at least ten feet away from Tárlach.

"Don't you worry," Tárlach began. "Loingsech knows what he's doing."

Loch wasn't so certain. The entire plan smelled of desperation to him. Everyone was supposed to traipse to some kind of shrine, and perform some kind of rite that no one understood — one that would wondrously remove their curse. The whole thing sounded like the incantations of a mad sailor who, far from his homeland, had been through too many restless seas to reason properly.

Oddly, despite his many grievances, Loch now believed that he was finally being led to his destiny. This was, after all, the Nechtain, the river he had chosen when he was a young one to go searching for the Water — and now, after turning his back on that quest, he was about to find the very shrine that had eluded him all this time.

This had been the river where, long ago, his mother had joined him to the Water. She had told him that he would one day be wise like the salmon and perform exceptional deeds for the Water Guild, but he knew that she had only seen in him what a mother's love allowed her to see. She could not have foreseen that her son would grow to lead the Roilers, pushing down anyone who stood in his way, yet now his choice to wear a lettered jacket nagged at him more than ever. Ever since Boann's arrival, doubt had been building in him, cracking his wall of arrogance and impelling him to consider more about the ways of his kin.

At the base of the falls he had been part of a group waking that may have enveloped every water Faery in the entire realm. This rapture, however fleeting, had haunted him ever since. If what Loingsech had said was true, Boann was really the one pulling the strings, and like it or not, she was commanding him to the shrine, along with everyone else. For now, the Water would *not* be on his terms.

"What's on your mind?" Tárlach asked.

"This Life I lead," Loch began, shaking his head. "It doesn't belong to me — or the Water — or the Elves. I couldn't control being forced to work for Ferrell, and I had no say in what Boann did to me either. No matter what I do — I'm blocked."

Tárlach paused for a moment, taking Loch's admission into account.

"There's a saying amongst the Elves," he replied. "The lathe may turn, but the hand that guides the headstock serves the master — not the forge."

"And that means?" Loch asked peevishly.

"That we all must serve *someone*," Tárlach replied knowingly.

"I'm tired of serving," Loch retorted. "*I'm* the one who should be served."

As Tárlach considered Loch, he was quiet. "Tell me, Roiler," he asked. "If Ferrell hadn't indentured you, where do you suppose you would be right now?"

"Back in Deuona, probably with my gang," Loch replied.

"Yes," Tárlach continued, "and you never would have seen Boann, or righted yourself with Baudwin by searching for him, or learned as much as you have from the Elves. Wouldn't you *rather* be here?"

"Of course not. . ." Loch replied gruffly, his voice trailing off. "I prefer to do things on *my* terms."

"And doesn't Ferrell do things on his terms as well?"

"Of course he does," Loch replied. "Just look at all the Elves beneath him who jump at his every command."

Tárlach shook his head. "Nay, Roiler. He serves Govannon, and even Govannon serves his subjects. None command completely. None can ever be completely in control, nor should they."

Mulling this over, Loch realized that the Elve was right. Not wanting to sound petulant, he decided not to defend his predicament any further.

"You told me before that you'd turned your back on the water," Tárlach continued, "but seeing you here with me now, I doubt that the water has done the same to you. If your water spirit has, through some device, demanded that you remain here until she's finished with you and everyone else, you must cling to the flame of her design like a hot coal. Stop fretting about the life you *insist* you should have had!"

Again Loch knew that Tárlach was right. More and more, he was taking a liking to this Elve. A feeling he rarely knew welled up in his chest. *If I can't <u>be</u> the master,* he thought, *I will master myself as best I can.* Perhaps in the end, even if Baudwin *had* been chosen by Boann, he would still find some meaning for himself. The Nechtain was, after all, his favorite river.

More time passed, and from the rear he could see flashes coming from the signaling tower on the *Bael Inse*. An elven lookout watched the strobes and then announced, "We're nearly at the fork the Faeries described. Soon we'll reach the shrine!"

Both ships neared a minor tributary forking off of the Nechtain, the first of many forks that would eventually split off to Lake Airmid or lead to River Deuona and then on to Wood Fern. This part of the river still flowed through water faery lands — the southernmost part before the trees grew thicker and thicker, near the border where the wood faery lands began. There was a loud *clack* in the wheelhouse as an Elve set the lever on the engine control to one quarter ahead. As the Timewaker slowed, Loch saw Rian leaving the quarterdeck to approach him.

The Druid of Guidance was lost in thought, the lines of his brow furrowed with concern. Uncharacteristically, he didn't meet Loch's gaze as he drew nearer. If Loch hadn't asked, "What's on your mind?" he might have passed by him. Abruptly, he stopped and regarded the Roiler, hesitating before speaking. Loch saw that his usual easygoing manner was beset with pessimism.

"There's something about this plan that I don't like," Rian began.

"Is there?" Loch asked.

"Yes. . ." Rian continued, haltingly. "It's not that I don't trust Loingsech. In fact, I trust him much more than Ferrell. It's just that there's something he didn't mention, which I'm sure he already knows about."

Rian said nothing more, and Loch heard only the high-pitched whine of the steam whistle.

"We must get on with it," Tárlach insisted, overhearing Rian's comment. "What has you in such a twist?"

Gravely, Rian regarded Loch and Tárlach. "We're supposed to invoke a rite of Glamorium," he began. "I cannot fathom how Loingsech plans to achieve this, but if anyone in the realm is able to, such a one would have to be a Baranthus Faery. You must both understand — I'm not afraid of Glamorium — I'm afraid of what may come to pass if Loingsech's plan actually works."

"And that is?" Loch asked.

"There's a shadow in Glamorium," Rian replied, "a very dangerous one. When Baudwin had a vision of Glamorium at the Engineerium, the shadow appeared to him."

Loch had no idea what Rian was talking about, yet he considered the druid to be wise, so he took what he said in stride.

Noting Loch's receptivity, Rian continued, "The shadow has been with us ever since the Great Befalling. Many visions of Glamorium have shown this — some kind of cold, noxious, inky black pool that seeks to drown the visions of those who have been graced by the *Dúrúnghlas*. I was there when this happened to Baudwin. The shadow sought to instill terror in him, and perhaps even corrupt him, should he have gotten trapped in its ruinous web."

"No wonder he ran away to Four Falls," Loch quipped snidely.

Rian scowled at him.

"A *vision* you say?" Tárlach interjected. "What harm could a vision really do? We've all had bad dreams before."

"You don't understand," Rian said. "A vision of the *shadow* may corrupt the heart of whomever sees it. I've heard of Elves, who, having seen such visions, afterwards become obsessed — in very strange and destructive ways — with *building*. Some race to the outskirts of the cities they dwell in, and begin constructing labyrinths. And they remain obsessed — until their constructions turn on them."

Rian then paused for a moment before asking, "Loch, do you know the difference between a maze and a labyrinth?"

Loch shook his head.

"A labyrinth has one continuous path to the center, but a maze has many paths inside that only lead to nowhere. The kin of these Elves report seeing them start to build a labyrinth, but as time goes on, they seek a path beyond their initial objective, and their creation becomes a maze. They make them larger and larger, and eventually they seal themselves inside, where they die of madness and starvation. This has happened more than a few times, and each time the Assembly tears down the maze, only to find rags on the ground, where those lost builders passed to Annwyn."

Loch was sobered by this story. He knew Rian wasn't a liar, and so he asked, "If the shadow is that dangerous, why then would Loingsech have us do this?"

"Because it's probably the only way," Rian replied, "and what makes it even more dangerous is that he's not simply seeking a vision of Glamorium. He intends to invoke it directly."

"How so?" Tárlach asked.

"When Baudwin touched Glamorium," Rian continued, "he was graced by a mere vision of Glamorium, but that is not what Loingsech has in mind. His intention is to invoke Glamorium *itself*. What this means is that we won't see its light come to us as if we were in a waking dream, we will see its magnificence — in its entirety — touching us directly, and if we are unlucky, the shadow will also be laid bare. That will be *far* more dangerous. No one I know of has ever experienced the shadow firsthand before. A rite such as this has not been performed since before most can remember. And what will happen is entirely unknown."

Loch now believed that he understood. A vision of a terrible thing was dangerous, but the terrible thing *itself* was far more dangerous — very much like the difference between a nightmare of a ravenous wolf, versus an actual ravenous wolf right in front of you.

"I don't know how to be a clear-sighted guide right now," Rian lamented. "What I'm most concerned about is what the Assembly will do when they learn of this. And of course, they will. I remember a hundred years ago in Platinum Spires when the Assembly exerted its influence by deciding what should and shouldn't be taught. As you can well imagine, there was a lot of dissension among the druids. We didn't want those *Northerners* telling us what we should teach the realm." Disdainfully, Rian shook his head, adding, "We had been the source of wisdom in *Tír Luí Lucharachán* for thousands of years, and so we protested, and for that Govannon imprisoned many high druids."

Rian reached for the chain around his neck. Vigorously, he rubbed the pendant, looking as if he hoped a light of reason would shine from the lantern etched in the Silver, illuminating them all. Sweat beaded his brow.

"Whatever it takes, we must break this curse," Loch declared flatly.

"None of us will get in trouble for doing this," Rian said. "And if Loingsech succeeds, I'm sure Govannon will give Ferrell a medal. The real danger is what the Assembly might do if the shadow takes us over. We're about to throw a log on a fire that could ignite the entire realm."

"I just don't know about all of this," Tárlach broke in. "You say no one has actually seen the shadow? Only in visions that came with Glamorium?"

"Yes," Rian replied.

"I wonder if Boann also meant for this to happen," Loch mused.

"Loch," Rian declared, "no one, not even Loingsech, knows what is about to take place — but I need to have you listen. You must understand that being a Roiler is now beside the point. Much more is happening than quarreling about our petty differences. Now that the entire realm is learning that Boann chose Baudwin, he will never be safe again. The Assembly will never trust what she might do with him. If we do manage to find him, then you will need to look after him — as one water Faery to another."

Loch wasn't sure about any of what Rian had said, so all he could do was to reply, "I will try my best to be honorable."

The answer seemed enough for Rian. "In the future," he added, his usual vigor returning, "that may be the hardest thing you'll ever have to do." Loch nodded his head, as if despite all of his own resistance, he knew that Rian had spoken the truth.

Before they could speak any further, they heard a Water Guard cry out, "The tributary is becoming too shallow! We're to board the longboats and make our way to shore."

There was a great deal of movement on the ship, and soon Rian, Loch, and Tárlach found themselves surrounded by others whom they didn't want hearing their conversation. And so they stopped talking, and instead prepared themselves to head to the shrine.

⚘

Matha watched the crew on the *Bael Inse* drop an anchor, built with large thick hooks that dug into the river bottom so the current couldn't carry the ship away. Almost everyone was on deck preparing to disembark. With a *kerunk,* the crane on the back of the *Bael Inse* swiveled around, and the longboat was lowered into the Water. Soon everyone was aboard the longboats, rowing to shore.

After the crews unloaded the longboats and dragged them onto the gravelly bank and unloaded them, both Elves and Faeries began to make their way up a bluff leading to a thick covering of trees. As they went, both sides stayed close to one another so they wouldn't stumble and go careening down the hill. But this also meant that most Elves and Faeries couldn't hear each other. Farther up the line, Matha could make out some of what the Elves were saying, but immediately behind him, conversation wasn't possible.

Steadily, they followed the dirt path up the side of the bluff. In the distance Matha spotted two immense boulders on either side of the path. Were his eyes playing tricks on him? They looked very much like the ones he and Baudwin had seen at the Springs of Coventina, and he wondered if they also had similar markings. After all that had happened since the day Boann had washed them out of the shrine, it seemed he was encountering the same discovery. "Look!" he said, pointing to the boulders. Sensing his excitement, the Faeries went to study them. Most of the Elves hadn't heard Matha speak, but seeing the Faeries gawking at the boulders, they too turned their attention to them.

Soon both Elves and Faeries were standing on either side of the path directly in front of the boulders. Matha broke from the group to take an even closer look, then stopped in his tracks, remembering that if he strayed too far from an Elve, he would tumble over. Turning, he saw Ferrell already dividing up his guards so they would cover the area and prevent anyone from falling down.

Looking closely at one of the boulders, Matha made out the relief of an Elven gent in profile, holding a hammer and with a Sun above his head — the symbol of Silver Forge. *Remarkable!* he thought, chuckling. *Are we going to find the same wonders in this shrine that Baudwin and I found at the Springs of Coventina where we followed the bluethroat — the thief that was actually a guide?*

Looking about, he sensed that every blade of grass, every leaf that fell from every tree to the ground, every stream where the otters dug their dens, and every concurrence of the Water had somehow ushered them to this place. By

Boann's will they had come, and on nature's ground they now tread — an eternal confluence that could not be diminished. And no matter how many bolts the Elves tightened, how many lumber rollers they drove, how many orders they followed, and how many lands they occupied, they as well would *still* have found themselves in this place, in this moment — because there was a greater purpose at play, a tapestry woven into the heavens that all the Fae in *Tír na nÓg* were bound to as cleavers and weavers. Regardless of whatever notions about their metals and their elements they might carry around in their heads, their true, essential role superseded all. And so Matha knew right then and there that their wills — however imbalanced — were subject to a far greater weaving, and all everyone could do was wait for the threads to reveal themselves.

This is far more than mere coincidence, he thought, although he knew Ferrell would probably disagree with him. To have so many wise and knowledgeable ones end up here as a group under such duress meant that this was meant to happen. As he thought again of Baudwin, a small hope welled up inside of him. *Perhaps our discoveries at the Springs of Coventina boded well for both Elves __and__ Faeries — so the Elves may learn that Loingsech's foolish errand isn't so foolish after all.*

Matha noticed interest and excitement stirring amongst the Fae. As gradually the burden of their afflictions became more bearable, they keenly studied the monuments.

"So, these be greetin' stones," Loingsech declared, catching up to Matha. "This shrine is similar in construction to the shrines of Baranthus, and was built thousands of years ago by the Elves of Silver Forge for the water Faeries. Long ago, the Elves gifted the Faeries with stoneworks such as these, as was the custom."

On the other side of the path, Ferrell and Maeve were inspecting the other boulder, which bore the relief of a water Faery in profile facing the Elve on the other boulder, with a Moon above her head, and a water droplet in her cupped hands — the symbol of water Faeries. Having heard what Loingsech had said, Ferrell replied, "That's certainly a laudable sentiment, but no one is certain anymore why these edifices were built."

Hearing this, Matha nodded knowingly at Loingsech.

Loingsech ignored the comment, choosing to shrug off Ferrell's skepticism. Speaking quietly to the Faeries near him he added, "He probably believes that long ago a bunch of Faeries came here lookin' for excitement, and then chiseled up the rocks after suckin' on too much sweet-vine."

Matha laughed, as did Loch, Seamus, and Lugh who were standing nearby.

"Inside, ye'll see the same theme of unity throughout the shrine," Loingsech continued, "much like all shrines of this kind from this time. Only the Assembly would ignore what's right in front of their faces. If any of ye Elves are from Silver Forge," he called out to the other side, "I want to thank ye *now* for this great gift."

Ferrell responded by shaking his head at Loingsech, but Kelven, who stood next to Ferrell, gave Matha a reassuring look. There was no more debate after that, and as the group left, Matha asked Loingsech in a low whisper, "Do you believe that we can *really* trust them to cooperate? They don't even believe the reason for why this place was built."

"Sure," Loingsech whispered back, "but if I'm right about all this, they won't have a choice *but* to cooperate."

Loch, who had been standing near them the entire time, then leaned in to speak. In a low voice he began, "I'm not calling you a liar, but what you say sounds unbelievable. Still, I'm just as desperate as the Elves to be free of all of this. On the other hand. . ." he whispered, hesitating as he spoke to make sure no Elve could hear him. "On the other hand, I believe that Ferrell is hiding what really happened with Boann in the drainworks of Four Falls. She could be *anywhere*, and if we don't tread carefully, we may find ourselves washed out of this shrine, just as we were in Coventina."

"Aye, we'll be careful," Loingsech replied, "and I know Ferrell wasn't bein' forthright about what happened to her. One way or another, we'll find out soon enough."

And so the group continued up the path. Below them Matha saw a gully with a stream that ran to the Nechtain where the boats were moored. At the top of the bluff a grove of hawthorns obscured their view. *Baudwin and I saw oaks, not hawthorns,* Matha thought, fondly remembering his friend. Venturing into the grove along a path that was now completely overgrown, they eventually made their way to a large formation covered with vines. As they reached the vines, Matha could see that the exterior of the shrine closely resembled the one at the Springs of Coventina. The ruins formed a square, and on each side were three granite oval entrances. Fieldstones placed between the ovals formed low, but level, connecting walls.

Eagerly, Matha rushed ahead of everyone and into the shrine. He had difficulty maintaining his balance, but one of Ferrell's guards followed him in, so he managed not to fall over. Looking about, he was again quite taken by how similar his surroundings were to the shrine at the Springs of Coventina. The scent of water lilies and honeysuckle vines enveloped him, as did the sound of Water spilling over rocks and logs. In the center of the sanctum stood a stone well, encircled by twelve rings of seats. Four aisles, precisely and beautifully crafted, divided the twelve rings into quarters. *Spring crocuses, summer roses, fall acorn shells, and winter holly leaves,* he thought — *all made of the same clear, white quartz.* Sadness pierced his heart as he remembered how excited he and Baudwin had been to discover these very same motifs of the seasons at Coventina. How sorely he missed his friend! Only yesterday, it seemed, they had chased that bluethroat to a place just like this, and discovered so many secrets — too precious to ever forget.

Cautiously, he made his way to the place where Baudwin had sat — a crystal seat fashioned in the shape of winter holly leaves — opposite the seats shaped into summer roses. Gently, he sat down on the seat, placing one arm on a leaf to his left and the other arm on a leaf to his right — *just as Baudwin did,* he thought. And just as they had done before, Matha became very still. Unlike the other time, the silence did not quiet him from within.

"Oh, Baudwin!" he cried out, remembering his friend's laughter when he had first discovered the crystal summer roses. "What songs does summer sing *now* — with you gone?"

"Summer sings of a new accord!" Loingsech proclaimed. Having entered the shrine, the sea Faery was already making his way down an aisle, seemingly very much at home in his surroundings. As soon as he reached Matha, he made a sign of the Water, bowing to the shrine.

"Don't forget to make a sign and bow when ye enter," he instructed Matha. With that, Matha stood up from his seat and also bowed, his hair almost brushing the crystal seat in front of him.

"I remember finding a shrine just like this with Baudwin," Matha began. "We came upon so many mysteries that day. The well was filled with offerings — myriad pieces of blue topaz, pearls, shards of green quartz, and gold — and we also found a glamorium poem etched into a tablet made of blue-green agate."

As Matha spoke, many others were also making their way down the aisles. He saw Ferrell coming, with a number of guards behind him. Stoically, the Luminary took in his surroundings, but to Matha's surprise, he paused for a moment to glide his hand over a crystal seat shaped like a spring crocus. The Elve had a look of admiration on his face as he marveled at the fine artisanship.

"Why were the offerings left?" Matha asked.

"Well," Loingsech replied, "they may have dropped a jewel in the Water for many a reason, but for me, when a special dreamin' comes, I rise from my bed, and after I've figured out the meanin' with my kin, I make my way to one of the wells in Baranthus and throw in a bit of azurite, or a pearl or two — a way of givin' thanks and showin' respect to the Water for bringin' me the dream."

Now Maeve had joined Ferrell. Surprisingly, she didn't seem interested in making sarcastic comments about Loingsech's talk about offerings, choosing instead to take in the artisanship of the crystal seats. "No seams, Ferrell," she declared, pointing to a number of crystal crocuses. "Not crafted by any means that the Four Branches possess."

The Luminary nodded his head, for he obviously had been mulling over the same thing. Looking closely at his own seat, Matha saw that the entire construction had no seams where the base was connected to the holly leaf seat, backrest, or arms.

"Was the seat made from only one piece of crystal?" Matha asked Ferrell and Maeve, who stood right across the aisle from him, studying the crystal acorn shells. Both turned to look at him, but said nothing. He could tell that they found their surroundings enchanting, and were somewhat at a loss for words.

"Yes," and then, uncharacteristically, Ferrell hesitated, before continuing. "This kind of quartz originates from Gleam, so the Elves of Silver Forge who made this place must have moved the crystal all the way from there, which, I assume, would have taken countless wagons, and of course, numerous grand horns. I myself can't imagine so many grand horns presenting themselves for such an arduous service, regardless of how many sacks of privet berries the Elves offered them," he added chuckling.

"Grand horns to get 'em from Four Falls to here," Loingsech declared, his voice booming. "But sailin' barges to take 'em from Gleam to Four Falls. I've made that voyage too many times to count."

"You mean too many times to *flaunt*," Ferrell added.

Matha thought more about what Ferrell and Loingsech had just said. There must have been almost one hundred seats for each season, and each seat was almost identical to the next, except for the differences in the motifs. This probably meant that the Elves had to have hauled nearly four hundred of these blocks and carved each seat perfectly, from a single piece. This endeavor was indeed remarkable, and Matha wondered why the Elves would go to such lengths, instead of hauling in smaller blocks and assembling each seat from a number of pieces.

"But this means," Matha countered, "that they had to have carved the seats from *hundreds* of individual blocks. Why would they go to all that effort?"

"The Luminary must know," Loingsech replied, "for here in this place, there is only one logical deduction that an Elve could make."

"You're asking the wrong question," Ferrell replied, speaking carefully. They weren't carved at all. Look very closely — at the stonework."

Matha did so, and saw no traces of chiseling. He also noticed the uniformity of the quartz — each seat was identical to the next. He was reminded then of the rainbow flute at Curios & Marvels, each part a color of the rainbow, all of them seamlessly connected to each other. Long ago, such things had somehow been made, but how was still a mystery.

"Legend says that Boann created *Teampall Easa*," Loingsech continued. "She shaped the marble with Water, but we know the Elves of Silver Forge built this place, not her. The Elves couldn't command the currents, so they must have used some other method to shape the quartz we now sit on."

"Does that mean that long ago the Elves possessed abilities like those of Boann?" Matha wondered aloud.

Loingsech simply raised an eyebrow at him, and looking at Ferrell and Maeve, Matha saw that they didn't object. Obviously, they both suspected the same thing, as Matha could also tell that they must have seen this kind of artisanship before.

"Ferrell," Matha began, "You've seen this before — haven't you? Why then all the secrecy? At *Curios & Marvels* Edmund had a story to explain everything, but nothing sounded true. Why does the Assembly hide the truth about these places?"

Loingsech stared at Ferrell, his eyes gleaming, wondering what the Luminary would say. To even ask him such a thing — put so bluntly — might have been seen as insolent, but Matha was a Faery of the Water, and in many ways an innocent. His earnestness alone disarmed the Luminary, and so Ferrell replied:

"These things are shaped this way in many places in *Tír Luí Lucharachán.* No one knows why, but the obvious should not be discounted. Clearly, they were not made by any tools we now possess, but the rest is for the Assembly to interpret."

Matha was irked by Ferrell's weak response, but catching a quick glance from Loingsech, he said nothing more. Maeve also remained silent.

"There be a legend that Brión[5] the Brave lost a bet that he could entice a fair elven lady after a Yule festival," Loingsech began, "but she shunned him, and he became so cross that he stamped his feet at the base of the Tadlachs, and all the fair stones in the lands broke into the forms his elven lady adored, so that he could finally win her affection."

"A beautiful tale," Ferrell chuckled, "but a tall tale all the same."

"What then, is *your* story?" Matha asked again.

Ferrell and Maeve only stared at Matha, their countenances as icy-looking as the crystal seats they stood next to. Matha sorely wished to know more, but thought better of pestering Ferrell with more questions. Surprisingly, he and Maeve had been somewhat forthright about how the seats were crafted, yet suspected that their candor was brief because they were also baffled. Ferrell didn't seem to completely believe the Assembly's account of the shrines. There was much more about them than met the eye, and Ferrell seemed to be hiding from the truth, just as the spirits of his ancestors could have been hiding amongst the pillars of the shrine — laughing at him.

---

[5] Pronounced [BRI-an]

Now many more entered the shrine. First came Loch, the Roiler, and so unlike the time before, when he had arrogantly attacked Matha and Baudwin, he was now simply taken by his surroundings. He didn't say much of anything, and to Matha, he seemed unnerved to be in a shrine so similar to the one at Coventina. When he approached the well, he did so warily, as if fearing the Water would again come gushing up from the center and wash him away.

Kelven then came along with Seamus. Making a sign of the Water they both bowed before the shrine, as did Criofan who stood with them. All three seemed quite relieved to have finally arrived. "Blessings to the Water!" Seamus offered. "What a wonderful sight," he added, surveying his surroundings. I must say that the shrine in Coventina eluded me my entire Life, so being here is quite an honor." Turning to Loingsech he added, "I would like to thank Loingsech for bringing us here, and Ferrell, for being willing to come to this place."

"In this most unexpected, yet hallowed fork in our journey, may the Water bless us all," Kelven said reverently. He then produced a glass vial of Water from his pocket and raised the blue-green treasure above his head. "I've kept this on me since leaving Deuona — drawn by me from the Water by the dam. I ask you, Loingsech, will you accept this blessed Water to invoke the ceremony?"

"Aye, I will," Loingsech replied, smiling.

Criofan made his way over to Matha and sat down. "So *this* is where the two of you found yourselves? And you got into a fight with him, he added, pointing to Loch, "and I missed out on all the fun."

Criofan shot a wink at Loch who smirked back at him. "Hey, Roiler," he added, "if we all come to blows again, don't blame me when the Water washes you away."

"There will be none of that!" Lugh announced behind them. Following along, his eyes shifted to and fro, tense with excitement, as they drank in the serene splendor of the sanctum. Matha was then reminded of Lugh's appearance when he had first met him at the Garden of Sprockets. Now, instead of being filled with perturbation, he was filled with amazement.

Lugh then affirmed, "I am *with* the Water! What a wondrous place! Why, Boann, did you wait so long before granting me this *assurance* of your majesty? Why didn't you bring me here — when I was young — so I could better serve you now?"

Rian and Tárlach were the last to enter the shrine. Tárlach had brought his squirrels with him, but Seamus had decided to leave Moonrise in his cage on the *Bael Inse*. Furtively, Tárlach glanced around him, his eyes darting to and fro, but when he spotted the well, his worries seemed to melt, and to Matha, he seemed intrigued. This was, after all, a water shrine, and he held the Water in highest regard.

Looking about with an air of reverence, Rian then asked Matha, "And a place just like this is where you found the tablet?"

"Indeed," Matha replied. "Just like this."

"What again, were the words?" Rian asked.

Matha recited:

You may wish for many things

Or never want for much

But that which holds the Truth you seek

Is something you must touch

"Whatever do those words mean?" Matha asked Loingsech.

"They mean for ye to reach out and touch somethin' greater than yerself," Loingsech replied, "regardless of what ye think ye be wantin'. The real lesson ye must get is that ye are no different than a blade of grass, or the sky above ye, and even no different than the Elves standing over there."

Hearing this, Ferrell and Maeve both looked askance at Loingsech, as if he was completely off his widget. Seeing their expressions, Rian said, "What he says is true. I told Baudwin that he must let the truth touch him. He was learning the lessons of the Triquetra, and after considerable contemplation, he was granted a vision of Glamorium. He looked within and touched something far greater than himself."

"Sure," Loingsech continued, "but now, we'll be placin' our attention not on ourselves, but on each other, for in this ceremony we be establishin' trust between one another — the Faeries and Elves, of course. This most basic and common rite has been held in shrines such as these for millennia."

"How will we do this?" Criofan asked.

"I'll be showin' ye," Loingsech said. "This way."

And so, everyone soon found themselves gathered around the well in the center of the shrine. Loingsech had the Elves stand in one group, while the Faeries stood in another, both sides close, but not too close, so they could still hear each other and not be stricken by the curse. He then explained, "The rite we be needin' to perform is to establish trust, but before we begin, we be needin' to consider the true meanin' of the Triquetra. So only then will I explain where to stand and how we'll conduct ourselves. But now, I must ask the Elves — who among ye will lead yer half of the ceremony?"

There were many unsure glances. Tárlach looked as if a tide was about to strike him, and on his shoulder, Bandy gave only a curious chirp. Maeve barely paid attention, for to her, the entire exercise was folly. Ferrell appeared to want to try, but didn't have the confidence to volunteer. The rest of the guards looked as if they would rather be anywhere but where they were.

Rian, the Druid of Guidance, then took a step forward. "I will lead," he said. "But I cannot lie. I truly have little sense of what to do."

"Ye have *plenty* of sense," Loingsech countered. "Ye simply need to be pointed in the right direction. Now — all of ye — listen carefully. Before we conduct the ceremony, we must first be rightly aware of the true nature of Glamorium. For ye see, the Triquetra teaches us what we must learn — and that is Honesty, Truth, and the Promise of Rebirth. Without recognizing these, just as surely as ye know yer element or yer metal, ye cannot harness Glamorium at all!"

"Enough!" Maeve exclaimed. "Ferrell, they seek to pervert the meaning of the Triquetra — Scrutiny, Certainty, and the Promise of the Future." Hearing this, the Elves around her gave a loud hurrah, but Loingsech only scowled.

"Nay nay nay!" Loingsech exclaimed. "The ceremony will never work if we don't stop buttin' horns like a bunch of obstinate sheep! You Elves have been misled into believin' that your version of the Triquetra is more important."

"Careful — sea squid," Maeve warned, wagging her finger. "You're violating the laws of the Assembly by calling the Triquetra anything else!"

Slowly, but firmly, Ferrell pushed down her arm. "For just this one occasion," he began, "and in the interest of cooperation, we will humor them."

"Very well then," Maeve scoffed, "because it's not like what we're about to do is going to work anyway."

"Honesty, Truth, and the Promise of Rebirth," Matha said. "What do you want us to understand?"

"That ye cannot *touch* Glamorium unless yer worthy," Loingsech replied. "And ye cannot be worthy, unless yer Honest with yerself, know the Truth of the realm, and understand that through the Promise of Rebirth, ye'll face yer Death and, in doing so, be reborn into something way beyond what ye think ye know," Loingsech said. "Most must live a lifetime to learn these things, but for now, we'll place our attention on just being Honest, for Honesty is what we'll need in this rite, if we are to weave the first cord in the knot of the Triquetra."

After a long pause, Loingsech then said, "Before we go any further, I must first ask ye all — why is trust so important?"

Kelven then spoke. "If we can't trust one another, then we can't live in harmony."

Seamus added, "And if we can't trust one another, then we'll always fight."

Lugh was doubtful. "You're telling us that we must trust one another? That's even funnier than trying to get those beavers to stop building their dams. Fat chance of *them* ever really trusting *us*," he added, pointing at the Elves.

"Trusting you Faeries would be much easier if you just followed the rules," Ferrell snapped back.

Loingsech raised his hands to signal to everyone that he now held the floor. "If we can't be trustin' one another, then we can't be speakin' to one another properly, let alone be cooperatin'. This most basic rite was what the Faeries and Elves used to perform, before the Faeries passed their dreams to the Elves. Without trust, we cannot hope to work together."

"You make what you say sound so easy," Criofan declared flatly.

"As once it was," Loingsech said, "but don't ye forget, everythin' always gets down to *intention,* doesn't it? Whether it be honin' like the Faeries or temperin' like the Elves, without right intention, ye can't even begin to trust one another. I know that our trials have been difficult for everyone, but we *must* persist."

"What do you know of our difficulties?" Maeve retorted.

"I be knowin' some," Loingsech began. "I be knowin' that Govannon, despite being unpopular with the Faeries, is a hero to most of ye Elves, and for good reason. He brought ye prosperity after a terrible time of sufferin'."

"That suffering was worse than you'll *ever* understand!" Maeve exclaimed. "Do you know why Govannon holds Ferrell in such high regard?"

"He fought with him at the siege of the Clock City," Loingsech replied.

"Yes, of course, but the *other* reason?"

The Faeries all gave puzzled looks. None knew what Maeve was referring to, and so she continued, "He, amongst very few, was willing to fight with Govannon against the nobles who had managed the planting in the Southern Isle so badly that many Elves found themselves starving to death. The nobles hid their mistakes by not reporting the extent of their incompetence. Instead, they hoarded whatever crops were available, leaving many Elves to wither and pass to Annwyn. And these were the very same nobles who had sworn their fealty to the council, which had once been a great beacon in the elven lands, but had long since fallen to corruption and disarray.

"And Brandon," she continued sarcastically, "the *great* King of the Elves and father to Govannon and Belanus, had become so irresolute and distanced from his homeland that he did nothing. He merely turned a blind eye to all the suffering. Almost no one was willing to help Govannon, but Ferrell and some others did. Vastly outnumbered, Govannon defied his father's order and led an uprising — and when he did, who was there to help? *Ferrell* was, and together they slew those rank incompetents, raided the granary, and soon no one was starving. Ferrell and those like him are the ones to whom we give our thanks — not to a bunch of boneheaded blunderers, or you ill-informed, compliant Faeries, who still supported the council afterwards. Luckily, Brandon forgave Govannon upon his return to Mist Valley."

Matha had never heard any of this before. He wondered why the Faeries were so complicit in supporting a council that allowed Elves to starve, but he assumed that Maeve's account was probably quite biased, and that the Southern Isle meant the large island below the Calming Reach in *Tír Luí Lucharachán*.

"There's more to that story," Lugh began. "We couldn't just interfere with your affairs, and the council assured us that the problem was being remedied. We are not heartless. I'm sure that had we known how terribly the Elves were suffering we'd have sent shipments to them. Isn't that right, Loingsech?"

"Sure," Loingsech agreed. It didn't seem as if he wanted to discuss such affairs, and Matha sensed that the sea Faery was trying to rein in the discussion. "There was an embargo, and I couldn't have gotten into port, even if I had known."

"That so-called *embargo* was simply a way to cover up the problem," Maeve continued. "Who needs food, if no one is starving? A benevolent gift from the nobles of the Southern Isle," she added sarcastically. "And, I might add, since when are *you* afraid of smuggling? Aiding Four Falls came so easily, did it not? Why should I trust a smuggler who chooses his fights in such a one-sided manner? Why should I trust any of you Faeries anyway? And especially, why should Ferrell? You don't know of our struggles, and you certainly don't know anything about Govannon."

"And I don't care to understand either," Lugh declared. "You Elves are the *occupiers* in *Tír Éirí Sióg.*"

A silence passed over the group, like a deadly cloud of contagion. *Any plan of a ceremony is now doomed,* Matha thought, *as are we.* How could any of them now speak of the virtues of Glamorium, or how to conduct a ceremony, with so much distrust between them? And how could Faery and Elve ever reconcile, with such a bitter history and so much suffering and resentment?

Matha sighed, unsure of what to do next. Addressing the concord of something so complicated seemed well-nigh impossible. Were they now doomed to stumble about and shout at each other for eternity — forever cursed?

"Let's put all hurt feelings behind us," Matha implored, as he stepped away from his crystal seat. "We must not forget why we've come to this sacred place."

"Aye," Loingsech began, "he be right. I'll now tell ye more about the ceremony." Pointing to the ground, he asked, "Do ye see the glyphs circlin' the base of this well?"

Everyone looked down at the carvings, a series of interlocking circles etched together, like links in a chain. Each center of each interlocking circle contained a glyph, first faery, and then elven, all the way around the well. Matha noted that they were the same as the ones he had seen in the other shrine with Baudwin.

"We must all stand together like this," Loingsech continued, motioning to everyone, "and go around the well one by one, first Faery, then Elve, joinin' together with our arms, so we're linked — just like the circles. I be leadin' the Faeries and Rian be leadin' the Elves, but don't forget that once we're closer to one other, we won't be able to hear each other, so if you get confused, look to your leader for help. Before we speak honestly to one another, I will recite the sacred words to invoke Glamorium."

"How are you going to invoke Glamorium?" Ferrell asked, looking about. "We don't have nary a piece."

With that, Loingsech produced something from a pocket in his jacket, raising his hand for all to see. There was no mistaking what he was holding — a fine pendant made of Glamorium in the shape of a double S spiral. The green metal shimmered brightly in the Sun.

"How beautiful, indeed!" Rian exclaimed.

"So lustrous, and yet so —" Maeve added, her voice trailing, as she spied the treasure. Matha sensed she was looking to find something wrong, but couldn't.

"*Wondrous,*" Seamus remarked. "So much like the egg that Baudwin brought home."

"I remember," Rian said, winking at Seamus.

"With this pendant," Loingsech began, "I'll invoke Glamorium, and if all goes as we hope when we are honest with ourselves, we will then have greater respect for one another. Please seriously consider what you say, and don't let your heart dwell on past grievances. Instead, remember the greater good."

"But will this actually work?" Ferrell asked.

"Sure, if ye let yer heart lead the way," Loingsech replied. "Don't forget, the Assembly has much to gain from this. Wouldn't ye like to tell yer kin the tale of how ye invoked Glamorium and saved us all from that spirit ye think is so dangerous and vile? Think of the honors Govannon will bestow upon ye."

"Then we may as well try," Ferrell said.

"Very good then," Loingsech said. "And now, Rian, if ye would please come to me, ye and I will invoke Glamorium. According to *gnàs*, for this to happen, an Elve of strong character must bond with a Faery of similar character, until goodwill prevails, and both can see the other in themselves. While there may be others here who might do just as well, I choose ye."

Rian was standing far enough away to hear Loingsech, and so Rian approached him. As soon as he was close enough to grasp the pendant, Loingsech offered the glimmering treasure to him and said, "A time for all places." He then waited to hear Rian's response, but Rian was unable to hear what Loingsech said, so none came.

An uncomfortable silence ensued, as everyone waited to see what, if anything, would happen. Maeve glared at Ferrell as if to say, "I told you so!" and Ferrell nodded back at her.

Everyone stood glumly, assuming the ceremony had failed before it had even begun. And then Tárlach, who was standing far from Rian and had heard Loingsech, cleared his throat and announced, "A place for all time."

Hearing this, the rest of the Elves who stood far from Rian took Tárlach's cue, and with great enthusiasm also announced, "A place for all time!"

Having finally understood Loingsech's message, Rian took a final step toward him, and with great accord, repeated, "A place for all time."

Hearing Rian and the Elves, the Faeries then chorused, "A time for all places!"

The exchange was now complete. Having made the appropriate greeting, Loingsech and Rian were now holding the pendant between them, and Elves and Faeries alike were much closer to seeing the other in themselves. Everyone had been quite distressed at the beginning, but now seemed genuinely pleased that they were able to solve the hearing problem so simply.

Genuine cooperation had prevailed.

Loingsech then motioned for the entire group to form a circle around the well. One by one, he pointed first for Ferrell to stand next to him on his left, and then Matha next to Ferrell, and then Maeve next to Matha, and then Criofan next to Maeve, continuing with Rian, then Seamus, then Tárlach, then Kelven, then an elven Water Guard, then Loch, then another elven Water Guard, then Lugh, and finally one last elven Water Guard. Looking across the well, Loingsech nodded at Rian, who now stood directly opposite him.

The guards who had been selected by Loingsech were chosen because they were Water Guards. Loingsech explained that this was to show respect to the Water.

"Now," Loingsech began, "we must prove ourselves worthy of Glamorium's splendor. I beseech you all to *honestly* share some part of yourself. If we all are honest enough, then perhaps we will be graced."

Without hesitation, Loingsech then spoke. "I'll be more honest with the Assembly — assuming that they will be more honest with me." Matha knew that only some of the Elves could hear him, and so Rian repeated his words.

Ferrell then joined in. "I will honestly tell the entire truth of what has come to pass here. I will not spare any details from Govannon, nor will I alter any of the facts. And if any of the Elves from times long past are listening, please let this ceremony ease our strife." Matha could not hear him, as the curse made this impossible, and so Rian repeated his words and Matha heard them.

Now Matha's turn had come, and so he said, "I'll do my best not to be partial with my honesty, even if doing so means risking even greater conflicts. Maeve just told us of her grievance — that many turned a blind eye to the suffering in the Southern Isle — and I will make it my work to ensure that others are also honest about what happened. A crime such as this should not be buried out of cowardice."

Loingsech repeated the words so the rest could hear.

Maeve then spoke. Again, Matha could not hear her. "All of you Faeries here — I must say that you have grown some on me. Know now that I do not hold any of you river dwellers guilty of anything but being earnest — perhaps *too* earnest with your love of the old ways. I know most of you mean well, and that even if we don't see eye to eye, my intentions are not to do you any harm."

Again, Rian repeated the words so the rest could hear.

And so, each of those remaining in the circle took a proper turn at being honest with themselves. Criofan admitted that too often he tried to appear honest when he actually wasn't, even with those who were closest to him. Rian promised to be more honest with others, even if they weren't being honest with him. Seamus declared that he would encourage others to be honest without fearing retribution. Tárlach affirmed that honesty made him feel stronger and more at ease. Kelven confessed that sometimes he was afraid to be honest, fearing the judgment of others. Loch vowed to embrace the honesty of others without taunting or condemning them. Lugh agreed to rely upon his own integrity, instead of taking on false accounts from others. And the Water Guards spoke of their revitalized loyalty to the Water, having taken the example of the water Faeries much more to heart.

Whenever someone couldn't hear a particular admission, either an Elve or Faery who did hear would inform that one. Soon, everyone knew what everyone had said, and all seemed heartened by how simple and rewarding being honest had been. A few steps had now been taken that might lead to releasing the curse.

"Now," Loingsech instructed, "to thank each other for yer honesty, please turn respectfully to yer right and make either the sign of Faery or Elve, until ye've gone all around the circle."

Rian repeated the instructions for the group. Loingsech then tapped Ferrell on the shoulder. Ferrell turned to Matha, made a circle with his hands, his fingers touching at the top and his thumbs at the bottom, and said, "A place for all time."

Matha then turned to Maeve, crossed his hands in front of himself, with his right palm facing down, and his left hand pointed up, and said, "A time for all places."

Maeve nodded at him, smiling, her chin slightly tilted. Struck by a side of her he hadn't ever seen, he smiled back. Truly, she was radiant, as if the majesty of Gold Haven was pouring from her very being. Turning back to Ferrell, he saw him smiling as well. Respectfully, the Luminary bowed his head, and once again Matha was struck by his countenance. *What would he be like at home during a much simpler time, next to a fire, perhaps with a book?* he wondered.

As the rest of them were experiencing the exact kind of moment that Matha, Maeve, and Ferrell had just had, everyone became excited. A current of joy ran through them, and suddenly they linked arms and began to do a spirited step dance around the well. *Now we're linked like the circles at the base of the shrine,* Matha thought, amazed. Forming a second circle behind them were a number of Faeries and Elves, each one holding a fife, flute, trumpet, tambourine, or drum. *And now we have music!* he thought elatedly, for he knew that both Elves and Faeries often carried their instruments under their coats, ready at a moment's notice to play them. This certainly was such a time. Around the well the two circles danced, both going in opposite directions.

Curiously, Matha noticed that the music could be heard coming from anyone in any place, unlike their speech. He'd not been a part of such levity since the important meeting. The Faeries tripped lightly, arm in arm with the Elves, and the Elves stomped and stomped to the fast-moving rhythm of the music. All smiled exuberantly, their faces lifted to the sky. Gazing to his left, Matha peered at Maeve, who deftly moved her feet in time to the fifes and drums, and to his right was Ferrell, having shed his Luminary posture to simply delight in the joy of the dance. *Maeve is so refined when she moves, and Ferrell so rustic,* he thought.

Memories of Baudwin filled his mind, and what they had discussed at the shrine of Coventina. Baudwin had asked him why there was a Sun at the shrine but no Moon: "We water Faeries do not revere the Sun — we revere the Moon. It could also be that the Faeries and Elves weren't simply cooperating to build this place, but *communing* with each other by doing some kind of Sun and water ritual."

And this was what they were all doing now, desperate to break Boann's horrible curse. Around and around the circles danced, ever more exhilarated by the music and the fragrance of the lilies and honeysuckle vines. Again, Matha remembered Baudwin. *We're actually communing!* he thought. *Perhaps because we have finally been honest enough with ourselves to respect one another — if only a little.*

"Elves — bow to the water!" Rian then shouted. Respectfully, the Elves bowed their heads to the Water as they whirled with the Faeries around the well.

"Faeries — bow to the Sun!" Loingsech then shouted, as the tempo of the drums increased. Immediately, the Faeries bowed their heads to the large topaz Sun in the vault above the well, their feet still flying and their faces bright with feeling.

Right after Loingsech said this, Matha saw Maeve attempt to hide some disdain, but she quickly became wide-eyed due to what happened next.

As everyone continued to twirl arm in arm around the well, something suddenly occurred that took them all by surprise. Watching Maeve, Matha saw her eyes grow wide with astonishment. As if on cue, the entire group stopped dancing to gaze inside the well. Up out of the shimmering pile of offerings

— blue topaz, pearls, shards of green quartz and gold — shot a ray of intense cobalt-blue Light, and down from the yellow topaz Sun shot a ray of golden yellow Light. Midway between the Water and the Sun, exactly where the two rays became one, the Light glowed a scintillating iridescent green. Awed by the sight, the musicians stopped playing, and a hush fell over the group.

Matha could see that Ferrell and Maeve were taken completely off guard, but spying Loingsech, he could also tell that the sea Faery seemed more pleased than surprised by what was taking place. Mesmerized by the luminous green Light swirling between the blue and yellow rays, everyone waited for him to speak.

"O revered shrine of the Sun and the Water!" he began. "The Water and the Sun have accepted us, by blessin' us with a rare gift — the Light of Glamorium — the *Dúrúnghlas.* For this, we be truly grateful, but our purpose in bein' here is not as yet fulfilled. Please accept our pleas to enter into a sacred rite before ye. We Elves and Faeries now present ourselves in an accord that had long since fallen away, but now, we be beseechin' ye. Let this rite of trust succeed! Let the Light we see, and the Triquetra, heal us with Honesty, Truth, and the Promise of Rebirth!"

Rian repeated these words.

In unison, both Elves and Faeries uttered a resounding *Ahhhhhhh,* and as they did, the green Light shone even brighter. Seeing this, Loingsech handed his pendant to the guard standing to his right. "Pass this pendant around the circle, so all may touch Glamorium. Do so quickly, while the green Light shines."

At first the guard hesitated, as he could not hear him, but Rian spurred him on.

And so each of the Fae held Glamorium for a moment, going clockwise around the circle, until all had done so. Matha wondered if anything more would happen, but thus far there was no effect. He could only surmise that once the time was right, the ceremony would then make Glamorium known to them all at once. When the pendant came back to Loingsech, he passed it the other way around the circle, saying, "As we go, we must recite the poem."

Rian, who stood opposite Loingsech on the other side of the well, said the same: "We must recite the poem."

Everyone began, and soon all were singing earnestly:

<blockquote>
You may wish for many things
Or never want for much
But that which holds the Truth you seek
Is something you must touch
</blockquote>

All the while, the green Light shined and shimmered between the blue and yellow Light inside the well.

"*Draíocht!*" Loingsech cried.

And "*Draíocht!*" Rian cried as well.

Loingsech again called out "*Draíocht!*", then Ferrell, then Matha, Maeve, Criofan, Rian, Seamus, Tárlach, Kelven, a guard, Loch, another guard, Lugh, and all the musicians in the second circle. Soon this word was on every lip as the pendant was passed around the circle yet another time.

Seemingly in response, a great thrumming resounded from all around them. The green Light inside the well disappeared, leaving only blue and yellow, and Loingsech's pendant began to glow a verdant green. Rising from the palm of his hand, the pendant then hovered, suspended by an unknown force just above his hand.

Still the sea Faery and the Druid of Guidance continued to cry "*Draíocht!*" as the pendant rose higher and higher into the air. From both sides of the double-spiraled pendant an almost blinding beam of verdant Light then shot out, forming a large, umbrella-like circle just above the heads of the Elves and Faeries. Transfixed, all they could see was the great green beam of Light, still emanating from the double spiral.

"Now," Rian declared, "comes not a vision of Glamorium — but Glamorium *itself.*"

Matha sensed a kind of waking overcome him, but not like a waking of the Water. Now, instead of hearing the thoughts and sensing the feelings of only water Faeries, he also knew the thoughts and feelings of the Elves around him. *Only a Glamorium waking would include everyone*, he thought. And then he felt something he had never known before — a sense of unity without distinction. In his heart, he did not feel separate from anyone around him. The appearances that divided everyone had vanished. The Elves held the same standing as he, as their essences were now laid bare. The illusions his mind had clung to were dispelled, and his longings extinguished. Seeing and being this, he felt an enduring peace — untouched by suffering of any kind.

For too long the strife of the realm had consumed them, but in this moment he knew they'd fought needlessly. Glamorium had come to them directly and shown that their actions were born of ignorance and propelled by a reasoning tethered to personal selfhood. In this moment he knew the truth — that there was only the Great Emerald Light.

Matha then turned to regard Ferrell, who regarded him as well, but in the other he saw only himself, and in himself, he saw only the other. He couldn't tell whether he was a Faery looking at an Elve, or whether an Elve was looking at a Faery. In that moment there was nothing — no separation or distinction — and his mind, normally abuzz with futile efforts to touch the world around him, was now muted, laid low by a greater force. Released from its ceaseless machinations, his mind was now but a minor servant.

He knew then that Ferrell saw the same, and turning to face Maeve, he saw her gaze at him, her anger and strife now eclipsed by something far greater.

O how he wished with every fiber of his being that this could always be! What great concord had come to them in that moment, and why, he wondered, could Life not *always* be thus? How had the realm become so distorted that conflict was inevitable? Why had everyone been drawn to such a painful and arduous path, only to be graced with a glimpse of this now? There were no answers to his questions, and all seemed futile to even ask.

How long the group remained engulfed in the emanations of Glamorium none could say, for then, the Elves had no sense of time, and the Faeries sensed both all space and no space. Matha could have left his Life behind, but before too long the verdant Light above their heads began to fade, and the pendant that was still floating above Loingsech's outstretched hand slowly began to lower back to his palm. The ceremony was now complete.

Matha heard the voice of an Elve, so close to him that at first he didn't notice that the curse had been lifted. "I have touched the heart of the mountains," Ferrell said, tears streaming from his eyes.

And from Maeve, Matha heard, "How could we have ever forgotten this?"

Soon everyone noticed that they could hear each other at a distance. Indeed, Glamorium had healed them, just as Loingsech said it would.

⚶

Rejoicing that the curse had been lifted, all gave thanks to Glamorium — again and again. Gathered close to the well, they chattered joyously about what had transpired, but before they could share even more, a shockwave emanated from the glamorium pendant that Loingsech now wore around his neck.

The shock began as a globe of dark energy, a small rather innocuous-looking orb that quickly expanded into a menacing cloud, growing larger and larger, until its malignancy had run through the entire shrine, moving above and around all of them. The cloud dissipated, and the smell of lilies and honeysuckle was abruptly overcome by a foul odor none could name. The Air turned cold and heavy with the weight of the stench.

At first, what was happening was not clear to most, but as the smell reached their nostrils, they immediately felt disoriented. Just as quickly, the euphoria of Glamorium faded away. Seamus grabbed at his heart — as the feeling within him was so intense that he couldn't utter a word. Around them, the roosting birds all fled from the trees, and the insects went silent. Matha stared at Ferrell, who was lost in a dark recollection — now triggered in him by the sudden shock that had run through them.

"What in all the metals of *Tír na nÓg* was *that?*" Ferrell asked.

Seamus observed, "I haven't known that feeling since. . . the Great Befalling."

"Yes," Kelven added, "the feeling is just as it was then, yet I'm not as bewildered as I was then. . . Nor as confounded. . . And yet, the quality is the same."

"If that was the great shock — now returned — we are in dire peril!" Rian exclaimed. Matha could sense the terror in him, and soon Loch was by his side, trying to reassure the druid. Loch's kindness toward Rian seemed peculiar to Matha, yet as soon as the Roiler spoke, Matha gained some clarity.

"Rian warned Tárlach and me!" Loch exclaimed. "Everyone — be on your guard! The shadow of Glamorium falls upon us!"

Confusion and worry clouded both sides, and Matha surmised that the elders among them were readying themselves for the ordeal they had endured long ago. Only they — not those born after them — knew the danger they were facing. Loingsech then cast his pendant on the ground, as if he had been bitten by a venomous spider. Still reeling from the shock — which had bored through him the deepest — he stumbled, almost falling, as he had been at the center of the attack.

Everyone looked now at the pendant, which just a few moments ago had been so cherished but now infected everyone with a sinister sense of foreboding and doom. The double-spiral S had clanked upon the ground, hitting the stonework near the base of the well. All looked on in horror, but before anyone could utter a word, a black miasma seeped from the edges of the pendant, rising up like a snake emerging from its burrow.

Matha saw the cloud of black rise, inky and cold with slithery veins racing over the mass. He watched — aghast — as the vapors separated into fearsome, yet curious-looking tendrils that began weaving in the Air in front of him. The shapes were of gears and sprockets, and as they interlocked with one another, they moved eerily in unison, forming the inside of a machine of some sort. *The moving parts might look beautiful,* he thought, *if they weren't all so tarnished.* He made out what appeared to be the inside of a broken-down steamway machine, strangely hoary and decayed, like ancient oak trees with dripping moss and gnarled limbs.

"What is it doing?" Matha asked, at once mesmerized and revolted by the sight.

"How *stunning!*" Maeve exclaimed. "See how it creates such a sublime machine — forged from Gold *and* Silver!"

"That's not what I'm seeing," Matha said, taken aback. "Surely a machine — but foul and perhaps even lethal."

Matha knew then that Maeve was seeing something similar to what he saw, but to her it was much more beautiful. This indeed was curious, but much sadder to him was that the euphoria of Glamorium had completely vanished, leaving him with only an intensely painful feeling of separation from everyone around him. Where he had previously known oneness without distinction, now he knew only division without oneness. Looking about, he saw that everyone was trapped once again in their own isolated world, alone and afraid. He then sensed the Water inside of him, and although he was still unjoined from his current, where once the Water had flowed within him with such grace, he now felt only a swirling vortex, causing his feelings to whirl about, like a frog trapped in a tide pool.

"This is terrible!" he said aloud.

"How can such a wondrous thing be *terrible*?" Maeve asked. "The gears and sprockets must be part of some machine it seeks to build. All of you guards! Commit this to memory so we might build this wonder in the factories of the Clock City!"

Maeve then turned to Ferrell. "This must be a gift! Surely, Govannon will be most pleased, but we must remember all the intricacies well." Boldly, Maeve approached the gearworks floating in the air. Enchanted, she peered into the construction, trying to make out how the mechanism worked.

"Maeve — be careful!" Ferrell warned.

"Are you blind to all of its splendor?" she asked Ferrell.

"No," Ferrell replied, his voice heavy with apprehension, "but I don't see Gold or Silver. . . more like a dull leaden color." Turning to face her he added, "Don't forget how the great shock weakened us so long ago."

Now Matha realized that everyone saw the shadow somewhat differently, which he found quite puzzling. Why wasn't everyone seeing the same thing?

Many theories were bandied about, amidst cries of fear and wonder. The Faeries — including Loch — were witnessing mostly the same thing, but the Elves saw something closer to what Maeve was describing, though not as stunningly as she.

As they all continued talking, Matha warily studied the spectacle before them, wondering if the strange, exaggerated contraption would turn on them all, but all the workings did was reconfigure themselves slowly, yet methodically, as if the gears and cogs were creating some kind of device whose purpose was as yet unclear. Matha noticed other things that resembled the inside of a steamway engine, but had no idea of what they did. A terrifying thought then struck him: *Whatever this thing is seeks to intrigue and poison us and make us into slaves, so we will forget ourselves and never even remember what just happened!*

Maeve reached out to touch the mass, but Ferrell quickly grabbed her wrist. "Stop!" he shouted, almost panicking. "Have you lost your senses?"

"Oh no! I've lost nothing and gained *much* more!" she roared, a crazed gleam in her eye. She tried to pull her hand away from him, but Ferrell's grip was strong, and as he ordered his guards to restrain her, she began raving.

"It's a gift! Let us touch it! Let us *own* it!"

Rian then intervened. "Ferrell — you must listen! Being near to whatever this thing is has made my thoughts race with blinding speed. I sense the metal in me shaping into something I cannot understand or control."

"Surely," Loingsech chimed in, "I be feelin' that the Water is movin' so strongly in me that I can't tell up from down, or good from bad."

Standing next to Loingsech, Criofan nodded, his alarm palpable. "There's something not right about this, as if I've been rejoined to the Water — but in a *foul* way."

As if they had been listening, the shadows in the air began to reconfigure themselves. The dark gears and somber ashen cogs had vanished, and instead Matha saw the shape of a beautiful fountain, dark and glistening, with inky Water shooting up.

"Now I see a fountain," Matha said, perplexed.

"I see a fine grinder," Tárlach spoke.

"A beautiful cooking pot," Kelven said, "brass and stout."

"I see beautifully cut glowstones," Seamus said. "They even appear to shine."

"A mechanical loom," Ferrell said. "The kind I'm sure my beloved would have cherished."

The fountain Matha saw reminded him of the one back in Deuona, in the center of his family shrine. He wondered how this strange manifestation could create such an exact copy. Had its workings seen into his mind somehow, and everyone else's as well — thereby showing them what they wanted to see?

"Why did it change?" Matha asked, aloud. "What does it want from us?"

"I don't trust it," Loingsech declared, pacing about. "It's showin' me a sculpture from Baranthus — a large and beautiful eternity knot, made long ago." Grimacing, he closed his eyes. "But seein' it doesn't make me feel better — in fact, I feel sick."

"That's because you see only a sculpture. I see the most beautiful magniglow dynamo I've ever laid my eyes on!" Maeve exclaimed.

"Nay!" Loingsech replied. "Yer not seein' a dynamo — ye just *want* it to be a dynamo — just like I wouldn't have minded lookin' at the sculpture from my homeland, even though I know it's too good to be true."

Maeve rounded on Loingsech, "Too good to be true, is it?" Staring fixedly ahead, she asked, "What could be truer than *this*?"

"Glamorium was truer — *far* truer," Loingsech retorted. "How quickly ye've forgotten the wondrous nature of the ceremony we just had — so lost are ye in the grip of whatever this thing is."

As if the image Matha saw was listening to their every word, suddenly the fountain became even more beautiful, the stonework smoother, the Water sparkling with bluish Light shooting small sparkles into the Air above the basin.

"It's changing," Matha said, "right before my eyes, as if it wants to *live* inside of me somehow."

"Everyone, be careful," Rian warned. "I fear what we are seeing is the shadow of Glamorium."

At this the Faeries became increasingly wary, but the Elves didn't share their concern. Turning again to consider the mesmerizing configuration of cogs, bolts, and gears, whirling and grinding in her sight, Maeve gasped. "Ferrell," she murmured, "this machine looks far more complex than any dynamo I've ever seen. If only Sprin were here, surely he could build whatever this is. We must find a way to bring it back with us."

"Nay — ye won't!" Loingsech hollered. Astounded, Matha watched him race to the glamorium pendant lying on the ground and bravely snatch up the glimmering green object. Holding the double S spiral at arm's length, he deftly moved toward the image in front of him. "All of ye now — watch this!" he shouted. "Soon all ye'll be seein' is the shadows of Annwyn comin' for ye!"

All awaited breathlessly to see what Loingsech would do next. "Begone, corruptin' foulness! *Draíocht!*" he shouted. "Never will ye overshadow Glamorium!"

As Loingsech brought the pendant closer to the floating image, Matha saw the beautiful fountain melt away, as if recoiling from the pendant itself. In turn, everyone, including both Faeries and Elves, saw the same — as each of their visions vanished in an instant.

"Stop that!" Maeve cried. "You're ruining *everything!*"

Echoing Maeve's frustration, the vision in the air coalesced into a black orb, expanding into a sepulchral cloud that grimly passed through everyone before quickly vanishing. As the darkness consumed Loingsech, the sea Faery gasped with shock and dropped the pendant on the ground. Matha now felt the darkness inside of himself as well, especially in the reaches of his own mind. His thoughts were much heavier, and thinking was far more difficult.

His mind strained as he thought then of the Elves, wanting to blame them for everything. This was — after all — entirely their fault. They'd come to Deuona with their plans for *Tír Éirí Sióg*, and then it was they who'd angered Boann. *Who knows what they really wanted with Baudwin*, he thought. An Elve who schemed and built was an Elve who instilled misery and guilt into all who did not share his vision for *Tír na nÓg*. Shocked by the torrid nature of his meandering thoughts, Matha tried to calm himself, but to no avail. They kept racing, as if something else was thinking *for* him. A short time later, much to his despair, he found himself bereft of feeling and utterly worn out.

Matha huddled on the ground, rocking back and forth, trying his best to pull himself together. He sensed a division between the Faeries and Elves that was starker than he had ever known, and his first impulse was to blame the Elves. The shadow in Glamorium — the forging shadow, if these wretched Fae knew its true name — raged inside of him, and all he could do was assume that everything wrong in the realm was *their* fault. He was not himself, and he knew this, but he didn't care. He continued to ruminate about who most deserved his blame. *Of course*, he thought. *Maeve. Yes, surely, she was more at fault than any other.*

He looked for her.

There she was, madly pacing about the shrine, searching for her vision of the magniglow dynamo. Behind the well she looked, but she couldn't find any trace of a gear or a housing. Matha wanted to tell her exactly why she couldn't find it, but for a moment he simply enjoyed watching her desperation.

"You there!" he shouted. Maeve was startled at first, unused to the tone of the Faery's voice. "Yes, *you!*"

She then turned to him.

"I see you're still looking for it," Matha taunted, "but it's *gone!* Gone somewhere else, somewhere far away from you, and you'll never find it. More important, you'll never be satisfied even if you do!" he added.

"Oh don't be silly!" Maeve countered. "It's here because it wants me to bring it to Govannon. He knows better than you what to do with such a gift. It's *he* who will realize its potential — not some feckless bumpkin!"

Matha would not be deterred. "You're so *wrong!*" he shouted. "It chooses only the one who sees it for what it truly is. That's it!" As Matha spoke these words, he felt compelled to upset her, yet he didn't understand what was driving him. "That's the problem with all you Elves," he scoffed. "Always telling us Faeries what to *think* about everything. Especially the metals!"

Maeve laughed, undaunted. "That reminds me so much of what Govannon said to me once. He said that the problem with you Faeries is that you're always telling the Elves what they should *feel* about everything. Especially the elements!"

"That's because we don't trust you!"

"We don't trust you either!"

Now their argument had garnered the attention of everyone around them, and they too were caught up in the growing divide, and they too were compelled to speak their minds. Soon the Faeries were huddled around Matha, and the Elves were huddled around Maeve, and both sides were shouting at each other.

"You *miserable* ingrates!" Ferrell barked. "If you were a little more forward thinking, perhaps the vision we just saw would have yielded more of its secrets!"

"I'll show you gratitude," Seamus said. "When I'm through boxing you in the head, you'll thank me afterwards for knocking some sense into you!"

Back and forth they traded insults. Tárlach then announced, "The *real* boon of Glamorium was the vision Maeve saw afterwards — one that none of you Faeries could hope to understand."

Rian then parted his arms and stood before them all. Matha hoped he would be a voice of reason, but instead the druid announced, "Come now, let me clarify what's really happening here. All of this ruckus can be settled, if we simply understand the vision we all just witnessed. You see, the vision was really a *dream*, and as Baudwin so clearly informed us at the Grand Unveiling, the dreams now belong to the Elves. And I agree with him completely — it is now high time for the Faeries to seriously consider the dreams of the Elves. Maeve, after all, was the one who saw the greatest potential in the vision, and so we must heed her and the ordered path we now must walk."

"The best path to walk would be a far different one from this," Kelven guffawed.

Somewhere deep inside, Matha managed to regain a part of himself. From the edge of his awareness, he knew something was very wrong. Everyone had utterly lost their composure, and he believed that the shadow in Glamorium was to blame. Unknown to him, it had been named the forging shadow by those who had fled the realm long ago. Its grip was tightening upon them, rendering them unable to be fair-minded or even-handed about anything. Seeing that the situation was becoming too fraught for even Rian to mediate, Matha shuddered. Rian didn't sound like himself — at all — and Matha worried that he as well would again be pulled into enmity. Still worse was that trapped within the clutches of the shadow, neither side had the slightest bit of empathy for the other. With every passing moment, the tension between not caring and desperately needing to care kept building inside of him.

Thankfully, he then remembered some words of wisdom from his mother, Brigh: "At their worst, disputes are an endless tug of war. If the scales tip too far, one side places an even heavier weight on the pan, but only a fool keeps adding more weight, and only the wise see the folly in measuring."

With this understanding, Matha felt the grip of the shadow ease, but looking around, he could see that this was not true for anyone else. The bickering only intensified, and he feared that soon the Fae would come to blows in the shrine, violating its sanctity. Desperately, he wondered what he could say or do to calm the crowd. He uttered phrases of concord, but his words fell upon deaf ears. Everyone had completely lost sight of the glamorium rite and all deference to *gnàs*. Wondering if there was anything he could do to remind them, he then noticed something — purely by happenstance — although perhaps more on purpose than he knew. As probably the only one who hadn't fully succumbed to the shadow, he was the only possible bearer of hope, and so a small measure of grace was bestowed upon him. Set into the masonry of the well was an arch-shaped niche with a scalloped top. He knew what had to be there. Quickly, he went and found a tablet just like the one he had seen so long ago when he had gone adventuring with his dear friend Baudwin at the Springs of Coventina.

Written on the tablet were the same glyphs that read:

You may wish for many things
Or never want for much
But that which holds the Truth you seek
Is something you must touch

Beneath the glyphs was the symbol of Glamorium — two side-by-side spirals making an *S* shape, with a line beginning in the center of one, and extending to the center of the other.

"All of you — stop right now!" he shouted, holding up the tablet to the discordant crowd. "Truth cannot emerge from such divisive talk. Have the Fae ever been so divided that they lose all sense of decency and decorum? Bring back to your minds the glorious gift we were all just granted. And remember, the curse is *lifted.* How can we speak thus, after having just so recently received the ability to speak properly at all? Stop, I say! Touch the Truth that is inside you and abandon this foolish strife!"

Matha believed his words might have some effect, but so consumed with their grievances were all those around him that he'd offered them only a momentary diversion. And then he caught sight of Loch, who of all those present in the shrine was standing still; as the rest of them continued their acrimonious taunts and bickering, Loch went unnoticed.

Maeve then stepped up to Matha, who assumed that perhaps she had come to reconcile. But before he could say one word, she grabbed the tablet out of his hands — so quickly that he could barely react.

Holding the tablet high above her head, she shrieked, "Real authority does *not* come from silly etchings!" She then threw the tablet to the ground with all her might, and just as before, the blue-green agate shattered into pieces. All Matha could do was to cry out in grief.

No one cared. This time Matha didn't even have Baudwin to stand with him, and he wondered then if he might as well give up all caring.

A hand grasped his shoulder — Loch's hand.

"Rian warned me that this might happen," Loch began, "and I myself can barely keep from joining in the terrible fracas that boils all around us. Long ago, I believed that if I searched for this shrine that the Water would come to me, but I never did find the Water. And then I thought that by being led here to this place that the Water would finally come to me, but now I realize that I was mistaken. I'm not to be chosen by the Water, but I will do my best to right this wrong, and also the wrong I committed that day when you and I and Baudwin were in a shrine just like this one."

Loch then knelt on the ground, gathering and placing all the pieces of blue-green agate together like a jigsaw puzzle, enabling them to read the words again. He then looked up to face everyone.

"This is *not* the way!" he cried, his voice breaking with emotion. "Listen to Matha!"

Although heartened that Loch had taken his side, Matha still knew that they would not listen. Their energies now spent, the crowd meandered about, as the shadow in Glamorium continued to work its way through them.

Matha then looked at Ferrell, who seemed agitated but oddly elated. He certainly didn't seem to be himself — at all.

"Maeve," Ferrell began, "whatever is happening, is working! I know we'll find Baudwin and set everything right again with the Faeries. All we need to do is get moving. Yes — we must move forward. Onward and upward! We have to get back to the ship!"

"Back to the ship?" Loingsech railed, his eyes blazing. "Why would ye be doin' a thing like *that* at a time like this? I know why — ye want to have a go at the supplies! Gettin' a little peckish, are we?"

Matha also knew that this didn't sound at all like Loingsech — more like one who had drunk too much fermented honey batter and was now addled. The Faeries all seemed to be in the same state, lost in an odd kind of stupor, while the Elves seemed clear-headed, but crazed with determination, as they tried to decide what to do next.

Pain throbbed in Matha's head. "This just isn't right. . . whatever it is — such a terrible reversal of the bliss we just knew."

He then saw Rian busily stacking stones on the ground — one on top of another. Repeatedly, the druid made his way in and out of the shrine, coming and going with one stone, and then another and another, stacking them higher and higher, apparently building a wall of some kind.

"Hey there, Rian," Seamus chortled. "With this whole shrine around us, do you really need to outdo your ancestors?"

"He can't help himself — he's an Elve," Criofan quipped. "They build in their sleep." He paused to look lazily about. "Speaking of which, I could really use a nap." Criofan then went and slumped onto a quartz crocus, his head tilted back — oblivious to everything around him.

Matha thought he might do the same, and join his good friend. The shadow of Glamorium was now inside him, and his thoughts were no longer entirely his own. But then he thought of how irresponsible it would be to simply leave this strife as is. His parents would never forgive him for not trying to find a solution. For years they had drummed responsibility into him, and he couldn't give up so easily.

Matha then felt Loch by his side again, a hand on his shoulder, earnestly squeezing him. Loch was panicked — something Matha had never seen before.

"Just as Rian told us," the Roiler said, "the shadow in Glamorium... the shadow is driving us mad. If we don't find a way to stop it, Rian will build a maze of some kind, trapping himself until he starves to Death. And the rest of us Faeries will just wither away."

Matha was having an increasingly difficult time paying attention, but couldn't help but notice Loingsech, sitting on the ground, staring up at the sky. Quickly, he ran over to him.

"Loingsech!" he exclaimed. "What do we do?"

Loingsech did not reply.

"Everyone is losing their minds — either in hopeless dithering or senseless wandering!" Matha shouted. "Whatever do we do?"

Loingsech stared at Matha, barely aware of his surroundings. "Losin' our minds?" he asked. "Isn't that the cure we all sought? The great gift of the *Dúrúnghlas*?" Blankly, he kept staring at the sky, unaware of what was happening.

Not knowing what to do, Matha glanced down at the glamorium pendant on the ground. He ran over to it, picked it up, and brought it back to Loingsech.

"Loingsech!' he exclaimed. "You *must* stop this! Tell me the words!"

"The words?" Loingsech asked.

"Yes — to invoke Glamorium!"

"Sorry — won't work," Loingsech replied sadly. "That *is* the problem, is it not? What's brought us all to this point — until now. You can't just stick yer hand in oily Water, and expect to pull it out all clean and rosy."

Matha froze. *If all of this happened because of the ceremony,* he thought, *and if, by invoking Glamorium they had brought this shadow upon themselves, or the sundering shock — or whatever it was — then there had to be a way to defeat, or at least to stop, the shadow — at least for now.*

Calming himself, he thought even harder. Despite his skills with concord, he couldn't hope to lead a ceremony on his own. The Faeries were lost in a strange kind of stupor and the Elves were driven to distraction, and he was amazed that he could still think — at all. Here he was, still unjoined, and weakened to such an extreme, with no one to turn to. He looked at Tárlach, who sat idly talking to his squirrels, but oddly, they didn't seem interested in anything he had to say. *They sense he's mad,* Matha thought. *They would probably sooner see him doused in a river, than speak to him again.*

Again, he stopped short, this time listening only to himself. Idly, he looked at the broken tablet on the ground that Loch had pieced back together. These words stuck out to him:

You may wish for many things

That's what I must do, he thought, his mind racing. He wasn't even completely sure why he'd run to the well. The entire thing seemed idiotic, but perhaps the Water alone could still help him. For a moment Maeve tried to block his way. She had sensed his earnestness and sought to quell it, but Loch rushed to his side and shoved her out of the way.

"Whatever you have to do — make it quick!" The Roiler shouted.

And so without a moment's hesitation, holding the double S spiral closely to his heart, he made a wish.

He then hurled the shimmering green pendant into the Water below.

Matha expected that nothing would happen, assuming that a desperate wish from a desperate fool would surely not be answered. The problem was that he just didn't feel worthy of help — or mercy. He looked down, searching. The pendant had disappeared into the soft blue-green Light, lost amongst countless other treasures at the bottom of the well. Faintly, he hoped that somehow Boann might come to his aid, but if Ferrell hadn't lied, she was far from being able to help anyone.

As everyone around him grew madder and madder, Matha kept his eyes on the Water. The Elves had now formed a group and were busily stacking stones in order to wall themselves off, and the Faeries were sitting around, frightened and befuddled.

When he was a young one, Brigh had told him that uttering a sacred wish would keep that wish from coming true. He could feel the grip of the shadow of Glamorium tightening, making his thoughts harder and harder to control. *What I wish now* he thought, *hardly even matters.*

Solemnly, he bowed his head, cupped his hands over his heart and made a sign of the Water. With trembling voice, he made his wish: "My wish is not for the Faeries or the Elves, or for you to chase this horrible shadow away. My only wish is that whatever small hope remains not be extinguished, so that there will always be someone — somewhere — who might still make their way in this realm."

Matha's small utterance traveled past the ancient mossy stones and deeply down into the well, its tiny vibration finally suffusing the Water. Strangely, he then felt the forging shadow sweep into his mind, causing him to lose all awareness of the moment. Indeed, he had never felt so lost — or so alone.

High up in the trees, a bluethroat chirped a melody to the Water — *chat chack, chat chack* — sounding strained and subdued. All was silent, and the Water then responded in kind.

From deep inside the well, Matha heard a thrumming, perhaps, he thought, produced by a being of some kind, or perhaps even by the Water itself. He knew that none present could have identified what they were hearing — even if they were present enough to see the Water stir, which they were not.

Staring into the well, Matha sensed that the glamorium pendant was surrounded by a nexus of rushing Water. He had thrown something both beautiful and hideous — something truly wonderful and terrible — into the heart of the shrine, and the Water itself would now remedy this. If the Water could *think* in order to judge, which it couldn't — at least not in the same way that the Fae did — then it would not accept something as injurious to its sanctity as this shadow. Nor would the Water allow suffering like this to continue, and so this most revered element of the water Faeries took pity on all the wretched Fae in the shrine.

Up and up went its currents — up like the high chord of the bluethroat as it sang its somber melody. Up rose the Water, purging the shrine of all foulness, and mourning the beauty that it now also had to eject.

The forging shadow fought back, but given that its nature was to subjugate the living, it could gain no purchase against a primordial force like the Water. There was no hook, no thinking, desiring being it could corrupt, and this lack of selfhood left the forging shadow vulnerable.

Up and out the Water surged from the well, once commanded by a great being — Boann herself — and now rushing out for the sake of the realm alone. Up and out it continued to flow, drenching the Elves and knocking over their mad creations — easily scattering all the stones they had laid so precisely. Rising further, the Water crashed over them as well, causing them to panic as the currents took them by surprise.

The Water then flooded the crystal seats, where most of the Faeries sat, stupefied. They too were drenched, and as the Water swirled around them, the grip of the forging shadow loosened, and they felt restored to their former selves.

But the forging shadow would not surrender control of their minds without a fight. In response, the Water created an even faster-moving vortex. With perfect precision, the waves guided the Elves and Faeries so they would not crash into the stonework and be crushed — even sweeping Tárlach's terrified squirrels to safety.

For a moment Matha's thoughts cleared, and although he couldn't comprehend what he had been swept up in, somehow he knew that his wish had been granted.

Round and round the Fae swirled in the vortex of the Water. Through sheer will, Matha grabbed onto a stone fixture on a wall. A bold, strong shape rushed past him, and he grasped the end of its dark leather jacket. *Loch!* The Roiler held fast to him, as they desperately tried to stay above the Water.

The current began moving even faster, sweeping the Fae out of the shrine. Barely able to hold on, Matha shouted to Loch, "The Water and *only* the Water protects us!"

Matha then let go of both Roiler and wall. He could have held on longer, but chose not to. He had no fear of the current — the current was his Life.

Soon everyone — both Elves and Faeries — was shooting out of the shrine, past roots and vines and through portals, tumbling and twisting in the Water as they went. All were ejected and dumped simultaneously, then left scattered about like rotting twigs.

At the same time, as the Water swirled around the pendant, the grip of the forging power loosened, until finally, it was forced back to the dormant place whence it had spawned. At least for now, everyone was free of the grip of its paralyzing shadow.

Sprawled out on the ground, Matha thought then of Baudwin, yearning with all of his heart to know what had become of his dear friend.

Chapter 35
WATER AND THE WOODS

A great current ran through River Nechtain, moving in a way that startled fish and made birds flee to the safety of nearby branches. No longer flowing downstream past forested bends to the great falls — as the river had always done — this current took all creatures by surprise. Instead, it traveled upstream, covering the river with a voluminous blanket and leaving behind a frothy wake, as if the keels of a flotilla had just cut through the Water.

Those who spotted the current saw a cocoon-shaped nexus at its center. They gawked and pointed at the whirling shape that passed them by in mere seconds. Many shouted, wondering what could make the Water move so strangely. What was its purpose? Some surmised that the Moon had gone mad and was railing away, upsetting the natural flow of the river until the currents forgot which way they were meant to flow. Others assumed that the Elves were testing a horrendous new invention, whose purpose only the Assembly knew.

The Faefries were the only ones who sensed another purpose. Racing along the riverbanks, the young ones shouted, "The Water yearns for a new direction!" Their parents could only wonder if this might be true, even though they couldn't understand why.

Lying inside the watery ethers was one who knew that a new direction had been forced upon him. Baudwin was now trapped inside an inescapable bubble which was moving at great speed. He wasn't sure how long he had been there. A day, two days, perhaps more? As the Water carried him farther and farther upstream, he fell in and out of awareness, dreaming again and again of voyages far to the west, above the Glittering Tundra. There, elven crews wore winter garb, their decks slick with ice. Heavily gloved hands held spyglasses as they scanned Sea Thuaidh. On Baudwin's behalf they searched, sailing in a grand voyage to fulfill Ferrell's promise. Forging a bond between Elve and Faery alike, they would have to save him now — or so he dreamed.

Inside the bubble Baudwin awakened. The dream had ended, and now only shocking imprisonment greeted him. Barely able to see or hear, he didn't know how he was able to breathe, but always some small pocket of Air greeted his lips, as if a faithful river creature of some kind swam beside him, breathing into his mouth and then swimming away.

His torment mounting, Baudwin could barely remember what had happened to him. He had been in Four Falls making an important speech, and then *she* had appeared, and now he was swept away, against his will.

Again she humiliated me, he thought, stricken by his confinement.

Fiercely, he struggled to escape, soon finding that his efforts were in vain. He tried to move his limbs, but could not control them. *Indeed, I am powerless,* he thought. Vaguely, he sensed sunlight shining from above into the Water. Some steady force was propelling him up and then down, avoiding obstacle after obstacle as the cocoon enclosing him shot farther up the Nechtain, leaving a surging layer of Water over the river.

From afar, he could make out the piping of river creatures. The sound they made was unfamiliar to him. It was like a clicking, and he thought perhaps they might be dolphins, but he could barely see, and soon the clicking was gone.

Baudwin then fell into a long, deep trance. Moments before losing awareness, he'd been sure that a bout could suddenly end his Life. Inside his watery prison he might as well have been a dragonfly trapped in a corked bottle — slowly suffocating. He now found the Air perilously hard to breathe. Even worse, this time there would be no one to come to his aid, and no way to undo the hold the Water had on him. No longer was he dreaming, yet still the paralyzing fear of suffering one last fatal bout lingered, which only increased his misery. As the nexus continued its rush upstream, Baudwin fell into oblivion — lost to his fate — with no relief in sight.

⟲⟳

Baudwin was awakened by a tickling sensation across his face. Opening his eyes a sliver, he surmised that he was on the shore of a river, somewhere very far from Four Falls. His body felt like a soggy ashen mound of flesh and bones, covered with duckweed and algae, barely able to breathe. Again, he felt a tickling against his face. As he turned his head to the side, a sharp pain shot through his neck. He groaned, ready to give up his efforts entirely. And then he saw a face staring at him, one with beady black eyes, a stubby black nose, and long whiskers.

A river otter had come to greet him.

Baudwin attempted to sit up, but his limbs were as limp as sand poured from a bucket. How exhausted he was, and oddly thirsty, despite having been the Water's prisoner for so long. And also so alone, for the Water that had brought him here had disappeared, — its mission now complete. Where he was now remained a mystery.

Sensing his weakness, the otter nuzzled him again. Tickled by the whiskers, Baudwin groaned. "Come now — don't torture me so when I can hardly move."

Baudwin found his senses so weak that he could barely use them. The otter nuzzled him more fiercely, this time brushing against his nose and letting out a high-pitched squeal. Hearing the sound, Baudwin recoiled, his ears throbbing with pain. From the corner of his eye he could make out at least half a dozen more otters. All gave a squeal, and soon they were circling him, nudging him to get up.

"I simply cannot move," he groaned, closing his eyes. "I'm much too weak. Too tired. . . too ruined. . ." His skin felt parched under the hot Sun, and his eyes so pained by the Light that he to keep them closed. Holding his sides in pain, he thought, *What a bitter end — to be so utterly helpless, with a raft of otters jeering at me.*

Excitedly, the otters squealed all the more. Baudwin strained, barely able to interpret their squeals

"Meet someone?" he mumbled testily. "Who? What do you mean 'go into the forest?' I can't even sit up. Just leave me be!"

At this the otters squealed even more. One of them approached him holding a piece of something long and green in its mouth. Feeling the twine-like object drop onto his face, he sensed sweet-vine. *Why is there no smell?* he wondered, worried. His nose did not seem to be working. Next, he heard the muffled flapping of a bird, delivering more sweet-vine for the otters to give him. He could barely turn his head to look.

Why even bother, he thought, *when I can't so much as move my arms?*

The otter that had first greeted him then took the sweet-vine in its teeth, holding the end with its paws. Clenching its jaws, it held the vine over Baudwin's mouth. Soon, sugary syrup glided out of the vine onto Baudwin's face. He opened his mouth, lapping up as much as he could.

The feeding was messy and ridiculous, but after a few vines, Baudwin felt his thirst abating. The otters then brought a large leaf to block the Sun's rays from reaching his face. Exhausted from the effort of drinking, he again passed out.

By the time Baudwin awoke, the Sun was setting. Lifting his head he saw a grand horn peering down at him. The otters were still around him, chattering.

"Meet the wise one?" Baudwin mumbled. "Now? Where?"

The otters didn't reply. The grand horn then knelt on the ground as the otters tugged at Baudwin, trying to push him onto its sturdy back.

"Stop," Baudwin groaned, his strength faltering. "I can't move, and you aren't strong enough to. . ."

And indeed he was right. They weren't strong enough, but there were now several goats with them, gently pushing him with their strong necks and curved horns. After much prodding and hoisting, they eventually rolled Baudwin onto the grand horn's back.

As the grand horn stood up, Baudwin felt that he might fall off, but the goats were able to hold him steady. Soon, a number of large birds carrying thick vines in their beaks began to tie him down, flying under the tall legs of the grand horn and then over its back, again and again. They continued until their handiwork was finished and Baudwin was firmly secured.

"Now you've got me tied up tight as a bundle of yule logs," he muttered.

The grand horn flared its nostrils and began to carry him off into the forest. "Thank you for the sweet-vine," he called to the otters, his voice strengthened by the drink.

The otters gurgled at him until he was out of sight.

Clop clop clop went the grand horn's giant hooves. In the shade of the forest, still feeling weak and helpless, Baudwin was silent. He wondered how it was that a bout hadn't ended his Life when the Water had him trapped. Now that he seemed to be saved, he also wondered about those he had left behind and how frightened they must be — unjoined and lost. And then, with all of his senses waning, he passed out.

ᘯᘀᘰ

When he finally came to on Tinedía,[1] Baudwin found himself lying in a bed with soft flannel sheets, his head resting on fluffy pillows scented with lavender. Gingerly, his fingers grazed the edge of the bed, wondering if the frame was like the one he had at home in Deuona — lined with a canal of Water. Listlessly, he withdrew his hand. There was no Water. Always this simple comfort had afforded him better sleep, and never had such a small stream triggered any bouts, but here there was no canal, which meant he was probably not in the home of a water Faery.

Anxiously, he realized that he couldn't hear or smell much of anything. He figured his senses had finally failed him altogether, having been barely open at the riverbank. Only a vague sense of touch remained. Worse, he could no longer see a thing. *Trapped for days by the Water, and now my senses are gone,* he thought miserably. Surely there was no reason to continue in such agony.

And then he felt two hands slowly massaging his ears. Though too weak to move, the sensation on his lobes brought back some of his hearing, and he began to relax.

After some time, he heard the voice of an old faery lady speaking to him.

"Time to awaken — my dear — you must wake up," she said cheerily, as she continued to massage his ears. "You're among friends."

---

[1] Pronounced [CHIN-UH-THEE-UH] Fireday, equivalent to Sunday, the seventh day of the week

Baudwin stirred and let out a groan. For so long he had been trapped, swaddled by the Water in Boann's inescapable grasp, and now he still couldn't move a muscle. All he heard were the thoughts racing through his head. *Something is not right! Did a bout claim my senses? My eyes!* A surge of fear arose in his guts as he reached for them.

Firmly, a hand stopped him.

"Your eyes have been closed for a very long time," the faery lady said, withdrawing a vial of Water from her apron pocket. "Let me put some healing Water on them." Carefully, she dabbed each eye. "Now wait. We must not rush."

In delirium, Baudwin asked, "Is that you, Brigh? What happened? What. . ."

"Shush — you must not speak. I'll explain later, but first you must drink this."

"Who are you?" Baudwin rasped.

"I'm not Brigh," the faery lady replied. "Now — no more questions! Heather, my grand horn, brought you here. The otters found you. Never have I seen my friends of the river so willing to give up their playtime to minster to the needs of a water Faery. If you wish to regain your senses, you'd be wise to follow my instructions. Your questions must wait for now, or they will slow the process of restoration."

Restoration? Baudwin was so upside down and inside out that he couldn't find a way to take stock of what was happening. Nor could he find a reason to allow her to help him. "Don't bother with me," he grumbled. "Nothing about me is worth restoring."

"Don't be silly," the faery lady said brightly. "You're here, aren't you? No one comes to me by mere happenstance," she added, proudly. "I'm very important in these Woods. Just ask my friends, the woodland creatures."

"Then I may be your first," Baudwin mumbled, "for I am one who is beyond help."

"Nonsense," she countered, her voice light and caring. She continued massaging his ears. "I'm here to perform the restoration, as you will be helpless otherwise."

Restoration, Baudwin wondered again. Whoever she was, her voice was kind and reassuring, and she seemed to know what she was doing. He relinquished his struggle, for as weak as he was, he had little choice but to heed her instructions.

She continued her work, carefully touching his forehead and temples.

"Very good," she said. "You're beginning to regain your senses. This will be easy if you just keep still. Otherwise, not. Remember — no questions until we're finished."

Baudwin wanted to tell her to stop, that she mustn't continue because, bereft as he was, he no longer had the will to continue. But, utterly exhausted, he simply nodded, keeping his eyes closed.

"Here's some healing salve," she said. "Your lashes are stuck fast. Now let me rub some on. After I gently wipe your eyes, you may open them — slowly — but do not speak."

Baudwin did as he was told, and as he opened his eyes, he was surprised to see the face that greeted him — heart-shaped and kind, with pale green, softly wrinkled skin and teary brown eyes peering sympathetically into his. Judging by her manner, he thought she must be a wood Faery, one who took the old ways to heart.

"You're very. . ." he tried to speak, drifting off.

"*Old,*" she said, agreeably. "If what you see before you is a faery lady more than seven and fifty, then that is good, because that is what you should see. Nod if this is so."

Baudwin nodded that indeed this was so. As he spoke, a tear fell down his cheek, followed by many more. *Am I grateful to see again,* he wondered, *or simply full of regret?* Confused, he closed his eyes tightly, and a shudder of despair went through him.

"Now, now, dear, you must not give up," the faery lady said.

"Why not?" Baudwin asked, his voice quavering. "What reason do I have to —"

"If only to *hear* again," the faery lady replied. "The songs of the birds, the murmurings of the trees, and the sounds of all the other forest creatures."

"And the splashing of the fish in the Water," Baudwin added.

"Yes," she agreed. "Now, please listen. You can hear me only because I am holding your head in my hands. I'm now about to let go. When I do, you won't be able to hear me. At this point, if you don't speak, I will restore your hearing right away. Nod if you understand."

Baudwin wasn't interested in hearing the sounds of the forest. Hearing and seeing meant that he would be more *here* than there, and part of him simply wanted to slip away to Annwyn — once and for all. Despite this, he nodded, if only to escape the crushing feelings weighing down his heart.

"Good," she said. "Let's begin." She let go of his head.

Baudwin flinched, as all sounds of the forest and the river disappeared. Then she held his head again.

"Easy, lad," she said. "Easy — this will pass." Baudwin heard no concern in her voice, which he found comforting.

"Do you hear the silence?" she asked, still holding his head.

Baudwin nodded that he did.

"I'm now going to perform a restoration," she explained, before taking her hands away from his head. "As I do this, you must stay still."

The old faery lady cupped her hands over Baudwin's ears, pressing firmly, and then swung her arms up toward the ceiling, repeating this many times. Each time, she cupped her hands over his ears longer than the time before.

Baudwin lost count of the cuppings until the final one, when suddenly, sounds of the wind in the trees, the rustle of leaves and the chirping of birds filled his ears.

"I can hear again!" he said, surprised at how happy he was to hear the birds. "And you're not touching me."

"Then you must also hear me reminding you not to talk," came the swift rebuke. "Simply listen to the chirping of the birds. Water Faeries must course with the Water, but you are in the Woods now, so my feathered friends will have to suffice. Besides," she added, chuckling, "you don't want your senses to get confused like an owl that can't see in the Dark."

She knows our ways, he thought, his despair lessening.

"Close your eyes — no peeking!" she exclaimed, as she placed something in his mouth. "Now tell me what you taste."

Baudwin rolled the round morsel over his tongue, puzzled at first. "Sour cherry," he replied.

"How wonderful — now you can taste again! Tasting is like smelling with the tongue, I often say. Can you smell this?" she asked, as she placed a whorl of arrowhead flowers under his nose.

"Yes, but faintly," Baudwin replied, stirring slightly.

"Indeed," she said, adding, "We can't have you without a sense of smell. You would never again enjoy the aroma of your favorite food."

Baudwin smiled gratefully.

"I must make sure that all of your senses are restored. You've been in a very deep trance — neither here nor there — so as you wake up, you must be very careful. You're lucky the otters rescued you — and in the nick of time, I would say."

Baudwin waited as she took stock of him again.

"All is well now," she announced. "Now you need only food and rest."

Smiling faintly, Baudwin nodded off to sleep, as having his senses restored had been surprisingly tiring.

Later, he awoke, and this time, as he opened his eyes, he took in more details of the room. Unlike his sleeping room in Deuona, the dresser had leaf-shaped brass handles, instead of waves, and he didn't see shades of blue anywhere. Instead, there were lots of browns and greens, including a mosaic of a tree on the wall, surrounded by flowers and rabbits, and many kinds of foliage painted on the furniture.

The door then opened, and there before him stood the same faery lady he had seen before, wearing a forest green apron over a paisley green dress with a matching shawl that hugged a very round frame. Her two thick gray braids were cinched together at her heart with a large gold bead.

Seeing her again, Baudwin realized the truth. "You're a wood Faery."

"Yes," she replied, smiling brightly.

His senses restored and his strength renewed, Baudwin then realized with a start that he had heard this voice before.

"You sound so familiar," he began cautiously, in case he was mistaken. "Have we met before?"

"In my seven hundred and sixty-six years I have met many Baudwin," she replied. "But never until now have I understood someone so well that I hadn't *actually* met."

Baudwin stared at her blankly, unable to understand her inference.

"That sounds rather strange," he said. "How can you possibly understand someone that you never actually met?" Still feeling hopeless and bereft, he added, "And why me — someone who isn't worth meeting *or* understanding?"

Hearing this, the old faery lady shook her head and then approached her dresser where a number of pinecones were on display. She had painted the tips of the seed scales with gold and lacquered each one, so they all shone.

"Tell me," she began, "when you look at this pinecone, do you see the tree that will grow from its seed?"

"No," Baudwin replied, as he knew far more about the ways of the Water than those of the Woods.

"*I* can," she continued. "I can see the splendid pine tree that will grow from one of its seeds." Picking up a pine cone, she tapped a seed scale until a winged seed fell into her hand. "There," she said, showing the seed to Baudwin. "I will plant this in my yard to honor our meeting. This tree will grow fine and strong — its branches will be straight, the trunk stout, and its bark will attract many generations of woodpeckers, looking for beetles. Even more important is that a great silver eagle will build a nest there, knowing that this tree was planted on such a special occasion. The eagle will pipe a beautiful call unlike any other in nature to remind all the animals that you and I shared a great moment here."

"You can really see that?" Baudwin asked, his spirits lifting.

"Naturally!" she replied, her eyes brightening. "For I am of the Wood, and can foresee the growth of all living things. The budding of every seed and the burrowing of every animal are but windows into the future."

Baudwin was struck by this. "Your ways of the Wood are indeed wise," he said.

She smiled at him.

Baudwin then remembered the voice that had spoken to him at the Springs of Coventina — long ago, after his journey had begun and the Water had come to him. Someone sounding kind and understanding — a female voice — had told him he had reached a new beginning, and that he was now swimming in the same current with her, and that she was very old and very wise.

"I remember now — you spoke to me!" he exclaimed. "At the Springs! I *know* it was you!"

The wood Faery did a curtsy, her gray braids with the gold bead swinging back and forth.

"Indeed, that was me," she replied, "and I spoke to you afterwards as well."

Baudwin then remembered another dream — the one he'd had in the Cyhiraeth — after he had been wounded at the Four Rivers Faire. That same female voice — not Boann's — had spoken reassuringly to him, saying, "Only along your own path will you find yourself, and in finding yourself will you know your true path. Do not lose heart."

"I remember you speaking to me again and again," Baudwin said, "but who *are* you?"

"My name is Sibéal[2], daughter of Niamh,"[3] she replied. "I was charged with watching over you, knowing that somehow your fate would bring you here when you were ready."

So many faery ladies and spirits have taken such an interest in me, he thought wonderingly — *I, without a mother.*

Baudwin had so many questions that he barely knew where to begin, so he began with the most obvious one.

"You spoke to me at the Springs of Coventina, but you weren't the one who made the Water rise later at the shrine. That was Boann. Tell me — do you know her? Did you direct her to wash us all away?"

At this, Sibéal let out a dramatic-sounding laugh, uproarious and full. How different her voice sounded from his water Faery cousins.

"Direct Boann to wash you away?" she asked incredulously. "Tell me, Baudwin, could you direct an ocean wave? Or order the Moon to shine through the clouds, so that we might dance under its Light? You would have better luck telling an Elve how to smith a furnace than directing Boann to do *anything*."

"But," Baudwin insisted, "Boann sent me here. . . She. . ."

"Of *course* she did," Sibéal cut in, "but not at my beckoning. She serves another."

"Who?"

"I cannot say."

---

2   Pronounced [SHI-beel]
3   Pronounced [NEEV]

"You must. . . you must tell me. I. . ."

"That I cannot do."

The tone of Sibéal's voice then changed, from that of helpful nurturer to somber instructor. "Tell me, Baudwin, when Boann sent you here, what did she say to you?"

Baudwin fumed at the memory. "She said I was a fool! She doubted my worthiness! She was terrible, and she whisked me away without a word. My father and grandfather are probably sick with worry!"

"Boann can be an unfathomable and formidable guide," Sibéal said. "She would flood the land, drowning us all, if in so doing she believed that she had cleared the way to a better realm."

"Well, she almost drowned me," Baudwin put in, resentfully.

"Yes," Sibéal said, peering down at Baudwin as he lay abed.

"And has that made you feel any more or *less* worthy?"

"Worthy?" Baudwin asked, surprised. "Of what?" Having felt so miserable upon his arrival, he couldn't understand why she would want him to consider such a matter now. "What in all of *Tír na nÓg* must I be worthy of? Tell me now — or let me pass to Annwyn, where as sure as the Moon travels through all its phases — I will go!"

"Baudwin, you cannot wield Glamorium if you are not worthy, which is the only way you will ever find your mother — Shaela."

"How do you know her name?" Baudwin asked.

"In addition to being old and wise," Sibéal replied, smiling, "I also see many things."

"Then you must be like Esther," Baudwin said. "Do you have the Sight?"

"Indeed," Sibéal replied. "And do you know what the Sight is showing me now?"

Baudwin shook his head.

"Only that a young water Faery must put aside his anger, and *honestly* ask himself why he might not be worthy of Glamorium."

"I don't even have any," Baudwin retorted. "How can I be worthy of something I don't even possess?!"

"Baudwin," Sibéal probed, her tone now more charitable, "do you really believe that in all the eons the Fae have dwelled in this realm that only those who possessed Glamorium were worthy of its wielding?"

Baudwin hesitated. He wasn't sure he was worthy, so he thought of those who had to be. Seamus had never owned any Glamorium, but Baudwin knew very well that his grandfather was worthy. He was a Guild Leader — wise and respected — and surely that mattered. Even the Grand Eldress herself probably didn't possess any, and she certainly had to be worthy.

"Yes, I see what you mean," Baudwin replied, as he continued to ponder the subject. "Owning is not the same as being worthy."

Sibéal let out a chuckle. "So, you *are* willing to learn! Very often the most impoverished are the ones who are the most worthy, for they endure hardship willingly and this, among other things, is what leads to the ability to wield Glamorium."

Baudwin waited to hear more.

"And here is something perhaps even more interesting for you to know," she added, as she pulled up Baudwin's blanket and fluffed his pillow. "The Elve who promised to help you. I've seen him placing his attention on you for some time now. Ferrell — yes, that's his name. How well do you know him?"

"I know he's an important Luminary who serves Govannon."

"Yes, he's an important Luminary, a courageous warrior and, some might even add, a great leader. But did you know that he was once poorer than perhaps anyone you have ever known?"

Hearing this, Baudwin remembered riding to see the Show Wheel with Ferrell. From the looks of the ornate carriage they had traveled in, Ferrell seemed quite well off. His indigo uniform handsomely sewn and pressed, with enough gold adornments to make most Faeries jealous — not to mention the roseberry libation from his flask that he served in crystal glasses — could not have been more impressive. Whatever Ferrell wanted, whether to have a fleet built or a magniglow exhibit erected, the means were always within his grasp. Baudwin couldn't believe that he had ever been poor.

"I never imagined that," he said.

"What I say is true," Sibéal continued. "He was born in the Chinewilds, to a very indigent family. He never had enough to eat or to wear, or enough of a roof over his head to keep him safe and warm. Those who raised him had their hearts hardened by their struggle, so he didn't receive the love he needed either. Unlike them, however, his deprivation didn't keep him from taking control of his destiny. And so, as the seasons went on, he strove to create a new Life for himself. Giving up wasn't in his nature. The poverty he endured made him who he was — determined and proficient. You should never underestimate him, because you don't know what he's capable of. A great ally he is — and an even worse enemy. Even Boann had to face the truth of that. . ."

With that, Sibéal's voice trailed off as if she was trying to make sense of something very important to her, but could not detect a trace of what it was.

Something in her story about Ferrell made Baudwin stir. "I must get up," he said, flinging away the covers and swinging his legs over the side of the bed. Slowly, he stood. "I haven't been on my feet in so long," he said. "The floor does feel rather good."

"I'm glad to see you doing so much better," Sibéal said, as she glided over to steady him. "Might we do a little walking?"

As Baudwin took a few tentative steps, she continued, "Say what you will about Ferrell, but he did prove himself to the Elves. Having been very, very poor, he rose up through the ranks, as Elves do, to became Govannon's favorite."

"What of it?" Baudwin asked absently, as he turned to walk the other way.

"If he were here," Sibéal replied, "he wouldn't want to hear you bleating on about not having Glamorium. That's the least of your problems, Baudwin."

"I did learn to be more honest," he insisted. "I *wanted* to be worthy. She even said I *was* more honest. But she never gave me back my Glamorium!"

"So do you feel worthy of trying again?" Sibéal asked. "One final trial before you give up entirely and run back to the Elves for help?"

One final trial? Baudwin wondered. *Can't she see that I'm finished?*

"I didn't ask to come here."

"No one asks for the hardship Life brings to them. Did the Fae ask for the Great Befalling to strike? Did Belanus ask for the upheaval that robbed him of his kingdom? When a hawk strikes a fleeing rabbit, did the rabbit ask to be hunted? In this realm you can play only the hand that fate deals you, and you're lucky to be given the chance to make something of your destiny as most about you are miring themselves in distractions and delusions. Are you going to leave this place mired in your own?"

Baudwin thought about what would happen if he did just leave this place. He could go back home or find Ferrell again. Everyone had to be terribly worried about him. Leaving would be so simple. And he wasn't at all convinced that he should trust this wood Faery. Apparently, she had been trying to help him for some time now, but he could sense that she was concealing a lot from him. The promise of Glamorium was incredible, its visions inspiring beyond words, but since then he had seen nothing but misery and hardship, and now he was being asked to soldier on and endure even more.

Baudwin looked again at Sibéal. Perhaps her intentions weren't sinister at all. In fact, if he didn't know better, he'd have guessed that she spent most of her time outside, carving birdhouses and singing to trees all day long. Yet she did seem to know a great deal about him. *And she knows my mother's name,* he thought.

He recalled Boann speaking through Esther to him, saying, "You'll find one who will send you to her, but before you do, you must first —"

"Travel as the salmon does. . ." he mused.

"Whatever are you talking about?" Sibéal asked.

"I was told by Esther that I had to travel as the salmon does, and then I would find someone who would send me to my mother, Shaela."

"Ah! And tell me, have you traveled like a salmon?"

Baudwin knew that he had. He had traveled upstream, just like a salmon returning to spawn, swimming ceaselessly against the current, pulled by the power of the Water.

"Indeed I have — just like one. Only I was trapped in a bubble. Now, I'm here — and I found you."

"And what else did Esther tell you?"

"Nothing more. Boann then took over Esther's reading. She spoke of a gate that would open only when a talisman was wielded by one who had enough command of the two lessons."

"And what might they be?" Sibéal asked.

Before answering, Baudwin mulled over what he had just said.

"Boann said that the first lesson was Honesty and the second, Truth," he replied, struck by yet another thought. "Which must be the reason I'm here."

Sibéal nodded.

"The gate," he began, as he stopped his walking to look out the window. "I'm to open a gate. Is the test you have for me to see if I can open the gate? So I can find my mother?"

At this, Sibéal nodded again. "Yes, and that talisman is located nearby — deep within the great ruins of the long-ago Age of Gold, ruins left by Sláine[4] of Copper Caves. Above these ruins I have built my dome home."

Baudwin now saw that everything that Esther and Boann told him had come to pass. He could not abandon the opportunity Sibéal offered. He had to try one more time.

"Please tell me more about Sláine," he said.

"You see," Sibéal continued, "she was the first ruler in the Age of Gold, which came after the even greater Age of Platinum. So much had been lost with the passage of that Golden Age that she decided to conserve as many of our traditions as possible. And so she built a place beneath our very feet from which to discover who is worthy. That is why I dwell here, Baudwin. I am the steward of what is below."

Baudwin had made up his mind. "Then let this be so!" he declared. "One final trial."

"Good," Sibéal replied. "But first you must rest. When you're strong enough, I will take you there."

๑๖๑

After several days of eating warm food and sleeping well, Baudwin was ready to proceed. Sibéal came for him, and they made their way down the stairs

---

4   Pronounced [SLAN-ya]

of her dome home, out the door, and into deep Woods. Erelong, directly ahead in a clearing, they came upon a great stone edifice that looked very much like the entrance to an ancient temple. The entire building seemed out of place, having been built in neither the water nor the wood faery style which would have suited the region.

Looking more closely, Baudwin was surprised to see that the stone roof was pointed and not domed. Four columns supported a triangular sky-piercing pediment. A procession of Elves in worn relief decorated one side of the pediment, moving in profile and gazing upward as they went. On the other side, a procession of Faeries also moved together in profile, gazing upward. Baudwin turned his attention to what they all were looking at — a large pentagram, and above that a symbol of the Triquetra — both embossed in stone.

To Baudwin it seemed as if the group was on some kind of pilgrimage as most were in traveling garb. Peering more closely at their weathered countenances, he saw earnestness and sincerity, as if Life held no other purpose than the meaning of the symbols hovering above them.

Baudwin also sensed another quality in them — their focus on reclaiming something that they had lost. Touched, he asked, "Why do they look so forlorn?"

"This place was built so that they could remember what had once been commonplace," Sibéal replied. "At the beginning of the Age of Gold, many feared they were losing the best parts of the Age of Platinum. Sláine and her subjects devoted their lives to preserving as much as they possibly could, which is likely why she chose a pentagram as her symbol."

"What does it mean?" Baudwin asked, pointing to the five-pointed star.

"The pentagram symbolizes protection. Sláine marked all of her structures with them."

"Will this one protect me?" Baudwin asked, wondering what lay in store for him.

"Perhaps so — perhaps not," Sibéal said. "It all depends on you."

Baudwin looked again at the relief work. "Back then, the Elves wanted to protect the old ways, but now they would never build something like this. How would Govannon receive Sláine if they met?"

Sibéal didn't respond. Instead, she produced a large muffin from her knapsack. "Here, dear," she said. "Eat this. You must be famished."

Baudwin's stomach had indeed been rumbling. The morning was late, and he hadn't taken a bite since the day before, so he devoured the muffin with great dispatch.

"Sláine built many of these kinds of places," Sibéal began. "Some are hidden away, and others are in plain sight, but not recognized, like this one. No one is entirely sure of what her intentions were, but I believe she was trying to spread as much of the old ways as possible, and enshrine what was lost. She must have seen that the turning of the ages would eventually lead us to where we are now."

"And where is that?" Baudwin asked as he munched on his muffin. The taste was especially pleasing, and he hoped for more.

"We're at a crossroads," Sibéal said, leading him to the entrance of the building. "Soon you will understand why you were brought here."

As they entered the edifice, Baudwin saw a stone elven weave, framing the door. On the lintel, the face of an elven lady carved in green Connemara marble gazed serenely down at them. Her countenance was regal and unvarying.

"Is that Queen Sláine?" he asked.

"Yes," Sibéal replied as she handed him another muffin. "That is her likeness."

"Was she a just ruler?" Baudwin asked, still eating hungrily.

"Yes, she is well well-regarded by history," Sibéal replied.

Now they had entered a common room of some kind. Baudwin saw no furniture, simply old stonework, worn and wondrous. In the center stood a statue of an elven lady, but sadly damaged, as an arm was missing.

"How unfortunate," Baudwin said.

"Yes," Sibéal agreed, "but the rest of what lies beneath us has been well preserved and protected."

Baudwin assumed that they would continue along one of the many hallways, but instead Sibéal approached a wall. There she placed her hand on a stone pentagram, turning the center. There was a loud *kerchunk* as she set some kind of mechanism in motion. She pushed ever so gently on the wall, and a slab of the stonework opened up. "The way is down these stairs," she directed, as she adjusted her stout form to descend the flight.

Making their way down the dark staircase, Sibéal produced a jar from her knapsack. Inside, Baudwin saw many large glow bugs with fat abdomens. She opened the lid and sprinkled some breadcrumbs inside. "Come now, my little ones — time to shine!" In response, the glow bugs began shining brightly as they hungrily devoured the food.

"Couldn't you just use a glowstone?" Baudwin asked.

"I suppose I could," Sibéal replied, "but then I couldn't take my brood for a walk, now could I?" Rolling her eyes, she chuckled. "I always forget that you water Faeries don't live as closely with forest creatures as we do."

"We talk to them, just like you do."

"Yes, but we have *deeper* conversations," Sibéal replied with a wink.

They continued down the spiraling staircase to the bottom, then entered what to Baudwin seemed like a kind of antechamber. To his surprise, shafts of

Light shone in wide translucent rays from skylights in the ceiling that ran all across the top of the building.

"This is where we must part ways," Sibéal said, facing Baudwin. "Inside, you will find three challenges. The first is a trial of Honesty. You will see many objects. You must choose the most beautiful one and place your choice on the center pedestal. When you see that you are ready, announce your answer to Sláine, as if she stood before you."

"And if I fail?" Baudwin asked, suddenly gripped with terrible uncertainty about the task before him.

"Then a great venomous toad will come and send you to Annwyn," she replied.

"What!" Baudwin exclaimed, his face pale with dread.

Sibéal chuckled. "I was only joking, my dear. But, if you place the wrong object on the pedestal, the way will remain closed. Nothing placed thereafter will work until the Moon has waxed and waned again."

"An *entire* month?" Baudwin asked.

"Yes," Sibéal replied flatly, "and in times long past the stewards never granted anyone a second chance."

"And what is the second trial?" Baudwin asked.

"You must take up arms against a giant beetle that I keep within, fed by fallen animals that I throw down the shaft."

Now Baudwin knew that she was putting him on. "Well, if that's the case, then I'm sure I will succeed," he joked. "Beetles are certainly no match for my skill with a quarrel staff."

Sibéal then became quite serious. "Far more difficult than facing venomous toads and devouring beetles is having the courage to face ourselves," she began, "which is something few come to respect, and only the most worthy ever accomplish."

Baudwin noticed the change in Sibéal's demeanor. In the short time since she had rescued him from the river's shore, she had not seemed so solemn.

"The second trial is one of Truth, Baudwin." She placed her hand firmly on his shoulder. "And if you are not able to discern the Truth, you may find yourself in mortal danger. You will find yourself in a place where you must find the true Light. I cannot tell you any more about the second trial. You will have to discover that for yourself. But should you fail, you will be trapped inside, and I will not be able to save you, for when you enter, the way will close behind you, and the way out must be solved by you — and you alone."

"I could pass to Annwyn in there?" Baudwin asked, as the gravity of his circumstance began to dawn on him.

"Yes, but only if you can't find the Truth of the Light within yourself."

With this, Baudwin suddenly felt quite unsure of himself. All of his feelings of trepidation and despair came rushing back.

"What is it?" Sibéal asked, sensing his reluctance.

"I'm not really afraid to pass to Annwyn," Baudwin replied. "If I must, then I must." Pausing several moments he then added, "I just don't know if I'm really ready for this — this *trial*." Lowering his eyes, he stood still, as if his doubts had turned him to stone.

"Baudwin," Sibéal asked, sensing his deep dread, "do you know why the otters that rescued you are so happy all the time?"

Baudwin looked at her, unsure of what to say, his usual cheerfulness entirely absent.

"Our friends of the river do not separate what is pleasant from what is painful. Instead, they simply meet the Water, regardless of their plight, living moment to moment, swimming and cavorting in the river — from which arises their constant joy."

Baudwin remembered the many times he had seen these delightful creatures when he was searching for the Water. Indeed, they were always so fiercely playful and happy, without concern — the present moment their only joy. *Perhaps there is something that I must learn from them,* he thought.

"You're right," he said. "I must be as the otters are."

"Good," Sibéal said. "And now I must inform you about the final trial — the Promise of Rebirth. Should you succeed with the first two, a wondrous gift awaits you. All you must do is solve a puzzle."

Baudwin was ready to begin. "So, this is all that I must do?" he asked. "Find the talisman — and then my mother too?"

"Your mother is not within these walls, but the talisman is. Should you succeed in bringing it back to me, I will explain much more. The talisman is waiting for you — a sacred object guarded by this place — so that the worthy may harness the Great Emerald Light."

Sibéal then turned to leave, saying, "Now I have told you everything that I can. You must go through that room. Once you do, the way behind you will close."

And so, Baudwin headed through the doorway, unable to retreat from where he had been, and equally uncertain of where his steps would take him. He tried his best not to worry about his fate, and instead be like a true water Faery — one to whom the Water had come and was now possessed with an otter's faith.

Chapter 36

THE RITE OF PASSAGE

Baudwin found himself in a long, dark passage. Guardedly he walked, watching out for any danger that might be lurking in the shadows. Gazing over his shoulder at the wall, he noticed a row of evenly spaced glowstones shaped like oak leaves. *Just like the flowers in the tunnel to the Engineerium*, he thought, feeling a small measure of comfort. As he passed he soundly tapped each one. Soon the entire passage was glowing softly with orange-copper Light. Relieved, he studied the niches, some of which were empty and others not. *Nothing but old statues*, he thought, *prisoners of time.*

Looking behind him, he saw that the room where he had left Sibéal was now sealed shut by a stone door that had closed when he entered — set into motion by some elven mechanism whose workings escaped him. He wondered if he called out to her, she would even hear him. "Likely not," he mumbled.

As he continued to make his way down the passage, tapping the glowstones kept him from feeling as if he were trapped in an eerie cavern. After a while the hallway emptied into a large room — just as Sibéal had said — with a pedestal in the center. He couldn't see well until he tapped more glowstones that had been placed around the room by the ancients.

Looking about, he was stunned to see what lay before his eyes — shelf after shelf laden with fine objects — candelabras, goblets, plates, and bowls made of gold and silver, bracelets, diadems, necklaces, and rings studded with every kind of precious gem, fine tapestries and statues, and, to his surprise, even weapons. Strewn about everywhere were chests of gold coins, ornate vases, and pieces of furniture constructed of the finest metals.

On the ceiling a mosaic of a Triquetra stood watch. On the right side of the Triquetra, the glyph for Honesty was a different color — bright red instead of gold — which made it stand out from the other two glyphs. Baudwin quickly surmised that the red glyph symbolized the trial of Honesty.

Stepping toward the pedestal, he looked more closely. The top was waist-high, made of stone, with a ring of unusual markings around the perimeter. *If only Matha were here*, he thought. *Perhaps he could figure them out.* The utter silence of the room packed with so many things, yet empty of another living being, only reminded him of how alone he was with his decision. Looking past the pedestal, he saw a sealed stone doorway at the end of the room, which Sibéal had said would open should he choose the correct object.

Now I must choose, he thought, struck by the seriousness of the task that lay before him. One mistake and there would be nothing he could do to save himself from yet another failure. *Banjaxed!* he thought angrily. *Haven't I failed enough?* How he wished he could escape once and for all.

For a moment he felt frozen — unable to move — but then found his courage again. *Seamus would never forgive me if I didn't try to do my best right now,* he thought. *After all, the Water did come to me.* He looked around at all the lovely objects. Indeed, they were all very fine, and many reminded him of those he had seen in Curios & Marvels at the Engineerium in Deuona. He picked up a golden bowl, blowing off the dust to study the intricate weaves embossed into the sides and how they sparkled in the Light. *This is certainly beautiful,* he thought.

Baudwin put the bowl down and then picked up a silver knife, with intricate carvings of flowers studded with gems and crescent Moons on the handle. The knife was tarnished, but with a little polishing he knew how brightly it would shine. *Which object is more beautiful,* he wondered, *the golden bowl or the silver knife?* Was it unfair to say that the knife was less beautiful because it was tarnished? And even if it were polished, who could say for certain that it was more or less beautiful than the bowl?

"No — no — no —" he said, putting down the knife. There had to be something even more beautiful — something that *really* stood out. He searched and searched, until inside a small golden chest on a shelf he found a gorgeous rose-shaped pendant with a huge ruby at its center, surrounded by petals made of emeralds and diamonds, hanging from a chain of gold and pearls. *Surely, he thought, <u>this</u> is the most beautiful object.* But then something else caught his eye. On the same shelf next to the small chest was a pair of brass knitting needles. He picked them up to examine them more closely.

"What are a pair of knitting needles compared to a necklace like this?" he asked himself.

Casually, he rubbed the knitting needles between his fingers. He didn't knit, and neither did Seamus or Kelven, but Elva his neighbor did all the time. Every year she made fine sweaters which she gave as gifts at Yule — always digging for compliments when she did. She probably would love to own knitting needles like these — such a good weight, and crafted by an Elve in some faraway land. He figured that she would agree the necklace was more beautiful, but then he also recalled her saying that everyday objects were what Faeries cherished the most.

Baudwin put down the knitting needles. Again he scanned the shelves. Yes, he saw many more beautiful objects, but also many plain ones that he had overlooked before — a pair of bronze pliers and a cane made of petrified wood — also an abacus with gemmed beads, and a blowing horn trimmed with gold. Having to consider so many works of art made him feel light-headed, so he sat down on an ornate chair and tried to take stock of where he stood.

Which object here is actually the most beautiful? he wondered. He looked and looked, but nothing made sense.

"If I choose what I believe to be most beautiful, then someone else might say that it's less so," he said. "What then — honestly — is the *most* beautiful of them all?"

Baudwin then spotted something else — a stunning wreath of polished oak, with gold and silver leaves and berries made of red jasper and green agate. He had often seen similar wreaths, but they were made by collecting the bounty of the forest. Faeries often placed them around their shrines at the equinoxes — Ostara and Mabon — and the solstices — Litha and Yule — to celebrate the turning of the seasons and harmony among the Fae.

On those days, both Elves and Faeries would set the worries of the realm aside and walk together in processions. Arm in arm they would go, and depending upon the season they would gather flowers, leaves, nuts, and berries, trading with each other as they went, and selecting what was best to make a wreath. When a Faery found something for an Elve, the Elve appreciated the Faery for finding the time, and when an Elve found something for a Faery, the Faery appreciated the Elve for making the space. Having ended their walk, they would then go home and create their wreaths.

Baudwin knew that the wreaths meant more than outward beauty — also harmony and accord — and to him the wreath he was holding truly was the most beautiful object in the room. Picking it up, he headed to the pedestal. *Surely, I've chosen correctly,* he thought. But as he was about to place his choice on the pedestal, he stopped.

Across from him was a mirror. There he saw himself — frozen — his arm extended, holding the wreath. He hadn't seen his reflection since before he was whisked away from Four Falls. Now, he looked much older, and the signature sparkle in his eyes seemed dulled, the burdens of his journey having weighed so heavily upon him.

"What if I do this and nothing happens?" he asked. "What if I fail? Is this *honestly* the most beautiful object here?"

Baudwin then tried to recall what Rian his elven friend had said about honesty — that being honest began with being honest with oneself. "One who is honest is never a fool," Rian had said, chuckling. "If you're being honest with me, then perhaps you're learning to be honest with yourself, and that is very good."

Baudwin knew then that honesty with himself — self-honesty — was the key to his decision. He looked again at the wreath and found himself hesitating. "I can't honestly say that this object is the most beautiful," he began. "Who am I to judge such things? Who could ultimately say that one thing is even slightly more beautiful than another?"

Exasperated, he fell silent. Nothing in the room could ever be the most beautiful. Baudwin sat on the chair looking idly about. The silence around him was suffocating, and he wondered if he pounded on the stone door — back down the hall — if Sibéal would even hear him. Was there another way out? His nervousness turned to agitation and feelings of doom. If he didn't solve this puzzle, the way forward would be blocked for a month, so he assumed that placing the wrong object on the pedestal meant that the doorway behind him would open again, and he would have to return empty-handed.

Or so he hoped.

Baudwin looked again at the wreath and then around the room, now knowing that nothing made by the Fae could be deemed the most beautiful. Studying the mosaic of the Triquetra above him, his eyes then fell on another mosaic on the wall — one that he hadn't noticed — with a figure in the center. *Sláine,* he thought, remembering what Sibéal had told him about her. She was standing in profile, her hand cupped as she reached outward. Above her hand was a glyph.

At first Baudwin wasn't sure what the glyph meant. Again, he wished Matha was there to tell him. Looking closely, he remembered something Matha had said, and he was able to decipher the meaning. *It's the ancient glyph for Fire,* he thought, grateful for his friend's instruction.

Above the glyph was another Triquetra, just like the one in the mosaic on the ceiling, and again the glyph for Honesty was accented in red. *Fire and Honesty,* he thought.

And then he stopped.

"No — not Fire *and* Honesty," he exclaimed. "The Fire *of* Honesty!"

Now Baudwin knew the answer. The most beautiful thing was not an object, but the Fire that burns within, when one is truly honest. *This is what the mosaic means,* he thought. A detail so easy to miss in a room filled with so many fine works of art. He looked about him. Baudwin had never liked Fire, and clearly remembered Ferrell telling him not to flinch when the Four Elven Orders had performed their fire dance at the Show Wheel. Water Faeries shied away from the leaping flames, but he knew that somewhere, there had to be Fire that he could place on the pedestal. *Perhaps,* he wished, *I could set the wreath afire,* but as the leaves were made of metal, he quickly dismissed the notion as silly.

Baudwin considered ripping a glowstone from the wall, but glowstones only glowed — they didn't flame.

"The Fire of Honesty. . . " Baudwin repeated, his voice trailing off. He knew now that nothing in the room was the most beautiful, and then the answer came to him. And so, he strode to the pedestal, and following Sibéal's instructions he made his statement to Sláine:

"There is no object in this room that is any more beautiful than any other. For a time, each one may honestly be thought of as the most beautiful, but these judgments are transitory. For me to choose one over the other would be folly. Only the Fire that burns within, the Fire of Honesty itself, is *truly* beautiful — and not because it is, in fact, *the* most beautiful, but because the Fire of Honesty transcends beauty — by taking us *beyond* knowing. So, all I can do is ask this pedestal to judge me accordingly — to measure the Fire of Honesty that burns within me, and if that Fire is bright enough, I humbly ask that I may be led to the next trial."

Much to Baudwin's amazement, the mosaic with the depiction of Sláine then began to glow. Looking across the pedestal at the wall, he saw that a number of red glowstones that he hadn't noticed before had begun to light up her profile. Shining brightly, they illuminated the glyph for Fire above her cupped hand, as well as her gown and the pearls in her hair — all of which glowed a fiery red. The pedestal before him also glowed an even brighter red, the Light emanating in scarlet rays from a glowstone in its center.

The doorway exit from the room leading to the second test then opened, revealing the passage to the second trial.

❧

Baudwin stepped into another stone passage, relieved that he had passed the first trial but still anxious about what lay before him. The trial of Truth was not something he felt prepared to master, especially remembering what Boann had said to him at Esther's reading in the Cyhiraeth Quarter:

"Through the lessons of Honesty, you must face this Truth: That to truly see who you are, you must let go of who you *think* you are!" Waiting a moment for him to absorb the blow, she had added, "And *that* is how you die before you die!"

"If I die before I die, does that mean that I will not *actually* die?" Baudwin asked aloud. Only his voice bouncing off the panels of the hoary carvings of sacred processions and ancient leaders replied back to him. Feeling terribly smaller than his surroundings, he tried his best not to listen to his fears.

Finally the passage ended, and he found himself in a room with a high ceiling that rose and rose, with eight sides tapering to the top. In the center of the ceiling, Light poured through a large circular opening. Baudwin noticed that the room was octagonal. On the far side he spotted a single dark door.

Sibéal had told him that somewhere in this place he would have to find the true Light. "The Truth of the Light within," he muttered.

Craning his neck to study the circular opening in the ceiling, he could not make out what was up there — just a very bright white Light that rained down to the floor, making the center of the room glow. *Surely if I am to discover the Truth, I must climb up there,* he thought, so he readied himself for the trial before him.

All around him were stackable objects, including a number of interlocked wooden boxes. *Simple enough,* he thought. The means to climb up were at his disposal — perhaps *too* easily.

Baudwin picked up a box. Its construction was light but seemed sturdy enough. Carefully he stepped on the top, which easily supported his weight. *Perhaps,* he thought, *I can stack them — one on top of the other — and climb my way to the circle of Light.*

Baudwin began to stack them near the center of the room, one atop another, aiming to create a makeshift staircase. To begin, he put two down — side by side — and then he picked up another, hopped on the first and dropped it on the second box. Then he hopped back down repeating this again and again, slowly building a higher and higher structure.

With great caution, he lifted his head to the Light.

The ceiling was still nerve-rackingly high above him. The boxes were stacked, but a sudden shift in weight could bring everything below him tumbling down. Even for a good acrobat such as he, the jump was very risky. If he didn't grab the lip of the opening in the ceiling he might fall and break a leg. Or his neck. There would be no help for him then.

Baudwin raised his arms above his head. He was so near and yet still so far. Looking down at the boxes below, he saw there were none left to stack. He braced himself to jump, but stopped.

"What a pile of boar droppings!" he shouted. "And as for finding the Truth — the Truth is that I'm *more* terrified than I was at the Hop and Hit, when I was losing to Loch!"

This was no exaggeration, for his spine felt as tight as an overwound spring. He stopped, consumed with dread. "At least at the Hop and Hit I would have hit the Water if I fell, not a stone floor built by a long-passed eccentric queen!"

Baudwin then considered all the other questors who may have come this way. Few, if any, were likely to have been well-trained acrobats, so this gave him an advantage. If anyone could make the jump, it was he. He prepared to take an enormous leap, but before he did, he heard a loud *crack,* and the boxes beneath his feet began to wobble.

Below him, one of the boxes had crumbled, and his makeshift staircase was swaying. Skillfully, Baudwin kept his balance as everything fell forward. Farther and farther the boxes went, and at the last moment he skillfully jumped off. The opening in the ceiling was well out of reach, so now all he could do was try and save himself before he crashed to the floor.

Down he fell, knowing that he could easily break every bone in his body. But luckily the boxes had fallen forward, and his jump had carried him toward the wall, his momentum allowing him to grab onto a ledge that circled the room. Slowly, he climbed from the ledge to the stone frame of the doorway, finding small handholds in the stonework as he headed for the floor.

Splayed among the boxes that had fallen every which way, Baudwin took stock of his body: Nothing broken — not even his spirit. *What to do next?* He then noticed something he hadn't seen before. There were several heaps of ragged clothes on the ground. He had been so focused on the ceiling that he hadn't noticed these rags. He picked up a pair of boots. The canvas barely held together between his fingers, and he wondered who had left them here. With a chill, he realized that many must have passed to Annwyn, leaving their garments behind.

Looking over his shoulder, he could see that the doorway he had entered from had sealed itself shut. Sweat beaded his brow. Until now, he thought that Sibéal had been bluffing — that she could rescue him at any moment and that surely, she had a means to open the door. The piles of rags told a different story.

Queasy with indecision, he paced about. Not only had he failed, but he was also trapped. His plan to scale the boxes hadn't worked, and with a broken box, the distance to the ceiling would be even greater. He knew he had to find another way.

Baudwin studied the single dark doorway opposite the one that was sealed shut. He had no idea what awaited inside. *Surely, I'm doomed,* he thought, anxiety coursing through him.

Considering his next move, he then remembered Rian's words, "If all you seek is Light without the shadow, then all you will find is shadow without the Light."

"Very well then, Rian," he said. "I'll stop climbing to the Light."

Baudwin chose to go through the door. As he made his way in the dark passage, a dank smell greeted his nose, making him gag. Sibéal had warned him that he could get lost or even perish, but he knew he had no choice but to continue. Seeing only blackness, he moved slowly, waiting for his eyes to adjust. Finally, he was able to barely make out the way before him.

Baudwin wondered why Sláine had gone to such lengths to build these passages. None of this seemed practical, but he sensed that soon enough he would find out why. Growing up in Deuona, he had frequently played in a hedge maze, tended by Criofan's neighbor, Molua.[1] The maze covered several acres, and finding his way out had always been a rigorous test of his memory. Remembering this, Baudwin hoped he had only to navigate one long corridor, so he wouldn't get lost. *That was fun,* he thought. *This is torture.*

Ahead, he saw something he could barely make out, perhaps a figure of some kind. Nervously he wondered what awaited him as he approached. Relieved, he stopped. *Just another statue of Sláine,* he thought, running his fingers over its contours.

Below the feet, he could make out the imprint of a plaque with glyphs carved into the center. They were ancient, but not as old as the ones at the ruins of Coventina, so he could decipher them. After a few moments, he read:

Your hope will keep you going

Though you haven't got a chance

Soon the Truth that is your healer

Will pierce you like a lance

Shuddering, Baudwin recoiled from the statue and continued on his way. As he went, he mulled the failure of his attempt to reach the Light. Something then struck him that stopped him in his tracks. *The hole of Light in the ceiling was simply a diversion,* he thought, *so that eventually, the Fae might decide to enter the dark passage.* All of the wooden boxes were there to trick the unwary. He wondered how many had jumped and broken their necks or, having come to such a nasty end and unable to pass the trial, had simply starved to Death.

The Fae of long ago were harsh stewards, he thought. No place he knew of in Deuona could end a Faery's life, simply for failing a challenge. The passage seemed to be growing ever darker as he walked, and for a moment he thought of going back, but he knew there was no way out. He had no choice but to press on and bravely face whatever his fate proved to be.

⚘

Baudwin had walked some distance until suddenly, something glared beneath his feet, casting a soft white Light around him. Looking down, he saw that he had stepped on some glowstones that were set into the path. The whole setup seemed quite peculiar to him. Never in Deuona had he seen glowstones used this way. Looking up, he saw why.

Before him was what appeared to be an orb of Darkness. Blacker than obsidian, it hung by a thick bronze chain close to the wall. No Light reflected from the surface. As Baudwin touched the orb, his fingers passed through,

---

[1] Pronounced [MUL-oo-a]

not altering the surface in the least. Quickly, he pulled them away, worried about what might happen if he kept probing. He was simply a water Faery who struggled enough to understand his own element, yet despite this, he could sense that what he was looking at was a different element altogether. Somehow, he suspected that the dark Faeries had hung this near the wall, but for what reason, he couldn't tell.

Baudwin had never met a single dark Faery. Certainly, he sensed their presence when he had been in the Cyhierath Quarter with his friends, exploring its gloomy foreboding streets until Esther had drawn them all to her. The dark Faeries had all vanished after the Great Befalling, but he could still tell that what he saw before him was their element — the Dark purely presented — just as clearly as he would have recognized Earth, Air, Fire, Wood, or Light. The dark Faeries had left this here with Sláine, even placing glowstones to guide him and previous questors too, so they would not miss this part of the trial.

Baudwin had never seen anything as mysterious-looking as this orb. *A rainbow of Light has all the colors,* he thought, *but this is absent anything that shines.* Surely, any Faery would be as terrified of this as he was. The hole in the ceiling had inspired him to build a flight of stairs to reach the Light, but he suspected that this orb would draw him into a place he was not prepared to go — the workings of Darkness itself, and perhaps even his own shadow. Could he bear to see the parts of himself that had coalesced around all of his awful thoughts and feelings? How mightily Baudwin wished that he *had* reached the Light so he wouldn't have to confront the Darkness that stood before him now. *This can't be what I'm meant to do,* he thought. And yet, he also felt mesmerized by the sight. However unnerved he might be, he decided to let the Darkness guide him.

As if to confirm his expectation, the Darkness in the orb receded, forming into patches of color. *My gaze made it change,* Baudwin thought. He gasped, unable to believe what was taking shape.

Before him was a portrait of himself, with his friends Criofan and Matha, almost one hundred years ago. Baudwin could both see and hear them, as if he were watching them perform on a stage. They were playing a game of fox den — where they first had to decide where the den should be — perhaps under a pile of leaves or in a log. One of them then had to be the fox and the others had to separate from the fox and outrun him, so they could get back to the den without getting caught.

In this instance, Baudwin was the fox, and his friends were trying to sneak past him to get to the den. However, Baudwin quickly got very upset with them, because in his view, they were running too far out of bounds, circling around and around him, which made catching them too hard.

"You're the fox!" Criofan and Matha kept shouting. "We must run!"

Rattled, Baudwin realized that the orb was showing him this memory, which meant that the Darkness knew the story in his mind. He remembered just how resentful he had felt that day, because his friends weren't playing with him on his terms. Furiously, he shrieked at them from the top of his lungs and then went storming off.

Now the orb shifted again, showing him sitting on a stone wall, feeling sad and dejected. His two friends had left him, and they wouldn't speak to him for at least a week.

"I was ungracious with both of you," Baudwin acknowledged as he studied the orb, but now, he didn't feel too badly. This incident had happened when they were much younger, and he had apologized to his friends long ago. He wondered why the orb had shown him this particular memory, then surmised that this was part of the trial of Truth. Surely, he was meant to face the Truth within himself, and so he readily accepted what he had just seen.

I certainly could have treated them better, he thought. *They were just excited to play with me.*

And then the orb shifted back to black.

The glowstone beneath his feet was still shining. Baudwin waited awhile, but didn't see the orb change again. He assumed that he was meant to continue onward, and so farther down the passage he went.

As he did, the passage narrowed. Again his steps were shrouded in Darkness, crushing him with dread. Not a sound could be heard, and in this void any horrible thing could be awaiting him. A sudden drop into a pit could end his Life. Even worse, he feared he might run into a spirit far meaner than Boann. He remembered how she had appeared to him as a serpent, with yellow eyes and a gaping jaw. If he stumbled right now into her mouth, he wouldn't even know what had hit him.

"STOP IT!" he cried aloud, for he was terrifying himself with his thoughts. There was no sense in making his trial harder than it had to be.

A short distance down the passage, more glowstones lit beneath his feet, and again he saw another dark orb. He looked, waiting for the Darkness to change, and then another image came into view.

Unlike the first, this one was of a joyous memory. He was with Criofan and Matha and they were wearing their acrobat costumes, bowing onstage to huge applause at the Beltane festival. Thirty years prior they had put on the show, when Baudwin had been about one and seventy, ten years after he had begun looking for the Water. Everyone in town had come to watch them. To celebrate the summer season, they had turned the stage into an enormous garden. With others in their troupe, they performed as ants and spiders, creeping in and out of rows of vegetables, building bridges and spinning webs, and then as bees and butterflies, buzzing and flitting among berries and flowers, their costumes shimmering in the Light. They had put on quite a show and the crowd could not stop applauding. What a fun time they had, and for Baudwin this Truth was very easy to accept — but then the orb shifted.

He then saw himself with Criofan and Matha, a couple of days after the performance, practicing their tricks in a nearby clearing. They had attached a tightrope to walk between two trees, and they had also been jumping and tumbling, and juggling balls, clubs, and rings. Baudwin was leaning against a tree with his arms crossed, and Criofan and Matha seemed upset with him.

Now he remembered this day. His friends had asked him if he wanted to help find a tree stump to carve a spiral for a neighbor who was soon to receive a new Faefry. According to custom, young gents were asked to find such stumps and move them to other neighboring ones. In this way, family members could begin the carving.

Baudwin remembered how low he had felt on that particular day, coming on the heels of his great performance. The exaltation he had felt during the show was now nothing more than a memory, leaving him adrift in a deep, never-ending emptiness. How he abhorred the feeling, but instead of confiding in his friends, he chose instead to lash out at them — blaming them for his unhappiness. They shouldn't want anything more of him — they should want to help him get more of what *he* wanted — more excitement, more pleasure. And so he railed at them, like a petulant Faefry, a performer who hated others because he wasn't getting all the applause he deserved. Why couldn't they have asked him to stump-hunt at *another* time? And then he remembered how Kelven had scolded him, telling him that the newborn didn't get to choose their own arrival, and that he should help his friends find the stump.

"Why are we carving a stump?" Baudwin had shouted at his father. "We're *water* Faeries! Let the wood Faeries play with stumps!" He was far too angry to see how selfish and immature he was being — mean and nasty — without kindness, unable to treat others with the respect they deserved. Stunned, Kelven shook his head and walked away.

Looking at this memory, Baudwin hung his head. "Yes, it was all my fault, and my triumph at the show made my head swell. I couldn't stand not having the joy continue — on and on. I shouldn't have been so mean to them — being unjoined was no excuse."

The orb then shifted again to black, but this time Baudwin didn't wait to see if there would be another change. He knew what this was — part of the trial of Truth — and so he had to keep going. The Darkness had shown him an even darker part of himself. As he left the orb, the glowstones beneath his feet went out.

Again as he moved down the passage he wondered how many of the orbs he would have to face. This walk couldn't go on forever, and he certainly hoped the trial wouldn't require too much more of him. He had, after all, told Loch at the important meeting that he wasn't afraid to face the Darkness in his own heart. And Loch, not he, would have been the one to fail here — or so he now told himself.

Step by step he continued, his boots echoing like dull hammers as they struck the stonework. *If I linger here too long,* he thought, *surely I will shrivel up, like a dried mushroom.* There was little moisture in the Air, which made him quite uncomfortable, but he took assurance that the passage had to lead somewhere, and that eventually he would triumph.

Nevertheless, he was very short of breath, so to calm himself he pressed his back against the wall and slid to the ground. Next to him was a pedestal attached to the wall, with a gap beneath its base. Idly, he stretched his arm to the stone floor, and as he did, his hand grazed something that felt like a rock beneath the pedestal.

Baudwin picked it up — an object as large as his fist but flatter and smoother. With no idea of what he held, he stood up. Searching around the pedestal, he found a small glowstone, which he tapped. A statue lit up on the pedestal, but what most captured his attention was the object in his hand.

A moonstone, he thought, utterly surprised — just like the glassy black orb Ayamonn had given to him at the Moonstone Rushes, although this one looked even more finely crafted. Baudwin couldn't help wondering who the giver and the receiver could have been of such an exquisitely polished treasure. Faeries were usually the ones who gifted Elves with moonstones, and this one could easily have been carved by the most masterful gem cutter in the realm. His moonstone could not begin to compare.

Baudwin then remembered what Ayamonn had taught him that day at the rushes — how he could actually peer into a moonstone to determine who the owner had been. He looked deeply at the surface. Perhaps this inspection was a foolish waste of time, but he couldn't help himself.

Closing his eyes, Baudwin placed all his attention on the moonstone. He knew that to find a memory, he need only to attune himself to its stirrings, so the color would turn from black to white. That was the secret. When Lugh had let him hold his moonstone at the rushes, he had told Baudwin to simply close his eyes and the memories would come. Now, he did just that, wondering who had owned this moonstone, and what memories it had held before being lost.

Opening his eyes, Baudwin saw that the surface was indeed beginning to turn from black to white. *Just like that day at the rushes,* he thought, intrigued. He closed his eyes again until he felt a memory stirring in the stone. A vision came to him — rough and murky. Baudwin didn't have much to go on, but he suspected that the memory he was seeing was not that of a Faery but rather of an Elve.

Baudwin could make out two figures walking side by side in silhouette, one quite tall and the other considerably shorter. Baudwin studied them both, noting that the taller figure was farther away, and the shorter one closer to Baudwin.

"My Prince," the shorter figure inquired, "are you certain you want to continue? These strange orbs reveal only the bitterest of memories. I fear for your safety and well-being. I've bypassed the mechanics of the doorways behind us. Please — let us leave this place."

As the two kept walking, Baudwin examined the shorter figure in more detail. His face was framed with coppery locks, oily and unkempt, but he was an intelligent-looking fellow, one not used to losing debates that required facts and figures, yet he seemed harried and strained to the point of exhaustion. Hurrying along, he gestured constantly, almost entangling his hands in the copper timepiece that hung from a chain around his neck.

Baudwin then turned his attention to the taller figure, who moved steadily, seemingly disinterested in the shorter one's entreaties. "Don't fear for me, Sprin," he replied, his voice as confident as an eagle's cry. "These trials were created to test the unworthy, and I have *surely* proved myself worthy so far — have I not?"

The short Elve is Sprin, Baudwin thought, *but who is the taller one?* He also wondered why Sprin had been allowed to accompany this tall Elve in the first place. The trial was meant to be undertaken alone.

"You certainly did pass the first trial," Sprin replied obsequiously, trying to persuade the other Elve, "as I knew you would. You proclaimed yourself to Sláine on the pedestal, and did not choose any object as the most beautiful in the room. But at the next trial you will have to face the Truth *inside* yourself, and who can say what rules must be followed — or if they are even fair? Please, my Prince, let us leave this place. I'm sure that we will find the power that you seek elsewhere."

My Prince, Baudwin pondered. *Whoever can he be?*

"No," the Prince replied adamantly, his voice feigning concern for Sprin. "This is where everything begins — and everything ends. When I learned of what was down here, I knew I would be the one to enter the passage and succeed at the trials." The Prince then produced a glowstone rod from his coat, which illuminated the passage. Glancing over his shoulder at Sprin, he added, "In time, I shall master the glamorium artifact I seek, but only after I claim it for myself."

The Prince then turned to look at Sprin, and seeing his face head-on, Baudwin took a deep breath. *Surely, I've seen him before,* he thought, *but <u>where</u>?* Who was this rather charming, yet sinister-looking Elve, his lips pursed, his features exuding such a calculating and decidedly superior manner?

Stunned, Baudwin then remembered. *I saw his face on the seal at the Four Rivers Faire!* Quickly, he remembered the debate between Seanán, of Gold Haven and Fearghus, of the Clock City, about the Eternal Movement and the Rise of Time — the one that had sparked the terrible riot. They had flipped a seal to determine who would begin — city or face — and the face of *Govannon* had won.

He — the Prince — looks <u>exactly</u> like him! Baudwin thought. *He must be Govannon.*

Unaltered by Baudwin's realization, the memory in the moonstone continued to reveal itself. "My Prince," Sprin began, "that is not the way. We are supposed to shroud ourselves in Darkness and gaze at the orbs to prepare ourselves. That is what the ancient texts described, and I shouldn't even be accompanying you. You are to go in alone."

Hearing this, Baudwin wondered whether Govannon would abide by the ancient rules or insist on forging ahead with his own.

Baudwin then heard Govannon reveal, "I've gazed into the darkness long enough. The memories of these orbs do not frighten me, and the lessons they teach have grown monotonous. I have faced the foulness of my father's reign, and that certainly has inured me to seeing the blackness in everything. I've never considered myself that much of a hypocrite that I couldn't see my own failings. So enough. A true ruler makes his own way, and I will make mine."

Baudwin was so dumbfounded seeing Govannon that he could barely consider what he had just heard him say. *Govannon, the King of the Elves. Whatever had <u>he</u> been doing there?* And then Baudwin saw Govannon point down the passage, which was now illuminated by the rod he carried.

"There — you see?" Govannon asked. "This passage will soon end, and my real trial is about to begin."

"Yes," Sprin confirmed, "but please, my Prince, surely we must proceed cautiously in this place if we are to survive its secrets."

Baudwin detected a note of forced sincerity in Sprin's voice, as if he didn't trust Govannon's judgment but needed to appear as if he did, to avoid being castigated. Baudwin waited to see what Govannon would say next.

"I agree," Govannon replied, "which is why I insist that you wait for me here. I expect the next trial to be intensely personal and perhaps quite frightening, and I cannot have my best adviser running away in terror, so you must remain here and wait."

"Alone in the dark?" Sprin asked, his anxiety mounting. "Govannon — let me stay with you!"

Baudwin then heard a laugh, arrogant and proud. "Sprin, don't I always treat you fairly? Here, take this." Baudwin saw Govannon hand the glowstone rod to Sprin. "I will be back shortly — have no fear."

The memory then faded, or rather Baudwin let it fall away, for he couldn't believe his ears. He was himself again, staring at the darkened moonstone in his hands. *How can this be Govannon's moonstone?* he wondered. The King of the Elves himself — the one who still ruled in the Clock City far to the west — had lost this here. But why? Baudwin could hardly believe what he had just seen, but he knew that what he held was real. Yet, what strange happenstance had made him find this here, and for what purpose, he did not know. He wondered what Ferrell might think of this discovery, and whether or not he should even tell him, if they were to meet again.

Pondering what he had just witnessed, Baudwin tucked the moonstone into his pocket. Govannon had stated that he was seeking a glamorium artifact, which meant that he had probably been searching for the same talisman that Sibéal had instructed Baudwin to find. Baudwin wondered whether or not Govannon had succeeded. If he had, then the talisman was gone. *Or, was there more than one?* he wondered. There was only one way to be certain, so he continued on.

After walking a short distance, a glowstone lit up under his feet, and Baudwin faced the third dark orb on the wall. In the moonstone memory, Govannon had dismissed looking at this one, but Baudwin wanted to respect the trial, and so he waited. Sure enough, the orb began to shift. As the image came into view, he was even more convinced that the dark Faeries had left their element here.

Baudwin saw himself at the Springs of Coventina, sitting on a rock soaking wet, brooding after yet another failure to find the Water. He wasn't exactly sure when this had happened, but then the image shifted. Seamus approached him, which rekindled his memory. *This happened about twenty years ago,* he thought, *when I was about ready to give up.*

Baudwin now recalled more of the memory. He had been especially sullen that day and had barely even looked at his grandfather, who had walked miles from their home to surprise him with a visit. He listened carefully, as the orb showed him more.

"Why so glum, my lad?" Seamus asked.

"I don't see the point, Grandfather," Baudwin complained bitterly. "I'm not joined, so the Water isn't going to hear my plea."

Seamus sat down next to Baudwin, draping his arm around his shoulder as if to bolster him like the trunk of an oak. "There's no need to be joined for the Water to listen," he said, his voice low and steady. "The Water listens as soon as a Faefry springs from the aethers, so surely the Water hears you now."

Baudwin turned to look at his grandfather. "Why then, will the Water not come to me? I've been trying for so long — almost twenty years. How much longer must I go on?"

"You must try for as long as it takes," Seamus replied.

Watching the orb, Baudwin saw himself turn away from his grandfather. As he stared at the ground, his clothes were still sopping wet, and his hair was a tangled mess. Listlessly, he picked up a stone and tossed it into the Water.

"I'm just so tired, Grandfather."

Watching the orb, Baudwin remembered how much strength Seamus had always given him, helping him to be confident so that he would not falter, but in that moment, Seamus hadn't been able to buttress him any further. They sat for quite a while in silence. Yet, just when Baudwin assumed that Seamus had nothing more to say, his grandfather had spoken.

"You've always been the sort of Faery who feasts when the stew is hot, and flees when the porridge is cold," Seamus began. "You're not the same as me. My weakness is different — and that's a fine thing — but the true test for you isn't whether or not the Water will come to you."

"Whatever is *that* supposed to mean?" Baudwin asked.

"Baudwin, you must stand fast when you fear the pain will overwhelm you," Seamus continued. "You must have *fortitude*. To have the courage to endure no matter what Life brings you is the source of your strength."

Hearing this, Baudwin recoiled. "Endure? I *have* been enduring!" As he shouted, a number of frogs leaped back into their pond, and a bluethroat quavered in reprimand.

"Yes," Seamus replied, "and if you are to learn the lesson fully, you must endure even more."

"How long will that take? Grandfather — I'm *so* tired of this."

Seamus then squeezed his grip on Baudwin's shoulder, until Baudwin turned to him. Firmly, he pressed his palm into the center of his grandson's chest.

"Until Annwyn calls you home, Baudwin."

Baudwin remembered how much this had startled him. And he remembered the next part very clearly. The orb continued showing him the memory.

"But. . ." Baudwin began haltingly, as his grandfather waited. "But that means I could be trying to find the Water until I'm your age? Is that what you're telling me?"

Seamus nodded.

"But that's not fair!"

Seamus shook his head. "It's not supposed to be fair, Baudwin. It's not supposed to be gratifying, either."

Seamus's assertion had put Baudwin on a razor's edge. He remembered how easily he then could have given up by deciding not to listen to Seamus anymore, but somewhere inside him his thoughts quieted down. Every fiber of his being knew that Seamus's words had to be true, and so, reluctantly, he had acquiesced.

"Well, if I must, I must. . ." Baudwin said, meeting his grandfather's kind, uncompromising gaze. "I will have fortitude to the bitter end. . ."

Seeing the orb, Baudwin knew that his younger self had not been sure that he could live up to such a powerful commitment, but in the end, Seamus had been right. Baudwin's fortitude *had* carried him through — right to where he now stood. Despite not being joined, he had learned the lesson of endurance by heeding his grandfather's instruction — words that still burned fiercely in his heart.

The orb's image then faded to black.

"To the bitter end it shall be then, Grandfather," Baudwin said, as he made his way down the passage to where Govannon himself had once strode. He would face the next trial with all of his strength.

⬥

With almost no time to shore up his reserves, Baudwin found himself in a place unlike any he had ever seen — a large cavern, with limestone walls and an arch-shaped marble ceiling. *Such irony,* he thought, *that Sláine and her followers had sweated and strained to build a way here, which in and of itself needed no building.* Resting deep within the Earth, the cavern was indeed a wonder — no doubt a sanctuary of hidden mysteries protected for thousands of years by the dark Faeries themselves. Searching about, he found several glowstone sconces, which he quickly lit.

Looking about in the dim Light, all he saw was bare Earth with a cobblestone path. His eyes followed the path to the center of the cavern, where four stone pillars had been carved out of the limestone to reach from ceiling to floor. *And this is how they ended their toils,* he thought, as he studied the massive columns, *leaving the moss to grow and the damp Air to linger.*

Baudwin approached one of the pillars and ran his fingers over the smooth, clammy surface. Looking past the pillars, he sensed that the orbs may not have prepared him for what lay ahead. *I must be strong,* he reminded himself, wondering if the dark Faeries had asked the Elves to build the pillars to instill courage in the questors. Carefully, he made his way past them to learn what his trial would be.

Before him was a large dark pool. Kneeling down, he discovered that whatever filled the pool was not Water. Inspecting the surface, he saw that the element was of the Dark, and that the pool had to be its natural fount. Baudwin surmised that out of respect, Sláine and her followers had gone to great lengths to enshrine it — so far from elven lands. Thousands of dedicated stonemasons had to haul and shape the materials to build the steps and passages — all so they would eventually lead a chosen few to face their darkest fears. *Chosen because they had no other choice — like me,* he thought with a wry smile.

Timidly, Baudwin dipped his finger into the pool, and quickly pulled it back. He stood up, startled. Whatever was in the pool couldn't be called wet. Much to his surprise, an odd residue remained on his finger, which dripped to the ground, only to recede back into the pool. *This element certainly has a will of its own,* he thought. He felt no pain or discomfort, but didn't trust the dark fount enough to poke his finger in again.

Baudwin remembered the day his quest had first begun at the Springs of Coventina and how he had touched the Water, feeling its icy wetness against his palm. How he had dived into the Water — and how *finally* the Water had come to him. After hearing all the voices of his tribe, Sibéal had spoken to him, telling him, "You are on your way."

But, what way am I on now? he wondered as he pondered Sibéal's most recent clue — that he must find the Light of Truth within. Water had come to him then, and Light needed to come now, but all he saw before him was a murky pool — ominous, yet strangely inviting.

Baudwin gasped.

As if the pool was responding to his touch, he saw shapes begin to form in the murky Darkness. First they were indistinct clumps that appeared to be void of substance, but quickly, they solidified. Kneeling again, he saw the shape of the back of a head, with long tresses that looked like decaying river moss plastered against a neck supported by broad yet wasted-looking shoulder blades. The head turned suddenly, and he was greeted by a pale face, lifeless and spoiled.

Baudwin let out a cry.

He believed that he was viewing the body of a deceased gent — but who or why he was there he couldn't tell.

Shocked, he stood up. And then — much to his horror — he saw what appeared to be even more lifeless bodies in the pool. Some were old, others were young, but all — whether Elves or Faeries — had a ghastly aura around them, which made him suspect that they were more spirit than flesh. If they were indeed spirits, his deduction made sense. The Fae who passed to Annwyn vanished soon, if not immediately after, their death, leaving their clothes behind, but these bodies lingered. Whether real or not, he wondered what they were doing there.

Searching for clues to make sense of this morbid spectacle, Baudwin found, right before the steps leading into the pool, some old glyphs etched into the floor.

They read:

O piteous one!
Submerge thyself
And affirm the Truth
Lest the shadows you fear
Condemn you to the mire
Where corpses wail
And blind ones see only Darkness

Reading this, Baudwin blanched. "Oh come now!" he shouted, his words bouncing off the cavern walls and the stalactites hanging above his head. "Surely you don't expect me to go in *there!*" He looked again at the spectral bodies in the dark pool. The sickly glow emanating from their skin enabled him to see them in the inky mire. Desperately, he tried to find another way — anything other than what the Darkness was calling him to do — but he couldn't. Unsure of what to do, he sat down on the cavern floor.

And then he realized that there was one other way.

Baudwin removed Govannon's moonstone from his pocket, assuming that if Govannon had come to this very place he might learn from him. He readied himself to use the moonstone, but, shuddering, then hesitated. For some reason, reading the memories the first time had left him feeling poisoned. Something about Govannon himself made harnessing his memories quite unsettling, so much so that Baudwin recoiled at the notion. Although this was the moonstone of a king, he had already decided that he had seen enough. But as he looked again at the lifeless bodies in the pool, he reasoned that using the moonstone had to be the best alternative.

And so, he closed his eyes as he had done before, and tried to harness the memory, imagining Govannon standing in this very place. The moonstone turned from black to white as slowly, a memory stirred. Painfully, a vision came to him.

Before him Baudwin again saw Govannon. The future king was gazing into the pool. Beneath his confident demeanor, he appeared uneasy — even frightened — but also puzzled, as he continued to look into the Darkness. Just as Baudwin had seen before, numerous ghastly-looking bodies swirled in the mire, but Govannon appeared not to care, as he was lost in thought. The Prince then studied the same glyphs that Baudwin had seen etched into the floor. After reading them, he quickly strode into the pool. The bodies vanished. *Obviously, the poem hadn't daunted him,* Baudwin thought. The pool reached Govannon's waist — nothing else stirred.

Baudwin then heard Govannon utter, "O great Queen from the time of Gold — builder of the vaults, and storer of treasures past. I've come to you in dire need. The Fae suffer from the incompetence of my father's rule. The Elves no longer know why they must build, nor can they properly hone their intentions. Instead, they argue and fight, while the common folk wither. Please — I beseech you! Dark Faeries who guard the secrets within, I must now prove myself worthy of an ancient treasure hidden in these walls — one that I must wield to save my realm and my kin from certain ruination. Please — Sláine — I beseech you! Let me pass this trial and become a beacon to the Fae."

Baudwin was immediately inspired by this Elve. To him, he sounded noble and fair. *It's no wonder that Ferrell serves him so diligently,* he thought. Govannon sounded so earnest that Baudwin believed he would gladly kneel before him, should they ever meet. However, looking at him more closely, he couldn't help but notice a beguiling, yet disturbing quality in his demeanor. Certainly, when he spoke, his features settled into a handsome face — vibrantly engaging all to whom he spoke. Yet when he stopped speaking, these same features appeared dull and empty, as if everything he had just said meant nothing to him. Baudwin couldn't tell which of the two faces revealed the Truth of who he was.

Govannon waited.

In the dark ether before him, a lucid image appeared. Baudwin knew that he was witnessing a memory within a memory — first from Govannon's moonstone and now in the pool where Govannon stood. Just as the three dark orbs had shown Baudwin his past, the image in the pool was now showing Govannon a memory of his past.

Fascinated, Baudwin watched.

The pool showed Govannon standing on a balcony in a grand palace, looking down on a courtyard full of thousands of onlookers. Next to Govannon stood another gent. Both were dressed in royal regalia. Baudwin surmised that they were in one of the larger elven cities in the West — perhaps Silver Forge, Copper Caves, or Gold Haven. The stonework of the palace had a golden luster, with ornate relief of flowers, leaves, and vines. The road below them sparkled. The grounds were immaculately kept. Golden leaves fell from the trees, covering the stone pathways in a shimmering carpet. Enthralled by the splendor, Baudwin guessed that they had to be in Gold Haven.

From behind Govannon and the gent standing next to him, Baudwin heard a voice call out, "Belanus. Where are you?"

Baudwin saw the gent turn, realizing that he had to be Belanus.

"Father!" Belanus exclaimed. "What a fine day this is! So many have gathered below. I hardly feel worthy."

"But you *are* worthy!" exclaimed the voice as he drew closer to Belanus. Baudwin saw that he was wearing a crown, so he knew that the Elve had to be King Brandon, striding in with his wife, Queen Chelsea, at his side.

"This crowd has come to congratulate you," King Brandon exclaimed, "for your fine service to the Eternal Movement."

Baudwin then saw Govannon smile at King Brandon — his father — and Belenus — his brother. Evenly, he masked his feelings, so that neither of them would detect the slightest hint of his displeasure.

Baudwin also noticed that as Govannon watched the memory of his father and his brother, he scowled, and so, eager to learn more, Baudwin continued to watch the memory unfold.

"You have rekindled their faith — haven't you, young Prince," King Brandon crowed. "Your pilgrimage to Platinum Spires was a success! You found the artifacts that revealed the origins of the Eternal Movement — proving that our way has always been the *true* way. As you also stood up to all those who sought to pervert the meaning of time, the crowd is now praising you."

King Brandon then put his arm around his son's shoulder. "Turn now, and wave to the crowd. For today is *your* day!"

The image of King Brandon and Belanus then went dark.

Baudwin waited silently, immersed in what remained of Govannon's memory in the moonstone, watching as Govannon seethed with bitterness and rage. "Always the favorite of Father," Govannon griped. "*Always* eager to please and never question."

Baudwin wondered if the memory of the moonstone was over, and then from the pool another image appeared before Govannon. Again, he was in Gold Haven, this time standing on a stage in a huge courtyard. A drape covered something on the stage. Govannon stood next to the drape, addressing the crowd. Baudwin saw King Brandon, Queen Chelsea, and Prince Belanus in a royal box — watching and waiting.

There were also many others in attendance — ladies and gents, and nobles and dignitaries from all over *Tír Luí Lucharachán*. Baudwin even saw Faeries — not just earth, water, air, and wood — but also dark, light, and even fire Faeries. Baudwin was mesmerized at the sight. He had never seen the latter three kinds of Faeries before, and he then realized that this memory had occurred before the Great Befalling, before they had gone missing. He wanted to see more of the Faeries, but the image shifted into something else.

Govannon pulled back the drape.

Baudwin saw a huge water clock on the stage, with a cone at least eight feet high, marked with lines and numbers and set into a two-column frame. *Just like the one in Seanán's tent at the Four Rivers Faire, he thought — only this one is made of gold.* Bronze piping fed Water to the magnificent clock, which dripped slowly from the bottom of the cone, accurately measuring the time.

Next to the water clock sat a mechanical clock, steadily ticking away. Baudwin then heard a great booing from the crowd, followed by a lot of commotion. Abruptly, King Brandon left his royal box and strode over to question Govannon. "What is the *meaning* of this?" he asked. "Why have you put that next to the water clock?"

"Father," Govannon replied, "I felt it only right and proper that we pay homage to *both* the Eternal Movement and the Rise of Time. Do you not agree?"

"No," King Brandon replied. "I do *not* agree. We've had this discussion before, have we not? This is *not* our way. Our kingdom has always used only water or sun clocks. You were to renovate the old one in order to pay respect, and instead you created *that*," he added, scowling at the mechanical clock.

"But Father," Govannon implored, "I only meant to pay respect to both. *Both* deserve respect!"

Baudwin could see that King Brandon was not going to listen. Soon, Govannon's memory shifted to the King's guards wielding great sledgehammers and pounding the mechanical clock to smithereens. The golden hands of the fine creation were torn off. Gears and cogs were smashed and scattered, until the inner workings were nothing but a broken heap of scrap. Baudwin saw that Govannon looked ashen, but remained composed, his feelings coiled inside him like a snake not quite ready to strike.

In front of everyone present, King Brandon then spoke. "On this auspicious occasion, we have been sadly misled. Only the Eternal Movement was to be honored, but instead my well-meaning but misguided son created a spectacle of himself. For that I must beg you all for forgiveness, and you, my son, must apologize."

However, Govannon did no such thing. Angrily, he strode away from the courtyard, stunning the crowd with his arrogance.

The vision in the dark pool ended. Baudwin continued to witness the memory in Govannon's moonstone. Still standing in the pool, the Prince looked defiant, having relived the memory of his father scolding him.

"I was fair with them!" he shouted, his words booming against the walls of the cavern. "I put both the *new* and the *old* side by side! What fault is there in that?" He raged, but the pool did not stir, and the closed stone doorway at the end of the room did not budge.

Baudwin then knew that Govannon had not passed the trial.

Govannon shouted again, "I did only what I thought best for the future of the kingdom! Change shall *not* be thwarted! If I hadn't brought the Rise of Time before them, someone far less capable than I would have done so. Surely this means that I have faced the darkness within — for I am the *light* of the realm!"

Again, there was no response. Baudwin gasped, as the lifeless bodies in the pool appeared again and swirled toward Govannon. Their eyes still closed, they encircled him in the pool, grasping and clawing.

He's condemned himself to the mire, Baudwin thought, remembering the poem he had read earlier. Looking more closely at the bodies, he noticed that their sickly aura glowed even more intensely. He knew then that they had to be specters. Now they grabbed Govannon by the legs to pull him under.

"No!" Govannon raged. "The Rise of Time shall *not* be denied!"

And so, he unsheathed his sword, and stabbed at the lifeless wretches. Hacking off arm after arm, leg after leg, head after head, the furious slashing continued until only floating torsos remained, with nothing left to thwart him.

Curiously, Govannon picked up a dismembered arm, which still glowed a sickly-looking green. Shrieking, he quickly dropped it, grasping his own arm instead. Writhing in pain, he then grabbed at all of his limbs, and Baudwin suspected that his slashing of the specters had also slashed him. In some way, they were part of him.

Surely, they are the shadows of his misery, he thought.

Baudwin half expected the dismembered limbs and heads to keep fighting, but then Govannon shouted, "The future of the realm will be shaped by *my* hand! Time will rise, ushering in a new Platinum Age! I will *not* be thwarted! I command you now — give to me my birthright!"

Baudwin recoiled in shock as, much to his amazement, the dark pool answered Govannon. Another vision appeared in the murky ethers.

Govannon watched — awed — as a vision of a gateway appeared before him. As the vision grew, he saw a grand bridge, longer than the eye could see, made of every color of the rainbow. In a flash, Govannon then saw a building with a large statue of a hooded man holding a spear high above his head. The vision then descended into the building, sinking deeper and deeper through aged corridors and vaults, until at the very bottom, where the foundations were laid, he could see a spear — a great spear — with a wooden shaft and a dark metal tip upon a pedestal of crystal.

Eagerly, Govannon reached for the spear, but his arm went through the vision into the dark ethers. He pulled his hand away, still staring at the image.

"What *is* that?" he asked aloud. "That bridge. . . that's the *Rainbow* Bridge. Yes! And that spear must be what will lead me to my destiny!"

And then, the vision ended. Govannon strode out of the pool. So excited was he that he paid no mind to the fact that the other door had remained sealed tightly shut. Shouting for Sprin to follow, he raced out of the room. He stumbled and tripped, and stumbled and tripped, until the moonstone fell from his pocket, sliding under a pedestal. And then the memory — the last memory the stone ever held — ended.

Baudwin then found himself — alone again — holding Govannon's moonstone, wondering what would come next.

⚜

Baudwin stared at the spectral bodies still floating in the dark ethers. He knew his time had come to step in, but if the bodies turned on him, he had no sword to defend himself — not even a quarrel staff. *I would be much better off if I were armed like Govannon,* he thought. The Prince had made his own rules in this place, but Baudwin also knew that he had failed. Although he had received a vision from the pool to guide his destiny, he had not crossed the far door and had left empty-handed.

Baudwin was determined to succeed. The memory in Govannon's moonstone had given him a clue. If he faced the Truth of any vision he saw, he would pass the trial, and so he stepped into the pool. The black ether was up to his waist, sloshing against him as he moved. Unsettled by the strange wetness, his spine tensed. So far, none of the spectral bodies had moved, so he waded out to the center of the pool. Looking down, expectantly, he waited.

Surrounded by the dark ethers, he took a measure of himself. *So far, I have been through much more than I ever bargained for,* he thought. He was still exhausted from his journey upriver. His sleep at Sibéal's had barely refreshed him, and his muscles still ached, but truly what wore on him most was how much he had failed. His glamorium egg had been taken, and he had fled from his home to the Four Rivers Faire, only to end up beaten and defeated under a bridge in the Cyhiraeth Quarter. To put himself on track again, he had plotted with Lugh to join the Elves at the Engineerium — but only as an indentured servant. Loch — not he — had helped to save the downtrodden Faeries in the Cyhiraeth Quarter. Boann had interrupted his plan to share the dreams of the Elves with the Faeries — by judging him harshly and casting him away from his tribe. He feared that he may even have lost some of the love of his father and grandfather for siding with the Elves.

Every failure stabbed at him, but here was his one last chance to redeem himself. One final opportunity to make everything work out. He looked again at the ether.

"I have come to prove myself!" he shouted at the pool.

Yet nothing changed, and the spectral bodies remained motionless. The Air was still, and not a sound reverberated off the imposing rock formations of the cavern.

When Baudwin had witnessed Govannon step into the pool, a vision had come quickly to the Prince, but for Baudwin, nothing stirred. He began to worry. Perhaps he wasn't important enough for the pool to answer him, or perhaps Govannon's vision had been the pool's last reply.

Unsure of what to do, Baudwin paused — waiting and waiting. If the Sun outside the cavern was low, he wouldn't have known, for he had lost all sense of time. He reflected more on his failures. Had he come all this way for nothing?

Baudwin looked down at one of the spectral bodies. The contorted face seemed only to mock him, as if he was now forever a prisoner of the Darkness.

"Well then!" he shouted. "Perhaps I *am* just a failure!"

Still, nothing changed.

Baudwin thought then of his home and of his tribe. He longed to simply be back with them — to be home with his father and grandfather, as if this misadventure had never happened. Seamus and Kelven had told him at the Grand Unveiling that he could stop whenever he wanted — that this Life of searching didn't have to be his only Life. But then, Boann had whisked him away, and now — again — he was facing defeat.

He seethed. He raged. He balled his fists and slammed them down — the dark ether splashing, the spectral bodies bobbing around him like bloated buoys, unable to save him from his fate.

"*I will not fail!*" he shouted defiantly. He then remembered how the Water had come to him at the Springs of Coventina, and so he shouted — as if he was hearing all the voices of his tribe and all of his ancestors were a witness to him, and every drop of rain that had ever fallen in the realm was nourishing the roots of his soul. He shouted for the destitute Fae of the Cyhiraeth and the Guild, and for the dreams of the Faeries and the Elves — together.

"I will *not*! I will *not*!" he shouted, again and again.

As if they knew the Truth of his conviction, the ethers then began to stir.

Baudwin tensed. The spectral bodies in the pool began to move, but not toward him. Instead, they floated away, joining together strangely as they went. With a gasp, Baudwin watched them merge into a large black mass. A dark silhouette then rose from the ether, shapeless at first, but then turning into a feminine form. Looking more closely, he saw that oddly, the form appeared to be a moorhen. Her arms were covered with dark brown feathers, ragged and molting. Her face had a pointed orange beak, and small, dull brown eyes, dark and despondent. *I've seen her before,* he thought.

And then he remembered. She was the lady-bird from the vision he had had with Rian at the Engineerium, after Rian had given him the glamorium egg. First he had seen a beautiful faery lady standing in a stream of Water and

Light, and then she had turned into a pitiful-looking bird, just like the one he now saw before him.

The lady-bird then turned her eyes to him, cooing piteously. She was frozen with terror, and her feathers shivered. She cooed again and again, and so, he went and embraced her, holding her to him.

"If you are my mother," he said, "then let us leave this place."

Baudwin tried to pull her from the pool, but then black claws emerged from the ethers and seized her, pulling her down. Baudwin bellowed.

"*No!*" he shouted.

He pulled with all his strength — harder and harder until he feared the joints on his fingers would break. He pulled until his breath burned in his chest like Fire.

Baudwin then looked into her eyes. They had changed color, and were now bright turquoise — just like his. She <u>must</u> *be my mother,* he thought.

Somehow, he managed to get to the edge of the pool — still holding her — while the dark claws pulled her the other way. Frantically, he tried to lift her from the pool, but as she began to slip, his grasp stripped the dark feathers from her arms. He then grabbed her around her middle, but the strength of the claws was greater than his, and slowly, she sank into the ether.

Tears filled his eyes — tears of rage and sorrow.

"Please — *no!*" he shouted. She had now almost completely disappeared beneath the ether. Only her arms and her face could he see, and her eyes begging for deliverance.

"What is happening?" he shouted.

As his strength failed him, her eyes filled with sorrow, and she let out a pitiful coo — and then she was gone.

Baudwin jumped back into the pool. The bodies had all vanished, and where the lady-bird had gone he did not know. There were no words left for him — nothing he could utter was worthy of his sorrow.

How cruel the pool had been to him. To give him such a tormenting vision, instead of guiding him to see through the Darkness. How much easier Govannon's trial had been, for despite his failure, he had not left empty-handed — for him was the vision of a marvelous spear, and the Rainbow Bridge beckoning him to cross.

Baudwin strode out of the pool to the far door, which was still sealed firmly shut.

"I am NOT a failure!" he roared, pounding and pounding on the bare stone with the little strength that he had left. "Failing does NOT make me a failure! The Light of Truth is known to me — dwelling FOREVER in every fiber of my being! For eternity! FOREVER!"

At this, the Darkness in the pool then answered him. As Govannon had railed at the ether, so too had Baudwin, and now, for sharing this most truthful cry from his heart, he was rewarded in kind by the merit of his intention.

The door opened, and Baudwin, astonished, fell to his knees. *Yes!* he thought. *I have passed the trial!* And indeed he had. Now, but one more remained before he could claim the talisman.

⚬✝⚬

Baudwin found himself traveling down yet another passage. Plodding ahead, he reflected upon what had just transpired. The lady-bird — that frightened, feathered effigy of his mother — had come again. The first time had been with Rian when Glamorium had graced him with a vision, and the forging shadow had stolen her away. But this time the Darkness of the Fae had presented her to him, and then taken her away, leaving him to face an illusion he himself did not know he carried. And now — unburdened — his steps were light and steady.

I'm not a failure, he thought, and now, having passed two trials, he was not as daunted by what might come next. He would disarm any traps and vanquish any specters that confronted him, and his heart would dispel any obstacle in his way. Nevertheless, as he pondered his last ordeal, a barb was pricking him.

I couldn't save her, he thought. *But who was she?*

Indeed, she had been dragged under, taken again, but it was now clear to him that the lady-bird wasn't real. She was a conjured hallucination, a trick of shadow and smoke. The pool had read his fears, and then offered him the obstacle that he had to overcome. The same had been true with Govannon — who had faced the tongue-lashing of his father, but had ultimately failed to find the Truth within himself, even though he believed that he had succeeded.

Baudwin wondered about this. Perhaps the pool had wanted Govannon to face his arrogance, but seeing his resistance, had shown him another way. Eager for glory, Govannon had left to fetch a spear that lay somewhere over the Rainbow Bridge. Baudwin again remembered Esther's reading, where she had told him that he too would cross a bridge and leave the realm behind. Would he eventually go the same way that Govannon had? He wasn't sure, but the notion intrigued him. There was one thing that he was certain of — the talisman was just one step away, and would be the means by which he would find his *real* mother.

As he made his way along, he pondered more about why the door had finally opened. Whoever had conceived the trial had wanted questors to consider not only their failings, but how they regarded themselves for having tried at all. *A small part of the Light of Truth within,* he thought. *Such simple wisdom,* he marveled, *so often buried beneath layers of suffering and implacable beliefs about oneself and others. I must always hold onto that part,* he vowed — *no matter what.*

And so he continued on, now drawn by a faint circle of Light that seemed to be calling to him from the end of the passage — much like the Light in the tunnel to the Engineerium. However, this time, he did not rush to reach the circle as he had with his friends that day, bursting with high expectations.

Baudwin paused for a moment, remembering what Brigh had told him at the Ceremony of the Joining, when he had been a young one:

"The rapids are not the shallows, and the shallows are not the rapids. Let neither rule you — a steady heart will always carry you through."

A steady heart will always carry you through, he thought, smiling. *Because the rapids are not better than the shallows, and the shallows are not inferior to the rapids. And high expectations are like rapids,* he thought, amazed. Despite being unjoined, he could finally understand what she had told him so long ago.

Remembering even more of the second trial, his understanding deepened. He had tried to build a staircase to reach the circle of Light, and failed. *I was in the depth of the shallows,* he thought — *such despair.* As he approached the circle of Light at the end of the passage, his heart was now more constant than he had ever felt.

Baudwin stepped through the opening and found himself in a large spring-grotto, cooled by rushing waterfalls within limestone walls lush with hanging plants. Moss carpeted the floor, and on either side of him a flight of stone stairs descended to a large pool of Water. High above him an opening in the ceiling painted the grotto with golden rays of afternoon sunlight. Near him on the cave wall stood a giant statue of Sláine greeting all who entered.

Gazing down on him, she looked like a benevolent figurehead on a ship, watching over all who stepped into the pool. Unlike other depictions thus far, Baudwin saw that she was at peace — serene as a swan gliding through the clouds — and elegantly dressed, with her hair billowing around her like smoke in the wind. This did not surprise him, for he figured that anyone having come through such an ordeal and passing all the trials would certainly welcome her serenity — as well as their own.

Across the pool Baudwin saw a pebbled shore. Rising up from the embankment was a mound, and on that mound he could make out some kind of stonework — a plinth near a large square-shaped stone box, but he couldn't make out anything more. Ever more confident that this trial would not prove too great a hardship, and yearning for a reprieve, he made his way down the steps.

As he moved, his muscles protested, sore from the struggle of pulling the lady-bird from the clutches of the dark ethers. His entire body still ached, and as he took each step, his calves burned. Yet, steadily down and down he went.

Now he was at the bottom of the steps, standing beneath the statue of Sláine. Looking up at her, he shouted, "Thank you — my dear lady!"

All that separated him from the mystery on the mound was the pool. Never did swimming daunt a water Faery — and certainly not now — for the distance wasn't very great. For a moment he wondered if he might have a bout, but there was no stopping him, and so he waded into the Water.

With a hearty breaststroke he made his way across, and as he swam, he could tell that this was no ordinary pool. The Water was sacred — touched by but a few — and it also held a boon: The Promise of Rebirth.

As he was now about halfway across, Baudwin knew for certain that he would be spared from a bout. Here he could meet the Water without fear. He could frolic in its shallows, and when the Sun gave way, dance beneath the Light of the Moon. For this was a pool more blessed than any he had ever known — a place where those haunted by unworthiness could find themselves worthy, and in so doing, begin anew.

Having reached the shore, Baudwin made his way up the mound, until finally, he saw what Sláine had built. Carved into the pedestal was a Triquetra — just like the one he had seen at Curios & Marvels — with a glyph for Glamorium at the center and a triangular glyph at each point. The glyphs at the points were made of copper and represented the three realms, *Tír na nÓg*, Danu, and Fios. They also stood out noticeably from the rest of the carving.

On a placard at the base of the pedestal were glyphs that read:

"When the realms are one — the triad will open the way."

Baudwin then went to the large stone box, which was fashioned with rounded corners and ornate gold work bordering the sides. He guessed that elven masons of Copper Caves must have crafted the box, and not Faeries. Cameos of Faeries and Elves made of carved shells and colored stones were set into the top. Were they a wise council that had overseen the building of this place? Baudwin didn't know, but he suspected as much.

In the center of the box near the top was a large triangular indentation. Baudwin wondered what should go there — perhaps a key of some sort. Mindful of the glyphs he had just read, he traced the indentation with his hand and turned the riddle over in his mind.

"When the realms are one. . ." he said, as he headed back to the stone Triquetra. Once there, he ran his fingers over the copper glyph — *Tír na nÓg* — and felt a slight jiggle.

"The triad will open the way," he said, completing the riddle.

With a start he realized that if he applied enough pressure, he could pull the copper glyph away from the Triquetra. *The glyphs are meant to be removed,*

he thought, holding the first one in his hands. The triangular glyph looked too small to fill the indentation on the stone box. Regardless, he went back to the box. Placing the glyph in the indentation, he then realized that the other two glyphs — Danu and Fios — would fit as well.

Soon he had them both in his hand. As he placed them in the indentation, they formed a new glyph:

The realms are now one! he rejoiced.

Astonished, Baudwin heard a *kerchunk* as the locking mechanism of the box gave way, and the top opened.

Joy of joys! he thought, looking inside. Before him was a gorgeous talisman — a circle of Glamorium interlocking with a gold Triquetra.

Baudwin cradled the talisman in his hand, careful not to touch the Glamorium. He couldn't fathom when the piece might have been crafted — many thousands of years ago, he guessed. A treasure like this could buy all the fineries in Deuona, and even rival much of what the Elves had hoarded in Gleam. He wondered if his friends would be happy for him, or what Ferrell might say. Would the Luminary even allow him to keep such a fine treasure?

One thing he did know for certain was that — finally — he had succeeded. Glamorium was again his! All along, Boann had meant for him to come this way. She had taken away his egg, and spurred him on a path to this place. He still wasn't certain he could trust her completely, but surely, this had been her will all along.

Baudwin had many questions to ask Sibéal, and so, after carefully placing the Triquetra into his pocket, he made his way out of the spring-grotto. Now all the doors were open to him, and his path was clear. Soon, he was among the trees again, heading back to her cottage.

☙❦❧

Near Sibéal's dome home, a charming concert was about to begin. Among the reddish catkins and small cones of an alder tree were patches of red, white, green, and brown. The conductor held up her baton, and the patches turned to face her. With a wave of her hand, a melodious song then sprang from every throat, as many beaks opened and closed among the branches. Red cardinals sang — *what cheer, what cheer, what cheer* — their red crests rising and falling with a flourish. White doves struck the backs of their wings together — making a staccato whir — while also cooing in rhythm with the cardinals. Greenfinches sang quickly, repeating a liquid-like stream of whistles and trills, and brown thrashers accompanied them all with high-pitched chirps.

Joyfully, Sibéal smiled as she waved her arms from side to side. "Come now, greenfinches," she said, "and hop in time!"

Seeing the greenfinches move together as one, she smiled, saying, "Very good! Now your turn, cardinals," she continued. "Make your crests into a wave! Keep our spirits high! Cheerful crests mean that our friend is safe and happy — even if he is far away."

The crests on the cardinals' heads then rose in a line, moving one at a time from head to head like a rising wave. And then they fell, moving one at a time from head to head, like a crashing wave, repeating this over and over.

"Excellent!" Sibéal exclaimed.

But I'm _not_ far away Baudwin thought, as he approached the uplifting symphony. *In fact, I'm finally here!* His heart was ready to burst with his good news, but remembering his manners, he leaned against a tree, waiting for the song to end.

One of the greenfinches hopped onto a small branch, and it snapped. Cocking their heads at the greenfinch, the other birds began chattering.

"Now now," Sibéal admonished. "You mustn't laugh. You wouldn't like your branch breaking during a performance — would you?"

Apologetically, the other birds bowed their heads.

"That's better," Sibéal said. "We mustn't be impolite." One of the thrashers chittered loudly, staring straight at Baudwin.

"Oh?" Sibéal asked. "Right behind me, you say?"

Sibéal turned, and saw Baudwin. "The Fae of the hour has arrived," she announced, "which means he must not be empty-handed."

"Indeed!" Baudwin exclaimed, beaming proudly. Producing the talisman from his pocket, he then offered her the shining treasure.

"How remarkable," Sibéal began, as she came closer, "and locked down there for who knows how long. I haven't seen its like since before the Great Befalling."

Baudwin could barely contain himself. "I have so many questions," he began, "that I don't even know where to begin."

As Baudwin spoke, the birds on the branches showed great interest. They flew to a tree close to where he stood, alighting in groups. Eagerly, they looked at him, waiting to hear more.

"Ask then," Sibéal said.

"Where is my mother?"

"She dwells now across the Rainbow Bridge — in Fios — the realm of the Luminous Ones."

"Why is she there — and why did she leave?"

At this, Sibéal became somber. "The Great Befalling was just too difficult for her to bear, Baudwin — agonizing for so many. She *had* to leave. Some of the Fae cannot linger here under such conditions. If she hadn't crossed the bridge to Fios, she surely would have perished."

A pair of mated doves let out long mournful *coos.*

"After the befalling, the realm was in chaos," Sibéal continued, "and so she asked that I direct you to her when the time was right, and she also asked that Boann prepare you as well."

"*Boann* helped her?" Baudwin asked.

"Indeed she did," Sibéal said. "She oversees not just the Water but the realm itself."

Baudwin wanted to learn more, but was even more keen on knowing how he was supposed to find his mother. "In Four Falls, a scryer told me that I had to cross a bridge, and go through a gate. Is that how I will find her?"

"Yes," Sibéal began, "this talisman is the only way I know of that can take you through. The Rainbow Bridge was damaged in the Great Befalling. Its resonance was disrupted, so now only one who wields a talisman such as this can travel across. It's also needed to activate the glimmer gate."

"I saw a gate," Baudwin said. "And I found a moonstone down there. You won't believe it, but it was Govannon's moonstone, and —"

"*Govannon's* moonstone?" Sibéal cut in.

At this the birds in the branches became quite agitated. Feathers ruffled, and heads bobbed. They chattered, but Sibéal waved her hand and they were quiet.

"How do you know?" Sibéal asked. "Did a memory come to you?"

"Yes, and I'm sure it was his." Baudwin recounted the memory to her, sparing no detail.

"So he was there before I was charged with this place," Sibéal mused, "and he failed the trial, but found some other path. I don't know what spear that is, but I do wonder."

Baudwin could tell that Sibéal was shocked at his discovery, but he had questions of his own. "Where is the glimmer gate? How do I use the talisman to make it work?"

Sibéal straightened up as she spoke. "That question is the most pressing one — is it not? Glimmer gates were made many thousands of years ago during the Age of Platinum. Back then anyone could traverse them freely, but now everything is much more difficult. Now, we must use a talisman like this one, and only one who wields it properly will be able to pass through the gate."

Sibéal paused to see if Baudwin was following what she said. "But as difficult as that is, finding a glimmer gate may be even harder. Govannon destroyed or sealed off most of them, and the rest are lost, but in each important city of the Fae, if you search hard enough, you may find one."

"Is there one near Four Falls?" Baudwin asked eagerly.

"Very likely lost somewhere in the drain works," Sibéal replied, "and you could spend a very long time searching down there, only to discover that it was already destroyed."

Hearing this, Baudwin was crestfallen. "Are you telling me this is all for nothing?" he asked. Attempting to console him, a cardinal hopped onto his shoulder. Staring into the distance, Baudwin stroked its feathers. How he missed Moonrise.

"You must take heart, Baudwin," Sibéal said. "There is still one way — but it will not be easy."

"I'll face any challenge!" Baudwin exclaimed. "After what I just went through, how difficult could it be?"

"Perhaps less difficult," Sibéal replied, "but in some ways even more so. The only glimmer gate I know of is near my home city of Wood Fern — lost somewhere in the Thicket of the Moons. There is a great tree there — the parent tree of the ones planted on the Island of the Falls. After the Great Befalling, the tree became sick, along with the nearby groves. All the roots and branches are like iron now — petrified — thick with a heavy dread that stifles the Life out of any living thing that tries to venture in."

"How then, can I hope to succeed?" Baudwin asked.

"Many have attempted to heal this tree, which is sacred to the wood Faeries. They blame the Elves, for they believe that the Great Befalling was all their doing."

"Was it?" Baudwin asked, open to the possibility.

"No one knows for sure," Sibéal said, "but the wood Faeries believe that the Elves put a malaise on the realm due to their over-fascination with their contraptions. I, myself, do not believe that this could be, but they do."

"How then, can I heal the tree?" Baudwin asked.

"Govannon is ever eager to curry favor with the Faeries," Sibéal continued. "He has launched a mission to win us all over. Ever since the Elves occupied *Tír Éirí Sióg,* he has been driven to win over the Faeries, and so he lent us one of the most precious treasures from Gleam — *glaschloch beatha,*[2] also known as the Lea Torch, a Spectramight artifact crafted by the great elven King Sitric. Anyone who is skilled enough to make use of the crystal would heal the tree, opening the way to the glimmer gate."

"Spectramight?" Baudwin asked.

"Spectramight is an ancient wonder of the Elves, made up of crystals of every color of the rainbow that can be harnessed to shape the waking-dream of the realm. Govannon has lent *glaschloch beatha* to the elders of Wood Fern. Every year they hold a festival to see if any Faery or Elve can harness its power and heal the tree. The next festival will soon be upon us, and now that you are here, I believe that the grove can be healed. No one has succeeded as yet, but there is one who may know of a way."

"Who?" Baudwin asked.

"There is a wood spirit that dwells near Wood Fern. Since *glaschloch beatha* is a green Spectramight crystal — the color of Life — the wood spirit may know how it can be used. Long ago, the Elves mastered these crystals and elementals were naturally attracted to the crystal of their color, forming a kinship between the wielders and what they wielded."

"*Another* spirit. . ." Baudwin groaned. "The last one almost sent me and half the Fae of Four Falls to Annwyn."

"Yes, and this one may be even more dangerous to you than Boann. You are not of the same element and share no direct kinship. You must understand that Boann is of your tribe, which may be one of the few reasons why she didn't fell you like an oak."

At this, the birds twittered nervously, hiding their heads under their wings.

---

[2] Pronounced [GLAHS-chlockh BYAH-huh] a green stone of Life, the light of the Sun

"Then — must I go to Wood Fern?" Baudwin asked, still holding the talisman. "If so, how do I wield this?"

"When you get to Wood Fern, you'll learn much more from the wood spirit," Sibéal replied, "but for now, I will help you to begin."

Taking the talisman from him, she began, "May the Fire of Honesty burn in my heart." Holding it to her forehead, she continued, "So I may discover the Light of Truth within." Bringing the talisman to her heart, she ended, "And always hold dear the Promise of Rebirth."

She then handed the talisman to Baudwin, saying, "Now you must try."

And try Baudwin did. Holding the talisman with both hands, he began, "May the Fire of Honesty burn in my heart." Holding it to his forehead, he continued, "So I may discover the Light of Truth within." Bringing the talisman back to his heart, he concluded, "And always hold dear the Promise of Rebirth."

As he uttered those last words, the talisman began to glow green. Seeing this, Sibéal continued, "Now to open the gate, you must say: Gate that glimmers brightly, with the Light of the green *Dùrùghlas, — open to the realm of the Luminous Ones.*"

Baudwin repeated the words, his eyes shining. Gazing at Sibéal, he saw a look of fear cross her face.

"Emerald bright — cease your Light!" she cried.

Baudwin was perplexed by her fear, until he saw a blackness enveloping the talisman. Quickly, the hollowing wave moved up his arm.

"Speak the words!" Sibéal cried.

"Emerald bright — cease your Light!" Baudwin declared, and with that the green glow of the talisman subsided, and the blackness, which had almost reached his face, vanished.

"I've seen that before!" Baudwin exclaimed. "That's the shadow in Glamorium."

"Yes," Sibéal said, her fright turning to dread. "This is also why you must use the glimmer gate near Wood Fern. If the Thicket of the Moons is healed by *glaschloch beatha,* this may ward off the shadow of Glamorium long enough to let you pass through quickly. There is no way to stop the shadow that I know of, so do not wield the talisman until you are ready. Keep it safe. Also know that Govannon's guards will not want anyone to venture into the thicket once it has been healed, so you will have to devise your own way through."

Baudwin was indeed thrilled that his mother was alive and well, but the task before him seemed even more difficult than any thus far. The wood spirit could smite him. The shadow of Glamorium could consume him. Govannon's guards could imprison him, and he didn't even know how his family and friends were faring.

"This all sounds so impossible," he said smiling, "but as my grandfather Seamus always said, when every other element is found lacking, the Water *alone* finds a way."

"And how might that be?" Sibéal asked.

"Because, as my grandfather also likes to say:

> The Earth stops, when the last pick drops
> The Air stalls, when the last leaf falls
> The Fire dies, when the last Fae cries,
> But the Water stays — like the full Moon's rays."

"And the Wood?" Sibéal asked, raising her eyebrows.

"The Wood stops, when the last tree plops," Baudwin improvised, laughing.

"The nerve!" Sibéal chortled.

They both laughed, and the birds in the branches chirped, and for the first time since leaving Deuona, Baudwin felt at home again. Naturally, he had many more questions for Sibéal, but sensing his exhaustion she gave him a hearty supper and ordered him to bed. She would tell him more when he awoke.

Baudwin did as he was told, and when he finally lay down, he saw that Sibéal had lined the oval bedframe around him with gourds of Water. He fell asleep almost instantly, with only his dreams to greet him. And downriver, near the forks at the glamorium temple of the Nechtain, a great green Light had lit up the sky, summoned by friends and foes alike. Little did they know that in their desperation, they had awakened the eye that sees what others do not see — blessing the Shiny folk and promising hope and resolution for all of *Tír na nÓg*.

And as Baudwin dreamed never could he have imagined that his greatest joy would flow from his greatest sorrow, nor that the Water would also actually will this to be so.

The end of *Secrets of the Rainbow Bridge:
The Fire of Ionracas*[3] *Book One*

For the continuation of this story arc please read *Secrets
of the Rainbow Bridge: The Fire of Ionracas Book Two*

www.sotrb.com

---

[3] Pronounced [UN-ruh-cuss] honesty

Thank you for reading Secrets of the Rainbow Bridge: The Fire of Ionracas Book One. Please bear in mind that this is only the beginning of the series. If you enjoyed reading about Baudwin's adventure, we humbly ask that you write a review on Amazon, or the website you purchased this from.

Organic reviews help us reach other like-minded readers who have similar interests as your own. We are a small indie publisher, and grow when people leave reviews, so please share what you thought of our book. Also visit our website to see more artwork, and information about our upcoming audiobook.

Thank you!
The SOTRB team

CAST IN ORDER OF APPEARANCE
OR FIRST MENTION

Aurali [AURA-lie]	Light faery lady, and Keeper of the Light
Scannlan [SCAN-lan]	Dark faery gent of Scáth
Baudwin [BOD-win]	Son of Kelven, water faery gent of Deuona, and Guilder
Seamus [SHAY-mus]	Son of Conn, water faery gent of Deuona, and Guild Leader
Kelven [KEL-ven]	Son of Seamus, water faery gent of Deuona, Guilder, and Primary of Water
Matha [MA-ha]	Son of Niall, water faery gent of Deuona, and Guilder
Criofan [CRI-fin]	Son of Congal, water faery gent of Deuona, and Guilder
Brigh [BREE]	Mother of Matha, water faery lady of Deuona, Guilder, and Primary of Concord
Loch [LOCK]	Water faery gent of Deuona, and Roiler Leader
Riona [REE-oh-na]	Elven lady of Copper
Donal [DHO-nil]	Water faery lad of Deuona
Gavin [GAV-en]	Elven gent, Druid of Lore, and Master of Silver
Lugh [LOU]	Son of Donovan, water faery gent of Four Falls, and Guild Leader
Ferrell [FAIR-ell]	Elven gent of the Chinewilds, Luminary, and Master of Gold
Glas [Gloss]	Elven gent, and proprietor of Magniglow Booth
Edmund [ED-mund]	Elven gent, Druid of Lore, and Master of Silver
Teigue [Tayg]	Cousin of Loch, water faery lad of Deuona, and Roiler

Elva [EL-vah]	Neighbor of Baudwin, wife of Eolann, water faery lady of Deuona, and Eddy
Eolann [Oh-lan]	Neighbor of Baudwin, husband of Elva, water faery gent of Deuona, and Eddy
Ida [EE-da]	Grandmother of Conor, water faery lady of Deuona
Conor [KON-ner]	Grandson of Ida, water faery lad of Deuona
Mailee [MAY-lee]	Water faery lassie of Deuona
Earc [Ear-k]	Water faery gent of Deuona, and Roiler
Carina [Ka-REEN-ah]	Water faery lady of Deuona, and racer
Brecc [BRECK]	Water faery gent of Deuona, and racer
Rian [Ry-an]	Son of Martin, elven gent, Druid of Guidance, and Master of Silver
Daibhi [DAY-bhee]	Husband of Una, elven gent, and clock maker
Una [OO-na]	Wife of Daibhi, elven lady
Cristin [KRIS-tin]	Elven lady, proprietor of Hammer Comb
Laserian [La-ZER-ee-an]	Elven gent, inventor of Jab and Jump
Rohan [RO-hawn]	Faery gent, improver of Hop and Hit
Bran [BRAN]	Elven gent, son of Laserian
Liam [LEE-am]	Faery gent, son of Rohan
Niall [NIEL]	Father of Matha, water faery gent of Deuona, Guilder, and Primary of Concord
Congal [CONN-ell]	Father of Criofan, water faery gent of Deuona, Guilder, and Primary of Commerce
Moira [MOY-ra]	Mother of Criofan, water faery gent of Deuona, Guilder, and Primary of Commerce
Aengus [ANG-us]	Friend of Niall, cousin of Finn and water faery gent of Deuona
Gobán [gub-BAWN]	Friend of Aengus, and water faery gent of Deuona
Càel [KALE]	Friend of Gobán, and water faery gent of Deuona
Finn [FIN]	Cousin of Aengus, and water faery gent of Deuona
Fraech [FREK]	Rian's brother, and elven gent
Artgal [ART-ghal]	Elven gent, and carpenter
Almha [ALM-ha]	Water faery lady of Deuona
Finola [Fin-O-lah]	Water faery lady of Deuona

Liber [LEE-ber]	Brother of Lugh, water faery gent of Deuona, and Eddy
Lachtin [LOCK-tin]	Water faery gent of Four Falls
Caitlin [KATE-lin]	Daughter of Brigh, water faery lady of Dueona
Declan [DECK-lan]	Farmer
Finbar [FIN-var]	Cow keeper
Boann [BOH-un]	Water spirit, Guardian of the Shiny Folk, babbler in the brook, whisperer in the well, rusher of the rivers, Creator of Teampall Easa, and A Chroí Istigh
Govannon [GO-VAAN-ahn]	Son of Brandon, brother of Belanus, elven gent of Mist Valley, King of the Elves, ruler of *Tír na nÓg*, and Master of Platinum
Belanus [BELL-UN-US]	Son of Brandon, brother of Govannon, elven gent of Mist Valley, and former King of the Elves
Earnan [ERN-nan]	Wood faery gent of Wood Fern
Tárlach [TAR-lock]	Elven gent of Pine Reach, and measurer of the water
Fearghus [FER-gus]	Son of Mochuda, elven gent of the Clock City
Seanán [SHAN-awn]	Son of Berach, elven gent of Gold Haven
Mochuda [MUK-oo-da]	Father of Fearghus, elven gent of Gold Haven
Berach [BAR-ock]	Father of Seanán, elven gent of Gold Haven
Ayamonn [AY-mon]	Son of Tassach, water faery gent of Four Falls, and Guild Leader of the Danu Quarter
Tassach [TASS-ock]	Father of Ayamonn, water faery gent of Four Falls
Padhra [PAR-ra]	Water faery gent of Four Falls, Guild Leader of the Cyhiraeth Quarter
Donagh [DUN-na]	Water faery gent of Four Falls, Guild Leader of the Condatis Quarter
Abaigeal [ABI-gale]	Mother of Lugh, water faery lady of Four falls
Cairbre [KAR-bra]	Dark faery gent, defender of the Onyx Shell Keep
Esther [EIS-tir]	Water faery lady of Four Falls, scryer
Martin [MAIR-tin]	Father of Rian, elven gent
Conn [KON]	Great grandfather of Baudwin

Loingsech [LUNG-shuk]   Sea faery of Baranthus,
                         Captain of the Bael Inse
Lí Ban [LEE Bahn]   Water spirit, alternate name for Boann
Meave [MAYV]   Daughter of Eibhlin, elven lady of
                         Gold Haven, and Master of Gold
Eibhlin [EV-leen]   Mother of Meave, elven lady of Gold Haven
Bethaill [BEV-el]   Former elven queen of Mist Valley
Sorcha [SOR-ka]   Former elven queen of Platinum Spires
Grania [GRAN-ya]   Former elven queen of Silver Forge
Mor [MORE]   Former elven queen of Copper Caves
Étain [AID-een]   Former elven queen of Gold Haven
Brión [BRI-an]   Legendary elven gent
Sibéal [SHI-beel]   Daughter of Niamh, wood faery lady
Niamh [NEEV]   Mother of Neev, wood faery lady
Sláine [SLAN-ya]   Former elven queen of Copper Caves
Molua [MUL-oo-a]   Criofan's neighbor, water
                         faery gent of Deuona

A NOTE ABOUT CAPITALIZATIONS

I n Secrets of the Rainbow Bridge we capitalize characters, and proper nouns, including places, titles, and geographical locations. We have also chosen to capitalize certain other words to emphasize the world building. In some contexts, we also drop capitalizations, so they aren't too overwhelming for you — dear reader — to take in.

As you consider all of this, you need not worry about memorizing *anything*. All of this will become second nature to you, as you read the book.

So to begin, we always capitalize Faery and Elve when they appear as *nouns*. For example:

The Faeries met to talk about the upcoming solstice festival. The Elves decided to build a new lumber roller.

However, we do not capitalize Faery or Elve when they appear as adjectives. For example: The faery lady went to the Solstice festival. The elven gents decided to build a new lumber roller.

In our world the Faeries consider the elements to be sacred, and they are Earth, Water, Air, Fire, Life (or Wood), Death, Light and Dark. When these words appear as *nouns* within a particular context or point of view that pertains to a Faery we capitalize them. Some examples are:

The Faery walked on the Earth. The Faery drew Water from the well. The Faery breathed in the Air. The Faery danced around the Fire. The Faery lived a Life filled with good deeds, (or lived in the Woods). The Faery escaped an untimely Death. The Faery saw a rainbow of Light. The Faery hid like a beaver in the Dark.

However, when Earth, Water, Air, Fire, Life, (or Wood), Death, Light and Dark appear as *adjectives* we never capitalize them. Some examples are:

The earth Faery walked to the tree. The water Faery took the bucket to the well. The air Faery breathed in the smell. The fire Faery tossed the ball of flame. The life (or wood) Faery raced through the trees. The death Faery made a strange wish. The light Faery especially liked the color red. The dark Faery disappeared mysteriously.

Also, if, in the above examples, we change the word Faery to *Elve* (because the context or the point of view pertains to an Elve, or the ways of the Elves) we do not capitalize the elements. Some examples are:

The Elve walked on the earth. The Elve drew water from the well. The Elve breathed in the air. The Elve danced around the fire. The Elve lived a life filled with good deeds (or lived in the woods). The Elve escaped an untimely death. The Elve saw a rainbow of light. The Elve hid like a beaver in the dark.

In our world, the Elves consider the metals to be sacred, and they are Copper, Silver, Gold, and Platinum. When these words appear as *nouns* within a particular context or point of view that pertains to an Elve, we capitalize them. Some examples are:

The Elve made a large sprocket out of Copper. The Elve wore a belt made of Silver. The Elve owned a clock made of Gold. The Elve held a crown made of Platinum.

However, when Copper, Silver, Gold, and Platinum appear as *adjectives* we never capitalize them. Some examples are:

The Elve crafted a copper sprocket. The Elve wore a silver belt. The Elve owned a gold clock. The Elve held a platinum crown.

And, if, in the above examples, we changed the word Elve to *Faery*, (because the context or the point of view pertains to a Faery, or the ways of the Faeries) we do not capitalize the metals. Some examples are:

The Faery looked at the sprocket made of copper. The Faery wore a belt made of silver. The Faery owned a clock made of gold. The Faery held a crown made of platinum.

Also, Faeries regard the Moon as sacred, and Elves regard the Sun as sacred, and both Elves and Faeries consider Glamorium to be a sacred metal, so we always capitalize Sun, Moon, and Glamorium when they appear as nouns, regardless of whether the context or point of view is that of a Faery or an Elve. Some examples are:

The Faeries revere the Moon. The Elves know the Faeries love the Moon. The Elves revere the Sun. The Faeries know the Elves love the Sun. Both Elves and Faeries revere Glamorium.

However, whenever Moon, Sun and Glamorium appear as *adjectives*, we have also chosen not to capitalize them as capitalizations appear rather frequently throughout our book, and we don't want our readers to experience "capitalization fatigue."

So, we don't capitalize Faery, when we say faery festival, or Elve when we say elven contraption, or Glamorium, when we say glamorium pendant.

For the most part we follow these rules regarding not capitalizing adjectives, although a few exceptions may appear here and there. One is that we chose to capitalize the word *Connemara*, as both a noun and an adjective, so as not to annoy or upset our Irish friends.

Here are a few more examples of how our capitalization rules work together:

The water Faery picked up the piece of copper and drank some Water. The Elve with the copper-colored shirt picked up a piece of Copper and drank some water. As the Light of the Moon shined on the table, the Faery looked at the light shining from the elven lamp.

All of this said, there is something else to consider about capitalizations which is: The Elve and Faery swam in the Water, holding pieces of Copper. Here both Elve and Faery are capitalized, along with Water and Copper, because the point of view is shared by an Elve and a Faery.

Finally, sometimes the narration is ambiguous about whose point of view it is, and in that case we make a judgement call ourselves. For example:

The Water willed this to be so.

DAYS OF THE WEEK

Earth Day – Crédía – CRAY-THEE-UH

Water Day – Uiscedía – ISH-KUH-THEE-UH

Air Day – Aerdía – AIR-THEE-UH

Fire Day – Tinedía – CHIN-UH-THEE-UH

Life (Wood) Day – Adhmaddía – EYE-MUD-THEE-UH

Dark Day – Dorchadía – DORCHUH-THEE-UH

Light Day – Solasdía – SOLACE-THEE-UH

www.ingramcontent.com/pod-product-compliance
Lightning Source LLC
Chambersburg PA
CBHW051122300726
48981CB00021B/515/J

9798988042907